ISBN 978-0-260-12620-7
PIBN 10929369

# THE CENTURY
## ILLUSTRATED MONTHLY
# MAGAZINE

VOL. LIII.
NEW SERIES, VOL. XXXI.
NOVEMBER, 1896, TO APRIL, 1897

THE CENTURY CO., NEW YORK
MACMILLAN & CO. LTD., LONDON

THE DE VINNE PRESS.

# INDEX

TO

# THE CENTURY MAGAZINE

VOL. LIII NEW SERIES: VOL. XXXI.

---

## POETRY.

PAINTED BY WILLIAM HOGARTH. SEE "TOPICS OF THE TIME." ENGRAVED BY T. COLE, IN THE NATIONAL GALLERY, LONDON.

THE SHRIMP-SELLER.

# THE CENTURY MAGAZINE

VOL. LIII. NOVEMBER, 1896. No. 1.

## ELECTION DAY IN NEW YORK.

WITH PICTURES BY JAY HAMBIDGE.

ELECTION-DAY morning is the earliest of the year. The polls open at six o'clock—long before daylight in that late and cloudy month of November. At three the policemen who are to serve at the polls (nearly three thousand of them on the last occasion) are aroused and sent to breakfast. An hour later they reassemble, are paraded before the desks of the station-houses, instructed, and despatched to their polls, taking with them all the ballot-boxes, ballots, and other furniture, for the safety of which they are held responsible.

As six o'clock approaches men may be seen plunging in and out of all-night restaurants, where they snatch a hasty breakfast, and then hurry away through the chilly gloom. These are inspectors and other officials who have early work to do.

The polling-place used to be generally some small shop belonging to a faithful adherent of the dominant party, who received fifty dollars from the city for the use of his premises during the four days of registration and one day's voting. The same place was likely to be occupied, and the same inspectors and clerks often served, year after year, partly for the pay (thirty-six dollars), but largely because the service carries with it exemption from jury duty for a year, and gives a man a certain distinction among his neighbors. Cigar shops were favorite places, but shoe shops, barber shops, undertakers' rooms, and even stables, were taken. In almost every case they used to be too small, and were dark, ill ventilated, and inconvenient. At one place a watcher met with (and stopped) the practice of leading horses in and out through the voting inclosure. The new police board has broken up the old custom of choosing these places for political reasons.

Before the polls open the small closets or «booths» in which the voters prepare their ballots, and which are built of canvas stretched upon light frames, hinged together so as to be collapsible, are unfolded and set up, one being provided for each fifty voters on the list. The ballot-boxes, which have two glass sides and a solid cover perforated by a narrow slit, are opened, proved to be empty, relocked by the chairman of the Board of Inspectors, and then arranged upon tables. Outside of all is set up a «guard-rail,» as a legal rather than an actual barrier to the approach within it of unprivileged persons. The ballot clerks set in order their ballots ready to be dealt out, while the poll clerks open their registry books containing the names of men supposed to be electors, and prepare to record each vote. Finally, any watchers present take their places within the rail, where they may scrutinize every proceeding. To the intelligence, vigilance, and courageous protests of these watchers all over the city the handsome result against misrule in 1894, and the freedom from illegal election methods, were very largely due, and they will be a regular institution hereafter.

On the stroke of six the poll is declared open, and the voting immediately begins, the name and address of each applicant being called out by the inspector as soon as the voter presents himself. If he is reported as properly registered, and no one challenges his right, the ballots are given him, their number is recorded by the clerks and every one else interested, and he retires to a booth to select in secret the ticket or tickets he wishes to vote. This done, he returns, hands his ballots to the inspectors, so folded that no one can see their purport, the fact that he has voted is proclaimed and recorded, and he leaves the inclosure. If challenged, he «swears in» his vote, or refuses to do so, according as he is willing or not to take the responsibility of an oath.

Here is where the watchers are of particular service. Registration lists have been scrutinized in advance, and suspected names looked up. Where a doubt remains, the man is challenged as soon as he appears. In a few cases earlier investigation has justified the issue of a judicial warrant, and he is arrested the moment he attempts to vote; but often he is able to show that the supposed falsification is somebody's error, and soon establishes his innocence. In many cases, as where the alleged inhabitants of a low lodging-house are challenged by wholesale, the protester is satisfied by the man taking an oath as to his right to the franchise, since prosecution and serious punishment may follow if subsequent proof of perjury is obtained. Now and then, when there is good reason to believe the applicant a fraud, he will be warned to take care, and told that he will be immediately investigated and punished if he has sworn falsely. As the Police Department issues annually a book containing a full compendium of the election laws, which is spread broadcast, there is no excuse for ignorance. Such a warning usually scares a rascal away, and his tale prevents others trying the same game. Of the twenty-three men registered from one lodging-house known to the writer at a recent election, only sixteen presented themselves, and two of these did not vote. The year before thirty-five had voted from the same house.

DRAWN BY JAY HAMBIDGE.

OUTSIDE THE POLLING-PLACE.

Meanwhile the great city is waking up. This is a legal holiday, but the smaller provision stores open their doors for a few hours,

DRAWN BY JAY HAMBIDGE.

A WARD HEELER.

perhaps an alderman, or maybe even a candidate, and these others are his «workers,» who share his chances, hopeful of recognition if he succeeds, failing which they will desert to the opposition, and possibly «squeal,» or betray damaging secrets against him. He is now making a round of the polls in his district to be sure that his representatives are on duty near by, and are properly distributing his pasters to every one who can be induced to take and use them. The use of pasters, by the way, is abrogated under the new ballot law.

Often a small portable closet of rough boards is set up on the sidewalk, in which the paster peddler ensconces himself like an old woman in a French bath-chair; and these little cabins, with three or four party men about each, form a notable feature of election-day scenes. They are made of fresh lumber, yellow, and oozing with amber resin; they are covered with lithographed portraits

for thousands of their customers never have eatables on hand for more than one meal at a time. Men are trotting from corner to corner extinguishing the gas-lamps, and the electric lights pale and go out by platoons, street after street. Surface and elevated cars pass with increasing frequency, but are half empty; milk-dealers rattle about. Toward the polling-places come groups of strong, active, but rather seedy men, talking the polyglot slang of the school of the curbstone.

One, better dressed, cleaner shaved, strides briskly around the corner, and is instantly attended to. He shakes hands with everybody, calling each by his Christian name—or a part of it, for time is precious this morning. Now and then he throws his arm about the neck of a henchman, and whispers a sentence or two in his ear, whereupon the recipient of the favor hurries away. This nabob is the leader of the district on one side, or

DRAWN BY JAY HAMBIDGE.

A CANDIDATE.

DRAWN BY JAY HAMBIDGE.

THE FLOATING VOTE.

and red-and-blue posters announcing their special candidates; they are the nuclei of groups of gossiping loungers, and often are upset in the rush of a fight which must be concluded before the peddler and his pasters can crawl out. In the worst era of municipal politics they were numerous and close to the polls, but almost disappeared in 1894.

Elsewhere the city has a Sabbath quiet; but if you go to the ferries or to the Grand Central depot an hour or two later, you see there plenty of people—well-dressed women and prosperous, clerkly-looking men, especially parties of the younger sort, armed with gun-cases or dress-suit valises, or perhaps both. These are going out of town for a day's pleasure: shooting in New Jersey or up the Hudson; fox-hunting on Long Island; Country Club sports in Westchester County or at Tuxedo; visiting with rural or suburban friends. It is fair to suppose that many of the above have voted, but a similar throng left town on Saturday and won't be back until Wednesday. In 1894 this fashionable irruption did not enliven the outgoing trains to any noticeable extent, and to the men who stayed in town to vote the Tiger may charge thousands of the flakes that snowed him under in that memorable political blizzard.

Another class rejoice in this holiday as an opportunity to sit at home enjoying domestic comfort, reading in slippered ease the postponed book, or fondling the pet hobby. The «people» call them «silk-stockings,» and have no fear of their beautifully modulated expressions of censure, because they rarely back it up by a vote.

Down at the polls they cannot understand this frame of mind. A certain number of citizens, to be sure, come, deposit their votes as quickly as possible, and go away with an attitude of having performed a disagreeable duty. But to the many who are more or less visible there all day this is the most important occasion of the year, and there is hardly anything they would not rather do than miss it. To be sure, it may be worth a few dollars to them, directly or indirectly; but plainly they look further than this, and

DRAWN BY JAY HAMBIDGE.

THE FLOATING VOTE.

have a hazy sense of the dignity of the act, comparable to the fetish-worshiper's notion of religion. They are not the ignorant, foreign, dollar-a-day laborers, stupid and besotted with liquor, but men earning wages enough to enable them to pay their footing in the bar-room club, and having sufficient brains to make them serviceable to their «captain.» Alert with the keenness of the streets, knowing everybody, and feeling above none, they are wholly devoted to «the cause» as long as they get fair treatment.

It is these men who make the voting-places picturesque. In rough garb and with lordly swagger, they sandwich themselves between neat and dignified lawyers, merchants, and clergymen, proudly sensible of their equality at the polls. Sometimes the motley line reaches out of doors and down the street. As soon as one has voted he joins the loiter-

DRAWN BY JAY HAMBIDGE.

ARREST OF A REPEATER

ers outside, and pompously lights a cigar, scornful of the black pipe more familiar to his teeth.

In the afternoon the brisk captain, who has been dodging all day from poll to poll, obtains an approximate list of those of his side who have not yet voted, and despatches workers to «bring them out.» They search their haunts, and presently return with recruits. Some of these delinquents have simply been tardy, others are sick or lame or blind, and are gently conducted to the polls, perhaps in a carriage, placed in the line, and carefully assisted to the ballot-box. The attention he gets on election day is a genuine comfort to many a poor devil kicked about all the rest of the year. Now and then a henchman seizes a captain and whispers portentously in his ear. A moment later he hurries off, looking very important, and soon reappears with a companion, who is sent on alone, while he himself stays back at the corner. This means that some voter has been ascertained to be out of town or sick abed, and that a willing and thrifty stranger has come to vote (illegally) in his name. This is only one of many tricks election officers and watchers must guard against toward the end of the day, and sometimes at a cost to the latter of no small courage; for whisky emboldens the roughest workers to try to «stand on his head» any one who interferes with them.

The day wears on—Sunday without the churches, a gray day in every sense of the word. In the lower wards, where folk are close enough together to feel one another's warmth, and where it really matters whether Mike O'Farron or Barney Cadigan is to be alderman or coroner, each cross-roads has an excited crowd; but up-town the side streets are deserted, and even Broadway and Fifth Avenue are dead.

The first to break the silence are the boys crying the afternoon papers; but there is nothing in them except clever guesswork, unless the tension of factions at some polling-place, or the wild foolishness of a tipsy worker, has brought on a fight or two. Election-day rows are now remarkably rare in New York.

Loiterers increase about the polling-places, and voters crowd forward, fearful lest they be too late. The weary inspectors and clerks most now work harder than ever, and the watchers watch their very best. This is the time when the schemer gathers results—gets in his fine work, as he would tell you. Men present themselves with specious claims, politicians bulldoze, and it is only the most determined guardian of the purity of the ballot who in this last hour can withstand the pressure. It happened in several districts, in 1894, when the voter was called upon to fold and select from twenty-three ballots, that there was not time enough in the day for all those entitled to the franchise to reach the ballot-box, and voting twice in one place was out of the question.

The moment the polls close the liquor-saloons open, but the excessive drunkenness and brawling common in former years are not now seen. Five o'clock editions of the newspapers are issued, but have little to tell, for everywhere the clerks are still busily counting the votes. The streets overflow with boys who hardly wait for the earliest darkness to institute their picturesque part of the day's doings. The New York citizen begins to break election-day laws as soon as he can toddle about the block. Bonfires are strictly prohibited, yet thousands of them redden the air and set all the windows aglow before seven o'clock.

Antiquarians inform us that this custom is nothing but a survival in America of the old English celebration of burning Guy Fawkes on the 5th of November, in recollection of the Gunpowder Plot of 1605, which the children have transferred to the movable feast of our election day. Maybe so. At any rate, for weeks beforehand the lads, large and small, rich and poor, have begged, borrowed, or stolen every burnable thing they could lay their hands on, and have kept their treasure as well as they could. Knowing by sad experience the untruth of the aphorism, «There is honor among thieves," they usually persuade some one to let them store these combustibles in his back yard or still safer cellar. From hundreds of such repositories the lads bring their treasures, heap them up in the middle of the street, and fight off raiders until they are safely blazing. Women and children swarm out of the huge tenements and cluster about the scene, where the youngsters are leaping and whooping and waving brands, like the true fire-worshipers they are. The smallest boys and girls have saved a box and a board or two, or beg some fuel from good-natured big brothers, and start little blazes of their own, with a headless ash-barrel for a chimney. Everywhere are dancing, merriment, singing, and shouting. The great heaps throw out a terrific heat, glare upon the highest windows, and illuminate the whole sky, while showers of sparks whirl up and down the narrow streets

DRAWN BY JAY HAMBIDGE.

A CAMPAIGN PARADE AT NIGHT.

DRAWN BY JAY HAMBIDGE.

THE WOLF AND THE LAMB.

in the autumn wind, yet rarely do serious damage. But boxes and barrels are slight, and the flames die down long before the enthusiasm of the boys and their applauding friends is exhausted. Now begins criminal foraging and senseless waste. Lumber-piles, scaffolding, new buildings, kitchen chairs, wheelbarrows, and sometimes even serviceable wagons, are seized by marauders and thrown on the fires, unless carefully guarded, so that each year sees not only a great waste of good fuel among the poor, but the destruction of much valuable timber and household furniture. This work of hoodlums cannot easily be stopped, because just then nearly all the police are in the polling-places watching the canvass.

The counting of the votes has been in the past more fruitful of trickery and falsification than any other part of the election process. In 1893 the canvassers in certain districts reduced the matter to its lowest terms by simply reporting a unanimous vote on their side, and then going out to fling up their hats for the rest of the night. In the subsequent election competent and incorruptible men supervised the canvass so strictly that the percentage of fraud was so small, if any existed, as never to be heard of. This watching at the count not only prevented intentional lying, but saved accidental mistakes. In one case the board of inspectors confessed they did not know how to count the votes, and submitted entirely to the guidance of a well-informed watcher.

The counting is done in public, and is often an interesting sight. Every organization and each candidate may send a representative to observe it, though nobody but the inspectors is permitted to touch the ballots. The straight tickets are first counted in tens by the four men in succession, and a tally is kept by at least two assistants. Each name is credited with as many votes as there are tickets for his side. Then one inspector reads off those tickets which are «split,» or have pasters attached, or upon which names have been erased or new names written, and each candidate is credited with a vote every time his name appears. When this is finished the most prominent office is taken up, and the sum of the votes for each candidate is ascertained. The result is immediately announced, but the official announcement and record are made in this wise:

The election bureau of the police board is the official recipient of the returns from the

DRAWN BY JAY HAMBIDGE.

EMBLEMS OF VICTORY.

DRAWN BY JAY HAMBIDGE.

BRINGING UP FUEL FOR THE BONFIRES.

voting precincts. This bureau furnishes each poll with blanks for the official record, and also with four sets of small blanks for each office. As soon as the count for any office is finished the four inspectors sign all four blanks, and a policeman takes them to police headquarters, and quickly returns for others. Thus the count goes on until it is completed —sometimes not before midnight.

Meantime there have gathered in a large room at police headquarters all the commissioners, the superintendent, and a great number of newspaper reporters with pencils sharpened at both ends, while the walls are lined with messenger and telephone boys. As soon as a report is brought it is read out by the superintendent, taken down by the newspaper men, and forwarded to their editors as rapidly as possible. By eight o'clock the returns come thick and fast, and nothing is heard but the scratching of pencils and the footsteps of racing messengers. The commissioners soon go to their private offices, for they know that anxious candidates will speedily be calling to learn their fate, although a very fair idea has spread abroad by nine or ten o'clock as to how the State and city have «gone» on the principal issues. In the case of the election of November, 1894, everybody knew that Tammany was beaten long before that hour.

But the fun of the street, which is now beginning, is not for that band of reporters at headquarters, nor for those other bands of writers in the newspaper offices down-town, who, with almost superhuman diligence and endurance, are tabulating and putting into type and commenting upon these returns for delectation of the public next morning.

The tenement-house districts have been alive with people since sundown, dancing about the fires. They have learned long ago the outlines of the result, and those on the successful side are rejoicing in their tumultuous way, sure of the support of all the boys. As the evening advances the excitement spreads to Broadway and up-town. The newspapers will issue extras every hour or so from 9 P. M. to two in the morning, but they do not hesitate to give all this news away upon their bulletins as fast as they get it.

The crowd knows this, and gathers early in City Hall Park and Newspaper Square to read the messages written upon glass «slides,» and magnified upon broad screens outside the buildings by means of a stereopticon. At first these bulletins are vague and partial, but toward midnight they increase in breadth and importance. At intervals the operator presents a summing up like this:

> 418 *districts out of a total of* 600 *in Ohio give John Smith, Dem.,* 117,926, *and James Brown, Rep.,* 180,460.

or:

> *Georgia elects the whole Democratic ticket by an estimated plurality of* 20,000.

When he has nothing to report the operator displays a portrait of a candidate, or an impromptu cartoon, exhibiting in comical allegory the success of his man, or his side, and the discomfiture of the other fellow. Of late a favorite bit of fun has been to throw upon the screen a question like this:

«What 's the matter with Cleveland?»

Promptly comes the answer from ten thousand throats:

«He 's all right!»

Then shines out:

«Who 's all right?»

And the windows rattle with the acclamation:

«C-l-e-v-e-l-a-n-d!»

As the principal dailies are published side by side in Park Row, and include political opponents, the populace is treated not only to the whole truth of the figures, but to all the portraits and both sides of the jokes, and the laughter is gaily impartial. Over all the scene in recent years glow the huge red or white beacons on the summit of the dome of one of these buildings, signaling the probable result to curious eyes miles away across the rivers.

Elsewhere eager minds are seeking the facts. Telephone and telegraph operators find the night a very busy one. At all the theaters the returns are read to the audience between the acts, and variety players bring out fresh laughter by impromptu «gags» at the expense of the losing politicians.

Temporary wires have been extended into the offices of the principal organizations, and there the leaders assemble and receive a constant stream of visitors and telegrams. The Republicans always assemble at the Fifth Avenue Hotel, where a jubilant crowd of substantial citizens soon takes possession of the corridors if that party wins. The Hoffman boils over with equally well-groomed and hilarious Democrats when they are in the ascendant.

But the greatest of these indoor jollifications is that at Tammany Hall. Early in the evening the spacious auditorium becomes packed with tribesmen, a brass band is stationed in the gallery, the wives and daughters of prominent braves appear in the boxes, and the big and little sachems, wiskinskies, and all the rest, gather about a mythical council-fire on the stage. A member with a stentorophonic voice reads telegrams from the district leaders and police headquarters, against a storm of cheerful yells and witticisms when the news is favorable, and of hoots and catcalls when it is not.

DRAWN BY JAY HAMBIDGE.

CAMPAIGN SONGS IN AN ELECTION-NIGHT CROWD.

DRAWN BY JAY HAMBIDGE.

CART-TAIL ORATORY.

In 1894 the society had its special wire, as usual, and a reader, a band, and a big audience, but nothing but failure to report. For a long time no orator was willing to go upon the stage, and when one or two did screw up the courage, their remarks evoked only groans and muttered imprecations. The band struck up at last, but could find nothing better to offer than «Massa 's in the cold, cold ground»; and the gleeful shout that greeted this disconsolate selection showed that the hall had been captured by enemies, who had come to twist the tail of the Tiger in his inmost cage. At this the wiskinskies retired, the musicians fled, and the discomfited braves sneaked out of side entrances to avoid the derisive crowd in Fourteenth street bent upon taking their scalps.

By ten o'clock Madison Square and upper Broadway are thronged and noisy. A search-light on the tapering tower of the Madison Square Garden swings its beam north and south, east or west, with the varying reports, according to an advertised code of signaling. Now and then the light is thrown down, and reveals the stirring thousands of men and women that stand in the plaza, all gazing with upturned faces upon the bulletins displayed at Fifth avenue and Twenty-third street.

The cable cars plow lanes through the shadowy masses, with clangorous gongs, but the horse-cars are simply swallowed up, the people dodging from under the noses of the horses as they wade slowly along, only to close in behind the car. An inarticulate murmur of satisfaction or discontent, and noise of shuffling feet, follow the display of each new bulletin, swelling loud and louder as later and more certain messages are spread upon the huge placard.

The crowd is a good-natured one, and patronizes liberally the «extra» boys, the peddlers of toy brooms and tiny feathered roosters, to be pinned to coat, or buys peanuts, candy, and cheap cigars from itinerant venders. To hundreds in it the contest may be a matter of serious personal importance, but though there is plenty of badinage, one hears little acrid discussion, and witnesses no rowdyism. As soon as it becomes apparent which side has won, arrive those strange companies of youths who seem preserved from year to year for this single appearance. They are fashionably attired, and look like college students, but are not, and whence they come and whither they go between times is an unsolved mystery. Blowing tin horns in impious disharmony, waving brooms over their shoulders, symbolic of the «clean sweep,» trailing behind a leader in single file or by twos, they dive into the masses of people, wind in and out and round about, singing some campaign song, or shouting in chorus a partizan slogan.

DRAWN BY JAY HAMBIDGE.

CONFERENCE OF LEADERS IN A NEW YORK WARD CLUB.

It is stark midnight before the bulletins cease, and the people begin to pack the street-cars, or troop homeward afoot through the moonlit avenues and crossways.

*Ernest Ingersoll.*

# CAMPAIGNING WITH GRANT.

BY GENERAL HORACE PORTER.

MY FIRST MEETING WITH GRANT—CONFERENCE AT THOMAS'S HEADQUARTERS—GRANT'S MANNER OF WRITING DESPATCHES—OPENING THE «CRACKER LINE»—GRANT SALUTED BY THE ENEMY—GRANT'S PERSONAL APPEARANCE—A HIGHER GRADE CREATED FOR GRANT—GRANT'S FIRST MEETING WITH LINCOLN—IN COMMAND OF ALL THE ARMIES—INTERVIEW WITH STANTON—GRANT IN A COMMUNICATIVE MOOD—AT GENERAL MEADE'S HEADQUARTERS—GRANT'S NARROW ESCAPE FROM CAPTURE—HIS ENORMOUS RESPONSIBILITY—GRANT'S PERSONAL STAFF.

## EDITORIAL PREFACE.

FROM A WARTIME PHOTOGRAPH.

GENERAL HORACE PORTER.

WITH the exception of Abraham Lincoln, no leader in the Civil War has been so much written about as the man who emerged from the struggle wearing the laurels of chief hero. From his first engagement at Belmont to the dawn of peace at Appomattox, no officer on the Union side was more completely in the public view than General Grant. His simple, direct personality was in no way concealed by the vapors of notoriety; his momentous official duties were pursued without ostentation; his acts were always so important that they overshadowed curiosity as to what he was; he had a way of doing his own writing, and of excluding from it all consciousness of himself as a personage. For these reasons, creditable to him, the ratio of personal flavor to important statement in the literature relating to his deeds was small until, at the last, he wrote his immortal «Memoirs,» which nevertheless are perhaps more modest as cast in the mold of the personal pronoun than Cæsar's «Commentaries» veiled in the third person.

So it has come to pass that, while little or nothing remains to be said of the acts of Grant the general, only broad outlines have been given to the public of the man within the armor. As a civilian, Grant the President and first citizen became better known; but what manner of man was he while shouldering the responsibility of carnage, and standing in the deadly breach? In this respect he is fully revealed in the papers begun with this number of THE CENTURY, and there is reason to doubt that any very substantial addition will be made to the world's knowledge of Grant in the field after their publication. Certainly the «Official Records» have little more to say, and it is not known that any other member of his military family kept notes of incidents and conversations relating to the daily activity of the commanding general during the crucial last year and a half of the war.

General Porter's talents and training, no less than his opportunities, fitted him for the added service of personal historian to his chief. As the son of a governor of Pennsylvania, he inclined in youth to a public career, and, securing an appointment to West Point, was graduated number three in the class of 1860. With a special taste for mechanics, shown by several useful inventions while still a boy, he chose the ordnance branch of the military service, and won his first brevet for «gallant and meritorious services» in the field as chief of ordnance and artillery in the reduction of Fort Pulaski; he served as chief of ordnance in the transfer of the Army of the Potomac from the Peninsula, and in the Antietam campaign, at the close of which he was transferred to the West, and served in that important capacity with Rosecrans at Chickamauga and Chattanooga.

It was during the investment of Chattanooga by Bragg that Captain Porter was brought into close relations with General Grant, who, on the transfer of the Captain to special duty in the Ordnance Bureau at Washington, sought in the following letter to have him attached permanently to his own staff:

CHATTANOOGA, TENN., Nov. 5, 1863.

MAJ.-GEN. H. W. HALLECK, General-in-Chief of the Army.

Capt. Horace Porter, who is now being relieved as chief ordnance officer in the Department of the Cumberland, is represented by all officers who know him as one of the most meritorious and valuable young officers in the service. So far as I have heard from general officers there is a universal desire to see him promoted to the rank of brigadier-general and retained here. I feel no hesitation in joining in the recommendation, and ask that he may be assigned for duty with me. I feel the necessity for just such an officer as Captain Porter is described to be, at headquarters, and, if permitted, will retain him with me if assigned here for duty. I am, &c., U. S. GRANT, Major-general.

Six months later, when Grant went to Washington as general-in-chief, Colonel Porter was transferred to his personal staff as aide-de-camp. From that day until the end of Grant's first term as President, he was the companion as well as the faithful aide of his chief, and was charged with more than one important special mission, like the visit to Sherman preparatory to the march to the sea.

A literary taste, which was developed chiefly on the side of public speaking, enabled the staff-officer, when public ovations succeeded the toil of the camp, to respond on behalf of the victorious general, who had not yet accustomed himself to the brief and pithy speeches for which he afterward became celebrated. While a cadet in the National Military Academy, General Porter wrote a humorous book in verse descriptive of «West Point Life.» His arduous duties as private secretary, charged with executive business, began with the inauguration of President Grant in the spring of 1869. From that time to the present General Porter has been in great demand at army reunions and festivals for after-dinner speeches and serious addresses, and has gained increasing fame by his eloquence and ready wit. After General Grant's death, General Porter delivered a notable memorial address before the Union League Club, of which he is now president; he is also Commander of the New York Commandery of the Military Order of the Loyal Legion, and of the George Washington Post of the Grand Army of the Republic, Past Commander of the Society of the Army of the Potomac, President-general of the National Society of the Sons of the American Revolution, President of the Grant monument association, and a member of several historical and other societies. It was at a sluggish period in the progress of the movement to erect the Grant monument and tomb in Riverside Park that General Porter was placed at the head of the association, and largely through his effective appeals and practical management the popular subscription of over half a million dollars was made up, and the work energetically carried on, so that the inauguration will take place next spring on General Grant's birthday. In recognition of his contributions to literature Union College conferred upon him the degree of LL.D.

During the progress of THE CENTURY war series, General Porter contributed to this magazine two articles which evinced the historical value and anecdotal quality of the notes industriously jotted down by him during the whole time of his association with General Grant. The first article dealt with the relations of «Lincoln and Grant,» and the second was the remarkable paper on the battle of Five Forks and the surrender at Appomattox. Since then, in moments of leisure, General Porter has arranged his unique stores of anecdotes and memoranda; and THE CENTURY, which was the means of inciting General Grant to the writing of the four articles which became the structural part of his «Memoirs,» takes pleasure in offering to its readers the accurate personal portrait of the great commander that is drawn with a free and vigorous hand by General Porter in the series of papers begun in the following pages.

EDITOR OF THE CENTURY.

DRAWN BY CHARLES S. REINHART.

General Rawlins. Charles A. Dana. General Wilson. General W. F. Smith. General Grant. General Thomas. Captain Porter.

GENERAL GRANT AT THE HEADQUARTERS OF GENERAL THOMAS.

### MY FIRST MEETING WITH GRANT.

WHILE sitting in my quarters in the little town of Chattanooga, Tennessee, about an hour after nightfall on the evening of Friday, October 23, 1863, an orderly brought me a message from General George H. Thomas, Commander of the Army of the Cumberland, on whose staff I was serving, summoning me to headquarters. A storm had been raging for two days, and a chilling rain was still falling. A few minutes' walk brought me to the plain wooden, one-story dwelling occupied by the commander, which was situated on Walnut street, near Fourth, and upon my arrival I found him in the front room on the left side of the hall, with three members of his staff and several strange officers. In an arm-chair facing the fireplace was seated a general officer, slight in figure and of medium stature, whose face bore an expression of weariness. He was carelessly dressed, and his uniform coat was unbuttoned and thrown back from his chest. He held a lighted cigar in his mouth, and sat in a stooping posture, with his head bent slightly forward. His clothes were wet, and his trousers and top-boots were spattered with mud. General Thomas approached this officer, and, turning to me and mentioning me by name, said, «I want to present you to General Grant.» Thereupon the officer seated in the chair, without changing his position, glanced up, extended his arm to its full length, shook hands, and said in a low voice, and speaking slowly, «How do you do?» This was my first meeting with the man with whom I was destined afterward to spend so many of the most interesting years of my life.

The strange officers present were members of General Grant's staff. Charles A. Dana, Assistant Secretary of War, who had been for some time with the Army of the Cumberland, had also entered the room. The next morning he sent a despatch to the War Department, beginning with the words, «Grant arrived last night, wet, dirty, and well.»

On the 19th of October General Grant's command had been enlarged so as to cover the newly created military division of the Mississippi, embracing nearly the entire field of operations between the Alleghanies and the Mississippi River, and the Army of the Cumberland had thus been placed under his control. About a month before, that army, after having fought at Chickamauga one of the most gallantly contested and sanguinary battles in the annals of warfare, had fallen back and taken up a defensive position on the south side of the Tennessee River, inclosing within its lines the village of Chattanooga. The opposing forces, under General Bragg, had invested this position, and established such a close siege that the lines of supply had been virtually cut off, rations and forage were about exhausted, and almost the last tree-stump had been used for fuel. Most of the men were without overcoats, and some without shoes; ten thousand animals had died of starvation, and the gloom and despondency had been increased by the approach of cold weather and the appearance of the autumn storms.

General Grant, upon assuming the responsibilities of his new command, had fully realized the critical condition of the Army of the Cumberland, and had set out at once for its headquarters to take charge in person of its future operations. On his way to the front he had telegraphed General Thomas, from Louisville, to hold Chattanooga at all hazards, to which that intrepid soldier made the famous reply, «I will hold the town till we starve.»

General Grant had started, the day before the incident I have described, from Bridgeport, a place thirty miles below Chattanooga, where the Nashville and Chattanooga Railroad crosses the Tennessee River, and had ridden by way of Walden's Ridge, the only route left open by which communication could be had with the beleaguered town. We had been advised that he was on his way, but hardly expected that he would reach Chattanooga that night, considering the state of the weather, the wretched condition of the roads, or rather bridle-paths, over the mountain, and the severe injury to his leg which had been caused by a fall of his horse several weeks before, and from which he was still suffering. When he arrived he had to be lifted from his saddle, and was evidently experiencing much pain, as his horse had slipped in coming down the mountain, and had further injured the lame leg; but the general showed less signs of fatigue than might have been supposed after his hard ride of two days under such trying circumstances.

### CONFERENCE AT THOMAS'S HEADQUARTERS.

As soon as General Grant had partaken of a light supper immediately after his arrival, General Thomas had sent for several general officers and most of the members of his staff to come to headquarters, and the room soon contained an exceedingly interesting group. A member of General Thomas's staff quietly called that officer's attention to the fact that the distinguished guest's clothes were pretty wet and his boots were thoroughly soaked with rain after his long ride through the storm, and intimated that colds were usually no respecters of persons. General Thomas's mind had been so intent upon receiving the commander, and arranging for a conference of officers, that he had entirely overlooked his guest's travel-stained condition; but as soon as his attention was called to it, all of his old-time Virginia hospitality was aroused, and he at once begged his newly arrived chief to step into a bedroom and change his clothes. His urgings, however, were in vain. The general thanked him politely, but positively declined to make any additions to his personal comfort, except to light a fresh cigar. Afterward, however, he consented to draw his chair nearer to the wood fire which was burning in the chimney-place, and to thrust his feet forward to give his top-boots a chance to dry. The extent of his indulgence in personal comfort in the field did not seem to be much greater than that of bluff old Marshal Suvaroff, who, when he wished to give himself over to an excess of luxury, used to go so far as to take off one spur before going to bed.

At General Grant's request, General Thomas, General William F. Smith, his chief engineer, commonly known in the army as «Baldy» Smith, and others, pointed out on a large map the various positions of the troops, and described the general situation. General Grant sat for some time as immovable as a rock and as silent as the sphinx, but listened attentively to all that was said. After a while he straightened himself up in his chair, his features assumed an air of animation, and in a tone of voice which manifested a deep interest in the discussion, he began to fire whole volleys of questions at the officers present. So intelligent were his inquiries, and so pertinent his suggestions, that he made a profound impression upon every one by the quickness of his perception and the knowledge which he had already acquired regarding important details of the army's condition. His questions showed from the outset that his mind was dwelling not only upon the prompt opening of a line of supplies, but upon taking the offensive against the enemy. In this he was only manifesting one of his chief military characteristics—an inborn dislike to be thrown upon the defensive. Even when he had to defend a position, his method of warfare was always that of the «offensive-defensive.»

After talking over a plan for communicating with our base of supplies, or, as he called it in his conversation, «opening up the cracker line,» an operation which already had been projected and for which preliminary steps had been taken, he turned to me as chief of ordnance of the Army of the Cumberland, and asked, «How much ammunition is there on hand?» I replied, «There is barely enough here to fight one day's battle, but an ample supply has been accumulated at Bridgeport to await the opening of communications.»

At about half-past nine o'clock he appeared to have finished his search after information for the time being, and turning to a table, began to write telegrams. Communication by wire had been kept open during all the siege. His first despatch was to General Halleck, the general-in-chief at Washington, and read: «Have just arrived; I will write to-morrow. Please approve order placing Sherman in command of Department of the Tennessee, with headquarters in the field.» He had scarcely begun to exercise the authority conferred upon him by his new promotion when his mind turned to securing advancement for Sherman, who had been his second in command in the Army of the Tennessee.

It was more than an hour later when he retired to bed in an adjoining room to get a much-needed rest. As he arose and walked across the floor his lameness was very perceptible. Before the company departed he had made an appointment with Generals Thomas and Smith and several staff officers to accompany him the next day to make a personal inspection of the lines. Early on the morning of the 24th the party set out from headquarters, and most of the day was spent in examining our lines and obtaining a view of the enemy's position. At Brown's Ferry General Grant dismounted and went to the river's edge on foot, and made his reconnaissance of that important part of the line in full view of the enemy's pickets on the opposite bank, but, singularly enough, he was not fired upon.

### GRANT'S MANNER OF WRITING DESPATCHES.

BEING informed that the general wished to see me that evening, I went into the room he

PHOTOGRAPH TAKEN IN THE FIELD AT CITY POINT, VA., BY H. F. WARREN, MARCH 15, 1865. THE ORIGINAL PHOTOGRAPH IS IN THE POSSESSION OF THE BOSTONIAN SOCIETY, AND HANGS IN THE MEMORIAL HALL, OLD STATE HOUSE, BOSTON, MASS.

U. S. Grant

was occupying at headquarters, and found two of his staff-officers seated near him. As I entered he gave a slight nod of the head by way of recognition, and pointing to a chair, said rather bluntly, but politely, «Sit down.» In reply to a question which he asked, I gave him some information he desired in regard to the character and location of certain heavy guns which I had recently assisted in putting in position on the advanced portion of our lines, and the kind and amount of artillery ammunition. He soon after began to write despatches, and I arose to go, but resumed my seat as he said, «Sit still.» My attention was soon attracted to the manner in which he went to work at his correspondence. At this time, as throughout his later career, he wrote nearly all his documents with his own hand, and seldom dictated to any one even the most unimportant despatch. His work was performed swiftly and uninterruptedly, but without any marked display of nervous energy. His thoughts flowed as freely from his mind as the ink from his pen; he was never at a loss for an expression, and seldom interlined a word or made a material correction. He sat with his head bent low over the table, and when he had occasion to step to another table or desk to get a paper he wanted, he would glide rapidly across the room without straightening himself, and return to his seat with his body still bent over at about the same angle at which he had been sitting when he left his chair. Upon this occasion he tossed the sheets of paper across the table as he finished them, leaving them in the wildest disorder. When he had completed the despatch, he gathered up the scattered sheets, read them over rapidly, and arranged them in their proper order. Turning to me after a time, he said, «Perhaps you might like to read what I am sending.» I thanked him, and in looking over the despatches I found that he was ordering up Sherman's entire force from Corinth to within supporting distance, and was informing Halleck of the dispositions decided upon for the opening of a line of supplies, and assuring him that everything possible would be done for the relief of Burnside in east Tennessee. Directions were also given for the taking of vigorous and comprehensive steps in every direction throughout his new and extensive command. At a late hour, after having given further directions in regard to the contemplated movement for the opening of the route from Bridgeport to Chattanooga, and in the mean time sending back to be foraged all the animals that could be spared, he bid those present a pleasant good night, and limped off to his bedroom.

I cannot dwell too forcibly on the deep impression made upon those who had come in contact for the first time with the new commander, by the exhibition they witnessed of his singular mental powers and his rare military qualities. Coming to us crowned with the laurels he had gained in the brilliant campaign of Vicksburg, we naturally expected to meet a well-equipped soldier, but hardly anybody was prepared to find one who had the grasp, the promptness of decision, and the general administrative capacity which he displayed at the very start as commander of an extensive military division, in which many complicated problems were presented for immediate solution.

I had fallen into the habit of making careful notes of everything of interest which came under my own observation, and these reminiscences are simply a transcript of memoranda of events jotted down at the time they occurred.

### OPENING «THE CRACKER LINE.»

After remaining three days as General Thomas's guest, General Grant established his headquarters in a modest-looking two-story frame-house on the bluff near the river, situated on what is now known as First street. In the evening of the 26th I spent some time in the front room on the left side of the hall, which he used as his office, and in which several members of his staff were seated with him. It was a memorable night in the history of the siege, for the troops were being put in motion for the hazardous attempt to open the river route to our base of supplies at Bridgeport. The general sat at a table, smoking, and writing despatches. After finishing several telegrams and giving some directions to his staff, he began to describe the probabilities of the chances of the expedition down the river, expressing a confident belief in its success. General W. F. Smith, who had been so closely identified with the project, was given command of the movement. At midnight he began his march down the north bank of the river with 2800 men. At three o'clock on the morning of the 27th, Hazen started silently down the stream, with his pontoons carrying 1800 men; at five he made a landing at Brown's Ferry, completely surprising the guard at that point, and taking most of them prisoners; at seven o'clock Smith's force had been ferried across, and began to fortify a strong position; and at ten a bridge had been completed. Hooker's advance, coming up from Bridgeport, arrived the next afternoon, the 28th, at Brown's Ferry. The river was now open from Bridgeport to Kelley's Ferry, and the wagon road from that point to Chattanooga by way of Brown's Ferry, about eight miles in length, was in our possession. The success of the movement had been prompt and complete, and there was now established a good line of communication with our base. This changed condition of affairs had been accomplished within five days after General Grant's arrival at the front.

As soon as the enemy recovered from his surprise, he woke up to the importance of the achievement; Longstreet was despatched to retrieve, if possible, the lost ground. His troops reached Wauhatchie in the night of the 28th, and made an attack upon Geary's division of Hooker's forces. The fight raged for about three hours, but Geary succeeded in holding his ground against greatly superior numbers. During the fight Geary's teamsters had become scared, and had deserted their teams, and the mules, stampeded by the sound of battle raging about them, had broken loose from their wagons and run away. Fortunately for their reputation and the safety of the command, they started toward the enemy, and with heads down and tails up, with trace-chains rattling and whiffletrees snapping over the stumps of trees they rushed pell-mell upon Longstreet's bewildered men. Believing it to be an impetuous charge of cavalry, his line broke and fled. The quartermaster in charge of the animals, not willing to see such distinguished services go unrewarded, sent in the following communication: «I respectfully request that the mules, for their gallantry in this action, may have conferred upon them the brevet rank of horses.» Brevets in the army were being bestowed pretty freely at the time, and when this recommendation was reported to General Grant he laughed heartily at the humor of the suggestion. Our loss in the battle, including killed, wounded, and missing, was only 422 men. The enemy never made a further attempt to interrupt our communications.

The much-needed supplies, which had been hurried forward to Bridgeport in anticipation of this movement, soon reached the army, and the rejoicing among the troops manifested itself in lively demonstrations of delight. Every man now felt that he was no longer to remain on the defensive, but was being supplied and equipped for a forward movement against his old foe, whom he had driven from the Ohio to the Cumberland, and from the Cumberland to the Tennessee.

### GRANT SALUTED BY THE ENEMY.

As soon as communication had been opened with our base of supplies, General Grant manifested an eagerness to acquaint himself minutely with the position of the enemy, with a view to taking the offensive. One morning he started toward our right, with several staff-officers, to make a personal examination of that portion of the line. When he came in sight of Chattanooga Creek, which separated our pickets from those of the enemy, he directed those who had accompanied him to halt and remain out of sight while he advanced alone, which he supposed he could do without attracting much attention. The pickets were within hailing distance of one another on opposite banks of the creek. They had established a temporary truce on their own responsibility, and the men of each army were allowed to get water from the same stream without being fired upon by those on the other side. A sentinel of our picket-guard recognized General Grant as he approached, and gave the customary cry, «Turn out the guard—commanding general!» The enemy on the opposite side of the creek evidently heard the words, and one of his sentinels cried out, «Turn out the guard—General Grant!» The confederate guard took up the joke, and promptly formed, facing our line, and presented arms. The general returned the salute by lifting his hat, the guard was then dismissed, and he continued his ride toward our left. We knew that we were engaged in a civil war, but such civility largely exceeded our expectations.

In company with General Thomas and other members of his staff, I was brought into almost daily contact with General Grant, and became intensely interested in the progress of the plans he was maturing for dealing with the enemy at all points of the theater of war lying within his command. Early in November instructions came from the Secretary of War calling me to Washington, and in accordance therewith General Thomas issued an order relieving me from duty with his army.[1]

[1] HEADQUARTERS, DEPARTMENT OF THE CUMBERLAND, CHATTANOOGA, TENN., November 5, 1863.
*General Orders, No.* 261.

1. Captain Thomas G. Baylor, ordnance corps, having, pursuant to orders from the Secretary of War, relieved Captain Horace Porter from duty at these headquarters, is announced as chief of ordnance for this army, and will at once enter upon the discharge of his duties.

The general commanding takes this occasion to express his appreciation of the valuable service rendered

I had heard through personal letters that the Secretary wished to reorganize the Ordnance Bureau at Washington, and wished my services in that connection on account of my long experience in that department in the field. The order was interpreted as a compliment, but was distasteful to me for many reasons, although I understood that the assignment was to be only temporary, and it was at a season when active operations in the field were usually suspended. It was a subject of much regret to leave General Thomas, for I had become greatly attached to him, and had acquired that respect and admiration for the character of this distinguished soldier which was felt by all who had ever come in contact with him. «Old Pap Thomas,» as we all loved to call him, was more of a father than a commander to the younger officers who served under his immediate command, and he possessed their warmest affections. He and his corps commanders now made a written appeal to General Grant, requesting him to intercede and endeavor to retain me in the command. In the evening of the 5th of November I was sent for by General Grant to come to his headquarters. On my arrival, he requested me to be seated at the opposite side of the table at which he sat smoking, offered me a cigar, and said: «I was sorry to see the order of the Secretary of War calling you to Washington. I have had some other views in mind regarding your services, and I still hope that

DRAWN BY HARRY FENN.

1. HEADQUARTERS OF GENERALS THOMAS AND ROSECRANS, CHATTANOOGA; 2, GRANT'S HEADQUARTERS AT GERMANIA FORD (AFTER A PICTURE IN «REDEEMING THE REPUBLIC,» PUBLISHED BY HARPER AND BROTHERS); 3, 4, GRANT'S HEADQUARTERS AT CHATTANOOGA—INTERIOR AND EXTERIOR.

by Captain Porter during his connection with this army. His thorough knowledge of the duties of his position, his good judgment and untiring industry, have increased the efficiency of the army, and entitle him to the thanks of the general commanding. . . . By command of Major-general George H. Thomas.

C. GODDARD, Assistant Adjutant-general.

—EDITOR.

I may be able to secure the recall of the order, and to have you assigned to duty with me, if that would be agreeable to you.» I replied eagerly, «Nothing could possibly be more agreeable, and I should feel most highly honored by such an assignment.» He went on to say, «With this step in view, I have just written a letter to the general-in-chief,» which he then handed me to read.[1]

Hardly allowing me to finish my expressions of surprise and gratification, he continued: «Of course, you will have to obey your present orders and proceed to Washington. I want you to take this letter with you, and see that it is put into the hands of General Halleck; perhaps you will soon be able to rejoin me here. My requests are not always complied with at headquarters, but I have written pretty strongly in this case, and I hope favorable action may be taken.» I replied that I would make my preparations at once to start East, and then withdrew. The next day I called to bid the general good-by, and, after taking leave of General Thomas and my comrades on the staff, set out for the capital by way of the new line of communication which had just been opened.

### GRANT'S PERSONAL APPEARANCE.

A DESCRIPTION of General Grant's personal appearance at this important period of his career may not be out of place here, particularly as up to that time the public had received such erroneous impressions of him. There were then few correct portraits of him in circulation. Some of the earliest pictures purporting to be photographs of him had been manufactured when he was at the distant front, never stopping in one place long enough to be «focused.» Nothing daunted, the practisers of that art which is the chief solace of the vain had photographed a burly beef-contractor, and spread the pictures broadcast as representing the determined, but rather robust, features of the coming hero, and it was some time before the real photographs which followed were believed to be genuine. False impressions of him were derived, too, from the fact that he had come forth from a country leather store, and was famous chiefly for striking sledge-hammer blows in the field, and conducting relentless pursuits of his foes through the swamps of the Southwest. He was pictured in the popular mind as striding about in the most approved swashbuckler style of melodrama. Many of us were not a little surprised to find in him a man of slim figure, slightly stooped, five feet eight inches in height, weighing only a hundred and thirty-five pounds, and of a modesty of mien and gentleness of manner which seemed to fit him more for the court than for the camp. His eyes were dark-gray, and were the most expressive of his features. Like nearly all men who speak little, he was a good listener; but his face gave little indication of his thoughts, and it was the expression of his eyes which furnished about the only response to the speaker who conversed with him. When he was about to say anything amusing, there was always a perceptible twinkle in his eyes before he began to speak, and he often laughed heartily at a witty remark or a humorous incident. His mouth, like Washington's, was of the letter-box shape, the contact of the lips forming a nearly horizontal line. This feature was of a pattern in striking contrast with that of Napoleon, who had a bow mouth, which looked as if it had been modeled after a front view of his cocked hat. The firmness with which the general's square-shaped jaws were set when his features were in repose was highly expressive of his force of character and the strength of his will-power. His hair and beard were of a chestnut-brown color. The beard was worn full, no part of the face being shaved, but, like the hair, was always kept closely and neatly trimmed. Like Cromwell, Lincoln, and several other great men in history, he had a wart on his cheek. In his case it was small, and located on the right side just above the line of the beard. His face was not perfectly symmetrical, the left eye being a very little lower than the right. His brow was high, broad, and rather square, and was creased with several horizontal wrinkles, which helped to emphasize the serious and somewhat careworn look which was never absent from his countenance. This expression, however, was in no wise an indication of his nature, which was always buoyant, cheerful, and hopeful. His voice was exceedingly musical, and one of the clearest in sound and most distinct in utterance that I have ever heard. It had a singular power of penetration, and sentences spoken by him in an ordinary tone in camp could be heard at a distance which was surprising. His gait in walking might have been called decidedly unmilitary. He never carried his body erect, and having no ear for music or rhythm, he never kept step to the airs played by the bands, no matter how vigorously the bass drums emphasized the accent. When walking in company there was no attempt to keep

[1] For the letter, see page 17.—EDITOR.

step with others. In conversing he usually employed only two gestures; one was the stroking of his chin beard with his left hand; the other was the raising and lowering of his right hand, and resting it at intervals upon his knee or a table, the hand being held with the fingers close together and the knuckles bent, so that the back of the hand and fingers formed a right angle. When not pressed by any matter of importance he was often slow in his movements, but when roused to activity he was quick in every motion, and worked with marvelous rapidity. He was civil to all who came in contact with him, and never attempted to snub any one, or treat anybody with less consideration on account of his inferiority in rank. With him there was none of the puppyism so often bred by power, and none of the dogmatism which Samuel Johnson characterized as puppyism grown to maturity.

### A HIGHER GRADE CREATED FOR GRANT.

WHEN I reached Washington I went at once to headquarters, and endeavored to see the commander-in-chief for the purpose of presenting General Grant's letter, but found, after two or three attempts, that it would be impossible to secure an interview. I therefore gave the letter to Colonel Kelton, his adjutant-general, who placed it in General Halleck's hands. Not only was there no action taken in regard to the request which the letter contained, but its receipt was not even acknowledged. This circumstance, with others of its kind, made it plain that General Grant would never be free to make his selection of officers, and organize his forces as he desired, until he should be made general-in-chief. Elihu B. Washburne, the member of Congress from the Galena district in Illinois, General Grant's old home, soon introduced a bill creating the grade of lieutenant-general, and it was passed by both houses of Congress, with the implied understanding that General Grant was to fill the position. The highest grade in the army theretofore created during the war had been that of major-general. The act became a law on February 26, 1864, and the nomination of General Grant was sent to the Senate by Mr. Lincoln on the 1st of March, and confirmed on the 2d. On the 3d the general was ordered to Washington. I had set to work upon my duties in the Ordnance Bureau, and in the mean time had received several very kind messages from the general regarding the chances of my returning to the field.

### GRANT'S FIRST MEETING WITH LINCOLN.

ON the evening of March 8 the President and Mrs. Lincoln gave a public reception at the White House, which I attended. The President stood in the usual reception-room, known as the «Blue Room,» with several cabinet officers near him, and shook hands cordially with everybody, as the vast procession of men and women passed in front of him. He was in evening dress, and wore a turned-down collar a size too large. The necktie was rather broad and awkwardly tied. He was more of a Hercules than an Adonis. His height of six feet four inches enabled him to look over the heads of most of his visitors. His form was ungainly, and the movements of his long, angular arms and legs bordered at times upon the grotesque. His eyes were gray and disproportionately small. His face wore a general expression of sadness, the deep lines indicating the sense of responsibility which weighed upon him; but at times his features lighted up with a broad smile, and there was a merry twinkle in his eyes as he greeted an old acquaintance and exchanged a few words with him in a tone of familiarity. He had sprung from the common people to become one of the most uncommon of men. Mrs. Lincoln occupied a position on his right. For a time she stood on a line with him and took part in the reception, but afterward stepped back and conversed with some of the wives of the cabinet officers and other personal acquaintances who were in the room. At about half-past nine o'clock a sudden commotion near the entrance to the room attracted general attention, and, upon looking in that direction, I was surprised to see General Grant walking along modestly with the rest of the crowd toward Mr. Lincoln. He had arrived from the West that evening, and had come to the White House to pay his respects to the President. He had been in Washington but once before, when he visited it for a day soon after he had left West Point. Although these two historical characters had never met before, Mr. Lincoln recognized the general at once from the pictures he had seen of him. With a face radiant with delight, he advanced rapidly two or three steps toward his distinguished visitor, and cried out: «Why, here is General Grant! Well, this is a great pleasure, I assure you,» at the same time seizing him by the hand, and shaking it for several minutes with a vigor which showed the extreme cordiality of the welcome.

The scene now presented was deeply impressive. Standing face to face for the first time were the two illustrious men whose names will always be inseparably associated in connection with the war of the rebellion. Grant's right hand grasped the lapel of his coat; his head was bent slightly forward, and his eyes upturned toward Lincoln's face. The President, who was eight inches taller, looked down with beaming countenance upon his guest. Although their appearance, their training, and their characteristics, were in striking contrast, yet the two men had many traits in common, and there were numerous points of resemblance in their remarkable careers. Each was of humble origin, and had been compelled to learn the first lessons of life in the severe school of adversity. Each had risen from the people, possessed an abiding confidence in them, and always retained a deep hold upon their affections. Each might have said to those who were inclined to sneer at his plain origin what a marshal of France, who had risen from the ranks to a dukedom, said to the hereditary nobles who attempted to snub him in Vienna: «I am an ancestor; you are only descendants.» In a great crisis of their country's history both had entered the public service from the same State. Both were conspicuous for the possession of that most uncommon of all virtues, common sense. Both despised the arts of the demagogue, and shrank from posing for effect, or indulging in mock heroics. Even when their characteristics differed, they only served to supplement each other, and to add a still greater strength to the cause for which they strove. With hearts too great for rivalry, with souls untouched by jealousy, they lived to teach the world that it is time to abandon the path of ambition when it becomes so narrow that two cannot walk it abreast.

The statesman and the soldier conversed for a few minutes, and then the President presented his distinguished guest to Mr. Seward. The Secretary of State was very demonstrative in his welcome, and after exchanging a few words, led the general to where Mrs. Lincoln was standing, and presented him to her. Mrs. Lincoln expressed much surprise and pleasure at the meeting, and she and the general chatted together very pleasantly for some minutes. The visitors had by this time become so curious to catch a sight of the general that their eagerness knew no bounds, and they became altogether unmanageable. Mr. Seward's consummate knowledge of the wiles of diplomacy now came to the rescue and saved the situation. He succeeded in struggling through the crowd with the general until they reached the large East Room where the people could circulate more freely. This, however, was only a temporary relief. The people by this time had worked themselves up to a state of uncontrollable excitement. The vast throng surged and swayed and crowded until alarm was felt for the safety of the ladies. Cries now arose of «Grant! Grant! Grant!» Then came cheer after cheer. Seward, after some persuasion, induced the general to stand upon a sofa, thinking the visitors would be satisfied with a view of him, and retire; but as soon as they caught sight of him their shouts were renewed, and a rush was made to shake his hand. The President sent word that he and the Secretary of War would await the general's return in one of the small drawing-rooms, but it was fully an hour before he was able to make his way there, and then only with the aid of several officers and ushers.

The story has been circulated that at the conference which then took place, or at the interview the next day, the President and the Secretary of War urged General Grant to make his campaign toward Richmond by the overland route, and finally persuaded him to do so, although he had set forth the superior advantages of the water route. There is not the slightest foundation for this rumor. General Grant some time after repeated to members of his staff just what had taken place, and no reference whatever was made to the choice of these two routes.

### IN COMMAND OF ALL THE ARMIES.

THE next day, March 9, the general went to the White House, by invitation of Mr. Lincoln, for the purpose of receiving his commission from the hands of the President. Upon his return to Willard's Hotel, I called to pay my respects. Curiosity led me to look at the hotel register, and the modesty of the entry upon the book, in the general's handwriting, made an impression upon me. It read simply, «U. S. Grant and son, Galena, Ill.» His eldest boy, Fred, accompanied him.

The act which created the grade of lieutenant-general authorized a personal staff, to consist of a chief of staff with the rank of brigadier-general, four aides-de-camp, and two military secretaries, each with the rank of lieutenant-colonel. In our conversation the general referred to this circumstance, and offered me one of the positions of aide-de-camp, which I said I would accept very gladly.

The next day, the 10th, he paid a visit by rail to the headquarters of the Army of the Potomac, near Brandy Station, in Virginia, about seventy miles from Washington. He returned the day after, and started the same night for Nashville, to meet Sherman and turn over to him the command of the Military Division of the Mississippi. While in Washington General Grant had been so much an object of curiosity, and had been so continually surrounded by admiring crowds when he appeared in the streets, and even in his hotel, that it had become very irksome to him. With his simplicity and total lack of personal vanity, he did not seem able to understand why he should attract so much attention. The President had given him a cordial invitation to dine that evening at the White House, but he begged to be excused for the reason that he would lose a whole day, which he could not afford at that critical period. «Besides,» he added, «I have become very tired of this show business.»

On the 12th the official order was issued placing General Grant in command of all the armies of the United States.

### INTERVIEW WITH STANTON.

I SOON learned that the Secretary of War, in spite of General Grant's request to have me assigned to his staff, wanted to insist upon my continuing my duties in the department at Washington, and I resolved to have an interview with him, and to protest against such action. The Secretary had a wide reputation for extreme brusqueness in his intercourse even with his friends, and seemed determined, as an officer once expressed it, to administer discipline totally regardless of previous acquaintance. A Frenchman once said that during the Revolution, while the guillotine was at work, he never heard the name of Robespierre that he did not take off his hat to see whether his head was still on his shoulders; some of our officers were similarly inclined when they heard the name of Stanton. However, I found the Secretary quite civil, and even patient, and, to all appearances, disposed to allow my head to continue to occupy the place where I was in the habit of wearing it. Nevertheless, the interview ended without his having yielded. I certainly received a very cold bath at his hands, and to this day I never see the impress of his unrelenting features upon a one-dollar treasury note without feeling a chill run down my back.

General Grant returned to the capital on March 23. I went to Willard's to call upon him that evening, and encountered him on the stairs leading up to the first floor. He stopped, shook hands, and greeted me with the words, «How do you do, colonel?» I replied: «I had hoped to be colonel by this time, owing to your interposition, but what I feared has been realized. Much against my wishes, the Secretary of War seems to have made up his mind to keep me here.» «I will see him to-morrow, and urge the matter in person,» answered the general. He then invited me to accompany him to his room, and in the course of a conversation which followed said that he had had Sheridan ordered east to take command of the cavalry of the Army of the Potomac.

Sheridan arrived in Washington on April 4. He had been worn down almost to a shadow by hard work and exposure in the field; he weighed only a hundred and fifteen pounds, and as his height was but five feet six inches, he looked anything but formidable as a candidate for a cavalry leader. He had met the President and the officials at the War Department that day for the first time, and it was his appearance on this occasion which gave rise to a remark made to General Grant the next time he visited the department: «The officer you brought on from the West is rather a little fellow to handle your cavalry.» To which Grant replied, «You will find him big enough for the purpose before we get through with him.»

General Grant had started for the field on the 26th of March, and established his headquarters in the little town of Culpeper Courthouse in Virginia, twelve miles north of the Rapidan. He visited Washington about once a week to confer with the President and the Secretary of War.

I continued my duties in the department at Washington till my fate should be decided, and on the 27th of April I found that the request of the general-in-chief had prevailed, and my appointment was officially announced as an aide-de-camp on his personal staff.

The afternoon of April 29 I arrived at Culpeper, and reported to him for duty. A plain brick house near the railway station had been taken for headquarters, and a number of tents had been pitched in the yard to furnish additional accommodations.

### GRANT IN A COMMUNICATIVE MOOD.

THE next morning the general called for his horse, to ride over to General Meade's headquarters, near Brandy Station, about six miles distant. He selected me as the officer who was to accompany him, and we set out together on the trip, followed by two orderlies.

He was mounted upon his large bay horse, Cincinnati, which afterward became so well known throughout the army. The animal was not called after the family of the ancient warrior who beat his sword into a plowshare, but after our modern city of that name. He was a half-brother to Asteroid and Kentucky, the famous racers, and was consequently of excellent blood. Noticing the agility with which the general flung himself into the saddle, I remarked, «I am very glad to see that your injured leg no longer disables you.» «No,» he replied; «it gives me scarcely any trouble now, although sometimes it feels a little numb.» As we rode along he began to speak of his new command, and said: «I have watched the progress of the Army of the Potomac ever since it was organized, and have been greatly interested in reading the accounts of the splendid fighting it has done. I always thought the territory covered by its operations would be the principal battle-ground of the war. When I was at Cairo, in 1861, the height of my ambition was to command a brigade of cavalry in this army. I suppose it was my fondness for horses that made me feel that I should be more at home in command of cavalry, and I thought that the Army of the Potomac would present the best field of operations for a brigade commander in that arm of the service.»

He then changed the subject to Chattanooga, and in speaking of that battle interjected into his descriptions brief criticisms upon the services and characteristics of several of the officers who had taken part in the engagement. He continued by saying: «The difficulty is in finding commanding officers possessed of sufficient breadth of view and administrative ability to confine their attention to perfecting their organizations, and giving a general supervision to their commands, instead of wasting their time upon details. For instance, there is General G——. He is a very gallant officer, but at a critical period of the battle of Chattanooga he neglected to give the necessary directions to his troops, and concentrated all his efforts upon aiming and firing some heavy guns, a service which could have been better performed by any lieutenant of artillery. I had to order him peremptorily to leave the battery and give his attention to his troops.»

He then spoke of his experiences with Mr. Lincoln, and the very favorable impression the President had made upon him. He said: «In the first interview I had with the President, when no others were present, and he could talk freely, he told me that he did not pretend to know anything about the handling of troops, and it was with the greatest reluctance that he ever interfered with the movements of army commanders: but he had common sense enough to know that celerity was absolutely necessary; that while armies were sitting down waiting for opportunities to turn up which might, perhaps, be more favorable from a strictly military point of view, the government was spending millions of dollars every day; that there was a limit to the sinews of war, and a time might be reached when the spirits and resources of the people would become exhausted. He had always contended that these considerations should be taken into account, as well as purely military questions, and that he adopted the plan of issuing his ‹executive orders› principally for the purpose of hurrying the movements of commanding generals; but that he believed I knew the value of minutes, and that he was not going to interfere with my operations. He said, further, that he did not want to know my plans; that it was, perhaps, better that he should not know them, for everybody he met was trying to find out from him something about the contemplated movements, and there was always a temptation ‹to leak.› I have not communicated my plans to him or to the Secretary of War. The only suggestion the President made—and it was merely a suggestion, not a definite plan—was entirely impracticable, and it was not again referred to in our conversations. He told me in our first private interview a most amusing anecdote regarding a delegation of ‹cross-roads wiseacres,› as he called them, who came to see him one day to criticize my conduct in paroling Pemberton's army after the surrender at Vicksburg, who insisted that the men would violate their paroles, and in less than a month confront me anew in the field, and have to be whipped all over again. Said Mr. Lincoln: ‹I thought the best way to get rid of them was to tell them the story of Sykes's dog. «Have you ever heard about Sykes's yellow dog?» said I to the spokesman of the delegation. He said he had n't. «Well, I must tell you about him,» said I. «Sykes had a yellow dog he set great store by, but there were a lot of small boys around the village, and that 's always a bad thing for dogs, you know. These boys did n't share Sykes's views, and they were not disposed to let the dog have a fair show. Even Sykes had to admit that the dog was getting unpopular; in fact, it was soon seen that a prejudice was growing up against that dog that threatened to wreck all his future prospects in life. The boys, after meditating how they could get the best of him, finally fixed up a cartridge with a long fuse, put the cartridge in a piece of meat, dropped the meat in the road in front of Sykes's door, and then perched themselves on a fence a good distance off, holding the end of the fuse in their hands. Then they whistled for the dog. When he came out he scented the bait, and bolted the meat, cartridge and all. The boys touched off the fuse with a cigar, and in about a second a report came from that dog that sounded like a clap of thunder. Sykes came bouncing out of the house, and yelled, ‹What 's up! Anything busted?› There was no reply, except a snicker from the small boys roosting on the fence; but as Sykes looked up he saw the whole air filled with pieces of yellow dog. He picked up the biggest piece he could find, a portion of the back with a part of the tail still hanging to it, and after turning it round and looking it all over, he said, ‹Well, I guess he 'll never be much account again—as a dog.› And I guess Pemberton's forces will never be much account again—as an army.» The delegation began looking around for their hats before I had quite got to the end of the story, and I was never bothered any more after that about superseding the commander of the Army of the Tennessee.›»

The general related this anecdote with more animation than he usually displayed, and with the manifestation of a keen sense of the humorous, and remarked afterward, «But no one who does not possess the President's unequaled powers of mimicry can pretend to convey an idea of the amusing manner in which he told the story.»

This characteristic illustration employed by the President was used afterward in a garbled form by writers, in an attempt to apply it to other events. I give the original version.

### AT GENERAL MEADE'S HEADQUARTERS.

When we reached General Meade's camp, that officer, who was sitting in his quarters, came out and greeted the general-in-chief warmly, shaking hands with him before he dismounted. General Meade was then forty-nine years of age, of rather a spare figure, and graceful in his movements. He had a full beard, which, like his hair, was brown, slightly tinged with gray. He wore a slouched felt hat with a conical crown and a turned-down rim, which gave him a sort of Tyrolese appearance. The two commanders entered Meade's quarters, sat down, lighted their cigars, and held a long interview regarding the approaching campaign. I now learned that, two days before, the time had been definitely named at which the opening campaign was to begin, and that on the next Wednesday, May 4, the armies were to move. Meade, in speaking of his troops, always referred to them as «my people.» During this visit I had an opportunity to meet a number of old acquaintances whom I had not seen since I served with the Army of the Potomac on General McClellan's staff two years before. After the interview had ended I returned with the general to headquarters, riding at a brisk trot. His conversation now turned upon the commander of the Army of the Potomac, in the course of which he remarked: «I had never met General Meade since the Mexican war until I visited his headquarters when I came East last month. In my first interview with him he talked in a manner which led me to form a very high opinion of him. He referred to the changes which were taking place, and said it had occurred to him that I might want to make a change in the commander of the Army of the Potomac, and to put in his place Sherman or some other officer who had served with me in the West, and urged me not to hesitate on his account if I desired to make such an assignment. He added that the success of the cause was much more important than any consideration for the feelings of an individual. He spoke so patriotically and unselfishly that even if I had had any intention of relieving him, I should have been inclined to change my mind after the manly attitude he assumed in this frank interview.»

This was the first long personal talk I had with the general-in-chief, as our intercourse heretofore had been only of an official character, and the exhibition of the remarkable power he possessed as a conversationalist was a revelation. I began to learn that his reputed reticence did not extend to his private intercourse, and that he had the ability to impart a peculiar charm to almost any topic.

That evening a large correspondence was conducted in relation to the final preparations for the coming movements.

### GRANT'S NARROW ESCAPE FROM CAPTURE.

A few days before, an occurrence had happened which came very near depriving the armies of the services of General Grant in the Virginia campaign. On his return to headquarters after his last visit to the President in Washington, when his special train reached Warrenton Junction he saw a large cloud of dust to the east of the road. Upon making inquiries of the station master as to its cause, he learned that Colonel Mosby, who commanded a partizan Confederate force, called by his own people Mosby's «conglomerates,» and who had become famous for his cavalry raids, had just passed, driving a detachment of our cavalry before him. If the train had been a few minutes earlier, Mosby, like Christopher Columbus upon his voyage to this country, would have discovered something which he was not looking for. As the train carried no guard, it would not have been possible to make any defense. In such case the Union commander would have reached Richmond a year sooner than he finally arrived there, but not at the head of an army.

### HIS ENORMOUS RESPONSIBILITY.

GENERAL GRANT now held a command the magnitude of which has seldom been equaled in history. His troops consisted of twenty-one army-corps, and the territory covered by the field of operations embraced eighteen military departments, besides the region held by the Army of the Potomac, which had never been organized into a department. The total number of troops under his command, «present for duty, equipped,» was 533,000. In all purely military questions his will was at this time almost supreme, and his authority was usually unquestioned. He occupied the most conspicuous position in the nation, not excepting that of the President himself, and the eyes of all the loyal people in the land were turned to him appealingly as the one man upon whom their hopes were centered and in whom their chief faith reposed. The responsibilities imposed were commensurate with the magnitude of the undertaking which had been confided to him. While commanding all the armies of the nation, he had wisely decided to establish his headquarters with the Army of the Potomac, and give his immediate supervision to the operations of that force and the troops which were intended to coöperate with it in the State of Virginia. Telegraphic communication was then open with nearly all the armies.

### GRANT'S PERSONAL STAFF.

THE staff consisted of twelve officers only, and was not larger than that of some division commanders. The chief of staff was Brigadier-general John A. Rawlins. When the war broke out he was a practising lawyer in Galena, Illinois, and had gained some prominence in politics as a Democrat. After the firing upon Fort Sumter a public meeting was held in Galena, and Captain Grant being an ex-army officer, was called upon to preside. Rawlins attended the meeting, and made a stirring and effective speech, declaring it to be the duty of all good citizens to sink their political predilections, and urging them to pledge themselves to the support of the Union and the enforcement of the laws. General Grant was much impressed with the vigor and logic of the address, and when he was afterward assigned to the command of a brigade, he appointed Rawlins on his staff. He was at first aide-de-camp, afterward assistant adjutant-general, and finally chief of staff. The general had a high regard for him officially, and was warmly attached to him personally. Rawlins in his youth had worked on a farm, and assisted his father in burning charcoal, obtaining what education he could acquire at odd times in the district school and at a neighboring seminary. He was frank, honest, and resolute, and loyally devoted to his chief. He always had the courage of his convictions, and was capable of stating them with great force. He was plain and simple in manner, of a genial disposition, and popular with all the other members of the staff. He had never served in a military organization, nor made a study of the art of war; but he possessed natural executive ability of a high order, and developed qualities which made him exceedingly useful to his chief and to the service.

The rest of the staff consisted of the following officers:

Lieutenant-colonel C. B. Comstock, aide-de-camp, an officer of the United States corps of engineers, with a well-deserved reputation for scientific attainments, who had shown great efficiency while serving with General Grant in the Vicksburg campaign.

Lieutenant-colonel Horace Porter, aide-de-camp.

Lieutenant-colonel O. E. Babcock, aide-de-camp, an accomplished officer of engineers, who had gained an excellent reputation in several campaigns, in which he had been conspicuous for his good judgment and great personal courage.

Lieutenant-colonel F. T. Dent, aide-de-camp, a classmate of General Grant, and brother of Mrs. Grant. He had served with credit in the Mexican war, and in Scott's advance upon the city of Mexico had been severely wounded, and was twice promoted for gallant and meritorious conduct in battle.

The four officers just named were of the regular army, and were graduates of the West Point Military Academy.

Lieutenant-colonel Adam Badeau, military secretary, who had first gone to the field as a newspaper correspondent, and was afterward made an aide-de-camp to General W. T. Sherman. He was badly wounded in the foot at Port Hudson, and when convalescent was assigned to the staff of General Grant. He had had a good training in literature, and was an accomplished writer and scholar.

Lieutenant-colonel William R. Rowley, military secretary, was also from Galena. He entered an Illinois regiment as a lieutenant, and after the battle of Donelson was made a captain and aide-de-camp to General Grant. His gallant conduct at Shiloh, where he greatly distinguished himself, commended him still more highly to his commander. He resigned August 30, 1864, and was succeeded by Captain Parker.

Lieutenant-colonel T. S. Bowers, assistant adjutant-general, was a young editor of a country newspaper in Illinois when hostilities began. He raised a company of volunteers for the Forty-eighth Illinois Infantry, but declined the captaincy, and fought in the ranks. He was detailed as a clerical assistant at General Grant's headquarters in the Donelson campaign, and was soon made a lieutenant, and afterward a captain and aide-de-camp. His services in all the subsequent campaigns were highly appreciated by his chief.

Lieutenant-colonel W. L. Duff had been for a time acting chief of artillery under General Grant in the West, and was now assigned to duty as assistant inspector-general.

Captain Ely S. Parker, assistant adjutant-general, who was a full-blooded Indian, a grand nephew of the famous Red Jacket, and reigning chief of the tribes known as the Six Nations. His Indian name was Donehogawa. Colonel Parker had received a good education, and was a civil engineer employed upon the United States government building in Galena at the breaking out of the war. He commended himself to General Grant by his conduct in the Vicksburg campaign, and was there placed on his staff, and served in the adjutant-general's department.

Captain Peter T. Hudson, a volunteer officer from the State of Iowa, had served with the general in the West, and was retained as an aide-de-camp.

Lieutenant William McKee Dunn, jr., a beardless boy of nineteen, was assigned as an acting aide-de-camp to General Rawlins, but performed general staff duty at headquarters, and under many trying circumstances proved himself as cool and gallant as the most experienced veteran.

All the members of the staff had had abundant experience in the field, and were young, active, and ready for any kind of hard work.

(To be continued.)

*Horace Porter.*

## SANTO DOMINGO.

AFTER long days of angry sea and sky,
The magic isle rose up from out the blue
Like a mirage, vague, dimly seen at first,
At first seen dimly through the mist; and then—
Groves of acacia; slender, leaning stems
Of palm-trees weighted with their starry fronds;
Airs that, at dawn, had from their slumber risen
In bowers of spices; between shelving banks,
A river through whose limpid crystal gleamed,
Four fathoms down, the silvery, rippled sand;
Upon the bluff a square red tower, and roofs
Of cocoa fiber lost among the boughs;
Hard by, a fort with crumbled parapet.
These took the fancy captive ere we reached
The longed-for shores; then swiftly in our thought
We left behind us the New World, and trod
The Old, and in a sudden vision saw
Columbus wandering from court to court,
A mendicant, with kingdoms in his hands.

*Thomas Bailey Aldrich.*

# WHY THE CONFEDERACY FAILED.

## THE EXCESSIVE ISSUE OF PAPER MONEY—THE POLICY OF DISPERSION—THE NEGLECT OF THE CAVALRY.

BY THE SON OF A CONFEDERATE OFFICER.

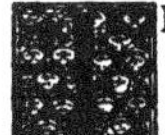

IF a person be asked the question, «Why did the seceding States fail to win independence in the war of 1861–65?» the chances are that he will give one of two answers. It is likely that he will say that it was never *intended* that they should win; that America was designed by almighty Providence for one great nation; that it is not divided by interior seas and other natural boundaries, but is essentially *one* country; and that any effort to divide it, not being a good cause, must fail. If he does not give such an answer as this, it is probable that he will say—especially if he is a Southerner—that the South was overpowered by the superior numbers and resources of the North.

Now, the first of these answers is not satisfying. Whatever happens is intended to happen. If the Southern States had succeeded in their effort to separate from the North and to set up a government for themselves, it could have been said with equal truth that it was intended to be so. As to the *oneness* of the country, Canada and Mexico are also a part of this one country; for hundreds of miles they are separated from it by imaginary lines only.

As to the other answer, all history teaches that in a war for independence superiority in numbers does not count. For instance, the little republic of Switzerland, surrounded by kingdoms and empires in arms, won its independence upward of six hundred years ago, and is independent to-day, yet it has, and has always had, only an army of militia. The little principality of Montenegro has been fighting the Turks since the fall of Constantinople, even before the discovery of America. The Dutch republic, and Scotland under Wallace and Bruce, and Prussia under Frederick II in the Seven Years' War, and America in the Revolution, all succeeded with greater odds of numbers against them than were opposed to the seceding States. And to-day Cuba, with only a million and a half of population, seems to be successfully fighting Spain with nearly twenty millions. No; in a war for independence numbers do not count, and it has not often happened in the history of the world that a people who have fought with such desperate valor as the Confederates displayed have failed to win independence.

As to material resources, there is no region under the sun more blessed in natural resources for waging war than the territory formed by the eleven seceding States. Within their own borders was to be found everything necessary for arming, equipping, feeding, and clothing their armies. The history of the industrial development of the South during the war has never yet been written. It is even more wonderful than that of its armies in the field, and is the most striking proof of that versatility and ingenuity which are peculiar to the American people. Before the war it was purely an agricultural people; there were no shipyards, dockyards, factories, or machine-shops to speak of. Within a few months after hostilities began these farmers and planters were building ironclads, marine boilers and engines, and torpedoes and torpedo-boats, and founding cannon and shells, and manufacturing muskets and rifles. When Sumter was fired upon there was not a powder factory in all the land. Soon almost every village had its piles of refuse for making saltpeter, and before the war ended the factories in Georgia and North Carolina could have supplied all the armies in the field with gunpowder. Cotton factories had also been built, and were all at work making cloth for the soldiers; and there was plenty of food in the South, though the soldiers failed to get their share of it, for corn had taken the place of cotton in the fields, and there was an abundance of cattle and hogs. In the last year of the war Sherman's army marched through the South, not starving, like Lee's men in the trenches before Petersburg, but living upon the fat of the land. No; there was no lack of men and warlike resources in the South; the causes of failure must be looked for elsewhere.

A few have intimated that the cause of failure was that the hearts of the Southern people were not really in the war, and therefore they did not persevere and support the government as they otherwise would have done. There was never a greater slander cast upon a brave people. It was the people's war. The party for the Union disappeared when the conflict began. The people proved that their hearts were in the struggle by their sacrifices and sufferings. And if further proof were necessary, their conduct toward the survivors of the Confederate army, and the dead of the lost cause, would be sufficient.

Then, if the South had the men and the warlike resources, and they were in earnest, how came it to pass that, unlike other brave peoples, they failed to win independence? How came their efforts to be so misdirected?

Three principal causes contributed to the fall of the Confederacy: (1) the excessive issue of paper money, (2) the policy of dispersion, and (3) the neglect of the cavalry.

1. The Confederate government was smothered and strangled to death with its own irredeemable paper money.

It has been proved beyond shadow of doubt and cavil that war cannot be waged with paper money. Our forefathers proved it in the war of the Revolution, and had not the French and the Dutch come to their rescue with real money, the American government, with its continental bills, would have been strangled like the Confederacy, and would likewise have «died a-borning.» However well or ill paper bills may answer for money in time of peace, in time of war they will not do. The «sinews of war» mean specie, and nothing but specie. And to get specie, and those things which specie will buy, there must be taxes, taxes, and taxes. A people who are unwilling to be taxed have no business to engage in war. The Southern people knew that war meant taxes, and they were willing to be taxed to carry on the war. The sacrifices they made, the eagerness with which they loaned their money to the government, bought its bonds, and took its paper money, showed that they were willing to be taxed.

But the Southern people were not fighting for independence only; they were contending as well for a certain theory of government. In order to be consistent with this theory, it was necessary for their leaders, in framing a constitution, to render it unlawful for the government to tax the lands and goods of the people except under conditions which made all taxation of property by the general government impossible. According to this theory, a government might lawfully order a man to shoulder his gun and march to the front to be shot at with cannon and rifle, but could not levy a tax upon his property to feed and clothe him while fighting for his country. The ports of the Confederacy were all blockaded, so there was really nothing that the government could do to raise money except issue bonds and paper bills. Of these, before the war ended, between one and two thousand millions of dollars—nominal value—had been emitted, the paper bills amounting to nearly one billion, or over one half of the whole. Nor does this include the millions of paper bills issued by state authority and by banks, of which it would be hard to give even an approximate estimate. During the same time, to the end of 1864, there was raised by taxation the pitiful sum of *forty-eight millions of dollars*, and that all paper money. It too might just as well have been printed, for the cost of collection would then have been saved. What more need be said to show why the Confederacy failed?

Ah, those beautiful paper bills, so nice and clean and pretty, but every one as deadly a foe to the South as an armed enemy! And how the people ran to get them! And how those printing-presses rumbled, all printing paper money! They shook the earth, and almost drowned the noise of the cannon wheels rolling to the front. A Southerner should hate the sight of one of those paper bills. Every one of them represents blood fruitlessly spilled, treasure wasted, and hopes blasted.

But in the beginning of the struggle no one seemed to suspect an enemy in that beautiful money. The government, at least, acted upon the theory that all it had to do to raise money was to print it. They did not seem to realize that, being the largest purchaser in the market, it was necessary for the government to keep down prices as much as possible; that every issue of bills must inevitably raise prices and render a new issue necessary; that every rise in prices must be followed by a new issue, until the bubble must collapse of its own expansion and redundancy.

At last the lesson was learned that a printing-press cannot take the place of a tax-collector in providing the sinews of war, but it was then too late; the giant was already prostrate and helpless. When it had come to pass that the armies were starving and freezing in camps and trenches, the government having not the means to buy them food and clothing or pay for their transportation, when it had come to pass that the War Department was compelled to pay a thousand of its paper dollars for a pair of army boots, when it had come to pass that a month's pay of a soldier would not buy him a single ration of bread and meat, the lesson was then learned; but it was too late. In the last gasp of the struggle the government attempted to abandon and throw off its make-believe money; but it was already buried, smothering and strangling under an avalanche, a mountain, of paper dollars.

2. The policy of dispersion.

The frontiers of the Confederacy extended over many thousands of miles. The policy which the government adopted in the beginning of the war, and upheld to the end, was that every foot of that frontier must be defended. To this end, the whole Confederacy was divided into military districts, and to each general there was given «a definite geographical command,» as the President of the Confederacy himself stated it. So the defense of the Confederacy was made purely a question of geography. Each general of a district was expected to drive back all enemies crossing his frontier, without much regard to what was going on in the other districts.

The better to carry out this idea, the capital itself was removed from Montgomery in the interior to Richmond near the frontier, «where it was expected that most of the fighting would take place.» And the defense of the shallow North Carolina sounds in the rear of Richmond was deemed of more importance than that of the passes of the Appalachians.

A policy more fatal to success could not have been adopted. The armies of the Confederacy were wrecked and wasted in the vain effort to defend its capital and the extended, indefensible frontier. Every great pitched battle of the war, unless Chickamauga be an exception, was fought within a day's march of the frontier, or of navigable water, which was in effect the frontier, because the Federals with their gunboats held all the navigable waters. Wherever the Federals chose to throw down the gauntlet of battle, the Confederates immediately picked it up. The fighting was glorious, magnificent: there has never been any better fighting in all the history of the world. But the Federals were always well fed and clothed, and never lacked for ammunition and army supplies, because the Confederates were willing to do the fighting almost within gunshot of the Federal gunboats and transports.

And so the great advantage which the Confederates could have had in the contest —that of «fighting from a center»—was deliberately thrown away. It never seemed to occur to those in authority that the battles for the Confederacy should be fought not upon the tidal waters of Virginia or upon the banks of the Mississippi—«that great inland sea»—and its navigable tributaries, but with concentrated armies on the flanks of the Appalachians.

When Bragg was sent through Cumberland Gap to occupy eastern Kentucky, the purpose was not to change the seat of war, but to make a «diversion,» to «relieve the pressure on the Mississippi.» But what could poor Bragg do, invading the rich and powerful North with his little army of thirty thousand men? And yet he has been blamed because he did not capture Cincinnati. He did very well, considering his opportunities. Even while Bragg was making his «diversion,» twice as many men as he had in all his army were scattered in garrisons along the Gulf coast, absolutely doing nothing. But the frontiers must be defended, and the capital too, if it took the last drop of Confederate blood! Such was the policy of dispersion.

A lesson might have been learned from the war of the Revolution; for in that war the capital of the country was changed no fewer than nine times, and the British armies marched from one end of the thirteen colonies to the other; yet America was not conquered: or from that greatest defensive war of ancient or modern times, wherein Frederick II of Prussia maintained the independence of his country against combined continental Europe. With the Austrian armies in his front, the French on his flanks, and the Russians and the Swedes pillaging his capital in his rear, not a battalion of his army would he risk merely to hold territory. For six of these seven bloody years he did not even see his capital. «Let the frontiers and the capital take care of themselves. The heart of Prussia is her army!» And so, attacking and retreating, marching and countermarching, delivering terrible blows whenever he could strike to advantage, always keeping his men together and preventing his enemies from concentrating, he fought on, furiously, desperately, until the fortune of war changed and the last foe was driven from his country. For himself he won the well-deserved title of «the Great.» Prussia he saved from the fate of Poland, and for all succeeding ages he showed how a defensive war against superior numbers ought to be fought. Such were the results of the policy of concentration.

It would have been better for the Confederacy if the government had thought that the «heart of the Confederacy was her army»: for territory may be abandoned and yet reoccupied, and a city may fall and yet be recaptured, but an army once lost is gone forever, a soldier once dead cannot be brought back to life. According to the policy of dispersion, however, it was not the army that was to be protected, but the territory and capital of the Confederacy. And so fifteen thousand men were lost at Fort Donelson in the effort to defend the frontier of Tennessee; thirty-two thousand men were lost at Vicksburg in the effort to defend the frontier of Mississippi; and thousands of brave men, untold and unnumbered, were lost in those terrible battles to defend Richmond, which was of no more value to the Confederacy than Norfolk or any other city upon tide-water. If every city upon the seaboard had been evacuated at the beginning of the war, the Confederates would have been the stronger and the Federals the weaker just to the extent of the garrisons which were necessary to hold them. In the war of the Revolution the British occupied every seaport from Maine to the Florida line; the only effect of it was to relieve the Americans of the trouble and expense of defending them.

From first to last the armies of the Confederacy were never concentrated. Of the six hundred thousand men in arms, there were never got together on a single battlefield more than seventy thousand available men. The scattered armies wasted away, were destroyed and captured piecemeal, trying to defend the frontiers; so that when Sherman was ready to march into the interior through Georgia and the Carolinas, there was no army to oppose him, and there were no frontiers to defend. The cause of the Confederacy was already lost. Such were the results of the policy of dispersion.

3. The neglect of the cavalry.

It is a fact worthy of remembrance, that all the greatest generals of ancient and modern times have put their greatest faith in their cavalry. It was his superb cavalry, and not the Macedonian phalanx, with which Alexander charged the Persian center at Arbela, and won the crown of Asia. It was Hannibal's Numidian horse which slaughtered those eighty thousand Romans at Cannæ, and carried the war to the very gates of Rome. It was Napoleon's powerful cavalry reserve at Austerlitz that enabled him to finish off that great victory with the capture of forty-three thousand Russian and Austrian prisoners, and a hundred pieces of artillery. And it is undoubtedly true, as the great captain himself stated, that his success at Dresden did not avail to save his throne, because the horses with which he had conquered Europe had perished in the snows of the Russian steppes.

The Prussians are the greatest soldiers of modern times, and they have never made the mistake of underrating cavalry. It was Blücher's terrible cavalry which changed the drawn battle of Waterloo into that dreadful rout, and which all that awful night after Waterloo pursued the flying French until, when the next day broke, of all those with whom Napoleon marched out to fight there was not an organized body remaining, except Grouchy's detached command. And in her last war it was the Prussian uhlans that made Germany's great victories so effective, and made possible Sedan with its two hundred thousand prisoners.

And so it has come to be considered an axiom that, however authorities may differ as to the relative value of the different arms of the service in battle, no great, decisive victory can be won without sufficient cavalry to press the pursuit; that the fruits of victory cannot be gathered, the harvest cannot be reaped, without sufficient fresh men on horseback to pursue the retreating enemy.

It might be expected that, as the Southerners were natural-born horsemen, «cavaliers from the cradle,» the mounted arm of the service would have been the strongest and the most valued and cherished; but strange as it seems, the contrary, the very contradictory, of that was true. From the beginning the cavalry was relatively the weakest, was underrated and neglected, and even ridiculed and derided. In jocularity rewards were offered for «a dead man with spurs on,» such a poor opinion had they of a soldier on horseback.

At the first great battle of the war, on the plateau of Manassas, the mounted men did not even fight as an organized body, but were divided, detailed, and attached two companies to each brigade, in imitation, perhaps, of the old Roman legion, a method of arranging cavalry in battle which was abandoned before the Christian era. And yet Johnston has been blamed because he did not capture the Federal army and the city of Washington too. And at all times after that the little band of horsemen never seemed to be considered as a constituent part of the fighting army. Nearly always they were separated from it on detached duty. At Gettysburg the Confederate cavalry was miles away when the battle began. They were not a factor in the great fight until the last day. If Lee had won, and had captured the heights of Gettysburg, it could not have been in effect more than a drawn battle, because he had not sufficient cavalry with which to press the pursuit.

And so, from the beginning to the end, either because the government could not learn the value of mounted troops, or was incapable of changing a policy once adopted, or for some inexplicable reason, the cavalry was underrated and neglected. The excuse cannot be offered that there were not sufficient horses in the Confederacy. A glance at the census of 1860 will show one that there were horses enough in Texas, or Georgia and North Carolina, to have mounted all the Confederate armies in the field, leaving enough to make the crops; and surely, if the government may lawfully «conscript» a man into the army, his horse or his neighbor's horse may also be conscripted. Almost at the very time when the general of the Army of Tennessee was begging for horses to draw his cannon, a Federal army was capturing nearly two thousand horses from the farmers in the valley of Virginia.

Nor can the excuse be made that «the country in which the armies generally operated was so densely wooded, broken, and difficult that cavalry could not be used to advantage»—by «cavalry» meaning not only those who usually fought on horseback, cavalry properly speaking, but all mounted troops. This was not true even in the war of the Revolution, when there were no roads at all, and nothing but grass to feed the horses. The little army with which Greene retreated so skilfully before Cornwallis along the Piedmont was nearly all cavalry, and Shelby's «back mountain men,» some of them even from Tennessee beyond the Alleghanies, who rode over the Blue Ridge to fall upon Ferguson at King's Mountain, were all mounted men, and Ferguson's army was captured to the last man.

The splendid work which Forrest did in the West was sufficient to show what might have been done had the cavalry branch of the Confederate service been organized. But neither Forrest nor his services were valued at their worth. For a time he was even removed from his command, and at all times he was left to shift for himself, to provide horses, arms, and equipments for his men.

If the country was too difficult for cavalry operations, how came it that the very men whom Jackson, in 1862, led victorious and triumphant up and down the valley of the Shenandoah—how came it that these same men, in 1864, when once defeated, were to be seen throwing away their guns and haversacks, and fleeing for their lives to the woods and the mountains? It was not all Early's fault. It was «Sheridan's terrible cavalry» that did it, as Early said. For the Federal government had at last learned what could be done with men on horseback. And so Sheridan was sent to join Grant, and Appomattox speedily followed.

Who can doubt, then, that if Lee had been provided with a reserve of twenty thousand fresh cavalry, under such a leader as Forrest, at Gaines's Mill, or the second Manassas, or Chancellorsville, the Army of the Potomac would not have survived to fight another battle? For, unless Sheridan be excepted, there was no cavalry general on either side in the war who could equal Forrest in the pursuit of a defeated army. Lord Wolseley has said, in his sketch of Forrest, that «Forrest's sixty-mile pursuit of Sturgis after their battle was a most remarkable achievement, and well worth attention by military students.»

But no; it was not to be. Perhaps, as has been said, it was not «intended» to be. A fatality seemed to attend the cause. At these battles, yes, and at Shiloh, at Chickamauga, at Malvern Hill, and at Fredericksburg, which are claimed as great victories for the Confederacy, what was the gain? A Federal army destroyed or captured? No. One hundred pieces of artillery, with ammunition and equipments, taken? No. Then what? The field of battle! «The Confederates fought gloriously, and won the field of battle!» And that was all they ever won with all their fighting. Always, on the next day, or at least within a few days afterward, the Federal army which they had defeated so «gloriously» was to be found drawn up in line of battle, and all the fighting had to be done over again. And so it was even to the end. The Confederates won many bloody fields of battle, thickly strewn with the bodies of their own dead and wounded as well as with those of their enemies, but from first to last they never gained a great victory, and the reason was because they were weak in cavalry.

But it is asked, «What doth it profit us to inquire into this? Anybody can criticize. Hindsights are better than foresights. It is not so easy to do as to know what had been good to do. Wherefore, then, seek to know why the Confederacy failed?»

All of which is very true. The study of the past would be profitless if it were indulged in only for the pleasure of finding fault. But we must keep in mind that it is history only that can furnish us a guide to the future, and that it is only by the study of the mistakes and successes of others who have gone before us that we can know how we should act under like circumstances.

Is not, then, the first cause of the failure of the Confederacy brought immediately home to us when we remember that the provision of the Confederate constitution which made it impossible for that government to raise money by taxation of property *was copied word for word from the Constitution of the United States* under which we are living to-day? In case of a war with a great naval power the United States would be just as helpless to raise money necessary to wage war, except by issuing bonds and paper bills, as was the Confederacy when its ports were blockaded from Norfolk to Galveston. For it is very certain that the sinews of war cannot be raised by a tax upon whisky, tobacco, and oleomargarine. It is property that must bear the brunt of war, and that is the first lesson that we may learn from the failure of the Confederacy.

No doubt the United States are strong enough to defend themselves, even though our generals should adopt a «policy of dispersion,» but surely we can learn another lesson from the failure of the Confederacy.

The Confederate leaders were educated at West Point. Was it not at West Point that they learned to depreciate the cavalry? Is it not the tradition, the fashion to-day, at West Point to underrate the cavalry? Are not the «honor men,» the «distinguished men of the class,» assigned to the engineers and artillery, while the dullards go to the cavalry?

Discussing the possibilities of a war with England, and the strength of the United States militia or national guard, some of our newspapers lately boasted that an army of a hundred thousand men could be thrown into Canada within a few weeks. How many of these men would be mounted on horseback? It is a very pertinent inquiry, for it requires from three to six months' training to make a cavalryman, and some of the States which furnish large contingents to the national guard have not a single troop of horse. If there is any lesson that the failure of the Confederacy can teach us, it is this: that an invasion of Canada—and I do not mean that such a thing is in the least probable or desirable—made without sufficient cavalry would be as barren of permanent results as it would be if made with an army of crossbowmen.

*Duncan Rose.*

## THE HEROIC AGE.

HE speaks not well who doth his time deplore,
Naming it new and little and obscure,
Ignoble, and unfit for lofty deeds.
All times were modern in the time of them,
And this no more than others. Do thy part
Here in the living day, as did the great
Who made old days immortal! So shall men,
Far-gazing back to this receding hour,
Say: «Then the time when men were truly men:
Though wars grew less, their spirits met the test
Of new conditions: conquering civic wrong;
Saving the state anew by virtuous lives;
Defying leaguèd fraud with single truth,
Not fearing loss, and daring to be pure.
When error through the land raged like a pest,
They calmed the madness caught from mind to mind,
By wisdom drawn from eld, and counsel sane;
And as the martyrs of the ancient world
Gave Death for man, so nobly gave they Life:
Those the great days, and that the heroic age.»

*G.*

# THE OLYMPIC GAMES OF 1896.

BY THEIR FOUNDER, BARON PIERRE DE COUBERTIN, NOW PRESIDENT OF THE INTERNATIONAL COMMITTEE.

WITH PICTURES BY A. CASTAIGNE.

THE Olympic games which recently took place at Athens were modern in character, not alone because of their programs, which substituted bicycle for chariot races, and fencing for the brutalities of pugilism, but because in their origin and regulations they were international and universal, and consequently adapted to the conditions in which athletics have developed at the present day. The ancient games had an exclusively Hellenic character; they were always held in the same place, and Greek blood was a necessary condition of admission to them. It is true that strangers were in time tolerated; but their presence at Olympia was rather a tribute paid to the superiority of Greek civilization than a right exercised in the name of racial equality. With the modern games it is quite otherwise. Their creation is the work of «barbarians.» It is due to the delegates of the athletic associations of all countries assembled in congress at Paris in 1894. It was there agreed that every country should celebrate the Olympic games in turn. The first place belonged by right to Greece; it was accorded by unanimous vote; and in order to emphasize the permanence of the institution, its wide bearings, and its essentially cosmopolitan character, an international committee was appointed, the members of which were to represent the various nations, European and American, with whom athletics are held in honor. The presidency of this committee falls to the country in which the next games are to be held. A Greek, M. Bikelas, has presided for the last two years. A Frenchman now presides, and will continue to do so until 1900, since the next games are to take place at Paris during the Exposition. Where will those of 1904 take place? Perhaps at New York, perhaps at Berlin, or at Stockholm. The question is soon to be decided.

It was in virtue of these resolutions passed during the Paris Congress that the recent festivals were organized. Their successful issue is largely owing to the active and energetic coöperation of the Greek crown prince Constantine. When they realized all that was expected of them, the Athenians lost courage. They felt that the city's resources were not equal to the demands that would be made upon them; nor would the government (M. Tricoupis being then prime minister) consent to increase facilities. M. Tricoupis did not believe in the success of the games. He argued that the Athenians knew nothing about athletics; that they had neither the adequate grounds for the contests, nor athletes of their own to bring into line; and that, moreover, the financial situation of Greece forbade her inviting the world to an event preparations for which would entail such large expenditures. There was reason in these objections; but on the one hand, the prime minister greatly exaggerated the importance of the expenditures, and on the other, it was not necessary that the government should bear the burden of them directly. Modern Athens, which recalls in so many ways the Athens of ancient days, has inherited from her the privilege of being beautified and enriched by her children. The public treasury was not always very well filled in those times any more than in the present, but wealthy citizens who had made fortunes at a distance liked to crown their commercial career by some act of liberality to the mother-country. They endowed the land with superb edifices of general utility—theaters, gymnasia, temples. The modern city is likewise full of monuments which she owes to such generosity. It was easy to obtain from private individuals what the state could not give. The Olympic games had burned with so bright a luster in the past of the Greeks that they could not but have their revival at heart. And furthermore, the moral benefits would compensate largely for all pecuniary sacrifice.

This the crown prince apprehended at once, and it decided him to lend his authority to the organizing of the first Olympic games. He appointed a commission, with headquarters in his own palace; made M. Philemon, ex-mayor of Athens and a man of much zeal and enthusiasm, secretary-general; and appealed to the nation to subscribe the necessary funds. Subscriptions began to come in from Greece, but particularly from London, Marseilles, and Constantinople, where there are wealthy and influential Greek colonies. The chief gift came from Alexandria. It was this gift which made it possible to restore the Stadion to its condition in the time of Atticus Herodes. The intention had been from the first to hold the contests in this justly celebrated spot. No one, however, had dreamed that it might be possible to restore to their former splendor the marble seats which, it is said, could accommodate forty thousand persons. The great inclosure would have been utilized, and provisional wooden seats placed on the grassy slopes which surround it. Thanks to the generosity of M. Averoff, Greece is now the richer by a monument unique of its kind, and its visitors have seen a spectacle which they can never forget.

Two years ago the Stadion resembled a deep gash, made by some fabled giant, in the side of the hill which rises abruptly by the Ilissus, and opposite Lycabettus and the Acropolis, in a retired, picturesque quarter of Athens. All that was visible of it then were the two high earth embankments which faced each other on opposite sides of the long, narrow race-course. They met at the end in an imposing hemicycle. Grass grew between the cobblestones. For centuries the spectators of ancient days had sat on the ground on these embankments. Then, one day, an army of workmen, taking possession of the Stadion, had covered it with stone and marble. This is the work that has now been repeated. The first covering served as a quarry during the Turkish domination; not a trace of it was left. With its innumerable rows of seats, and the flights of steps which divide it into sections and lead to the upper tiers, the Stadion no longer has the look of being cut out of the hill. It is the hill which seems to have been placed there by the hand of man to support this enormous pile of masonry. One detail only is modern. One does not notice it at first. The dusty track is now a cinder-path, prepared according to the latest rules of modern athletics by an expert brought over from London for the purpose. In the center a sort of esplanade has been erected for the gymnastic exhibitions. At the end, on each side of the turning, antiquity is represented by two large boundary-stones, forming two human figures, and excavated while the foundations were being dug. These were the only finds; they add but little to archæological data. Work on the Stadion is far from being completed, eighteen months having been quite insufficient for the undertaking. Where marble could not be placed, painted wood was hastily made to do duty. That clever architect M. Metaxas cherishes the hope, however, of seeing all the antique decorations restored—statues, columns, bronze quadrigæ, and, at the entrance, majestic propylæa.

When this shall be done, Athens will in truth possess the temple of athletic sports. Yet it is doubtful whether such a sanctuary be the one best suited to the worship of human vigor and beauty in these modern days. The Anglo-Saxons, to whom we owe the revival of athletics, frame their contests delightfully in grass and verdure. Nothing could differ more from the Athenian Stadion than Travers Island, the summer home of the New York Athletic Club, where the championship games are decided. In this green inclosure, where nature is left to have her way, the spectators sit under the trees on the sloping declivities, a few feet away from the Sound, which murmurs against the rocks. One finds something of the same idea at Paris, and at San Francisco, under those Californian skies which so recall the skies

DRAWN BY A. CASTAIGNE.

ON THE WAY TO THE STADION.

of Greece, at the foot of those mountains which have the pure outlines and the iridescent reflections of Hymettus. If the ancient amphitheater was more grandiose and more solemn, the modern picture is more *intime* and pleasing. The music floating under the trees makes a softer accompaniment to the exercises; the spectators move about at friendly ease, whereas the ancients, packed together in rigid lines on their marble benches, sat broiling in the sun or chilled in the shade.

The Stadion is not the only enduring token that will remain to Athens of her inauguration of the new Olympiads: she has also a velodrome and a shooting-stand. The former is in the plain of the modern Phalerum, along the railway which connects Athens with the Piræus. It is copied after the model of that at Copenhagen, where the crown prince of Greece and his brothers had an opportunity of appreciating its advantages during a visit to the King of Denmark, their grandfather. The bicyclists, it is true, have complained that the track is not long enough, and that the turnings are too abrupt; but when were bicyclists ever content? The tennis-courts are in the center of the velodrome. The shooting-stand makes a goodly appearance, with its manor-like medieval crenelations. The contestants are comfortably situated under monumental arches. Then there are large pavilions for the rowers, built of wood, but prettily decorated, with boat-houses and dressing-rooms.

WHILE the Hellenic Committee thus labored over the scenic requirements, the international committee and the national committees were occupied in recruiting competitors. The matter was not as easy as one might think. Not only had indifference and distrust to be overcome, but the revival of the Olympic games had aroused a certain hostility. Although the Paris Congress had been careful to decree that every form of physical exercise practised in the world should have its place on the program, the gymnasts took offense. They considered that they had not been given sufficient prominence. The greater part of the gymnastic associations of Germany, France, and Belgium are animated by a rigorously exclusive spirit; they are not inclined to tolerate the presence of those forms of athletics which they themselves do not practise; what they disdainfully designate as « English sports » have become, because of their popularity, especially odious to them. These associations were not satisfied with declining the invitation sent them to repair to Athens. The Belgian federation wrote to the other federations, suggesting a concerted stand against the work of the Paris Congress. These incidents confirmed the opinions of the pessimists who had been foretelling the failure of the fêtes, or their probable postponement. Athens is far away, the journey is expensive, and the Easter vacations are short. The contestants were not willing to undertake the voyage unless they could be sure that the occasion would be worth the effort. The different associations were not willing to send representatives unless they could be informed of the amount of interest which the contests would create. An unfortunate occurrence took place almost at the last moment. The German press, commenting on an article which had appeared in a Paris newspaper, declared that it was an exclusively Franco-Greek affair; that attempts were being made to shut out other nations; and furthermore, that the German associations had been intentionally kept aloof from the Paris Congress of 1894. The assertion was acknowledged to be incorrect, and was powerless to check the efforts of the German committee under Dr. Gebhardt. M. Kémény in Hungary, Major Balck in Sweden, General de Boutonski in Russia, Professor W. M. Sloane in the United States, Lord Ampthill in England, Dr. Jiri Guth in Bohemia, were, meantime, doing their best to awaken interest in the event, and to reassure the doubting. They did not always succeed. Many people took a sarcastic view, and the newspapers indulged in much pleasantry on the subject of the Olympic games.

EASTER MONDAY, April 6, the streets of Athens wore a look of extraordinary animation. All the public buildings were draped in bunting; multicolored streamers floated in the wind; green wreaths decked the house-fronts. Everywhere were the two letters « O. A., » the Greek initials of the Olympic games, and the two dates, B. C. 776, A. D. 1896, indicating their ancient past and their present renascence. At two o'clock in the afternoon the crowd began to throng the Stadion and to take possession of the seats. It was a joyous and motley concourse. The skirts and braided jackets of the *palikars* contrasted with the somber and ugly European habiliments. The women used large paper fans to shield them from the sun, parasols, which would have obstructed the view, being prohibited. The king and the queen drove up a little before three o'clock, followed by Princess Marie, their daughter, and her fiancé, Grand

DRAWN BY A. CASTAIGNE.

ARRIVAL OF THE WINNER OF THE MARATHON RACE.

Duke George of Russia. They were received by the crown prince and his brothers, by M. Delyannis, president of the Council of Ministers, and by the members of the Hellenic Committee and the international committee. Flowers were presented to the queen and princess, and the cortège made its way into the hemicycle to the strains of the Greek national hymn and the cheers of the crowd. Within, the court ladies and functionaries, the diplomatic corps, and the deputies awaited the sovereigns, for whom two marble arm-chairs were in readiness. The crown prince, taking his stand in the arena, facing the king, then made a short speech, in which he touched upon the origin of the enterprise, and the obstacles surmounted in bringing it to fruition. Addressing the king, he asked him to proclaim the opening of the Olympic games, and the king, rising, declared them opened. It was a thrilling moment. Fifteen hundred and two years before, the Emperor Theodosius had suppressed the Olympic games, thinking, no doubt, that in abolishing this hated survival of paganism he was furthering the cause of progress; and here was a Christian monarch, amid the applause of an assemblage composed almost exclusively of Christians, announcing the formal annulment of the imperial decree; while a few feet away stood the archbishop of Athens, and Père Didon, the celebrated Dominican preacher, who, in his Easter sermon in the Catholic cathedral the day before, had paid an eloquent tribute to pagan Greece. When the king had resumed his seat, the Olympic ode, written for the occasion by the Greek composer Samara, was sung by a chorus of one hundred and fifty voices. Once before music had been associated with the revival of the Olympic games.

DRAWN BY A. CASTAIGNE.

FENCING BEFORE THE

The first session of the Paris Congress had been held June 16, 1894, in the great amphitheater of the Sorbonne, decorated by Puvis de Chavannes; and after the address of the president of the congress, Baron de Coubertin, the large audience had listened to that fragment of the music of antiquity, the hymn to Apollo, discovered in the ruins of Delphi. But this time the connection between art and athletics was more direct. The games began with the sounding of the last chords of the Olympic ode. That first day established the success of the games beyond a doubt. The ensuing days confirmed the fact in spite of the bad weather. The royal family was assiduous in its attendance. In the shooting-

KING OF GREECE.

contest the queen fired the first shot with a flower-wreathed rifle. The fencing-matches were held in the marble rotunda of the Exposition Palace, given by the Messrs. Zappas, and known as the Zappeion. Then the crowd made its way back to the Stadion for the foot-races, weight-putting, discus-throwing, high and long jumps, pole-vaulting, and gymnastic exhibitions. A Princeton student, Robert Garrett, scored highest in throwing the discus. His victory was unexpected. He had asked me the day before if I did not think that it would be ridiculous should he enter for an event for which he had trained so little! The stars and stripes seemed destined to carry off all the laurels. When they ran up the «victor's mast,» the sailors of the *San Francisco*, who stood in a group at the top of the Stadion, waved their caps, and the members of the Boston Athletic Association below broke out frantically, «B. A. A.! rah! rah! rah!» These cries greatly amused the Greeks. They applauded the triumph of the Americans, between whom and themselves there is a warm feeling of good-will.

The Greeks are novices in the matter of

athletic sports, and had not looked for much success for their own country. One event only seemed likely to be theirs from its very nature—the long-distance run from Marathon, a prize for which has been newly founded by M. Michel Bréal, a member of the French Institute, in commemoration of that soldier of antiquity who ran all the way to Athens to tell his fellow-citizens of the happy issue of the battle. The distance from Marathon to Athens is 42 kilometers. The road is rough and stony. The Greeks had trained for this run for a year past. Even in the remote districts of Thessaly young peasants prepared to enter as contestants. In three cases it is said that the enthusiasm and the inexperience of these young fellows cost them their lives, so exaggerated were their preparatory efforts. As the great day approached, women offered up prayers and votive tapers in the churches, that the victor might be a Greek!

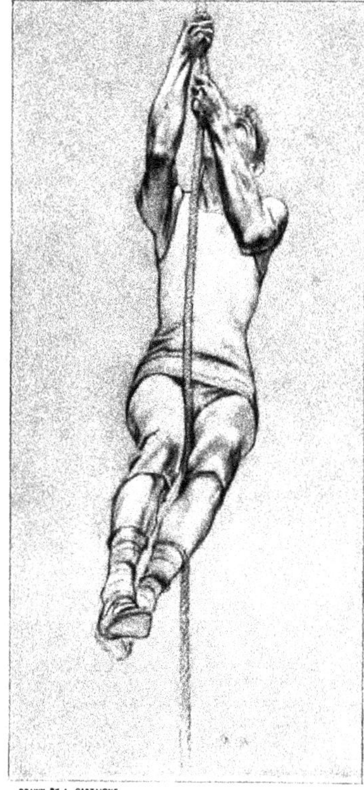

DRAWN BY A. CASTAIGNE

CLIMBING THE SMOOTH ROPE.

The wish was fulfilled. A young peasant named Louës, from the village of Marousi, was the winner in two hours and fifty-five minutes. He reached the goal fresh and in fine form. He was followed by two other Greeks. The excellent Australian sprinter Flack, and the Frenchman Lermusiaux, who had been in the lead the first 35 kilometers, had fallen out by the way. When Louës came into the Stadion, the crowd, which numbered sixty thousand persons, rose to its feet like one man, swayed by extraordinary excitement. The King of Servia, who was present, will probably not forget the sight he saw that day. A flight of white pigeons was let loose, women waved fans and handkerchiefs, and some of the spectators who were nearest to Louës left their seats, and tried to reach him and carry him in triumph. He would have been suffocated if the crown prince and Prince George had not bodily led him away. A lady who stood next to me unfastened her watch, a gold one set with pearls, and sent it to him; an innkeeper presented him with an order good for three hundred and sixty-five free meals; and a wealthy citizen had to be dissuaded from signing a check for ten thousand francs to his credit. Louës himself, however, when he was told of this generous offer, refused it. The sense of honor, which is very strong in the Greek peasant, thus saved the non-professional spirit from a very great danger.

Needless to say that the various contests were held under amateur regulations. An exception was made for the fencing-matches, since in several countries professors of military fencing hold the rank of officers. For them a special contest was arranged. To all other branches of the athletic sports only amateurs were admitted. It is impossible to conceive the Olympic games with money prizes. But these rules, which seem simple enough, are a good deal complicated in their practical application by the fact that definitions of what constitutes an amateur differ from one country to another, sometimes even from one club to another. Several definitions are current in England; the Italians and the Dutch admit one which appears too rigid at one point, too loose at another. How conciliate these divergent or contradictory utterances? The Paris Congress made an attempt in that direction, but its decisions are not accepted everywhere as law, nor is its defini-

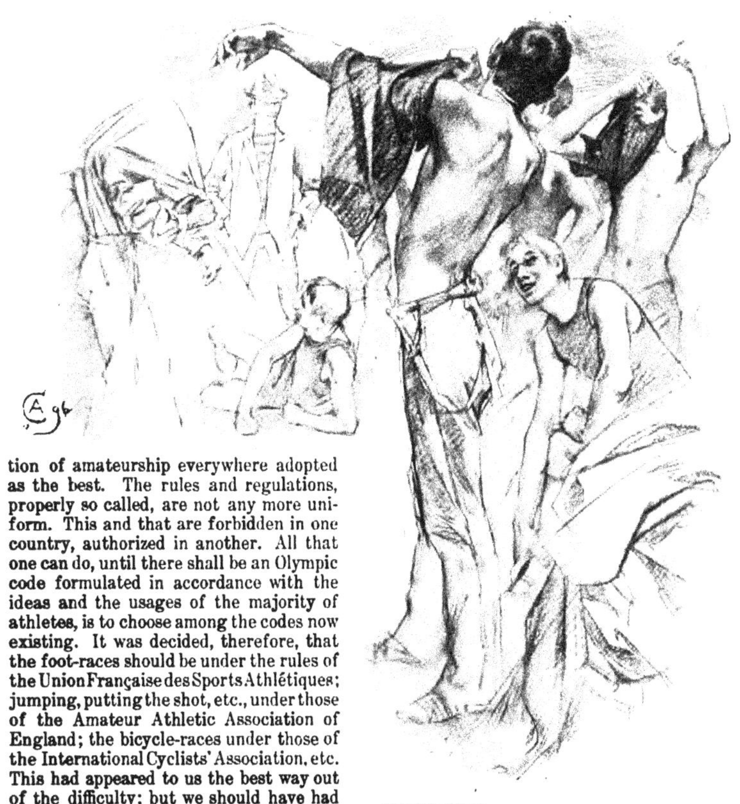

DRAWN BY A. CASTAIGNE.

MAKING READY.

tion of amateurship everywhere adopted as the best. The rules and regulations, properly so called, are not any more uniform. This and that are forbidden in one country, authorized in another. All that one can do, until there shall be an Olympic code formulated in accordance with the ideas and the usages of the majority of athletes, is to choose among the codes now existing. It was decided, therefore, that the foot-races should be under the rules of the Union Française des Sports Athlétiques; jumping, putting the shot, etc., under those of the Amateur Athletic Association of England; the bicycle-races under those of the International Cyclists' Association, etc. This had appeared to us the best way out of the difficulty; but we should have had many disputes if the judges (to whom had been given the Greek name of ephors) had not been headed by Prince George, who acted as final referee. His presence gave weight and authority to the decisions of the ephors, among whom there were, naturally, representatives of different countries. The prince took his duties seriously, and fulfilled them conscientiously. He was always on the track, personally supervising every detail, an easily recognizable figure, owing to his height and athletic build. It will be remembered that Prince George, while traveling in Japan with his cousin, the czarevitch (now Emperor Nicholas II), felled with his fist the ruffian who had tried to assassinate the latter. During the weight-lifting in the Stadion, Prince George lifted with ease an enormous dumb-bell, and tossed it out of the way. The audience broke into applause, as if it would have liked to make him the victor in the event.

Every night while the games were in progress the streets of Athens were illuminated. There were torch-light processions, bands played the different national hymns, and the students of the university got up ovations under the windows of the foreign athletic crews, and harangued them in the noble tongue of Demosthenes. Perhaps this tongue was somewhat abused. That Americans might not be compelled to understand French, nor Hungarians forced to speak German, the daily programs of the games, and even invitations to luncheon, were written in Greek. On receipt of these cards, covered with mysterious formulæ, where even the date was not

DRAWN BY A. CASTAIGNE.

ONE OF OUR BOYS.

clear (the Greek calendar is twelve days behind ours), every man carried them to his hotel porter for elucidation.

Many banquets were given. The mayor of Athens gave one at Cephissia, a little shaded village at the foot of Pentelicus. M. Bikelas, the retiring president of the international committee, gave another at Phalerum. The king himself entertained all the competitors, and the members of the committees, three hundred guests in all, at luncheon in the ball-room of the palace. The outside of this edifice, which was built by King Otho, is heavy and graceless; but the center of the interior is occupied by a suite of large rooms with very high ceilings, opening one into another through colonnades. The decorations are simple and imposing. The tables were set in the largest of these rooms. At the table of honor sat the king, the princes, and the ministers, and here also were the members of the committees. The competitors were seated at the other tables according to their nationality. The king, at dessert, thanked and congratulated his guests, first in French, afterward in Greek. The Americans cried «Hurrah!» the Germans, «*Hoch!*» the Hungarians, «*Eljen!*» the Greeks, «*Zito!*» the French, «*Vive le Roi!*» After the repast the king and his sons chatted long and amicably with the athletes. It was a really charming scene, the republican simplicity of which was a matter of wonderment particularly to the Austrians and the Russians, little used as they are to the spectacle of monarchy thus meeting democracy on an equal footing.

Then there were nocturnal festivities on the Acropolis, where the Parthenon was illuminated with colored lights, and at the Piræus, where the vessels were hung with Japanese lanterns. Unluckily, the weather changed, and the sea was so high on the day appointed for the boat-races, which were to have taken place in the roadstead of Phalerum, that the project was abandoned. The distribution of prizes was likewise postponed for twenty-four hours. It came off with much solemnity, on the morning of April 15, in the Stadion. The sun shone again, and sparkled on the officers' uniforms. When the roll of the victors was called, it became evident, after all, that the international character of the institution was well guarded by the results of the contests. America had won nine prizes for athletic sports alone (flat races for 100 and 400 meters; 110-meter hurdle-race; high jump; broad jump; pole-vault; hop, step, and jump; putting the shot; throwing the discus), and two prizes for shooting (revolver, 25 and 30 meters); but France had the prizes for foil-fencing and for four bicycle-races; England scored highest in the one-handed weight-lifting contest, and in single lawn-tennis; Greece won the run from Marathon, two gymnastic contests (rings, climbing the smooth rope), three prizes for shooting (carbine, 200 and 300 meters; pistol, 25 meters), a prize for fencing with sabers, and a bicycle-race; Germany won in wrestling, in gymnastics (parallel bars, fixed bar, horse-leaping), and in double lawn-tennis; Australia, the 800-meter and 1500-meter foot-races on the flat; Hungary, swimming-matches of 100 and 1200 meters; Austria, the 500-meter swimming-match and the 12-hour bicycle-

DRAWN BY A. CASTAIGNE.

THE KING PRESENTING THE REWARDS.

race; Switzerland, a gymnastic prize; Denmark, the two-handed weight-lifting contest.

The prizes were an olive-branch from the very spot, at Olympia, where stood the ancient Altis, a diploma drawn by a Greek artist, and a silver medal chiseled by the celebrated French engraver Chaplain. On one side of the medal is the Acropolis, with the Parthenon and the Propylæa; on the other a colossal head of the Olympian Zeus, after the type created by Phidias. The head of the god is blurred, as if by distance and the lapse of centuries, while in the foreground, in clear relief, is the Victory which Zeus holds on his hand. It is a striking and original conception. After the distribution of the prizes, the athletes formed for the traditional procession around the Stadion. Louës, the victor of Marathon, came first, bearing the Greek flag; then the Americans, the Hungarians, the French, the Germans. The ceremony, moreover, was made more memorable by a charming incident. One of the contestants, Mr. Robertson, an Oxford student, recited an ode which he had composed, in ancient Greek and in the Pindaric mode, in honor of the games. Music had opened them, and Poetry was present at their close; and thus was the bond once more renewed which in the past united the Muses with feats of physical strength, the mind with the well-trained body. The king announced that the first Olympiad was at an end, and left the Stadion, the band playing the Greek national hymn, and the crowd cheering. A few days later Athens was emptied of its guests. Torn wreaths littered the public squares; the banners which had floated merrily in the streets disappeared; the sun and the wind held sole possession of the marble sidewalks of Stadion street.

It is interesting to ask oneself what are likely to be the results of the Olympic games of 1896, as regards both Greece and the rest of the world. In the case of Greece, the games will be found to have had a double effect, one athletic, the other political. It is a well-known fact that the Greeks had lost completely, during their centuries of oppression, the taste for physical sports. There were good walkers among the mountaineers, and good swimmers in the scattered villages along the coast. It was a matter of pride with the young *palikar* to wrestle and to dance well, but that was because bravery and a gallant bearing were admired by those about him. Greek dances are far from athletic, and the wrestling-matches of peasants have none of the characteristics of true sports. The men of the towns had come to know no diversion beyond reading the newspapers, and violently discussing politics about the tables of the cafés. The Greek race, however, is free from the natural indolence of the Oriental, and it was manifest that the athletic habit would, if the opportunity offered, easily take root again among its men. Indeed, several gymnastic associations had been formed in recent years at Athens and Patras, and a rowing-club at Piræus, and the public was showing a growing interest in their feats. It was therefore a favorable moment to speak the words, «Olympic games.» No sooner had it been made clear that Athens was to aid in the revival of the Olympiads than a perfect fever of muscular activity broke out all over the kingdom. And this was nothing to what followed the games. I have seen, in little villages far from the capital, small boys, scarcely out of long clothes, throwing big stones, or jumping improvised hurdles, and two urchins never met in the streets of Athens without running races. Nothing could exceed the enthusiasm with which the victors in the contests were received, on their return to their native towns, by their fellow-citizens. They were met by the mayor and municipal authorities, and cheered by a crowd bearing branches of wild olive and laurel. In ancient times the victor entered the city through a breach made expressly in its walls. The Greek cities are no longer walled in, but one may say that athletics have made a breach in the heart of the nation. When one realizes the influence that the practice of physical exercises may have on the future of a country, and on the force of a whole race, one is tempted to wonder whether Greece is not likely to date a new era from the year 1896. It would be curious indeed if athletics were to become one of the factors in the Eastern question! Who can tell whether, by bringing a notable increase of vigor to the inhabitants of the country, it may not hasten the solution of this thorny problem? These are hypotheses, and circumstances make light of such calculations at long range. But a local and immediate consequence of the games may already be found in the internal politics of Greece. I have spoken of the active part taken by the crown prince and his brothers, Prince George and Prince Nicholas, in the labors of the organizing committee. It was the first time that the heir apparent had had an opportunity of thus coming into contact with his future subjects. They knew him to be patriotic and high-minded, but they did not know his other admirable and solid qualities. Prince

DRAWN BY A. CASTAIGNE.

THE PARADE OF THE WINNERS.

DRAWN BY A. CASTAIGNE.

THE NIGHT FESTIVAL AT THE PIRÆUS.

Constantine inherits his fine blue eyes and fair coloring from his Danish ancestors, and his frank, open manner, his self-poise, and his mental lucidity come from the same source; but Greece has given him enthusiasm and ardor, and this happy combination of prudence and high spirit makes him especially adapted to govern the Hellenes. The authority, mingled with perfect liberality, with which he managed the committee, his exactitude in detail, and more particularly his quiet perseverance when those about him were inclined to hesitate and to lose courage, make it clear that his reign will be one of fruitful labor, which can only strengthen and enrich his country. The Greek people have now a better idea of the worth of their future sovereign: they have seen him at work, and have gained respect for and confidence in him.

So much for Greece. On the world at large the Olympic games have, of course, exerted no influence as yet; but I am profoundly convinced that they will do so. May I be permitted to say that this was my reason for founding them? Modern athletics need to be *unified* and *purified*. Those who have followed the renaissance of physical sports in this century know that discord reigns supreme from one end of them to the other. Every country has its own rules; it is not possible even to come to an agreement as to who is an amateur, and who is not. All over the world there is one perpetual dispute, which is further fed by innumerable weekly, and even daily, newspapers. In this deplorable state of things professionalism tends to grow apace. Men give up their whole existence to one particular sport, grow rich by practising it, and thus deprive it of all nobility, and destroy the just equilibrium of man by making the muscles preponderate over the mind. It is my belief that no education, particularly in democratic times, can be good and complete without the aid of athletics; but athletics, in order to play their proper educational rôle, must be based on perfect disinterestedness and the sentiment of honor.

If we are to guard them against these threatening evils, we must put an end to the quarrels of amateurs, that they may be united among themselves, and willing to measure their skill in frequent international encounters. But what country is to impose its rules and its habits on the others? The Swedes will not yield to the Germans, nor the French to the English. Nothing better than the international Olympic games could therefore be devised. Each country will take its turn in organizing them. When they come to meet every four years in these contests, further ennobled by the memories of the past, athletes all over the world will learn to know one another better, to make mutual concessions, and to seek no other reward in the competition than the honor of the victory. One may be filled with desire to see the colors of one's club or college triumph in a national meeting; but how much stronger is the feeling when the colors of one's country are at stake! I am well assured that the victors in the Stadion at Athens wished for no other recompense when they heard the people cheer the flag of their country in honor of their achievement.

It was with these thoughts in mind that I sought to revive the Olympic games. I have succeeded after many efforts. Should the institution prosper,—as I am persuaded, all civilized nations aiding, that it will,—it may be a potent, if indirect, factor in securing universal peace. Wars break out because nations misunderstand each other. We shall not have peace until the prejudices which now separate the different races shall have been outlived. To attain this end, what better means than to bring the youth of all countries periodically together for amicable trials of muscular strength and agility? The Olympic games, with the ancients, controlled athletics and promoted peace. It is not visionary to look to them for similar benefactions in the future.

*Pierre de Coubertin.*

# HUGH WYNNE, FREE QUAKER:

## SOMETIME BREVET LIEUTENANT-COLONEL ON THE STAFF OF HIS EXCELLENCY GEORGE WASHINGTON.

BY DR. S. WEIR MITCHELL,

Author of «In War Time,» «When all the Woods are Green,» etc.

Yours very truly
S. Weir Mitchell

## PREFACE.

IT is now many years since I began these memoirs. I wrote fully a third of them, and then put them aside, having found increasing difficulties as I went on with my task. These arose out of the constant need to use the first person in a narrative of adventure and incidents which chiefly concern the writer, even though it involve also the fortunes of many in all ranks of life. Having no gift in the way of composition, I knew not how to supply or set forth what was outside of my own knowledge, nor how to pretend to that marvelous insight as to motives and thoughts which they affect who write books of fiction. This has always seemed to me absurd, and so artificial that, with my fashion of mind, I have never been able to enjoy such works, nor agreeably to accept their claim to such privilege of insight. In a memoir meant for my descendants, it was fitting and desirable that I should at times speak of my own appearance, and, if possible, of how I seemed as child or man to others. This, I found, I did not incline to do, even when I myself knew what had been thought of me by friend or foe. And so, as I said, I set the task aside, with no desire to take it up again.

Some years later my friend John Warder died, leaving to my son, his namesake, an ample estate, and to me all his books, papers, plate, and wines. Locked in a desk I found a diary, begun when a lad, and kept with more or less care during several years of the great war. It contained, also, recollections of our youthful days, and was very full here and there of thoughts, comments, and descriptions concerning events of the time, and of people whom we both had known. It told of me much that I could not otherwise have willingly set down, even if the matter had appeared to me as it did to him, which was not always the case; also, my friend chanced to be present at scenes which deeply concerned me, but which, without his careful setting forth, would never have come to my knowledge.

A kindly notice, writ nine years before, bade me use his journal as seemed best to me. When I read this, and came to see how full and clear were his statements of much that I knew, and of some things which I did not, I felt ripely inclined to take up again the story I had left unfinished; and now I have done so, and have used my friend as the third person, whom I could permit to say what he thought of me from time to time, and to tell of incidents I did not see, or record impressions and emotions of his own. This latter privilege pleases me, because I shall, besides my own story, be able to let those dear to me gather from the confessions of his journal, and from my own statements, what manner of person was the true gentleman and gallant soldier to whom I owed so much.

I trust this tale of an arduous struggle by a new land against a great empire will make those of my own blood the more desirous to serve their country with honour and earnestness, and with an abiding belief in the great ruler of events.

In my title of this volume I have called myself a «Free Quaker.» The term has no meaning for most of the younger generation, and yet it should tell a story of many sad spiritual struggles, of much heart-searching distress, of brave decisions, and of battle and of camp.

These Free Quakers were they who, insisting that they were still of the same mind as Penn and Fox as to modes of worship and religious beliefs in general, were also of opinion that resistance to the oppression of the crown was a duty not to be avoided. They have left their mark on the history of a stormy time, and none better served their country and their God.

At Fifth and Arch streets, on an old gable, is this record:

By General Subscription,<br>For The Free Quakers.<br>Erected A. D. 1783,<br>Of The Empire 8.

In the burying-ground across the street, and within and about the sacred walls of Christ Church, not far away, lie Benjamin Franklin, Francis Hopkinson, Peyton Randolph, Benjamin Rush, and many a gallant soldier and sailor of the war for freedom. Among them, at peace forever, rest the gentlefolks who stood for the king—the gay men and women who were neutral, or who cared little under which George they danced, or gambled, or drank their old Madeira. It is a neighborhood which should be forever full of interest to those who love the country of our birth.

*Hugh Wynne.*

DRAWN BY HOWARD PYLE.

«'DIDST THOU TELL THEM I TAUGHT THEE?'»

(SEE PAGE 62.)

A CHILD'S early life is such as those who rule over him make it; but they can only modify what he is. Yet, as all know, after their influence has ceased, the man himself has to deal with the effects of blood and breed, and, too, with the consequences of the mistakes of his elders in the way of education. For these reasons I am pleased to say something of myself in the season of my green youth.

The story of the childhood of the great is often of value, no matter from whom they are «ascended,» as my friend Warder used to say; but even in the lives of such lesser men as I, who have played the part of simple pawns in a mighty game, the change from childhood to manhood is not without interest.

I have often wished we could have the recorded truth of a child's life as it seemed to him day by day, but this can never be. The man it is who writes the life of the boy, and his recollection of it is perplexed by the siftings of memory, which let so much of thought and feeling escape, keeping little more than barren facts, or the remembrance of periods of trouble or of emotion, sometimes quite valueless, while more important moral events are altogether lost.

As these pages will show, I have found it agreeable, and at times useful, to try to understand, so far as in me lay, not only the men who were my captains or mates in war or in peace, but also myself. I have often been puzzled by that well-worn phrase as to the wisdom of knowing thyself; for with what manner of knowledge you know yourself is a grave question, and it is sometimes more valuable to know what is truly thought of you by your nearest friends than to be forever teasing yourself to determine whether what you have done in the course of your life was just what it should have been.

I may be wrong in the belief that my friend Warder saw others more clearly than he saw himself. He was of that opinion, and he says in one place that he is like a mirror, seeing all things sharply, except that he saw not himself. Whether he judged me justly or not, I must leave to others to decide. I should be glad to think that, in the great account, I shall be as kindly dealt with as in the worn and faded pages which tell brokenly of the days of our youth. I am not ashamed to say that my eyes have filled many times as I have lingered over these records of my friend, surely as sweet and true a gentleman as I have ever known. Perhaps sometimes they have even overflowed at what they read. Why are we reluctant to confess a not ignoble weakness, such as is, after all, only the heart's confession of what is best in life? What becomes of the tears of age?

This is but a wearisome introduction, and yet necessary; for I desire to use freely my friend's journal, and this without perpetual mention of his name, save as one of the actors who played, as I did, a modest part in the tumult of the war in which my own fortunes and his were so deeply concerned. To tell of my own life without speaking freely of the course of a mighty story would be quite impossible. I look back, indeed, with honest comfort on a struggle which changed the history of three nations, but I am sure that the war did more for me than I for it. This I saw in others. Some who went into it unformed lads came out strong men. In others its temptations seemed to find and foster weaknesses of character, and to cultivate the hidden germs of evil. Of all the examples of this influence, none has seemed to me so tragical as that of General Arnold, because, being of reputable stock and sufficient means, generous, in every-day life kindly, and a free-handed friend, he was also, as men are now loath to believe, a most gallant and daring soldier, a tender father, and an attached husband. The thought of the fall of this man fetches back to me, as I write, the remembrance of my own lesser temptations, and with a thankful heart I turn aside to the uneventful story of my boyhood and its surroundings.

I was born in the great city Governor William Penn founded, in Pennsylvania, on the banks of the Delaware, and my earliest memories are of the broad river, the ships, the creek before our door, and of brave gentlemen in straight-collared coats and broad-brimmed beaver hats.

I began life in a day of stern rule, and among a people who did not concern themselves greatly as to a child's having that inheritance of happiness with which we like to credit childhood. Who my people were had much to do with my own character, and what those people were, and had been, it is needful to say before I let my story run its natural and, I hope, not uninteresting course.

In my father's bedroom, over the fireplace, hung a pretty picture done in oils, by whom I know not. It is now in my library. It represents a pleasant park, and on a rise of land a gray Jacobean house with, at each side, low wings curved forward so as to embrace a courtyard shut in by railings and gilded gates. There is also a terrace with urns and flowers. I used to think it was the king's palace until, one morning, when I was still a child, Friend Pemberton came to visit my father with James Logan and a very gay gentleman, Mr. John Penn, he who was sometime lieutenant-governor of the province, and of whom and of his brother Richard great hopes were conceived among Friends. I was encouraged by Mr. Penn to speak more than was thought fitting for children in those days, and because of his rank I escaped the reproof I should else have met with.

He said to my father, «The boy favors thy people.» Then he added, patting my head, «When thou art a man, my lad, thou shouldst go and see where thy people came from in Wales. I have been at Wyncote. It is a great house, with wings in the Italian manner, and a fine fountain in the court, and gates which were gilded when Charles II came to see the squire, and which are not to be set open again until another king comes thither.»

Then I knew this was the picture up-stairs, and, much pleased, I said eagerly:

«My father has it in his bedroom, and our arms below it, all painted most beautiful.»

«Thou art a clever lad,» said the young lieutenant-governor, «and I must have described it well. Let us have a look at it, Friend Wynne.»

But my mother, seeing that James Logan and Friend Pemberton were silent and grave, and that my father looked ill pleased, made haste to make excuse, because it was springtime, and the annual house-cleaning was going on.

Mr. Penn cried out merrily: «I see that the elders are shocked at thee, Friend Wynne, because of these vanities of arms and pictures; but there is good heraldry on the tankard out of which I drank James Pemberton's beer yesterday. Fie, fie, Friend James!» Then he bowed to my mother very courteously, and said to my father, «I hope I have not got thy boy into difficulties because I reminded him that he is come of gentles.»

«No, no,» said my mother.

«I know the arms, madam, and well, too: quarterly, three eagles displayed in fesse, and—»

«Thou wilt pardon me, Friend Penn,» said my father, curtly. «These are the follies of a world which concerns not those of our society. The lad's aunt has put enough of such nonsense into his head already.»

«Let it pass, then,» returned the young lieutenant-governor, with good humor; «but I hope, as I said, that I have made no trouble for this stout boy of thine.»

My father replied deliberately, «There is no harm done.» He was too proud to defend himself, but I heard long after that he was taken to task by Thomas Scattergood and another for these vanities of arms and pictures. He told them that he put the picture where none saw it but ourselves, and, when they persisted, reminded them sharply, as Mr. Penn had done, of the crests on their own silver, by which these Friends of Welsh descent set much store.

I remember that when the gay young lieutenant-governor had taken his leave, my father said to my mother, «Was it thou who didst tell the boy this foolishness of these being our arms, and the like, or was it my sister Gainor?»

Upon this my mother drew up her brows, and spread her palms out,—a French way she had,—and cried: «Are they not thy arms? Wherefore should we be ashamed to confess it?»

I suppose this puzzled him, for he merely added, «Too much may be made of such vanities.»

All of this I but dimly recall. It is one of the earliest recollections of my childhood, and being out of the common was, I suppose, for that reason better remembered.

I do not know how old I was when, at this time, Mr. Penn, in a neat wig with side rolls, and dressed very gaudy, aroused my curiosity as to these folk in Wales. It was long after, and only by degrees, that I learned the following facts, which were in time to have a great influence on my own life and its varied fortunes.

In or about the year 1671, and of course before Mr. Penn, the proprietary, came over, my grandfather had crossed the sea, and settled near Chester on lands belonging to the Swedes. The reason of his coming was this. About 1669 the Welsh of the English church, and the magistrates, were greatly stirred to wrath against the people called Quakers, because of their refusal to pay tithes. Among these offenders was no small number of the lesser gentry, especially they of Merionethshire.

My grandfather, Hugh Wynne, was the son and successor of Godfrey Wynne of Wyncote. How he chanced to be born among these hot-blooded Wynnes I do not comprehend. He is said to have been gay in his early days, but in young manhood to have become averse to the wild ways of his breed, and to have taken a serious and contemplative turn. Falling in with preachers of the people called Quakers, he left the church of the establishment, gave up hunting, ate his game-cocks, and took to straight collars, plain clothes, and plain talk. When he refused to pay the tithes he was fined, and at last cast into prison in Shrewsbury Gate House, where he lay for a year, with no more mind to be taxed for a hireling ministry at the end of that time than at the beginning.

His next brother, William, a churchman as men go, seems to have loved him, although he was himself a rollicking fox-hunter; and seeing that Hugh would die if left in this duress, engaged him to go to America. Upon his agreeing to make over his estate to William, those in authority readily consented to his liberation, since William had no scruples as to the matter of tithes, and with him there would be no further trouble. Thus it came about that my grandfather Hugh left Wales. He had with him, I presume, enough of means to enable him to make a start in Pennsylvania. It could not have been much. He carried also, what no doubt he valued, a certificate of removal from the Quarterly Meeting held at Tyddyn y Garreg. I have this singular document. In it is said of him and of his wife Ellin («for whom it may concern»), that «they are faithfull and beloved Friends, well known to be serviceable unto Friends and brethren, since they have become convinced; of a blameless and savory conversation. Also are P'sons Dearly beloved of all Souls. His testimony sweet and tender, reaching to the quicking seed of life; we cannot alsoe but bemoan the want of his company, for that in difficult occasion he was sted-fast—nor was one to be turned aside. He is now seasonable in intention for Pennsylvania, in order into finding his way clear, and freedom in the truth according to the measure manifested unto him,» etc.

And so the strong-minded man is commended to Friends across the seas. In the records of the meetings for sufferings in England are certain of his letters from the jail. How his character descended to my sterner parent, and through another generation to me, and how the coming in of my mother's gentler blood helped in after days, and amid stir of war, to modify in me, this present writer, the ruder qualities of my race, I may hope to set forth.

William died suddenly in 1679, without children, and was succeeded by the third brother, Owen. This gentleman lived the life of his time, and dying in 1700 of much beer and many strong waters, left one son, Owen, a minor. What with executors and other evils, the estate now went from ill to worse. Owen Wynne second was in no haste, and thus married as late as somewhere about 1740, and had issue, William, and later, in 1744, a second son, Arthur, and perhaps others; but of all this I heard naught until many years after, as I have already said.

It may seem a weak and careless thing for a man thus to cast away his father's lands, as my ancestor did; but what he gave up was a poor estate, embarrassed with mortgages and lessened by fines until the income was, I suspect, but small. Certain it is that the freedom to worship God as he pleased was more to him than wealth, and assuredly not to be set against a so meager estate, where he must have lived among enmities, or must have diced, drunk, and hunted with the rest of his kinsmen and neighbors.

I have a faint memory of my aunt Gainor Wynne as being fond of discussing the matter, and of how angry this used to make my father. She had a notion that my father knew more than he was willing to say, and that there had been something further agreed between the brothers, although what this was she knew not, nor ever did for many a day. She was given, however, to filling my young fancy with tales about the greatness of these Wynnes, and of how the old homestead, rebuilded in James I's reign, had been the nest of Wynnes past the memory of man. Be all this as it may, we had lost Wyncote for the love of a freer air, although this did not much concern me in the days of which I now write.

Under the mild and just rule of the proprietary, my grandfather Hugh prospered, and in turn his son John, my father, to a far greater extent. Their old home in Wales became to them, as time went on, less and less important. Their acres here in Merion and Bucks were more numerous and more fertile. I may add that the possession of many slaves in Maryland, and a few in Pennsylvania, gave them the feeling of authority and position which the colonial was apt to lose in the presence of his English rulers, who, being in those days principally gentlemen of the army, were given to assuming airs of superiority.

In a word, my grandfather, a man of excellent wits and of great importance, was of the council of William Penn, and, as one of his chosen advisers, much engaged in his difficulties with the Lord Baltimore as to the boundaries of the lands held of the crown. Finally, when, as Penn says, «I could not prevail with my wife to stay, and still less with Tishe,» which was short for Lætitia, his daughter, an obstinate wench, it was to men like Markham, Logan, and my grandfather that he gave his full confidence, and delegated his authority; so that Hugh Wynne had become, long before his death, a person of so much greater condition than the small squires to whom he had given up his estate that he was like Joseph in this new land. What with the indifference come of large means, and the disgust for a land where he had been ill treated, he probably ceased to think of his forefathers' life in Wales as of a thing either desirable or in any way suited to his own creed.

Soon the letters, which at first were frequent, that is, coming twice a year, when the London packet arrived or departed, became rare; and if, on the death of my great-uncle William, they ceased, or if any passed later between us and the next holder of Wyncote, I never knew. The Welsh squires had our homestead, and we our better portion of wealth and freedom in the new land. And so ended my knowledge of this matter for many a year.

You will readily understand that the rude life of a fox-hunting squire, or the position of a strict Quaker on a but moderate estate in Merionethshire, would have had little to tempt my father. Yet one thing remained with him awhile as an unchanged inheritance, to which, so far as I remember, he only once alluded. Indeed, I should never have guessed that he gave the matter a thought but for that visit of Mr. John Penn, and the way it recurred to me in later days in connection with an incident concerning the picture and the blazoned arms.

I think he cared less and less as years went by. In earlier days he may still have liked to remember that he might have been Wynne of Wyncote; but this is a mere guess on my part. Pride spiritual is a master passion, and certain it is that the creed and ways of Fox and Penn became to him, as years created habits, of an importance far beyond the pride which values ancient blood or a stainless shield.

The old house, which was built much in the same fashion as the great mansion of my Lord Dysart on the Thames near to Richmond, but smaller, was, after all, his family home. The picture and the arms were hid away in deference to opinions by which, in general, he more and more sternly abided. Once, when I was older, I went into his bedroom, and was surprised to find him standing before the hearth, his hands crossed behind his back, looking earnestly at the brightly colored shield beneath the picture of Wyncote. I knew too well to disturb him in these silent moods, but hearing my steps, he suddenly called me to him. I obeyed with the dread his sternness always caused me. To my astonishment, his face was flushed and his eyes were moist. He laid his hand on my shoulder, and clutched it hard as he spoke. He did not turn, but, still looking up at the arms, said in a voice which paused between the words, and sounded strange:

«I have been insulted to-day, Hugh, by the man Thomas Bradford. I thank God that the Spirit prevailed with me to answer him in Christian meekness. He came near to worse things than harsh words. Be warned, my son. It is a terrible setback from right living to come of a hot-blooded breed like these Wynnes.»

I looked up at him as he spoke. He was smiling.

«But not all bad, Hugh, not all bad. Remember that it is something, in this nest of disloyal traders, to have come of gentle blood.»

Then he left gazing on the arms and the old home of our people, and said severely, «Hast thou gotten thy tasks to-day?»

«Yes.»

«It has not been so of late. I hope thou hast considered before speaking. If I hear no better of thee soon, thou wilt repent it. It is time thou shouldst take thy life more seriously. What I have said is for no ear but thine.»

I went away with a vague feeling that I had suffered for Mr. Bradford, and on account of my father's refusal to join in resistance to the Stamp Act; for this was in November, 1765, and I was then fully twelve years of age.

My father's confession, and all he had said following it, made upon me one of those lasting impressions which are rare in youth, but which may have a great influence on the life of a man. Now all the boys were against the Stamp Act, and I had at the moment a sudden fear at being opposed to my father. I had, too, a feeling of personal shame because this strong man, whom I dreaded on account of his severity, should have been so overwhelmed by an insult. There was at this period, and later, much going on in my outer life to lessen the relentless influence of the creed of conduct which prevailed in our home for me, and for all of our house. I had even then begun to suspect at school that non-resistance did not add permanently to the comfort of life. I was sorry that my father had not resorted to stronger measures with Mr. Bradford, a gentleman whom, in after years, I learned greatly to respect.

More than anything else, this exceptional experience as to my father left me with a great desire to know more of these Wynnes, and with a certain share of that pride of race which, to my surprise as I think it over now, was at that time in my father's esteem a possession of value. I am bound to add that I also felt some self-importance at being intrusted with this secret, for such indeed it was.

Before my grandfather left Wales, he had married a distant cousin, Ellin Owen, and on her death, childless, he took to wife, many years later, her younger sister, Gainor;[1] for these Owens, our kinsmen, had also become Friends, and had followed my grandfather's example in leaving their home in Merionethshire. To this second marriage, which occurred in 1713, were born my aunt, Gainor Wynne, and, two years later, my father, John Wynne. I have no remembrance of either grandparent. Both lie in the ground at Merion Meeting-house, under nameless, unmarked graves, after the manner of Friends. I like it not.

My father, being a stern and silent man, must needs be caught by his very opposite, and, according to this law of our nature, fell in love with Marie Beauvais, the orphan of a French gentleman who had become a Quaker, and was of that part of France called the Midi. Of this marriage I was the only surviving offspring, my sister Ellin dying when I was an infant. I was born in the city of Penn, on January 9, 1753, at 9 P. M.

## II.

I HAVE but to close my eyes to see the house in which I lived in my youth. It stood in the city of Penn, back from the low bluff of Dock Creek, near to Walnut street. The garden stretched down to the water, and before the door were still left on either side two great hemlock-spruces, which must have been part of the noble woods under which the first settlers found shelter. Behind the house was a separate building, long and low, in which all the cooking was done, and up-stairs were the rooms where the slaves dwelt apart.

The great garden stretched westward as far as Third street, and was full of fine fruit-trees, and in the autumn of melons, first brought hither in one of my father's ships. Herbs and simples were not wanting, nor berries; for all good housewives in those days were expected to be able to treat colds and the lesser maladies with simples, as they were called, and to provide abundantly jams and conserves of divers kinds.

There were many flowers, too, and my mother loved to make a home here for the wildings she found in the governor's woods. I have heard her regret that the most delicious of all the growths of spring, the ground-sweet, which I think they now call arbutus, would not prosper out of its forest shelter.

The house was of black and red brick, and double; that is, with two windows on each side of a white Doric doorway, having something portly about it. I use the word as Dr. Johnson defines it—a house of port, with a look of sufficiency, and, too, of ready hospitality, which was due, I think, to the upper half of the door being open a good part of the year. I recall also the bull's-eye of thick glass in the upper half-door, and below it a great brass knocker. In the white shutters were cut crescent openings, which looked at night like half-shut eyes when there were lights within the rooms. In the hall were hung on pegs leathern buckets. They were painted green, and bore, in yellow letters, «Fire» and «J. W.»

The day I went to school for the first time is very clear in my memory. I can see myself, a stout little fellow about eight years old, clad in gray homespun, with breeches, low shoes, and a low, flat beaver hat. I can hear my mother say, «Here are two big apples for thy master,» it being the custom so to propitiate pedagogues. Often afterward I took eggs in a little basket, or flowers, and others did the like.

«Now run! run!» she cried, «and be a good boy; run, or thou wilt be late.» And she clapped her hands as I sped away, now and then looking back over my shoulder.

I remember as well my return home to this solid house, this first day of my going to school. One is apt to associate events with persons, and my mother stood leaning on the half-door as I came running back. She was some little reassured to see me smiling, for, to tell the truth, I had been mightily scared at my new venture.

This sweet and most tender-hearted lady wore, as you may like to know, a gray gown, and a blue chintz apron fastened over the shoulders with wide bands. On her head was a very broad-brimmed white beaver hat, low in the crown, and tied by silk cords under her chin. She had a great quantity of brown hair, among which was one wide strand of

[1] Thus early we shed the English prejudice against marriage with a deceased wife's sister.

gray. This she had from youth, I have been told. It was all very silken, and so curly that it was ever in rebellion against the custom of Friends, which would have had it flat on the temples. Indeed, I never saw it so, for, whether at the back or at the front, it was wont to escape in large curls. Nor do I think she disliked this worldly wilfulness for which nature had provided an unanswerable excuse. She had serious blue eyes, very large and wide open, so that the clear white was seen all around the blue, and with a constant look as if of gentle surprise. And in middle life she was still pliant and well rounded, with a certain compliment of fresh prettiness in whatever gesture she addressed to friend or guest. Some said it was a French way, and, indeed, she made more use of her hands in speech than was common among people of British race.

Her goodness seems to me to have been instinctive, and to have needed neither thought nor effort. Her faults, as I think of her, were mostly such as arise from excess of loving and of noble moods. She would be lavish where she had better have been merely generous, or rash where some would have lacked even the commoner qualities of courage. Indeed, as to this, she feared no one, neither my grave father nor the grimmest of inquisitive committees of Friends.

As I came, she set those large, childlike eyes on me, and opening the lower half-door, cried out:

«I could scarce wait for thee! I wish I could have gone with thee, Hugh; and was it dreadful? Come, let us see thy little book. And did they praise thy reading? Didst thou tell them I taught thee? There are girls, I hear,» and so on—a way she had of asking many questions without waiting for a reply.

As we chatted, we passed through the hall, where tall mahogany chairs stood dark against the whitewashed walls, such as were in all the rooms. Joyous at escape from school and its confinement of three long, weary hours, from eight to eleven, I dropped my mother's hand, and running a little, slid down the long entry over the thinly sanded floor, and then slipping, came down with a rueful countenance, as nature, foreseeing results, meant that a boy should descend when his legs fail him. My mother sat down on a settle, and spread out both palms toward me, laughing, and crying out:

«So near are joy and grief, my friends, in this world of sorrow.»

This was said so exactly with the voice and manner of a famous preacher of our meeting that even I, a lad then of only eight years, recognized the imitation. Indeed, she was wonderful at this trick of mimicry, a thing most odious among Friends. As I smiled, hearing her, I was aware of my father in the open doorway of the sitting-room, tall, strong, with much iron-gray hair. Within I saw several Friends, large, rosy men in drab, with horn buttons and straight collars, their stout legs clad in dark silk hose, without the paste or silver buckles then in use. All wore broad-brimmed, low beavers, and their gold-headed canes rested between their knees.

My father said to me, in his sharp way: «Take thy noise out into the orchard. The child disturbs us, wife. Thou shouldst know better. A committee of overseers is with me.» He disliked the name Marie, and was never heard to use it, nor even its English equivalent.

Upon this, the dear lady murmured, «Let us fly, Hugh,» and she ran on tiptoe along the hall with me, while my father closed the door. «Come,» she added, «and see the floor. I am proud of it. We have friends to eat dinner with us at two.»

The great room where we took our meals is still clear in my mind. The floor was two inches deep in white sand, in which were carefully traced zigzag lines, with odd figures in the corners. A bare table of well-rubbed mahogany stood in the middle, with a thin board or two laid on the sand, that the table might be set without disturbing the patterns. In the corners were glass-covered buffets full of silver and Delft ware, and a punch-bowl of Chelsea was on the broad window-ledge, with a silver-mounted cocoanut ladle.

«The floor is pretty,» she said, regarding it with pride; «and I would make flowers, too, but that thy father thinks it vain, and Friend Pemberton would set his bridge spectacles on his nose and look at me until I said naughty words, oh, very! Come out; I will find thee some ripe damsons, and save thee cake for thy supper if Friend Warder does not eat it all. He is a little man, and eats much. A solicitous man,» and she became of a sudden the person she had in mind, looking somehow feeble and cautious and uneasy, with arms at length, and the palms turned forward, so that I knew it for Joseph Warder, a frequent caller, of whom more hereafter.

«What is so—solicitous?» I said.

«Oh, too fearful concerning what may be thought of him. Vanity, vanity! Come, let us run down the garden. Canst thou catch me, Hugh?» And with this she fled away, under the back stoop and through the trees, light and active, her curls tumbling out, while I hurried after her, mindful of damsons, and wondering how much cake Friend Warder would leave for my comfort at evening.

Dear, ever dear lady, seen through the mist of years! None was like you, and none as dear, save one who had as brave a soul, but far other ways and charms.

And thus began my life at school, to which I went twice a day, my father not approving of the plan of three sessions a day, which was common, nor, for some reason, I know not what, of schools kept by Friends. So it was that I set out before eight, and went again from two to four. My master, David Dove, kept his school in Vidall's Alley, nigh to Chestnut street, above Second. There were many boys and girls, and of the former, John Warder, and Graydon, who wrote certain memoirs long after. His mother, a widow, kept boarders in the great Slate-roof House near by, for in those days this was a common resource of decayed gentlewomen, and by no means affected their social position. Here came many officers to stay, and their red coats used to please my eyes as I went by the porch, where at evening I saw them smoking long pipes, and saying not very nice things of the local gentry, or of the women as they passed by, and calling «*Mohair!*» after the gentlemen, a manner of army word of contempt for citizens. I liked well enough the freedom I now enjoyed, and found it to my fancy to wander a little on my way to school, although usually I followed the creek, and where Second street crossed it lingered on the bridge to watch the barges or galleys come up at full of tide to the back of the warehouses on the northeast bank.

I have observed that teachers are often eccentric, and surely David Dove was no exception, nor do I now know why so odd a person was chosen by many for the care of youth. I fancy my mother had to do with the choice in my case, and was influenced by the fact that Dove rarely used the birch, but had a queer fancy for setting culprits on a stool, with the birch switch stuck in the back of the jacket, so as to stand up behind the head. I hated this, and would rather have been birched *secundum artem* than to see the girls giggling at me. I changed my opinion later.

Thus my uneventful life ran on, while I learned to write, and acquired, with other simple knowledge, enough of Latin and Greek to fit me for entrance at the academy which Dr. Franklin had founded in 1750 in the hall on Fourth street built for Whitefield's preaching.

At this time I fell much into the company of John Warder, a lad of my own age, and a son of that Joseph who liked cake, and was, as my mother said, solicitous. Most of the games of boys were not esteemed fitting by Friends, and hence we were somewhat limited in our resources; but to fish in the creek we were free; also, to haunt the ships and hear sea-yarns, and to skate in winter, were not forbidden. Jack Warder I took to because he was full of stories, and would imagine what things might chance to my father's ships in the West Indies; but why, in those early days, he liked me, I do not know.

Our school life with Dove ended after four years in an odd fashion. I was then about twelve, and had become a vigorous, daring boy, with, as it now seems to me, something of the fortunate gaiety of my mother. Other lads thought it singular that in peril I became strangely vivacious; but underneath I had a share of the relentless firmness of my father, and of his vast dislike of failure, and of his love of truth. I have often thought that the father in me saved me from the consequences of so much of my mother's gentler nature as might have done me harm in the rude conflicts of life.

David Dove, among other odd ways, devised a plan for punishing the unpunctual which had considerable success. One day when I had far overstayed the hour of eight, by reason of having climbed into Friend Pemberton's gardens, where I was tempted by many green apples, I was met by four older boys. One had a lantern, which, with much laughter, he tied about my neck, and one, marching before, rang a bell. I had seen this queer punishment fall on others, and certainly the amusement shown by people in the streets would not have hurt me, compared with the advantage of pockets full of apples, had I not of a sudden seen my father, who usually breakfasted at six, and was at his warehouse by seven. He looked at me composedly, but went past us, saying nothing.

On my return about eleven he unluckily met me in the garden, for I had gone the back way in order to hide my apples. I had an unpleasant half-hour, despite my mother's tears, and was sent at once to confess to Friend James Pemberton. The good man said I was a naughty boy, but must come later when the apples were red ripe, and I should take all I wanted, and I might fetch with me another boy, or even two. I never forgot this, and did him some good turns in after years, and right gladly, too.

In my own mind I associated David Dove

with this painful interview with my father. I disliked him the more because, when the procession entered the school, a little girl for whom Warder and I had a boy friendship, in place of laughing, as did the rest, for some reason began to cry. This angered the master, who had the lack of self-control often seen in eccentric people. He asked why she cried, and on her sobbing out that it was because she was sorry for me, he bade her take off her stays. These being stiff, and worn outside the gown, would have made the punishment of the birch on the shoulders of trifling moment.

As it was usual to whip girls at school, the little maid said nothing, but did as she was bid, taking a sharp birching without a cry. Meanwhile I sat with my head in my hands, and my fingers in my ears, lest I should hear her weeping. After school that evening, when all but Warder and I had wandered home, I wrote on the outside wall of the school-house with chalk, «David Dove Is A Cruel Beast,» and went away somewhat better contented.

Now, with all his seeming dislike to use the rod, David had turns of severity, and then he was far more brutal than any man I have ever known. Therefore it did not surprise us next morning that the earlier scholars were looking with wonder and alarm at the sentence on the wall, when Dove, appearing behind us, ordered us to enter at once.

Going to his desk, he put on his spectacles, which then were worn astride of the nose. In a minute he set on below them a second pair, and this we knew to be a signal of coming violence. Then he stood up, and asked who had written the opprobrious epithet on the wall. As no one replied, he asked several in turn, but luckily chose the girls, thinking, perhaps, that they would weakly betray the sinner. Soon he lost patience, and cried out he would give a king's pound to know.

When he had said this over and over, I began to reflect that, if he had any real idea of doing as he promised, a pound was a great sum, and to consider what might be done with it in the way of marbles of Amsterdam, tops, and certain much-desired books; for now this last temptation was upon me, as it has been ever since. As I sat, and Dove thundered, I remembered how, when one Stacy, with an oath, assured my father that his word was as good as his bond, my parent said dryly that this equality left him free to choose, and he would prefer his bond. I saw no way to what was for me the mysterious security of a bond, but I did conceive of some need to stiffen the promise Dove had made before I faced the penalty.

Upon this I held up a hand, and the master cried, «What is it?»

I said, «Master, if a boy should tell thee, wouldst thou surely give a pound?»

At this a lad called «Shame!» thinking I was a telltale.

When Dove called silence, and renewed his pledge, I, overbold, said, «Master, I did it, and now wilt thou please to give me a pound —a king's pound?»

«I will give thee a pounding!» he roared; and upon this came down from his raised form, and gave me a beating so terrible and cruel that at last the girls cried aloud, and he let me drop on the floor sore and angry. I lay still awhile, and then went to my seat. As I bent over my desk, it was rather the sense that I had been wronged than the pain of the blows which troubled me.

After school, refusing speech to any, I walked home, and ministered to my poor little bruised body as I best could. Now, this being a Saturday, and therefore a half-holiday, I ate at two with my father and mother.

Presently my father, detecting my uneasy movements, said, «Hast thou been birched to-day, and for what badness?»

Upon this, my mother said softly: «What is it, my son? Have no fear.» And this gentleness being too much for me, I fell to tears, and blurted out all my little tragedy.

As I ended, my father rose, very angry, and cried out, «Come this way!» But my mother caught me, saying: «No! no! Look, John! See his poor neck and his wrist! What a brute! I tell thee, thou shalt not! It were a sin. Leave him to me,» and she thrust me behind her as if for safety.

To my surprise, he said, «As thou wilt,» and my mother hurried me away. We had a grave, sweet talk, and there it ended for a time. I learned that, after all, the woman's was the stronger will. I was put to bed, and declared to have a fever, and given sulphur and treacle, and kept out of the paternal paths for a mournful day of enforced rest.

On the Monday following I went to school as usual, but not without fear of Dove. When we were all busy, about ten o'clock, I was amazed to hear my father's voice. He stood before the desk, and addressed Master Dove in a loud voice, meaning, I suppose, to be heard by all of us.

«David Dove,» he said, «my son hath been guilty of disrespect to thee and to thy office. I do not say he has lied, for it is my belief that thou art truly an unjust and cruel beast. As for his sin, he has suffered enough [I felt glad of this final opinion]; but a bargain was made. He, on his part, for a consideration of one pound sterling, was to tell thee who wrote certain words. He has paid thee, and thou hast taken interest out of his skin. Indeed, Friend Shylock, I think he weighs less by a pound. Thou wilt give him his pound, Master David.»

Upon this a little maid near by smiled at me, and Warder punched me in the ribs. Master Dove was silent a moment, and then answered that there was no law to make him pay, and that he had spoken lightly, as one might say, «I would give this or that to know.» But my father replied at once:

«The boy trusted thee, and was as good as his word. I advise thee to pay. As thou art master to punish boys, so will I, David, use thy birch on thee at need, and trust to the great Master to reckon with me if I am wrong.»

All this he said so fiercely that I trembled with joy, and hoped that Dove would deny him; but in place of this he muttered something about Meeting and Friends, and meanwhile searched his pockets, and brought out a guinea. This my father dropped into his breeches pocket, saying, «The shilling over will be for interest» (a guinea being a shilling over a king's pound). After this, turning to me, he said, «Come with me, Hugh,» and went out of the school-house, I following after, very well pleased, and thinking of my guinea. I dared not ask for it, and I think he forgot it. He went along homeward, with his head bent, and his hands behind his back. In common he walked with his head up and his chin set forward, as though he did a little look down on the world of other men; and this in truth he did, being at least six feet three inches in his stocking-feet, and with no lack of proportion in waist or chest.

Next day I asked my mother of my guinea; but she laughed gaily, and threw up her hands, and cried: «A bad debt—a bad debt, Hugh! Dost thou want more interest? My father used to say they had a proverb in the Midi, ‹If the devil owe thee money, it were best to lose it.› *Le diable!* Oh, what am I saying? *Mon fils*, forget thy debt. What did thy father say?» And I told it again, to her amusement; but she said at last very seriously:

«It has disturbed thy father as never before did anything since he would not join with Friend Bradford against the Stamp Act. I would I had seen him then, or this time. I like sometimes to see a strong man in just anger. Oh, *mon Dieu!* What did I say! I am but half a Quaker, I fear.» My mother never would turn away from the creed of her people, but she did not altogether fancy the ways of Friends.

«Eh, *mon fils*, sometimes I say naughty words. Give me a sweet little pat on the cheek for my badness, and always come to me with all thy troubles.» Then I kissed her, and we went out to play hide-and-find in the orchard.

As to my father, even his grim, sarcastic humor left him as years went on, and he became as entirely serious as I ever knew a man to be. I think on this occasion his after annoyance, which endured for days, was more because of having threatened Dove than for any other cause. He no doubt regarded me as the maker of the mischief which had tempted him for a moment to forget himself, and for many a day his unjust severity proved that he did not readily forgive. But so it was always. My mother never failed to understand me, which my father seemed rarely able to do. If I did ill, he used the strap with little mercy, but neither in these early years, nor in those which followed, did he ever give me a word of praise. Many years afterward I found a guinea in a folded paper laid away in my father's desk. On the outer cover he had written, «This belongs to Hugh. He were better without it.»

My mother scarce ever let slip her little French expletives or phrases in my father's hearing. He hated all French things, and declared the language did not ring true—that it was a slippery tongue, in which it was easy to lie. A proud, strong man he was in those days, of fixed beliefs, and of unchanging loyalty to the king. In his own house he was feared by his son, his clerks, and his servants; but not by my mother, who charmed him as she did all other men, and had in most things her desire.

Outside of his own walls few men cared to oppose him. He was rich and coldly despotic; a man exact and just in business, but well able, and as willing, to help with a free hand whatever cause was of interest to Friends. My aunt Gainor, a little his senior, was one of the few over whom he had no manner of control. She went her own way, and it was by no means his way, as I shall make more clear by and by.

Two days later I was taken to the academy, or the college, as some called it, which is now the university. My father wrote my name, as you may see it in the catalogue, and his own signature, with the date of June 4, 1765. Beneath it is the entry of John Warder and his father, Joseph; for Jack had also been removed from Dove's dominion because of what my father said to Joseph, a man always pliable, and advised to do what larger men thought good. Thus it came about that my friend Jack and I were by good fortune kept in constant relation. Our schoolmate, the small maid so slight of limb, so dark and tearful, was soon sent away to live with an aunt in Bristol, on the Delaware, having become an orphan by the death of her mother. Thus it came about that Darthea Peniston passed out of my life for many years, having been, through the accident of her tenderness, the means for me of a complete and fortunate change.

III.

THE academy was, and still is, a plain brick building, set back from Fourth street, and having a large graveled space in front and also at the back. The main school-room occupied its whole westward length, and upstairs was a vast room, with bare joists above, in which, by virtue of the deed of gift, any Christian sect was free to worship if temporarily deprived of a home. Here the great Whitefield preached, and here generations of boys were taught. Behind the western playground was the graveyard of Christ Church. He was thought a brave lad who, after school at dusk in winter, dared to climb over, and search around the tombs of the silent dead for a lost ball or what not.

I was mightily afraid of the academy. The birch was used often and with severity, and, as I soon found, there was war between the boys and the town fellows who lived to north and east. I was also to discover other annoyances quite as little to the taste of Friends, such as stone fights or snowball skirmishes. Did time permit, I should like well to linger long over this school life. The college, as it was officially called, had a great reputation, and its early catalogues are rich with names of those who made an empire. This task I leave to other pens, and hasten to tell my own personal story.

In my friend Jack Warder's journal there is a kind page or two as to what manner of lad I was in his remembrance of me in after years. I like to think it was a true picture.

« When Hugh Wynne and I went to school at the academy on Fourth street, south of Arch, I used to envy him his strength. At twelve he was as tall as are most lads at sixteen, but possessed of such activity and muscular power as are rarely seen, bidding fair to attain, as he did later, the height and massive build of his father. He was a great lover of risk, and not, as I have always been, fearful. When we took apples, after the fashion of all Adam's young descendants, he was as like as not to give them away. I think he went with us on these and some wilder errands chiefly because of his fondness for danger, a thing I could never comprehend. He still has his mother's great eyes of blue, and a fair, clear skin. God bless him! Had I never known him, I might perhaps have been, as to one thing, a happier man, but I had been less deserving of such good fortune as has come to me in life. For this is one of the uses of friends—that we consider how such and such a thing we are moved to do might appear to them. And this for one of my kind, who have had—nay, who have—many weaknesses, has been why Hugh Wynne counts for so much to me.

« We, with two other smaller boys, were at that time the only sons of Friends at the academy, and were, thanks to the brute Dove, better grounded in the humanities than were some, although we were late in entering.»

I leave this and other extracts as they were writ. A more upright gentleman than John Warder I know not, nor did ever know. What he meant by his weaknesses I cannot tell, and as to the meaning of one phrase, which he does not here explain, these pages shall perhaps discover.

Not long after our entrance at the academy, my father charged me one morning with a note to my aunt Gainor Wynne, which I was to deliver when the morning session was over. As this would make me late, in case her absence delayed a reply, I was to remain and eat my midday meal. My father was loath always to call upon his sister. She had early returned to the creed of her ancestors, and sat on Sundays in a great square pew at Christ Church, to listen to the Rev. Robert Jennings. Hither, in September of 1763, my aunt took me, to my father's indignation, to hear the great Mr. Whitefield preach.

Neither Aunt Gainor's creed, dress, house, nor society pleased her brother. She had early made clear, in her decisive way, that I was to be her heir, and she was, I may add, a woman of large estate. I was allowed to visit her as I pleased. Indeed, I did so often. I liked no one better, always excepting my mother. Why, with my father's knowledge of her views, I was thus left free, I cannot say. He was the last of men to sacrifice his beliefs to motives of gain.

When I knocked at the door of her house on Arch street, opposite the Friends' Meeting-house, a black boy dressed as a page let me in. He was clad in gray armozine, a sort of corded stuff, with red buttons, and he wore a red turban. As my aunt was gone to drive, on a visit to that Madam Penn who was once Miss Allen, I was in no hurry, and was glad to look about me. The parlor, a great room with three windows on the street, afforded a strange contrast to my sober home. There were Smyrna rugs on a polished floor, a thing almost unheard of. Indeed, people came to see them. The furniture was all of red walnut, and carved in shells and flower reliefs. Of tables there were so many, little and larger, with claw-feet or spindle-legs, that one had to be careful not to overturn their loads of Chinese dragons, ivory carvings, grotesque Delft beasts, and fans French, or Spanish, or of the Orient. There was also a spinet, and a corner closet of books, of which every packet brought her a variety. Up-stairs was a fair room full of volumes, big and little, as I found to my joy rather later, and these were of all kinds—some good, and some of them queer or naughty. Over the wide, white fireplace was a portrait of herself by the elder Peale, but I prefer the one now in my library. This latter hung, at the time I speak of, between the windows. It was significant of my aunt's idea of her own importance that she should have wished to possess two portraits of herself. The latter was painted by Sir Joshua Reynolds when she was in England in 1750, and represents her as a fine, large woman, with features which were too big for loveliness in youth, but in after years went well with her abundant gray hair and unusual stature; for, like the rest of us, she was tall, of vigorous and wholesome build and color, with large, well-shaped hands, and the strength of a man—I might add, too, with the independence of a man. She went her own way, conducted the business of her estate, which was ample, with skill and ability, and asked advice from no one. Like my father, she had a liking to control those about her, was restlessly busy, and was never so pleased as when engaged in arranging other people's lives, or meddling with the making of matches.

To this ample and luxurious house came the better class of British officers, and ombre and quadrille were often, I fear, played late into the long nights of winter. Single women, after a certain or uncertain age, were given a brevet title of «Mistress.» Mistress Gainor Wynne lost or won with the coolness of an old gambler, and this habit, perhaps more than aught beside, troubled my father. Sincere and consistent in his views, I can hardly think that my father was, after all, unable to resist the worldly advantages which my aunt declared should be mine. It was, in fact, difficult to keep me out of the obvious risks this house and company provided for a young person like myself. He must have trusted to the influence of my home to keep me in the ways of Friends. It is also to be remembered, as regards my father's motives, that my aunt Gainor was my only relative, since of the Owens none were left.

My mother was a prime favorite with this masterful lady. She loved nothing better than to give her fine silk petticoats or a pearl-colored satin gown; and if this should nowadays amaze Friends, let them but look in the «Observer,» and see what manner of finery was advertised in 1778 as stole from our friend Sarah Fisher, sometime Sarah Logan, a much-respected member of Meeting. In this, as in all else, my mother had her way, and, like some of the upper class of Quakers, wore at times such raiment as fifty years later would have surely brought about a visit from a committee of overseers.

Waiting for Aunt Gainor, I fell upon an open parcel of books just come by the late spring packet. Among these turned up a new and fine edition of «Captain Gulliver's Travels,» by Mr. Dean Swift. I lit first, among these famous adventures, on an extraordinary passage, so wonderful, indeed, and so amusing, that I heard not the entrance of my father, who at the door had met my aunt, and with her some fine ladies of the governor's set. There were Mrs. Ferguson, too well known in the politics of later years, but now only a beautiful and gay woman; Madam Allen; and Madam Chew, the wife of the attorney-general.

They were eagerly discussing, and laughingly inquiring of my father what color of masks for the street was to be preferred. He was in no wise embarrassed by these fine dames, and never, to my thinking, was seen to better advantage than among what he called «world's people.» He seemed to me more really at home than among Friends, and as he towered, tall, and gravely courteous in manner, I thought him a grand gentleman.

As I looked up, the young Miss Chew, who afterward married Colonel Eager Howard, was saying saucily: «Does not Madam Wynne wear a mask for her skin? It is worth keeping, Mr. Wynne.»

«Let me recommend to you a vizard with silver buttons to hold in the mouth, or, better, a riding-mask,» cried Aunt Gainor, pleased at this gentle badgering, «like this, John. See, a flat silver plate to hold between the teeth. It is the last thing.»

«White silk would suit her best,» cried Mrs. Ferguson, «or green, with a chin-curtain—a loo-mask. Which would you have, sir?»

«Indeed,» he said quietly, «her skin is good enough. I know no way to better it.»

Then they all laughed, pelting the big man with many questions, until he could not help but laugh as he declared he was overwhelmed and would come on his business another day. But on this the women would not stay, and took themselves and their high bonnets and many petticoats out of the room, each dropping a courtesy at the door, and he bowing low, like Mr. John Penn, as never before I had seen him do.

No sooner were they gone than he desired me to give him the note he had written to his sister, since now it was not needed, and then he inquired what book I was reading. Aunt Gainor glanced at it, and replied for me: «A book of travels, John; very improving, too. Take it home, Hugh, and read it. If you find in it no improprieties, it may be recommended to your father.» She loved nothing better than to tease him.

«I see not what harm there could be in travels,» he returned. «Thou hast my leave. Gainor, what is this I hear? Thou wouldst have had me sell thee for a venture threescore hogsheads of tobacco from Annapolis. I like not to trade with my sister, nor that she should trade at all; and now, when I have let them go to another, I hear that it is thou who art the real buyer. I came hither to warn thee that other cargoes are to arrive. Thou wilt lose.»

Aunt Gainor said nothing for a moment, but let loose the linen safeguard petticoat she wore against mud or dust when riding, and appeared in a rich brocade of gray silken stuff, and a striped under-gown. When she had put off her loose camlet over-jacket, she said: «Will you have a glass of Madeira, or shall it be Hollands, John? Ring the bell, Hugh.»

«Hollands,» said my father.

«What will you give me for your tobacco to-day, John?»

«Why dost thou trifle?» he returned.

«I sold it again, John. I am the better by an hundred pounds. Two tobacco-ships are wrecked on Hinlopen. An express is come. Have you not heard?»

«Farewell,» he said, rising. He made no comment on her news. I had an idea that he would not have been unhappy had she lost on her venture.

Joseph Warder was her agent then and afterward. She rarely lost on her purchases. Although generous, and even lavish, she dearly loved a good bargain, and, I believe, liked the game far more than she cared for success in the playing of it.

«Come, Hugh,» she said, «let us eat and drink. Take the book home, and put it away for your own reading. Here is sixpence out of my gains. I hope you will never need to trade, and, indeed, why should you, whether I live or die? How would the king's service suit you, and a pair of colors?»

I said I should like it.

«There is a pretty tale, Hugh, of the French gentlemen who, being poor, have to make money in commerce. They leave their swords with a magistrate, and when they are become rich enough take them back again. There is some pleasing ceremony, but I forget. The Wynnes have been long enough in drab and trade. It is time we took back our swords, and quitted bow-thouing and bow-theeing.»

I said I did not understand.

«Oh, you will,» said Aunt Gainor, giving me a great apple-dumpling. «Take some molasses. Oh, as much as you please. I shall look away, as I do when the gentlemen take their rum.»

You may be sure I obeyed her. As to much that she said, I was shocked; but I never could resist a laugh, and so we made merry like children, as was usual; for, as she used to say, «To learn when to laugh and when not to laugh is an education.»

When my meal was over, and my stomach and my pockets all full, Aunt Gainor bade me sit on her knees, and began to tell me about what fine gentlemen were the Wynnes, and how foolish my grandfather had been to turn Quaker, and give up fox-hunting and the old place. I was told, too, how much she had lost to Mr. Penn last night, and more that was neither well for me to hear nor wise for her to tell; but as to this she cared little, and she sent me away then, as far too many times afterward, full of my own importance, and of desire to escape some day from the threatened life of the ledger and the day-book.

At last she said, «You are getting too heavy, Hugh. Handsome Mrs. Ferguson says you are too big to be kissed, and not old enough to kiss,» and so she bade me go forth to the afternoon session of the academy.

After two weeks at the academy I got my first lesson in the futility of non-resistance, so that all the lessons of my life in favor of this doctrine were of a sudden rendered vain. We were going home in the afternoon, gay and happy, Jack Warder to take supper with me, and to use a boat my aunt had given me.

Near to High street was a vacant lot full of bushes and briers. Here the elder lads paused, and one said, «Wynne, you are to fight.»

I replied: «Why should I fight? I will not.»

«But it is to get your standing in the school, and Tom Alloway is to fight you.»

«This was a famous occasion in our lives,» writes my friend Jack; «for, consider, I, who was a girl for timidity, was sure to have my turn next, and here were we two little fellows, who had heard every First-day, and ever and ever at home, that all things were to be suffered of all men—and of boys, too, I presume. I was troubled for Hugh, but I noticed that while he said he would not fight he was buttoning up his jacket and turning back the cuff of one sleeve. Also he smiled as he said, ‹No, I cannot›; and many times since I have seen him merry in danger.

«For, of a truth, never later did he or I feel the sense of a great peril as we did that day, with the bigger boys hustling us, and Alloway crying ‹Coward!› I looked about for some man who would help us, but there was no one; only a cow hobbled near by. She looked up, and then went on chewing her cud. I, standing behind Hugh, said, ‹Run! run!›

«The counsel seemed good to me who gave it. As I think on it now, I was in great perplexity of soul, and had a horrible fear as to bodily hurt. I turned, followed by Hugh, and ran fleetly across the open ground and through the bushes. About midway I looked back. Two lads were near upon us, when I saw Hugh drop upon his hands and knees. Both fellows rolled over him, and he called out, as they fell to beating him, ‹Run, Jack!›

«But I was no longer so minded. I kicked one boy, and struck another, and even now recall how a strange joy captured me when I struck the first blow.»

There was a fine scrimmage, for no quarter was asked or given, and I saw my poor Jack's girl-face bloody. This was the last I remember clearly, for the lust of battle was on me, and I can recall no more of what chanced for a little than I could in later years of the wild melley on the main street of Germantown, or of the struggle in the redoubt at Yorktown.

Presently we were cast to right and left by a strong hand, and, looking up as I stood fierce and panting, I saw Friend Rupert Forest, and was overwhelmed with fear; for often on First-day I had heard him preach solemnly, and always it was as to turning the other cheek, and on the wickedness of profane language. Just now he seemed pleased rather than angered, and said, smiling:

«This is a big war, boys. What is it about?»

I said, «I must fight for my standing, and I will not.»

«I think thou wert scarcely of that mind just now. There will be bad blood until it is over.»

To this I replied, «It is Alloway I am to fight.»

To my surprise, he went on to say, «Then take off thy jacket, and stand up, and no kicking.»

I asked nothing better, and began to laugh. At this my foe, who was bigger and older than I, cried out that I would laugh on the other side of my mouth—a queer boy phrase of which I could never discover the meaning.

«And now, fair play,» said Friend Forest. «Keep cool, Hugh, and watch his eyes.»

I felt glad that he was on my side, and we fell to with no more words. I was no match for the practised fists of my antagonist; but I was the stronger, and I kept my wits better than might have been expected. At last I got his head under my arm, with a grip on his gullet, and so mauled him with my right fist that Friend Forest pulled me away, and my man staggered back, bloody, and white too, while I was held like a dog in leash.

«He hath enough, I think. Ask him.»

I cried out, «No! Damn him!» It was my first oath.

«Hush!» cried Forest. «No profane language!»

«I will not speak to him,» said I; «and—and—he is a beast of the pit.» Now this fine statement I had come upon in a book of Mr. William Penn's my father owned, wherein the governor had denounced one Mr. Muggleton.

Friend Forest laughed merrily. «Thou hast thy standing, lad.» For Alloway walked sullenly away, not man enough to take more or to confess defeat. Jack, who was still white, said:

«It is my turn now, and which shall it be?»

«Shade of Fox!» cried Friend Forest. «The war is over. Come, boys, I must see you well out of this.» And so reassuring us, he went down Fourth street, and to my home.

My father was in the sitting-room, taking his long-stemmed reed pipe at his ease. He rose as we followed Friend Forest into the room.

«Well,» he said, «what coil is this?» For we were bloody, and hot with fight and wrath, and, as to our garments, in very sad disorder.

Friend Forest very quietly related our

story, and made much of his own share in the renewal of our battle. To my surprise, my father smiled.

«It seems plain,» he said, «that the lads were not to blame. But how wilt thou answer to the Meeting, Rupert Forest?»

«To it, to thee, to any man,» said the Quaker.

«It is but a month ago that thy case was before Friends because of thy having beaten Friend Waln's man. It will go ill with thee —ill, I fear.»

«And who is to spread it abroad?»

«Not I,» said my father.

«I knew that,» returned the Friend, simply. «I am but a jack-in-the-box Quaker, John. I am in and out in a moment, and then I go back and repent.»

«Let us hope so. Go to thy mother, Hugh; and as to thee, John Warder, wait until I send with thee a note to thy father. There are liquors on the table, Friend Forest.»

My mother set us in order, and cried a little, and said:

«I am glad he was well beaten. Thou shouldst never fight, my son; but if thou must, let it be so that thy adversary repent of it. *Mon Dieu! mon Dieu! j'en ai peur;* the wild Welsh blood of these Wynnes! And thy poor little nose—how 't is swelled!»

Not understanding her exclamations, Jack said as much; but she answered:

«Oh, it is a fashion of speech we French have. I shall never be cured of it, I fear. This wild blood—what will come of it?» And she seemed—as Jack writes long after, being more observing than I—as if she were looking away into the distance of time, thinking of what might come to pass. She had, indeed, strange insight, and even then, as I knew later, had her fears and unspoken anxieties. And so, with a plentiful supper, ended a matter which was, I may say, a critical point in my life.

(To be continued.)

*S. Weir Mitchell.*

# THE BREATH OF HAMPSTEAD HEATH.

THE wind of Hampstead Heath still burns my cheek
As, home returned, I muse, and see arise
Those rounded hills beneath the low, gray skies,
With gleams of haze-lapped cities far to seek.
These can I picture, but how fitly speak
Of what might not be seen with searching eyes,
And all beyond the listening ear that lies,
Best known to bards and seers in times antique?
The winds that of the spirit rise and blow
Kindle my thought, and shall for many a day,
Recalling what blithe presence filled the place
Of one who oftentimes passed up that way,
By garden close and lane where boughs bend low,
Until the breath of Hampstead touched his face.

*Edith M. Thomas.*

# AN OBJECT-LESSON IN MUNICIPAL GOVERNMENT.

## SHOWING HOW PUBLIC AFFAIRS ARE CONDUCTED IN THE CITY OF BIRMINGHAM.

WITH PICTURES BY LOUIS LOEB.

T would be interesting, even to American readers, to develop with some fullness the personal side of a story so interesting as the redemption of a great community from the hands of incompetent men; but space will not permit more than the attempt to develop results, leaving out these most interesting details.

Joseph Chamberlain became mayor of Birmingham, England, November 10, 1873. On January 13, 1874, he proposed that the manufacture, supply, and sale, of gas should be taken under the control of the corporation.

### GAS- AND WATER-WORKS.

A bill authorizing the purchase and amalgamation of the gas-works was submitted to the ratepayers, carried through Parliament, and the city obtained possession of the property September 1, 1875, the entire cost amounting to £2,000,931. A Gas Committee was appointed, efficient men were employed as managers, and the manufacture of gas began. Almost the first thing the committee did was to reduce the price 3*d.* per thousand, making the new charge ranging from 2*s.* 9*d.* to 3*s.* 3*d.*

The conditions make the district of supply very large. For lighting purposes, districts more than ten miles from the town hall are dependent upon the corporation, and for many miles beyond the corporate limits the streets of the smallest villages and the main country roads are lighted. The price of gas varies according to quantity consumed, the highest charge being 2*s.* 10*d.* per thousand, and the lowest 2*s.* 6*d.* for consumers of more than 50,000 feet per quarter, the average price being just under 2*s.* 7*d.* Bills are subject to a discount of five per cent. if settled within thirty days. The price charged to the city —the gas committee merely supplying the gas to the Public Works Committee, which erects its own street-lamps, which it lights, extinguishes, and repairs—is slightly less than 1*s.* 3*d.* per thousand. Outlying towns or local authorities have the advantage of the reduction, while private consumers pay at the same rate, whether in or out of the city.

In order to facilitate lighting in courts, the corporation undertakes to treat such lamps as public, on the principle that a light is almost as valuable as a policeman. In 1880 the number of court-lamps was 4, consuming 60,000 cubic feet of gas, at an annual cost of £10; in 1894 the number of lamps had increased to 1784, burning more than 25,000,000 cubic feet, and the cost to £1,866 per annum. Of the 160,000 houses in the district of supply, only 60,000 have meters, and of these not more than three fourths are dwelling-houses. In England gas-fixtures are individual property, furnished by the tenant, and removable when he goes into another house, the landlord supplying only the connection with the street mains. The department now encourages landlords to connect their houses, to supply tenants with fixtures, and to put in prepayment, or penny-in-the-slot, meters, like those in the artisans' houses belonging to the corporation, all to be covered by the gross cost of the gas furnished at a rate of 3*s.* 4*d.* per thousand.

The success of the consolidated gas scheme has been much greater than was predicted. The total profits appropriated to public purposes during the twenty years ending in 1894 have been £532,298; the reserve fund for maintenance and extension of plant amounts to £100,000; and the sinking fund for the redemption of debt to £415,606; while the large expenditure for betterment does not appear in the capital account, but is found in annual expenditure.

One of the most difficult problems Birmingham had to solve was its water-supply. It occupies the unique position of a great city far from any considerable body of water, salt or fresh. Owing to its situation, there is no river of respectable volume within many miles; lying so near the source of streams, they have no opportunity to acquire volume or force. When the town had grown to such size as to render necessary a public water-supply, it was drawn from the river Tame.

When it was necessary, an enlarged supply was drawn from some small streams, and from a series of deep wells, the water from both being pumped to the heights necessary to secure distribution by gravitation. Even so late as 1872, two fifths of the people were dependent upon shallow wells, which had become so foul as greatly to increase the death-rate.

Attempts to obtain authority to buy the undertaking were futile, but public sentiment was irresponsive until, in December, 1874, Mr. Chamberlain moved a resolution for the purchase of the water company's property and rights. This was carried without opposition, as it was also at the resulting town-hall meeting of the ratepayers. Mr. Chamberlain, while the bill authorizing the purchase was passing through Parliament, laid down the proposition, since accepted as a principle by most of the municipalities of England, that «all regulated monopolies sustained by the state, in the interest of the inhabitants generally, should be controlled by the representatives of the people, and not left in the hands of private speculators.» Progress was rapid, and the bill received the royal assent within eight months after its introduction, and January 1, 1876, the city had possession of the water-supply.

The health authorities then began the wholesome policy, since followed, of condemning the wells which had done so much to increase the death-rate from its then normal 22 in the thousand to 28 or 29. So effective has this been that the rents, the supply, and the number of consumers, have all nearly doubled since 1876, while the price has been three times reduced and only once increased. The works have been extended, and the old plant has been replaced by new, so that the property would bring in the market far more than its original cost, about £1,350,000, since swelled to £2,443,903 by extensions and by the new water scheme. The use of private baths and water-closets is slight compared with cities in the United States.

In spite of the increased demand and constant efforts to meet it, the water committee reached the conclusion some years ago that it was dangerous to trust existing resources. As early as 1871 it was proposed that the supply should be drawn from the valleys of the Elan and the Claerwen, in mid-Wales, eighty miles due west. The elevation of the lowest proposed reservoir is about 800 feet above the sea, some 200 feet greater than the highest point in Birmingham, so that water may be brought by gravitation over mountains and hills, under or over rivers, and deposited in reservoirs without pumping—now one of the most expensive processes. The corporation now distributes water to an area of 83,192 acres, and for its future supply has already acquired in the Welsh mountains areas amounting to over 45,000 acres.

The cost of the first section, to be in operation in 1902, will be about £4,000,000, and it is estimated that this will meet all demands for twenty-five years, after which, when needed, pipes will be added, the whole sum authorized to be expended by the act of Parliament being £6,600,000. The water is said to be the best in the kingdom, pure and soft, a curious incidental feature being the claim that the substitution of soft water for the hard now in use will result in a saving of from £35,000 to £60,000 a year in the cost of soap.

No opportunity is afforded for jobbery or corruption, because the work is done under the immediate personal supervision of the Water Committee, composed of eight of the best business men in the Council, serving without a penny of remuneration. During the last four years the chairman of the committee, Alderman Lawley Parker, has devoted an average of three days a week to the work in hand, and during the next six years will give nearly the whole of his time to its completion. It is not surprising that few mistakes are made, or that no intimation of jobbery or waste is heard.

## DWELLING-HOUSES AND HEALTH SCHEMES.

One of the first things the reform element did, when it obtained control, was to get accurate knowledge of the districts containing slums or insanitary areas. Immediately after his first election as mayor, Mr. Chamberlain suggested a special inspection of every part of the town. In order to do this, each member of the Health Committee—busy men engaged in their own affairs—undertook the work in two wards. During the following two years each member gave such time as he could to this work, going into every part of the district assigned him, including dark, noisome courts and narrow passages, and among a population to which he was unaccustomed. The slums were found to be almost as bad as could be, considering the conditions. It was an overcrowded population in small houses, not in tenements. Houses were then built in courts, many of them back to back. In the most congested

DRAWN BY LOUIS LOEB. ENGRAVED BY M. HAIDER.

THE OLD MARKET.

districts they were very small. The English workingman wants to have his home as nearly next door to his work as possible, one of the difficult problems being to get this class distributed into suburbs; so workshops had held their own in the heart of the town, and the work-people had remained with them. The worst district was within a stone's throw of the principal business street, its center no more than 300 yards from the town hall, and almost midway between the two great railway stations.

In 1875, during the second year of Mr. Chamberlain's mayoralty, Parliament passed the Artisans' Dwellings Act, providing that in any town of more than 25,000 population the medical officer of health, either on his own motion or upon complaint, should make an official representation that an unhealthy area existed. It also provided that the local authorities should remedy the condition of the area thus reported; that the local government board, after inquiry, could approve the scheme devised, and make a provisional order embodying it; and when confirmed by Parliament, the condemned property might be purchased by agreement or arbitration, without paying an extra price for compulsory sale. After making the necessary improvements, the surplus land might be sold, but the city could not, without special authority from the local government board, enter upon the building of houses.

Birmingham was the first corporation to take advantage of this act. The medical officer of health, in accordance with law, made a report declaring the crowded central district insanitary. The new committee presented a scheme condemning over 90 acres of land, covered with 3744 houses, with a total population of 16,596. Of these, 3054 were artisans' houses, in which the number of inhabitants was 13,538. The key to the proposed improvement was the making of a new street, 22 yards wide and 851 yards long, through the condemned area, the widening of other streets, the destruction of many of the houses, the building of artisans' houses cutting a very small figure in the original estimates and plans. The gross cost was estimated at £1,308,221, and the net cost, deducting the value of the land not used for making new streets or widening old ones, £461,958. Work upon this scheme was begun in 1876, and continued until about 1882. The character of the central part of the city was entirely changed; but the example, united with the vigilant action of the Health Committee in enforcing the law, brought about an amelioration of conditions in every crowded quarter of the city.

For some years the corporation made no effort to build or to procure the building of artisans' houses on the surplus land. Sixty-two houses and twenty shops were built on one part by private capital; but the high price of land, and the stringent rules as to the kind of houses, made it difficult to get builders to take it up. The corporation had altered and repaired the existing houses where this was possible. It took down some of them, put in windows, enlarged and paved the courts, perfected the sanitary arrangements, and they have since been rented with success. In 1889 application was made for leave, under the act, to erect a block of artisans' dwellings, and during the next year twenty-two cottages were completed, at a cost of £4000, or an average of £181 each. These were at once let, care being taken that they should be occupied by the artisan classes, for whom they were intended, at inclusive rents—that is, all rates paid—of from 5*s.* to 7*s.* 6*d.* per week. In 1891 eighty-one additional dwellings were erected from different and perfected designs, at a cost of £14,000—an average of nearly £173 each. In general, these houses consist of a front living-room, 13 feet by 12 feet 6 inches, and a kitchen, 12 feet by 9 feet 6 inches, on the first floor, with bedrooms of the same size on the second floor, and an attic room 13 feet square—five in all. Each is furnished with ranges in the ground-floor rooms, and grates in the bedrooms, and has a separate water-closet and coal-bin, but no cellar. They are furnished with penny-in-the-slot machines supplying 25 cubic feet of gas, enough to keep one burner going four hours.

In carrying out the improvement scheme, there has been expended as capital £1,676,465, and for maintenance £354,607, a total of £2,031,072. For this the city has 45 acres of land, mostly let on leases for seventy-five years, many of them having only sixty years to run. The land, being centrally located, commands the highest rentals, and is occupied with the best business buildings of the town. These must be kept in perfect repair until the expiration of the leases, when they will become corporation property. The best estimates of the present actual sale value of the property included in the scheme are £2,250,000.

The effect upon the health-rate in the area covered by the scheme was immediate. For the three years, 1873–75, the average annual death-rate in nine of the worst streets in-

DRAWN BY LOUIS LOEB.

WORKINGMEN'S COTTAGES NEAR THE GAS-WORKS.

cluded in it was 53.2 per thousand of population. For the three years, 1879–81, the average death-rate in the same streets was only 21.3 per thousand.

When the work of regeneration was taken up, one of the pressing problems was the general sanitary condition. Fortunately, in 1872 Parliament passed a general act consolidating sanitary authorities, and greatly increasing their powers. Immediate advantage was taken of its provisions, and Dr. Alfred Hill, who had been borough analyst since 1859, was appointed medical officer of health, which place he still holds. In 1875 the report, based upon personal inspection by the members of the Sanitary Committee, was made to the Council. The conditions disclosed as existing in crowded districts were about as bad as could be. More than half of the buildings inspected had no back door, being built back to back, and the inhabitants of two fifths of them were dependent for their scanty supply of water upon wells liable to corruption from surface sources. The number of inspectors was found to be utterly inadequate. The report emphasized the fact that the public health had been declining for several years, and that sewerage and drainage, the paving of streets and foot-paths, and a thorough system of scavenging, were absolutely necessary. The work of doing all these was undertaken and carried out with such success that the death-rate of 26.8 in the thousand in 1874, and 26.3 in 1875, declined to 22.4 in 1876. This continued, with slight variations owing to local or temporary conditions, until, in 1888, the average had fallen to 18.2, since which time it has slightly increased, owing mainly to epidemics of influenza (the grippe), smallpox, and, during the last few years, of diarrheal affections among children. An average reduction of about 4 per thousand, or nearly 2000 per year, in the death-rate tells the story of hard and intelligent work.

One of the worst features under the old management was the disposal of the sewage. By way of remedy two systems have found adoption. Under one the Health Committee collects the offal of houses, and either destroys it or turns it into fertilizers. This is more offensive and less successful than it might be made, but is apparently a necessity until the pan system has been abandoned. A sewage-farm of nearly 1300 acres has been developed several miles from the city, some 400 feet lower in elevation. The sewage, first mixed with lime to prevent too rapid decomposition and to assist in the precipitation of the solid matter, is passed through a series of depositing tanks, during which process the mud is removed. The remainder is dug into the land, one third of which is dealt with each year, the effluent being discharged in a harmless state into the river Tame. Upon the other two thirds are grown early vegetables, and grain and hay for cows kept for milk and market. The net annual cost to the city is about £24,000.

### STREETS, PARKS, AND TRAMWAYS.

BIRMINGHAM has emphasized its ownership of the streets. Early in the present régime the policy was adopted of requiring new streets to be put into permanent condition, graded and macadamized, before acceptance. Most of the 257 miles of streets are paved with macadam varying from 6 to 18 inches in depth. It is well adapted for the less crowded residence districts, although somewhat costly to maintain. In the business quarter stone blocks are used, their average life being twenty-five years. This is done by the Public Works Committee, with laborers working by the day or week. Other streets in the same quarter are paved with wood blocks, insuring greater freedom from noise and more cleanliness. This is laid by contract, and is supposed to have an average life of fourteen years. Whatever material is used, the streets are kept in the best repair. Street-cleaning gangs meet in the business quarter at five o'clock each morning, sweep up and cart away the accumulated dirt, and water the streets before and after the operation, until those laid with wood look as if they had been carefully scrubbed. They are also kept clear of litter during the day. In residence districts they are swept once, twice, or three times a week, as required. As a result, they are everywhere kept so clean as to cause surprise. It cannot, however, be said that the foot-paths are so well kept, the practice of every man sweeping before his own door not being common, except for the removal of snow.

More to assert and maintain its control of the streets than for profit, the Council in 1871 assumed the building of tramway lines. These are constructed by the Public Works Committee, and let on leases to run twenty-one years, the lessee maintaining the pavement. Thus far they are a burden rather than a profit. When the property, including rolling-stock, engine-houses, storage-battery motors, and all fixtures, falls in, it is thought it will pay expenses. As the use of trams increases, —which it does slowly, and not by leaps and bounds as in American cities,—the property will doubtless become remunerative.

In 1871, though there were nominally three parks, containing a total area of 90 acres, there was really but one,—Aston Park, with its 49 acres, and Aston Hall (one of the best remaining examples of a Jacobean mansion, and to which Washington Irving has given a new lease of immortality by making it the model for those delightful studies of old-time life which radiate from « Bracebridge Hall »), —the others being little more than bare pieces of land, with no attractiveness, natural or artificial.

ASTON HALL PLAYGROUND.

In the face of many difficulties, something has been done to supply the lack of open spaces. Now there are seven parks, five recreation-grounds, and two gardens, fourteen in all, well distributed in the town and suburbs, with a total area of 350 acres. Two

DRAWN BY LOUIS LOEB. ENGRAVED BY H. DAVIDSON.

THE LIBRARY—NEWSPAPERS.

of these were the gift of a public-spirited woman, the late Miss Ryland, who refused even so much as to permit either of them to bear her name. These are highly creditable, containing pools, out-door swimming-baths, flower-beds, and the accessories of modern parks. Most of the others are play and recreation-grounds, well adapted for their purposes, and useful to the crowded population about them.

One feature rather surprising to an American is that every park is made for use. There is no fear lest the grass may be injured, but in every ground adapted for them are cricket-and football-fields, picnic-grounds, croquet-lawns, tennis-courts, bowling-greens, the use of which is permitted for a merely nominal payment.[1] Every park, large or small, has one or more concerts each week during the summer, paid for by a neighborhood subscription. Less need exists for large parks than in American cities of the same size, because the better class of houses all have ample gardens.

[1] It is easier to keep grass in good condition in the moist atmosphere of England.—EDITOR.

## FREE LIBRARIES, ART GALLERY AND SCHOOL, AND TECHNICAL SCHOOL.

LIBRARIES, free and subscription, have long had a place in Birmingham, and an attempt was made to take prompt advantage of the act permitting corporations to support free libraries. But public sentiment was lax in 1853, when, economy ruling the day, the proposition was defeated by failure to command the support of the requisite two thirds. This decision was not reversed until 1860, when the experiment was entered upon with success, with the result that a slow and steady growth followed until about 1872, when the forward sweep of public sentiment gave it a decided impetus. From the beginning the Council admitted outsiders into a share of its work, on the ground that it was technical, and to insure success needed men instructed in its mysteries. Samuel Timmins and J. Thackray Bunce have been on the committee from the beginning, though never members of the Council, and their services to the free libraries, covering more than thirty-four years of hard work, cannot be measured or exaggerated. With the librarian, Mr. J. D. Mullins, they have bought the books, organized and maintained the staff, enlarged the scheme as it became necessary, created the public sentiment which made expansion possible, and given ungrudging, unpaid attention to the task. The Central Lending Library was first developed, and the policy of starting branches, of which there are now seven, was entered upon. A reference library, opened in 1866 in a modest way, has grown until it is one of the best in the Old World, special attention being paid to the technical books relating to the trades of the district. As in providing for mental as well as for physical wants, the interests of the working-people have always been in mind, and, in return, this element has been the main reliance for support. In 1879, when the Central libraries were burned, the town arose as a man, and assisted in the raising of money to rebuild and to buy books, the working-people making collections in their shops. These subscriptions were so liberal that their success was greater than ever before. The growth from 1871 to 1894 has more than kept pace with the progress of the town. The number of volumes has risen from 57,857 to 187,443, and the annual issues from 436,445 to 1,126,830, the greater ratio of increase being shown in the reference library. Nowhere in the kingdom is there a more complete Shaksperian collection, and it attracts special students from far and wide. There are also special collections devoted to Byron, Cervantes, and Milton,—proof that bibliographical interest may be maintained even in an institution dependent on popular favor.

A school of art, with reference to the industries of the district, has been in existence since 1821. It was supported by private subscriptions until, by the liberality of three donors, steps were taken in 1881 which led to its transfer to the corporation, which assumed responsibility for its maintenance. It is housed in a building designed for the purpose,—the last work of John Henry Chamberlain,—and is fully equipped with a corps of well-qualified teachers. Since its transfer to the corporation it has been managed with conspicuous success. In addition to the central school, fourteen branches have been opened in School Board buildings, close relations having been established and maintained between the art schools and the elementary schools. The number of students during 1894 was 3536, and the training is based on industrial and decorative uses, upon the principle that if art can be applied to the ordinary affairs of life, it will naturally lead to development on higher and broader lines. Of the entire cost of £56,000, nearly three fifths have come by gifts from liberal citizens.

Closely related to the art school is the museum and art gallery, toward which a beginning was made as early as 1867, with about a dozen pictures, which had been presented from time to time. With these as a nucleus, the work was earnestly taken up when the forward movement began, but it was not until 1880 that substantial progress was made. In that year Mr. Richard (now Sir Richard) Tangye, one of the men whose benefactions to the libraries, art school, and art gallery are among the glories of the town, on behalf of himself and his brother, tendered £10,000 for the purchase of pictures and art objects. This was supplemented by other donors, until, when a fund of £17,000 had become available, it was intrusted to an Art Gallery Purchase Committee, composed of members of the Council, and eight representatives of donors and art organizations. The money thus raised has now been spent, and collections of pictures and objects of art, to the value of about £50,000, have been presented to the gallery and museum. Many of the great English artists of this century are represented by excellent examples; but more attention has been paid to the museum, wherein is gathered a notable collection of things for use, interest, and instruction. These are

DRAWN BY C. A. VANDERHOOF.

BIRMINGHAM MUNICIPAL TECHNICAL SCHOOL—SUFFOLK STREET ELEVATION.
ESSEX, NICOL & GOODMAN, ARCHITECTS.

housed in appropriate galleries built over the offices of the Gas Department, and out of the profits of that investment. All collections are open two hours for visitors on Sunday, and the average number for that day is about 2000. Admission is free at all times. The attendance, which rose to nearly 1,200,000 in 1886, declined to an average of about 900,000 during the last four years. Successful attention has been paid to cataloguing, so that the issues, at the price of a penny, are a wonder to the managers of other galleries. No attempt has been made to acquire the last picture by the artist who has just become the rage, the policy of making a representative collection having been followed. A collection has thus been made which gives a better idea of industrial and decorative art, and has more representative pictures than any other in England, outside of London.

Technical education was an important element in a district which was one of the busiest workshops in the world, and this was supplied for many years by the Midland Institute. But in 1890 Parliament passed a law making contributions, from local taxes collected by the imperial government, for the promotion of trade education. The Council, taking immediate advantage of the act, took over the Technical School, placing the management in the hands of a new committee. There was at once a marked increase in the number of students, and 80 classes were organized. In order not to exclude even the humblest, the fees were reduced to ten shillings, free scholarships were offered in connection with the board schools, and the facilities for study and experiment were improved. The courses were made progressive, so that the student might go from one branch to another. Prizes in the various branches taught were offered by employers, and close relations were established, and have been maintained, with the labor organizations.

The number of classes has increased in three years from 80 to 119, and the individual students from 794 to 1528, representing 120 occupations. This rapid growth has made necessary a new building, at a cost of about £80,000 for building and grounds. The fees have been so reduced that, while only £457 were collected from this source, £1094 were paid for chemicals, apparatus, and diagrams for the use of students. Thus another institution has been added to the educational facilities of the town, in which young mechanics may learn at night everything about the trades they pursue during the day. The Technical School Committee admits outside persons as members, an experiment which has already been tried successfully with the committees on free libraries and museum and art gallery, and also artisans, or their representatives.

### THE FINANCES.

PERHAPS the most difficult part of the work has been the management of the finances. Such vast sums have been necessary that many men have been forced to study ways and means. The resources at the beginning were small, the expenditure meager, and the debt insignificant, so that even the boldest might have been appalled at the prospect. The indebtedness in 1871, less sinking-fund and cash on hand, was only £546,393, and the average rate of interest something over four and a quarter per cent. The three great schemes entered upon in 1874 and 1875 alone increased this tenfold, while expenditure has gone forward steadily until the debt, aside from sinking-funds and money on hand, is £7,861,615, nearly fifteen times the amount due twenty-three years before, and the average rate of interest—unnaturally high because of the issue of perpetual irredeemable four-per-cent. annuities in payment for the gas and water schemes—is now about three and a half per cent. For capital expenditure, corporation stock to run sixty years is issued; that at three and a half per cent. is now worth 116, while the current issue at three per cent. is quoted at 105. A sinking-fund is provided for each item of indebtedness, arranged to pay both interest and principal in from ten years to a hundred.

The present capital account is represented by the net debt, and £1,825,726, the amount of sinking-funds provided from income, for debt redemption.

No rigid limit of indebtedness is fixed by law, but when it is desired to make a new loan, application is made to the local government board in London, which sends an inspector to report upon the necessity for the proposed improvement. If this is favorable, the borrowing powers are granted. If the city asks Parliament for a bill giving special authority to do anything, the mayor submits the matter to a meeting of ratepayers in the town hall, at which a poll may be demanded; *i.e.*, a vote «yes» or «no» by ballot. Each ratepayer under £50 annual value has then one vote, and an additional vote for each £50 up to £250, six in all. If he is owner as well as occupier, his votes are doubled for each qualification, until he may have twelve in all. This modified referendum has been resorted to five or six times since 1871, and in no case has a proposal to increase indebtedness failed to carry.

Money is raised by a borough rate and an improvement rate, both collected under arrangement by the poor-law overseers, and paid into the city treasury. The imperial authorities collect licenses from publicans, game-, tobacco-, and plate-dealers, appraisers, auctioneers, house-agents, pawnbrokers, and for armorial bearings, dogs, male servants, and for leave to kill game or carry guns, a proportion of the proceeds being returned to local authorities under the name of «exchequer contributions,» from which certain specified charges must be paid, the balance being turned into the city treasury. For 1893 the amount allotted to Birmingham was £91,569, the net amount carried to the relief of rates being £29,713. The receipts from the Gas Department were £595,709, from the Waterworks, £178,621, the income of the other committees, £234,812, leaving £460,920 for collection under the borough and improvement rates.

All accounts are examined by independent auditors, chartered accountants appointed by the Council or its committees, who must examine and certify to their correctness.

The average rates of all kinds, which were 14*s.* per head of population in 1871, have risen to 23*s.* 6*d.* in 1894, the profits from the gas and water schemes doing their full part in carrying on great improvements.

As work and responsibility have increased, the salaries of the principal officials have also grown. They are now: Town Clerk, £2200; City Surveyor, £1400; secretary of the Gas Department, £1250; chief engineer of the Water Department, £1200; City Treasurer, £1050; one engineer of the Gas Department, £1200; and the second, £1050; Medical Officer of Health, £1000; Chief of Police, £920; and the secretary of the Water Department, £600.

DRAWN BY LOUIS LOEB.

LOOKING UP NEW STREET.

THE CITY COUNCIL.

THE governing body, executive as well as legislative, is the City Council. The eighteen wards are each represented by four members, one having the title of alderman, and three that of councilor, all meeting in a single body. One is elected annually for each ward, so that two thirds of the councilors, and all the aldermen, have had experience. They are chosen by burgesses, who are male or female occupiers of any dwelling-house, shop, or manufactory, or of any land or tenement of the annual value of £10. The difference between burgesses and parliamentary electors is that women are admitted to the former. The parliamentary electors number 81,097, and burgesses and School Board electors 92,709, the difference representing with fair accuracy women voters. Members of Parliament are elected by districts, councilors from wards, and the School Board on a general ticket. No two classes are voted for at the same election, though practically the same machinery is employed. The expenditure permitted to municipal candidates is about £60 each. Vacancies in the Council are filled by special election. One alderman from each ward is elected by the Council for six years, half the terms ending every three years. As a rule they are reëlected indefinitely, party or factional considerations having little influence.

The Council is reorganized on the 9th of November of each year, when the General Purposes Committee, comprised of the mayor as chairman, and the chairman of each of the working committees,[1] nominates the committees for the ensuing year. Outside persons are appointed as additional members of the Museum and School of Art, Free Libraries, and Technical Schools Committees, who in practice control the technical work, the Council members retaining financial management.

Each member of a committee proposed is voted for separately. The wishes of individuals are rarely consulted until their names are presented, when they may decline and be excused. None may serve on more than two committees, nor be chairman of more than one. Every effort is made to secure the very best results. No precedents require the appointment of old members even to important committees, and a new member known to be capable and interested in some special work has no difficulty in obtaining an assignment that may enable him to do his best. But in practice the experienced men are reappointed without question. Each committee selects its own chairman.

The Council is a thoroughly representative body. Of the seventy-two members of the present Council, twenty-three are manufacturers, six are classified as gentlemen (men retired from business), six are provision merchants, five are brass and iron founders, solicitors, jewelers, and medical men respectively, three are merchants, there are two each of auctioneers, chemists, and drapers, while printers, teachers, butchers, bakers, glass-workers, tin-plate-workers, and newspaper managers each have one. So far as I can find out, but one publican has ever been in the Council, although this class had much influence prior to 1871.

No member has any privileges on a railway or public conveyance of any sort, even on the tramways belonging to the city, or admission to a theater or entertainment, and none is permitted to vote on a question when he has a personal interest. He is subject to a fine of £50, with loss of office, if he enters into any contract with the city, or sells an article of even the smallest value to the Council, or to any of its subsidiary or associated committees or departments. So strictly is this observed that a member of a committee, suspected of a desire to sell eligible property to the city, was forced to retire from public life.

When the work of a committee is to be discussed, it presents a report of all it has done since its affairs were last before the Council, setting out what it proposes. This report or agenda must be printed and sent to each councilor three full days before the meeting. In some cases, especially when a new scheme is proposed, each member is requested to make a personal investigation of the conditions with which it is proposed to deal.

Of the members of the Council in 1894, twenty-two had served for eleven years and more. One entered in 1852; another in 1855; one each in 1866 and 1867 respectively; two in 1870; one each in 1871, 1872, and 1873; two in 1874; one each in 1876, 1877, 1878, 1879, and 1880; and two each in 1881, 1882, and 1883. Of the prominent members who have either retired or died during the last twenty years, one, the late Thomas Avery, served continuously from 1862 to 1892; the late Sir

[1] The committees are as follows: Baths and Parks, Estates (custody of city property), Finance, General Purposes, Markets and Fairs, Health, Public Works, Watch (police and fire), Lunatic Asylums, Industrial School (reform school), Gas, Water, Improvement, Free Libraries, Museum and School of Art, Art Gallery Purchase, and Technical School.

Thomas Martineau from 1876 until his death in 1893; J. Powell Williams from 1877 to 1890; Joseph Chamberlain from 1869 to 1880; Jesse Collings from 1868 to 1886; and Richard Chamberlain, formerly M. P., from 1874 to 1886.

The time required of the principal members, chairmen of the leading committees, is from two to four business days per week, and of ordinary members from one to two days. A return sent me by the town clerk, showing the terms of service as chairman on some of the principal committees, is interesting. Alderman J. Powell Williams gave five and a half years to the chairmanship of the Finance Committee, and Alderman Clayton has devoted seven years to the same work. Alderman Cook has been chairman of the Health Committee, devoting himself unfailingly and unflinchingly to a most important and disagreeable work, for twenty years. Alderman Lawley Parker was nine years chairman of the Public Works Committee, and two years chairman of the Water Committee. Alderman Pollock has been chairman of the Gas Committee thirteen years, and the late Alderman Avery saw the same period of service as chairman of the Water Committee. Alderman Richard Chamberlain was five years chairman of the Improvement Committee, and Alderman George Baker has served eight years

### THE MAYOR.

AT the annual meeting on the 9th of November, the first business is the election of a mayor for the next year. He may be chosen from the body of citizens, but this has been done only once. As municipal work becomes intricate, it is more and more difficult for any man to be mayor without a Council training. In most cases, though not in all, the mayor has reached the title of alderman. If only a councilor, courtesy demands that he shall be elected to fill the first aldermanic vacancy. This may not occur during his mayoralty, but come when it may, he has a right to expect that he will be chosen. The choice of a mayor is made about the middle of July before his service is to begin. This is not done in public, but by a private meeting of all the members. The man himself is generally consulted, and given an opportunity to accept or decline, but a known seeker for the place is seldom selected. Just before the annual meeting, a requisition signed by a majority —and in some cases by all—is presented to the candidate, so that there has only once been a contest.

Immediately after his formal election, the mayor takes his place as president of the Council, and the appointment of the committees is proceeded with. A man may reach the mayoralty in from four to ten years, Joseph Chamberlain's case being an illustration of the shorter period. As a rule he is not thought of for mayor until his fitness for the place has been proved. Without exception, during the recent years the mayors have been men of good standing in business, none of large wealth, and none really poor.

There is no prescribed scale of expenditure for a mayor. He fixes his own standard of entertainment. He need invite nobody to his house, nor hold even an annual reception; but every mayor gives an annual entertainment or reception in the Council House, attended by from three to five thousand people. The cost of a year's service as mayor, under accepted conditions, is not less than £1000, nor more than £2000. The latter expenditure will be necessary only when a number of important official functions are held.

He has no staff except a private secretary, who is a permanent official, and has been in office many years. He cannot appoint or remove an official, however humble. His only new power is as president of the Council and in his membership of every committee. During his term he can give little attention to business or profession, his whole time being required for official work. As showing the work expected of the mayor, and actually done, the following return for the last four years may interest American readers. During the year 1890 the mayor was summoned to 416 meetings, either of the City Council or its committees, and attended 358; in 1891 he was summoned to 450, and attended 338; in 1892 he was summoned to 375, and attended 322; and in 1893 he was summoned to 387, and attended 342. The total number of meetings of the Council committees, subcommittees, and of public bodies in which the Council is represented, was from 1155 to 1201 during different years of this period.

At the end of his term the mayor returns by courtesy to the chairmanship of a committee. Of the twelve mayors of Birmingham now living, nine are still engaged in Council work. The fact that a member of the Council has been mayor makes him alderman in due time, allows him to choose his committee, and confers a sort of undefined dignity. Upon the expiration of his term he becomes deputy-mayor, on the principle that his recent experience fits him better than any other man for presiding over the Council, or as a substitute in ceremonial matters.

DRAWN BY LOUIS LOEB.

TOWN HALL—MASON COLLEGE—CHAMBERLAIN MEMORIAL—LIBERAL CLUB—COUNCIL HOUSE.

TOWN CLERK AND PERMANENT OFFICIALS.

THE oldest office in connection with local government is the town clerk. Originally he was the learned man—perhaps the only one among gilds and local magnates who could read and write. The town clerk has now become legal adviser of the mayor and Council and all committees. It is his duty to investigate carefully the law of every new scheme proposed; to conduct the litigation of the city, or to secure the public rights without it; to draft measures for submission to Parliament, and to prepare cases for submission. In addition he is the clerk to the Council, and sits with that body. He gives his opinion when asked, and in many cases is able thereby to shape its action. He assists the mayor at such public functions as the opening of the assizes, or the visit of a royal person. He directs the election machinery, and the clerks to the committees are part of his office.

DRAWN BY LOUIS LOEB. ENGRAVED BY H. DAVIDSON.

IN EDGBASTON (BIRMINGHAM).

The city has been fortunate in its officials, nearly all having been long in its service. They are not only efficient in the public duties assigned them, but take their part in the incidental work. The city surveyor has held his place since 1857, the treasurer since 1867, the medical officer of health since 1859, the chief constable since 1882, the secretary of the Gas Committee since 1875, the engineer of the Waterworks since that project was taken over, and for ten years before; the clerk of the Drainage Board since its organization, while the secondary officials have had a long and useful experience.

No civil-service examination is necessary for entrance into the clerical or labor force, appointments and removals being made by their superior officers or the committees. All assignments to duty are temporary, and if found unfitted the men are dropped without question. Laborers are taken on or off as needed, but permanence is the rule. Outside the Police and Fire Departments, there is no regular system of retirement, although a few pensions are paid to very old men, or to those injured while on duty.

Policemen are appointed as the result of a pass examination by the superintendent, supplemented by the most exacting inquiries covering their entire career. Police superannuation has gone on rapidly of late years, under a law permitting retirement on two thirds of their salary after twenty-six years' service. The police contribute two and a half per cent. of their salaries toward this fund, the burden upon the rates being very light thus far.

The question of political opinion does not enter into the selection of permanent officials or working force. Heads of departments are anxious to secure effectiveness in the force under them, as any deficiency would soon become apparent to the committees, in whom real responsibility is lodged. As is the case everywhere, there is some complaint that men grow old and practically useless, but this is generally dealt with by transfer to lighter work.

## POLICE COURT AND POOR-LAW AUTHORITIES.

THE police courts are held by one stipendiary magistrate, who is paid, and has the authority of two justices sitting together, and eighty-eight justices, who sit by twos or threes. Each sits on a certain day, generally once a fortnight, the sittings lasting from two to four hours. The mayor is chairman of the bench, remains a justice for one year after the expiration of his term, and is then generally appointed permanently. They may suspend a policeman, and report him to the police superintendent and the Watch Committee, but this power is seldom used. They sit by committee as a court for licensing public-houses, theaters, and concert-halls, and action in such cases is reviewed by the entire bench. Another committee inspects the prisons at regular intervals, and, in doing so, its members may go into the cells and question the prisoners, and they must read the Riot Act in time of commotion, if called upon to do so. These men hear with patience each case that comes before them, the accused getting the benefit of all doubts, without necessity for counsel. Justices, who are the leading men in the community,—one fourth of the present bench being members of the City Council,—have as advisers clerks who must be well instructed in the law, though without actual power in making a decision. The time required is considerable, but, as in all other cases, it is given with apparent ease, although probably not one in twenty is really a man of leisure. To be once a justice is to be always a justice, as it is an office that cannot be held for a time and then resigned. There is no escape from it, except by disgrace or death.

The details of poor-law administration do not fall within the limits of a study of municipal conditions, but the guardians and overseers in the three parishes or parts of parishes of which Birmingham[1] is composed number more than eighty. They lay and collect rates, producing something like £120,000 a year, which are expended under their control. Their machinery is used to collect the rates levied by the City Council. They constitute one more governing body the members of which give unpaid time and attention to public duties. From their ranks, as from a training-school, have come many men who afterward did good service in the Council or other bodies.

The task of developing a city from what was little more than a village is practically over. Much of the work remains to be completed, but no large new schemes are necessary. Progress has not been so rapid as to hinder assimilation to new surroundings and conditions. Civic patriotism and civic pride have more than kept pace with development. Although the work of execution is done by a few, its benefits are fully appreciated by the many. Reliance has been placed upon the new voters as the suffrage has been enlarged, and no proposition to restrict it has been suggested.

[1] AREAS AND POPULATION UNDER DIFFERENT BODIES OR COMMITTEES.

| | Acres. | Population June 1894 (estimated). |
|---|---|---|
| Birmingham | 12,705 | 492,301 |
| Drainage Board | 42,278 | 691,700 |
| Gas Department | 75,000 | 700,000 |
| Water Supply | 83,192 | 667,409 |

At no time, since the task of regenerating the city was taken up, has there been difficulty in procuring help from honest and efficient men. In the earlier days it was insisted that no man not fitted to become mayor should be sent to the Council. Many who entered that body between 1867 and 1873 did attain the mayoralty. The theory now is that if the Council can always have in it twenty-five of the leading business and professional men, with the remainder less prominent and less able, though no less honest and well meaning, the best standard of work may be maintained. This would give, roughly speaking, a man of high merit and ability for mayor, and one for chairman of each of the principal working committees, with a second for colleague. The members approved by long or conspicuous service, who were willing to do the work when the workers were few, are safe in control. There have been some conspicuous instances in which really useful men, with a record of well-recognized service for the city, have been defeated for nomination or election; but dishonest or unworthy men have never been preferred, as the Council does not contain one such. None of the vile influences of disorderly houses or saloons, none of the behests of bosses, no desire or intention to reward questionable personal or political service, has thus far entered into account in the choice of a single councilor. Sharp contests occur every year, but they are not between a good man and a disreputable one, or between two of the latter. So, while it is sometimes said that the Council is degenerating, it is difficult for an outsider to see in what this degeneracy consists. The average of ability and character is now so high that it is difficult to imagine the existence of conditions under which it could be kept permanently at a better standard. Judged by the efficient way in which public work is done, and the uniform desire among all kinds of people to maintain this position, there is every reason to believe that public sentiment is becoming more rather than less exacting concerning the way that the civic life shall be administered.

DRAWN BY LOUIS LOEB.

« ST. PHILIP'S »—COLMORE ROW.

I have seen no attack upon the honesty of the Council, or of any of its members. In the worst times, even when inefficiency was common, never was there a scandal about paving, street-cleaning, or public works, or corruption alleged about the management of the police. Criticism is heard about matters of opinion, this or that policy is pronounced a mistake, but no intimation is uttered that a man in a public place is using it to make money for himself or his friends. This, too, in spite of the fact that no people keep closer watch on their public bodies, and that nowhere is the ratepayer so universally a grumbler, with plaints to fill newspapers and echo from every platform. Even did opportunity permit, public sentiment is so exacting that a man less honest in a public capacity than in his private business could not remain in the Council for a day.

This conspicuous success has not been achieved in a day, or maintained without effort. The men who began the work learned everything possible about the needs of their community, and proceeded by speech and writing to explain them, and to demonstrate the necessity and policy of undertaking reforms. One class has not transacted the public business, leaving to another the management of charitable, religious, and educational institutions; all has been treated as part of the civic life that must be carried on. No close corporation has been possible. The leaders have come from every part of the kingdom, and it is a curious feature of an old country to find that so few are natives of the town. They live well, but without ostentation, and make no attempt to form an exclusive society.

Nor is it due to conditions unusually favorable. Elevation above the sea, remoteness from any body of water, a broken, uneven surface, and a turbulence accepted as a characteristic of the population, were serious defects to be remedied. On the other hand, the concentration of population, and the fact that the different elements of which it was originally composed have become thoroughly assimilated, the convenient suburbs, the democracy of the people, and the variety of the industries, have all made for good government.

*George F. Parker.*

# THE PARLOUS WHOLENESS OF EPHRAIM.

BY THE AUTHOR OF «THE CAT AND THE CHERUB,» ETC.

SOME of the people forgot the admonition about avoiding the main road, and they went by the Junkins place, and were seen by Zendy as she sat at the window sewing pieces of apples on a string. Cory Judd, who scorned riding, walked past without a look, which was perhaps because of his shame at his pride in his new clothes.

«Now, what 's Cory Judd all handsomed up for?» said Zendy. «Do you s'pose he 'll tramp clear to Boston, same 's he threatens?»

Ephraim sat in the wooden rocker with the «Book of Seven Hundred Ailments,» which was opened at Ailment No. 440.

«I dunno,» replied Ephraim. «You holler down and ask him 'bout that ‹Man-and-Beast Salve.› I 've got 440 sprouting out 'twixt my shoulder-blades, sure 's you live; and if it strikes in, it 'll lead to 441, and that 'll be my end. I 'm going to have another one them spells, for I believe I must of et something.»

«I sh' like to come and ketch myself a-hollering to Cory Judd!» said Zendy, casting a glance at the «Book of Ailments.» «You 've got forty-'leven salves. I s'pose the next book will be ‹The Complete Barnyard Physician.› Then you 'll be a-howling round with the pip, and the distemper, and conniption fits. If I was you I 'd tumble int' the cellar and git a new set of griefs; you ain't quite miserable enough these days. Now, I *do* wonder what Cory Judd's a-kiting so for. I sh' think 't was Fourth July, the way he 's slicked up.»

«Mebbe *I* sha'n't ever be slicking up any more,» replied Ephraim. «I 'm a pretty faded man, Zendy, and you don't two thirds realize it. Don't suspect you will till I 'm took. Here 's 201 I 've had for years, and 213, and 697, and I felt a touch of 149 this morning, just as plain as your face: ‹aching back, dull eye, shooting pains, pale tongue—›»

«‹Can't lie awake by night, no appetite after meals,›» interpolated Zendy. «Overwork 's what 's done it. Yesterday you cleaned a lamp-chimney, and day before you wound the old clock. If I was you I should n't set and watch me sewing apples; might tucker you out. Now, if there ain't the Spinneys in their new wagon, so washed and dressed they dasn't sneeze! Do you s'pose it 's Sabbath, and we 've mislaid a whole day from this week? What *do* you s'pose—?»

«Why can't ye yell to Elziry Spinney to tell her boy to pull some that yeller-dock root out back their house,» replied Ephraim. «I kinder hanker after it, and it drives off 622. I sh' think you could; might be my dying wish, for all you know. I can feel my liver palpitating 'bout twice too fast. Zendy, I 'm persuaded

I must of drunk some rain-water that wa'n't b'iled. I bet I 'm heaping full of them invisible phenomenons on page 1286—them you can't see without a burning-glass. I 've got a million of 'em plotting and planning inside of me. I tell ye, I can see the handwriting on the wall!»

«Well, I vow!» said Zendy. «If you ain't growing peskier and worse every day. You 're jus' well 's I be, and you have been these two years. I sh' think you 'd been blowed up in a railroad accident. All you think about is you. Now I sh' jus' like to know what the Spinneys—»

«Yuss, I *be* a-getting worse,» replied Ephraim. «See how fat I am. It 's the dropsy—578—jus' as noticeable as your nose. But I had n't spoke, because I don't git no sympathy. There ain't a bone in my body but what 's warped with neuraligy; but all you think about is the neighbors.»

«Well,» said Zendy, with a sigh, «swaller your forty-'leven medicines! You pour 'em all into one now, don't ye? Why don't you take some shingle-nails and cider, 'gainst the general debility breaking out on ye? Land sakes! if there ain't the Stapleses—and them all perked up, too! Ephrum, somebody 's having a time, and you and me ain't invited!»

«Pshaw!» said Ephraim, «Elziry was in yesterday, and she tells everything, and what she don't know 'bout what 's going on ain't so. I wish you had git-up-and-git enough to screech to Anne Staples, and git the whereabouts of that doctor feller that proscribes by mail.»

«I know what they 're doing,» said Zendy, suddenly. «Sed Staples told me some one told her she overheard 'Mandy Dame say 'Lisby Lemly's daughter give out she wa'n't going to have you to her wedding. Said you always mourned so much 'bout your ailments that it set the whole company 's solemn 's conference. Said she 'd show folks a wedding without one your speeches. Now, that 's just it; they 're having that wedding, and I bet the rest of 'em was 'shamed, and went round by the lane.»

Ephraim had put down the «Book of Ailments.»

«But you don't s'pose so?» he said, rising to peer after the wagon with the Staples family sitting starchly in it. «Now, folks would n't do that. I don't kinder believe folks would give a wedding nor any kind of time without me: you see, I always make a speech, you know. Besides, I give Jerushy Jane Lemly a muskrat skin once; and one time you worked her a fascinator.»

«Yuss; but she always did the most at our huskings,» said Zendy.

«Yuss; but she always et the most punkin-pie, too; so that 's even,» reasoned Ephraim. «You lemme git the paper; mebbe they 's a circus.»

«Circus! pshaw!» said Zendy. «You lemme git the telescope.»

Zendy disappeared up-stairs, while Ephraim vainly searched the weekly journal. Zendy was gone for what seemed a long time, and Ephraim called to her, having long professed that climbing to the second story was too much for him. He thought that the loud puffing with which he at length made the ascent was sufficient notification to Zendy of his unusual performance, and that she would express her surprise at his approach; but Zendy made no sign. The trap-door to the roof was open, and the marks of Zendy's shoes were on the dusty ladder.

«Zendy!» called Ephraim, «what do you see? Is it the wedding? Zendy! Zendy, you ain't fallen off the roof, have ye? Now, I wonder if that old fool has slid off and broke her neck,» wailed Ephraim in distress. «Zendy!»

«Um!» said Zendy, finally, from above. She was outside, sitting on the ridge-pole, holding the telescope pointed through the trees toward the barn of the Lemly place, a mile in the distance; but she would not tell what she saw.

«You 're too sick a man,» she said grimly. «If I was to tell, you 'd git a spell of 1177.»

«Well, I know,» said Ephraim. «Jerushy Jane is having that wedding, and I ain't invited. They think I 'm petered out, and could n't speechify to set 'em gaping, same 's I used to. Guess I could outwrastle with old Lemly right now. Zendy, you got to walk past the Lemly place, jus' same 's you did n't know we was slighted, and give 'em lief to put the thing down in black and white. They sha'n't say 't was forgitfulness, b' George! You go right 'long; do you hear?»

«Sha'n't do no such thing,» said Zendy. «I shall leave 'em be. I can see 'em one by one putting their teams int' the barn, jus' same 's they was 'shamed. Every one of 'em dressed up stiff 's a ramrod. There 's Elziry Spinney; did you ever see any one look so put together?»

Zendy refused to go and walk by the Lemly place. Ephraim argued that he could n't do it, because such an exertion would deliver him over to a number of numbers that always lurked in his constitution, as she ought to know. Zendy said that he could take the old pig and ride, which roused Ephraim's feelings to an uncommon pitch. He rapped his stick on the floor, and went down the stairs more quickly than he had come up, with unpleasant mutterings. Nevertheless, Zendy, sitting on the ridge-pole, was not prepared to see him issue from the house, and start with decided steps down the short stretch that led to the main road. And when, without stopping, he turned and set off toward the Lemly place, Zendy put the astonished telescope on him. Ephraim had departed without taking his several medicines; he had not in two years walked so far; if he had gone away it had been after much urging, so that people who asked him to be present at their weddings thought themselves under an obligation to him, and he had always driven in a degree of state. It had been rare to find him farther than the hen-house. Zendy was troubled.

«I don't kinder like it,» she said to herself. «I do s'pose he's kinder poorly, though not's much so's he thinks. It's unusual, and unusual breeds unusual; and I'm scared lest something 'll happen.»

What happened first was that Jerusha Jane Lemly, while the best friends were worrying over her skirts, looked up the road from her chamber window, and made an exclamation. The people she had seen driving into the barn completed the invited company, which had been made select by a number of omissions of Jerusha's choosing; but now the tone of the gathering was threatened by one she did not like.

«Heaps o' wonders!» said Jerusha. «If there ain't old Ephrum Junkins—pegging 'long the road 's though he 'd been made whole by faith! Ma! Ma! There's old Ephrum Junkins! Now, what you going to do? I sha'n't have him! I sha'n't, if I set up here till kingdom come!»

The echoing of this statement through the house brought consternation, as every one knew what Jerusha Jane would n't do when she said she would n't. Father Elisha at first mildly suggested that they might as well let Ephraim in, now that he had come so far; but Mother Lemly put her thumb on him. She issued warning to the people who were yet out-doors, and they vanished quickly at her command. The wedding guests inside suddenly found themselves whispering in the dark, with all the shades drawn, and information concerning the progress of Ephraim Junkins in great demand. Some of those outside, who had failed to get into the barn before it was locked, ran hither and thither, and finally put themselves away as best they could, and everybody was saying to himself, «Well, I *do* declare!» at such a situation. The most unconcerned person near by was Ephraim. When, after a few minutes, he reached the place, he apparently bade fair to pass on without having vouchsafed a glance, but when opposite the front door he paid it the compliment of a casual notice. At the same time seemed to arise a feeling that he ought to stop for a moment, and pay his respects to old Elisha Lemly, though the perfunctoriness of it was plainly portrayed on Ephraim's face for all who cared to see. Jerusha Jane, peeping through a pin-hole she had made in her chamber shade, saw Ephraim knocking at the kitchen door, just as had been his wont in the days before his ailments.

There was no answer to his knocks. Ephraim tried the barn, but all the doors were locked. Then he went around to the front door, to which a freshly trodden trail led through the long grass in the yard. Pinned to the door was an envelop bearing the scrawl:

«Lemly's folks all went away yesterday.»

«Now ain't that strange!» soliloquized Ephraim in a penetrating voice. «Old 'Lishy must have pulled up stakes and moved his family to the next county.»

The door of the long wagon shed had been so hastily fastened that Ephraim opened it with little difficulty, and the effort gave him a chance to prove that his strength had not so wholly departed as people might think. The sound caused considerable rustling in a pile of salt hay inside. In fact, old Silas Ludlow, who was much beholden to Ephraim Junkins for past services in the way of speechmaking — Silas being blessed with seven daughters—had, in endeavoring to hide his head, exposed one half of his person.

«Now, who 'd 'a' thought!» said Ephraim, surveying this considerable half. «If there ain't old Silas's pantyloons, all stuffed with salt hay so 's to keep! I 've known 'em for years by that patch, which don't appear except when he steps into his wagon down to the meeting-house. Gone and left his boots sticking into 'em—almost 's natural 's life; looks as though he was kinder anxious 'bout something when he left 'em there—kinder absent-minded and hurried-like. Now, what sights you do see when you 're all alone and no one to prove it!»

It was getting unduly warm inside the Lemly house, with only the scullery window open. Ezra Dame, who was shortly to be joined in holy matrimony to Jerusha Jane, if only the Lord would make a suitable disposition of Ephraim Junkins, was so embarrassed in his corner that he was smiling painfully; and it was especially hard on the two Lemly poor relatives, who toiled in the kitchen, cooking the wedding-dinner, and growing redder in the face and more hateful of Jerusha every minute. Ephraim had been investigating with leisurely thoroughness, and now he made his way to the front door and solemnly settled himself on the big stone step. In the parlor the impression gained that he had gone; but now he was plainly heard to say:

«Guess I 'll set and brood awhile.»

For some time Ephraim kept eating some choice apples he had discovered near the scullery window.

«Now I will say, this is a pretty tearful subject,» he began at length, in a voice as if he were talking to a large assemblage, but all the while looking at the envelop in his hand. «Here 's the whole Lemly fam'ly suddenly took right off the earth—clean sweep. Here 's me a-setting on the door-step, and here 's the old Lemly house shut 's tight 's a drum, and nary soul inside—nary one. Now, ain't that a pity! Here 's the barn-door closed, and old Lemly forgot and went off and left 'em all padlocked on the inside. I don't see how he ever got out himself, nor how he 's to git in. But I see through a crack they was as many 's fifteen of his neighbors' hosses crawled in there somehow or other, and it 's a wonder some of their owners ain't here looking for 'em. Strange that old Lemly should go 'way and leave these fancy Baldwins round! Dunno 's they 's anything I like so 's one of his late-ripe'ing Baldwins when they 're hard and green, same 's these; and this was off year for apples, too; and Simon Staples told me only yesterday how 'Lishy was saving the only few he had for some pet purpose, and here he 's gone away and left 'em! I sh'll have to take the rest of 'em home.

«'T is mighty sad to think of the whole Lemly tribe being wiped off the map of this township in one sundown,» continued Ephraim, turning to face the darkened windows, «especially that old, dried-up Jerushy Jane, her that we was all afraid would git spliced to that young nincompoop Ezry Dame. I 'm glad she 's quit without so, for that 's a sight of trouble saved. I 'm glad because that, while 't is generally thought that while Jerushy Jane—even her—deserves a mite better than such as him, also Ezry Dame he deserves a quick sight better than Jerushy Jane. For the Lord knows no one would think of marrying her if 't wa'n't for what her father has. *I* was scared least they would hitch up, and I be requested to make one them felicitating speeches, one such as no wedding has been complete without or thought of in these hereabouts for the last twenty-five years. For I should of had to git out of it the easiest I could, without hurting some one's feelings, not being cantankerous-like nor *mean-sneaking* out from a thing, as folks has been known to. But I 'd seen Jerushy Jane die an old maid, which by nature she was meant to do, 'fore I 'd git up and prognosticate lies 'bout her future happiness here or hereafter; for there ain't a person in this county that can see how any one is to be congratulated for marrying Jerushy Jane, nor any one for marrying Ezry Dame.»

In the parlor old Peter Hammond, while waiting for the ceremony to begin, had fallen asleep. Ezra Dame was so red that he thought his cheeks visible in the dark, a thought which made them redder.

«So they 's a sorter sweet sorrer in that,» pursued Ephraim, «though it does seem pretty tearful to have the whole Lemly fam'ly took out from under your feet like a stroke of lightning. They must of left in a hurry, for they did n't stop to take in the mats from the doors, but left out their best one, which I ain't seen before since I give it to Mother Lemly when she and 'Lishy had their silver wedding. Pretty expensive mat that was, as any one could see by comparing it to the one 'Lishy bought to give the minister when he was married. Mother Lemly, I hear, used this one for a tidy at first. She 'd never gone and left it lying loose like this unless 't was something happened; mebbe she heard of some one that was willing to marry Jerushy; and as for 'Lishy, Lord knows he would n't leave a hoss-hair round if he thought an angel might take it for a harp-string. And they left the scullery window open. Awful absent-minded,» said Ephraim, rising. «Thieves might break in and steal Jerushy's curls.»

The remainder of the late-ripening Baldwins had disappeared from the scullery window, but Ephraim did not seem to notice it. He took away the stick that held the sash up, and closed the window, leaving the two poor relatives to stifle in the kitchen. In the parlor the minister was staring devoutly at the points of sunlight that came through the window-shade, to which Ephraim was now addressing his meditations. Every one was unaware of Ephraim, and determined that every one else should perceive it.

«Beats all,» continued Ephraim, loudly, as he settled himself once more on the stone step, «how things without spiritual life shows how they miss Jerushy! 'T is jus' so everything that belongs to the fam'ly could speak. ‹Here,› says this envelop, which I see is postmarked this morning, and could n't of got here before this noon—‹here,› says it, ‹Ephrum Junkins must know 'bout this!› So it shakes the letter from its inwards, and runs and gits a pencil, and scratches on its back, ‹Lemly's folks all went away yesterday,› in a first-rate forgery of Mother Lemly's handwriting, and then climbs up and pins itself to the door. Jus' the same with the things out back. ‹Here,› says they, ‹Jerushy Jane 's gone off looking for some wooden pate to marry her; but we 'll git ourselves ready 'gainst her coming back unsuccessful, jus' same 's them two poor relations of hers, that does all the work and gits nothing for it but leavings and hard words, same 's they was here to slop round and get dinner.› So them late-ripe'ing Baldwins says to themselves, ‹Here, we 'd better git in out of the sun, or we 'll git mellered 'fore our time.› So they up and roll int' the house, same 's they had legs. Then the sink-pump begins to draw water—I can hear it a-snorting now; sounds jus' 's though old Peter Hammond was setting in the corner of the parlor winder, and had fell asleep waiting for something to happen. Then out back the shed some that wood that 'Lishy cut from Widder Cole's half-acre,—because she could n't pay the interest on the mortgage, and he knew the church would git her through the winter somehow,—some that wood takes the ax and chops itself to kindlings, and gits a match, and crawls int' the stove, and touches itself off, and roars like a turkey-red lion, as you can see by the smoke a-spilling out the chimney. ‹Jerushy Jane 'll be home 'for' long,› says everything. And the old black pot gits down off the hook, and waddles up to the sink and gits itself full of water, and climbs up on the stove, and sets down to git a-bubbling. And then the onions —I can smell 'em 's loud 's they was under my chin—well, they turn to and peel off their coats, and run and jump int' the pot, and squat down to bile!

«Still,» said Ephraim, very loudly, «I dunno why I sh'd be brooding here. The Lemlys ain't much to me. I always treated 'em considerate-like. When Mother Lemly come to me and said what a close-fisted old barn-rat 'Lishy was, I never told 'Lishy. When 'Lishy come to me and asked if 't was wicked to wish that Mother Lemly was enjoying a stay in heaven, I never told her. I give 'em both my honest sympathy; but they ain't anything to me, more than folks that live in the same town that I do. First thing I know, my folks from Boston will be arriving, and I dunno 's I 'd pick out jus' these steps to let 'em see me setting on, for my Boston folks are pretty tony and stylish, and rather particular 'bout who they see me with. I 'll make that stretch home in 'bout nine minutes.»

Ephraim straightened himself and walked briskly from the yard, and still more briskly, until he had gone from sight around a bend in the road. The exercise, far from fatiguing him, was exhilarating, and he kept on at the same gait, chuckling as he went. The stick with which he had plodded up the stairs to find Zendy lay forgotten in the Lemly yard. Ephraim grew more charmed with himself at every step.

Zendy was standing alone. The figure that seemed to be Ephraim was coming too fast for him, and when Ephraim was within call he did not seem himself, for the customary melancholy of his face was supplanted by a gleam of satisfaction. Zendy was troubled.

«What 's the matter?» she said. «Where you been? Where 's your stick? Ain't you tuckered?»

«Well, sir,» said Ephraim, radiantly, steaming past her, and taking the rise in front of the house at a pace which left her in the rear. «Well, sir, I jus' give it to 'em! Guess they won't forgit it. Is anybody follering me? 'Cause I ain't looked round; walked off jus' same 's I forgotten 'em at their own gate. You oughter heard me a-brooding aloud—offhand! ‹Onions took their coats off,› says I, ‹and jumped in and squat down to bile!› Plain 's your face! And Silas's Sunday pantyloons—he, hee! Well, sir, you 'll wish you 'd come!»

«There, Ephraim, there,» said Zendy, soothingly. «You ain't quite well, I 'm sure. You 're all tuckered, ain't ye? There, I should n't let myself git so excited. How 's your aches?»

«Tuckered?» said Ephraim. «Who 's tuckered? I 'll teach 'em I ain't no setting rooster, b' George! Think I 've lost my gift, do they? As for aches and pains, I ain't a single one—if I was to try. Dunno 's I ever shall have again. I 've shook my ills and give' up pills—and don't pay no more doctor's bills, eh, Zendy?»

«Ephrum Junkins,» said Zendy, solemnly, «you 've got to git right to bed! You 're a sick man, and you don't realize it one mite. I ain't seen you exert so these ten years. Don't you lemme hear 'nother word. You need every parcel of strength you got. Oh, Ephrum, why did n't you stay to home!»

«Go-to-bed pshaw!» said Ephraim. «I tell ye I 'm 's pert 's a sparrer. Could n't find no ache nor pain if I was to hunt.»

«That 's just what 's the matter,» said Zendy. «You 've come to the fair hilltop overlooking the valley of shadder of death, Ephrum, and here you be a-ready to go coasting down t' the bottom 's fast 's you know how! Don't you see how 't always is—them that 's ailing all of a sudden gitting up and hopping round out-doors and looking pert, and everybody saying how smart Ephrum Junkins is looking, and then all of a jump the Lord whisks your head off 's though 't was an ax! Ephrum—I dunno, Ephrum! There,» she said, recovering herself, «you go to bed, won't ye?»

«Pshaw!» said Ephraim. «Here I be as skittish as a yeller kitten. You sh'd see me kiting 'long the road 's though I was shot from a bow! Well, sir, they was fifteen hosses that crawled int' that barn, b' George; and they 'd locked themselves in—eh? I s'pose I set there 's much 's an hour, brooding to myself loud enough for the pigeons! I cal'late Jerushy Jane 'll live to see me—»

But the enthusiasm had spilled from Ephraim's voice.

«I *was* going to step off front the house 'bout time the wedding broke off, and chop that tree I been a-going to so long,» he added thoughtfully.

Zendy left him sitting still in the rocking-chair, gazing rather steadily at his thumbs. She ran down to the road, and caught the boy whom she had seen driving one of Lemly's teams.

«You hurry and find Dr. Payne,» she said. «He 's down to the wedding, I guess. You tell him to come up along 's fast 's he can, for Ephrum Junkins is took so that I misdoubt he 'll last the evening. You hurry, and I 'll give you a watermelon.»

When she came back Ephraim was silent, and she looked at him sadly and said nothing. He expected her to urge him again to retire, but she did not. At length Ephraim said:

«Of course, if you are any scared, Zendy, I s'pose I might just as well go. Still, it does seem kinder foolish, and I should n't tell any the neighbors 'bout it.»

«Hain't you the leetlest kind of an ache?» asked Zendy.

«No,» said Ephraim, with a shade of regret; «I can't truthfully git up and lie 'bout it. I ain't got the shadder of one.»

«It 's unusual,» said Zendy, «and unusual breeds unusual. You jump in 's quick 's you know how, and I 'll make a poultice, and some licorish tea, and I 'll stuff your ears with cotton so the crickets and roosters and things sha'n't keep you awake. And there, I 'd drink some hot water if I was you. Dunno 's I should be scared, Ephraim; mebbe it 'll pass off in the night.»

Ephraim lay in the depths of the feather-bed, with the blinds closed, while Zendy stirred about the adjoining kitchen. A streak of sunlight came through and found the wall beside him; all the world seemed wide awake and well, but Ephraim's lightsome spirits had departed. Presently he called:

«'T is kinder unusual, ain't it?»

«Well, mebbe,» said Zendy. «Still—»

«Still what?» said Ephraim, with the cotton in his ears. «Say, I guess you 'd better git out some that Mrs. Slopley's Sure Cure: 't won't do no harm, though I dunno 's they 's any cause for you to git worried, feeling so smart 's I do.»

«Oh, no,» said Zendy; «worrying will only make you worse.»

Ephraim lay staring at the ceiling, unpleasantly aware of his own fiber. He listened to the throbbing of his arteries, and asked himself if there was not something unusual in it—unusual bred unusual. People's hearts sometimes unexpectedly stopped, and then people give three gasps, and all was over.

«S'pose you set some that Greenson's Painkiller handy,» he called. «And if you sh'd see Dr. Payne, you might yell to him. I felt 's coltish 's a calf when I laid down here; but I dunno.»

The ticking of the clock seemed to keep time with his breathing—at least it had at first; but now surely the clock was getting ahead. His lungs might be gradually slowing down, and perhaps they would lag until by and by they would stop short—collapsed like an empty bellows.

«I dunno but you 'd better send for him, Zendy, so 's to keep you from worrying,» he managed to say without falling behind the clock.

«There, I should n't snort so,» said Zendy. «He 's a-coming.»

«What, you sent for him?» exclaimed Ephraim. «I wonder if you 've had one your presentiments? I should n't have such nonsense. Here I be, looking 's bright 's a new dollar—ain't I? What 's the use you trying to scare me so? There, ain't that clock gitting ready to stop? I ain't superstitious, but you kinder make me nervous running round the way you do.»

Zendy comforted him with the licorice tea for his inner man, and with something she put between his shoulders—a poultice the mustardy nature of which she concealed from Ephraim on account of his objection to being burned. The licorice tea began searching for the late-ripening Baldwins.

Lemly's boy had met the people as they were leaving after the wedding, and he mingled among them eager with the importance of his news, so that before dusk every one had heard of Ephraim's going to bed. Those who had known Ephraim and Zendy since early years came in to see if they could be of assistance, and they made a considerable gathering of people in their Sunday clothes.

«I ain't going to be caught napping,» exclaimed Zendy. «Here he ails and wails every minute for two years, and here he gits up suddenly, and tramps off somewhere, and says he ain't got an ache nor a pain, and wants to chop down trees! I jus' drove him to bed.»

Ephraim removed the cotton from one ear. The arrival of the visitors had for awhile turned his thoughts away from himself.

«Real nice of you to put your good clothes on jus' to come see us,» he heard Zendy say. They all sat in the kitchen, with the lamp casting a dimness over their faces, and they settled themselves as if they had come to see the affair to its end. Conversation languished, for everybody was thinking about the wedding, and no one dared to speak of it. Old Peter Hammond, who was deaf, was last, and Ephraim heard him say:

«What—nary an ache nor pain?»

«Nary a fly-bite,» called Ephraim. «I dunno 'f the Lord 's crowding a place for me on the other shore, but seems to me 't would of been just as well if I 'd first stepped out front and chopped that old apple-tree. Been going to these ten years, ever since the time Leviticus Brooks drove the pitchfork into his leg, and Alice Dame 's calf got hurt, too, and Joel Pitkin was 'lected.»

«He's beginning to reach back,» whispered Amanda Dame to Sarah Tower. «When they begin to reach back years and years, then I know they 're going out.»

This remark was repeated to the others, and for a while Ephraim heard nothing but an ominous murmur.

«Good deal of sickness and ailments round,» came the voice of Mother Margery Hook, at length breaking the funereal silence. «They do say May Tenny Warren won't last out the night, and she so young, too—you would n't expect. And then old Jeddy Marvin—that was born on same day 's Ephraim—he 's done a fearful night and ain't no better. I declare, I ain't got nothing fit to wear to a funeral.»

«You 'll have to go jus' to weddings till you git something new,» said Zendy, surveying Mother Margery's lavender trimmings. This remark caused another silence.

«Zendy!» called Ephraim. «You steep me some catnip, will ye?»

«What she said reminds me of old Josiah Codman,» came the voice of Hannah Swan. «Old Josiah, 'f you remember, rose up from a stroke and hoed a whole patch of beets. Come evening he was flat on his back, and stone cold before morning.»

Ephraim's mind went back to the clock, which now seemed to tarry behind his breathing. Perhaps his lungs would go faster and faster, until they burst with panting, and he lay stone dead.

«There was Jim Sweet's wife, too,» he heard Angy Brooks say. «She left the chronic sinking-fits and went to a dance. Said she 'd like to see the one that could outbob and fling with her! And she up and died in the middle of a jig. Most of the orthodox folks took it for a judgment.»

«Then Eunice Dexter, 'f you remember,» said Hannah Swan, «she that married the Spooner twins, one after the other. She got up and went to a husking, and died from eating Mother Hammond's pandowdy. I don't s'pose Ephrum 's et anything, has he?»

«No,» said Zendy, «he ain't et anything; he 's too scared to eat what fights him.» But Ephraim thought of the late-ripening Baldwins, and for some indefinable reason he wished he had not touched them.

«Zendy!» he called, «that boy ain't found Dr. Payne! Why 's he so slow?»

«Dr. Payne?» said Mother Margery Hook. «Gone to Boston—for a week.»

«Thunder!» said Ephraim, breaking out in a cold sweat. «Zendy, what you going to do?»

«And Dr. Wallace is away to Bucksport,» whispered Peter Hammond, loudly. «Still, I don't think a doctor would mend any, Zendy. I quit doctoring these ten years. Speaking of like cases,» Ephraim heard Peter say, «come to think of it, there was Ephrum's own father. 'T was jus' 'bout same 's this. Dunno 's any of you remember; but old Ephrum had been lain up with something he called typhoid-gout,—he doctored himself mostly,—and one day he rose off his lounge, where he 'd been most the time for several years, carving little clipper ships inside of ginger-pop bottles, rose off and took stick and stumped clear down to Cedar Creek, and made old Enoch Blood, that was keeping a blacksmith shop 'bout where the meeting-house now is—made him pone up seven dollars Enoch had owed him since he 'd married Thankful Spinney—with seven per cent. interest—and had them four boys. And old Ephrum came a-thumping home all smiling 's could be, and said he cal'lated to git out to work to his trade, which, if you rec'lect, was shipwright. Well, come lamplight—'bout this time, 's I remember—he was suddenly took with a cramp somewhere in his inwards, and old Ephrum jus' wriggled himself out of this world—you 'd heard him for miles. He had three doctors, but, Lord! the doctors could n't do him no good! So Ephrum need n't feel so bad.»

«Zendy,» called Ephraim, feebly, with beads upon his brow. «My inwards don't feel right. S'pose I take some Fam'ly Cure? I think mebbe I have a pain.»

Zendy absented herself for awhile, during which she conned the symptoms of Ephraim with a practised eye. Then she came out and whispered to the rest.

«His eyes are kinder staring, and his breath comes quick, and his hair kinder stands up; but, Lord! I ain't worried no more! He ain't going to sink. No, he ain't; I know Ephraim.»

«I dunno 's I sh'd be too hopeful,» Ephraim heard Mother Margery say; and Peter Hammond whispered very plainly, «Neither sh'd I—with that pain—so like his father.»

«Zendy!» called Ephraim, «440 's commencing to burn betwixt my shoulder-blades. I wish some of you 'd look into the book. Zendy ain't worth a hill of beans with it.»

Peter Hammond had the book in his grasp, and no one could get it away from him.

«Here 's 440,» said Peter, after a search which had led him to page 440 instead of to the ailment of that number. «Some kinder fits, it says; but, pshaw! Ephrum, it don't say they break out 'twixt your shoulder-blades.»

«Zendy, ain't you a gump!» cried Ephraim. «Give the book to some one that can spell numbers. Have I got to lay here and die! Oh, my back! Oh, but I 'm a sick man!»

Zendy returned to the chamber. Ephraim lay with his face pushed into the pillow.

«My time 's come!» he cried in muffled tones. «I can feel myself stiflin'. I 'm a-goin'; 201 's coming back; 697 's coming; 440 's bringin' on 441! I 'm a-goin'; good-by, Zendy, if I sh'd lose my mind!»

Zendy came and closed the door. The visitors stared expectantly.

«I guess you folks had better all go home,» she said, «unless you got some wedding or other to go to, for it kinder flusters Ephrum. He 's all right now. He 's got his aches and pains back, and he 's too strapping mad and scared with his ailments to be a-going to die. Good-night, all,» she said as she held the lamp, and they filed out into the dark. «I kinder put faith in that mustard and licorish.» But it was plain that they all thought Ephraim in a perilous state.

Ephraim was rolling and writhing in the billows of the feather-bed. Zendy hove a sigh of relief to see him, and she sat down and rested in the wooden rocker.

«There, if you ain't carrying on natural,» she said approvingly. «Just as like yourself as two peas. There, I dunno 's I 'd shout so.»

«I was ticketed to leave ye 'fore long!» cried Ephraim. «I kep' tellin' ye so, but I did n't git no sympathy; 440 has struck in! Zendy, why don't you git scared and do somethin'? Here I be on my dyin' bed, and you a-settin' there like a bump on a log! Oh, them apples—my back 's burnin' right off! Oh, Zendy, ain't you got no more feeling than I was a frog?»

The head of Cory Judd appeared at the open window.

«Heard Ephrum was took,» said Cory, who sometimes looked like an owl. «How 's he doing?»

«Oh, he 's doing real nice, thank ye,» said Zendy. «I guess he only et something.»

«Oh, yuss!» said Ephraim, savagely, rising in bed. «I was invited out to a wedding, and I et the door-knob off the door!»

*Chester Bailey Fernald.*

# AFTER BR'ER RABBIT IN THE BLUE-GRASS.

## A THANKSGIVING EVENT.

By the author of «Fox-Hunting in Kentucky.»

WITH PICTURES BY MAX F. KLEPPER.

OR little more than a month Jack Frost has been busy—that arch-imp of Satan who has got himself enshrined in the hearts of little children. After the clear sunset of some late October day, when the clouds have hung low and kept the air chill, he has a good night for his evil work. By dawn the little magician has spun a robe of pure white, and drawn it close to the breast of the earth. The first light turns it silver, and shows the flowers and jewels with which wily Jack has decked it, so that it may be mistaken for a wedding-gown, perhaps, instead of a winding-sheet. The sun, knowing better, lifts, lets loose his tiny warrors, and, from pure love of beauty, with one stroke smites it gold. Then begins a battle which ends soon in crocodile tears of reconciliation from dauntless little Jack, with the blades of grass and the leaves in their scarlet finery sparkling with the joy of another day's deliverance, and the fields grown gray and aged in a single night. On just such a morning, and before the fight is quite done, saddle-horses are stepping from big white barns in certain counties of the blue-grass, and, sniffing the cool air, are being led to old-fashioned stiles, from which a little later they bear master or mistress out to the turnpike and past flashing fields to the little county-seat several miles away. There in the court-house square they gather, the gentlefolk of country and town, and from that point they start into the country the other way. It is a hunting-meet. Br'er Rabbit is the quarry, and they are going for him on horseback without dog, stick, snare, or gun—a unique sport, and, so far as I know, confined wholly to the blue-grass. There is less rusticity than cosmopolitanism in that happy land. The townspeople have farms, and the farmers own stores; intercourse between town and country is unrestrained; and as for social position, that is a question one rarely hears discussed: one either has it unquestioned, or one has it not at all. So out they go, the hunters on horseback, and the chaperons and spectators in buggies, phaëtons, and rockaways, through a morning that is cloudless and brilliant, past fields that are sober with autumn, and woods that are dingy with oaks and streaked with the fire of sumac and maple. New hemp lies in shining swaths on each side, while bales of last year's crop are going to market along the white turnpike. Already the farmers are turning over the soil for the autumn sowing of wheat. Corn-shucking is just over, and ragged darkies are straggling from the fields back to town. Through such a scene move horse and vehicle, the riders shouting, laughing, running races, and a quartet, perhaps, in a rockaway singing some old-fashioned song full of tune and sentiment. Six miles out they turn in at a gate, where a big square brick house with a Grecian portico stands far back in a wooded yard, with a fish-pond on one side and a great smooth lawn on the other. Other hunters are waiting there, and the start is made through a blue-grass woodland, greening with a second spring, and into a sweep of stubble and ragweed. There are two captains of the hunt. One is something of a wag, and has the voice of a trumpet.

«Form a line, and form a good un!» he yells, and the line stretches out with a space of ten or fifteen feet between each horse and his neighbor on each side. The men are dressed as they please, the ladies as they please. English blood gets expression, as usual, in independence absolute. There is a sturdy disregard of all considerations of form. Some men wear leggings, some high boots; a few have brown shooting-coats. Most of them ride with the heel low and the toes turned according to temperament. The Southern woman's long riding-skirt has happily been laid aside. These young Dianas wear the usual habit; only the hat is a derby, a cap, sometimes a beaver with a white veil, or a tam-o'-shanter that has slipped down behind and left a frank bare head of shining hair. They hold the reins in either hand, and not a crop is to be seen. There are plenty of riding-whips, however, and sometimes one runs up the back of some girl's right arm; for that is the old-fashioned position for the whip when riding in form. On a trip like this, however, everybody rides to please his fancy, and rides anywhere but off his horse. The men are sturdy country youths, who in a few years will make good types of the beef-eating young English squire—sunburned fellows with big frames, open faces, fearless eyes, and a manner that is easy, cordial, kindly, independent. The girls are midway between the types of brunette and blonde, with a leaning toward the latter type. The extreme brunette is as rare as is the unlovely blonde, whom Oliver Wendell Holmes differentiates from her dazzling sister with locks that have caught the light of the sun. Radiant with freshness these girls are, and with good health and strength; round of figure, clear of eye and skin, spirited, soft of voice, and slow of speech.

DRAWN BY MAX F. KLEPPER.

«BILLY,» SHOUTS THE CAPTAIN, «I FINE YOU TEN DOLLARS.»

There is one man on a sorrel mule. He is the host back at the big farm-house, and he has given up every horse he has to guests. One of the girls has a broad white girth running all the way around both horse and saddle. Her habit is the most stylish in the field; she has lived a year in Washington, perhaps, and has had a finishing touch at a fashionable school in New York. Near her is a young fellow on a black thoroughbred—a graduate, perhaps, of Yale or Princeton. They rarely put on airs, couples like these, when they come back home, but drop quietly into their old places with friends and kindred. From respect to local prejudice, which has a hearty contempt for anything that is not carried for actual use, she has left her riding-crop at home. He has let his crinkled black hair grow rather long, and has covered it with a black slouch-hat. Contact with the outer world has made a difference, however, and it is enough to create a strong bond of sympathy between these two, and to cause trouble between country-bred Phyllis, plump, dark-eyed, bare-headed, who rides a pony that is trained to the hunt, as many of the horses are, and young farmer Corydon, who is near her on an iron-gray. Indeed, mischief is brewing among those four. At a brisk walk the line moves across the field, the captain at each end yelling to the men—only the men, for no woman is ever anywhere but where she ought to be in a Southern hunting-field—to keep it straight.

«Billy,» shouts the captain with the mighty voice, «I fine you ten dollars.» The slouch-hat and the white girth are lagging behind. It is a lovers' quarrel, and the girl looks a little flushed, while Phyllis watches smiling. «But you can compromise with me,» adds the captain, and a jolly laugh runs down the line. Now comes a «rebel yell.» Somewhere along the line a horse leaps forward. Other horses jump too; everybody yells, and everybody's eye is on a little bunch of cotton that is being whisked with astonishing speed through the brown weeds. There is a massing of horses close behind it; the white girth flashes in the midst of the mêlée, and the slouch-hat is just behind. The bunch of cotton turns suddenly, and doubles back between the horses' feet. There is a great crash, and much turning, twisting, and sawing of bits. Then the crowd dashes the other way, with Corydon and Phyllis in the lead. The fun has begun.

## II.

FROM snow to snow in the blue-grass Br'er Rabbit has two inveterate enemies,—the darky and the school-boy,—and his lot is a hard one. Even in the late spring and early summer, when «ole Mis'» Rabbit is keeping house, either one of her foes will cast a destructive stone at her if she venture into open lane or pasture. When midsummer comes even her tiny, long-eared brood is in danger. Not one of the little fellows is much larger than your doubled fist when the weeds get thick and high, and the elderberries are ripe, and the blackberries almost gone, but he is a tender morsel, and with the darky ranks in gastronomical favor close after the possum and the coon. You see him then hopping about the edge of hemp- and harvest-fields, or crossing the country lanes, and he is very pretty, and so innocent and unwary that few have the heart to slay him except his two ruthless foes. When the fields of grain are cut at harvest-time, both are on a close lookout for him. For as the grain is mown about him, he is penned at last in a little square of uncut cover, and must make a dash for liberty through stones, sticks, dogs, and yelling darkies. After frost comes, the school-boy has both eyes open for him, and a stone ready, on his way to and from his books, and he goes after him at noon recess and on Saturdays. The darky travels with a «rabbit-stick» three feet long in hand and a cur at his heels. Sometimes he will get his young master's bird-dog out, and give Br'er Rabbit a chase, in spite of the swearing that surely awaits him, and the licking that may. Then he makes a «dead fall» for him—a broad board supporting a heavy rock, and supported by triggers that are set like the lines of the figure 4; or he will bend the top of a young sapling to the ground, and make a snare of a string, and some morning there is innocent Br'er Rabbit strung up like a murderer. Sometimes he will chase him into a rock fence, and then what is a square yard or so of masonry to one fat rabbit? Sometimes Br'er Rabbit will take a favorite refuge, a hollow tree; for while he cannot climb a tree in the usual way, he can arch his back and rise spryly enough on the inside. Then does the ingenious darky contrive a simple instrument of torture—a long, limber stick with a prong or a split end. This he twists into Br'er Rabbit's fur until he can gather up with it one fold of his slack hide, and down comes the game. This hurts, and with this provocation only will the rabbit snap at the hunter's hand. If this device fails the hunter, he will try smoking him out; and if that fails, there is left the ax. Always, too, is the superstitious darky keen for the rabbit that is caught in a graveyard, by a slow hound, at midnight, and in the dark of the moon. The left hind foot of that rabbit is a thing to conjure with.

On Saturdays both his foes are after him with dog and gun. If they have no dog they track him in the snow, or they «look for him settin'» in thick bunches of winter blue-grass, or under briers and cut thorn-bushes that have been piled in little gullies; and alas! they «shoot him settin'» until the darky has learned fair play from association, or the boy has had it thumped into him at school. Then will the latter give Br'er Rabbit a chance for his life by stirring him up with his brass-toed boot and taking a crack at him as he lopes away. It will be a long time before this boy will get old enough or merciful enough to resist the impulse to get out of his buggy or off his horse, no matter where he is going or in how great a hurry, and shy a stone when a cottontail crosses his path. Indeed, a story comes down that a field of slaves threw aside their hoes and dashed pell-mell after a passing rabbit. An indignant observer reported the fact to their master, and this was the satisfaction he got.

«Run him, did they?» said the master, cheerfully. «Well, I'd have whipped the last one of them if they had n't.»

And yet it is not until late in October that Br'er Rabbit need go into the jimson-weeds and seriously «wuck he haid» (work his head) over his personal safety; but it is very necessary then, and on Thanksgiving day it behooves him to say his prayers in the thickest cover he can find. Every man's hand is against him that day. All the big hunting-parties are out, and the Iroquois Club of Lexington goes for him with horse and greyhound. And that is wild sport. Indeed, put a daredevil Kentuckian on a horse or behind him, and in a proper mood, and there is always wild sport—for the onlooker as well. It is hard to fathom the spirit of recklessness that most sharply differentiates the Southern hunter from his Northern brother, and that runs him amuck when he comes into contact with a horse, whether riding, driving, or betting on him. If a thing has to be done in a hunting-field, or can be done, there is little difference between the two. Only the thing must, with the Northerner, be a matter of skill and judgment, and he likes to know his horse. To him or to an Englishman the Southern hunter's performances on a green horse look little short of criminal. In certain counties of Virginia, where hunters follow the hounds after the English fashion, the main point seems to be for each man to «hang up» the man behind him, and desperate risks are run. «I have stopped that boyish foolishness, though,» said an aged hunter under thirty; «I give my horse a chance.» In other words, he had stopped exacting of him the impossible. In Georgia they follow hounds at a fast gallop through wooded bogs and swamps at night, and I have seen a horse go down twice within a distance of thirty yards, and the rider never leave his back. The same is true of Kentucky, and I suppose of other Southern States. I have known one of my friends in the blue-grass to amuse himself by getting into his buggy an unsuspecting friend, who was as sedate then as he is now (and he is a judge now), and driving him at full speed through an open gate, then whizzing through the woods and seeing how near he could graze the trunks of trees in his course, and how sharply he could turn, and ending up the circuit by dashing, still at full speed, into a creek, his companion still sedate and fearless, but swearing helplessly. Being bantered by an equally reckless friend one dark midnight while going home, this same man threw both reins out on his horse's back, and gave the high-strung beast a smart cut with his whip. He ran four miles, kept the pike by some mercy of Providence, and stopped exhausted at his master's gate.

A Northern visitor was irritated by the apparently reckless driving of his host, who is a famous horseman in the blue-grass.

«You lunatic,» he said, «you 'd better drive over those stone piles!» meaning a heap of unbroken rocks that lay on one side of the turnpike.

«I will,» was the grave answer, and he did.

This is the Kentuckian in a buggy. Imagine him on horseback, with no ladies present to check the spirit or the spirits of the occasion, and we can believe that the Thanksgiving hunt of the Iroquois Club is perhaps a little more serious business than playing polo, or riding after anise-seed. And yet there is hardly a member of this club who could sit in his saddle over the course at Meadowbrook or Chevy Chase, for the reason that he has never practised jumping a horse in his stride, and because when he goes fast he takes the jockey seat, which is not, I believe, a good seat for a five-foot fence; at the same time, there is hardly a country-bred rider in the blue-grass, man or woman, who would not try it. Still, accidents are rare, and it is yet a tenet in the creed of the Southern hunter that the safer plan is to take no care. On the chase with greyhounds the dogs run, of course, by sight, and the point with the huntsman is to be the first at the place of the kill. As the greyhound tosses the rabbit several feet in the air and catches it when it falls, the place is seen by all, and there is a mad rush for that one spot. The hunters crash together, and often knock one another down. I have known two fallen horses and their riders to be cleared in a leap by two hunters who were close behind them. One of the men was struck by a hoof flying over him.

«I saw a shoe glisten,» he said, «and then it was darkness for a while.»

But it is the hunting without even a dog that is interesting, because it is unique and because the ladies share the fun. The sport doubtless originated with school-boys. They could not take dogs or guns to school; they had leisure at «big recess,» as the noon hour was called; they had horses, and the rabbits were just over the school-yard fence. One day two or three of them chased a rabbit down, and the fun was discovered. These same boys, perhaps, kept up the hunt after their school-days were over, and gave the fever to others, the more easily as foxes began to get scarce. Then the ladies began to take part, and the sport is what it is to-day. The President signs a great annual death-warrant for Br'er Rabbit in the blue-grass when he fixes a day for Thanksgiving.

DRAWN BY MAX F. KLEPPER.

«‹I WILL,› WAS THE GRAVE ANSWER, AND HE DID.»

III.

AGAIN Br'er Rabbit twists, and Phyllis's little horse turns after him like a polo pony after a ball. The black thoroughbred makes a wide sweep; Corydon's iron-gray cuts in behind, and the whole crowd starts in a body toward the road. This rabbit is an old hand at this business, and he knows where safety lies. A moment later the horses come to their haunches at the pike fence. Br'er Rabbit has gone into a culvert under the road, and already a small boy and a yellow dog are making for that culvert from a farm-house near. Again the trumpet, «Form a line!» Again the long line starts. There has been a shifting of positions. Corydon is next the white girth and stylish habit now, and he looks very much pleased. The slouch-hat of the college man and Phyllis's bare head are together, and the thoroughbred's master is talking earnestly. Phyllis looks across the field and smiles. Silly Corydon! The slouch-hat is confessing his trouble and asking advice. Yes, she will help, as women will, out of pure friendship, pure unselfishness; sometimes they have other reasons, and Phyllis had two. Another yell, another rabbit. Off they go, and then, midway, still another cry and still another rabbit. The hunters part in twain, the thoroughbred leading one wing, the iron-gray the other. Watch the slouch-hat now, and you will see how the thing is done. The thoroughbred is learning what his master is after, and he swerves to the right; others are coming in from that direction; the rabbit must turn again; others that way, too. Poor Mollie is confused; whichever way her big, startled eyes turn, that way she sees a huge beast and a yelling demon bearing down on her. The slouch-hat swoops near her first, flings himself from his horse, and, in spite of the riders pressing in on him, is after her on foot. Two others swing from their horses on the other side. Mollie makes several helpless hops, and the three scramble for her. The riders in front cry for those behind to hold their horses back, but they crowd in, and it is a miracle that none of the three is trampled down. The rabbit is hemmed in now; there is no way of escape, and instinctively she shrinks frightened to the earth. That is the crucial instant; down goes her pursuer on top of her as though she were a foot-ball, and the quarry is his. One blow of the hand behind the long ears, or one jerk by the hind legs, which snaps the neck as a whip cracks, and the slouch-hat holds aloft the brush, a little puff of down, and turns his eye about the field. The white girth is near, and as he starts toward her he is stopped by a low «Ahem!» behind him. Corydon has caught the first rabbit, and already on the derby hat above the white girth is pinned the brush. The young fellow turns again. Phyllis, demure and unregarding, is there with her eyes on the horns of her saddle; but he understands, and a moment later she smiles with prettily feigned surprise, and the white puff moves off in her loosening brown hair. The white girth is betrayed into the faintest shadow of vexation. Corydon heard that eloquent little clearing of the throat

DRAWN BY MAX F. KLEPPER.

«DOWN GOES HER PURSUER ON TOP OF HER.»

with a darkling face, and, indeed, no one of the four looks very happy except Phyllis.

«Form a line!»

Again the rabbits jump,—one, two, three,—and the horses dash and crash together, and the men swing to the ground, and are pushed and trampled in a mad clutch for Mollie's long ears; for it is a contest between them as to who shall catch the most game. The iron-gray goes like a demon, and when Corydon drops the horse is trained to stop and to stand still. This gives Corydon an advantage which balances the superior quickness of the thoroughbred and the agility of his rider. The hunting-party is broken up now into groups of three and four, each group after a rabbit, and for the time the disgusted captains give up all hope of discipline. A horse has gone down in a gully. Two excited girls have jumped to the ground for a rabbit. The big mule threshes the weeds like a tornado. Crossing the field at a heavy gallop, he stops suddenly at a ditch, the girth of the old saddle breaks, and the host of the day goes on over the long ears.

DRAWN BY MAX F. KLEPPER.

«HE STOPS SUDDENLY AT A DITCH.»

When he rises from the weeds there is a shriek of laughter over the field, and then a mule-race, for, with a bray of freedom, the sorrel makes for home. Not a rabbit is jumped on the next circuit; that field is hunted out. No matter; there is another just across the meadow, and they make for it. More than a dozen rabbits dangle head downward behind the saddles of the men. Corydon has caught seven, and the slouch-hat five. The palm lies between them plainly, as does a bigger motive than the game. It is a matter of gallantry—conferring the brush in the field; indeed, secrets are hidden rather than betrayed in that way; so Corydon is free to honor the white girth, and the slouch-hat can honor Phyllis without suspicion. The stylish habit shows four puffs of down; Phyllis wears five—every trophy that the slouch-hat has won. That is the way Phyllis is helping a friend, getting even with an enemy, and putting down a rebellion in her own camp. Even in the meadow a rabbit starts up, and there is a quick sprint in the open; but Br'er Rabbit, another old hand at the hunt, slips through the tall palings of a garden fence. In the other field the fun is more furious than ever, for the rabbits are thicker and the rivalry is very close. Corydon is getting excited; once he nearly overrides his rival.

The field has gone mad. The girl with the white girth is getting flushed with something more than excitement, and even Phyllis, demure as she still looks, is stirred a little. The pony's mistress is ahead by two brushes, and the white girth is a little vexed. She declares she is going to catch a rabbit herself. The slouch-hat hears, and watches her thereafter uneasily. And she does spring lightly, recklessly, to the ground just as the iron-gray and the thoroughbred crash in toward her, and right between the horses' hoofs Br'er Rabbit is caught in her little black riding-gloves. Indeed, the front feet of a horse strike her riding-skirt, mashing it into the soft earth, and miss crushing her by a foot. The slouch-hat is on the ground beside her. «You must n't do that again!» he says with sharp authority.

«Mr. ——,» she says quietly, but haughtily, to Corydon, who is on the ground too, «will you please help me on my horse?»

The slouch-hat looks as red as a flame, but Phyllis whispers comfort. «That's all right,» she says wisely; and it is all right. Under the slouch-hat the white face meant fear, anxiety, distress. The authority of the voice thrilled the girl, and in the depths of her heart she was pleased: and Phyllis knew.

The sun is dropping fast, but they will try one more field, which lies beyond a broad pasture of blue-grass. Now comes the chase of the day. Something big and gray leaps from a bunch of grass and bounds away. It is the father of rabbits, and there is a race indeed—an open field, a straight course, and no favor. The devil take the hindmost! Listen to the music of the springy turf, and watch that thoroughbred whose master has stayed behind to put up the fence! He has n't had half a chance before. He feels the grip of knees as his master rises to the racing-seat, and knowing what that means, he lengthens. No great effort is apparent; he simply stretches himself close to the earth and skims it as a swallow skims a pond.

Within two hundred yards he is side by side with Corydon, who is leading, and Corydon, being no fool, pulls in and lets him go on. Br'er Rabbit is going up one side of a long, shallow ravine. There is a grove of locusts at the upper end. The hunters behind see the slouch-hat cut around the crest of the hill, and, as luck would have it, Br'er Rabbit doubles, and comes back on the other side of the ravine. The thoroughbred has closed up the gap that the turn made, and is not fifty yards behind. Br'er Rabbit is making either for a rain-washed gully just opposite, or for a brier-patch farther down. So they wait. The cottontail clears the gully like a ball of thistledown, and Phyllis hears a little gasp behind her as the thoroughbred too rises and cleaves the air. Horse and rabbit dash into the weedy cover, and the slouch-hat drops out of sight as three hunters ride yelling into it from the other side. There is a scramble in the bushes, and the slouch-hat emerges with the rabbit in his hand. As he rides slowly toward the waiting party, he looks at Phyllis as though to receive further orders. He gets them. Wily Phyllis shakes her head as though to say:

«Not me this time; *her*.»

And with a courtly inclination of the slouch-hat, the big brush goes in lieu of an olive-branch for peace.

The shadows are stretching fast; they will not try the other field. Back they start through the radiant air homeward, laughing, talking, bantering, living over the incidents of the day, the men with one leg swung over the pommel of their saddles for rest; the girls with habits disordered and torn, hair down, and a little tired, but all flushed, clear-eyed, and happy. The leaves, russet, gold, and crimson, are dropping to the green earth; the sunlight is as yellow as the wings of a butterfly; and on the horizon is a faint haze that foreshadows the coming Indian summer. If it be Thanksgiving, a big dinner will be waiting for them at the stately old farm-house, or if a little later in the year, a hot supper instead. If the hunt is very informal, and there be neither, which rarely happens, everybody asks everybody else to go home with him, and everybody means it, and accepts if possible. This time it is warm enough for a great spread out in the yard on the lawn and under the big oaks. What a feast that is—chicken, turkey, cold ham, pickles, croquettes, creams, jellies, «beaten» biscuit! And what happy laughter, and thoughtful courtesy, and mellow kindness!

Inside, most likely, it is cool enough for a fire in the big fireplace with the shining old brass andirons; and what quiet, solid, old-fashioned English comfort that light brings out! Two darky fiddlers are waiting on the back porch—waiting for a dram from «young cap'n,» as «young marster» is now called. They do not wait long. By the time darkness settles the fiddles are talking old tunes, and the nimble feet are busy. Like draws to like now, and the window-seats and the tall columns of the porch hear again what they have been listening to for so long. Corydon has drawn near. Does Phyllis sulk or look cold? Not Phyllis. You would not know that Corydon had ever left her side. It has been a day of sweet mischief to Phyllis.

DRAWN BY MAX F. KLEPPER.

«IN LIEU OF AN OLIVE-BRANCH.»

At midnight they ride forth in pairs into the crisp, brilliant air and under the kindly moon. The white girth turns toward town with the thoroughbred at her side, and Corydon and Phyllis take the other way. They live on adjoining farms, these two. Phyllis has not forgotten; oh, no! There is mild torture awaiting Corydon long after he shall have forgotten the day, and he deserves it. Silly Corydon! to quarrel over nothing, and to think that he could make her jealous over that—the white girth is never phrased, for Phyllis stops there. It is not the first time these two have crossed foils. But there is peace now, and the little comedy of the day, seen by nearly every woman and by hardly a man, comes that night to a happy end.

*John Fox, Jr.*

# THE CHINESE OF NEW YORK

## CONTRASTED WITH THEIR FOREIGN NEIGHBORS.

POPULAR opinion, when considering our foreign immigrants, has given the lowest rank among them to the Chinese. Whether or not this is a just conclusion is a matter which certainly admits of discussion. But it behooves us, as Americans who desire to see justice done to all, to consider the question from the standpoint of facts, and not of prejudice.

It is admittedly true that no city in America presents so varied a population as does New York. Here we have a quota of all the nationalities that have come to us, dwelling, to a very considerable extent, in colonies by themselves. Because of this colonization the native habits and customs, religious and domestic, are retained much longer, and the Americanization—I might almost say the civilization in some cases—is consequently slower and more laborious than in many cities. Here, also, the Chinese have congregated in sufficient numbers to form a settlement of their own, bearing the peculiar stamp of their nationality. For this reason, therefore, as a place for a comparison of the races when dwelling in America, New York City offers a peculiar advantage.

To judge a people accurately one should know something more of their inner life than can be learned from a tour of their colony, or from the police officers who stand guard at their doors. One should know the people by personal contact as well. From that point of view the writer is able to speak of the Chinese with the utmost freedom, and of the neighboring foreigners with a good degree of familiarity. The work of a city missionary has brought me to a considerable extent in contact with Italians, Russians, and Poles, Germans, Irish, and Chinese, and to a slight extent with Spaniards, Turks, French, and Scandinavians. But the comparisons which I wish to draw in this article are more particularly between the first-named classes, with whom I am best acquainted, and who make up the immediate environment of New York's Chinatown.

Chinatown, as it is called, is composed of three short blocks, two of which intercept each other at right angles, thus:

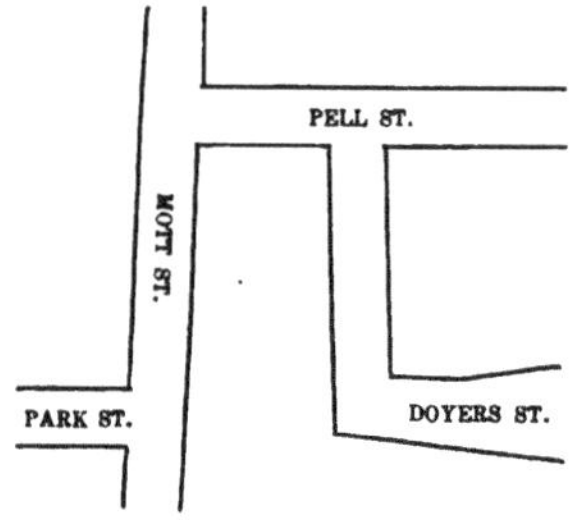


Its inhabitants are not by any means confined to the Chinese, for many Italians, a few negroes, and a few Irish people share the crowded tenements with them. For the most part the buildings are old and dilapidated, and those converted to Chinese use have been refitted with the flimsiest of wooden partitions, and are void of many of the most ordinary of modern conveniences.

In the streets surrounding Chinatown to the north and east the population seems even more dense, if that can be possible, and is made up in the northeast portion of Russian and Polish Hebrews, and to the west and north of Italians. Directly east of Chinatown is that greatest artery of the city, Third Avenue, or «The Bowery,» as the avenue is called from Chatham Square to Seventh street. This is the greatest field in the city for petty showmen and for lodging-house keepers. The street is lined from the terminus of the Brooklyn Bridge to the Cooper Union building with museums, theaters, beer-gardens, dance-halls, and dives of all sorts and degrees of degradation, while shops and stores, owned mostly by Jews, are sandwiched in between them. The upper stories of a large proportion of these buildings are used as lodging-houses and hotels for homeless men and boys, and are of all grades, from the seven-cents-per-night lodging to the fifty-cent «hotel.»

As to the moral status of the streets west and north of Chinatown, I need scarcely do more than mention that these are Mulberry, Baxter, and Bayard, and that within a stone's throw of Mott street is the notorious «Mulberry Bend,» for many years past the hiding-place of criminals, and the last and lowest resort of the abandoned and vicious of both sexes. The tales of «Mulberry Bend» that until recently assailed the ears of the missionary are absolutely unrelatable, and to be comprehended only by one used to the sight and knowledge of the lives of criminals and outcasts of the lowest possible character. Within the last few years the police have driven out the worst dives of the region, but the evil effects of those once-abounding evils are still to be seen there, and unfortunately tell sadly upon the Italians who have filled up the quarter. This, in brief, is the sort of life which surrounds Chinatown, and it is the purpose of this article to show whether or not the Chinese have found their element in its level, or whether, in spite of its stagnant, slimy, deadly influence, the Chinese character has asserted itself to be something better than its environment.[1]

The moral status of a people is sometimes indicated in their amusements. The beer-gardens of the Bowery, the dance-halls and vaudeville performances of its theaters, its museums and its saloons, are patronized by English-speaking peoples of recent foreign extraction, and also by thousands of foreigners who speak no tongue but their own. Among them you will find the Polish and Russian Jew, the German, the Italian, the ever-present and permeative Irishman, the Spaniard and Hungarian, in fact, representatives from every country which has sent us its immigrants—except the Chinese.

The people of Mulberry Bend and Baxter street are for the most part too poor to patronize the gaudy shows of the Bowery. They have no amusements, unless drinking beer in saloons and courtyards can be called an amusement. This does, indeed, seem to be the only pleasure these sad people know, and a wedding or christening is celebrated by an all-night carousal, when beer flows freely, and night is made hideous with their songs. Songs and drinking are kept up until daylight, when the men stumble to their own tenements to spend the day in a drunken stupor.

The amusements of Chinatown seem to consist of three things—the Chinese theater, opium-smoking, and social intercourse.

DRAWN BY F. H. LUNGREN.

PRESSING DOUGH.

Let us first consider the Chinese theater. In contrast with the vaudeville performance of the Bowery theaters and gardens is the Chinese play, steady, dignified, dramatic, rarely ever even humorous. Here, instead of some unnamable social scandal being utilized as the dramatic impulse of their play, the national history, the greatest fictions of Chinese literature, embodying innumerable moral precepts and examples, are the subjects for the actors' interpretation. The Chinese actor himself is the very embodiment of dignity, while the quintessence of etiquette marks his manners. He endeavors to conceal rather than betray emotion.

Do the Chinese dance? Never; neither in China nor in America, unless they have become so far denationalized as to be considered a foreign graft on the Western stalk, which occurs not once in a thousand cases. There is therefore no dance upon the Chinese stage. In all their performance, from beginning to end, there is nowhere any sort of a dance, from the likeness of the minuet of a century ago to the latest ballet step of to-

[1] A park has destroyed a part of the section. —EDITOR.

day. The Chinese look upon such a thing as entirely beneath the dignity of a Chinaman, and such a performance would be received with disgust and hisses.

A well-known New York daily newspaper recently made itself ridiculous, and lauded its own ignorance to the skies, by referring with beautiful serenity to the wickedness of the vaudeville performance in the Chinese theater. A vaudeville performance in a Chinese theater? There is no such thing. Even more than that: to a Chinaman it would be an insupportable scandal that women should appear upon the stage as freely as they do in America and Europe. Such a thing never was known either in China or in the Chinese theaters of America. A woman appears only when her husband or father is a member of the company, and then in the most insignificant parts, and her identity is suppressed rather than advertised. Women's parts in ninety-nine cases out of a hundred are taken by men, and these are enacted with a modesty and humility which we would fain see copied by the actresses of our stage to-day—ay, even by some of our women themselves. Could a little of the Chinese dignity, reticence, and womanly modesty be poured into American blood, it would be a good thing for the American people, and an admirable specific for the American «girl of the period.» There is therefore no comparison to be made, from a moral standpoint, between the Chinese stage and the vile, immodest, and frequently obscene performances which the white people of the Bowery put upon their boards. But there is one feature of New York amusements that is wholly unknown to the Chinaman, and that is the concert-garden. To congregate in a public place to drink intoxicating beverages, listen to sensuous music, and watch vulgar displays of the human figure; to be waited upon by young women of more than questionable character; to take part in profane and obscene talk: all this is beneath the dignity of a Chinaman, and nowhere in the Chinese quarter, from beginning to end, can such a place be found. But they are found on the Bowery, and Germans, Irishmen, Italians, and Jews fill the places to the doors.

If you made with me a complete tour of Chinatown, visiting every place where a Chinaman dwells, when you had returned you would sum up what you had seen about as follows:

Places where opium was smoked by Chinese in their own private apartments: about one fourth of the whole.

Places where opium was sold to white visitors who smoked and slept on the premises, and which is commonly called an «opium-joint»: possibly three in your whole tour.

Places where gambling was in progress: about one twentieth of the whole.

Places where men were pursuing the ordinary vocations of life: nearly three fourths.

The population of Chinatown on Sundays is about four or five thousand, on week-days very much less. The difference may be accounted for by the fact that on Sunday the Chinese from all parts of New York and Brooklyn, and from Long Island, New Jersey, and Connecticut towns, flock to Chinatown to visit their friends and to do business. Since the American Sunday does not permit laundry work on that day, the laundrymen seize upon it as a general recreation day, and go to Chinatown by hundreds. This, therefore, is the great business day of that region, and all the stores are open and every employee is constantly occupied.

Here the laundrymen buy all their dry groceries, their clothing, and their laundry supplies. Here, also, are the great family headquarters whither comes the mail from China, and where the Chinese meet to discuss the affairs of their people, and incidentally the various phases of American anti-Chinese legislation.

That Chinatown is not wholly a place of opium-joints and gambling-dens, as public prejudice would have you believe, is proved by a census of the streets which recently revealed sixty-five stores and eighteen gambling-places. Since our police do not read the Chinese language, the games of chance and the sale of opium may be openly advertised with perfect impunity, and they are constantly so advertised in red placards pasted on walls, doors, and windows. At the present writing very little opium is being offered for sale, and only trusted customers can obtain it. While in probably one fourth of the Chinese apartments opium is smoked daily or occasionally, yet it would be wholly unfair to infer that one fourth of the Chinese in this vicinity use the hateful drug. That is manifestly not the case. For instance, one may enter an apartment and find two or three men smoking, and twenty or thirty who are not smoking, but are visiting, laughing, jesting, or playing on musical instruments. Among no people from any quarter of the globe, nor among those from a long line of American parentage, have I seen an equally strong desire for one another's companionship. To go to see

DRAWN BY W. H. DRAKE.

IN A CHINESE THEATER.

his «cousin» is the Chinaman's great delight, and on Sunday they gather by the score in the apartments of their family or members of their clan, or in the business places of their particular friends. You rarely find a Chinaman dwelling alone, and that not from motives of economy only, but because they desire companionship. To them friendship is everything. A Chinaman trusts his friend or his relative to an extent that we would consider foolish, almost imbecile. This testimony is borne of the people not only by missionaries of New York, but by business men of the Pacific coast and by missionaries of long residence in China.

The Chinese are a merry, fun-loving people, in spite of their general air of indifference in the presence of strangers. They race up and down stairs, or sometimes through the streets, on a frolic, every man laughing until he is out of breath, pulling cues, stealing hats, and playing all manner of practical jokes on one another. I recently heard a great commotion in Doyers street on a hot Sunday afternoon, when the street was crowded with Chinamen, and, fearing trouble, hurried hastily to the place, only to find one man the butt of another's joke, trying to get away from his pursuer, while about five hundred laughing men joined in the fun, and finally administered good-natured justice to the perpetrator of the joke. At another time on Sunday afternoon I heard a sudden outcry and scuffle overhead, and the running of scores of feet. I ran into the hall, fearing that the building was on fire, and with a sickening dread at my heart for the Italian children in Bethany Sunday-school, which was then in session in the Mission rooms. I saw a man coming down-stairs, and asked him what was the matter. With a shrug of infinite disdain, he remarked: «Oh, my people too muchee laugh,» and passed on his way. It was only a school-boy joke played by one group of men on another, followed by a general mêlée, in which shouts and laughter, and the incessant clatter of wooden soles on board floors, made us think of «pandemonium let loose.» Some of the keenest and purest humor and some of the wittiest sallies I have ever heard have fallen from the lips of Chinamen in lower New York. I well remember the amused and contemptuous look with which a Chinaman once said, «Melican man savee [understand] Chinaman allee same number one fool. Chinaman savee Melican man allee same. Chinaman every time gettee top side Melican man»—which does not contain a reference to pugilism, but merely means that in a battle of wits the Chinaman «sees through» the American man, and will come out on the «top side.» They are very quick at repartee, and their black eyes will sparkle with amusement and fun if you jest with them, or when they start the ball rolling among themselves.

They dwell together for years in the same apartments, happy and comfortable. They minister to one another in sickness, bury a relative or neighbor when dead without calling on public charities for help, and in the case of a relative assume the support of the family of the dead man when he is gone. These people—these much-derided people—spend hours together in one another's apartments, conversing together, eating together, sometimes smoking the long water-pipe, always with a pot of steaming tea between them. In two years I have seen thousands of such groups, but never yet have I found these men drinking liquor together. I have found them playing games—sometimes, but not always, gambling; have found them playing their musical instruments, which are harmonious to them, however much they may lack of melody to other ears; or have found them reading or discussing the last Hong-Kong or Shanghai daily: but I repeat I have never found them drinking liquor, or in any degree under the influence of intoxicants.

The Chinaman celebrates his wedding, not by a drunken carousal, but by the finest feast that his pocket-book can command, to which not only his immediate relatives are invited, but all who have the slightest claim of friendship upon him. A Chinaman who was recently married in Mott street gave three large feasts in as many restaurants, entertaining several hundred people at each before he had gone the round of his acquaintances and friends. Yet this man was not one of the most prosperous ones. A child's birthday is likewise celebrated with a feast, the wife entertaining her friends in the family home, while her husband entertains his friends at his place of business or in a public restaurant.

I have said that a Chinaman trusts his friends to an extent that we would consider almost imbecile. Among them money is loaned without interest and without any written acknowledgment or witnesses. If a man is «short» and appeals to his cousin or his friend to help him, that friend will divide up without specifying a time for its repayment. If the man is sick or poor, the creditor, in all probability, will never mention the matter again, and will certainly not ask for its return while the debtor refrains from gambling or opium-smoking, and honestly does his best. I have known men to be for a time without employment, and while they were trying to obtain it, if they conformed to the strict moral code of Chinese law, they were helped by the various cousins with gifts of money sufficient to support them until work was obtained; and not only to support themselves, but their families also. And then, as «turn about is fair play,» they were expected to be equally generous with some one else.

One amusing incident of Chinese generosity recently occurred under my notice. A man who had been out of work for some time, and had been liberally helped by his friends, tried in every possible way to earn money. One day he found an attractive Newfoundland puppy up-town, and purchased the

DRAWN BY F. H. LUNGREN.

NIGHT IN CHINATOWN.

dog for a dollar. He brought it home for his wife and baby to see, gleefully announcing that he would sell the puppy for «two, t'ree dollar» to some of his countrymen. He soon afterward started out, with the dog under his arm, in search of his hoped-for customer. He was soon surrounded by admiring Chinese, and the first man who got the dog in his arms, quite unaware of his friend's financial scheme, begged him to give it to him. Thereupon the would-be dog-merchant cheerfully presented the canine to his friend, explaining to his wife afterward: «Of course, he askee dog, me give him. Me no got bad heart for friend.» It was perfectly proper that he should make a present of the dog at his friend's request, and he did so without hesitation.

Perhaps in these things I need not stoop to contrast the Chinese with the lower classes of Irish, Italians, Hebrews, or Germans, but may go somewhat higher, and compare them with the Americans, who are the outcome of generations of enlightenment, the progeny of ancestors of strict piety and principles of honesty and integrity, and may point out that in generosity and kindness to his brother the Chinese strangely outstrip us.

Some of our immigrants become paupers, or dependents on public or private charity in some form, and many others are, or become, criminals. The percentage of foreigners in our hospitals, asylums, and penal institutions is overwhelming. But the Chinese make little call upon us for philanthropy, and that only for medical help. Little by little these people are coming to see the superiority of our medical treatment, and in cases of severe sickness they will sometimes turn to our hospitals for help. But they ask no other aid from us. If a Chinaman needs any monetary assistance, his countrymen help him without burdening our public philanthropies. It is not uncommon for the men of one clan, or friends from different clans, to band together to establish a loan fund, every man giving so much toward it week by week. This is loaned to needy men, without security or interest; and when repaid it is loaned again, and thus many a man is carried through a sickness or set up in business, and outsiders are none the wiser.

Let us contrast these foreign immigrants from another point of view—that of their value in the labor-market.

Of late years there has been a constant cry against «Chinese cheap labor.» Whatever may have been the price put upon Chinese labor when the great railways of the West were built by these people, to-day it is evident to all who have studied the question that there is no such thing as «Chinese cheap labor.» Chinese laundries charge higher rates than domestic laundries. Chinese laundrymen command higher prices than laundresses of other nationalities. A Chinaman earns ordinarily from eight to fifteen dollars a week and his board and lodging. The white or colored laundress makes from four to ten dollars a week, without board or lodging. The Chinaman works from eight o'clock in the morning until one or two o'clock at night. Sometimes he washes, sometimes he starches, sometimes he irons; but he is always at it, not tireless, but persevering in spite of weariness and exhaustion. Other laborers clamor for a working-day of eight hours. The Chinaman patiently works seventeen, takes care of his relatives in China, looks after his own poor in America, and pays his bills as he goes along.

In the Chinese store ten dollars per week is the lowest sum paid for a man-of-all-work. In a Chinese restaurant the lowest wage paid to a kitchen-boy is twenty dollars per month and board. Chinese cooks will not go to American families for less than forty dollars per month, and they rarely ever stay for that sum. This, then, is Chinese cheap labor—a cheap labor of which ordinary people cannot avail themselves.

«But,» perhaps you may say, in considering this topic, «there are certainly many evils in Chinatown.»

So there are. Gambling is an evil, whether the gambler be a white, black, or yellow man. But to show you that the yellow gambler is at least no worse than the black or the white gambler, I will say that as a Christian missionary I am able to enter freely all the gambling-rooms of Chinatown, and go among the men, being treated everywhere with respect and courtesy, a thing which I could not do among any other people on the continent.

Again, opium-smoking is an evil—an evil offset by the use of intoxicants among our natives and among foreign peoples of other climes. Among the opium-smokers I can go with perfect freedom, bearing Christian literature, and with an invitation to our mission upon my lips. But I could not go into an American saloon with the same safety or impunity. Among the Chinese I am safe from fear of insult or annoyance, be they good or bad men. It is not so among our white peoples. There the missionary must curtail many efforts and walk with cautious steps. But you say, «There is the terrible ‹Hip Shing Tong,› the highbinders' society.» Yes, even in New York this branch of the evil society exists; but against that let me place the imported Mafia of Italy, the nihilism of Russia, the anarchism of Germany and Italy; and while we weigh one against the other, let us remember that while the Hip Shing Tong may sometimes become the instrument of private vengeance for personal wrongs, the anarchist club and the nihilist society hurl their death-dealing blows at great social and political institutions, and attack and destroy the pure and innocent without reason or cause.

«But,» you say, «personal purity is not the

rule in Chinatown.» I do not know if it be the rule or be not the rule. I know that there are many buildings in Chinatown for which a Chinaman would blush as quickly as an American. I know also that in these buildings lewd women have fastened themselves like leeches, fostering sin and guilt wherever they are. I know that on these thresholds Christian missionaries must halt for very shame, and that the Chinese who dwell within these buildings, knowing no other type of American womanhood than this, have small conception of purity and chastity. I know of no degree in such vice. It is the same heinous, shameful sin, whether the sinner be black or white, red or yellow. Only in this can the Chinese be said to be different from others: they are less brutal and violent to these women than are the men of whiter skin, and for this reason, and because of the love of opium which is so prevalent among this class, the women cling to the neighborhood, and refuse to leave unless effectually driven out by the police.

But from among the Chinese themselves have come many strong efforts to do away with these evils. Much good has been accomplished. In the coming years let us hope that much more may yet be done, and that the honor of thousands of respectable business men may not be impugned by the sins of their guilty countrymen.

Let us now examine the police records as to which nationality most often falls into the hands of the law. I append below a table based upon the police report for 1890, and the United States census for that year:

| NATIONALITY. | POPULATION. | NO. OF ARRESTS. | PERCENTAGE. |
|---|---|---|---|
| Italians | 39,951 | 4,757 | 11.9 |
| Irish | 190,418 | 21,254 | 11. |
| English and Scotch | 47,149 | 3,388 | 7. |
| Swedes and Norwegians | 8,644 | 526 | 6. |
| French | 10,535 | 549 | 5.2 |
| Russians and Poles | 55,549 | 2,624 | 4.7 |
| Natives of United States | 875,358 | 39,611 | 4.5 |
| Chinese [1] | 5,000 | 219 | 4.3 |
| Germans | 210,723 | 9,146 | 4.2 |
| Bohemians and Hungarians | 20,321 | 308 | 1.5 |

According to this table, six of the nations most largely represented in New York city,—viz., Italy, Ireland, Great Britain, Sweden and Norway, France, and Russia,—and even these United States themselves, send a larger contingent to our prisons than do the Chinese. It seems to me that this table is perhaps as conclusive an answer as can be given to the popular fancy that the Chinese are the worst sinners on our shores.

But let us contrast these people in the matter of conformity to American life and customs. Generally speaking, almost any other people find such conformity easier than do the Chinese. The difference between life in Europe and life in America is much less distinct than between life in Asia and in America. Of all who come here, the Chinese are the most conservative and the least pliable. Were it possible for them to attain to citizenship at the end of fifteen or even twenty-five years of residence here, it would doubtless act as an incentive to the better class among them to adopt American ideas and habits. I know of a certainty the high value which many of these Chinamen put upon American citizenship. At one time, a number of years ago, it was possible for a man to swear to his intention to become a citizen, and until the constitutional amendment was passed which forbade any State to naturalize them, many judges issued such papers. I well remember many instances in which Chinese have preserved these useless papers as their greatest treasures, and have showed them to me with pride, and their eyes glistened with joy while they told me how they would sometime be citizens of this great American country. Poor fellows, how little they realized the utter worthlessness of those bits of well-loved paper! But they are stamped as «aliens» by the Government, and are treated as aliens by our people.

The Chinese are a specially proud people. They ask neither our sympathy nor our help. If a Chinaman ever tells you his thoughts, or talks to you of himself or his people, it is because you have won his confidence to a considerable degree. They are also extremely sensitive, easily offended, and not easily

[1] The Chinese population of New York is a matter of conjecture. It is well known that it is next to impossible to obtain a correct census of these people, since their ignorance of our customs and doings makes them extremely suspicious and uncommunicative. The United States census in 1890 places the number at 2048. But a few months later a private canv ss of the laundries and of the stores of Chinatown—not including the buildings there used as residences, and which shelter many hundreds—showed a population of upward of 6000. The Chinese themselves estimate it at from 8000 to 10,000. When the certificates of residence were issued in 1894, over 6000 Chinese registered from one district alone. At the Morning Star Mission, every Sunday for three years past, we have distributed in an hour from 2000 to 4000 copies of the «Chinese News,» and that only in Chinatown. There has been nothing to cause either a great accession or diminution in the Chinese colony during the last five years, and hence it seems to me only a matter of justice to

DRAWN BY F. H. LUNGREN.

IN A CHINESE RESTAURANT.

placated. These qualities, added to their natural conservatism, may account somewhat for their lack of pliability, and slowness in adopting American habits and customs. Unfortunately the anti-Chinese riots of the West have not proved conducive to a great faith in our friendliness; neither have the numberless annoyances and insults to which

estimate this population at the exceedingly reasonable figure of 5000. If, however, the reader prefers to accept the census figure of 2048, the percentage of Chinese placed under arrest will be 10.6, which still leaves them second in rank to the Irish and third to the Italians.

they are constantly subjected in the streets of our Eastern cities won any greater confidence in us. The Chinaman is an alien, and he knows and feels he is an alien. It is useless for him to try to be an American, for he never can be one of us, whether he be a graduate of Yale or a humble laundryman, and therefore he does not try. He comes here, therefore, spends the best years of his life in the most unremitting labor, and with his few thousands of dollars goes back to China, to a land and a government that will own him; and so long as he lives he takes care of his wife and his children, his parents, and, if they be in need, his uncles and all the rest of the family that may have the slightest claim upon him.

Other people who come here gradually adopt the American dress and way of living. Their children, if not themselves, learn to speak English, are taken into American business houses, become naturalized, and in time they are an integral part of the great whole, and no one asks, «Did you come from Italy, or Sweden, or Germany, or Turkey, or Austria, or Scotland, or France, or Ireland, or Spain?» They are thenceforward, to all intents and purposes, Americans. Their nationality is not continually thrust upon us by their dress. Unquestionably a Chinaman in American dress is better treated, more respected, than a Chinaman in Chinese dress; and while in points of comfort the Chinese dress is probably to be preferred to the closer-fitting American suit, yet many Chinamen recognize this fact, and surrender their own clothes to don ours.

In the matter of living but few have adopted American beds. Our tables, chairs, and kitchen furniture they readily approve; but in ninety-nine cases out of a hundred they prefer the rude wooden platform spread with straw matting to the softer beds of the Americans. Not so the European immigrants. They will have all of these comfortable things that they can get. The Chinese do not comprehend some of the ordinary but most important sanitary arrangements in our buildings. (I am speaking now of the rank and file of the residents of Chinatown, not of the educated or the Christianized men.) Consequently in certain respects they are a problem to landlords and a menace to themselves and their neighbors in the matter of health. As a rule there is more regard for personal cleanliness among the Chinese than among either Italians, Jews, or the other races that fill lower New York. Not all are clean, but the majority are, and very much cleaner than the Italians or the Jews. A tour of Mulberry Bend or of Hester street reveals far more filth and disorder than a tour of Chinatown will reveal.

Not long ago I accompanied through Hester street a missionary from China, who has long resided in Canton. As we turned the corner and came into full view of the street, with its thronging crowd and heterogeneous merchandise, she suddenly exclaimed:

«This is China! The same crowds, the merchandise, the dirt! Only it is worse, for *there* no babes or women are to be seen.» We passed child after child, still too young to walk, lying upon the stone flagging of the pavement, or sitting upon the curb or in the roadway. From Hester street we passed to Mulberry Bend, where we saw much the same scene, but a less number of people. From both streets the odors were so foul and loathsome that upon our return to Chinatown my companion was overcome with illness. Returning to the quiet streets of the Chinese district, to their clean and orderly stores, to the well-behaved and unobtrusive inhabitants, seemed like coming from Bedlam to a city of peace.

We have now compared these peoples from the standpoint of morality, of cleanliness, and very briefly in those labor-markets in which they appear together as competitors. We have also seen them in their amusements, their domestic festivals, their social relations. It seems to me that the Chinese have not suffered by this comparison, but that they have rather risen in our estimation. Let us, then, accord our brother from the East an equal respect with the members of these other races, than whom certainly he is no worse.

*Helen F. Clark.*

# A SPECIAL PROVIDENCE.

BY THE AUTHOR OF «THE FLOATING BETHEL.»

RS. MELISSA ALLGOOD settled herself in her rocking-chair for a good talk. «I was telling you,» she began, «about Sister Belle Keen and Brother Singleton and me being a Holiness Band last summer, and preaching all around in middle Kentucky, and about Brother Singleton taking down so sick at Smithsboro, and Sister Belle getting her eyes opened, and marrying him, and taking him home.

«Well, that broke up the band; for of course a lone widow woman, going on thirty-four years old, can't go preaching over the country with nothing but a tent to keep her company, no matter how much heartfelt religion and sanctification she 's got. Anyhow, I felt like I 'd done about enough work for one summer, and like now was my time to rest awhile. Sister Belle she had made me keep fifteen dollars of the collection we took up the last night, and I knew I better be getting along home while I had the money to go on. So I stayed around a few days with the folks there at Smithsboro, and then started home. Smithsboro is pretty near up to Louisville, and I had to take a roundabout way to get home, going down by Bowling Green and Guthrie, and then up again to the Station.

«Most of Smithsboro was down at the noon train to see me off, and I hated bad to leave them all. Lots of the women folks had give me presents to carry home with me. My valise was so full I had to set on it to fasten it, and I had a big bandbox full of lunch—because them Smithsboro people said they could n't bear to think of me traveling hungry—and a large-sized basket, with a lot of young fruit-trees and rose and geranium plants, and others, that different ones had give me; and here, at the last minute, old Sister Macklin she brought me down to the train six cans of Indian peaches she had put up herself—those half-gallon glass cans. I did n't see how on earth I was going to get home with 'em all, especially the cans of peaches, and change cars at Guthrie; but I never was in a tight place yet that the Lord did n't help me out, and I had faith that somebody would be provided to pack them cans around when it come time to change cars, and rested easy on the promise. I set the cans down on the floor of the car underneath the seat, and piled the other things up on the seat in front of me to keep them from jostling the cans, and then I set back in perfect peace, and spread my Bible open in my lap, ready to read when I got tired looking at the folks in the car.

«There was n't much to look at, being all men folks, and it was a mighty hot day, and I had eat a big dinner, and look like I could n't keep from nodding to save my life. I reckon I must have fell asleep, for first thing I knew I was woke up by my head getting a hard bump against the side of the car. It made me so blind I could n't see for a minute, but when I could the first thing I laid eyes on was an old gentleman leaning over the back of my seat fanning me with a big palm-leaf fan, and trying to tuck a pillow behind my head. ‹Madam,› he says, ‹allow me to make you more comfortable. I hope you ain't suffering from that bump you got.› I set up straight, and took a good look at him. He was a real nice, pious-looking old gentleman, about sixty-five years old, with gray hair and whiskers, and mighty bland ways. I never saw anybody I liked the looks of any better. ‹I hope you 'll accept of this pillow,› he says, ‹to rest your head on. I find it a mighty useful thing to travel with.› I would n't have hurt the old man's feelings for anything; so I leaned back against it, and thanked him as polite as I could, and told him how much beholden I was to him for his kindness, and which nobody knew better how to appreciate than a lone widow woman like me. He leaned over the back of my seat, and fanned me the politest that ever was, and said, no, indeed; the obligations was all on his side; that when he met up with a young female like me, traveling over the wide, wide world without any natchul protector, or no strong arm to lean on, it raised his sympathies up to that point he considered it a blessed privilege to be any assistance to such a one, and especially, he said, when it happened to be a godly female like he could see I was, by my traveling with a Bible, and reading it so industrious. He said it was a sight that brought joy to his soul, in this generation of vipers, to see a righteous woman. Then, of course, I had to tell him all about my conversion, and getting sanctification, and feeling called to preach and save sinners, and about the meetings we'd been carrying on all the summer. Then he told me about his living down in Tennessee, and being an elder in the church, and said he'd just been up to Louisville on a little trip, but had found it a terrible ungodly place, and was glad to get out of it. The minute he said he lived down in Tennessee, I says to myself that instant, ‹Here 's my special providence the Lord has provided to help me change cars, and pack them cans at Guthrie,› and I just give thanks in my soul, and rejoiced.

«We talked on, and had a mighty entertaining conversation on religion. He said he could n't agree with me on sanctification; but I read Bible to him on that line, and expounded till he said he did n't know but what I was right—that if there ever was anybody truly sanctified and free from sin he believed it must be me. And I felt plumb happy over his being convinced, and over me being the one to lead him out of Babylon. Then he asked me a heap of questions, and seemed to take a real fatherly interest in me. Then he commenced telling about himself, and said he was a widower, and done lost three as dear companions as ever shed their rays on mortal man, and how the last one had been in glory just a year to the day, and how lonesome he was, his children being all married off. I felt awful sorry for him. It always did seem to me like a man was a mighty incomplete thing without a wife to steady him, and always reminded me of a young colt. You know there ain't a more foolish animal on earth than a colt. He 'll head off across a field, and after while he 'll bring up short, and wonder what he 's there for; then he 'll kick up, and strike away in another direction—don't seem to have any object in life. It 's the same way with a lone man, and any woman with feelings is bound to feel sorry for 'em. I could n't have felt more sorry for my own father than I did for that old man. I told him all my sympathies was with him. He said if ever there was a man needed sympathy he knew it was him; that look like he had more trouble than he could bear. I asked him what his particular trouble was, and he give a big groan, and said he was going to confide in me.

«He said he 'd been looking around for the last two or three months, it being natchul for a man that had had three such dear companions to feel the need of another when they was taken; that he 'd heard a heap about these matrimonial associations around over the country, that brings people together by advertising; and he said he felt led to put a card in one of them matrimonial newspapers, giving a description of himself and his intentions. He said the very next week he got an answer to it from a lady up at Louisville, ‹a widow, refined, thirty-two, and a brunette, without incumbrances, and willing to correspond with a view to matrimony.› Said that description suited him exactly. That he 'd always wanted to marry a Kentuckian, somehow, but look like the other three times he never quite made it, his other three dear companions having come from Georgia, Alabama, and Tennessee. But he said this time he made up his mind from the start that he 'd try for a Kentucky woman—that there was something mighty beguiling about them. Then he said her being a brunette suited him, too—that all his three other companions had been blue-eyed, and he felt like he 'd enjoy a little change and variety. Then he said her being without incumbrances was another good thing; that at his time of life he did n't feel warranted in taking a family to raise up. So he said he answered right back, and the letters commenced to fly pretty lively, and in two weeks' time all the arrangements was made, and the day set. He said, out of compliment to his last dear departed companion, he set the anniversary of her death for the wedding-day. He said he turned in then, and told all his connection and friends about his going to be married; and they made big arrangements about giving him a house-warming when he got back, and welcoming the bride, and saw him off on the train, and told him he could count on all of them being there, and more too, when he got back, to meet the bride. So he said he started off, rejoicing in his heart.

«He said he got to Louisville about five o'clock in the evening, and spruced himself up a little at the station,—clean collar and such,—and set out to hunt the widow. That he found the number all right,—a real nice-looking frame house,—and rung the bell; and who should come to the door but the widow herself? He said the sight of her just natchully paralyzed him; that he had made allowances for a woman's natchul good opinion of herself, and had n't set his expectations up too high. But he said she just laid it over all the women he had ever seen before; that none of them could n't compare with her. That her eyes was the blackest, and her teeth the whitest, and her cheeks the rosiest he ever did see, and she was as round and plump as a partridge, and never looked a day over twenty-nine. That he fairly held his breath to think of him marrying such a wife as that—that none of his three dear companions could n't hold a candle to her in looks.

That she treated him the politest and most affectionate that ever was, and hung up his hat for him, and took him in the parlor, and set and talked until supper about their wedding and plans and such, and then made him go out and eat supper with her and her kin that she was staying with. Said he never was treated as nice in his life; that she just honeyed him up and paid him more compliments than ever was, and looked at him like she thought he was just too sweet for anything. Said after supper she told him she had a heap of things to do—packing and such—to get ready for to-morrow, and she expect she'd have to send him down to his hotel right away to get a chance. He told her he was agreeable; that it was like pulling teeth to leave her that early in the evening, but he was n't the man to interfere with any woman's wedding plans, and go he would. She told him to see that he got there in plenty of time in the morning—that she was might'ly afraid he 'd keep her waiting, that she was going to have the preacher there at eight o'clock sharp, and did n't want the bridegroom to be behind time. That she just made eyes at him till he was plumb crazy, and then she kissed him good-by and sent him off.

«He said just as he got about half-way down the square from her house he met up with a big, tall man, with a red mustache and a broad-brimmed hat, and his pants tucked in his boots, and a leather belt on. Said the man was stopping before every house to look at the numbers, and that he knew the minute he laid eyes on the man that he was from Texas, from the way he walked all over the sidewalk. That he turned around, and looked at the man several times after he passed by him, and after while the man stopped in front of the widow's house, and looked at the number, and took a piece of paper out of his pocket and looked at that, and then opened the gate and went in. He said he knew in a minute it was some of the widow's Texas kin come up to her wedding, and was might'ly tickled over it.

«So he said he went to the hotel then, and stayed all night, and got up betimes in the morning so as he would n't be late for the wedding; that by five o'clock he was up and dressed in his wedding clothes, and then he had to set around and wait till half-past six before they 'd give him any breakfast, them city people being such late risers. That at seven he got a hack, and started out to the bride's. That when he got there, lo and behold! there was another carriage standing there at the gate, and not no common hack neither, but what he called a landau, with the top all throwed back, and a driver with a stove-pipe hat. Said he supposed it belonged to the bride's rich kin, and never worried no more about it, but got out of his hack and started up the walk. That just as he got to the bottom of the steps the front door opened, and out walked the widow, hanging on the arm of that red-headed Texas man, and smiling back over her shoulder at the folks inside. Said when she turned her head and laid eyes on him, she just give one scream, and dodged behind the Texas man, and hung on to his shoulders hollering and weeping. That the Texas man he looked plumb dazed, but he just natchully got two pistols out of his pockets to have 'em handy. That the old gentleman then he spoke up and asked what it was all about, and why, when a honorable man come to get his bride, folks wanted to meet him at the front door with pistols. Nobody could n't answer him, seemed like, till a man that looked like a preacher stepped out of the door, and asked him who it was that he expect to marry, and he told the preacher it was the lady there in the door, and the preacher said he just done married that lady to another gentleman, and there must be some mistake. Then the widow she bu'st out crying worse than ever, and said she knew she had promised to marry the old gentleman, but that was the evening previous, before she had seen the gentleman from Texas, and learned to love him with undying love. Said she been carrying on a correspondence with 'em both, and set the same wedding-day for both of 'em, thinking whichever she liked best when they got there she would take. Said she thought she liked the old gentleman when she saw him, but after she laid eyes on the Texas man, her present husband, she knew that her heart was his forever, so she had the wedding at seven in the morning instead of eight, thinking they 'd be off before the old gentleman come, so 's to save his feelings: and which they would have been off in five minutes more, and she hoped the old gentleman would forgive her, that she'd never do it again. ‹And then,› the old gentleman says, ‹her and the Texas man got in the landau and rode off, and the folks throwed old shoes and rice after 'em.›

«Look like the old man felt the worst about it that ever was. He just laid his head down on the back of my seat and groaned. ‹To think,› he says, ‹of me giving my heart into the hands of such a female as that—such a fickle, heartless, deceiving woman, and one with such poor taste! But he said what he was suffering from her treating him that scandalous way was n't by no means the worst of it; that it was having the world know a man's sorrows that was the hardest to bear. Said he could have stood it if nobody had knowed it but him; but when he thought about his children and kin and friends all fixing for such a big housewarming that evening, and the whole town being at the train to meet him and his bride, looked like his heart would certainly break in two. He said man was certainly born to trouble, as the sparks fly upward.

«I tried to cheer him up all I could, and told him he certainly had a heap to bear, but I never doubted it would be sanctified to him in the end, if he would bear it patient; that the Lord always provided a balm for wounded feelings, and bound up the broken heart. The old gentleman he leaned his elbow on the window-sill, and his head on his hand, and looked out of the window, the dolefulest you ever saw, and every now and then he'd fetch a groan. I felt awful sorry for him. I never could understand how a woman could have the heart to treat a man so bad.

«By and by he raised his head up again, like a new notion struck him. ‹The Lord will provide,› he says, ‹the Lord will provide,› kind of to himself, over and over. Then he took a good look at me. Then he leaned over the back of my seat again. ‹Sister Allgood, madam,› he says, ‹it ain't for me to say the Lord don't work in mysterious ways his wonders to perform, or that he deserts the righteous in their hour of need. No; as I have set here I have seen his wonderful works and intentions. As I set here I see the special providence he has provided for me. In you, madam, I see that special providence—that balm which is to bind up my wounds. In you I see the wife sent to me from heaven, and just in the nick of time. I see now that it never was intended for me to marry a black-eyed woman. Blue eyes I know and have tried, and am going to stick to them. Yes; in them eyes of yours I behold truth and constancy and affection. And the train stops thirty minutes for supper at Guthrie, and I'll get a preacher there to marry us, and when I get off the train at my home I 'll have a bride for them to welcome and housewarm, and won't have my head bowed to the dust in humiliation and broken heart.›

He laid his hand on my shoulder. I was just natchully struck dumb, and could n't have said a word if I'd had a chance. ‹Don't speak,› he says; ‹a woman is always opposed to making up her mind in a hurry; but it's all right. This is a special providence, and the will of God. I know all you would say—a woman can't help being coy and bashful. But never mind; it's all right.› He patted me on the shoulder. ‹But, brother,—› I says. ‹Don't mention it,› he says. ‹Do you reckon such frivolous things as clothes enters into my calculations?› ‹It ain't clothes, brother,› I says; ‹it 's—› ‹It is short notice,› he says, ‹but I could n't love you better if I had knowed you a thousand years. You need n't have no fears about my affection, or about me making a good husband. If my three dear departed companions could rise up here in this car and give their testimony, it would convince you.› ‹Yes, sir,› I says; ‹I don't doubt it would; but—› ‹Of course I ain't as young as I used to be; but my folks are a long-lived family, and don't age soon. My father died at ninety, hale and hearty, and my grandfather at ninety-five, spry as a kitten. No, madam; a man is as old as he feels; and I assure you I don't feel a day over forty. We will have a long life to live together.›

«And so that old man went on, and I could n't get in a word edgewise, for every time I'd start to say anything he'd take the words out of my mouth. Look like he never seemed to have no earthly idea maybe I did n't *want* to marry him. I commenced to get plumb scared and trembly. I actually got afraid that old man would overpersuade me to marry him against my will. Seem like there was n't anything on earth I could do or say but just set there and listen to him talk. It was awful—I did n't know what in the world to do, and just set there in a cold perspiration.

«At last the train stopped at a station, and a mighty nice-looking old lady got on—the only lady besides me in the car. Then I felt better. I told the old gentleman I was very tired, and felt like I must have a little rest, and if he would go into the smoking-car and take a smoke for a while, I would try to rest myself. He said certainly, but he wanted me to understand he could n't stay away from me long, and would make that pipe a short one. As soon as he was out of the car I run over and set down by the old lady, and told her as quick as I could what a trouble I was in, and how I never knew how on earth to get rid of the old gentleman. She felt awful sorry for me, and told me not to cry; that we 'd fix it up all right, and there was n't no real danger. She said she reckoned the old man's mind was a little turned by his trouble, but she 'd see that I got away from him all right at Guthrie. That I would have to wait ten minutes at Guthrie for my train going north, and his train would wait there half an hour for supper before going south, and the thing for her and me to do would be to get him started off to hunt a preacher so 's he would n't be on hand when my train left, and I would get off all right on my train for home. She said it would be as easy as falling off a log. She said for me to send him to her to make inquiries about a preacher, and she would fix him so he would n't get back under half an hour. She told me to treat him just the same as I had, when he come back from the smoking-car, and not to rile him or cross him any.

«So when he come back in the car I did like she said. He never seemed to expect me to say anything anyhow, so I just let him go ahead and talk and plan and rejoice, though I felt like an awful hypocrite.

«Finally we got to Guthrie about six o'clock that evening, and the old gentleman helped me and my bandbox and valise and basket and cans off the nicest kind, and took me to the waiting-room. Then he said he must hurry out and get the preacher that was to make him the happiest man on earth, and for me not to stir till he come back. I told him he better inquire where to find a preacher, and I expect that lady setting over the other side of the room might know something about the preachers down this way. So he went over and asked her, and I felt like a whited sepulcher. Then he started off a-running.

«Them ten minutes before my train come seemed to me more like ten years. I just set there and shook, I was so afraid the old gentleman would meet up with a preacher on the way, and get back before my train started, or that my train would be late. But finally my train whistled, and the old lady she picked up my valise and bandbox, and I jerked up the basket of fruit-trees and the six cans of peaches, and we made for the train. The folks that was inside the car all had to get out before I could get in, and looked to me like I would certainly go raving, distracted crazy, they were so slow. But at last the very last one come down the steps, and I had just set foot on the lowest step, and the conductor was bracing me from behind—me not being able to catch hold of anything on account of my arms being so full—when I heard a yell that fairly knocked the life out of me, so 's I could n't move hand or foot, but was just petrified where I was at, and if the conductor had n't been boosting me like he was I reckon I 'd have fell off that step like a bag of meal. I cast one eye down the station platform, and there come the old gentleman, his coat-tails flying, and him yelling every step of the way, and the preacher he had got trying to keep up with him. ‹Lord, help!› I says; ‹Lord, help!› I knew if the Lord did n't help me I was gone. Then I turned them fruit-trees and them six cans of Indian peaches loose, and grabbed hold of the railing, and got the strength from heaven to climb up the steps of that car and on to the platform of it. The glass cans rolled down, and bu'sted as they fell, and the peaches just went all over the depot platform there, and when the old gentleman come a-tearing along, he never did a thing but slip up on them peaches and fall all over himself. And just then the train it commenced to pull out, and the conductor jumped on with my valise and bandbox, and the last I seen of the old gentleman he was still a-squirming around in them Indian peaches in his wedding-clothes, trying to get on his feet, and still a-yelling. And I just rejoiced and give thanks and shouted, because I knew I had been mightily delivered. And of course I felt awful sorry for the old gentleman; but, like the Bible says, ‹Am I my brother's keeper?› And how could anybody expect me to be keeper to a crazy man, anyhow?

«I 've had a many a experience with widowers in my time, and got mighty little respect for 'em anyway, but that was the narrowest escape I ever had, or ever hope to have.»

*Lucy S. Furman.*

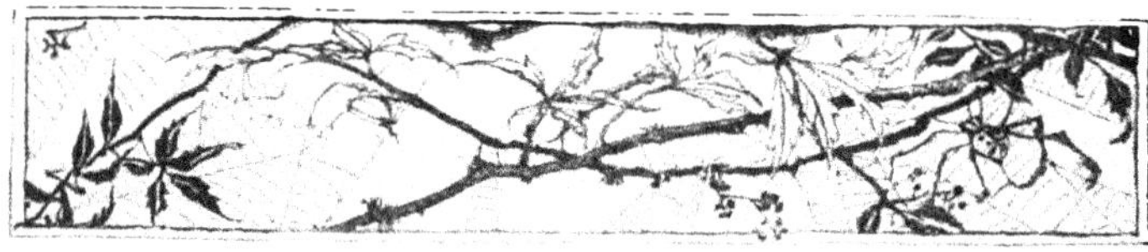

# THE NATIONAL HERO OF FRANCE:

## JOAN OF ARC.

DEPICTED AND DESCRIBED BY BOUTET DE MONVEL.

No artist has treated more sympathetically than M. Boutet de Monvel the incidents of the life of Joan of Arc. It was a privilege to see recently, in his studio, the exquisite series of water-color designs in which he has depicted the career of the child-saint and warrior. It is at our request that the artist has undertaken to put into words his impressions of that marvelous career; the result being the brief paper herewith printed, portraying with the same sympathetic touch the leading incidents of Joan's life. The illustrations are reproductions of some of the original designs, printed in advance of their publication in France. The article has been translated for THE CENTURY by the American artist Will H. Low, a friend of Boutet de Monvel, and the writer of the article in THE CENTURY for June, 1894, descriptive of his work.—EDITOR.

HAVING undertaken to write a brief paper on Joan of Arc, I must at the outset plead for the indulgence due to a workman handling unaccustomed tools. Without pretension as a writer or historian, I shall simply endeavor to render the impression left upon me by the two years which I have spent face to face with our great national heroine.

The sentiment which in me dominates all others in the consideration of the life and career of Joan of Arc is one of wonder. I find there a sequence of occurrences which, outside of all questions of religious belief or faith, are equally and incontestably above or outside the laws of human possibility. It is as though a monument, resplendent in beauty and grandeur, were suddenly fashioned from a grain of sand.

To understand this phenomenal apparition, we must first consider the ruins from which it rose. Imagine France, at the beginning of the fifteenth century, a nation in an embryonic state, a confusion of provinces, a chaotic reunion of fiefs, in which rivalry, covetousness, and violence ran counter to one another. Added to the exhaustion caused by a century of conflict with the English, internecine quarrels were rife, and misery in the shape of hunger, cold, and disease claimed even more victims than the pitiless weapons of war. Sunken deep in this slough of despond, the unfortunate country was without hope of deliverance, lacking the energetic hand to guide, or the example of patriotic devotion to follow. On the one hand, the victorious English, possessing already half the kingdom, joined to the advantage of powerful organization the prestige of fifteen years' uninterrupted success; on the other, a lost cause, demoralized soldiers deserting their arms, a powerless nobility whose only thought was to dispute jealously the remaining vestiges of royal favor, and for supreme hope a king without courage or will, dissipating in festivities the last resources drained from his remaining provinces. Renouncing all hope, the king, in fact, nourished the intention of escaping into Dauphiné, perhaps farther still over the Pyrenees into Spain, thus abandoning his kingdom, the rights which he claimed, and the duties which he had studiously evaded.

It was otherwise ordained. The nation, expiring under the heel of the oppressor, was to be saved; a hand was to lift her, to restore strength to her exhausted body and courage to her despairing heart.

To accomplish this task was needed a sturdy arm, a mind skilled to command, one of the great captains who at rare intervals in the world's history has appeared with much of the suddenness and all the force of a thunderbolt. There was needed a heroic soldier or an imperious prince—a soldier or a prince, as these alone at that time had the right to command or to act.

Once more it was otherwise ordained. In that class of the people who were as the beasts of the field, in a remote village of Lorraine, a girl of thirteen appeared. Tears were in her eyes; in the innermost parts of her being she had felt the quickening of a new birth unforetold—the birth of patriotism. To her had come the archangel Michael with the message of the «great pity which was for the kingdom of France.» He had marked her forehead with the seal of her divine mission, and had said, «Thou shalt save France.» «Messire,» answered the child, «I am but a poor child of the fields; neither know I to mount a horse, nor yet to lead the men-at-arms.» «God will aid thee,» the angel had responded.

And the child believed. For five years she cherished in her heart this daring thought, living in the solitude of her secret, of which she spoke to none, not even to her confessor. At last, in her eighteenth year, the celestial voice brought the message, «Thine hour has come; thou must depart.» Then this girl, timid, pious, and tender, left all that she loved; she set forth without looking back, guided by the superior power which led her on; she went, announcing to all that she was sent of the Lord God to save the kingdom of France.

The first to whom she bore this message was the Sire de Baudricourt. «The girl is mad,» said he, and ordered her marched home to have her folly whipped out of her. But Joan insisted that she must be conducted to the presence of the king. «I will go,» she pleaded, «if I wear my legs down to the knees.» Her conviction was so strong that it gained the sympathy of the poor about her. To these humble beings, for whom everything is difficulty and impossibility in life, imagination opens a rich field where all dreams seem credible. They believed the dream of Joan, and lent their aid to the accomplishment of her miracle. This help and complicity of the people she was to find everywhere on her road. The king and the nobles accepted her because she served their purpose; the people believed in her and lent her their strength. Thus from the first step of her undertaking her situation was clearly outlined, as it was to be to the end—to martyrdom. The poor people gave from their poverty to buy her a horse and vestments of war, and a squire, Jean de Metz, won by the popular enthusiasm, offered to accompany her with a few men. They set out for Chinon, where the court was assembled. The way was long and beset with danger, but Joan upheld the courage of her companions. «Fear nothing,» she said; «the Lord God has chosen my route; my brothers in paradise guide me on the way»; and in safety they arrived at Chinon. There new obstacles arose; it was difficult to obtain access to the king, jealously guarded from all outside influence by his favorite La Trémoille. But, as in a fairy-tale, doors were opened, walls fell before her magic, and one evening the young peasant entered the great hall where, among the courtiers, disguised in a modest costume, stood the king, whom she had never seen. Without hesitation she walked straight to the king, and, falling on her knees, proffered her request with so much grace and ardor that Charles VII was moved.

But imposture, witchcraft, even, was suspected, and before a decision was arrived at learned doctors and ecclesiastics were called on to examine her and scrutinize her conscience. To all the subtleties of her examiners she answered with so much simplicity, so much profundity of good sense, that they were confounded. «There is more in the book of God than in yours,» she said; and added, «I know not *a* from *b*, but I am sent of the Lord God.»

Meantime popular enthusiasm increased; the common people believed in her sanctity and the holiness of her mission. The court, in its distress, decided that, as a last resort, it was well to utilize this spontaneous aid. A small force was given to Joan, who, under the direction of experienced men of war, was assigned the task of delivering the city of Orléans, which for eight months had withstood the assaults of the English, but was on the point of succumbing.

Before us now opens a new chapter of this miraculous legend, difficult of belief were it not thoroughly substantiated. The simple girl, high-hearted and sincere, the young peasant who had led but sheep to pasture, was now to march at the head of men of war, and, amid the clash of arms, to become a consummate general.

In the campaign of France, the most admirable effort of his career, Napoleon, suddenly appearing on the field where his conscripts struggled against an overwhelming force, said proudly, «My presence here adds to the army a hundred thousand men.» It was true, and the same might well be said of Joan; for to her army she was as the will is to brute force, as energy to inertia. And not only had she the moral effect upon her followers which is the mark of a great captain, but from the first the more practical qualities which are commonly the fruit of experience.

At this epoch, when the art of war was in a rudimentary state, when hazard was counted the chief element of success, Joan was to discover and practise strategic measures as new to her time as were those which gave Bonaparte victory over Austria at the time of the Italian campaign. First of the warriors of the

DRAWN BY BOUTET DE MONVEL.

JOAN HEARS THE VOICES.

She willingly drew away from her little comrades to meditate, and she heard celestial voices — « holy voices » she called them. With an exalted mind the child grew up, guarding in the depths of her heart the secret of her celestial conversations.

middle ages, Joan appreciated the advantages to be gained by reiterated attacks on an enemy already shaken and demoralized, without leaving him the time between action to recover and reorganize. And this was not the effect of happy accident; during the entire campaign, in every circumstance, she again and again gave proof of the superiority of her intelligence; and this despite all difficulties, in the face of the ill-will of her officers,—jealously indignant of being superseded by a mere girl of low origin,—hampered by the indolence of the king, and carrying on her frail shoulders the weight of all decisions and the responsibility of all initiative effort. To the chiefs who sought to make decisions without consulting her she proudly asserted, « Hold your counsel together; I will hold mine with the Lord God, and his will prevail.» The ardor of her prayers moved at last the coward indolence of the king, and she succeeded in making him share her enthusiasm, warming his cold heart at the fire which burned within her.

In battle her courage was peerless, and well it was that it was so, for each success was dearly bought, her indomitable energy alone inspiring her faint-hearted followers. When her troops threatened retreat, it was by throwing herself into the thickest of the fight, crying, «They are ours!» that she turned defeat to victory. Often wounded, she disdained the pain of her mangled flesh, and remained on the field as an example to her men. A gracious woman withal, her pity was even greater than her courage, braving and receiving blows, but never returning them. She had but one weapon, her banner, for her sword never left its scabbard. Later she was to say that she «loved her banner a thousand times more than her sword.» At night, when the heat of battle was assuaged, her tears fell at the thought of the wounded and the dead. «I have never seen French blood shed without my hair standing on end,» was one of her naïve utterances. The enemy commanded her pity as well, and she was as often seen assisting the dying English as her own people. Thus she was not only the mind which directs, she was likewise the heart filled with sympathy, the soul solicitous of the welfare of other souls, intuitively understanding that the soldier who fights the best is he whose heart is pure. In the same spirit she lightened the burden of the army by curtailing useless luggage, and she drove away the disreputable women who had followed the camp, and with them the debauchery and disorder which they had brought. On the other hand, she gently admonished her soldiers to clear their conscience, to be virtuous and religious as well as brave.

The influence she exercised on her surroundings, the prestige of her success, the idolatry of the people, never spoiled the charm of her simple nature. To the end she was the humble girl rendering to God the glory of each action. «I bring to you,» was her message to the besieged citizens of Orléans, «the best aid of all—the aid of the King of heaven; it does not come to you through me, but from the Lord himself, who, moved by the prayers of St. Louis and Charlemagne, has taken pity on your city.» Could any one keep in the background with more charming ingenuity?

Her religious faith was her chief support; inspired of God, she felt herself strong with the force which he lent her. In her ardent, steadfast, and regular piety, she had touching returns to the humility of her past life, wishing to be informed of the day when beggars received communion, in order that she might share it with them. Her pity went broadcast to all suffering, but her love was reserved for the poor and disinherited; they were her brothers, among whom she had been born. The king could ennoble her, could give her squires, pages, and rich vestments, but never a breath of pride rose within her heart. Consequently her influence on the people was great, and wherever she passed, throngs of the lowly pressed about her. Men, women, and children, in their anxiety to approach, to kiss her hands or the hem of her garment, crowded so thickly that accidents occurred; those in the foremost row were pushed under her horse's feet. «She is holy,» they exclaimed; and the belief that she could accomplish miracles grew apace. Strange legends sprang up: one had seen the holy band of archangels militant surrounding her in battle, and across the country swarms of white butterflies had been seen to follow her banner; the villagers who asked for arms with which to accompany her were directed to take the crosses from above the graves in the churchyards, and they turned to swords in their hands. She was in popular belief the virgin whose coming was foretold by rustic seers, and who was predestined to save the kingdom—perhaps an angel descended from paradise. Medals were struck bearing her effigy, and rude portraits of her were hung in village churches. Later, when, on trial for her life, her judges imputed to her as a crime this outpouring of popular enthusiasm, she humbly protested: «Many came to me, but they kissed my hands as little as I could help; the poor came to me because I did not repulse them.» When reproached with having permitted this adulation of the people to assume the character of idolatry, she answered, «I might not, in truth, have escaped such sin had not God helped me,» again rendering to divine power her sustaining modesty throughout the popular frenzy.

Although the scope of this study is too slight to permit their detailed narration, I must enumerate the principal events comprised between the date of Joan's arrival before Orléans, April 29, 1429, and the moment when she was taken prisoner at Compiègne, May 24, 1430.

The 29th of April Joan crossed the Loire before the city of Orléans. Lacking enough boats, her army was forced to return to Blois, whence, passing through the Beauce, they rejoined their leader before the city. On the morning of the 4th of May the little army entered Orléans, and in the afternoon the

DRAWN BY BOUTET DE MONVEL.

JOAN'S ENTRANCE INTO THE COUNCIL.

The chiefs of the army met at the house of the chancellor of the Duke of Orléans to deliberate on plans. Joan had not been asked to the meeting. Full of indignation, Joan entered. «You have held counsel among yourselves,» said she; «I have held counsel with the Lord. Be sure that his will will be done, and that your plans will perish.»

fort of St. Loup was captured. The next day was given up to prayer, repose, and preparations, and on the two following days the forts of the Augustins and the Tourelles were successively taken. On the 8th of May the English evacuated the remaining strongholds, and left the city, which, after having been in their possession for eight months, was thus recaptured in four days. In order to profit by the discomfiture of the English after their first defeat, Joan returned at once to Chinon, determined to take the king to Rheims, in order that his coronation might take place and fulfil the prophecy of the archangel. Charles VII hesitated. The country was still infested by the English, who were in force on the banks of the Loire, and Joan decided to push them back in the direction of Paris before setting forth toward Rheims in the east. Her troops met at Selles; on the 11th of June they took the outlying faubourg, and the next day became masters of the city of Jargeau. On the 15th the French captured the bridge at Meung, and went on to Beaugency, which, attacked on the morrow, capitulated the next day. On the 18th Joan exterminated the English army led by Talbot to the rescue of Beaugency. The whole region was freed from the invader, and the moral effect of the rapidity with which Joan had achieved her second successful campaign was great. She returned at once to the king, determined at any cost to break the bonds of his apathy. The English had imprudently neglected to crown their young king, and it was important to profit by their neglect, in order that Charles might be first in the field as the anointed king of France.

Ten days of entreaty at last decided Charles to move, and on the 29th of June the royal army set forth. On the way the cities opened their gates, and on the 16th of July the king entered his city of Rheims. The next day the ceremony of coronation took place. At the moment when Charles VII was anointed, Joan threw herself at his feet, kissing his knees, and with tears streaming down her cheeks cried through her sobs, «O gentle king, now is done the pleasure of God, who willed that I should conduct you to your city of Rheims, there to receive your holy anointment, that all may know that you are the true king, and to you is the kingdom of France!»

On her banner Joan had embroidered the image of Christ with the names Jesus, Maria. On April 28 the small army set forth. Joan, with floating banner, led the march, all singing the «Veni Creator.»

DRAWN BY BOUTET DE MONVEL.

JOAN AT THE HEAD OF THE ARMY.

Thus in less than three months the territory won by the English by years of conflict was freed. But Joan did not consider her mission at an end; she still desired to deliver Paris, the capital of his kingdom, into the hands of her king.

Faithful to her principles, she urged haste, desiring to profit by the popular enthusiasm and by the demoralization of the English forces. The march toward Paris was one of triumph. Soissons and Laon opened their doors, and in turn Château-Thierry, Provins, Coulommiers, Crécy-en-Brie, Compiègne, and Beauvais welcomed their king. Joan, however, judged their progress too slow, though no effort of hers sufficed to accelerate the march, the indecision and indolence of the king acting as effectual obstacles to rapid and decisive action. At last, on the 23d of August, devoured by impatience, Joan left the main army, accompanied by the Duc d'Alençon and a strong body of men-at-arms, and marched toward Paris. Menaced with abandonment by the entire army, which wished to follow Joan, Charles decided at last to move.

It was already too late to surprise Paris, which had had ample time to prepare its defense. Nevertheless, Joan impetuously led a first assault, in which she was wounded by an arrow which pierced her thigh. Remaining on the field, she directed that the ditches surrounding the walls be filled to afford passage for her men, whom she encouraged to scale the walls. Unfortunately, night was falling; against her will she was forced on her horse,

Joan arrived in time to rally the French, who were retreating; and leading them again to the attack, she took the Fort of St. Loup.

DRAWN BY BOUTET DE MONVEL.

JOAN LEADS THE ATTACK AT ST. LOUP.

and the order given to retreat to La Chapelle. Early the next morning, despite her wound, Joan ordered the attack, assuring all that the city would capitulate; but Charles VII countermanded the order. He had been dragged about with his army long enough, and sighed for the luxurious ease of his castles on the Loire. He desired repose, and, deaf to all entreaty, ordered a retreat. This was not only a grave mistake from a military or political point of view: it was, above all, fatal to the ascendancy of Joan, who by it ceased to be considered invincible. She submitted meekly to her king, and the army retired slowly into Touraine, where it was disbanded. The court party, led by La Trémoille, had triumphed in suspending military operations and reducing Joan to inactivity. They were well content, for of a truth this peasant began to be of too great importance, and it was not difficult to bring the king, fatigued with the efforts which she had imposed on him, to their way of thinking. In November Joan succeeded in getting together a few soldiers, and at the head of her small force renewed the combat. St. Pierre le Moutier was first captured, and she then proceeded to lay siege to La Charité, but as it was strong and well fortified, this proved too great a task. Her little army was without food and without aid, and, the king refusing to help her in any way, she was forced to retreat. Fretting under inaction, Joan at last left the court without permission, and in April, 1430, at Lagny-sur-Marne, associated herself with the predatory troops, who kept up a species of guerrilla warfare with the English. By a lucky stroke she made at once an important capture of one Franquet d'Arras, a Frenchman in the English service; and then learning that Compiègne was seriously menaced by the Burgundians and the English, she directed her troops to its support. At daybreak on May 24, 1430, she entered Compiègne. To the soldiers who accompanied her she added as many from the garrison as was prudent, and with this small force bravely attacked the Burgundians, hoping to defeat them, and then fall back on the English and disperse them in turn. At first she was successful, but the English, closing in, threatened to cut off her retreat, at which her troops murmured, and pressed her to regain the city. «Silence!» was her answer; «if you will, the day is ours; think only of what is before us.» But her brave spirit was overruled, and a retreat was ordered. Forced to follow, she marched last and supported the retreat. The English succeeded in throwing their force to the base of the castle, whereat Guillaume de Flavy, fearing that they might enter the city, ordered the drawbridge raised. Joan, surrounded by the few men who were faithful to her, arriving at this moment, found entrance to the stronghold impossible. At the foot of the walls in the moat five or six archers threw themselves upon her. «Surrender, and give us thy faith,» they demanded. «I have sworn my faith to another, and will keep my word,» was her reply, still struggling until they pulled her from her horse by the long skirt which she wore. Thus she was made prisoner by the soldiers of Jean de Luxembourg, while the governor of Compiègne, Guillaume de Flavy, witnessed the drama from his battlements without effort to save her.

DRAWN BY BOUTET DE MONVEL

JOAN A PRISONER BEFORE THE DUKE OF BURGUNDY.

The shame of his inaction stains his name indelibly, if, indeed, Joan's capture was not secretly planned. He was related to La Trémoille, and perhaps, like the king and his court, was not sorry to rid himself of too zealous a champion. That such was the unavowed desire of the court, or of certain members of it, is amply proved by the letter in which Regnault de Chartres, archbishop of Rheims, announces the capture of Joan to his diocese. Her defeat is presented as a direct judgment of God, «inasmuch as she would accept no advice, but acted according to her good pleasure, by which she had fallen into the sin of pride, and had not done that which the Lord had ordained.» This was the ingratitude, these were the calumnies, with which were rewarded her admirable devotion and incalculable services.

Joan was a prisoner; her martyrdom approached. As she had fallen into the hands of Jean de Luxembourg, a man of high birth but a soldier of fortune, ransom would not have been difficult; but to the eternal shame of the King of France, no effort was made, was even considered. The English ardently desired to lay hands on her; ten thousand *livres tournois* was the price put upon her head, and, securely guarded, she was carried in triumph to Rouen.

It was not only a personal vengeance which the English desired: in their eyes Joan represented the force of France. She was the sorceress who struck their troops dumb with terror; once disposed of, victory would again be theirs. From their point of view, therefore, it was important to establish as a fact that the powers of darkness had lent their aid, to account for the course which events had taken.

To bring about this shameful end, it was necessary to find a judge devoted to this view and devoid of scruple. The man was ready at hand in the person of Cauchon, bishop of Beauvais. He assembled about him a certain number of ecclesiasts and doctors of the University of Paris, and in January, 1431, the trial of Joan began.

The poor girl, alone and abandoned by all, could oppose only her simplicity to the perfidious quibbles and outrageous insinuations of judges resolved to condemn her. She was condemned before trial, but what a triumphant defeat—the triumph of sincerity, of uprightness, of noble sentiment, and of delicate modesty! In the midst of so much ignominy her virtue shone with so bright a luster that a number of her judges, whose past vileness had been counted a guaranty of their servility, left the court in sheer disgust at the work imposed upon them.

The questions addressed to Joan, and her answers day by day, have been transmitted in the records of the court. To read them is to understand the brutal ferocity with which she was tortured, until, turning on her accuser, she cried, «You call yourself my judge; be careful what you do, for I am indeed sent by the Lord, and you place yourself in great danger.»

To answers almost sublime succeeded answers filled with naïve ingenuity. Questions were plied, traitorously conceived, concerning the visions which had come to her, and the celestial voices which she heard, and which throughout her mission had counseled and guided her. But on this point she was firmly silent. It was as though it were a secret which she was forbidden to betray. She consented to take an oath to speak nothing but the truth, but concerning her visions she made a reservation. «You could cut my head off before I would speak,» she protested. At night, in the darkness of her dungeon, St. Catherine and St. Margaret appeared to her, and celestial voices comforted her. She avowed that she had seen them «with the eyes of her body, . . . and when they leave me,» she added, «I wish that they would take me with them.»

«When St. Michael appears to you, is he naked?» asked the bishop.

«Do you think, then, that God cannot clothe his saints?»

«And your ‹voices›—what do they say to you?»

«That I answer you without fear.»

«What more?»

«I cannot tell all; I am more afraid to displease them than I am to answer you.»

Insisting, the judge asked:

«But is it displeasing to God to tell the truth, Joan?»

«My ‹voices› have told me certain things not for you, but for the king»; adding quickly, «Ah! if my king knew them, he would be more easy at dinner. I would like to go without mine till Easter if he could but know them.»

For her king, who had so cowardly abandoned her, she retained a passionate worship. He was the personification of France; he was her banner. One day during the trial Guillaume Everard accused the King of France of heresy, whereat, trembling with indignation, Joan cried out: «By my faith, sire, with all reverence due to you, I dare say and swear, under peril of my life, that he is the most Christian of all Christians, he who best loves the law and the church; he is not what you say.» In such a cry we feel that she uttered all her heroic soul.

She was asked if St. Catherine and St. Margaret loved the English.

«They love those whom the Lord loves, and hate those whom he hates.»

«Does the Lord hate the English?»

«Of the love or the hate of the Lord for the English I know nothing. I only know that they will be put out of France, save those who perish here.»

As she declared that she «had nothing done save by the grace of God,» the bishop asked her a perfidious and insidious question, one which no living being could truly answer:

«Joan, do you believe yourself in a state of grace?»

To say no was to avow herself unfit to be the instrument of divine power; to answer yes was to commit the mortal sin of pride—in a word, the sin which would put her outside of the pale of grace. She cut the Gordian knot with a simplicity most Christianlike.

«If I am not, please God may make me so; if I am, may God so keep me.»

The judges were disconcerted. Once more they touched upon sorcery; her standard, they pretended, must have been bewitched.

«No,» she answered simply; «I only said, ‹Go in among the English!› and I took it there.»

«But why was your banner carried into the

cathedral of Rheims, at the coronation, while those of other captains were stacked outside?»

«It had been in the thick of the fray; it was justice that it should be in the place of honor.»

She retained the garb of a man, and they shamed her, affecting to be ignorant of the fact that it was her best safeguard against the brutality of her jailers, who were with her day and night. For that matter, it was not alone these menials whom she had cause to dread: an English lord had attempted her dishonor, and when, after a desperate struggle, she had repulsed him, chained as she was to the wall of her dungeon, he had not hesitated to strike her. Hence, when her judges had insisted that she wear the costume of her sex, she had pleaded blushingly «that at least the skirt should be long.»

To condemn the saint as a sorceress seemed beyond their powers; the task was too monstrous; but in the armor of her mysticism there was perhaps a flaw where their weapon could penetrate. It might well be imputed a crime that she believed herself in direct communication with the powers above, without the intervention of the church. She was asked if she would accept the judgment of the church for all that she had said or done, and she answered that she «loved the church, and desired its support with all her heart, but for that which she had done she placed her confidence in the King of heaven, whose mission she had fulfilled»; adding, «in truth, our Lord and the church are but one.»

Then she was told that she must distinguish between the church triumphant—God, the saints, and the souls redeemed—and the church militant—the pope, the bishops, and the clergy, enlightened by the Holy Ghost. Would she submit her case to the church militant?

«I am come of God, of the Virgin Mary, of the saints, and the victorious church of heaven; to that church I submit all, myself and my actions, all that I have done or yet may do.» How could this girl, whose heart was pure and simple, who had lived with her eyes fixed on heaven, stoop to the distinctions of narrow theologians? On this point she was firm, though they pressed her close. «I submit to the church militant,» she pleaded, «if it does not ask the impossible, our Lord God's service coming first.»

Joan's judges had refused her all religious consolation. One day, on her way back from the seat of judgment, she knelt in front of a chapel door and prayed fervently.

DRAWN BY BOUTET DE MONVEL.

JOAN PRAYS AT THE CHAPEL DOOR.

When reproached with heresy, she protested, «I am a good Christian; I have been baptized, and will die a good Christian.»

The trial was too long to suit the English; their impatience became more and more marked. «Priests, you are not earning your money!» was the shout when the court rose. More haste was demanded of their servility. But the ignominy of the judges and executioners gave good measure. Joan was condemned as a heretic, backslider, apostate, and idolatress. May 30, 1431, she was burned at the stake on the place of the Old Market at Rouen. «Bishop, I die by your hand,» she said to the Bishop of Beauvais, as she mounted the funeral pyre, and she died murmuring the name of Jesus.

Her death was so touching that her judges and executioners wept, and the English present fled, crying loudly, «We are lost; we have burned a saint!»

Such is the summary recital of the brief apparition of Joan of Arc in the dark history of her epoch, a gleam of daybreak through the night of brutality and violence of the middle ages. For us—Frenchmen—Joan of Arc is the most perfect figure of our history, the one altar before which men of all opinions bend the knee, the patron saint of our country. If we look with the eye of reason on this miracle of virtues, of grace, and of gifts suddenly revealed in the being of a simple peasant girl, and bursting forth into actions so extraordinary, and if we search for an explanation, we must consider that the country was crazed by misery and suffering, and fallen to such a depth of distress that nothing but supernatural aid seemed able to save it. It was enfeebled to a point favorable to every hallucination. Joan had grown up in this environment; she had suffered with the suffering about her; the soul of her people vibrated within her; and when the angel appeared, the child could but give herself to the dream which was thus brought to her. And the people followed her, believing as she believed. The child was of the elect, her soul open to all pity, to all devotion, to all enthusiasms; and these virtues, which would have remained hidden in the obscurity of her humble life, flourished and became resplendent in the bright daylight of her larger existence. In the shock of succeeding events her virtues became more exalted, became purified to the degree of absolute perfection. The saint becomes a hero, an immaculate hero. There are those who scoff at the visions; but what to us is the question of their reality? One thing is undoubted—to her they were real. It is true that she was exalted, was mystical; but her mysticism was militant; it was realized in the sphere of human actions and human interests. Her exaltation modified in no degree the fine equilibrium of health; on the contrary, it developed in her the active qualities, her admirable common sense, her quickness of thought and action. With her there is no suspicion of fevered thought; all her acts and all her words are redolent with the grace of calm simplicity. At times she speaks as though by divine inspiration, and in certain of her responses to her judges at Rouen we imagine we hear the voice of the child Jesus when he confounded the doctors in the temple.

To close, I must endeavor, after having tried to render the moral side of our national heroine, to give an idea of what I imagine may have been her appearance as she walked this earth.

While at work on my series of designs, I have often been asked to describe my conception of the personal appearance of Joan of Arc. At this question I have always seen before me a figure which little by little has grown more distinct, until now it is as though I saw Joan, to use her own words, «with the eyes of my body.» Of actual evidence nothing remains; no portrait exists, nor has there come down to us the smallest shred of her vestments or fragment of her arms. We know that she was tall and well proportioned, that her physiognomy was agreeable; but all this is vague. Some have it that she was fair, others that she was dark. Her hair was, in all probability, neither the one nor the other, but of a shade between the two, which would account for the difference of opinion. To me she must have been somewhat fair, as thus she seems more feminine. Judith had black hair; Jeanne Hachette, who from the ramparts opposed the enemy with her battle-ax, was dark; but Joan of Arc had such a tender breast, so much pity—I find in her so much of womanly grace in contrast with her decision in the hour of action—that I can see her only blonde: not the blonde of the fair-haired races of the North, but the blonde chestnut of our France. She was not in any sense *pretty;* we must not forget that warlike companions, men not overburdened with scruples, testified that she never inspired the thought of gallantry. If not pretty, however, she had probably the beauty of the peasant: a firmly, well constructed head; her eyes were bluish gray, not too light, for they flashed fire at times; her nose was somewhat heavy, but with sensitive nostrils; and her mouth strongly marked, with full red lips. Her complexion was browned by exposure, rich and healthy in color; her carriage free and somewhat boyish, for she was a girl of the fields, free as air, and her limbs were vigorous, and her chest was deep. She never knew fatigue, say the chronicles of her time. We know that she was tall and well proportioned, but although tall for a woman, she seemed small, when dressed as a man, in comparison with her soldiers. For the same reason her strong features were by comparison delicate, and her boyish carriage became more womanly when her figure was incased in armor. Side by side with the brutal soldiers she appeared feeble and delicate. Her force, then, was entirely moral, and art must preserve for her this character, though without exaggeration. The danger of presenting a creature bloodless or hysterical must be avoided. She must be able to act not for a mere instant, under the influence of momentary nervous exaltation, but continuously, with the rhythmic regularity of a well-constituted body. No; she was not what is ordinarily termed beautiful, but she became so at certain moments—beautiful with the beauty of a soul which was noble and true.

*Maurice Boutet de Monvel.*

# THE WHITE SPIDER.

BY THE AUTHOR OF «TWO RUNAWAYS.»

«IT is absurd! There never was a ghost!» The statement, emphatic, almost petulant, came from the lips of a girl.

«Edith, my dear, you can be positive without discourtesy.» The grandmother's voice was courtesy itself.

«But not so charming, grandmother. When Edith is positively discourteous she is superb.»

«Gallantry from my brother! Think of it! But thanks, Tom, if you are in earnest.» He sat on the steps, and blew a smoke circle into the soft autumn evening, and looked lazily through it at the full moon mounting in the eastern sky.

«Never more so in my life, sis. But about ghosts?»

«Ask mama.»

«I have never seen one,» said the placid little lady appealed to; «but the testimony of the Scriptures is certainly in favor of the proposition that disembodied spirits have appeared on earth.»

Several couples promenading the white-columned porch paused, their attention arrested by the theme. The discussion grew animated.

«Professor,» said Tom, with his drawl, and the easy familiarity of a lifelong acquaintance, «you have just about time to make your escape. It is coming.»

The professor, sitting near the Madeira-vine, had fallen into a reverie. His friend and host next to him, availing himself of the privilege of age and wearied with evolution into which the learned guest had wandered, was sleeping peacefully in the white oak rocker.

«What is coming, Tom?» The professor returned smilingly to the present.

«Ghost-story! But perhaps you believe in ghosts too.»

«Well, yes; perhaps so.»

«Oho! Seen any?»

«Yes; at least I have seen one!»

«Oh, professor!» This shout was followed by a rush of feet and a clatter of chairs drawn near; then by a general laugh. It had all been comically sudden. No one ever knew where the professor was going to begin in a subject, and as usual he took all by surprise.

«I am afraid you have frightened my little friend out there, or perhaps it is Tom's smoke annoys him. There, he is at work again.»

All eyes followed the direction of the speaker's gaze. The angle of the moon's rays was just right to bring into view the wonderful web of the wood-spider, so called, a four-pointed star eight or ten feet in diameter, with concentric circles spun in the center, the star-points resting on rays of cedar and madeira and a trellis corner. Each strand was a silver cable wet with dew. It shone against the Georgian sky like diamond tracings upon a window-pane. The tiny artist was distinctly visible as he began to hurry about, strengthening his structure with guys, and building with a confident intelligence too subtle for analysis.

«I was thinking about my ghost and watching yonder little fellow before the excitement began, for my ghost was also a spider!»

«How delightfully horrible! But don't mind me!» This from the skeptic with the cigar. The professor took him at his word, and continued:

«There are ghosts and ghosts: ghosts of the imagination, ghosts of ruined castles, ghosts of dead hopes, ghosts of the intellect, having their own particular hours to walk and corridors to walk in. These are vivid in proportion to the activity of the brain that is conscious of them, for of all effects ghosts are most dependent upon environment.»

The earnest, measured tones of the speaker changed the mood of the party. Even the irreverent cynic was listening.

«The ghost to which I refer,» he continued, «is a family affair, and he has been with us for a number of generations—an intellectual heirloom, I suppose I may say, but none the less a ghost. His existence is a mystery deeper than life, and far beyond the range of science. Fix your attention upon the little fellow out there, while I follow his example, and prepare my web; for with his structure, as he hangs between heaven and earth at the mercy of his environment, he is the best existing type of the mind itself—that intelligence from which radiate the gossamer threads of heredity, of memory, and of hope, binding it to the past and future—an intelligence centered in its web of nerves that make it as a part of the present to glow with the radiance of its prisms, to suffer with the violence of its storms, to break at last, and to pass away.»

The professor bent his head, and was silent. Out in the moonlight the spider made his rounds under the gaze of the wondering group, but nearer at hand something far more wonderful was occurring. All were aware of it, but no eye could follow the prototype the old man had just outlined, as it began with mysterious power to prepare for a finer structure. The dreamer alone might, in still moments of solitude, faintly see its radiating lines reaching half a century back, and to the stars the other way, and here and there gray guy-strands that held fast to things unknown in the vastness of lateral distances. A generation has passed since that night, and still the marvelous snare he spread with the swiftness of light itself holds fast the fluttering wings of fancy.

«It is a serial,» said the professor, looking up and smiling, «begun in one of the back numbers of our family, and, as the weeklies say, ‹continued in our next.›

«My early childhood was more or less troubled by fear of spiders. I had an inexpressible abhorrence for the creatures, and so sensitive was my physical mind to their presence that I would be made aware of the nearness of one of them by some subtle influence before it became visible. The antipathy was complete; I do not believe that at ten years of age I would have touched a spider for all the gold in the world. I could not have done it.

«At this time I was living with my grandfather, a noted physician, and one day was made desperately ill by imprudent eating, and was given large doses of opium to relieve the pain. Succumbing at length to the drug, I fell into a deep slumber of many hours' duration. Now note the fact: upon awakening, I began to see a white spider miles away, in the center and at one end of a horn-shaped web, the outer circle of which held me prisoner. He approached by traveling around upon the widening circles of his web, himself growing larger, until, reaching the outer line, he sprang at my throat. His body at this stage was as large as a keg, and covered with bristles; his eyes shone like electric lights; his crab-like legs were armed with hooks and pincers; and his mouth was a red cavern ending in a beak of enormous size and apparent strength. I screamed and leaped from the bed, but was put back and soothed. Again I saw the spider miles away begin the widening circles; again he leaped at me, and I from the bed. This continued at lengthening intervals for hours. No explanation from my grandfather could restrain me. I knew that I was suffering from a hallucination, but whenever the spider leaped I got out of his way. Finally I saw him travel in circles that did not increase; then, after a while, he receded, faded away, and I slept.

«The vision was due, of course, to the drug, but it troubled my grandfather greatly, and one day he gave me these facts.

«When my grandfather was a boy, in the family there was an old negress named Nancy, who for years had nursed the children. She had many good qualities, but there was one fault, overlooked just as it is in modern nurses to-day: she controlled wayward children through their imagination and fears. On the plantation at that time was a very deep well covered by an old house, intended and used by his parents as a place for keeping fresh meats and butter in warm weather, but then abandoned. It had become to the negroes and the white children a mysterious and dreadful place. They were accustomed to peep down into that dark well through cracks in the floor to see the white spider which old Nancy said was there. Grandfather's childish imagination, more vivid, perhaps, than those of the others, stimulated by her description of the beast, made the place a veritable pit of horror, and in his mind became fixed the image of a great white spider with enormous body, flaming eyes, and beak of bronze.

«Grandfather, after reaching the age of manhood, began the study of medicine, making nerve-disease a specialty, and incidentally became interested in mental phenomena. You can imagine, perhaps, his feelings when one night he heard my father, then a mere child, and never for a moment under the influence of Nancy or any one connected with the plantation, talking in his sleep about a white spider with fiery eyes. He was too wise to attempt to make the child recall anything of the dream,—a very serious matter, by the way, to ponder on one's dreams,—but the train of thought set in motion by the incident led him, when visiting the old home, to question the then very aged nurse about the white spider of his youth. Her experience, as given, comprised about all the clear impressions she at that time retained of her savage life in Africa. I can give you only the bare outlines, as related to me by grandfather after my sickness. There was a god by the great lakes, mighty and terrible, who controlled the destinies of her people, and whose form was that of a white spider. He lived in a cave under the mountain, the entrance to which was as large as a barn. Across the mouth of this cave he spun his web—ropes that shone like silver—covered with a glue so strong that no living thing once caught by it could release itself. The web narrowed like an ox-horn far into the cave, and at the end of it dwelt the god making the thunder and lightning which brought the rain. When he was pleased rain fell on the whole country; when he was dissatisfied no rain fell, and the country suffered. Those who looked into the black cave saw only his two eyes shining like stars far away, or flashing like the lightning one sees between the low clouds and the horizon in summer. But if the web was touched he felt it, and if a word was spoken he heard it; so you perceive, my young friends, that in the heart of Africa a heathen god had set up a telegraph and telephone system centuries before our inventions were dreamed of.

«No one, however, had seen this god and lived, except the priests. To him, through these priests, all the people made sacrifice once a year. At the beginning of the dry season the priests went before the cave and offered a human victim—a female child. Naturally the girlhood of females in the tribe was unhappy, for the child the priests demanded was doomed. The welfare of all the people depended upon the sacrifice, and the custom was too old to be resisted. At the appointed time these men took the victim, journeyed northward, and, after certain rites before the cave, at midnight cast her upon the web. Then, in the far depths of the den, the thunder began to roll, and the two stars to move in widening circles, the light growing in intensity until, in the glare of those fearful eyes, the white spider was seen to dash out upon his prey, seize it by the throat, and return to his lair. The priests always fled to a safe distance while this was going on.

«The old woman, as a girl, was selected for the honor of this sacrifice, and taken in charge by the priests, to be fed and prepared for the monster. During the week that intervened, you well understand, the ghost that had dwelt with the tribe so long made his home in her poor childish brain. She was carried away at last, but when almost in the mountains was seized by slave-traders, and presto! the priests, Nancy, and the ghost were in Georgia.

«This is the purport of her story. At your leisure you may unravel the spider-myth of the poor Africans,—perhaps Mr. Ruskin can help you,—and if you find that it goes back beyond the flood, don't be surprised. But to continue the adventures of my ghost. When I left him he was in the brain-structure of my father, who was then a lad, and had erected there a wonderful web. Well, he grew up, my father did, and my grandfather explained the phenomenon to him as best he could, and cautioned him against repeating the story. He obeyed, or at least never did he mention the subject to me; so that when I developed acquaintance with the old-time cave-god, it was by an esoteric process, and the consciousness of this fact was what troubled my grandfather, who was doubtful as to the extent this ghost would grow in succeeding generations, and what the effect would be. Armed with his explanation, however, and acting under his advice, I went to work to lay this specter, and grappled with him manfully. I began the study of spiders, and became familiar with all their habits. I even succeeded in accustoming myself to the handling of them, but I confess that even now the touch is invariably accompanied by a queer thrill of the nerves. By the time I had reached manhood I was so far free from my antipathy that when I dreamed of the white spider his antics were merely funny, and we were always on good terms. Then my boy came along, and, as you know, perhaps, at an early age made a name for himself as a naturalist. One of the first things that brought him before the scientific world was his treatise upon spider venom, in which he showed how senseless is the popular prejudice against some of the tribe of *Arachnida*, and how beautiful is the art of the geometric members. The boy never seemed to dream of spiders, though he may have done so, but from his earliest babyhood exhibited a remarkable fondness for them. He had located about the premises many old settlers that he fed daily. His first discovery was announced to me at eight years of age. You may get the result that he obtained by dropping a spider into a glass pickle-jar and then covering it with gauze. It will fill the jar with web, but not spun in circles. Just why a spider that has never built anything but a circular web should, when confined, set up one without any apparent plan whatever puzzled the boy for months; but finally he solved the problem to his own satisfaction. He noticed that half a bottle of borax-and-camphor hair-wash, when shaken, became filled with air-bubbles of peculiar shapes, and that the spider-web in the jar needed only films from strand to strand to represent exactly the same geometrical forms. What was the correlation between the two? It was this. The bubbles represented air seeking expansion in globular form, that is, circles in every direction. The space was insufficient, and crowding was the result. The lines between the aggregation of bubbles represented the lines of equal pressure. The spider's peculiar web was the result of his persevering attempts to spin a circular web. The transparent glass cylinder deceived him, stopped him in every direction, and finally left him exhausted of silk and weary and puzzled in the midst of a skeleton that represented the dividing lines of bubbles. The same spider in the same jar, after it had been painted black, spun a circular web. This exhibition of nature working by physical laws through simple elements on the one hand, and through the instinct of an animal to produce a similar form, is very curious and interesting. But think of the source of the mental stimulus that put the boy's mind in harmony with it all, and enabled him to read the secret! It was the specter of the cave enlightening the nineteenth century.

« His second great discovery was that the funnel or ox-horn web of the wood-spider was intended to convey sound. It was both a telephone and a telegraph system. The whir of the fly's wing across the hollow log is known to the spider whose web leads within! The lightest touch of a strand thrills and brings him to the front. If the slight brush of a wing on this web sends a vibration back into the log, what must be the sound that falls upon the victim when the terrible beast rushes across the same strands to quench his thirst for blood! And what suggested to the poor Africans the idea that thunder roared in the cave when the white god came forth?

« The laws of vibration are now well understood. There is a particular note from a vibrating string that will cause impalpable dust upon a disk to assume the shape of a cornucopia; and if the note arranges the dust in such shape, it is clear that the shape ought to be the best conductor of the note. It is not impossible that the log-spider's web is built to catch a particular note, and that the note comes only from the vibrating wings of his own particular prey. My son used to say that, knowing the note, if he knew the insect for which the web was planned he could tell the number of vibrations of its wings. But in this age the spider seems to take almost anything that comes to him. Mr. Darwin might say that it is a case of the survival of the fittest, and that the original prey has become extinct. However this may be, you will see how the African ghost has walked in the family, and how he is working. I doubt not that many African myths stalk in this Southern land, and that one effect of slavery will be the flashing of equatorial colors upon the public mind. This is one way nature has of getting closer to people who have wandered too far from her.

« But to resume. The virus of the original fear lost its strength in my generation, as you will soon perceive, and finally bloomed in beauty—not an unusual thing in nature. The sap that makes the stem, the leaf, the thorn, dies in an expiring effort, and lo! the imperial rose. The fields are full of such sunsets. Poems are sunsets. The art galleries of the world are sunsets. Who has ever painted the sunrise of genius? Were I an artist commissioned to the task, I could but imagine the gray gloom of an African cave with twin stars fixed in its depths. I will tell you how the sunset has already been painted.

« My two grandchildren were educated abroad, as you all know. Their mother was of French descent, and upon the death of my son, influenced by the mental drift of her children, a boy and girl, concluded to make her permanent home in France. The boy developed a most decided talent for architecture, and was given every possible advantage in the best institutes. In his final year he sent me a water-color design that had received the highest award; indeed, the examining committee pronounced it, in points of originality, delicacy, and brilliancy of execution, the finest work ever submitted to them by a student. It represented a cathedral window, circular in form, a brilliant blending of rainbow hues along a silvery network geometrically developed. I did not need to ask him whence came the idea, nor will you when you have seen the sunrise through the dew upon yon little palace in the air.

«That window illumines the chancel of one of the greatest cathedrals in France. Last year, when I visited that country, it was to dissuade my granddaughter from her resolution to become a nun; but, as you are all aware, my efforts met with no success; she passed into the sisterhood of the Sacred Heart. When the ceremony took place, it was in the cathedral I have mentioned. I knelt by the artist brother in deep distress, but this he did not share with me, being himself a devout Catholic. The occasion seemed to him one of holy triumph; and gradually, under the influence of the music and the scene, I too became reconciled to the inevitable. It was while in this frame of mind that I suddenly became aware that the ceremony had progressed to the point where the novitiate prostrates herself prone upon her face. There, in white, lay my child, a sacrifice. Above her shone with the splendor of the passing sun the fairy window. I gazed upon the boy by my side. His eyes were fixed upon his work, and his lips moved. I dared not ask him if he saw beyond its lines the faint brain-picture I beheld of a different offering in the dark depths of Africa. I opened wide my own eyes to let it fade the quicker, conscious that one of life's strangest cycles was being completed, and that the spider-myth was at last passing into its sunset.»

The old man ceased speaking, and in profound silence all eyes were fixed upon the web in the ambient air; and as thus they gazed the angle of light became narrower. A change crept over the lines of the structure. It grew dim, as the lines of a dream half seen upon awakening, and then swiftly, as if withdrawn by an invisible hand, it blended with the somber tones of the background, and was seen no more. It was the professor's voice that broke the silence, but so low, so solemn, it seemed unnatural: «So fade all sunsets; so dies the light on land and sea; so pass away all the fairy pictures of the mind. But the sun shall rise again, the light on land and sea grow white, and on the filmy skies of unformed minds the hand that paints the blossoms of the field and tints the rose may flash the pictures of the past.»

*Harry Stillwell Edwards.*

## THE YOUNG TENOR.

I WOKE; the harbored melody
  Had crossed the slumber bar,
And out upon the open sea
  Of consciousness, afar
Swept onward with a fainter strain,
As echoing the dream again.

So soft the silver sound, and clear,
  Outpoured upon the night,
That Silence seemed a listener
  O'erleaning with delight
The slender moon, a finger-tip
Upon the portal of her lip.

*John B. Tabb.*

# A ROSE OF YESTERDAY.[1]

BY F. MARION CRAWFORD,

Author of «Mr. Isaacs,» «Saracinesca,» «Casa Braccio,» etc.

I.

WONDER what he meant by it,» said Sylvia, turning again in her chair, so that the summer light, softened and tinted by the drawn blinds, might fall upon the etching she held.

«My dear,» answered Colonel Wimpole, stretching out his still graceful legs, leaning back in his chair, and slowly joining his nervous but handsome hands, «nobody knows.»

He did not move again for some time, and his ward continued to scrutinize Dürer's Knight. It was the one known as «The Knight, Death, and the Devil,» and she had just received it from her guardian as a birthday present.

«But people must have thought a great deal about it,» said Sylvia, at last. «There must be stories about what it means. Do tell me; I'm sure you know.»

She laid the unframed print upon her knees, still holding it by the edges, lest the fitful breeze that came in through the blinds should blow it to the floor. At the same time she raised her eyes till they met the colonel's.

Her earnest young face expressed something like veneration as she gazed at him, and perhaps he thought that it was undeserved, for he soon looked away with a faint sigh. She sighed too, but more audibly, as though she were not ashamed of it. Possibly she knew that he could not guess what the sigh meant, and the knowledge added a little pain to what she felt just then, and had felt daily of late. She began to study the etching again.

«To me,» she said softly, «the Knight is a hero. He is making Death show him the way, and he has made the Devil his squire and servant. He will reach the city on the hill in time, for there is still sand enough in the hour-glass. Do you see?» She held out the print to the colonel. «There is still sand enough,» she repeated. «Don't you think so?»

Again, as she asked the question, she looked at him; but he was bending over the etching, and she could see only his clear profile against the shadows of the room.

«He may be just in time,» he answered quietly.

«I wonder which house they lived in, of those one can see,» said Sylvia.

«Who are ‹they›? Death, the Devil, and the Knight?»

«No; the Knight and the lady, of course —the lady who is waiting to see whether he will come in time.»

The colonel laughed a little at her fancy, and looked at her as the breeze stirred her brown hair. He did not understand her, and she knew that he did not. His glance took in her brown hair, her violet eyes, her delicately shaded cheek, and the fresh young mouth, with its strange little half-weary smile that should not have been there, and that left the weariness behind whenever it faded for a time. He wondered what was the matter with the girl.

She was not ill; that was clear enough, for they had traveled far, and Sylvia had never once seemed tired. The colonel and Miss Wimpole, his elderly maiden sister, had taken Sylvia out to Japan to meet her father, Admiral Strahan, who had been stationed some time with a small squadron in the waters of the far East. He had been ordered home rather suddenly, and the Wimpoles were bringing the girl back by way of Europe. Sylvia's mother had been dead three years, and had left her a little fortune. Mrs. Strahan had been a step-sister, and no blood relation, of the Wimpoles; but they had been as a real brother and a real sister to her, and she had left her only child to their care during such times as her husband's service should keep him away from home. The girl was now just eighteen.

Colonel Wimpole wondered whether she could be destined for suffering, as some women are, and the thought linked itself to the chain of another life, and drew it out of his heart, that he might see it and be hurt; for he had known pain in himself, and through one he loved. He could not believe that Sylvia was fore-fated to sorrow, but the silent weariness that of late was always in her face meant something which he feared to learn, but for which he felt himself vaguely responsible, as though he were not doing his duty by her.

He was a man of heart, of honor, and of

[1] Copyright, 1896, by F. Marion Crawford.

conscience. Long ago, in his early youth, he had fought bravely in a long and cruel war, and had remained a soldier for many years afterward, with an old-fashioned attachment for arms that was dashed with chivalry, till at last he had hung up his sword, accepting peace as a profession. Indeed, he had never loved anything of war except its danger and its honor; and he had loved one woman more than either, but not against honor, nor in danger, though without much hope.

He had lived simply, as some men can and as a few do live, in the midst of the modern world, parting with an illusion now and then, and fostering some new taste in its place, in a sort of innocent and simple consciousness that it was artificial, but in the certainty that it was harmless. He was gentle in his ways, with the quiet and unaffected feeling for other people which not seldom softens those who have fought with their hands in the conviction of right, and have dealt and received real wounds. War either brutalizes or refines a man; it never leaves him unchanged. Colonel Wimpole had traveled from time to time, more for the sake of going to some one place which he wished to see than of passing through many places for the sake of traveling. There is a great difference between the two methods. Wherever he went, he took with him his own character and his slightly formal courtesy of manner, not leaving himself at home, as some people do, nor assuming a separate personality for Europe, like a disguise; for, such as he was, he was incapable of affectation, and he was sure that the manners which had been good enough for his mother were good enough for any woman in the world, as indeed they were, because he was a gentleman, that is, a man, and gentle at all points, excepting for his honor. But no one had ever touched that.

He looked what he was, too, from head to foot. He was a tall, slender man of nervous strength, with steady gray eyes, high features, smooth, short, and grizzled hair; simple and yet very scrupulous in his dress; easy in his movements; not old before his time, but having already something of the refinement of age upon the nobility of his advanced manhood; one of whom a woman would expect great things in an extremity, but to whom she would no longer turn for the little service, the little fetching and carrying, which most women expect of men still in prime. But he did such things unasked, and for any woman, when it seemed natural to do them. After all, he was only fifty-three years old, and it seems to be established that sixty is the age of man's manumission from servitude, unless the period of slavery be voluntarily extended by the individual. That leaves ten years of freedom, if one live to the traditional age of mankind.

But Sylvia saw no sign of age in Colonel Wimpole. In connection with him, the mere word irritated her when he used it, which he sometimes did quite naturally; and he would have been very much surprised could he have guessed how she thought of him, and what she was thinking as she sat looking from him to Dürer's Knight, and from the etched rider to the living man again. For she saw a resemblance which by no means existed, except, perhaps, between two ideals.

The Knight in the picture is stern and strong and grim, and sits his horse like the incarnation of an unchanging will, riding a bridled destiny against Death and evil to a good end. And Death's tired jade droops its white head and sniffs at the skull in the way, but the Knight's charger turns up his lip and shows his teeth at the carrion thing, and arches his strong neck, while the Knight looks straight before him, and cares not, and his steel-clad legs press the great horse into the way, and his steel-gloved hand holds curb and snaffle in a vise. As for the Devil, he slinks behind, an evil beast, but subdued, and following meekly, with a sort of mute animal astonishment in his wide eyes.

And beside Sylvia sat the colonel, quiet, gentle, restful, suggesting, just then, nothing of desperate determination, and not at all like the grim Knight in feature. Yet the girl felt a kinship between the two, and saw one and the same heroism in the man and in the pictured rider. In her inmost heart she wished that she could have seen the colonel long ago, when he had fought, riding at death without fear. But the thought that it had been so very long ago kept the wish down below the word-line in her heart's well. Youth clothes its ideals with the spirit of truth, and hides the letter out of sight.

But in the picture Sylvia looked for herself, since it was for a lady that the knight was riding, and all she could find was the big old house up in the town, on the left of the tallest tower. She was waiting somewhere under the high gabled roof, with her spinning-wheel or her fine needlework, among her women. Would he ever come? Was there time before the sand in Death's hour-glass should run out?

«I wish the horse would put his forefoot down and go on!» she said suddenly.

Then she laughed, though a little wearily.

How could she tell the colonel that he was the Knight, and that she was waiting in the tall house with the many windows? Perhaps he would never know, and forever the charger's forefoot would be lifted, ready for the step that was never to fall upon the path.

But Colonel Wimpole did not understand. It was unlike her to wish that an old print should turn into a page from a child's movable picture-book.

«Why do you wish that the horse would go on?» he asked half idly.

«Because the sand will not last if he waits,» said Sylvia, quietly; and as she spoke a third time of the sand in the hour-glass she felt a little chill at her heart.

«There will always be time,» answered the colonel, enigmatically.

«As there will always be air, I suppose, and that will not matter to us when we are not here to breathe it any more.»

«That is true. Nothing will matter very much a hundred years hence.»

«But a few years matter much more than a hundred.» Her voice was sad.

«What are you thinking of?» asked Colonel Wimpole, changing his position so as to see her face better.

He resented her sadness a little, for he and his sister were doing their best to make her happy. But Sylvia did not answer him; she bent her white forehead to the faint breeze that came through the closed green blinds, and she looked at the etching. The colonel believed that she was thinking of her dead mother, whom she had loved. He hesitated, choosing his words; for he hated preaching, and yet it seemed to him that Sylvia mourned too long.

«I was very fond of your mother too, my dear,» he said gently, after a time. «She was like a real sister to us. I wish I could have gone instead, and left her to you.»

«You?» Sylvia's voice startled him; she was suddenly pale, and the old print shook in her hands. «Oh, no!» she cried half passionately. «Not you—not you!»

The colonel was surprised for a moment; then he was grateful, for he felt that she was very fond of him. He thought of the woman he loved, and that he might have had such a daughter as Sylvia, but with other eyes.

«I am glad you are fond of me,» he said. «You are very good to me, and I know I am a tiresome old man.»

At that word one beat of the girl's heart sent resentful blood to her face.

«You are not old at all!» she cried. «And you could not be tiresome if you tried! And I am not good to you, as you call it!»



The girl's young anger made him think of summer lightning, and of the sudden flashing of new steel drawn silently and swiftly from the sheath into the sunshine.

«Goodness may be a matter of opinion, my dear,» said he, «but age is a matter of fact. I was fifty-three years old on my last birthday.»

«Oh, what do years matter?» Sylvia rose quickly, and turned from him, going toward the window.

The colonel watched her perfectly graceful movements. She wore gray, with a small black band at her throat, and the soft light clung to the lovely outline of her figure and to her brown hair. He thought again of the daughter that might have been born to him, and even of a daughter's daughter. It seemed to him that his own years might be a greater matter than Sylvia would admit. Yet, as their descending mists veiled hope's height, he was often glad that there should not be as many more as there had been. He said nothing, and there was a dream in his eyes.

«You are always saying that you are old. Why?» Sylvia's voice came from the window, but she did not turn. «It is not kind,» she said, still more softly.

«Not kind?» He did not understand.

«It is not kind to me. It is as though I did not care. Besides, it is not true!»

Just then the conviction had come back to her voice, stronger than ever, strengthening the tone just when it was breaking. She had never spoken to him in this way. He called her.

«Sylvia! will you come here, my dear?» She came, and he took her fresh young hands. «What is it? Has anything happened? Are you unhappy? Tell me.»

At his question the violet eyes slowly filled, and she just bent her head once or twice as though assenting.

«You are unhappy?» He repeated his question, and again she nodded sadly.

«But happy too—often.»

There was not room for happiness and sorrow together in her full eyes. The tear fell, and gladness took its place at his touch. But he looked, and remembered other hands, and began to know the truth. Love's unforgotten spirit came, wafting a breath of other days.

He looked, and wondered whom the girl had chosen, and was glad for her happiness while he grew anxious for its life. She was so young that she must have chosen lately and quickly. In a rush of inward questioning his mind ran back through the long journey they had made together, and answers came in many faces of men that glided before him. One of them stopped him and held his thought, as a fleeting memory will—a young officer of her father's flagship, lean, brown, bright-eyed, with a strong mouth and a rare smile. Sylvia had often talked with him, and the boy's bright eyes used to watch her from a distance when he was not beside her. Quiet of speech he was, and resolute, bred in the keen air of a northern sea, of the few from among whom fate may choose the one. That was the man.

The colonel spoke then as though he had said much, glad and willing to take the girl's conclusion.

«I know who it is,» he said, as if all had been explained. «I am glad, very glad.»

His hands pressed hers more tightly, for he was a man of heart, and because his own life had failed strangely he knew how happy she must be, having all he had not. But the violet eyes grew wide and dark and surprised, and the faint color came and went.

«Do you really, really know at last?» she asked very low.

«Yes, dear; I know,» he said, for he had the sure conviction out of his sympathy for the child.

«And you are glad? Glad as I am?»

«Indeed I am! I love you with all my heart, my dear.»

She looked at him a moment longer, and then her sight grew faint, and her face hid itself against his coat.

«Say it! say it again!» she repeated, and her white fingers closed tightly upon his sleeve. «I have waited so long to hear you say it!»

An uneasy and half-distressed look came to his face instantly as he looked down at the brown hair.

«What?» he asked. «What have you waited to hear me say?»

«That—the words you said just now.» Her face still hidden, she hesitated.

«What did I say? That I loved you, my dear?»

She nodded silently against his coat.

«But I have always loved you, Sylvia, dear,» he said, while a wondering fear stole through him.

«You never told me; and I did not dare tell you—how could I? But now you understand. You know that the years mean nothing, after all, and that there is still sand in the hour-glass, and you and I shall reach the end of the road together—»

«Sylvia!» His voice rang sharply and painfully as he interrupted her.

He was a little pale, and his gray eyes were less steady than usual, for he could not be mistaken any longer. He had faced many dangers bravely, but the girl frightened him, clinging to his sleeve and telling her half-childish love for him. Then came the shock to his honor, for it seemed as though it must somehow have been his fault.

She looked up and saw his face, but could not understand it, though she had a prevision of evil, and the stealing sickness of disappointment made her faint.

«I did not know what you meant, my child,» he said, growing more pale, and very gently pushing her back a little. «I was thinking of young Knox; I thought you loved him. I was so sure that he was the man.»

She drew back now of her own will, staring.

«Knox? Mr. Knox?» She repeated the name, hardly hearing her own words, half stunned by her mistake. «But you said—you said you loved me—»

«As your father does,» said Colonel Wimpole, very gravely. «Your father and I are just of the same age. We were boys together. You know it, my dear.»

She was a mere child, and he made her feel that she was. Her hands covered her face in an instant as she fled, and before the door had closed behind her the colonel heard the first quick sob.

He had risen to his feet, and stood still, looking at the door. When he was alone he might have smiled, as some men might have done, not at Sylvia, indeed, though at the absurdity of the situation; but his face was sad, and he quietly sat down again by the table, and began to think of what had happened.

Sylvia was very foolish, he said to himself, as he tried to impose upon his mind what he thought should have been his conviction. Yet he was deeply and truly touched by her half-childish love, and its innocence seemed pathetic to him, while he was hurt for her pain and, most of all, for her overwhelming confusion.

At the same time came memories and visions, and his head sank forward a little as he sat in his chair by the table. The vision of hope was growing daily more dim, but the remembrance of the past was as undying as what has been is beyond recall.

Sylvia would wake from her girlish dream, and in the fullness of young womanhood would love a man of her own years. The colonel knew that. She would see that he was going in under the gateway of old age, while she was on the threshold of youth's morning. A few days, or a few months, or at most a few years more, and she must see that he was an old man. That was certain.

He sighed, not for Sylvia, but because age is that deadly sickness of which hope must perish at last. Time is a prince of narrow possessions, absolute where he reigns at all, cruel upon his people, and relentless; for beyond his scanty principality he is nothing, and his name is not known in the empire of eternity. Therefore, while he rules he raises the dark standard of death, taking tribute of life, and giving back a slow poison in return.

Colonel Wimpole was growing old, and though the woman he still loved was not young, she was far younger than he, and he must soon seem an old man even in her eyes; and then there would not be much hope left. Sadly he wondered what Sylvia saw in him which that other woman, who had known him long, seemed to have never quite seen. But such questioning could find no satisfaction.

He might have remained absorbed in his reflections for a long time had he been left alone, but the door opened behind him, and he knew by the steady and precise way in which it was opened and shut that his sister had entered the room.

«Richard,» she said, «I am surprised.» Then she stood still and waited.

Miss Wimpole was older than her brother, and was an exaggeration of him in petticoats. Her genuine admiration for him was curiously tempered by the fact that when they had been children, she, as the elder, had kept him out of mischief, occasionally by force, often by authority, but never by persuasion. When in pinafores the colonel had been fond of sweets. Miss Wimpole considered that he owed his excellent health to her heroic determination to save him from destruction by jam. Since those days she had been obliged to yield to him on other points, but the memory of victory in the matter of preserves still made her manner authoritative.

She was very like him, being tall, thin, and not ungraceful, though as oddly precise in her movements and gestures as she was rigid in her beliefs, faithful in her affections, and just in her judgments. She had loved a man who had been killed in the war, and being what she was, she had never so much as considered the possibility of marrying any one else. She was much occupied in good works, and did much good, but she was so terribly accurate about it as to make Sylvia say that she was like a public charity that had been brought up in good society.

The colonel rose as she spoke.

«What is the matter?» he asked. «Why are you surprised?»

«What have you been saying to Sylvia, Richard?» inquired Miss Wimpole, not moving.

It would have been hard to hit upon a question more certain to embarrass the colonel. He felt the difficulty of his position so keenly that, old as he was, a faint color rose in his cheeks. No answer occurred to him, and he hesitated.

«She has locked herself up in her room,» continued Miss Wimpole, with searching severity, «and she is crying as though her heart would break. I heard her sobbing as I passed the door, and she would not let me in.»

«I am very sorry,» said the colonel, gravely.

«You do not seem much concerned,» retorted his sister. «I insist upon knowing what is the matter.»

«Girls often cry,» observed Colonel Wimpole, who felt obliged to say something, though he did not at all know what to say.

«Sylvia does not often cry, Richard, and you know it. You must have said something very unkind to her.»

«I hope not,» answered the colonel, evasively.

«Then why is she sobbing there, all by herself? I should like you to answer that question.»

«I am sorry to say that I cannot. When she is herself again, you had better ask her.»

Colonel Wimpole thought this good diplomacy. Since he meant not to tell his sister the truth, and was incapable of inventing a falsehood, he saw no means of escape except by referring Miss Wimpole directly to Sylvia.

«Richard,» said the maiden lady, impressively, «I am surprised at you.» And she turned away rather stiffly. «I thought you had more confidence in me,» she added as she reached the door.

But Colonel Wimpole made no further answer, for he saw that she had accepted his silence, which was all he wanted. When he was quite sure that she was in her own room, he went and got his hat and stick, and slipped quietly out of the hotel.

## II.

COLONEL WIMPOLE did not like Lucerne, and as he strolled along the shady side of the street he unconsciously looked up at the sky or down at the pavement rather than at the houses and the people. He disliked the tourists, the buildings, the distant scenery, and the climate, and could give a reason for each separate aversion. Excepting the old tower, which was very much like a great many other old towers, he maintained that the buildings were either flat and dull or most modernly pretentious. The tourists were tourists, and that alone condemned them beyond redemption. The climate was detestable, and he was sure that every one must think so. As for the scenery, with its prim lake, its tiresome snow mountains, and its toy trees, he said that it was little better than a perpetual chromolithograph, though at sunset it occasionally rose to the dignity of a transparent «landscape» lamp-shade. The colonel's views of places were not wholly without prejudice. Being a very just man where men and women were concerned, he allowed himself to be as unfair as he chose about inanimate things, from snow mountains to objects of art.

It was the pretension of Switzerland, he said, to please and to attract. Since it neither attracted him nor pleased him, he could not see what harm there could be in saying so. The Rigi's feelings could not be hurt by a sharp remark, nor could Mount Pilatus be supposed to be sensitive. He never abused Switzerland where any Swiss person could hear him. The same things, he said, were true of objects of art. If they failed to please, there could be no reason for their existence, or for not saying so, provided that the artist were not present. As for the latter, the charitable colonel was always willing to admit that he had done his best. It was gratuitous to suppose that any man should wilfully do badly what he could do well.

The colonel strolled slowly through the back streets, keeping in the shade. The day was hot, and he felt something like humiliation at having allowed himself to yield to circumstances and come out of the house earlier than usual. He would certainly not have acknowledged that he had been driven from the hotel by the fear of his sister's curiosity, but he would have faced a hotter sun rather than be obliged to meet her inquisitive questions again.

It was true that, being alone, he had to meet himself and discuss with himself the painful little scene which had taken place that afternoon; for he was not one of those people who can get rid of unpleasant difficulties simply by refusing to think about them. And he examined the matter carefully as he went along, staring alternately at the sky and at the pavement, while his stick rang sharply in time with his light but still military step. He did not see the people who passed, but many of them looked at him, and noticed his face and figure, and set him down for a gentleman and an old soldier, as he was.

At first sight it seemed ridiculous that Sylvia should be in love with him; then it seemed sad, and then it seemed childish. He remembered the tragedy of Ninon de l'Enclos and her son, and it was horrible, until he recalled an absurd story of a short-sighted young man who had fallen in love with his grandmother because his vanity would not allow him to wear spectacles. At this recollection Colonel Wimpole smiled a little, though he was obliged to admit that Sylvia's eyes had always been very good. He wished, for a moment, that he were quite old already, instead of being only at the edge of old age. It would have been more easy to laugh at the matter. He was glad that he was not ten years younger, for in that case he might have been to blame. As he was turning into the main street he caught sight of his own reflection in the big plate-glass window of a shop. He stopped short, with a painful sensation.

Had the image been that of a stranger he should have judged the original to be a young man. The figure he saw was tall and straight and active, dressed in the perfection of neatness and good taste. The straw hat shaded the upper part of the face, but the sunlight caught the well-cut chin and gilded the small, closely trimmed mustache.

The colonel was extremely annoyed, just then, by his youthful appearance. He stopped, and then went close to the plate-glass window, till he could see his face distinctly in it against the shadows of the darkened shop. He was positively relieved when he could clearly distinguish the fine lines and wrinkles and gray hairs which he saw every morning in his mirror when he shaved. It was the sunshine playing with shadow that had called up the airy reflection of his departed youth for a moment. Sylvia could never have seen him as he had appeared to himself in the window.

He looked a little longer. A lady in black was talking with the shopkeeper, and a short young man stood beside her. Colonel Wimpole's fingers tightened suddenly upon the familiar silver knob of his stick, his face grew a little pale, and he held his breath.

The lady turned quietly, walked to the window, followed by the shopkeeper and the young man, and pointed to a miniature which lay among a great number of more or less valuable antiquities and objects of art, all of them arranged so as to show them to an undue advantage. She stood quite still, looking down at the thing she wanted, and listening to what the shopkeeper said. The colonel, just on the other side of the thick plate-glass, could hear nothing, though he could have counted the heavy lashes that darkly fringed the drooping lids as the lady kept her eyes upon the miniature. But his heart was standing still, for she was the woman he had loved so long and well, and he had not known that she was to pass through Lucerne. The short young man beside her was her son, and Colonel Wimpole knew him also, and had seen him from time to time during the nineteen years of his life. But he scarcely noticed him now, for his whole being was intent upon the face of the woman he loved.

She was dark, though her hair had never been jet-black, and her complexion had always reminded the colonel of certain beautiful roses of which the smooth, cream-colored petals are very faintly tinged with a warm blush that bears no relation to pink, but which is not red either—a tint without which the face was like marble, which could come in a moment, but was long in fading as a northern sunset, and which gave wonderful life to the expression while it lasted. The lady's features were bold and well-cut, but there were sad lines of lifelong weariness about the curved mouth and deep-set eyes; and there was a sort of patient, but not weak, sadness in all her bearing—the look of those who have tired, but have not yielded, who have borne a calm face against a great trouble from without, and a true heart against a strong temptation from within.

She was neither tall nor short, neither heavy nor light in figure, a woman of good and strong proportions; and she was dressed in black, though one small jeweled ornament and a colored ribbon in her hat showed that she was not in mourning.

The elderly man at the window did not move as he watched her, for he felt sure that she must presently look up and meet his eyes; then he would go in. But it did not happen just in that way, for her son recognized him first: a dark youth, very squarely built, with a heavy face, and straight eyebrows that met over his nose. When he saw the colonel he smiled, lifted his hat, and spoke to his mother. The lady started perceptibly, and seemed to press the handle of her black parasol to her side. Several seconds passed after that before the fringed lids were lifted and the two looked at each other fixedly through the thick glass. A soft, slow smile smoothed and illuminated the lady's face, but Colonel Wimpole felt that he was paler than before, and his lips moved, unconsciously pronouncing a name which he had never spoken carelessly during two-and-twenty years. Nor, in that long time, had he ever met Helen Harmon suddenly face to face without feeling that his cheeks grew pale and that his heart stood still for a moment.

But his pulse beat quite regularly again when he had entered the shop and stood before her, extending his hand to meet hers, though he felt that he was holding out his heart to meet her heart, and he was full of unexpected happiness. So, in dim winter days, the sun shines out in a sudden glory, and spring is in the air before her time for an hour; but afterward it is cold again, and snow falls before night. Many a far glimpse of the flower-time had gladdened the colonel's heart before now, but the promised summer had never come.

The two stood still for a moment, hand in hand, and their eyes lingered in meeting just a second or two longer than if they had been mere friends. That was all that a stranger could have seen to suggest that Richard Wimpole had loved Helen Harmon for twenty-two years, and the young man at her side did not even notice it. He shook hands with the colonel in his turn, and was the first to speak.

«One meets everybody in Lucerne,» he observed in a rather tactless generalization.

«I certainly did not hope to meet you,» answered the colonel, smiling. «It is true that the cross-roads of Europe are at Lucerne if they are anywhere. My sister and I are taking Sylvia Strahan home from Japan. Of course we stopped here.»

«Oh, of course,» laughed young Harmon; «everybody stops here. We have been here ever so long, on our way to Carlsbad, I believe.»

His mother glanced at him nervously before she spoke, as though she were not sure of what he might say next.

«I am thinking of buying a miniature,» she said. «Will you look at it for me? You know all about these things; I should like your advice.»

The dealer's face fell as he stood in the background, for he knew the colonel, and he understood English. But as he spoke, Mrs. Harmon was thinking more of Wimpole than of the miniature, and he, when he answered, was wondering how he could succeed in being alone with her for one half-hour, one of those little half-hours on which he lived for weeks and months after they were past.

Mrs. Harmon's manner was very quiet, and there was not often any marked change in her expression. Her rare laugh was low, regretful, and now and then a little bitter. Sometimes, when one might have expected a quick answer, she said nothing at all, and then her features had a calm immobility that was almost mysterious. Only now and then, when her son was speaking, she was evidently nervous, and at the sound of his voice her eyes turned quickly and nervously toward his face, while the shadows about the corners of her mouth deepened a little, and her lips set themselves. When he said anything more witless than usual, she was extraordinarily skilful and quick to turn his saying to sense by a clever explanation. At other times she generally spoke rather slowly, and even indolently, as though nothing mattered very much. Yet she was a very sensible woman, and not by any means unpractical in daily life. Her tragedy, if it were one, had been slow and long drawn out.

First, a love which had been real, silent, and so altogether unsuspected, even by its object, that Richard Wimpole had never guessed it to this day. Then a marriage thrust upon her by circumstances, which she had accepted at last in the highest nobility of honest purpose. After that much suffering, most scrupulously covered up from the world, and one moment of unforgotten horror. There was a crooked scar on her forehead, hidden by the thick hair which she drew down over it; when she was angry it turned red, though there was no other change in her face. Then a little while, and her husband's mind had gone. Even then she had tried to take care of him, until it had been hopeless and he had become dangerous. The mercy of death seemed far from him, and he still lived, for he was very strong. And all along there had been the slowly increasing certainty of another misfortune. Her son, her only child, had been like other children at first, then dull and backward, and in the end, as compared with grown men, deficient. His mind had not developed much beyond a boy's, and though he was unusually strong, he had never learned to apply his strength, and did not even excel in athletic sports. One might have been deceived at first by a sharp glance of his eyes, but they were not bright with intelligence. The young man's perfect physical health alone made them clear and keen as a young animal's, but what they saw produced little reaction of understanding or thought.

Nor was that all that Helen Harmon had borne. There was one other thing, hardest of any to bear. By an accident she had learned at last that Richard Wimpole had loved her, and she had guessed that he loved her still. He had fancied her indifferent to him, and Harmon had been his friend in young days. Harmon had been called fast even then, but not vicious, and he had been rich. Wimpole had stood aside and had let him win, being diffident, and really believing that it might be better for Helen in the end. He thought that she could make anything she chose of Harmon, who was furiously in love with her.

So the two had made the great mistake, each meaning to do the very best that could be done. But when Harmon had gone mad at last, and was in an asylum, without prospect of recovery, and Helen found herself the administrator of his property for her son, it had been necessary to go through all his disordered papers, and she had found a letter of Wimpole's to her husband, written long ago. Had it been a woman's letter she would have burned it unread. But it was a duty to read every paper which might bear upon business matters from the beginning, and she naturally supposed that Harmon must have had some reason for keeping this one; so she read it.

It had been written in the early days of her husband's courtship. He too had been generous then, with impulses of honor in which there had been, perhaps, something of vanity, though they had impelled him to do right. There had been some conversation between the friends, and Harmon had found out that Wimpole loved Helen. Not being yet so far in love as he was later, he had offered to go away and let the young colonel have a chance, since the latter had loved her first. Then Wimpole had written this letter which she found twenty years later.

It was simple, grateful, and honorably conceived; it said what he had believed to be the truth: that Helen did not care for him, that Harmon was quite as good as he in all ways, and much richer, and it finally and definitely refused the offer of «a chance.» There was nothing tragic about it, nor any high-flown word in its short, clear phrases; but it had decided three lives, and the finding of it after such a long time hurt Helen more than anything had ever hurt her before.

In a flash she saw the meaning of Wimpole's life, and she knew that he loved her still, and had always loved her, though in all their many meetings throughout those twenty years he had never said one word of it to her. In one sudden comprehension she saw all his magnificent generosity of silence. For he had partly known how Harmon had treated her; every one knew something of it, and he must have known more than any one except the lawyer and the doctor whom she had been obliged to consult.

And yet, in that quick vision, she remembered too that she had never complained to him, nor ever said a word against Harmon. What Wimpole knew, beyond some matters of business in which he had helped her, he had learned from others or had guessed. But he had guessed much. Little actions of his, under this broad light of truth, showed her now that he had often understood what was happening when she had thought him wholly in ignorance.

But he, on his side, found no letter, nor any unexpected revelation of her secret; and still, to him, she seemed only to have changed indifference for friendship, deep, sincere, lasting, and calm.

She kept the old letter two days, and then, when she was alone, she read it again, and her eyes filled, and she saw her hands bringing the discolored page toward her lips. Then she started, and looked at it, and she felt the scar on her forehead burning hot under her hair, and the temptation was great, though her anger at herself was greater. Harmon was alive, and she was a married woman, though he was a madman. She would not kiss the letter, but she laid it gently upon the smoldering embers, and then turned away that she might not see it curling and glowing and blackening to ashes on the coals. That night a note from the director of the asylum told her that her husband was in excellent bodily health, without improvement in his mental condition. It was dated on the first of the month.

After that she avoided the colonel for some time; but when she met him, her face was again like marble, and only the soft, slow smile and the steady, gentle word showed that she was glad to see him. Two years had passed since then, and he had not even guessed that she knew.

He often sought her, when she was within reach of him, but their meeting to-day, in the fashionable antiquary's shop at the cross-roads of Europe, was altogether accidental, unless it were brought about by the direct intervention of destiny. But who believes in destiny nowadays? Most people smile at the word «fate,» as though it had no meaning at all. Yet call «fate» the «chemistry of the universe,» and the skeptic's face assumes an expression of abject credulity, because the term has a modern ring and smacks of science. What is the difference between the two? We know a little chemistry; we can get something like the perfume of spring violets out of nauseous petroleum, and a flavor of strawberries out of stinking coal-tar. But we do not know much of the myriad natural laws by which our bodies are directed hither and thither, mere atoms in the everlasting whirlpool of all living beings. What can it matter whether we call those rules chemistry or fate? We shall submit to them in the end, with our bodies, though our souls rebel against them eternally. The things that matter are quite different, and the less they have to do with our bodies the better it is for ourselves.

Colonel Wimpole looked at the miniature, and saw that it was a modern copy of a well-known French one, ingeniously set in an old case, to fit which it had perhaps been measured and painted. He looked at the dealer quietly, and the man expressed his despair by turning up his eyes a very little, while he bent his head forward and spread out his palms, abandoning the contest; for he recognized the colonel's right to advise a friend.

«What do you think of it?» asked Mrs. Harmon.

«That depends entirely on what you mean to do with it, and how much you would give for it,» answered the colonel, who would not have let her buy an imitation under any circumstances, but was far too kind-hearted to ruin the shopkeeper in her estimation.

«I rather liked it,» was the answer. «It was for myself. There is something about the expression that pleases me. The lady looks so blindly happy and delighted with herself. It is a cheerful little thing to look at.»

The colonel smiled.

«Will you let me give it to you?» he asked, putting it into her hand. «In that way I shall have some pleasure out of it, too.»

Mrs. Harmon held it for a moment, and looked at him thoughtfully, asking herself whether there were any reason why she should not accept the little present. He was not rich, but she had understood from his first answer that the thing was not worth much after all, and she knew that he would not pay an absurd price for it. Her fingers closed quietly upon it.

«Thank you,» she said; «I wanted it.»

«I will come back this afternoon and pay for it,» said the colonel to the dealer, as the three went out of the shop together a few moments later.

During the little scene young Harmon had looked on sharply and uneasily, but had not spoken.

«How are those things made, mother?» he asked, when they were in the street.

«What things?» asked Mrs. Harmon, gently.

«Those things—what do you call them?

Like what Colonel Wimpole just gave you. How are they made?»

«Oh! miniatures? They are painted on ivory with very fine brushes.»

«How funny! Why do they cost so much money, then?»

His questions were like those of a little child, but his mother's expression did not change as she answered him, always with the same unvarying gentleness.

«People have to be very clever to paint them,» she said. «That is why the very good ones are worth so much. It is like a good tailor, my dear, who is paid well because he makes good coats, whereas a man who only knows how to make workmen's jackets earns very little.»

«That 's not fair,» said young Harmon. «It is n't the man's fault if he is stupid, is it?»

«No, dear, it is n't his fault; it 's his misfortune.»

It took the young man so long to understand this that he said nothing more, trying to think over his mother's words, and getting them by heart, for they pleased him. They walked along in the hot sun, and then crossed the street opposite the Schweizerhof, and got into the shade of the foolish-looking trees that have been stuck about, like Nuremberg toys, between the lake and the highway. The colonel had not spoken since they had left the shop.

«How well you are looking!» he said suddenly, when young Harmon had relapsed into silence. «You are as fresh as a rose.»

«A rose of yesterday,» said Helen Harmon, a little sadly.

Quite naturally, Colonel Wimpole sighed as he walked along at her elbow, for though he did not know that she had ever loved him, he remembered the letter he had written to the man she had afterward married, and he was too much a man himself not to believe that all might have been different if he had not written it.

«Where are you stopping?» he asked, when they had gone a few steps in silence.

Mrs. Harmon named a quiet hotel on the other side of the river.

«Close to us,» observed the colonel, just as they reached the new bridge.

They were half-way across when an exclamation from young Harmon interrupted their conversation, which was, indeed, but a curiously stiff exchange of dry information about themselves and their movements past, planned, and probable. For people who are fond of each other, and meet rarely, are, first of all, anxious to know when they may meet again. But the boy's cry of surprise made them look round.

«Jukes!» he exclaimed loudly. «Jukes!» he repeated more softly, but very emphatically, as though solely for his own benefit.

«Jukes» was his only expression when pleased and surprised. No one knew whether he had ever heard the word, or had invented it, and no one could ever discover what it meant, nor from what it was derived. It seemed to be what Germans call a «nature-sound,» by which he gave vent to his feelings. His mother hated it, but had never been able to induce him to substitute anything else in its place. She followed the direction of his eager glance, for she knew by his tone that he wanted what he saw.

She expected to see a pretty boat, or a big dog, or a gorgeous poster. Archie had a passion for the latter, and he often bought them and took them home with him to decorate his own particular room. He loved best the ones printed in violent and obtrusive colors. The gem of his collection' was a purple woman on a red ground with a wreath of yellow flowers.

But Mrs. Harmon saw neither advertisement, nor dog, nor boat. She saw Sylvia Strahan. She knew the girl very well, and knew Miss Wimpole, of course. The two were walking along on the other side of the bridge, talking together. Against the blaze of the afternoon sun reflected from the still lake they could hardly have recognized the colonel and the Harmons, even if they had looked that way.

«It 's Sylvia, mother,» said Archie, glaring at the girl. «But is n't she grown! And is n't she lovely? Oh! ju-u-ukes!»

His heavy lips thickened outward as he repeated the mysterious ejaculation, and there was more color than usual in his dark face. He was but little older than Sylvia, and the two had played together as small children, but he had never shown any especial preference for her as a playmate. What struck him now was evidently her beauty. There was a look in his eyes, and a sort of bristling of the meeting eyebrows, that reminded Helen of his father, and her white lids quivered for an instant at the recollection, while she felt a little chill run through her.

The colonel also saw.

«Shall we cross over and speak to them,» he asked in a low voice, «or shall we just go on?»

«Let us go on,» answered Helen; «I will go and see them later. Besides, we have passed them now. Let us go on and get into the shade; it is so dreadfully hot here.»

«Won't you stop and speak to them, mother?» asked Archie Harmon, in a tone of deep disappointment. «Why, we have not seen them for ever so long!»

«We shall see them by and by,» answered his mother. «It 's too hot to go back now.»

The young man turned his head and lagged a little, looking after the girl's graceful figure, till he stumbled awkwardly against a curbstone. But he did not protest any more. In his dull way he worshiped his mother as a superior being, and hitherto he had always obeyed her with a half-childish confidence. His arrested intelligence still saw her as he had seen her ten years earlier, as a sort of high and protecting wisdom, incarnate for his benefit, able to answer all questions, and to provide him with unlimited pocket-money wherewith to buy bright-colored posters and other gaudy things that attracted him. Up to a certain point he could be trusted to himself, for he was almost as far from being an idiot as he was from being a normally thinking man. He was about as intelligent and about as well informed as a rather unusually dull school-boy of twelve years or thereabouts. He did not lose his way in the streets, nor drop his money out of his pockets, and he could speak a little French and German, which he had learned from a foreign nurse, enough to buy a ticket or order a meal. But he had scarcely outgrown toys, and his chief delight was to listen to the stories his mother told him. She was not very inventive, and she told the same old ones year after year. They always seemed to be new to him. He could remember faces and names fairly well, and had an average recollection of events in his own life; but it was impossible to teach him anything from books; his handwriting was the heavy, unformed scrawl of a child, and his spelling was one long disaster.

So far, at least, Helen had found only his intellectual deficiency to deal with, and it was a perpetual shame to her, and a cause of perpetual sorrow and sympathy. But he was affectionate and docile enough, not cruel, as some such beings are, and certainly not vicious, so far as she could see. Dull boys are rarely mischievous, though they are sometimes cruel, for mischief implies an imagination which dullness does not possess. Archie Harmon was never violent, but he occasionally showed a strength that surprised her, though he never seemed to care about exhibiting it. Once she had fallen and hurt her foot, and he had carried her up many stairs like a child. After that she had felt now and then as men must feel who tame wild beasts and control them.

He worshiped her, and she saw that he looked with a sort of pity on all other women, young or old, as not worthy to be compared with her in any way. She had begun to hope that she might be spared the humiliation of ever seeing him in love, despised or pitied, as the case might be, by some commonplace pretty girl with white teeth and pink cheeks. She feared that, and she feared lest he should some day taste drink and follow his father's ways to the same hideous end. But as yet he had been like a child.

It was no wonder that she shuddered when, as he looked at Sylvia Strahan, she saw something in his face which had never been there before, and heard that queer word of his uttered in such a tone. She wondered whether Colonel Wimpole had heard and seen, too, and for some time the three walked on in silence.

«Will you come in?» asked Mrs. Harmon, as they reached the door of her hotel.

The colonel followed her to her little sitting-room, and Archie disappeared, for the conversation of those whom he still, in his own thoughts, regarded as «grown-up people» wearied him beyond bearing.

«My dear friend,» said Colonel Wimpole, when they were alone, «I am very glad to see you!»

He held one of her hands in his while he spoke the conventional words; his eyes were a little misty, and there was a certain tone in his voice which no one but Helen Harmon had ever heard.

«I am glad, too,» she said simply, and she drew away her hand from his with a sort of deprecation which he only half understood, for he knew only that half of the truth which was in himself.

They sat down, as they had sat many a time in their lives, at a little distance from each other, and just so that each had to turn the head a little to face the other. It was easier to talk in that way, because there was a secret between them, besides many things which were not secrets, but of which they did not wish to speak.

«It is terribly long since we last met,» said the colonel. «Do you remember? I went to see you in New York the day before we started for Japan. You had just come back from the country, and your house was in confusion.»

«Oh, yes, I remember,» replied Mrs. Harmon. «Yes, it is terribly long, but nothing is changed.»

«Nothing?» The colonel meant to ask her about Harmon, and she understood.

«Nothing,» she answered gravely. «There was no improvement when the doctor wrote on the first of last month. I shall have another report in a day or two; but they are all exactly alike. He will just live on, as he is now, to the end of his life.»

«To the end of his life,» repeated the colonel, in a low voice, and the two turned their heads and looked at each other.

«He is in perfect health,» said Mrs. Harmon, looking away again.

She drew out a long hat-pin and lifted her hat from her head with both hands, for it was a hot afternoon, and she had come into the sitting-room as she was. The colonel noticed how neatly and carefully she did the thing. It seemed almost unnecessary to do it so slowly.

«It is so hot,» she said, as she laid the hat on the table.

She was pale now, perhaps with the heat of which she complained, and he saw how tired her face was.

«Is this state of things really to go on?» he asked suddenly.

She moved a little, but did not look at him.

«I am not discontented,» she said; «I am not—not altogether unhappy.»

«Why should you not be released from it all?» asked the colonel.

It was the first time he had ever suggested such a possibility, and she looked away from him.

«It is not as though it had all been different before he lost his mind,» he went on, seeing that she did not answer at once. «It is not as if you had not had fifty good reasons for a divorce before he finally went mad. What is the use of denying that?»

«Please do not talk about a divorce,» said Mrs. Harmon, steadily.

«Please forgive me if I do, my dear friend,» returned the colonel, almost hotly, for he was suddenly convinced that he was right, and when he was right it was hard to stop him. «You have spent half your life in sacrificing all of yourself. Surely you have a right to the other half. There is not even the excuse that you might still do him some good by remaining his wife in name. His mind is gone, and he could not recognize you if he saw you.»

«What should I gain by such a step, then?» asked Helen, turning upon him rather suddenly. «Do you think I would marry again?» There was an effort in her voice. «I hate to talk in this way, for I detest the idea of divorce, and the principle of it, and all its consequences. I believe it is going to be the ruin of half the world in the end. It is a disgrace, in whatever way you look at it!»

«A large part of the world does not seem to think so,» observed the colonel, rather surprised by her outbreak, though in any case excepting his own he would have agreed with her.

«It would be better if the whole world thought so,» she answered with energy. «Do you know what divorce means in the end? It means the abolition of marriage laws altogether; it means reducing marriage to a mere experiment, which may last a few days, a few weeks, or a few months, according to the people who try it. There are men and women already who have been divorced and married again half a dozen times. Before the next generation is old that will be the rule and not the exception.»

«Dear me!» exclaimed Colonel Wimpole, «I hope not!»

«I know you agree with me,» said Mrs. Harmon, with conviction. «You only argue on the other side because—» She stopped short.

«Why?» He did not look at her as he asked the question.

«Because you are my best friend,» she answered, after a moment's hesitation, «and because you have got it into your head that I should be happier. I cannot imagine why. It would make no difference at all in my life —now.»

The last word fell from her lips with a regretful tone, and lingered a little on the air like the sad singing of a bell's last note, not broken by a following stroke. But the colonel was not satisfied.

«It may make all the difference, even now,» he said. «Suppose that Harmon were to recover.»

Helen did not start, for the thought had been long familiar to her, but she pressed her lips together a little, and let her head rest against the back of her chair, half closing her eyes.

«It is possible,» continued the colonel. «You know as well as I do that doctors are not always right, and there is nothing about which so little is really certain as insanity.»

«I do not think it is possible.»

«But it is, nevertheless. Imagine what it would be if you began to hear that he was better and better, and finally well, and, at last, that there was no reason for keeping him in confinement.»

Mrs. Harmon's eyes were quite closed now, as she leaned back. It was horrible to her to wish that her husband might remain mad till he died, yet she thought of what her own life must be if he should recover. She was silent, fighting it out in her heart. It was not easy. It was hard even to see what was right to wish, for in every human being there is the prime right of self-preservation, against which no argument avails, save that of a divinely good and noble cause to be defended. Yet the moral wickedness of praying that Harmon might be a madman all the rest of his life frightened her. Throughout twenty years and more she had faced suffering and shame without flinching, and without allowing herself one thought of retaliation or hatred. She had been hardened to the struggle, and was not a woman to yield if it should begin again; but she shrank from it now, as the best and bravest may shrink at the thought of torture, though they would not groan in slow fire.

«Just think what it might be,» resumed Colonel Wimpole. «Why not look the facts in the face while there is time? If he were let out he would come back to you, and you would receive him, for I know what you are. You would think it right to take him back because you promised long ago to love, honor, and obey him; to love, to honor, and to obey—Henry Harmon!»

The colonel's steady gray eyes flashed for an instant, and his gentle voice was suddenly thick and harsh as he pronounced the last words. They meant terribly much to the woman who heard them, and in her distress she leaned forward in her seat and put up her hands to her temples, as though she had pain, gently pushing back the heavy hair that she wore so low on her forehead. Wimpole had never seen her so much moved, and the gesture itself was unfamiliar to him. He did not remember ever to have seen her touch her hair with her hands, as some women do. He watched her now as he continued to speak.

«You did all three,» he said. «You honored him, you loved him, and you obeyed him for a good many years. But he neither loved, nor honored, nor cherished you. I believe that is the man's part of the contract, is it not? And marriage is always called a contract, is it not? And, in any contract, both parties must do what they have promised, so that if one party fails, the other is not bound. Is not that true? And, Heaven knows, Harmon failed badly enough!»

«Don't! Please don't talk in that way! No, no, no! Marriage is not a contract; it is a bond, a vow—something respected by man because it is sacred before God. If Henry failed a thousand times more, I should be just as much bound to keep my promise.»

Her head sank still more forward, and her hands pushed her hair straight back from the temples.

«You will never persuade me of that,» answered the colonel. «You will never make me believe—» He stopped short, for as he watched her he saw what he had never seen before, a deep and crooked scar high on her forehead. «What is that?» he asked suddenly, leaning toward her, his eyes fixed on the ugly mark.

She started, stared at him, dropping her hands, realized what he had seen, and then instantly turned away. He could see that her fingers trembled as she tried to draw her hair down again. It was not like her to be vain, and he guessed at once that she had some reason other than vanity for hiding the old wound.

«What is that scar?» he asked again, determined to have an answer. «I never saw it before.»

«It is a—I was hurt long ago—» She hesitated, for she did not know how to lie.

«Not so very long ago,» said the colonel. «I know something about scars, and that one is not many years old. It does not look as though you had got it in a fall, either. Besides, if you had, you would not mind telling me, would you?»

«Please don't ask me about it! I cannot tell you about it—»

The colonel's face was hardening quickly. The lines came out in it, stern and straight, as when, at evening, a sudden frost falls upon a still water, and the first ice-needles shoot out, clear and stiff. Then came the certainty, and Wimpole looked as he had looked long ago in battle.

«Harmon did that,» he said at last, and the first curse that followed was not the less fierce because it was unspoken.

Helen's hands shook violently now, for no one had ever known how she had been wounded. But she said nothing, though she knew that her silence meant her assent. Wimpole rose suddenly, straight as a rifle, and walked to the window, turning his back upon her. He could say things there under his breath, which she could not understand, and he said them earnestly.

«He did not know what he was doing,» Helen spoke at last, rather unsteadily.

The colonel turned on his heels at the window, facing her, and his lips still moved slowly, though no words came. Helen looked at him, and knew that she was glad of his silent wrath. Not realizing what she was thinking of, she wondered what sort of death Harmon would have died if Richard Wimpole had seen him strike her to the ground with a cut-glass decanter. For a moment the cloak of mercy and forgiveness was rent from head to heel. The colonel would have killed the man with those rather delicate-looking hands of his, talking to him all the time in a low voice. That was what she thought, and perhaps she was not very far wrong. Even now, it was as well for Harmon that he was safe in his asylum on the other side of an ocean.

It was some time before Wimpole could speak. Then he came and stood before Helen.

« You will stay a few days? You do not mean to go away at once? » he said, with a question.

« Yes. »

« Then I think I will go away now, and come and see you again later. »

He took her hand rather mechanically and left the room. But she understood, and was grateful.

(To be continued.)

*F. Marion Crawford.*

# AMERICA AND ENGLAND.

1895–1896.

I.

HAST thou forgot the breasts that gave us suck,
  And whence our likeness to our fathers came,
  Though from our arms twice stooping with the same
Great blow that Runnymede and Naseby struck?
Out of thy heart the imperial spark we pluck
  Which in our blood is breaking into flame;
  Oh, of one honor make not double shame;
Give not the English race to wanton luck!

Thy reef of war across our seaboard thrown,
  Fortress and arsenal against us stored—
Trust not in them! the awful summons blown,
  High o'er the long sea-blaze and battle poured
Through all the marches of the open North,
  On our uplifted arms thy Child rides forth.

II.

Mother of nations, of them eldest we,
  Well is it found, and happy for the state,
  When that which makes men proud first makes them great,
And such our fortune is who sprang from thee,
And brought to this new land from over sea
  The faith that can with every household mate,
  And freedom whereof law is magistrate,
And thoughts that make men brave, and leave them free.

O Mother of our faith, our law, our lore,
  What shall we answer thee if thou shouldst ask
How this fair birthright doth in us increase?
  There is no home but Christ is at the door;
Freely our toiling millions choose life's task;
  Justice we love, and next to justice peace.

III.

What is the strength of England, and her pride
  Among the nations, when she makes her boast?
  Has the East heard it, where her far-flung host
Hangs like a javelin in India's side?
Does the sea know it, where her navies ride,
  Like towers of stars, about the silver coast,
  Or from the great Capes to the uttermost
Parts of the North like ocean meteors glide?

Answer, O South, if yet where Gordon sank,
  Spent arrow of the far and lone Soudan,
There comes a whisper out of wasted death!
  O every ocean, every land, that drank
The blood of England, answer, if ye can,
  What is it that giveth her immortal breath?

IV.

Then the West answered: «Is the sword's keen edge
  Like to the mind for sharpness? Doth the flame
  Devour like thought? Many with chariots came,
Squadron and phalanx, legion, square, and wedge;
They mounted up; they wound from ledge to ledge
  Of battle-glory dark with battle-shame;
  But God hath hurled them from the heights of fame
Who from the soul took no eternal pledge.

«Because above her people and her throne
  She hath erected reason's sovereignty;
Because wherever human speech is known
  The touch of English breath doth make thought free;
Therefore forever is her glory blown
  About the hills, and flashed beneath the sea.»

V.

First of mankind we bid our eagles pause
  Before the pure tribunal of the mind,
  Where swordless justice shall the sentence find,
And righteous reason arbitrate the cause.
First of mankind, whom yet no power o'erawes,
  One kin would we confederate and bind;
  Let the great instrument be made and signed,
The mold and pattern of earth's mightier laws!

Crown with this act the thousand years of thought,
  O Mother-Queen, and wheresoever roams
Thy sea-flown brood, and bulwarked states hath wrought
  Far as the loneliest wave of ocean foams,
Thy children's love with veneration brought
  Shall warm thy hearthstone from their million homes.

*G. E. Woodberry.*

# TOPICS OF THE TIME

### General Grant's Fame.

WITH most actors on the stage of public affairs, the height of reputation is reached when they retire to private life or are buried with all the honors. They are useful to their time, but their acts are not more significant to posterity than the deeds of their successors in the current affairs of state. They leave behind them no record of greatness—in the case of some, perhaps, because they were not called upon to act in a great crisis; and if they die in the sanctity of a great reputation, their fame fades away like a repeating echo. But when true greatness has put itself on record, the grave becomes but the portal of a new earthly existence; thereafter it serves mankind as a standard of duty and character.

Down to the very grave there were fellow-actors ready to deny General Grant every claim to greatness. When the posthumous testimony of his «Memoirs» appeared they relented a little, partly in pitying respect for the heroic circumstances in which his public testament was written. Every year of the decade since his death has witnessed the steady growth of popular interest in his life, and of admiration for what he did and was. When his worthy monument, grandly placed, is formally dedicated on his birthday in the coming spring, his fame will be commensurate with the extraordinary honor thereby paid to the memory of a great soldier.

It must always be a gratification to the American people that the first one, apparently, to perceive the greatness of Grant, the man of action, was that other type of American greatness, Lincoln, the man of ideas. Testimony to his early insight, and that of one of Grant's fellow-generals, is given in the «Open Letters» of this number of THE CENTURY; and in General Porter's recollections of the personal Grant there will be found data of the highest value and authenticity for a better understanding of his character.

### Old English Masters.

HOGARTH'S «Shrimp Girl,» the frontispiece of this number of THE CENTURY, is printed as the first example of the new series of «Masters,» engraved from the originals by the distinguished American engraver, Timothy Cole. The present unusual interest in the art of the great English painters will give the new series of wood-engravings special acceptability. Mr. Cole has taken up this work in the same spirit manifested in his exquisite and unique reproduction of the Old Italian and of the Old Dutch masters. His literary collaborator is Professor John C. Van Dyke. Not only have some of the best known pictures of the English school been selected from the public collections for reproduction, but permission has been obtained in behalf of THE CENTURY for the engraving of some of the finest examples of English art in the hands of private owners.

### The Better New York.

AT a time when civic patriotism is being so generally awakened in America, and the people are rescuing their municipalities from the hands of political adventurers and jobbers, the careful study made by United States Consul Parker of the government of Birmingham, and printed in this number of THE CENTURY, will be found particularly interesting by inhabitants of the metropolitan districts, as they are now engaged in the work of unifying and remodeling their local government. It should be understood, of course, that our conditions are different, and that every detail of the Birmingham plan is not necessarily a precedent for us. But this one phase of the Birmingham system should not fail to be impressed upon American communities—namely, the necessity of carrying on the local government by means of the best morality and intelligence that the city is fortunate enough to possess. While the Greater New York may be said to exist in law, it will be several years before it will affect the political life of the city; but the Better New York is already an accomplished fact. It represents something more than a material reality, for it embodies the intellectual force of a moral victory.

Until 1893, when, as a climax of degradation, the public reception to a descendant of Columbus was made ridiculous by the leadership of a Tammany mayor, supported at his right hand by the city's most notorious promoter of gambling, another member of the Reception Committee in a box near by being the most conspicuous murderer in public office, it was natural that the country should regard New York chiefly as an exemplar of municipal jobbery. But when, in the following year, the city not only turned the criminal element out of office, but also sent a few of the lesser malefactors to prison, the country was quick to recognize the existence of the forces which have rapidly created the Better New York.

The traits of the Better New York are pleasing and obvious. One feature is as impressive to those who are native to the city as to the thousands who continuously succeed one another as visitors. It is a feature which is lowest in the scale of progress, yet first in physical importance—the never-ending drudgery of municipal housekeeping, the cleaning of the streets. The last manful effort at reform brought to that task a man educated in the art of sanitary improvement, skilled through military experience in the handling of organized forces of men, and, above all, willing to make a personal sacrifice for the sake of showing that it was unnecessary for New York to wallow in its own filth. The never-to-be-effaced result is a city as clean as that city of model neatness, Paris, and possibly even more exemplary as regards the streets that are the breathing-places as well as the highways of the poor; for Colonel Waring applied his rigorous system, by preference, to the quarters which his predecessors had always neglected, in their scheme of producing the greatest apparent effect with the least possible effort by devoting themselves to Broadway and Fifth Avenue. Not since the first review of the paid fire-department, a third of a century ago, has anything been seen in New York so significant of a new era of permanent improvement as the first parade of «Waring's angels.» That public inspection of the first street-cleaning force of the city was a complete vindication of every detail of the new organization, and especially of the white duck uniforms; for one who undertakes the mission of a cleaner should himself have a sense of personal cleanliness.

Another material sign of the Better New York is the improved condition of the streets and parks. It will be claimed for the Tammany régime that these reforms were of their devising, and it is a fact that all the credit they have deserved was in that direction. It used to be said in the days of the Tweed martyrdom that the Tammany «boss» had conferred great blessings on the city by his encouragement of lavish expenditure on the streets and parks. But Tweed deserved no credit. In order to steal by his method, which was merely an exaggeration of the surviving Tammany method, he had to spend the public money lavishly for an obvious public necessity. That some good was attained in the parks depended on his carrying out the plans of honest experts, who then and since have been at the head of the profession of landscape architecture in this country. In fact, there is not a detail in the making of the Better New York, from the construction of the city hall, in the first decade of the century, to the application of honest business methods in municipal affairs under Mayor Strong, that may not be credited to educated men, having special training for their professional or business duties.

In the way of moral improvement no better evidence of advance is needed than the Tammany resistance offered, within and without the police force, to the intelligent and courageous efforts that have been made by President Roosevelt and his colleagues to correct the scandalous evils of that department. In spite of laws obstructive to effective organization, and notwithstanding crafty misrepresentation as to prevailing crime, life and property are safer in the Better New York than during the previous era of blackmail; and the conduct of the various kinds of purveyors of vice has never been so restrained, and so little invasive of public order and decency.

In addition to all this, civil service reform has made immense strides; unsavory tenement-house districts are being cleaned out and small parks are letting in light and air, while the housing of the people is constantly improving.

A city without adequate means of spreading and preserving the knowledge of civilization is a misnomer. To the relatively backward metropolis has come, at last a new system of school management, equal, under intelligent and honest direction, to the higher demands of the age. Her two universities are taking on the material as well as the intellectual aspects of greatness. Her scientific and art museums possess treasures of world-wide importance; the halls of her professional, technical, and art schools are thronged by thousands of talented students; a great public library commensurate with the city's intelligence and wealth awaits only a roof large enough to cover it; architecture and sculpture are offering to wealth and to patriotism the means of monumental grandeur; in short, the Better New York appeals to the pride of the nation with a force which the Greater New York may enhance by political honor.

### Cheap Money in Two Wars.

IN the very striking paper which we publish in this number of THE CENTURY on «Why the Confederacy Failed» there is a lesson in national finance that is none the less impressive because it is so familiar. It is the same lesson that has been taught, at frequent intervals during the past four hundred years, by every nation that has had the short-sightedness to tamper with its standard of value. «The Confederate government,» says the writer, «was smothered and strangled to death with its own irredeemable paper money.» He does not say that this was the sole cause of the failure of the Southern rebellion, but he places it first among three causes which he enumerates. His argument in support of his views speaks for itself. There may be difference of opinion on his second and third causes, but on his first there is likely to be none among men whose opinion is best worth having. No cause, however deserving, could have succeeded on such a financial basis as that on which the war of secession was conducted. The war of the revolution, as Mr. Rose points out, would have failed had not the French and Dutch come to the rescue of Washington and his army with real money.

On this point Washington's own words are conclusive. The crisis came in the spring of 1781, the seventh year of the war. The continental money had then become so worthless as to make useless further employment of it as a means of defraying the expenses of the war. John Laurens, one of Washington's aides-de-camp, was selected to go to Paris, to press upon the French government the needs of the army, and raise a new loan. Washington wrote to him on the eve of his departure: «Be assured, my dear Laurens, day does not follow night more certainly than it brings with it some additional proof of the impracticability of carrying on the war without the aids you are directed to solicit. . . . In a word, we are at the end of our tether, and now or never our deliverance must come.» About the same time Hamilton wrote to General Greene that public credit was so totally lost that nobody would furnish aid even in the face of impending ruin. To the appeals of Laurens France responded with a loan of four millions of livres; the French king granted six millions more as a free gift, and also guaranteed in Holland a loan of ten millions more, making in all twenty million livres, or about five million dollars. This real money put such new life into the American army that Cornwallis was forced to surrender a few months later, and independence was won.

It is the opinion of most financial authorities that the greenbacks, instead of being a help to the North during the war of the rebellion, were a hindrance, and that we won in spite of them rather than because of them. Certain it is that they added enormously to the cost of the war. Mr. Henry C. Adams, in his work on «Public Debts,» shows that the war cost us over $800,000,000 more than it would had we not issued the greenbacks and thus gone off the gold standard. If the government had relied on increased taxation for funds to prosecute the war, it would have remained on the gold basis, and would have bought all its supplies on the same basis. At the same time it would have maintained its credit unimpaired, and would have been able to borrow all the additional money it needed at much better rates than it actually paid. As it was, it paid an average premium of 50 per cent. on all its purchases for nearly three years and a half. The total expenditure of the four years of the war was over $3,350,000,000, of which Mr. Adams estimates that $2,500,000,000 consisted of purchases in the open market, where the greenback dollar bought only 66 cents' worth of goods. In other words, we spent $2,500,000,000 and got in return only $1,630,000,000 worth of property. The difference, $870,000,000, was the unnecessary cost to the taxpayers which the greenback entailed.

It has been demonstrated with mathematical accuracy, in tables published recently by the National Bureau of Labor, that a heavy share of this unnecessary burden fell upon the laboring classes. These tables show that when, in 1865, prices stood at 217 as compared with 100 in 1860, wages had reached only 143; that is, while prices had more than doubled, wages had risen less than one half. This has been the case invariably when a nation has indulged in the experiment of cheapening its money. Wages have always been the last to respond to the new order of things, and prices the first. So convinced was Secretary Chase, who was the author of the greenback currency, of the mistake that was made in issuing it, that, as chief justice of the Supreme Court, he subsequently expressed strong disapproval of his own act as secretary of the treasury. Speaking of the legal-tender quality of the greenbacks, he said that that quality did not add anything to their value or usefulness, and added: «The legal-tender quality was only valuable for purposes of dishonesty. Every honest purpose was answered as well, or better, without it.»

As our readers will remember, we have pointed out in this department of THE CENTURY that legal-tender money, from the first appearance of it in history, has been inferior money, and that the conferring of that quality upon it has been for the purpose of forcing it into circulation against the public will.[1] The best test of any money is, Will it circulate without this quality? Nobody claims that gold needs it. The international trade of the world has been carried on from its beginning without any legal-tender money. The gold-standard advocates to-day have urged repeatedly, as the solution of the silver controversy, that we have free coinage of both gold and silver, with no legal-tender quality upon either, and let the people decide which they prefer as money; but the silver advocates will not listen to this. They demand the free coinage of silver at 16 to 1, or at about half the value of silver, and declare that it must also be made legal tender in payment of all debts. This was the experiment which was tried with the continental and greenback money, and which failed in both cases. It succeeded best with the greenbacks because the North succeeded in the war, and because of the North's enormous resources and wealth; but even then the value of the greenbacks could not be kept from falling to 36 cents on a dollar, their average value during the war being only 50 cents. They expressed at all times the amount of public confidence in the government's ability to keep its promises to pay all its obligations in gold. The Confederate money had no legal-tender quality, but it had value so long as there was public confidence in the South in the triumph of the Southern cause. It began to depreciate the moment that confidence began to wane.

The lesson of these experiences at the present time is obvious. If it should be decreed that a silver dollar worth 53 cents should be legal tender for all debts public and private, and that an unlimited amount of such dollars should be issued, the inevitable result would be that gold would go to a premium, and we should be on a silver standard, with all prices doubled. The wage-earner would find no immediate change in his income, but he would discover that everything he bought cost him twice as much. The difference between a silver dollar worth only 53 cents and a paper dollar worth nothing would be that whereas the latter might ultimately be reduced through government bankruptcy to absolute worthlessness, the silver dollar would not fall below its bullion price. It would always sell for the amount of silver it contained, and this would go up and down with the market value of silver bullion. But it would, by being made a forced standard of value, entail a vast amount of harm upon the nation, subject all wage-earners to enormous loss, and, by destroying the credit of the government, bring us into disgrace with the civilized world, dealing a staggering blow to our prosperity and development, from which we should not recover for a quarter of a century.

1 See "Cheap-Money Experiments," 3d edition, THE CENTURY Co.: chapter on "Legal-tender Money in History."

### The Rise of General Grant.

ON the 24th day of May, 1861, from his humble home at Galena, U. S. Grant, then a private citizen of Illinois engaged with his father in the leather trade, despatched a letter to the adjutant-general of the regular army, offering his services to the government during the impending civil war. Although the good offices of an influential person were volunteered, we are told by Grant in the «Memoirs» that he declined all indorsement for permission to fight for his country. So, without support and probably with but little hope, he sent forward the application which has just been found in the files of the War Department, and of which a facsimile is herewith printed for the first time. Aside from extrinsic reasons, I think the reader will agree with me that this letter is a striking paper, by reason of its trenchant conciseness in setting forth that which the writer with undoubted anxiety wished to make known to the military authorities. But in the eyes of the world, the distinction to which Grant subsequently rose gives to it its chief interest, and a value far beyond the ordinary.

While evidently the composition of a man of firm purpose,—one having complete confidence in himself,—there is yet about this application a modest diffidence which is a true index to a great personality. In directness and precision it is remarkable, like all his writings denoting a well-ordered intellect. I have seen letters of six or eight pages, written by Grant amid the wearing excitement of a gigantic and doubtful campaign, without an erasure or interlineation, yet couched in clear, strong English which it is a pleasure to read. There are a score of such in the Was Department archives.

The result of this effort was typical of the attitude of the higher authorities toward Grant throughout the earlier months of his career. The application bore no fruit, it was not even answered by the usual courteous note which says nothing. While others from civil life were made major-generals, brigadiers, and colonels, and at once received high commands, the man who modestly thought he might be competent by reason of his education and past service to command a regiment remained unnoticed. Fortunately for the country, Governor Yates took note of Grant's capacity and merits, and conferred upon him the command of an unruly regiment. Thus, ignored at Washington, the future chief, through the local authorities, got his foot upon the first rung of the ladder.

It is very singular, considering Grant's early appearance upon the stage with an important geographical command, and the further and more dominant fact of his conspicuous successes, that the Union military authorities were so belated in «catching on» to the promising officer Yates had discovered. It is not at all surprising that the general public, with its eyes admiringly fixed on the star performers at the great military headquarters, should overlook the silent man who did not have the trick of advertising his own performances. The people were wistfully looking for the Napoleon they never doubted was concealed somewhere about, ready to spring forth to the supreme command full-fledged, and put down the rebellion in a single brilliant campaign; and not until after McClellan's signal failure did they reluctantly abandon this hope and begin to look around for practical possibilities

Grant's first military success, vastly important as it was to the cause, to the administration, and to General Halleck's personal fortunes, received but scant notice in high quarters other than in the form of criticism. Even Mr. Lincoln, always generous, and quick to notice successful officers, made no sign. The spontaneous acclaim which greeted lesser exploits of other generals was never heard in the early days in connection with Grant's achievements, and it is a queer fact that, from first to last, they never aroused any enthusiasm for Grant personally. While there were fugitive manifestations of gratitude, there was no popular and official shouting of the kind that, strangely enough, greeted the comparatively barren action of Murfreesboro', for instance, which Halleck effusively asseverated entitled Rosecrans to the «admiration of the world.»

The capture of Donelson, so timely to check the rising European ardor for intervention, was not heralded as a Grant victory. True, the magnitude and far-reaching effects of the blow were fully appreciated by both government and people, but Grant somehow at the time seemed to be dissociated from it. His glory was largely appropriated by others, or cunningly belittled, and for a time he was even deprived of his command. If for a brief moment there was an incipient outbreak threatening to make a hero of the right man, it was at once chilled into silence by Halleck's equivocal reports to McClellan of «disorders» that prevailed after the Confederate surrender, of «insubordination» on Grant's part—wholly unwarranted, as it afterward transpired, but tending none the less to strengthen some vague stories of Grant's «habits» that now began to be bruited about, set afloat nobody knows exactly how. Answering, McClellan—reminding one of Artemus Ward's willingness to sacrifice all his wife's relations to put down the rebellion—telegraphed Halleck not to hesitate to arrest Grant if discipline demanded such an extraordinary proceeding

In the light of what occurred afterward, and of our present minute knowledge of the characters and careers of these three personages, could one well imagine anything more absurdly grotesque than this: two mere theorists, organizers of dress parades as it were, sitting

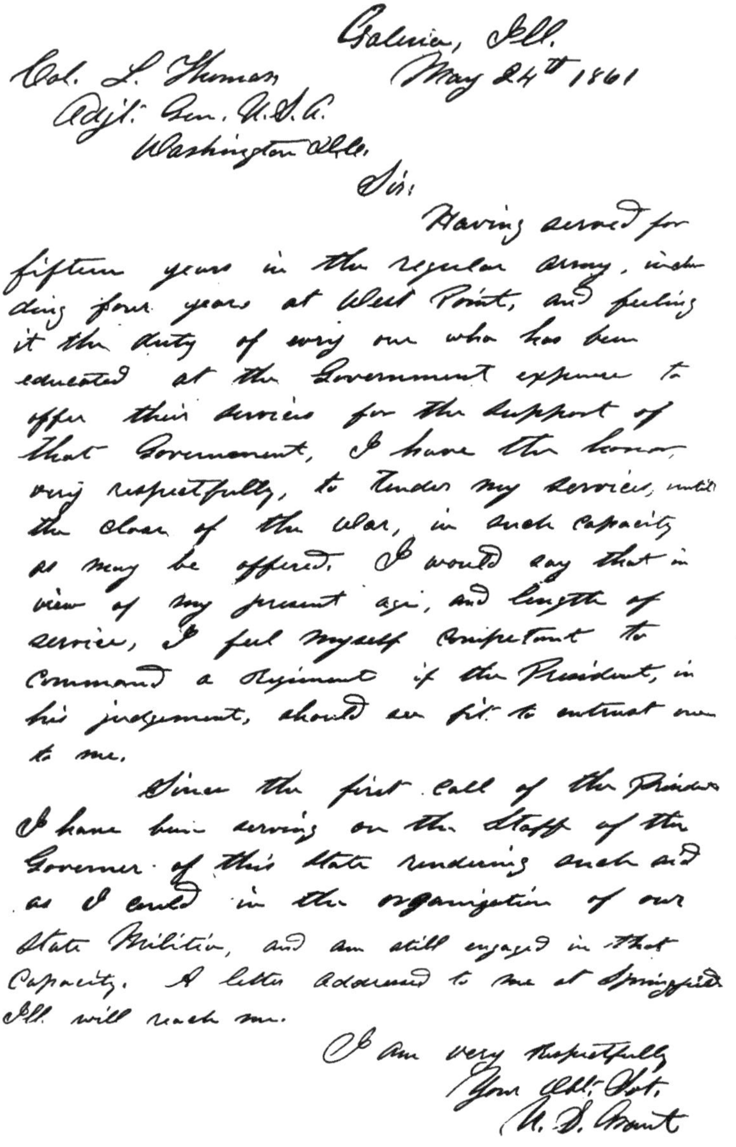

Galena, Ill.
May 24th 1861

Col. L. Thomas
Adjt. Gen. U.S.A.
Washington D.C.

Sir:

Having served for fifteen years in the regular Army, including four years at West Point, and feeling it the duty of every one who has been educated at the Government expense to offer their services for the support of that Government, I have the honor, very respectfully, to tender my services, until the close of the War, in such capacity as may be offered. I would say that in view of my present age, and length of service, I feel myself competent to command a Regiment if the President, in his judgement, should see fit to entrust one to me.

Since the first call of the President I have been serving on the Staff of the Governer of this State rendering such aid as I could in the organization of our State Militia, and am still engaged in that capacity. A letter addressed to me at Springfield Ill. will reach me.

I am very respectfully
Your Obt. Svt.
U. S. Grant

FACSIMILE OF GENERAL GRANT'S APPLICATION FOR A COMMAND IN 1861.

in solemn judgment upon the man of action in the very midst of a triumphant campaign? Had either McClellan or Halleck at that day won such a victory as Donelson, —an improbable speculation,—he would instantly have been glorified by resolutions of high civic bodies, and showered with congratulatory telegrams. Grant modestly announced the victory to his immediate superior, and, as we have seen, Halleck did the rest. There were no congratulations for Grant. It is doubtful if subsequently there was not a covert attempt to forestall his promotion.

Again, after Shiloh, the original scandal about Grant's «habits» was revived with variations, supplemented with the more cruel falsehood that he had stolidly permitted his army to be surprised and cut to pieces, and was saved from utter annihilation only by the arrival of Buell. The malignancy with which he was pursued is almost past comprehension. He came near being submerged by the storm. A second time Grant was temporarily deprived of his command, much in the same indirect manner, by the same jealous influence, and probably for the same sinister purpose. I doubt if Colonel McClure's ingenious explanation of Grant's temporary effacement is the complete story of that episode.

Shiloh was the first battle-field of the war where carnage rose to the gruesome dignity of the grand scale, and the nerves of the supersensitive were greatly shaken at the spectacle. The battle was a trial of strength between the two armies at the unexpected invitation of the Confederate commander, in which at the close of the first day he was clearly worsted. Six months later, after McClellan and Pope had familiarized the country with lost or drawn battles and the aspect of rivers of human blood, Shiloh would have been hailed for what it actually was,—a real as well as a technical Union victory,—and no attention whatever paid to the butcher's bill, which was equally large on the other side. Ultimately a better understanding of that battle prevailed, accompanied as a natural sequence by a dawning popular comprehension of Grant's scope of usefulness; there was gradual growth of a quiet, yet firm confidence in him as a commander.

Dealing with all sorts of commanders, and particularly with the bad sort—always most in evidence—that failed to accomplish anything of moment except to bring the government into disrepute with the people, in the natural course of events President Lincoln eventually began to note this one man of a genus distinct from his other generals, who always brought victory and honor instead of defeat and humiliation, who needed no urging to go forward, and who accomplished more with less relative means than any other man in the service; and thus noting, his honest heart was glad. And thenceforward Lincoln stood by Grant through thick and thin—one of the very greatest tributes that could be paid to the worth of any man of that epoch. It may be said that this was easy because Grant was almost uniformly successful; yet there was one short period following Shiloh when the President's powerful support was necessary to save him from obscurity. Even then the President had not come to a full appreciation of Grant's sterling qualities as a commander.

Colonel McClure records that just after Shiloh he went to Washington, at the instance of the sentimentalists, to secure Grant's removal from command. After listening in gloomy silence to McClure's earnest representations concerning the Western general's unpopularity, intemperance, and incompetence, which were steadily dragging the administration down to ruin, and every possible appeal for an immediate change, the President straightened himself up and with earnest decision said, «I can't spare this man; *he fights.*» This closed the conference; Colonel McClure perceived that Mr. Lincoln's resolution was unalterable.

Grant never had a personal following in the country at large, like that of McClellan or Rosecrans, by whom their important services were, without question or criticism, accepted at their own valuation and even exaggerated. His battles and victories—some of them equal to the most brilliant in the annals of war—were received by the public either with cold, analytical reserve, or at best in measured terms of praise. Yet, as I have said, it was looking and longing for a military idol. Why, then, it should fight off Grant's fame until the final test, should begrudgingly yield to him its plaudits only at the eleventh hour, goes beyond my comprehension; it is rather a matter of astonishment that he was not fairly overwhelmed with cheap honors and lip-service. This strange, half-hearted manner on the part of the public of tendering its applause for magnificent offerings of victory may have been one of the «mysteries of Grant» of which General Badeau tells us, but it was more probably the result of the systematic attacks made with a purpose to prevent his rise. They were so plausibly and persistently urged as to mislead many honest men; for a time it was generally believed that his successes were the result, perhaps, of mere blundering luck.

General Horace Porter has said that General Grant's «unassuming manner, and absolute loyalty to his superiors and to the work in which he was engaged, inspired loyalty in others, and gained him the devotion of the humblest of his subordinates.» And on his own part, Grant's tenacious loyalty to friendship was so unfeigned and marked a characteristic as to be a positive eccentricity. Herein we have the key to one of the great forces of his character: he was endowed with that singular quality which, without effort, bound to himself with hooks of steel the unhesitating confidence, the unqualified love, of every one who was thrown into intimate personal or official association with him. One and all, those who knew him most thoroughly became his unquestioning adherents. This is a most extraordinary fact in connection with one who, apparently repellent to the world at large, was almost throughout his public career the victim of the malevolent calumny of designing cabals, always decried, misunderstood, and underestimated. Yet he was unobtrusive, avoided personal controversies, and shunned politics; solicited no favors; never annoyed his superiors or the government with importunities or demands of any kind, except for permission to press forward; and interfered with nobody except the enemy. The antithesis developed in these attributes of Grant's personality is so remarkable as to have fixed the attention of abler students of ethnology than myself.

But Grant was not prone to lavish his friendships indiscriminately. He was not lacking in penetration, nor was he a dull student of mankind. The official records, and especially those made by himself, leave no room for doubt that he had a keen discernment of character, but more especially of those elements that make the good soldier. After he attained to the dignity of exercising his own choice, he seldom erred in the selection of agents to carry on military operations. The rise of Sherman, McPherson, Sheridan, Schofield, Ord, Terry, and of some younger men like James H. Wilson and Emory Upton, aside from their high intrinsic merits, was largely owing to Grant's appreciation. On the other hand, he had but little patience with slow and inefficient officers, and none whatever with worthless ones; and he did not lack the moral nerve to put them aside whenever the necessity occurred or opportunity offered.

The deeper one dives into the official archives, the more his admiration and respect for Grant increases. His own letters and reports are the strongest evidence of a thoroughly honest and upright nature, as well as of his singleness of purpose and his comprehensive ability. There is no posing for effect, no waste of words in fine writing; everything is simple, earnest, and straightforward. His style is admirable; not an undignified line, nor a base or cunning motive, can be detected in all his multitudinous correspondence, public and private. Of course the greater part of the mass was written without expectation or design that it would ever see the light, and hence is all the more valuable and reliable as an index to a character which has been somewhat of a puzzle to superficial observers.

In Vol. XXXI, Part II, of the War Records, at page 402, there is a striking letter bearing upon Grant's personal and military character which, having never been exploited in the public press, may prove interesting to the reader in connection with the foregoing speculations. It has additional value from its authorship and its entirely voluntary character. General Hunter could have no other motive than to write the truth in a confidential communication of this nature. Previous to the battle of Missionary Ridge, Hunter, then temporarily out of employment, but having the personal good-will of both the President and the Secretary of War, was sent west on a tour of inspection. After visiting Grant at Chattanooga, he reported to Secretary Stanton as follows:

LOUISVILLE, KY., December 14, 1863.

HON. E. M. STANTON,
Secretary of War, Washington.

DEAR SIR: I arrived at Chattanooga a month since, and was received by General Grant with the greatest kindness. He gave me his bed, shared with me his room, gave me to ride his favorite war-horse, read to me his despatches received and sent, accompanied me on my reviews, and I accompanied him on all his excursions and during the three days of battle. In fact, I saw him almost every moment, except when sleeping, of the three weeks I spent in Chattanooga.

I mention these, to you, otherwise very unimportant facts, to show you that I had a first-rate opportunity of judging of the man. He is a hard worker, writes his own despatches and orders, and does his own thinking. He is modest, quiet, never swears, and seldom drinks, as he only took two drinks during the three weeks I was with him. He listens quietly to the opinions of others and then judges promptly for himself; and he is prompt to avail himself in the field of all the errors of his enemy. He is certainly a good judge of men, and has called around him valuable counselors.

Prominent as General Grant is before the country, these remarks of mine may appear trite and uncalled for; but having been ordered to inspect his command, I thought it not improper for me to add my testimony with regard to the commander. I will also add that I am fully convinced the change of commanders was not made an hour too soon, and that if it had not been made just when it was we should have been driven from the Valley of the Tennessee, if not from the whole State. . . .

I have the honor to be, very respectfully,
Your most obedient servant,
D. HUNTER, Major-General.

While another general, encamped in middle Tennessee with seventy thousand men,—the largest available army in the West,—was answering the government's eager promptings to move against an inferior enemy with urgent requests for reinforcements, and meanwhile doing nothing, Grant was energetically prosecuting a campaign for the reduction of Vicksburg with a force no more than equal to the enemy he was to overcome, and twenty-five thousand less than Rosecrans's army.

The contrast in the character and attitude of the two chief commanders in the West during the spring and early summer of 1863 must have been an object-lesson to the Washington military authorities, and certainly not to the disadvantage of Grant; for it only served to emphasize, to bring into bolder relief, his high qualifications for the most important and trying duties. He made no requisitions or demands whatever upon the President, not even for time; as soon as opportunity offered, without pressing, he at once took the field with what force he had, depending on conditions and the development of events to denote to the government his necessities as they occurred.

Before the government was fairly aware that the campaign was inaugurated, Grant, confounding the enemy by his well-dissembled movements, had swiftly beaten Pemberton at every point, and had him safely «holed up» in Vicksburg. It was evident that Pemberton must eventually succumb unless he was relieved, and also plain that outside relief was hopeless if Grant was strongly reinforced. It is noteworthy that, while Grant energetically began to concentrate all the available troops in his own department in the trenches before the city, he still made no appeal or representations to Washington; he let the situation speak for itself. During the entire two months' campaign Grant sent to Washington no more than two or three communications. The President found no occasion to bother him with orders, suggestions, or appeals to beat up the enemy; neither did Grant importune the President for reinforcements and munitions. He, nevertheless, got all he needed, and soon had Vicksburg environed with eighty thousand men.

Among the reinforcing troops sent to Vicksburg were two divisions of the Ninth Corps from General Burnside's command in the Department of the Ohio. Upon Pemberton's surrender, Grant notified the President that he would immediately return to Burnside the borrowed troops, of which fact the Secretary of War in turn notified Burnside; but Grant changed his mind, and sent them out with Sherman against General Johnston. After waiting some time, Burnside became very impatient; he finally complained to the President that Grant was not «toting fair,» and was still detaining his troops. Thereupon Mr. Lincoln sent to General Burnside the following reply:

WAR DEPARTMENT, WASHINGTON, D. C., July 27, 1863.

Major-General BURNSIDE, Cincinnati, O.

Let me explain. In General Grant's first despatch after the fall of Vicksburg, he said, among other things, he would send the Ninth Corps to you. Thinking it would be pleasant to you,

I asked the Secretary of War to telegraph you the news. For some reasons, never mentioned to us by General Grant, they have not been sent, though we have seen outside intimations that they took part in the expedition against Jackson. General Grant is a copious worker and fighter, but a very meager writer or telegrapher. No doubt he changed his purpose in regard to the Ninth Corps for some sufficient reason, but has forgotten to notify us of it.

A. LINCOLN.[1]

Under the circumstances, and in the light of his experience of the previous two years with army commanders, Mr. Lincoln's characterization of Grant was a panegyric. Some of them had been exactly the reverse—very copious writers and telegraphers, but meager workers and fighters.

These two letters, together with his original tender of service, show the characteristics which were the foundation of Grant's final rise to the supreme command unquestioned, and afterward to an unexampled personal influence. He was no politician; his success was due solely to solid merit. The coy maiden, Fame, was won as Vicksburg was reduced—only after a long siege. When Lee surrendered at Appomattox Grant was only forty-three years old. With a genius for war, in spite of every obstacle, by courage and uncomplaining persistence, from comparative obscurity Grant raised himself to the highest pinnacle of an honorable ambition. His name will stand on the same plane with Lincoln and Washington. Slow to mature, but at last securely fixed, his fame will survive as long as the records of the period last; and it will grow as the centuries pass, and the power of the nation he served increases, as it must increase, beyond the grandeur of Rome or any other known in history.

*Leslie J. Perry.*

WAR RECORDS OFFICE, Washington.

[1] See Hay and Nicolay's «Complete Works of Abraham Lincoln.»

**Tramps and Whipping-posts.**

A LETTER from Frankfort, Indiana, expresses dissent from the whipping-post communication printed in this department. The writer, the Rev. Demetrius Tillotson, referring to the law to make vagrancy a crime, says:

«It would be necessary only that employment be found that would enable the individual to secure food and shelter to make such a law practical. The establishment of food and shelter depots patterned after those in General Booth's social scheme, where the individual is compelled to work before he can eat, would be more Christian, less expensive in the end to society, and far more effectual than the whipping-post. No remedy, however, will ever be effectual until the sources of supply are destroyed.

«Eighty per cent. of the tramps in the United States have been produced, either directly or indirectly, through the influence of the saloon; and until this evil is done away with no permanent cure can be expected.»

**The Maxim.**

ONE golden drop, from countless roses pressed,
Hands down an Orient garden to the West:
From age to age a proverb thus survives,
The lasting essence of unnumbered lives.

*Dora Read Goodale.*

**To the Hero of a Scientific Romance.**

IF you wish, go be a pig,
In and out of season;
But don't bore us with a big
Philosophic reason.

*R.*

**Finance at the Lyceum.**

YES, sir; down at our lyceum we discussed the finance cause,
An' some needed legislatin' fer revisin' of the laws.
Silas Simpkins spoke fer fi-at (this, o' course, was 'fore Si died),
An' a little cuss named Taylor 'lowed he 'd take the other side
(One o' them Oak Valley Taylors—got a sorter snappy eye).
So the rest of us jest lis'ened, though we mos'ly favored Si;
Fer he use' to talk an' whittle while the seasons went an' came,
An' we knew that he was loaded fer the biggest kind o' game.

Si riz first, an' he orated fer about a half a' hour;
An' I recollec' he stated that the nation had the power
To pervide us all with greenbacks long 's their printin'-press 'ud run;
An' he told about a ratio which he called sixteen to one,
An' some gole-bugs; an' he said he would n't take no gold in his,
Fer he 'lowed a paper dollar was the best one that they is—
(Er a silver)—an' concludin', Si said p'intedly, said he,
«If the banks won't take yer fi-at, you jes' bring it roun' to *me*.»

Wal, that little Taylor feller had been lis'nin' all the while,
An' he riz when Si had finished, with a sorter knowin' smile,
An' he said that Si was crafty, but he 'lowed that *he* 'ud vote

Fer to make a legal-tender out of ev'ry feller's note
Jest es big es he could write it, an' a law to make it good,
With pervision fer renewin' jest es often es he would.
This, he said, 'ud save the printin'. Then he closed his argiment,
An' we left without adjournin', a-reflectin' es we went.

*Albert Bigelow Paine.*

DRAWN BY PETER NEWELL.

A RUMOR.

«The inmates of the Insane Asylum have broken out!»
«No, you don't say!»
«Yes, with the measles.»

### A Fatal Climax.

JIM RODES, better known as «Spooky» Rodes, was one of the left-overs after the first mining-fever subsided in California. He lived for over twenty years in Tuolumne County, and though he never rose above the station of hanger-on in a mining-camp, he attained a local fame unique and unenvied.

Rodes had no particular place of habitation. He was like a bird of passage, flitting from place to place, and taking philosophically such fare as fell in his way. He owned a decrepit nag, which served to carry him over the rough country roads, for Jim had no intention of subjecting his shoes to unneenssary wear and tear.

The old man passed his winters down in the foot-hill country, and in the spring made a yearly visit to the mountains, where he remained until the snow and frost drove him back to a more congenial clime.

«Spooky» began his yearly visits at the house of one Andy Simons. He tied his horse under the giant oak which the thrifty Simons used for barn and stable, and took up his abode in the three-roomed house. There was already a large family, but that did not discourage Jim. There was always plenty of bacon and potatoes at Andy's, and a full stomach was more to Jim than a palace. He would prolong his visit one, two, three weeks, as long as the hostess would tolerate him; and finally, when his welcome was worn threadbare, and even the baby began to offer infantile snubs, Jim saddled his horse and moved along.

«Spooky» Rodes was a generous soul. He presented Mrs. Simons with a fine new butter-mold upon his arrival, and now that he intended visiting the Twillers, the nearest neighbors, he saw no harm in quietly pocketing the half-dozen plated spoons, the pride of Mrs. Simons's heart, and carrying them as an offering to the Lares and Penates in the Twiller household.

Thus Jim moved about the circle of his acquaintances, and in moving carried with him many little articles of value or virtu. Indeed, the good people of Tuolumne had come to know so well Jim's give-and-take code of etiquette that on his arrival spoons were consigned to the bottom of the flour-barrel, new linen was stowed away on the rafters, and a general counting up took place at night. But even with this vigilance, Jim managed to make offerings to his various hostesses ranging in value from soft-soap to plated ware.

Jim had had some thrilling experiences—at least, he could tell about them in a way to thrill his audiences. They would sit listening with open mouths and straining ears until Jim had reached his climax; then, drawing long breaths of relief, they would sink back into their chairs, as he led them gently down by easy steps to a place where he could satisfactorily conclude his story.

But Jim's high sense of the fitness of things once led him into a grievous snare which obliged him to choose between himself and an artistic climax. Like a true raconteur, he sacrificed himself, but brought down upon his head the derision of a younger and more irreverent generation, by whom he was ever after known as «Spooky» Rodes.

Jim was making his annual visit at the Twillers'. Supper was over, and the men were tilted back against the house with pipes and tobacco, while the women-folk «rid» the table and pared the potatoes for breakfast.

«I reckon,» said Jim, meditatively, «thet none o' ye hev hearn tell on thet experunce I hed with the Injuns. I reckon it war nigh on thirty year ago, when I war crossin' the plains, thet the experunce thet I 'm 'bout to tell ye happened. I war ridin' a fiery black hoss, an' I got clear ahead o' the train,—more 'n ten mile ahead, I reckon,—when all to onct I heerd behind me the dernedest yell. I jerked a look backwards, an' seen a band o' thirty or forty Injuns a-comin' it towards me, with their bows all a-aimin', an' their toes dug into their hosses' flanks; an' sez I, ‹It 's all up with ye, Jim Rodes.› But I reckoned it 'd pay to sell my life dear, so I clapped my spurs into my hoss's flanks, an' 'way we went.

«Right afore us war one o' them tremenjous big cañons ye 've hearn tell on back on the plains—the Grand Cañon, or the Royal George, or somethin' like thet. Well, I did n't see much diff'runce, so I put my hoss right for the cañon, an' pell-mell up we went—the cañon gittin' narrower an' narrower every minute, an' the walls on the sides just risin', I reckon, nigh about a thousand feet. Anyways, no sun ever got down to the bottom, an' 't war gloomy as the grave, an' them Injun devils whoopin' it up behind. On they came, boys. I could hear their hosses snortin', an' the arrows whizzed by my ears like a swarm o' bees. Off went my hat, my coat-sleeves were ripped open, old hoss's ears bleedin' with the arrows, an' the walls gittin' closer an' closer together, an' it gittin' powerful dark too; an' then we dashed past a big rock, an' oh, Lordy! there I saw a sight to make my hair stand on end an' the cold sweat to run offen me; an' oh, Lordy! there, right in front o' me, about twenty yards ahead, the walls come together, all but jest wide enough for a waterfall a thousand feet high to come tumbling down; an' oh, Lordy!—»

«Great Scott!» cried an anxious listener, «what did you do?»

«Why, oh, Lordy! them Injuns come tearin' on behind, an' I jest plowed my spurs into the old hoss, an' on, an' on, an' on—»

«What about that waterfall?» cried the youngest Twiller boy.

«What in thunder did the Injuns do to ye?» cried Twiller.

«Why—why—the waterfall—an'—an' the Injuns,» stammered Jim—«why, dernital, they killed me!»

*Stella Walthall Belcher.*

**Mrs. Brown Visits the Capital.**

«YES; I 've actchully been to Washington on a visit. I 'm jes back, an' I 'm 'most fagged out, too. I went to visit sister Malvina. She married Lemuel Jones, you know. He 's a butcher there.

«Do tell you about my visit—how I enjoyed it, an' what I saw?

«Well, I had a nice time—a mighty nice time. I wish you could have been along an' seen the sights. There was a forty-nine-cent store there that jes beat anything you ever laid your two eyes on. You never seen sech bargains in all your born days. You know them muffin-pans that Silas Reed wants seventy-five cents apiece for, up at the cross-roads? Well, I could jes git all I wanted at forty-nine cents a pair. Now what do you think o' that?

«An' them glass pitchers like Miranda Johnson 's got—she paid a dollar apiece for 'em in butter an' eggs this very spring, mind you; an' I bought the very same pair like hers for forty-nine cents apiece. Jes think o' that; forty-nine cents apiece!

«Did I see the Corcoran Art Gallery? Yes, I s'pose I did; but I did n't go in. Sister said there war n't nothin' but a lot o' picture-paintin's in there, so I did n't go in, though I am right fond o' photygraphs an' the like. Well, as I was sayin', I never did see sech bargains as they had at that forty-nine-cent store. I saw some winder-shades that were jes beautiful. They had them big bokays o' roses on 'em, 'most as natural as real. I bought a pair for the dinin'-room for only forty-nine cents. War n't that dirt-cheap?

«Did I visit the Capitol? La! yes; me an' sister Malvina spent 'most two hours there. I never was so tired out walkin' around a place in all my life. That reminds me. My feet was well-nigh blistered, an' I jes had to go to the forty-nine-cent store an' buy me a pair o' carpet slippers to wear about the house. I 've got 'em on now; they 're so comfortable-lookin' an' easy, an' I only

DRAWN BY MAUDE COWLES.

«'I 'VE GOT 'EM ON NOW.'»

paid forty-nine cents for 'em. Silas Reed asked a dollar an' ten cents for a pair that war n't near as nice as these I 've got on.

«Oh, yes; of course I went to the White House an' shook hands with the President; everybody does that. An' let me tell you, he had on a black necktie jes the dead match to one I bought Hosea at the forty-nine-cent store. I don't believe you could tell 'em apart.

«Smith an' Son's Institute, did you say? I reckon I saw that too; but there was such a lot o' big buildin's, I can't half remember the names of 'em all. They had little books with pictures in 'em of sech at the forty-nine-cent store, but there was so many other things to buy I did n't git one.

«Dear me! Yes; we went clean up to the top of Gen'r'l Washington's monument. It was awful high, an'—would you believe me?—you could even see the flag that was wavin' over the forty-nine-cent store from up there. Sister Malvina pointed it out.

«What! you ain't goin' a'ready? Well, you must run in ag'in soon; I 've got a lot o' things more to tell you. I want to show you the cutest trick you ever saw. It 's a new-fangle thing to take pies out of the oven without burnin' your fingers clean to the bone. I bought it an' a dozen nice pie-pans at the forty-nine-cent store jes before I started home.»

*Emma Cleveland Wood.*

### My Cyclone-proof House.

Two or three months ago, when I was just deciding to build a house, I saw in our local paper a description of a cyclone-proof dwelling. Now, if there is anything I dislike, it is to have a full-blooded, centripetal twister come cavorting through the air and wipe my dwelling off the earth. It annoyed me to go down cellar for a bottle of raspberry jam, only to find that while I was below my house was flipped into Dugan's potato-patch, and deposited there tails up, heads down, and not a thing left on my lot except my neighbor's hencoop and the wind-proof, fire-proof, water-proof eight-per-cent. mortgage that I put on the lot myself four years ago next August, and which could not be blown off with four tons of dynamite.

Having such a deep-rooted hatred of the cyclone, I was naturally much taken with the account of the cyclone-proof house, and I had one built on my lot. The house was as simple as it was perfect. The principal feature was a sort of circular track or rail on which the house could revolve, a fin or rudder being placed over the kitchen in such a manner that it must necessarily catch the wind and swing the house around on the circular track. In this way the front of the house was always in the teeth of any strong breeze. And here came in the practical part of the scheme: for in the front room over the hall was a port-hole from which protruded a small cannon. This cannon discharged loaded bombs at any approaching cyclone-cloud. The explosion of the bomb in the bosom of the cloud was said to rip the airy devastation into flinders.

When my house was completed it was a source of pride to me, and a source of wondering curiosity to the townsfolk. On the first breezy day I operated the revolving device, and found it worked perfectly. The house is supposed to front north, and the breeze came strongly from the south, and my pulses thrilled with pleasure as the house swung slowly and grandly around in the wind.

But, unfortunately, the wind stayed from the south until nightfall, when it died, leaving my house in a most peculiar position, with the front porch adjacent to the hog-pen, and the kitchen within three feet of the front gate. I prayed earnestly for wind for a week, but none arose, and during that time my house was the joke of the village. At the end of the week I rented Silas Bogg's ox-team, and pulled the house into its normal position; and it was indeed a great comfort to be able to empty the dish-water without having to carry it from the kitchen through the dining-room and parlor, and out at the front door into the back yard.

However, the real test of the house did not occur until about a month thereafter. To tell the truth, I am a little timid in a storm since our house was blown into Dugan's field; and as for my wife, she would rather break her neck falling down the cellar stairs than risk it in a May zephyr. This timidity accounts for our loss of presence of mind the night it stormed. We were in bed and asleep, and I was dreaming I was at sea on a very dizzy vessel, when my wife shook me and said a fearful storm was coming; and, in fact, the house was spinning round like a top, now making six or eight revolutions to the right, and then suddenly whirling to the left, like a half-witted kitten with a fit. The wind seemed to have no stability, and veered constantly, and I could not see a yard from the window where I stood ready to fire the cyclone-bomb at first sight of the monster. My wife stood at my side, and gazed with me out of the window into the blackness. Suddenly she gave a cry of alarm. «There! there!» she shrieked; and I too saw the cyclone-cloud rising dark and ominous before us. In a thought I had fired the cannon; the bomb sped on its way, and I heard it explode with a terrific crash. For a moment we waited in breathless anxiety, and then she fell into my arms, sobbing, «Oh, Henry, Henry! we are saved!»

And we were.

The cyclone did n't catch us that night. It could n't. In fact, there was no cyclone. It was just a plain, every-day blow—a little one-horse, two-for-a-nickel wind.

But I had tried the cyclone-bomb gun. The next morning I went out to see what I had been gunning at. It was my barn! In the dark I dare say it resembled a cyclone, but by day it resembled a pile of kindling-wood. I had simply shot a first-class red barn into atoms, and had slaughtered a good, steady, five-year-old family horse, and a nice spotted Jersey cow with two toes on each foot and burs in her tail.

Cyclone-proof houses? *No!* No, *sir!* Not for Uncle Harry! I have had my experience. I am only glad the wind was from the south instead of from the west when I fired the fatal bomb. Had it been from the west, I should have knocked the internal effects clean out of my neighbor Murphy's home, to say nothing of neighbor Murphy himself.

And, by the way, if you hear of any one who would like to purchase a cyclone-proof house, he can get one from me at reduced rates, and I will throw in a sixty-foot lot with a hearty mortgage on it, and a brand-new red barn on which softly rests a brand-new mechanic's lien.

*Ellis Parker Butler.*

### Protest.

Who say my hea't ain't true to you?
  Dey bettah heish dey mouf;
I knows I loves you th'oo an' th'oo,
  In watah time er drouf.
I wish dese people 'd heish dey talkin'—
Don't mean no mo' dan chickens squawkin'.
I guess I knows whah I is walkin';
  I knows de no'f f'om souf.

I does not love Elizy Brown;
  I guess I knows my min'.
You 's allus got to bring me down
  'Bout evahthing you fin'.
Ef dese hyeah folks will keep on fillin'
Yo' haid wif nonsense, an' you 's willin',
I bet some day dey 'll be a killin'
  Somewhah erlong de line.

O' co'se I buys de gal ice-cream;
  Whut else I gwine to do?
I knows jes' how de thing 'ud seem
  Ef I 'd be sho't wif you.
On Sunday you 's at chu'ch a-shoutin',
Den all de week you spen' a-poutin';
I 's mighty tiahed o' all dis doubtin',
  I tell you 'cause I 's true!

*Paul Laurence Dunbar.*

THE DE VINNE PRESS, NEW YORK.

STUDY FOR THE HEAD OF CHRIST.

IN THE PAINTING OF «THE LAST SUPPER,» BY P. A. J. DAGNAN-BOUVERET.

*CHRISTMAS NUMBER.*

THE CENTURY MAGAZINE

VOL. LIII. DECEMBER, 1896. No. 2.

# A GROUP OF AMERICAN GIRLS.

## EARLY IN THE CENTURY.

A REGRET frequently uttered by middle-aged persons is that in youth they had not paid more heed to the reminiscences of their elders. I also utter this regret, although, having always been intensely interested in the tales which my grandparents told of the events and friends of their early days, I have in this respect less to mourn than most.

Especially was I enchanted by the accounts given by my grandmother of her girlhood on the banks of the Hudson, and of her one winter in New York society, in 1806–7, culminating in a voyage up the Hudson in Fulton's first steamboat, the *Clermont*, in August, 1807. After an evening at my grandmother's, I often wrote out the things she had told me, as nearly as possible in her own words, and have since had the good fortune to find some letters which have helped me to piece together a connected narrative of this period of her life. The grandmother referred to was Helen, second daughter of Gilbert R. Livingston of Red Hook (now Tivoli) on the Hudson. In 1809, being then nineteen years of age, she married William Mather Smith, Esq., of Sharon, Connecticut, only son of Governor John Cotton Smith of that State.

My grandmother often said that it was fortunate for herself and sisters that they were not born a few years earlier than they were; for in the troublous times immediately succeeding the American Revolution things were not made very pleasant for the defeated party.

Unlike the rest of the Livingstons, most of whom had, in one way or another, taken an active part with the resisting colonies, my grandmother's father espoused the principles of his wife's family, the Kanes, and remained loyal to the king. Mr. Livingston was one of those who emigrated to Nova Scotia, returning to the States only after the conclusion of the war. It does not appear that he was ever actually in field service against his country, but it is certain that he held a captain's commission in the British army, and that a pension from the crown was paid to him and afterward to his widow. Of course Mr. Livingston's property interests suffered heavily (a thing which, her republican descendants never failed to remind my grandmother, was richly deserved), and would have suffered still more but for the fact that their kindred welcomed back the humbled recusants, and relinquished to them much which might have been legally withheld. Red Hook was really Reade's Hoeck, named after the Reade family, which held large estates there, and the head of which had married the favorite sister of Captain Livingston.[1] At this place several farms and a fairly handsome residence had belonged to the father of Captain Livingston. These were now allotted to him, and his British military title was politely ignored by his kindly neighbors, who would not willingly remind his young family of what was felt to be their father's disgraceful adherence to the cause of his country's oppressors, though there were many Livingstons, and so many bearing the names of Robert, Gilbert, John, and Philip, that titles were extremely useful to distinguish one from another. For this reason we shall here give to Captain Livingston his despised title.

The vicinity of the new home to Clermont, the country-seat of Captain Livingston's father's cousin, Robert R., better known as Chancellor Livingston, was a great blessing to the young sons and daughters of the late Tory. Members of this large family filled some of the most important positions in the States of New Jersey and New York and in the General Government; but perhaps the chancellor filled the largest place of all in the public esteem. Whether as an orator, as a magistrate, or as an ambassador to foreign courts, he has had few superiors, and American society has probably never known a more high-minded, courtly, and accomplished gentleman.

Chancellor Livingston had been attached heart and soul to the cause of the colonies, and it is said that he admitted that it might have been much harder for him to forgive the course taken by the «British Livingston» had it not been for the personal beauty of the latter's sons and daughters. It is a family tradition that when the question was mooted of how the families of the late Tories were to be received in the new society, the chancellor declared that, «seeing the wrong-headed creatures *would* have such deucedly pretty daughters, there was nothing else to be done but to let bygones be bygones»—a humorous turn by which he doubtless thought to conciliate some of those who were inclined to take less lenient views. Traditions from many sources show that personal beauty of a rare sort did indeed belong to such Tory families as the De Lanceys and the Kanes, as well as to that of Captain Livingston. Family traditions are so apt to be misleading on some points, and especially so on this, that sometimes one is led to wonder whether the artists of those days were positively incapable of seizing a resemblance, or whether tradition has not been overkind. But there are those yet living who can recall the fine features and exquisite complexion—with hardly a wrinkle at the age of seventy-six—of the late Mrs. Henry Beeckman (the «Sister Kate» of the following notes), and the noble, intellectual beauty and majestic grace of Mrs. David Codwise («Sister Patty»), as for several years after she had reached seventy she continued to preside at the anniversaries of the New York Female Bible Society, and at the early meetings of the managers of the Woman's Hospital, which her enthusiastic efforts did much to establish.

In the early part of this century Clermont was considered one of the finest residences in North America, and its owner maintained a style of living hardly in consonance with the strictly republican principles which he had hazarded all to maintain. But it must be remembered that social equality was at no time held to be either possible or desirable by the majority of the leaders among those who fought to achieve independence from the rule of Great Britain. They fully believed in and desired political equality and all civil rights for all; but the notion of social equality was peculiar to those who, like Jefferson, had been under the influence of the enthusiasts of the first French Revolution.

The chancellor was fond of riding, and was on horseback a great deal; but when he made calls upon the families of his friends he drove in a great gilded coach drawn by four perfectly black, or four perfectly white, or four dappled-gray horses, according to the weather, using the blacks when the day was bright and dry, the whites when it was gloomy and dry, and the grays in rain and mud. I find in my notes that «grandmother says that rarely more than two or three days passed, when the chancellor was staying at Clermont, that his coach did not drive to our door. Sometimes he would step out from it, tall, stately, magnificent in carriage, but gracious and winning in manner, and ascend our steps to the porch, where, at the first news of his approach, we all speedily assembled to greet him, as was fitting, seeing that he was so great a man, and we but his juniors, whom it pleased him to have taken under his protection. But more often the coach came

[1] One of the daughters of Mr. and Mrs. Henry Reade married Mr. Hooker of Poughkeepsie; another married Nicholas William Stuyvesant; a third married Philip Kearny of Kearny Manor, near Newark, N. J., and was the grandmother of General Kearny, the «fighting Phil» of the war of the rebellion.

PAINTED BY GILBERT STUART, 1796. ENGRAVED BY R. G. TIETZE. IN POSSESSION OF JOHN H. LIVINGSTON, CLERMONT, NEW YORK.

CHANCELLOR ROBERT R. LIVINGSTON.

empty, an outrider bearing a polite note from the chancellor to our mother, begging the pleasure of the society of any two or four of her sons or daughters whom she might be pleased to spare to him for the day. Needless to say that we were always delighted to accept. The chancellor's wife was not living, but one or the other of his two married daughters was nearly always at home to act as hostess, and he had always, besides, some matron or elderly spinster of the family connection. Generally there was more than one, as all esteemed it an honor to be invited to spend a few months at Clermont, and it was an agreeable way for him to discharge his duty to such female members of the clan as might not be otherwise so well provided for.»

At about this point in her narrative my grandmother always expatiated upon the fact that «any one who aspired to the title of

FROM A MINIATURE IN POSSESSION OF THE AUTHOR. ENGRAVED BY H. DAVIDSON.

WILLIAM MATHER SMITH AT 21.

gentleman would have found himself irretrievably disgraced if he allowed a female member of his family, even as remote as a third or fourth cousin, to do aught for her own support or to accept assistance from any one not a relative,» and would add that «the cases in which such a dependent was allowed to feel herself such were rare indeed. Certainly at Clermont those ladies were always treated by their host (and consequently by all others) as if they were the true owners of the place, and he but the most obliged of their guests.» Sometimes, tradition declares, they would get to imagine that this was the actual state of affairs! In such a case the host has been known to write to some other relative, not well provided with the sinews of war, inclosing a liberal draft, and requesting that an urgent invitation might be immediately forwarded to «Cousin Sally» or «Betty» to arrive by a certain day. After an interval a letter of recall to Clermont was issued, and the experiment tried anew, usually with a more agreeable result.

All of Captain Livingston's descendants always spoke of their visits at their «Cousin Chancellor's» as the «fairy days» of their youth. His grounds, extending a mile or more along the river-front, were beautifully laid out and cared for; his fine and spacious house, «built in the shape of a letter H, the long arms of which were over a hundred feet in length, without counting the four pavilions which terminated them,» was elegantly furnished, mainly with articles brought from Paris shortly after the French Revolution, when the returning *émigrés* were glad to sell to a wealthy American the wonderfully carved and inlaid pieces of furniture, and the costly tapestries, which until then had been used only by the great courts of Europe and the nobles attached to them. I remember in particular that my grandmother and aunts often mentioned a buhl writing-desk, and four corner cabinets of the same, which had been the property of the Cardinal de Rohan whose «wicked vanity and presumption» were the cause of the «*affaire* of the diamond necklace,» which did so much toward pushing poor Marie Antoinette on to the scaffold which was even then building for her, though all unseen. There was also at Clermont a spinet said to have belonged to the ill-fated Princesse de Lamballe, adorned with paintings by Mme. Lebrun. Another article of much interest was

FROM A MINIATURE IN POSSESSION OF THE AUTHOR. ENGRAVED BY W. A. HIRSCHMANN.

HELEN LIVINGSTON (MRS. WILLIAM MATHER SMITH) AT 32.

Caps were then worn by all matrons from the birth of their first child. At this time the caps were elaborate structures of fine lace, trimmed with gauze ribbons in bows kept stiff by «ribbon-wires.»

a snuff-box containing a portrait of Napoleon by Isabey, presented to Chancellor Livingston as the latter was leaving France in 1804. In showing it the recipient used always to say: «I value it, of course, he is so great a man; but the picture is n't in the least like him. None of his pictures are. To paint him would take as great a genius as himself.»

DRAWN BY B. WEST CLINEDINST.

«HE DROVE IN A GREAT GILDED COACH.»

The chancellor used to relate the history of each piece to his delighted young relatives, and they found it all as «interesting as any story-book, and more, for Cousin Chancellor was an eloquent man, with the gift of touching hearts; and as he walked about with us, with perhaps a hand kindly resting on one of our young shoulders (not for support, but for friendliness, for he was but sixty and not at all infirm, though so deaf that he had had to relinquish public life), and told us tale after tale, pausing by this table or that chair, as his mind traveled back over all the events he had taken part in, and the grand people he had known and perhaps personally helped in their great troubles, we would forget everything but the charm of his voice, and weep or smile at his will.»

There were few conservatories and not many greenhouses in America at that time; but the chancellor had both, and all were well stocked with rare things, under the care of a Scotch head gardener, who was far more pompous and assuming than the owner of it all, and often begrudged the liberal orders which he was obliged to fill for less fortunate neighbors, to whom the earliest melons and the choicest grapes, oranges, and lemons were always sent.

Clermont was nearly always filled with guests, and these were among the most distinguished persons of our own country, as well as of those foreigners who visited our shores. Many a bearer of an ancient and

FROM A MINIATURE IN POSSESSION OF ROBERT FULTON BLIGHT, ESQ. ENGRAVED AND BORDER DESIGNED BY FRANK FRENCH.

MRS. ROBERT FULTON.

honored name of the old French *noblesse* (no longer owning anything but his name) was here received and sheltered for months, and even years, by the chancellor, who, strong republican as he was, sincerely pitied the sufferers from the French Revolution, and, as he used often to say, «loved all Frenchmen for the sake of those who had fought for us.» For several years one of these refugees gratefully insisted upon acting as teacher of his own language, dancing, and fencing to such of his patron's young relatives as chose to avail themselves of his instructions. His pupils grew very fond of him, and always mentioned him with gratitude.

The Clermont dinners were grand affairs even when there was no state occasion, and the daughters of Captain Livingston were not allowed to attend them very often, as their mother feared that «so much grandeur would foster worldly pride in their hearts,» which she was far too strict a Calvinist to wish to do. «And truly,» said Mrs. Smith, «it must be confessed that, though personally Cousin Chancellor was as kindly and gentle to the lowliest as he was magnificent to the loftiest in station, and was ever a stanch republican in politics, there was little that savored of republican simplicity in the retinue of liveried servants always employed about him, and in the general sumptuousness and state of his manner of living.»

All of the Livingstons had large quantities of silverware, a good deal of it having come

FROM A PORTRAIT IN POSSESSION OF ROBERT FULTON BLIGHT, ESQ. ENGRAVED BY R. G. TIETZE.

ROBERT FULTON.

over from Scotland with the first Robert, whom it is now the fashion to call «Robert the Founder,» and much having been acquired by later generations. «But,» said Mrs. Smith, «all the silver of all the other branches put together would not equal the amount in daily use at Cousin Chancellor's, and among it all there was not a single silver knife or fork; yet now you think you could not dine without them. Three-tined steel forks, and steel knives with silver handles, were then the highest style.» China in plenty, including many most beautiful specimens of Sèvres, filled the glazed closets about the great dining-room; but it was kept carefully locked away for service only on very stately occasions, solid silver plate being employed for all daily uses. In those days people were not so much afraid of thieves as of breakage.

But to the young people, especially to Helen, the chief attraction of Clermont, after its owner and his wonderful tales, was the library. In Mrs. Lamb's «History of New York» it is stated that this consisted of more than four thousand volumes, and was then held to be the finest private library in the State. Mrs. Smith and her brother made a catalogue of it for their cousin, and «found it to number more than six thousand books (not volumes), besides quantities of pamphlets.»

The room itself was a grand one, lofty and well lighted, its broad windows overlooking the Hudson and the cloud-capped Catskills beyond it, and all the wall-spaces filled from floor to ceiling with the best books of the day, not only in English and the learned languages, but in Spanish and French, both of which tongues the chancellor read and spoke with ease, a most unusual accomplishment for an American of his day. «Indeed,» said Mrs. Smith, «his knowledge of French was so perfect that I have seen him move a group of French persons to weep or smile at his pleasure as readily as in his younger days he had swayed and borne away the victory from such famous opponents as Alexander Hamilton and Aaron Burr.» To add to the pleasantness of this room, both the orangery and the conservatory opened into it, and it was in these surroundings that the young sons and daughters of Captain Livingston, and some of their cousins, had many a lesson in literature, elocution, and singing from the gifted and eccentric but courtly and kindly Scottish gentleman known as Lord Ogilvie, who, without money or price, devoted himself for many years to the instruction of young gentlemen and ladies in this new country, knowing that it could yet afford but few opportunities, and generously wishing that the scions of the young republic should lack none of the graces of a polite education. «A strange man he was in many ways,» said my grandmother, «but gifted beyond any I have ever known in his own favorite lines.» He was always welcomed at Clermont, and made it his headquarters for several years, going and coming as he willed, sometimes appearing at breakfast, after an absence of months, as unceremoniously as if he had been only a few hours away, and disappearing again after months of sojourn as silently as an Indian brave. «Odd enough he was, but a most rare and lovable man; and though plain of face, endowed with remarkable manly beauty of form and grace of manner.»

FROM A MINIATURE IN POSSESSION OF HER DAUGHTER, MRS. HELEN LIVINGSTON GRAHAM, CHICAGO. ENGRAVED AND BORDER DESIGNED BY FRANK FRENCH.

«SISTER KATE» (MRS. BEECKMAN) AT 19.

It is to be wished that we could gather more information in regard to this gentleman. Mrs. Smith thought it probable that his title of «lord» was bestowed upon him in this country, either through a misunderstanding of the Scottish designation of «laird,» or in a sort of half-tender, half-ironical courtesy. At any rate, he always accepted it with grave politeness, as if it were his right; and it may have been. If his antecedents were known to his host, the confidence was sacredly kept.

My friend Miss Susan Hayes Ward of Newark, New Jersey, tells me that her grandmother, Mrs. William A. Hayes of South Berwick, Maine, when Miss Susan Lord, heard Lord Ogilvie read the then new poem of «Marmion» in Portsmouth. She was enraptured with the poem, and the next morning hastened to the book-store to buy a copy. Here she was heard by the reader of the previous evening, who, in grateful appreciation of her enthusiasm, begged to present her with a copy of the book. A little later than this Lord Ogilvie took great pains to instruct Miss Lord, who was a fine musician for the place and time, in the proper pronunciation of the Scotch songs which she sang. Mrs. Hayes always loved to recall anecdotes concerning her voluntary tutor. Miss Ward has heard that Lord Ogilvie was at one time in Virginia and Kentucky, pursuing his original but highly valuable kind of educational mission work. Surely there should be more traces left of this remarkable man. Who was he? What led him here? How long was he in America? What became of him? At the time of his stays at Clermont he was, in my grandmother's estimation, «quite an elderly man»; but she was then so young that a man of forty would have seemed old to her. He may have been the heir of the Lord Ogilvie who, with his «clan regiment of six hundred men from Strathmore and Airlie,» was «out

N BY B. WEST CLINEDINST.

«THE GIRLS WERE OBLIGED TO STUDY.»

in Forty-five," at Prestonpans. In that case his estates would have been confiscated. He was certainly violently opposed to the house of Hanover, and endued his pupils with an exaggerated love of the «martyred» Queen of Scots and Charles I, while his affection for this country seemed to be rather on account of the humiliation it had inflicted upon England than for any sympathy with republican ideas.

At this date schools where girls could receive «the elements of a polite education» were few in number; even the ability to write a passably well-spelled letter was not common; so that the exceptional advantages offered at Clermont gave to the daughters of Captain Livingston a recognized superiority over most of their contemporaries—at least over those who had not had the advantage of attending the celebrated school of Mrs. Isabella Graham, at which were taught, «by competent instructors, reading, writing, spelling, arithmetic, grammar, geography, deportment, plain sewing, embroidery, cloth-work, filigree-work, japanning, drawing, painting, music, dancing, and French.» What the so-called accomplishments amounted to may be a matter of doubt, but there is no question that some of the finest women that New York has ever known received their training at Mrs. Graham's school.

ENGRAVED AND BORDER DESIGNED BY FRANK FRENCH.

«SISTER PATTY»
(MRS. CODWISE) AT 32.

During the season when Clermont was open, and its many guests were coming and going, riding, driving, boating, hunting, and exchanging dinners and dancing parties with «neighbors» whose country-seats sparsely lined the Hudson from Yonkers to Albany, the instructions of Lord Ogilvie and the French tutor were somewhat desultory; and during this season of gaiety the careful mother did not wish to have her sons and daughters too much under its influence. So for these months they were kept pretty constantly at home, under the authority of a theological student who acted as tutor in fitting the boys for college, and of an elderly governess who taught the girls all that she knew about the three R's, fine sewing, embroidery, and (not least) «deportment.» By this term was understood the practice of the etiquette of the time: the art of entering and leaving a room; the gradations of the courtesy, whether intended to express the reverence due to an acknowledged superior or the politeness proper for one's equals, and the different greetings to be extended to all grades of one's social inferiors; how to preside at table and the art of carving were also included in «deportment.» For majestic and graceful carriage the three daughters of Captain Livingston who have already been mentioned, as well as Susan, afterward Mrs. John Constable of Schenectady, were justly noted all their lives; and they themselves attributed this advantage to the training of their old governess, which at the time they had heartily disliked. The girls were obliged to study their lessons with their backs and their arms as far as the elbows strapped flat to an upright board. On one side of the school-room were shelves at various heights, to accommodate the eyes of the students whether sitting or standing, on which the books were fastened open before them. The back-boards were worn during the entire school day, except when the free use of the hands was required, as in writing and sewing. In all weathers both boys and girls took a great deal of exercise in the open air, not being deterred from competing with one another in all sorts of active sports. The girls did not skate or shoot, save with bow and arrows, but in all else they freely joined their brothers and cousins; and these made a group of not less than forty who lived near enough to one another to be considered as neighbors in the days when rides and drives of fifteen or twenty miles were frequently taken in order

DRAWN BY B. WEST CLINEDINST.

«CARRYING LADEN BASKETS ON THEIR HEADS.»

to breakfast at the houses of kindred. When the weather was too inclement for outdoor pastimes dumb-bell exercises, and games of «battledore and shuttlecock» and «graces,» were played in the large and well-ventilated garret.

In that day «stays» were *de rigueur*, but Mrs. Livingston boldly declared that she would none of them either for herself or for her daughters; that if they took a proper amount of healthful exercise they would need nothing of the sort. At least two of her daughters, Mrs. Smith and Mrs. Codwise, never wore, and did not need, the support of even the corset, which is so vast an improvement upon that fearful instrument of torture known in their youthful days as «stays.» Part of the elastic grace of carriage which so distinguished them was undoubtedly due to the practice, required by their mother, of carrying laden baskets on their heads. Prizes, in the form of little treats, were offered to the girl who should be able to run farthest on a level, or to mount and descend flights of stairs the greatest number of times during each week, bearing on her head a basket full of light and breakable articles, without mishap. Mr. John Kane, the father of Mrs. Livingston, had observed the easy and majestic carriage imparted by this sort of burden-bearing to the peasant women of Italy and the slaves of the West Indies, and insisted that his descendants should have the benefit of the practice.

What the sewing and embroidery of that day were everybody knows because so many specimens of feminine handiwork remain, but less is known of the games and exercises which did much to develop the fine physiques so often admired in the women of the early part of this century. It was not until the next generation, when schools became plentier and home education less rigorous, that physical training fell into neglect.

In the autumn of 1806 there arose a great commotion in the hearts of two of the family of Captain Livingston: Kate and Helen were invited to spend the winter in «the society of the metropolis.» It was felt that Helen, being only seventeen, was a little too young; but it was right that Kate should be introduced into the great world, and it was thought that, though Helen was the younger, her superior sedateness would prove a check upon the sometimes thoughtless gaiety of the elder sister.

The journey itself was then a matter of some moment. It was to be taken in the chancellor's sloop, which made what were then called «regular» trips up and down the Hudson, carrying farm produce for sale in New York, and bringing back all the articles that might be needed in so large an establishment as Clermont, or in the homes of the chancellor's relatives. This, of course, included everything that could not be raised on the farm or made in the house. At that time, it will be remembered, several trades were always carried on in every house of pretension, and all the linen and woolen fabrics for ordinary household use were made at home. All, or nearly all, the goods not so made were imported, and at prices which were practically prohibitive to all but the very wealthy. As the «regularity» of the sloop's trips depended upon the winds, it was not uncommon for cargoes and passengers to have to wait a week or more after all was in readiness, and of course in winter navigation was closed.

On this private trading-sloop were accommodations for from eight to sixteen passengers. That is, there were two little state-rooms in the stern, in each of which four persons could sleep by making two beds on the floor and slinging two hammocks above them. The state-rooms were always reserved for ladies, if any were present, while the gentlemen were provided with similar beds and hammocks in the tiny main cabin. All these were gathered up by the servants and cleared away at an early hour, in order to leave space for the breakfast-table to be laid.

The beds and bedding did not belong to the sloop, but were provided by the passengers, who also brought provisions and servants. The crew was always provisioned for a ten days' voyage, but the passengers seldom took more than enough for four days, as it was expected that, in case of getting becalmed, they could always be rowed ashore and spend the time of waiting in visiting some of their friends on the river's bank; for all the «gentle people» knew one another, at least by repute, and hospitality was a virtue universally practised. It was a usual thing for a vessel flying some well-known pennant to be hailed from the shore, and begged to come to anchor to allow the passengers to attend some festivity that might be going on in the vicinity.

When Kate and Helen Livingston started for New York in November, 1806, they were accompanied only by their Aunt Reade, one of her daughters, and her son Robert; so they were not overcrowded in their tiny cabins. The party was provided with three straw-beds (there were then no springs), three feather-beds, pillows, good store of

DRAWN BY B. WEST CLINEDINST.

THE FIRST STEAMBOAT ON THE HUDSON.

blankets (because there was no means of heating the little vessel), and a fine variety of cooked food, for these trips were like prolonged picnics. The facilities for cooking consisted only of what are called «charcoal-kettles,» something like those which plumbers use for heating solder. A supply of tin foot-stoves was always kept on board. These could be filled with lighted charcoal, and were often required, whether in the cabin or on deck. Little cooking was attempted, save the making of tea and coffee, the baking of «shortcake» or griddle-cakes, or the frying of bacon or a mess of fresh fish.

The voyage from Clermont to New York sometimes occupied seven or eight days; four days and nights was considered an average trip, and forty-eight hours a remarkably

BY B. WEST CLINEDINST.

«A SUPPLY OF TIN FOOT-STOVES WAS ALWAYS KEPT ON BOARD.»

quick one, although in a few instances the run had been made in less than twenty hours. On this occasion the time was from one Monday morning till the next Sunday morning; but twenty-four hours had been taken by a stop-over at Van Cortlandt Manor, the chancellor's boat having been hailed, and its passengers pressingly invited to stop for a dinner, an evening of dancing, and a morning of hunting. The families of Livingston and Van Cortlandt being connected, it would have been esteemed discourteous to decline unless some pressing business could be pleaded in excuse. It was at the dance that evening that «Sister Kate» first met her future husband, a Mr. Cuyler, although she was not married until two or more years later, and after Helen. Mr. Cuyler was killed by a hunting accident not very long after his marriage, and a few years later his young widow married Mr. Henry Beeckman, a wealthy and most upright and lovable man.

I am not able to say exactly where the two sisters stayed during their New York winter, only knowing that it was at the house of one of their mother's brothers, of whom she had two, and perhaps three, then living in the city. It was probably at the house of Mr. John Kane.

It would be desirable to locate the house at which the sisters stayed on account of a little incident concerning Washington Irving which was often told by my grandmother. As related in his biography, Mr. Irving had suffered an irreparable loss in the death of his fiancée, Miss Matilda Hoffman, daughter of Mr. Josiah Ogden Hoffman, in whose law office Mr. Irving had been a student.

The windows of the room which the sisters occupied overlooked the cemetery in which the body of Miss Hoffman was laid to rest. New York was but a small place then, hardly more than a big village, in fact, and everybody in society knew everybody else. Hence the sisters were constantly meeting Washington Irving, although he shunned all the gaieties he could. He was never gloomy, but never gay, and his romantic sorrow attracted the unspoken sympathy of all, but of none more than of the two country girls who used to watch from behind their curtains for the twilight hour, at which he always slipped quietly in through the cemetery gate, and sought the shadow beneath which lay the grave of her whom he loved so well. The cemetery was surrounded by a high wall and a hawthorn hedge, so that one walking in the grounds would remain unseen, save from neighboring windows, and of these there were only those of the Kane house, which overlooked it. So here, all unaware of the gentle, sympathetic espionage of the two sisters, the handsome, sad-faced mourner came almost daily, in all weathers, to lay his tribute of flowers, and to stand, sometimes for a few moments only, but oftener for a half-hour or longer, with bowed, uncovered head, as if communing with the departed. One night he did not come, and after his usual time had long passed by, Helen shyly sought the place and left there a few flowers of her own. The next night he came as usual. Finding flowers which were not his own, he seized them and made as if about to throw them away. «But,» said my grandmother, «he was too gentle for that, and laid them back again, putting his own flowers at his loved one's feet. I never took any more.»

This small incident was the only one ever related of that winter in which appeared the slightest tinge of sadness. In general all was rose-colored to the two young country girls launched into society with every advantage which youth, cultivation, beauty, and high connections could bestow. Riches they did not possess, but they were too happy to care for that. Their wardrobe strikes one as having been decidedly limited, but at that time it was held that simplicity should rule the attire of all young girls, so they did not feel abashed in the fresh, sheer white India-muslin gowns, relieved with broad sashes, which were their only evening wear. These were made with low, square-cut necks, and full sleeves gathered into a puff a little above the elbow. The so-called Empire styles were then prevalent, and probably in an exaggerated form, as is apt to be the case when fashions have to be copied at a distance not only of thousands of miles, but also of a year or more of time. The skirts were short, showing not only the thin slipper, but the clocked silk stockings well above the ankle, and were so very scant that it required skill to dance in them without rending the slight fabric. Neither of the sisters had a silk dress. Gowns of that material were hardly considered suitable for unmarried women under twenty-five years of age. Gowns of pretty flowered chintz were worn at home, except in extremely cold weather, when a heavy but soft material known as «stuff» was permitted. For driving or walking each sister had a gown of dark crimson broadcloth. These were made with close sleeves coming a little below the elbow, where, as well as around the neck and the bottom of the skirt, was an edging of swan's-down, changed later in the season for a border of marten fur. Long pelisses of crimson cloth, lined and trimmed with the marten fur, and great muffs and tippets of the same were worn in all suitable weather. The crimson velvet bonnets were large and scoop-like things, adorned with an abundance of white ostrich plumes, but not by any means as exaggerated in size as those worn a few years later.

In a fragment of a letter written by Helen to her mother, she says that «we last night attended a great party at Cousin Stuyvesant's; one hundred and twenty-five persons were present, and all of us related to each other.» Of course this was nothing remarkable, because the few great families of the colonies had intermarried so freely. The «Livingston clan» alone might easily have numbered as many, no less than twelve families bearing the name having their winter residences within a short distance of one another, and most of them not far from Trinity Church. Of these, besides the chancellor, there were the families of his two brothers, John R., a man of singular cultivation and intellectual power, and Henry, familiarly known as «Colonel Harry,» who had gained distinction in Washington's army. Not far away were the houses of their sisters, Janet, the widow of General Montgomery; Gertrude, wife of Governor Morgan Lewis; and a third, the wife of General Armstrong. Brockholst Livingston, son of New Jersey's patriotic war governor, was a judge in the city, and very popular in society; and his brilliant sisters, one of whom was the wife of Chief-Justice John Jay, were often there. Though with very few outside sources of amusement, this charming coterie missed nothing; for, embracing as it did the most brilliant minds of the time, it had the added charm of that perfect freedom which can spring from kinship alone. Toward the close of this winter Helen writes: «We have attended a dinner or an evening party on every week-day this four months, and sometimes both.» As the fashionable dinner hour was three in the afternoon, this did not imply such late home-coming as the same thing would now do. «We were not often at the same house more than once in each month, and were always at the house of a relative. All have vied with each other in efforts to make it pleasant for us. I did not know there were so many agreeable people in the world. We have been perfectly happy.»

One of the chief amusements was to drive in sleighs for a long distance out of town, and, returning, stop at the house of some friend living «out of the city» to dinner or supper. One of the houses which the sisters most frequently visited in this way was that of their father's sister, Mrs. Hake,[1] who had built «an elegant country-seat on the New Bowery Road.» This «country-seat» was not far from the corner of Houston street! Another favorite place was the house of Mr. Archibald Gracie, which must have seemed a long way off, being on the East River, at Eighty-eighth street, opposite Hell Gate.

After the close of the winter's festivities the sisters were not allowed to return immediately to the home at Red Hook. There was a little round of visits to be paid among their kindred, including some of the De Lanceys (with whom most of the Livingstons were not on very good terms on account of their Tory principles), and winding up with a delightful fortnight at Liberty Hall, the residence of the family of the late Governor William Livingston, at Elizabethtown, New Jersey. Writing from here, Helen says:

> My dear mother will be glad to know that we are soon to return home. Cousin Chancellor has a wonderful new boat which is to make the voyage up the North River some day soon. It will hold a good many passengers, and he has, with his usual kindness to us, invited us to be of the party. He says it will be something to remember all our lives. He says we need not trouble ourselves about provision, as his men will see to all that. In the mean time we are enjoying ourselves very much, everybody is so kind and cordial.
>
> This house is immense and quite full of visitors. Last evening many assembled, and we amused ourselves in various ways. There were many beautiful young ladies present, but not one was so beautiful as Sister Kate. She was compelled to sing «My Face is my Fortune» three times over, and many slyly made the remark that *she* needed no other. Cousin Robert Reade played on the flute to accompany her, whereat Mr. C—— looked very black, because he cannot play the flute, and drank so much wine that he became noisy and had to be taken away.

This last sentence turns the search-light upon the one great blot on the otherwise charming society of the early years of the present century. The adulteration of liquors had by no means reached its present point, hence there were not so many cases of violence resulting from their use; but the habit of drinking wines, and even brandy and rum (whisky does not yet appear), was so well-nigh universal, and excess was so common, that it excited the gravest apprehension in

[1] The husband of Mrs. Hake had been a commissary-general in the British army, and was the claimant of an English title and estates. I do not know whether he was living at this time. Their daughter Maria married General Frederick de Peyster.

all thoughtful minds. In time this resulted in the great moral wave called the temperance movement; but in 1807 it had not arrived, and such scenes as the one referred to in the foregoing quotation were so sadly common as to attract little attention. The wife of Captain Livingston, descended on the mother's side from the stanch Connecticut families of Kent and Whiting, had inherited rigid principles which were far from popular in the jovial set into which she had married. But as a result of them, all of her four sons became model young men at a time when it was unfashionable to be so. She had declared that, «to gain her consent, suitors for the hands of her daughters must, of course, be well born and well brought up, but the only other point upon which she would insist was that they should be men of good moral character, and above all be strictly temperate.» She was often told that she would thus leave her daughters to the then so much dreaded fate of spinsterhood; but the prophets were mistaken. All of her daughters married, and married well in all senses. The husband of Helen became one of the most active and efficient temperance reformers in a day when to enroll himself on that side meant social ostracism.

The «new boat» of the letter was the now celebrated *Clermont*, the steamboat of Robert Fulton, which in August, 1807, made the first successful steam voyage up the astonished Hudson, and demonstrated to the world that a new force had been discovered by which old methods in nearly all lines were to be revolutionized.

Very likely, with all their loving confidence in the wisdom of the chancellor, the sisters embarked with some distrust of his new boat's making good its promise to get them home in less than three days, even if both wind and tide should prove unfavorable; but they were not afraid of anything worse than delay, though most of their friends feared for them. During the nine years that had passed since «Robert R. Livingston and Robert Fulton had first secured the concession to navigate the waters in New York State for twenty years, providing they should build a boat of not less than twenty tons, that would go not less than four miles an hour against wind and tide,» the subject had been so often talked over in their presence that the sisters were already quite intelligent upon it, and laughed at the fears of their timorous friends.

The embarkation was from a dock «near the State prison» (which was in «Greenwich village» on the North River), and was witnessed by a crowd of «not less than five hundred persons.» Many were friends of the passengers, who bade them farewell with as much solicitude as if they were going to Madagascar, especially trembling with apprehension at the «terrible risk run by sailing in a boat full of fire.»

The adventurous voyagers, who were the guests of Robert Fulton and Chancellor Livingston, were about forty in number, including but few ladies.[1] Among the latter, besides our two young sisters and their aunt, Mrs. Thomas Morris (daughter-in-law of Robert Morris, the financier of the Revolution), were at least one of the chancellor's two daughters, four of the many daughters of his brothers John R. and Colonel Harry, and a young lady who was more interested in the result of this memorable experiment than any one save the inventor himself. In all the biographies of Fulton, Miss Harriet Livingston is called the chancellor's niece, but she was really his cousin. She was a beautiful, graceful, and accomplished woman, and had long given her heart to Robert Fulton. The fair Harriet was at this time about two-and-twenty, and «as deeply in love with her handsome, gifted lover as any girl well could be.» There were many distinguished and fine-looking men on board the *Clermont*, but my grandmother always described Robert Fulton as surpassing them all. «That son of a Pennsylvania farmer,» she was wont to say, «was really a prince among men. He was as modest as he was great, and as handsome as he was modest. His eyes were glorious with love and genius.»

A little before reaching Clermont, when the success of the voyage was well assured, the betrothal was announced by the chancellor in a graceful speech, in the course of which he prophesied that the «name of the inventor would descend to posterity as that of a benefactor to the world, and that it was not impossible that before the close of the present century vessels might even be able to make the voyage to Europe without other motive power than steam.»

This hardy prediction was received with but moderate approval by any, while smiles of incredulity were exchanged between those who were so placed that they could not be seen by the speechmaker or the inventor. John R. was heard to say, in an aside to his cousin John Swift Livingston, that «Bob had many a bee in his bonnet before now, but this

[1] In none of the lives of Fulton is it mentioned that any ladies were present on this first trip; but the facts are as here stated.

steam folly would prove the worst one yet.» Both the chancellor's brothers lived to see the ocean regularly traversed by steam vessels, but the prophet himself, and the inventor, both passed away before the realization of their dreams.

If the lodgings on board the sloop which brought our two girls to New York in the previous autumn had struck us as uncomfortable, we should have been still less pleased with those on the first steamboat. Even four years later,—June, 1811,—when Gouverneur Morris, «with true public spirit,» ventured to «intrust himself to the mercies» of the new-fangled craft, he found «the lodging so uncomfortable» that he «could stay in bed but a short time,» though «the evening was cool,» and so remained on deck until reaching Albany, «which was not until midnight, having left New York eleven hours before.» This was a great advance over the speed attained on the first trip.

My grandmother always described the *Clermont* as «the very ugliest craft that could well be imagined.» It was decked over but a short distance at stem and at stern. In the center, exposed to the view of all, was the strange-looking machinery; only the boiler was roofed over. The fuel was dry pine-wood, and the smoke seemed excessive.

On the same afternoon on which the *Clermont* left her dock upon her adventurous trip she fell in with numbers of sailing craft coming and going, to which she was an object of unmitigated astonishment, if not of actual alarm. It is related that when the crews of some of these vessels saw this queer-looking, sailless thing approaching steadily, and gaining on them in spite of contrary wind and tide, they abandoned their vessels and took to the woods, being convinced that this shapeless and smoke-vomiting monster must have come straight from the infernal regions.

When about opposite Fishkill the *Clermont* was met by the *Admiral*, a private sloop, with which, its pennant being known as that of Mr. Jacob Evertson of Pleasant Valley, the *Clermont* exchanged signals. On board it was Helen Livingston's future husband, a grandson of Mr. Evertson, and then unknown to her. It was not until several months later that they became acquainted. My grandfather always declared that no sight of his life ever seemed to him so strange as that of this ungainly craft, «looking precisely like a backwoods sawmill mounted on a scow and set on fire,» while all the stern of the scow was crowded with a party of gaily dressed gentlemen and ladies singing a song which, as long as he lived, seemed to him to be the sweetest in the world—«Ye Banks and Braes o' Bonnie Doon.»

For Helen Livingston there remained hardly one more year of happy girlhood, free to go and come, dance and be merry, in the old innocent girlish fashion; for at that time betrothal was as sacred as marriage itself, and much more restrictive of privileges. That is, the freedom of girlhood was lost, and that of the matron had not come. If the lover were present, of course these restrictions were not felt, but in his absence the poor girl had little more liberty than a Hindu widow. She must not accept even the most ordinary attentions from any man, must dance with no one except her father or brother, and she must always wear, conspicuously displayed hanging from her neck, face outward, the miniature of her future husband. These miniatures were often skilfully painted on ivory, and were usually oval in shape and about three and a half inches by two and a half in size, without counting the gold frames, which were sometimes quite heavy. The broad remarks which it was considered in order for even chance acquaintances to address to the fiancée upon sight of this badge of appropriation were intolerable to Helen Livingston, and rather than subject herself to them she resolutely refrained from accepting an invitation even to her loved «Cousin Chancellor's» during the few months of her engagement, which ended in a happy marriage in the spring of 1809. On one occasion, when a large and most interesting company of American and foreign guests was expected at Clermont, Helen vainly sought her mother's permission to attend without wearing the telltale portrait. Finding that this would not be allowed, and realizing that her sister's disappointment would be great, «Sister Patty,» only fifteen, but already tall and stately, heroically volunteered to wear the obnoxious picture, personating its rightful owner. But the innocent fraud was not permitted, and as Helen would not go if obliged to wear the miniature, she was compelled to relinquish the coveted pleasure. Of course the boy lover—he was barely twenty-one—was in no way responsible for this custom, which he subsequently often, and justly, characterized as odious; and I think that he never liked to see the miniature which had been the means of depriving of ever so small a pleasure the woman whom he idolized through a long life.

*Helen Evertson Smith.*

# ONE OF THE TWELVE.

## A CHRISTMAS CAROL.

FROM THE PROVENÇAL OF ROUMANILLE,
AFTER LITERAL TRANSLATION BY MRS. CATHARINE A. JANVIER.

«GREAT stir among the shepherd folk;
To Bethlehem they go,
To worship there a God whose head
On straw is laid full low;
Upon the lovely new-born Child
Their gifts will they bestow.

«But I, who am as poor as Job—
A widowed mother I,
Who for my little son's sweet sake
For alms, to all, apply—
Ah, what have I that I can take
The Child of Love most high?

«Thy cradle and thy pillow too,
My little lamb forlorn,
Thou sorely needest them—no, no,
I cannot leave thee shorn!
I cannot take them to the God
That in the straw was born.»

Oh, miracle! The nursing babe—
The babe e'en as he fed—
Smiled in his tender mother's face,
And, «Go, go quick!» he said;
«To Jesus, to my Saviour, take
My kisses and my bed.»

The mother, all thrilled through and
through,
To Heaven her hands did raise;
She gave the babe her breast, then took
The cradle—went her ways, . . .
And now, at Bethlehem arrived,
To Mary Mother says:

«O Mary, Pearl of Paradise,
That Heaven on earth hath shed,
O Virgin Mother, hear the word
My little babe hath said:
‹To Jesus, to my Saviour, take
My kisses and my bed.›

«Here, Mary, here the cradle is;
Thy need is more than mine;
Receive, and in it lay thy Son,
Messiah all-divine!
And let me kiss, upon my knees,
That darling Babe of thine!»

The blessed Virgin, then, at once,
Right glad of heart, bent low,
And in the cradle laid her Child,
And kissed him, doing so.
Then with his foot St. Joseph rocked
The cradle to and fro.

«Now, thanks to thee, good woman,
thanks,
For this that thou hast done.»—
Thus say they both, with friendly looks.
«Of thanks I merit none;
Yet, holy Mother, pity me,
For sake of thy dear Son.»

Since then a happy soul was hers;
God's blessing on her fell;
One of the Twelve her child became,
That with our Lord did dwell.
Thus was this story told to me,
Which I afar would tell.

*Edith M. Thomas.*

[BEGUN IN THE NOVEMBER NUMBER.]

# A ROSE OF YESTERDAY.[1]

BY F. MARION CRAWFORD,

Author of «Mr. Isaacs,» «Saracinesca,» «Casa Braccio,» etc.

## III.

HEN Archie Harmon disappeared, and left the colonel and his mother together, she supposed that he had gone to his room to sleep, for he slept a great deal, or to amuse himself after his fashion, and she did not ask him where he was going. She knew what his favorite amusement was, though he did his best to keep it a secret from her.

There was a certain mysterious box, which he had always owned, and took everywhere with him, and of which he always had the key in his pocket. It took up a good deal of space, but he could never be persuaded to leave it behind when they went abroad.

To-day he went to his room, as usual, locked the door, took off his coat, and got the box out of a corner. Then he sat down on the floor and opened it. He took out some child's building-blocks, some tin soldiers, much the worse for wear, for he was ashamed to buy new ones, and a small and gaudily painted tin cart, in which an impossible lady and gentleman of papier-mâché, dressed in blue, gray, and yellow, sat leaning back with folded arms and staring, painted eyes. There were a few other toys besides, all packed away with considerable neatness, for Archie was not slovenly.

He sat cross-legged on the floor, a strong grown man of nearly twenty years, and began to play with his blocks. His eyes fixed themselves on his occupation, as he built up a little gateway with an arch, and set a red-legged French soldier on each side of it for sentinels. He had played the same game a thousand times already, but the satisfaction had not diminished. One day in a hotel he had forgotten to lock the door, and his mother had opened it by mistake, thinking it was that of her own room. Before he could look round she had shut it again, but she had seen, and it had been like a knife-thrust. She kept his secret, but she lost heart from that day. He was still a child, and was always to be one.

Yet there was perhaps something more of intelligence in the childish play than she had guessed. He was lacking in mind, but was not an idiot; he sometimes said and did things which were certainly far beyond the age of toys. Possibly the attraction lay in a sort of companionship which he felt in the society of the blocks, and the tin soldiers, and the little papier-mâché lady and gentleman. He felt that they understood what he meant, and would answer him if they could speak, and would expect no more of him than he could give. Grown people always seemed to expect a great deal more, and looked at him strangely when he called Berlin the capital of Austria, and asked why Brutus and Cassius murdered Alexander the Great. The toy lady and gentleman were quite satisfied if their necks were not broken in the cunningly devised earthquake which always brought the block house down with a rush when he had looked at it long enough, and was already planning another.

Besides, he did all his best thinking among his toys, and had invented ways of working out results at which he could not possibly have arrived by a purely mental process. He could add and subtract, for instance, with the bits of wood, and, by a laborious method, he could even do simple multiplication, quite beyond him with paper and pencil. Above all, he could name the tin soldiers after people he had met, and make them do anything he pleased, by a sort of rudimentary theatrical instinct that was not altogether childish.

To-day he built a house as usual, and, as usual, after some reflection as to the best means of ruining it by taking out a single block, he pulled it down with a crash. But he did not at once begin another. On the contrary, he sat looking at the ruins for a long time in a rather disconsolate way, and then all at once began to pack all the toys into the box again.

«I don't suppose it matters,» he said aloud. «But of course Sylvia would think me a baby if she saw me playing with blocks.»

And he made haste to pack them all away, locking the box and putting the key into his pocket. Then he went and looked through the half-closed blinds into the sunny street, and he could see his red bridge not far away.

«I don't care what mother thinks!» he exclaimed. «I 'm going to find her again.»

He opened the door softly, and a moment later he was in the street, walking rapidly toward the bridge. At a distance he looked well. It was only when quite near to him that one was aware of an undefinable ungainliness in his face and figure—something blank and meaningless about him, that suggested a heavy wooden doll dressed in good clothes. In military countries one often receives that impression. A fine-looking infantry soldier, erect, broad-shouldered, bright-eyed, spotless and scrupulously neat, comes marching along, and excites one's admiration for a moment. Then, when close to him, one misses something which ought to go with such manly bearing. The fellow is only a country lout, perhaps, hardly able to read or write, and possessed of an intelligence not much beyond the highest development of instinct. Drill, exercise, and the fear of black bread and water under arrest have produced a fine piece of military machinery, but they could not create a mind, nor even the appearance of intelligence, in the wooden face. In a year or two the man will lay aside his smart uniform and go back to the class whence he came. One may give iron the shape and general look of steel, but not the temper and the springing quality.

Archie Harmon looked straight ahead of him as he crossed the bridge, and followed the long street that runs beside the water, past the big hotels and the gaudy awnings of the still provincially smart shops. At first he only looked along the pavement, searching among the many people who passed. Then, as he remembered how Colonel Wimpole had seen him through a shop window, he stopped before each of the big plate-glass ones, and peered curiously into the shadows within.

At last, in a milliner's, he saw Sylvia and Miss Wimpole, and his heavy face grew red and his eyes glared oddly as he stood motionless outside, under the awning, looking in. His lips went out a little as he pronounced his own especial word very softly:

«Jukes!»

He stood first on one foot and then on the other, like a boy at a pastry-cook's, hesitating while devouring with his eyes. He could see that Sylvia was buying a hat. She turned a little each way as she tried it on before a big mirror, putting up her hands and moving her arms in a way that showed all the lines of her perfect figure.

Archie went in. He had been brought up by his mother, and chiefly by women, and he had none of that shyness about entering a women's establishment, like a milliner's, which most boys and many men feel so strongly. He walked in boldly, and spoke as soon as he was within hearing.

«Miss Sylvia! I say! Miss Sylvia—don't you know me?»

The question was a little premature, for Sylvia had barely caught sight of him when he asked it. When she had recognized him, she did not look particularly pleased.

«It 's poor Archie Harmon, my dear,» said Miss Wimpole, in a low voice, but quite audibly.

«Oh, I have not forgotten you!» said Sylvia, trying to speak pleasantly as she gave her hand. «But where in the world did you come from? And what are you doing in a milliner's shop?»

«I happened to see you through the window, so I just came in to say how do you do. There 's no harm in my coming in, is there? You look all right. You 're perfectly lovely.»

His eyes were so bright that Sylvia felt oddly uncomfortable.

«Oh, no,» she answered, with an indifference she did not feel. «It 's all right—I mean—I wish you would go away now, and come and see us at the hotel, if you like, by and by.»

«Can't I stay and talk to you? Why can't I stay and talk to her, Miss Wimpole?» he asked, appealing to the latter. «I want to stay and talk to her. We are awfully old friends, you know; are n't we, Sylvia? You don't mind my calling you Sylvia, instead of Miss Sylvia, do you?»

«Oh, no! I don't mind that!» Sylvia laughed a little. «But do please go away now.»

«Well, if I must—» he broke off, evidently reluctant to do as she wished. «I say,» he began again with a sudden thought, «you like that hat you 're trying on, don't you?»

Instantly Sylvia, who was a woman, though a very young one, turned to the glass again, settled the hat on her head, and looked at herself critically.

«The ribbons stick up too much, don't they?» she asked, speaking to Miss Wimpole, and quite forgetting Archie Harmon's presence. «Yes, of course they do. The ribbons stick up too much,» she repeated to the milliner in French.

A brilliant idea had struck Archie Harmon. He was already at the desk, where an aggrieved-looking young woman in black received the payments of passing customers.

«She says the ribbons stick up too much,»

he said to the young person at the desk. «You get them to stick up just right, will you?—the way she wants them. How much did you say the hat was? Eighty francs? There it is. Just say that it's paid for when she asks for the bill.»

The young woman in black raked in the note and the bits of gold he gave her, catching them under her hard, thin thumb on the edge of the desk, and counting them as she slipped them into her little drawer. She looked rather curiously at Archie, and there was still some surprise in her sour face when he was already on the pavement outside. He stopped under the awning again, and peered through the window for a last look at the gray figure before the mirror, but he fled precipitately when Sylvia turned, as though she were going to look at him. He was thoroughly delighted with himself. It was just what Colonel Wimpole had done about the miniature, he thought; and then, a hat was so much more useful than a piece of painted ivory.

In a quarter of an hour he was in his own room again, sitting quietly on a chair by the window, and thinking how happy he was, and how pleased Sylvia must be by that time.

But Sylvia's behavior, when she found out what he had done, would have damped his innocent joy if he had been looking through the windows of the shop, instead of sitting in his own room. Her father, the admiral, had a hot temper, and she had inherited some of it.

«Impertinent young idiot!» she exclaimed, when she realized that he had actually paid for the hat, and the angry blood rushed to her face. «What in the world—» She could not find words.

«He is half-witted, poor boy,» interrupted Miss Wimpole. «Take the hat, and I will manage to give his mother the money.»

«‹Betty Foy and her idiot boy› over again!» said Sylvia, with all the brutal cruelty of extreme youth. «‹We who have seen the idiot in his glory›—» As the rest of the quotation did not apply, she stopped and stamped her little foot in speechless indignation.

«The young gentleman doubtless thought to give Mademoiselle pleasure,» suggested the milliner, suavely. «He is doubtless a relation—»

«He is not a relation at all!» exclaimed Sylvia, in English, to Miss Wimpole. «My relations are not idiots, thank Heaven! And it's the only one of all those hats that I could wear! Oh, Aunt Rachel, what shall I do? I can't possibly take the thing, you know! And I must have a hat. I've come all the way from Japan with this old one, and it is n't fit to be seen.»

«There is no reason why you should not take this one,» said Miss Wimpole, philosophically. «I promise you that Mrs. Harmon shall have the money by to-night, since she is here. Your uncle Richard will go and see her at once, of course, and he can manage it. They are on terms of intimacy,» she added rather primly, for Helen Harmon was the only person in the world of whom she had ever been jealous.

«You always use such dreadfully correct language, Aunt Rachel,» answered the young girl. «Why don't you say that they are old friends? ‹Terms of intimacy› sounds so severe, somehow.»

«You seem impatient, my dear,» observed Miss Wimpole, as though stating a fact about nature.

«I am,» answered Sylvia. «I know I am. You would be impatient if an escaped lunatic rushed into a shop and paid for your gloves, or your shoes, or your hat, and then rushed off again, goodness knows where. Would n't you? Don't you think I am right?»

«You had better tell them to send the hat to the hotel,» suggested Aunt Rachel, not paying the least attention to Sylvia's appeal for justification.

«If I must take it, I may as well wear it at once, and look like a human being,» said Sylvia. «That is, if you will solemnly promise to send Mrs. Harmon the eighty francs at once.»

«I promise,» answered Miss Wimpole, solemnly; and as she had never broken her word in her life, Sylvia felt that the difficulty was at an end.

The milliner smiled sweetly, and bowed them out.

«All the same,» said Sylvia, as she walked up the street with the pretty hat on her head, «it is an outrageous piece of impertinence. Idiots ought not to be allowed to go about alone.»

«I should think you would pity the poor fellow,» said Miss Wimpole, with a sort of severe kindliness that was genuine but irritating.

«Oh, yes! I will pity him by and by, when I 'm not angry,» answered the young girl. «Of course—it's all right, Aunt Rachel, and I'm not depraved nor heartless, really. Only, it was very irritating.»

«We had better not say anything about it to your uncle Richard, my dear,» continued Miss Wimpole. «He is so fond of Archie's mother that he would feel very badly about it.»

«Would he?» asked Sylvia, in surprise. «About herself, I should understand; but about that boy! I can't see why he should mind.»

«He ‹minds,› as you call it, everything that has to do with Mrs. Harmon,» was the reply.

Sylvia glanced at her companion, but said nothing, and they walked on in silence for some time. It was still hot, for the sun had not sunk behind the mountains; but the street was full of people, who walked about indifferent to the temperature, because Switzerland is supposed to be a cold country, and they therefore thought that it was their own fault if they felt warm. This is the principle upon which nine people out of ten see the world when they go abroad. And there was a fine crop of European and American varieties of the tourist taking the air on that afternoon, men, women, and children. The men, who had huge field-glasses slung over their shoulders by straps, predominated, and one, by whom Sylvia was particularly struck, was arrayed in blue serge knickerbockers, patent leather walking-boots, and a very shiny high hat. But there were also occasional specimens of what she called the human being—men in the ordinary garments of civilization, and not provided with opera-glasses. There were, moreover, young and middle-aged women in short skirts, boots with soles half an inch thick, complexions in which the hue of the boiled lobster vied with the deeper tone of the stewed cherry, bearing alpenstocks that rang and clattered on the pavement; women who, in the state of life to which heaven had called them, would have gone to Margate or Staten Island for a Sunday outing, but who had rebelled against providence, and forced the men of their families to bring them abroad. And the men generally walked a little behind them, and had no alpenstocks, but carried shawls and paper bundles, badges of servitude, and hoped that they might not meet acquaintances in Lucerne, because their women looked like angry cooks, and had no particular luggage. Now and then a smart old gentleman with an eye-glass, in immaculate gray or white, threaded his way along the pavement, with an air of excessive boredom; or a young couple passed by, in the recognizable newness of honeymoon clothes, the young wife talking perpetually, and evidently laughing at the ill-adorned women, while the equally young husband answered in monosyllables, and was evidently nervous lest his bride's remarks should be overheard and give offense.

Then there were children, conspicuous among them the vulgar little children of the not long rich, repulsively disagreeable to the world in general, but pathetic in the eyes of thinking men and women. They are the sprouting shoots of the gold-tree, beings predestined never to enjoy, because they will be always able to buy what strong men fight for, and will never learn to enjoy what is really to be had only for money; and the measure of value will not be in their hands and heads, but in bank-books, out of which their manners have been bought with mingled affection and vanity. Surely, if anything is more intolerable than a vulgar woman, it is a vulgar child. The poor little thing is produced by all nations and races, from the Anglo-Saxon to the Slav. Its father was happy in the struggle that ended in success. When it grows old, its own children will perhaps be happy in the sort of refined existence which wealth can bring in the third generation. But the child of the man grown suddenly rich is a living misfortune between two happinesses—neither a worker nor an enjoyer; having neither the satisfaction of the one nor the pleasures of the other; hated by its inferiors in fortune, and a source of amusement to its ethic and esthetic betters.

Sylvia had never thought much about the people she passed in a crowd. Thought is generally the vault of suffering of some kind, bodily or intellectual, and she had but little acquaintance with either. She had traveled much, and had been very happy until to-day, having been shown the world on bright days and by pleasant paths. But to-day she was not happy, and she began to wonder how many of the men and women in the street had what she had heard called a «secret care.» Her eyes had been red when she had at last yielded to Miss Wimpole's entreaties to open the door, but the redness was gone already, and when she had tried on the hat before the glass she had seen with a little vanity, mingled with a little disappointment, that she looked very much as usual, after all. Indeed, there had been more than one moment when she had forgotten her troubles, because the ribbons on the new hat stuck up too much. Yet she was really unhappy, and sad at heart. Perhaps some of the people she passed, even the women with red faces, dusty skirts, and clattering alpenstocks, were unhappy too.

She was not a foolish girl, nor absurdly romantic, nor full of silly sentimentalities, any more than she was in love with Colonel Wimpole in the true sense of the word. For she knew nothing of its real meaning, and, apart from that meaning, what she felt for him filled all the conditions proposed by her imagination. If one could classify the ways by which young people pass from childhood to young maturity, one might say that they are brought up by the head, by the imagination, or by the heart, and one might infer that their subsequent lives are chiefly determined by that one of the three which has been the leading-string. Sylvia's imagination had generally had the upper hand, and it had been largely fed and cultivated by her guardian, though quite unintentionally on his part. His love of artistic things led him to talk of them, and his chivalric nature found sources of enthusiasm in lofty ideals, while his own life, directed and moved as it was by a secret, unchanging, and self-sacrificing devotion to one good woman, might have served as a model for any man. Modest, and not much inclined to think of himself, he did not realize that although the highest is quite beyond any one's reach, the search after it is always upward, and may lead a good man very far.

Sylvia saw the result, and loved it for its own sake with an attachment so strong that it made her blind to the more material sort of humanity which the colonel seemed to have outgrown, and which, after all, is the world as we inherit it, to love it, or hate it, or be indifferent to it, but to live with it, whether we will or not. He fulfilled her ideal, because it was an ideal which he himself had created in her mind, and to which he himself nearly approached. Logically speaking, she was in a vicious circle, and she liked what he had taught her to like, but liked it more than he knew she did.

Sylvia glanced at Miss Wimpole sideways. She knew her simple story, and wondered whether she herself was to live the same sort of life. The idea rather frightened her, to tell the truth, for she knew the aridity of the elderly maiden lady's existence, and dreaded anything like it. But it was very simple, and logical, and actual. Miss Wimpole had loved a man who had been killed. Of course she had never married, nor ever thought of loving any one else. It was perfectly simple. And Sylvia loved, and was not loved, as she told herself, and she also must look forward to a perpetually gray life.

Then, suddenly, she felt how young she was, and she knew that the colonel was almost an old man, and her heart rebelled. But this seemed disloyal, and she blushed at the word «unfaithful,» which spoke itself in her sensitive conscience with the cruel power to hurt which such words have against perfect innocence. Besides, it was as though she were quarreling with what she liked because she could not have it, and she felt as though she were thinking childishly, which is a shame in youth's eyes.

Also, she was nervous about meeting him again, for she had not seen him since she had fled from the room in tears, though he had seen her on the bridge. She wished that she might not see him at all for a whole day, at least, and that seemed a very long time.

Altogether, when she went into the hotel again she was in a very confused state of mind and heart, and was beginning to wish that she had never been born. But that was childish too.

## IV.

HELEN HARMON was glad when the colonel was gone. She went to a mirror, fixed to the wall between the two windows of the room, and she carefully rearranged her hair. She could not feel quite herself until she knew that the scar was covered again, and hidden from curious eyes. Then she sat down, glad to be alone. It had been a great and unexpected pleasure to see Wimpole, but the discovery he had made, and the things he had said, had disturbed and unnerved her.

There had been conviction in his voice when he had said that Harmon might recover, and the possibility of a change in her husband's condition had crossed her mind more than once. She felt that a return to such a state of things as had made up her life before he had become insane would kill her by slow torture. It was of no use any longer to tell herself that recovery was impossible, and to persuade herself that it was so by the mere repetition of the words. Words had no more weight now.

She thought of her freedom since that merciful deliverance. It was not happiness, for there were other things yet to be suffered, but it was real freedom. She had her son's affliction to bear, but she could bear it alone, and go and come with him as she pleased. She contrasted this liberty with what she had borne for years.

The whole history of their married life came back to her, the gradual progress of it from first to last, if indeed it had yet reached the end, and was not to begin again.

First there had been the sort of half-contented resignation which many young women feel during the early months of married life, when they have made what is called by the world a good match, simply because they saw no reason for not marrying, and because they were ashamed to own that they cared for a man who did not seem to be attached to them. Sometimes the state lasts throughout life, a neutral, passionless, negative state, in which the heart turns flat and life is soon stale; a condition in which many women, not knowing what pain is, grow restless, and believe that it must be pleasanter to be hurt than to feel nothing.

Henry Harmon had been handsome, full of life and nerve and enthusiasm for living, a rider, a sportsman, more reckless than brave, and more brave than strong-minded, with a gift for being, or seeming to be, desperately in love, which had ultimately persuaded Helen to marry him in spite of her judgment. He turned pale when he was long near her, his eyes flashed darkly, his hands shook a little, and his voice trembled. An older woman might have thought it all rather theatrical, but he seemed to suffer, and that moved Helen, though it did not make her really love him. Women know that weakness of theirs, and are more afraid of pitying an importunate suitor than of admiring him. So Helen married Harmon.

Disillusionment came as daylight steals upon dancers in a ball-room. At first it was not so painful as might have been imagined, for Helen was not excessively sensitive, and she had never really loved the man in the least. He grew tired of her, and left her to herself a good deal. That was a relief, at first, for after she had realized that she did not love him she shrank from him instinctively, with something very like real shame; and to be left alone was like being respected.

« Mrs. Blank's husband is neglecting her, » says one.

« She does not seem to care; she looks very happy, » answers another.

And she is temporarily happy, because Mr. Blank's neglect gives her a sense of bodily relief, for she knows that she has made a mistake in marrying him. It was so with Helen, and as she was not a changeable, nor at all a capricious person, it might have continued to be so. But Harmon changed rapidly in the years that followed. From having been what people called fast, he became dissipated. He had always loved the excitement of wine. When it failed him, he took to stronger stuff, which presently became the essential requisite of his being. He had been said to be gay, then he was spoken of as wild, then as dissipated. Some people avoided him, and every one pitied Helen. Yet although he ruined his constitution, he did not wreck his fortunes, for he was lucky in all affairs connected with money. There remained many among his acquaintances who could not afford to disapprove of him, because he had power.

He drank systematically, as some men do, for the sake of daily excitement, and Helen learned to know tolerably well when he was dangerous, and when he might be approached with safety. But more than once she had made horrible mistakes, and the memories of them were like dreams out of hell. In his drunkenness her face recalled other days to him, and forgotten words of passion found thick and indistinct utterance. Once she had turned on him, white and desperate in her self-defense. Then it was that he struck her on the forehead, with a cut-glass decanter snatched from her toilet-table. When she came to herself, hours afterward, it was daylight. Harmon was in a drunken sleep, and the blood on his face was hers.

She shuddered with pain from head to foot when she thought of it. There had come strange lapses of his memory, disconnected speech, even hysterical tears, following senseless anger, and then he had ceased to recognize any one, and had almost killed one of the men who took care of him, so that it was necessary to take him to an asylum, struggling like a wild beast. Twice, out of a sense of duty, she had been to see whether he knew her, but he knew no one, and the doctors said it was a hopeless case. Since then she had received a simple confirmation of the statement every month, and there seemed to be no reason for expecting any change, and she felt free.

Free was the only word she could find, and she applied it to herself in a sense of her own, meaning that she had been liberated from the thraldom in which she had lived so many years face to face with his brutality, and hiding it from the world as best she could, protecting and defending his name, and refusing pity as she would have refused money had she been poor. People might guess what she suffered, but no one should know it from her, and no one but herself could tell the half of what she underwent.

Yet, now that it was all over, Wimpole suggested that it might begin again, unless she took measures to defend herself. But her heart revolted at the idea of a divorce. She wondered, as she tried to test herself, whether she could be as strong if the case really arose. It never occurred to her to ask whether her strength might not be folly, for it lay in one of those convictions by which unusual characters are generally moved, and conviction never questions itself.

It was not that in order to be divorced she must almost necessarily bring up in public, and prove by evidence, a certain number of her many wrongs. The publicity would be horrible. Every newspaper in the country would print the details, with hideous headlines. Even her son's deficiency would be dragged into the light. She should have to explain how she had come by the scar on her forehead, and much more that would be harder to tell, if she could bring her lips to speak the words.

Nevertheless, she could do it, and bear everything for a good cause; if, for instance, Archie's future depended upon it, or even if it could do him some good. She could do it all for his sake. But even for his sake she would not be divorced, not even if Harmon were let out of the asylum and came back to her.

Some people, perhaps many, could not understand such a prejudice, or conviction, now that all convictions are commonly spoken of as relative. But will those who do not understand Helen Harmon consider how the world looked upon divorce as recently as five-and-twenty years ago? Nothing can give a clearer idea of the direction taken by social morality than the way in which, during the lifetime of people now barely in middle age, half the world has become accustomed to regard marriage as a contract, and not as a bond.

Twenty-five or thirty years ago divorces were so rare as to be regarded in the light of very uncommon exceptions to the general rule. The divorce law itself is not yet forty years old in England, nor twenty years old in France. In Italy there is no civil divorce whatever at the present day, and the Catholic Church only grants what are not properly divorces, but annullations of marriage, in very rare cases, and with the greatest reluctance.

Even in America every one can remember how divorce was spoken of and thought of until very recently. Within a few years it was deemed to be something very like a disgrace, and certainly a profoundly cynical and immoral proceeding. To-day we can most of us count in our own acquaintance half a dozen persons who have been divorced and been married again. Whatever we may think of it in our hearts, or whatever our religious convictions may be on the subject, it has become so common that when we hear of a flagrant case of cruelty or unfaithfulness, by which a man or woman suffers, the question at once rises to our lips, «Why does she not divorce her husband?» or, «Why does he not divorce his wife?» We have grown used to the idea, and if it does not please us, it certainly does not shock us. It shocked our fathers, but we are perfectly indifferent.

Of course there are many, perhaps a majority, who, though not Roman Catholics, would in their own lives put up with almost anything rather than go to the divorce court for peace. Some actually suffer much, and ask for no redress. But there are very many who have not suffered anything at all, excepting the favorite «incompatibility of temper,» and who have taken advantage of the loose laws in certain States to try a second matrimonial experiment. In what calls itself society there seems still to be a prejudice against a third marriage for divorced persons, but at the present rate of advance in civilization this cannot last long, and the old significance of the word «marriage» will be quite lost before our youngest grandchildren are dead: in other words, by the end of the next century, at the furthest.

There are various forms of honorable political dreaming and of dishonorable political mischief-making nowadays, which we are accustomed to call collectively «socialism.» Most of these rely for their hope of popular success upon their avowed intention of dividing property and preventing its subsequent accumulation. Marriage is an incentive of such accumulation, because it perpetuates families, and therefore keeps property together by inheritance. Therefore all forms of socialism are at present in favor of divorce, as a means of ultimately destroying marriage altogether. A proverb says that whosoever desires the end, desires also the means. There is more truth in the saying than morality in the point of view it expresses. But there are those who desire neither the means nor the end to which they lead, and a struggle is coming the like of which has not been seen since the beginning of the world, and of which we who are now alive shall not see the termination.

The Civil War in the United States turned upon slavery incidentally, not vitally. The cause of that great fight lay much deeper. In the same way the Social War which is coming will turn incidentally upon religion, and be perhaps called a religious war hereafter; but it will not be declared for the sake of faith against unbelief, nor be fought at first by any church, or alliance of churches, against atheism. It will simply turn out that the men who fight on the one side will have either the convictions or the prejudices of Christianity, or both, and that their adversaries will have neither. But the struggle will be at its height when the original steady current of facts which led to inevitable strife has sunk into apparent insignificance under the raging storm of conflicting belief and unbelief. The disadvantage of the unbelievers will lie in the fact that belief is positive and assertive, whereas unbelief is negative and argumentative. It is indeed easier to deny than to prove almost anything. But that is not the question. In life and war it is generally easier to keep than to take, and besides, those who believe «care,» as we say, whereas those who deny generally «care» very little. It is probable, to say the least of it, that so long as the socialists of the near future believe assertively that they have discovered the means of saving humanity from misery and poverty, and fight for a pure conviction, they will have the better of it; but that when they find themselves in the position of attacking half of mankind's religious faith, having no idea, but only a proposition, to offer in its place, they will be beaten.

That seems far from the question of divorce, but it is not. Before the battle the opposing forces are encamped and intrenched at a little distance from each other, and each tries to undermine the other's outworks. Socialism, collectively, has dug a mine under Social Order's strongest tower, which is called marriage, and the edifice is beginning to shake from its foundations, even before the slow-match is lighted.

To one who has known the world well for a quarter of a century, it seems as though the would-be destroyers of the existing order had forgotten, among several other things, the existence of woman, remembering only that of the female. They practically propose to take every woman's privileges in exchange for certain more or less imaginary «rights.» There is no apparent justice in the «conversion,» as it would be called in business. If woman is to have all the rights of man, which, indeed, seem reducible to a political vote now and then, why should she keep all the privileges which man is not allowed? But tell her that when she is allowed to vote for the President of the United States once in four years, no man shall be expected to stand up in a public conveyance to give her a seat, nor to fetch and carry for her, nor to support her instead of being supported by her, nor to keep her for his wife any longer than he chooses, and the «conversion» looks less attractive.

The reason why women have privileges instead of rights is that all men tacitly acknowledge the future of humanity to be dependent on woman from generation to generation. Man works or fights, and takes his rights in payment therefor as well as for a means of working and fighting to greater advantage. And while he is fighting or working, his wife takes care of his children almost entirely. There is not one household in a hundred thousand, rich or poor, where there is really any question about that. It sounds insignificant, perhaps, and it looks as though anybody could take care of two or three small children. Those who have tried it know better, and they are women. Now and then rich mothers are too lazy to look after their children themselves. To do them such justice as one may, they are willing to spend any amount of money in order to get it well done for them, but the result is not encouraging to those who would have all children brought up «by the state.» Even if it were so, who would bring them up? Women, of course. Then why not their own mothers? Because mothers sometimes—or often, for the sake of argument—do not exactly know how. Then educate the mothers, give them chances of knowing how, let them learn, if you know any better than they, which is doubtful, to say the least of it.

Moreover, does any man in his senses really believe that mothers, as a whole, would submit, and let their children be taken from them to a state rearing-house, to be brought up under a number on a ticket by professional baby-farmers, in exchange for the «right» to vote at a presidential election, and the «right» to put away their husbands and take others as often as they please, and the «right» to run for Congress? Yet the plan has been proposed gravely.

There seems to be a good deal to be said in favor of the existing state of things, after all, and particularly in favor of marriage, and therefore against divorce; and it is not surprising that woman, whose life is in reality far more deeply affected by both questions than man's life is, should have also the more profound convictions about them.

Woman brings us into the world, woman is our first teacher, woman makes the world what it is, from century to century. We can no more escape from woman, and yet continue to live our lives as they should be lived, than we can hide ourselves from nature. We are in her care or in her power during more than half our years, and often during all, from first to last. We are born of her, we grow of her, as truly as trees and flowers come of the mother earth and draw their life from the soil in which they are planted. The man who denies his mother is a bad man, and the man who has not loved woman is a man in darkness.

Man is not really unjust to woman in his thoughts of her either, unless he be a lost soul, but he has little reason in respect of her nor any justice in his exactions. Because within himself he knows that she is everything and all things for the life and joy of men, therefore he would seem perfect in her eyes; and he rails against whatsoever in her does not please him, as a blot upon the luster of his ideal, which indeed he would make a glorified reflection of his own faults. When he is most imperfect, he most exacts her praise; when he is weakest, she must think him most strong; when he fails, she must call failure victory, or at the least she must name it honorable defeat; she must not see his meanness, but she must magnify the smallest of his generosities to the great measure of his immeasurable vanity therein; she must see faith in his unfaithfulness, honor in his disgrace, heroism in his cowardice, for his sake; she must forgive freely and forgettingly such injury as he would not pardon any man; in one word, she must love him, that in her love he may think and boast himself a god.

It is much to ask. And yet many a woman who loves a man with all her heart has done and daily does every one of those things, and more; and the man knows it, and will not think of it lest he should die of shame. And, moreover, a woman has borne him, a woman has nursed him, a woman taught him first; a woman gives him her soul and her body when he is a man; and when he is dead, if tears are shed for him, they are a woman's.

If we men are honest, we shall say that we do not give her much for all that, not much honor, not much faith. We think we do enough if we give her life's necessities and luxuries in fair share to the power of our poverty or wealth; that we give much, if we love her; too much, if we trust her altogether.

It is a wonder that women should love, seeing what some men are and what most men may be when the devil is in them. It is a wonder that women should not rise up in a body and demand laws to free them from marriage, for one half the cause that so many of them have.

But they do not. Even in this old age of history they still believe in marriage, and cling to it, and in vast majority cry out against its dissolution. No man ever believes in anything as a woman who loves him believes in him. Men have stronger arms, and heads for harder work, but they have no such hearts as women. And the world has been led by the heart in all ages.

Even when the great mistake is made, many a woman clings to the faith that made it, for the sake of what might have been, in a self-respect of which men do not dream. Even when she has married with little love, and taken a man who has turned upon her like a brute beast, her marriage is still a bond which she will not break, and the vow made is not void because the promise taken has been a vain lie. Its damnation is upon him who spoke it, but she still keeps faith.

So, when her fair years of youth lay scattered and withered as blown leaves along the desert of her past, Helen Harmon, wisely or unwisely, but faithfully, and with a whole heart, meant to keep that plighted word, which is not to be broken by wedded man and woman «until death shall them part.»

## V.

Miss Wimpole was walking up and down the little sitting-room in considerable perplexity. When she was greatly in doubt as to her future conduct, she puckered her elderly lips, frowned severely, and talked to herself with an occasional energetic shaking of the head. She always did up her hair very securely and neatly, so that this was quite safe. Women who are not sure of their hair-pins carry their heads as carefully as a basket of eggs, and do not bend their necks if they have to stoop for anything.

Talking to one's self is a bad habit, especially when the door is open, whether one be swearing at something or examining one's own conscience. But Miss Wimpole could not help it, and the question of returning the price of the hat to Archie Harmon's mother was such a very difficult one that she had forgotten to shut the door.

«Most impossible situation!» she repeated aloud. «Most terrible situation! Poor boy! Half idiotic—father mad. Most distressing situation! If I tell his mother, I shall hurt her feelings dreadfully. If I tell Richard, I shall hurt his feelings dreadfully. If I tell nobody, I shall break my promise to Sylvia, besides putting her in the position of accepting a hat from a young man. Ridiculous present, a hat! If it had only been a parasol! Parasols are not so ridiculous as hats. I wonder why! Perfectly impossible to keep the money, of course. Even Judas Iscariot—dear me! Where are my thoughts running to?

Shocking! But a terrible situation. It was dear, too—eighty francs! We must get it into Mrs. Harmon's hands somehow—»

« Why must you get eighty francs into Mrs. Harmon's hands? » inquired the colonel, laying his hat upon a chair.

The door had been open, and he had heard her talking while he was in the corridor. She uttered an exclamation as she turned and saw him.

« Oh—well—I suppose you heard me. I must really cure myself of talking when I am alone! But I was not saying anything particular.»

« You were saying that you must manage to pay Mrs. Harmon eighty francs. It is very easy, for she happens to be here, and I have just seen her.»

« Oh, I know she is here! » cried Miss Wimpole. « I know it to my cost! She and that —and her son, you know.»

« Yes, I know. But what is the matter? What is the trouble? »

« Oh, Richard! you are so sensitive about anything that has to do with Mrs. Harmon.»

« I? » The colonel looked at her quietly.

« Yes. Of course you are, and it is quite natural, and I quite understand, and I do not blame you in the least. But such a dreadful thing has happened. I hardly know how I can tell you about it. It is really too dreadful for words.»

Wimpole sat down and fanned himself slowly with the Paris « Herald.» He was still rather pale, for his nerves had been shaken.

« Rachel, my dear,» he said mildly, « don't be silly. Tell me what is the matter.»

Miss Wimpole walked slowly once round the room, stopped at the window and looked through the blinds, and at last turned and faced her brother with all the energy of her seasoned character.

« Richard,» she began, « don't call me silly till you hear. It's awful. That boy suddenly appeared in a shop where Sylvia was buying a hat, and paid for it and vanished.»

« Eh? What 's that? » asked Wimpole, opening his eyes wide. « I don't think I quite understood, Rachel. I must have been thinking of something else just then.»

« I dare say you were,» replied his sister, severely. « You are growing dreadfully absent-minded. You really should correct it. I say that when Sylvia was buying a hat, just now, Archie Harmon suddenly appeared in the shop and spoke to us. Then he asked Sylvia whether she liked the hat she was trying on, and she said she did. Then he went off, and when we wished to pay we were told that the hat had been paid for by the young gentleman. Now—»

The colonel interrupted and startled his sister by laughing aloud at this point. He could not help it, though he had not felt in the least as though he could laugh at anything for a long time when he had entered the room. Miss Wimpole was annoyed.

« Richard,» she said solemnly, « you surprise me.»

« Does it not strike you as funny? » asked the colonel, recovering.

« No. It is—it is almost tragic. But perhaps,» she continued, with a fine point of irony, « since you make so light of the matter, you will be good enough to return to Mrs. Harmon the price of the hat purchased by her half-witted boy for your ward.»

« Don't call him half-witted, Rachel, said the colonel. « It 's not so bad as that, you know.»

« I cannot agree with you,» replied his sister. « Only an idiot would think of rushing into a shop where a lady is buying something, and suddenly paying for it. You must admit that, Richard. Only an idiot could do such a thing.»

« I have done just such a thing myself,» observed Wimpole, thoughtfully, for he remembered the miniature he had bought for Helen that afternoon. « I suppose I was an idiot, since you say— »

« I said nothing of the kind, my dear! How can you accuse me of calling you an idiot? Really, Richard, you behave very strangely to-day. I don't know what can be the matter with you. First you manage to make Sylvia cry her eyes out— Heaven knows what dreadful thing you said to her! And now you deliberately accuse me of calling you an idiot. If this sort of thing goes on much longer, there will be an end of our family happiness.»

« This is not one of my lucky days,» said the colonel, resignedly, and he laid down the folded newspaper. « How much did the hat cost? I will return the money to Mrs. Harmon, and explain.»

Miss Wimpole looked at him with gratitude and admiration in her face.

« It was eighty francs,» she answered. « Richard, I did not call you an idiot. In the first place, it would have been totally untrue, and in the second place, it would have been —what shall I say?—it would have been very vulgar to call you an idiot, Richard. It is a vulgar expression.»

« It might have been true, my dear, but I certainly never knew you to say anything vulgar. On the other hand, I really did not assert that you applied the epithet to me. I applied it to myself, rather experimentally. And poor Archie Harmon is not so bad as that, either.»

«If he is not idiotic—or—or something like it, why do you say ‹poor› Archie?»

«Because I am sorry for him,» returned the colonel. «And so are you,» he added presently.

Miss Wimpole considered the matter for a few seconds; then she slowly nodded, and came up to him.

«I am,» she said. «Richard, kiss me.»

That was always the proclamation of peace, not after strife, for they never quarreled, but at the close of an argument. It was done in this way. The colonel rose, and stood before his sister; then both bent their heads a little, and as their cool gray cheeks touched, each kissed the air somewhere in the neighborhood of the other's ear. They had been little children together, and their mother had taught them to «kiss and make friends,» as good children should, whenever there had been any difference; and now they were growing old together, but they had never forgotten, in nearly fifty years, to «kiss and make friends» when they had disagreed. What is childlike is not always childish.

The colonel resumed his seat, and there was silence for a few minutes. The folded newspaper lay on the table unread, and he looked at it, scarcely aware that he saw it.

«I think Archie Harmon must have fallen in love with Sylvia,» he said at last. «That is the only possible explanation. She has grown up since he saw her last, and so has he, though his mind has not developed much, I suppose.»

«Not at all, I should say,» answered Miss Wimpole. «But I wish you would not suggest such things. The mere idea makes me uncomfortable.»

«Yes,» assented the colonel, thoughtfully. «We will not talk about it.»

Suddenly he knew what he was looking at, and he read the first head-lines on the paper, just visible above the folded edge. The words were «Harmon Sane,» printed in large capitals. In a moment he had spread out the sheet.

The big letters only referred to a short telegram lower down. «It is reported, on good authority, that Henry Harmon, who has been an inmate of the Bloomingdale Insane Asylum for some years, is recovering rapidly, and will shortly be able to return to his numerous friends in perfect mental health.»

That was all. The colonel searched the paper from beginning to end in the vain hope of finding something more, and read the little paragraph over and over again. There was no possibility of a mistake. There had never been but one Henry Harmon, and there could certainly be but one in the Bloomingdale asylum. The news was so sudden that Wimpole felt his heart stand still when he first read it, and as he thought of it he grew cold, and shivered as though he had an ague.

It had been easier to think of Harmon's possible recovery before he had seen that scar on Helen's forehead. For many years he had borne the thought that the woman he had silently loved so long was bound to a man little better than a beast; but it had never occurred to him that she might have had much to bear of which he had known nothing, even to violence and physical danger. The knowledge had changed him within the last hour, and the news about Harmon now hardened him all at once in his anger, as hot steel is chilled when it has just reached the cutting temper, and does not change after that.

The colonel was as honorable a man as ever shielded a woman's good name or rode to meet an enemy in fair fight. He was chivalrous with all the world, and quixotic with himself. He had charity for the ways of other men, for he had seen enough to know that many things were done by men whom no one would dare to call dishonorable, which he would not have done to save his own life. He understood that such a lasting love as his was stronger than himself, yet he himself had been so strong that he had never yielded even to its thoughts, nor ever allowed the longing for a final union with Helen at all costs to steal upon his unguarded imagination.

He was not tempted beyond his strength, indeed, and in his apparent perfection that must be remembered. In all those years of his devoted friendship Helen had never let him guess that she could have loved him once, much less that she loved him now, as he did her, with the same resolution to hide from her inward eyes what she could not tear from her inmost heart. But it is never fair to say that if a man had been placed in a certain imaginary position he might have been weak. So long as he has not broken down under the trials and burdens of real life, he has a right to be called strong.

The colonel set no barrier, however, against the devotion to Helen's welfare which he might honorably feel and show. In day-dreams over old books he had envied those clean knights of a younger time, who fought for wives not theirs so openly and bravely and so honestly that the spotless women for whom they faced death took luster of more honor from such unselfish love. And for Helen's sake he had longed for some true circumstance of mortal danger in which to prove once more how well and silently an honest man can die to save an innocent woman.

But those were dreams. In acts he had done much, though never half of what he had always wanted to do. The trouble had all come little by little in Helen's existence, and there had not been one great deciding moment in which his hand or head could have saved her happiness.

Now it seemed as though the time were full, and as if he might at last, by one deed, cast the balance by the scale of happiness. He did not know how to do it, nor whither to turn, but he felt, as he sat by the table with the little newspaper in his hand, that unless he could prevent Harmon from coming back to his wife his own existence was to turn out a miserable failure, his love a lie, and his long devotion but a worthless word.

His first impulse was to leave Lucerne that night, and reach home in the shortest possible time. He would see Harmon and tell him what he thought, and force from him a promise to leave Helen in peace—some unbreakable promise which the man should not be able to deny, some sort of bond that should have weight in law.

The colonel's nostrils quivered, and his steady gray eyes fixed themselves and turned every light as he thought of the interview, and of the quiet, hard words he should select. Each one of them should be a retribution in itself. He was the gentlest of men, but under great provocation he could be relentless.

What would Harmon answer? The colonel grew thoughtful again. Harmon would ask him, with an intonation that would be an insult to Helen, what right Wimpole had acquired to take Helen's part against him, her lawful husband. It would be hard to answer that. He had no right of his own to fight her battles, least of all against the man she had married.

He might answer by reminding Harmon of old times. He might say that he at least resigned the hope of that right, when Harmon had been his friend, because he had believed that it was for Helen's happiness.

That would be but a miserably unsatisfactory answer, though it would be the truth. The colonel did not remember that he had ever wished to strike a man with a whip until the present moment. But the sight of the cut on Helen's forehead had changed him very quickly. He was not sure that he could keep his hands from Harmon if he should see him. And slowly a sort of cold and wrathful glow rose in his face, and he felt as though his long, thin fingers were turning into steel springs.

Miss Wimpole had taken up a book and was reading. She heard him move in his chair, and looked up and saw his expression.

«What is the matter with you, Richard?» she inquired, in surprise.

«Why?» He started nervously.

«You look like the destroying angel,» she observed calmly. «I suppose you are gradually beginning to be angry about Sylvia's hat, as I was. I don't wonder.»

«Oh, yes—Sylvia's hat; yes, yes, I remember.» The colonel passed his hand over his eyes. «I mean, it is perhaps the heat. It 's a warm day. I'll go to my room for a while.»

«Yes, do, my dear. You behave so strangely to-day—as if you were going to be ill.»

But the colonel was already gone, and was stalking down the corridor with his head high, his eyes as hard as polished gray stones, and his nervous hands clenched as they swung a little with his gait.

His sister shook her head energetically, then slowly and sadly, as she watched him in the distance.

«How much more gracefully we grow old than men!» she said aloud, and took up her book again.

(To be continued.) *F. Marion Crawford.*

## DISTANCES.

WE marvel that the silence can divide
  The living from the dead; yet more apart
Are they who all life long dwell side by side,
  But never heart by heart.

*Florence D. Snelling.*

(*BEGUN IN THE NOVEMBER NUMBER.*)

# HUGH WYNNE, FREE QUAKER:

## SOMETIME BREVET LIEUTENANT-COLONEL ON THE STAFF OF HIS EXCELLENCY GENERAL WASHINGTON.

BY DR. S. WEIR MITCHELL,

Author of «In War Time,» «When all the Woods are Green,» etc.

WITH PICTURES BY HOWARD PYLE.

SYNOPSIS OF FIRST PART.

[HUGH WYNNE tells why he desired to write the story of his life, and how the diary of his friend John Warder enabled him to compass this end. He relates why his people came out of Wales and gave up an estate to win freedom to worship God as Quakers please. Of his school life in Philadelphia, about 1760 and later, he speaks; of the books he read, and of his mother, a French Quaker; and also of his aunt Gainor Wynne, a maiden lady of wealth, who early went back to the Church of England and was all for resistance to the crown. Hugh speaks of John Wynne, his father, as a stern man and an exemplary Quaker, strongly loyal to the king. Between these two conflicting influences Hugh Wynne's young life was passed. He leaves school to attend the academy, which now is the University of Pennsylvania. He has his first fight, and is thereby discouraged as to the value of non-resistance to oppression.]

IV.

AFTER this my days went by more peacefully. The help and example of Jack assisted me greatly in my lessons, which I did little relish. I was more fond of reading, and devoured many books as I sat under our orchard trees in the spring, or nestled up to the fire on the long winter evenings, coiled on the settle, that its high back might keep off drafts. My aunt lent me an abundance of books after that famous «Travels» of Mr. Gulliver. Now and then my father looked at what she gave me, but he soon tired of this, and fell asleep in the great oak chair which Governor Penn gave my grandfather.

Many volumes, and some queer ones, I fell upon in my aunt's house, but, save once, as to the naughtiness of Mrs. Aphra Behn, she never interfered. We liked greatly a book called «Peter Wilkins,» by one Paltock, full of a queer folk who had winged «graundees,» a sort of crimson robe made of folds of their own skin. None read it now. My dear Jack fancied it much more than I.

I was nigh to fifteen before we read «Robinson Crusoe,» but even earlier I devoured at my aunt's «Captain Jack» and «The History of the Devil.» As to the first book, it filled us with delight. Jack and I used to row over to Windmill Island, on the great Delaware, and there at the south end we built a hut, and slew bullfrogs, and found steps on the sand, I being thereafter Friday, and Jack my master. We made, too, a sail and mast for my boat, and, thus aided, sailed of Saturdays up and down the noble river, which I have always loved.

A still greater joy was to go in our chaise with my mother to the governor's woods, which extended from Broad street to the Schuylkill, and from Callowhill to South street. There we tied the horse, and under the great trees we found in spring arbutus, even beneath the snow, and later fetched thence turkey-foot ferns, and wild honeysuckle, and quaker-ladies, with jack-in-the-pulpits, and fearful gray corpse-lights hid away in the darker woods. In the forest my mother seemed even younger than at home, and played with us, and told us quaint tales of her French people, or fairy-stories of Giant Jack and others, which were by no means such as Friends approved.

In our house one same stern, unbending rule prevailed. I have been told by my aunt Gainor Wynne that when he was young my father was not always so steadfast in conduct as to satisfy Friends. When I was old enough to observe and think, he had surely become strict enough; but this severity of opinion and action increased with years, and showed in ways which made life difficult for those near to him. In fact, before I attained manhood the tinted arms and the picture of Wyncote were put away in the attic room. My mother's innocent love of ornament also became to him a serious annoyance, and these peculiarities seemed at last to deepen whenever the political horizon darkened. At such times he became silent, and yet more keen than usual to detect and denounce anything in our home life which was not to his liking.

The affairs of a young fellow between the ages of childhood and younger manhood can have but meagre interest. Our school life went on, and while we worked or played, our elders saw the ever-increasing differences between king and colonies becoming year by year more difficult of adjustment. Except when some noisy crisis arose, they had for us lads but little interest.

Most people used the city landings, or lightered their goods from ships in the stream. We, however, had a great dock built out near to the mouth of Dock Creek, and a warehouse. Hither came sloops from my father's plantation of tobacco, near Annapolis, and others from the «permitted islands,» the Cape de Verde and the Madeiras. Staves for barrels, tobacco, and salt fish were the exports, and in return came Eastern goods brought to these islands, and huge tuns of Madeira wine. Rum, too, arrived from New England, and salted mackerel. What else my father imported, of French goods or tea, reached us from England, for we were not allowed to trade with the continent of Europe nor directly with India.

Once my father took me with him to Lewes, near Cape Hinlopen, on one of his ships, and to my joy we were met there by Tom, our black slave, with horses, and rode back during two days by Newcastle and Chester. As I rode ill, of course, and was sore for a week, my father thought it well that I should learn to ride, and this exercise I took to easily. Just before I was sixteen my aunt gave me a horse, and after we had separated abruptly a few times, and no harm to any, I became the master, and soon an expert rider, as was needful in a land where most long journeys were made on horseback.

It seems to me now, as I look back, that the events of life were preparing me and my friend Jack for what was to follow. Our boating made every part of the two rivers familiar. Now that I had a horse, Jack's father, who would always do for him readily what my Aunt Gainor did for me, yielded to his desire to ride; and so it was that we began, as leisure served, to extend our rides to Germantown, or even to Chestnut Hill. Thus all the outlying country became well known to both of us, and there was not a road, a brook, or a hill, which we did not know.

Until this happy time I had been well pleased to follow my aunt on a pillion behind her servant Cæsar, but now I often went with her, perched on my big horse, and got from my aunt, an excellent horsewoman, some sharp lessons as to leaping, and certain refinements in riding that she had seen or known of in London.

A Captain Montresor—he who afterward, when a major, was Howe's engineer—used to ride with her in the spring of '69. He was a tall, stout man of middle age, and much spoken of as likely to marry my Aunt Gainor, although she was older than he, for, as fat Oliver de Lancey said years after, «There is no age to a woman's money, and guineas are always young.» My aunt Gainor Wynne was still a fine gentlewoman, and did not look her years. As to this question of age, she was like a man, and so in fact she was in some other ways. She would tell any one how old she was. She once informed Mr. de Lancey that she was so much more of a man than any British officer she knew that she did not see how she could decently marry any of them.

I think it was about this time that I saw a little scene which much impressed me, and which often recurs to my memory. We—that is, Mr. Montresor, and my Aunt Gainor and I—on a Saturday afternoon rode over by the lower ferry and up Gray's Lane, and so to Mr. Hamilton's country-seat. «The Woodlands,» as it was called, stood on a hill amid many beautiful trees and foreign shrubs and flowers. Below it ran the quiet Schuylkill, and beyond, above the governor's woods, could be seen far away Dr. Kearsley's fine spire of Christ Church. No better did Master Wren himself ever contrive, or more proportioned to the edifice beneath it.

On the porch were Mr. Hamilton and Mrs. Penn, with saucy gray eyes, and Mrs. Ferguson. A slim young girl, Rebecca Franks, was teasing a cat. She teased some one all her days, and did it merrily, and not unkindly. She was little and very pretty, with a dark skin. Did she dream she should marry a British soldier, —a baronet and general,—and end her days in London well on in the century yet to come?

Andrew Allen, whose father, the chief justice, took his wife Margaret from this house, sat on the steps near Miss Franks, and beside her little Peggy Shippen, who already gave promise of the beauty which won for her so pitiful a life. Nothing in this garden of gay women and flowers foretold the tragedy of West Point. I think of it now with sad wonder.

In one or another way these people became known in our annals. Most of them were of the more exclusive party known as the governor's set, and belonged to the Church of England. With the Galloways, Cadwaladers, Willings, Shippens, Chews, and others, they formed a more or less distinct society, affecting London ways, dining at the extreme hour of four, loving cards, the dance, fox-hunting, and to see a main of game-cocks. Among them—not of them—came and went certain of what were called «genteel» Quakers—Morrises, Pembertons, Whartons, and Logans. They had races too,—that is, the governor's set,—and one of my delights was, on the way to the academy, to stop in Third street, above Chestnut, and see the race-horses in the Widow Nichols's stables at the sign of the Indian Queen.

But I have left the laughter of the last century echoing among the columns of Andrew Hamilton's home. The guests were made welcome, and had a dish of tea or a glass of punch; and those desiring no more bohea set a spoon across the cup, and fell into groups. My aunt opened the velvet bag which hung at her waist, to pay Mrs. Ferguson a small gambling debt of the night before.

« Ah, here! » she cried gaily, « Mr. Montresor, this is for you. One of Mr. Grenville's stamps; I kept two. I was lucky enough to get them from Master Hughes, the stamp officer—a great curiosity. You shall have one.»

Mr. Montresor bowed. « I will keep it,» he said, « until it comes into use again.»

« That will be never,» said Andrew Allen, turning.

« Never! » repeated Miss Wynne. « Let us hope, sir, it may be a lesson to all future ministers.»

« A man was wanted in New York in place of Mr. Gage,» cried Mrs. Ferguson. « As to those New England Puritans, they were in rebellion before they came over, and have been ever since.»

« And what of New York, and this town, and Virginia? » said my Aunt Gainor, with her great nose well up.

« I would have put an end to their disloyal ways, one and all,» cried Mrs. Ferguson.

« It is curious,» said Mr. Galloway, « that the crown should be so thwarted. What people have more reason to be contented? »

« Contented! » said Miss Wynne. « Already they talk of taxes in which we are to have no voice. Contented! and not a ship dare trade with France! It amazes me that there is a man in the plantations to sit quiet under it.»

« I am of your opinion, madam,» said Mr. Macpherson, « and I might go still further.»

« They consider us as mere colonials, and we may not so much as have a bishop of our own. I would I had my way, sir.»

« And what would you do, Mistress Wynne? » asked Mr. Chew.

« I would say, ‹ Mr. Attorney-General, give us the same liberty all the English have, to go and come on the free seas! › »

« And if not? » said Montresor, smiling.

« And if not,» she returned, « then—» and she touched the sword at his side. I wondered to see how resolute she looked.

The captain smiled. « I hope you will not command a regiment, madam.»

« Would to God I could! »

« I should run,» he cried, laughing. And thus pleasantly ended a talk which was becoming bitter to many of this gay company.

Destiny was already sharpening the sword we were soon to draw, and of those who met and laughed that day there were sons who were to be set against fathers, and brothers whom war was to find in hostile ranks. A young fellow of my age, the son of Mr. Macpherson, sat below us on the steps with the girls. He was to leave his young life on the bastion at Quebec, and, for myself, how little did I dream of what I should get out of the devil-pot of war which was beginning to simmer!

Very soon I was sent with Rebecca Franks and Miss Chew to gather flowers. Miss Franks evidently despised my youth, and between the two little maids I, being unused to girls, had not a pleasant time, and was glad to get back to the porch, where we stood silent until bidden to be seated, upon which the girls curtseyed and I bowed, and then sat down to eat cakes and drink syllabub.

At last my aunt put on her safeguard petticoat, the horses came, and we rode away. For a while she was silent, answering the captain in monosyllables; but just beyond the ferry his horse cast a shoe, and went so lame that the officer must needs return to Woodlands leading him, there to ask a new mount.

For yet a while my aunt rode on without a word, but at last she began to rally me as to Miss Chew. I had to confess I cared not for her or the other, or, indeed, for maids at all.

« It will come,» said she. « Oh, it will come soon enough. Peggy Chew has the better manners. And, by the way, sir, when you bow, keep your back straight. Mr. Montresor has a pretty way of it. Observe him, Hugh. But he is a fool, and so are the rest; and as for Betty Ferguson, I should like to lay a whip over her back like that,» and she hit my horse sharply, poor thing, so that I lost a stirrup and came near to falling.

When the beast got quiet I asked why these nice people, who had such pleasant ways, were all fools.

« I will tell you,» she said. « There are many and constant causes of trouble between us and the king. When one ends, like this Stamp Act, another is hatched. It was the best of us who left England, and we are trained to rely on ourselves, and have no need of England. You will live to see dark days, Hugh—just what, God alone can tell; but you will live to see them, and your life will have to answer some questions. This may seem strange to you, my lad, but it will come.»

What would come I knew not. She said

no more, but rode homeward at speed, as she liked best to do.

Thus time went by, until I was full sixteen, having been at the college a year later than was usual. I had few battles to fight, and contrived to keep these to myself, or to get patched up at my Aunt Wynne's, who delighted to hear of these conflicts, and always gave me a shilling to heal my wounds. My dear, fair-haired Jack Aunt Gainor thought a girl-boy, and fit only to sell goods, or, at best, to become a preacher. His father she used and disliked.

Meanwhile we had been through Horace and Cicero,—and Ovid for our moral improvement, I suppose,—with Virgil and Sallust, and at last Cæsar, whom alone of them all I liked. Indeed, Jack and I built over a brook in my Aunt Gainor's garden at Chestnut Hill a fair model of Cæsar's great bridge over the Rhine. This admired product of our ingenuity was much praised by Captain Montresor, who was well aware of my aunt's weakness for a certain young person.

My father's decisions came always without warning. In the fall of 1769 I was just gone back to the academy, and put to work at mathematics and some Greek under James Wilson, at that period one of the tutors, and some time later an associate judge of the Supreme Court. This great statesman and lawyer of after-days was a most delightful teacher. He took a fancy to my Jack, and, as we were inseparable, put up with my flippancy and deficient scholarship. Jack's diary says otherwise, and that he saw in me that which, well used, might make of me a man of distinction. At all events, he liked well to walk with us on a Saturday, or to go in my boat, which was for us a great honour. My father approved of James Wilson, and liked him on the holiday to share our two-o'clock dinner. Then, and then only, did I understand the rigour and obstinacy of my father's opinions, for they ofttimes fell into débate as to the right of the crown to tax us without representation. Mr. Wilson said many towns in England had no voice in Parliament, and that, if once the crown yielded the principle we stood on, it would change the whole political condition in the mother-land; and this the king would never agree to see. Mr. Wilson thought we had been foolish to say, as many did, that, while we would have no internal taxes, we would submit to a tax on imports. This he considered even worse. My father was for obedience and non-resistance, and could not see that we were fighting a battle for the liberty of all Englishmen. He simply repeated his opinions, and was but a child in the hands of this clear-headed thinker. My father might well have feared for the effect of Mr. Wilson's views on a lad of my age, in whose mind he opened vistas of thought far in advance of those which, without him, I should ever have seen.

John Wynne was, however, too habitually accustomed to implicit obedience to dream of danger, and thus were early sown in my mind the seeds of future action, with some doubt as to my father's ability to cope with a man like our tutor, who considerately weighed my father's sentiments (they were hardly opinions), and so easily and courteously disposed of them that these logical defeats were clear even to us boys.

Our school relations with this gentleman were abruptly broken. One day in late October of 1769, we went on a long walk through the proprietary's woods, gathering for my mother boughs of the many-tinted leaves of autumn. These branches she liked to set in jars of water in the room where we sat, so that it might be gay with the lovely colours she so much enjoyed. As we entered the forest about Eighth street Mr. Wilson joined us, and went along, chatting agreeably with my mother. Presently he said to me: «I have just left your father with Mr. Pemberton, talking about some depredations in Mr. Penn's woods. He tells me you boys are to leave school, but for what I do not know. I am sorry.»

Jack and I had of late expected this, and I, for one, was not grieved, but my friend was less well pleased.

We strolled across to the Schuylkill, and there, sitting down, amused ourselves with making a little crown of twisted twigs and leaves of the red and yellow maples. This we set merrily on my mother's gray beaver, while Mr. Wilson declared it most becoming. Just then Friend Pemberton and my father came upon us, and, as usual when the latter appeared, our laughter ceased.

«I shall want thee this afternoon, Hugh,» he said. «And what foolishness is this on thy head, wife? Art thou going home in this guise?»

«It seems an innocent prettiness,» said Pemberton, while my mother, in no wise dismayed, looked up with her big blue eyes.

«Thou wilt always be a child,» said my father.

«Je l'espère,» said the mother; «must I be put in a corner? The *bon Dieu* hath just changed the forest fashions. I wonder is He a Quaker, Friend Pemberton?»

«Thou hast ever a neat answer,» said the gentle old man. «Come, John, we are not yet done.»

My father said no more, and we boys were still as mice. We went homeward with our mirth quite at an end, Jack and Wilson leaving us at Fourth street.

In the afternoon about six—for an hour had been named—I saw my aunt's chaise at the door. I knew at once that something unusual was in store, for Mistress Wynne rarely came hither except to see my mother, and then always in the forenoon. Moreover, I noticed my father at the window, and never had I known him to return so early. When I went in he said at once:

«I have been telling thy aunt of my intention in regard to thee.»

«And I utterly disapprove of it,» said my aunt.

«Wait,» he said. «I desire that thou shalt enter as one of my clerks; but first it is my will that, as the great and good proprietary decreed, thou shouldst acquire some mechanic trade, I care not what.»

I was silent; I did not like it. Even far later certain of the stricter Friends adhered to a rule which was once useful, but was now no longer held to be of imperative force.

«I would suggest shoemaking,» said my Aunt Gainor, scornfully, «or tailoring.»

«I beg of thee, Gainor,» said my mother, «not to discontent the lad.»

«Concerning this matter,» returned my father, «I will not be thwarted. I asked thee to come hither, not to ridicule a sensible decision, but to consult upon it.»

«You have had all my wisdom,» said the lady. «I had thought to ask my friend Charles Townsend for a pair of colours; but now that troops are sent to Boston to override all reason, I doubt it. Do as you will with the boy. I wash my hands of him.»

This was by no means my father's intention. I saw his face set in an expression I well knew; but my mother laid a hand on his arm, and, with what must have been a great effort, he controlled his anger, and said coldly: «I have talked this over with thy friend Joseph Warder, and he desired that his son should share in my decision as to Hugh. Talk to him, Gainor.»

«I do not take counsel with my agent, John. He does as I bid him. I could shift his opinions at a word. He is a Tory to-day, and a Whig to-morrow, and anything to anybody. Why do you talk such nonsense to me? Let me tell you that he has already been to ask me what I think of it. He feels some doubt, poor man. Indeed, he is disposed to consider. Bother! what does it matter what he considers?»

«If he has changed his mind, I have not. Joseph hath ever a coat of many colours.»

«I shall tell him,» she cried, laughing. The Quaker rule of repression and non-resistance by no means forbade the use of the brutal bludgeon of sarcasm, as many a debate in Meeting could testify. She rose as she spoke, and my mother said gently:

«Thou wilt not tell him, Gainor.»

Meanwhile I stood amazed at a talk which so deeply concerned me.

«Shall it be a smithy?» said my father.

«Oh, what you like. The Wynnes are well down in the world—trade, horseshoeing. Good evening.»

«Gainor! Gainor!» cried my mother; but she was gone in wrath, and out of the house.

«Thou wilt leave the academy. I have already arranged with Lowry, in South street, to take thee. Three months should answer.»

To this I said, «Yes, yes,» and went away but little pleased, my mother saying, «It is only for a little time, my son.»

## V.

SAYS my friend Jack in his journal:

«The boys were in these times keen politicians whenever any unusual event occurred, and the great pot was like soon to boil furiously, and scald the cooks. Charles Townsend's ministry was long over. The Stamp Act had come and gone. The Non-importation Agreement had been signed even by men like Andrew Allen and Mr. Penn. Lord North, a gentle and obstinate person, was minister. The Lord Hillsborough, a man after the king's heart, had the colonial office. The troops had landed in Boston, and the letters of Dickinson and Vindex had fanned the embers of discontent into flame.

«Through it all we boys contrived to know everything that was happening. I had a sense of fear about it, but to Hugh I think it was delightful. A fire, a mob, confusion, and disorder appeal to most boys' minds as desirable. My father was terrified at the disturbance of commerce, and the angry words which began to be heard. As to Mr. John Wynne, he coolly adjusted his affairs, as I have heard, and settled down with the Friends, such as Waln and Shoemaker and Pemberton and the rest, to accept whatever the king might decree.»

Jack and I talked it all over in wild boy fashion, and went every day at six in the morning to Lowry's on South street. At first we both hated the work, but this did not last; and once we were used to it, the business had for fellows like ourselves a certain charm. The horses we learned to know and understand. Their owners were of a class with which in those days it was not thought seemly for persons of our degree to be familiar; here it was unavoidable, and I soon learned how deep in the hearts of the people was the determination to resist the authority of the crown.

The lads we knew of the gay set used to come and laugh at us as we plied the hammer or blew the bellows; and one day Miss Franks and Miss Peggy Chew, and I think Miss Shippen, stood awhile without the forge, making very merry. Jack got red in the face, but I was angry, worked on doggedly, and said nothing. At last I thrashed soundly one Master Galloway, who called me a horse-cobbler, and after that no more trouble.

I became strong and muscular as the work went on, and got to like our master, who was all for liberty, and sang as he struck, and taught me much that was useful as to the management of horses, so that I was not long unhappy. My father, pleased at my diligence, once said to me that I seemed to be attentive to the business in hand; and as far as I remember, this was the only time in my life that he ever gave me a word of even the mildest commendation.

As for Jack, it was what he needed. His slight, graceful figure filled out and became very straight, losing a stoop it had, so that he grew to be a well-built, active young fellow, rosy, and quite too pretty, with his blond locks. After our third month began, Lowry married a widow, and moved away to her farm up the country and beyond the Blue Bell tavern, where he carried on his business, and where he was to appear again to me at a time when I sorely needed him. It was to be another instance of how a greater Master overrules our lives for good.

Just after we had heard the news of the widow, my father came into the forge one day with Joseph Warder. He stood and watched me shoe a horse, and asked Lowry if I had learned the business. When he replied that we both might become more expert, but that we could make nails, and shoe fairly well, my father said:

«Take off these aprons, and go home. There will be other work for both of you.»

We were glad enough to obey, and, dropping our leathern aprons, thus ended our apprenticeship. Next week Tom Lowry, our master, appeared with a fine beaver for me, saying, as I knew, that it was the custom to give an apprentice a beaver when his time was up, and that he had never been better served by any.

My Aunt Gainor kept away all this time, and made it clear that she did not wish my black hands at her table. My father, no doubt, felt sure that, so far as I was concerned, she would soon or late relent. This, in fact, came about in midwinter, upon her asking my mother to send me to see her. My father observed that he had no will to make quarrels, or to keep them alive. My mother smiled demurely, knowing him as none other did, and bade me go with her.

In her own room she had laid out on the bed a brown coat of velveteen, with breeches to match, and stockings with brown clocks, and also a brown beaver, the back looped up, all of which she had, with sweet craftiness, provided, that I might appear well before my Aunt Gainor.

«Thou wilt fight no one on the way, Hugh. And now, what shall be done with his hands, so rough and so hard? Scrub them well. Tell Gainor I have two new lilies for her, just come from Jamaica. Bulbs they are; I will care for them in the cellar. I was near to forget the marmalade of bitter orange. She must send; I cannot trust Tom. Thy father had him whipped at the jail yesterday, and he is sulky. Put on thy clothes, and I will come again to see how they fit thee.»

In a little while she was back again, declaring I looked a lord, and that if she were a girl she should fall in love with me, and then—«But I shall never let any woman but me kiss thee. I shall be jealous. And now, sir, a bow. That was better. Now, as I curtsey, it is bad manners to have it over before I am fully risen. Then it is permitted that *les beaux yeux se rencontrent. Comme çà. Celà va bien.* That is better done.»

«What vanities are these?» said my father at the door she had left open.

She was nowise alarmed. «Come in, John,» she cried. «He does not yet bow as well as thou. It would crack some Quaker backs, I think. I can hear Friend Waln's joints creak when he gets up.»

«Nonsense, wife! Thou art a child to this day.»

«Then kiss me, *mon père.*» And she ran to him and stood on tiptoe, so engaging and so pretty that he could not help but lift up her slight figure, and, kissing her, set her down. It was a moment of rare tenderness. Would I had known or seen more of them!

«Thou wilt ruin him, wife.»

As I ran down the garden she called after me: «Do not thou forget to kiss her hand. To-morrow will come the warehouse; but take the sweets of life as they offer. Adieu.» She stood to watch me, all her dear heart in her eyes, something pure, and, as it were, virginal in her look. God rest her soul!

It was late when I got to my aunt's, somewhere about eight, and the hum of voices warned me of her having company. As I entered she rose, expecting an older guest, and, as I had been bid, I bowed low, and touched her hand with my lips, as I said:

«Dear Aunt Gainor, it has been so long!» I could have said nothing better. She laughed.

«Here is my nephew, Mr. Etherington»—this to an English major; «and, Captain Wallace of the king's navy, my nephew.»

The captain was a rough, boisterous sailor, and the other a man with too much manner, and, as I heard later, risen from the ranks.

He saluted me with a lively thump on the shoulder, which I did not relish. «Zounds! sir, but you are a stout young Quaker!»

«We are most of us Quakers here, captain,» said a quiet gentleman, who saw, I fancy, by my face that this rude greeting was unpleasant to me.

«How are you, Hugh?» This was the Master of the Rolls, Mr. John Morris. Then my aunt said, «Go and speak to the ladies—you know them»; and as I turned aside, «I beg pardon, Sir William; this is my nephew, Hugh Wynne.» This was addressed to a high-coloured personage in yellow velvet with gold buttons, and a white flowered waistcoat, and with his queue in a fine hair-net.

«This is Sir William Draper, Hugh; he who took Manilla, as you must know.» I did not, nor did I know until later that he was one of the victims of the sharp pen of Junius, with whom, for the sake of the Marquis of Granby, he had rashly ventured to tilt. The famous soldier smiled as I saluted him with my best bow.

«Fine food for powder, Mistress Wynne, and already sixteen! I was in service three years earlier. Should he wish for an ensign's commission, I am at your service.»

«Ah, Sir William, that might have been, a year or so ago, but now he may have to fight General Gage.»

«The gods forbid! Our poor general!»

«Mistress Wynne is a rank Whig,» put in Mrs. Ferguson. «She reads Dickinson's ‹Farmer's Letters,› and all the wicked treason of that man Adams.»

«A low demagogue!» cried Mrs. Galloway. «I hear there have been disturbances in Boston, and that because one James Otis has been beaten by our officers, and because our bands play ‹Yankee Doodle› on Sundays in front of the churches—I beg pardon, the meetings—Mr. Robinson, the king's collector, has had to pay and apologise. Most shameful it is!»

«I should take short measures,» said the sailor.

«And I,» cried Etherington. «I have just come from Virginia, but not a recruit could I get. It is like a nest of ants in a turmoil, and the worst of all are the officers who served in the French wars. There is, too, a noisy talker, Patrick Henry, and a Mr. Washington.»

«I think it was he who saved the wreck of the king's army under Mr. Braddock,» said my aunt. «I can remember how they all looked. Not a wig among them. The lodges must have been full of them, but their legs saved their scalps.»

«Is it for this they call them wigwams?» cries naughty Miss Chew.

«Fie! fie!» says her mamma, while my aunt laughed merrily.

«A mere Potomac planter,» said Etherington, «'pon my soul—and with such airs, as if they were gentlemen of the line.»

«Perhaps,» said my aunt, «they had not had your opportunities of knowing all grades of the service.»

The major flushed. «I have served the king as well as I know how, and I trust, madam, I shall have the pleasure to aid in the punishment of some of these insolent rebels.»

«May you be there to see, Hugh,» said my aunt, laughing.

Willing to make a diversion, Mrs. Chew said, «Let us defeat these Tories at the card-table, Gainor.»

«With all my heart,» said my aunt, glad of this turn in the talk.

«Come and give me luck, Hugh,» said Mrs. Ferguson. «What a big fellow you are! Your aunt must find you ruffles soon, and a steenkirk.»

With this I sat down beside her, and wondered to see how eager and interested they all became, and how the guineas and gold half-joes passed from one to another, while the gay Mrs. Ferguson, who was at the table with Mrs. Penn, Captain Wallace, and my aunt, gave me my first lesson in this form of industry.

A little later there was tea, chocolate, and rusks, with punch for the men; and Dr. Shippen came in, and the great Dr. Rush, with his delicate, clean-cut face under a full wig. Dr. Shippen was full of talk about some fine game-cocks, and others were busy with the spring races in Centre Square.

You may be sure I kept my ears open to hear what all these great men said. I chanced to hear Dr. Rush deep in talk behind the punch-table with a handsome young man, Dr. Morgan, newly come from London.

Dr. Rush said, «I have news to-day, in a letter from Mr. Adams, of things being unendurable. He is bold enough to talk of separation from England; but that is going far, too far.»

« I think so, indeed,» said Morgan. « I saw Dr. Franklin in London. He advises conciliation, and not to act with rash haste. These gentlemen yonder make it difficult.»

« Yes; there is no insolence like that of the soldier.» And this was all I heard or remember, for my aunt bade me run home and thank my mother, telling me to come again and soon.

The plot was indeed thickening, and even a lad as young as I could scent peril in the air. At home I heard nothing of it. No doubt my father read at his warehouse the « Pennsylvania Journal,» or more likely Galloway's gazette, the « Chronicle,» which was rank Tory, and was suppressed in 1773. But outside of the house I learned the news readily. Mr. Warder took papers on both sides, and also the Boston « Packet,» so that Jack and I were well informed, and used to take the gazettes when his father had read them, and devour them safely in our boat, when by rare chance I had a holiday.

And so passed the years 1770, 1771, and 1772, when Lord North precipitated the crisis by attempting to control the judges in Massachusetts, who were in future to be paid by the crown, and would thus pass under its control. Adams now suggested committees of correspondence, and thus the first step toward united action was taken.

These years, up to the autumn of 1772, were not without influence on my own life for both good and evil. I was of course kept sedulously at work at our business, and, though liking it even less than farriery, learned it well enough. It was not without its pleasures. Certainly it was an agreeable thing to know the old merchant captains, and to talk to their men or themselves. The sea had not lost its romance. Men could remember Kidd and Blackbeard. In the low-lying dens below Dock Creek and on King street, were many, it is to be feared, who had seen the black flag flying, and who knew too well the keys and shoals of the West Indies. The captain who put to sea with such sailors had need to be resolute and ready. Ships went armed, and I was amazed to see, in the holds of our own ships, carronades, which out on the ocean were hoisted up and set in place on deck; also cutlasses and muskets in the cabin, and good store of pikes. I ventured once to ask my father if this were consistent with non-resistance. He replied that pirates were like to wild beasts, and that I had better attend to my business; after which I said no more, having food for thought.

These captains got thus a noble training, were splendid seamen, and not unused to arms and danger, as proved fortunate in days to come. Once I would have gone to the Madeiras with Captain Biddle, but unluckily my mother prevailed with my father to forbid it. It had been better for me had it been decided otherwise, because I was fast getting an education which did me no good.

« Indeed,» says Jack in his diary, « I was much troubled in the seventies» (he means up to '74, when we were full twenty-one) « about my friend Hugh. The town was full of officers of all grades, who came and went, and brought with them much licence and contempt for colonists in general, and a silly way of parading their own sentiments on all occasions. Gambling, hard drinking, and all manner of worse things became common and more openly indulged in. Neither here nor in Boston could young women walk about unattended, a new and strange thing in our quiet town.

« Mistress Gainor's house was full of these gentlemen, whom she entertained with a freedom equalled only by that with which she spoke her good Whig mind. The air was full of excitement. Business fell off, and Hugh and I had ample leisure to do much as we liked.

« I declare that I deserve no praise for having escaped the temptations which beset Hugh. I hated all excess, and suffered in body if I drank or ate more than was wise. As to worse things than wine and cards, I think Miss Wynne was right when she described me as a girl-boy; for the least rudeness or laxity of talk in women I disliked, and as regards the mere modesties of the person, I have always been like some well-nurtured maid.

« Thus it was that when Hugh, encouraged by his aunt, fell into the company of these loose, swaggering captains and cornets, I had either to give up him, who was unable to resist them, or to share in their vicious ways myself. It was my personal disgust at drunkenness or loose society which saved me, not any moral or religious safeguards, although I trust I was not altogether without these helps. I have seen now and then that to be refined in tastes and feelings is a great aid to a virtuous life. Also I have known some who would have been drunkards but for their heads and stomachs, which so behaved as to be good substitutes for conscience. It is sometimes the body which saves the soul. Both of these helps I had, but my dear Hugh had neither. He was a great, strong, masculine fellow, and if I may seem to have said that he wanted refined feelings, that is not so, and to him, who will never read these lines, and to myself, I must apologise.»

I did come to see these pages, as you know. I think he meant that, with the wine of youth, and at times of other vintages, in my veins, the strong paternal blood, which in my father only a true, if hard, religion kept in order, was too much for me. If I state this awkwardly it is because all excuses are awkward. Looking back, I wonder that I was not worse, and that I did not go to the uttermost devil. I was vigourous, and had the stomach of a temperate ox, and a head which made no complaints. The morning after some mad revel I could rise at five, and go out in my boat and overboard, and then home in a glow, with a fine appetite for breakfast; and I was so big and tall that I was thought to be many years older than I was.

I should have been less able unwatched to go down this easy descent, had it not been for a train of circumstances which not only left me freer than I ought to have been, but, in the matter of money, made it only too possible for me to hold my own amid evil or lavish company. My aunt had lived in London, and in a society which had all the charm of breeding, and all the vices of a period more coarse than ours. She detested my father's notions, and if she meant to win me to her own she took an ill way to do it. I was presented to the English officers, and freely supplied with money, to which I had been quite unused, so long as my father was the only source of supply. We were out late when I was presumed to be at my Aunt Gainor's; and to drink and bet, or to see a race or cockfight, or to pull off knockers, or to bother the ancient watchmen, were now some of my most reputable amusements. I began to be talked about as a bit of a rake, and my Aunt Gainor was not too greatly displeased; she would hear of our exploits and say «Fie! fie!» and then give me more guineas. Worse than all, my father was deep in his business, lessening his ventures, and thus leaving me more time to sow the seed of idleness. Everything, as I now see it, combined to make easy for me the downward path. I went along it without the company of Jack Warder, and so we drew apart; he would none of it.

When my father began to withdraw his capital my mother was highly pleased, and more than once in my presence said to him: «Why, John, dost thou strive for more and more money? Hast thou not enough? Let us give up all this care and go to our great farm at Merion, and live as peaceful as our cattle.» She did not reckon upon the force with which the habits of a life bound my father to his business.

I remember that it was far on in April, 1773, when my Aunt Gainor appeared one day in my father's counting-house. Hers was a well-known figure on King street, and even in the unpleasant region alongshore to the south of Dock street. She would dismount, leave her horse to the groom, and, with a heavily mounted, silver-topped whip in hand, and her riding-petticoat gathered up, would march along, picking her way through mud and filth. Here she contrived to find the queer china things she desired, or in some mysterious way she secured cordials and such liquors as no one else could get.

Once she took my mother with her, and loaded her with gods of the Orient and fine China pongee silks.

«But, Hugh,» said the dear lady, «*ce n'est pas possible de vous la décrire. Mon Dieu!* she can say terrible words, and I have seen a man who ventured some rudeness to me—no, no, *mon cher*, nothing to anger you; *il avait peur de cette femme*. He was afraid of her—her and her whip. He was so alarmed that he let her have a great china mandarin for a mere nothing. I think he was glad to see her well out of his low tavern.»

«But the man,» I urged; «what did he say to thee, mother?»

«*N'importe, mon fils*. I did want the mandarin. He nodded this way—this way. He wagged his head as a dog wags his tail, like Thomas Scattergood in the Meeting. *Comme çà*.» She became that man in a moment, turning up the edge of her silk shawl, and nodding solemnly. I screamed with laughter. Ever since I was a child, despite my father's dislikes, she had taught me French, and when alone with me liked me to chatter in her mother language. In fact, I learned it well.

On the occasion of which I began just now to speak, my Aunt Gainor entered, with a graver face than common, and I rising to leave her with my father, she put her whip across my breast as I turned, and said, «No; I want you to hear what I have to say.»

«What is it, Gainor?»

«This business of the ship ‹Gaspee› the Rhode Island men burned is making trouble in the East. The chief justice of Rhode Island, Hopkins, has refused to honour the order to arrest these Rhode-Islanders.»

«Pirates!» said my father.

«Pirates, if you like. We shall all be pirates before long.»

«Well, Gainor, is that all? It does not concern me.»

«No; I have letters from London which inform me that the Lord North is but a puppet, and as the king pulls the wires he will dance to whatever tune the king likes. He was a nice, amiable young fellow when I stayed at my Lord Guilford's, and not without learning and judgment. But for the Exchequer—a queer choice, I must say.»

«It is to be presumed that the king knows how to choose his ministers. Thou knowest what I think, Gainor. We have but to obey those whom the Lord has set over us. We are told to render unto Cæsar the things which are Cæsar's, and to go our ways in peace.»

«The question is, What are Cæsar's?» said my aunt. «Shall Cæsar judge always? I came to tell you that it is understood in London, although not public, that it is meant to tax our tea. Now we do not buy; we smuggle it from Holland; but if the India Company should get a drawback on tea, we shall be forced to take it for its cheapness, even with the duty on it of threepence a pound.»

«It were but a silly scheme, Gainor. I cannot credit it.»

«Who could, John? And yet it is to be tried, and all for a matter of a few hundred pounds a year. It will be tried not now or soon, but next fall when the tea-ships come from China.»

«And if it is to be as thou art informed, what of it?»

«A storm—a tempest in a teapot,» said she.

My father stood still, deep in thought. He had a profound respect for the commercial sagacity of this clear-headed woman. Moreover, he was sure, as usual, to be asked to act in Philadelphia as a consignee of the India Company.

She seemed to see through her brother, as one sees through glass. «You got into trouble when the stamps came.»

«What has that got to do with this?»

«And again when you would not sign the Non-importation Agreement in '68.»

«Well?»

«They will ask you to receive the tea.»

«And I will do it. How can I refuse? I should lose all their India trade.»

«There will soon be no trade to lose. You are, as I know, drawing in your capital. Go abroad. Wind up your affairs in England; do the same in Holland. Use all your ships this summer. Go to Madeira from London. Buy freely, and pay at once so as to save interest; it will rise fast. Come home in the fall of '74 late. Hold the goods, and, above all, see that in your absence no consignments be taken. Am I clear, John?»

I heard her with such amazement as was shared by my father. The boldness and sagacity of the scheme impressed a man trained to skill in commerce, and ever given to courageous ventures.

«You must sail in October or before; you will need a year. No less will do.»

«Yes—yes.»

I saw from his look that he was captured. He walked to and fro, while my Aunt Gainor switched the dust off her petticoat or looked out of the window. At last she turned to me. «What think you of it, Hugh?»

«Mr. Wilson says we shall have war, aunt, and Mr. Attorney-General Chew is of the same opinion. I heard them talking of it last night at thy house. I think the king's officers want a war.» I took refuge, shrewdly, in the notions of my elders. I had no wiser thing to say. «I myself do not know,» I added.

«How shouldst thou?» said my father, sharply.

I was silent.

«And what think you, John?»

«What will my wife say, Gainor? We have never been a month apart.»

«Let me talk to her.»

«Wilt thou share in the venture?» He was testing the sincerity of her advice. «And to what extent?»

«Five thousand pounds. You may draw on me from London, and buy powder and muskets,» she added, with a smile.

«Not I. Why dost thou talk such folly?»

«Then Holland blankets and good cloth. I will take them off your hands at a fair profit.»

«I see no objection to that.»

My aunt gave me a queer look, saying, «The poor will need them. I shall sell them cheap.»

It was singular that I caught her meaning, while my father, reflecting on the venture as a whole, did not.

«I will do it,» he said.

«Then a word more. Be careful here as to debts. Why not wind up your business, and retire with the profit you will make?» It was the same advice my mother had given, as I well knew.

«Hast thou been talking to my wife?» he said.

«No,» she replied, surprised; «may I?»

«Yes. As to going out of business, Gainor, I should be but a lost man. I am not as well-to-do as thou dost seem to think.»

«Stuff and nonsense!» cried my aunt. «I believe Thomas Willing is no better off in what you call this world's gear, nor Franks, nor any of them. You like the game, and, after all, what is it but a kind of gambling? How do you know what hands the ocean holds? Your ventures are no better than my guineas cast down on the loo-table.» These two could never discuss anything but what it must end in a difference.

«Thou art a fool, Gainor, to talk such wicked nonsense before this boy. It is not worth an answer. I hear no good of Hugh of late. He hath been a concern to James Pemberton and to my friend Nicholas Waln, and to me—to me. Thy gambling and idle red-coats are snares to his soul. He has begun to have opinions of his own as to taxes, and concerning the plain duty of non-resistance. As if an idle dog like him had any right to have an opinion at all!»

«Tut! tut!» cried Miss Wynne.

«I am not idle,» I said, «if I am a dog.»

He turned and seized me by the collar. «I will teach thee to answer thy elders.» And with this he shook me violently, and caught up a cane from a chair where he had laid it.

And now, once again, that disposition to be merry came over me, and, perfectly passive, I looked up at him and smiled. As I think of it, it was strange in a young fellow of my age.

«Wouldst thou laugh?» he cried. «Has it gone that far?» and he raised his stick. My Aunt Gainor jerked it out of his hand, and, standing, broke it over her knee as if it had been a willow wand.

He fell back, crying, «Gainor! Gainor!»

«My God! man,» she cried, «are you mad? If I were you I would take some heed to that hot Welsh blood. What would my good Marie say? Why have you not had the sense to make a friend of the boy? He is worth ten of you, and has kept his temper like the gentleman he is.»

It was true. I had some queer sense of amusement in the feeling that I really was not angry; neither was I ashamed; but an hour later I was both angry and ashamed. Just now I felt sorry for my father, and shared the humiliation he evidently felt.

My aunt turned to her brother, where, having let me go, he stood with set features, looking from her to me, and from me to her. Something in his look disturbed her.

«You should be proud of his self-command. Cannot you see that it is your accursed repression and dry, dreary life at home that has put you two apart?»

«I have been put to scorn before my son, Gainor Wynne. It is thy evil ways that have brought this about. I have lost my temper and would have struck in anger, when I should have reflected, and, after prayer, chastised this insolence at home.»

«I heard no insolence.»

«Go away, Hugh, and thou, Gainor. Why dost thou always provoke me? I will hear no more!»

«Come, Hugh,» she said; and then: «It seems to me that the boy has had a good lesson in meekness, and as to turning that other cheek.»

«Don't, Aunt Gainor!» said I, interrupting her.

«Oh, go!» exclaimed my father. «Go! go, both of you!»

«Certainly; but, John, do not mention my news or my London letter.»

«I shall not.»

«Then by-by. Come, Hugh.»

## VI.

THERE must have been in this troubled country many such sad scenes as I have tried to recall. Father and son were to part with hot words, brother to take sides against brother. My unpleasant half-hour was but prophetic of that which was to come in worse shape, and to last for years.

My Aunt Gainor said, «Do not tell your mother,» and I assuredly did not.

«He will tell her. He tells her everything, soon or late. I must see her at once. Your father is becoming, as the French say, impossible. The times, and these wrangling Friends, with their stupid testimonies, irritate him daily until he is like a great, strong bull, such as the Spaniards tease to madness with little darts and fireworks. You see, Hugh, events are prickly things. They play the deuce with obstinate people. Your father will be better away from home. He has never been in England, and he will see how many, like Mr. Pitt and Colonel Barré, are with us. I have been a bit of a fool about you, and your father is more or less right. We must abjure sack and take physic.»

«What?» said I.

«To be plain, we must—that is, you must—play less and drink less, and in your father's absence look sharply, with my help, to his business.»

I was to need other doctors before I mended my ways. I said my aunt was right, and I made certain good resolutions, which were but short-lived and never reached adult maturity of usefulness.

My aunt walked with me north between the warehouses, taverns, and ship-chandlers on the river-front, and so across the bridge over Dock Creek, and up to Third street. She said I must not talk to her. She had thinking to do, and for this cause, I suppose, turning, took me down to Pine street. At St. Peter's Church she stopped, and bade me wait without, adding, «If I take you in I shall hear of it; wait.»

There was a midday service at this time, it being Lent. I waited idly, thinking of my father, and, as I before said, vexed and sorry and ashamed by turns. Often now I pause before I enter this sacred edifice, and think of that hour of tribulation. I could hear the fine, full voice of the Rev. Dr. Duché as he intoned the Litany. He lies now where I stood, and under the arms on his tomb is no record of the political foolishness and instability of a life otherwise free from blame. As I stood, Mrs. Ferguson came out, she who in days to come helped to get the unlucky parson into trouble. With her came my aunt.

«I said a prayer for thee, Hugh,» she whispered. «No; no cards in Lent, my dear Bess. Fie! for shame! This way, Hugh»; and we went east, through Pine street, and so to the back of our garden, where we found a way in, and, walking under the peach-trees, came to where my mother sat beneath a plum-tree, shelling peas, her great Manx cat by her side.

She wore a thin cap on top of the curly head, which was now wind-blown out of all order. «Come, Gainor,» she cried, seeing us; «help me to shell my peas. Thou shalt have some. They are come in a ship from the Bermudas. What a pretty pale green the pods are! I should like an apron of that colour.»

«I have the very thing, dear. Shall it be the minuet pattern or plain?»

«Oh, plain. Am I not a Friend? *Une Amie? Ciel!* but it is droll in French. Sarah Logan is twice as gay as I, but John does not love such vanities. *Quant à moi, je les adore.* It seems odd to have a colour to a religion. I wonder if drab goodness be better than red goodness. But what is wrong, Gainor? Yes; there is something. Hugh, thy collar is torn; how careless of me not to have mended it!»

Then my Aunt Gainor, saying nothing of my especial difficulty, and leaving out, too, her London news, related with remarkable clearness the reasons why my father should go overseas in the early fall and be gone for a year. The mother went on quietly shelling the peas, and losing no word. When Gainor had done, the bowl of peas was set aside, and my mother put back her curls, fixed her blue eyes on her sister-in-law, and was silent for a moment longer. At last she said: «It were best, for many reasons best. I see it,» and she nodded her head affirmatively. «But my son? my Hugh?»

«You will have him with you at home. Everything will go on as usual, except that John will be amusing himself in London.»

At this the little lady leaped up, all ablaze, so to speak. Never had I seen her so moved. «What manner of woman am I, Gainor Wynne, that I should let my husband go alone on the seas, and here and there, without me? I will not have it. As to my boy, he is my boy; God knows I love him; but my husband comes first now and always, and thou art cruel to wish to part us.»

«But I never wished to part you. Go with him, Marie. God bless your sweet heart! Leave me your boy; he cannot go. As God lives, I will take care of him!»

Upon this the two women fell to weeping in each other's arms, a thing most uncommon for my Aunt Gainor. Then they talked it all over, as if John Wynne were not: when it would be, and what room I was to have, and my clothes, and the business, and so on—all the endless details wherewith the cunning affection of good women knows to provide comfort for us, who are so apt to be unthankful.

It amazed me to see how quickly it was settled, and still more to learn that my father did not oppose, but fell in with all their plans.

Now, back of all my weaknesses and folly I had, as I have said, some of the sense of honour and proud rectitude of my father, who strictly abided by his creed and his conscience. I returned no more that day to the counting-house, but, saying to my mother I had business, I went off, with a hunk of bread, to my boat, and down the creek to the Delaware. I pulled out, past our old playground on the island, and far away toward the Jersey shore, and then, as the sun fell, drifted with the tide, noting the ruddy lines of the brick houses far away, and began to think.

The scene I had gone through had made a deep impression. It has been ever so with me. Drinking, gaming, betting, and worse, never awakened my conscience or set me reflecting, until some sudden, unlooked-for thing took place, in which sentiment or affection was concerned. Then I would set to work to balance my books and determine my course. At such times it was the dear mother who spoke in me, and the father who resolutely carried out my decision.

The boat drifted slowly with the flood-tide, and I, lying on the bottom, fell to thought of what the day had brought me. The setting sun touched the single spire of Christ Church, and lit up yellow squares of light in the westward-looking windows of the rare farm-houses on the Jersey shore. Presently I was aground on the south end of Petty's Island, where in after-years lay rotting the *Alliance*, the remnant ship of the greatest sea-fight that ever was since Grenville lay in the *Revenge*, with the Spanish fleet about him. I came to ground amid the reeds and spatter-docks, where the water-lilies were just in bud. An orchestra of frogs, with, as Jack said, fiddles and bassoons in their throats, ceased as I came, and pitched headlong off the broad green floats. Only one old fellow, with a strong bass voice, and secure on the bank, protested loudly at intervals, like the owl in Mr. Gray's great poem, which my Jack loved to repeat.

At last he—I mean my frog—whose monastery I had disturbed, so vexed me, who wanted stillness, that I smacked the water with the flat of an oar, which he took to be a hint, and ceased to lament my intrusion.

I was now well on to twenty, and old enough to begin at times to deal thoughtfully with events. A young fellow's feelings are apt to be extreme, and even despotic, so that they rule the hour with such strength of sway as may be out of proportion to the cause. I might have seen that I had no just cause to blame myself, but that did not help me. The mood of distressful self-accusation was on me. I had no repeated impulse to smile at what, in my father's conduct, had appeared to me a little while ago odd, and even amusing. I could never please him. I had grinned as I always did when risks were upon me. He never understood me, and I was tired of trying. What use was it to try? I had one of those minutes of wishing to die, which come even to the wholesome young. I was aware that of late I had not, on the whole, satisfied my conscience; I knew this quite too well; and now, as I lay in the boat discontented, I felt, as the youthful do sometimes feel, as if I were old, and the ending of things were near. It was but a mood, but it led up to serious thought. There are surely hours in youth when we are older than our years, and times in age when we are again young. Sometimes I wonder whether Jack was right, who used to say it may be we are never young or old, but merely seem to be so. This is the queer kind of reflection which I find now and then in Jack's diary, or with which he used to puzzle me and please James Wilson. Of course a man is young or is old, and there's an end on't, as a greater man has said. But Jack has imagination, and I have none.

I asked myself if I had done wrong in what I had said. I could not see that I had. With all my lifelong fear of my father, I greatly honoured and respected him, finding in myself something akin to the unyielding firmness with which he stood fast when he had made up his mind.

That this proud and steadfast man, so looked up to by every one, no matter what might be their convictions religious or political, should have been humiliated by a woman, seemed to me intolerable; this was the chief outcome of my reflections. It is true I considered, but I fear lightly, my own misdoings. I made up my mind to do better, and then again the image of my father in his wrath and his shame came back anew. I turned the boat, and pulled steadily across the river to our landing.

My father was in the counting-house in his own room, alone, although it was full late. «Well?» he said, spinning round on his high stool. «What is it? Thou hast been absent, and no leave asked.»

«Father,» I said, «if I was wrong this morning I wish to ask thy pardon.»

«Well, it is full time.»

«And I am come to say that I will take the punishment here and now. I did not run away from that.»

«Very good,» he replied, rising. «Take off thy fine coat.»

I wished he had not said this of my coat. I was in a heroic temper, and the sarcasm bit cruelly, but I did as I was bid. He went to the corner, and picked up a rattan cane. To whip fellows of nineteen or twenty was not then by any means unusual. What would have happened I know not, nor ever shall. He said: «There, I hear thy mother's voice. Put on thy coat.» I hastened to obey him.

The dear lady came in with eyes full of tears. «What is this, John, I hear? I have seen Gainor. I could not wait. I shall go with thee.»

«No,» he said; «that is not to be.» But she fell on his neck, and pleaded, and I, for my part, went away, not sorry for the interruption. As usual she had her way.

I remember well this spring of '73. It was early by some weeks, and everything was green and blossoming in April. My father and mother were not to sail until the autumn, but already he was arranging for the voyage, and she as busily preparing or thinking over what was needed.

When next I saw my Aunt Gainor, she cried out: «Sit down there, bad boy, and take care of my mandarin. He and my great bronze Buddha are my only counsellors. If I want to do a thing I ask Mr. Mandarin—he can only nod yes; and if I want not to do a thing I ask Buddha, and as he can neither say no nor yes, I do as I please. What a wretch you are!»

I said I could not see it; and then I put my head in her lap, as I sat on the stool, and told her of my last interview with my father, and how for two days he had hardly so much as bade me good-night.

«It is his way, Hugh,» said my aunt. «I am sorry; but neither love nor time will mend him. He is what his nature and the hard ways of Friends have made him.»

I said that this was not all, nor the worst, and went on to tell her my latest grievance. Our family worship at home was, as usual with Friends in those days, conducted at times in total silence, and was spoken of by Friends as «religious retirement.» At other times, indeed commonly, a chapter of the Bible was read aloud, and after that my father would sometimes pray openly. On this last occasion he took advantage of the opportunity to dilate on my sins, and before our servants to ask of Heaven that I be brought to a due sense of my iniquities. It troubled my mother, who arose from her knees in tears, and went out of the room, whilst I, overcome with anger, stood looking out of the window. My father spoke to her as she opened the door, but she made no answer, nor even so much as turned her head. It brought to my memory a day of my childhood, when my father was vexed because she taught me to say the Lord's Prayer. He did not approve, and would have no set form of words taught me. My mother was angry too, and I remember my own amazement that any one should resist my father.

When I had told my aunt of the indignity put upon me, and of the fading remembrance thus recalled, she said, «John Wynne has not changed, nor will he ever.» She declared that, after all, it was her fault—to have treated me as if I were a man, and to have given me too much money. I shook my head, but she would have it she was to blame, and then said of a sudden: «Are you in debt, you scamp? Did John pray for me?» I replied that I owed no one a penny, and that she had not been remembered. She was glad I was not in debt, and added: «Never play unless you have the means to pay. I have been very foolish. That uneasy woman, Bessy Ferguson, must needs tell me so. I could have slapped her. They will have thy sad case up in Meeting, I can tell thee.»

«But what have I done?» I knew well enough.

«Tut! you must not talk that way to me; but it is my fault. Oh, the time I have had with your mother! I am not fit, it seems, to be left to take care of you. They talk of leaving you with Abijah Hapworthy—sour old dog! I wish you joy of him!»

«Good heavens!» I exclaimed; for among my aunt's gay friends I had picked up such exclamatory phrases as, used at home, would have astonished my father.

«Rest easy,» said Mistress Wynne; «it is not to be. I have fought your battle, and won it. But I have had to make such promises to your father, and—woe is me!—to your mother, as will damn me forever if you do not help me to keep them. I can fib to your father and not care a snap, but lie to those blue eyes I cannot.»

«I will try, Aunt Gainor; indeed I will try.» Indeed, I did mean to.

«You must, you must. I am to be a sort of godmother-in-law to you, and renounce for you the world, the flesh, and the devil; and that for one of our breed! I shall be like a sign-post, and never go the way I point. That was Bessy Ferguson's malice. Oh, I have suffered, I can tell you. It is I, and not you, that have repented.»

«But I will; I do.»

«That is all very well; but I have had my whipping, and you got off yours.»

«What do you mean, aunt?»

«What do I mean? Here came yesterday Sarah Fisher, pretty gay for a Quaker, and that solemn Master Savory, with his sweet, low voice like a nice girl's tongue, and his gentle ways. And they are friends of thy people, who are distressed at thy goings on; and Nicholas Waln has seen thee, with two sons of Belial in red coats, come out of the coffee-house last month at evening, singing songs such as are not to be described, and no better able to take care of yourself than you should be. They did think it well and kind—hang 'em, Hugh!—to consider the matter with me. We considered it—we did, indeed. There be five people whose consciences I am to make you respect. And not one of them do I care for but Mother Blue-eyes. But I must, I must! It was all true, sir, what Friend Waln said; for you had reason enough left to come hither, and did I not put you to bed and send for Dr. Chovet, who grinned famously, and said, ‹*Je comprends,*› and went to call on your father on a hint from me, to declare you were *enrhumé*, and threatened with I know not what? In fact, he lied like a gentleman. You made a noble recovery, and are a credit to the doctor. I hope you will pay the bill, and are ashamed.»

I was, and I said so.

«But that is not all. These dear Quakers were the worst. They were really sorry, and I had to put on my best manners and listen; and now everybody knows, and you are the talk of the town. Those drab geese must out with the whole naughtiness, despite the company which came in on us, and here were Mr. Montresor and that ape Etherington grinning, and, worst of all, a charming young woman just come to live here with her aunt, and she too must have her say when the Quakers and the men were gone.»

«And what did she say?» I did not care much. «And what is her name?»

«Oh, she said the Quakers were rather outspoken people, and it was a pity, and she was sorry, because she knew you once, and you had taken her part at school.»

«At school?»

«Yes. She is Darthea Peniston, and some kin of that Miss de Lancey whom Sir William Draper will marry if he can.»

«Darthea Peniston?» I said, and my thoughts went back to the tender little maid who wept when I was punished, and for whom I had revenged myself on Master Dove.

«Quite a Spanish beauty,» said my Aunt Wynne; «a pretty mite of a girl, and not more money than will clothe her, they say; but the men mad about her. Come and see her to-morrow if you are sober.»

«O Aunt Gainor!»

«Yes, sir. I hear Mr. Montresor has leave from Anthony Morris to invite you to ‹The Colony in Schuylkill› to-morrow. It is well your father has gone to visit Mr. Yeates at Lancaster.»

«I shall behave myself, Aunt Gainor.»

«I hope so. The Fish House punch is strong.»

I went home thinking of Miss Darthea Peniston, and filled with desire to lead a wiser life. It was full time. My aunt's lavish generosity had, as I have said, given me means to live freely among the officers, who were, with some exceptions, a dissolute set. To be with them made it needful to become deceitful and to frame excuses, so that, when I was supposed to be at my aunt's, or riding, I was free that past winter to go on sleighing-parties or to frequent taverns, pleased with the notice I got from men like Montresor and the officers of the Scots Greys.

I have dwelt not at all on these scenes of dissipation. It is enough to mention them. My father was wrapped up in his business, and full of cares both worldly and spiritual; for now Friends were becoming politically divided, and the meetings were long and sometimes agitated.

My mother was neither deceived nor unconcerned. She talked to me often, and in such a way as brings tears to my eyes even now to think of the pain I gave her. Alas! it is our dearest who have the greatest power to wound us. I wept and promised, and went back to my husks and evil company.

I have no wish to conceal these things from my children. It is well that our offspring when young should think us angels; but it were as well that when they are older they should learn that we have been men of like passions with themselves, and have known temptation, and have fought, and won or lost, our battles with sin. It is one of the weaknesses of nations, as well as of children, that they come to consider their political fathers as saints. I smile when I think of the way people nowadays think of our great President, as of a mild genius, incapable of being moved to anger or great mirth, a man unspotted of the world. But some day you shall see him as my friend Jack and I saw him, and you will, I trust, think no worse of him for being as human as he was just.

The day of my more honest repentance was near, and I knew not that it was to be both terrible and of lasting value. I sometimes reflect upon the curious conditions with which my early manhood was surrounded. Here was I, brought up in the strictest ways of a sect to which I do no injustice if I describe it as ascetic. At home I saw plain living, and no luxury, save as to diet, which my father would have of the best money could buy. I was taught the extreme of non-resistance, and absolute simplicity in dress and language. Amusements there were none, and my father read no books except such as dealt with things spiritual, or things commercial. At my aunt's, and in the society I saw at her house, there were men and women who loved to dance, gamble, and amuse themselves. The talk was of bets, racing, and the like. To be drunk was a thing to be expected of officers and gentlemen. To avenge an insult with sword or pistol was the only way to deal with it. My father was a passive Tory, my aunt a furious Whig. What wonder that I fell a victim to temptation?

(To be continued.)

*S. Weir Mitchell.*

DRAWN BY HOWARD PYLE.

«'I WILL TEACH THEE TO ANSWER THY ELDERS.'»

(SEE PAGE 204.)

# A PAINTER OF MOTHERHOOD.

## VIRGINIE DEMONT-BRETON.

CHEVALIÈRE DE LA LÉGION D'HONNEUR.

THE maternal instinct is the predominant quality, the motive force, in the character and work of the strongest woman figure-painter in France, Virginie Demont-Breton. No woman combines so high a grade of subject with such force and knowledge of technical rendering; not only are her subjects poetical and full of pathos and reality, but they are put upon the canvas with a master's hand.

Virginie Demont-Breton, Presidente de l'Union des Femmes Peintres et Sculpteurs, chevalière de la Légion d'Honneur, membre de l'Académie Royale d'Anvers, membre de l'Ordre de Nichan Iftichan, all of which honors have been bestowed upon her in the last two or three years, is the daughter of the well-known painter Jules Breton.

She is the only woman painter since Rosa Bonheur to receive the cross of the Legion of Honor, so rarely given to women. She chooses greater subjects than her illustrious senior, in that these subjects are human; and her talent is more versatile and tender. Her color and harmony of tones please the most critical; her mothers speak to all and her children to those who have had children of their own. They are not impossible, idealized dream-children and dream-mothers, but real ones such as one knows. Though the beautiful Joan of Arc child, on her knees in the field, has an inspired look in her face, she is nevertheless like many French peasant children to be met along any roadside in summer; the mother aiding the tottering steps of her twins is doing only what all nurses and mothers do; in «Dipped in the Sea» the child is but struggling as all others do when plunged into the waves.

Virginie Demont-Breton has deep-set blue eyes, a strong, well-cut nose, soft curly hair, and a broad brow not out of proportion to the rest of her face. She is short and slight; every movement shows energy. The portrait of her exhibited in the Salon of 1895 is excellent in every way.

Mme. Demont-Breton comes of a family of artists; her mother's father, Félix de Vigne, was an artist of considerable reputation. When Jules Breton first went to Félix de Vigne for advice, the latter had, among other children, a little girl of seven, Élodie, who in after years became Mme. Jules Breton.

Her story has been written by her husband. He has told how he asked her to be his wife while she was sitting to him for her portrait, and of her calmness: she showed no emotion, and seemed almost to have expected it. The surprise could not have been less had he asked her to change her position or move her hand to right or left.

The child born to them in 1859 was Virginie, who grew up in a happy home in Courrières, a hamlet in the north of France, near the Belgian frontier. Virginie, in turn, married Adrien Demont, a young painter who came to her uncle Émile Breton from time to time for lessons and criticism. But her romance should be told in her own words, as she told it to me.

«I was only fourteen years old when I first saw my uncle's pupil Adrien; I saw him only once, but for a year after I thought often of the handsome fellow of nineteen, with his sketches under his arm. I had thought so often of him that when at the end of a year I saw him again I was enraptured. In a few hours he was gone, and the next time we met I was sixteen. He appeared at intervals to consult my uncle about his work, but my feelings were such that I wondered with fear whether he had even given me a thought. I realized what it would be to me if, as was just possible, he was almost ignorant of my existence.

«Again the third time he came and went. Soon after my father was questioning me about many things, and about my feelings for my young playmates. He named first one, then another. I was surprised when he asked, as if by chance, what I thought of my uncle's pupil Adrien Demont. He had only to look to realize what the mere mention of this name was to me.

«It soon transpired that he had asked my father for me, and we became engaged—an engagement which was to last for three years and more. But they were not long; we saw each other every two weeks, and wrote between times, just as, I am told, young people who love each other do in America.»

Adrien Demont is stalwart and tall, with the head of a poet and the energy of a man of action.

As a child Virginie Breton had always a pencil in hand, and at fourteen years of age

PAINTED BY VIRGINIE DEMONT-BRETON.

«DIPPED IN THE SEA.»

began studying under her father, with whom she drew and painted until, at nineteen, she came to Paris with her mother. Here, in the Luxembourg quarter, they took a small apartment, and in three months' time she finished the first three pictures she ever exhibited. They were exhibited that year, and received honorable mention. Several of the jury were for giving her a medal, but her father begged that it should be only an honorable mention the first year, as a medal might turn her head and prevent her from working seriously.

Success followed immediately upon her first exhibition, and an American bought her first Salon picture.

About this time her marriage with Adrien

Demont was celebrated, and the crowning happiness of her life came when, five years later, her first child was born. In connection with this there is an interesting incident.

On a May day in 1886, in the little cemetery of Écouen, eight miles from Paris, Jules Breton and a number of artists gathered together about the grave of their confrère Édouard Frère. After the ceremony the artists who lived in the village divided among themselves their brothers who had come from a distance, and carried them off to luncheon. Jules Breton and a number of others fell to the lot of the English painter Todd, who entertained them at a table spread under an arbor in his garden. A large company sat down; they spoke in low tones of the departed, of the loss to them, and their sympathy for the family. When they had satisfied their hunger, conversation became general, and for the moment all forgot that they were eating funeral meats.

Jules Breton sat at the head of the long table; he was silent most of the time, but there was a happy look in his odd blue eyes and a bright expression on his face, which were explained when at dessert he told that his only daughter had honored him by making him a grandfather that day. The guests exclaimed, «The king is dead—long live the king!» as they raised their glasses and drank to future painters.

Mme. Virginie Demont looks back to her earliest childhood to find the first traces of the maternal instinct, the power in almost all of her important pictures. She cannot remember a time when she did not think of children—of her own children that were to be. The children who now exist influenced her life long before they were born. When she became a mother the little ones resembled strongly the children she had depicted in her paintings years before. She has lately written: «Maternity is the most beautiful, the healthiest glory of woman; it is a love dream in palpable form, and comes smilingly to demand our tenderness and our kisses; it is the inexhaustible source whence feminine art draws its purest inspirations.»[1]

Love is the inspiring motive of almost every one of her pictures. When it is not a mother's love which inspires her, it is love of country, as in her picture of «Jean Bart,» where the officer of marines so inspires the fishermen of Dunkirk with a love for their country that one and all enlist for the coming struggle with Holland.

Virginie Demont-Breton has a lovely home at Montgeron, a village of a thousand inhabitants ten or more miles from Paris. Pretty little roads and lanes separate simple villas, each with more or less ground about it, surrounded by railing or stone wall. The Seine winds back and forth not very far away; the swamp willows along the border of the river, whether in early spring with their crimson tops or in their fresh green summer dress, are always pretty; the poplars are trimmed to within a few feet of their tops, and stand in long rows, wind-beaten, and full of character with their peculiar lightness and grace.

To this pretty but simple country house in Montgeron the Demonts have added fine twin studios. The house stands surrounded by trees, with alleys and pretty vistas in several directions. The watch-dog is jealous of all who enter, and the little girls, when not in the house with their mother, are driving their donkey, or fishing in the pond not far off, or playing under their own apple-trees. The Bohemian spirit, the spirit of shiftlessness, of letting well enough alone, of forgetfulness of the morrow, is lost in the mother and wife.

The walls of the twin ateliers, designed by an uncle of Adrien Demont, attest to the industry of both husband and wife. The gray walls are covered with narrow shelves, which rise tier upon tier to the top of the studios; upon these shelves stand hundreds of studies for many of the pictures long since hung in public museums or private collections. Each studio is approached by a winding carved-wood stairway, which forms pretty balconies. It is on this stair that Salgado has posed Mme. Demont-Breton for his successful portrait. Each studio is supplied with its upper and side lights; husband and wife work side by side.

In Mme. Demont's studio the walls are covered with studies and pictures of children of all ages and conditions, from the infant in arms to older ones clinging about the mother's knee. Some are asleep, others taking first steps, others digging in the sand or dipping in the waves. Each figure of each picture is studied over and over, first in one attitude, then in another, in one drapery, then in another, first in one combination of colors, then in another, until the general harmony is gained. The love of childhood in all its phases is depicted everywhere. The Virgin and Child is a frequent theme with Virginie Demont, and her career can scarce close before she gives to the world a Holy Family worthy to hang side by side with the best examples of the masters of Italian, Flemish, or Spanish art.

Many of her important works have found places in different Continental museums,

[1] «Woman in Art,» by Virginie Demont-Breton, in «La Revue des Revues,» March 1, 1896.

PAINTED BY VIRGINIE DEMONT-BRETON.

«TWINS.»

while others are owned by Englishmen and Americans. But all this success has not turned the artist's head. She is fond of a good story, and is a charming hostess in her country home, where her little girls already show their colored drawings, and are likely to follow in the footsteps of their parents and forefathers for several generations. The village schoolmaster comes to give them lessons each week, but the great twin ateliers are their school-room. Here they know each study and group of studies; they run to fetch certain ones on demand, just as if finding their dolls and playthings for inspection. When the mother's or the father's memory is at fault, the children are appealed to, to tell where and when a certain picture was exhibited, and where others are now.

In a fifteen years' residence in Montgeron the artists know none of their neighbors. They are jealous of anything that can mar the home life or the seclusion of working hours. But they are well known and often seen elsewhere, for Mme. Demont-Breton is president of the Union des Femmes Peintres et Sculpteurs, which has a large annual exhibition; and since accepting this position she has worked intelligently to enlarge and remodel this growing society.

DRAWN BY VIRGINIE DEMONT-BRETON.

«THE FIRST CHRISTMAS.»

For six months in the year she is at her summer home at Wissart, a small fishing-village in the north of France, between Boulogne and Calais. Here the home is built on the top of a high hill, and is square on all sides and on top; the walls are of stone three feet thick, to keep out the wind and damp. The garden is on the roof, and the rocky hillside, where sheep are pastured and over which the sea-birds sweep, is left untouched up to the very door-sill.

Wissart has in summer about a hundred visitors, some of whom go to be within reach of Mme. Demont's instruction. The coast is rugged and dangerous, with here and there a brilliant white sand-heap in a little cove; the winds are fierce and the storms dangerous. It is at Wissart that she finds the sands and rocks for her backgrounds and settings; it is among the Wissart fisherfolk that she finds her models; it is their solitary, touching lives which ofttimes inspire her.

Here Virginie Demont's life is devoted to unremitting work, either at her art or in ameliorating the condition of some of the fisherfolk so dear to her heart. Many of the inhabitants she has known since their birth, and she is never more interesting than when recounting the romances of their fateful lives. Nothing shows more clearly their love for her and their sense that she belongs to them than their joy when she received the cross of the Legion of Honor. The morning that the news came they went in a spontaneous procession to her house, with the national flag floating at their head. They took whatever flowers their little gardens afforded, and culled wild ones as they went along. The summer visitors, following their lead, had also a meeting on the beach, to bear witness to their appreciation of the well-merited honors bestowed upon her. The following Sunday was declared a public holiday; the townspeople, with the village pastor at their head, with painters, school-children, fishermen, and fishwives, went in procession to the house on the hill. The children of the fishermen hitched themselves to a small triumphal car, and drew the two little girls in triumph before their mother, the new *chevalière*. From the house they went to the market-place. Here, before the town hall, under the national flag, the representative painters, lawyers, and others among the summer visitors, spoke for the fisherfolk and for themselves. Carrier-Belleuse spoke of her great heart and talent, her grandeur of subject and simplicity of character, her faultless touch and her tenderness; of her life divided equally between love of home and love of art; of her youth, and her people's love.

Mme. Demont has written a volume of stories the scenes of which are laid along this rugged coast. She is welcome in every cottage, and all woes are poured into her ear. When a boat goes ashore in a winter storm, and lives are lost, it is her friends who have perished. Some have posed for her pictures, and others have been at her beck and call for any work she gave them the pleasure of doing for her. Her motherly heart has led her to found a society for their relief, for caring for the aged and infirm in the long winters, for forwarding a little money to furnish the young fellows with fishing-tackle or other means of earning their own livelihood.

It is to Mme. Demont-Breton that the Minister of Public Instruction has finally accorded the promise, so long a matter of discussion, that women shall be allowed to enter the classes of the École des Beaux-Arts, the government school of painting, sculpture, architecture, music, etc. The state has recognized her merit, her fellow-artists in Belgium have signified their esteem, the women painters and women sculptors of France have chosen her to be their leader, and the government of Algiers has added its quota; honors are arriving from every direction; and all this recognition has come before she has reached the age of forty.

CHIEF PICTURES BY MME. DEMONT-BRETON,

EXHIBITED AT THE SALON OF THE CHAMPS-ELYSÉES, WITH THEIR PRESENT LOCATION.

| | | |
|---|---|---|
| 1881 | «Fisherwife bathing Child» Medal 3d class | Museum, Amsterdam |
| 1882 | «A Family» | Museum, Douai |
| 1883 | «The Beach» Medal 2d class | Museum, Luxembourg |
| 1884 | «The Calm» | |
| 1885 | «First Steps» | New York |
| " | «Old Tars» | Museum Gand, Belgium |
| 1887 | «Making Bread» in Dauphiny | |
| " | «Dance of an Infant» | |
| 1888 | «The Bath» | |
| " | «Twins» | Museum, Sydney, N. S. W. |
| 1889 | «Father is Away» | Minneapolis |
| " | «The Wave» (World's Exhibition) | Rochester, N.Y. |
| 1890 | «Child in a Garden» | |
| 1891 | «The Messiah» | Philadelphia |
| " | «Giotto» | Paris |
| 1892 | «Dipped in the Sea» | New York |
| " | «The Blue Country» | Chicago |
| 1893 | «The Fireside» | New York |
| " | «Joan of Arc» | Museum, Lille |
| 1894 | «Jean Bart» | Museum, Dunkirk |
| " | «The Fisherman's Son» | New York |
| 1895 | «Stella Maris» | New York |
| " | «Mistletoe» | |
| 1896 | «Ishmael» | |

Many others—gold medals at world's fairs, etc.—are not in this list. Illustrations, portraits, and smaller pictures are not mentioned.

*Lee Bacon.*

DRAWN BY CHARLES STANLEY REINHART.

GRANT'S HEADQUARTERS IN THE WILDERNESS.

# CAMPAIGNING WITH GRANT.

BY GENERAL HORACE PORTER.

PREPARATIONS FOR A GENERAL ADVANCE—GRANT'S REASONS FOR MOVING BY THE LEFT FLANK—HIS INSTRUCTIONS TO HIS STAFF—GRANT'S NUMERICAL STRENGTH OFFSET BY LEE'S STRATEGICAL ADVANTAGE—CROSSING THE RAPIDAN—THE HEADQUARTERS MESS—ON THE EVE OF BATTLE—LONGSTREET'S ESTIMATE OF GRANT—AN EARLY BREAKFAST AT HEADQUARTERS—GRANT AND MEADE PITCH TENTS IN THE WILDERNESS—GRANT HEARS OF THE DEATH OF AN OLD COMRADE—A CONFERENCE BETWEEN GRANT AND MEADE—GRANT'S PREPARATION FOR THE SECOND DAY IN THE WILDERNESS—HANCOCK FLUSHED WITH VICTORY—GRANT AT A CRITICAL MOMENT—THE CRISIS OF THE WILDERNESS—GRANT'S DEMEANOR ON THE FIELD—HIS PECULIARITIES IN BATTLE—GRANT'S CONFIDENCE IN SUCCESS—THE GENERAL-IN-CHIEF AS AID TO A DROVER—CONFUSION CAUSED BY A NIGHT ATTACK—GRANT ADMINISTERS A REPRIMAND—GRANT AFTER THE BATTLE—THE WILDERNESS A UNIQUE COMBAT.

## PREPARATIONS FOR A GENERAL ADVANCE.

HE night of May 3 will always be memorable in the recollection of those who assembled in the little front room of the house occupied as headquarters at Culpeper. The eight senior members of the staff seated themselves that evening about their chief to receive their final instructions, and participated in an intensely interesting discussion of the grand campaign, which was to begin the next morning with all its hopes, its uncertainties, and its horrors. Sherman had been instructed to strike Joseph E. Johnston's army in northwest Georgia, and make his way to Atlanta. Banks was to advance up the Red River and capture Shreveport. Sigel was ordered to make an expedition down the valley of Virginia, and endeavor to destroy a portion of the East Tennessee, Virginia, and Georgia Railroad. His movement was expected to keep Lee from withdrawing troops from the valley, and reinforcing his principal army, known as the Army of Northern Virginia. Butler was directed to move up the James River, and endeavor to secure Petersburg and the railways leading into it, and, if opportunity offered, to seize Richmond itself. Burnside, with the Ninth Corps, which had been moved from Annapolis into Virginia, was to support the Army of the Potomac. The subsequent movements of all the forces operating in Virginia were to depend largely upon the result of the first battles between the Army of the Potomac and the Army of Northern Virginia. General Grant felt, as he afterward expressed it in his official report, that our armies had acted heretofore too independently of one another—«without concert, like a balky team, no two ever pulling together.» To obviate this, he had made up his mind to launch all his armies against the Confederacy at the same time, to give the enemy no rest, and to allow him no opportunity to reinforce any of his armies by troops which were not themselves confronted by Union forces.

## GRANT'S REASONS FOR MOVING BY THE LEFT FLANK.

THE general sat for some time preparing a few final instructions in writing. After he had finished he turned his back to the table, crossed one leg over the other, lighted a fresh cigar, and began to talk of the momentous movement which in a few hours was to begin. He said: «I weighed very carefully the advantages and disadvantages of moving against Lee's left and moving against his right. The former promised more decisive results if immediately successful, and would best prevent Lee from moving north to make raids, but it would deprive our army of the advantages of easy communication with a water base of supplies, and compel us to carry such a large amount of ammunition and rations in wagon-trains, and detach so many troops as train guards, that I found it presented too many serious difficulties; and when I considered especially the sufferings of the wounded in being transported long distances overland, instead of being carried by short routes to water, where they could be comfortably moved by boats, I had no longer any hesitation in deciding to cross the Rapidan below the position occupied by Lee's army, and move by our left. This plan will also enable us to coöperate better with Butler's forces, and not become separated too far from them. I shall not give my attention so much to Richmond as to Lee's army, and I want all commanders to feel that hostile armies, and not cities, are to be their objective points.» It was the understanding that Lee's army was to be the objective point of the Army of the Potomac, and it was to move against Richmond only in case Lee went there. To use Grant's own language to Meade, «Wherever Lee goes, there you will go also.» He of course thought it likely that Lee would fall back upon Richmond in case of defeat, and place himself behind its fortifications; for he had said to Meade, in his instructions to him, «Should a siege of Richmond become necessary, ammunition and equipments can be got from the arsenals at Washington and Fort Monroe»; and during the discussion that evening he rose from his seat, stepped up to a map hanging upon the wall, and with a sweep of his forefinger indicated a line around Richmond and Petersburg; and remarked: «When my troops are there, Richmond is mine. Lee must retreat or surrender.»

### HIS INSTRUCTIONS TO HIS STAFF.

HE then communicated verbal instructions to his staff, which gave the key to his method of handling troops in actual battle, and showed the value he placed upon celerity and the overcoming of delays in communicating orders. He said to us: «I want you to discuss with me freely from time to time the details of the orders given for the conduct of a battle, and learn my views as fully as possible as to what course should be pursued in all the contingencies which may arise. I expect to send you to the critical points of the lines to keep me promptly advised of what is taking place, and in cases of great emergency, when new dispositions have to be made on the instant, or it becomes suddenly necessary to reinforce one command by sending to its aid troops from another, and there is not time to communicate with headquarters, I want you to explain my views to commanders, and urge immediate action, looking to coöperation, without waiting for specific orders from me.» He said he would locate his headquarters near those of Meade, and communicate his instructions through that officer, and through Burnside, whose command at this time was independent of the Army of the Potomac; but that emergencies might arise in which he himself would have to give immediate direction to troops when actually engaged in battle.

He never made known his plans far in advance to any one. It was his invariable custom to keep his contemplated movements locked up in his own mind to avoid all possibility of their being mentioned. What impressed every one most was the self-reliance displayed in perfecting his plans, and his absolute faith in their success. His calm confidence communicated itself to all who listened to him, and inspired them with a feeling akin to that of their chief.

The discussion did not end till long past midnight. As usual on the eve of a battle, before the general retired he wrote a letter to Mrs. Grant. I did not know the nature of the contents of the letters to his wife until after the war, when Mrs. Grant, in speaking of them, said that they always contained words of cheer and comfort, expressed an abiding faith in victory, and never failed to dwell upon the sad thought which always oppressed him when he realized that many human lives would have to be sacrificed, and great sufferings would have to be endured by the wounded. The general's letters to his wife were very frequent during a campaign, and no pressure of official duties was ever permitted to interrupt this correspondence.

### GRANT'S NUMERICAL STRENGTH OFFSET BY LEE'S STRATEGICAL ADVANTAGE.

THE Rapidan separated the two hostile forces in northern Virginia. Lee's headquarters were at Orange Court-House, a distance of seventeen miles from Culpeper. The Army of the Potomac consisted of the Second Corps, commanded by Hancock; the Fifth, commanded by Warren; the Sixth, commanded by Sedgwick; and the cavalry corps under Sheridan. Besides these, there was Burnside's separate command, consisting of the Ninth Army Corps. These troops numbered in all about 116,000 present for duty, equipped. The Army of Northern Virginia consisted of three infantry corps, commanded respectively by Longstreet, Ewell, and A. P. Hill, and a cavalry corps commanded by J. E. B. Stuart. Its exact strength has never been accurately ascertained, but from the best data available it has been estimated at between 75,000 and 80,000 present for duty, equipped.

Those familiar with military operations, and unprejudiced in their judgment, will concede that, notwithstanding Lee's inferiority in numbers, the advantages were, nevertheless, in his favor in the approaching campaign. Having interior lines, he was able to move by shorter marches, and to act constantly on the defensive at a period of the war when troops had learned to intrench themselves with marvelous rapidity, and force the invading army continually to assault fortified positions. The task to be performed by the Union forces was that of conducting a moving siege. The field of operations, with its numerous rivers and creeks difficult of approach, its lack of practicable roads, its dense forests, its impassable swamps, and its trying summer climate, debilitating to Northern troops, seemed specially designed by nature for purposes of defense. Lee and his officers were familiar with every foot of the ground, and every inhabitant was eager to give them information. His army was in a friendly country, from which provisions could be drawn from all directions, and few troops had to be detached to guard lines of supply. The Union army, on the contrary, was unfamiliar with the country, was without accurate maps, could seldom secure trustworthy guides, and had to detach large bodies of troops from the main command to guard its long lines of communication, protect its supply-trains, and conduct the wounded to points of safety. The Southern Confederacy was virtually a military despotism, with a soldier at the head of its government, and officers were appointed in the army entirely with reference to their military qualifications. Since Lee had taken command he had not lost a single battle fought in the State of Virginia, and the prestige of success had an effect upon his troops the importance of which cannot easily be overestimated. His men were made to feel that they were fighting for their homes and firesides; the pulpit, the press, and the women were making superhuman efforts to «fire the Southern heart»; disasters were concealed, temporary advantages were magnified into triumphant victories, and crushing defeats were hailed as blessings in disguise. In the North there was a divided press, with much carping criticism on the part of journals opposed to the war, which was fitted to discourage the troops and destroy their confidence in their leaders. There were hosts of Southern sympathizers, constituting a foe in the rear, whose threats and overt acts often necessitated the withdrawal of troops from the front to hold them in check. In all the circumstances, no just military critic will claim that the advantage was on the side of the Union army merely because it was numerically larger.

### CROSSING THE RAPIDAN.

The campaign in Virginia was to begin by throwing the Army of the Potomac with all celerity to the south side of the Rapidan, below Lee's position. The infantry moved a little after twelve o'clock in the morning of May 4. The cavalry dashed forward in advance under cover of the night, drove in the enemy's pickets, secured Germanna Ford, and also Ely's Ford, six miles below, and before six o'clock in the morning had laid two pontoon bridges at each place, and passed to the south side of the river. Warren's corps crossed at Germanna Ford, followed by Sedgwick's, while Hancock's corps made the passage at Ely's Ford. At 8 A. M. the general-in-chief, with his staff, started from headquarters, and set out for Germanna Ford, following Warren's troops. He was mounted upon his bay horse «Cincinnati,» equipped with a saddle of the Grimsley pattern, which was somewhat the worse for wear, as the general had used it in all his campaigns from Donelson to the present time. Rawlins was on his left, and rode a «clay-bank» horse he had brought from the West named «General Blair,» in honor of Frank P. Blair, who commanded a corps in the Army of the Tennessee. General Grant was dressed in a uniform coat and waistcoat, the coat being unbuttoned. On his hands were a pair of yellowish-brown thread gloves. He wore a pair of plain top-boots, reaching to his knees, and was equipped with a regulation sword, spurs, and sash. On his head was a slouch hat of black felt with a plain gold cord around it. His orderly carried strapped behind his saddle the general's overcoat, which was that of a private soldier of cavalry. A sun as bright as the «sun of Austerlitz» shone down upon the scene. Its light brought out in vivid colors the beauties of the landscape which lay before us, and its rays were reflected with dazzling brilliancy from the brass field-pieces and the white covers of the wagons as they rolled lazily along in the distance. The crisp, bracing air seemed to impart to all a sense of exhilaration. As far as the eye could reach the troops were wending their way to the front. Their war banners, bullet-riddled and battle-stained, floated proudly in the morning breeze. The roads resounded to the measured tread of the advancing columns, and the deep forests were lighted by the glitter of their steel. The quick, elastic step and easy, swinging gait of the men, the cheery look upon their faces, and the lusty shouts with which they greeted their new commander as he passed, gave proof of the temper of their metal, and the superb spirit which animated their hearts. If the general's nature had been as emotional as that of Napoleon, he might have been moved to utter the words of the French emperor as his troops filed past him in moving to the field of Waterloo: «Magnificent, magnificent!» But as General Grant was neither demonstrative nor communicative, he gave no expression whatever to his feelings.

With the party on the way to the front rode a citizen whose identity and purposes soon became an object of anxious inquiry among the troops. His plain black, funereal-looking citizen's clothes presented a sight not often witnessed on a general's staff, and attracted no little attention on the part of the soldiers, who began to make audible side remarks, evincing a searching curiosity to know whether the general had brought his private undertaker with him, or whether it was a parson who had joined headquarters so as to be on hand to read the funeral service over the Southern Confederacy when the boys succeeded in getting it into the «last ditch.» The person was Mr. E. B. Washburne, member of Congress from General Grant's district, who had arrived at headquarters a few days before, and had expressed a desire to accompany the army upon the opening campaign, to which the general had readily assented.

A short time before noon the general-in-chief crossed one of the pontoon bridges at Germanna Ford to the south side of the Rapidan, rode to the top of the bluff overlooking the river, and there dismounted, and established temporary headquarters at an old farm-house with Dutch gables and porch in front. It was rather dilapidated in appearance, and looked as if it had been deserted for some time. The only furniture it contained was a table and two chairs. Meade's headquarters were located close by. General Grant sat down on the steps of the house, lighted a cigar, and remained silent for some time, quietly watching Sedgwick's men passing over the bridge. After a while he said: «Well, the movement so far has been as satisfactory as could be desired. We have succeeded in seizing the fords and crossing the river without loss or delay. Lee must by this time know upon what roads we are advancing, but he may not yet realize the full extent of the movement. We shall probably soon get some indications as to what he intends to do.»

A representative of a newspaper, with whom the general was acquainted, now stepped up to him and said, «General Grant, about how long will it take you to get to Richmond?» The general replied at once: «I will agree to be there in about four days—that is, if General Lee becomes a party to the agreement; but if he objects, the trip will undoubtedly be prolonged.» The correspondent looked as if he did not see just how he could base any definite predictions upon this oracular response.

I happened to be looking over a field map at the time, and, at the general's request, handed it to him. He examined it attentively for a few minutes, and then returned it without making any remarks. The main roads were pretty well represented on our maps. The Germanna road runs a little east of south; five miles from the Rapidan it is crossed by a road running east and west, called the Orange turnpike; a mile beyond it intersects the Brock road, which runs north and south; and a mile farther on the Brock road is crossed by the Orange plank-road running east and west. There were also some narrow cross-roads cut through the woods in various places.

About one o'clock word came from Meade that our signal officers had succeeded in deciphering a message sent to General Ewell, which read as follows: «We are moving. Had I not better move D. and D. toward New Verdierville? (Signed) R.» The general manifested considerable satisfaction at receiving this news, and remarked: «That gives just the information I wanted. It shows that Lee is drawing out from his position, and is pushing across to meet us.» He now called for writing material, and placing a book upon his knee, laid the paper upon it, and wrote a despatch to Burnside at Rappahannock Station, saying: «Make forced marches until you reach this place. Start your troops now in the rear the moment they can be got off, and require them to make a night march.»

### THE HEADQUARTERS MESS.

A COLD lunch was then eaten off a pine table in the dining-room of the deserted house. Later in the afternoon our tents arrived, and were pitched near the house, and a little before dark the «mess» sat down to dinner. The table had been laid under the fly of a large tent of the pattern known as the «hospital tent.» Perhaps no headquarters of a general in supreme command of great armies ever presented so democratic an appearance. All the officers of the staff dined at the table with their chief, and the style of conversation was as familiar as that which occurs in the household of any private family. Nothing could have been more informal or unconventional than the manner in which the mess was conducted. The staff-officers came to the table and left it at such times as their duties permitted, sometimes lingering over a meal to indulge in conversation, at other times remaining to take only a few mouthfuls in all haste before starting out upon the lines. The chief ate less and talked less than any other member of the staff, and partook only of the plainest food.

## ON THE EVE OF BATTLE.

A CAMP-FIRE of dry fence-rails had been built in front of the general's tent, not because the evening was particularly cold, but for the reason that the fire lighted up the scene and made the camp look more cheerful. General Meade came over to headquarters after dinner, and took a seat upon a folding camp-chair by our fire, and he and General Grant entered into a most interesting discussion of the situation, and the plans for the next day. The general-in-chief offered Meade a cigar. The wind was blowing, and he had some difficulty in lighting it, when General Grant offered him his flint and steel, which overcame the difficulty. The general always carried in the field a small silver tinder-box, in which there was a flint and steel with which to strike a spark and a coil of fuse, which was easily ignited by the spark, and not affected by the wind. The French would call it a *briquet*. While the two generals were talking, and a number of staff-officers sitting by listening, telegrams were received from Washington saying that Sherman had advanced in Georgia, Butler had ascended the James River, and Sigel's forces were moving down the valley of Virginia. These advances were in obedience to General Grant's previous orders. He said: «I don't expect much from Sigel's movement; it is made principally for the purpose of preventing the enemy in his front from withdrawing troops to reinforce Lee's army. To use an expression of Mr. Lincoln's, employed in my last conversation with him, when I was speaking of this general policy, ‹If Sigel can't skin himself, he can hold a leg while somebody else skins.› It is very gratifying to know that Hancock and Warren have made a march to-day of over twenty miles, with scarcely any stragglers from their commands.» Telegrams were now sent to Washington announcing the entire success of the crossing of the Rapidan, and saying that it would be demonstrated before long whether the enemy intended to give battle on that side of Richmond. Meade soon after retired to his headquarters, and a little while before midnight General Grant entered his tent and turned in for the night. Its only furniture consisted of a portable cot made of a coarse canvas stretcher over a light wooden frame, a tin wash-basin which stood on an iron tripod, two folding camp-chairs, and a plain pine table. The general's baggage was limited to one small camp trunk, which contained his underclothing, toilet articles, a suit of clothes, and an extra pair of boots.

## LONGSTREET'S ESTIMATE OF GRANT.

GENERAL LONGSTREET, then commanding a corps in Lee's army, told me, several years after the war, that the evening on which news was received that Grant intended to give personal direction to the army which was to operate against Lee, he had a conversation on the subject at Lee's headquarters. An officer present talked very confidently of being able to whip with all ease the western general who was to confront them, at which Longstreet said: «Do you know Grant?» «No,» the officer replied. «Well, I do,» continued Longstreet. «I was in the corps of cadets with him at West Point for three years, I was present at his wedding, I served in the same army with him in Mexico, I have observed his methods of warfare in the West, and I believe I know him through and through; and I tell you that we cannot afford to underrate him and the army he now commands. We must make up our minds to get into line of battle and to stay there; for that man will fight us every day and every hour till the end of this war. In order to whip him we must outmanœuver him, and husband our strength as best we can.»

## AN EARLY BREAKFAST AT HEADQUARTERS.

AFTER the officers at headquarters had obtained what sleep they could get, they arose about daylight, feeling that in all probability they would witness before night either a fight or a foot-race—a fight if the armies encountered each other, a foot-race to secure good positions if the armies remained apart.

General Meade had started south at dawn, moving along the Germanna road. General Grant intended to remain in his present camp till Burnside arrived, in order to give him some directions in person regarding his movements. The general sat down to the breakfast-table after nearly all the staff-officers had finished their morning meal. While he was slowly sipping his coffee, a young newspaper reporter, whose appetite, combined with his spirit of enterprise, had gained a substantial victory over his modesty, slipped up to the table, took a seat at the farther end, and remarked, «Well, I would n't mind taking a cup of something warm myself, if there 's no objection.» Thereupon seizing a coffee-pot, he poured out a full ration of that soothing army beverage, and, after helping himself to some of the other dishes, proceeded to eat breakfast with an appetite which had evidently been stimulated by long hours of fasting. The general paid no more attention to this occurrence than he would have paid to the flight of a bird across his path. He scarcely looked at the intruder, did not utter a word at the time, and made no mention of it afterward. It was a fair sample of the imperturbability of his nature as to trivial matters taking place about him. General Grant sent a message to Meade at 8 : 24 A. M., saying, among other things, «If an opportunity presents itself for pitching into a part of Lee's army, do so without giving time for dispositions.» It will be observed from this despatch, and many others which follow, that nearly all of our commanding officers in the field indulged in a certain amount of colloquialism in their communications. Perhaps it seemed to them to make the style less stilted, to give more snap to their language, and express their meaning more briefly. It certainly savored less of the «pomp» and more of the «circumstance» of war than the correspondence of European commanders.

Sheridan's cavalry had been assigned to the duty of guarding the train of four thousand wagons, and feeling out to the left for the enemy. The head of Burnside's leading division was now seen crossing the river; but as General Grant was anxious to go to the front, he decided not to wait to see Burnside in person, but to send him a note instead, urging him to close up as rapidly as possible upon Sedgwick's corps. This communication was depatched at 8:41 A. M., and the general immediately after directed the staff to mount and move forward with him along the Germanna road. After riding a mile, an officer was seen coming toward us at a gallop, and was soon recognized as Colonel Hyde of Sedgwick's staff. He halted in front of General Grant and said: «General Meade directed me to ride back and meet you, and say that the enemy is still advancing along the turnpike, and that Warren's and Sedgwick's troops are being put in position to meet him.» The general now started forward at an accelerated pace, and, after riding four miles farther along the Germanna road, came to the crossing of the Orange turnpike. Here General Meade was seen standing near the roadside. He came forward on foot to give General Grant the latest information. The general now dismounted, and the two officers began to discuss the situation.

### GRANT AND MEADE PITCH TENTS IN THE WILDERNESS.

It had become evident that the enemy intended to give battle in the heart of the Wilderness, and it was decided to establish the headquarters of both generals near the place where they were holding their present conference, at the junction of these two important roads. As this spot became the central point from which nearly all the orders of the commander were issued during one of the most desperate battles in the annals of history, a description of the location is important, in order to give the reader a clear understanding of the memorable events which took place in its vicinity.

A little to the east of the cross-roads stood the old Wilderness tavern, a deserted building surrounded by a rank growth of weeds, and partly shut in by trees. A few hundred yards to the west, and in the northwest angle formed by the two intersecting roads, was a knoll from which the old trees had been cut, and upon which was a second growth of scraggy pine, scrub-oak, and other timber. The knoll was high enough to afford a view for some little distance, but the outlook was limited in all directions by the almost impenetrable forest with its interlacing trees and tangled undergrowth. The ground upon which the battle was fought was intersected in every direction by winding rivulets, rugged ravines, and ridges of mineral rock. Many excavations had been made in opening iron-ore beds, leaving pits bordered by ridges of earth. Trees had been felled in a number of places to furnish fuel and supply sawmills. The locality is well described by its name. It was a wilderness in the most forbidding sense of the word.

The headquarters wagons had followed the staff, the tents were soon pitched, and a camp was established on low ground at the foot of the knoll just described, between it and the Germanna road. Grant and Meade had, in the mean time, taken up their positions on top of the knoll and stood there talking over the situation; Warren had joined them, and had communicated the latest news from his front. As soon as General Grant learned the situation, he followed his habitual custom in warfare, and, instead of waiting to be attacked, took the initiative and pushed out against the enemy. Warren had been directed to move out in force on the Orange turnpike, Getty's division of Sedgwick's corps was put into position on Warren's left, and as soon as it was found that the enemy was advancing on the Orange plank-road, orders were sent to Hancock to hurry up his troops, and take up a position on the left of Getty. While these preparations were progressing, General Grant lighted a cigar, sat down on the stump of a tree, took out his penknife, and began to whittle a stick. He kept on his brown thread gloves, and did not remove them once during the entire day. Everything was comparatively quiet until the hour of noon, when the stillness was suddenly broken by the sharp rattle of musketry and the roar of artillery. These sounds were the quick messengers which told that Warren had met the enemy and begun the conflict. He encountered Ewell's corps, and drove it nearly a mile, but was soon compelled to fall back and restore the connection which had been lost between his divisions.

Warren then had a conference with General Grant, who proposed that they should ride out to the front. He called for his horse, which had remained saddled, and directed me and another of the aides to accompany him. As General Warren was more familiar with the ground, he rode ahead. He was mounted on a fine-looking white horse, was neatly uniformed, and wore the yellow sash of a general officer. He was one of the few officers who wore their sashes in a campaign, or paid much attention to their dress. The party moved to the front along a narrow country road bordered by a heavy undergrowth of timber and bristling thickets. The infantry were struggling with difficulty through the dense woods, the wounded were lying along the roadside, firing still continued in front, and dense clouds of smoke hung above the tops of the trees. It was the opening scene of the horrors of the Wilderness.

### GRANT HEARS OF THE DEATH OF AN OLD COMRADE.

After having learned from personal inspection the exact character of the locality in which the battle was to be fought, General Grant returned to headquarters, in order to be able to communicate more promptly with the different commands. News had been received that Hill's corps of Lee's army was moving up rapidly on the Orange plank-road. Grant was now becoming impatient to take the initiative against the enemy, and staff-officers were sent with important orders to all parts of the line. It was soon seen that the infantry would have to fight it out without much aid from the artillery, as it was impossible to move many batteries to the front, owing to the difficult nature of the ground. Hancock, with great energy, had thrown forward two of his divisions to support Getty, who had already attacked Hill. I was sent to communicate with Hancock during this part of the engagement. The fighting had become exceedingly severe on that part of the field. General Alexander Hays, one of the most gallant officers in the service, commanding one of Hancock's brigades, finding that his line had broken, rushed forward to encourage his troops, and was instantly killed. Getty and Carroll were severely wounded, but both refused to leave the field, and continued to command their troops throughout the fight. After remaining for some time with Hancock's men, I returned to headquarters to report the situation to the general-in-chief, and carried to him the sad intelligence of Hays's death. General Grant was by no means a demonstrative man, but upon learning the intelligence I brought, he was visibly affected. He was seated upon the ground with his back against a tree, still whittling pine sticks. He sat for a time without uttering a word, and then, speaking in a low voice, and pausing between the sentences, said: «Hays and I were cadets together for three years. We served for a time in the same regiment in the Mexican war. He was a noble man and a gallant officer. I am not surprised that he met his death at the head of his troops; it was just like him. He was a man who would never follow, but would always lead in battle.»

### A CONFERENCE BETWEEN GRANT AND MEADE.

Wadsworth's division of Warren's corps was sent to support Hancock; but it encountered great difficulty in working its way through the woods, and darkness set in before it could get within striking distance of the enemy. Sedgwick had some fighting on the right of Warren, but no important results had been accomplished on his front. About eight o'clock in the evening the firing died away, and the troops in the immediate presence of the enemy lay on their arms to await the events of the morning.

Sheridan had left a force in the rear sufficient to protect the trains, and had formed the rest of his command so as to confront the enemy's cavalry, which had been moved around by the right of the enemy's line. He had some severe fighting on our extreme left. When we sat down at the mess-table at headquarters that evening, the events of the day were fully discussed, and each staff-officer related to the general in detail the scenes which had occurred upon the particular portion of the front which he had visited. Soon after we had risen from the table and left the mess-tent, Meade walked over from his headquarters, and he and the general-in-chief seated themselves by the camp-fire, and talked over the events of the day and the plans for the morrow. Mr. Washburne and our staff-officers made part of the group. The general manifested intense anxiety in regard to relieving the wounded, and the medical officers and the commanders of troops were urged to make every possible effort to find the sufferers and convey them to the rear. Even in daylight it would have been a difficult undertaking to penetrate the thickets and carry the wounded to a place of safety, but at night it was almost impossible, for every time a lantern was shown, or a noise made, it was certain to attract the fire of the enemy. However, those who had been slightly wounded made their own way to the field-hospitals, and by dint of extraordinary exertions, great numbers of the seriously injured were brought to positions where they could be cared for.

During the conversation General Grant remarked: «As Burnside's corps, on our side, and Longstreet's, on the other side, have not been engaged, and the troops of both armies have been occupied principally in struggling through thickets and fighting for position, to-day's work has not been much of a test of strength. I feel pretty well satisfied with the result of the engagement; for it is evident that Lee attempted by a bold movement to strike this army in flank before it could be put into line of battle and be prepared to fight to advantage; but in this he has failed.»

The plan agreed upon that night for the coming struggle was as follows: Hancock and Wadsworth were to make an attack on Hill at 4:30 A. M., so as to strike him if possible before Longstreet could arrive to reinforce him. Burnside, who would arrive early in the morning with three divisions, was to send one division (Stevenson's) to Hancock, and to put the other two divisions between Wadsworth and Warren's other divisions, and attack Hill in flank, or at least obliquely, while Warren and Sedgwick were to attack along their fronts, inflict all the damage they could, and keep the troops opposed to them from reinforcing Hill and Longstreet. Burnside's fourth division was to guard the wagon-trains. This division was composed of colored troops, and was commanded by General Ferrero. General Meade, through whom all orders were issued to the Army of the Potomac, was of the opinion that the troops could not be got into position for the attack as early as half-past four o'clock, and recommended six; but General Grant objected, as he was apprehensive that this might give the enemy an opportunity to take the initiative. However, he agreed to postpone the time till five o'clock, and the final orders were given for that hour. Meade now arose, said good night, and walked over to his headquarters. Before eleven o'clock the general-in-chief remarked to the staff: «We shall have a busy day to-morrow, and I think we had better get all the sleep we can to-night. I am a confirmed believer in the restorative qualities of sleep, and always like to get at least seven hours of it, though I have often been compelled to put up with much less.» «It is said,» remarked Washburne, «that Napoleon often indulged in only four hours of sleep, and still preserved all the vigor of his mental faculties.» «Well, I, for one, never believed those stories,» the general replied. «If the truth were known, I have no doubt it would be found that he made up for his short sleep at night by taking naps during the day.» The chief then retired to his tent, and his example was followed by all the officers who could be spared from duty. The marked stillness which now reigned in camp formed a striking contrast to the shock and din of battle which had just ceased, and which was so soon to be renewed.

### GRANT'S PREPARATION FOR THE SECOND DAY IN THE WILDERNESS.

AT four o'clock the next morning, May 6, we were awakened in our camp by the sound of Burnside's men moving along the Germanna road. They had been marching since 1 A. M., hurrying on to reach the left of Warren. The members of the headquarters mess soon after assembled to partake of a hasty breakfast. The general made rather a singular meal preparatory to so exhausting a day as that which was to follow. He took a cucumber, sliced it, poured some vinegar over it, and partook of nothing else except a cup of strong coffee. The first thing he did after rising from the table was to call for a fresh supply of cigars. His colored servant «Bill» brought him two dozen. After lighting one of them, he filled his pockets with the rest. He then went over to the knoll, and began to walk back and forth slowly upon the cleared portion of the ridge. While listening for Hancock's attack on the left, we heard the sound of heavy firing on the right, and found that the enemy had attacked Sedgwick and Warren. Warren afterward had one brigade pretty roughly handled, and driven back some distance; but no ground was permanently lost or gained by either side on that part of the line. Promptly at five o'clock the roar of battle was heard in Hancock's front, and before seven he had broken the enemy's line, and driven him back in confusion more than a mile. The general now instructed me to ride out to Hancock's front, inform him of the progress of Burnside's movement, explain the assistance that officer was expected to render, and tell him more fully the object of sending to his aid Stevenson's division of Burnside's corps.

### HANCOCK FLUSHED WITH VICTORY.

I MET Hancock on the Orange plank-road, not far from its junction with the Brock road, actively engaged in directing his troops, and restoring the confusion in their alinement caused by the desperate fighting and the difficult character of the ground. All thought of the battle which raged about us was to me for a moment lost in a contemplation of the dramatic scene presented in the person of the knightly corps commander. He had just driven the enemy a mile and a half. His face was flushed with the excitement of victory, his eyes were lighted by the fire of battle, his flaxen hair was thrust back from his temples, his right arm was extended to its full length in pointing out certain positions as he gave his orders, and his commanding form towered still higher as he rose in his stirrups to peer through the openings in the woods. He was considered the handsomest general officer in the army, and at this moment he looked like a spirited portrait from the hands of a master artist, with the deep brown of the dense forest forming a fitting background. It was itself enough to inspire the troops he led to deeds of unmatched heroism. He had been well dubbed «Hancock the Superb.» This expression dated back to the field of Williamsburg. At the close of that battle, General McClellan sent a telegram to his wife in New York announcing his victory, and as she and Hancock were old friends, he added the words, «Hancock was superb.» The newspapers got hold of the despatch, and the designation was heralded in prominent head-lines throughout the entire press. The description was so appropriate that the designation clung to him through life.

Along the line of Hancock's advance the enemy's dead were everywhere visible; his wounded strewed the roads; prisoners had been captured, and battle-flags had been taken: but Hancock was now compelled to halt and restore the contact between his commands. Before nine o'clock, however, he was pushing out again on the Orange plank-road, and another fierce fight soon began.

Sheridan had become engaged in a spirited contest with Stuart's cavalry on the left at Todd's tavern, in which our troops were completely victorious. The sound of this conflict was mistaken for a time for an attack by Longstreet from that direction, and made Hancock anxious to strengthen his exposed left flank. His embarrassments were increased by one of those singular accidents which, though trivial in themselves, often turn the tide of battle. A body of infantry was reported to be advancing up the Brock road, and moving upon Hancock's left and rear. A brigade which could ill be spared was at once thrown out in that direction to resist the threatened attack. It soon appeared that the body of infantry consisted of about seven hundred of our convalescents, who were returning to join their commands. The incident, however, had caused the loss of valuable time. These occurrences prevented Hancock from further taking the offensive.

After waiting for some time, and hearing nothing of Burnside's contemplated assault, I told Hancock I would ride over to Burnside, explain to him fully the situation on the left, and urge upon him the importance of making all possible haste. Upon reaching his position, I found that he was meeting with many difficulties in moving his men into position, and was making very little progress. I explained the absolute necessity of going to the relief of Hancock, and Colonel Comstock and I labored vigorously to help to find some means of getting the troops through the woods. Seeing the difficulties in the way, I returned to General Grant to let him know the true situation, and that an early attack from that quarter could not be depended upon.

### GRANT AT A CRITICAL MOMENT.

WARREN'S troops were driven back on a portion of his line in front of general headquarters, stragglers were making their way to the rear, the enemy's shells were beginning to fall on the knoll where General Grant was seated on the stump of a tree, and it looked for a while as if the tide of battle would sweep over that point of the field. He rose slowly to his feet, and stood for a time watching the scene, and mingling the smoke of his cigar with the smoke of battle, without making any comments. His horse was in charge of an orderly just behind the hill, but he evidently had no thought of mounting. An officer ventured to remark to him, «General, would n't it be prudent to move headquarters to the other side of the Germanna road till the result of the present attack is known?» The general replied very quietly, between the puffs of his cigar, «It strikes me it would be better to order up some artillery and defend the present location.» Thereupon a battery was brought up, and every preparation made for defense. The enemy, however, was checked before he reached the knoll. In this instance, as in many others, the general was true to the motto of his Scottish ancestors of the Grant clan: «Stand fast, Craig Ellachie.»

About eleven o'clock the battle raged again with renewed fury on Hancock's front. He had been attacked in front and on the flank by a sudden advance of the enemy, who, concealed by the dense wood, had approached near at several points before opening fire. This caused some confusion among Hancock's troops, who had become in great measure exhausted by their fighting since five o'clock in the morning, and they were now compelled to fall back to their breastworks along the Brock road. The enemy pressed on to within a few hundred yards of the intrenchments, but did not venture to assault. In this attack Longstreet was badly wounded, and the Confederate general Jenkins was killed, both having been accidentally shot by their own men. We suffered a severe loss in the death of the gallant General Wadsworth. After Longstreet's removal from the field, Lee took command of his right in person, as we learned afterward, and ordered that any further assault should be postponed till a later hour.

Colonel Leasure's brigade of Burnside's corps now executed a movement of striking brilliancy. It had been sent to Hancock, and posted on the left of his line, and was ordered by him to sweep along his front from left to right. Leasure moved out promptly, facing to the right, with his right flank about a hundred yards from our line of breastworks, and dashed along the entire front with such boldness and audacity that the portions of the enemy he encountered fell back without attempting to make any serious resistance.

General Grant was becoming more anxious still about Burnside's attack, and I soon after galloped over to the latter with instructions to move on without a moment's delay, and connect with Hancock's right at all hazards. I found his troops endeavoring to obey orders as best they could, but, in struggling through underbrush and swamps, all efforts to keep up their alinement were futile. General Burnside, when I met him this time, was dismounted and seated by the roadside. A champagne basket filled with lunch had been brought up, and at his invitation I joined him and some of his staff in sampling the attractive contents of the hamper. In doing so we acted upon the recognized principle of experienced campaigners, who always eat a meal wherever they can get it, not knowing where the next one is to come from. It was called «eating for the future.»

A little after noon Burnside's advance became engaged for about a quarter of an hour, but did not accomplish any important result. I worked my way out on foot to his extreme front line at this time, to obtain a more accurate knowledge of the difficulties which impeded the advance of his troops, and then returned again to headquarters to report the situation.

### THE CRISIS OF THE WILDERNESS.

ABOUT half the army was now under Hancock's command, and it was probable that he would need still more reinforcements, and the general-in-chief was devoting a good deal of thought to our right, which had been weakened. At 10:30 A. M. Sedgwick and Warren had been ordered to intrench their fronts and do everything possible to strengthen their positions. A portion of the wagon-train guards had been ordered to report to Sedgwick for duty on his front. Every one on the right was on the alert, and eager to hear particulars about the fighting on the left. The various commands had been advised from time to time of the events which occurred, for it was General Grant's invariable custom to have commanding officers on different points of the line promptly informed of what occurred at other points.

Generals Grant and Meade, after discussing the situation, now decided to have Hancock and Burnside make a simultaneous attack at 6 P. M. It was then supposed that Burnside would certainly be in position by that hour to unite in such an assault. I started for Hancock's front to confer with him regarding this movement, and just as I joined his troops, the enemy, directed by Lee in person, as we afterward discovered, made a desperate assault upon our line. It began at 4:15 P. M. The woods in front of Hancock had now taken fire, and the flames were communicated to his log breastworks and abatis of slashed timber. The wind was, unfortunately, blowing in our direction, and the blinding smoke was driven in the faces of our men, while the fire itself swept down upon them. For a time they battled heroically to maintain their position, fighting both the conflagration and the enemy's advancing columns. At last, however, the breastworks became untenable, and some of the troops who had displayed such brilliant qualities during the entire day now fell back in confusion. The enemy took advantage of the disorder, and, rushing forward with cheers, succeeded in planting some of his battle-flags upon our front line of breastworks; but Hancock and all the staff-officers present made strenuous exertions to rally the men, and many of them were soon brought back to the front. General Carroll's brigade was now ordered to form and retake the line of intrenchments which had been lost. These gallant troops, led by the intrepid Carroll in person, dashing forward at a run, and cheering as they went, swept everything before them, and in a few minutes were in possession of the works. Both the attack and counter-attack were so handsomely made that they elicited praise from friend and foe alike. Some of Hancock's artillery was served with great efficiency in this engagement, and added much to the result. At five o'clock the enemy had been completely repulsed, and fell back, leaving a large number of his dead and wounded on the field.

Burnside made an attack at half-past five, but with no important results. The nature of the ground was a more formidable obstruction than the enemy. Warren and Sedgwick had been engaged during part of the day, and had prevented the enemy in front of them from withdrawing any troops, but notwithstanding their gallant fighting they had substantially gained no ground.

### GRANT'S DEMEANOR ON THE FIELD.

WHILE the most critical movements were taking place, General Grant manifested no perceptible anxiety, but gave his orders, and sent and received communications, with a coolness and deliberation which made a marked impression upon those who had been brought into contact with him for the first time on the field of battle. His speech was never hurried, and his manner betrayed no trace of excitability or even impatience. He never exhibited to better advantage his peculiar ability in moving troops with unparalleled speed to the critical points on the line of battle where they were most needed, or, as it was sometimes called, «feeding a fight.» There was a spur on the heel of every order he sent, and his subordinates were made to realize that in battle it is the minutes which control events. He said, while waiting for Burnside to get into position and attack: «The only time I ever feel impatient is when I give an order for an important movement of troops in the presence of the enemy, and am waiting for them to reach their destination. Then the minutes seem like hours.» He rode out to important points of the line twice during the day, in company with General Meade and two officers of the staff. It was noticed that he was visibly affected by his proximity to the wounded, and especially by the sight of blood. He would turn his face away from such scenes, and show by the expression of his countenance, and sometimes by a pause in his conversation, that he felt most keenly the painful spectacle presented by the field of battle. Some reference was made to the subject in camp that evening, and the general said: «I cannot bear the sight of suffering. The night after the first day's fight at Shiloh I was sitting on the ground, leaning against a tree, trying to get some sleep. It soon began to rain so hard that I went into a log-house near by to seek shelter; but I found the surgeons had taken possession of it, and were amputating the arms and legs of the wounded, and blood was flowing in streams. I could not endure such a scene, and was glad to return to the tree outside, and sit there till morning in the storm.» I thought of this remark while sitting by his bedside twenty-one years afterward, when he, in the last days of his fatal illness, was himself undergoing supreme physical torture.

### HIS PECULIARITIES IN BATTLE.

As the general felt that he could be found more readily, and could issue his orders more promptly, from the central point which he had chosen for his headquarters, he remained there almost the entire day. He would at times walk slowly up and down, but most of the day he sat upon the stump of a tree, or on the ground, with his back leaning against a tree. The thread gloves remained on his hands, a lighted cigar was in his mouth almost constantly, and his penknife was kept in active use whittling sticks. He would pick up one small twig after another, and sometimes holding the small end away from him would rapidly shave it down to a point; at other times he would turn the point toward him and work on it as if sharpening a lead-pencil; then he would girdle it, cut it in two, throw it away and begin on another. We had long been accused of being a nation of whittlers, and this practice on the part of such a conspicuous representative American seemed to give color to the charge. He seldom indulged in this habit in subsequent battles. The occupation played sad havoc with the thread gloves, and before nightfall several holes had been worn in them, from which his finger nails protruded. After that day the gloves disappeared, and the general thereafter went without them in camp, and wore the usual buckskin gauntlets when on horseback. It was not till the Appomattox campaign that another pair of thread gloves was donned. There was a mystery about the use of those gloves which was never entirely solved. The impression was that Mrs. Grant had purchased them, and handed them to the general before he started from Washington, and that, either in deference to her, or because he had a notion that the officers in the Eastern armies were greater sticklers for dress than those in the armies of the West, he wore the gloves continuously for the first three days of his opening campaign in Virginia; that is to say, as long as they lasted under the wear and tear to which he subjected them.

#### GRANT'S CONFIDENCE IN SUCCESS.

His confidence was never for a moment shaken in the outcome of the general engagement in the Wilderness, and he never once doubted his ability to make a forward movement as the result of that battle. At a critical period of the day he sent instructions to have all the pontoon bridges over the Rapidan in his rear taken up, except the one at Germanna Ford. A short time after giving this order he called General Rawlins, Colonel Babcock, and me to him, and asked for a map. As we sat together on the ground, his legs tucked under him, tailor fashion, he looked over the map, and said: «I do not hope to gain any very decided advantage from the fighting in this forest. I did expect excellent results from Hancock's movement early this morning, when he started the enemy on the run; but it was impossible for him to see his own troops, or the true position of the enemy, and the success gained could not be followed up in such a country. I can certainly drive Lee back into his works, but I shall not assault him there; he would have all the advantage in such a fight. If he falls back and intrenches, my notion is to move promptly toward the left. This will, in all probability, compel him to try and throw himself between us and Richmond, and in such a movement I hope to be able to attack him in a more open country, and outside of his breastworks.» This was the second time only that he had looked at the maps since crossing the Rapidan, and it was always noticeable in a campaign how seldom he consulted them, compared with the constant examination of them by most other prominent commanders. The explanation of it is that he had an extraordinary memory as to anything that was presented to him graphically. After looking critically at a map of a locality, it seemed to become photographed indelibly upon his brain, and he could follow its features without referring to it again. Besides, he possessed an almost intuitive knowledge of topography, and never became confused as to the points of the compass. He was a natural «bushwhacker,» and was never so much at home as when finding his way by the course of streams, the contour of the hills, and the general features of the country. I asked him, one day, whether he had ever been deceived as to the points of the compass. He said: «Only once—when I arrived at Cairo, Illinois. The effect of that curious bend in the river turned me completely around, and when the sun came up the first morning after I got there, it seemed to me that it rose directly in the west.»

#### THE GENERAL-IN-CHIEF AS AID TO A DROVER.

During a lull in the battle late in the afternoon, General Grant, in company with two staff-officers, strolled over toward the Germanna road. While we stood on the bank of a small rivulet, a drove of beef cattle was driven past. One of the animals strayed into the stream, and had evidently made up its mind to part company with its fellows and come over to our side. One of the drovers yelled out to the general, who was a little in advance of his officers: «I say, stranger, head off that beef critter for me, will you?» The general, having always prided himself upon being a practical farmer, felt as much at home in handling cattle as in directing armies, and without changing countenance at once stepped forward, threw up his hands, and shouted to the animal. It stopped, took a look at him, and then, as if sufficiently impressed with this show of authority, turned back into the road. The general made no comment whatever upon this incident, and seemed to think no more about the salutation he had received than if some one had presented arms to him. He knew, of course, that the man did not recognize him. If he had supposed the man was lacking in proper military respect, he would perhaps have administered to him the same lesson which he once taught a soldier in the Twenty-first Illinois, when he commanded that regiment. An officer who had served under him at the time told me that Colonel Grant, as he came out of his tent one morning, found a strapping big fellow posted as sentinel, who nodded his head good-naturedly, smiled blandly, and said, «Howdy, colonel?» His commander cried, «Hand me your piece,» and upon taking it, faced the soldier and came to a «present arms»; then handing back the musket, he remarked, «That is the way to say ‹How do you do› to your colonel.»

### CONFUSION CAUSED BY A NIGHT ATTACK.

It was now about sundown; the storm of battle which had raged with unabated fury from early dawn had been succeeded by a calm. The contemplated general attack at six o'clock had been abandoned on account of the assault of the enemy on Hancock's front, and the difficulty of perfecting the alinements and supplying the men with ammunition. It was felt that the day's strife had ended, unless Lee should risk another attack. Just then the stillness was broken by heavy volleys of musketry on our extreme right, which told that Sedgwick had been assaulted, and was actually engaged with the enemy. The attack against which the general-in-chief during the day had ordered every precaution to be taken had now been made. Meade was at Grant's headquarters at the time. They had just left the top of the knoll, and were standing in front of General Grant's tent talking to Mr. Washburne. Staff-officers and couriers were soon seen galloping up to Meade's headquarters, and his chief-of-staff, General Humphreys, sent word that the attack was directed against our extreme right, and that a part of Sedgwick's line had been driven back in some confusion. Generals Grant and Meade, accompanied by me and one or two other staff-officers, walked rapidly over to Meade's tent, and found that the reports still coming in were bringing news of increasing disaster. It was soon reported that General Shaler and part of his brigade had been captured; then that General Seymour and several hundred of his men had fallen into the hands of the enemy; afterward that our right had been turned, and Ferrero's division cut off and forced back upon the Rapidan. General Humphreys, on receiving the first reports, had given prompt instructions with a view to strengthening the point of the line attacked. General Grant now took the matter in hand with his accustomed vigor. Darkness had set in, but the firing still continued. Aides came galloping in from the right, laboring under intense excitement, talking wildly, and giving the most exaggerated reports of the engagement. Some declared that a large force had broken and scattered Sedgwick's entire corps. Others insisted that the enemy had turned our right completely, and captured the wagon-train. It was asserted at one time that both Sedgwick and Wright had been captured. Such tales of disaster would have been enough to inspire serious apprehension in daylight and under ordinary circumstances. In the darkness of the night, in the gloom of a tangled forest, and after men's nerves had been racked by the strain of a two days' desperate battle, the most immovable commander might have been shaken. But it was in just such sudden emergencies that General Grant was always at his best. Without the change of a muscle of his face, or the slightest alteration in the tones of his voice, he quietly interrogated the officers who brought the reports; then, sifting out the truth from the mass of exaggerations, he gave directions for relieving the situation with the marvelous rapidity which was always characteristic of him when directing movements in the face of an enemy. Reinforcements were hurried to the point attacked, and preparations made for Sedgwick's corps to take up a new line, with the front and right thrown back. General Grant soon walked over to his own camp, seated himself on a stool in front of his tent, lighted a fresh cigar, and there continued to receive further advices from the right.

### GRANT ADMINISTERS A REPRIMAND.

A general officer came in from his command at this juncture, and said to the general-in-chief, speaking rapidly and laboring under considerable excitement: «General Grant, this is a crisis that cannot be looked upon too seriously. I know Lee's methods well by past experience; he will throw his whole army between us and the Rapidan, and cut us off completely from our communications.» The general rose to his feet, took his cigar out of his mouth, turned to the officer, and replied, with a degree of animation which he seldom manifested: «Oh, I am heartily tired of hearing about what Lee is going to do. Some of you always seem to think he is suddenly going to turn a double somersault, and land in our rear and on both of our flanks at the same time. Go back to your command, and try to think what we are going to do ourselves, instead of what Lee is going to do.» The officer retired rather crestfallen, and without saying a word in reply. This recalls a very pertinent criticism regarding his chief once made in my presence by General Sherman. He said: «Grant always seemed pretty certain to win when he went into a fight with anything like equal numbers. I believe the chief reason why he was more successful than others was that while they were thinking so much about what the enemy was going to do, Grant was thinking all the time about what he was going to do himself.»

### GRANT AFTER THE BATTLE.

HANCOCK came to headquarters about 8 P. M., and had a conference with the general-in-chief and General Meade. He had had a very busy day on his front, and while he was cheery, and showed that there was still plenty of fight left in him, he manifested signs of fatigue after his exhausting labors. General Grant, in offering him a cigar, found that only one was left in his pocket. Deducting the number he had given away from the supply he had started out with in the morning showed that he had smoked that day about twenty, all very strong and of formidable size. But it must be remembered that it was a particularly long day. He never afterward equaled that record in the use of tobacco.

The general, after having given his final orders providing for any emergency which might arise, entered his tent, and threw himself down upon his camp-bed. Ten minutes thereafter an alarming report was received from the right. I looked in his tent, and found him sleeping as soundly and as peacefully as an infant. I waked him, and communicated the report. His military instincts convinced him that it was a gross exaggeration, and as he had already made every provision for meeting any renewed attempts against the right, he turned over in his bed, and immediately went to sleep again. Twenty-one years thereafter as I sat by his death-bed, when his sufferings had become agonizing, and he was racked by the tortures of insomnia, I recalled to him that night in the Wilderness. He said: «Ah, yes; it seems strange that I, who always slept so well in the field, should now pass whole nights in the quiet of this peaceful house without being able to close my eyes.»

It was soon ascertained that although Sedgwick's line had been forced back with some loss, and Shaler and Seymour had been made prisoners, only a few hundred men had been captured, and the enemy had been compelled to withdraw. General Grant had great confidence in Sedgwick in such an emergency, and the event showed that it was not misplaced.

The attack on our right, and its repulse, ended the memorable battle of the Wilderness. The losses were found to be: killed, 2246; wounded, 12,037; missing, 3383; total, 17,666. The damage inflicted upon the enemy is not known, but as he was the assaulting party as often as the Union army, there is reason to believe that the losses on the two sides were about equal. Taking twenty-four hours as the time actually occupied in fighting, and counting the casualties in both armies, it will be found that on that bloody field every minute recorded the loss of twenty-five men.

As the staff-officers threw themselves upon the ground that night, sleep came to them without coaxing. They had been on the move since dawn, galloping over bad roads, struggling about through forest openings, jumping rivulets, wading swamps, helping to rally troops, dodging bullets, and searching for commanding officers in all sorts of unknown places. Their horses had been crippled, and they themselves were well-nigh exhausted. For the small part I had been able to perform in the engagement, the general recommended me for the brevet rank of major in the regular army, «for gallant and meritorious services.» His recommendation was afterward approved by the President. This promotion was especially gratifying for the reason that it was conferred for conduct in the first battle in which I had served under the command of the general-in-chief.

### THE WILDERNESS A UNIQUE COMBAT.

THERE were features of the battle which have never been matched in the annals of warfare. For two days nearly 200,000 veteran troops had struggled in a death-grapple, confronted at each step with almost every obstacle by which nature could bar their path, and groping their way through a tangled forest the impenetrable gloom of which could be likened only to the shadow of death. The undergrowth stayed their progress, the upper growth shut out the light of heaven. Officers could rarely see their troops for any considerable distance, for smoke clouded the vision, and a heavy sky obscured the sun. Directions were ascertained and lines established by means of the pocket-compass, and a change of position often presented an operation more like a problem of ocean navigation than a question of military manœuvers. It was the sense of sound and of touch rather than the sense of sight which guided the movements. It was a battle fought with the ear, and not with the eye. All circumstances seemed to combine to make the scene one of unutterable horror. At times the wind howled through the tree-tops, mingling its moans with the groans of the dying, and heavy branches were cut off by the fire of the artillery, and fell crashing upon the heads of the men, adding a new terror to battle. Forest fires raged; ammunition-trains exploded; the dead were roasted in the conflagration; the wounded, roused by its hot breath, dragged themselves along, with their torn and mangled limbs, in the mad energy of despair, to escape the ravages of the flames; and every bush seemed hung with shreds of blood-stained clothing. It was as though Christian men had turned to fiends, and hell itself had usurped the place of earth.

(To be continued.)

*Horace Porter.*

# SOUVENIRS OF A VETERAN COLLECTOR.

THE late William T. Walters of Baltimore, whose admirable collection of pictures and Barye bronzes is known to many art-lovers in the United States, went to Europe in 1861, and resided there for a number of years. Before that time he had been interested in art, and had purchased pictures by some of the American painters then in vogue. In Paris he met his friend Mr. George A. Lucas of Baltimore, a graduate of West Point, and an engineer, who knew some of the Barbizon painters and their artist friends, and, making their acquaintance, Mr. Walters was so much impressed with the merit of their works that he thought they might find purchasers in America. He thus appears as one of the earliest American amateurs who predicted the success of Millet, Rousseau, Corot, Diaz, and others of the famous group. Mr. Samuel P. Avery was at this time practising his profession of engraving in New York, and toward the close of our civil war he decided, at Mr. Walters's suggestion, to go into business as a dealer in works of art. Mr. Walters bought pictures in France, Mr. Avery sold them at auction in New York, and they divided the profits. This was the beginning of the long career that made Mr. Avery the best-known dealer of his time in America, and which came to a close eight years ago, when he retired. He has since been prominent in art matters in New York, being one of the trustees of the Metropolitan

Paris le 23 Juin 1879.

Adieu, mon vieux Sphinx,
au revoir. monsieur Avery.
Luc Olivier Merson
23 Juin 1879

DRAWN AND WRITTEN BY LUC OLIVIER MERSON.

Museum, and devoting much of his time to its affairs. His advice is highly valued. His friends include about all of our prominent collectors,—except, perhaps, some of those who have come to the front in the West of late years,—the book-loving coterie of the Grolier Club, and the trustees of Columbia University, in which he founded an architectural library. But his friends and acquaintances are not confined to his earlier associates and veterans among the connoisseurs. In the social meetings of the Architectural League, at the Century Club, and other places of congregation of the art world, he is often seen, and is as ready with his appreciation of a new movement as he is apt with his reminiscences of an old one.

DRAWN AND WRITTEN BY JULES BRETON.

Imagine a Corot sold in New York for one hundred and ten dollars! Yet this was the price obtained for one that Mr. Avery sold in 1863. Among the first pictures that he received from Mr. Walters were some genre subjects by Édouard Frère, and two landscapes by Corot. The Frères found ready purchasers, but the Corots were not so easily understood. These two were the first that were brought to this country, and they had cost five hundred francs apiece. Both the price and the profit now seem incredibly small, but they show how modest were the beginnings of a business that afterward involved many thousands of dollars. Mr. Avery had charge of the Fine Arts Department in the American section of the Paris Exposition of 1867, and from that time on his trips abroad were frequent. His acquaintance with French, German, and British artists grew wider with each succeeding year, and some of his acquaintances became his friends. Though not an autograph-collector, it occurred to him to get the sign-marks of the many painters he had met, and it is not remarkable that when he had the sketches and souvenirs they had given him bound in a tasteful volume, its pages should be full of interest. Some of these artistic *cartes de visite* were made on the spur of the moment, and possess the impromptu quality of a bit of conversation; others consist of a sentiment or a greeting. There are carefully finished drawings in the book, and sketches made with a few hasty lines. The pages are dotted with the autographs of many of the greatest men in modern art.

One of the first of the French artists whose acquaintance Mr. Avery made was Jules Breton. He wrote to him at his home at Courrières in Picardy in 1867, with reference to a commission for a picture that Mr. John Taylor Johnston wished to give him, and Breton replied that he would meet him on a given day at twelve o'clock at the Universal Exposition, in front of Meissonier's pictures. He did not appoint the rendezvous before his own works, as he might have done. Mr. Avery and Mr. Lucas were at the appointed place, and promptly at the hour Mr. Lucas, who knew Breton, said, «There he comes.» He was accompanied by his wife and daughter—his only child, then five or six years of age, accompanied by her *nounou*, with cap and cloak and flowing ribbons. Breton, hale and hearty, wore a checked waistcoat with pearl buttons, such as are worn in the country districts, and the whole party had the unaffected air of good people from the provinces. The distinguished painter has always kept his simplicity of dress and manner. He accepted the commission from Mr. Johnston, agreeing to paint a picture with two figures for twenty-five hundred francs, and from that time on Mr. Avery saw him frequently. Though they have no longer matters of business to write about, their relations continue, and the famous French artist does not forget his friend in America. He has given Mr. Avery copies of his books (for Jules Breton has published several volumes of prose and verse), with a few lines expressing his friendship on the fly-leaves, and this year he sent him « Un Peintre Pay-

Mon cher Monsieur Avery voici un méchant croquis d'une des figures de mon bon tableau, Le Renseignement, que vous avez tiré d'Allemagne pour mon ami Mr Vanderbilt. J'aurais voulu le faire meilleur, mais tel qu'il est qu'il laisse sur votre livre le souvenir du plaisir que j'ai eu d'avoir ce tableau et quelque grâce de le savoir entre les mains d'un amateur aussi distingué.

à vous bien cordialement

1880 21 juillet E Meissonier

DRAWN AND WRITTEN BY MEISSONIER.

san,» his latest production, bearing in his handwriting the dedication, «Témoignage bien affectueux à son fidèle ami.» One morning, in Paris, Mr. Avery went to Breton's hotel, —a small but comfortable hostelry near the Luxembourg, which the painter's father and mother before him had made their stopping-place in the great capital,—and, though it was but nine o'clock, found that the painter had already set out for the meeting of the Salon jury. Breton had been up at six o'clock, for, like a good many other artists in France, he is an early riser. He returned to the hotel about eleven, and Mr. Avery breakfasted with him. When Breton took up the album to write the verses, «Courrières,» on the page, his little daughter prompted him as he spoke them while he wrote, for she knew them all. At the bottom of the page he sketched with the pen a silhouette of Courrières from memory, with the field, the houses, and the church tower. When Jules Breton's little daughter

DRAWN BY ÉDOUARD DETAILLE.

grew up she became a painter, and married a painter, M. Adrien Demont. Mr. Avery bought her first picture. (See page 210.—EDITOR.)

Meissonier writes: « I thank Mr. Avery for his visit to Poissy, and I am so much the more flattered since he informs me he has just purchased my small ‹Republican Sentinel of the Army of the Var.› I take pleasure in repeating to him what I said to my friend M. Petit, who ceded him the picture; it is the first time I sign a canvas with which I am absolutely satisfied.» This is dated at Poissy, August 29, 1875. Later on, July 21, 1880, he writes: « Dear Mr. Avery: Here is a bad sketch (*méchant croquis*) of one of the figures in my good picture, ‹Le Renseignement,› which you have got back from Germany for my friend Mr. Vanderbilt. I wish I could have done better, but such as it is, I leave it in your book as a souvenir of my pleasure in having seen the picture again, and of knowing it is in the hands of so distinguished an amateur. Very cordially yours, E. MEISSONIER.» The way in which « Le Renseignement » was « rescued » forms an interesting story. The picture shows Marshal Saxe, with a body of troops, interrogating a peasant at a crossroads in the forest, and taking notes. In 1880 Mr. William H. Vanderbilt was sitting to Meissonier for his portrait, and Mr. Avery and Mr. Lucas were invited by the artist to come to his studio during the sittings, as Mr. Vanderbilt did not speak French. One day Mr. Vanderbilt asked, «What picture does M. Meissonier think is the best he ever painted?» Meissonier, replying through Mr. Lucas, spoke of two, the celebrated «1814» and «Le Renseignement.»[1] The latter picture, he said, with a sigh and a deeply felt «hélas!» was in Germany, in the hands of the enemies of France. It had been painted for the Exposition of 1867, and was bought by M. Petit, who asked fifty thousand francs for it. Mr. Walters had offered forty-five thousand francs, but a German banker in Paris, M. Mayer, paid the price and got the picture. He was a well-known collector, and his family home was in Dresden. When the war of 1870 broke out, M. Mayer left Paris, and took the picture with him. Mr. Avery had seen his gallery every time he went to Dresden, and knew the picture. The conversation in the studio continued, and Avery and Lucas agreed that «Le Renseignement» was, indeed, a wonderful canvas. Petit had tried to buy it back, but could not get it. It was thought it would be impossible to get Mayer to sell it, but Avery, authorized by Mr. Vanderbilt, resolved to try. He did not wish to make a trip to Dresden at the time, so he wrote to Mayer that a friend of his wanted the picture, but not as a matter of business. It was not to buy to sell again. The banker replied that he had often been importuned to sell the picture, but had invariably refused; yet, now that he felt himself growing old (he had then reached the age of eighty), and that as after his death his family might not care to keep it, he would take a certain price for it. He added that he might change his mind overnight, for he found it hard to decide to sell. Avery lost no time in telegraphing, and the next day received the canvas by parcels post; the marvelous picture was actually in his room in the hotel! A draft on London was sent to Dresden at once, and the deed was done. Mr. Vanderbilt and his two fellow-conspirators now set about arranging a surprise for Meissonier. The next day was to be the last sitting for the portrait, and when they arrived at the studio one of them carried a

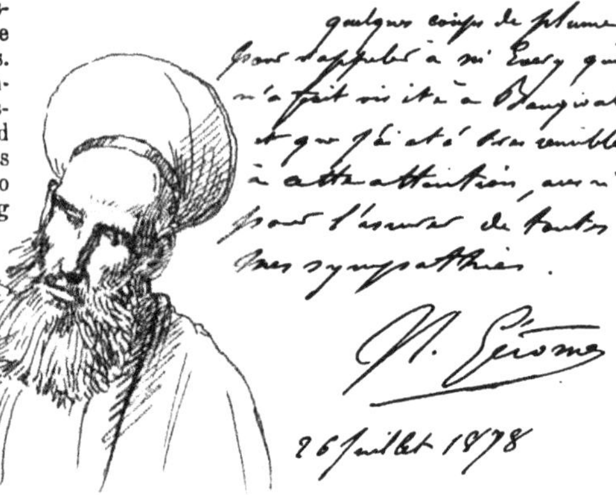


DRAWN AND WRITTEN BY J. L. GÉRÔME.

DRAWN AND WRITTEN BY M. MUNKACSY.

[1] Engravings of these pictures appeared in THE CENTURY for July and August, 1896.

parcel, which was placed in a safe corner. The sitting proceeded, and at last Meissonier said the portrait was finished; there was not another touch to be added. «Now you may see me sign,» he announced, and the act was accomplished with a due observance on the part of the company of the importance of the moment. The artist then went into another room to put the little portrait in a frame he had ready for it. «Le Renseignement» was quickly taken from the corner, set in a frame on the easel, and the three men stood by to see what Meissonier would do. «When he came in and suddenly saw the picture,» says Mr. Avery, «he almost went crazy in his joy. He got down on his knees before it so that he could look at it closely, and cried out, ‹*Oh, mon bon tableau! Oh, mon bon tableau!*› and with difficulty found words to express his delight. He loved his picture that he never expected to see again, and his heart was full.» Of course when it became known that «Le Renseignement» was in France again, there were accounts in the newspapers of how it had come about, and in Berlin and in Paris the stories were equally wide of the truth. One paper said that Mrs. Vanderbilt, the wife of a multimillionaire from America, had gone to Dresden, bought the picture, and carried it off in her arms. Another said that a rich English lord had gone to Mayer's, and counted out bank-notes on the table before him until he told him to stop and take the picture.

Mr. Vanderbilt and Mr. Avery went down to By one morning to see Mme. Rosa Bonheur at her country place on the outskirts of the Forest of Fontainebleau. Her well-appointed trap met them at the station, and carried them to the house in time for luncheon. Mme. Bonheur poured out their wine for them herself, and they talked of the forest and the beautiful surroundings of her home. «Yes,» she said; «but I hear them cutting down trees in the forest sometimes, and every blow of the ax hurts my heart.» She had met Mr. August Belmont, and had received commissions from him to paint two pictures when he was United States minister at The Hague. She had told him that she was exceedingly busy and could n't paint them very soon, and he had said: «How long must I wait? One year—two years? I am getting old, and I want them soon.» She asked him how old he was, and when he said, «Seventy-one,» she replied, «That is my age, too.» So she shook hands with him, and told him she would paint the pictures for him at once. Mme. Bonheur related this incident to her visitors, and added: «Mr. Belmont is a great Democrat, is n't he? When will he be elected President of the United States?» She evidently thought his chances were very good, but Mr. Vanderbilt told her he thought they were about as good as his own, and his he considered painfully small; so Mme. Bonheur was enlightened on American politics. «At this time,» says Mr. Avery, «she did not seem at all old. She had a refined, womanly face and a very sweet voice. Her temperament was bright and gay, and her manner charming.»

DRAWN BY MENZEL.

Gérôme writes in the album accompanying

a drawing, «A few strokes of the pen to remind Mr. Avery of the visit he made me at Bougival, with which attention I am much flattered, as well as to assure him of my many sympathies.» Munkacsy makes a formula sketch of himself, as a souvenir of Mr. Avery's first visit to him in Paris in 1878, and writes on another page, in New York in 1886, when he visited Mr. Avery. Jules Lefebvre, in 1878, accompanies a sketch of the figure in one of his pictures with the lines: «Good-by, Mignon! You are now safe in an asylum for which I have to thank Mr. Avery. Don't forget me!» Olivier Merson, in a similar vein, in 1879, writes: «Adieu, my old sphinx. Au revoir, Mr. Avery.» Van Marcke, on July 4, 1876, writes: «I am very much pleased to have met Mr. Avery to-day. His visit coincides with a great day, the anniversary of America's independence. I congratulate him on that great event with a hearty shake of the hand.» «And it was Van Marcke who remembered the day,» says Mr. Avery, «for I had not mentioned it.» «I swear on this Spaniard's head,» writes Jules Worms, referring to his sketch in the book, «to do all in my power to please our excellent friend Mr. Avery.» «A knowing hand has Mr. Avery,» writes a celebrated painter and etcher, «for he places it upon the choicest things. His kind visit to my studio proves this—he deprives me of my unique proofs. Nevertheless, I remain his truly devoted L. Flameng.» «I shall be glad to be presented to the American public by Mr. Avery, and hope soon to seize this happy occasion,» is signed by the great artist Paul Baudry. He wrote amid the scaffoldings and ladders in the foyer of the opera-house, where he was at work on his famous ceilings; but events prevented him from painting the promised picture. After his seven years' work in the opera-house he went to Egypt to rest, and other great works taking his time afterward, the commission was never executed. «Here is my autograph,» says Madrazo, laconically, but he painted a portrait of Mr. Avery in oil in one sitting that is a marvel. «Here is a souvenir of our young Vestal, who is to wake up in America next year,» writes Hector Leroux. And so on through the pages follow the messages and sentiments of half the celebrated painters in France—Corot, Daubigny, Millet, Cabanel, Bouguereau, Detaille, De Neuville, Dagnan-Bouveret, Vibert, Jules Jacquemart, Charles Muller, Hébert, Clairin, Berne-Bellecour, Jacquet, Boulanger, Ziem, and many more.

DRAWN AND WRITTEN BY SEYMOUR HADEN.

Amusing stories are told of Ziem, who lived in a house at the top of the rue Lepic on Montmartre. His house was his castle in the literal sense of the word. It was difficult to obtain admission, for the painter had an upper window out of which he always looked when the bell rang, and interrogated his would-be visitors. He had a basket which he let down

Sor Avery.
Muy Sor mio:
Deseoso de tener
noticias de V. y sa=
ber el parecer del cuadro último que
le remití aprovecho la ocasion para
felicitarle el nuevo año y que sea
para V. de prosperidad
Siempre de V. le sa=
luda su afmo amigo Domingo
Paris 17 Enero 1882

DRAWN AND WRITTEN BY DOMINGO.

by a cord to receive packages or messages, and he slept in a wonderful swinging-bed. His house was a veritable museum, illuminated Persian manuscripts being part of his collection. Some of these were worth thousands of francs, but it was impossible to persuade him to sell any of them. In place of a newel-post on his stairway stood the prow of a gilded gondola, and, closely immured in his studio, he painted pictures of Venice, and bade defiance to all who came to disturb his peace.

Georges Clairin had just come back from Algiers when Mr. Avery saw him in 1871, not long after the siege of Paris. He had brought with him Henri Regnault's dog and painting-

ENGRAVED BY PETER AITKEN.

Maurice Leloir
Paris 1887

Quand ce petit commissionnaire
Aura sur la rive étrangère
Transporté tout ce chargement,
Espérons, si l'on est content,
Qu'il en viendra reprendre autant

DRAWN AND WRITTEN BY LOUIS LELOIR.

traps, and told how he and some other comrades, who were in the same company of the national guard with Regnault, went to the battle-field of Buzenval after the sortie from Paris, and turned over the fallen French soldiers by night trying to find the body of their friend. The way the bodies all lay, Clairin said, showed that they had fallen with their faces toward the Germans, and Regnault's was found like the rest.

Louis Leloir put a delightful water-color in the album, a porter in Henri Quatre costume, loaded with pictures and crossing the seas from France to America in seven-league

DRAWN AND WRITTEN BY M. RICO.

boots, besides an inscription in verse. Maurice Leloir, the talented brother of this lamented painter, has a line in the book too, but he has recently sent to Mr. Avery a present that the latter rightly values very highly. It is an édition de luxe of «The Sentimental Journey,» and the artist has retouched all the black-and-white drawings, of which there are some hundreds in the book, with water-color, and has painted on the false title a beautiful little picture. A dedication expresses the kindly sentiments always felt by the artist and his brother, and testifies to their pleasant relations with Mr. Avery.

In 1880, when the trustees of the Metropolitan Museum wished to have a portrait painted of their president Mr. John Taylor Johnston, Mr. Avery, on their behalf, called on Bonnat, whom they had selected as the artist, to give him the commission. M. Bonnat, however, at the mention of an order, expressed his regret that he could not possibly undertake to paint Mr. Johnston at the time, as he had so many important commissions on hand that he was obliged to have three different sittings every day, and to begin at seven o'clock in the morning, in order to get through his day's work: the Duc d'Aumale and other prominent men were among the sitters. But when it was explained to him that the portrait was to be for an American museum of art, the genial gentleman, who deservedly by his record and his attainments occupies the position of official head of the French school, said that that put a different face on the matter—that he would find time in spite of his overwhelming engagements; and he did.

While the preëminence of French art in the last thirty or forty years makes the contributions in Mr. Avery's book from the painters in and about Paris the most interesting, and these artists appear in his recollections as the chief figures, his relations with those in other places were close, and marked by many pleasant incidents. Madrazo, Domingo, Rico, Palmaroli, and Escosura, the Spaniards, were identified with Paris. So too was Castiglione, the Italian; Otto von Thoren, the Austrian; Gallait, the Belgian; Schreyer, the German; and Josef Israels, the Dutchman. «Rico made a charming little sketch in my book in no time,» comments Mr. Avery, «for he happened to get it just as he was starting on a journey. He wrote, ‹I have no time for more, as the train leaves at eight.›» Under his clever sketch of an orchestra and choir Domingo indites his wishes for a happy New Year, and «greetings to you always from your faithful friend.» Von Thoren writes a sentiment: «Though your subject be stupid, if you can render it with feeling it will make its mark.» Israels says, «I have always much sympathy with America and its inhabitants.» One day, when Mr. Avery and his wife were at the studio of Israels, Mrs. Avery asked him about a picture which she had seen and admired, giving its title as «The Widow.» «Which widow can it be?» said the painter. «My dear madam, I have made so many widows, I cannot tell.» When the picture was more fully described, he remembered it, and exclaimed: «Oh, yes, I know. That is one of my *good* widows.»

Among the German and Austrian artists Mr. Avery counts many friends. In the album,

SKETCH BY DAGNAN-BOUVERET, FROM «UN ACCIDENT.»

DRAWN BY ROSA BONHEUR.

among others, are the names of Menzel, Piloty, Meyer von Bremen, Knaus, Lindenschmidt, Diez, Gabriel Max, Löfftz, Carl Becker, Defregger, Munthe, Preyer, and Braith. Menzel tore a leaf from his sketchbook for the album. Defregger says, «Life is serious, art is gay.» Max writes, «Think very often of the beautiful Starenberg Lake,» on the borders of which he lived, and the picturesqueness of which he was anxious to have appreciated. He had a study in his house, in which he worked with great interest in comparative anatomy, dissecting monkeys and other animals, and enjoying a wide reputation in the scientific world. Piloty, Löfftz, Lindenschmidt, and others were painting in one of King Ludwig's splendid palaces. They talked of the mysteries of the place, and gave the difficulties of their work for the mad king as an excuse for not having finished pictures they had promised. Preyer, the still-life painter, once so famous for the downy surface of his peaches, is an interesting figure. He was a man of various attainments, much esteemed by his fellow-citizens in Düsseldorf, and had been mayor of the town. He was a dwarf not over three feet high, with curly hair and a great beard. He lived to be over eighty years of age, and had two children, a tall son and daughter. He sat in a high chair at the head of his table, and offered his hospitality with dignity, but sometimes after dinner, his wife, who was a woman of ordinary height, would lift him up bodily and set him on the mantel. He knew all the American painters who had studied at Düsseldorf, such as Worthington Whittredge, Eastman Johnson, and Ehninger, and was much interested in all that concerned the United States.

Of course any one having to do with the purchase of pictures must know the London market, and though before our present fashion for English works of the earlier school not many pictures by British artists were bought by American amateurs, and though scarcely any by the Englishmen of to-day are brought over, there are some notable exceptions. Mr. Avery, for instance, gave Sir John Millais a commission for Mr. Vanderbilt. The picture he painted was «Lucia di Lammermoor and Edgar,» and the artist made it a condition of the order that the engraver should keep the canvas two years. It was delivered by the engraver at the end of that period, and Mr. Avery wrote to Sir John that he should like to show it to him, so that he might see if it was in perfect condition before its departure for New York. He found Millais working on portraits of Gladstone and Carlyle, and the talk turned on the traits of the two men. It appeared that Mr. Gladstone asked questions, and evinced a desire to learn about painting from the artist's point of view, and showed deference to his opinions. Carlyle, on the other hand, was very dogmatic, gave his opinions as final, thought there could be no question as to their validity, and also proved to be such an impatient sitter that the portrait had to be abandoned.

Millais, Holman Hunt, Nicol, and Seymour Haden are among the English names in the album, and that of George Cruikshank also

*Presented to Mrs. Saml. P. Avery by the Artist.*
*George Cruikshank—on his 84th birth day Sept.*
*27—1876.*

appears. But Mr. Avery has a unique souvenir from the hand of the famous artist of «Punch,» in the form of a business card which the latter etched for him. Cruikshank made the plate when he was eighty-one years of age, and presented the original drawing to Mrs. Avery on his eighty-fourth birthday. The old gentleman remarked that he could make such a card for a dealer in New York, but it would never do to perform the same service for one in London. I doubt, though, whether any London dealer has had such unique and pleasant experiences with the painters from whom he bought pictures, and so perhaps none would have been entitled to so great a favor.

*William A. Coffin.*

## SLEEP AND GRIEF.

AH, if oblivion of sleep would last
  Through one short hour of wakefulness, that so
  The heart might rest a little while and know
That it was resting! But, however fast

We may awaken, pain has still the start,
  And sits beside the bed, and overhangs
  The opening eyes, that it may sink its fangs
In the first stirring of the tortured heart!

*Charles Buxton Going.*

THE MOTT STREET BARRACKS.

The rear buildings on the right have been condemned by the Board of Health under the Tenement House Laws of 1895. The death-rate from 1890–1895, inclusive, was 45.87.

# LIGHT IN DARK PLACES.

## A STUDY OF THE BETTER NEW YORK.

By the author of «How the Other Half Lives,» «The Children of the Poor,» etc.

[NOTHING could be more in the spirit of the Christmas season than the story of the light that has come into the dark places of the metropolis of the New World through wise legislation and firm execution of the laws, nor could any one more appropriate be selected for the telling of the story than the hard-working daily journalist who has for so many years been a part of almost every important judicious and statesmanlike effort for the amelioration of the condition of the masses of the people of New York. A large portion of the legislative reforms of which he speaks have been merely the endorsement of the words «*Be it enacted*» upon the hopes of good and earnest men like Jacob A. Riis. The successful philanthropic career of Mr. Riis is indeed an exemplary object lesson, for he is not among those who let their sympathies and emotions run away with their judgment; he has worked for practicable and just measures of improvement, with «a warm heart and a cool head.»—EDITOR.]

ONE summer night, ten or a dozen years ago, there was stir and excitement on the East Side. For the first time in its experience, except when ordered by Jupiter Pluvius, whose work was not thorough, Hester street was to have a bath. The newspapers had heralded it, the public had discussed it and laughed at it a little. Everybody agreed that it was time, for the offense of Hester street was rank indeed; but few believed that it would do much good. Good or bad, it was something new, and the East Side turned out, as to a circus parade, to see New York's dirtiest street washed.

The fire-engines were turned into it, with men and hose, and the water was turned on in every hydrant. All night they pumped and squirmed, and Hester street became a black and rushing river, with mud-geysers at every corner, as the culverts were clogged with the black deposits scratched semi-occasionally for years by ineffectual brooms. The dwellers in the old tenements along the market highway of Jewtown looked on in awe and wonder; landlords whose cellars shared in the superabundance of the strange element wailed and wrung their hands; and the curious crowds hooted and ran before the advancing flood. When at length it was over, the last engine uncoupled and gone, and the morning sun shone upon the rough pavement, long hidden from the sight of man, the sneers of the scoffers were seen to be justified. The scrubbing had improved the top, but it needed to go deeper; more drastic measures were needed to cleanse this Augean stable. The experiment, I believe, was not repeated.

The recollection of that night came back to me as I sat at my office window in Mulberry street, on one of the hot evenings of last August, and saw the block invaded by firemen bent on their merciful mission of cooling the tenement streets—where death stalked early and late in that terrible week—by washing down the pavements. They were preceded by bands of noisy youngsters, stripped to the shirt, who jumped and reveled in the streaming gutters, and came out clean, tumbling over one another with shouts of laughter, while their elders, perched on door-step and curb, cheered them on. And when the noisy procession had moved into the next street, expected and received there by fresh bands of revelers awaiting their chance for a good washing-up, the smooth roadway was already coming out clean and dry as any floor, and in the air, but now so heavy and hot, there was a fresh breath, as if a breeze from the sea, slumbering out beyond the sands, had passed that way. The girls of the block were forming for a dance. And in the attuning of Mulberry street to the better day I measured the span between then and now—a span of asphalt pavements and of unpolitical street-sweeping.

The experience of New York that it pays to provide decently paved streets for the poor tenant whose children have heretofore had no other playground, and to put a man, instead of a «voter,» behind every broom, must rank among the great discoveries in local

DRAWN BY JAY HAMBIDGE.

BONE ALLEY.

To be removed to make way for a new East Side small park, under the Tenement House Laws of 1895.

municipal affairs of the last decade. That it was a part of the business of the community to see to it that its masses were properly housed, had impressed itself earlier upon its consciousness by dint of much argument and the persuasion of disastrous epidemics, for which its overcrowded rookeries were justly held to blame, and nail after nail had been driven into the structure of tenement-house law, erected to neutralize as far as might be the mischief which could never be wholly undone; but it is only within a year that they have been clinched by the enactment of a law permitting the seizure and demolition of unsanitary property as a menace to the public, and the determination of the Health Board to enforce it to the letter. Thus all the most important steps which have contributed to the making over, as it were, of the metropolis on the eve of its throwing off provincial fetters, and becoming in truth the Greater and Better New York of the twentieth century, fall within the half-score years since it first undertook, in the face of much ridicule, to wash its dirtiest street.

I do not think that, as a class, New-Yorkers have taken a just pride in their city in the past, and I am sure they have thereby lost something well worth having. Perhaps, in a measure, this failure can be laid at the door of the official corruption that has disgraced it; perhaps in even a larger sense the failure is to blame for the corruption. Let that pass. I have seen some of the world's great cities, some of them famed for their beauty, and this I know, that I have come back each time more impressed with the conviction that there is none of them that can compare with New York in point of natural advantages and real attractiveness. When, two or three years ago, I had returned from a summer spent in northern Europe, I used to go every day for a month from my office in Mulberry street over to the corner of Broadway and Houston street, on purpose to look up and down Broadway, and get the view of that royal thoroughfare, to Grace Church on the north, with every detail of its beautiful gray spire standing forth clear and distinct in the sparkling October air, and south two full miles to the tall buildings about Bowling Green. I did not tire of admiring the brilliancy of the atmosphere, which seemed little less than a revelation after the heavy sultriness of London's streets, or Hamburg's, or Copenhagen's. I have never seen such sunsets on sea or land as are to be had any fine summer evening from the rear end of an East River ferry-boat, with the towers and roofs of the city, clear in outline and color, without the smudge of Chicago or London or Cincinnati, against a background of orange and pink and purple, blending in warm and changing tints as the sun sinks deeper behind the Palisades. And where is there a view like that of our matchless harbor, sailing up through the Narrows on a bright morning? The vaunted waterways of foreign ports become tame beside this majestic stream, in which the navies of the world might lie at anchor, with elbow-room and to spare. The picture is not without its reverse, of course,—where is there one that has none? —and it may be that in our new eagerness to render it tolerable we have not given ourselves time sufficiently to admire that which is really admirable. If so, we have at least the knowledge to comfort us that the effort has borne fruit. The Better New York is already a creditable and gratifying fact.

Go back the span of a man's life. Charles Dickens had come and gone, and the smart of his strictures lingered yet. How well deserved they were only those who have delved in the musty legislative records of forty and fifty years ago can know. «There are annually cut off from the population by disease and death enough human beings to people a city, and enough human labor to sustain it,» reported a Senate committee sent down to find out what ailed New York. The death-rate had risen, under the fearful crowding and uncleanliness of the tenements, from one in 41.83 in 1815 to one in 27.33 in 1855, a year when no unusual epidemic afflicted the city. The Society for Improving the Condition of the Poor printed in its annual report: «Crazy old buildings crowded with rear tenements in filthy yards, dark, damp basements, leaking garrets, shops, outhouses and stables converted into dwellings, though scarcely fit to shelter brutes, are habitations of thousands of our fellow-beings in this wealthy Christian city.» The city, says its historian, Mrs. Martha Lamb, «was a general asylum for vagrants.» The Health Department was not yet organized. It is thirty years since it began its campaign of education. In very truth it was that, and the beginning had to be made with the a-b-c. One of its ordinances of that first winter of 1867 prohibited owners of swine from letting them forage in the streets. Up to that time they had roamed unmolested. As late as 1879,—only seventeen years ago,—official reports, read in the churches, sought to trace the cause of the juvenile crime that was rampant to the wretched tenement homes of children brought up in «an atmosphere of actual darkness, moral and physical»; and one of the famous physicians of the day, speaking of the heavy infant mortality, exclaimed indignantly that if one could only see the air breathed by these unfortunates in their tenements, «it would show itself to be fouler than the mud of the gutters.» Those were the days when slums like Mulberry Bend and Gotham Court, worse in degree but not in kind than Bone Alley and the Mott street barracks in the picture, flourished practically unchecked, though they figured in the health-reports with reason as «dens of death.» The time had not yet come when they could be dealt with as their record warranted. The rights of property were yet held superior to the life of the community, and the battle of reform had to be fought warily against heavy odds of prejudice and indifference, lest the labor of years be upset in a day by legislatures and courts, which had yet to be brought into line with the new way of thinking. The slum landlord's day was not yet at an end.

But the appeal to the public conscience told at last. With that attack in the churches, which had not been without blame, the new era began. That year a public competition evolved the present type of tenement, far from perfect, but an immense improvement upon the wicked old barracks. The sanitary reformers got the upper hand, and their work told. The death-rate came down slowly. It is to-day, at the end of thirty years, quite twenty-five per cent. lower than it was when the Health Department was organized, and New York has been redeemed from a reproach for which there was no excuse, for no city in the world has such natural opportunities for good sanitation. The immense stride it has taken was measured by the mortality during the unprecedented hot spell of last summer. It was never so great, as, indeed, there never was an emergency like it since records were kept. During the ten days it lasted the heat craved many more victims than the last cholera epidemic during its whole season. Yet, beyond those killed by the direct effects of the sun, the mortality was singularly low; the infant mortality—ever the finger that points unerringly to the sore spots in a community, if any there be—was so noticeably low as to cause a feeling almost of exultation among the sanitary officials. And it was shown, by comparison with earlier hot spells, that the population yielded more slowly to the heat. Where it had taken two or three days to reach the climax of sunstroke, it now took five. The people, better housed, better fed, and breathing clean air in clean streets, had acquired a power of resistance to which the past had no parallel. The sanitarians had proved their case.

With what toil and infinite patience only those who stood near watching the fight can know. Often they were accused of faint-heartedness, charged by men hot for results with indifference, even with treachery. They might have been at times over-cautious, but they gained their end. It took them twenty long years to persuade the ash-bins and barrels that befouled street and landscape to come off the sidewalk out of sight, while Colonel Waring cleared the streets of trucks in a week, riding rough-shod over the supposed rights of a thousand truckmen, and Mayor Grant made an end of the disfiguring telegraph-poles—in the teeth of the experts' declaration that it could not be done—by a curt command. It seems incredible to-day, hardly a year after the great street-sweeper wrought his monumental reform, that there were times when the firemen could not get at burning buildings because of the trucks with which the streets were barricaded at night. Yet I have known personally more than one such instance. It is to be remembered, however, in making such comparisons, that but for the slower methods of the health-officers in the days when every step was a lesson to be learned by a half-hostile community, those later iconoclasts might not have commanded to such purpose. Public opinion had first to be made. Sanitary methods of to-day are not slow. They are quite up to the mark.

The point of submitting New York's case to a jury was reached a dozen years ago. The judgment of the first Tenement-House Commission (1884)—two thirds of the people of the metropolis by this time lived in tenements—was reversed to some extent by the landlord, the courts, and the legislature, though it was far from intemperate; but for all that its work set the community a long step ahead. By the time the laws recommended by the latest commission were enacted the change wrought in public sentiment was complete. The earlier commission had suggested the opening of a street through the worst tenement block in the city as a means of letting the air and the sunlight into it. The legislature amended this by condemning the whole block as unfit to stand. The second Commission (1894) unhesitatingly demanded the seizure of enough property to make at least two small parks in the thickest crowd on the East Side, without reference to the character of the property, as but scant and tardy justice to the poor tenant; and it put on the statute-book the declaration that a house unfit to live in was a threat to the community, and that as such the community had a right to destroy it in self-defense. All the power of the landlord was exerted against it in vain. While I am writing this he is making his last stand in the courts against what he loudly bewails as robbery, forgetting that, if the case of unfitness is fairly made out, it was he who all along was the despoiler, alike of his tenant and of his city's fair fame. The Board of Health has seized, for condemnation, a hundred of the worst rear tenements, which the Commission denounced as veritable infant slaughter-houses, and the end of the slum is in sight.

For upon the road which New York has been treading this half-score years there is at last no turning back. The streets evacuated by the trucks have been occupied by the children, the truckman's with the rest, for the want of better playgrounds, and the truckman has abandoned the fight; and where they crowd thickest, playgrounds of their own are being fitted up for them in school and park. «Hereafter no school-house shall be constructed in the city of New York without an open playground attached to or used in connection with the same,» says one of the briefest but most beneficent laws ever enacted by the people of the State of New York. It is all there is of it, but it stands for a good deal. No child of New York, poor or rich, shall hereafter be despoiled of his birthright —a chance to play; and as for the streets, does any one imagine that New-Yorkers will ever be persuaded to barter away their clean and noiseless pavements and pure air for the whirling dust-clouds, the summer stenches, and the winter sloughs of old, seasoned with no matter what mess of political pottage? If so, he is grievously mistaken. Colonel Waring has shown us that the streets of New York can be cleaned, and any future city government, no matter how corrupt or despotic, will have to reckon with him. And right well the enemy knows it: he may not refrain from picking our pockets in future, but he will at least have to do it with due regard to the decencies of life.

Mulberry Bend is gone, and in its place have come grass and flowers and sunshine. Across the Bowery, where 324,000 human beings were shown to live out of sight and reach of a green spot, four of the most crowded blocks have been seized for demolition, to make room for the two small parks demanded by the Tenement-House Commission. Bone Alley, redolent of filth and squalor and wretchedness, is to go, and the children of that teeming neighborhood are to have a veritable little Coney Island, with sand-hills and shells, established at their very doors. Who can doubt the influence it will have upon young lives heretofore framed in gutters? I question whether the greatest wrong done the children of the poor in the past has not been the esthetic starvation of their lives rather than the physical injury. Against the latter provision has been made by stringent tenement-house laws, by the vigorous warfare upon child-labor, by the extension of the law's protection to stores as to factories, and by the restriction of the sweat-shop evil. In the park to be laid out by the Schiff fountain, in the shadow of the Hebrew Institute,— one of the noblest of charities,—a great public bath is to rise upon the site of the present rookeries, harbinger of others to come. All about, new school-houses are going up, on a plan of structural perfection and architectural excellence at which earlier school-boards would have stood aghast. The first battle for the schools has been fought and won, and though there be campaigning ahead without stint on that score, the day is in sight when every child who asks shall find a seat provided for him in the public school, and when that scandal of the age, the mixing of truants and thieves in a jail, shall have finally ceased, even as it is now forbidden by law.

The Mott street barracks are on their last legs. The rear houses were cleared by order of the Board of Health last June, and even the saloon-keeper who collected the rents admitted to me, when it was well over, that it was a good thing. These tenements were among the first to be seized under the sanitary expropriation law. They were nearly the worst in the city, and hopeless from structural defects. The rift between the front and rear buildings—it hardly deserves the name of gap—is just six feet ten inches wide. Through it came whatever of sunlight and air reached the rear houses, for they backed up against the rear tenements on Elizabeth street, so that one could put his hand through the dark little windows on the stairs, and touch the wall of the neighbor's house, hardly a foot away. The rent rose as one went up, instead of the reverse, for the good reason that there was some air at the top, while down at the bottom there was none, nor light either. In this rookery lived 360 tenants, all Italians except two families, when the police census of 1888 was taken. Forty of them were babies. The infant death-rate of the barracks that year was 325 per thousand; that is to say, nearly one third of the forty babies died. The general infant death-rate for the whole tenement-house population that year was 88.38. By 1891, by persistent nagging, the number of tenants had been reduced to 238,—the barracks were directly under the windows of the Health Board, and gave the officials much concern by their open defiance of health laws,—but there were more babies than ever. That year the infant death-rate in the barracks was 106.38; in the whole tenement population, 86.67. In the interval of four years, fifty-one funerals had gone out from the barracks, thirty-five of them with white hearses. The old houses had been touched up with much paint and whitewash and a gorgeous tin cornice with the year 1890 in raised letters a foot long, and had changed owners; but it was all of no avail. The same summer that saw a conference of experts and philanthropists gathered in New York to discuss better means of housing the propertyless masses, and saw plans evolved that look toward grappling with the whole problem in a humane and liberal spirit, witnessed also the seizure of the barracks as typical of the worst devised by a heedless past. It was as it should be. The tenant was having his innings at last. The undertaker had had his, and made the most of it.

With the stale-beer dives gone, the police-station lodging-rooms, awful parody on municipal charity, closed for good and all,[1] and the tramp on the run; with the almshouse successfully divorced from the jail at last, poverty from crime on the official register; with the new gospel of enforcement of law preached in high places, our youth taught that laws are not made only to be broken when their restraint is felt, their elders drilled in Jefferson's lesson that «the whole art of government consists in the art of being honest» until they grasp its meaning fully; and with the business of city government slipping slowly but surely out of the grasp of politics in this groove, the Better New York is coming—has come—to stay, we may hope, for all time.

Has anything been lost in the change—anything of picturesqueness, of originality? Nothing that was worth the keeping. New World poverty is not often picturesque. It lacks the leisurely setting, the historic background. Starvation by steam is not popular. Tenement-house squalor never had other interest than the human one, demanding instant remedy in action. The tragedy of life is as eloquent in rags as in silk, but the rags are not indispensable. A patch here and there will do no harm. The poor we shall have with us still, even though we improve their homes, and with them their chances. Nothing has been lost, but something has been gained besides this. So much thought and effort has not been bestowed upon improving the part of the community that could not help itself without reacting upon the part that could. The gentler feelings have appealed to the gentler arts, and, it may be, have been wrought upon in their turn. The esthetic has blossomed on the avenue, as philanthropy delved, ever more determined, in the slums. Better architectural ideals obtain. Up-town the hideous monotony of the all-pervading brownstone high-stoop residence of our fathers is being relieved by graystone and granite, with individuality in the design, by peaked roofs, even by tiles. An organization of citizens, among whom is counted the Mayor of New York, is formed in a night to plant shade-trees in our home streets, the while the reformer down-town is busy letting light into dark halls, and finding ways and means of diverting the surplus from the congested districts to homes in the country lanes of the Greater New York. Our public gardens blossom forth season after season with a wealth of color and of fragrance unsurpassed, and into the tall unsightliness of some of the tower-like structures that have shot up in their sky-scraping ambition all over town, there is coming, here and there, hint of character and design. Even the twenty-five-foot lot has found its mission; the nightmare of earlier architects has become the opportunity of their successors.

So moves the world. The task is not finished, the transformation not yet complete. But much has been done—so well done that no New-Yorker of to-day need hang his head for his home city, but may hold it up proudly, and proclaim, with Saul of Tarsus, that he is indeed «a citizen of no mean city.»

*Jacob A. Riis.*

[1] The introduction of the beer-pump into general use contemporaneously with the downfall of Mulberry Bend, closed the dives by depriving them of their stock in trade—the dregs left in the kegs by the old way of tapping them. The Police Board closed the lodging-rooms. There was not much choice between them. What there was, was rather in favor of the dives.

# BREAKING HIS OWN WILL.

WITH PICTURES BY MAUDE COWLES.

«I'LL tell ye how it was about Uncle Eliphelet Wilkerson's comin' back from the dead. In my opinion, he did it purpose to disapp'int them as 'lotted on his bein' laid by fer good, and out o' their way. Seems it wa'n't enough fer him to be dictatin' to folks whilst he was livin', but he must have a hand in 't after he was dead and buried.»

The speaker, a well-preserved woman of seventy, sat knitting and talking with the garrulity of age to a pretty grandniece, who, with the sweet wiles of youth, was drawing from her the story of her life.

«He outlived all his folks, Uncle 'Liphe' did; in my opinion, he wore 'em all out. I 've took notice that cross-tempered folks is sure to live long ag'in as them as is wanted in this world. Then ag'in, Uncle 'Liphe' drawed a pension from the war o' 1812, and drawin' a pension tends towards long livin', so I 've heard folks say. Them two things kep' Uncle 'Liphe' a-livin' along and tormentin' folks long past his time, spite o' the fact that he was always complainin' and swallerin' doctor's stuff enough to kill any two peaceable-disposed men if they was any sech stren'th in it as them doctors would have you believe.

«When he was upwards of seventy-five, and the last o' his folks died and lef' him alone, he come over to see me, and wanted I should come and live weth him. I was livin' alone, the same 's him. 'S I was upwards of forty, they was them as took it upon 'em to call me an ol' maid, and speak o' me as ‹the ol' Markam girl,› and all this 'n' that. They don't no one like havin' sech remarks passed about 'em, least of all them as had chances in their time as well as the next one, and more so 'n some that has got married and made a poor job on 't into the bargain. It worked me considerable, fer I was well-appearin', if I do say it, and smart to work, and they was them that would 'a' jumped at the chance o' gittin' me yit if I 'd be'n willin' to take up weth sech as they was—widowers weth strings o' young ones, ol' men that was lookin' to be nursed, and them o' my own age that did n't have no objections to a comfortable home and a likely woman to do fer 'em while they took life easy. But I made up my mind I 'd ruther be ‹the ol' Markam girl› all my days, much as it went ag'inst my feelin's, than take up weth any o' that stripe. Fact o' the business is, I 'd been disapp'inted when I was a young woman, and the man I was disapp'inted in was one of the pick, tall, well-appearin', pleasant-spoken, and mild-mannered as you could wish to see in a man, though he was one that could speak up fast enough if they was any call fer it. My feelin's was sot on him when I was a young woman and he was comin' to see me constant, and carryin' on me round, and settin' up weth me nights. But they was more 'n one young feller a-follerin' on me up in them days, and it ruther turned my head, there bein' so many on 'em to pick and choose amongst. So I begun a-makin' 's if I did n't care nothin' fer him, purpose to hector him, though all the time I was sot on havin' him, and had n't no more idee o' throwin' on him over 'n the end than you have o' goin' wethout your nex' meal o' victuals. Well, I got rightly punished fer my presumption, fer one evenin' when I 'd been a-carryin' on, as I made a practice o' doin' them times, purpose to try him, he took up his hat and left, and never come inside the house ag'in. Them was tough times fer me along fer a spell, I can tell ye. The more he tried to make it appear that he did n't want me nohow, the more fierce I was to git him back, though I was at a loss to know how to bring it about. But he was put out weth me, and he begun a-makin' up to Melviny Slocum that he liked nex' to me, and in the course of a couple o' months they was married. When it first come to my ears that he was promised to another, seemed like something begun a-pullin' and a-tearin' on my heart-strings. But I was bound I 'd keep up appearances, come what would, fer I could n't bear the idee o' him and Melviny gittin' wind o' my feelin's, so I carried my head high when I was out among folks, spite o' the fact that all the time my heart was a-gnawin' and a-achin' fit to break in two; and when it come night, and they wa'n't no one round, I took on dreadful. Then was when I took up tailorin' to sort o' take my mind off. I put sights o' hard feelin's into them stitches, but I calc'late that was better than carryin' on 'em around weth me.

«Well, it run along, and in the course o'

time I got hardened, as folks does in this world, let it be what it may. But I had n't no stomic' nohow fer any o' the young fellers that kep' on a-makin' up to me, and I used 'em so hard that they soon fell off. It run along very dull till the widowers and ol' men sot in. They had an eye out fer stiddiness, which the young fellers don't trouble their heads about. But they could n't none on 'em hold a candle to him as I 'd been disapp'inted in havin', or so it seemed to me. In the course o' time I was forced to live alone, which I had n't calc'lated on, pa and ma bein' dead, and the boys married and gone. Well, it got so 't seemed like I could 'a' put up weth 'most anythin' in the shape of a human critter that would pass a few words weth me evenin's, when the wind was whistlin' and the clock tickin' fit to drive you ravin' distracted. So it come about that I listened to what Uncle 'Liphe' said to me about comin' to live weth him. He talked fair, Uncle 'Liphe' did; he said he 'd keep a hired girl, and he 'd find my clothin', and he 'd leave me the farm when he died. When folks is a-livin' along peaceful they 're ginerally possessed to think they can better themselves, and so it was weth me. I knowed 'Liphelet Wilkerson, if he was my uncle, was as disagreeable a' old critter as could be found far and near. I 've heard tell his wife, when she was livin', used to make a practice o' goin' round cryin' weth her ol' sunbunnet drawed down over her face a good share of the time, on account o' the remarks he passed upon her; but she was a poor-sperited woman, and I had n't no idee o' breakin' my heart over what no man said to me, least of all Uncle 'Liphe'. So I packed up my things and went over there, thinkin' 't would be fine havin' nothin' to do, and how I 'd be sot up fer life when the ol' man died and lef' me the place, which was big and sightly, and well pervided weth all the furniture and beddin' heart could wish fer.

« If I was to undertake to tell ye all I went through weth that man, I could n't bring to mind the half on 't. Fer dictatin' they wa'n't his equal, and fer hectorin' on ye, day in and day out, I never see the beat. Fault-findin' wa'n't no name fer it; if he was put out, he 'd yell at ye like some wild critter, and I never see sech another hen-hussy in all my born days. They wa'n't a kittle put onto the stove but what he must stick his nose in 't. But what worked me worst of all was the way he 'd turn around when they was company come to the house, and be so smooth-spoken as to hold out the idee he wa'n't never no other way.

« Many 's the day I 've wished m'self back in my little house a-hummin' to m'self over my tailorin', weth no one to come in and find fault weth me. But I kep' a-puttin' up weth it from day to day and from year to year, best way I could, plannin' how I 'd come into the property some o' these days, and that would pay me some fer what I 'd be'n through. I did n't git no pay no other way, fer he was close-fisted, Uncle 'Liphe' was, along with all the rest, and never a cent did I git fer my clothin', so that I had to dip into my savin's to look decent. His bein' plain-spoken saved him more 'n one penny, fer some did n't like to ask him fer what was their due. Then ag'in, there was the girl. She was a trial to me from the start, fer she wa'n't neat about the work, and he made much of her, purpose to torment me, or so I suppose. One o' his notions was that folks was born equal, which is true enough, only it ain't no reason why they should be fools, and he would n't set down to table till that girl got done bakin' pancakes. If they 's any one thing I do hate above another, it 's soggy pancakes, and I wa'n't never one to stan' at bakin' on 'em m'self fer others to eat. But he took it in his head I was puttin' upon the girl, because I wanted she should bake the cakes while we was to breakfast. Sech works sot her up till they wa'n't no livin' weth her, so I let her go, and told him I 'd do the work m'self if he 'd pay me fer it, same as he did her. Well, he did n't stan' up no more while the pancakes was bakin', and it run along a spell, and then he give me to understan' that I 'd git my pay if I got the place when he died. I did n't care to have no words weth him, and I did n't really want nothin' should fall to me without deservin' on 't, so I did n't say no more, but went on a-dippin' into my savin's that I 'd laid up ag'inst my old age. But the tryin'est thing of all was a way he had o' throwin' on 't up to me constant that I was a disapp'inted woman. No woman likes to have the name o' bein' disapp'inted. It makes you feel fer all the world like a piece o' caliker that keeps a-gittin' cheaper, because it 's so humbly they don't no one want it. It come hard, but that was Uncle 'Liphe' all over. If they was a sore spot in you anywhere, he was sure to spy it out and keep a-pokin' at it everlastin'.

« Fer years I had n't see' but little of him — him I mean that it always has and always will seem to me was out o' the common run. We passed the time o' day now and ag'in, but nothin' more, and I had an idee all the time that he thought light on me fer triflin' weth him when we was young together. Melviny she had died long before that; she had n't no constitootion, poor thing, and he never married ag'in. I did n't never hear how he took it, losin' on her, nor how it was weth him, only sech things 's he 'd took a lumber job, and he 'd paid off the mortgage on his farm, and he 'd gone North as a delegate to the convention, and sech as that, which wa'n't no noos sech as my heart wished to hear. But I heard his name spoke more 'n I wanted, fer Uncle 'Liphe' owed him a spite fer plain speakin'; Uncle 'Liphe' always calc'lated to do all the plain-speakin' himself, and he never let pass a chance to say an ill word on him, if 't was a possible thing.

« You must know Uncle 'Liphe' made a practice o' goin' about a good deal, which was a mercy fer me, fer it give me some rest, spite o' the fact that I was always a-dreadin' his comin' back. He would n't hear nothin' to havin' no one to drive fer him, fer he did n't want it to appear he was too old fer sech things; if they was one thing he hated above another, it was to be took fer an old man. His horse was old, 'most as old according as he was, and she was the hatefullest old mare I ever laid eyes on. Seemed like she 'd lived weth him so long she 'd ketched it of him. She wa'n't afraid of the cars, nor steam-mills, nor thrashin'-machines, nor nothin' that sensible critters nat'rally dislikes; but once in a while, when you 'd made out to forgit her capers, she ups and scares at some little fool stone or stump, and whirls around in the road, all you could do and say. Well, it come about one time that she dumped Uncle 'Liphe' out, and then she stood lookin' at him, 's much as to say, ‹ Well, I 've shook your cussin' old breath out 'n ye this time,› which she had done, and no mistake. They picked him up and fetched him home, and he got over it after a spell o' groanin' and complainin'; fer, 's luck would have it, they wa'n't none o' his bones broke. Folks told Uncle 'Liphe' he had n't never ought to ride behind that air horse ag'in, but he did n't pay no heed to what any one had to offer about the old mare, though he was far from wishin' to die—he loved to torment folks too well fer that; and the upshot was, he wanted I should drive him. I told him to git the hired man to do it, but he would n't hear to that; he wanted he should be a-workin', and he made it appear to me, 's he often did, that it was to my interest to be savin', fer it would all come to me when he died. He stuck and hung till I give in and went weth him, and I 'm free to say I never enjoyed ridin' less, that I can call to mind. The old mare she conducted herself very good fer a spell, till she thought I 'd forgot her capers. Then one day she give a jump and begun to whirl round. Well, I was lookin' out fer her, and I hauled on t' other line 's hard 's I could, layin' the whip onto her all the time. But it did n't do no good; she was a-turnin' the wagon over in spite of me, when I see a man comin' from t' other way, and I hollered to him to come 'n' help. 'T wa'n't more 'n a second before he had hold o' that possessed old animal's head, and we was saved from bein' spilled out. Well, what must Uncle 'Liphe' do, but inst'id of returnin' thanks, he begun a-jawin' at me.

«‹ You ol' fool!› sez he, or words to that effect; ‹ you don't know no more about drivin' than you do about anythin' else,› sez he; ‹ fer stoopidness I never see your beat,› sez he; and more o' the same sort, fer he would n't never have it his horse was to blame.

« I could 'a' gone through the floor, or the ground, fer there wa'n't no floor there; fer I see by now that the man that had stopped the horse was Hiram Hardin', him that I 've be'n a-tellin' on ye I was disapp'inted in havin' years ago. But Hiram spoke up very sudden, he did, and he sez, sez he:

«‹ Who be you usin' them words to, Mr. Wilkerson?› sez he.

«‹ I 'm a-talkin' to Mari',› sez Uncle 'Liphe', very spiteful; ‹ they ain't no sense in a woman o' her years bein' so all-fired useless,› sez he, knowin' them words would mortify me 's much 's any, and meanin' they should.

«‹ You hain't no call to hold sech language about Mari',› Hiram makes answer; ‹ and you know well enough you hain't. If she wa'n't better disposed than the most o' folks, she would n't 'a' put up weth you 's long 's she has.›

« Well, Uncle 'Liphe' shut up his head that time, fer he did n't never calc'late to show out before folks. As fer me, them words o' Hiram's drawed the tears to my eyes. I never had no patience weth poor-sperited women that could n't bear up under nothin' wethout sheddin' tears, and I wa'n't never one to go around cryin' under no old sunbunnet after I 'd be'n misused, but I wa'n't hardened to kindness. When he come up and inquired very anxious whether I was hurt, I made out to put a bold face on 't, and smiled whilst I said ‹ No,› though the water was a-standin' in my eyes all the time.

« Strange to say, after that I was jest as bad as any young fool. My thoughts was sot on Hiram, night and day, same as they used to be when I was a young woman, in place o' bein' on the cookin' and the bakin' and the apple-dryin' and the soap-b'ilin', which would 'a' be'n more becomin' in one o' my years. I've took notice that folks that is gittin' on in life sets a sight by them as was dear to 'em when they was young, same as they like victuals the way their mother cooked 'em. I think, like enough, they was other men to be found jest as good and better 'n Hiram Hardin'; but Hi' was, and always has be'n, the only man fer me far and near.

«It stood to nater 't that tormentin' ol' man should git it into his head they was somethin' up weth me, and he brought me up sharp fer forgittin', which I did, I 'm bound to say, beyond everything. Betwix' him and my feelin's, which wa'n't at rest, I was all wore out, and come near leavin' on him more than once, and would certain if it had n't 'a' be'n fer my havin' dipped into my savin's, and worked so long fer him wethout nothin' to show fer it, that I thought I best stick it out and git my pay out o' what Uncle 'Liphe' lef' me in his will, which he was free in his promises of when I talked o' leavin'. Though he used me so hard, Uncle 'Liphe' could n't bear the thoughts o' my goin', fer he had n't no other near relations, wethout it was Obidiar Woodbury. Obidiar was his cousin, and Obidiar's wife was always a-schemin' and a-contrivin' to git the ol' man's property wethout bein' forced to do fer the disagreeable old critter herself, which was a job no one courted. Obidiar's wife was a cur'us woman as I ever see. She would patch and darn underclothin' till it was a shame to behold, but when she took a notion to have a silk dress or gold-bowed spec's, she 'd dip in and have the best they was goin'. She made a practice o' puttin' on the worst she had when she come over to see Uncle 'Liphe', purpose to hold out the idee that they was needy; and she 'd go on, she would, about how contrivin' and savin' she was forced to be, and all this and that, to work upon the ol' man's feelin's, if he ever had any, which I have my doubts on. Them was tryin' days fer me, when Obidiar's wife come over, fer I can't abide sech schemin' folks nohow. She 'd set and talk to the ol' man dreadful feelin' about his complaints, which he had more on than I can bring to mind; and she 'd flatter him up, she would, till it would turn your stomic' listenin' to her. Sometimes she 'd bring him presents, but I took notice they was always somethin' that did n't cost her nothin', like a flowered cup and saucer which was give' away weth a pound o' tea at the store to town. Uncle 'Liphe' was smooth-spoken when she was there, as he made a practice o' bein' when they was visitors in the house; but when she was well out o' sight he run on about her dreadful.

«Like enough, I 'd got over dwellin' on the thoughts o' Hiram Hardin' if it had n't 'a' be'n, long about this time, he took to droppin' in now and ag'in to pass the time o' day weth Uncle 'Liphe'. That ol' man could n't bear the thoughts on him, and yit he 'd set and talk to him about the crops and politics and his ailments, which wa'n't off'n his mind long at a time. Fact o' the business was, Uncle 'Liphe', fer all he was so mean-actin', sensed enough to want folks should think well on him; and like enough it was because it come so hard fer him to be agreeable to them as did n't live weth him that made him so waspish to home. 'S I said, Hiram kep' a-comin' now and ag'in, and the sight on him, weth his smilin' eyes, and the kind words he let drop, sot me a-thinkin' and a-feelin' more 'n was becomin', mebbe. They did n't nothin' escape Uncle 'Liphe's notice, and he hectored me about Hiram till I did n't know which way to turn. At the same time I did n't have no idee Hiram had any intentions in comin'. I was dreadful careful not to let on what was a-goin' on in my mind; but knowin' Uncle 'Liphe', I kep' a-frettin' lest he should say somethin' that would bring me out, fer I do think the meanest thing entirely is fer a woman to be throwed at a man when she ain't be'n asked fer.

«Well, sure enough, it turned out jest as I 'spected. Whether it was that the ol' man got tired of havin' Hiram comin' there, or whether it was that he was afraid of his gittin' me away, I never could rightly make out; but one evenin' when Hiram was there he sot out to show out. He found fault about the weather; he found fault about politics, which was always in the wrong, accordin' to his tell; and he found fault weth me, whichever way I turned. I could n't set nor stand but what he wa'n't suited. Hiram he tried to turn him off, but they wa'n't no turnin' Uncle 'Liphe'; come what would, he 'd have his say out. He run out ag'inst one thing and another, and purty soon he begun a-complainin' how sick he was, and how he was handled when he had his spells, and how he did n't have no one to care fer him as he had ought to be cared fer, and all this 'n' that.

«‹Folks tells me,› sez he, ‹I had ought to be thankful to have Mari' to do fer me. I don't know how it 's come, but the idee 's got around that Mari' 's smart to work, when the

DRAWN BY MAUDE COWLES.

«‹I CAN'T ABIDE SUCH SCHEMIN' FOLKS NOHOW.›»

fact o' the business is, she ain't no housekeeper, and never was.›

« ‹They 's some as would be dreadful glad to git her to keep house for 'em if you 're tired on her yourself,› sez Hiram, a-lookin' at me in his smilin' way. Weth that the tears come to my eyes, which was a way I had when folks made much on me. You could n't make me give no sign, jawin' at me; but give me a kind word and I could n't control my feelin's nohow. Uncle 'Liphe' wa'n't long in bringin' me to my senses, though; fer he spoke up, he did, and he sez, sez he:

«‹If it 's you that 's a-wantin' on her, she 'll go fast enough; fer it 's well known she 's be'n a-pinin' fer you this twenty year, ever sence the time you give her the go-by when she was a girl.›

« Well, I flared up when I heard that. I said they wa'n't a word o' truth in what he said—which I could say honest, fer pinin' wa'n't my style, whatever my feelin's might be. Hiram he looked at me ruther sudden, he did, and I thought he took note how red I was in the face, and he sez to me, sez he:

«‹Mr. Wilkerson's a-jokin' on ye, Mari',› sez he; ‹that 's his way.›

«‹His hard words I can stan',› sez I; ‹but his jokes I can't put up weth nohow.›

« Weth that Uncle 'Liphe' speaks up and sez, sez he: ‹You 'll put up weth anything, and I know it, to git the place when I'm dead.

You 're jes so mean-sperited. The property is all you 're after, and you know 's much.›

«‹By George!› sez Hiram, jumpin' to his feet, and comin' to stan' by me t' other side of the fire, ‹I would n't put up weth no sech talk as that, Mari',› sez he, ‹not fer no one. They 's them as can treat you better 'n that, by a long shot, if you 'll but listen to 'em,› sez he, catchin' at my hand and holdin' on it, spite of all I could do 'n' say.

«‹If it 's my property you 're after, you 've gone the wrong way about to git it,› yells Uncle 'Liphe', 'most black in the face by now; ‹fer I sha'n't leave one cent on 't to Mari' if she 's fool enough to take up weth any sech a feller as you be.›

«‹I don't want none o' your cussed property,› sez Hiram, 's black in the face as Uncle 'Liphe', and madder, if sech a thing could be; ‹I 'd sooner have Mari' weth nothin' to her name than any other woman weth a kingdom at her back!›

«‹Them 's fine words,› yells Uncle 'Liphe', ‹but you can't face me down that way. I know what I see weth my own eyes. Looks likely, when a feller leaves a girl alone 's long as she 's poor and doin' tailorin' fer a livin', and begins to make up to her when he sees a chance to git the best farm in the county—looks likely he ain't a-lookin' out fer somethin'! When I see sech doin's I have my own idees.›

«‹Have 'em,› roars Hiram, ‹fer Satan himself could n't hender, oncet you took a notion›; and then he turns to me and speaks very gentle, and sez, sez he, ‹Could you make out to care fer me, Mari', 'nough to take up weth me, now I ain't no longer young?› sez he. ‹I 'd give more 'n I can tell to make up fer what 's past,› sez he.

«Now I had it in my mind, all this time, that Hiram was a-takin' on me fer pity, and I could n't stan' that nohow, so I sez, sez I: ‹I 'm as much to blame fer what 's past as you be, and mebbe more, and I hain't no hard feelin's, but I guess I can put up weth Uncle 'Liphe' his time out.›

«Hiram's face fell, and Uncle 'Liphe' he spoke up, he did, and he sez, sez he: ‹I knowed Mari' wa'n't fool enough to run no resk o' losin' the property, so you can whistle somewheres else fer a woman,› sez he, ruther triumphant.

«‹Thunder and lightnin'!› yells Hiram, ‹you beat all I ever see; and it 's a blasted shame fer any woman to have to put up weth sech words, let her be who she may, let alone Mari' Markam, that 's the best woman God ever made!›

«Weth that the tears come to my eyes ag'in, which I 'd ruther they had n't, fer I never did think cryin' sot well on a woman; and Hiram he turns to me, and he sez, sez he, ‹Mari',› sez he, ‹had you any feelin's fer me in the old days when you and me was keepin' company? Sometimes it come acrost me you had, and then ag'in I thought defferent.›

«‹Why do you ask?› sez I, not willin' to give m'self away till I knowed where I stood.

«‹I ask,› sez he, ‹fer the reason that them as has oncet had sech feelin's towards each other can have them ag'in if it so happens they ain't nothin' to come betwix' 'em.›

«‹I 'd like to know, before I make any answer,› sez I, ‹whether you 're a-puttin' that question to me because you feel fer me, sitooated as I be here, or whether it 's because I 'm more to you than another?›

«‹You 're more to me 'n I can tell,› sez he; ‹and you always have be'n, though God knows I cared fer Melviny as a man should fer his woman. I 'd 'a' made up to you long ago, Mari',› sez he, ‹if you 'd give' me any 'casion to think that you had them feelin's towards me sech as my heart could wish. Give me my answer, Mari',› he sez, wethout stoppin' to give me time to draw a breath, fer all the world 's if he was a young feller once more.

«‹Well,› sez I, laughin', ‹I was a fool when I was a young woman, and so I be now, and they ain't no gittin' round it.›

«Them words told him all he wanted to know, and he put his arm around me and laughed out hearty. All this time, you must know, old Uncle 'Liphe' was a-runnin' on fit to deefen you, and it 's nat'ral to suppose he said every mean thing he could muster up; but Hiram and me we never heard a word on 't, and we wa'n't none the worse off, I 'll be bound. Hiram acted redic'lous, I must say, fer he hugged me and kissed me right in the face an' eyes o' that ol' sourgrass; do what I could, they wa'n't no stoppin' him, and to cap all, he takes my hand and steps up to Uncle 'Liphe' and begun a-thankin' on him fer bringin' on us together ag'in after so many years; and come to look at it one way, we was beholden to him, fer every time we got ketched in our talk he give us a start. The old man did n't think much on his works, fer he was fairly foamin', he was so put out.

«‹Mari' need n't never look to git nothin' out o' me,› sez he, a-sputterin', ‹after the way she 's performed.›

«‹That don't make no odds,› sez Hiram, very good-natered, fer sech was his feelin's, owin' to how things had come around after so many years; ‹I 've got enough fer both on us,› sez he, ‹and you can change your will to-night if you 're a mind to.›

«‹They ain't no call fer that,› bu'st out Uncle 'Liphe'; ‹fer the property 's all made over to Obidiar, anyhow!›

«And so it turned out. That contrairy old critter had be'n deceivin' on me all along to git me to do fer him fer nothin'. Well, it did n't make much odds to me then. I was took up weth other things. When folks gits what 's be'n a-wantin' in their lives fer a matter o' twenty years, they don't stop to think much about property, however much they may wish fer 't afterwards. Hiram wanted I should set the weddin'-day right off—I never see a man so impatient; but I wa'n't willin' to leave Uncle 'Liphe' wethout a soul to care fer him, bad as he 'd used me—the more so that it would seem like when I did n't have no hopes o' gittin' the property I had n't no feelin's fer the poor ol' soul that I 'd done fer eight year and more; so I stayed on and waited fer him to git some one to take my place, fer he would n't hear to Obidiar's wife, and he threatened strong o' marryin' some woman that would take up weth him for the sake o' gittin' a widder's pension when he was gone, which would 'a' be'n puttin' upon the gov'ment shameful. I was at a stan' what to do betwix' Hiram and him, when Uncle 'Liphe' was took down weth the pneumony. We pulled him through, though he was upwards of eighty-four; but he did n't really gain, and he sot in his chair day in and day out, a-snarlin' at man and beast. I never see the beat; 's long as he had stren'th lef' in him to breathe, he had stren'th to jaw. But he did n't do no complainin' now that he was sick enough to git all the notice he craved, and he really seemed to take comfort in folks remarkin' how bad he looked, and how poor he was in his hands, and all this 'n' that.

«Uncle 'Liphe' had some cur'us notions. One was that the most o' folks was buried alive, and it beats all how many stories he found in the papers about folks comin' to life after they was dead. It 's my belief they make up them stories when they hain't nothin' else to print. But Uncle 'Liphe' he would n't hear to nothin' else but that they was sights o' folks buried alive. Finally he got up the idee that we—me and the neighbors that sot up weth him nights—was hangin' round waitin' fer the chance to hustle him off before he 'd breathed his last. He give it out, 'most the last talkin' he did, that he wanted we should bury him up in the further medder and leave the grave open weth a little house built over it. The house was to be locked so the doctors could n't git his body, which was another of his notions; and the strangest thing of all was, they was to be two keys, and one on 'em was to be laid beside him in the coffin. He was so afraid o' bein' laid away too soon, poor ol' soul, that he would n't lay in a bed, but died a-settin' in his chair. Well, we laid him out nice in his broadcloth clothes. Then Obidiar's wife come over, and nothin' would do but she must take the lead in everything. She made her calc'lations that the property was comin' to her, or to him, which come to the same thing, and she would n't let me have no say about nothin'. I suppose, like enough, she wanted to git at the readin' o' the will, and git possession of the things in the house, which she seemed to think I 'd swaller; but anyway, she sot out to have the funeral the nex' day, spite o' the fact that I was strong ag'inst it on account o' Uncle 'Liphe's notion, though he had n't said nothin' about bein' kep'. The doctor upheld her, and she had her way, as she commonly did, and the poor ol' man was hurried off in a way that wa'n't decent, accordin' to my idees. We laid him in his grave and built a little shed over him, and I will say it was the most unchristian way o' buryin' a man I ever see. The buildin' looked fer all the world like them little houses they build over rams fer pumpin' water, and it stood out there, bare and lonesome, fer the ol' man was pertic'ler they should n't be no trees feedin' on him, and he said he heard tell their roots grew a long way a-feelin' fer a grave. The idee come to me, when I stood there lookin' at Uncle 'Liphe's grave and feelin' kind o' sober 'bout his dyin' 's he had, that mebbe the ol' man made his calc'lations to rise once in a while to git a peek at Obidiar, and see if he farmed it to suit him. It would come hard, if he see the fences runnin' down and the alders gainin' ground, not to be able to jaw.

«They was the greatest goin's on in that air house after the funeral you ever see. All the ol' man's distant relations—he had n't none so near as me—come a-flockin' round to see what they could make out o' the poor ol' critter and his belongin's. They was a-pokin' and a-spyin' and a-layin' hands on everything they sot eyes on. Obidiar's wife was took up weth me; fer as soon as that air will was read, and she see that the property fell to her man, she sot herself to watch every motion I made. Seems she took it in her head that I was like her, and did n't have no other object but to git all I could. She follered me up every step I took, till I was

DRAWN BY MAUDE COWLES.

«THE OL' MAN'S DISTANT RELATIONS.»

ravin' distracted. Greedy wa'n't no name fer the way she acted. I was a-packin' my trunk to leave where I wa'n't no longer wanted, and nothin' would do but she must stan' by me and watch everything I put in 't, fer fear I 'd go off weth the beddin' and the silver. I never see the beat. Though I was goin' to git married to Hiram, and my heart was content, yit I must say I had my hard feelin's about the years and the stren'th and the money I 'd spent there, and nothin' to show fer it; but I had n't no more thought o' techin' what did n't belong to me than nothin' in the world. They was them that wa'n't so partic'ler, fer whilst Obidiar's wife was took up weth watchin' me, them other relations persuaded themselves they had as good a right to things as her, and they helped themselves to towels and piller-cases and spoons, and anything else that come handy. It was sickenin', I can tell ye; seemed fer all the world like crows hangin' around to devour a dead critter.

«Well, in the very height of it all Uncle 'Liphe' come back from the dead! Seems like he had to be on hand to have one more jab at his feller-critters. It come about this way. I stepped into the kitchen to git somethin', and there he stood a-peerin' into one o' the kittles to see what they was goin' to be fer dinner—hen-hussyin' as usual, jest as nat'ral as you please. I was so took back I give a squeal and come nigh fallin' over, but he turned round, he did, and called me a fool, or words to that effect, and that brought me round, fer I begun to feel 's if he had n't never died. If he 'd said somethin' pious, now, I should 'a' be'n frightened out o' my wits, fer I 'd 'a' be'n sure he was a ghost; but I knowed they would n't no sperit use no sech language as Uncle 'Liphe' made a practice o' doin'.

«Jest at this p'int they come to words in the settin'-room, fer it so happened that Obidiar's wife ketched them folks at their doin's, and she let out on 'em. It 's well known that when a passel o' women-folks gits their tempers up, they 'll make the winders shake, and so they did now. When it come over Uncle 'Liphe' what was a-goin' on, he looked 's well pleased as I ever see him, and he stood there a spell a-listenin'. They had it hot and heavy in t' other room, and they let out on each other to beat all; Obidiar's wife accusin' them relations o' stealin', and they accusin' her o' hustlin' off the ol' man wethout hardly givin' him time to git cold, so her man d come into the property sooner. Uncle 'Liphe' took it all in, which wa'n't hard, fer you could 'a' heard them women to the barn, and then he put along into the settin'-room. Well, you better believe them relations o' hisn was took back when they laid eyes on him. They lef' off a-rummagin' and a-squabblin' mighty sudden, I can tell you; and when they got over their scare they begun a-talkin' fair, and a-fawnin' on the ol' man fit to turn your stomic'. But he made short work on 'em. He sot there in his chair, after he 'd took somethin' warm to drink, and he told 'em he 'd come back to see how they performed. Then he ups and makes 'em empty out their bags and their passels, right before his eyes, and then he clears 'em out in short order. Next he falls upon Obidiar's wife fer hustlin' him off 's she did, and he brings her up purty sharp, I can tell ye. She stuck and hung to git him to let her stay, and she told all the lies that she could muster up on sech short notice, but they wa'n't never no use in lyin' to Uncle 'Liphe'. You might jest as well save yourself the trouble, fer he see through things to beat anythin'. They wa'n't no way out on 't; she had to go, and Obidiar weth her, but he did n't never count, fer he was led by her in all he did and said.

«By this the doctor come, fer we 'd sent fer him; and he looked tur'ble foolish when he see Uncle 'Liphe' a-settin' there as waspish as ever, spite o' his havin' given it out so certain 't he was dead. The ol' man give him a taste o' his tongue, and sent him about his business. I looked fer my turn to come next, but beyond callin' on me a blasted fool, and other sech expressions as had come as nat'ral to me by now as my own name, he did n't let out on me at all. Inst'id o' that, he sent fer a lawyer and a jestice, and he tore up his ol' will and burned it, and he made a deed o' the hull place to me; he would n't hear to no more wills, fer he said them relations o' hisn would dispute 'em, and try to make it out he wa'n't alive and in his right mind, spite o' the fact that they was all-fired certain he was, jedgin' by the way they made tracks fer home.

«‹There,› he says, when all was done, ‹I hain't a doubt but what you 'll marry that air smooth-spoken, long-favored, mean-actin' Hiram Hardin', spite of all I 've done fer you. You always was a fool, Mari', and I can prove it. If you wa'n't a fool, how did it come you stood by and see them women a-makin' off weth the things you be'n a-handlin' this nine year, and never raised a finger to help yourself to nothin'? That was the simplest piece o' work I ever heard tell on.›

«Then the ol' man went to bed, and died peaceful, after lingerin' on a spell. He did n't ask fer no ram-shed to be put up over him this time, and we made sure he was dead before we laid him away. But it was long before I could git over lookin' to see him peerin' into the kittles every time I come into the kitchen.

«Hiram and me got married in the end, and I think like enough we be'n as big a couple o' old fools as ever struck this part o' the country; but we lost so much time when we was young that we was obliged to make the most of our chances if we looked to git our share of happiness in this world.»

*Elizabeth Eggleston Seelye.*

DRAWN BY MAUDE COWLES.

«THERE HE STOOD A-PEERIN' INTO ONE O' THE KITTLES.»

# THE BLIND GIRL.

## A CHRISTMAS CAROL.

FROM THE PROVENÇAL OF ROUMANILLE,
AFTER LITERAL TRANSLATION BY MRS. CATHARINE A. JANVIER.

IT was the day whereon a Virgin Mother mild
In Bethlehem bore
Unto this sinful world a little helpless Child.
He shivered sore,
For only on some straw spread upon the cold earth
The Blest One lay,
Whileas the angels who had hailed his holy birth
Sped swift away

To tell the joyful news to shepherds, who thereon
Came to the place—
Women and men—in eager haste to gaze upon
That wondrous face.
But one of them, the mother of a poor blind child,
Was last to go,
For that her little suffering daughter, weeping wild,
Implored her so.

« Why wilt thou, mother dear, that I stay here alone
Among the sheep?
Whilst thou art cherishing that holy Little One
Thy child will weep.»
« Soul of my soul,» the mother said, « thy piteous tears
Melt all my heart;
But if thou wilt with patience, quieting thy fears,
Let me depart,

« To-morrow, when the pleasant twilight cometh, we
Shall meet again,
And I will tell thee all that I shall hear and see—
Glad thou 'lt be then!
Willingly would I take thee, dearest, if but so
Thou 'dst see his face,
Although the way is long and cold and hard to go
To that blest place.»

« I know that to the grave alone through darkness drear
My way must be.
Oh lovely golden face! Oh Godlike Babe most dear
I may not see!
But are eyes needed to believe and to adore,
My mother? Oh,
I still could touch his little hand, if nothing more,
Might I but go!»

Down at the mother's knees she prayed and wept, until
The mother's heart
Was cloven, and she answered, « Have thou then thy will;
My life thou art!»
And when they to the manger came, and the child knelt,
With love and awe,
As on her thrilling heart his little hand she felt,
Her Lord she saw!

*Margaret Vandegrift.*

SEE "OPEN LETTERS."  ENGRAVED BY HENRY WOLF.

«CHARITY,» BY WALTER GAY.

# In Bethlehem of Judea

I.

I HEARD the bells of Bethlehem ring—
Their voice was sweeter than the priests';
I heard the birds of Bethlehem sing
Unbidden in the churchly feasts.

II.

They clung and sung on the swinging chain
High in the dim and incensed air;
The priests, with repetitions vain,
Chanted a never-ending prayer.

III.

So bell and bird and priest I heard,
But voice of bird was most to me—
It had no ritual, no word,
And yet it sounded true and free.

IV.

I thought child Jesus, were he there,
Would like the singing birds the best,
And clutch his little hands in air
And smile upon his mother's breast.

*R. W. Gilder.*

Bethlehem, Holy Week, 1896.

# THE CHRISTMAS KALENDS OF PROVENCE.

BY THOMAS A. JANVIER,

SÒCI DÒU FELIBRIGE,

Author of «An Embassy to Provence,» etc.

WITH PICTURES BY LOUIS LOEB.

FANCY you 've journeyed down the Rhône,
  Fancy you 've passed Vienne, Valence,
Fancy you 've skirted Avignon—
  And so are come *en pleine* Provence.

Fancy a mistral cutting keen
  Across the sunlit wintry fields,
Fancy brown vines, and olives green,
  And blustered, swaying cypress shields.

Fancy a widely opened door,
  Fancy an eager outstretched hand,
Fancy—nor need you ask for more—
  A heart-sped welcome to our land.

Fancy the peal of Christmas chimes,
  Fancy that some long-buried year
Is born again of ancient times—
  And in Provence take Christmas cheer.

I.

IN my own case, this journey and this welcome were not fancies but realities. I had come to keep Christmas with my friend M. de Vièlmur according to the traditional Provençal rites and ceremonies in his own entirely Provençal home: an ancient dwelling which stands high up on the westward slope of the Alpilles, overlooking Arles and Tarascon and within sight of Avignon, near the Rhône margin of Provence.

The Vidame—such is M. de Vièlmur's ancient title, derived originally not from a minor overlord but directly from the sovereign counts of Provence—is an old-school country gentleman who is amiably at odds with modern times. While tolerant of those who have yielded to the new order, he himself is a great stickler for the preservation of antique forms and ceremonies; sometimes, indeed, pushing his fancies to lengths that fairly would lay him open to the charge of whimsicality, were not even the most extravagant of his crotchets touched and mellowed by his natural goodness of heart.

The château of Vièlmur has remained so intimately a part of the middle ages that the subtle essence of that romantic period still pervades it, and gives to all that goes on there a quaintly archaic tone. The donjon, a prodigiously strong square tower dating from the twelfth century, partly is surrounded by a dwelling in the florid style of two hundred years back, the architectural flippancies of which have been so tousled by time and weather as to give it the look of an old beau caught unawares by age and grizzled in the midst of his affected youth.

In the rear of these oddly coupled structures is a farm-house with a dependent rambling collection of farm-buildings, the whole inclosing a large open court to which access is had by a vaulted passageway that on occasion may be closed by a double set of ancient iron-clamped doors. As the few exterior windows of the farm-house are grated heavily, and as from each of the rear corners of the square there projects a crusty tourelle from which a raking fire could be kept up along the walls, the place has quite the air of a testy little fortress—and a fortress it was meant to be when it was built three hundred years ago (the date, 1561, is carved on the keystone of the arched entrance) in the time of the religious wars.

But now the iron-clamped doors stand open on rusty hinges, and the courtyard has that look of placid cheerfulness which goes with the varied peaceful activities of farm labor and farm life. Chickens and ducks wander about it chattering complacently, an aged goat of a melancholy humor stands usually in one corner lost in misanthropic thought, and a great flock of extraordinarily tame pigeons flutters back and forth between the stone dovecote rising in a square tower above the farm-house and the farm well.

This well—inclosed in a stone building surmounted by a very ancient crucifix—is in the center of the courtyard, and it also is the center of a little domestic world. To its curb come the farm animals three times daily; while as frequently, though less regularly, most of the members of the two households come there too; and there do the humans—notably, I have observed, if they be of different sexes—find it convenient to rest for a while together and take a dish of friendly talk. From the low-toned chattering and the soft laughter that I have heard now and then of an evening I have inferred that these nominally chance encounters are not confined wholly to the day.

The château stands, as I have said, well up on the mountain-side; and on the very spot (I must observe that I am here quoting its owner) where was the camp in which Marius lay with his legions until the time was ripe for him to strike the blow that secured southern Gaul to Rome.

## II.

In the dominion of Vièlmur there is an inner empire. Nominally, the Vidame is the reigning sovereign; but the power behind his throne is Misè Fougueiroun. The term «Misè» is an old-fashioned Provençal title of respect for women of the little bourgeoisie—tradesmen's and shopkeepers' wives and the like—that has become obsolescent since the Revolution and very generally has given place to the fine-ladyish «Madamo.» With a little stretching, it may be rendered by our English old-fashioned title of «Mistress»; and Misè Fougueiroun, who is the Vidame's housekeeper, is mistress over his household in a truly masterful way.

This personage is a little round woman, still plumply pleasing, although she is rising sixty, who is arrayed always with an exquisite neatness in the dress—the sober black and white of the elder women, not the gay colors worn by the young girls—of the Pays d'Arles; and although shortness and plumpness are at odds with majesty of deportment she has, at least, the peremptory manner of one long accustomed to command.

By my obviously sincere admiration of the château and its surroundings, and by a discreet word or two implying a more personal admiration,—a tribute which no woman of the Pays d'Arles ever is too old to accept graciously as her due,—I was so fortunate as to win Misè Fougueiroun's favor at the outset; a fact of which I was apprised on the evening of my arrival—it was at dinner, and the housekeeper herself had brought in a bottle of precious Château-neuf-du-Pape—by the cordiality with which she joined forces with the Vidame in reprobating my belated coming to the château. Actually, I was near

DRAWN BY LOUIS LOEB

AT THE WELL.

a fortnight behind the time named in my invitation, which had stated expressly that Christmas began in Provence on the feast of Saint Barbara, and that I was expected not later than that day—December 4.

«Monsieur should have been here,» said the housekeeper with decision, «when we planted the blessed Saint Barbara's grain. And now it is grown a full span. Monsieur will not see Christmas at all!»

But my apologetic explanation that I never even had heard of Saint Barbara's grain only made my case the more deplorable.

«Mai!» exclaimed Misè Fougueiroun, in the tone of one who faces suddenly a real calamity. «Can it be that there are no

Christians in Monsieur's America? Is it possible that down there they do not keep the Christmas feast at all?»

To cover my confusion, the Vidame intervened with an explanation which made America appear in a less heathenish light. «The planting of Saint Barbara's grain,» he said, «is a custom that I think is peculiar to the south of France. In almost every household in Provence, and over in Languedoc too, on Saint Barbara's day the women fill two, sometimes three, plates with wheat or lentils, which they set afloat in water and then stand in the warm ashes of the fireplace or on a sunny window-ledge to germinate. This is done in order to foretell the harvest of the coming year, for as Saint Barbara's grain grows well or ill so will the harvest of the coming year be good or bad; and also that there may be on the table when the Great Supper is served on Christmas eve—that is to say, on the feast of the winter solstice—green growing grain in symbol or in earnest of the harvest of the new year that then begins.

«The association of the Trinitarian Saint Barbara with this custom,» the Vidame continued, «I fear is a bit of makeshift. Were three plates of grain the rule, something of a case would be made out in her favor. But the rule, so far as one can be found, is for only two. The custom must be of pagan origin, and therefore dates from far back of the time when Saint Barbara lived in her three-windowed tower at Heliopolis. Probably her name was tagged to it because of old these votive and prophetic grain-fields were sown on what in Christian times became her dedicated day. But whatever light-mannered goddess may have been their patroness then, she is their patroness now; and from their sowing we date the beginning of our Christmas feast.»

It was obvious that this explanation of the custom went much too far for Misè Fougueiroun. At the mention of its foundation in paganism she sniffed audibly, and upon the Vidame's reference to the light-mannered goddess she drew her ample skirts primly about her and left the room.

The Vidame smiled. «I have scandalized Misè, and to-morrow I shall have to listen to a lecture,» he said; and in a moment continued: «It is not easy to make our Provençaux realize how closely we are linked to older peoples and to older times. The very name for Christmas in Provençal, Calèndo, tells how this Christian festival lives on from the Roman festival of the winter solstice, the January Kalends; and the beliefs and customs which go with its celebration still more plainly mark its origin.»

III.

In the early morning a lively clatter rising from the farm-yard came through my open window, along with the sunshine and the crisp freshness of the morning air.

In the courtyard there was more than the ordinary morning commotion of farm life, and the buzz of talk going on at the well and the racing and shouting of a parcel of children all had in it a touch of eagerness and expectancy. While I still was drinking my coffee—in the excellence and delicate service of which I recognized the friendly hand of Misè Fougueiroun—there came a knock at my door, and, upon my answer, the Vidame entered, looking so elate and wearing so blithe an air that he easily might have been mistaken for a frolicsome middle-aged sunbeam.

«Hurry! Hurry!» he cried, while still shaking both my hands. «This is a day of days—we are going now to bring home the *cacho-fiò*, the Yule log! Put on a pair of heavy shoes—the walking is rough on the mountain-side. But be quick, and come down the moment that you are ready. Now I must be off. There is a world for me to do.»

When I went down-stairs, five minutes later, I found him standing in the hall by the open doorway. «Come along!» he cried. «They all are waiting for us at the Mazet,» and he hurried me down the steps to the terrace and so around to the rear of the château, talking away eagerly as we walked.

«It is a most important matter,» he said, «this bringing home of the *cacho-fiò*. The whole family must take part in it. The head of the family—the grandfather, the father, or the eldest son—must cut the tree; all the others must share in carrying home the log that is to make the Christmas fire. And the tree must be a fruit-bearing tree. With us it usually is an almond or an olive. The olive especially is sacred. Our people, getting their faith from their Greek ancestors, believe that lightning never strikes it. But an apple-tree or a pear-tree will serve the purpose, and up in the Alp region they burn the acorn-bearing oak. What we shall do to-day is an echo of Druidical ceremonial—of the time when the Druid priests cut the Yule oak and with their golden sickles reaped the sacred mistletoe; but old Jan here, who is so stiff for preserving ancient customs, does not know that this custom, like many others that he stands for, is the survival of a rite.»

While the Vidame was speaking we had

turned from the terrace and were nearing the Mazet—which diminutive of the Provençal word *mas*, meaning farm-house, is applied to the farm establishment at Vièlmur partly in friendliness and partly in indication of its dependence upon the great house, the château. At the arched entrance we found the farm family awaiting us: Old Jan, the steward of the estate, and his wife Elizo; Marius, their elder son, a man over forty, who is the active manager of affairs; their younger son Esperit, and their daughter Nanoun; and the wife of Marius, Janetoun, to whose skirts a small child was clinging while three or four larger children scampered about her in a whir of excitement over the imminent event by which Christmas really would be ushered in.

When my presentation had been accomplished we set off across the home vineyard, and thence upward through the olive-orchards, to the high region on the mountain-side where grew the almond-tree which the Vidame and his steward in counsel together had selected for the Christmas sacrifice.

Nanoun, a strapping red-cheeked, black-haired bounce of twenty, ran back into the Mazet as we started, and joined us again, while we were crossing the vineyard, bringing with her a gentle-faced fair girl of her own age, who came shyly. The Vidame, calling her Magali, had a cordial word for this newcomer, and nudged me to bid me mark how promptly Esperit was by her side. «It is as good as settled,» he whispered. «They have been lovers since they were children. Magali is the daughter of Elizo's foster-sister, who died when the child was born. Then Elizo brought her home to the Mazet, and there she has lived her whole life long. Esperit is waiting only until he shall be established in the world to speak the word. And the scamp is in a hurry. Actually, he is pestering me to put him at the head of the Lower Farm!»

The Vidame gave this last piece of information in a tone of severity; but there was a twinkle in his kind old eyes as he spoke which led me to infer that Master Esperit's chances for the stewardship of the Lower Farm were anything but desperate, and I noticed that from time to time he cast very friendly glances toward these young lovers, as our little procession, mounting the successive terraces, went through the olive-orchards along the hillside upward.

Presently we were grouped around the devoted almond-tree, a gnarled old personage, of a great age and girth, having that pathetic look of sorrowful dignity which I find always in superannuated trees, and now and then in people of gentle natures who are conscious that their days of usefulness are gone.

Even the children were quiet as old Jan took his place beside the tree, and there was a touch of solemnity in his manner as he swung his heavy ax and gave the first strong blow, that sent a shiver through all the branches, as though the tree realized that death had overtaken it at last. When he had slashed a dozen times into the trunk, making a deep gash in the pale red wood beneath the brown bark, he handed the ax to Marius, and stood watching silently with the rest of us while his son finished the work that he had begun. In a few minutes the tree tottered, and then fell with a growling death-cry, as its brittle old branches crashed upon the ground.

Whatever there had been of unconscious reverence in the silence that attended the felling was at an end. As the tree came down everybody shouted. Instantly the children were swarming all over it. In a moment our little company burst into the flood of loud and lively talk that is inseparable in Provence from gay occasions, and that is ill held in check even at funerals and in church. They are the merriest people in the world, the Provençaux.

## IV.

MARIUS completed his work by cutting through the trunk again, making a noble cacho-fiò near five feet long—big enough to burn, according to the Provençal rule, from Christmas eve until the evening of New Year's day.

We returned homeward, moving in a mildly triumphal procession that I felt to be a little tinctured with ceremonial practices come down from forgotten times. Old Jan and Marius marching in front, Esperit and the sturdy Nanoun marching behind, carried between them the Yule log slung to shoulder-poles.

Our procession took on grand proportions, I should explain, because our Yule log was of extraordinary size. But always the Yule log is brought home in triumph. If it is small, it is carried on the shoulder of the father or the eldest son; if of a goodly size, these two carry it together; or a young husband and wife may bear it between them—as we actually saw a thick branch of our almond borne away that afternoon—while their children caracole around them or lend little helping hands.

Being come to the Mazet, the log was stood

on end in the courtyard in readiness to be taken thence to the fireplace on Christmas eve. I fancied that the men handled it with a certain reverence; and the Vidame assured me that such actually was the case. Already, being fully destined for the Christmas rite, it had become in a way sacred; and along with its sanctity, according to the popular belief, it had acquired a power which enabled it sharply to resent anything that smacked of sacrilegious affront.

DRAWN BY LOUIS LOEB.

BRINGING HOME THE «CACHO-FIÒ» (YULE LOG).

On the other hand, when treated reverently and burned with fitting rites, the Yule log brings upon all the household a blessing; and when it has been consumed even its ashes are potent for good.

The home-bringing ceremony being thus ended, we walked back to the château together—startling Esperit and Magali standing hand in hand, lover-like, in the archway; and when we were come to the terrace, and were seated snugly in a sunny corner, the Vidame told me of a very stately Yule log gift that was made anciently in Aix—and very likely elsewhere also—in feudal times.

In Aix it was the custom, when the counts of Provence still lived and ruled there, for the magistrates of the city each year at Christmas-tide to carry in solemn procession a huge cacho-fiò to the palace of their sovereign; and there formally to present to him—or, in his absence, to the grand seneschal on his behalf—this their free-will and good-will offering. And when the ceremony of presentation was ended the city fathers were served with a collation at the count's charges, and were given the opportunity to pledge him loyally in his own good wine.

Knowing Aix well, I was able to fill in the outlines of the Vidame's bare statement of fact, and also to give it a background. What a joy the procession must have been to see! The gray-bearded magistrates, in their velvet caps and robes, wearing their golden chains of office; the great log, swung to shoulder-poles and borne by leathern-jerkined henchmen; surely drummers and fifers, for such a ceremonial would have been impossibly incomplete in Provence without a *tambourin* and *galoubet;* doubtless a brace of ceremonial trumpeters; and a seemly guard in front and rear of steel-capped and steel-jacketed halberdiers. All these marching gallantly through the narrow, yet stately, Aix streets; with comfortable burghers and well-rounded matrons in the doorways looking on, and pretty faces peeping from upper windows and going all a-blushing because of the overbold glances of the men-at-arms! And then fancy the presentation in the great hall of the castle; and the gay feasting; and the merry wagging of gray-bearded chins as the magistrates cried all together, «To the health of the count!» and tossed their wine!

V.

As Christmas day drew near I observed that Misè Fougueiroun walked thoughtfully and seemed to be oppressed by heavy cares. It was the same just then with all the housewives of the region; for the chief ceremonial event of Christmas in Provence is the *Gros Soupa* that is eaten upon Christmas eve, and of even greater culinary importance is the dinner that is eaten upon Christmas day—wherefore does every woman brood and labor that her achievement of these meals may realize her high ideal. Especially does the preparation of the Great Supper compel exhaustive thought. Being of a vigil, the supper necessarily is «lean,» and custom has fixed unalterably the principal dishes of which it must be composed. Thus limited straitly, the making of it becomes a struggle of genius against material conditions.

Because of the Vidame's desolate bachelorhood, the kindly custom long ago was established that he and all his household every year should eat their Great Supper with the farm family at the Mazet—an arrangement that did not work well until Misè Fougueiroun and Elizo (after some years of spirited squabbling) came to the agreement that the former should be permitted to prepare the delicate sweets served for dessert at that repast. Of these the most important is *nougat*, without which Christmas would be as barren in Provence as Christmas would be in England without plum-pudding or in America without mince-pies.

But it was the making of the Christmas dinner that mainly occupied Misè Fougueiroun's mind—a feast pure and simple, governed by the one jolly law that it shall be the very best dinner of the whole year. What may be termed its by-laws are that the principal dish shall be a roast turkey, and that nougat and *poumpo* shall figure at the dessert. Why poumpo is held in high esteem by the Provençaux I am not prepared to say. It seemed to me a cake of only a humdrum quality; but even Misè Fougueiroun spoke of it in a sincerely admiring and chop-smacking way.

Ordinarily the Provençal Christmas turkey is roasted with a stuffing of chestnuts, or of sausage-meat and black olives; but the high cooks of Provence also roast him stuffed with truffles, making so superb a dish that Brillat-Savarin has singled it out for praise.

Of the minor dishes served at the Christmas dinner it is needless to speak. There was nothing ceremonial about them; nothing remarkable except their excellence and their profusion. Indeed, the distinctiveness of a Provençal Christmas—unless the New-Year ceremonial be considered as a part of it—ends on Christmas eve with the midnight mass.

VI.

But in spite of their eager natural love for all good things eatable, the Provençaux also are poets, and along with the cooking, another matter was in train that was wholly of a poetic cast. This was the making of the *crèche*, a representation with odd little figures and accessories of the personages and scene of the Nativity, the whole at once so naïve and so tender as to be possible only among a people blessed with rare sweetness and rare simplicity of soul.

In a way, the crèche takes in Provence the place of the Christmas tree, of which Northern institution nothing is known here; but it is closer to the heart of Christmas than the tree, being touched with a little of the tender beauty of the event which it represents in so quaint a guise. Its invention is ascribed to Saint Francis of Assisi. The chronicle of his order tells that this seraphic man, having first obtained the permission of the holy see, represented the principal scenes of the Nativity in a stable, and that in the stable so transformed he celebrated mass and preached to the people. All this is wholly in keeping with the character of Saint Francis; and certainly the crèche had its origin in Italy in his period, and in the same conditions which formed his graciously fanciful soul. Its introduction into Provence is said to have been in the time of John XXII, the second of the Avignon popes, who came to the pontificate in the year 1316, and by the fathers of the Oratory of Marseille: from which center it rapidly spread abroad through the land until it became a necessary feature of the Christmas festival both in churches and in homes.

Obviously, the crèche is an offshoot from the miracle-plays and mysteries which had their beginning a full two centuries earlier. These also survive vigorously in Provence in the «Pastouralo,» an acted representation of the Nativity that is given each year during the Christmas season by amateurs or professionals in every city and town and in almost every village.

In the farm-houses, and in the dwellings of the middle class, the crèche is placed always in the living-room, and so becomes an intimate part of the family life. On a table set in a corner is represented a rocky hillside rising in terraces tufted with moss and grass and

DRAWN BY LOUIS LOEB.

THE BLIND GIRL.

(SEE PAGES 262 AND 283.)

little trees, and broken by foot-paths and a winding road. This structure is very like a Provençal hillside, but it is supposed to represent the rocky region around Bethlehem, and it is dusted with flour to represent snow. At its base, on the left, embowered in laurel or in holly, is a wooden or pasteboard representation of the inn; and beside the inn is the stable: an open shed in which are grouped little figures representing the several personages of the Nativity. In the center is the Christ-child, either in a cradle or lying on a truss of straw; seated beside him is the Virgin; Saint Joseph stands near, holding in his hand the mystic lily; with their heads bent down over the Child are the ox and the ass —for those good animals helped with their breath through that cold night to keep him warm. In the foreground are the two *ravi*—a man and a woman in awed ecstasy, with upraised arms—and the adoring shepherds. To these are added on Epiphany the figures of the Magi—the kings, as they are called always in French and in Provençal—with their train of attendants, and the camels on which they have brought their gifts. Angels (pendent from the farm-house ceiling) float in the air above the stable. Higher is the star, from which a ray (a golden thread) descends to the Christ-child's hand. Over all, in a glory of clouds, is the figure of Jehovah attended by a white dove.

These are the essentials of the crèche, and in the beginning, no doubt, these made the whole of it. But for nearly six centuries the delicate imagination of the Provençal poets and the cruder, but still poetic, fancy of the Provençal people have been enlarging upon the simple original—with the result that two-score or more figures often are found in the crèche of to-day.

Either drawing from the quaintly beautiful medieval legends of the birth and childhood of Jesus, or directly from their own quaintly simple souls, the poets from early times have been making Christmas songs—noëls, or *nouvè* as they are called in Provençal—in which new subordinate characters have been created in a spirit of frank realism, and these have materialized in new figures surrounding the crèche. At the same time the fancy of the people, working with a still more naïve directness along the lines of associated ideas, has been making the most curiously incongruous and anachronistic additions to the group.

To the first order belong such creations as the blind man, led by a child, coming to be healed of his blindness by the Infant's touch; or that of the young mother hurrying to offer her breast to the New-born (in accordance with the beautiful custom still in force in Provence), that its own mother may rest a little before she begins to suckle it; or that of the other mother bringing the cradle of which her own baby has been dispossessed, because of her compassion for the poor woman at the inn whose Child is lying on a truss of straw.

But the popular additions, begotten of association of ideas, are far more numerous and also are far more curious. The hilltop, close under the floating figure of Jehovah, has been crowned with a windmill, because windmills abounded anciently on the hilltops of Provence; and to the mill, naturally, has been added a miller who is riding down the road on an ass with a sack of flour across his saddle-bow that he is carrying as a gift to the Holy Family. The adoring shepherds have been given flocks of sheep, and on the hillside more shepherds and more sheep have been put for company. The sheep, in association with the ox and the ass, have brought in their train a whole troop of domestic animals—including geese and turkeys and chickens and a cock on the roof of the stable; and in the train of the camels has come the extraordinary addition of lions, bears, leopards, elephants, ostriches, and even crocodiles! The Provençaux being from of old mighty hunters (the tradition has found its classic embodiment in Tartarin), and hillsides being appropriate to hunting, the figure of a fowler with a gun at his shoulder has been introduced; and as it is well, even in the case of a Provençal sportsman, to point a gun at a definite object, the fowler usually is so placed as to aim at the cock on the stable roof. He is a modern, yet not very recent, addition, the fowler, as is shown by the fact that he carries a flint-lock fowling-piece. Drumming and fifing being absolute essentials to every sort of Provençal festivity, a conspicuous figure always is found playing on a tambourin and galoubet. Itinerant knife-grinders are an old institution here, and in some obscure way—possibly because of their thievish propensities—are associated intimately with the devil; and so there is either a knife-grinder simple, or a devil with a knife-grinder's wheel. Of old it was the custom for the women to carry distaffs and to spin out thread as they went to and from the fields or along the roads (just as the women nowadays knit as they walk), and therefore a spinning-woman always is of the company. Because child-stealing was not uncommon here formerly, and because Gipsies still are plentiful, there are three Gipsies lurking about the inn all ready to steal the Christ-child away. As the innkeeper naturally would come out to investigate the cause of the commotion in his stable-yard, he is found with the others, lantern in hand. And, finally, there is a group of women bearing as gifts to the Christ-child the essentials of the Christmas feast: codfish, chickens, *carde*, ropes of garlic, eggs, and the great Christmas cakes, poumpo and *fougasso*.

Many other figures may be, and often are, added to the group, of which one of the most delightful is the Turk who makes a solacing present of his pipe to Saint Joseph. But all of these which I have named have come to be now quite as necessary to a properly made crèche as are the few which are taken direct from the Bible narrative; and the congregation surely is one of the quaintest that ever poetry and simplicity together devised.

VII.

ON the morning of the day preceding Christmas a lurking, yet ill-repressed, excitement pervaded the château and all its dependencies. In the case of the Vidame and Misè Fougueiroun the excitement did not even lurk: it blazed forth so openly that they were as a brace of comets—bustling violently through our universe and dragging into their erratic wakes, away from normal orbits, the whole planetary system of the household and all haply intrusive stars.

Although the morning still was young, work on the estate had ended for the day, and about the door of the kitchen more than a score of laborers were gathered.

Misè Fougueiroun—a plump embodiment of Benevolence—stood beside a table on which was a great heap of her own fougasso, and big baskets filled with dried figs and almonds and celery, and a genial battalion of bottles standing guard over all. One by one the vassals were called up—there was a strong flavor of feudalism in it all—and to each, while the Vidame wished him a «Bòni fèsto!» the housekeeper gave his Christmas portion: a fougasso, a double handful each of figs and almonds, a stalk of celery, and a bottle of *vin cue*, the cordial that is used for the libation of the Yule log and for the solemn Yule cup; and each, as he received his portion, made his little speech of friendly thanks—in several cases most gracefully turned—and then was off in a hurry for his home.

VIII.

As we passed the Mazet in our afternoon walk we stopped to greet the new arrivals there, come to make the family gathering complete: two more married children, with a flock of their own little ones, and Elizo's father and mother—a bowed little rosy-cheeked old woman and a bowed lean old man, both well above eighty years. There was a lively passage of friendly greetings between them all and the Vidame; and it was quite delightful to see how the bowed little old woman kindled and bridled when the Vidame gallantly protested that she grew younger and handsomer every year.

A tall ladder stood against the Mazet, and the children were engaged in hanging tiny wheat-sheaves along the eaves—the Christmas portion of the birds.

IX.

OUR march, out through the rear door of the château and across the courtyard to the Mazet, was processional. All the household went with us. The Vidame gallantly gave his arm to Misè Fougueiroun; I followed with her first officer, a saucebox named Mouneto, so plumply provoking and charming in her Arlesian dress that I will not say what did or did not happen in the darkness as we passed the well! A little in our rear followed the house servants, even to the least; and in the Mazet already were gathered, with the family, the few work-people of the estate who had not gone to their own homes. For the Great Supper is a patriarchal feast, to which in Christian fellowship come the master and the master's family and all of their servitors and dependents on equal terms.

A broad stream of light came out through the open doorway of the farm-house, and with it a great clatter and buzz of talk, that increased tenfold as we entered, and a cry of «Bòni fèsto!» came from the whole company at once. As for the Vidame, he so radiated cordiality that he seemed to be the veritable spirit of Christmas (incarnate at the age of sixty, and at that period of the present century when stocks and frilled shirts were worn), and his joyful old legs were near to dancing as he went among the company with warm-hearted greetings and outstretched hands.

X.

THE crèche, around which the children were gathered in a swarm, was built up in one

BY LOUIS LOEB.

MAGALI.

(SEE PAGE 281.)

corner, and our coming was the signal for the first of the ceremonies, the lighting of the crèche candles, to begin. In this all the children had a part, making rather a scramble of it: for there was rivalry as to which of them should light the most, and in a moment a constellation of little flames covered the Bethlehem hillside and brought into bright prominence the Holy Family and its strange attendant host of quite impossible people and beasts and birds.

The laying of the Yule log followed—a ceremony so grave that it has all the dignity of, and really is, a religious rite. The buzz of talk died away into silence as Elizo's father, the oldest man, took by the hand and led out into the courtyard where the log was lying his great-grandson, the little Tounin, the youngest child: it being the rule that the nominal bearers of the cacho-fiò to the hearth shall be the oldest and the youngest of the family—the one personifying the year that is dying, the other the year new-born. Sometimes, and this is the prettiest rendering of the custom, the two are an old, old man and a baby carried in its mother's arms, while between them the real bearers of the burden walk.

In our case the log actually was carried by Marius and Esperit; but the tottering old man clasped its forward end with his thin, feeble hands, and its hinder end was clasped by the plump, feeble hands of the tottering child. Thus, the four together, they brought it in through the doorway and carried it thrice around the room, circling the supper-table and the lighted candles; and then, reverently, it was laid before the fireplace, that still sometimes is called in Provençal the *lar*.

There was a pause, while the old man filled out a cup of vin cue, and a solemn hush fell upon the company, and all heads were bowed, as he poured three libations upon the log, saying with the last: «In the name of the Father, and of the Son, and of the Holy Ghost!» and then cried with all the vigor that he could infuse into his thin and quavering old voice:

Cacho-fiò,
Bouto-fiò!
Alègre! Alègre!
Dièu nous alègre!
Calèndo vèn! Tout bèn vèn!
Dièu nous fague la gràci de vèire l'an que vèn,
E se noun sian pas mai, que noun fuguen pas mens!

Yule log,
Catch fire!
Joy! Joy!
God gives joy!
Christmas comes! All good comes!
May God give us grace to see the coming year,
And if we are not more, may we not be less!

As he ended his invocation he crossed himself, as did all the rest; and a great glad shout was raised of «Alègre! Alègre!» as Marius and Esperit, first casting some fagots of vine-branches on the bed of glowing coals, placed the Yule log upon the fire. Instantly the vines blazed up, flooding the room with brightness; and as the Yule log glowed and reddened everybody cried:

Cacho-fiò,
Bouto-fiò!
Alègre! Alègre!

again and again—as though the whole of them together of a sudden had gone merry-mad!

In the midst of this triumphant rejoicing the bowl from which the libation had been poured was filled afresh with vin cue, and was passed from hand to hand and lip to lip,—beginning with the little Tounin, and so upward in order of seniority until it came last of all to the old man,—and from it each drank to the new fire of the new year.

One of my Aix friends, the poet Joachim Gasquet, has described to me the Christmas-eve customs which were observed in his own home: the Gasquet bakery, in the Rue de la Cépède, that has been handed down from father to son through so many hundreds of years that even its owners cannot tell certainly whether it was in the fourteenth or the fifteenth century that their family legend of good baking had its rise.

In the Gasquet family it was the custom to eat the Great Supper in the oven-room: because that was the heart, the sanctuary, of the house; the place consecrated by the toil which gave the family its livelihood. On the supper-table there was always a wax figure of the infant Christ, and this was carried just before midnight to the living-room, off from the shop, in one corner of which the crèche was set up. It was the little Joachim whose right it was, because he was the youngest, the purest, to carry the figure. A formal procession was made. He walked at its head, a little chap with long curling golden hair, between his two grandfathers; the rest followed in the order of their age and rank: his two grandmothers, his father and mother, Monsieur Auguste (a dashing blade of a young baker then) with the maid-servant, and the apprentices last of all. A single candle was carried by one of his grandfathers into the dark room—the illumination of which, that

DRAWN BY LOUIS LOEB.

AT THE STROKE OF MIDNIGHT.

night, could come only from the new fire kindled before the crèche. Precisely at midnight—at the moment when all the clocks of Aix striking together let loose the Christmas chimes—the child laid the holy figure in the manger, and then the candles instantly were set ablaze.

Sometimes there would be a thrilling pause of half a minute or more while they waited for the bells: the child, with the image in his hands, standing before the crèche in the little circle of light; the others grouped behind him, and for the most part lost in dark shadow cast by the single candle held low down; those nearest to the crèche holding matches ready to strike so that all the candles might be lighted at once when the moment came. And then all the bells together would send their voices out over the city heavenward; and his mother would say softly, «Now, my little son!» and the room would flash into brightness suddenly—as though a glory radiated from the

DRAWN BY LOUIS LOEB.

«ELIZO'S OLD FATHER.»

Christ-child lying there in the manger between the ox and the ass.

XI.

WHILE our Yule-log ceremonial was in progress, the good Elizo and Janetoun, upon whom the responsibility of the supper rested, evidently were a prey to anxious thoughts. They whispered together, and cast uneasy glances toward the chimney, into the broad corners of which the various cooking-vessels had been moved to make way for the cacho-fiò; and barely had the cup of benediction passed their lips when they precipitated themselves upon the fireplace, and replaced the pots and pans for a final heating upon the coals.

The long table had been set before our arrival and was in perfect readiness, covered with a fine white linen cloth, sacredly reserved for use at high festivals, that fairly sparkled in the blaze of light cast by the overhanging petroleum lamp. Yet the two ceremonial candles, one at each end of the table, also were lighted.

Beside these candles were the harvest harbingers, the plates on which was growing Saint Barbara's grain, so vigorous and so freshly green that old Jan rubbed his hands together comfortably as he said to the Vidame, «Ah, we need have no fears for the harvest that is coming in this blessed year!» In the center of the table, its browned crust slashed with a cross, was the great loaf of Christmas bread, *pan Calendau;* on which was a bunch of holly tied with the white pith of rushes—the «marrow» of the rush, that is held to be an emblem of strength. Old Jan, the master of the house, cut the loaf into as many portions as there were persons present, with one double portion over to be given to some poor one in charity—«the portion of the good God.» It is of a miraculous nature, this blessed bread: the sailors of Provence carry morsels of it with them on their voyages, and by strewing its crumbs upon the troubled waters stay the tempests of the sea.

For the rest, the table had down its middle a line of dishes—many of them old faïence of Moustiers, the mere sight of which would have thrilled a collector's heart—heaped with the nougat and the other sweets over the making of which our housekeeper and her lieutenants so soulfully had toiled. And on the table in the corner were fruits and nuts and wines.

Grace always is said before the Great Supper—a simple formula ending with the prayer of the Yule log that if another year there are no more, there may be no less. It is the custom that this blessing shall be asked by the youngest child of the family who can speak the words—a pretty usage which sometimes makes the blessing go very queerly indeed. Our little Tounin came to the front again in this matter, exhibiting an air of grave responsibility which showed that he had been well drilled; and it was with quite a saintly look on his little face that he folded his hands together and said very earnestly: «God bless all that we are going to eat, and if we are no less next year, may we be no more!» at which everybody looked at Janetoun and laughed.

In our seating a due order of precedence was observed. Old Jan, the head of the family, presided, with the Vidame and myself on his right and with Elizo's father and mother on his left; and thence the company went downward by age and station to the foot of the table, where were grouped the servants from the château and the workmen on the farm. But no other distinction was made. All were served alike and all drank together as equals when the toasts were called. The servers were Elizo and Janetoun, with Nanoun and Magali for assistants; and these four, although they took their places at the table when each course had been brought on, had rather a Passover time of it: for they ate, as it were, with their loins girded and with full or empty dishes imminent to their hands.

As I have said, the Great Supper must be «lean,» and is restricted to certain dishes which in no circumstances can be changed; but rich leanness is possible in a country where olive-oil takes the place of animal fat in cooking, and where the accumulated skill of ages presides over the kitchen fire. The principal dish is the *raïto*—a ragout made of delicately fried fish served in a sauce flavored with wine and capers—whereof the tradition goes back around twenty-five hundred years, to the time when the Phocæan housewives brought with them to Massalia (the Marseille of to-day) the happy mystery of its making from their Grecian homes. But this excellent dish was not lost to Greece because it was gained by Gaul: bearing the same name, and made in the same fashion, it is eaten by the Greeks of the present day. It usually is made of dried codfish in Provence, where the cod is held in high esteem; but is most delicately toothsome when made of eels.

The second course of the Great Supper also is fish, which may be of any sort and served in any way—in our case it was a perch-like variety of dainty pan-fish, fresh from the Rhône. A third course of fish sometimes is served, but the third course usually is snails cooked in a rich brown sauce strongly flavored with garlic. The Provençal snails, which feed in a *gourmet* fashion upon vine-leaves, are peculiarly delicious, and there was a murmur of delight from our company as the four women brought to the table four big dishes full of them; and for a while there was only the sound of eager munching, mixed with the clatter on china of the empty shells. To extract them we had the strong thorns, three or four inches long, of the wild acacia; and on these the little brown morsels were carried to the avid mouths and eaten with a bit of bread sopped in the sauce; and then the shell was subjected to a vigorous sucking, that not a drop of the sauce lingering within it should be lost.

To the snails succeeded another dish essentially Provençal, carde. The carde is a giant thistle that grows to a height of five or six feet, and is so luxuriantly magnificent both in leaf and in flower that it deserves a place among ornamental plants. The edible portion is the stem—blanched like celery, which it much resembles, by being earthed up—cooked with a white sauce flavored with garlic. The garlic, however, is a mistake, since it overpowers the delicate taste of the carde; but garlic is the overlord of all things eatable in Provence. I was glad when we passed on to the celery, with which the first section of the supper came to an end.

The second section was such an explosion of sweets as might fly into space should a comet collide with a confectioner's shop—nougat, fougasso, a great poumpo, compotes, candied fruits, and a whole nightmare herd of rich cakes on which persons not blessed

DRAWN BY LOUIS LOEB.

THE ANGEL AND THE SHEPHERD.

(SEE PAGE 283.)

with the most powerful organs of digestion surely would go galloping to the country of dreadful dreams. Of the dessert of nuts and fruit the notable features were grapes and winter melons.

With the serious part of the supper we drank the ordinary small wine diluted with water; but with the dessert was paraded a gallant company of dusty bottles containing ancient vintages which through many ripening years had been growing richer by feeding upon their own excellence in the wine-room of the Mazet or the cellar of the château.

## XII.

BUT the material element of the Great Supper is its least part. What entitles it to the augmenting adjective is its soul—that subtle essence of peace and amity for which the word Christmas is a synonym in all Christian lands. It is the rule of these family gatherings at Christmas-time in Provence that the heartburnings and rancors which may have sprung up during the year then shall be cut down; and even if sometimes they quickly grow again, as no doubt they do now and then, it makes for happiness that they shall be thus banished from the peace-feast of the year. When the serious part of the supper had been disposed of and the mere palate-tickling period of the dessert had come, I was much interested in observing that the talk, mainly carried on by the elders, was turned with an obviously deliberate purpose upon family history, and especially upon the doings of those who in the past had brought honor upon the family name.

The chief ancestral glory of the family of the Mazet is its close blood-relationship with the gallant André Etienne, that drummer of the fifty-first demi-brigade of the Army of Italy who is commemorated on the frieze of the Panthéon, and who is known and honored as the «Tambour d'Arcole» all over France. It was delightful to listen to old Jan's telling of the brave story: how this André, their own kinsman, swam the stream under the enemy's fire at Arcola with his drum on his back and then drummed his fellow-soldiers on to vicvictory; how Bonaparte awarded him the drumsticks of honor, and later, when the Legion of Honor was founded, gave him the cross; how they carved him in stone, drumming the charge, up there on the front of the Panthéon in Paris itself; how Mistral, the great poet of Provence, had made a poem about him that had been printed in a book; and how, only two years ago, they set up his marble statue in Cadenet, the little town, not far from Avignon, where he was born!



Old Jan was not content with merely telling this story—like a true Provençal he acted it: swinging a supposititious drum upon his back, jumping into an imaginary river and swimming it with his head in the air, swinging his drum back into place again, and then —*zóu!*—starting off at the head of the fifty-first demi-brigade with such a rousing play of drumsticks that I protest we fairly heard the rattle of them, along with the spatter of Austrian musketry in the face of which André Etienne beat that gallant *pas de charge!*

It set me all a-thrilling; and still more did it thrill those other listeners who were of the Arcola hero's very blood and bone. They clapped their hands and they shouted. They laughed with delight. And the fighting spirit of Gaul was so stirred within them that at a word. I verily believe they would have been for marching in a body across the southeastern frontier!

Elizo's old father was rather out of the running in this matter. It was not by any relative of his that the drumsticks of honor had been won; and his thoughts, after wandering a little, evidently settled down upon the strictly personal fact that his thin old legs were cold. Rising slowly from the table, he carried his plate to the fireplace, and when he had arranged some live coals in one of the sconces of the waist-high andirons he rested the plate above them on the iron rim; and so stood there, eating contentedly, while the warmth from the glowing Yule log entered gratefully into his lean old body and stirred to a brisker pulsing the blood in his meager veins. But his interest in what was going forward revived again—his legs being, also, by that time well warmed—when his own praises were sounded by his daughter in the story of how he stopped the runaway horse on the very brink of the precipice at Les Baux; and how his wife all the while sat steady beside him in the cart, cool and silent and showing no sign of fear.

When Elizo had finished this story she whispered a word to Magali and Nanoun that sent them laughing out of the room; and presently Magali came back again arrayed in the identical dress which had been worn by the heroine of the adventure—who had perked and plumed herself not a little while her daughter told about it—when the runaway horse so nearly had galloped her off the Baux rock into eternity. It was the Provençal costume, with full sleeves and flaring cap, of sixty years back; but a little gayer than the strict Arles dress of that period, because her mother was not of Arles, but of Beaucaire. It was not so graceful, especially in the head-dress, as the costume of the present day; nor nearly so becoming—as Magali showed by looking a dozen years older after putting it on. But Magali, even with a dozen years added, could not but be charming.

By long experience, gained on many such occasions, the Vidame knew that the culminating point of the supper would be reached when the family drummer swam the river and headed the French charge at Arcola. Therefore had he reserved until a later period, when the excitement incident to the revival of that honorable bit of family history should have subsided, a joy-giving bombshell of his own that he had all ready to explode. An American or an Englishman never could have fired it without something in the way of speechmaking; but the Vidame was of a shy temper, and speechmaking was not in his line. When the chatter caused by Magali's costuming had lulled a little, and there came a momentary pause in the talk, he merely reached diagonally across the table and touched glasses with Esperit and said simply: «To your good health, Monsieur the Superintendent of the Lower Farm!»

It was done so quietly that for some seconds no one realized that the Vidame's toast brought happiness to all the household, and to two of its members a lifelong joy. Esperit, even, had his glass almost to his lips before he understood to what he was drinking; and then his understanding came through the finer nature of Magali, who gave a quick, deep sob as she buried her face in the buxom Nanoun's bosom and encircled that astonished young person's neck with her arms. Esperit went pale at that; but the hand did not tremble in which he held his still raised glass, nor did his voice quaver as he said with a deep earnestness: «To the good health of Monsieur le Vidame, with the thanks of two very happy hearts!»—and so drained his wine.

A great danger puts no more strain upon the nerves of a man of good fiber than does a great joy; and it seemed to me that Esperit's absolute steadiness, under this sudden fire of happiness, showed him to be made of as fine and as manly stuff as went to the making of his kinsman who beat the pas de charge up the slope at Arcola at the head of the fifty-first demi-brigade.

But nothing less than the turbulence of the whole battle of Arcola—not to say of that whole triumphant campaign in Italy—will suffice for a comparison with the tumult that arose about our supper-table when the meaning of the Vidame's toast fairly was grasped by the company at large. I do not think that I could express in words, nor by any less elaborate method of illustration than a kinetoscope, the state of excitement into which a Provençal will fly over a matter of absolutely no importance at all; how he will burst forth into a very whirlwind of words and gestures about some trifle that an ordinary human being would dispose of without the quiver of an eye. And as our matter was one so truly moving that a very Dutchman through all his phlegm would have been stirred by it, such a tornado was set a-going as would have put a mere hurricane of the tropics to open shame.

Naturally, the disturbance was central over Esperit and Magali and the Vidame. The latter—his kind old face shining like the sun of an Easter morning—gave back with a good will on Magali's cheeks her kisses of gratitude, and exchanged embraces and kisses with the elder women, and went through such an ordeal of violent hand-shaking that I trembled for the integrity of his arms. But as for the young people, whom everybody embraced over and over again with a terrible energy—that they came through it all with whole ribs is as near to being a miracle as anything that has happened in modern times!

Gradually the storm subsided, though not without some fierce after-gusts, and at last worked itself off harmlessly in song, as we returned to the ritual of the evening and took to the singing of noëls—the Christmas canticles which are sung between the ending of the Great Supper and the beginning of the midnight mass.

## XIII.

THE Provençal noëls—being some real, or some imagined, incident of the Nativity told in verse set to a gay or tender air—are the crèche translated into song. The simplest of them are direct renderings of the Bible narrative. Our own Christmas hymn, «While Shepherds Watched their Flocks by Night,» is precisely of this order; and, indeed, is of the very period when flourished the greatest of the Provençal noël-writers; for the poet laureate Nahum Tate, whose laurel this hymn keeps green, was born in the year 1652 and had begun his mildly poetic career while Saboly still was alive.

But most of the noëls—*nouvè* they are called in Provençal—are purely imaginative:

quaintly innocent stories created by the poets, or taken from those apocryphal scriptures in which the simple-minded faithful of patristic times built up a warmly colored legend of the Virgin's life and of the birth and childhood of her Son. Sometimes, even, the writers stray away entirely from a religious base and produce mere roistering catches or topical songs.

The Provençaux have been writing noëls for more than four hundred years. One of the oldest belongs to the first half of the fifteenth century and is ascribed to Raymond Féraud; the latest are of our own day—by Roumanille, Crousillat, Mistral, Girard, Gras, and a score more. But only a few have been written to live. The memory of many once famous noël-writers is preserved now either mainly or wholly by a single song.

The one assured immortal among these musical mortalities is Nicolas Saboly,[1] who was born in Monteux, close by Avignon, in the year 1614; who for the greater part of his life was chapel-master and organist of the Avignon church of St. Pierre; who died in the year 1675; and who was buried in the choir of the church which for so long he had filled with his own heaven-sweet harmonies.

Saboly's music has a «go» and a melodic quality suggestive of the work of Sir Arthur Sullivan; but it has a more tender, a fresher, a purer note, even more sparkle, than ever Sullivan has achieved. In his gay airs the attack is instant, brilliant, overpowering,—like a glad outburst of sweet bells, like the joyous laughter of a child,—and everything goes with a dash and a swing. But while he thus loved to harmonize a laugh, he also could strike a note of infinite tenderness. In his pathetic noëls he drops into thrillingly plaintive minors which fairly drag one's heart out—echoes or survivals, possibly (for this poignant melody is not uncommon in old Provençal music), of the passionately longing love-songs with which Saracen knights once went a-serenading beneath castle windows here in Provence.

Nor is his verse, of its curious kind, less excellent than his music. By turns, as the humor takes him, his noëls are sermons, or delicate religious fancies, or sharp-pointed satires, or whimsical studies of country-side life. One whole series of seven is a history of the Nativity (surely the quaintest and the gayest and the tenderest oratorio that ever was written!) in which, in music and in words, he is at his very best. Above all, his noëls are local.

This naïve local twist is not peculiar to Saboly. With very few exceptions all Provençal noëls are packed full of the same delightful anachronisms. It is to Provençal shepherds that the herald angel appears; it is Provençaux who compose the *bregado*, the pilgrim company, that starts for Bethlehem; and Bethlehem is a village always within easy walking-distance here in Provence. Yet is it not wholly simplicity that has brought about this shifting of the scene of the Nativity from the hill-country of Judea to the hill-country of southeastern France. The life and the look of the two lands have much in common; and most impressively will their common character be felt by one who walks here by night beneath the stars.

[1] The admirable edition of Saboly's noëls, text and music, published at Avignon in the year 1856 by François Seguin, is to be reissued for this present Christmas by the same publisher in definitive form. It can be obtained through the Librairie Roumanille, Avignon.

## XIV.

It was with Saboly's «Hòu, de l'houstau!» that our singing began. It is one of the series in his history of the Nativity and is the most popular of all his noëls: a dialogue between Saint Joseph and the Bethlehem innkeeper, that opens with a sweet and plaintive long-drawn note of supplication as Saint Joseph timorously calls:

> O-o-oh, there, the house! Master! Mistress!
> Varlet! Maid! Is *no* one there?

And then it continues with humble entreaties for shelter for himself and his wife, who is very near her time; to which the host replies with rough refusals for a while, but in the end grants grudgingly a corner of his stable in which the wayfarers may lie for the night.

Esperit and Magali sang this responsively; Magali taking Saint Joseph's part—in which, in all the noëls, is a strain of feminine sweetness and gentleness. Then Marius and Esperit, in the same fashion, sang the famous «C'est le bon lever,» a dialogue between an angel and a shepherd, in which the angel, as becomes so exalted a personage, speaks French, while the shepherd speaks Provençal.

«It 's high time to get up, sweet shepherd,» the angel begins; and goes on to tell that «in Bethlehem, quite near this place,» the Saviour of the world has been born of a virgin.

«Perhaps you take me for a common peasant,» the shepherd answers, «talking to me like that! I am poor, but I 'd have you to know that I come of good stock. In old times my great-great-grandfather was mayor of our village! And who are you, anyway, fine sir! Are you a Jew or a Dutchman? Your jargon makes me laugh. A virgin mother! A child god! No, never were such things heard!»

But when the angel reiterates his strange statement the shepherd's interest is aroused. He declares that he will go at once and steal this miraculous child; and he quite takes the angel into his confidence—as though standing close to his elbow and speaking as friend to friend. In the end, of course, he is convinced of the miracle, and says that he «will get the ass and set forth» to join the worshipers about the manger at Bethlehem.

There are many of these noëls in dialogue; and most of them are touched with this same quality of easy familiarity with sacred subjects, and abound in turns of broad humor, which render them not a little startling from our nicer point of view. But they never are coarse, and their simplicity saves them from being irreverent; nor is there, I am sure, the least thought of irreverence on the part of those by whom they are sung. I noticed, though, that these lively numbers were the ones which most hit the fancy of the men; while the women as plainly showed their liking for those of a finer spirit in which the dominant qualities were pathos and grace.

Of this latter class is Roumanille's rarely beautiful noël, «The Blind Girl» («La Chato Avuglo»),[1] that Magali sang with a tenderness which set the women to crying openly, and which made the older men cough a little and look suspiciously red about the eyes. Of all the modern noëls it has come closest to and has taken the strongest hold upon the popular heart—this pathetic story of the child «blind from her birth,» who pleads with her mother that she also may go with the rest to Bethlehem, urging that though she cannot see the «lovely golden face» she still may touch the Christ-child's hand.

And when, all thrilling, to the stable she was come
She placed the little hand of Jesus on her heart—
And saw him whom she touched!

I am persuaded, so thoroughly did they all enjoy their own caroling, that the singing of noëls would have gone on until broad daylight had it not been for the intervention of the midnight mass. But the mass of Christmas eve—or, rather, of Christmas morning—is a matter not only of pleasure, but of obligation. Even those upon whom churchly requirements at other times rest lightly rarely fail to attend it; and to the faithful it is the most touchingly beautiful, as Easter is the most joyous, church festival of the year.

By eleven o'clock, therefore, we were under way for our walk of a mile or so down the long slope of the hillside to the village.

Presently some one started a very sweet and plaintive noël, fairly heart-wringing in its tender beseeching and soft lament, yet with a consoling undernote to which it constantly returned. I think, but I am not sure, that it was Roumanille's noël telling of the widowed mother who carried the cradle of her own baby to the Virgin, that the Christ-child might not lie on straw.[2] One by one the other voices took up the strain, until in a full chorus the sorrowingly compassionate melody went thrilling through the moonlit silence of the night.

And so, singing, we walked by the white way onward, hearing as we neared the town the songs of other companies coming up, as ours was, from outlying farms. And when they and we had passed in through the gateways—where the townsfolk of old lashed out against their robber infidel and robber Christian enemies—all the black, little narrow streets were filled with an undertone of murmuring voices and an overtone of clear, sweet song.

## XV.

On the little Grande Place the crowd was packed densely. There the several streams of humanity pouring into the town met and mingled, and thence in a strong current flowed onward into the church. Coming from the blackness without,—for the tall houses surrounding the Grande Place cut off the moonlight and made it a little pocket of darkness,—it was with a shock of splendor that we encountered the brightness within. All the side-altars were blazing with candles, and as the service went on, and the high altar also flamed up, the whole building was filled with a soft radiance—save that strange luminous shadows lingered in the lofty vaulting of the nave.

After the high altar, the most brilliant spot was the altar of Saint Joseph, in the west transept; beside which was a magnificent crèche, the figures half life-size, beautifully modeled and richly clothed. But there was nothing whimsical about this crèche: the group might have been, and very possibly had been, composed after a well-painted «Nativity» by some artist of the late Renaissance.

The mass was the customary office; but at

[1] See page 262.

[2] See page 181.

the offertory it was interrupted by a ceremony that gave it suddenly an entirely medieval cast, of which I felt more fully the beauty, and the strangeness in our time, because the Vidame sedulously had guarded against my having knowledge of it in advance. This was nothing less than a living rendering of the adoration of the shepherds, done with a simplicity to make one fancy the figures in Ghirlandajo's picture were alive again and stirred by the very spirit that animated them when they were set on canvas four hundred years ago.

By some means only a little short of a miracle, a way was opened through the dense crowd along the center of the nave from the door to the altar, and up this way with their offerings real shepherds came—the quaintest procession that anywhere I have ever seen. In the lead were four musicians, playing upon the tambourin, the galoubet, the very small cymbals called *palets*, and the bagpipe-like *carlamuso;* and then, two by two, came ten shepherds wearing the long, brown, full cloaks, weather-stained and patched and mended, which seem always to have come down through many generations and which never by any chance are new; carrying tucked beneath their arms their battered felt hats browned, like their cloaks, by long warfare with sun and rain; holding in one hand a lighted candle and in the other a staff. The two leaders, dispensing with staves and candles, bore garlanded baskets; one filled with fruit—melons, pears, apples, and grapes—and in the other a pair of doves, which with sharp, quick motions turned their heads from side to side as they gazed wonderingly on their strange surroundings with their bright, beautiful eyes.

Following came the main offering—a spotless lamb. Most originally, and in a way poetically, was this offering made. Drawn by a mild-faced ewe, whose fleece had been washed to a wonder of whiteness and who was decked out with bright-colored ribbons in a way to unhinge with vanity her sheepish mind, was a little two-wheeled cart—all garlanded with laurel and holly, and bedizened with knots of ribbon and pink paper roses and glittering little objects such as are hung on Christmas trees in other lands. Lying in the cart placidly, not bound and not in the least frightened, was the dazzlingly white lamb, decked like the ewe with knots of ribbon and wearing about its neck a red collar brilliant to behold. Now and then the ewe would turn to look at it, and in response to one of these wistful maternal glances the little creature stood up shakily on its unduly long legs and gave an anxious baa. But when a shepherd bent over and stroked it gently, it was reassured; lying down contentedly again in its queer little car of triumph, and thereafter through the ceremony remaining still.

Behind the car came ten more shepherds, and in their wake a long double line of country-folk, each with a lighted candle in hand. There is difficulty, indeed, in keeping this part of the demonstration within bounds, because it is esteemed an honor and a privilege to walk in the procession of the offered lamb.

Slowly this strange company moved toward the altar, where the ministering priest awaited its coming; and at the altar steps the bearers of the fruit and the doves separated, so that the little cart might come between them and their offering be made complete, while the other shepherds formed a semicircle in the rear. The music was stilled, and the priest accepted and set upon the altar the baskets; and then extended the paten that the shepherds, kneeling, might kiss it in token of their offering of the lamb. This completed the ceremony. The tambourin and galoubet and palets and carlamuso all together struck up again, and the shepherds and the lamb's car passed down the nave between the files of candle-bearers and so out through the door.

Within the last sixty years or so this naïve ceremony has fallen more and more into disuse. But it still occasionally is revived—as at Barbentane in 1868, and Rognonas in 1894, and repeatedly within the last decade in the sheep-raising parish of Maussane—by a curé who is at one with his flock in a love for the customs of ancient times. Its origin assuredly goes back far into antiquity; so very far, indeed, that the airs played by the musicians in the procession seem by comparison quite of our own time: yet tradition ascribes the composition of these airs to the good King René, whose happy rule over Provence ended more than four centuries ago.

## XVI.

WHEN the stir caused by the coming and going of the shepherds had subsided, the mass went on, with no change from the usual observance, until the sacrament was administered, save that there was a vigorous singing of noëls. It was congregational singing of a very enthusiastic sort,—indeed, nothing short of gagging every one of them could have kept those song-loving Provençaux still,—but it was led by the choir, and choristers took the solo parts. The most notable number was the famous noël in which the crowing of a cock alternates with the note of a nightingale; each verse beginning with a prodigious cock-a-doodle-d-o-o! and then rattling along to the gayest of gay airs. The nightingale was not a brilliant success; but the cock-crowing was so realistic that at its first outburst I thought that a genuine barnyard gallant was up in the organ-loft. I learned later that this was a musical *tour de force* for which the organist was famed. A buzz of delight filled the church after each cock-crowing volley; and I fancy that I was alone in finding anything odd in so jaunty a performance within church walls. The viewpoint in regard to such matters is of race and education. The Provençaux, who are born laughing, are not necessarily irreverent because even in sacred places they sometimes are frankly gay.

Assuredly, there was no lack of seemly decorum when the moment came for the administration of the sacrament, which rite on Christmas eve is reserved to the women, the men communing on Christmas day. The women who were to partake—nearly all who were present—wore the Provençal costume, but of dark color. Most of them were in black, save for the white *chapelle*, or kerchief, and the scrap of white which shows above the ribbon confining the knotted hair. But before going up to the altar each placed upon her head a white gauze veil, so long and so ample that her whole person was enveloped in its soft folds; and the women were so many, and their action was with such sudden unanimity, that in a moment a delicate mist seemed to have fallen and spread its silvery whiteness over all the throng.

Singly and by twos and threes these palely gleaming figures moved toward the altar, until more than a hundred of them were crowded together before the sanctuary rail. Nearest to the rail, being privileged to commune before the rest, stood a row of black-robed sisters—teachers in the parish school—whose somber habits made a vigorous line of black against the dazzle of the altar, everywhere aflame with candles, and by contrast gave to all that sweep of lustrous misty whiteness a splendor still softer and more strange. And within the rail the rich vestments of the ministering priests, and the rich cloths of the altar, all in a flood of light, added a warm color-note of gorgeous tones.

Slowly the rite went on. Twenty at a time the women, kneeling, ranged themselves at the rail, rising to give room to others when they had partaken, and so returning to their seats. For a full half-hour those pale, lambent figures were moving ghost-like about the church, while the white-veiled throng before the altar gradually diminished until at last it disappeared, fading from sight a little at a time, softly, as dream-visions of things beautiful melt away.

Presently came the benediction, and all together we streamed out from the brightness of the church into the wintry darkness, being by that time well into Christmas morning, and the moon gone down. But when we had left behind us the black streets of the little town, and were come out into the open country, the star-haze sufficed to light us as we went onward by the windings of the spectral white road; for the stars shine very gloriously in Provence.

We elders kept together staidly, as became the gravity of our years; but the young people, save two of them, frolicked on ahead and took again with a will to singing noëls; and from afar we heard through the night stillness, sweetly, other home-going companies singing these glad Christmas songs. Lingering behind us, following slowly, came Esperit and Magali, to whom that Christmas-tide had brought a lifetime's happiness. They did not join in the joy-songs, nor did I hear them talking. The fullest love is still.

And peace and good-will were with us as we went along the white way homeward beneath the Christmas morning stars.

*Thomas A. Janvier.*

## DOUBT.

I.

THOU Christ, my soul is hurt and bruised;
With words the scholars wear me out:
Brain of me weary and confused,—
Thee, and myself, and all I doubt.

II.

And must I back to darkness go
Because I cannot say their creed?
I know not what I think; I know
Only that thou art what I need.

*R.*

# ONE MAN WHO WAS CONTENT.

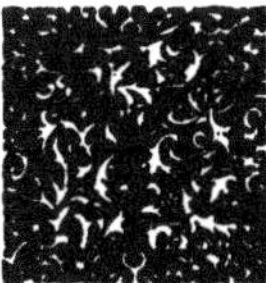

OU, a young man, have asked me, an old man, to tell you something of my private life, because you think that I may thus assist your understanding of life in general. You say that I have had a great public career, honorable as well as influential and prolonged, and that I have lived in this without family ties or intimate social habitudes, yet seeming to possess a contented spirit. Has my contentment, you inquire, been but the natural, predicable result of the labors and successes which the eye of the world has seen, or has it sprung from another source? Has it been identical with happiness? Do I think, indeed, that true happiness is within men's reach; and if it is, what is the true secret of its acquisition?

As best I can, I shall try to answer your questions. That is, I shall try to paint my own portrait, believing that the record of any life, even if briefly given, must contain the germs of instructiveness. But I beg you not to draw too many general inferences from a single sequence of facts and feelings. When we say many men, we mean many temperaments no less than many minds. Each temperament puts its own interpretation and its own valuation upon the thing we call success, and aspires to its own ideal of contentment, of happiness; and therefore the philosophies formulated, tested, and approved by any one man may have small value for another, except as prompting the development of a creed of a very different kind.

I.

When I was a lad there were two things which I felt I should require of life, and as I grew older I knew that they were indeed the things which I should try to obtain from life. I desired the love of a woman, and I desired the power to sway the thoughts and deeds of men.

I already possessed health, vigor, and good looks, an excellent social standing, and much money. I valued them all, but mainly as means toward the compassing of my chief aims, and no lesser aims divided my aspirations. I had traveled enough to blunt the edge of curiosity and to open my mind for the comprehension of our own and other lands, and I was willing to travel no more. Idleness wearied me, and pleasure, in the vulgar sense, did not appeal to me. Knowledge of all sorts seemed desirable, of course, but as a help along my path, not as its goal. And literature, music, art, converse with agreeable men and charming women—these I prized as I prized sleep, as inestimable sources of refreshment. But even if any by-paths had seemed more attractive than chanced to be the case, I should have been willing to concentrate and to limit myself, and to deny myself in many directions, if only I might attain the twin summits which were the Delectable Mounts of my imagination.

These, however, were not the mole-hills which bear their names in the imagination of most mortals. Many men take wives, find them useful and pleasing, never regret their choice, and call themselves happy at home; and many achieve conspicuous station, are counted influential and even powerful, and feel satisfied abroad. But I wanted, in my outer life, to stand on the very top of whichsoever ladder I might choose to climb, with no man standing higher. And in my inner life I wanted to sound the deepest seas of human emotion; I wanted to be justified in feeling, no matter what I might hear or read of the potency and joy of love, «This I have experienced, and it did not vanish like a morning cloud; this, the most that any man has known of love, I too have known, and not as a dream, but as a truth and a fact.»

Among the many paths which may lead toward public influence I chose the political path, and as its best beginning I selected the practice of the law. I had a good opening in my native town (one of the most important towns in an important State), and made diligent use of all its opportunities. I won the confidence of my fellow-townsmen and the notice of a much wider circle, and before I was thirty I had achieved political place and a prominence which seemed to guarantee political progress of a rapid and creditable kind. And then I met the woman who became my wife.

Of course I had not been able to work toward her discovery as I had worked toward the accomplishment of my other aim in life. For the chance to find her I had been obliged to rely upon the graciousness of fate. Yet I had felt that here, too, at least in passive ways, I might give fate assistance. I had kept the image of the woman whom I should love, and the hope of its incarnation, always fresh and clear in my mind, and had held myself safe from all entanglements which might prevent my claiming her when she should appear, or make my perception of her advent less than instantaneously vivid. But, at the same time, I had never allowed myself to picture, as the woman whom I must have, a woman who must be of this or that particular type, physically, mentally, emotionally, or even morally. Somewhere, I believed, there lived a woman who had been planned and made and meant for me, and some day I should find her and know her, own her, and be content in her possession. But I had seen too much of men's loves and marriages, as compared with their schemes for love and marriage, to think that any one may predict what kind of woman will eventually take him captive; and I did not wish to prepare a disappointment for myself, or a need to reconstruct a shattered ideal. So I did not venture to affirm that the woman of my love must be well born, or beautiful, or very amiable, or very intellectual. I did not ask myself whether she should be intensely or but delicately responsive to my passion. And I did not insist to myself that she must be ignorant of life's dangers, or even so wholly innocent of life's plausible mistakes that our one-sided and hypocritical conventionalities would grant her right to be called unimpeachably virtuous. How was I to know with what special qualities of person, mind, or soul might be bound up the spirit which should prove to be my spirit's mate? How was I to guess through what pleasant paths of quietude, ease, and virtue, or along what fiery ways of temptation and misfortune, fate might see fit to conduct this spirit ere we should be allowed to meet? I believed that, in the essence of her nature, the woman of my love would be good, as goodness is defined by the wise gods in heaven, and by truly wise men and women upon earth. If, in addition, she should have a past without mistakes, it would be well. But it would also be well if she should have a past to be redeemed; my knowledge of this fact would be only a part of the price I should be willing to pay for the best blessing that life could bring me.

As I have said, I found the woman for whom I was waiting. I married her, and I was content. It matters not who she was. It matters not what she was. If I should try to describe her, I could make no one understand; and if I could, I would not take the trouble. None are living now who knew her. She belongs to the past—to the grave and to me. It is enough that she was made for me, and I for her, and that we found each other and were content.

After my marriage my outward activities went on almost as before. There was room enough in my life, I thought, for two great and satisfying things—for love and work, for emotion and ambition. I believed that I was savoring them to the full, and I wanted nothing else. Every moment that I could spare from my work I devoted to my wife; every thought that I could tear away from my love I bestowed on my career; and I was entirely happy. The present gave me all that I asked of it, and the future seemed convincingly to promise all that I hoped from it. I had actually achieved full success, I thought, in one direction, and I saw it shining before me in the other; and so I said to myself, «Some men have failed in life, but not I; and I have wanted more than most men desire.»

## II.

THEN, at the end of a year, there came a sudden shock, a crisis, and a radical change of existence. My wife was very ill; for a while her recovery seemed hopeless, and I stood in the center of a black and reeling world, conscious of little and sure of nothing except an enormous agony which wrenched and tore and sickened every fiber of my body as well as of my soul. After a time a little light dawned, the earth grew steadier beneath my feet, and once again I could see, although as in a glass darkly, that there were other men in the world besides myself, other things besides my pain. In the reaction I thought that the shining of the perfect day was to come again. But it was not so. I was told:

«She will live, and she may live for many years. But all will depend upon you—upon what you do with her, and what you do for her. Here she cannot remain. Her former existence she cannot resume. She must be taken away from cities and their physical strains, and from active lives and their mental strains. For a time, and probably until the end, she must live where nature can minister to her body and soul, and where love can give all its strength to the tendance of her mind and heart; where she will be watched and fostered like a delicate vine; and, above all, where she will have nothing to think about but the mere fact of pleasurable living: no hopes, or cares, or responsibilities, personal or vicarious; nothing new to expect, and therefore nothing to fear beyond the wholly inescapable accidents of mortality. It is not merely that her frame is exquisitely frail. Her reason hangs by a thread, and only absolute peace, physical and mental, can preserve it for her and for you.»

At first I understood no more than the blessed fact that I might save her. But soon I began to realize that this saving would mean the cutting away of one half of my own existence. Yet, of course, I did not stop to choose; I did not even think of choosing. There was only one thing to do—to begin the task of rescue. I found a new home in a distant part of the country, where nature was beautiful and soothing, and where there sounded no reverberation from the struggles of mankind. There we began our new life, and there I wrestled with myself to put the old behind me, with its fullness of satisfaction and its richer fullness of promise.

I wrestled with myself, but not to find mere resignation. This has never seemed to me a virtue. To say «I am resigned» is to acknowledge defeat at the hands of life, to accept it, and in passive endurance to give up the fight for happiness. A brave soul cannot do this, because it would be ashamed; and a wise soul cannot, because it feels that, as it must continue in the world, simple common sense commands it to gather all of good that the world may still present. To dwell in resignation is to look forward with nothing more than patience. But the brave man, the wise man, holds to his birthright of hope, and looks forward to a time when, although he does not yet understand the way, in some sure way he will reconquer and reëstablish contentment. He does not accept defeat at the hands of life; he merely accepts the fact that one of his weapons has been wrested from him. He does not sink into a resigned surrender, but rises to a determined renunciation, and sharpens the blades of the weapons which he still retains. He resolves to readjust himself to life's new denials and demands. If needs must, he will curtail his ambitions or change them entirely, but he will not consent to live unpricked by any spur. He will conceive of happiness in a different shape, but will not agree to its elimination. If his old existence is shattered he will mold a scheme for a new one, and will mold himself over into a new creature fitted to draw contentment from it. He will not be dominated by fate. He will say to fate: «Take away what you choose, and still I shall not be denuded; do your worst, and still I shall not be defeated; still I shall be successful, for still I shall find something to desire which I shall be able to secure.»

These were the things that I said to myself in our new home, out under the warm stars at night, and looking from my window at the cool blue dawning of the day. And gradually I did what I thought that a man should do: I reconquered contentment. I put my past quite out of my mind, with all that it implied for the future in regard to a public career. I formed a new present and a new future with the elements of existence that were left me, and again I was happy, in a different and, you may say, in a narrower manner, yet really happy again. That which had been one of my two aims in life—the development and enjoyment of a deep affection—was now my only aim. But now I felt that it might suffice to fill the whole horizon of my life, for the menacing hand of death had emphasized its value; and for such fragments of time and thought as it could not absorb I found a novel use.

I determined to see what pleasure and profit could be drawn from mental exercise, pursued for its own sole sake. I framed this resolve with a clear conscience, knowing that practical work for the benefit of others was no longer possible; and with a lively hope, remembering how many men in all ages of the world had acted upon a like resolve with infinite gratification. Out in our wilderness books were of course my only helpers; but in them I sought for guides to philosophic thought, for clues to the understanding of human life, alike in its broadly historical and its intimately personal phases, and for springs of more purely esthetic enjoyment.

Soon these new aspirations and resources became established ambitions and satisfying habits; my days grew full, and my soul regained the sense that it possessed what it desired. Then I discovered that, if we fight any battle well, victory may have an unanticipated richness. I discovered that a new chance to gain the power for which I once had longed might be born of my very determination to abandon its pursuit. I found myself looking forward again to a day when I might influence the minds of men, not, as I once had hoped, through spoken words and overt acts, but through books which should make manifest the lessons I was learning from experience, and from the novel exercise of my powers of abstract thought.

First among the lessons which experience taught me came a knowledge of the difference between things that we have lost—lost through our own fault or weakness—and those that have merely been taken from us; between things that have turned to dust in our grasp and those that we have merely been compelled to lay away in the dust of that grave which is called renunciation. To let slip what we prize, or to find that it disappoints us—this is failure; and the memory of failure must sadden, even if it does not blacken, every day we have still to live. But to have what we prize taken away by fate, and to feel that, if we could have retained it always, it would never have disappointed us—this is not failure. It is only deprivation. And though deprivation must sadden the days which follow it closely, it need not blacken them, and it need not even sadden the days of a farther future. Nay, it irradiates these as soon as we learn to picture our life, not as it would have been if we could have kept our ravished treasures, but as it would have been if we had never possessed them. The past is as much a part of our lives as the present or the future, and in one way it is the very best part, for fate can lay no blighting finger upon it. When we realize this, then the joy of having had grows more to us day by day. Those who have had, and have been deprived, are fools or weaklings if they think of themselves as the true types of sorrow. Fate's cruelest work is not the pain of deprivation, but the consciousness that this pain has been escaped because of a lifelong poverty. In a sense Rachel must always go mourning for her children; but unless she is deplorably feeble in spirit, she does not bestow upon herself the same deep pity that she gives to women who have never borne a child. And as in a Rachel's later life may dwell, radiant and comforting, proud memories of her stalwart sons, so eventually the high ambitions of my early years took their place in mine. They had been slain, but through no fault of my own. I believed that they would never have disappointed me if they had been allowed to live; and therefore I still could say that, even in this direction, fate had not defrauded or denuded me.

This was one truth that I perceived in our new home—the beautiful truth that *having had* means *having* until the end of our days. And as my time and thoughts were more and more absorbed by the great passion which still played a living part in my existence, a second great truth was as distinctly learned. I saw that only by giving ourselves up wholly to one powerful feeling can its profoundest depths be sounded; I saw that I had made a great mistake when I thought, in our old home, that I knew the woman whom I loved, and lived in close communion with her, and fully grasped the meaning of mutual affection. Now, day by day and month by month, her health improved, and my fear that she might be taken from me vanished away. The threatened mental trouble had had a purely physical cause, and as her body strengthened, her mind grew calm and steady, and in our days of constant intellectual exercise progressed step by step with mine. Community in action, in interests, thoughts, emotions, could not be closer between man and woman, between any soul and any other soul, than it now became between my wife and me in our peaceful, our isolated yet populous twin solitude. And as this community (not to be achieved except in such a solitude) deepened and broadened, grew more intense, and at the same time more delicate and subtile, so it was, concordantly, with the love upon which at first it had been founded. From the first I had thought this a perfect love, but now I recognized a change—not as from a river-bed scantily filled to one that was fully filled, but as from a river brimming with pure water when it was small to the same stream spreading out and growing more profound, and keeping full to the edge meanwhile, until it became a king among the streams of the earth. Then I realized that, in truth, there could never have been time and room enough in my life, or in any life, for the tender, constant nourishing which alone can ripen the richest harvest of human love, and for the strenuous pursuit of any active outside aim. By the sacrifice of my coming success in a public career I had bought, and in the only possible way, complete success of that other sort which from the first I had counted equally desirable.

### III.

For seven years we lived on thus in our new home, until I almost forgot that I had ever been a man of a different kind, leading a life of a different temper; until the day when, without an hour of warning, without a word or a cry of farewell, the woman I loved was taken from me. The world did not again grow black to my vision and unsteady beneath my feet. It grew silent, still, and pallid, every feature of it clearly visible, but without meaning, value, or life—a world of stone, in the center of which I sat, a figure of stone. The suddenness and the hopelessness of this second shock left me paralyzed. Only, I had still the power to know that I was paralyzed, and to feel the horror of it, and mingled with this a dreadful fear of the greater horror of the time when my nerves and sinews should again begin to perform their work. I sat as though weighed upon by a weight of a million tons; and I held my breath, conscious that if I tried to move it would bring me a keener sense of the burden. I sat as in a dream, and a dream of agony unendurable; I knew that the dream was fact, and that the agony had to be endured; but I tried, by keeping passive, dumb, and rigid, to preserve as long as I could the semi-semblance of unreality.

Whether, in this paralyzed, icy, shuddering mood which came over me when I saw that the woman I loved was dead, I suffered more or suffered less than in the mood of hot and blinding terror which had enwrapped me, seven years before, when I was told that she would die, this I cannot say. Who is to compare and appraise the extremes of different tortures, as of burnings by fire and of tearings with surgeons' tools? Hope, of course, had been intermixed with fear in the first tormenting, while in the second there was nothing but despair. Yet I do not know which was worse, the sudden plunging from hope into terror, or the deadly persistence of blank desperation. Who, indeed, can decide which is more awful—a hell of intermittent flames, or one that is sheathed in steadily grinding ice? No man. Not even the man who has gone down for a time into the heart of the one and the other.

Just how soon I cannot remember, but slowly I came up out of hell, through the anguish of awakening sensibility, into a living world, yet a world of arctic solitude. And once again I went out under the stars of night and into the dawnings of days, to take needful counsel with myself.

It was the same struggle once again, harder, bitterer, grimmer, and now to be fought out alone, yet the same in kind. Not to be cowardly and not to be reasonless—this seemed again the great commandment; to refuse to be defeated, and to refuse to let aught that remained of good in the world slip through a nerveless hand. And the great help seemed again the vitality of remembrance, the fact that what we have once possessed is our own for ever and ever. For eight years I had possessed a woman whom I loved with a fullness to which few lovers can ever have attained. Should I, therefore, through all my future years feel myself more miserable than men who had never loved? Was I more lonely to-day than they? If all the years of my life had been as the years of theirs, should I to-day be sitting in the ashes of despair? And if not, why should I consent to dwell among them in that actual to-day which was glorified by the radiance of the words, *Lo, I have had?* Lonely I was indeed, yet I could look back into chambers of intimate companionship unimaginable by the average human heart. Surely the windows of these chambers would always stand open; their light would always continue to shine from behind me along my darkened path; and that path might again be made to lead through valleys of renunciation out upon uplands where the sun of contentment should rise once more.

These are the thoughts upon which I pondered in my second and far more terrible need, when not merely one half of my life, but much more than one half of my very self, seemed to have been lopped away. I laid them diligently to my torn and fainting soul, I strengthened myself upon them, and I began to act as they bade me. Of course I went forth into the active world again. As before, I would have no commerce with resignation, with passive patience. I wanted to learn again to renounce and then again to achieve, to possess. I wanted to fill again, as fully as I could, the vacant spaces in my mind and soul, not to sit alone and learn to endure the prospect of my vacant heart. I summoned back my old ambitions, my old desires for a great public career; and they came, grayly, unalluringly at first, but soon with an increasing charm of genuine interest and hope. I went forth into the world again, back to my native State. Not again to my native town—that I could not have borne. But I believed that, even after seven years, in the capital of my State, where I had sat for a while in the legislative body, there would still be some to remember me, to welcome me, and to help me to a new place and a new chance.

This proved to be the truth, and I threw myself again into legal and political life. I worked with extraordinary diligence, for I had an extraordinary task before me. I had a void to fill such as few men can even faintly picture. I knew that I should never reach the frame of mind which is called forgetting, and not for an instant did I wish to reach it: that would have meant assisting fate to denude and defraud me. But neither did I wish remembrance to surge forever uppermost in my mind: that would have meant assisting fate to conquer me. And only by working with all the force of all my faculties during all the hours that I did not need for sleep and for vigorous bodily exercise, could I keep the blood of my wounded heart from flooding and drowning the brain upon which alone I could now rely to win me back the sense that it was worth my while to be alive.

But this sense did come back to me. The ambition which I had encouraged as a possible panacea became a palatable food, and then an intoxicating draught; and the labor it prescribed crowded out of my thoughts all envy of other men, all need for other occupations, all desire for what are called amusements—everything except a deep and solid fund of memories, to which I turned a hundred times a day with pride, with comfort, yes, and with actual joy, and of which I was always proudly, joyfully conscious, even when my definite thoughts were concerned with alien things. Again I prospered, became well known and well esteemed, and was chosen for public place and honor. And step by step I passed from the council-chambers of my city and my State into those of the nation's capital.

You know what my record in this capital has been. You know the conspicuous part I played throughout the War of the Rebellion and the distracted years that followed; and you know how, in later, quieter, but not less critical years, my influence has deepened and expanded. Many believe that at one time I aspired to higher chairs and titles than those which I have held so long: but this is not true; my ambition was then fully satisfied. I was content to possess the substance of power, and cared nothing for its signs. I preferred great usefulness to the exalted station which may often limit personal endeavor, and valued personal freedom more than the high prerogatives which must often express the will of other men. And these feelings have never changed. No man in my party has, for as long a time, been as influential as I. None has owed his influence more entirely to his personal qualities, his individual force. None, I believe, has exerted it in more beneficent ways. And thus, as mine has been the party in power and place, no man has stood higher than I upon the ladder which very long ago I resolved to climb.

Did this success make me happy again? Yes; if happiness means the feeling that life is well worth having; if it means contentment with life, gratitude for life, an eager desire that, just as it stands, life may be prolonged. Bitter and but dimly hopeful days I knew during many months after the death of my wife, and sad and isolated hours I have often counted since. Indeed, ever and always since her death I have lived alone. Yet my soul has not been lonely, because it has perpetually communed with satisfying recollections. For many years there has not been a night when I have gone to my bed unthankful for the day's experience set against the shining background of a vanished but still living past; and there have been few mornings when I have awakened feeling less than glad that a new day was breaking. I have enjoyed the doing of my work in all its phases. And I have rested from it in the cheering sense that it has been important work well done, that more of it will always be waiting to be done, and that back in the past, safe beyond peradventure, lies garnered that other rare success, that other inestimable joy, for which in my youth my soul cried out.

## IV.

When I reflect upon this strenuous part of my life, I see that the lessons it has taught me are the same that I had already learned in my seven years of dual solitude. It has reiterated the hard yet bracing truths that if we would be strong we must concentrate our strength, and that our full development may sometimes be attained only through the elimination of some precious element from our lives. But it has also accentuated the beautiful, the consoling truth that things eliminated are not things destroyed. With a wife at my side whose love I wished to retain and enjoy, I could never have thrown myself into a public career with the energy which, I now perceive, was needed to insure me high success. Nor, again, could I have compassed this energy had I never possessed my wife; the full development of all my powers required the anguish of deprivation, leaving behind it a huge void which I could not permit to remain unfilled. On the other hand, such intensities of solitary labor would not have been endurable ungilded by the memory of the companionship I had once enjoyed. And, of course, my power to rule the minds and deeds of men has been largely the result of the years of enforced seclusion which enlightened and disciplined my own mind, and gave me control of the written and the spoken word. The books about life which I then foresaw have never been produced; but their substance has gone into my personal activity, and through this into the thinking and doing of many thousands of my fellows.

You may say that other men, although urged by less insistent goads than I, and forced less sternly to a concentration of their strength, have equaled or surpassed me in achievement. But I think this merely means that, with a fiercer pressure of some sort, they might have gone still farther and done still better. All success is reducible to terms of power, and there is no limit to possible power. No man has ever had so much that we cannot imagine him as having more. And, I believe, most men who have paid lightly for their share of power would have acquired a larger share if, in one way or another, fate had asked as heavy a price from them as from me. I feel that I have indeed been successful, not because I have done all that with my chances a man might do, but because I have done absolutely all that with my abilities was possible to me.

This, then, is the source of my contented spirit—the feeling that all my sufferings, all my struggles, have been worth while. And this is the source of my happiness—the sense that I have really lived the life of a man; that I have wanted and obtained, aspired and realized, possessed and enjoyed, fought with my special fate and gained the victory. Some men, I am aware, may be of a different temper; I am only trying to paint myself. All I wish is to explain that the bitterest possible hour for me would have been an hour which convinced me that I had never possessed, never achieved, and that now it was too late to hope.

Does all this imply that I can look back upon my days and say that, as fate decreed them for me, so I would have decreed them for myself if with open eyes I could have determined their course? Naturally, my soul protested and revolted while the two great crises of my life were passing. But afterward? During my seven years of satisfied affection, could I honestly have affirmed that I was glad my early scheme of existence had been shattered? Or would I have turned back eagerly to that scheme if I had felt it again consistent with the welfare of the woman whom I loved? And during my later years would I have abandoned my career of public usefulness to regain this woman? Or could I say that I was truly content that she had died?

Sometimes I have asked these questions of myself. But the only answer has been an immense feeling of relief that to questions such as they we are never obliged to frame replies. And from this feeling of relief has sprung the knowledge that, after all, the best features of human life are those commonly declared to be its worst. We rebel because we are supplied with the materials from which we must develop success and evolve contentment—because the brute clay of existence and the helpful straw are alike apportioned to us, and in measures which, from day to day, we cannot foresee; and we lament because, once our bricks are made, it is impossible to improve them. But even thus, and even when our dole of straw is very small, we are still far better off than we should be in a world where we were bidden to select, as well as utilize, both the clay and the straw. Curse as we may the force called fate, it is the only force which could make our impotence effective. If we could look forward and control our opportunities, or if we could look backward and believe that anything might have been which actually has not been, then, indeed, the unborn might be afraid of birth.

Yes, rebel and lament as we may, the best elements in our lives are the protecting invisibility of the future and the justifying inevitableness of the past. It is really because of these that almost all men can endure to live. And I, for one, am content to have lived, I am glad to have lived, even though it has been with often aching hands beneath a burning sky; for I have molded many bricks and have built them into beautiful and serviceable walls. I envy no man who has sat unbruised in one of the world's dimmer, cooler, idler corners, waiting for death to show him some justification for his record of empty days.

*M. G. Van Rensselaer.*

## ABASHED.

STRAIGHT at the noonday summer sun
I dared to gaze unflinching as an eagle might;
Then sudden ceased, my powers undone:
With down-dropt eyelids and in shame,
I fancied the Eternal Flame
Of Justice thus my sinful soul should pierce and blight.

*Clifford Westmore Lake.*

## «THEM OLD CHEERY WORDS.»

PAP he allus ust to say,
  «Chris'mus comes but onc't a year!»
Liked to hear him that-a-way,
  In his old split-bottomed cheer
By the fireplace here at night—
Wood all in, and room all bright,
Warm and snug, and folks all here:
«Chris'mus comes but onc't a year!»

Me and Lize, and Warr'n and Jess
  And Eldory home fer two
Weeks' vacation; and, I guess,
  Old folks tickled through and through,
Same as we was,—«Home onc't more
Fer another Chris'mus—shore!»
Pap 'u'd say, and tilt his cheer,
«Chris'mus comes but onc't a year!»

Mostly pap was ap' to be
  Ser'ous in his «daily walk,»
As he called it; giner'ly
  Was no hand to joke er talk.
Fac's is, pap had never be'n
Rugged-like at all—and then
Three years in the army had
Hepped to break him purty bad.

Never flinched, but frost and snow
  Hurt his wound in winter. But
You bet mother knowed it, though:
  Watched his feet, and made him putt
On his flannen; and his knee,
Where it never healed up, he
Claimed was «well now—mighty near—
Chris'mus comes but onc't a year!»

«Chris'mus comes but onc't a year!»
  Pap 'u'd say, and snap his eyes.
Row o' apples sputter'n' here
  Round the hearth, and me and Lize
Crackin' hicker'-nuts; and Warr'n
And Eldory parchin' corn;
And whole raft o' young folks here.
«Chris'mus comes but onc't a year!»

Mother tuk most comfert in
  Jest a-heppin' pap. She 'd fill
His pipe fer him, er his tin
  O' hard cider; er set still
And read fer him out the pile
O' newspapers putt on file
Whilse he was with Sherman. (She
Knowed the whole war history!)

Sometimes he 'd git het up some.
  «Boys,» he 'd say, «and you girls, too,
Chris'mus is about to come;
  So, as you 've a right to do,
Celebrate it! Lots has died,
Same as Him they crucified,
That you might be happy here.
Chris'mus comes but onc't a year!»

. . . .

Missed his voice last Chris'mus—missed
  Them old cheery words, you know.
Mother helt up tel she 'd kissed
  All of us—then had to go
And break down! And I laughs: «Here!
‹Chris'mus comes but onc't a year!›»
«Them 's his very words,» sobbed she,
«When he asked to marry me.»

«Chris'mus comes but onc't a year!»
  «Chris'mus comes but onc't a year!»
Over, over, still I hear,
  «Chris'mus comes but onc't a year!»
Yit, like him, I 'm goin' to smile
And keep cheerful all the while;
Allus Chris'mus there—and here
«Chris'mus comes but onc't a year!»

*James Whitcomb Riley.*

# FOR VALUE RECEIVED.

BY THE AUTHOR OF «STORIES OF THE FOOT-HILLS,» ETC.

A SOFT yellow haze lay over the San Jacinto plain, deepening into purple where the mountains lifted themselves against the horizon. Nancy Watson stood in her cabin door, and held her bony, moistened finger out into the tepid air.

«I believe there 's a little breath of wind from the southeast, Robert,» she said, with a desperate hopefulness; «but the air does n't feel rainy.»

«Oh, I guess the rains 'll come along all right; they gener'ly do.» The man's voice was husky and weak. «Anyway, the barley 'll hold its own quite a while yet.»

«Oh, yes; quite a long while,» acquiesced his wife, with an eager, artificial stress on the adjective. «I don't care much if the harvest is n't earlier 'n usual; I want you to pick up your strength.» She turned into the room, a strained smile twitching her weather-stained face. She was glad Robert's bed was in the farthest corner away from the window. The barley-field that stretched about the little redwood cabin was a pale yellowish green, deeper in the depressions, and fading almost into brown on the hillocks. There had been heavy showers late in October, and the early-sown grain had sprouted. It was past the middle of November now, and the sky was of that serene, cloudless California blue which is like a perpetual smiling denial of any possibility of rain.

«Is the barley turning yellow any?» queried the sick man, feebly.

Nancy hesitated.

«Oh, not to speak of,» she faltered, swallowing hard.

Her husband was used to that gulping sob in her voice when she stood in the door. There was a little grave on the edge of the barley-field. He had put a bit of woven-wire fence about it to keep out the rabbits, and Nancy had planted some geraniums inside the small inclosure. There were some of the fiery blossoms in an old oyster-can at the head of the little mound, lifting their brilliant smile toward the unfeeling blue of the sky.

«There 's pretty certain to be late rains, anyway,» the man went on hoarsely. «Leech would let us have more seed if it was n't for the mortgage.» His voice broke into a strained whisper on the last word.

Nancy crossed the room, and laid her knotted hand on his forehead.

«You hain't got any fever to-day,» she said irrelevantly.

«Oh, no; I 'm gettin' on fine; I 'll be up in a day or two. The mortgage 'll be due next month, Nancy,» he went on, looking down at his thin gray hands on the worn coverlet; «I calc'lated they 'd hold off till harvest if the crop was comin' on all right.» He glanced up at her anxiously.

The woman's careworn face worked in a cruel, convulsive effort at self-control.

«It ain't right, Robert!» she broke out fiercely. «You 've paid more 'n the place is worth now; if they take it for what 's back, it ain't right!»

Her husband looked at her with pleading in his sunken eyes. He felt himself too weak for principles, hardly strong enough to cope with facts.

«But they ain't to blame,» he urged; «they lent me the money to pay Thomson. It was straight cash; I guess it 's all right.»

«There 's wrong somewhere,» persisted the woman, hurling her abstract justice recklessly in the face of the evidence. «If the place is worth more, you 've made it so workin' when you was n't able. If they take it now, I 'll feel like burnin' down the house and choppin' out every tree you 've planted!»

The man turned wearily on his pillow. His wife could see the gaunt lines of his unshaven neck. She put her hand to her aching throat and looked at him helplessly; then she turned and went back to the door. The barley *was* turning yellow. She looked toward the little grave on the edge of the field. More than the place was worth, she had said. What was it worth? Suppose they should take it. She drew her high shoulders forward and shivered in the warm air. The anger in her hard-featured face wrought itself into fixed lines. She recrossed the room, and sat down on the edge of the bed.

«How much is the mortgage, Robert?» she asked calmly. The sick man gave a sighing breath of relief, and drew a worn account-book from under his pillow.

«It 'll be $287.65, interest an' all, when it 's due,» he said, consulting his cramped figures. Each knew the amount perfectly well, but the feint of asking and telling eased them both.

«I 'm going down to San Diego to see them about it,» said Nancy; «I can't explain things in writing. There 's the money for the children's shoes; if the rains hold off they can go barefoot till Christmas. Mother can keep Lizzie out of school, and I guess Bobbie and Frank can 'tend to things outside.»

A four-year-old boy came around the house wailing out a grief that seemed to abate suddenly at sight of his mother. Nancy picked him up and held him in her lap while she took a splinter from the tip of his little grimy outstretched finger; then she hugged him almost fiercely, and set him on the door-step.

«What 's the matter with gramma's baby?» called an anxious voice from the kitchen.

«Oh, nothing, mother; he got a sliver in his finger; I just took it out.»

«He 's father's little soldier,» said Robert, huskily; «he ain't a-goin' to cry about a little thing like that.»

The little soldier sat on the door-step, striving to get his sobs under military discipline and contemplating his tiny finger ruefully.

An old woman came through the room with a white cloth in her hand.

«Gramma 'll tie it up for him,» she said soothingly, sitting down on the step, and tearing off a bandage wide enough for a broken limb. The patient heaved a deep sigh of content as the unwieldiness of the wounded member increased, and held his fat little fingers wide apart to accommodate the superfluity of rag.

«There, now,» said the old woman, rubbing his soft little gingham back fondly; «gramma 'll go and show him the turkeys.»

The two disappeared around the corner of the house, and the man and woman came drearily back to their conference.

«If you go, Nancy,» said Robert, essaying a wan smile, «I hope you 'll be careful what you say to 'em; you must remember they don't *think* they 're to blame.»

«I won't promise anything at all,» asserted Nancy, hitching her angular shoulders; «more 'n likely, I 'll tell 'em just what I think. I ain't afraid of hurtin' their feelin's, for they hain't got any. I think money 's a good deal like your skin: it keeps you from feelin' things that make you smart dreadfully when you get it knocked off.»

Robert smiled feebly, and rubbed his moist, yielding hand across his wife's misshapen knuckles.

«Well, then, you had n't ought to be hard on 'em, Nancy; it's no more 'n natural to want to save your skin,» he said, closing his eyes wearily.

«ROBERT WATSON?»

The teller of the Merchants' and Fruit-growers' Bank looked through the bars of his gilded cage, and repeated the name reflectively. He did not notice the eager look of the woman who confronted him, but he did wonder a little that she had failed to brush the thick dust of travel from the shoulders of her rusty cape.

The teller was a slender, immaculate young man, whose hair arose in an alert brush from his forehead, which was high and seemed to have been polished by the same process that had given such a faultless and aggressive gloss to his linen.

He turned on his spry little heel and stepped to the back of the inclosure, where he took a handful of long, narrow papers from a leather case, and ran over them hastily. Nancy did not think it possible that he could be reading them; the setting in his ring made a little streak of light as his fingers flew. She watched him with tense earnestness; it seemed to her that the beating of her heart shook the polished counter she leaned against. She hid her cotton-gloved hands under her cape for fear he would see how they trembled.

The teller returned the papers to their case, and consulted a stout, short-visaged man, whose lips and brow drew themselves together in an effort of recollection.

The two men stood near enough to hear Nancy's voice. She pressed her weather-beaten face close to the gilded bars.

«I 'm Mrs. Watson. I came down to see you about it; my husband 's been poorly and could n't come. We 'd like to get a little more time; we 've had bad luck with the barley so far, but we think we can make it another season.»

The men gave her a bland, impersonal attention.

«Yes?» inquired the teller, with tentative sympathy, running his pencil through his upright hair, and tapping his forefinger with it nervously. «I believe that 's one of Bartlett's personal matters,» he said in an undertone.

The older man nodded, slowly at first, and then with increasing affirmation.

«You 're right,» he said, untying the knot in his face, and turning away.

The teller came back to his place.

«Mr. Bartlett, the cashier, has charge of that matter, Mrs. Watson. He has not been down for two or three days: one of his children is very sick. I 'll make a note of it, however, and draw his attention to it when he comes in.» He wrote a few lines hurriedly on a bit of paper, and impaled it on an already overcrowded spindle.

«Can you tell me where he lives?» asked Nancy.

The young man hesitated.

«I don't believe I would go to the house; they say it 's something contagious—»

«I 'm not afraid,» interrupted Nancy, grimly.

The teller wrote an address, and slipped it toward her with a nimble motion, keeping his hand outstretched for the next comer, and smiling at him over Nancy's dusty shoulder.

The woman turned away, suddenly aware that she had been blocking the wheels of commerce, and made her way through the knot of men that had gathered behind her. Outside she could feel the sea in the air, and at the end of the street she caught a glimpse of a level blue plain with no purple mountains on its horizon.

Someway, the mortgage had grown smaller; no one seemed to care about it but herself. She had felt vaguely that they would be expecting her and have themselves steeled against her request. On the way from the station she had thought that people were looking at her curiously as the woman from «up toward Pinacate» who was about to lose her home on a mortgage. She had even felt that some of them knew of the little wire-fenced grave on the edge of the barley-field.

She showed the card to a boy at the corner, who pointed out the street and told her to watch for the number over the door.

«It is n't very far; 'bout four blocks up on the right-hand side. Yuh kin take the street-car fer a nickel, er yuh kin walk fi' cents cheaper,» he volunteered, whereupon an older boy kicked him affectionately, and advised him in a nauseated tone to «come off.»

Nancy walked along the smooth cement pavement, looking anxiously at the houses behind their sentinel palms. The vagaries of Western architecture conveyed no impression but that of splendor to her uncritical eye. The house whose number corresponded to the one on her card was less pretentious than some of the others, but the difference was lost upon her in the general sense of grandeur.

She went up the steps and rang the bell, with the same stifling clutch on her throat that she had felt in the bank. There was a little pause, and then the door opened, and Nancy saw a fragile, girl-like woman with a tear-stained face standing before her.

«Does Mr. Bartlett live here?» faltered the visitor, her chin trembling.

The young creature leaned forward like a flower wilting on its stem, and buried her face on Nancy's dusty shoulder.

«Oh, I 'm so glad to see you,» she sobbed; «I thought no one ever *would* come. I did n't know before that people were so afraid of scarlet fever. They have taken my baby away for fear he would take it. Do you know anything about it? Please come right in where she is, and tell me what you think.»

Nancy had put her gaunt arm around the girl's waist, and was patting her quivering shoulder with one cotton-gloved hand. Two red spots had come on her high cheek-bones, and her lips were working. She let herself be led across the hall into an adjoining room, where a yellow-haired child lay restless and fever-stricken. A young man with a haggard face came forward and greeted her eagerly. «Now, Flora,» he said, smoothing his wife's disordered hair, «you don't need to worry any more; we shall get on now. I 'm sure she 's a little better to-day; don't you think so?» He appealed to Nancy, wistfully.

«Yes; I think she is,» said Nancy, stoutly, moving her head in awkward defiance of her own words.

«There, Flora, that 's just what the doctor said,» pleaded the husband.

The young wife clung to the older woman desperately.

«Oh, do you think so?» she faltered. «You know, I never *could* stand it. She 's all—well, of course there 's the baby—but—oh—you see—you know—I never could bear it!» She broke down again, sobbing, with her arms about Nancy's neck.

«Yes, you can bear it,» said Nancy. «You can bear it if you have to, but you ain't a-goin' to have to—she 's a-goin' to get well. An' you 've got your man; you ought to recollect that»—she stifled a sob—«he seems well an' hearty.»

The young wife raised her head and looked at her husband with tearful scorn. He met her gaze meekly, with that ready self-effacement which husbands seem to feel in the presence of maternity.

«Have you two poor things been here all alone?» asked Nancy.

«Yes,» sobbed the girl-wife, this time on her husband's shoulder; «everybody was afraid,—we could n't get any one,—and I don't know anything. You 're the first woman I 've seen since—oh, it 's been *so* long!»

«Well, you 're all nervous and worn out and half starved,» announced Nancy, untying her bonnet-strings. «I 've had sickness, but I 've never been this bad off. Now, you just take care of the little girl, and I 'll take care of you.»

It was a caretaking like the sudden stilling of the tempest that came to the little household. The father and mother would not have said that the rest and order that pervaded the house, and finally crept into the room where the sick child lay, came from a homely woman with an ill-fitting dress and hard, knotted hands. To them she seemed the impersonation of beauty and peace on earth.

That night Nancy wrote to her husband. The letter was not very explicit, but limited expression seems to have its compensations. There are comparatively few misunderstandings among the animals that do not write at all. To Robert the letter seemed entirely satisfactory. This is what she wrote:

I have not had much time to see about the Morgage. One of their children is very sick and I will have to stay a few days. If the cough medisine gives out tell mother the directions is up by the Clock. I hope you are able to set up. Write and tell me how the Barley holds on. Tell the children to be good. Your loving wife,

NANCY WATSON.

«Nancy was always a great hand around where there 's sickness,» Robert commented to his mother-in-law. «I hope she won't hurry home if she 's needed.»

He wrote her to that effect the next day, very proud of his ability to sit up, and urging her not to shorten her stay on his account. «Ime beter and the Barly is holding its own,» he said, and Nancy found it ample.

«This Mrs. Watson you have is a treasure,» said the doctor to young Bartlett; «where did you find her?»

«Find her? I thought you sent her,» answered Bartlett, in a daze.

«No; I could n't find any one; I was at my wit's end.»

The two men stared at each other blankly.

«Well, it does n't matter where she came from,» said the doctor, «so she stays. She 's a whole relief corps and benevolent society in one.»

Young Bartlett spoke to Nancy about it the first time they were alone.

«Who sent you to us, Mrs. Watson?» he asked.

Nancy turned and looked out of the window. «Nobody sent me—I just came.»

Then she faced about.

«I don't want to deceive nobody. I come down from Pinacate to see you about some —some business. They told me at the bank that you was up at the house, so I come up. When I found how it was, I thought I 'd better stay—that 's all.»

«From Pinacate—about some business?» queried the puzzled listener.

«Yes; I did n't mean to say anything to you; I don't want to bother you about it when you 're in trouble an' all wore out. I told them down at the bank; they 'll tell you when you go down.» And with this the young man was obliged to be content.

It was nearly two weeks before the child was out of danger. Then Nancy said she must go home. The young mother kissed her tenderly when they parted.

«I 'm so sorry you can't stay and see the baby,» she said, with sweet young selfishness; «they 're going to bring him home very soon now. He 's *so* cute! Archie dear, go to the door with Mrs. Watson, and remember—» She raised her eyebrows significantly, and waited to see that her husband understood before she turned away.

The young man followed Nancy to the hall.

«How much do I owe— » He stopped, with a queer choking sensation in his throat.

Nancy's face flushed.

«I always want to be neighborly when there 's sickness,» she said; «'most anybody does. I hope you 'll get on all right now. Good-by.»

She held out her work-hardened hand, and the young man caught it in his warm, prosperous grasp. They looked into each other's eyes an instant, not the mortgager and the mortgagee, but the woman and the man.

«Good-by, Mrs. Watson. I can never—» The words died huskily in his throat.

«Papa,» called a weak, fretful little voice.

Nancy hitched her old cape about her high shoulders.

«Good-by,» she repeated, and turned away.

ROBERT leaned across the kitchen table, and held a legal document near the lamp.

«It 's marked ‹Satisfaction of mortgage› on the outside,» he said in a puzzled voice; «and it must be our mortgage, for it tells all about it inside; but it says,»—he unfolded the paper, and read from it in his slow, husky whisper,—«‹The debt—secured thereby—having been fully paid—satisfied—and discharged.› I don't see what it means.»

Nancy rested her elbows on the table, and looked across at him anxiously.

«It must be a mistake, Robert. I never said anything to them except that we 'd like to have more time.»

He went over the paper again carefully.

«It reads very plain,» he said. Then he fixed his sunken eyes on her thoughtfully. «Do you suppose, Nancy, it could be on account of what you done?»

«Me!» The woman stared at him in astonishment.

Suddenly Robert turned his eyes toward the ceiling, with a new light in his thin face.

«Listen!» he exclaimed breathlessly, «it 's raining!»

There was a swift patter of heralding drops, and then a steady, rhythmical drumming on the shake roof. The man smiled, with that ineffable delight in the music which no one really knows but the tiller of the soil.

Nancy opened the kitchen door and looked out into the night.

«Yes,» she said, keeping something out of her voice; «the wind 's strong from the southeast, and it 's raining steady.»

Nancy Watson always felt a little lonesome when it rained. She had never mentioned it, but she could not help wishing there was a shelter over the little grave on the edge of the barley-field.

*Margaret Collier Graham.*

# THE BLOSSOM OF THE SOUL.

THOU half-unfolded flower
  With fragrance-laden heart,
What is the secret power
  That doth thy petals part?
What gave thee most thy hue—
The sunshine, or the dew?

Thou wonder-wakened soul!
  As Dawn doth steal on Night
On thee soft Love hath stole.
  Thine eye, that blooms with light,
What makes its charm so new—
Its sunshine, or its dew?

*Robert Underwood Johnson.*

# OUR GREAT PACIFIC COMMONWEALTH.

## A STUDY OF ULTIMATE CALIFORNIA.

CALIFORNIA is widely celebrated, but little known. Its unique climate and productions, and the dramatic incidents of its early history, have been deeply impressed upon the popular imagination wherever the name of the republic is spoken. These circumstances have given it rank among the most famous of American States, yet its problems and its future are inscrutable enigmas to all who have not studied the subject at close range, and to many who have. The anomaly that one of the States most talked of should be one of the least understood is not difficult to explain.

In the first place, California is known not by what millions of people have seen, but by what millions have read. Europe is better known by contact to Americans than California. A prominent American author recently «discovered» California, and filled the newspapers with the interesting and suggestive impressions it had made upon his mind. He had been to Europe twenty times, and to the Pacific coast once, which is once oftener than many other distinguished travelers of the Eastern seaboard. Still further, the Anglo-Saxon race is dealing with new conditions in California. Coming from dense forests, from a land of heavy rainfall, and from a temperate climate where winters are long and stern, it settled in treeless deserts, in a land of slight and peculiar rainfall, and under a sky that never knows the winter. Finally, California is in its infancy, having recently celebrated its forty-sixth birthday as an American commonwealth. Born in a paroxysm of speculation,—one of the wildest the world has seen,—it has outlived a trying experience of lesser economic epilepsy, and come to the threshold of its true career strengthened and purified by the extraordinary process. In less than half a century several far-reaching changes have swept through the industrial and social life of the State, swiftly altering the conditions of labor and of business. Even for those living in the midst of these events, it has been difficult to read their significance and estimate their influence on the ultimate character of the place and people. What wonder, then, that to the outside world California has meantime appeared like a jumble of gold, palms, and oranges, of gilded millionaires and hopeless paupers, of enviable farmers living luxuriously on small sections of paradise, and of servile alien laborers herded in stifling tenements? Such are the conflicting aspects of the Golden State to those who view it from afar. What are the facts?

### THE SPECULATING FARMER.

THE great farmer of California is the successor of the gold-hunter. Both were speculators of the thoroughbred type; both looked with contempt upon the matter of making a living, and dreamed only of making a fortune. Of homes and institutions they were neither architects nor builders, for they sought only to take the wealth from the soil and spend it elsewhere. The miner leaves nothing to commemorate the place where he has gathered gold save crumbling hovels and empty tin cans. The five-thousand-acre wheat-farmer leaves no monument beyond fields of repulsive stubble and the shanties of his «hoboes.» These social forces belong rather more to barbarism than to civilization.

The rise of horticulture brought no material change in these conditions. As with the miner and wheat-farmer, so with the fruit-grower the aim was to get rich quickly, and the method was speculation. Certain districts were devoted almost exclusively to prunes, others to wine-grapes, others to raisins, and yet others to oranges. Fruit-land rose to almost fabulous prices, and was readily bought by those who had been taught to believe that they could realize profits ranging from one hundred to one thousand dollars per acre for certain crops. Exceptional instances justified this prediction, and everybody seemed to prefer to found expectations upon these instances rather than upon average returns. It is not difficult to understand why a man who counts upon an income of five to ten thousand dollars from ten acres, or double that amount from twenty acres, should turn his back upon common things, and devote his land exclusively to the crops which promise such gilded profits.

### WHEN PROSPERITY IS A BLIGHT.

THIS was the general policy, and it conferred great prosperity upon some classes, particularly the Chinese and Italian market-gardeners, who raised food for the orchard-farmers to eat. There were years, however, when the fruit of trees and vines brought very large returns. Wherever the policy of single crops is pursued, whether it be wheat, corn, or cotton, raisins, prunes, or oranges, there are occasional years of well-nigh riotous prosperity. But such years are frequently more disastrous in their results than sober periods of depression. They feed the flame of speculation and raise false industrial ideals. Under the spell of such times, the people depart still further from the safe path of self-sufficient agriculture, buying more land to devote to the favorite crop, expanding their living expenses, and running into debt. When this spirit becomes the breath of industry no human laws can avert disaster. A true industrial system is like a noble river fed by eternal snows: it never floods its banks with an excessive flow, and never sinks below its normal stage. It ebbs and flows with the regular tides of the great commercial ocean to which it is tributary, but alike at high water and at low it bears the ships of men upon its tranquil bosom.

### THE CIVILIZING POWER OF IRRIGATION.

THE evolutionary process of the last twenty years has wrought out some very valuable lessons for the future of California. It has demonstrated that irrigation is essential to the highest standard of civilization. The census of 1890 revealed the fact that two thirds of the gain in rural population stood to the credit of eight counties where irrigation prevailed. The counties which rely upon rainfall had about reached a standstill or scored a loss. The people have always been divided on the question as to whether irrigation is necessary. Those who oppose urge that it breeds malaria and injures the quality of the fruit. Those who favor insist that it is essential to the most scientific agriculture, and to the maintenance of dense population. The last twenty years have answered the question forever. The answer consists of a comparison between the south and the north. The one was born of the irrigation canal; the other of the mining-camp and the wheat-ranch. The one is characterized by a high civilization; the other by a low one.

### THE HOLLAND OF THE SOUTH.

WHAT Holland was to the life of Europe in the fourteenth, fifteenth, and sixteenth centuries, southern California is to the life of the Pacific coast at the end of the nineteenth century. The industrial impulse which the men of the Netherlands caught from their conquest of the sea, the men of the southern valleys caught from their conquest of the desert. «Curbing the ocean and overflowing rivers with their dikes,» says one of the closest students of Dutch history, «they came to love the soil, their own creation, and to till it with patient, almost tender care.» So they became the fathers of scientific farming in Europe. They wrought a marvelous revolution in the methods of cultivating the soil. «When Catherine of Aragon wished for a salad, she was compelled to send for it across the Channel by a special messenger.» The civilization founded upon this wonderful agriculture maintained its high character through the whole range of their economic life. The habits of skilful industry which grew from the intensely cultivated soil conferred the same prosperity when adapted to the workshop and the store. The thread of coöperation spun from their common labor on the dikes ran through the entire industrial fabric of the crowded little nation. The influence of neighborly association involved in the conditions of existence on farms of petty size colored and shaped their social life. As it was in Holland, so it is in southern California.

The men of the southern valleys made the small farm unit supreme. With marvelous patience and intelligence they worked out the highest methods of watering and tilling the soil known to the world. Tempering their speculative instincts with love of home, they developed towns and surroundings of rare beauty and comfort, and made them centers of high social and intellectual life. To compare these conditions with those which prevail in the great wheat- and cattle-ranches of the north, where labor is mostly servile, and where beauty has never laid its hand upon the home or dooryard, is like comparing Holland to Paraguay. Although the south has by no means escaped the evils of the single crop, it has vindicated irrigation and the small farm, and the extraordinary social possibilities inherent in both. These are the valuable lessons which may be set against the failures and disappointments of the last two decades.

### CALIFORNIA'S FUTURE MILLIONS.

WITH a population estimated by Governor Budd in 1896 at less than one million and a quarter, California has a territory nearly as large as that of France. It is inferior to France neither in climate, soil, natural resources, nor sea-coast, and its capacity for sustaining a dense population is fully as great as that of the European republic. The latter supports more than thirty-eight millions. If, then, the comparatively few inhabitants of the California of to-day are not equally prosperous, it is because they have failed to make the best use of their opportunities. With the same rate of increase in the next century as in that of the immediate past, the United States will contain in 1996 a total population of over five hundred and eighty millions. Nothing is more certain than that California must receive its full share of these future millions. It seems hardly less certain that they will realize there the highest destiny of the race. But how?

Notwithstanding the supreme attractions of its rural life, more than seventy-seven per cent. of California's total increase in the last decade covered by the national census settled in towns and cities. As a result, the urban life of this far, new State is as badly congested as that of the old communities of the East. But the possibilities of agriculture, of manufacture, and of mining are relatively untouched. Ultimate California remains to be fashioned from these undeveloped materials. The tendencies of future growth are revealed by the teaching of the past, and not less by its failures than by its successes—not less by the fury of old speculations than by the calm current of these saner times. The future tides of population in the Golden State must first spend their energy upon the soil. It is the creation of a new and ampler civilization that is involved, and agriculture must be its foundation. But if those now engaged in cultivating the soil can scarcely maintain themselves, what hope is there for new recruits in the industry? The question is natural, but the answer is conclusive. There is no hope for them if they engage in speculation, but there is an absolute guaranty of a living and a competence, to be enjoyed under the most satisfying and ennobling social conditions, if they work upon sound industrial lines. These lines are clearly disclosed by the light of past experience.

### THE SETTLER'S OPPORTUNITY.

THREE classes of products should enter into the calculations of the new settler in California: the things he consumes; the things California now imports from Eastern States and foreign countries; the things which Eastern communities consume, but can never hope to produce, and of which California possesses virtually a monopoly. In the first list is almost everything which would appear in an elaborate dinner menu, from the course of olives to the course of oranges, nuts, and raisins, and excluding only the coffee. This policy of self-sustenance has been ignored to a startling degree in the mad struggle for riches, but the coming millions of farmers can be sure of a luxurious living only by stooping to collect it from the soil.

### MILLIONS FOR NEEDLESS IMPORTS.

IN the second list are many of the commonest articles of consumption, which California might readily produce at home, but for which it sends millions of dollars abroad each year. The imports of pork and its products range as high as eight or ten millions each year. Condensed milk is not only a very important article of consumption in mining-camps and great ranches, but is largely shipped abroad for the Asiatic trade. It is brought across the continent from New Jersey. California also sends beyond its borders from twenty to twenty-five millions annually for the item of sugar, which should not only be produced in sufficient quantities to supply consumption, but for export as well. It is a curious fact that many of the finest fruit preserves sold in San Francisco bear French and Italian labels, and that the supply of canned sweet corn comes mostly from Maine. Essential oils made from the peelings of citrus fruits are also imported. It is not uncommon to find orange marmalade which has been prepared in Rochester, New York, the oranges having been shipped eastward, and the manufactured product westward, at a cost of two transcontinental freights. Imports are by no means confined to things which require capital and machinery for their manufacture. Chickens, turkeys, and eggs are largely brought from outside. A single commission-house in San Francisco imports five hundred thousand chickens every year. Thus a good many thousands of the new settlers can profitably be employed in feeding much of the present population of the State, which includes a large proportion of those who are speculating on wheat and fruit, sheep, cattle, and hogs.

### PRODUCTS FOR EXPORT.

HAVING made perfectly sure of his living, and disposed of his surplus for cash in the home market, the settler still has left a promising field in the list of things which nine tenths of the American people consume but cannot produce. Among these products are oranges, lemons, and limes. Florida competition in this line has been temporarily destroyed, if not permanently injured. Mexico is, perhaps, a rising competitor; but there is little reason to fear that California cannot hold its own against all foreign producers. Even more promising is the olive culture; for while the orange is an article of luxury, the olive must ultimately become here as elsewhere an important article of food. Californians are just beginning to pickle the ripe olives. The difference between a green olive and a ripe one is precisely the difference between a green and a ripe apple. In Spain the people subsist largely on olives, but not on green ones. All who have eaten the ripe fruit which is now being pickled in California will agree that it is conservative to say that when the American public become acquainted with this product, its consumption will be enormously increased. This will be true, because in its new form the olive is as nutritious as it is palatable, and the people will learn to depend upon it as an article of diet. In the production of deciduous fruits, such as peaches, apricots, cherries, and nectarines, California has much competition, and is to have much more in the future. There are irrigated valleys throughout the Pacific Northwest, the intermountain region, and the now undeveloped Southwest, which are beginning to produce marvelous fruits of this kind. The same is true of olives, almonds, and walnuts in a much more restricted way. The California wine industry is promising to-day, and the culture of grapes for this purpose profitable. Planters who depend for their entire income upon the cultivation of these export crops will necessarily suffer all the evils of speculative farming, but those who have founded their industry upon the plan of self-sufficiency will always have a surplus income from this third source, and in years of high prices it will be large. It is thus that the agricultural basis of California will be indefinitely broadened in order to sustain future millions.

### THE FACTORY AND THE MINE.

Upon this foundation manufactures, mining, and an enlarged commerce will rest. The first cannot be long delayed. California will not permanently endure the enormous waste involved in shipping its wool and hides across the continent to Eastern mills, tanneries, and workshops, and in shipping back again the manufactured cloth and shoes. The factories must inevitably grow up near the raw material and the consumers. Expediency and the economy of nature alike demand it. This important part of California's civilization remains almost wholly to be developed. Its growth will open new avenues for employment and new outlets for the products of the soil.

The mining industry is also in its youth. To use a common phrase, but a true one, «the surface of the ground has only been scratched.» Old methods have been outlived, and the conditions of the industry are changing in vital ways; but the work of taking gold and silver, copper, lead, and iron, from the foot-hills and mountains of California has only been begun. The day of the individual miner, working with his pan in the gravel bed of the stream, is mostly past. The conditions of hydraulic mining were materially altered by legislation because of the injury done by polluting the rivers and filling their channels; but quartz-mining is in a state of rapid development, and is destined to assume prodigious proportions. It will add untold millions to the wealth of the community, increasing the demand for labor, and widening the markets of the farmer.

### THE FUTURE INDUSTRIAL ORGANIZATION.

Nature has unquestionably provided the foundation of a marvelous industrial life in which millions of people will finally participate. To-day these resources are undeveloped. There is but one force that can awaken the sleeping potentialities into a manifold and fruitful life. That force is human labor. Looking down the years of the future, it is possible to predict, with the accuracy of mathematics, that human labor will coin from these vacant valleys and rugged mountain-sides billions upon billions of money. The wealth to be so created will build many beautiful homes, capitalize banks, factories, and railroads, and send great steamships across the Pacific to foreign shores. To whom shall these things belong when labor has made them from the materials which nature provided? Upon the answer to that question hang the destinies of California.

The seed of the California of the past was in the little group of feverish gold-hunters who camped by Sutter's mill in 1849. It bore the gaudy weed of speculation, with its bitter harvest of misfortune and discontent for the many, accentuated only by the superfluous riches which it gave to the few. The seed of the California of the future is in the irrigation canals owned and administered by small landed proprietors; in the fruit-exchanges which are supplanting the commission system and securing to the producer the rewards of his labor; in the coöperative creameries and canning-factories which, in the face of deficient capital and unfair competition, are slowly fighting their way to the sure ground of abiding prosperity; in the multitudinous and uniformly successful manufacturing and mercantile associations which Mormon genius has planted in the valleys of Utah; in the banks, insurance companies, and loan and building societies which, all over the Union and all over the world, have vindicated the possibilities of associated man.

### SOIL FOR NEW INSTITUTIONS.

INDUSTRIAL organization is the only shield against the evil possibilities of concentrated wealth. In a settled country, where the roots of old institutions are deeply planted, and where vested interests have fastened upon all the sources of natural wealth, the application of this principle is surrounded by serious difficulties. But in a country where, in a comparative sense, all remains to be made, there is a fair field for its development. Such is the fortunate situation of California and of nearly one half of the continent to-day. It is mostly a blank page which awaits the makers of history. Its institutions are to be formulated, founded, and realized by the men of the future. Without raising a hostile hand against a vested right or privilege, without enacting a single new law, and without doing violence to any rational sentiment, the millions that are yet to occupy the fairest portion of the national domain may win precious victories for humanity.

Those who come to till the soil may own the numerous small industries which consume and concentrate their crude products either by setting aside a portion of their original investment, or by dedicating a part of their subsequent income to the purpose. This has been done on a great scale in Utah and in some foreign countries, and is being done in a small way in various parts of the West. They can go further under the same principle, and establish industries less closely related to the soil. The problem of distributing their products even to the remotest markets is already in process of rapid solution. Only the possession of the iron highway by private capital now balks their perfect triumph, and even the railway system may some day be made subservient to the interests of production. The mines are mostly within the reach of the organized community; they are located on public lands. They require only well-directed labor to bring them to a stage where they readily command either capital or credit sufficient to obtain the necessary machinery. The labor that does the work requires to be fed only with that which grows from the soil. The properly organized community would furnish both the labor and the sustenance. Thus the earnings of mines, like the rewards of the farm and factory, would be distributed among those whose labor created them.

All this has been done, and will be done in a much larger way, without resort to socialism or any other daring scheme of revolutionary character. It involves but two principles —the joint-stock company and the New England town meeting. These are applicable, if not to great aggregations of people, at least to small communities. The system which they represent rests upon individual independence. The society which they serve finds its unit in the family and the home. There is a point beyond which the individual cannot go without associating his labor with that of others, either as wage-earner or share-owner. Under the system now growing up in the West, the stock company, composed of many petty capitalists, takes the place of the employer. It is a legitimate and natural economic development, and perhaps the most hopeful one of recent times.

### THE FIELD FOR GROWTH.

IT is interesting to consider what portions of California will receive the bulk of the future population. The coast region presents a frontage of over one thousand miles to the sea. Though narrowly hemmed in by mountains, it contains many fertile agricultural valleys which have long been occupied. The chief industries are dairying, stock-raising, and general farming, with some mining; in a few districts, notably the Santa Clara Valley, fruit-raising has assumed large proportions. While the coast region will inevitably enjoy a gradual increase of population, we must look elsewhere to find a field which invites the immigration of millions, and offers hopeful ground for the growth of new institutions.

What is popularly known as southern California is a narrowly restricted district reaching eastward from Los Angeles for about one hundred miles, and southward to San Diego. Like the coast region, its character is fixed, though on widely different lines. Its population is already comparatively dense, and its future growth will be measured by the water-supply for irrigation, the limitations of which seem already in sight. It is an impressive fact that the seven counties of the south received sixty-one per cent. of the whole increase of rural population between 1880 and 1890. This marvelous showing was chiefly due to the superior public spirit of the locality, and to the attractive institutions which grew out of it. But its very success in the past places limitations upon the country as a field for future expansion. Land values have risen high, and the water-supply has become almost as precious as gold. A curious development of colonization in this locality is a new community to which desirable families are admitted upon condition that they will expend not less than two hundred and fifty thousand dollars each for improvements. It is reassuring to reflect, however, that the millionaire colonists can accomplish little more with their abundant capital than humbler settlers may do with their united labor. The sun, the sky, the earth, and the waters will be as kind to one class as to the other. While it should not be inferred that none but the very rich can settle in the south, it is perfectly true that this charming district is not within the field of the largest future developments.

Where, then, is the field to accommodate the hosts who will come when the population of California begins to approximate that of France? It lies principally in four great and distinct bodies, which may be named, in the order of their importance, as follows: the Sacramento Valley, stretching north from the Bay of San Francisco to the feet of snowy Shasta; the San Joaquin Valley, reaching south from the great bay to the place where the two mountain-ranges meet at the pass of Tehachapi; the intermountain valleys on the eastern slope of the Sierra, extending over the boundary into Nevada; and the Colorado Desert, in the extreme southeastern part of the State, on the borders of Mexico.

### THE SACRAMENTO VALLEY.

THE first of these, the valley of the Sacramento, received an addition of only two thousand to its rural population, out of a total of nearly ninety-seven thousand for the State, between 1880 and 1890. The fault lay neither with the soil nor the climate, which are equal to those of any part of California, but with economic conditions. The country is held in vast estates, principally devoted to the cultivation of grain, which has been a losing industry for several years. Where horticulture has been adopted it has frequently been done upon a great scale. The vast orchards and vineyards of Mrs. Stanford, of General Bidwell, and of A. T. Hatch are striking instances of this tendency. When General N. P. Chipman, himself a distinguished resident of the Sacramento Valley, called attention to the startling revelations contained in the census figures, the matter was widely dicussed, but with little result. The public spirit which has given the southern counties their splendid place in the life of the Pacific coast is distinctly lacking in the north. The truth is that it cannot be cultivated on wheat-fields or in mining-camps. It comes with irrigation, with the subdivision of the land into thousands of diminutive holdings, with a citizenship composed of a multitude of small proprietors.

These conditions are exactly reversed in the northern valley, with pitiful results. The same forces would make the same civilization in both localities, for the physical foundation is practically identical. The southern valley lies open to the sea, the breezes from which mercifully temper the summer heat. In other respects, the advantages are all on the side of the Sacramento. It is far greater in area; its water-supplies are both more abundant and more reliable; its surrounding advantages, notably in the way of mines and timber, are much superior. Finally, it possesses the inestimable blessing of a mighty river, navigable for a distance of two hundred miles, and capable of being much improved. This is a factor of the highest import. It furnishes cheap transportation by boat, and materially lessens railroad charges. Furthermore, it gives the valley a comprehensive system of drainage from Shasta to the sea. The wonderful mineral riches of this locality will be rapidly developed. They are by no means confined to gold, for what promises to be one of the greatest copper-mines in the world has recently been opened in Shasta County, with the aid of British capitalists. It is from the foot-hills on the eastern side of the Sacramento Valley that the earliest oranges and lemons seek the market. They command high prices, and are mostly sold on the coast from San Francisco to British Columbia. It is in this imperial valley, and in the foot-hills and mountains which rise above it in splendid pictures on each side, that a large proportion of the future millions will find homes and prosperity.

### THE SAN JOAQUIN VALLEY.

THE San Joaquin Valley is even larger, and in many respects resembles its northern sister. It is not as fortunate, however, in extent of water-supply, navigation facilities, or natural drainage. Here irrigation and the small farm had begun to make themselves felt, and the single county of Fresno gained more than five times as much in population in the last census decade as the entire Sacramento Valley. Both irrigation and small farming have here been attended with misfortunes which have injured them in public esteem. Perhaps the earliest triumph of the new woman in this generation was that of Miss Austin and her three associates—all schoolteachers of San Francisco—who founded the wonderful Fresno raisin industry. Investing their savings in a ranch, and then boldly venturing upon a culture in which few had faith, they demonstrated that raisins equal to those of Spain could be produced in the San Joaquin. They were rewarded with handsome profits, and later thousands of people shared in the benefits of their demonstration. But speculation and the fallacy of the single crop followed as natural consequences, bringing hard times, mortgages, and disappointment in their train. In the mean time unskilful irrigation without proper drainage wrought harm in various ways. All of these misfortunes are being overcome, but it is not easy for the great valley to undo the injury which its reputation has suffered in the last few years. Nevertheless, the country of the San Joaquin contains great possibilities, and will sustain a dense population. Its contiguous mountains are richly endowed with mines and great timber, as well as with the sublimest scenery.

THE FALL OF WHEAT A BLESSING.

THE valleys of the Sacramento and San Joaquin have been, and are yet, the grain-fields of the Pacific coast. Many of their residents have bemoaned the fall in the price of wheat as the greatest of calamities. The truth is that for California it is the first of blessings. The fall in wheat prices has broken the land monopoly which kept labor servile, and gave the most fruitful of countries to four-footed beasts rather than to men. Not until nearly all great ranches had been mortgaged to their full capacity, not until the failure of prices had made the debts intolerably burdensome and brought their owners face to face with disaster, was it possible to open the country for its best and highest uses. With the supremacy of wheat will go the shanty and the «hobo» laborer, to be followed in time by the Chinaman. In their places will come the home and the man who works for himself. Civilization will bloom where barbarism has blighted the land. There are localities where the cultivation of grain can be pursued, but the semi-tropical valleys of California were plainly intended for better things.

Irrigation, drainage, and cheap transportation are closely related as economic problems in the great interior valleys. William Hammond Hall, the former State engineer, has predicted that within fifty years the waters which rise in the mountains and meander through these valleys to the sea will all be utilized to moisten and fertilize the soil, and then be turned into canals, serving the double purpose of drainage and transportation. He claims that it is feasible, from an engineering standpoint, to construct such works, and to propel trains of freight-boats by electricity at a speed of six miles an hour. If this shall be done, the gain to the State will be beyond all calculation, provided the works be owned by the public. It is by no means an idle dream when considered in connection with ultimate California.

EAST OF THE SIERRA.

THE third field of future development is the desert country lying east of the Sierra Nevada. This is almost unknown to the outside world, and is reached only by lines of narrow-gage railway running northwest and southwest from Reno, Nevada. It lies in two large bodies, the more northerly of which is in Lassen and Modoc counties. This enjoys large water-supplies and fertile soil, with abundant resources of timber and mineral. The country is of a sage-brush character, and most of the land is still open to entry by citizens. The altitude ranges from four thousand feet upward, and the climate is distinctly that of the temperate zone. The more southern body east of the Sierras lies largely in Inyo County. Here the climate is milder, though temperate rather than semi-tropical. A large population will occupy these districts in the future.

THE COLORADO DESERT.

THE most famous of waste places in America, the Colorado Desert, is popularly regarded as an empire of hopeless sterility, the silence of which will never be broken by the voices of men. But the great desert is the life-work of the Colorado River. The scientific men of the University of Arizona have analyzed these waters, and found that the actual commercial value of the fertilizing matter which would be deposited upon each acre by irrigation amounts, in the course of a year, to $9.07. What, then, is the potential value of the land which this river has created in centuries? The products of the region include oranges and the dates of commerce. The place is more like Syria than any other part of the United

States, and the daring imagination may readily conceive that here a new Damascus will arise, more beautiful than that of old.

With the occupation of the Colorado Desert, and of the great peninsula which adjoins it, a powerful impulse will be given to agriculture, mining, and commerce in a vast region now little peopled. One of the inevitable consequences will be the rise of San Diego to the proportions of a large city —probably the largest in the southern part of the coast.

LAND OF THE COMMON PEOPLE.

THE future of California will be very different from its past. It has been the land of large things—of large estates, of large enterprises, of large fortunes. Under another form of government it would have developed a feudal system, with a landed aristocracy resting on a basis of servile labor. These were its plain tendencies years ago, when somebody coined the epigram, «California is the rich man's paradise and the poor man's hell.» But later developments have shown that whatever of paradise the Golden State can offer to the rich it will share, upon terms of marvelous equality, with the middle classes of American life. Over and above all other countries, it is destined to be the land of the common people. This is true because, owing to its peculiar climatic conditions, it requires less land to sustain a family in generous comfort. For the same reason cheaper clothing and shelter, as well as less fuel, suffice, while it is possible to realize more perfectly the ideal of producing what is consumed. Moreover, it is a natural field for the application of associative industry and the growth of the highest social conditions. Indeed, the country has distinctly failed as a land of big things, and achieved its best successes in the opposite direction. Its true and final greatness will consist of the aggregate of small things—of small estates, of small enterprises, of small fortunes. Progress toward this end is already well begun. It must go on until the last great estate is dismembered and the last alien serf is returned to the Orient. Upon the ruins of the old system a better civilization will arise. It will be the glory of the common people, to whose labor and genius it will owe its existence. Its outreaching and beneficent influence will be felt throughout the world.

*William E. Smythe.*

# WHAT LANGUAGE DID CHRIST SPEAK?

INTRODUCTORY NOTE.

IT is by no accident that Mrs. Agnes Smith Lewis, the author of the following article, has won the credit of having made one of the greatest biblical discoveries of the century. She had been a student of the Syriac language, and could talk Arabic and Greek. It was with the plan of getting access to the treasures of the monastery of St. Katherine that she went to Mount Sinai, where Tischendorf had found the magnificent Sinaitic manuscript of the Greek Bible, and where Professor Palmer had failed to complete his attempted catalogue of the library. Her ability to talk with the Greek monks in their own language, and her wonderful tact and generalship, secured their good will; and she was not slow in discovering, under a late and worthless monkish biography, the faded letters of an ancient Syriac text of the four gospels. The leaves were stuck together, but she separated them by the steam of a tea-kettle, and took four hundred photographs, which she brought to England, where they proved to be a peculiar and very old version of the gospels of extraordinary interest. She has since visited the monastery again, with her sister, Mrs. Gibson, who made a catalogue of the six hundred Arabic manuscripts, while she catalogued the two hundred Syriac manuscripts, and made other important discoveries. A volume published by her last year contains a translation of the famous manuscript which bears her name.

*William Hayes Ward.*

THIS subject has awakened considerable interest of late years, owing partly to the discoveries of ancient biblical manuscripts which have recently been made, and partly to a growing desire on the part of Christians to realize how truly the Son of God became man, subject by virtue of his manhood to the same conditions of life, and to most of the same limitations, as ourselves. For, however many miracles he wrought, these were all for the benefit of others; and not once in the canonical gospels do we find it recorded that he used his divine creative energy to lessen the burden which his true manhood imposed upon him. It is not to be denied that we can appreciate the meaning of our Lord's gracious words as they reach us through an English translation; but that a translation often fails to give the exact force of the original is felt by every earnest student of Greek as soon as he begins to read the New Testament. Few of my readers are likely to fall into the mistake attributed to a Scotch minister of the last century, who introduced an apt quotation from the Psalms by, «As King David said in his own beautiful Saxon»; or to that other worthy who exclaimed in the heat of a theological argument, «Do ye mean to say that Paul spoke Greek?» Yet the question as to what was the mother-tongue of Jesus is not yet altogether settled, some holding that it must have been Greek, because three out of the four gospels are supposed to have been written in that language; and others that it was a Semitic tongue, probably Aramaic or Syriac, which was at that time the vernacular of Palestine.

We shall try to place before our readers some considerations which have induced the most learned biblical critics of our day to adopt the latter hypothesis. But we must preface it with a short account of the Syriac language, taken partly from the introduction to the first edition of my translation of the Syriac gospels from the palimpsest manuscript which I had the happiness of discovering in the Convent of St. Katherine on Mount Sinai in 1892, and partly from the works of the many writers who have lately discussed the subject in Great Britain, in France, and in Germany. Syriac, or more properly Christian Aramaic, was the first language into which the New Testament was translated; and as the Greek text itself was written by men who habitually thought in Syriac, the early versions in this tongue have a closer affinity with the original text than those of any other can possibly have, not excepting the Old Latin. Aramaic was once popularly supposed to be a corrupt form of Hebrew, but that is a mistake. It is a language quite as regularly formed, and with a grammar quite as distinct, as either Hebrew or Arabic. Almost our first record of its use is from the lips of Laban. In Gen. xxxi. 47 we read that when Laban and Jacob set up a heap of stones as a witness of the covenant between them, Jacob called it, in good Hebrew, Galeed, and Laban, in equally good Aramaic, Jegar-sahadutha. From this some have concluded that Aramaic was the vernacular of Mesopotamia, the cradle of Abraham's family, and that it was brought into Palestine by the captives who returned from Babylon. Others say that, while it has an undoubted affinity with the Semitic of Babylonian cuneiform inscriptions, it was the language of the kingdom of Syria, which flourished in the territory stretching between the Euphrates and the Lebanon from about B. C. 1600 to B. C. 600, and that it was through this channel that it made its way into Palestine.

It is not easy to ascertain when Hebrew ceased to be the language of the common people; but that it had so ceased in the period immediately before our Lord's advent there can be little doubt. The Talmud, which was written about that time, shows clearly that the rabbis were accustomed to speak to the common people in Aramaic. Many of the legal documents necessary to civil life, such as contracts of sale, receipts, marriage certificates, bills of divorcement, were drawn up in that language.[1] Even some of the prayers of the synagogue, such as were intended to be understood by women and children, were translated into this, the vulgar tongue.

Our difficulty of proving this is increased by the ambiguous sense in which the word «Hebrew» is used in the New Testament. Strictly speaking, it ought to be applied to that language only in which the Pentateuch was written; but it was used carelessly also for Aramaic, as being the language spoken by the Hebrews in contradistinction to the cosmopolitan tongue of the Greeks. The «great silence» which followed the very beginning of St. Paul's address to the people, as recorded in Acts xxi. 40, was assuredly not produced by the sound of classical Hebrew, but by the familiar accents to which the miscellaneous crowd were accustomed in everyday life. We do not mean to say that the language of the Torah and of the prophets was quite unknown to them all; they heard it solemnly read every Sabbath day in their synagogues, and they used it in the blessings which they invoked over their meals. But it is, to say the least, more than doubtful if they could have followed the extempore arguments addressed to them by St. Paul had he spoken to them in the sacred classical tongue.

[1] Arnold Meyer, «Jesu Muttersprache,» p. 39; Dalman, p. 12.

It is also clear from this narrative that the mob of Jerusalem would not have understood a discourse in Greek.

It is believed by students of the works of Philo and of Josephus, both of whom were contemporaries of our Lord, that by the phrases τῇ πατρίῳ γλώσσῃ and ἑβραΐζων these writers meant Aramaic.[1] Josephus wrote his «Jewish War» first of all in his native dialect, and he confesses to the labor and delay (ὄκνος καὶ μέλλησις) which he had when translating it into Greek.[2] If a highly educated man, as he was, experienced this difficulty, how very unlikely is it that the fishermen of Bethsaida and the peasants of Galilee would have followed the Sermon on the Mount if addressed to them in Greek! God does not multiply miracles needlessly, and we may be certain that there were no pre-Pentecostal facilities granted to the crowds which hung upon our Lord's lips, nor even to his immediate disciples. But before going further we must explain that the early Aramaic Christians adopted the name of Syrians bestowed on them by the Greeks because they, the Aramaia, did not wish to be confounded with the Armaia (the heathen). The country of Aram was henceforth known as Syria, and its language as the Syriac.

We are on surer ground when we come to the indications in the text of the gospels which point to these narratives having been produced in a Syriac rather than in a Greek or a Hebrew atmosphere.

We have, first of all, the various Aramaic phrases actually embodied in the Greek text as having been uttered by our Lord, such as «Ephphatha» («Be opened»), «Talitha, cumi» («Maiden, arise»), where the word *cumi* might be Hebrew or Syriac or Arabic, but where *talitha* is purely Syriac. And the last despairing cry of our Lord on the cross, «Eloi, Eloi, lama sabachthani?» is not translated in the Sinaitic palimpsest, for the good reason that it is a natural part of the Syriac text.

Take next the names of persons and places in the New Testament. The Syriac word for «son» is *bar*, and so we have Bartholomew, Barabbas, Bar-Jesus, Bar-Jona, Barnabas, Bar-Timæus. Had Hebrew been the spoken tongue, these names would have run Ben-tholomew, Ben-Jesus, etc. We have also «Cepha» (a stone, feminine gender), «Boanerges,» *i. e.*, *Beni-rogaz* (sons of thunder), «Sapphira» (the beautiful), «Thoma» (the twin), «Martha» (the mistress), «Tabitha» (the gazelle), «Bethsaida» (house of fishing), «Nazareth» (watch), «Gethsemane» (an oil-press), «Golgotha» (place of a skull), «Aceldama» (the field of blood). It may as well be explained that the final syllable of most of these names, *a*, is a distinctively Syriac termination. The words «mammon» (Matt. vi. 24) and «raca» (Matt. v. 22) and «abba» are Syriac also.

[1] Meyer, «Jesu Muttersprache,» p. 40.
[2] «Bell. Jud.,» proem 1.

Nor are other indications wanting that our Lord spoke in Syriac. Semitic peoples delight in puns and in assonances or jingles of words. We need not go far to prove this. The Koran derives much of its supposed sanctity from this cause alone. Babylonian royal decrees and Arabic legal documents are all enlivened by it; and in the Syriac version of our Lord's discourses it seems as if one word had sometimes suggested another. We give the following instances: John viii. 34—«He who committeth sin is the slave of sin.» Here the word for «commit» and the word for «slave» are both regular forms of the triliteral verb *'bad*. There is a similar play on the same word in Luke vii. 8: «I say to my slave, Do this, and he doeth it.»

Matthew xxvii. 6: *dmaya ennōn da dmā* (the price of blood).

In Matthew x. 12, 13 we have: «And when ye come into an house, give peace to it [that is, salute it]. And if the house be worthy, your peace shall rest upon it: and if not, your peace shall return unto you.» In the Greek text ἀσπάσασθε (salute) has no verbal relation to εἰρήνη (peace). We therefore conclude that our Lord gave this direction in a Semitic tongue, and used either the Hebrew *shalōm* or the Syriac *shalma*.

In Matthew xi. 17 Dr. Jahn has pointed out an assonance between the words *raqadtun* (danced) and *arqadtun* (lamented), while Dr. Nestle observes another in the *anichkun* (I will give you rest) of verse 28 and the *danich ana* (for I am meek) of verse 29.

The alliteration, *memoth tamōth*, of Mark vii. 10 can be reproduced in an English idiom, «die the death,» though it is absent from the Greek.

In John xii. 32, «And I, if I be lifted up from the earth, will draw all men unto me,» the word «lifted up» has the secondary sense of «be crucified.»

In John xx. 10 there is in the Greek text an expression, ἀπῆλθον . . . πρὸς ἑαυτούς, which is not classical, and may perhaps be a translation of the Syriac *ezal lahūn;* and in John xx. 19 the curious grammar of τῇ μιᾷ τῶν σαββάτων is at once explained by the Syriac *had beshaba*. These last two examples may have sprung from the evangelist's thoughts being habitually in Syriac.

St. Paul may have been thinking in Aramaic when he wrote to the Romans (xiii. 8): «Owe no man any thing, but to love one another.» Here the word *hāb* (owe) is not the same as *habb* (love), but the sound is very similar. And in the Palestinian Syriac the words addressed by the risen Saviour to Mary Magdalene are so rhythmical that we feel as if they must be the very accents that fell from his lips: «Attatha, ma at bakia, leman at ba'ia?» («Woman, why weepest thou? whom seekest thou?») Perhaps the most interesting indications that our Lord's discourses were delivered in Syriac are, however, those passages where the Syriac text helps to clear up some apparent ambiguity in the Greek one. I give some instances from Dr. Arnold Meyer's very instructive work, «Jesu Muttersprache.» Let us hope that they may be only the first specimens from a field of research where the diligence of Syriac students will in the future be more amply rewarded.

The seeming discrepancy between the word *δόξητε* (think) of Matthew iii. 9 and *ἄρξησθε* (begin) of Luke iii. 8 disappears when we find that the Syriac word for «ye begin» is *tishrun*, and that for «ye think» might be *tesharrun*.

In Matthew xxiv. 51, says Dr. Meyer, *διχοτομήσει* (cut in pieces) is hardly a suitable punishment; certainly a Jewish householder would scarcely have treated his servants in such a fashion. And how could the servant afterward howl and gnash his teeth? But in the Sinaitic palimpsest, and in the Palestinian Syriac version, we find the verb *f'lag* used, which means both «to cut in pieces» or «to divide (*i. e.*, appoint) a portion.» If we elide the words *αὐτὸν καὶ* in the Greek—words which have perhaps been supplied by some too zealous editor—we get the simple and natural meaning, not that the servant was cut to pieces, but simply that his portion was appointed with the hypocrites, whoever these may signify. Take another of our Lord's hard sayings, Matthew viii. 22: «But Jesus said unto him, Follow me, and let the dead bury their dead.» Four of the Syriac versions, to wit, the Sinai palimpsest, the Peshito, the Palestinian Syriac, and the Philoxenian, have, «Let the buriers [*i. e.*, grave-diggers] bury their dead.» Dr. Meyer suggests that our Lord's meaning may have been, «Care not thou about the mortal part of thy father—a grave-digger will be found for *that*; but preach thou the kingdom of God; it is coming soon, and it suffers no delay.»

A suggestion about this very difficult passage is worth noting, by whom made we cannot tell. It is that the phrase «bury my father» simply meant that the young man wished, like other Jews, to live at home until his father died, and that there was no question about the latter's impending dissolution; that, in fact, he was using a common Jewish idiom.

We might give a few more instances in which textual critics think that the Syriac sheds light upon the Greek texts: but some of these questions are still under discussion, so we have limited ourselves to those only which appear to admit of the least doubt, and of which those who know neither Greek nor Syriac can understand the reasonable character.

The great Reformation of the sixteenth century was accompanied by a burning zeal to study the text of Scripture in the light of the languages in which its various books were written. Nay, we may even say that this zeal was a proximate cause of the intellectual and religious upheaval. Even strong partizans of the Church of Rome were fired with it, without being in the least aware where others would naturally be led. The nineteenth century has witnessed another period of enthusiasm for textual criticism, and many distinguished scholars in America and in Europe have spent years of labor in the comparison of ancient manuscripts, so as to discover if any corruptions have crept into the received text, and to know what the evangelists and the apostles really wrote. The spade of the archæologist may be expected to throw more light upon the Old Testament, while in regard to the New fresh materials for research are continually being brought to light. Not the least of these are the manuscripts of the various versions produced in the Syriac Church, the Curetonian, the Sinaitic palimpsest, the Peshito, the Palestinian, the Philoxenian, and the still undiscovered Syriac text of Tatian's «Diatessaron,» or harmony of the four gospels, composed between A. D. 160 and A. D. 170. Apart from the interesting variations which some of these versions show, they have the supreme value of being perfectly independent witnesses to the genuineness and accuracy of the oldest Greek manuscripts, with which they are in constant and substantial agreement.

One objection which has been urged against the probability of our Lord's discourses having been delivered in Syriac is this. We have the authority of tradition and the evidence of Papias (A. D. 110) as reported by Eusebius,[1] for believing that St. Matthew's gospel was originally written in Aramaic, but that the

[1] Eus., «H. E.,» iii., chap. 39, p. 16.

gospels of Mark, of Luke, and of John were written in Greek; and there is always some loss of force or of delicacy of expression in the very best translation. To this we reply that no shorthand writer took down the teachings of Jesus; they were written in the form we now have them, entirely from memory, years after his ascension. It is probable that the Sermon on the Mount, for instance, as recorded by St. Matthew, contains the gist of many separate discourses delivered at different times and to different audiences. Had the teachings of three years been preserved in their totality, the world itself would not have contained the books that would have been written.

Other objections have been urged upon my consideration by a Jewish friend. He says: «While we find that Hillel (B. C. 75-A. D. 5), who came from Babylon, spoke sometimes in Aramaic, his colleague Shammai spoke always in Hebrew. In ‹Jerushalmi Sotah,› 24*b*, we have reported a prophecy of Samuel Hakaton, which he predicted before his death (about 110 A. D.). It runs: ‹Simeon and Ishmael are destined for the sword, the people for a prey, and there will be many distresses.› He said it in the Aramaic language, and they knew not what he said. If we allow that Aramaic was the language of the people, then the whole of what we call the New Hebrew must have been an invention of the rabbis, a mere artificial language, which I can hardly believe.»

Of these arguments, the story about Samuel Hakaton seems to me the most forcible. It can, however, be explained away when we recollect that there were at least two dialects of Aramaic, the eastern and the western. Few writers in modern times, whether Jewish or Christian, who have examined the subject, have come to any other conclusion but that Aramaic was the language of Palestine during the first century of the Christian dispensation, and it would take many tales to outweigh the fact of those few of our Lord's sayings which are reported in that language. These objections, however, will serve to show the difficulties with which the subject is still beset.

Some of our readers there may be who find it difficult to understand why, since God has revealed to us his will in a book, or rather in a library of inspired books, as the Bible truly is, he has not at the same time given us an infallible text. How much labor would have been saved had we possessed the autographs of four evangelists! To this we answer that, had one such autograph existed, some branch of the Christian church, possibly every branch, ourselves included, would have made an idol of the writer's parchment, while neglecting its teaching altogether. We can only seek to comprehend the ways of Providence in one sphere by observing them in another. Man is the heir of all things; yet he is sent into the world to depend for food, clothing, and all the comforts and adornments of life, on his wits. How greatly is he thereby differentiated from the brutes! How immeasurably is the educated man, and especially the scientific investigator, raised above the savage simply as the result of his own efforts! Is it not possible that he who gave the Word of Life designs to quicken our interest in it by arousing afresh in each successive generation of Christians the desire to approach nearer to its sources, to remove the undergrowth of legend and tradition which has sometimes obstructed its free course, and that we are saved from the danger of finding it trite by the feeling that we possess a divine treasure which, though a gift, is not entirely independent of our own exertions for the measure in which it shall minister to our edification?

*Agnes Smith Lewis.*

# TOPICS OF THE TIME

### The Christmas Century.

THE CENTURY has the desire to greet its readers Christmas after Christmas with «Christmas numbers» that have not only some of the gaiety of the holiday, but also a hint of its deeper meanings. How well this desire may have been accomplished this year it is for our readers themselves to determine; but we feel like making note of our own satisfaction in one Christmas «feature,» which seems to us to have about it more of the genuine flavor of the season than anything of the kind we have come upon this many a long day. Indeed, one's memory runs back to Irving's «Bracebridge Hall» for a fit companion to the gay and tender pleasantries of Mr. Janvier's delightful paper on the «Christmas Kalends of Provence,» to which Mr. Loeb has fitted such fine and sympathetic pictures. In a sense, Keats has put the charm of Provence into one famous line:

Dance and Provençal song and sunburnt mirth!

But the charm of this unique land is so many-sided,—in its history, its literature, its sunny landscape, its people, its customs, its temperament,—that, in fact, the story has not been fully told in all the books that have been written about it by native and foreign writers. Mr. Janvier's present contribution seems to us particularly vivid and successful. He recreates the atmosphere of a beautiful land and season; he makes us see and feel a foreign world, but one that is foreign only in its exterior aspects—a world of good feeling and happy, kindly living which is native and homelike to every human heart.

### The Approach of a New Era.

THE rumor of an agreement on the subject of arbitration by the governments of Great Britain and the United States comes as a happy forerunner of the Christmas season, and thrills the hearts of all humane and Christian people with the impatient expectancy of a great and noble event. There is every reason to hope that, in contrast with the gloomy Christmas season of last year, the present Christian festival may be marked by a glorious and historic advance toward the practical attainment of an era of «peace on earth and good will to men.»

There could hardly be a more cogent proof of the popular demand for an amicable adjustment of international difficulties than the subsidence for a long period both of active interest in the Venezuelan affair, and of alarm over the outcome of that once absorbing controversy. It is easy to see from outcropping events that this was not popular indifference; rather, it was a strong conviction that, in the face of the overwhelming demand on both sides of the sea for a peaceable adjustment of the question,—and indeed for a system of peaceable adjustment of all such questions,—those charged with the diplomatic affairs of the two countries could not fail to rise to the extraordinary responsibility under which they have rested. In no narrow sense it may be said that the peace of the English-speaking world has been for the time in their hands. They have had it in their power to make the closing years of the century illustrious by a diviner interpretation of Christian brotherhood than has ever found expression in the diplomacy of the world. No greater fame could fall to the portion of any statesman than to have been effectively enlisted in this cause of humanity.

On the other hand, opposition from any quarter, though it might now seem conclusive, could be only temporary. The record of the influential friends of arbitration is both long and important. In both lands the clergy, the educational institutions, the press, the commercial interests, the bar, the workingmen, and the chosen representatives of the people have expressed themselves in favor of this extension of the judicial system with a unanimity not disclosed on any other international question, and scarcely on any national question of the first rank. An official who seeks approval for supporting such a treaty has but to look about him to find it among the eminent of every profession. None have been more outspoken in its favor than the practitioners and expounders of the law. Some, including the distinguished Lord Chief Justice of England, have, indeed, suggested limitations of scope, but all have most warmly favored the principle of such an understanding. It would not be strange if there should be some difficulties in the adjustment of the system—some inherent ones, and some to be found as the scheme goes into practice; but these are the conditions of all progress, and may safely be intrusted to the highest legal school and experience. The chief thing is to make a beginning on the basis of permanence: Injustice and embarrassment may for a time, or at times, result; but what is war but the most monstrous system of injustice and embarrassment? Civilization advances by the balancing of a reformatory system against an existing system. It is not until one is convinced of the national peril involved in the old method of distributing spoils of office that he becomes a civil-service reformer; it is not until one appreciates the lawlessness of literary piracy that he accepts a copyright law containing comparatively small defects. So, in the face of the settled conviction of England and America that war between the two countries should be taken out of the category of the *easily possible* and placed in that of the *barely possible*, it is unpatriotic, inhuman, unchristian to hesitate at trifles in the progress of the principle. It is not too much to say that the whole English-speaking world, whether religious or non-religious, without regard to opinion on the Venezuelan affair, is looking forward to the establishment of a permanent tribunal, and will not only overlook any shortcomings of detail, but will be impatient of their influence in delaying the consummation desired.

Daniel Webster, in the only speech made during his visit to England which has been preserved,—that of July 18, 1839, before the National Agricultural Society at Oxford,—set forth in a notable passage the feeling that is at the basis of the present popular conviction on this subject. Mr. Webster said:

> With regard to whatsoever is important to the peace of the world, its prosperity, the progress of knowledge and of just opinions, the diffusion of the sacred light of Christianity, I know nothing more important to the promotion of those best interests of humanity, and the cause of the general peace, amity, and concord, than the good feeling subsisting between the Englishmen on this side of the Atlantic and the descendants of Englishmen on the other.
>
> Some little clouds have overhung our horizon. I trust they will soon pass away. I am sure that the age we live in does not expect that England and America are to have controversies carried to the extreme upon any occasion not of the last importance to national interests and honor.
>
> We live in an age when nations as well as individuals are subject to a moral responsibility. Neither government nor people — thank God for it!—can now trifle with the general sense of the civilized world; and I am sure that the civilized world would hold your country and my country to a very strict account if, without very plain and apparent reason deeply affecting the independence and great interests of the nation, any controversy between them should have other than an amicable issue.
>
> I will venture to say that each country has intelligence enough to understand all that belongs to its just rights, and is not deficient in means to maintain them; and if any controversy between England and America were to be pushed to the extreme of force, neither party would or could have any signal advantage over the other, except what it could find in the justness of its cause and the approbation of the world.

The progressive opinion of the world not only has reached, but has passed Mr. Webster's position, and the time has now come to embody that opinion in law.

### Are Our Lawmakers Deteriorating?

STUDENTS of democracy in all parts of the world have been giving much attention during recent years to the quality of modern legislators. Not only in this country, but in all parliamentary countries, the work of legislation has been passing out of the hands of the kind of men who controlled it fifty years ago. It was formerly in the hands of men who were truly the representatives of the intelligence, morality, and property of the land; for their standing in their respective communities was of the best. In the early American State legislatures it was the country squire, the prosperous farmer, the leading man in the town, who was sent to the legislature. He legislated there for the best interests of the community which had sent him. Being a man of property himself, he guarded jealously the interests of property, and thus legislated in the interest of public order, wise economy, and the general welfare. From the cities leading business men and lawyers were sent, who, actuated by similar influences and motives, legislated in the same direction.

In course of time the rural constituencies have diminished in importance and changed in character. The cities have advanced to a predominating influence, and their political and nominating machinery has passed into the hands of men who too often represent the lowest, rather than the best, elements of the community. The professional politician, the man who gets his living out of politics, has penetrated everywhere. Instead of being a man who has won his way to prominence by success in business or agriculture or in a professional career, he is more likely to be a man who has failed in private life and has gone into politics as an easier way to get a living.

The consequence is that the work of legislation, in many instances, has passed out of the hands of the men who own the property which makes up the wealth of the State, and into the hands of those who have little or none of that wealth. In other words, those who have nothing are legislating for those who have all. It must be exceptional if men who have no property to be taxed are wise and discriminating about the ways in which taxes are levied. Too often a man who has no property of his own is eager to attack the property of other people, either with the hope of personal benefit, or with the belief that he can thus gain favor with the ignorant or the disorderly elements of the population.

But the man of property in a legislative body who is an obstacle to legislation in the obvious interest of the people is quite as objectionable as the adventurer who uses his legislative position for selfish or demagogic ends. In fact, the «successful man» is far from being the only one capable of legislating for the whole people. It is intelligence and character that are needed, be the legislator as rich as Crœsus or as poor as a church mouse.

The growing power of political machines and bosses has contributed materially to the decline in the quality of legislators. It has come to be more and more the practice each year for the boss or the political machine to select the men who are to be the party's candidates for the legislature. The first condition of such choice is that the man shall obey orders. As only men of inferior character will consent to accept this condition, the result is that few really capable legislators are chosen. A nomination is often given to a man who is in financial difficulties, with the expectation on his part that he can turn it to such profit as to rid himself of his burdens. In the large cities he often pays an «assessment» for the privilege of the nomination, and reaches the legislature with the expectation of recouping himself out of his opportunities as a lawmaker.

The consequences of this change in the quality of legislators are familiar to all observers. Not only have the men of business, of professional eminence, of high character, in all walks of life separated themselves from the work of making laws, but the interests which they would properly represent in the halls of legislation have in some cases adopted the practice of obtaining by purchase the legislation which they desire.

The remedy for this condition of affairs is obvious, and has been applied in many States. It has happened repeatedly that when a legislature became so bad that its doings were intolerable, its successor has contained men of a higher and more useful character. The people have recognized that the fault lay in their own indifference or negligence, and have exerted themselves to secure the nomination and election of better men. This can be done in every State if the people will arouse themselves to their duty in the matter. The great cities, with their ignorant and their depraved voters, are the most difficult fields in which to work; but there is not one of these in which the honest and intelligent people cannot triumph by uniting and making the necessary effort. Popular government cannot be trusted to take care of itself. Respectable citizens cannot neglect their public duties, decline to take an active part in politics or to hold public office, and expect their government to be intelligent and honest. If they do not take charge of their public affairs, the other elements of the population will take charge of them, and, having obtained possession, will administer them in their own way.

### The Flag — a Symbol or a Fetish?

MUCH has been said within recent years about the teaching of patriotism in the public schools of the United States. To the end that it might be encouraged, many of the schools have been provided with flags, and in a considerable number formal exercises take place from time to time, when the flag is paraded, saluted, and the pupils pledge allegiance to it. The sight is always impressive and gratifying.

Yet it may properly be asked whether there be not some danger lest the enthusiasm thus aroused expend itself upon the sign rather than upon the thing signified; that is to say, whether our patriotic endeavors may not, unless wisely directed, produce a sentimental attachment to an emblem instead of creating a type of civic life whereby the emblem is genuinely glorified. It is of the highest importance that our children and youth should be taught that the nation expects them to devote property and life, if need be, to her defense, and that they must regard the integrity of the state as their peculiar care. But the possible danger which lurks in teaching patriotism primarily by means of this beautiful symbol is that it encourages the pupil to look for an international rather than a domestic field wherein to display his devotion. When a Spanish mob, incensed by what it considers bitter provocation, tears the Stars and Stripes in pieces, or an Irish poet sings of «bastard freedom» and a «fustian flag,» he is duly roused. The flag seems to him to have been immediately and grossly insulted, and he resents the insult; but so long as it waves undisturbed by any hostile hand or mocking word, he is tempted to feel that it is safe, even though corruption, greed, and partizanship bear sway under its very shadow. He is so convinced that where the sign is deliberately dishonored the thing signified must be insulted as to take for granted the wholly different proposition that so long as the flag is outwardly respected the state must be secure.

Under scarce any form of government can this fallacy produce more lamentable results than in a great republic. It was long since wisely observed that «the danger to a small republic comes from without; to a great republic it comes from within.» Indeed, any one who rereads the «Knights» of Aristophanes must be struck with the cogent application of its sarcasm to latter-day politics. *Mutatis mutandis*, Cleon and the Sausage-seller are with us still, striving as best they may to outbid each other in the favor of Demos—making small account, to be sure, of what Demos really needs, but fertile in devices for pleasing his ear, tickling his palate, fostering his self-love, and befogging his judgment. Now, as then, too, each is prodigal of protestations that he and he alone is truly loyal to the good name of his master, and that if Demos will but put the household quite unreservedly into his keeping, he will give especial attention to its social dignity and influence among the neighbors. One remembers the eulogy upon Colonel Yell of Yellville, «that though it was true his books did not balance, none could doubt that his heart beat warmly for his native land.» It serves to remind us that the deeper a man's hands go into the public pocket, the louder may become his vociferations of devotion to the flag, and the fiercer his indignation against any who may insult it. Nothing, indeed, can suit his purposes better than to foster a worship of the sign so blind and fatuous as to brand as unpatriotic all inquiry into the reality signified.

The recent history of biblical research has afforded us an admirable example of the tendency of means to usurp the place of ends. The Bible contained so sacred and necessary a revelation that in their reverence for its high office men confounded the Book and the message. A notion spread abroad that all searching examination of the sacred volume was an implied insult to it. Simply as a volume, or a collection of literature, it became sacrosanct, and men who would have shrunk in horror from the suggestion of idolatry fell perilously little short of worshiping it. To treat it as one might treat any other intelligent and trustworthy literature savored of heresy. And it is only after a long struggle that the Church has come to see that wise and candid study, with the aid of the best appliances, is the truest expression of reverence for the essence of the message. In a somewhat different fashion the emblem of the cross has genuine significance, and is worthy of man's reverence only as it represents the spirit and mind of Christ. It may become the merest fetish that ever misled and blinded human souls.

It is a matter of commonest experience that the higher the moral quality of any emotion, sentiment, or theory of life, the more dangerous the husk of it is likely to prove when emptied of ethical content. There is a distinct tendency in some quarters to-day to treat everything as glorious which the flag can be made to cover, and to denounce as unpatriotic all critical inquiry into the real ethical conditions of national life. The mass of Americans have yet to realize that patriotism is less an impulse than a duty, and that the man who makes most searching inquisition into the failings and possible iniquities that mar our public life, pleading for simple, unambiguous public speech, and the sternest and most uncompromising integrity in public act, may prove to be a truer patriot than he whose love of country never goes beyond the flag, which he bespatters with tawdry adjectives, and degrades by meaninglessly flaunting it in the face of sister nations.

The sapient remark of Guyau that «defense against the attacks of barbarians from within is as essential to our democracies as defense against the foe from without,» has a profound significance for American citizens. What the rising generation needs in the way of civic training is an intelligent acquaintance with the economy of our governmental system; the awakening of an unselfish and never-ceasing devotion to the duties of citizenship; a clear discernment between truth and cant in political speech; and a conception of patriotism that shall be ethical as well as emotional. By all means let the flag be kept in the schools and honored there; but let renewed effort be made to teach the pupils that its glory is precisely commensurate with the true nobility of that national life which it symbolizes.

### The Frontispiece.

DAGNAN-BOUVERET'S picture, «The Last Supper,» was perhaps the most notable of the paintings seen in this year's spring exhibition in Paris. In it a great religious theme is treated with all the skill of modern Parisian art, but with none of its sensationalism. The name of Dagnan-Bouveret, indeed, is a guaranty of serious intention no less than of high artistic accomplishment.

No copy has yet been put forth of the painting; but by arrangement with and through the courtesy of Boussod, Valadon & Co., we are able to present to the readers of THE CENTURY a copy of the study for the head of the central figure. This head of Christ, which thus appears as the frontispiece of the Christmas CENTURY, is an important addition to the imaginative presentations of this most sacred and most difficult of all subjects.

### The Higher Education for Women.

MR. ROMANES has lately given utterance to the theory that women of unusual mental powers are deserving of heart-felt pity; that they are destined to be very unhappy themselves, and to be exceedingly obnoxious to all those of either sex who may have the misfortune to know them. As a matter of fact, we do not find that those women who have actually been distinguished for their mental powers have done anything to confirm this theory. They have every one had the perversity to lead remarkably happy lives, and to have bound to themselves by the strongest ties of friendship the greatest and best of their contemporaries. Mrs. Somerville had rare social powers, and she met with a rare degree of social success. Mme. Kovalévsky, the famous Russian mathematician, is described as exerting a remarkable fascination upon all who surrounded her, and children in particular, it is said, were very sensitive to her charms. Sophie Germain had a wide circle of friends, who all spoke with enthusiasm of the charm and grace of her conversation, of the self-forgetfulness and the modesty of her character. Maria Mitchell had the love and reverence of class after class of enthusiastic young girls, and whoever had once been her pupil remained her devoted friend for life.

But this theory of Mr. Romanes is one which does not need confirmation by facts. It is one of those theories which the strong intuitive powers of his sex can perceive to be true at a glance, and to which the dicta of experience are absolutely immaterial. The slower-going reasoning powers of women, not seeing this hypothesis borne out by the facts, cannot help asking by what theoretical arguments it is supported; but on this point Mr. Romanes does not offer any assistance. He fails to give us any reason why clear and straightforward habits of thinking, which are admitted to be an element of agreeableness in a man, should be of an opposite character in women. I admit that there is something rather attractive about the mental powers of children. I admit that frivolity and inconsequence have a certain charm in a fair young girl; she is so very charming that everything about her is seen in an enchanted light. But is it to be supposed that if a good, clear understanding were added to her other attractions, she would be any less the mistress of all hearts than she is now? I do not believe that intelligence is a blemish in a woman any more than I believe that gentleness and virtue are blemishes in men. It is not to be supposed that a good intellect will always insure a woman's being lovable; but at the same time, it should not be forgotten that there are disagreeable women even among the very weakest-minded. It is true that a small amount of cleverness, a degree of learning which does not rise above pedantry, may make a person of either sex unadapted to lending charm to human intercourse; but that large mental powers, generously cultivated by the best attainable means, have not the effect of making both men and women more valuable for friendship, and more charming for love, is a proposition so nonsensical that it would not seem possible for any fair-minded person to hold it. It is an opinion that can be accounted for only when it is entertained by those men whose overweening vanity makes it impossible for them to find happiness except in an atmosphere of feminine adulation.

Neither can it be supposed that the possession of a feeble intellect, or of one which has been allowed to grow up wholly in a state of nature, is an absolutely certain guaranty of a well-ordered house and of well-trained children. There was once a race, the name of which has not been preserved in history, whose women had very soft and flabby muscles. A lover of reform proposed to introduce bodily exercises among them, in order to develop in them a greater degree of strength. «No,» said some; «that would unfit her for her duties as wife and mother. It is only her weakness that causes her to love her children. Make her strong, and she will insist upon digging the cabbages, and milking the cows, and all our children will die of neglect in early infancy.» So the change was not introduced, and the surrounding nations, being equally favorably situated in other respects, and having stronger women, gradually gained upon this short-sighted race, until it was crowded out of existence. There can be no doubt that that nation which first adds the well-trained mental powers of its women to the sum total of its intelligence will add vastly to its power for dealing with all those difficult questions which are pressing for solution. And there is no walk of life so uncomplicated that its problems cannot be better met, and hence the level of intelligence in citizenship be distinctly raised, by fitting out brains with knowledge, and with the mental force requisite for its application. There was a time when living was a simpler matter than it is now. Each generation was content to carry on its life as its fathers and mothers had done before it, and the pattern having once been set, it did not require much head to reproduce it. But the simplest kind of life cannot now be carried on by brains that are weak and flabby. No head of a household can sleep well at night unless she has knowledge enough to superintend her plumber. She cannot regulate her expenditures with easy conscience unless she can disentangle many far-reaching questions of political economy. She is forced to choose whether she will make her influence felt on questions of public and social reform, of temperance, of socialism,—on all the rocks on which our civilization is in danger of being shattered,—or whether she will join the ranks of those who are indifferent to the welfare of their kind. No one can form sound opinions in these days, and support them in such a way that they will carry weight, unless he has had his thinking powers hardened and tempered and sharpened by the very best processes that have yet been invented to that end.

The moral of my argument is very plain. Let women have the best education that can be given them. Permit them to make the most of their intellectual powers, however humble those powers may be. Because women excel men in virtue, they have not laid down the rule that men shall not be encouraged to practise the few small virtues that they are capable of. Preachers do not urge men to shun gentle manners, lest they should unsex themselves. Why not let each half of the human race cultivate whatever qualities it has, instead of crushing some of them altogether, because it is possible that they are too small already? Women have now entered the fields of organized charity, of prison reform, of management of schools. If they are bent upon occupying themselves with such grave concerns as these, why not put them in the way of getting that scientific knowledge without which they will do far more harm than good? Why not make it easy for every girl who has the right amount of ability for it to train her faculties as she thinks best? There are not many of either sex upon whom it is worth while to expend the higher education. For those women who deserve it we ask the best that can be had. Throw open to them the rich existing endowments which have long enough been lavished exclusively upon young men. Organize some method for picking out the clever girls from among those who cannot afford to go to college, and provide them with scholarships. Do not let the colleges reserved for women be crippled for lack of means. But above all, make them free of those postgraduate courses which are the flower of our great institutions of learning. Here and there will appear a woman of exceptional powers which it had been a pity if the world had lost. None will be injured by too much learning; all will be strengthened and ennobled, and we shall have fitted them, so far as in us lies, to leave behind them a world made better by their having lived in it.

*Christine Ladd Franklin.*

### A Lock of Napoleon's Hair.

A RARE relic of the first Napoleon is in the possession of Mr. C. H. Bagley, of Abilene, Kansas. It is a lock of hair cut from the Emperor's head after he was dressed for burial on the island of St. Helena. Mr. Bagley is a native of the island, as were his ancestors for several generations. Mrs. Lowd, the nurse of Napoleon, was acquainted with the entire family and was a close friend of his mother. For fifteen years preceding the removal of the Emperor's body to France Mr. Bagley's father was the captain of the guard of the tomb. When the family, in 1860, left the island for America, Mrs. Lowd, as a farewell memento, gave to Mrs. Bagley half of the most precious of her possessions—this lock of hair. She said that on the night of the Emperor's lying in state she crept in to take a last farewell of the man she had nursed, and to whom she was much attached, both for his kindnesses to her and because of his position. She longed for a lock of his hair, and made a request of General Bertrand that she be allowed to clip a tiny strand. He acceded, and she did so. For forty years she had cherished it, and then gave half of it to her dearest friend; the remainder is in the possession of Mrs. Lowd's daughter, still on the island. Two years later Mrs. Bagley died, and the lock was handed down to her eldest son, the present owner, who was seventeen years old when he left the island, and has a distinct remembrance of the hale old nurse and of the farewell visit. She was about seventy years old at the time of his departure. The lock consists of twenty-four hairs, black-brown, with one that shows a tinge of gray. It is sealed up in a bottle and kept in a case, with a piece of the coffin, some velvet from the pall, plaster from the room in which the Emperor died, a bit of wood from the original willow-tree over the grave, and some mortar that held the granite on which the head of the coffin rested. Three grown children, who were present at the receiving of the lock, made affidavits to the truth of the statements recorded, and these are filed with the relics. There is no doubt of the authenticity of the lock of hair, and of the other interesting though less valuable relics. The hair is particularly notable, as it is probably the only bit of that which was mortal of the great Emperor now on this continent.

ABILENE, KANSAS. *Charles Moreau Harger.*

[Not the only. The writer in his youth was present when was opened probably one of the lockets containing Napoleon's hair which were distributed, by the Emperor's direction, at his death. A single hair was given to the writer; he tied a bit of silk thread about it and placed it for safe keeping in his watch; the watch was left with a watchmaker for repair. The next day he went back to the shop and asked if a small piece of thread had been found inside the watch. «Yes; I blew it out.» «Then you blew out a piece of Napoleon Bonaparte,» said the writer.—EDITOR.]

### «The Century's» American Artists Series.

WALTER GAY. (SEE PAGE 263.)

MR. WALTER GAY was born in Boston, Massachusetts, forty years ago. When twenty years of age he left that city for Paris, where he entered as a student the atelier of Bonnat. His first *envoi* to the Salon was three years later, since which time he has been a regular contributor to that exhibition. His honors are: honorable mention, Paris Salon, 1885; medal of the third class, 1888; medal of the second class and *hors concours*, 1889.

Mr. Gay is one of the few foreigners who have been fortunate enough to have a work bought by the French government for the Luxembourg, and his «Mass in Brittany» received many votes for the grand medal of honor in 1892.

Mr. Gay's pictures display in an eminent degree the faculty of infusing the picturesque into common things. The movements of the figures are apt and right; they are always doing something, and are not simply posed models. The chief distinction of his paintings lies in the diffused light and vibration of atmosphere. Their color, somewhat sad and cold, is admirably wedded to the subjects, which lean to the pathetic. Mr. Gay tends to the naturalistic, but his naturalism is always gracious.

*W. Lewis Fraser.*

**Ronda.**

A LETTER from L. W. Hopkinson states that she did not find the inhabitants of Ronda as «grisly and ghoulish» as Mrs. Pennell states in her account of «Midsummer in Southern Spain,» published in the September CENTURY. Our correspondent says that she and her mother visited Ronda twice in March, 1895—two women without courier or *valet de place*, and ignorant of the Spanish language. Although the town was swarming with young conscripts, they walked freely about the place, together and separately, without receiving molestation or ill-will from man, woman, or child. They found the «America» scrupulously clean, and with an English-speaking landlord.

DRAWN BY JAY HAMBIDGE.

EM'LINE.

**The «Settin' Out» at Big'low's.**

WITH PICTURES BY JAY HAMBIDGE.

«YOU don't mean to tell *me* you never heard tell of a settin' out, do you? Well, it 's plain to be seen as you don't belong in these here parts, then. Why, settin' out 's a'most as common as courtin', an' everybody knows that 's been common ever since Adam 'n' Eve.

«Settin' out is when two fellers is dead gone on the same gal. That does happen awful frequent, you know; an' most likely they happens to meet at her house some night, both makin' a courtin'. Well, then, neither of them two fellers will go fust. They both sits an' talks, an' talks an' sits, an' each tries to tire the other out. The fust one to git tired an' go home is sot out, an' he don't never show up after that at that gal's house. That 's what settin' out is. An' a feller that comes foolin' round a gal after he 's been sot out, he gits sot down on hard by the gal, I kin tell you.

«Ever hear of the settin' out at Big'low's? No? Well, I thought everybody in the State had heard tell o' that. Go ahead an' smoke, an' I 'll tell it to you. I don't mind smoke; my old man nigh smokes me to death, an' I kind o' git used to it.

«You see, old Tom Big'low, that lives in the big house down acrost from Burr Oak school-house, he had a mighty purty gal. Her name was Em'line, an' she was the belle of these parts for sure. Lots of black hair, brown eyes, an' pinky skin, an' all that. An' a hustler, too. 'S fine a gal at a churn or at bakin' as I ever see. Everybody said Em'line would make a fine wife, an' all the young fellers was after her hard; but none of 'em was in it 'longside of Jim Doolan an' Hi' Morgan.

«It seemed mighty clear to all of us that them two held the inside track, an' it only needed a settin' out to see which one was to git Em'line.

«Course everybody knew Em'line rather favored a young feller down at the Corners, a story-writer or some sech thing as had come into these parts to look at us an' write us up into fool stories, which ought to be made shut of by law, goodness knows, they are so redic'lous, an' not a bit as we really are. But we all knew old Tom Big'low 'd never let Em'line throw herself away on no such trash; an' Em'line understood that pretty well, too. You see, old Tom Big'low is the richest man in the county, an' the meanest, an' he had

DRAWN BY JAY HAMBIDGE.

«‹JIM AND HI' SOT THERE.›»

swore by goodness gracious that Em'line should n't marry nobody but either Jim Doolan or Hi' Morgan.

«Well, that was in the winter of '75› an' I was takin' care of the Big'low house like, helpin' Em'line, Missus Big'low bein' laid up with rheumatiz in her back. So one night there comes a jingle of sleigh-bells in the yard, an' in comes Jim Doolan. Old Tom makes him to home, an' Jim sits down by the fire opposite Em'line, an' begins to talk about the huskin' at his house, which was set for the next Thursday.

«Almost before he gits started talkin', there comes some more bells in the yard, an' in comes Hi' Morgan, an' he looks at Jim kind o' cross like, an' he takes the other chair by the fire, an' Em'line moves over between them, so 's to be nice an' impartial; an' there them two fellers sits scowlin', while old Tom brings in some cider an' apples an' sets 'em on the table.

«Well, I sees it 's goin' to be a settin' out, an' liable to last 'most till mornin'; so I takes up my knittin', an' says good night, an' goes up to my room, for I knew young folks don't like to have their courtin's spoiled by outsiders. An' in a little while I hear old Tom come up an' go into his room, an' I knew the settin' out had begun in earnest. An' so it had. Em'line told me all about it the next year.

«Fust, for a while Jim an' Hi' sot there an' just glared at each other like they saw a bull-snake, an' Em'line she sot there waitin' for one or the other to speak; but neither of them showed signs of beginnin', so at last Em'line ups an' says, ‹Dad has put some cider on the table, boys; mebby you 'd like some.›

«‹Thanks, I *would* like some,› they both says at once; so Em'line she pours out a glass an' hands it to Jim, bein' as he come fust. Then she fills it again an' gives it to Hi'; but he pushes it back, an' says as stiff as tacks, ‹If you please, Miss Em'line, I 'd rather not drink from *his* glass.›

«That makes Jim kind o' huffy, an' he says, ‹Perhaps you think I poisoned it, *Mr.* Morgan.›

«‹Well,› says Hi', ‹I know as you 'd like to, whether you done it or not; but I *am* a bit partic'ler who I drinks after.›

«Well, Em'line she sees they are goin' to quarrel all evenin', so she gits her sewin' (some fancy stuff, which I don't take no stock in, for my part), an' she starts to sewin'; an' them two fellers just sits quiet like an' scowls at each other, not either of 'em sayin' a word for fear the other would take him down.

«After about an hour this way Em'line begins to yawn pretty frequent, an' Jim says: ‹Mr. Morgan, I think perhaps Miss Em'line means to hint that she an' I would rather be alone. Perhaps you are thinkin' of goin' home.›

«‹Not at all,› says Hi'; ‹on the contrary, I 'm havin' a very nice time indeed, an' I mean to stay just as long as Miss Em'line will 'low me.› An' with that he settles himself back in his chair like he was goin' to stay all night, an' closes his eyes contented like; an' Jim puts a couple of sticks on the fire, an' then *he* fixes himself back in his chair an' closes his eyes like he was contented.

«Well, Em'line sits there sewin', 'n' them two fellers sits there waitin', an' the fire gits warm, an' the clock on the fire-mantel keeps up a steady tickin', an', fust thing they knows, both them fellers is sound asleep.

«That way it goes on till ten o'clock, an' 'leven o'clock, an' twelve o'clock, an' Jim an' Hi' both snorin' to beat all. 'Bout half after twelve there is a little noise on the shutter, like a scratchin', an' Em'line gits up an' puts down her sewin', an' goes over to Jim an' shakes him gentle like. Jim he wakes up right away, an' so does Hi'. ‹'Scuse me,› says Em'line, ‹but I 'm afraid I heard the cat in the kitchen, an' I 'll just go an' see. An' I want to git a warmer wrap to put on, as it 's gittin' cool in here. You gentlemen just set still, an' I 'll be back by and by.› Then she kind o' smiles at both to oncet, an' goes out.

«Well, Jim an' Hi' they sits there an' glares at each other, an' glares an' glares like they thought they could kill each other by ugly looks. An' there they sot, an' after while they hears the kitchen door open into the yard, an' Em'line sayin', ‹Scat, there! Git out, you cat!› An' then they sot an' sot *an'* sot, but Em'line did n't seem to be very anxious to come back, an' in a while they goes to sleep again, an snores like a dry axle goin' uphill.

«Well, there they sets until old Tom comes down to feed the stock, an' finds 'em there sleepin' like infants. So he wakes up Jim, an' Hi' he wakes up too, an' both of 'em look round dazed like at the bright room an' the lamp burnin' yaller on the table, an' they don't hardly know where they are. Then old Tom ups an' says, ‹Where 's Em'line?› An' Jim looks kind of foolish, an' says, ‹I guess we hain't been very entertainin', an' she must have gone to bed,› an' with that he gits up and gits his hat. ‹Good mornin', Mr. Big'low,› he says; ‹give Miss Em'line my regards, an' tell her I 'll call again this evenin',› an' with that he goes.

«Then Hi' he gits up and says, ‹If you please, Mr. Big'low, give Miss Em'line my compliments, an' tell her I 'll call this evenin', too,› an' he takes his hat an' goes.

«Well, about that time I comes down, an' old Tom he sends me up to wake up Em'line, an' I go up to her room, when, law sakes! her bed hain't been touched! Course there was old Ned to pay then! An' what d' you think? While them two fellers was a-snorin' like a cow tryin' to swaller a corn-cob, that story-writer had come with a sleigh, an' Em'line had eloped with him! Yes, sir, right under them two fellers' noses!

«That was the great settin' out at Big'low's. Everybody in the county knows all about it, an' Jim an' Hi' had to go over into Illinoy to git away from the chaff of the other fellers. They 'd 'a' been joked to death if they had n't.

«Let me tell you one thing: when my old man was a-settin' out with me ag'in' Dick Haines, you 'd better believe he did n't do no snorin'; no, nor Dick either. If my old man had, he would n't 'a' been my old man now. Why, if he had, I actually believe I 'd have been willin' to have run away with a story-writer myself, though I must say they is mostly poor-doin' critters, an' do misrepresent us country people most awful in their fool stories.»

*Ellis Parker Butler.*

**The Mistaken Vocation of Shakspere's Heroines.**

«My subject,» said the lecturer, as she stepped gracefully upon the platform of the Twentieth-Century Woman's Club, «will commend itself to you, my sisters, as one which women alone can fully appreciate. I have chosen it because the world needs to hear a loud and convincing protest from the progressive Womanhood of this new era against Shakspere's attitude with respect to his heroines. Doubtless you have been taught in youth, as I was, to consider him as an unsurpassed delineator of female character; doubtless *Rosalind* and *Juliet*, *Portia* and *Cordelia*, *Ophelia* and *Imogen*, *Viola* and *Beatrice*, have been held up before you as the ideals of a perfect Womanhood. Doubtless, also, you have believed it all, and never stopped to think that Shakspere himself was but a man, and that his commentators have been men without being Shaksperes. The masculine conception of feminine character has thus been forced upon us. Shall we submit? [Cries of «No!» «No!»] Or shall we test the poet by the higher criticism of advanced Womanly thought? [Cries of «Yes!» «Yes!» and enthusiastic applause.]

«Let us, then, examine the pretensions of Shakspere. I do not deny that he shows in many cases a remarkable appreciation of the superlative qualities of woman. I will go further: I will admit that many of his heroines, in themselves, are ideally conceived. But—partly in deference to the opinions of his benighted age, now happily far behind us [cheers], and partly through his own ignorance and his own prejudices—I charge him, before the tribunal of cultivated modern Womanhood, with criminal injustice in placing his heroines in every play at a disadvantage. Hampered by a tyrannical plot, and bound to uncongenial or overbearing heroes, their energies are fettered and their true sphere closed against them. I am prepared to give convincing examples of what I assert [Cries of «Hear!» «Hear!»]—examples which will show you that the whole structure of Shakspere's dramas rests upon the disfranchisement of those heroines whom he is falsely supposed to idealize. [Great excitement.]

«I will begin with the four great tragedies, so called, ‹Hamlet,› ‹Macbeth,› ‹Othello,› and ‹Lear.› The tragedy is not, as some have falsely asserted, in the nature of the heroes of these plays, but in the misplacement of the heroines. Take, for instance, the gentle, obedient *Ophelia*. What cruelty to place her in such an unsuitable position as she is unjustly forced to occupy! The woman for *Hamlet*, ladies, was *Lady Macbeth!* [Wild applause.] His weak irresolution would have vanished with that intrepid counselor by his side. ‹Hie thee hither,› she would have said,

> ‹That I may pour my spirits in thine ear,
> And chastise with the valour of my tongue
> All that impedes thee!›

Could he have hesitated before his just revenge with her reproachful words in his ears?

> ‹Was the hope drunk
> Wherein you dressed yourself? hath it slept since,
> And wakes it now, to look so green and pale
> At what it did so freely? . . . Art thou afeard
> To be the same in thine own act and valour
> As thou art in desire? . . . Nor time nor place
> Did then adhere, and yet you would make both:
> They have made themselves, and that their fitness now
> Does unmake you!›

It is sixteen to one, my sisters, that *Hamlet* would have killed the king half an hour after *Lady Macbeth* came to court. [Cheers.] Yet the only use that Shakspere makes of this heroic woman is to urge forward a hesitating criminal to his doom. [Groans and hisses.] *Macbeth* was not a bad man—only a weak one. He needed a woman like *Portia* to manage him. If those celebrated remarks,

> 'The quality of mercy is not strained,
> It droppeth as the gentle rain from heaven
> Upon the place beneath; it is twice blessed,' etc.,

had been made to him by the lady of Belmont, he would have let *Duncan* go unharmed, and probably been an ornament to the highest circles of Scottish society until the end of his days. And *Portia* certainly would have been much more in her element ruling the Highland clans, and laying down the law as the thane's lady, than as the wife of an ordinary Venetian citizen, who had to borrow money from his friend to get married on! [A voice, «Down with *Bassanio!*»] Or, going further, if we study *Othello's* character, we find that either *Beatrice* or *Juliet* would have had no trouble whatever with him. *Juliet* would have convinced him beyond the possibility of a doubt as to her single-hearted and boundless affection for him alone:

> 'My bounty is as boundless as the sea,
> My love as deep; the more I give to thee,
> The more I have, for both are infinite';

while *Beatrice*, by her quick wit, would have dispersed his jealousies like a summer cloud, laughed away his suspicions, and teased him out of his authority. 'Would it not grieve a woman to be overmastered with a piece of valiant dust? to make an account of her life to a clod of wayward marl?' she would have protested saucily; and she would have exposed *Iago* mercilessly with the help of her keen eye and clever tongue. [Great applause.] As for *Lear*, *Rosalind* in *Cordelia's* place would have had far more tact than needlessly to offend her choleric old father.

> 'If with myself I hold intelligence,
> Or have acquaintance with my own desires;
> . . . . . . .
> Never so much as in a thought unborn
> Did I offend your highness,'

she would have protested tenderly; and I venture to say that she would have been more than a match afterward, single-handed, for *Regan* and *Goneril* combined. In a word, ladies, with these heroines in their appropriate places, there would have been no tragedies at all among Shakspere's works! [Prolonged applause.]

«And what holds good with the great dramas, my hearers, I repeat with regard to the lesser ones. If *Miranda* or *Ophelia* had been in *Juliet's* place, they would never have disobeyed their fathers for a moment, or dreamed of falling in love against orders. *Paris* would have been accepted without a murmur, and, on the whole, would probably have made a much better husband for either of them than *Romeo*, who was notoriously fickle. *Julius Cæsar*, if he had had *Brutus's Portia*, or even *Isabella*, to wife, instead of that submissive *Calpurnia*, would in all likelihood have obeyed her warning and stayed at home that day, and there would have been no fatality to mark the ides of March; while a wife like *Imogen* or *Cordelia*, frank, yet tenderly loyal, would have cured *Timon of Athens* of his foolish misanthropy, and made a good citizen out of him in no time. [«Hear!» «Hear!»]

«In view of these plain facts, my sisters, can we longer accept William Shakspere as an authority? [Cries of «No!» «No!»] Shall we keep him upon our bookshelves, and read him to our girls? [A voice, «Never!»] Shall we not regard him, rather, as well-meaning, but inadequate—blind to the true powers of Woman and the illimitable wideness of her sphere?» Here the lecture concluded amid continued feminine applause, and cries of «Down with Shakspere!»

*Priscilla Leonard.*

**Parted.**

De breeze is blowin' 'cross de bay,
My lady, my lady;
De ship hit teks me far away,
My lady, my lady.
Ole Mas' done sol' me down de stream;
Dey tell me 't ain't so bad 's hit seem,
My lady, my lady.

O' co'se I knows dat you 'll be true,
My lady, my lady;
But den I do' know whut to do,
My lady, my lady.
I knowed some day we 'd have to pa't,
But den hit put' nigh breaks my hea't,
My lady, my lady.

De day is long, de night is black,
My lady, my lady;
I know you 'll wait twell I come back,
My lady, my lady.
I 'll stan' de ship, I 'll stan' de chain,
But I 'll come back, my darlin' Jane,
My lady, my lady.

Jes wait, jes b'lieve in whut I say,
My lady, my lady;
D' ain't nothin' dat kin keep me 'way,
My lady, my lady.
A man 's a man, an' love is love;
God knows ouah hea'ts, my little dove;
He 'll he'p us f'om his th'one above,
My lady, my lady.

*Paul Laurence Dunbar.*

DRAWN BY E. W. KEMBLE

A THANKSGIVING ORDER, AFTER THE GAME.

CHARLEY LEFTGUARD: «Let your kick-off be cream soup; a touch-down of roast beef next; with a ten-yard gain of duck to follow; wind up with coffee for goal.»

THE DE VINNE PRESS, NEW YORK.

PAINTED BY FRANZ VON LENBACH

ENGRAVED BY HENRY WOLF.

# THE CENTURY MAGAZINE

VOL. LIII. JANUARY, 1897. No. 3.

## LENBACH: THE PAINTER OF BISMARCK.

DRAWN BY OTTO H. BACHER.

LENBACH'S HOUSE, GARDEN, AND PRIVATE MUSEUM.

EVERY one who has visited Munich carries away a recollection of that quarter of the town made beautiful by the broad streets and magnificent Greek buildings which date from the reign of the art-loving Ludwig I. Here, where it receives an added charm from the beauty of its environment, is the studio of Franz von Lenbach, one of the finest in the world, rivaling, if not surpassing, those of the great English and French painters. Built after the plan of a Roman villa, with a beautiful garden and fountain in front, it forms, with the neighboring private museum, an imposing group, a worthy addition to the symmetrical and beautiful structures about it.

The great steps, half the width of the house, lead from the ground to the studio in the second and the top story, giving to the whole a palatial appearance. Ascending the broad stairway, on each side of which are blossoming orange-trees, one reaches the fine loggia, round the marble pillars of which twine great masses of purple passion-flowers; from this one may pass on into the spacious and somberly rich studio beyond.

In appearance Lenbach is typical of his

race, with tall, heavily built figure, near-sighted blue eyes, and thin sandy hair. His manner is marked by an extreme simplicity and an entire absence of ceremony, amounting at times to a sort of mental withdrawal from those about him. Only after a nearer acquaintance one realizes that the seemingly careless glance with which he receives his many visitors takes in with unerring precision their physical, social, and mental dimensions. He is essentially a self-made man. Born of humble parents a half-century ago in a little village eight miles from Munich, he early showed marked artistic ability, and for a time was pupil at the Akademie. He began almost immediately to make copies of the masterpieces in the Alte Pinakothek, by which he was enabled to support himself, while at the same time he was forming his own taste.

During the years of his early manhood he made journeys to Spain and Italy, where the cult of the old masters, which so distinguishes him, was encouraged and strengthened. It is one of his cardinal beliefs that the true breath of inspiration is drawn from them, and at this the formative period of his art he made numberless copies from the Italian and Spanish schools, as well as from those of the Netherlands. The Schack Gallery has many rooms hung with paintings by him after the immense canvases of Correggio, Titian, Rubens, etc.; also portraits from Velasquez and Rembrandt. His constant and unvarying advice to young colleagues, toward whom his critical kindness is well known, is, «Study the old masters.» As a boy he spent long hours seeking out their color-formulas, analyzing their compositions, or searching after the spiritual verities embodied in them. For the English school of the eighteenth century he also has a great admiration, and some of his portraits recall the graceful and poetic creations of Gainsborough, Reynolds, Romney, or Lawrence.

DRAWN BY OTTO H. BACHER

THE FOUNTAIN IN THE GARDEN.

In the early part of his career his name was somewhat associated with that of Piloty, though, with his deeply ingrained idealist tendencies, he could never have been alto-

FROM A PHOTOGRAPH FROM LIFE. ENGRAVED BY HENRY WOLF.

LENBACH AND HIS CHILD.

THE CORRIDOR LEADING TO THE BISMARCK ROOM.

gether in sympathy with this great exponent of the realist movement in Germany.

To Lenbach what counts is insight and «the breath of life.» He believes that artists, like poets, are born, not made; that each must work out his own salvation in the way his genius best prompts; and that, after all, it is but little the master can do for the pupil. Imbued with these sentiments, it was only natural that he should cut loose from the established German schools. To exceptional genius and unusual methods of study he has added a lifelong habit of unflagging industry. For years he worked in an unpretentious back building on the site where he has now erected the magnificent house of which his brother, well known in his special branch, was architect. The studio is divided into three spacious rooms, and occupies the whole of the second story. The ceilings are richly decorated with medallions and bas-reliefs in dark woods picked out with gold; the walls, also dark in tone, are hung with valuable tapestries, and copies of well-known pictures made during his *Wanderjahre*, with here and there an authenticated work of an old master. An unceasing and discriminating collector, Lenbach has filled his house and studio with objects of esthetic and historic interest. There are marble statues and friezes of ancient Greece and Rome, busts and bas-reliefs dating from the Renaissance, crucifixes and reliquaries breathing the mystical afflatus of the middle ages, priceless and historic brocades, rugs, and hangings from the East—everything, from the beautiful shell grotto adjoining the studio, with its elaborate mosaics, to a rare bit of brocade from some suppressed monastery, giving evidence of the unerring taste of the master. The whole building is illuminated by a complete system of electric lights, enabling him to paint, as he often does, until far into the night. He is in consequence a late riser, breakfasting at ten, and rarely going to his work before eleven o'clock.

His studio is in a way a reflex of his domestic and private life. Noticeable by their number and beauty are sketches of his one child, a little girl of three, who is perfectly at home there, and always welcomed by her father, who invariably lays down palette or crayon at her approach. As beautiful as she is precocious, her silvery blond hair and delicate, rose-leaf face are a spot of color in the somber richness of the great rooms. She knows the names of many of the pictures, and it is a pretty sight to see her pointing out the various portraits in her soft voice and uncertain accents: «das Bismarck,» «das Helmholtz,» «das der alte Kaiser,» and so on. She upsets palette and oil-cans, steps on pastel stumps with impunity, and the choicest bibelots are given her as playthings. The great artist seems to find his chief happiness in portraying the loveliness of this child. A phantom-like delicacy of touch is specially apparent in these pictures.

In glancing about, one sees portraits of nearly all the contemporaneous great men of Germany, and many celebrities of other lands. Statesmen and diplomats, artists and musicians, women whose beauty has made them preëminent, scientists and litterateurs, many of them warm personal friends, bear testimony to Lenbach's power as a man as well as an artist. Portraits of the imperial house abound—the old Kaiser and members of his immediate family, among them that fine one of the Emperor Frederick which portrays him in the flush of expectancy and strength, clad in his white uniform, with a great star upon his breast. There are numerous and finely characteristic portraits of Bismarck and Von Moltke, his intimate friendship with the latter being too well known to need more than a passing mention. Wagner and Liszt are there, with something of the fire of the special genius of each caught and fixed on the canvas; also striking and gracefully individual portraits of Sembrich and Duse. Of the latter there are several done with his little girl, and the dark intentness of the great tragedienne is in strange and startling contrast to the almost ethereal brightness of the child. Lady de Grey's loveliness is offset by Monaldeschini's Southern intensity, and Paul Heyse's poetic head is seen near a picture of the Queen of England. Noticeable, also, is a fine portrait of Prince Rudolph of Liechtenstein done in dark tones, and near it is a characteristic one of the Pope. Among others is an interesting and powerful likeness of Professor Edward Emerson, which had one of the places of honor in this year's exhibit.

Lenbach has all his life been a great producer. This has been made possible in part by his rapid methods of work. He obtains his fine results with astonishingly few lines. One may see him put in a life-size head in pastel or oil in an hour, which, though linearly slight, is yet complete, revealing with marvelous precision the form and individuality of the sitter. His portraits are mostly bare of accessories, the greater number being, in fact, simply heads, the dress indicated by some slight suggestion of coat or drapery, which is soon lost in a background always subordinate. His work is never marred by over-perfecting. Possessing the rare quality of knowing when to stop, he seems specially to delight in a sort of happy play of half-veiled effects, which arrest the eye and arouse the imagination. The end of the studio where he works is lighted by a window of scarcely more than ordinary size, and even then he sometimes closes the lower half of the folding blinds.

His pastel sketches are unusual, being so slight sometimes that they seem the unsubstantial fabric of a dream, and yet the essentials, life and individuality, are in every one. As he himself said of them, «A breath, yet all must be there.» His memory for form and expression is prodigious, and he may often be found working at a portrait in a rapid and introverted way, without the sitter.

A CORNER OF THE BISMARCK ROOM.

PAINTED BY FRANZ VON LENBACH. ENGRAVED BY HENRY WOLF.

PROFESSOR EDWARD EMERSON.

Lenbach's views on life in general are revealed only in snatches, for he speaks but little of himself, and his conversation on any topic is rarely sustained, though in the phrases he lets fall here and there he betrays a simple and profound appreciation of the best of all ages. In literature his tendency is toward the classics. Seneca and Epictetus may be seen on the table near his easy-chair. The modern literary movements represented by the French psychological school and the various schools of the realists are absolutely alien to his temper of mind; modern metaphysics, with its hair-splitting analyses, has little interest for him. He cares little for forms and conventions, and, though acquainted with courts,

PHOTOGRAPHED BY FREDERICK BRUCKMANN. ENGRAVED BY HENRY WOLF.

FRANZ VON LENBACH. PAINTED BY HIMSELF.

has nothing of the courtier. A few years ago he was knighted by the Bavarian king, but he seldom uses his title. He has shown absolute independence of thought and action in a country the institutions of which have been considered to necessitate certain concessions toward people born to position, and an unswerving fidelity to the people and causes he has elected to uphold; these traits have probably been among the elements of his success.

The French consider him academic, and he, on his side, considers that, ethically, modern French art is all wrong; and one can see how he, pure idealist that he is, would shrink from the absolute literalness shown in their choice and handling of subjects. Their power he admits, and their learning; but he feels that their desire to show how well they can paint makes them forget that art, to be great, must be significant, expressive of some truth, moral or esthetic. He holds that the technic they carry to such a high degree of perfection is often used by them as an end, not a means, and is not only unworthy, but pernicious, in that it deceives and corrupts the beholder, accustoming and training him to the letter instead of the spirit. The sensational and realistic have no charm for him. The province of art is, he believes, to portray the beautiful, and not only the relatively beautiful but the absolutely beautiful. Though he does not exhibit in Paris himself, he nevertheless is very much interested in the pictures that the French send every year to the Munich exposition.

Lenbach often says that if it were not for the barrier of language he would rather have built his studio in London, which he considers the center of the civilized world.

In conclusion, it would perhaps be interesting to say a word of the painter's annual special exhibit at the Glaspalast, where his pictures are shown under nearly the same conditions of light and shade in which they were painted. The space allotted to him is divided into three rooms, the first a dim antechamber with only two pictures, hung opposite a large divan where one may sink down and forget the glare and fatigue of the main galleries. Here everything breathes repose and harmony. The ceiling is of dark inlaid wood, from which hang some rich old embroidered canopies; the walls are of a *fade* red, with here and there a piece of fine tapestry, and there is a discriminating use of screens, antique carved chairs, and various *objets d'art*.

A CORNER OF THE STUDIO.

For the better preservation of his great collection, Lenbach has built his private museum, and to this the public is daily admitted between the hours of one and three. It is the repository of countless marbles, carvings, and hangings of great beauty and value. In this is the magnificent suite of rooms, with tessellated floors and Japanese brocade hangings of the seventeenth century, known as the Bismarck suite, from its having been occupied by the chancellor during several of his visits to Munich.

Among the thirty pictures shown at Lenbach's last exhibit was his striking new portrait of Bismarck. The eyes are specially fine, with their steadfast intensity of look. Leaning on his sword, wearing a superb helmet, and wrapped in a paletot with a vivid yellow collar, one does not notice at first sight that this portrait of the Iron Chancellor, despite the insignia of power and the brilliant bits of color, makes him out older and sterner, with the lines of thought and care deepened about the mouth and eyes—those eyes that have kept so long and vigilant a watch over the destinies of Germany.

Viewed as a whole, Lenbach's art strikes one, above all, as honest. Here are no tricks of the brush, no specious strokes to deceive the eye into thinking it beholds truth where the work is but meretricious, no sensational juxtaposition of light and shade, no abnormal craving after something new. His work is pursued on great and long-acknowledged principles, modified only so far as the individual genius of every artist inevitably modifies the medium of expression. His portraits, in the eyes of which shine the soul, the mind, and the character of the sitter, bear testimony that his art is a faithful, if sometimes idealized, portrayal of nature. They testify to his peculiar gift of seizing and fixing those subtle traits that, more than form or feature, make us different one from another.

*Edith Coues.*

DRAWN BY OTTO H. BACHER.

SHELL GROTTO ADJOINING THE STUDIO.

# SPEECH AND SPEECH-READING FOR THE DEAF.[1]

THE majority of people will, I presume, be surprised to learn that there are to-day more than 2500 deaf children in this country who are not only taught to speak and understand the speech of others, but are taught as wholly by means of speech as the children of our public schools.

The children of our school always have quite enough to tell and to ask, but when they first return after their summer vacation they are filled with news almost to bursting. They chatter all at once if we will let them, and pull us this way and that in their endeavors to monopolize our attention. This year two little chaps were specially amusing. Each was eager to relate the adventures of the summer, and one with a roguish laugh placed his hand over the mouth of the other while he told me that he stepped in a bees' nest, and the bees stung him and hurt him very much; that he fell into a brook and got wet all over—« but my shoes did not get wet.» « Why did n't your shoes get wet? » I asked. « Because they were on the grass,» was the reply. My time was exhausted before their stock of information, and I fled in desperation, leaving them to tell their experiences to one another.

Can such children be called deaf-mutes? Had they been educated by the sign method their only means of conveying information to people in general or obtaining it from them would have been the laborious medium of pencil and paper, for very few people understand the language of signs. People soon weary of writing their conversation on the street, in a carriage, even in a room and at a table. A gentleman who had lost his hearing at seventeen, and then learned the sign language and was educated at the college for deaf-mutes in Washington, once said to me, « I found that people who came full of interest, and with many things to tell me, seemed to freeze up and close the fountains of their expression when I presented them with a pencil and tablet. So I learned lip-

[1] See also « Open Letter » on Helen Keller at Cambridge.

reading after I left Washington, and now I can talk with you or any one else, and I keep up more easily with the times. I knew I should lose my speech, as others have before, if I did not use it constantly, so all the time I was in Washington I read aloud to myself for hours in my room. I learned poetry, and recited it when alone, and in that way kept up my speech by my own efforts.»

Thanks to the pure oral method, and the pressure brought to bear by its advocates upon the schools of the old style, the day has almost passed when in any institution for the deaf such force of character is necessary in a boy to overcome the neglect of his instructors. It will soon seem incredible that such a statement as the following of Dr. Alexander Graham Bell could *ever* have been true. He says: «I have seen a boy who became deaf at twelve years of age, and who had previously attended one of our public schools, go into an institution for the deaf and dumb (where articulation was taught an hour or so a day) talking as readily as you or I, and come out a deaf-mute.»

To-day not only may those who have lost their hearing after acquiring language and speech be educated by speech, and taught to understand it on the lips of others, but also those who have been born deaf or become so in infancy. Little by little the teaching of speech and speech-reading has been forced upon the schools of the old type, sometimes by the public demand, and sometimes through the receptive intelligence of the principals. In 1866 there were 26 schools for the deaf in this country, in none of which was the oral method practised, and in only two or three was an hour or two a day given to the attempt to teach articulation to a favored few. To-day there are 89 schools, and in all but 7 articulation is taught, in 60 the oral method is used, and in 26 is employed exclusively.

The earliest recorded attempt to found a school where the deaf could be educated was made in the early part of the seventeenth century by the learned John Butler, a contemporary of Milton and Bacon. He, however, says of the project: «I soon perceived, by falling into discourse with some rationall men about such a designe, that the attempt seemed so paradoxicall, prodigious, and Hyperbolicall, that it did rather amuse than satisfie their understandings.» Indeed, it was not until more than a century later, when De l'Épée, Heinicke, and Braidwood founded schools in France, Germany, and Great Britain respectively, that any permanent institutions were established for the education of the deaf.

It is a very rare occurrence when a deaf person is mute for any other reason save the lack of the instruction which a hearing child receives through his ears. Recognizing this fact, and that speech is the most distinctive gift of man, Heinicke and Braidwood devoted themselves to the training of the vocal organs of their pupils, and to teaching them to read the speech of others by noting the movements of the lips and tongue. On the other hand, the good Abbé de l'Épée based his method of instruction upon the fact that all human beings, when deprived of speech, either through deafness or ignorance of the language spoken about them, resort to signs to make known their wants. All savage races have a code of signs by which they can communicate with one another and with the surrounding tribes. He therefore conventionalized and systematized signs, and invented new ones when natural gestures failed to convey the idea.

With this system of conventionalized signs, brought to this country by Dr. Thomas H. Gallaudet, a school was opened in Hartford, Conn., in the year 1817. It had been found, however, that the sign language did not solve the problem of giving the deaf a means of communication with the world in general. Very few people understood this language, while its construction, so far as there was any, and its conciseness—a single gesture frequently representing a complete sentence of spoken vernacular—rendered it unfit for representing grammatically constructed language. The method of spelling the words with the fingers by means of a finger alphabet was then pressed into service in conjunction with signs. This is the same as writing in foreign characters on the blackboard or upon paper, except that it is more rapid and more convenient. In this way the reading and writing of grammatical English could be taught, and both the manual alphabet and the sign language are employed in certain schools to-day.

For many years after the founding of the Hartford school no speech was taught there, though to-day the teaching of articulation is an important factor in their work. In 1867, largely through the efforts of Horace Mann, who some years previously had visited the schools of Europe, two institutions were established in this country where the deaf could not only be taught to speak, but be taught by speech without the use of the manual alphabet or the sign language. One of these was in New York City and the other in Northampton, Mass., and they are to-day large and flourishing institutions. After the establishment of these institutions there sprang up in this country, in the ranks of the teachers of the deaf, a division which already existed in Europe. On the one side were the ardent

DRAWN BY IRVING R. WILES. ENGRAVED BY E. H. DEL'ORME.

READING THE SHADOW.

advocates of the sign language as a means of instruction and explanation, while on the other were the opponents of signs, who employed the manual alphabet, writing, and speech only. The controversy has been waged with more or less energy ever since; but like all the ideas of a cruder and less advanced age, the sign language has been gradually crowded out, until now it is entirely excluded from many schools and used but sparingly in others. A single argument brought forward by the son of a distinguished advocate of the ancient method in support of this language is enough to indicate its ultimate fate, though it has served a noble purpose in its day. He says: «It is a fact worth noting that the signs used by the Indians of North America are identical in many instances with those employed by the deaf-mutes of to-day.» No one will question the truth of this observation, nor deny that it is worth noting; but we have reached a stage in the world's history when we can lay aside the tools of savagery. Through progress in enlightenment we are fortunately able now to give our deaf children a better means of communication with men than that employed by the American Indian or the African savage. It is a friendly struggle, in which the old-school advocates of the sign language are the defensive party and the oralists the aggressors. Both are, however, engaged in the great work of ameliorating the condition of an unfortunate class, and have much that is common ground where they can clasp hands with hearty approval.

In the schools for the deaf in the United States to-day three systems of instruction are used. The methods employed are, in the first system, signs and the manual alphabet; second system, speech and the manual alphabet; third system, speech only. Writing is of course employed in all the systems.

In 1817 there was but one school for the deaf in the United States, and it contained only 20 pupils; in 1870 there were 34 schools, and, in round numbers, 4000 pupils under instruction; while to-day there are 89 schools and 9000 pupils in attendance. In 1884, 27 per cent. of all pupils were given instruction in articulation; in 1895, 55 per cent. In 1870, 3 per cent. of the 4000 children under instruction were taught by means of speech alone in the pure oral method; while in 1895, 28 per cent. of the 9000 then in the schools were being educated by the pure oral method. It is beginning to be realized that all children should at least have a trial under this method, though their instructors may see fit to change to another system later. The State of Pennsylvania has taken the matter into its own hands, and has passed a law declaring that a State appropriation for the education of the deaf shall not be available unless facilities are provided for giving each pupil a trial under the pure oral method.

Formerly if a taxpayer was so unfortunate as to have a deaf child, he paid the regular school tax, but derived no benefit from it, as the State provided no school for the education of his deaf child. To-day in most States this injustice no longer exists, and a man can have his child educated free of cost by either the sign or oral system. In most schools the pupils are received when six years old, and retained for a period varying from six to twelve years. Owing to the desirability of continuous supervision in the education of the deaf, and the fact that many of the pupils come from long distances, most of the institutions are boarding-schools. The intercourse of the pupils with one another is therefore much more intimate than in an ordinary public school; as these are really boarding public schools, many parents of means and refinement hesitate to send their children to them. To meet this demand for a refined, cultivated home and school combined, a small school has lately been opened in New York. The instruction ranges here from the kindergarten through the college preparatory course. One special disadvantage of the public institutions is that, by reason of the small appropriation per pupil, the classes must of necessity be large, and it is here that a private school has a great advantage; for while still retaining the very desirable and almost necessary stimulus of association with others in the class, and the companionship that is needed for the best development of the child, it keeps the numbers small, and gives a greater opportunity for individual instruction.

It is generally supposed that the deaf have a tendency to moroseness and melancholy. This is least true of the orally educated adult, and among the children in the oral schools is not true at all. I know of no happier or more contented lot of children than are to be found in these schools. The visitor who expects to enter a place of silent halls, quiet play-rooms, and noiseless yards is much surprised to hear peals of childish laughter, and cries and shouts, as the children romp and frolic out of school hours.

As this is an article on the speech and speech-reading of the deaf, those so-called «combined» schools where only an hour or two a day is devoted to the teaching of speech and speech-reading may be passed by with a brief reference. Their results in teaching the congenitally deaf to speak and understand the speech of others are unsatisfactory, for a pupil cannot be expected to acquire those difficult arts with his share, perhaps a tenth or twentieth, of an hour per day. One might much better expect to learn to speak Greek fluently by studying it twenty minutes a day, and devoting the rest of the time exclusively to writing and reading English. I therefore pass on to the oral method, which alone can give the pupil a practical and working knowledge of speech, both uttered and read from the lips.

To most people the task of educating a deaf child seems very formidable, and yet in reality it is but little more so than that of educating a hearing child. In proportion to the amount that he has to learn, the deaf pupil progresses at about the same rate as his hearing brother. It must be remembered that the great majority of deaf pupils who

DRAWN BY IRVING R. WILES. A LESSON IN VIBRATION. ENGRAVED BY ROBERT VARLEY.

unless the mother takes great pains to preserve it by constantly talking to the child and encouraging it to speak. The preservation of this speech is well worth the time and trouble expended. As soon as the parents of a child discover that it is deaf, no matter at what age, they should seek the advice of some competent educator of the deaf.

One of the first lessons that the child has to learn upon entering school is to watch the lips of his teacher and attach a meaning to their movements. All directions and commands are, from the very outset, spoken, and the foundation of speech-reading is laid in the first half-hour, when the child learns to recognize his name on the teacher's lips. The amount of spoken language that a child has learned to understand before he can speak or write is considerable.

enter schools at six years of age have almost as much to learn as a hearing child of two. The deaf child has to be taught at school what the hearing child picks up while playing at home. At the end of six years the deaf pupil has more than kept his relative position; he has, as a general thing, gained a little on his brother, for though they are still separated from each other, the distance is less than at the beginning of their school lives.

If the mothers of deaf children could all be made to realize the importance and helpfulness of persistent, watchful training of the senses and faculties of their little children even before they are old enough to go to school, the work of educating the deaf would be much easier and the results more satisfactory. In most instances the child, though not more than three or four years old, can be taught to understand many simple-spoken phrases. If hearing was lost through sickness after some progress had been made in learning to talk, this speech will fade away

The first few months of the school life are devoted chiefly to exercises for the development and training of those senses still possessed by the child, which must do the work of the missing sense in addition to their own, and in cultivating in him the habits of obedience, attention, and concentration, without which he can make no progress. The attention on the part of the deaf child in the class-room must be closer than is required of a hearing pupil; for if his eyes wander from the teacher's lips he immediately loses the connection, since his ears do not tell him what is being said. The habits formed in the earliest classes are of fundamental importance, and a great responsibility rests upon the teachers of the lowest grades. Before the actual teaching of speech the attention of the child must be aroused, his interest awakened, the spirit of observation, imitation, and obedience cultivated, and the senses of sight and touch rendered alert. This is attained by a series of introductory exercises nearly in the form of play. The games are arranged to train the sight to rapid and accurate recognition of objects, colors, number, forms, and movements, and to develop in the sense of touch a swift and delicate discrimination between forms, surfaces, textures, weights, and finally vibrations. The eyes must do the work of the ears in comprehending the speech of others, and the tactile sense must come to the rescue in the training and guiding of the pupil's own organs of speech. The ability to distinguish differences of vibration by touch is the objective point of all tactile training, and the exercises bearing directly upon this are conducted with musical instruments such as the guitar, zithern, and piano, and then applied to the vibrations of the voice as felt in the chest, throat, and head. The child stands beside the teacher, and places the ends of his fingers upon the head of the guitar that she holds on her knees. She strikes a low note, and the child, watching, feels the vibration of the instrument. She then strikes a high note, and, repeating this, calls his attention to the difference. He is then made to shut his eyes while she causes one of the strings to vibrate. He soon learns to tell by the feeling whether it was a high or low note that was sounded. The next step is to place his hand upon her throat while she sings high and low notes alternately. By and by he acquires the ability to recognize the difference in tone by feeling her throat. The same thing is repeated with the zithern and the piano, and when the utterance of articulate sounds is begun; this power of recognizing tones by the sense of touch is used to guide the child in modifying his voice as may be necessary—in raising it if it is too deep, or lowering it if it is too shrill. He gradually learns to tell by the feeling in his own head and chest, not only whether he is speaking loudly, but also whether his voice is high or deep.

The introduction of diagrams representing the positions of the vocal organs in uttering the various sounds marks a new and entertaining step in advance for the children. The teacher calls one of the little ones to her, and, leaning his head against the blackboard, draws its outline with the chalk, to the immense amusement of the class, each one of whom insists upon having his profile added to the collection. Next day they are drawn with open mouth, exposing the teeth to view, and soon the teacher erases the top and back of the head, leaving only the lines of the nose, lips, and chin. The children are now given hand-glasses, and with the keenest interest identify the upper and lower teeth, tongue, hard and soft palates as they are added. They are now ready for a game which they greatly enjoy—assuming the different positions which the diagrams picture to them.

DRAWN BY IRVING R. WILES. ENGRAVED BY C. W. CHADWICK.

FIRST STEP LEADING TO THE DIAGRAM.

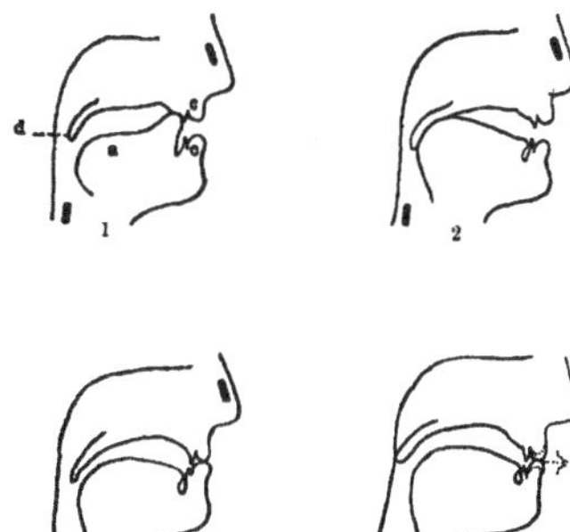

1, Diagram for N. a, tongue; d, uvula; ▮, voice or vibration; cc, lips. 2, Diagram for Ng; 3, Diagram for M; 4, Diagram for P. (Dotted lines show second position with expulsion of breath indicated by arrow.) Diagrams furnished by the author.

Each illustration represents the positions of the organs for a single elementary sound, and where a change is made in uttering the sound the second position is indicated by dotted lines. By the use of these graphic representations, and by imitation of the movements of the teacher's organs, the children are gradually taught to make all the separate sounds at will. As soon as a sound is mastered it is combined with others. In this way the different sounds acquire a definiteness and accuracy that it is hard to attain by any other means. It very rarely happens that a child fails to make some sound at the same time that he attempts to assume the positions indicated by the diagrams and by his teacher's tongue and lips. It does happen sometimes, however, that a pupil will go through these exercises noiselessly, and, even after recognizing the vibrations produced in the teacher's throat by voice, seems unable to produce those vibrations himself at will. The teacher must then watch her opportunity, and when the boy next laughs or cries, or makes some sound in his play, instantly call his attention to it. Sometimes it is a matter of weeks, but success is sure in the end, provided, of course, there be no physical defect of the organs.

So the work goes on, changing from day to day and from week to week, until, in the words of one of the most brilliant teachers of the entering grade, «At the end of three months the class are ready for the work of acquiring language. Their stock in trade, besides some twenty nouns *taught as rewards of merit* [the italics are mine], consists of the ability to write a legible hand, to pronounce simple English, to read from the lips the more common directions given in school and at the table, and, most important of all, the foundation of habits of concentration and attention.»

The hearing child just learning to talk is quite unintelligible at first, but gradually the organs learn their lesson, and utterance grows distinct. But the ear is the guide and critic of these early attempts. The deaf child, however, hears no sound, and sees only the slight movements of the lips and tongue, and can never learn to speak by his own unaided observation and imitation of those motions. The teacher must furnish the correction and training that the ear ordinarily supplies. The teaching of speech to a totally deaf child who has never spoken is truly a wonderful achievement. He has no conception of sound, and can never have; for the only sense by which he can be taught the existence of such a thing is that of touch, which simply gives him a knowledge of the motions that accompany sound, but are no more the sound itself than the vibrations that produce heat are the sensation we call warmth. To train the deaf child's organs to take their proper positions for the utterance of words as unconsciously as those of a hearing person is a very slow process. The development of any set of reflex actions is a laborious task even where mistakes can be recognized and corrected by the learner himself; in this case, however, the learner cannot correct his own errors, but must rely upon the alert ear of his teacher to keep him from acquiring a wrong set of reflex actions and forming habits that it will be almost impossible to break up.

Side by side with articulation comes the task of teaching language. Imagine yourself in a country whose speech you did not know, and whose inhabitants did not understand yours. Imagine, in addition, that you were suddenly deprived of your hearing. How well do you think you would succeed in learning the new language? Yet the congenitally deaf child is under even a greater disadvantage than this. He is not only in a foreign land the language of which he does not understand, but, to begin with, he has no conception of what language is. He has no language of his own which can be used as a framework on which and by which to build the new. If he is more than two years old, he may have invented for himself a few natural, gestural signs to indicate isolated objects or the simple needs of his body, such as hungry, tired, thirsty; but these signs can no more be called a language than the different movements of a dog's tail and ears which indicate his feelings or his wants can be dignified by that name. He has no conception of a structurally connected means of expression. Is it any wonder, then, if, after some years of instruction, the teacher occasionally finds a sentence like this, written by a boy in his journal after coming to school one cold March morning: «The wind is very blew, and I am a little shiver»? Or this substitution of act for implement: «The man chopped the ground with his dig, and the dog hurrahed with his wag»? The irregularities and inconsistencies of English grammar and spelling make it much harder, of course, to teach the deaf, and no class of people would be more greatly benefited by a strictly phonetic spelling and an exceptionless grammar than they. That the deaf child is not frightened by these irregularities is shown by the reply of a bright little girl when asked to give the principal parts of some irregular verbs. Several were given correctly, and then she began on another: «Eat—ate»—she paused for a moment in thought, and then added, «swallowed.»

Perhaps you would like to step into an intermediate-class room for a few minutes. The children are nine or ten years old and have been in school between three and four years—only four years removed from dumbness and utter ignorance even of the existence of language!

You notice that they are seated with their backs to the light, which falls full upon the teacher as she stands or sits before them. They are, perhaps, looking toward the newcomers, and the teacher taps the floor with her foot to attract their attention to herself. They do not hear the sound, but feel the vibration and recognize it as their call.

DRAWN BY IRVING R. WILES. ENGRAVED BY F. H. WELLINGTON.

DISTINGUISHING BETWEEN HIGH AND LOW PITCH.

After the ceremony of introduction is finished, they will, if permitted, put you through a catechism as to the location of your home, how far away it is, how you reach it, and how long it takes, until a stop is put to their questions. When you have thus been used as an exercise in geography, arithmetic, and language, the interrupted lesson is resumed.

The chances are that in this class it will be a simple language lesson. Language, being the key which unlocks the treasure-house of knowledge, must take precedence over all else. No one who has not taught deaf children has any idea of the difficulty of giving them an adequate understanding and command of English. Nearly every school exercise, then, is a language exercise in some form, perhaps appearing under names like «geography» and «history,» but often undisguised. The teacher is constantly on the alert to correct grammar, expression, and articulation, to supply words for ideas indicated, and also to work in information while the interest of the class is aroused. It is frequently necessary, in correcting articulation in the lower classes, to resort to mechanical manipulation of the pupil's tongue and lips, to placing the hand upon the teacher's throat, nose, and chest, and to phonetic analysis. The lesson is conducted as much by speech on the part of both pupil and teacher as though it was not a school for the deaf. You may not understand all the children readily at first. The speech of a congenitally deaf child is never natural, and varies widely in intelligibility, but can always be made such that those who have occasion frequently to listen to him will soon come to understand him, and that is a vast improvement over dumbness. In many cases much more than this can be accomplished.

DRAWN BY IRVING R. WILES. THE DIFFERENCE BETWEEN B AND P. ENGRAVED BY JOHN W. EVANS.

An interesting exercise, and one in which the children take the keenest interest, is a sort of «twenty-questions» game, in which the visitor, perhaps, if he feels so inclined, otherwise the teacher, is the one questioned, and a pupil the interrogator. An object, the nature of which is known to the class, but not to the person being questioned, is hidden in a box, which is intrusted to one of their number. I remember once it was a bright-eyed little girl of eight years, with dimpled, roguish face, who stood in front of me, the mysterious box held tightly in her little hands, and while the eager eyes of the others were fastened on our lips, propounded these questions:

«How many are there?» I said six at random, and hit wide of the mark, for they all cried in chorus, «Oh, no!» I then made a sudden drop to one, and was greeted with applause and a delighted «Yes» from my interlocutor. «What color is it?» I was next asked. I guessed a great many colors, and was finally successful in winning the applause with brown. I then insisted upon knowing whether it was good to eat, and was assured that it was, and she then asked me what it was made of. I began to suspect that it was a ginger cooky, and so enumerated the constituents that, to the best of my knowledge, go to make up that delight of the childish heart. I frequently met with assenting applause, but not in each ingredient, and finally discovered that it was a piece of spice-cake.

The instruction, begun as I have briefly indicated, is carried on until the children have been given a good common-school education, the subjects which they are taught being reading, writing, arithmetic, geography, history, English literature, physiology, natural philosophy, elementary chemistry, botany, drawing, and sometimes geometry and algebra. In many schools a course in industrial training is added, such as wood- and iron-working, wood-carving, clay-modeling, and painting. Truly the world has made great progress since the giving of even the most rudimentary education to the deaf seemed to «rationall» men, «paradoxicall, prodigious, and Hyperbolicall.»

Speech-reading in an oral school begins, as I have said, with a child's first school hour, and never ends. They learn to read the lips before they can speak or have any language whatever. At that stage it is only the reading of a labial instead of a manual sign. The

PHOTOGRAPHED BY A. MARSHALL.

Helen A. Keller

child very quickly learns that a certain sequence of motions of the lips and tongue means «Come here,» and he comes when he sees those motions, though he has no conception of the words. A beckoning gesture of the finger would bring him also, but is, of course, much less desirable, as it can never lead up to spoken words. By and by he learns to connect the words «Come here» with the familiar labial sign, and can write and speak them himself. In this way little children learn to understand many simple things that are said to them before they have the vocabulary to represent the ideas, and they thus early acquire the habit of watching the lips, and realizing that some definite idea is obtainable from their motions. Indeed, a school has been recently founded for the training of little children in speech and speech-reading before they are of school age, and remarkable success is being attained with the little ones. But speech-reading in its general application must be accompanied by a knowledge of language, spoken or written. Given language, speech-reading becomes a comparatively simple thing. There is no reason why every person (of good health) who has become deaf after the acquirement of language should not learn to understand conversation by the movements of the mouth. With proper instruction and practice, this accomplishment, which is almost a necessity, is within the reach of every deaf person. Even in the case of people who are only hard of hearing, it is a great advantage to be able to understand their friends without requiring them to raise their voices to a pitch that is wearisome both to the speaker and to those who may be near. The art of speech-reading in its wider applications is comparatively new, and those who have devoted thought and study to the methods of teaching it are few in number; but I feel sure that as an art it is destined to become more and more common, particularly among the adult deaf. To prove to yourself, however, that it is no easy thing to acquire the ability to read the lips, and that it is only *comparatively* that we speak of it as a simple matter, take the hand-glass from your dressing-table, and, sitting down with your back to some bright light, the reflection of which is thrown full upon your lips, speak a few sentences, words, and letters, and see how soon you think you could learn to understand even your native language by the aid of the eye alone. Better yet, put some cotton in your ears, and get a friend to speak to you in a whisper. Let him speak the words «night,» «tight,» «died,» «tide,» «nine,» «tine,» «dine,» for instance, and see if you can by the closest scrutiny discover any difference between the visible motions which produce them. Perhaps you will thus gain some idea of the difficulties a speech-reader must surmount. There are many words which cannot be distinguished from one another in appearance, but the speech-reader can, as a rule, distinguish between them by the context. «Come again to-morrow. . . .» The speech-reader would know that «night» was the only one of the above list that would make sense. The expert speech-reader often runs ahead of the speaker, and knows what is coming, in the same manner that a listener frequently knows what a speaker is going to say before his sentence is half completed, for thought is swifter than speech. In the same way the speech-reader comprehends the full sentence, though he may see only a part of it, since he supplies that which, though it escaped his eye, he knows must have been uttered. I have heard Dr. Alexander Bell compare speech-reading to reading a line of print with the lower half of the letters covered by a slip of paper. The eye sees only a portion of the letters, but the mind readily supplies the remainder, and reads the words. An excellent proof that the speech-reader sees only a portion of the words and supplies the intervening parts from his own consciousness is found in shadow reading. Several times I have arranged the light in such a way as to throw a sharp profile of the speaker upon some white background, and have seen a skilful speech-reader standing behind the speaker repeating sentences spoken deliberately, simply from the motions of the shadow. I have even seen this done when the speaker was a gentleman with a rather heavy mustache and beard, though the mustache was not, of course, allowed to fall over the lower lip.

Many people, and I am sorry to say some teachers of the deaf, fail to realize, in practice at least, that speech is not as clearly visible to the eye as it is audible to the ear, and think that by speaking slowly, word by word, and opening their mouth to the widest extent, they will render the task of the speech-reader easier. As a matter of fact they render it all the more difficult. A child in school may learn to understand a teacher who mouths his words in this manner, but this ability is of no value to him when he leaves school. Indeed, perfectly natural, deliberate speech is easier to understand than the exaggerated form of articulation which people are apt to use the moment they know they are talking to a totally deaf person. People who depend entirely upon their speech-reading for understanding others have requested me, when introducing them to strangers, not to say that they were deaf, because they find it easier to read the lips when the person speaking is not aware that he is being

DRAWN BY IRVING R. WILES. ENGRAVED BY E. H. DEL'ORME.

TEACHING THE WORD «HAT.»

understood in that way. I have in my acquaintance a young man educated wholly by this method, who travels a great deal, and picks up acquaintances on the steamer or on the train just as people do who possess all their faculties. I have in mind, also, a congenitally deaf girl of fourteen who is not considered unusually bright, yet whose speech is clearly intelligible to strangers after the first ten minutes, who is intelligent on the topics of the day, and whose conversational repertoire is much larger and more entertaining than that of many young ladies of twenty and over that I have met in metropolitan society.

Helen Keller is a household name both in America and foreign lands. She is blind as well as deaf. That the walls of silence and darkness which shut her from the world have been broken down, that her soul has been set free, and the seal of silence taken from her lips, seems miraculous to those who know not how it was done. The limits of this article will permit only the briefest outline of her story.

Rendered both deaf and blind at nineteen months by severe illness, she passed the first seven years of her life in silence, darkness, and ignorance. Who could have suspected the exquisite soul imprisoned in that mute and darkened body? A bright, patient, loving woman came, and the miracle began.

There was only one possible avenue of approach to the beleaguered soul. The sense of touch remained, and to that the teacher, Miss Annie M. Sullivan, addressed her efforts. Through finger-spelling the child at length obtained the idea of language, and with this key other doors could be unlocked. Having naturally a fine mind, she learned rapidly when once started, and developed a phenomenal memory.

While Helen received information only through manual spelling and in limited amount, she never forgot. To tell her something was like writing it in a book. When you wished the fact again months or even years afterward, you had only to ask for it. But later, as she began to read books, to meet more people, and to receive impressions through more channels and in larger numbers, her memory ceased to be so absolutely reliable.

Until she was eleven years of age her only means of communication was by finger-spelling. Then at her own urgent request she was given lessons in speech by Miss Fuller, principal of the Horace Mann School. The rapidity with which she acquired the ability to speak was unprecedented. She soon abandoned finger-spelling as a means of expression, and has ever since used speech alone.

But others still had to communicate with her by their fingers. She then expressed a strong wish to learn to read the lips by touching them with her fingers. For the purpose of attempting this difficult task and to get special training in speech she came to the Wright-Humason School in New York city. During the two years that she remained there she succeeded in acquiring the power of understanding people when they spoke to her, and at the same time pursued regular courses of study in arithmetic, history, physical geography, French, and German. She has read much of the best literature, and is very intelligent on the topics of the day. Her own speech is now excellent, and she has entered a girls' school in Cambridge, Massachusetts, where she is taking a course preparatory for Radcliffe College.

When being spoken to she places her index-finger lightly upon the lips, while the other fingers rest upon the cheek, the middle one touching the nose. Her thumb is upon the larynx. This position gives her the greatest possible information concerning the elements of which speech is composed.

The public are always interested in results. What, then, is a conservative statement of the results obtained by the oral method aside from the general education? It gives to those deaf from infancy a speech that is intelligible to their immediate friends, and in varying degrees to strangers. It enables them to understand conversation on ordinary topics wherever the lips are clearly visible. It restores them to the society of their fellows in very much larger measure than is possible without speech and speech-reading. I do not claim that they are on the same footing as hearing people. They cannot be; their speech is never perfectly natural, and they can never take part in general conversation as those in the possession of their hearing. The orally educated deaf are found in many of the callings of life, such as journalism, civil engineering, architecture, designing, business, and the trades. They have written for publication on various subjects, in a clear, forcible, and interesting style; but I am not aware that any of them have ever attained literary prominence. The realm of poetry is practically closed to them. They appreciate the beauty of its expression, but though they are frequently quick to catch the rhythm of motion, and are fond of dancing, the rhythm and swing of words seem to escape them. There has been, I think, but one deaf poet, and his poems were chiefly remarkable in the light of his infirmity. So much for the most conservative view. On the other hand, there are many deaf people in this country who have acquired all their speech and speech-reading by instruction after becoming deaf, who go into society, entertain in their own homes, and are entertained in the homes of others, as freely as any members of the community. There are many with whom a stranger might talk for an hour without suspecting that they were deaf, accounting for their slight peculiarity of speech by supposing all the time that they were foreigners. Methods are being constantly improved, and it is to be expected that still better results will be obtained hereafter. Meanwhile experience has demonstrated that by the use of speech as a medium of instruction, the deaf can be successfully educated, and taught to speak and understand the speech of others; and I believe the time is coming when this will be the only way in which they are taught.

*John Dutton Wright.*

DRAWN BY CHARLES STANLEY REINHART.

"HAIL TO THE CHIEF!"

# CAMPAIGNING WITH GRANT.

BY GENERAL HORACE PORTER.

GRANT'S THIRD DAY IN THE WILDERNESS—HAIL TO THE CHIEF!—A NIGHT ALARM—A MIDNIGHT RIDE—GRANT ROUGHS IT WITH HIS TROOPS—OUT OF THE WILDERNESS—SHERIDAN ORDERED TO CRUSH «JEB» STUART—A CHAPTER OF ACCIDENTS—GRANT IN FRONT OF SPOTSYLVANIA—THE DEATH OF SEDGWICK—ARRIVAL OF DESPATCHES—«I SHALL TAKE NO BACKWARD STEPS»—COMMUNICATING WITH BURNSIDE—GRANT ATTACKS THE ENEMY'S CENTER—HOW A FAMOUS MESSAGE WAS DESPATCHED—NEWS FROM THE OTHER ARMIES—AN EVENTFUL MORNING AT HEADQUARTERS—TWO DISTINGUISHED PRISONERS—HOW THE «ANGLE» WAS CAPTURED—SCENES AT THE «BLOODY ANGLE.»

### GRANT'S THIRD DAY IN THE WILDERNESS.

THE next morning, May 7, General Grant was almost the first one up. He seated himself at the camp-fire at dawn, and looked thoroughly refreshed after the sound sleep he had enjoyed. In fact, a night's rest had greatly reinvigorated every one. A fog, combined with the smoke from the smoldering forest fires, rendered it difficult for those of us who were sent to make reconnaissances to see any great distance, even where there were openings in the forest. A little after 6 A. M. there was some artillery firing from Warren's batteries, which created an impression for a little while that the enemy might be moving against him; but he soon sent word that he had been firing at some skirmishers who had pushed down to a point near his intrenchments and discharged a few shots. At 6:30 A. M. the general issued his orders to prepare for a night march of the entire army toward Spotsylvania Court House, on the direct road to Richmond. At 8:30 Burnside pushed out a skirmishing party to feel the enemy, and found that he had withdrawn from a portion of his line. Skirmishing continued along parts of Warren's front till 11 A. M. In fact, each army was anxious to learn promptly the position and apparent intentions of the other, so as to be able to act intelligently in making the next move in the all-absorbing game. The enemy was found to be occupying a strongly intrenched line defended by artillery, and at an average distance from our front of nearly a mile.

While sitting at the mess-table taking breakfast, I asked the general-in-chief: «In all your battles up to this time, where do you think your presence upon the field was most useful in the accomplishing of results?» He replied: «Well, I don't know»; then, after a pause, «perhaps at Shiloh.» I said: «I think it was last night, when the attack was made on our right.» He did not follow up the subject, for he always spoke with great reluctance about anything which was distinctly personal to himself. The only way in which we could ever draw him out, and induce him to talk about events in his military career, was to make some misstatement intentionally about an occurrence. His regard for truth was so great that his mind always rebelled against inaccuracies, and in his desire to correct the error he would go into an explanation of the facts, and in doing so would often be led to talk with freedom upon the subject.

An officer related to the general an incident of the attack the night before, which showed that even the gravest events have a comical side. In the efforts to strengthen our right, a number of teamsters had been ordered into the ranks and sent hurriedly to the front. As they were marching past their teams, one of the men was recognized by his favorite «lead» mule, who proceeded to pay his respects to him in a friendly hee-haw, which reverberated through the forest until the sound bid fair to rival the report of the opening gun at Lexington, which fired the «shot heard round the world.» The teamster turned to him and cried: «Oh, you better not laugh, old Simon Bolivar. Before this fight 's through I bet they 'll pick you up and put you into the ranks, too!»

After leaving the breakfast-table, the general lighted a cigar and took his seat on a camp-stool in front of his tent. In a conversation with the staff he then began to discuss the operations of the day before. He expressed himself as satisfied with the result in the main, saying: «While it is in one sense a drawn battle, as neither side has gained or lost ground substantially since the fighting began, yet we remain in possession of the field, and the forces opposed to us have withdrawn to a distance from our front and taken up a defensive position. We cannot call the engagement a positive victory, but the enemy have only twice actually reached our lines in their many attacks, and have not gained a single advantage. This will enable me to carry out my intention of moving to the left, and compelling the enemy to fight in a more open country and outside of their breastworks.»

An old officer who was passing by, an acquaintance of the general's, now stepped up to the group. He had recently been ordered in from the plains, and his wild tales of red-handed slaughter in the land of the savages had already made him known in the army as the «Injun-slayer.» An aide remarked to him, «Well, as you 've been spoiling for a fight ever since you joined this army, how did yesterday's set-to strike you by way of a skirmish?» «Oh!» was the reply, «you had large numbers engaged, and heavy losses; but it was n't the picturesque, desperate hand-to-hand fighting that you see when you 're among the Injuns.» «No; but we got in some pretty neat work on the white man,» said the aide. «Yes; but it did n't compare with the time the Nez Percés and the Shoshonee tribes had their big battle,» continued the veteran. «Why, how was that?» cried all present in a chorus. «Well, you see,» explained the narrator, «first the Nez Percés set up a yell louder than a blast of Gabriel's trumpet, and charged straight across the valley; but the Shoshonees stood their ground without budging an inch, and pretty soon they went for the Nez Percés and drove 'em back again. As soon as the Nez Percés could catch their breath they took another turn at the Shoshonees, and shoved them back just about where they started from. By this time the ground between 'em was so covered by the killed and wounded that you could n't see as much as a blade of grass. But still they kept on charging back and forth across that valley, and they moved so fast that when their lines of battle passed me, the wind they made was so strong that I had to hold my hat on with both hands, and once I came mighty near being blown clear off my feet.» «Why, where were *you* all this time?» asked several voices. «Oh,» said he, «I was standing on a little knoll in the middle of the valley, looking on.» «Why,» remarked an officer, «I should think they would have killed you in the scrimmage.» Then the face of the veteran of the plains assumed an air of offended innocence, and in a tone of voice which made it painfully evident that he felt the hurt, he said, «What?—the Injuns! Lord, they all knew *me!*» The general joined in the smiles which followed this bit of sadly mutilated truth. Similar Munchausenisms, indulged in from time to time by this officer, demonstrated the fact that he had become so skilled in warping veracity that one of his lies could make truth look mean alongside of it, and he finally grew so untrustworthy that it was unsafe even to believe the contrary of what he said.

At 3 P. M. despatches were received by way of Washington, saying that General Butler had reached the junction of the James and Appomattox rivers the night of the 5th, had surprised the enemy, and successfully disembarked his troops, and that Sherman was moving out against Johnston in Georgia, and expected that a battle would be fought on the 7th.

### HAIL TO THE CHIEF!

ALL preparations for the night march had now been completed. The wagon-trains were to move at 4 P. M., so as to get a start of the infantry, and then go into park and let the troops pass them. The cavalry had been thrown out in advance; the infantry began the march at 8:30 P. M. Warren was to proceed along the Brock road toward Spotsylvania Court House, moving by the rear of Hancock, whose corps was to remain in its position during the night to guard against a possible attack by the enemy, and afterward to follow Warren. Sedgwick was to move by way of Chancellorsville and Piney Branch Church. Burnside was to follow Sedgwick, and to cover the trains which moved on the roads that were farthest from the enemy.

Soon after dark, Generals Grant and Meade, accompanied by their staffs, after having given personal supervision to the starting of the march, rode along the Brock road toward Hancock's headquarters, with the intention of waiting there till Warren's troops should reach that point. While moving close to Hancock's line, there occurred an unexpected demonstration on the part of the troops, which created one of the most memorable scenes of the campaign. Notwithstanding the darkness of the night, the form of the commander was recognized, and word was passed rapidly along that the chief who had led them through the mazes of the Wilderness was again moving forward with his horse's head turned toward Richmond. Troops know but little about what is going on in a large army, except the occurrences which take place in their immediate vicinity; but this night ride of the general-in-chief told plainly the story of success, and gave each man to understand that the cry was to be «On to Richmond!» Soldiers weary and sleepy after their long battle, with stiffened limbs and smarting wounds, now sprang to their feet, forgetful of their pains, and rushed forward to the roadside. Wild cheers echoed through the forest, and glad shouts of triumph rent the air. Men swung their hats, tossed up their arms, and pressed forward to within touch of their chief, clapping their hands, and speaking to him with the familiarity of comrades. Pine-knots and leaves were set on fire, and lighted the scene with their weird, flickering glare. The night march had become a triumphal procession for the new commander. The demonstration was the emphatic verdict pronounced by the troops upon his first battle in the East. The excitement had been imparted to the horses, which soon became restive, and even the general's large bay, over which he possessed ordinarily such perfect control, became difficult to manage. Instead of being elated by this significant ovation, the general, thoughtful only of the practical question of the success of the movement, said: «This is most unfortunate. The sound will reach the ears of the enemy, and I fear it may reveal our movement.» By his direction, staff officers rode forward and urged the men to keep quiet so as not to attract the enemy's attention; but the demonstration did not really cease until the general was out of sight.

### A NIGHT ALARM.

WHEN Hancock's headquarters were reached, the party remained with him for some time, awaiting the arrival of the head of Warren's troops. Hancock's wound received at Gettysburg had not thoroughly healed, and he suffered such inconvenience from it when in the saddle that he had applied for permission to ride in a spring ambulance while on the march and when his troops were not in action. He was reclining upon one of the seats of the ambulance, conversing with General Grant, who had dismounted and was sitting on the ground with his back against a tree, whittling a stick, when the sound of firing broke forth directly in front. Hancock sprang up, seized his sword, which was lying near him, buckled it around his waist, and cried: «My horse! my horse!» The scene was intensely dramatic, and recalled vividly to the bystanders the cry of Richard III on the field of Bosworth. Grant listened a moment without changing his position or ceasing his whittling, and then remarked: «They are not fighting; the firing is all on one side. It takes two sides to start a fight.» In a few minutes the firing died away, and it was found that the enemy was not advancing. The incident fairly illustrates the contrast in the temperaments of these two distinguished soldiers.

### A MIDNIGHT RIDE.

AT 11 o'clock word came to Grant and Meade that their headquarters escorts and wagons were delaying the advance of Warren's corps, and they decided to move on to Todd's tavern in order to clear the way. The woods were still on fire along parts of the main road, which made it almost impassable, so that the party turned out to the right into a side road. The intention was to take the same route by which the cavalry had advanced, but it was difficult to tell one road from another. The night was dark, the dust was thick, the guide who was directing the party became confused, and it was uncertain whether we were going in the right direction or riding into the lines of the enemy. The guide was for a time suspected of treachery, but he was innocent of such a charge, and had only lost his bearings. Colonel Comstock rode on in advance, and hearing the sound of marching columns not far off on our right, came back with this news, and it was decided to return to the Brock road. General Grant at first demurred when it was proposed to turn back, and urged the guide to try and find some cross-road leading to the Brock road, to avoid retracing our steps. This was an instance of his marked aversion to turning back, which amounted almost to a superstition. He often put himself to the greatest personal inconvenience to avoid it. When he found he was not traveling in the direction he intended to take, he would try all sorts of cross-cuts, ford streams, and jump any number of fences to reach another road rather than go back and take a fresh start. If he had been in the place of the famous apprentice boy who wandered away from London, he would never have been thrice mayor of that city, for with him Bow Bells would have appealed to deaf ears when they chimed out, «Turn again, Whittington.» The enemy who encountered him never failed to feel the effect of this inborn prejudice against turning back. However, a slight retrograde movement became absolutely necessary in the present instance, and the general yielded to the force of circumstances. An orderly was stationed at the fork of the roads to indicate the right direction to Warren's troops when they should reach that point, and our party proceeded to Todd's tavern, reaching there soon after midnight. It was learned afterward that Anderson's (Longstreet's) corps had been marching parallel with us, and at a distance of less than a mile, so that the apprehension felt was well founded.

### GRANT ROUGHS IT WITH HIS TROOPS.

THE general and staff bivouacked upon the ground. The night was quite chilly, and a couple of fires were lighted to add to our comfort. General Grant lay down with his officers beside one of the fires, without any covering; when asleep, an aide quietly spread an overcoat over him. For about four hours we all kept turning over every few minutes so as to get warmed on both sides, imitating with our bodies the diurnal motion of the earth as it exposes its sides alternately to the heat of the sun. When daylight broke it was seen that a low board structure close to which the general-in-chief had lain down was a pig-pen; but its former occupants had disappeared, and were probably at that time nourishing the stomachs of the cavalry troopers of the invading army. Unfortunately, the odors of the place had not taken their departure with the pigs, but remained to add to the discomfort of the bivouackers. Sheridan's cavalry had had a fight at this place the afternoon before, in which he had defeated the opposing force, and the ground in the vicinity, strewn with the dead, offered ample evidence of the severity of the struggle.

At daylight on the morning of the 8th active operations were in progress throughout the columns. General Sheridan had ordered his cavalry to move by different roads to seize the bridges crossing the Po River. General Meade modified these orders, and directed a portion of the cavalry to move in front of Warren's infantry on the Spotsylvania Court House road. The enemy were felling trees and placing other obstacles in the way, in order to impede the movement, and the cavalry was afterward withdrawn and the infantry directed to open the way.

About sunrise General Grant, after taking off his coat and shaking it to rid it of some of the dust in which he had lain down, shared with the staff-officers some soldiers' rations, and then seated himself on the ground by the roadside to take his morning smoke.

### OUT OF THE WILDERNESS.

SOON afterward he and General Meade rode on, and established their respective headquarters near Piney Branch Church, about two miles to the east of Todd's tavern. It was Sunday, but the overrunning of the country by contending armies had scattered the little church's congregation. The temple of prayer was voiceless, the tolling of its peaceful bell had given place to the echo of hostile guns, and in the excitement which prevailed it must be confessed that few recalled the fact that it was the Sabbath day.

A drum corps in passing caught sight of the general, and at once struck up a then popular negro camp-meeting air. Every one began to laugh, and Rawlins cried, «Good for the drummers!» «What 's the fun?» inquired the general. «Why,» was the reply, «they are playing, ‹Ain't I glad to get out ob de wilderness!›» The general smiled at the ready wit of the musicians, and said, «Well, with me a musical joke always requires explanation. I know only two tunes: one is ‹Yankee Doodle,› and the other is n't.»

Charles A. Dana, Assistant Secretary of War, joined us during the forenoon, coming from Washington by way of Rappahannock Station, and remained at headquarters most of the time through the entire campaign. His daily, and sometimes hourly, despatches to the War Department, giving the events occurring in the field, constituted a correspondence which is a rare example of perspicuity, accuracy, and vividness of description.

### SHERIDAN ORDERED TO CRUSH «JEB» STUART.

SHERIDAN had been sent for by Meade to come to his headquarters, and when he arrived, between eleven and twelve o'clock that morning, a very acrimonious dispute took place between the two generals. Meade was possessed of an excitable temper which under irritating circumstances became almost ungovernable. He had worked himself into a towering passion regarding the delays encountered in the forward movement, and when Sheridan appeared went at him hammer and tongs, accusing him of blunders, and charging him with not making a proper disposition of his troops, and letting the cavalry block the advance of the infantry. Sheridan was equally fiery, and, smarting under the belief that he was unjustly treated, all the hotspur in his nature was aroused. He insisted that Meade had created the trouble by countermanding his (Sheridan's) orders, and that it was this act which had resulted in mixing up his troops with the infantry, exposing one cavalry division to great danger, and rendering ineffectual all his combinations regarding the movements of the cavalry corps. Sheridan declared with great warmth that he would not command the cavalry any longer under such conditions, and said if he could have matters his own way he would concentrate all the cavalry, move out in force against Stuart's command, and whip it. His language throughout was highly spiced and conspicuously italicized with expletives. General Meade came over to General Grant's tent immediately after, and related the interview to him. The excitement of the one was in singular contrast with the calmness of the other. When Meade repeated the remarks made by Sheridan, that he could move out with his cavalry and whip Stuart, General Grant quietly observed, «Did Sheridan say that? Well, he generally knows what he is talking about. Let him start right out and do it.» By one o'clock Sheridan had received his orders in writing from Meade for the movement. Early the next morning he started upon his famous raid to the vicinity of Richmond in rear of the enemy's army, and made good his word.

After the interview just mentioned, the general-in-chief talked for some time with officers of the staff about the results of the battle of the previous days. He said in this connection: «All things in this world are relative. While we were engaged in the Wilderness I could not keep from thinking of the first fight I ever saw—the battle of Palo Alto. As I looked at the long line of battle, consisting of three thousand men, I felt that General Taylor had such a fearful responsibility resting upon him that I wondered how he ever had the nerve to assume it; and when, after the fight, the casualties were reported, and the losses ascertained to be nearly sixty in killed, wounded, and missing, the engagement assumed a magnitude in my eyes which was positively startling. When the news of the victory reached the States, the windows in every household were illuminated, and it was largely instrumental in making General Taylor President of the United States. Now, such an affair would scarcely be deemed important enough to report to headquarters.» He little thought at that moment that the battles then in progress would be chiefly instrumental in making the commander himself President of the United States.

### A CHAPTER OF ACCIDENTS.

THE movements of the opposing armies now became one of the most instructive lessons in the art of modern warfare. They showed the closeness of the game played by the two great masters who commanded the contending forces, and illustrated how thoroughly those skilled fencers had carte and tierce at their fingers' ends. They demonstrated, also, how far the features of a campaign may be affected by accidents and errors. In the Wilderness the manœuvers had been largely a game of blindman's-buff; they now became more like the play of pussy-wants-a-corner. Anderson had been ordered by Lee, on the evening of May 7, to start for Spotsylvania Court House the next morning; but Anderson, finding the woods on fire, and no good place to go into camp, kept his troops in motion, continued his march all night, and reached Spotsylvania in the morning. The cavalry which Sheridan had placed at the bridges over the Po River might have greatly impeded Anderson's march; but owing to conflicting orders the movements of the cavalry had been changed, and Anderson occupied a position at Spotsylvania that morning as the result of a series of accidents. When Lee found our wagon-trains were moving in an easterly direction, he made up his mind that our army was retreating, and telegraphed on the 8th to his government at Richmond: «The enemy has abandoned his position, and is moving toward Fredericksburg.» He sent an order the same day to Early, then commanding Hill's corps, saying: «Move by Todd's tavern along the Brock road as soon as your front is clear of the enemy.» It will be seen that in this order he directed a corps to move by a road which was then in full possession of our forces, and Early did not discover this fact till he actually encountered Hancock's troops at Todd's tavern. Early was then compelled to take another road. It was after these movements that General Grant uttered the aphorism, «Accident often decides the fate of battle.»

At 11:30 A. M. General Grant sent a telegram to Halleck, saying: «The best of feeling prevails. . . . Route to the James River . . . not yet definitely marked out.» In talking over the situation at headquarters, he said: «It looks somewhat as if Lee intends to throw his army between us and Fredericksburg, in order to cut us off from our base of supplies. I would not be at all sorry to have such a move made, as in that case I would be in rear of Lee, and between him and Richmond.»

### GRANT IN FRONT OF SPOTSYLVANIA.

THAT morning, May 8, the troops under Warren encountered those of Anderson's corps, who were intrenched near Spotsylvania. Warren attacked, but was not able to make much progress, and decided to strengthen his own position and wait until other troops came to his assistance before giving battle. His men had suffered great hardships. They had been under fire for four days, and had just made a long night march to reach their present position. Late in the afternoon Warren and Sedgwick were ordered to attack with all their forces, but it was nearly dark before the assault could be made, and then only half of Sedgwick's command and but one of Warren's divisions participated. There was no decided result from this day's fighting.

Late in the afternoon of the 8th headquarters were moved south about two miles, and camp was pitched in the angle formed by the intersection of the Brock road with the road running south from Piney Branch Church. Lee had by this time comprehended Grant's intentions, and was making all haste to throw his troops between the Union army and Richmond, and take up a strong defensive position. Most of the officers of the staff had been in the saddle since daylight, communicating with the corps commanders, designating the lines of march, and urging forward the troops; and as soon as the tents were pitched that night all who could be spared for a while from duty «turned in» to catch as many winks of sleep as possible.

Every one at headquarters was up at daylight the next morning, prepared for another active day's work. Hancock was now on the right, Warren next, then Sedgwick; Burnside was moving down to go into position on the extreme left. The general expressed his intention to devote the day principally to placing all the troops in position, reconnoitering the enemy's line, and getting in readiness for a combined attack as soon as proper preparations for it could be made. The country was more open than the Wilderness, but it still presented obstacles of a most formidable nature. Four rivers run in a southeasterly direction. Some early pioneer, ingenious in systematic nomenclature, and who was evidently possessed of a due regard for «helps to human memory,» had named the streams respectively, beginning with the most southerly, the Mat, the Ta, the Po, and the Ny, and then deployed these terms in single line, closed them in until they were given a touch of the elbow, and called the formation the Mattapony, the name by which the large river is known into which the four smaller ones flow.

Spotsylvania Court House lies between the Po and the Ny. While these streams are not wide, their banks are steep in some places and lined by marshes in other. The country is undulating, and was at that time broken by alternations of cleared spaces and dense forests. In the woods there was a thick tangled undergrowth of hazel, dwarf pine, and scrub-oak.

### THE DEATH OF SEDGWICK.

A LITTLE before eight o'clock on the morning of May 9, the general mounted his horse, and directed me and two other staff-officers to accompany him to make an examination of the lines in our immediate front. This day he rode a black pony called «Jeff Davis» (given that name because it had been captured in Mississippi on the plantation of Joe Davis, a brother of the Confederate president). It was turned into the quartermaster's department, from which it was purchased by the general on his Vicksburg campaign. He was not well at that time, being afflicted with boils, and he took a fancy to the pony because it had a remarkably easy pace, which enabled the general to make his long daily rides with much more comfort than when he used the horses he usually rode. «Little Jeff» soon became a conspicuous figure in the Virginia campaign.

We proceeded to Sedgwick's command, and the general had a conference with him in regard to the part his corps was to take in the contemplated attack. Both officers remained mounted during the interview. The gallant commander of the famous Sixth Corps seemed particularly cheerful and hopeful that morning, and looked the picture of buoyant life and vigorous health. When his chief uttered some words of compliment upon his recent services, and spoke of the hardships he had encountered, Sedgwick spoke lightly of the difficulties experienced, and expressed every confidence in the ability of his troops to respond heroically to every demand made upon them. When the general-in-chief left him, Sedgwick started with his staff to move farther to the front. Our party had ridden but a short distance to the left when General Grant sent me back to Sedgwick to discuss with him further a matter which it was thought had not been sufficiently emphasized in their conversation. While I was following the road I had seen him take, I heard musketry-firing ahead, and soon saw the body of an officer being borne from the field. Such a sight was so common that ordinarily it would have attracted no attention, but my apprehensions were aroused by seeing several of General Sedgwick's staff beside the body. As they came nearer I gave an inquiring look. Colonel Beaumont, of the staff, cast his eyes in the direction of the body, then looked at me with an expression of profound sorrow, and slowly shook his head. His actions told the whole sad story. His heroic chief was dead. I was informed that as he was approaching an exposed point of the line to examine the enemy's position more closely, General McMahon, of his staff, reminded him that one or two officers had just been struck at that spot by sharp-shooters, and begged him not to advance farther. At this suggestion the general only smiled, and soon after had entirely forgotten the warning. Indifferent to every form of danger, such an appeal made but little impression upon him. His movements led him to the position against which he had been cautioned, and he had scarcely dismounted and reached the spot on foot when a bullet entered his left cheek just below the eye, and he fell dead. As his lifeless form was carried by, a smile still remained upon his lips. Sedgwick was essentially a soldier. He had never married; the camp was his home, and the members of his staff were his family. He was always spoken of familiarly as «Uncle John,» and the news of his death fell upon his comrades with a sense of grief akin to the sorrow of a personal bereavement.

I rode off at once to bear the sad intelligence to the general-in-chief. For a few moments he could scarcely realize it, and twice asked, «Is he really dead?» The shock was severe, and he could ill conceal the depth of his grief. He said: «His loss to this army is greater than the loss of a whole division of troops.» General Wright was at once placed in command of the Sixth Corps.

### ARRIVAL OF DESPATCHES.

At daylight on May 9 Burnside had moved down the road from Fredericksburg, crossed the Ny, driven back a force of the enemy, and finally reached a position within less than two miles of Spotsylvania. By noon it was found that the Confederate army occupied an almost continuous line in front of Spotsylvania, in the form of a semicircle, with the convex side facing north. The demonstrations made by Lee, and the strengthening of his right, revived in General Grant's mind the impression that the enemy might attempt to work around our left, and interpose between us and Fredericksburg; and preparations were made in such case to attack Lee's left, turn it, and throw the Union army between him and Richmond. At noon a package of despatches from Washington reached headquarters, and were eagerly read. They announced that Sherman's columns were moving successfully in northwestern Georgia, that Resaca was threatened, and that Joe Johnston was steadily retreating. A report from Butler, dated the 5th, stated that he had landed at City Point, and reports of the 6th and 7th announced that he had sent out reconnoitering parties on the Petersburg railroad, and had despatched troops to take possession of it; that he had had some hard fighting, and was then intrenching, and wanted reinforcements. General Grant directed the reinforcements to be sent. Sigel reported that he had not yet met the enemy, and expected to move up the Shenandoah Valley and try to connect with Crook. General Grant did not express any particular gratification regarding these reports, except the one from Sherman, and in fact made very few comments upon them.

### «I SHALL TAKE NO BACKWARD STEPS.»

Hancock had crossed the Po, and was now threatening Lee's left. On the morning of the 10th Hancock found the enemy's line strongly intrenched, and no general attack was made upon it. Lee had realized the danger threatened, and had hurried troops to his left to protect that flank. Grant, perceiving this, decided that Lee must have weakened other portions of his line, and at once determined to assault his center.

At 9:30 A. M. the general-in-chief sat down in his tent at his little camp-table, and wrote with his own hand, as usual, a despatch to Halleck which began as follows: «The enemy hold our front in very strong force, and evince a strong determination to interpose between us and Richmond to the last. *I shall take no backward steps. . .*» The last sentence, which I have italicized, attracted no notice at the time on the part of those who read it, but it afterward became historic and took a prominent place among the general's famous sayings.

It was now suggested to him that it would be more convenient to move our camp farther to the left, so as to be near the center, where the assault was to take place, and orders were given to establish it a little more than a mile to the southeast, near the Alsop house. The tents were pitched in a comfortable-looking little dell, on the edge of a deep wood, and near the principal roads of communication.

### COMMUNICATING WITH BURNSIDE.

At half-past ten on the morning of May 10 the general-in-chief called me to where he was standing in front of his tent, spoke in much detail of what he wanted Burnside to accomplish, and directed me to go to that officer, explain to him fully the situation and the wishes of the commander, and remain with him on the left during the rest of the day. As I was mounting the general added: «I had started to write a note to Burnside; just wait a moment, and I'll finish it, and you can deliver it to him.» He stepped into his tent, and returned in a few minutes and handed me the note. I set out at once at a gallop toward our left. There were two roads by which Burnside could be reached. One was a circuitous route some distance in rear of our lines; the other was much shorter, but under the enemy's fire for quite a distance. The latter was chosen on account of the time which would thereby be saved. When the exposed part of the road was reached, I adopted the method to which aides so often resorted when they had to take the chances of getting through with a message, and when those chances were not particularly promising—putting the horse on a run, and throwing the body down along his neck on the opposite side from the enemy. Although the bullets did considerable execution in clipping the limbs of the trees and stirring up the earth, they were considerate enough to skip me. The horse was struck, but only slightly, and I succeeded in reaching Burnside rather ahead of schedule time. His headquarters had been established on the north side of the river Ny. I explained to him that a general attack was to be made in the afternoon on the enemy's center by Warren's and Hancock's troops, and that he was to move forward for the purpose of reconnoitering Lee's extreme right, and keeping him from detaching troops from his flanks to reinforce his center. If Burnside could see a chance to attack, he was to do so with all vigor, and in a general way make the best coöperative effort that was possible.

A little while before, the heroic Stevenson, commander of his first division, had been struck by a sharp-shooter and killed. He had served with Burnside in the North Carolina expedition, and the general was much attached to him. He felt his loss keenly, and was profuse in his expressions of grief.

The forward movement was ordered at once. Burnside was in great doubt as to whether he should concentrate his three divisions and attack the enemy's right vigorously, or demonstrate with two divisions, and place the third in rear of Mott, who was on his right. I felt sure that General Grant would prefer the former, and urged it strenuously; but Burnside was so anxious to have General Grant make a decision in the matter himself that he sent him a note at 2:15 P. M. He did not get an answer for nearly two hours. The general said in his reply that it was then too late to bring up the third division, and he thought that Burnside would be secure in attacking as he was.

I had ridden with General Burnside to the front to watch the movement. The advance soon reached a point within a quarter of a mile of Spotsylvania, and completely turned the right of the enemy's line; but the country was so bewildering, and the enemy so completely concealed from view, that it was impossible at the time to know the exact relative positions of the contending forces. Toward dark Willcox's division had constructed a line of fence-rail breastworks, and held pretty securely his advanced position.

I had sent two bulletins to General Grant describing the situation on the left, but the orderly who carried one of the despatches never arrived, having probably been killed, and the other did not reach the general till quite late, as he was riding among the troops in front of the center of the line, and it was difficult to find him. I started for headquarters that evening, but owing to the intense darkness, the condition of the roads, and the difficulty of finding the way, did not arrive till long after midnight.

### GRANT ATTACKS THE ENEMY'S CENTER.

THE same day, May 10, had witnessed important fighting on the right and center of our line. Hancock moved his troops back to the north side of the Po. Barlow's division, while withdrawing, became isolated, and was twice assaulted, but each time repulsed the enemy. The losses on both sides were heavy. Wright had formed an assaulting force of twelve regiments, and placed Colonel Emory Upton in command. At 4 P. M. Wright, Warren, and Mott moved their commands forward, and a fierce struggle ensued. Warren was repulsed with severe loss, and Mott's attack failed; but Upton's column swept through the enemy's line, carrying everything before it, and capturing several guns and a number of prisoners. Unfortunately the troops ordered to his support were so slow in reaching him that he had to be withdrawn. The men had behaved so handsomely, however, and manifested such a desire to retake the position, that General Grant had additional troops brought up, and ordered another assault. Again a rush was made upon the enemy's line, and again the same gallantry was shown. Many of our men succeeded in getting over the earthworks, but could not secure a lodgment which could be held; and as the assaults at other points were not made with the dash and spirit exhibited by Upton, his troops were withdrawn after nightfall to a position of greater security, in which they would not be isolated from the rest of the forces. He was compelled to abandon his captured guns, but he brought away all his prisoners. Upton had been severely wounded. General Grant had obtained permission of the government before starting from Washington to promote officers on the field for conspicuous acts of gallantry, and he now conferred upon Upton the well-merited grade of brigadier-general. Colonel Samuel S. Carroll was also promoted to the rank of brigadier-general for gallantry displayed by him in this action.

Lee had learned by this time that he must be on the lookout for an attack from Grant at any hour, day or night. He sent Ewell a message on the evening of the 10th, saying: «It will be necessary for you to reëstablish your whole line to-night. . . . Perhaps Grant will make a night attack, as it was a favorite amusement of his at Vicksburg.»

While the general-in-chief was out on the lines supervising the afternoon attack, he dismounted and sat down on a fallen tree to write a despatch. While thus engaged a shell exploded directly in front of him. He looked up from his paper an instant, and then, without the slightest change of countenance, went on writing the message. Some of the Fifth Wisconsin wounded were being carried past him at the time, and Major E. R. Jones of that regiment said, and he mentions it in his interesting book of reminiscences published since, that one of his men made the remark: «Ulysses don't scare worth a d—n.»

### HOW A FAMOUS MESSAGE WAS DESPATCHED.

THE 11th of May gave promise of a little rest for everybody, as the commander expressed his intention to spend the day simply in reconnoitering for the purpose of learning more about the character and strength of the enemy's intrenchments, and discovering the weakest points in his line, with a view to breaking through. He sat down at the mess-table that morning, and made his entire breakfast off a cup of coffee and a small piece of beef cooked almost to a crisp; for the cook had by this time learned that the nearer he came to burning up the beef the better the general liked it. During the short time he was at the table he conversed with Mr. Elihu B. Washburne, who had accompanied headquarters up to this time, and who was now about to return to Washington. After breakfast the general lighted a cigar, seated himself on a camp-chair in front of his tent, and was joined there by Mr. Washburne and several members of the staff. At half-past eight o'clock the cavalry escort which was to accompany the congressman was drawn up in the road near by, and all present rose to bid him good-by. Turning to the chief, he said: «General, I shall go to see the President and the Secretary of War as soon as I reach Washington. I can imagine their anxiety to know what you think of the prospects of the campaign, and I know they would be greatly gratified if I could carry a message from you giving what encouragement you can as to the situation.»

The general hesitated a moment, and then replied: «We are certainly making fair progress, and all the fighting has been in our favor; but the campaign promises to be a long one, and I am particularly anxious not to say anything just now that might hold out false hopes to the people»; and then, after a pause, added, «However, I will write a letter to Halleck, as I generally communicate through him, giving the general situation, and you can take it with you.» He stepped into his tent, sat down at his field-table, and, keeping his cigar in his mouth, wrote a despatch of about two hundred words. In the middle of the communication occurred the famous words, «*I propose to fight it out on this line if it takes all summer.*» When the letter had been copied, he folded it and handed it to Mr. Washburne, who thanked him warmly, wished him a continuation of success, shook hands with him and with each of the members of the staff, and at once mounted his horse and rode off. The staff-officers read the retained copy of the despatch, but neither the general himself nor any one at headquarters realized the epigrammatic character of the striking sentence it contained until the New York papers reached camp a few days afterward with the words displayed in large headlines, and with conspicuous comments upon the force of the expression. It was learned afterward that the President was delighted to read this despatch giving such full information as to the situation, and that he had said a few days before, when asked by a member of congress what Grant was doing: «Well, I can't tell much about it. You see, Grant has gone to the Wilderness, crawled in, drawn up the ladder and pulled in the hole after him, and I guess we 'll have to wait till he comes out before we know just what he 's up to.»

### NEWS FROM THE OTHER ARMIES.

THE general was now awaiting news from Butler and Sheridan with some anxiety. While maturing his plans for striking Lee, he was at the same time keeping a close lookout to see that Lee was not detaching any troops with the purpose of crushing Butler's or Sheridan's forces. This day, May 11, the looked-for despatches arrived, and their contents caused no little excitement at headquarters. The general, after glancing over the reports hurriedly, stepped to the front of his tent, and read them aloud to the staff-officers, who had gathered about him, eager to learn the news from the coöperating armies. Butler reported that he had a strongly intrenched position at Bermuda Hundred, in the angle formed by the James and Appomattox rivers; that he had cut the railroad, leaving Beauregard's troops south of the break, and had completely whipped Hill's force. Sheridan sent word that he had torn up ten miles of the Virginia Central Railroad between Lee's army and Richmond, and had destroyed a large quantity of medical supplies and a million and a half of rations. The general-in-chief expressed himself as particularly pleased with the destruction of the railroad in rear of Lee, as it would increase the difficulty of moving troops suddenly between Richmond and Spotsylvania for the purpose of reinforcing either of those points. As usual, the contents of these despatches were promptly communicated to Generals Meade and Burnside.

### PREPARING TO ATTACK THE «ANGLE.»

THE result of the day's work on our front was to discover more definitely the character of the salient in Lee's defenses on the right of his center. It was in the shape of a V with a flattened apex. The ground in front sloped down toward our position, and was in most places thickly wooded. There was a clearing, however, about four hundred yards in width immediately in front of the apex. Several of the staff-officers were on that part of the field a great portion of the day. At three o'clock in the afternoon the general had thoroughly matured his plans, and sent instructions to Meade directing him to move Hancock with all possible secrecy under cover of night to the left of Wright, and to make a vigorous assault on the «angle» at dawn the next morning. Warren and Wright were ordered to hold their corps as close to the enemy as possible, and to take advantage of any diversion caused by this attack to push in if an opportunity should present itself. A personal conference was held with the three corps commanders, and every effort made to have a perfect understanding on their part as to exactly what was required in this important movement. Colonels Comstock and Babcock were directed to go to Burnside that afternoon, and to remain with him during the movements of the next day, in which he was to attack simultaneously with Hancock. The other members of the staff were sent to keep in communication with the different portions of Hancock's line. The threatening sky was not propitious for the movement, but in this entertainment there was to be «no postponement on account of the weather,» and the preparations went on regardless of the lowering clouds and falling rain. All those who were in the secret anticipated a memorable field-day on the morrow.

Hancock's troops made a difficult night march, groping their way through the gloom of the forests, their clothing drenched with rain, and their feet ankle-deep in Virginia mud. A little after midnight they reached their position, and formed for the attack at a distance of about twelve hundred yards from the enemy's intrenchments.

I had been out all night looking after the movements of the troops which were to form the assaulting columns. After they had all been placed in position I started for headquarters, in obedience to instructions, to report the situation to the general-in-chief. He counted upon important results from the movement, although he appreciated fully the difficulties to be encountered, and was naturally anxious about the dispositions which were being made for the attack. The condition of the country was such that a horseman could make but slow progress in moving from one point of the field to another. The rain was falling in torrents, the ground was marshy, the roads were narrow, and the movements of the infantry and artillery had churned up the mud until the country was almost impassable. In the pitchy darkness one's horse constantly ran against trees, was shoved off the road by guns or wagons, and had to squeeze through lines of infantry, who swore like «our army in Flanders» when a staff-officer's horse manifested a disposition to crawl over them. By feeling the way for some hours I reached headquarters about daylight the next morning, May 12.

### AN EVENTFUL MORNING AT HEADQUARTERS.

WHEN I arrived the general was up and sitting wrapped in his overcoat close to a camp-fire which was struggling heroically to sustain its life against the assaults of wind and rain. It had been decided to move headquarters a little nearer to the center of the lines, and most of the camp equipage had been packed up ready to start. The general seemed in excellent spirits, and was even inclined to be jocose. He said to me: «We have just had our coffee, and you will find some left for you»; and then, taking a critical look at my drenched and bespattered clothes and famished appearance, added, «But perhaps you are not hungry.» To disabuse the chief's mind on this score, I sent for a cup of coffee, and drank it with the relish of a shipwrecked mariner, while I related the incidents of the embarrassments encountered in Hancock's movement, and the position he had taken up. Before I had quite finished making my report the stillness was suddenly broken by artillery firing, which came from the direction of Burnside's position. A few minutes after came the sound of cheers and the rattle of musketry from Hancock's front, telling that the main assault upon the «angle» had begun. No one could see a hundred yards from our position on account of the dense woods, and reports from the front were eagerly awaited. It was nearly an hour before anything definite was received, but at 5:30 an officer came galloping through the woods with a report from Hancock saying he had captured the first line of the enemy's works. This officer was closely followed by another, who reported that many prisoners had been taken. Fifteen minutes later came the announcement that Hancock had captured two general officers. General Grant sent Burnside this news with a message saying, «Push on with all vigor.» Wright's corps was now ordered to attack on the right of Hancock. Before six o'clock a message from Hancock's headquarters reported the capture of two thousand prisoners, and a quarter of an hour later Burnside sent word that he had driven the enemy back two miles and a half in his front. Hancock called for reinforcements, but Grant had anticipated him and had already ordered troops to his support. The scene at headquarters was now exciting in the extreme. As aides galloped up one after the other in quick succession with stirring bulletins, all bearing the glad tidings of overwhelming success, the group of staff-officers standing about the camp-fire interrupted their active work of receiving, receipting for, and answering despatches by shouts and cheers which made the forest ring. General Grant sat unmoved upon his camp-chair, giving his constant thoughts to devising methods for making the victory complete. At times the smoke from the struggling camp-fire would for a moment blind him, and occasionally a gust of wind would blow the cape of his greatcoat over his face, and cut off his voice in the middle of a sentence. Only once during the scene he rose from his seat and paced up and down for about ten minutes. He made very few comments upon the stirring events which were crowding so closely upon one another until the reports came in regarding the prisoners. When the large numbers captured were announced, he said, with the first trace of animation he had shown, «That 's the kind of news I like to hear. I had hoped that a bold dash at daylight would secure a large number of prisoners. Hancock is doing well.» This remark was eminently characteristic of the Union commander. His extreme fondness for taking prisoners was manifested in every battle he fought. When word was brought to him of a success on any part of the line, his first and most eager question was always, «Have any prisoners been taken?» The love for capturing prisoners amounted to a passion with him. It did not seem to arise from the fact that they added so largely to the trophies of battle; and was no doubt chiefly due to his tenderness of heart, which prompted him to feel that it was always more humane to reduce the enemy's strength by captures than by slaughter. His desire in this respect was amply gratified, for during the war it fell to his lot to capture a larger number of prisoners than any general of modern times.

### TWO DISTINGUISHED PRISONERS.

MEADE had come over to Grant's headquarters early, and while they were engaged in discussing the situation, about 6:30 A. M., a horseman rode up wearing the uniform of a Confederate general. Halting near the camp-fire, he dismounted and walked forward, saluting the group of Union officers as he approached. His clothing was covered with mud, and a hole had been torn in the crown of his felt hat, through which a tuft of hair protruded, looking like a Sioux chief's war-lock. Meade looked at him attentively for a moment, and then stepped up to him, grasped him cordially by the hand, and cried, «Why, how do you do, general?» and then turned to the general-in-chief and said, «General Grant, this is General Johnson—Edward Johnson.» General Grant shook hands warmly with the distinguished prisoner, and exclaimed, «How do you do? It is a long time since we last met.» «Yes,» replied Johnson; «it is a great many years, and I had not expected to meet you under such circumstances.» «It is one of the many sad fortunes of war,» answered General Grant, who offered the captured officer a cigar, and then picked up a camp-chair, placed it with his own hands near the fire, and added, «Be seated, and we will do all in our power to make you as comfortable as possible.» Johnson sat down, and said in a voice and with a manner which showed that he was deeply touched by these manifestations of courtesy, «Thank you, general, thank you; you are very kind.» He had been in the corps of cadets with General Meade, and had served in the Mexican war with General Grant, but they probably would not have recognized him if they had not already heard that he had been made a prisoner. I had known Johnson very well, and it was only four years since I had seen him. We recognized each other at once, and I extended a cordial greeting to him, and presented the members of our staff. He was soon quite at his ease, and bore himself under the trying circumstances in a manner which commanded the respect of every one present. General Hancock had already provided him with a horse to make his trip to the rear with the rest of the prisoners as comfortably as possible. After some pleasant conversation with Grant and Meade about old times and the strange chances of war, he bade us good-by, and started under escort for our base of supplies. General George H. Steuart was also captured, but was not sent in to general headquarters on account of a scene which had been brought about by an unseemly exhibition of temper on his part. Hancock had known him in the old army, and in his usual frank way went up to him, greeted him kindly, and offered his hand. Steuart drew back, rejected the offer, and said rather haughtily, «Under the present circumstances, I must decline to take your hand.» Hancock, who was somewhat nettled by this remark, replied, «Under any other circumstances, general, I should not have offered it.» No further attempt was made to extend any courtesies to his prisoner, who was left to make his way to the rear on foot with the others who had been captured.

While Generals Grant and Meade were talking with General Johnson by the camp-fire, a despatch came in from Hancock, saying, «I have finished up Johnson, and am now going into Early.» General Grant passed this despatch around, but did not read it aloud, as usual, out of consideration for Johnson's feelings. Soon after came another report that Hancock had taken three thousand prisoners; then another that he had turned his captured guns upon the enemy and made a whole division prisoners, including the famous Stonewall Brigade. Burnside now reported that his right had lost its connection with Hancock's corps. General Grant sent him a brief, characteristic note in reply, saying, «Push the enemy with all your might; that 's the way to connect.»

The general-in-chief showed again upon that eventful morning the value he placed upon minutes. Aides were kept riding at a full run carrying messages, and the terseness, vigor and intensity manifested in every line of his field orders were enough to spur the most sluggish to prompt action.

### HOW THE «ANGLE» WAS CAPTURED.

AFTER giving such instructions as would provide for the present emergencies, the general ordered the pony «Jeff Davis» to be saddled, and started for the front. He left an adjutant-general behind, with orders to forward to him promptly all communications. The staff rode with the general, and after a while reached a clearing on a piece of elevated ground from which a view of portions of the line could be obtained. It was found, upon learning the details of the assault upon the «angle,» that, notwithstanding the fatigues and hardships to which the troops had been subjected, they had moved forward with the step of veterans, and had marched half-way across the open ground which separated them from the well-defended earthworks in their front with a steady pace and unbroken alinement. At that point they sent up cheers which rent the air, and the columns dashed forward at a run, scattering the enemy's pickets before them in their swift advance. A brisk fire was opened by the Confederate line from a position to the left, but, unheeding it, and without firing a shot, the assaulting column tore away the slashed timber and other obstacles in its path, and rushed like a mighty torrent over the intrenchments. A desperate hand-to-hand encounter now followed, in which men fought like demons, using their bayonets and clubbed muskets when in too close contact to load and fire. The main assault fell on Johnson's division of Lee's army. Lee was led to believe that there was an intention to attack his left, and he had sent most of Johnson's artillery to strengthen that flank. Johnson had his suspicions aroused during the night that there were preparations under way for attacking his front, and had induced Lee to order the artillery back. By a strange coincidence, it arrived just as Johnson's line was carried, and before the guns could fire a shot they fell into Hancock's hands. Besides capturing Generals Steuart and Johnson, he took nearly four thousand prisoners, thirty pieces of artillery, several thousand stands of small arms, and about thirty colors. His troops swept on half a mile, driving the enemy before them in confusion, and did not pause till they encountered a second line of intrenchments. The enemy was now driven to desperation, and every effort was bent toward retaking his lost works. Reinforcements were rushed forward by Lee as soon as he saw the threatening condition of matters at the «angle»; and a formidable counter-movement was rapidly organized against Hancock. As our troops were upon unknown territory, and as their formations had been thrown into considerable confusion by the rapidity of their movements, they withdrew slowly before the attack to the main line of works they had captured, and turning them against the enemy, held them successfully during all the terrific struggle that followed.

By six o'clock A.M. Wright was on that portion of the field, and his men were placed on the right of the «angle.» Scarcely had he taken up this position when the Confederates made a determined and savage attack upon him; but despite their well-directed efforts they failed to recapture the line. Wright was wounded early in the fight, but refused to leave the field. Hancock had placed some artillery upon high ground, and his guns fired over the heads of our troops and did much execution in the ranks of the enemy. Warren had been directed to make an attack before eight o'clock, in order to prevent the enemy from massing troops upon the center in an effort to retake the «angle,» but he was slow in carrying out the order. Although the instructions were of the most positive and urgent character, he did not accomplish the work expected of him. A little before eleven o'clock General Grant became so anxious that he directed General Meade to relieve Warren if he did not attack promptly, and to put General Humphreys in command of his corps. General Meade concurred in this course, and said that he would have relieved Warren without an order to that effect if there had been any further delay. General Grant said to one or two of us who were near him: «I feel sorry to be obliged to send such an order in regard to Warren. He is an officer for whom I had conceived a very high regard. His quickness of perception, personal gallantry, and soldierly bearing pleased me, and a few days ago I should have been inclined to place him in command of the Army of the Potomac in case Meade had been killed; but I began to feel, after his want of vigor in assaulting on the 8th, that he was not as efficient as I had believed, and his delay in attacking and the feeble character of his assaults to-day confirm me in my apprehensions.» This was said in a kindly spirit, but with an air of serious disappointment. Longstreet's troops had continued to confront Warren, knowing that to lose that part of the enemy's line would expose the troops at the «angle» to a flank attack, and the obstacles to a successful assault were really very formidable. Warren was blamed not so much for not carrying the line in his front as for delays in making the attack.

The general now started for another part of the field, and kept moving from point to point to get a close view of the fighting on different parts of the line. Once or twice he called for a powerful field-glass belonging to Badeau. This was rather unusual, for the general never carried a glass himself, and seldom used one. He was exceptionally far-sighted, and generally trusted to his natural vision in examining the field. Badeau's near-sightedness made him very dependent on his glass. A few days before, while he was using it, a battery commander who was passing attempted a professional joke by remarking, «I say, Badeau; can you see Richmond?» «Not quite,» answered the colonel; «though I hope to some day.» «Better have the barrels of your glass rifled so that it will carry farther,» suggested the artillerist.

Before riding far the general came to a humble-looking farm-house, which was within range of the enemy's guns, and surrounded by wounded men, sullen-looking prisoners, and terror-stricken stragglers. The fences were broken, the ground was furrowed by shells; and the place presented a scene which depicted war in its most repulsive aspect. An old lady and her daughter were standing on the porch. When the mother was told that the officer passing was the general-in-chief, she ran toward him, and with the tears running down her cheeks, threw up her arms and cried, «Thank God! thank God! I again behold the glorious flag of the Union, that I have not laid eyes on for three long, terrible years. Thank the Lord that I have at last seen the commander of the Union armies! I am proud to say that my husband and my son went from here to serve in those armies, but I have been cut off from all communication, and can get no tidings of them. Oh, you don't know, sir, what a loyal woman suffers in this land; but the coming of the Union troops makes me feel that deliverance is at last at hand, and that the gates have been opened for my escape from this hell.» The general was so touched by this impassioned speech, and felt so firmly convinced that the woman was telling the truth, that he dismounted and went into the yard, and sat for a little time on the porch, to learn the details of her story, and to see what he could do to comfort and succor her. She gave an account of her persecutions and sufferings which would have moved the sternest heart. The general, finding that she was without food, ordered a supply of rations to be issued to her and her daughter, and promised to have inquiries set on foot to ascertain the whereabouts of her husband and son. She was profuse in her expressions of gratitude for these acts of kindness. Her story was afterward found to be true in every particular.

SCENES AT THE «BLOODY ANGLE.»

I HAD been anxious to participate in the scenes occurring at the «angle,» and now got permission to go there and look after some new movements which had been ordered. Lee made five assaults, in all, that day, in a series of desperate and even reckless attempts to retake his main line of earthworks; but each time his men were hurled back defeated, and he had to content himself in the end with throwing up a new line farther in his rear.

The battle near the «angle» was probably the most desperate engagement in the history of modern warfare, and presented features which were absolutely appalling. It was chiefly a savage hand-to-hand fight across the breastworks. Rank after rank was riddled by shot and shell and bayonet-thrusts, and finally sank, a mass of torn and mutilated corpses; then fresh troops rushed madly forward to replace the dead, and so the murderous work went on. Guns were run up close to the parapet, and double charges of canister played their part in the bloody work. The fence-rails and logs in the breastworks were shattered into splinters, and trees over a foot and a half in diameter were cut completely in two by the incessant musketry fire. A section of the trunk of a stout oak-tree thus severed was afterward sent to Washington, where it is still on exhibition at the National Museum. We had not only shot down an army but also a forest. The opposing flags were in places thrust against each other, and muskets were fired with muzzle against muzzle. Skulls were crushed with clubbed muskets, and men stabbed to death with swords and bayonets thrust between the logs in the parapet which separated the combatants. Wild cheers, savage yells, and frantic shrieks rose above the sighing of the wind and the pattering of the rain, and formed a demoniacal accompaniment to the booming of the guns as they hurled their missiles of death into the contending ranks. Even the darkness of night and the pitiless storm failed to stop the fierce contest, and the deadly strife did not cease till after midnight. Our troops had been under fire for twenty hours, but they still held the position which they had so dearly purchased.

My duties carried me again to the spot the next day, and the appalling sight presented was harrowing in the extreme. Our own killed were scattered over a large space near the «angle,» while in front of the captured breastworks the enemy's dead, vastly more numerous than our own, were piled upon each other in some places four layers deep, exhibiting every ghastly phase of mutilation. Below the mass of fast-decaying corpses, the convulsive twitching of limbs and the writhing of bodies showed that there were wounded men still alive and struggling to extricate themselves from their horrid entombment. Every relief possible was afforded, but in too many cases it came too late. The place was well named the «Bloody Angle.»

The results of the battle are best summed up in the report which the general-in-chief sent to Washington. At 6:30 P.M., May 12, he wrote to Halleck as follows: «The eighth day of battle closes, leaving between three and four thousand prisoners in our hands for the day's work, including two general officers, and over thirty pieces of artillery. The enemy are obstinate, and seem to have found the last ditch. We have lost no organization, not even that of a company, whilst we have destroyed and captured one division (Johnson's), one brigade (Doles's), and one regiment entire of the enemy.» The Confederates had suffered greatly in general officers. Two had been killed, four severely wounded, and two captured. Our loss in killed, wounded, and missing was less than seven thousand; that of the enemy, between nine and ten thousand, as nearly as could be ascertained.

(To be continued.)

*Horace Porter.*

# NAPOLEON'S INTEREST IN THE BATTLE OF NEW ORLEANS.

WITH A DESCRIPTION OF THE BATTLE, BY GENERAL JACKSON.

WHEN the news reached Europe of the battle at Chalmette, commonly known as the battle of New Orleans, and of the terribly disastrous results to the English army, the account at first was not credited. That a trained force from the picked regiments of the British army, schooled in war, with commanders of the distinction that Pakenham and Keene enjoyed, should meet with such a defeat at the hands of a «militia general,» was hardly to be believed under any circumstances; but that out of a force of 6000 strong there should be a loss of 2117 killed and wounded on the British side, while the Americans had only 6 killed and 7 wounded, was held to be impossible. The Duke of Wellington was particularly savage in his denunciation of the «Yankee lie,» as he termed the first vague reports that reached him of the terrible and unexpected defeat. When, however, the facts touching the result of the fight were substantiated, Europe was amazed.

The news reached the Emperor Napoleon, then in exile at Elba, some time in February. He was intensely interested to know how such a defeat had been effected, and through Colonel Saint-Maur, a former soldier of the Empire then living in southwest Louisiana, the details of the battle were furnished to General Bertrand, who communicated them to the Emperor. When Napoleon learned that the American riflemen had mainly done the deadly work, he immediately desired that all the information touching these riflemen, their weapon, and their method of fighting should be obtained and sent him. «Such an arm,» he said, «would surely be as effective in Europe as in America. The French army should have some *tirailleurs* capable of using it. Surely the gift of marksmanship is not confined to the American alone.»

Through Stephen Girard, four American rifles that had been used at New Orleans, and some targets shot by Coffee's Kentuckians, were sent to the Emperor after his arrival in Paris on his return to power. The weapons were very different from any ever seen in Europe. Up to that time the Tyrolean and German riflemen were the most famous sharp-shooters the Continent had ever known. Their rifles were short compared with the American arm, very large in caliber, and handsomely finished and mounted. Those from America were from forty-two to forty-eight inches in the barrel, and full-stocked—that is, the wood of the gun extended the full length of the barrel, which was heavy, weighing from nine and a half to ten and a half pounds. The workmanship of the entire piece was rude and unattractive; but with this weapon—unwieldy to European eyes—the American backwoodsmen conquered the great wilderness lying from the Alleghanies to the Gulf of Mexico.

One feature of «the deadly American gun,» as Napoleon called it, was its extreme accuracy. The targets sent to him, it was certified, had been shot at from seventy-five to one hundred and twenty-five yards. At the distance first named ten bullets had been put into a square four inches by four and a half. The farthest-distance shots were made at a six-inch square with two black lines crossing at the center. All the bullets of this firing were well inside the square. This was the most wonderful sharp-shooting of which Napoleon had ever seen proof. The severe simplicity of the American rifle greatly impressed him; but this was explained in the following fashion by Mr. Laurens of South Carolina: «Silver is too scarce and valuable to use on the hunting-rifle for its ornamentation; but the reason an experienced woodsman of our country would not venture into an Indian campaign with an ornamented rifle is that all white metal glitters. An Indian's eye might detect the gleam of silver on a rifle when he would not discover its owner in any other way; so no experienced scout ever permits his men to take the field in an Indian campaign with anything among their accoutrements that will reflect the sun's rays.»

Napoleon derived his best idea of the battle at Chalmette from a personal letter from General Jackson to Mr. James Monroe, which fully described the fight, and was carefully translated into French, and then was printed, and sent to the Emperor.

Monroe had been American minister to the court of the French Republic in 1803, when Bonaparte was consul; and it was Monroe's sturdy Americanism that had brought about the purchase from France of the Louisiana territory, out of which fourteen States have been added to the Union. A firm friendship grew up between the young French general and the American statesman, which ended only with Bonaparte's death. To the late Judge Gayarré of Louisiana I was indebted for information as to the existence of this letter, and in 1866 General George W. Monroe of Kentucky, a grandnephew of President Monroe, allowed it to be copied. It is as follows:

The battle [said General Jackson] commenced at a very little before 7 A. M., January 8, 1815, and as far as the infantry was concerned it was over by 9 A. M. My force was very much mixed. I had portions of the Seventh and Forty-fourth regular infantry regiments, Kentucky and Tennessee riflemen, creoles, United States marines and sailors, Baratarian men,—one of them, Captain Dominique You, commanded part of my artillery (and a famous gunner he was),—and two battalions of free negroes. I had in the action about 6000 men. The British strength was almost the same as mine, but vastly superior in drill and discipline. Of their force my riflemen killed and wounded 2117 in less than an hour, including two general officers (both died on the field, each a division commander), seven full colonels, with seventy-five line and staff officers. I lost 6 killed and 7 wounded.

As to tactics, there were very little in use on either side. We had some works of earth fronting the river, but the Kentucky and Tennessee riflemen, who sustained the main attack, had protected themselves by a work about two feet and a half high, made of logs placed two feet apart, and the space between filled in with earth. This work began at the Mississippi River, and ended in the swamp, being at a right angle with the river.

Thinking this the weakest portion of our line, and seeing ununiformed men behind the trifling defenses, General Pakenham thought it the best thing to begin his attack by carrying this part of my line with the bayonet. On the 3d of January I had ordered that each rifleman's powder-horn be filled, and enough lead for one hundred bullets issued, besides good material for bullet-patching. Coffee reported to me on the 7th that this order had been obeyed, and every man had cleaned up his rifle and put a new flint into the hammer; so we were as ready as we could be for the attack.

There was a very heavy fog on the river that morning, and the British had formed and were moving before I knew it. The disposition of the riflemen was very simple. They were told off in numbers one and two. Number one was to fire first, then step back and let number two shoot while he reloaded. About six hundred yards from the riflemen there was a great drainage canal running back from the Mississippi River to the swamp in the rear of the tilled land on which we were operating. Along this canal the British formed, under the fire of the few artillery pieces I had near enough to them to get their range. But the instant I saw them I said to Coffee, whom I directed to hurry to his line, which was to be first attacked: «By——, we have got them; they are ours!» Coffee dashed forward, and riding along his line, called out, «Don't shoot till you can see their belt-buckles.» The British were formed in mass, well closed up, and about two companies front.[1]

The British, thus formed, moved on at a quick step, without firing a shot, to within one hundred yards of the kneeling riflemen, who were holding their fire till they could see the belt-buckles of their enemies. The British advance was executed as though they had been on parade. They marched shoulder to shoulder, with the step of veterans, as they were. At one hundred yards' distance from our line the order was given, «Extend column front.»[2] «Double quick, march! *Charge!*» With bayonets at the charge, they came on us at a run. I own it was an anxious moment; I well knew the charging column was made up of the picked troops of the British army. They had been trained by the duke himself, were commanded by his brother-in-law, and had successfully held off the ablest of Napoleon's marshals in the Spanish campaign. My riflemen had never seen such an attack, nor had they ever before fought white men. The morning, too, was damp; their powder might not burn well. «God help us!» I muttered, watching the rapidly advancing line. Seventy, sixty, fifty, finally forty yards, were they from the silent kneeling riflemen. All of my men I could see was their long rifles rested on the logs before them. They obeyed their orders well; not a shot was fired until the redcoats were within forty yards. I heard Coffee's voice as he roared out: «Now, men, aim for the center of the cross-belts![3] Fire!» A second after the order a crackling, blazing flash ran all along our line. The smoke hung so heavily in the misty morning air that I could not see what had happened. I called Tom Overton and Abner Duncan, of my staff, and we galloped toward Coffee's line. In a few seconds after the first fire there came another sharp, ringing volley. As I came within one hundred and fifty yards of Coffee, the smoke lifted enough for me to make out what was happening.

[1] This would have made the massed column sixty files deep.

[2] That is, the English front was increased from 120 files to 240, so that a greater portion of the American works might be attacked at once. It was a fatal move for the English, as it increased the number of targets for the deadly rifles.

[3] The place where the two belts then in use by the British army for carrying the cartridge-box and the bayonet crossed on the breast.

The British were falling back in a confused, disorderly mass, and the entire first ranks of their column were blown away. For two hundred yards in our front the ground was covered with a mass of writhing wounded, dead, and dying redcoats. By the time the rifles were wiped[1] the British line was reformed, and on it came again. This time they were led by General Pakenham in person, gallantly mounted, and riding as though he was on parade. Just before he got within range of Coffee's line I heard a single rifle-shot from a group of country carts we had been using, about one hundred and seventy-five yards distant, and a moment thereafter I saw Pakenham reel and pitch out of his saddle. I have always believed he fell from the bullet of a free man of color, who was a famous rifle-shot, and came from the Atakappas region of Louisiana. The second advance was precisely like the first in its ending. In five volleys the 1500 or more riflemen killed and wounded 2117 British soldiers, two thirds of them killed dead or mortally wounded. I did not know where General Pakenham was lying, or I should have sent to him, or gone in person, to offer any service in my power to render.

I was told he lived two hours after he was hit. His wound was directly through the liver and bowels. General Keene, I hear, was killed dead. They sent a flag to me, asking leave to gather up their wounded and bury their dead, which, of course, I granted. I was told by a wounded officer that the rank and file absolutely refused to make a third charge. «We have no chance with such shooting as these Americans do,» they said.

[1] The old-time rifleman always ran a wad of tow down his barrel after each shot, to keep it from becoming foul and to insure accuracy.

This concludes the material part of General Jackson's letter. It was in the feverish glories of the Hundred Days that Napoleon came into possession of Mr. Monroe's translation. There was no doubt about the facts. There happened to be abroad then in France two or three American gentlemen who were accustomed to the use of the rifle. One of them selected a weapon out of the four sent from America to the French emperor, and in Napoleon's presence did some really excellent sharp-shooting at one hundred yards.

Had Napoleon won Waterloo, it is possible that he would have organized a corps of sharp-shooters and armed them with the American rifle, which was capable of a more deadly accuracy than any European arm of the kind, not excepting even the rifle of Switzerland. General Jackson repeated the compliment of Napoleon to the typical American weapon to General William Selby Harney, then a field-officer of dragoons, who in turn related the incident to the writer.

*William Hugh Robarts.*

## ENNUI.

A WIDE, bare field 'neath blinding skies,  
Where no tree grows, no shadow lies,  
Where no wind stirs, where no bee flies.

A roadway, even, blank, and white,  
That swerves not left, that swerves not right,  
That stretches, changeless, out of sight.

Footprints midway adown its dust;  
Two lagging, leaden feet, that just  
Trail on and on, because they must.

*Grace Denio Litchfield.*

(BEGUN IN THE NOVEMBER NUMBER.)

# HUGH WYNNE, FREE QUAKER:

## SOMETIME BREVET LIEUTENANT-COLONEL ON THE STAFF OF HIS EXCELLENCY GENERAL WASHINGTON.

BY DR. S. WEIR MITCHELL,

Author of «In War Time,» «When all the Woods are Green,» etc.

WITH PICTURES BY HOWARD PYLE.

### SYNOPSIS OF NOVEMBER AND DECEMBER PARTS.

[HUGH WYNNE tells why he desired to write the story of his life, and how the diary of his friend John Warder enabled him to compass this end. He relates why his people came out of Wales and gave up an estate to win freedom to worship God as Quakers please. Of his school life in Philadelphia, about 1760 and later, he speaks; of the books he read, and of his mother, a French Quaker; and also of his aunt Gainor Wynne, a maiden lady of wealth, who early went back to the Church of England and was all for resistance to the crown. Hugh speaks of John Wynne, his father, as a stern man and an exemplary Quaker, strongly loyal to the king. Between these two conflicting influences Hugh Wynne's young life was passed. He leaves school to attend the academy, which now is the University of Pennsylvania. He has his first fight, and is thereby discouraged as to the value of non-resistance to oppression.

Is apprenticed to a farrier, after the custom of the early Friends, who would have all learn a trade. Of the society of that time. Enters his father's counting-house. Of his temptations. His father is persuaded to go with his wife to England in the autumn, to avoid being consignee of the tea. Of a quarrel with his father. Of Hugh's lapses from virtue, and of what Friends said of them. How he was influenced by his aunt against the king, and how all his home teaching had been of non-resistance and of the duty of obedience to the crown.]

### VII.

HE next day, having seen to matters of business in the morning, I set out after dinner in my finest clothes to join my friends. I fear that I promised my mother to be careful, and to be at home by nine o'clock.

I met Captain Montresor at the London Coffee-house at High and Front streets, and, having taken a chaise, drove out through the woods to the upper ferry, and thence to Eglesfield, the seat of Mr. Warner, from whom the club known then as «The Colony in Schuylkill» held under a curious tenure the acre or two of land where they had built a log cabin and founded this ancient and singular institution. Here were met Anthony Morris, who fell at Trenton; Mr. Tench Francis, sometime Attorney-General; Mifflin; and that Galloway who later became a Tory, with Mr. Willing, and others of less note, old and young. I was late for the annual ceremony of presenting three fish to Mr. Warner, this being the condition on which the soil was held, but I saw the great pewter dish with the Penn arms, a gift from that family, on which the fish were offered.

It was a merry and odd party; for, clad in white aprons, the apprentices, so called, cooked the dinner and served it; and the punch and Madeira went round the table often enough, as the «king's health» was drunk, and «success to trade,» and «the ladies, God bless them!»

I liked it well, and, with my aunt's warning in mind, drank but little, and listened to the talk, which was too free at times, as was the bad custom of that day, and now and then angry; for here were some who were to die for their country, and some who were to fail it in the hour of need.

Despite my English friends, and thanks to Mr. Wilson and my Aunt Gainor, I was fast becoming an ardent Whig, so that the talk, in which I had small share, interested me deeply. At last, about seven, the pipes having been smoked and much punch taken, the company rose to go, some of them the worse for their potations.

We drove into town, and at the coffee-house put up and paid for our chaise. I said good-by to Mr. Montresor, who, I think, had been charged by Miss Wynne to look after me, when a Captain Small, whom I knew, stopped me. He was well known as one of the most reckless of the younger officers, a stout, short man, rather heroically presented long afterward, in Trumbull's picture of the «Death of Warren,» as trying to put aside the bayonets. As I paused to reply, I saw Jack Warder standing on the other side of the street. He nodded, smiling, and made as if he were about to cross over. He had many times talked with me seriously this winter, until I had become vexed, and told him he was a milksop. After this I saw little of him. Now I was annoyed at the idea that he was spying upon my actions, and therefore, like a fool, merely nodded, and, turning my back on him, heard Mr. Small say: «You must not go yet, Mr. Wynne. We are to have supper upstairs, and you will like to see a gentleman of your name, Mr. Arthur Wynne, of the Grenadiers. He tells me he is of distant kin to you.»

Montresor said I had better go home, but Etherington asked if I wanted my bottle and nurse; and so at last, partly from pride and partly out of curiosity to see this other Wynne, I said I would remain long enough to welcome the gentleman and take a social glass. When we entered the room upstairs, I found a supper of cold meats and, as usual, punch and liquors. There were two dozen or more officers in undress jackets, their caps and swords in the corners, and also two or three of the younger men of the Tory or doubtful parties.

Several officers called to me to sit with them, for I was a favourite, and could troll a catch or sing parts fairly well. My companion, Small, said, «This way, Wynne,» and, followed by Montresor and the colonel of the Scots Greys, whose name I forget, we moved to a table remote from the door. Here Montresor, pushing past Small, said: «Captain Wynne, I have the honour to present to you Mr. Hugh Wynne, one of your family, I hear.»

Upon this there rose to greet me a gentleman in undress uniform. He was tall and well built, but not so broad or strong as we other Wynnes; certainly an unusually handsome man. He carried his head high, was very erect, and had an air of distinction, for which at that time I should have had no name. I may add that he was dressed with unusual neatness, and very richly; all of which, I being but a half-formed young fellow, did much impress me.

He looked at me so steadily as we came near that it gave me a rather unpleasant impression; for those who do not meet the eye at all are scarcely less disagreeable than those who too continually watch you, as was this man's way. I was rather young to be a very careful observer of men's faces, but I did see that Captain Wynne's bore traces of too convivial habits.

As I recall his dark, regular features, I remember, for we met often afterward, that the lower part of his face was too thin, and that in repose his mouth was apt not to remain fully shut, a peculiarity, as I now think, of persons of weak will.

My first feeling of there being something unpleasing about him soon left me. He rose, and, with graciousness and the ease and manner of one used to the best society, moved around the table and took my hand.

«I am but a far-away kinsman,» he said, «but I am charmed to make your acquaintance. You are like the picture of old Sir Robert at Wyncote, where I was last year for the otter-hunting.»

I greeted him warmly. «And art thou living at Wyncote?» I asked rather awkwardly.

«No; I do not live at home. I am but a cadet, and yours is the elder branch.» Then he added gaily: «I salute you, sir, as the head of our old house. Your very good health!» And at this, with a charm of manner I have seen but rarely, he put a hand on my shoulder, and added: «We must be friends, Cousin Wynne, and I must know your father, and above all Mistress Wynne. Montresor never ceases talking of her.»

I said it would give me pleasure to present him; then, delighted to hear of Wyncote, I sat down, and, despite a warning look from Montresor, began to take wine with this newly found kinsman.

Mr. Arthur Wynne was a man fully ten years my senior. He had served in the Guards, and in the Indies, and was full of stories of court and camp and war, such as every young fellow of spirit likes to hear.

Captain Montresor lingered awhile, and then, finding it vain to persist in his purpose, gave it up, and fell to talking with one of his fellow-officers, while I went on questioning my cousin as to the Wynnes to their uttermost generation. Either he cared little about them, or he knew little, for he seemed much to prefer to tell queer stories about the court ladies, and my Lord Chesterfield's boor of a son, who had such small manners and such a large appetite, and of Sir Guy Carleton, whom he was about to join in Canada. He advised me to get a pair of colours as my aunt had once desired, and seemed surprised when I paraded my friend Mr. Wilson's opinions as my own, and talked of taxation and the oppression under which commerce had to be carried on. In fact, as to this I knew something; but in this, as in other matters, he deferred to me as one does to a well-informed talker of one's own age, now setting me right with admirable courtesy, and now cordially agreeing.

What with his evident desire to be friendly, and the wine I was taking, I fell an easy prey to one who rarely failed to please when he was so minded. Too well amused to reflect that the hours were swiftly passing, I sat, taking glass after glass mechanically. As the night went on we had more punch, and the dice began to rattle on the tables, despite the landlord's remonstrance, who feared to fall into the hands of the law and lose his licence. But a lively major called out that here was licence enough, and hustled him out of the room, calling for more rum-punch, and stronger.

Meanwhile the smoke grew thick and thicker. Here and there a song broke out, and the clink of coin and the rattle of dice went on. When at last Montresor came to our table and said he was going, and would I come, too, I rose, and, bidding my kinsman good-by, went with the captain. I heard him swear as he found the door locked. No one seemed to know who had the key, and not at all ill-pleased, and past feeling regret, I turned back and stood over a table where some officers were throwing a main.

Then I saw in a corner a poor fellow who used to be an usher at the academy, and who, having taken to drink, had lost his place. Now he was a sort of servitor in the coffee-house, and had gotten locked up in the room and could not escape. He had taken refuge in a corner at a deserted table, and, sitting unnoticed, was solacing himself with what was left of a bowl of punch. A sense of not altogether maudlin pity came upon me, and I went over and sat down beside him. No one took any heed of us. The air was heavy with pipe-smoke, oaths, mad catches of song, clink of glasses, and rattle of dice noisily cast, with here and there a toast cried; so that it was hard to see for the smoke, or to hear a man speak.

«Why, Savoy! How camest thou here?» I said.

«The devil fetched me, I guess.»

He was far gone in liquor. «I am like Mr. Sterne's starling: ‹I can't get out.› Ever read Mr. Sterne's—what is it?—oh, his ‹Sentimental Journey›?»

Here was one worse than I, and I felt inclined to use what Friends call a precious occasion, a way being opened.

«This is a sad business, Savoy,» I said.

«Dre'ful,» he returned. «*Facilis descensus taverni.* No use to talk to me. I am tired of life. I am going to die. Some men shoot themselves, some like the rope, and some cold water. You know what Bishop what's-his-name—I mean Jeremy Taylor—says about ways to die: ‹None please me.› But drink is the best. I mean to drink myself dead—dead—d—dead,» and here he fell on to my shoulder. Letting him down easily, I loosed his neckerchief, and stood beside him, pitiful and shocked. Then in a moment I felt that I was drunk. The room whirled, and with an effort I got to the open window, stumbling over legs of men, who looked up from their cards and cursed me.

Of what chanced after this I knew for a time but little until I was in one instant sobered. This was an hour later, and nigh to twelve o'clock. What took place I heard from others; and as it concerns a turning-point in my life, I shall try to relate it as if I myself had been conscious all the while.

The better for air, I went over to a table in the center of the room not far from the door. Leaning heavily on Captain Small's shoulder, I threw on the table the last gold joe my aunt had given me with her final lesson in morals.

«Best in three, Etherington.»

«Take it,» he cried.

I threw double sixes, he threes, and I deuce ace. Then he cast some numbers as good. Certainly the devil meant to have me. I threw a third time; a six and a five turned up, and he an ace and a four. I had won, «Double or quits,» I said; «one throw.» I won again, and at this I went on until the pile of gold grew beneath my eyes, amid laughter, curses, and all manner of vileness. Presently I heard the colonel exclaim, «This won't do, gentlemen,» and I felt some one trying to draw me from the table. It was Captain Wynne. I cried out: «Hands off! no liberties with me! I am the head of thy house; thou art only a cadet.» He laughed as I pushed him aside.

«You said double or quits,» cried the stout major. How he got into the game I knew not.

«It is a mere boy! for shame!» cried the colonel. «I forbid it.»

«I am a gentleman,» I said. «Thou canst order thy officers; thou canst not order me,» and as I spoke I cast so hard that I crushed the box. I heard some one cry, «A —— pretty Quaker! By George, he has lost! A clean hundred pounds!» Even in this drunken revel there was a pause for a moment. I was, after all, but a tipsy lad of twenty, and some were just not far enough gone to feel that it might look to others an ugly business. The colonel said something to Major Milewood as to disrespect, I hardly know what; for at this moment there was a loud knocking at the door. In the lull that followed I heard the colonel's voice.

Then the tumult broke out anew. «By Jove, it is a woman!» cried Wynne. «I hear her. Wine and women! A guinea to a guinea she 's pretty!»

«Done!» cried some one.

«Here 's the key,» said the major; «let 's have her in.»

«*Place aux dames*,» hiccoughed a cornet.

The colonel rose, but it was too late. Wynne, seizing the key, unlocked the door and threw it wide open, as my mother, followed by Jack Warder, entered the room, and stood still a moment, dazed.

Captain Wynne, leering and unsteady, caught at her waist, exclaiming, «By George! she might be younger, but I 've won. A toast! a toast! A Quaker, by George!»

Whether I was sobered or not, I know not. I can only say that of a sudden I was myself and strangely quiet. I saw the dear lady, brave, beautiful, and with her curls falling about her neck, as she shrank back from the man's touch.

«Come, Hugh,» she said.

«Yes, mother,» I said; «but first—» and I struck Captain Wynne full in the face, so that, unprepared as he was, he fell over a table and on to the floor.

Every one started up. There was instant silence.

In a moment he was on his feet, and, like myself, another man. Turning, he said, with amazing coolness, wiping the blood away, for I was strong, and had hit hard: «Madam, I beg your pardon; we have been behaving like beasts, and I am fitly punished. As to you, Mr. Wynne, you are a boy, and have undertaken to rough it with men. This shall go no further.»

«It shall go where I please,» I cried.

«No, no; Hugh, Hugh!» said my mother.

«We will talk it over to-morrow,» said the captain; and then, turning, «I mean, gentlemen, that this shall stop here. If any man thinks I am wrong, let him say so. I shall know how to settle accounts with him.»

«No, no,» said the colonel; «you are right, and if any officer thinks otherwise, I too am at his service.» In the silence which came after he added, «Permit me, madam»; and offering his arm to my mother, we following, they went downstairs, Jack and I after them, and so into the street and the reproachful calm of the starlit April night.

## VIII.

«Even so far away as now,» says Jack, writing in after-days, «it grieves me to think of that winter, and of this mad scene at the London Coffee-house. When I saw Hugh go in with the officers, I waited for an hour, and then went away. Returning later, I learned that he was still upstairs. I felt that if I stayed until he came forth, although he might not be in a way to talk to me, to know that I had waited so long might touch him and help him to hear me with patience. I walked to and fro until the clock had struck twelve, fearful and troubled like a woman. Sometimes I think I am like a woman in certain ways, but not in all.

«There were many people who loved Hugh, but, save his mother, none as I did. He had a serious kindliness in his ways, liking to help people, and for me at certain times and in certain crises a reassuring directness of swift dealing with matters in hand, most sustaining to one of my hesitating nature. His courage was instinctive, mine the result of obedience to my will, and requiring a resolute effort.

«I think of him always as in time of peril, throwing his head up and his shoulders back, and smiling, with very wide-open eyes, like his mother's, but a deeper blue. The friendship of young men has often for a partial basis admiration of physical force, and Hugh excelled me there, although I have never been considered feeble or awkward except among those of another sex, where always I am seen, I fear, to disadvantage.

«Just after twelve I saw a woman coming hastily up Front street. As she came to a pause in the light which streamed from the open door, I knew her for Madam Marie, as she had taught me to call her. She wore a *calèche* hood, fallen back so that I saw her hair, half tumbled from under the thin gauze cap worn on the top of the head by most Quakers. She was clad quite too slightly, and had for wrap only a light, gray silk shawl.

«‹*Mon Dieu!*› she exclaimed, ‹I had to come. Jack, is he here? *Il faut que je monte*, I must go upstairs.› In excitement she was apt to talk French, and then to translate. ‹Let me go,› said I; but she cried out, ‹No, no! come!›

«There were many rough folks without, and others called together by the noise above, and no wonder. I said, ‹Come in; I will go up with thee.› She pushed me aside, and, with staring eyes, cried, ‹*Où est l'escalier?*› As we went through the coffee-room, the loungers looked at her with surprise. She followed me without more words, ran by me on the stairs, and in a moment beat fiercely on the door, crying, ‹*Ouvrez!* open! quick!› Then there was that madhouse scene.»

And this was how it came about, as Jack has here told, that, still hot and angry, but much sobered, I, her son, walked beside my mother till we came to our door, and Jack left us, saying:

«Wilt thou see me to-morrow?»

I said, «Yes. God bless thee! Thou art the real son,» and we entered.

Then it was sweet to see her; she said no word of reproach except, « *Il ne faut pas me donner ton baiser ce soir.* No, no; I am not to be kissed.» And so I went, sorrowful and still dizzy, up to my sleepless couch.

At the first gray light of dawn I rose, and was soon away half a mile from shore in my boat. As I came up from my first plunge in the friendly river, and brushed the water from my eyes, I do assure you the world seemed different. The water was very cold, but I cared nothing for that. I went home another and a better man, with hope and trust and self-repose for company. That hour in the water at early morn forever after seemed to me a mysterious separation between two lives, like a mighty baptismal change. Even now I think of it with a certain awe.

I pulled home as the sun rose, and lingered about until our servants came in for the early worship of the day. Soon I had the mother's kiss, and underwent a quick, searching look, after which she nodded gaily, and said, « *Est-ce que tout est bien, mon fils?* Is all well with thee, my son?» I said, « Yes—yes.» I heard her murmur a sweet little prayer in her beloved French tongue. Then she began to read a chapter. I looked up amazed. It was the prodigal's story.

I stood it ill, thinking it hard that she should have made choice of that reproachful parable. I stared sideways out at the stream and the ships, but lost no word, as, with a voice that broke now and then, she read the parable to its close. After this should have come prayer, silent or spoken; but, to my surprise, she said, « We will not pray this morning,» and we went in to breakfast at once.

As for me, I could not eat. I went out alone to the garden and sat down. I knew she would come to me soon. It seemed to me a long while. I sat on the grass against a tree, an old cherry, as I remember, and waited.

I can see her coming toward me under the trees, grave and quiet and sweet. The great beauty, Sarah Lukens, who married in mid-war the gallant Lennox, used to say of my mother that she put some sugar into all her moods; and it was true. I have seen her angry. I had rather have faced my father in his wildest rage than her. Why was she not angry now? She had vast reason for displeasure. After men have become wise enough to understand woman, I protest there will remain the mother, whom no man will ever comprehend.

« What a beautiful day, Hugh! And thou hadst a good swim? Was it cold? Why may not girls swim? I should love it.»

Next she was beside me on the grass, my head on her bosom, saying, with a little sob, as if she had done some wrong thing:

« I—I did not choose it, dear; indeed I did not. It came in order with the day, as my father reads; and I—I did not think until I began it, and then I would not stop. It is strange for it so to chance. I wonder where that prodigal's mother was all the while? Oh, thou art better than that wicked, wicked prodigal. I never would have let him go at all—never if I could have helped it, I mean. *Mon Dieu!* I think we women were made only for prayer or for forgiveness; we can stop no sin, and when it is done can only cry, ‹Come back! come back! I love you!›»

If I cried on that tender heart, and spoke no word, and was but a child again, I am sure that it was of all ways the best to tell her that never again should she be hurt by any act of mine.

« See, there is Judith at the door, wondering where I am,» she said, « and what is to be for dinner. I must go and get ready the fatted calf. Ah, I would not have left one alive. Yes, yes, I can jest, because I am no more afraid, *mon fils*, nor ever shall be.»

Upon this I would have said something of my deep shame, and of the swine among whom I had wallowed.

« No,» she cried; « *c'est fini, mon cher.* It is all over. The swine will eat alone hereafter.» And so would hear no more, only adding, « As for me, I want to be told once how brave I was. Jack said so; indeed he did. I *was* brave, was I not?»

« Don't, dear mother! please! I cannot bear it.» Somehow this plea, so childlike, to be praised for what must have cost so much, quite overcame me.

« Yes, yes,» she said; « I understand thee, and I shall always. How strong thou art, *mon fils!* I was proud of thee, even in that sty of pigs in red coats. And he behaved like a gentleman, and hath wondrous self-command. I would see him again; who is he?»

I told her his name.

« *Que c'est drôle.* That is curious. Thy cousin! No doubt we shall see him to-day, and thy father. I shall tell him all—all. He must know.»

« Yes, he must know,» I said; « but I will tell him myself.»

« He will be angry, but that is part of thy punishment.»

Then I told her, too, I had lost an hundred pounds, as I believed, and she said:

« That is, after all, the least. There are pearls of my sister's I never wear. Thy aunt must take them and pay this debt. Go now to thy business as if nothing had happened, and I will send thee the pearls by Tom. No, no; it is to be as I say; I must have my way.»

What could I do? I kissed her, and we parted. I made no promises, and she asked for none. I like to think of how, after all, I left with her this sense of quiet trust.

I have said that the daily march of events never so influenced my life as did critical occasions. This was surely one of them. I do not now regret the knowledge of a baser world which I thus acquired. It has been of use to me, and to some with whose lives I have had to deal.

Of the wrath of my father, when I humbly confessed my sins, it is not needful to speak at length. For business calamities he was ready enough, and lacked not decision; but in this matter he was, as I could see, puzzled. He strode up and down, a great bulk of a man, opening and shutting his hands, a trick he had in his rare moments of doubt or of intense self-repression.

«I know not what to do with thee,» he said over and over; «and thou didst strike the man, thy cousin? Well, well! and hurt him, I am told? And he did not return the blow!»

I had not said so. Thus I knew that other busy tongues had been at work. For my life, I could not see whether he looked upon the blow as my worst iniquity, or deep in his heart was hardly grieved at it.

«Thou didst strike him? I must consider of thee; I must take counsel. Go! thou wilt bring my gray hairs in sorrow to the grave.» And so I left him, still striding to and fro, with ever the same odd movement of his hands. He took counsel, indeed, and for me and for him the most unwise that ever a troubled man could have taken. It was some days before this unpleasant scene took place, and meanwhile I had seen my aunt.

She was taking snuff furiously when I entered, and broke out at once, very red in the face, and walking about in a terrible rage. My mother used to say that the first thing one saw of my Aunt Gainor was her nose. It had been quite too much of a nose for the rest of her face until gray hair and some change wrought by time in the architecture of her fine head helped to make it more in harmony with the rest of her features. Somehow it arrested my attention now, and Heaven knows why it seemed to me more odd than ever.

«This is a fine repentance, indeed! What are you staring at, you fool? Here has been that wild curlew Bess Ferguson with an awful tale of how you have gambled and lost an hundred pounds, and half killed an unlucky cousin. Who the deuce is the man? A nice godchild you are! A proper rage I am in, and Dr. Rush tells me I am never to let myself get excited! As to Mrs. Galloway, duels and murder are the least of her talk; and, upon my word, you know no more of the small sword than of—I know not what. I must send you to Pike for lessons. When is it to be?»

«My dear aunt,» I cried, «I wish all these Tory cats of yours were dead!»

At this she broke into laughter, and sat down.

«Cats! and did n't they miaow! But that sweet girl Jack Warder has been here too; sent, I suppose, by that dear Jesuit, your mother. How he blushes! I hear you behaved like a gentleman even in your cups. I like the lad; I did not use to. He is a manly miss. Sit down, and tell me all about it. Bless me! how hot I am!»

Upon this I knew I had won my battle, and went on to tell the whole story. When I produced my pearls, of which I was horribly ashamed, she broke out anew, declaring we were all mere traders, and did we think her a pawnbroker? and ended by giving me an hundred pounds, and bidding me to be careful and pay at once, as it was a debt of honour. «As to the pearls, let Madam Marie keep them for thy wife.»

Thus ended a sorry business. It was to be told, and I have told it; but none, not even my mother or Jack, knew how deep a mark it left upon my character, or how profoundly it affected my life.

My friend Jack shall say the requiescat of this chapter of my life, which I have so unwillingly recorded. There was one more thing needed to complete its misery. Says Jack:

«Hugh Wynne and I fell quite apart that winter of '72 and '73. It was my fault.» This I do not understand. «Came then that hideous night in April, and all the rest; and Hugh I saw the day after, and begged him to forgive me because I had so easily deserted him. I took him later a kind message from Mr. James Wilson; for our small city knew it all. Friends looked at him as one disgraced, except Friend Rupert Forest, who, to my amusement, seemed to enjoy to hear the whole story, saying, ‹Alas! alas!› and yet, as I saw, far more pleased than distressed. It brought to my mind the battle he had set us to fight out when we were boys. For a week or two Hugh was dispirited, but after that, when the colonel had called, and his cousin Arthur Wynne began to be more and more with him, he took heart, and faced our little world, and would let no one except myself say a word to him of the time of his downfall. This I think I never did, save perhaps once, and that long after.

«There was no need to preach. Converted devils make the best saints. I never was as good as Hugh, because I lacked courage to be wicked. Hugh was no saint, but he drank no more for a long while, and was ever after moderate. As to cards and dice, it was much the same.»

What Jack has here written is all nonsense. He was a better man than I, and never was nor could have been a bad one.

IX.

I HAVE said that one event had to be recorded before I completed the story of that episode of which I was weary of hearing. My father —and it was against all his habits in regard to most matters—reminded me almost daily of my misdeeds. He hoped I did not drink any more, and he would even look at the square flasks on the shelf to see, as I suspected, if they had been used. To be prayed for was worst of all, and this he did more than once. It was all of it unwise, and but for my mother I should have been even more unhappy. I can see now that my father was this while in distress, feeling that he must do something, and not knowing what to do.

In his business life there had always been a way opened, as Friends say. He did not see that what I needed was what it was not in his nature to give, and thus it came about that we drew apart, and perhaps neither then nor at any later time were, or could ever have been, in the kindlier relation which makes the best of friendships that of the grown-up son with the elderly father.

At last, after a month or more, when it was far on in June, he ceased to trouble me, and to walk up and down, opening and shutting his hands, as he recounted my sins. He had reached an unfortunate decision, of which I was soon to feel the results.

In the mean time my cousin Mr. Arthur Wynne had come into very close intimacy with all our family circle. As he had much to do with my later life, it is well to return a little, and to detail here what followed after the night of my mother's visit to the coffee-house.

Next day, in the evening, came the colonel of the Scots Greys, and desired to see me in the sitting-room, my father being still in Lancaster.

«Mr. Wynne,» he said, «Captain Wynne has asked me to call in reference to that unhappy business of last night. He begs to make his excuses to Mrs. Wynne in this letter, which may I ask you to deliver? And after this action on his part I trust you will see your way to regret the blow you struck.»

I was quiet for a moment, feeling that I must be careful what answer I made. «I cannot feel sorry,» I said; «I do not regret it.»

«That is a pity, Mr. Wynne. You should remember that Mr. Arthur Wynne could not have known who the lady was. A blow is a thing no gentleman can, as a rule, submit to; but this has been discussed by Sir William Draper and myself, and we feel that Mr. Arthur Wynne cannot challenge a boy of eighteen.»

«I am twenty,» I replied.

«Pardon me—of twenty, who is his cousin. That is the real point I would make. You have the best of it. You were right, quite right; but, by St. George, you are a hard hitter! Mr. Wynne would have come in person, but he is hardly fit to be seen, and a sign-painter is just now busy painting his eyelids and cheek, so as to enable him to appear out of doors.»

The colonel treated me with the utmost respect, and, as a young fellow naturally would be, I was embarrassed more than a little, but not at all dissatisfied with the condition of my cousin. I said awkwardly that if he was willing to forget it I supposed I ought to be.

«I think so,» said the colonel. «Suppose you leave it with me, and in a day or two talk it over with him. Indeed, he is a most charming gentleman, and a worthy member of a good old house.»

I said I would leave it with the colonel, and upon this he said, «Good-by, and come and dine with the mess some day, but don't hit any more of us»; and so, laughing, he went away, leaving me flattered, but with the feeling that somehow he had gotten the better of me.

My mother declared it was a beautiful letter, writ prettily, but ill-spelled (neither George the king nor our own George could spell well). She would not let me see it. I did years afterward. In it he spoke of me as a boy, and she was cunning enough to know that I should not like that.

It was a week before we saw Mr. Arthur Wynne. My father had meanwhile vented his first wrath on me, and I was slowly getting over the strong sense of disgust, shame, contrition, and anger, and had settled down earnestly to my work. I hardly recognised the man who came in on us after supper, as my mother and I sat in the orchard, with my father in a better humour than of late, and smoking a churchwarden, which, you may like to know, was a long clay pipe. The smoke sailed peacefully up, as I sat looking at its blue smoke-rings. (How often have I seen them float from the black lips of cannon, and thought of my father and his pipe!)

We discussed the state of trade, and now and then I read aloud bits from the Boston «Packet» of two weeks back, or my mother spoke of their September voyage, and of what would be needed for it, a voyage being looked upon as a serious affair in those times.

«I found your doors hospitably open,» said the captain, appearing, «and the servant said I should find you here; so I have taken my welcome for granted, and am come to make my most humble excuses to Mrs. Wynne.»

We all rose as he drew near, my mother saying in my ear as he approached, «It is Arthur Wynne. Now, Hugh, take care!»

This newly found cousin was, like all of us, tall, but, as I have said, not quite so broad as we other Wynnes. He was of swarthy complexion from long service in the East, and had black hair, not fine, but rather coarse. I noticed a scar on his forehead. He shook hands, using his left hand, because, as I learned, of awkwardness from an old wound. But with his left he was an expert swordsman, and, like left-handed swordsmen, the more dangerous.

«We are glad to see thee, Cousin Wynne,» said my mother.

As for me, I saw marks of my handiwork still on his cheek; I took his greeting with decent cordiality, and said, «Sit down; wilt thou smoke a pipe, Cousin Arthur?»

He said he did not smoke, and set himself, with the address of a man used to a greater world than ours, to charm those whom no doubt he considered to be quite simple folk. In a few minutes the unpleasantness of the situation was over. He and my father were at one about politics, and I wisely held my peace. He let fall a discreet sentence or two about the habits of soldiers, and his own regrets. As to me, he said, laughing:

«Your son is not quite of your views as a Friend in regard to warfare.»

«My son is a hasty young man,» said my father, and I felt my mother's touch on my arm.

Our cousin was in no way upset by this. He said, «No, no, cousin; he is young, but not hasty. I was fitly dealt with. We are hot-blooded people, we Wynnes. The ways of Friends are not our ways of dealing with an injury; and it was more—I wish to say so—it was an insult. He was right.»

«There is no such thing as insult in the matter,» said my father. «We may insult the great Master, but it is not for man to resent or punish.»

«I fear as to that we shall continue to differ.» He spoke with the utmost deference. «Do you go to Wyncote? I hear you are for England in the autumn.»

«No; I shall be too full of business. Wyncote has no great interest for me.»

«Indeed? It might perhaps disappoint you—a tumble-down old house, an embarrassed estate. My brother will get but a small income when it falls to him. As to my father, he fights cocks and dogs, rides to hounds, and, I grieve to say, drinks hard, like all our Welsh squires.»

I was surprised at his frank statement. My mother watched him curiously, with those attentive blue eyes, as my father returned:

«Of a certainty, thou dost not add to my inducements to visit Wyncote. I should, I fear, be sadly out of place.»

«I am afraid that is but too true, unless your head is better than mine. We are a sad set, we Wynnes. All the prosperity, and, I fear, much of the decency, of the family crossed the ocean long ago.»

«Yet I should like to see Wyncote,» said I. «I think thou didst tell me it is not thy home.»

«No; a soldier can hardly be said to have a home; and a younger brother, with a tough father alive, and an elder brother on an impoverished estate, must needs be a wanderer.»

«But we shall make thee welcome here,» said my father, with grave kindness. «We are plain people, and live simply; but a Wynne should always find, as we used to say here, the latch-string outside.»

With a little more talk of the Wynnes, the captain, declining to remain longer, rose, and, turning to me, said, «I hear, Cousin Hugh, that you refused to say that you were sorry for the sharp lesson you gave me the other night. I have made my peace with your mother.»

«I shall see that my son behaves himself in future. Thou hast heard thy cousin, Hugh?»

I had, and I meant to make it up with him, but my father's effort as a peacemaker did not render my course the more easy. Still, with the mother-eyes on me, I kept my temper.

«I was about to say thou hast done all a man can do,» said I.

«Then let us shake hands honestly,» he replied, «and let bygones be bygones.»

I saw both my parents glance at me. «I should be a brute if I did not say yes, and mean it, too; but I cannot declare that I am sorry, except for the whole business.» And with this I took his left hand, a variety of the commonplace ceremony which always, to my last knowledge of Captain Wynne, affected me unpleasantly.

He laughed. «They call us in Merionethshire the wilful Wynnes. You will find me a good friend if you don't want the things I want. I am like most younger brothers, inclined to want things. I thank you all for a pleasant hour. It is like home, or better.» With this he bowed low to my mother's curtsey, and went away, chatting as I conducted him to the door, and promising to sail with me, or to fish.

Naturally enough, on my return I found my parents discussing our newly found relative. My mother thought he talked much of himself, and had been pleasanter if he had not spoken so frankly of his father. My father said little, except that there seemed to be good in the young man.

«Why should we not forgive that in him which we must forgive in our own son?»

My father had some dreadful power to hurt me, and to me only was he an unjust man; this may have been because my wrong-doing troubled both his paternal and his spiritual pride. I was about to say that there was little likeness between my sin and that of my cousin; but I saw my mother, as she stood back of my father's great bulk, shake her head, and I held my tongue. Not so she.

«If thou hadst been a woman in my place, John Wynne, thou wouldst be far from saying the thing thou hast said.»

Never had I heard or seen in our house a thing like this. I saw, in the fading light, my father working his hands as I have described, a signal of restrained anger, and, like anything physically unusual in one we love, not quite pleasant to see. But my mother, who knew not fear of him nor of any, went on, despite his saying, «This is unseemly—unseemly, wife.»

«Thou art unjust, John, to my son.»

«Thy son?»

«Yes; mine as well as thine. I have faith that thou, even thou, John, wouldst have done as my boy did.»

«I? I?» he cried; and now I saw that he was disturbed, for he was moving his feet like some proud, restrained horse pawing the grass. At last he broke the stillness which followed his exclamations: «There is but one answer, wife. Both have been brutes, but this boy has been kept near to godly things all his life. Each First-day the tongues of righteous men have taught him to live clean, to put away wrath, to love his enemies; and in a day—a minute—it is gone, and, as it were, useless, and I the shame of the town.»

I hoped this was all; but my mother cried. «John! John! It is thy pride that is hurt. No, it is not seemly to dispute with thee, and before thy son. And yet—and yet—even that is better than to let him go with the thought that he is altogether like, or no better than, that man. If thou hast a duty to bear testimony, so have I.» And thus the mother of the prodigal son had her say. No doubt she found it hard, and I saw her dash the tears away with a quick hand, as she added, «If I have hurt thee, John, I am sorry.»

«There is but one answer, wife. Love thy enemy; do good to them that despitefully use thee. Thou wilt ruin thy son with false kindness, and who shall save him from the pit?»

I turned at last in a storm of indignation, crying, «Could I see my mother treated like a street-wench or a gutter-drab, and lift no hand? I wish I had killed him!»

«You see, wife,» said my father. «Yes, even this was to be borne.»

«Not by me!» I cried, and strode into the house, wondering if ever I was to be done with it.

The day after no one of us showed a sign of this outbreak. Never had I seen the like of it among us; but the Quaker habit of absolute self-repression and of concealment of emotion again prevailed, so that at breakfast we met as usual, and, whatever we may have felt, there was no outward evidence of my mother's just anger, of my father's bitterness, or of my own disgust.

## X.

I WAS not yet to see the end of my iniquity, and was to feel the consequences in ways which, for many a day, influenced my life and actions.

It was toward the end of June. The feeling of uneasiness and dread was becoming more and more felt, not only in commerce, which is so sensitive, but also in the social relations of men. The king's officers were more saucy, and, like all soldiers, eager for active service, imagining an easy victory over a people untrained in war. Such Tory pamphleteers as the foul-tongued Massachusetts writer, Daniel Leonard, were answering «Vindex» (Mr. Adams) and the widely read letters of «An American Farmer.» The plan of organised correspondence between the colonies began to be felt in some approach to unity of action, for at this time the outspoken objection to the views of the king and his facile minister was general, and even men like Galloway, Chew, the Allens, and

John Penn stood with varying degrees of good will among those who were urging resistance to oppression. As yet the too mighty phantom of independence had not appeared on the horizon of our stormy politics, to scare the timid, and to consolidate our own resistance.

I worked hard with my father at our lessening and complicated business, riding far into the country to collect debts, often with Jack, who had like errands to do, and with whom I discussed the topics which were so often, and not always too amiably, in question at my Aunt Gainor's table. I was just now too busy to be much with my old favourites, the officers. Indeed, I was wise enough to keep away from them.

My cousin I saw often, both at my aunt's, as I shall relate, and elsewhere; for he came much to our house, and my father found it agreeable to talk over with him the news of the day. My mother did not like him as well, but she held her peace, and, like every other man, he was attracted by her gaiety, and quaint way of looking at men and things.

Mr. Wilson I saw at times, as he still had, I know not why, a fancy for me, and loved well to sail with me of evenings over to Kaighn's Point to fish, or down to Gloucester to bob for crabs. I owed him much. A profound knowledge of law, variety of reading, and a mind which left broadly on our after-history the marks of his powerful intellect, were at my service. He used to caution me how I spoke of his opinions to others, and he would then discuss with freedom politics and the men whose figures were fast rising into distinctness as leaders to be listened to and trusted. Many of them he knew, and thus first I heard clearly what manner of persons were Patrick Henry and the Adamses, Dickinson, Peyton Randolph, and others less prominent. In this way I came to be more and more confirmed in the opinions my Aunt Gainor so resolutely held, and also more careful how I expressed them. Indeed, although but twenty years of age, I was become quite suddenly an older and graver man. Mr. Wilson surprised me one day by saying abruptly, as he pulled up a reluctant crab, «Do you never think, Hugh, that we shall have war?»

I was indeed amazed, and said so. Then he added: «It will come. My place will not be in the field, but, whether you like it or not, you will see battles. You were made for a soldier, Hugh, Quaker or no Quaker.»

I thought it odd that two people as different as my Aunt Gainor and he should have the same belief that we were drifting into war. She had said to me the night before that she had known Lord North as a boy, and that the king was an obstinate Dutchman, and would make his minister go his way, adding, «When it comes you will be in it; you can't escape.»

No one else whom I knew had any such belief. Wilson's views and prediction sent me home thoughtful enough.

That evening my father said to me, «We go to Merion to-morrow, Hugh.» It was there we spent our summers. «To-morrow will be Fourth-day. It is our last day of Meeting in the town. There will, perhaps, be some wise words said as to present confusions, and I wish thee to hear them, my son.»

I said, «Yes; at seven, father?» I was, however, astonished; for these occasional night Meetings in the middle of the week were but rarely attended by the younger Friends, and, although opened with such religious observances as the society affected, were chiefly reserved for business and questions of discipline. I had not the least desire to go, but there was no help for it.

Our supper took place at six on this Wednesday, a little earlier than usual, and I observed that my father drank several cups of tea, which was not his habit. Few people took tea since the futile tax had been set upon it; but my father continued to drink it, and would have no concealment, as was the custom with some Whigs, who in public professed to be opposed to the views of the crown as to the right to collect indirect taxes.

Seeing that I did not drink it, and knowing that I liked nothing better than a good dish of tea, he asked me why I did not partake of it. Not willing to create new trouble, I said I did not want any. He urged the matter no further, but I saw he was not well pleased. We set off soon after in silence, he walking with hands behind his back clasping his gold-headed cane, his collarless coat and waistcoat below his beaver, and the gray hair in a thick mass between. He wore shoes, fine drab short-clothes, and black silk stockings, all without buckles; and he moved rapidly, nodding to those he met on the way, to the Bank Hill Meeting-house, in Front street, above Arch.

It was a simple brick building, set on a bank a few feet above the level of the roadway. The gables and shutters were painted white, as was also the plain Doric doorway, which had a pillar on each side. I judged by the number of both sexes entering that it was an unusual occasion. There were many drab-coated men, and there were elderly women, in gowns of drab or gray, with white silk shawls and black silk-covered cardboard bonnets. Here and there a man or woman was in gayer colours or wore buckles, and some had silver buttons; but these were rare. The Meeting-room was, so to speak, a large oblong box with whitewashed walls. A broad passage ran from the door to the farther end; on the right of it sat the men, on the left the women; against the remoter wall, facing the rude benches, were three rows of seats, one above the other. On these sat at the back the elders, and in front of them the overseers. The clerk of the Meeting had a little desk provided for him. Over their heads was a long sounding-board.

To me the scene had been familiar for years; but to-day it excited my attention because of an air of expectation, and even of excitement, among the few more youthful Friends. I saw, as we entered, furtive glances cast at my father and me; but as to this I had grown to be of late more or less indifferent, and had no anticipation of what was to follow later.

I had become, since my sad downfall, a more serious and thoughtful young man, and far better fitted to feel the beauty and the spirituality of these Meetings than I had been before. When the doors were closed I sat silent in prayer; a great stillness fell upon one and all of the three or four hundred people here met together.

As I waited, with long-trained patience, for full twenty minutes, a still deeper quiet came upon the figures seated on each side of the aisle. For a time none of the men uncovered, but soon a few took off their broad hats, having remained with them on their heads long enough to satisfy custom by this protest against the ways of other men. The larger number kept their hats on their heads. Then a strange incident took place: a woman of middle age, but gray, her hair fallen about her shoulders, entered noisily, and, standing before the elders, cried out in a loud voice, as though in affliction and sore distress: «See to your standing; the Lord is about to search and examine your camp. Ho, ye of little faith and less works, the hand of God is come upon you—the mighty hand of punishment!» As she spake thus wildly she swayed to and fro, and seemed to me disordered in mind. Finally she passed across the space in front of the overseers, to the women's side, and then back again, repeating her mad language. My Aunt Gainor's great bronze Buddha was not more motionless than they who sat on the elders' seats. At last the woman faced the Meeting, and went down the aisle, waving her hands, and crying out, «I shall have peace, peace, in thus having discharged my Lord's errand.» The many there met did justice to their discipline. Scarce a face showed the surprise all must have felt. No one turned to see her go out, or seemed to hear the door banged furiously after her. The covered heads remained silent and almost motionless; the rows of deep bonnets were almost as moveless. Fully ten minutes of perfect silence followed this singular outburst. Then I saw the tall, gaunt figure of Nicholas Waln rise slowly, a faint but pleasant smile on his severe face, while he looked about him and began:

«Whether what ye have heard be of God I cannot say. The time hath troubled many souls. The woman, Sarah Harris, who has, as some are aware, borne many sweet and pleasing testimonies to Friends in Wilmington, I know not. Whether what ye have heard be of God or but a rash way of speech, let us feel that it is a warning to Friends here assembled that we be careful of what we say and do. It hath been horne in upon me that Friends do not fully understand one another, and that some are moved to wrath, and some inclined to think that Friends should depart from their ways and question that which hath been done by the rulers God hath set over us. Let us be careful that our General Epistles lean not to the aiding of corrupt and wicked men, who are leading weak-minded persons into paths of violence.» And here he sat down.

A moment later got up Thomas Scattergood, grim and dark of visage. None of his features expressed the slightest emotion, although even from the beginning he spoke with vehemence and his body rocked to and fro.

«The days are darkening; the times are evil. Our master, set over us by God, has seen fit to tax certain commodities that means may be raised for the just government of these colonies, where we and our fathers have prospered in our worldly goods, under a rule that has left us free to worship God as seems best to us. And now we are bid by men, not of our society, ungodly self-seekers, sons of darkness, to unite with them in the way of resistance to the law. There have even been found here among us those who have signed agreements to disobey such as are set over us, unmindful of the order to render to Cæsar that which is his. Let there be among Friends neither fear nor any shortcoming. Let us bear testimony against evil-doers, whether they be of us or not. Let us cut down and utterly cast forth those who depart from righteousness. Are they not of the scum which riseth on the boiling pot? There is a time for Friends to remonstrate, and a time to act. I fear lest these too gentle counsels of Friend Waln be out of time and out of place. Away with those who, hearing, heed not. Let them be dealt with as they should be, with love for the sinner, but with thought as to the evil which comes of unscourged examples, so that when again we are met in the Quarterly Meeting there shall be none among us to stir up discord, and we can say to other Meetings: ‹As we have done, so do ye. Make clean the house of the Lord.›»

The night was now upon us, and the ringing tones of the speaker were heard through the darkness before he sat down. While all waited, two Friends lighted the candles set in tin sconces against the pillars of the gallery, and, in the dim light they gave, the discussion went on.

Then I saw that Arthur Howell was about to speak. This able and tender-minded man usually sat in Meeting with his head bent, his felt hat before his eyes, wrapped in thought, and lifted above all consideration of the things of this earth. As he began, his rich, full voice filled the space, and something in its pleading sweetness appealed to every heart. He spoke as one who, having no doubt, wondered that any one else should doubt, and he brought the discussion to a decisive point at once.

«It is well,» he said, «that all should be convinced by those who, from age and influence among Friends, have the best right of speech. Nevertheless, since this is a Meeting for discipline, let all be heard with fairness and order. Men have gone astray. They have contended for the asserting of civil rights in a manner contrary to our peaceable profession and principles, and, although repeatedly admonished, do not manifest any disposition to make the Meeting a proper acknowledgment of their outgoings. Therefore it is that we bear our testimony against such practices, and can have no unity with those who follow them until they come to a sense of their errors. Therefore, if this be the sense of our Meeting, let the clerk be moved to manifest the feelings of the Meeting to these members, signing on our behalf, for the matter hath already been before us twice, and hath been deeply and prayerfully considered by ourselves; and I am charged to tell Friends that these members who have thus gone astray are unwilling to be convinced by such as have sought to bring them to a better mind. This hath been duly reported, and overseers having thus failed, it doth only remain to abide by the sense of our Meeting. But this I have already said: the matter hath been prayerfully considered.»

After this, others spoke, but all elder Friends understood that the business had been disposed of, and little attention was given to those who rose after Friend Howell sat down. Indeed, that they were ill-advised to speak at all was plainly to be read in the countenances of many.

This was my first experience of an evening Meeting, and even to one acquainted with all the ways of Friends the scene was not without its interest. The night was now dark outside. The tallow dips ran down and flared dismally. A man with snuffers went to and fro, and the pungent odours of candles, burned out and to be replaced, filled the room.

In the quiet which followed Arthur Howell's refined and distinct accents, I looked at the row of placid faces where the women sat, some rosy, some old, all in the monastic cell of the bonnet, which made it as impossible to see, except in front, as it is for a horse with blinders. I wondered how this queer head-gear came to have been made, and recalled my aunt's amusement at the care exercised as to its form and material. Few there, I think, let their thoughts wander, and in front of me the row of drab coats and wide felt or beaver hats remained almost motionless.

At last James Pemberton, the esteemed clerk of the Meeting, rose. «I am moved,» he said, «by the Spirit to declare that the sense, and also the weight, of the Meeting is that Cyrus Edson and William Jameson be advised, in accordance with the instructed wish of Friends.»

He then sat down. There was no vote taken. Even had a majority of those present been hostile to the proposed action, it is improbable that any protest would have been made. The clerk's statement that the weight of the Meeting was affirmative, would have been held to settle the matter, as it appeared best to a limited number of those recognised, through their piety and strict living, to be competent to decide for the rest.

I was now assured that this was all, and looked to see two of the elders shake hands, which is the well-recognised signal for the Meeting to break up; but as the elders did not move, the rest sat still and waited. By and by I saw Nicholas Waln extend his hand to my father, who, looking steadily before him, made no sign of perceiving this intention to dismiss Friends. A still longer pause followed. As I learned afterward, no further speaking was anticipated. No one stirred. For my part, I was quite ready to go, and impatiently awaited the signal of dismissal. A minute or two passed; then I was aware of a short, neatly built man, who rose from a bench near by. His face was strong, irregular of feature, and for some reason impressed me. I could see even in the indistinct light that he flushed deeply as he got up on his feet. He received instant attention, for he went past me, and, standing in the passageway, was quiet for a moment. He was, I think, not over thirty, and seemed embarrassed at the instant attention he received. For a few minutes he appeared to seek his words, and then, quite suddenly, to find them in eloquent abundance.

«It is not usual,» he said, «for disowned members of the society to openly protest. Neither are these our brothers here to-day. Nor, were they with us, are they so skilled with the tongue as to be able to defend themselves against the strong language of Thomas Scattergood or the gentle speech of Arthur Howell. I would say a word for them, and, too, for myself, since nothing is more sure than that I think them right, and know that ye will, before long, cast out me, to whom your worship is sweet and lovely, and the ways of Friends for the most part such as seem to me more acceptable than those of any other Christian society. Whether it be that old memories of persecution, or too great prosperity, have hardened you, I do not know. It does seem to me that ye have put on a severity of dress and life that was not so once, and that undue strictness hath destroyed for us some of the innocent joys of this world. I also find unwholesome and burdensome that inner garment of self-righteousness in which ye clothe yourselves to judge the motives of your fellow-men.

«So far as the law went against such views as you entertained, none did more resist them, in your own way, than did you; but now the English across the seas tell us that the liberty our fathers sought on these shores is to be that which pleases a corrupt and pliant ministry, and not that which is common to men of English blood. Some brave men of our society say: ‹Let us make a stand here, lest worse things come. Let us refuse to eat, drink, or wear the articles they assume to tax, whether we will or not.› There is no violence. Believe me, there will be none if we are one throughout the colonies. But if not—if not—if grave old men like you, afraid of this mere shadow of passive resistance, dreading to see trade decay and the fat flanks of prosperity grow lean—if you are wholly with our oppressors, passively with them, or, as some believe, actively, then—then, dear friends, it will be not the shadow, but the substance, of resistance that will fall in blood and ruin on you and on all men—on your easy lives and your accumulated gains.

«Ay, look to it! There is blood on the garments of many a man who sits fearfully at home, and thinks that because he does nothing he will be free of guilt when the great account is called.»

On this a rare exception to the tranquillity of Meeting occurred. Daniel Offley, by trade a farrier, rose and broke in, speaking loudly, as one used to lift his voice amid the din of hammers: «Wherefore should this youth bring among us the godless things of worldly men?» His sonorous tones rang out through the partial obscurity, and shook, as I noticed, the scattered spires of the candle flames. «This is no time for foolish men to be heard, where the elders are of a mind. The sense of the Meeting is with us. The weight of the Meeting is with us. The king is a good king, and who are we to resist? Out with those who are not of our ways! Let the hammer fall on the unrighteous, lest the sheep be scattered, and the Shepherd leave them.»

At this queer mixture of metaphors I saw the previous speaker smile as he stood in the aisle. Next I heard the gentle voice of James Pemberton break in on the uncouth speech of the big farrier.

«It is the custom of Friends that all men who feel to be moved to tell us aught shall be heard. Friend Wetherill, we will hear thee to an end.» He spoke with the courteous ease of a well-bred gentleman, and the smith sat down.

Friend Wetherill paused a moment, looking to left and right along the lines of deeply interested and motionless faces. Then he continued: «On what you and others do in these days depends what shall come upon us. Let no man deceive you, not even the timid counsel of gray hairs or the wariness of wealth. The guinea fears; the penny fights: and the poor penny is to-day deeply concerned. You take shelter under the law of Christ, to live, as far as possible, at peace with all men. As far as possible? It should at times be felt that Paul's limitation is also a command. Do not resist him who would slay a child or wrong a woman—that is how you read the law of God.

«It is extremes which bring ruin to the best Christian societies, and if the mass of men were with you, civil order would cease, and the carefully builded structure of civilisation would perish. You are already undergoing a process of dry decay, and as you dry and dry, you harden and shrink, and see it not. A wild woman has told you to set your camp in order. See to it, my friends; see to it!»

For not less than a minute the speaker remained silent, with bended head, still keeping the wonderfully steady attention of this staid assembly. Very slowly he lifted his face, and now, as he began again, it was with a look of tender sweetness: «It was far back in Second-month, 1771, I began to be encompassed by doubts as to the course Friends were taking. To-day I am assured in spirit that you are wrong in the support you gave, and, let me say, are giving, to an unjust cause. I think I take an innocent liberty to express myself on this occasion, also according to the prospect I have of the matter. There is something due to the king, and something to the cause of the public. When kings deviate from the righteous law of justice in which kings ought to rule, it is the right, ay, and the religious duty, of the people to be plain and honest in letting them know where. I am not a person of such consequence as to dictate; but there is in me and in you a court to which I confidently appeal. I *have* appealed to it in prayer as to what my course shall be. I obey my conscience. Take heed that you do not act rashly.»

Here again, after these calm words, he paused, and then said, with emphatic sternness: «As my last words, let me leave with you the admonition of the great founder of this colony. ‹I beseech you,› he says, ‹for the sake of Christ, who so sharply prohibited making others suffer for their religion, that you have a care how you exercise power over other men's consciences. My friends, conscience is God's throne in man, and the power of it his prerogative!› These are solemn words. Whether you leave me to live among you, free to do what seems right to me, or drive me forth, who have no wish to go, now and always I shall love you. That love you cannot take away, nor weaken, nor disturb.»

I was sorry when the melody of this clear voice ceased. The speaker, wiping the moisture from his brow, stood still, and, covering his face with his hands, was lost in the prayer which I doubt not followed.

A long interval of absence of all sound came after he ceased to speak. No one replied. The matter was closed, a decision reached, and the clerk instructed. I knew enough to feel sure that those manly tones of appeal and remonstrance had failed of their purpose.

At this moment I saw an elderly man on the seat before me rise, and with deliberateness kneel in prayer; or, as Friends say, Israel Sharpless appeared in supplication. At first, as he began to be heard, Friends rose here and there, until all were afoot and all uncovered. The silence and reverent bended heads, and the dim light, affected me as never before. Many turned their backs on the praying man, an odd custom, but common. As he prayed his voice rose until it filled the great room; and of a sudden I started, and broke out in a cold sweat, for this was what I heard:

«O Lord, arise, and let Thine enemies be scattered. Dip me deeper in Jordan. Wash me in the laver of regeneration. Give me courage to wrestle with ill-doers. Let my applications be heard.

«Father of mercy, remember of Thy pity those of the young among us who, being fallen into evil ways, are gone astray. We pray that they who have gambled and drunk and brought to shame and sorrow their elders may be recovered into a better mind, and sin no more. We pray Thee, Almighty Father, that they be led to consider and to repent of deeds of violence, that those among us whom the confusion of the times has set against the law and authority of rulers be better counselled; or, if not, strengthen us so to deal with these young men as shall make pure again Thy sheepfold, that they be no longer a means of leading others into wickedness and debauchery.» I heard no more. This man was a close friend of my father. I knew but too well that it was I who was thus reproved, and thus put to shame. I looked this way and that, the hot blood in my face, thinking to escape. Custom held me. I caught, as I stared, furtive glances from some of the younger folk. Here and there some sweet, gentle face considered me a moment with pity, or with a curiosity too strong for even the grim discipline of Friends. I stood erect. The prayer went on. Now and then I caught a phrase, but the most part of what he said was lost to me. I looked about me at times with the anguish of a trapped animal.

At last I saw that my gentle-voiced speaker, Wetherill, was, like myself, rigid, with upheld head, and that, with a faint smile on his face, he was looking toward me. Minute after minute passed. Would they never be done with it? I began to wonder what was going on under those bent gray hats and black bonnets. I was far away from penitence or remorse, a bruised and tormented man, helpless, if ever a man was helpless, under the monotonous and silent reproach of some hundreds of people who had condemned me unheard. It did seem as if it never would end.

At last the voice died out. The man rose, and put on his hat. All resumed their seats and their head-coverings. I saw that Friend Scattergood extended a hand to my father, who was, as I have not yet stated, an elder. The grasp was accepted. Elders and overseers, both men and women, rose, and we also. I pushed my way out, rudely, I fear. At the door James Pemberton put out his hand. I looked him full in the face, and turned away from the too inquisitive looks of the younger Friends. I went by my father without a word. He could not have known what pain his method of saving my soul would cost me. That he had been in some way active in the matter I did not doubt, and I knew later that my opinion was but too correct.

Hastening down Front street with an overwhelming desire to be alone, I paused at our own door, and then, late as it was, now close to ten, I unmoored my boat, and was about to push off when I felt a hand on my shoulder. It was Samuel Wetherill.

«Let me go with thee, my boy,» he said. «We should talk a little, thou and I.»

I said: «Yes. Thou art the only man I want to see to-night.»

There were no more words. The moon was up as I pulled down Dock Creek and out on my friendly river.

«Let thy boat drift,» he said. «Perhaps thou art aware, Hugh Wynne, how grieved I was; for I know all that went before. I somehow think that thou hast already done for thyself what these good folk seemed to think was needed. Am I right?»

«Yes,» I said.

«Then say no more. James Wilson has spoken of thee often. To be loved of such a man is much. I hear that thou hast been led to think with us, and that, despite those wicked wild oats, thou art a young man of parts and good feelings, thoughtful beyond thy years.»

I thanked him almost in tears; for this kindly judgment was, past belief, the best remedy I could have had.

«I saw thy great suffering; but in a year, in a month, this will seem a thing of no import; only, when thou art calm and canst think, hold a Meeting in thy own heart, and ask thy quiet judgment, thy conscience, thy memory, if prayer be needed; and do it for thyself, Hugh.»

I said, «Thank thee,» but no more. I have ever been averse to talking of my relations to another world, or of what I believe, or of what I am led thereby to do in hours of self-communion. I sat wishing my father were like this, a tender-hearted yet resolute man.

Seeing me indisposed to speak, he went on: «If we could but keep the better part of Friends' creed, and be set free to live at peace with the law, to realise that to sit down quietly under oppression may be to serve the devil, and not God! Thou knowest, as well as I, that divers Friends have publicly avowed the ministry, and allege that whatever they may do is a just punishment of rebellion. We are going to have a serious settlement, and it will become us all, Hugh, young and old, to see that we are on the right side, even if we have to draw the sword. And thou and I shall not be alone of Friends. There are Clement and Owen Biddle, and Christopher Marshall, and more.»

I was surprised, and said so.

«Yes, yes,» he said; «but I talk to thee as to a man, and these things are not to be spread abroad. I trust I have been to thee a comfort; and, now the moon is setting, let us go home.»

I thanked him as well as I knew how. He had indeed consoled me.

When I came in my father had gone to bed, but my mother was waiting to see me. She caught me in her arms, and, weeping like a child, cried: «Oh, I have heard! He did not tell me beforehand, or I should have forbade it. Thou shouldst never have gone—never! It was cruel! *Mon Dieu!* how could they do it!»

It was I who now had to comfort, and this helped me amazingly, and yet added to my just anger; for why must she, who was innocent, be thus made to suffer? My father, when he came in, had asked for me. He had met my cousin, who had seen me going down Front street, and had hinted that I meant to find comfort at the coffee-house among the officers. She knew better, and had said her mind of this kinsman and his ways; upon which my father had gone angry to his bed. I was beginning to have an increasing distrust and dislike of Arthur, and the present news did not lessen either feeling. So at last here was an end of the consequences of my sad night at the coffee-house.

(To be continued.)

*S. Weir Mitchell.*

DRAWN BY HOWARD PYLE.

«THERE WAS INSTANT SILENCE.»

(SEE PAGE 365.)

# PUBLIC SPIRIT IN MODERN ATHENS.

BY D. BIKÉLAS.[1]

WITH PICTURES BY A. CASTAIGNE.

DRAWN BY A. CASTAIGNE.

A BYZANTINE CORNER.

I.

DURING the war for Greek independence the seat of government was moving from place to place, according to circumstances, until it was fixed at Nauplia under Capo d'Istria's short-lived presidency. It was in that city that young King Otho landed in 1832, amid the acclamations of the regenerated nation joyfully welcoming its first sovereign. Two years later the capital of the newly created kingdom was transferred from Nauplia to Athens—a measure imposed upon the counselors of the youthful king alike by her geographical position and her glorious name.

On the eve of the revolution in 1821 the population of Athens was said not to exceed 8000 souls. During the war she played an important part. Exposed to all the ravages of that long and merciless contest, many times taken and retaken, the town had then reached the lowest point of decay. When the Turks were strongest in the surrounding plain, where almost incessant fighting was going on, the inhabitants took refuge in the neighboring islands of Salamis and Ægina, as the ancient Athenians had done at the approach of Xerxes, returning with the tide of victory to their ruined dwellings. When the Turks had finally gone scarcely 2000 Greeks were left in the three hundred dilapidated houses piled at the foot of the Acropolis. As to the Piræus, a rickety building which had served as a custom-house was the only one to be seen on the desolate banks of the unfrequented port.

When, a few years later, it was decided to transfer the capital, signs of improvement had already begun to appear; the population had once more reached some 8000, and new houses had been erected here and there. The best one, now serving as a police office, was secured as a royal residence pending the construction of the palace, which, begun in 1834, was finished only four years later. If the aim of its German architect was, by the unpretending simplicity of the façade, to escape dangerous comparison with the monuments of antiquity, it must be allowed that he fully succeeded. The north part, adorned with an Ionic colonnade, by far the best part of the structure, can be seen only from the garden. In spring this garden, or park, with its vigorous verdure, is delightful when the orange-trees are in blossom and the nightingales sing in the shade. It shows what the poor soil of Attica is capable of when properly cared for.

Ancient Athens spread round the Acropolis, especially on the hills facing the south, which are now uninhabited. The new town lies to the north of the antique citadel—an extension of the cluster of houses already existing at the foot of the rock when the war was ended. Two main intersecting streets were laid out—Æolus street, starting from below the Acropolis and running northward, and Hermes street, leading from the royal palace toward the Piræus. The capital was

[1] American readers will be interested to know that Mr. Bikélas as the leading literary man of Greece, was chairman of the Greek Committee in charge of the Olympian Games of 1896. The present paper was written by him in English.—EDITOR.

SOCRATES IN THE STREETS OF ATHENS, B. C. 400.

thus designed to lie in the valley between the Acropolis on one side and Mount Lycabettus on the other. No ambition of future development is traceable in the original plan. The ground chosen, and the width of the main streets, tend to show that the founders of the new city little dreamed of its rapid extension. Squeezing herself out of her narrow confines, the city has gradually scaled the foot of Lycabettus and spread beyond the valley on both sides, principally in a southwesterly direction. If the extension had been in a straight line toward the sea, Athens would now be nearing a junction with the Piræus; but both towns, as if avoiding each other, extend in parallel lines, and one must look to a probably distant future for the day when they shall be connected by rows of houses, instead of the long walls of ancient days.

The fashionable quarters of the capital are to be found in the new additions to the primitive plan—the Neapolis, as it is called. Large thoroughfares have there been opened, fine buildings erected, both public and private; and Athens, already the finest city in the east of Europe, bids fair to become, if no stop be put to her progress, one of the handsomest cities on the Mediterranean.

Under King Otho's reign progress was comparatively slow. At the accession of King George, in the year 1863, the population did not exceed 45,000. The advance has been more rapid since then, especially during the last twenty years of material prosperity, which has lately been interrupted, let us hope temporarily, by the financial entanglements of the Greek government. During that period the immigration of well-to-do Greeks from abroad has not been one of the least causes of this development. In 1879 the census showed a population of nearly 64,000; in 1889, 114,000; and to-day, judging by the vital and building statistics, the number of inhabitants, if it does not exceed, cannot fall short of 130,000. The progress of the newly created town of Piræus is not less remarkable. From 5000 or 6000 souls, which had already gathered there some thirty years ago, its population had grown to 34,000 in 1889, and is now estimated at more than 50,000. Together the two towns number as many inhabitants as they probably possessed in the fourth century B. C. The sources of information as to the population of ancient Athens are indeed vague; but from a passage of Xenophon giving the number of families as 10,000, and from a passage of Athenæus indicating the proportion of slaves to freemen at the time of Demetrius Phalereus, it may be calculated that at that epoch the population of Athens, including that of the Piræus, was about 180,000. The area included within the walls of both towns seems rather to confirm this estimate. The surrounding country was thickly populated—much more so than at any succeeding period; but it is more than probable that the inhabitants of Athens proper and of her seaport never exceeded 200,000.

DRAWN BY A. CASTAIGNE.

THE PNYX.

DRAWN BY A. CASTAIGNE.

A GREEK SHEPHERD.

The progress of the modern capital of Greece will not astonish American readers; but Athens in no way resembles New York or Chicago, nor is Greece America. Between the two countries there is no point of comparison whatsoever. The Americans, springing from and connected with a powerful European nation, began their career with all the advantages and few of the drawbacks of civilization. They had only to confront the physical obstacles to their possession of the extensive territories which attracted and rewarded their enlightened energy, and immigration accelerated the formation of a glorious commonwealth. The Greeks, emerging from ages of debasing serfdom, had no political or social or intellectual preparation for the work of regeneration. After having achieved by dint of desperate efforts the independence of a part only of their land and race, they had to undergo a series of revolutions before settling down into an organized body politic. Moreover, the belief that the national unity is not yet complete has tended, and long may tend, to retard the work of internal development. Neither these considerations, nor the fact that the whole country was a scene of desolation at the close of the war of independence, must be lost sight of in forming a judgment as to the progress thus far effected.

The revival of education was the first care of the Greeks on feeling once more free. In this they received from America welcome help, of which the grateful memory is far from being lost. The names of Dr. and Mrs. Howe of Boston, and of Mr. and Mrs. Hill, who made Athens their home, are not forgotten in Greece. In the schools opened by the latter, and in those of the Rev. Mr. King, six hundred girls were receiving education as early as 1835. Those schools were mainly supported by the practical generosity of American ladies. It may have been forgotten in America that this was the first example of the union of bodies representing different religious denominations in a common good work. A Greek society was soon formed, with the same object—that of female education. One of the ornaments of modern Athens is the fine school building erected for that society at the expense of a wealthy Greek whose name it bears (Arsakeion). This is but one among the many institutions due to the patriotism of Hellenes residing abroad, but nobly vying with each other in the embellishment of the capital which symbolizes the unity of the race.

First in date and in importance of these institutions is the university. At the time of its foundation academic instruction would seem to have been superfluous, elementary schools being the crying need of Greece; but such was not the feeling of the people. A seat of high culture in the capital of the new kingdom, open to all Greeks within and without its boundaries, was an assertion of national life, a bond of union, and a banner of hope. The new building, the first important one erected in Athens apart from the royal residence, was begun in 1839, and completed only in 1864, though one of its wings was occupied by the university as early as 1841. More than three thousand students, coming from all parts of Hellendom, and distributed among four faculties, now yearly justify the optimism of the original promoters. The cost of the edifice was covered by private contributions. «Each year,» says Professor Pantasides, the historian of the university, «the rectors, in their annual reports, announced gifts showing the interest taken in the establishment by all classes. One offered his field, another his house or books or apparatus. Most of the contributors gave money; side by side with the wealthy donor who brought his tens of thousands came an itinerant grinder with twenty drachmæ; a man-servant sent twenty-eight drachmæ and five lepta, and an old soldier of the war of independence, having only his now useless weapons, gave them to the fund.»

The university, situated on a commanding site in the center of the new town, is flanked by buildings not less imposing, due to the munificence of Greeks living abroad. Baron Sina of Vienna, whose father had already built the beautiful observatory on the hill above the Pnyx, is the founder of the marble palace on the left.

On the right of the university another building of equal magnificence, now approaching completion, is being built at the expense of Mr. Vagliano, a Greek merchant of London. This will serve for the national library. The collection of books now requiring and deserving such a home had very modest beginnings. The nucleus, it will interest Americans to know, was a gift of fifty-two volumes from their countryman Governor Winthrop of Massachusetts, in the year 1837. The collection, then stored in the tiny medieval church just behind the new metropolitan church of Athens, was removed to the upper story of the uni-

DRAWN BY A. CASTAIGNE

A VIEW FROM THE TEMPLE OF THESEUS.

DRAWN BY A. CASTAIGNE.

AT THE SHRINE (THE ACROPOLIS IN THE DISTANCE).

versity building on its completion, when the little church, one of the most interesting Byzantine monuments in Athens, was once more opened to worship.

These three buildings of dissimilar styles, but all inspired by ancient Greek art, constitute a group of which any city might be proud. They are the chief ornaments of University street, in which also stand the Arsakeion school already referred to; the Ophthalmic Hospital, a structure in the Byzantine style, likewise erected by private contribution; the Roman Catholic church; and a series of handsome mansions, all surpassed in beauty by the residence of the late Dr. Schliemann. When the few gaps still remaining in this street shall be filled, it will be one of the finest in Europe.

The list would be long were we to enumerate all the buildings or institutions due to private munificence. Among these the traveler will not fail to notice, in the Patissia street, the school of arts, called Metzoveion, after its founders, three cousins from the still unemancipated town of Metzovon, in Epirus. In the upper story of this were exhibited the collections of the Archæological Society, now removed to the Central Museum close by, of which hereafter. In the same building are housed the collections of the Ethnological and Historical Society of Greece, mainly devoted to the revolutionary period.

At the other end of University street, past

DRAWN BY A. CASTAIGNE

DISTANT VIEW OF THE ACROPOLIS AT SUNSET.

the row of elegant mansions in Kephissia street, lies the seminary founded by Rizaris, an Epirote, and opposite it the model hospital, Evangelismos, patronized by the queen. One of its wings was built at the expense of M. Syngros, the founder of the museum at Olympia, who has also endowed Athens with other philanthropic institutions, such as the poor-house, near the Evangelismos Hospital, and the model prison outside Athens, in the direction of the Piræus. To him is likewise due the home of the Female Industrial Institute, where a society of Athenian ladies provides work and tuition to hundreds of poor girls and women, and where foreign visitors will be glad to find varied specimens of national industry.

Appropriate mention has already been made in THE CENTURY of the immense amphitheater of the Stadion which has been restored at the expense of a Greek, M. Avérof, in view of the revival of the Olympic games.[1] About a million drachmæ were spent to prepare the Stadion for the recent celebration of the games. The generous donor, who had already deserved by other gifts an eminent place among the benefactors of Greece, has undertaken to complete its restoration in marble, at the cost of at least double the amount already spent.

Close to the Stadion, on this side of the Ilissus, stands the palace destined for the industrial exhibitions of Greece. This is one of the numerous gifts the Greek nation owes to the two Zappas, who were both born in Epirus, and who both died in Rumania, and whose testamentary dispositions caused an interruption of diplomatic relations between Rumania and Greece, the government of the former denying the right of Greece to take possession of the landed property of the testators, in spite of the opinions of eminent European jurists, and of the offer of Greece to settle the dispute by arbitration. In front of this building, called Zappeion after the name of its founders, a park has been laid out, which in a few years, when the young trees shall have grown, will be one of the finest promenades possible. With the rock of the Acropolis on the right, and on the left the hills above the Ilissus encircling the Stadion, but not hiding the flanks and summit of Mount Hymettus, the view plunges thence through the majestic group of the columns of Jupiter's temple, along the sloping plain, down to the Ægean, the graceful lines of the isle of Ægina closing the horizon. When the sun sets in a sky of fathomless clearness, or sometimes dappled with purple cloudlets, the beauty of the hues reflected on Hymettus and on the ruined marble monuments is beyond the reach of description.

Of the three mountains inclosing the plain of Athens, Mount Parnes is the highest (4640 feet); Mount Pentelicus (3641 feet), with its regular triangular shape suggesting the

[1] See «The Olympic Games of 1896,» THE CENTURY for November, 1896.

DRAWN BY A. CASTAIGNE.

A GIRL FROM ELEUSIS.

pediment of a temple, is the most imposing; but the thyme-covered, honey-producing Hymettus (3368 feet) has always been most intimately associated with Athens. It lies nearer to the city, and from almost all the streets and all the windows looking eastward can be seen its curved line marking the blue sky above, except on the rare gray days, when clouds resting on its top are an infallible sign of rain. The various hues of the mountains and the smaller hills forming an inner circle around Athens, combined with the view of the sea, lend an additional effect of airiness and buoyancy to the aspect. In the long, straight streets of the new town, open from end to end, nothing impedes the view on either side.

In praising Athens, we must not draw a veil over her defects. Such improvements as are indispensable to a modern city have not kept pace with her growth in extent and affluence. The stages of this progress can be

IN THE ANTIQUE CEMETERY.

seen in the structural inequalities even of contiguous dwellings. These dwellings may be chronologically divided into three categories: those of the first settlers, when all were poor, and the main necessity was at any rate to be housed; those of the thrifty citizens, who felt the want of more space and greater convenience, but had little regard for external appearance or interior comfort, and considered carpets and plate-glass a luxury, and even chimneys of small consequence; and those of the wealthy immigrants, who gave an impulse to the building of elegant houses among all who, thanks to increasing prosperity, could afford to imitate them. The proximity of the quarries of Hymettus and Pentelicus enables Athens to supply herself with a building material which no other city could have at equal cost. Marble, in itself an embellishment, is profusely used, and loses none of its brilliancy in the dry atmosphere, whose transparency makes pleasant to the eye even the light colors spread on the stone walls, which in other latitudes would hardly be bearable. The agreeable effect thus obtained is increased by the trees in some of the streets and squares, as well as in the gardens of the better class of houses. But Athens might and would be more verdant still were it not for the lack of abundant water. This want was felt in antiquity as well: to it may partly be ascribed the epidemics recorded by ancient historians in times of war, when the number of inhabitants was increased by those of the surrounding country seeking refuge within the walls. Antoninus Pius endowed Athens with a perfect system of waterworks. They consisted of subterranean galleries collecting the waters of the neighboring mountains. To these old Roman aqueducts, successively discovered, repaired, and utilized, Athens still owes her scanty supply of water. Projects for increasing the supply are ever talked of, but will be deferred so long as the municipal finances remain no better than the national. Meanwhile, the macadamized roads between the fine sidewalks are hardly watered. This fact and the nature of the soil, notorious for its thinness since the days of Thucydides, account for the dust, which is the greatest blemish of Athens. An English lady was heard to admire the picturesqueness of its whirling clouds; but even were that single representative of an optimistic minority on a fine day, succeeding one of rain, to see the town and the clear outline of the distant mountains through a dustless atmosphere, she could not help regretting that the same effects are not artificially attainable.

On the whole, Athens will show to best advantage if visited after Constantinople and other towns in Turkey, as the standard of comparison will be fairer than that afforded by the great capitals of the West. It must not be forgotten that, if one of the most ancient, she is at the same time one of the newest among European towns; nor ought the long period of her decline ever to be lost sight of when comparing her with other towns.

The traveler who, remembering that long period of Turkish sway, counts on receiving an Oriental impression from the aspect of Athens is doomed to disappointment. Even the national garb is fast disappearing. It may still be worn by a few elderly Athenians. These, and a peasant here and there selling milk or cheese, recall the day when their dress was the national one. It is, however, the uniform of certain soldiers of light infantry, who may be seen parading the streets or mounting guard at the palace, in all the

DRAWN BY A. CASTAIGNE.

THE ACADEMY OF ATHENS.

white splendor of the fustanelle. The wide blue trousers of the Ægean islanders are not less rare, nor is there much chance of seeing them at the Piræus, among the craft from the various islands moored along the quays. The uglier and cheaper product of the slop-shop has replaced the picturesque drapery of the olden time. The monotony of the modern costume is broken only by the priests, with their long black robes and their peculiar hats.

## II.

THE foreign visitor will naturally first visit the Acropolis and the museums. His red Baedeker or Murray in hand, he will set out on his pilgrimage, and than either book no better guide could he have. The work of the archæological cicerone is well done in both, and it were idle to repeat here what is so easily found elsewhere.

The Acropolis, most beautiful, most renowned, and most sacred of rocks, will attract the traveler's eye even before he enters the Piræus; it is visible from almost every street within, and from every point outside of Athens; but nowhere is it seen to better advantage than from near the small church of St. Demetrius, on the height between the two hills crowned respectively by the monument of Philepappus and by the observatory, or from the windows of the latter, whence the view of the Propylæa and the façade of the Parthenon, in all their majesty of form and color, is undisturbed by modern buildings. The slope leading up to the entrance of the antique fortress, planted with pine-trees and aloes dating from the time of Amelia, the first queen of Greece, forms a zone of verdure setting off the brightness of the sun-gilt marbles above. On the other side of the rock the remnants of the old Turkish town and more recent hovels, piled one above another, rise with defacing effect to the very base of the Acropolis. These are condemned, and will have to be pulled down sooner or later. The plans are ready, and only await an administration which shall have the money, the will, and the power to carry them out. The steep base of the rock will then be cleared of the accumulated rubbish and of the unsightly dwellings, and more relics of antiquity will, it is hoped, be brought to light. Plantations will cover the cleared ground, and through them the road now leading to the gate of the Acropolis will be continued all round toward Hadrian's arch. The Acropolis itself will thus gain in height and beauty.

However admirable even now its external appearance, the view from within is not less impressive; the setting is worthy of the jewel. No sight can surpass in reposeful grandeur the panorama one commands in skirting the edge of the rock. The mountains inclosing the plain with its olive grove, the blue sea on the south shut in by the isles of Ægina and Salamis and by the distant mountains of the Morea, and, nearer, the columns of the Olympian Jupiter and of the Theseion, all arched by the transparent Attic sky, unite to form one harmonious picture, the natural features of which are heightened by the magic of the memories of old. In other countries, and elsewhere in Greece, may be seen landscapes that stir the admiration of the beholder; but nowhere are to be found more graceful lines or brighter coloring than one sees from the steps of the Parthenon, between the columns of the Propylæa, when the sun goes down:

> Not, as in northern climes, obscurely bright,
> But one unclouded blaze of living light!

Byron's verses come naturally to the mind on the spots which so well inspired him. The elegant choragic monument of Lysicrates stood within the courtyard of the now demolished convent of the Capuchins where the poet resided. Byron's statue, the gift of a Greek, the late M. Demetrius Schilizri, has recently been erected close by, near Hadrian's arch and the ruined temple of Jupiter.

The concatenation of present and past events caused Mr. Freeman, the historian and many others with him, to protest against the zeal of archæologists, who are apt to overlook the historical interest of postclassical monuments; and he and they continued vainly to protest against each successive obliteration of the traces left by the various occupants of the Acropolis. No doubt a line ought to be drawn somewhere; but where? When the Turks left Athens, the columns of the Propylæa half protruded from the roof of a storehouse, the Erechtheum was an exploded powder-magazine, and tumble-down houses covered the Acropolis. People are still living old enough to remember certain of the Turkish houses serving as museums, and fragments of sculpture and architecture scattered haphazard about the ruined temples. The removal of the former and the setting in order of the latter were on no account to be condemned; but the demolition of the Frankish tower, the destruction of the old entrance to the citadel and of its gates bearing Turkish inscriptions, and the leveling of the bastion connected with Odysseus's achievements,

DRAWN BY A. CASTAIGNE.

CONSTITUTION PLACE, THE ROYAL PALACE IN THE BACKGROUND.

during the revolution, were contestable measures. The defenders of the point of view of general history have, however, been silenced by the success with which the work of destruction has been crowned. Had it been less thorough, the statues buried by the ancients before Pericles's renovation of the Parthenon would not have been found, nor could the monuments themselves have been studied with the same advantage; but the gain thus secured should not be an encouragement to further depredations. No wiser limit could be put to such work than that suggested by Lord Bute in his address at a meeting of the subscribers to the British school at Athens (1892). «I am not arguing,» said he, «that when one historical monument hopelessly interferes with another, the inferior should not be removed; what I do say is that such removal should only be effected after the greatest consideration, with the greatest care and caution, after making the most accurate record of what is to be destroyed, and with the careful preservation and transference, if need be, to another site of the historical monuments disturbed.»

It is true that foreign archæologists cannot be expected to care much for anything beyond the immediate object of their study and researches, and that the Greeks themselves, from the very dawn of their independence, have regarded the relics of their glorious past as the main link between their country and the rest of the civilized world. The Archæological Society is one of the oldest and most useful institutions of modern Greece. The central museum, thanks to M. Cavvadias, the general ephor of antiquities, and to his excellent staff of young Greek archæologists, has become one of the finest in existence, not only for the value, but also for the methodical arrangement of its contents. Among these will especially be noticed the splendid series of funereal sculptures, and of Tanagra and Myrina figurines, the rare specimens of archaic art, and, above all, the unique treasure of Mycenæ found by an adoptive citizen of the United States, the late M. Schliemann. If the traveler feels some disappointment at not seeing in the museum the «Hermes» of Praxiteles, let him consider that a journey to Olympia is quickly and easily made, and that much may be said in favor of local museums, especially when adjacent to the monuments to which many of the objects they contain once belonged.

The world-wide interest in Grecian antiquities has been demonstrated by the establishment and development of the foreign archæological schools in Athens. Thanks to them, the capital is becoming the real center for the study of ancient art. The French set the example in 1845; the German school was founded next; the American school, housed in close neighborhood to the English one at the northeastern extremity of the town, displays, in keeping pace with the other schools, a spirit of emulation which has been rewarded by excellent results, and which promises still better for the future. Between this school and Athens a new bond of sympathy has been created by the recent death of its former director, Professor Merriam, who lies buried in the land he had learned to love so well.

These foreign schools, while tending to make Athens once more a seat of learning, serve also as social centers for visitors of the nationalities they respectively represent, and so help to facilitate intercourse between strangers, learned Greeks, and Athenian society in general. The directors, in addition to their appointed duties, perform others of an international nature, and the traveler, whether he come only to study the monuments, or, like Ulysses, «to see the cities of men, and to know something of their minds,» will not find their protection or guidance less useful than that of the accredited representative of his country. So exceptional an advantage should lend additional attraction to Athens, and yet the number of foreigners, and particularly of Americans, though increasing from year to year, is chiefly limited to a chosen few.

The main cause of discouragement to travelers, as well as to the formation of a numerous foreign colony in Athens, is the relative difficulty of access. This will be remedied when the railway now begun between Athens and Salonica shall have united Greece with the European system. In the interim, the voyage of three days and a half from Marseilles to the Piræus, by the large and comfortable French steamers of the Messageries Company, is rather too long for bad sailors. By way of Brindisi and Patras the voyage is not so long, but it might be shortened and made more agreeable by means of a direct line of larger and better steamers in regular correspondence with the railways both in Italy and in Greece.

Of late years internal communication has been greatly facilitated by the construction of railways and carriage-roads, but without as yet effecting any sensible improvement in provincial hotels, which in general still leave much to be desired. There is, of course, something that gratifies the spirit of adven-

DRAWN BY A. CASTAIGNE.

IN THE OLD QUARTER.

ture in conquering the difficulties which beset the traveler in some parts of Greece; and doubtless many will regret the vulgarization of classic scenes by the «personally conducted.» It will be long, however, before Taygetus, Parnassus, or Pindus is desecrated by funicular railways, or Greece becomes as stale as Switzerland. Without aiming so largely to increase traveling facilities, the Greek government would consult the best interests of the country by rendering it more accessible and more penetrable; and it should seek, moreover, to increase the attractions of the capital. The impulse once given, foreigners would begin to settle there, and the rest might be left to the law of supply and demand. The hotels in Athens are good, and at least two of them rank among the best in Europe. The letting of furnished apartments has not yet been greatly developed, but the Greeks are not likely to overlook a business so profitable. Life in Athens will be found easy and not expensive. The court (to whose social functions foreigners diplomatically presented find easy entrance), hospitable society, historic interest, picturesque environment, and a good climate are among the attractions that Athens offers to those who shall prefer her as a place of residence to one or another of the favored cities of Europe.

Surrounded by a zone of hills, beyond which rise the mountains, and looking southward to the sea, Athens enjoys a climate that is at once continental and insular. The mean temperature is less variable than that of a continent, and more so than that of an island, in the same latitude. The spring and autumn are delightful, and the winters are mild, the mercury seldom falling below zero, which it has not touched once during twenty-two of the winters since 1840. Snow very rarely falls in the plain, though it yearly whitens the mountain-tops; fogs and frost are equally rare, and, upon the whole, the daily variations of temperature are less than those observed in most European towns, including Paris, Milan, Florence, and even Nice.[1] The summer is long, but in the very hottest months, July and August, the sea-breeze which sweeps across the Ægean tempers the heat and diminishes that dryness of the air to which are due the extraordinary tenuity and limpidity of the ambient atmosphere, the wonderful blue of the Attic sky, and the optical illusion which makes distant objects seem near.

Sooner or later Athens is sure to become a winter resort not less favored than any on the Mediterranean, and the permanent home of many foreigners. The opinion thus confidently expressed is strengthened by the fact that few who have lived for some length of time within her gates pass out of them without regret, or fail to reënter them with pleasure.

[1] The mean temperature is in winter 8.90° centigrade, 47.50° Fahrenheit; in spring, 15.37° centigrade, 59° Fahrenheit; in summer 25.96° centigrade, 78.50° Fahrenheit; in autumn 18.70° centigrade, 65° Fahrenheit; January and February are the coldest months (8.04° and 8.63° centigrade respectively); July and August the hottest (26.99° and 26.63° centigrade). The mean annual rainfall is 0.4059, and the moisture of the air is put at 74.3 for the winter; 64.9 for the spring; 49.3 for the summer; 65.2 for the autumn. These details are due to the kindness of M. Eginitis, the learned director of the observatory at Athens.

*D. Bikélas.*

# THE PARTHENON BY MOONLIGHT.

I.

THIS is an island of the golden Past
  Uplifted in the tranquil sea of night.
This is true Athens! How the heart beats fast
  When climbs the pilgrim to this gleaming height:
The crown and glory of consummate form;
  The jewel of all the world, most nobly set;
High Beauty's shrine, outwearing every storm;
  Shattered, but not undone; thrice lovely yet.

II.

Ah, Heaven, what tragic waste! Is Time so lavish
  Of dear perfection, thus to see it spilled?
'T was worth an empire; now behold the ravish
  That laid it low. The soaring plain is filled
With the wide-scattered letters of one word
  Of loveliness that nevermore was spoken;
Nor ever shall its like again be heard:
  Not dead is art—but that high charm is broken.

III.

Now moonlight builds with swift and mystic art
  And makes the ruin whole—and yet not whole,
But exquisite, though crushed and torn apart.
  Back to the temple steals its living soul:
In the star-silent night it comes all pale—
  A spirit breathing beauty and delight,
And yet how stricken! Hark! I hear it wail,
  Self-sorrowful, while every wound bleeds white.

IV.

And though more sad than is the nightingale
  That mourns in Lycabettus' fragrant pine,
That soul to mine brings solace; nor shall fail
  To heal the heart of man while still doth shine
Yon planet, doubly bright in this deep blue;
  Yon moon that brims with fire these violet hills:
For Beauty is of God, and God is true,
  And with his strength the soul of mortal fills.

*R. W. Gilder.*

# THE LIGHTS OF SITKA.

BY THE AUTHOR OF «THE CAT AND THE CHERUB,» ETC.

'T WAS the little gunboat *Lexington*, with sixes in the fore and aft of her, and a row of invidjus pop-guns arrayed in her side. 'T was a new cruise, and we laid several days waiting word, with the newspapers stirring up wars by the day. First we was bound for China, says they, to pull up the roots of the emperor's pigtail for being a pagan; and next we was sailing for Samoa, to boulyverse the nigger on uts throne; and the same day they had us running down forty knots an hour to Chile, to blow off the peaks off the Andes, and conquer the country with a file of bluebottle marines. And any of us that was right in uz mind give ut no thought, the sea being the sea, and wishes crank craft in a gale; but there was two aboard that was cross-eying themselves with their noses in the newspapers, one a bo'sun's mate named Oliver Peck, which no one would trust um in the shadow of a candle, and the other a pink little lad named Ellerson, that was new to uz drill, and homesick as the divil in heaven. 'T was only a crazy twist of good fortune, says they, that would steam us to a place called Corvana; which I never heard of ut before, but they said 't was the prettiest port south of paradise. Ut was circumstantial that them two, which distasted each other like oil and water, should wilt for sake of the small spot; and 't was me luck to find why. We up for Puget Sound, for the mayor of Corvana was having a party in uz back grass-yard, to celebrate the fifth anniversary of the town, and git umself reëlected, and the *Lexington* was to let no foreign power interfere with the Highland fling.

Then little Ellerson turned flipflops clean round the capstan, and old Peck was that pleased that I seen um smile. But when I drew me first bead on Corvana I filled ut with hard words, for 't was three streets and a moth-eaten wharf of a town, that looked like 't was robbed from the floor of the sea. But what was gnawing old Peck and young Ellerson was plain: 't was a young girl, and I seen her countenance standing on the pier.

She was a diamond! She was that sweet and true ye could find ut in her face; and little, and trimmed in black, with the scrap of a hanky slung in her belt, and two feet, begad! like kittens peeping from under a door-step. Her eyes was that baby-blue ut made ye think of a fine day at home, no matter where ye lived, and her mouth that inviting ye wished there was more of ut. And every time ye looked at her ye looked at her again. And when ye seen the beating of her heart that Ellerson should be first ashore, ye asked yourself, What would she be to that rubber-faced Oliver Peck?

One day would be little Ellerson's liberty, and the next would be Peck's, each steaming up the same street, and never back till the tick of boat-time. And with Peck ashore little Ellerson would be blue as a sounding-lead, and with Ellerson ashore Peck would be ugly as umself. And seeing that the black-hearted bo'sun's mate had ut in for the lad, I laid alongside of little Ellerson, whence many a pleasant cross-parlance we had. Especially would he take uz pipe of an evening, and smoke up uz thoughts about womenkind, which to him was angels from heaven by virtue of white starch. 'T was painful and pretty to hear, for every woman that is bad, he would say, is bad because of some evil man with a stovepipe, he would say, and none so bad but the spark of saints and martyrs is lurking inside. And I talked to um awkward, for divil an answer I knew when I thought of me female reminiscences in ten different tongues. But he stuck by me close, and would take comfort in ut, and Clarence O'Shay would set staring at uz remarks like a wooden owl. Till one day little Ellerson says, would we be going ashore with um to pay uz respects to a fine-looking lady? And we polished ourselves to the occasion.

'T was a little house the big of a horse-car, and the grandmother sat laid up in a wheel-chair, with posies climbing all over the porch. Then Ellerson stood the two of us in a row, and says he:

«These is me two shipmates. The squat one, with the two little bandy legs, and the look like a mile-stone,» says he, «is Mr. O'Shay; and the spider-legged one, with uz hands dangling at uz knees, is Mr. Lannigan —Sudden Lannigan, they call um; and together the two invented the tricks of the trade. Consider yourself knocked down to 'em,» says he.

And with that the young girl hauled off with a broken tea-pot, and give us tea from ut with no apologies, but her smiles made ye feel at home in your stockings. And Clarence O'Shay would be all the time looking at her with uz mouth hanging open like a bag, so that I first lacked the parts of speech with me embarrassment at um; but the girl stood by, and would talk of the sea, which even the name of ut scared her.

«For I hear once,» says she, «that the sea was all sweet as tea, but 't was made salt by the sailors' wives a-weeping on the shores of ut.»

And she would be asking many inquiries, saying, was the *Lexington* free from sinking qualities, and when was the next war, and how many of us would be killed at the first discharge of our guns? And I says, have no fear, for the foreign dis'greements of Uncle Sam was all in uz own living-space—which I slapped O'Shay between uz shoulder-pits to wake from uz hypnotism. «Ut 's Heaven's own truth—every inch of ut!» says he, coming to umself. And on the way I expostulated to um the meaning of ut. And when was we going there again? says he; but I told um the little girl was Ellerson's. For of Peck she spoke never a word, though Oliver umself was forever praising the charms of her.

Then come the cogitation of the powers what next to do with the ship; and the Secretary-grandmother of the Navy called in the President to um, and the cabinet, and the Supreme Court, and they all sat screwing their eyebrows on ut for ten days, till the old man got uz telegraph from Washington, saying, «Go where ye please.» Whereby the skipper says to umself, «We 'll take a cargo of time to Alaska,» that being the paradise free from statesmen.

And the day before we sailed I went by request to the little girl. Straight up in the wind she came, with eyes flying red signals, though she tried to smuggle the reason of ut. Mr. Ellerson, says she, was such a true friend of the family, says she, and so hard to part with um! War was coming, says she, for the newspapers said ut, though 't was not yet decided who we should fight. And would n't I hold little Ellerson behind me door to protect the enemy from hurting um? And with that she let loose with her weeping like the breaking of a dike, and I stood shifting me feet and fingering me cap, and saying, I 'm a dom fool, till I laid hold of the parts of speech.

«*I* 'll bring um to ye!» then says I, shaking me fist at her. «There 's a deal more ink to be spilt than blood,» says I; «and most of the fighting is after dark, by them big-head reporter men with glasses.»

«I knowed ye 'd do ut,» says she, sopping the tears; «for ut 's you that 's strong and brave and wise,» says she; «and you would n't let um come to harm, would ye?»

And I says, not by the chin of St. Patrick would the divil umself harm a hair of uz head. And I got under steerageway, badly with me emotions.

And when we hove up and begun to show heels to Corvana, there she was, standing on the pier, so blasted fine! Her little pocket doily was swabbing of her eyes one by one, till O'Shay filled uz pipe with oakum by mistake; and Oliver Peck was waving uz fin from the stern; but her dry light was glued to the forrard six, forninst which was leaning little Ellerson, sometimes smiling, sometimes snuffling to umself. I looked along the swash of us, and took me last sight at the little girl waving her hanky the big of a postage-stamp, with the pink setting sun shrinking in uts size behind her, and I gulped, and I says to meself, «It 's Lannigan will bring um home safe and sound to ye, or Lannigan will break a nerve!»

We lost one man by French leave at Corvana, which give a new station-bill, with Ellerson at Peck's command. And at fire-drill I seen Peck working um up, dealing um all the vituperation that should be evenly distributed among the boys. And that night I wiggled me thumb at old Peck, and says I, «Luff, ye beggar, or I 'll expostulate to ye!»

So that night little Ellerson freed umself about her, and I 'll never forget the velvet of uz voice with the little girl's name. She was orphan on one side, says he, and on the other her father was lost at sea. Small pence they had, with the grandmother laid up in ordinary and kept afloat by the apothecary; and the one that hauled 'em out of the mud once or twice, and would take the girl for salvage, was Oliver Peck umself—that was husband to her aunt that died. «But for me,» the snake would whisper to her, «ye 'd long been sent to the divil for bread. For the world is that hard,» he would say in the ear of the innocent lass, «that no man will lift uz hand for ye on respectable terms—no man except me, that will give ye me name and a decent life,» says he. And she, the poor little skiff, was drifting to ut, though she 'd rather charm vipers than look the black Satan of a Peck between uz eyes. And she grew white, and promised to marry um, when along come little Ellerson.

From the sight of um, the pink little saint, 't was all over with Oliver. First she put in for a stay of proceedings, and then she rose up and would die before she 'd be spliced to um. And Peck swore to her, and says, begad! he 'd fix the two of 'em for doing um out of uz own; and little Ellerson offered to fight um abaft the court-house; but says Peck, «You 're a boy.» Then ut was Ellerson that had the right of line, and she took on weight, and looked like a new-painted posy, when of a sudden Ellerson had lost uz billet on the Puget Sound boat; and the marrying must be postponed, with Peck laying off and on, and mentioning umself again, being softy, and saying 't was a child's fascination she had for the lad, no doubt; that must now enlist for want of a job. And Peck made the young greenhorn take money for reaching Mare Island to present umself, which divil knows how, but he paid ut back from uz first two months, though the obligation left um strangely with one that hated um.

And when the *Lexington* dropped into Corvana ut was several months gone by. The little girl met um with the eyes of long nights awake, and says she, «I 'll not be promised to ye no longer, for I 'll not load ye with one that has nothing, and could only be a weight to your spirits,» says she, «and maybe would make a poor wife anyway.» And first little Ellerson kissed her, and then mildly he cussed her, and then he kissed her again; but not an inch would she be budging, saying only that Peck she would not marry, and saying no more. But when the last parting come, she up and kissed um smack on uz forehead, and give um a push in the chest, and run in and slammed the door in uz face; and by this he took main reliance in favor of her loving um, though he was doubtful if whether she would n't have kissed um in uz mouth if so, and would wonder if maybe she had n't aimed at uz mouth anyway, but missed ut by firing too soon at the wrong elevation. Then, in a while, the lad was afraid the girl might tire of life and so marry old Peck, and uz mouth hauled down with every turn of the screw. For he says how Peck was beseeching her every day at Corvana, and how, when she followed the ship to Seattle by rail, old Peck would easy git ashore for uz, being petty officer's mate, though for Ellerson 't would be hard, since the ship would only lay to for twenty-four hours—the time ut takes a navy officer to telegraph uz last ten words to the department. But I says to um, «Ye 'll go ashore by accident»; for I knowed old Peck would be prevaricating umself to freedom, which he did.

'T was a smoke-fog night on the Sound, and the sun went below looking the color of an amber mouthpiece, and then come dry blackness without a drop of dew on a hand-rail; and if ye put your hand out ten feet before ye 't was invisible. From a boatman I chartered a bit of a soap-box, and at the right time I sent little Ellerson by the board, with instructions to keep uz head inside of uz box till ut floated from sight. And he went. I can hear um this minute, with uz eager young smile looking in me ear. «God bless ye, old man!» says he; «'t was Heaven sent ye to be me friend.» And with that he dropped away soft in the tide, swimming with uz head in the box, like the man in front of the stage at the opera. He went off diagonizing toward the shore, and I knowed in an hour the little girl would be weeping on uz collar.

And scarce had the fog swallowed um when off come the launch, with old Peck smiling satisfied to umself, and he walked about forrard, wishing Ellerson would see um in uz content; and he would be all the time singing to umself a heaving lay, which the sound of ut is photographed on me mind as though with a chisel:

> He had a wife at Callao,
> At Rio dee Janeerio,
> At Rotterdam and Tokio,
> At Cairo, Cannes, and Malta.
> A wife he had at Killisnoo,
> At Singapore and Sebeeroo,
> At Mozambique and Timbuctoo,
> At Boston and Gibraltar.
>
> A single-hearted man was *he*;
> You need not speak of bigam*ie*;
> Because uz wife was Rosylie,
> And she sailed with um on the sea.

And at eight bells he went on duty aft, and I stowed meself in the dark near um, at risk of reprimand for being there off watch. «Where 's Ellerson?» says Peck. «Gone ashore in imitation of a cake of soap,» says I; «and the one that peaches on um will settle with me and with the ancestors that 's left behind me!» Then old Peck dropped uz humming, and gripped the chain-rail till ut creaked, and I heard the profanation escaping from um like the after-gas from a rifle;

and in a minute says he, «Ye 'll be sorry some day for putting your nose in places that don't fit ut.» And says I, «I 'll operate me own nose.» And he said no more, though we waited four hours in the dark; but the black snake was conniving in uz heart.

'T was near midnight when I heard little Ellerson's whistle floating on the tide, and the navigator that was officer of the deck that night was getting ready for uz relief, and would be going to fondle uz charts, being a crank fresh from the Hydrygravic Office. I leaned over and give a sneeze, which was the countersign between me and Ellerson; but then Oliver Peck worked uz trick on me. «There 's an incandescent died last night in the chart-house, sir,» says he; «and the man with the store-room key is in the hammick, sir.» And the navigator says, «Then send one to wake um up and git a new lamp,» which Peck turned to me, as being uz support there by rights, and says, «Git the lamp,» and I hurried to do ut, having no choice, for Peck had the call on me. But I would not rob the sleep of the carpenter's mate, robbing instead the nearest lamp-cage between decks; and I says to meself, «Ye misunderstood the order, and ye thought 't was for the captain's smoking-room.» And so with the lamp I made a dive for the place, which was a bit of a coop in her stern-frames, and by midnight the quietest place aboard. The ports was too small for me head. But I heard the loud whisper of little Ellerson, that thought ut was me, though 't was Peck, leaning over above.

«Hurrah!» says the lad; «she 's mine!» says he. «We 'll be spliced next year, and take the chances of life together. And ut 's you, old man, that 's to blame for me good luck!»

And then says Peck, with a voice like a stone, «I did n't know ut. Maybe ye think I 'm Sudd Lannigan!» and the lad in the water give an «Oh!» with confusion that ye could hear ut in the dark. «Bring along the box as ye come,» says Peck, growling; «I 'd be going ashore that way meself. Take a stiff hand on ut, now!» says he, throwing um the halyard end. And I heard um hard hauling ut in over the scupper, and uz grunting, and the dripping of the soap-box in the dark, and I says to meself, little Ellerson was being hoisted aboard, box and all. And then I thought of meself, and made out from the smoking-room in me stocking-feet; and as I went I seen Ellerson's leg swing by the port, with the box tied to uz toe, and the next second I heard a splash in the water, as of the box, and I says to meself, little Ellerson had fooled um, and glad I was.

I put me lamp in uts place in the chart-house in the nick of time, and I went forrard, looking for Ellerson. But uz hammick was yet in uts place in the berthing, and I seen no signs of um, and I hunted the living-space through, and the platforms, and every place that would hold um. Then I tumbled up again, and made me way, at the risk of reprimand, back to the poop. «Where is he?» says I to Peck, that was standing hand-hold to the rail. «Where is who?» says Peck, giving a jump because I come upon um barefoot, and looking ready to deal me one. «The lad, of course,» says I. «How do I know where he is?» says Peck, in a way that was new to um. «Am I detailed to nestle um?» says he, jerking ut out; and I stood looking at um, steaming with the lust of smashing uz head. «The boy just passed forrard,» then says Peck, looking at the deck; «and he talked of getting uz coin and slipping uz cable. I suppose he 's swum ashore by this. Now leave me alone, man,» says Peck; «for I 'm off me feed this night!»

And I trotted back and searched for the boy once more in every place a man could fit, living or dead; and a whirling set up in me head, for there was divil a sign of um, and uz coin still in the toe of uz boot in uz bag. Then I set down to reason, being frightened at the conundrum of ut, and me eyes sticking out at me head. «Bad—bad ut smells!» says I to meself; «for ye heard uz whistle, and ye seen uz head floating back invisible, and then ye heard uz voice, and seen uz foot with ut tied to the box; then ye heard a splash! Ah, ye blithering fool!» I yelled to meself, in a whisper; «if he come aboard at all he was wet to uz skin with water, and tracks of um is plain on the deck! And if not, then what was the splash?» Then I rose in the air, and charged with all me feet for the poop of her, no matter what officer stood in me way, but only praying mé legs to git there, with me breath playing tricks and me heart between me teeth; but the deck stuck to me soles like fly-paper. «Ye 'll never git there at all!» says I to meself, with groans, and I let out me full contents of imprecation. And as I come thundering over the ladder to the poop I seen a vision in the middle of the dark astern of her. I seen a dear little lass trimmed all in black, with a little white hanky flying from her fingers; and she stood on the pier, and grew smaller and smaller till she was ten thousand miles away; and I heard her voice saying in me ear acrost the water, «Ut 's you that 's strong and brave and wise, and you would n't let um come to harm, *would* ye?» Me insides give way. I dropped on me knees by the flag-staff, feeling and feeling for just one drop of water. And I let out a yell. The planks was dry as a stone. «I 'm a dom fool!» says I; «a dom —dom fool!» I howled, breaking with tears, and slamming me head on the deck. Then two blue-breeches came running, and hauled me away to the prison abaft the sick-bay. And me next distinct recollection I never knowed.

WHEN I come to meself I was sitting on the capstan, and the ship lagging along between terra firma and Vancouver's Island. And Clarence O'Shay says to me, «I 'm detailed to watch that ye do no harm to the bo'sun's mate. For some says ye 've been bit by a water-dog and have hydrophobia; and some says ye 've gone crazy, and your intelligence loose and dangling inside of ye. And now,» says he, «if you 're crazy, out with ut and say so—between friends,» says he; «and if not I 'll smoke me pipe.»

I seen a ring around the paymaster's clerk auctioneering off the kit of a blue-jacket. «'T is another deserter,» says O'Shay: «little Ellerson, that Peck says jumped off the bill-boards last night.» And I seen little Ellerson's white uniform hanging up, with «D. D. E.» on ut in stencil. «'T is ‹D. D.› he is now!» says I to meself, and I gulped and went below; and I sent O'Shay to buy what was left, which ut cost me double for O'Shay's bidding so stubborn ag'in' umself.

In a week, by easy stops, the ship set down for a stay at Sitka, in a fine berth abreast the ranch. Never a word did I say to old Peck all that time, for he kept the whites of uz eyes to umself, and I seen uz face change like a tree in the fall; for he loaded up with Victoria smuggle at Killisnoo, and was half seas over the rest of the time, yet taking but small content in uz liquor. And him, that was celebrated for keeping uz own company, would now be asking to go along with the boys, spearing salmon with 'em, and fishing for Siwash girls in the ranch; and ut looked that he was afraid to be alone with umself, as though he was scared he would say something to umself if he got the chance. One day I come acrost um behind uz back in the copper-green Grecian church, bowing uz head before the blessed Virgin, and he give a start as though stabbed, and coughed himself red for uz foolishness; till by and by he took with a Siwash girl, and would be spending uz time and wages on her, to the comment of the place. 'T was by this he twice overstayed uz liberty, and was deprived for ut, and went profaning to umself, with me eyes fastened on um trying to see um through. And not one of them days but I asked meself, could ut be any way that little Ellerson had slipped the ship without coming aboard, and could he be still living? And not a night but I seen in me dreams the little girl standing on the pier, and asking me the same question—with me snuffling in me sleep till they says, «Sudd Lannigan is plumb in the day, but crazy by midnight.» And I says to meself, Would one man murder another and live along and along, and never pay for ut, by virtue of no one to prove ut, with little Ellerson's body floating boot up to a soap-box, and so never observed? And me memory was gnawing me vitals, and the divil's own downheartedness stewing in me mind.

'T was the third time old Peck overstayed, and was deprived for ut two days when he ached hard to meet uz Siwash, that I seen a red petticoat waving in the afternoon from the little island next Japonski. And I seen a note carried ashore for um, and I says, something 's up. Then me fate took me in uts two hands and held me aboard, though I had full leave to go where I pleased; and I stowed meself barefoot in the curl of the anchor, pretending to smoke to meself. The moon was darting zigzag among the clouds, with Oliver Peck eying ut with hard looks from near by. I peeped over the side, and seen a canoe dropping down in the tide, held by a long line from another behind ut. Then Peck laid down by the edge, and in a minute the dugout fouled the anchor-chain, and he rolled over the side and went down the chain. And when he turned round he seen another man with um, and ut was me; and never a word had I spoke to um up to this since we left Seattle.

First he looked hard in the dark to make me out, and I grabbed the paddle and helped the tide, with him groping in the bottom for another, which there was none. And with one hand I hauled in the long line and fastened the end of ut to the anchor-stone. The moon give a peep out, and says he suddenly, «'T is you, Sudd Lannigan!» And says I, «'T is you, Oliver Peck!»

«Where do we be going at?» says he.

«Divil I know,» says I.

«It ain't your hands, then,» says he, «that's handling that paddle?»

«No,» says I; «'t is the hand of God.»

And says he, «What may that mean?»

«Divil I know,» says I, paddling fast. I knowed he was staring at me in the dark, conniving as cool as uz thoughts would let um.

«'T is a fine boat behind ye,» says he, pointing to the excursion steamer from Puget Sound that lay at the pier. There was lights and music and dancing aboard of her, and a handsome sight she was; and I never turned me head.

«'T is strange you 're not aboard, dancing with the swells,» says he, in a minute, with a sneer.

«Not so,» says I; «for I loaned me claw-hammer to the Prince of Wales, and he never give ut back.»

«Ha, ha!» says Peck, laughing as though he was paid for ut; «ye 've a fine stowage of wit, Lannigan, and it 's an accomplished man ye are!»

«True,» says I, «for I can play ‹Yankee Doodle› with one hand, and listen to ‹God Save the Queen› with me other ear.»

Then he held uz mouth, and I kept paddling, saying never a word, but watching um take points on the island toward where we was headed, doubtful in the dark as to which one ut was. And in ten minutes we breasted a jut of rock and pines, and heard a female voice hail us with «*Klahow yah!*» And says Peck:

«'T is right in here I 'll be going ashore, thank ye.»

But I looked at um, and paddled steady, with never a word.

«Right in here, man!» says he, loud enough, and the wish to deal me one breaking in uz voice.

But I kept her headed where she was, and the tide took us rushing by the point, and Oliver let out a swear.

«Look here, Lannigan,» says he; «I 'm a mild-mannered man—I 'm a good-natured man; but there 's an end to trifling; and I 'll be going ashore on that island, and that 's all of ut—see?» says he, with a strain of uz voice.

But I said never a word. And uz hand dropped on the gun'le, and he took again to conniving. The tide was galloping with the wind in uts rear, and the dugout humming betwixt one island and another till the lights of Sitka disappeared, and by a few easy twists of her prow I lost um uz bearings. The cedars grew black down to the sea, with their feet on the rocks that swashed with the breakers, and dense they was, like a wall that shut ye away from time. Peck leaned over and scanned the shore, where the water was a hundred feet sheer, and by moonlight I seen the sweat on uz face and the look as of one counting uz chances.

«'T is this island,» says I, «where a man starved to death, near in plain sight of Sitka.»

And he thought a minute, and says he: «And 't is here, I believe, that one man knocked the other from the dugout, and drownded um, and then went where he dom'd pleased.»

«Indeed?» says I, paddling past ut. «And which of the two was ut?»

Which Peck made no reply; but I seen the inside of um as though he was glass, with the hate and the divil-craft surging in uz heart like the bilge in a pump. I rounded a point, and turned up an arm of the sea, with the water laying dim for two miles beyond us, and the high mountains towering on top of us, like ye might have been ten thousand miles from the history of man. 'T was that still ye could hear the lapping of the water on the shore, though the wind was stopped by the point, and the place laid as smooth as a table. And when a loon flew over us, and give a shout with uz fright, ye could hear the shout bounce back from the heart of the trees like the laughter of fifty jim*panzees*, till Oliver Peck coughed to cheer umself with the sound of uz voice, and then was scared by uts echo. And I steered up in the darkness twenty feet from the shore of the wilderness, till the trees shut out the moon and most of the sky.

«Ha, ha!» says Peck, of a sudden; «'t is a fine excursion we 're having! And so let ut go at that, and no malice between us, for I never felt that gay as this minute! I could kill and eat two species of the human race! Show me a man that 's looking for trouble, will ye, Lannigan?»

And in the middle of ut come a long howl of a she-bear that had lost her cub—a howl like the last despair.

«What 's that?» says he, gripping the gun'le.

«Hark!» says I, dropping the paddle; «'t is the voice of a hand that 's laid hold of the bottom of us! Hark!» says I. And I leaned over the stern and dropped the anchor-stone without uz knowing ut, and the she-bear let out another howl, like 't was in the air forninst us.

«Paddle, man—paddle!» says Peck, with uz tongue sticking to uz lips. «This is no place—»

«Hark!» says I; «'t is a voice walking on the bottom! Listen, listen! 'T is little Ellerson. ‹Ellerson, Ellerson, Ellerson!› ut says.

And then, ‹Peck, Peck, Oliver Peck!› What does ut mean?» says I.

«What 's that to me?» says Peck, like a cur in a corner. «What 's ut to me? I 've no relations with um. He run off at Seattle; he took off to be deceiving the woman that promised to marry me. What are ye looking at *me* for? You 're crazy!»

And he seized the paddle and worked ut like wild, sending the spray all over us. But we stayed stuck and fast, for we was anchored. And the howling of the she-bear—long, squealing, and divilish ut was, like the ghost of a sick locomotive lost in the hills—the howling of ut made um bend to ut, to the broiling of uz wits.

«What is ut? What is ut?» says he, with the beads on uz brow.

«'T is Ellerson,» says I. «'T is Ellerson saying he wants you. He says he wants the man that stove uz head in and dropped um overboard to drown. What does ut mean, man?» says I. «Who stove uz head in? Was ut you, ye white-livered snake?» says I, crawling at um. And I seen in the dark uz hands go over uz head, stripping the lanyard of uz jack-knife. «Was ut you that robbed um from the little girl standing on the pier?» says I. «He 's down at the bottom,» says I, darting me thumb at the side; «and he says 't was you that took uz life!»

«Go tell um 't is true, then!» says Peck, with a yell like a savage. «*That* for ye!» says he.

And he made a swing at me with the paddle, which ut broke to splinters on me arm; and I give a duck, and the canoe overturned, and we dropped in the ice-water, hugging like brothers, with the sea absorbing the profanity of ut, and then the top of the water rising above us in bubbles, and divil a sound. For we was forty feet below, with the sandy bottom roiling under our toes, while we carved with knives. And the business me and Peck had together was transacted then and there, for I rose up flabbergasting round the water a bit, and then laid hold of the bottom of the canoe, with the moon looking on ut as peaceful as a garden, when I heard a small sound, and I looked down in the water, and I seen something bubbling up from below. Ut was uz soul. And the moon went behind uts clouds, and I set and think.

DIVIL a word I said to meself till I seen the lights of Sitka. The dugout I righted; but the paddle had gone by the board, and 't was two hours of swimming with ut ahead of me, in a dead calm, before the tide took a hand and let me steer with me feet, with the prow of the boat stuck high in the air. I seen the lights of Sitka reflected in the still water for four miles,—all the lights from the houses and the swell steamer, and the beacon on Baranoff Castle, and the light from the Mission of Christ,—and every one of them was pointing straight at me.

«Ye killed a man!» says they. «Look at ye—ye killed a man!»

«Aye,» says I, «and small consolation. But ut won't bring um back to her,» says I. «She 's standing on the pier there, trimmed all in black, with a little white hanky slung in her belt. And she 's waving her hand to me; and I hear her speaking acrost the waters with a voice that breaks in two at each word, and she says, ‹I 'm waiting, I 'm waiting!› she says; ‹for ut 's you that 's strong and brave and wise, and you *would n't* let um come to harm, *would* ye?› »

«And ye killed a man!» says the lights of Sitka.

«Yes, and I did,» says I; «but it won't bring back little Ellerson, and she 'll never see um again till the coming of judgment day, and the squaring of the log.»

CLARENCE O'SHAY was sitting forrard, uz feet embracing the jack-staff, and uz pipe smoking in uz teeth.

«Hair and hide of ye is wet to the skin,» says he, as I laid me hand on her bow, with the moon white-shining as innocent as a maid. «And your bugle 's broke, and a bloody stab on the shoulder, and your pants one leg flapping in the wind. What 's the answer to ut?»

«One of me legs mutinied,» says I, «and I brung ut aboard by force. And the Lord have mercy on me soul!»

*Chester Bailey Fernald.*

# A GIRL OF MODERN TYRE.

BY THE AUTHOR OF «MAIN TRAVELLED ROADS,» «PRAIRIE SONGS,» ETC.

WITH PICTURES BY T. DE THULSTRUP.

HARTLEY.

ALBERT LOHR was studying the motion of the ropes and lamps, and listening to the rumble of the wheels and the roar of the ferocious wind against the pane of glass that his head touched. It was the midnight train from Marion rushing toward Warsaw like some savage thing unchained, creaking, shrieking, and clattering through the wild storm which possessed the whole Mississippi Valley.

Albert lost sight of the lamps at last, and began to wonder what his future would be. «First I must go through the university at Madison, then I'll study law, go into politics, and perhaps some time I may go to Washington.»

In imagination he saw that wonderful city. As a Western boy, Boston to him was historic, New York was the great metropolis, but Washington was the great American city, and political greatness the only fame.

The car was nearly empty: save here and there the wide-awake Western drummer, and a woman with four fretful children, the train was as deserted as it was frightfully cold. The engine shrieked warningly at intervals, the train rumbled hollowly over short bridges and across pikes, swung round the hills, and plunged with wild warnings past little towns hid in the snow, with only here and there a light shining dimly.

One of the drummers now and then rose up from his cramped bed on the seats, and swore dreadfully at the railway company for not heating the cars. The woman with the children inquired for the tenth time, «Is the next station Lodi?»

«Yes, ma'am, it is,» snarled the drummer, as he jerked viciously at the strap on his valise; «and darned glad I am, too, I can tell yeh! I 'll be stiff as a car-pin if I stay in this infernal ice-chest another hour. I wonder what the company think—»

At Lodi several people got on, among them a fat man and a very pretty daughter abnormally wide awake, considering the time of night. She saw Albert for the same reason that he saw her—they were both young and good-looking.

He began his musings again, modified by this girl's face. He had left out the feminine element; obviously he must recapitulate. He 'd study law, yes; but that would not prevent going to sociables and church fairs. And at these fairs the chances were good for a meeting with a girl. Her father must be influential—county judge or district attorney; this would open new avenues.

He was roused by the sound of his name.

«Is Albert Lohr in this car?» shouted the brakeman, coming in, enveloped in a cloud of fine snow.

«Yes; here!» shouted Albert.

«Here 's a telegram for you.»

Albert snatched the envelop with a sudden fear of disaster at home; but it was dated «Tyre»:

> Get off at Tyre. I 'll be there.
>
> HARTLEY.

«Well, now, that 's fun!» said Albert, looking at the brakeman. «When do we reach there?»

«About 2:20.»

«Well, by thunder! A pretty time o' night!»

The brakeman grinned sympathetically. «Any answer?» he asked at length.

«No; that is, none that 'u'd do the matter justice,» Albert said, studying the telegram.

«Hartley friend o' yours?»

«Yes; know him?»

«Yes; he boarded where I did in Lacrosse.»

When he came back again, the brakeman said to Albert, in a hesitating way:

«Ain't going t' stop off long, I s'pose?»

«May an' may not; depends on Hartley. Why?»

«Well, I 've got an aunt there that keeps boarders, and I kind o' like t' send her one when I can. If you should happen to stay a few days, go an' see her. She sets up first-class grub, an' it would n't kill anybody, anyhow, if you went up an' called.»

«Course not. If I stay long enough t' make it pay I 'll look her up sure. I ain't no Vanderbilt to stop at two-dollar-a-day hotels.»

The brakeman sat down opposite Albert, encouraged by his smile.

«Y' see, my division ends at Lacrosse, and I run back and forth here every other day, but I don't get much chance to see them, and I ain't worth a cuss f'r letter-writin'. Y' see, she 's only aunt by marriage, but I like her; an' I guess she 's got about all she can stand up under, an' so I like t' help her a little when I can. The old man was killed in the army, an' that left the old lady t' rustle f'r her livin'. Dummed if she ain't sandy as old Sand. They 're gitt'n' along purty—»

The whistle blew for brakes, and seizing his lantern, the brakeman slammed out on the platform.

«Tough night for twisting brakes,» suggested Albert, when he came in again.

«Yes—on the freight.»

«Good heavens! I should say so. They don't run freight such nights as this?»

«Don't they? Well, I guess they don't stop for a storm like this if they 's any money to be made by sending her through. Many 's the night I 've broke all night on top of the old wooden cars, when the wind cut like a razor. Shear the hair off a cast-iron mule —*woo-o-o!* There 's where you need grit, old man,» he ended, dropping into familiar speech.

«Yes; or need a job awful bad.»

The brakeman was struck with this idea. «There 's where you 're right. A feller don't take that kind of a job for the fun of it. Not much! He takes it because he 's got to. That 's as sure 's you 're a foot high. I tell you, a feller 's got t' rustle these days if he gits any kind of a job—»

«*Toot, too-o-o-o-t, toot!*»

The station passed, the brakeman did not return, perhaps because he found some other listener, perhaps because he was afraid of boring this pleasant young fellow. Albert shuddered with a sympathetic pain as he thought of the men on the tops of the icy cars, with hands straining at the brake, and the wind cutting their faces like a sand-blast. His mind went out to the thousands of freight-trains shuttling to and fro across the vast web of gleaming iron spread out on the mighty breast of the Western plains. Oh, those tireless hands at the wheel and throttle!

He looked at his watch; it was two o'clock; the next station was Tyre. As he began to get his things together, the brakeman came in.

«Oh, I forgot to say that the old lady's name is Welsh—Mrs. Robert Welsh. Say I sent yeh, and it 'll be all right.»

«Sure! I 'll try her in the morning—that is, if I find out I 'm going to stay.»

«Tyre! *Tyre!*» yelled the brakeman, as with clanging bell and whizz of steam the train slowed down and the wheels began to cry out in the snow.

Albert got his things together, and pulled his cap firmly down on his head.

«Here goes!» he muttered.

«Hold y'r breath!» shouted the brakeman.

Albert swung himself to the platform before the station—a platform of planks along which the snow was streaming like water.

«Good night!» called the brakeman.

«*Good* night!»

«All-l abo-o-o-ard!» called the conductor somewhere in the storm; the brakeman swung his lantern, and the train drew off into the blinding whirl, and the lights were soon lost in the clouds of snow.

No more desolate place could well be imagined. A level plain apparently bare of houses, swept by a ferocious wind; a dingy little den called a station—no other shelter in sight; no sign of life save the dull glare of two windows to the left, alternately lost and found in the storm.

Albert's heart contracted with a sudden fear; the outlook was appalling.

«Where 's the town?» he yelled savagely at a dimly seen figure with a lantern—a man evidently locking the station door, his only refuge.

«Over there,» was the surly reply.

«How far?»

«'Bout a mile.»

«A mile!»

«That 's what I said—a mile.»

«Well, I 'll be blanked!»

«Well, y' better be doing something besides standing here, 'r y' 'll freeze t' death. I 'd go over to the Arteeshun House an' go t' bed if I was in your fix.»

«Oh, y' would!»

«I would.»

«Well, where *is* the Artesian House?»

«See them lights?»

«I see them lights.»

«Well, they 're it.»

«Oh, would n't your grammar make Old Grammati-cuss curl up, though!»

«What say?» queried the man, bending his head toward Albert, his form being almost lost in the snow that streamed against them both.

«I said I guessed I 'd try it,» grinned the youth, invisibly.

«Well, I would if I was in your fix. Keep right close after me; they 's some ditches here, and the foot-bridges are none too wide.»

«The Artesian is owned by the railway, eh?»

«Yup.»

«And you 're the clerk?»

«Yup; nice little scheme, ain't it?»

«Well, it 'll do,» replied Albert.

The man laughed without looking around.

«Keep your longest cuss-words till morning; you 'll need 'em, take my word for it.»

In the little bar-room, lighted by a vilely smelling kerosene-lamp, the clerk, hitherto a shadow and a voice, came to light as a middle-aged man with a sullen face slightly belied by a sly twinkle in his eyes.

«This beats all the winters I ever *did* see. It don't do nawthin' but blow, *blow*. Want to go to bed, I s'pose. Well, come along.»

He took up one of the absurd little lamps and tried to get more light out of it.

«Dummed if a white bean would n't be better.»

«Spit on it!» suggested Albert.

«I 'd throw the whole business out o' the window for a cent,» growled the man.

«Here 's y'r cent,» said the boy.

«You 're mighty frisky f'r a feller gitt'n' off'n a midnight train,» replied the man, tramping along a narrow hallway, and talking in a voice loud enough to awaken every sleeper in the house.

«Have t' be, or there 'd be a pair of us.»

«You 'll laugh out o' the other side o' y'r mouth when you saw away on one o' the bell-collar steaks this house puts up,» ended the clerk as he put the lamp down.

«‹Sufficient unto the day is the evil thereof,›» called Albert after him, and then plunged into the icy bed.

He was awakened the next morning by the cooks pounding steak down in the kitchen, and wrangling over some division of duty. It was a vile place at any time, but on a morning like this it was appalling. The water was frozen, the floor like ice, the seven-by-nine glass frosted so that he could n't see to comb his hair.

«All that got me out of bed,» said Albert to the clerk, «was the thought of leaving.»

«Got y'r teeth filed?» said the day clerk, with a wink. «Old Collins's beef will try 'em.»

The breakfast was incredibly bad—so much worse than he expected that Albert was forced to admit he had never seen its like. He fled from the place without a glance behind, and took passage in an omnibus for the town, a mile away. It was terribly cold, the thermometer twenty below zero; but the sun was very brilliant, and the air still.

The driver pulled up before a very ambitious wooden hotel entitled «The Eldorado,» and Albert dashed in and up to the stove, with both hands holding on to his ears.

As he stood there, frantic with pain, kicking his toes and rubbing his ears, he heard a chuckle,—a slow, sly, insulting chuckle,—turned, and saw Hartley standing in the doorway, visibly exulting over his misery.

«Hello, Bert! that you?»

«What 's left of me. Say, you 're a good one, ain't yeh? Why did n't you telegraph me at Marion? A deuce of a night I 've had of it!»

«Do yeh good,» laughed Hartley, a tall, alert, handsome fellow nearly thirty years of age.

After a short and vigorous «blowing up,» Albert said: «Well, now, what 's the meaning of all this, anyhow? Why this change from Racine?»

«Well, yeh see, I got wind of another fellow going to work this county for a ‹Life of Logan,› and thinks I, ‹By jinks! I 'd better drop in ahead of him with Blaine's «Twenty Years.»› I telegraphed f'r territory, got it, and telegraphed to stop you.»

«You did it. When did yeh come down?»

«Last night, six o'clock.»

Albert was getting warmer and better-natured.

«Well, I 'm here; what yeh going t' do with me?»

«I 'll use yeh some way; can't tell. First thing is to find a boarding-place where we can work in a couple o' books on the bill.»

«Well, I don't know about that, but I 'm going to look up a place a brakeman gave me a pointer on.»

«All right; here goes!»

Scarcely any one was stirring on the streets. The wind was pitilessly cold, though not strong. The snow under the feet cried out with a note like glass and steel. The windows of the stores were thick with frost, and Albert gave a shudder of fear, almost as if he were homeless. He had never experienced anything like it before.

Entering one of the stores, they found a group of men sitting about the stove, smoking, chatting, and spitting aimlessly into a huge spittoon made of boards and filled with sawdust. Each man suspended smoking and talking as the strangers entered.

«Can any of you gentlemen tell us where Mrs. Welsh lives?»

There was a silence; then the clerk behind the counter said:

«I guess so. Two blocks north and three west, next to last house on left-hand side.»

«Clear as a bell!» laughed Hartley, and they pushed out into the cold again, drawing their mufflers up to their eyes.

«I don't want much of this,» muttered Bert through his scarf.

The house was a large frame-house standing on the edge of a bank, and as the young men waited they could look down on the meadow-land, where the river lay blue and still and as hard as iron.

A pale little girl ten or twelve years of age let them in.

«Is this where Mrs. Welsh lives?»

«Yes, sir.»

«Will you ask her to come here a moment?»

«Yes, sir,» piped the little one. «Won't you sit down by the fire?» she added, with a quaint air of hospitality.

The room was the usual village sitting-room: a cylinder heater full of wood at one side of it; a rag carpet, much faded, on the floor; a cabinet organ; a doleful pair of crayon portraits on the wall, one supposedly a baby—a figure dressed like a child of six months, but with a face old and cynical enough to be forty-five. The paper on the wall was of the hideous striped sort, and the chairs were nondescript; but everything was clean—so clean it looked worn more with brushing than with use.

A slim woman of fifty, with hollow eyes and a patient smile, came in, wiping her hands on her apron.

«How d' ye do? Did you want to see me?»

«Yes,» said Hartley, smiling. «The fact is, we 're book-agents, and looking for a place to board.»

«Well—a—I—yes, I keep boarders.»

«I was sent here by a brakeman on the midnight express,» put in Bert.

«Oh, Tom,» said the woman, her face clearing. «Tom 's always sending us people. Why, yes; I 've got room for you, I guess—this room here.» She pushed open a folding-door leading into what had been her parlor.

«You can have this.»

«And the price?»

«Four dollars.»

«Eight dollars f'r the two of us. All right; we 'll be with you a week or two if we have luck.»

The woman smiled and shut the door. Bert thought how much she looked like his mother in the back—the same tired droop in the shoulders, the same colorless dress, once blue or brown, now a peculiar drab, characterless with much washing.

«Excuse me, won't you? I 've got to be at my baking; make y'rselves at home.»

«Now, Jim,» said Bert, «I 'm going t' stay right here while you go and order our trunks around—just t' pay you off f'r last night.»

«All right,» said Hartley, cheerily going out. After getting warm, Bert sat down at the organ and played a gospel hymn or two from the Moody and Sankey hymnal. He was in the midst of the chorus of «Let your lower lights,» etc., when a young woman entered the room. She had a whisk-broom in her hand, and stood a picture of gentle surprise. Bert wheeled about on his stool.

«I thought it was Stella,» she began.

«I'm a book-agent,» said Bert, rising with his best grace; «I might as well out with it. I 'm here to board.»

«Oh!» said the girl, with some relief. She was very fair and very slight, almost frail. Her eyes were of the sunniest blue, her face pale and somewhat thin, but her lips showed scarlet, and her teeth were fine. Bert liked her, and smiled.

«A book-agent is the next thing to a burglar, I know; but still—»

«Oh, I did n't mean that, but I *was* surprised. When did you come?»

«Just a few moments ago. Am I in your way?» he inquired, with elaborate solicitude.

«Oh, no! Please go on; you play very well, I think. It is so seldom young men play.»

«I had to at college; the other fellows all wanted to sing. You play, of course.»

«When I have time.» She sighed. There was a weary droop in her voice; she seemed aware of it, and said more brightly:

«You mean Madison, I suppose?»

«Yes; I 'm in my second year.»

«I went there two years. Then I had to quit and come home to help mother.»

«Did you? That 's why I 'm out here on this infernal book business—to get money.»

She looked at him with interest now, noticing his fine eyes and waving brown hair.

«It 's dreadful, ain't it? But you 've got a hope to go back. I have n't. At first I did n't think I could live; but I did.» She ended with a sigh, a far-off expression in her eyes.

There was a pause again. Bert felt that

she was no ordinary girl, and she was quite as strongly drawn to him.

«It almost killed me to give it up. I don't s'pose I'd know any of the scholars you know. Even the teachers are not the same. Oh, yes —Sarah Shaw; I think she 's back for the normal course.»

«Oh, yes!» exclaimed Bert, «I know Sarah. We boarded on the same street; used t' go home together after class. An awful nice girl, too.»

«She 's a worker. She teaches school. I can't do that, for mother needs me at home.» There was another pause, broken by the little girl, who called:

«Maud, mama wants you.»

Maud rose and went out, with a tired smile on her face that emphasized her resemblance to her mother. Bert could n't forget that smile, and he was still thinking about the girl, and what her life must be, when Hartley came in.

«By jinks! It 's *snifty*, as dad used to say. You can't draw a long breath through your nostrils; freeze y'r nose solid as a bottle,» he announced, throwing off his coat with an air which seemed to make him an old resident of the room.

«By the way, I 've just found out why you was so anxious to get into this house, hey?» he said, slapping Bert's knee. «Another case o' girl.»

Bert blushed; he could n't help it, notwithstanding his innocence in this case. Hartley went on.

«Oh, I know you! A girl in the house; might 'a' known it,» Hartley continued, in a hoarse whisper.

«I did n't know it myself till about ten minutes ago,» protested Bert.

Hartley winked prodigiously.

«Don't tell me! Is she pretty?»

«No—that is, *you* would n't call her so.»

«Oh, the deuce I would n't! Don't you *wish* I would n't? I'd like to see the girl I would n't call pretty, right to her face, too.»

The girl returned at this moment with an armful of wood.

«Let *me* put it in,» cried Hartley, springing up. «Excuse me. My name is Hartley, book-agent: Blaine's ‹Twenty Years,› plain cloth, sprinkled edges, three dollars; half calf, three-fifty. This is my friend Mr. Lohr of Madison, German extraction, soph at the university.»

The girl bowed and smiled, and pushed by him toward the door of the parlor. Hartley followed her in, and Bert could hear them rattling away at the stove.

«Won't you sit down and play for us?» asked Hartley, after they returned to the sitting-room, with the persuasive music of the book-agent in his fine voice.

«Oh, no! It 's nearly dinner-time, and I must help about the table.»

«Now make yourselves at home,» said Mrs. Welsh, appearing at the door leading to the kitchen; «if you want anything, just let me know.»

«All right. We will; don't worry. We'll be trouble enough. Nice people,» said Hartley, as he shut the door of their room and sat down. «But the girl *ain't* what I call pretty.»

By the time the dinner-bell rang they were feeling at home in their new quarters. At the table they met the other boarders: the Brann brothers, newsdealers; old man Troutt, who kept the livery-stable (and smelled of it); and a small, dark, and wizened woman who kept the millinery store. The others, who came in late, were clerks.

Maud served the dinner, while Stella and her mother waited upon the table. Albert was accustomed to this, and made little account of the service. He did notice the hands of the girl, however, so white and graceful; no amount of work could quite remove their essential shapeliness.

Hartley struck up a conversation with the newsdealers, and left Bert free to observe Maud. She was not more than twenty, he decided, but she looked older, so careworn and sad was her face.

«They 's one thing ag'in' yeh,» Troutt, the liveryman, was bawling to Hartley: «they 's jest been worked one o' the goldingedest schemes you *ever* see! 'Bout six munce ago s'm' fellers come all through here claimin' t' be after information about the county and the leading citizens; wanted t' write a history, an' wanted all the pitchers of the leading men, old settlers, an' so on. You paid ten dollars, an' you had a book an' your pitcher in it.»

«I know the scheme,» grinned Hartley.

«Wal, sir, I s'pose them fellers roped in every man in this town. I don't s'pose they got out with a cent less 'n one thousand dollars. An' when the book come—wal!» Here he stopped to roar. «I don't s'pose you ever see a madder lot o' men in your life. In the first place, they got the names and the pitchers mixed so that I was Judge Ricker, an' Judge Ricker was ol' man Daggett. Did n't the judge swear—oh, it was awful!»

«I should say so.»

«An' the pitchers that wa'n't mixed was so goldinged *black* you could n't tell 'em from niggers. You know how kind o' lily-livered

Lawyer Ransom is? Wal, he looked like ol' black Joe; he was the maddest man of the hull b'ilin'. He throwed the book in the fire, and tromped around like a blind bull.»

«It was n't a success, I take it, then. Why, I should 'a' thought they 'd 'a' nabbed the fellows.»

«Not much! They was too keen for that. They did n't deliver the books theirselves; they hired Dick Bascom to do it f'r 'em. Course Dick wa'n't t' blame.»

«No; I never tried it before,» Albert was saying to Maud, at their end of the table. «Hartley offered me a good thing to come, and as I needed money, I came. I don't know what he 's going to do with me, now I 'm here.»

Albert did not go out after dinner with Hartley; it was too cold. Hartley let nothing stand in the way of business, however. He had been at school with Albert during his first year, but had gone back to work in preference to study.

Albert had brought his books with him, planning to keep up with his class, if possible, and was deep in a study of Cæsar when he heard a timid knock on the door.

«Come!» he called, student fashion.

Maud entered, her face aglow.

«How natural that sounds!» she said.

Albert sprang up to help her put down the wood in her arms. «I wish you 'd let me bring the wood,» he said pleadingly, as she refused his aid.

«I was n't sure you were in. Were you reading?»

«Cæsar,» he replied, holding up the book. «I am conditioned on Latin. I 'm going over the ‹Commentaries› again.»

«I thought I knew the book,» she laughed.

«You read Latin?»

«Yes, a little—Vergil.»

«Maybe you can help me out on these *oratia obliqua*. They bother me yet. I hate these ‹Cæsar saids.› I like Vergil better.»

She stood at his shoulder while he pointed out the knotty passage. She read it easily, and he thanked her. It was amazing how well acquainted they felt after this; they were as fellow-students.

The wind roared outside in the bare maples, and the fire boomed in its pent place within. The young people forgot the time and place. The girl sank into a chair almost unconsciously as they talked of Madison,—a great city to them,—of the Capitol building, of the splendid campus, of the lakes and the gay sailing there in summer and ice-boating in winter, of the struggles of «rooming.»

«Oh, it makes me homesick!» cried the girl, with a deep sigh. «It was the happiest, sunniest time of all my life. Oh, those walks and talks! Those recitations in the dear, chalky old rooms! Oh, *how* I would like to go back over that hollow door-stone again!»

She broke off, with tears in her eyes. He was obliged to cough two or three times before he could break the silence.

«I know just how you feel. I know, the first spring when I went back on the farm, it seemed as if I could n't stand it. I thought I 'd go crazy. The days seemed forty-eight hours long. It was so lonesome, and so dreary on rainy days! But of course I expected to go back; that 's what kept me up. I don't think I could have stood it if I had n't had hope.»

«I 've given it up now,» she said plaintively; «it 's no use hoping.»

«Why don't you teach?» asked Albert, deeply affected by her voice and manner.

«I did teach here for a year, but I could n't endure the noise; I'm not very strong, and the boys were so rude. If I could teach in a seminary—teach Latin and English, I should be happy, I think. But I can't leave mother now.»

She began to appear a different girl in the boy's eyes; the cheap dress, the check apron, could not hide her pure intellectual spirit. Her large blue eyes were deep with thought, and the pale face, lighted by the glow of the fire, was as lovely as a rose. Almost before he knew it, he was telling her of his life.

«I don't see how I endured it as long as I did,» he went on. «It was nothing but work, work, and mud the whole year round; it 's just so on all farms.»

«Yes, I guess it is,» said she. «Father was a carpenter, and I 've always lived here; but we have people who are farmers, and I know how it is with them.»

«Why, when I think of it now it makes me crawl! To think of getting up in the morning before daylight, and going out to the barn to do chores, to get ready to go into the field to work! Working, wasting y'r life on dirt. Goin' round and round in a circle, and never getting out.»

«It 's just the same for us women,» she corroborated. «Think of us going around the house day after day, and doing just the same things over an' over, year after year! That 's the whole of most women's lives. Dish-washing almost drives me crazy.»

«I know it,» said Albert; «but a fellow has t' do it. If his folks are workin' hard, why, of course he can't lay around and study. They ain't t' blame. I don't know that anybody 's t' blame.»

«No, I don't; but it makes me sad to see mother going around as she does, day after day. She won't let me do as much as I would.» The girl looked at her slender hands. «You see, I'm not very strong. It makes my heart ache to see her going around in that quiet, patient way; she 's so good.»

«I know, I know! I 've felt just like that about my mother and father, too.»

There was a long pause, full of deep feeling, and then the girl continued in a low, hesitating voice:

«Mother 's had an awful hard time since father died. We had to go to keeping boarders, which was hard—very hard for mother.» The boy felt a sympathetic lump in his throat as the girl went on again: «But she does n't complain, and she did n't want me to come home from school; but of course I could n't do anything else.»

It did n't occur to either of them that any other course was open, nor that there was any heroism or self-sacrifice in the act; it was simply *right*.

«Well, I'm not going to drudge all my life,» said the boy at last. «I know it 's kind o' selfish, but I can't live on a farm; it 'u'd kill me in a year. I 've made up my mind to study law and enter the bar. Lawyers manage to get hold of enough to live on decently, and that 's more than you can say of the farmers. And they live in town, where something is going on once in a while, anyway.»

In the pause which followed, footsteps were heard on the walk outside, and the girl sprang up with a beautiful blush.

«My stars! I did n't think—I forgot—I must go.»

Hartley burst into the room shortly after she left it, in his usual breeze.

«Hul-*lo!* Still at the Latin, hey?»

«Yes,» said Bert, with ease. «How goes it?»

«Oh, I 'm whooping 'er up! I 'm getting started in great shape. Been up to the courthouse and roped in three of the county officials. In these small towns the big man is the politician or the clergyman. I 've nailed the politicians through the ear; now you must go for the ministers to head the list—that 's your lay-out.»

«How 'm I t' do it?» said Bert, in an anxious tone. «I can't sell books if they don't want 'em.»

«Yes, yeh can. That 's the trade. Offer a big discount. Say full calf, two-fifty; morocco, two-ninety. Regular discount to the clergy, yeh know. Oh, they're on to that little racket —no trouble. If you can get a few of these leaders of the flock, the rest will follow like lambs to the slaughter. Tra-la-la—who-o-o-*ish*, whish!»

Albert laughed at Hartley as he plunged his face into the ice-cold water, puffing and wheezing.

«Jeemimy Crickets! but ain't that water cold! I worked Rock River this way last month, and made a boomin' success. If you take hold here in the—»

«Oh, I 'm all ready to do anything that is needed, short of being kicked out.»

«No danger of that if you 're a real book-agent. It 's the snide that gets kicked. You 've got t' have some savvy in this, just like any other business.» He stopped in his dressing to say, «We 've struck a great boarding-place, hey?»

«Looks like it.»

«I begin t' cotton to the old lady a'ready. Good 'eal like mother used t' be 'fore she broke down. Did n't the old lady have a time of it raisin' me? Phewee! Patient! Job was n't a patchin'. But the test is going t' come on the biscuit; if her biscuit comes up t' mother's I 'm hern till death.»

He broke off to comb his hair, a very nice bit of work in his case.

## II.

THERE was no discernible reason why the little town should have been called Tyre, and yet its name was as characteristically American as its architecture. It had the usual main street lined with low brick or wooden stores—a street which developed into a road running back up a wide, sandy valley away from the river. Being a county town, it had a courthouse in a yard near the center of the town, and a big summer hotel. The valley was peculiarly picturesque. Curiously shaped and oddly distributed hills rose out of the valley sand abruptly, forming a sort of amphitheater in which the village lay. These square-topped hills rose to a common level, showing that they were not the result of an upheaval, but were the remains of the original stratification left standing after the vast scooping action of the post-glacial floods.

The abrupt cliffs and lone huge pillars and peaks rising out of the valley level here and there showed the original layers of rock unmoved. They looked like vast ruined castles ancient as hills, on the massive tops of which time had sown sturdy oaks and cedars. They lent a certain air of romance to the valley at all times; but when in summer vines clambered over their rugged sides and underbrush softened their broken lines, it was not at all difficult to imagine them the remains of an unrecorded, very warlike people.

Even now, in winter, with yellow-brown and green cedars standing starkly upon their summits, the hickories and small ashes blue-black with their masses of fine bare limbs meshed against the snow, these towers had a distinct charm. The weather was glorious winter, and in the early morning when the trees glistened with frost, or at evening when the white light of the sun was softened and violet shadows lay along the snow, the whole valley was a delight to the eye, full of distinct and lasting beauty, part of the beautiful and strange Mississippi River scenery.

In the campaign which Hartley began Albert did his best, and his best was done unconsciously, for the charm of his manner (all unknown to himself) was the most potent factor in securing consideration.

«I 'm not a book-agent,» he said to one of the clergymen to whom he went first; «I 'm a student trying to sell a good book and make a little money to help me complete my course at the university.»

He did not go to the back door, but walked up to the front, asked to see the minister, and placed his case at once before him. He had a sureness of air and a leisurely utterance quite the opposites of the brazen timidity and rapid, parrot-like tone of the professional. He secured the clergymen of the place to head his list, much to the delight and admiration of Hartley.

«Good! Now corral the alumni of the place. Work the fraternal racket to the bitter end. Oh, say! there 's a sociable to-morrow night; I guess we 'd better go, had n't we?»

«Go alone?»

«Alone? No! Take some girls. I 'm going to take neighbor Picket's daughter; she 's homely as a hedge-fence, but I 'll take her—great scheme!»

«Hartley, you 're an infernal fraud!»

«Nothing of the kind—I 'm business,» ended Hartley, with a laugh.

After supper the following day, as Albert was still lingering at the table with the girls and Mrs. Welsh, he thought of the sociable, and said on the impulse:

«Are you going to the sociable?»

«No; I guess not.»

«Would you go if I asked you?»

«Try me and see!» answered the girl, with a laugh, her color rising.

«All right. Miss Welsh, will you attend the festivity of the evening under my guidance and protection?»

«Yes, thank you.»

«I 'll be ready before you are.»

«No doubt; I 've got to wash the dishes.»

«I 'll wash the dishes; you go get ready,» said the self-regardless mother.

Albert felt that he had one of the loveliest girls in the room as he led Maud down the floor of the vestry of the church, filled with laughing young people moving about or seated at the long tables. Maud's cheeks were full of delicate color and her eyes shone with maidenly delight as they took seats at the table to sip a little coffee and nibble a bit of cake.

«I suppose they *must* have my fifteen cents some way,» said Albert, in a low voice, «and I guess we 'd better sit down.»

Maud introduced him to a number of young people who had been students at the university. They received him cordially, and in a very short time he was enjoying himself very well indeed. He was reminded rather disagreeably of his office, however, by seeing Hartley surrounded by a laughing crowd of the more frolicsome young people. He winked at Albert, as much as to say, «Good stroke of business.»

The evening passed away with songs, games, and recitations, and it was nearly eleven o'clock when the young people began to wander off toward home in pairs. Albert and Maud were among the first of the young folks to bid the rest good night.

The night was clear and cold, but perfectly still, and the young people, arm in arm, walked slowly homeward under the bare maples, in delicious companionship. Albert held her arm close to his side.

«Are you cold?» he asked in a low voice.

«No, thank you; the night is lovely,» she replied; then added with a sigh, «I don't like sociables so well as I used to—they tire me out.»

«We stayed too long.»

«It was n't that; I 'm getting so they seem kind o' silly.»

«Well, I feel a little that way myself,» he confessed.

«But there is so little to see here in Tyre at any time—no music, no theaters. I like theaters, don't you?»

«I can't go half enough.»

«But nothing worth seeing ever comes into these little towns—and then we 're all so poor, anyway.»

The lamp, turned low, was emitting a terrible odor as they entered the sitting-room.

«My goodness! it 's almost twelve o'clock. Good night.» She held out her hand.

«Good night,» he said, taking it, and giving it a cordial pressure which she remembered long.

«Good night,» she repeated softly, going up the stairs.

Hartley came in a few moments later, and found Bert sitting thoughtfully by the fire, with his coat and shoes off, evidently in deep abstraction.

«Well, I got away at last—much as ever.»

«Great scheme, that sociable, eh? I saw your little girl introducing you right and left.»

DRAWN BY T. DE THULSTRUP

«‹WHERE 'S THE TOWN?›» (SEE PAGE 402.)

«Say, Hartley, I wish you 'd leave her out of this thing; I don't like the way you speak of her when—»

«Phew! You don't? Oh, all right! I 'm mum as an oyster—only keep it up! Get in all the church sociables, and all that; there 's nothing like it.»

HARTLEY soon had canvassers out along the country roads, and was working every house in town. The campaign promised to lengthen into a month, perhaps longer. Albert especially became a great favorite. Every one declared there had never been such book-agents in the town: such gentlemanly fellows, they did n't press anybody to buy; they did n't rush about and «poke their noses where they were not wanted.» They were more like merchants with books to sell. The only person who failed to see the attraction in them was Ed Brann, who was popularly supposed to be engaged to Maud. He grew daily more sullen and repellent, toward Albert noticeably so.

One evening about six, after coming in from a long walk about town, Albert entered his room without lighting his lamp, lay down on the bed, and fell asleep. He had been out late the night before with Maud at a party, and slumber came almost instantly.

Maud came in shortly, hearing no response to her knock, and after hanging some towels on the rack went out without seeing the sleeper. In the sitting-room she met Ed Brann. He was a stalwart young man with curling black hair, and a face heavy at its best, but set and sullen now. His first words held a menace:

«Say, Maud, I want t' talk to you.»

«Very well; what is it, Ed?» replied the girl, quietly.

«I want to know how often you 're going to be out till twelve o'clock with this book-agent?»

Perhaps it was the derisive inflection on «book-agent» that woke Albert. Brann's tone was brutal—more brutal even than his words, and the girl turned pale and her breath quickened.

«Why, Ed, what 's the matter?»

«Matter is just this: you ain't got any business goin' around with that feller with my ring on your finger, that 's all.» He ended with an unmistakable threat in his voice.

«Very well,» said the girl, after a pause, curiously quiet; «then I won't; here 's your ring.»

The man's bluster disappeared instantly. Bert could tell by the change in his voice, which was incredibly great, as he pleaded:

«Oh, don't do that, Maud; I did n't mean to say that; I was mad—I 'm sorry.»

«I'm *glad* you did it *now*, so I can know you. Take your ring, Ed; I never 'll wear it again.»

Albert had heard all this, but he did not know how the girl looked as she faced the man. In the silence which followed she looked him in the face, and scornfully passed him and went out into the kitchen. He did not return at supper.

Young people of this sort are not self-analysts, and Maud did not examine closely into causes. She was astonished to find herself more indignant than grieved. She broke into an angry wail as she went to her mother's bosom:

«Mother! mother!»

«Why, what 's the matter, Maudie? Tell me. There, there! don't cry, pet! Who 's been hurtin' my poor little bird?»

«Ed has; he said—he said—»

«There, there! poor child! Have you been quarreling? Never mind; it 'll come out all right.»

«No, it won't—not the way you mean,» the girl cried, lifting her head; «I've given him back his ring, and I 'll never wear it again.»

The mother could not understand how the wounding brutality in the man's tone had fallen upon the girl's spirit, and Maud felt in some way as if she could not explain sufficiently to justify herself. Mrs. Welsh consoled herself with the idea that it was only a lovers' quarrel—one of the little jars sure to come when two natures are settling together—and that all would be mended in a day or two.

But there was a peculiar set look on the girl's face that promised little for Brann. Albert, being no more of a self-analyst than Maud, simply said, «Served him right,» and dwelt no more upon it for the time.

At supper, however, he was extravagantly gay, and to himself unaccountably so. He joked Troutt till Maud begged him to stop, and after the rest had gone he remained seated at the table, enjoying the indignant color in her face and the flash of her infrequent smile, which it was such a pleasure to provoke. He volunteered to help wash the dishes.

«Thank you, but I 'm afraid you 'd be more bother than help,» she replied.

«Thank you, but you don't know me. I ain't so green as I look, by no manner o' means. I 've been doing my own housekeeping for four terms.»

«I know all about that,» laughed the girl. «You young men rooming do precious little cooking, and no dish-washing at all.»

«That 's a base calumny! I made it a point to wash every dish in the house, except the spider, once a week; had a regular cleaning-up day.»

«And about the spider?»

«I wiped that out nicely with a newspaper every time I wanted to use it.»

«Oh, horrors! Mother, listen to that!»

«Why, what more could you ask? You would n't have me wipe it *six* times a day, would you?»

«I wonder it did n't poison yeh,» commented Mrs. Welsh.

«Takes more 'n that to poison a student,» laughed Albert, as he went out.

The next afternoon he came bursting into the kitchen, where Maud stood with her sleeves rolled up, deep in the dish-pan, while Stella stood wiping the dishes handed to her.

«Don't you want a sleigh-ride?» he asked, boyishly eager.

She looked up with shining eyes.

«Oh, would n't I! Can you get along, mother?»

«Certainly, child; the air 'll do yeh good.»

«W'y, Maud!» said the little girl, «you said you did n't want to when Ed—»

Mrs. Welsh silenced her, and said:

«Run right along, dear; it 's just the nicest time o' day. Are there many teams out?»

«They 're just beginning t' come out,» said Albert. «I 'll have a cutter around here in about two jiffies; be on hand, sure.»

Troutt was standing in the sunny doorway of his stable when the young fellow dashed up to him.

«Hello, Uncle Troutt! Harness the fastest nag into your swellest outfit instanter.»

«Aha! Goin' t' take y'r girl out, hey?»

«Yes; and I want 'o do it in style.»

«I guess ol' Dan 's the idee, if you can drive him; he 's a ring-tailed snorter.»

«Fast?»

«Nope; but safe. Gentle as a kitten and as knowin' as a fox. Drive him with one hand—left hand,» the old man chuckled.

«Troutt, you 're an insinuating old insinuator, and I 'll— »

Troutt laughed till his long faded beard flapped up and down and quivered with the stress of his enjoyment of his joke. He ended by hitching a vicious-looking sorrel to a gay, duck-bellied cutter, saying as he gave up the reins:

«Now, be keerful; Dan 's foxy; he 's all right when he sees you 've got the reins, but don't drop 'em.»

«Don't you worry about me; I grew up with horses,» said the over-confident youth, leaping into the sleigh and gathering up the lines. «Stand aside, my lord, and let the cortège pass. Hoop-la!»

The brute gave a tearing lunge, and was out of the doorway like a shot before the old man could utter a word. Albert thrilled with pleasure as he felt the reins stiffen in his hands, while the traces swung slack beside the thills.

«If he keeps this up he 'll do,» he thought.

As he turned up at the gate Maud came gaily down the path, muffled to the eyes.

«Oh, what a nice cutter! But the horse—is he gentle?» she asked, as she climbed in.

«As a cow,» Albert replied. «Git out o' this, Bones!»

The main street was already full of teams, light sleighs, bob-sleighs filled with children, and here and there a man in a light cutter alone, out for a race. Laughter was on the air, and the jingle-jangle of bells. The sun was dazzling in its brightness, and the gay wraps and scarfs lighted up the street with flecks of color. Loafers on the sidewalks fired a fusillade of words at the teams as they passed:

«Go it, Bones!»

«‹Let 'er *go*, Gallagher!›»

«Ain't she a daisy!»

But what cared the drivers? If the shouts were insolent they laid them to envy, and if they were pleasant they smiled in reply.

DRAWN BY T. DE THULSTRUP.

«‹I NEVER 'LL WEAR IT AGAIN.›»

Albert and Maud had made two easy turns up and down the street, when a man driving a span of large black-hawk horses dashed up a side street and whirled in just before them. The man was a superb driver, and sat with the reins held carelessly but securely in his left hand, guiding the team more by his voice than by the bit. He sat leaning forward with his head held down in a peculiar and sinister fashion.

«*Hel*-lo!» cried Bert; «that looks like Brann.»

«It is,» said Maud.

«Cracky! that's a fine team—black-hawks, both of them. I wonder if ol' sorrel can pass 'em.»

«Oh, please don't try,» pleaded the girl.

«Why not?»

«Because—because I 'm afraid.»

«Afraid of what?»

«Afraid something 'll happen.»

«Something *is* goin' t' happen; I 'm goin' t' pass him if old Bones has got any *git* to him.»

«It 'll make him mad.»

«Who mad? Brann?»

«Yes.»

«Well, s'pose it does, who cares?»

The teams moved along at an easy pace. Some one called to Brann:

«They 're on y'r trail, Ed.»

There was something peculiar in the tone, and Brann looked behind for the first time, and saw them. He swore through his teeth, and turned about. He looked dogged and sullen, with his bent shoulders and his chin thrust down.

There were a dozen similar rigs moving up or down the street, and greetings passed from sleigh to sleigh. Everybody except Brann welcomed Albert with sincere pleasure, and exchanged rustic jokes with him. As they slowed up at the upper end of the street and began to turn, a man on the sidewalk said confidentially:

«Say, cap', if you handle that old rack-o'-bones just right, he 'll distance anything on this road. When you want him to do his best let him have the rein; don't pull a pound. I use to own 'im—I know 'im.»

The old sorrel came round «gauming,» his ugly head thrown up, his great red mouth open, his ears back. Brann and the young doctor of the place were turning together a little farther up the street. The blacks, superbly obedient to their driver, came down with flying hoofs, their great glossy breasts flecked with foam from their champing jaws.

«Come on, fellers!» yelled Brann, insultingly, as he came down past the doctor, and seemed about to pass Albert and Maud. There was hate in the glare of his eyes.

But he did not pass. The old sorrel seemed to lengthen; to the spectators his nose appeared to be glued to the glossy side of Brann's off black.

«See them blacks trot!» shouted Albert, in ungrammatical enthusiasm.

«See that old sorrel shake himself!» yelled the loafers.

The doctor came tearing down with a spirited bay, a magnificent stepper. As he drew along so that Bert could catch a glimpse of the mare's neck, he thrilled with delight. There was the thoroughbred's lacing of veins; the proud fling of her knees and the swell of her neck showed that she was far from doing her best. There was a wild light in her eyes.

These were the fast teams of the town. All interest was centered in them.

«Clear the track!» yelled the loafers.

«The doc's good f'r 'em.»

«If she don't break.»

Albert was pulling at the sorrel heavily, absorbed in seeing, as well as he could for the flung snowballs, the doctor's mare draw slowly, foot by foot, past the blacks. Suddenly Brann gave a shrill yell and stood up in his sleigh. The gallant little bay broke and fell behind; Brann gave a loud laugh; the blacks trotted on, their splendid pace unchanged.

«Let the sorrel out!» yelled somebody.

«Let him loose!» yelled Troutt on the corner, quivering with excitement. «Let him go!»

Albert remembered what the fellow had said; he let the reins loose. The old sorrel's teeth came together with a snap; his head lowered and his tail rose; he shot abreast of the blacks. Brann yelled:

«Sam—Saul, *git!*»

«See them trot!» shouted Bert, lost in admiration; but Maud, frightened into silence, had covered her head with the robe to escape the blinding cloud of flying snow. The sorrel drew steadily ahead; he was passing when Brann turned.

«Durn y'r old horse!» he yelled through his shut teeth, and laid the whip across the sorrel's hips. The blacks broke wildly, but, strange to say, the old sorrel increased his speed. Again Brann struck at him, but missed him, and the stroke fell on Bert's outstretched wrists. He turned to see what Brann meant by it; he did not see that the blacks were crowding him to the gutter; his hands felt numb.

«Look *out*, there!»

Before he could turn to look, the cutter seemed to be blown up by a bomb, and he rose in the air like a vaulter; he saw the traces part, he felt the reins slip through his hands, and that was all; he seemed to fall an immeasurable depth into a black abyss. . . . The next that he knew was a curious soft murmur of voices, out of which a sweet, agonized girl-voice broke, familiar but unrecognized:

«Oh, where 's the doctor! He 's dead—oh, he 's dead! *Can't* you hurry!»

Next came a quick, authoritative voice, still far away, and a hush followed it; then an imperative order:

«Stand out o' the way! What do you think you can do by crowding on top of him?»

«Stand back! stand back!» other voices called.

Then he felt something cold on his head: they were taking his cap off and putting snow on his head; then the doctor (he knew him now) said:

«Let me take him!»

DRAWN BY T. DE THULSTRUP.

"'CAN YOU HEAR US? ALBERT, DO YOU KNOW ME?'"

«Oh, can't I do something?» said the sweet voice.

«No—nothing.»

Then there came a strange fullness in his head. Shadows lighted by dull red flashes passed before his eyes; he wondered, in a slow, dull way, if he were dying. Then this changed; a dull, throbbing ache came into his head, and as this grew the noise of voices grew more distinct and he could hear sobbing. Then the dull, rhythmic red flashes passed slowly away from his eyes, and he opened his lids, but the glare of the sunlight struck them shut again; he saw only Maud's face, agonized, white, and wet with tears, looking down into his. He felt the doctor's hands winding bandages about his head, and he felt a crawling stream of blood behind his ear, getting as cold as ice as it sank under his collar.

They raised him a little more, and he opened his eyes on the circle of hushed and excited men thronging about him. He saw Brann, with wild, scared face, standing in his cutter and peering over the heads of the crowd.

«How do you feel now?» asked the doctor.

«Can you hear us? Albert, do you know me?» called the girl.

His lips moved stiffly, but he smiled a little, and at length whispered slowly, «Yes; I guess—I 'm all—right.»

«Put him into my cutter; Maud, get in here, too,» the doctor commanded, with all the authority of a physician in a small village. The crowd opened, and silenced its muttered comments as the doctor and Troutt helped the wounded man into the sleigh. The pain in his head grew worse, but Albert's perception of things grew in proportion; he closed his eyes to the sun, but in the shadow of Maud's breast opened them again and looked up at her. He felt a vague, child-like pleasure in knowing she was holding him in her arms; he felt the sleigh moving; he thought of his mother, and how it would frighten her if she knew.

The doctor was driving the horse and walking beside the sleigh, and the people were accosting him. Albert could catch their words now and then, and the reply:

«No; he is n't killed, nor anything near it; he 's stunned, that 's all; he is n't bleeding now. No; he 'll be all right in a day or two.»

«Hello!» said a breathless, hearty voice, «what the deuce y' been doing with my pardner? Bert, old fellow, are you there?» Hartley asked, clinging to the edge of the moving cutter, and peering into his friend's face. Albert smiled.

«I 'm here—what there is left of me,» he replied faintly.

«Glory! how 'd it happen?» he asked of the girl.

«I don't know—I could n't see—we ran into a culvert,» replied Maud.

Albert felt a steady return of waves of pain, but did not know that they were waves of returning life. He groaned, and tried to rise. The girl gently but firmly restrained him. Hartley was walking beside the doctor, talking loudly. «It was a devilish thing to do; the scoundrel ought 'o be jugged!»

Albert groaned, and tried to rise again. «I 'm bleeding yet; I 'm soaking you!»

The girl shuddered, but remained firm.

«No; we 're 'most home.»

She felt no shame, but a certain exaltation, as she looked into the curious faces she saw in groups on the sidewalk. The boys who ran alongside wore in their faces a look of awe, for they imagined themselves in the presence of death.

Maud gazed unrecognizingly upon her nearest girl friends. They seemed something alien in that moment; and they, gazing upon her white face and unrecognizing eyes, spoke in awed whispers.

At the gate the crowd gathered and waited with deepest interest, with a sort of shuddering pleasure. It was all a strange, unusual, and enthralling romance to them. The dazzling sunshine added to the wonder of it all.

«Ed Brann done it.»

«How?» asked several.

«With the butt-end of his whip.»

«That 's a lie! His team ran into Lohr's rig.»

«Not much; Ed crowded him into the ditch.»

«What fer?»

«'Cause Bert cut him out with Maud.»

«Come, get out of the way! Don't stand there gabbing,» yelled Hartley, as he took Albert in his arms, and, together with the doctor, lifted him out of the sleigh.

«Goodness sakes alive! Ain't it terrible! How is he?» asked an old lady, peering at him as he passed.

On the porch stood Mrs. Welsh, supported by Ed Brann.

«She 's all right, I tell you. He ain't hurt much, either; just stunned a little, that 's all.»

«Maud! child!» cried the mother, as Maud appeared out of the crowd, followed by a bevy of girls.

«Mother, *I 'm* all right!» she said as gaily as she could, running into the trembling arms outstretched toward her; «but oh, poor Albert!»

After they disappeared into the house the crowd dispersed. Brann went off by way of the alley; he was not prepared to meet their questions; but he met his brother and several others in his store.

«Now, what in —— you been up to?» was the fraternal greeting.

«Nothing.»

«Welting a man on the head with a whipstock ain't anything, hey?»

«I did n't touch him. We was racing, and he run into the culvert.»

«Hank says he saw you strike—»

«He lies! I was strikin' the horse to make him break.»

«Oh, yeh was!» sneered the older man. «Well, I hope you understand that this 'll ruin us in this town. If you did n't strike him, they 'll say you run him into the culvert, 'n' every man, woman, 'n' child 'll be down on you, and *me* f'r bein' related to you. They all know how you feel towards him for cuttin' you out with Maud Welsh.»

«Oh, don't bear down on him too hard, Joe. He did n't mean t' do any harm,» said Troutt, who had followed Ed down to the store. «I guess the young feller 'll come out all right. Just go kind o' easy till we see how he comes out. If he dies, why, it 'll haf t' be looked into.»

Ed turned pale and swallowed hastily. «If he should die!» He would be a murderer; he knew that hate was in his heart. He shivered again as he remembered the man's white face with the bright red stream flowing down behind his ear and over his cheek. It almost seemed to him that he *had* struck him, so close had the accident followed upon the fall of his whip.

III.

ALBERT sank into a feverish sleep that night, with a vague perception of four figures in the room—Maud, her mother, Hartley, and the young doctor. When he awoke fully in the morning his head felt prodigiously hot and heavy.

It was early dawn, and the lamp was burning brightly. Outside, a man's feet could be heard on the squealing snow—a sound which told how still and cold it was. A team passed with a jingle of bells.

Albert raised his head and looked about. Hartley was lying on the sofa, rolled up in his overcoat and some extra quilts. He had lain down at last, worn with watching. Albert felt a little weak, and fell back on his pillow, thinking about the strange night he had passed—a night more filled with strange happenings than the afternoon.

His sleep had been broken by the most vivid and exciting dreams, and through these visions had moved the figures of Hartley, the doctor, and Maud and her mother. He had a confused idea of the night, but a very clear idea of the afternoon. He could see the sidewalks lined with faces, the sun shining on the snow, the old sorrel's side-flung head and open mouth; the sleigh rose under him again, and he felt the reins burn through his hands.

As the light grew in the room his mind cleared, and he began to feel quite like himself again. He lifted his muscular arm and opened and shut his hand, saying aloud in his old boyish manner:

«I guess I 'm all here.»

«What 's that?» called Hartley, rolling out of bed. «Did you ask for anything?»

«No—yes; gimme some water, Jim; my mouth is dry as a powder-mill.»

«How yeh feelin', anyway, pardner?» said Hartley, as he brought the water.

«First-rate, Jim; I guess I 'll be all right.»

«Well, I guess you 'd better keep quiet.»

Albert rose partly, assisted by his friend, and drank from the glass a moment; then fell back on his pillow.

«I don't feel s' well when I sit up.»

«Well, don't, then; stay right there where you are. Oh-um!» gaped Hartley, stretching himself; «it 's about time f'r breakfast, I guess. Want y'r hands washed and y'r hair combed?»

«I guess I ain't reduced to *that* yet.»

«Well, I guess y' *be*, old man. Now keep *quiet*, or have I got t' make yeh?» he asked in a threatening tone which made Albert smile. He wondered if Hartley had n't been sitting up most of the night; but if he had, he showed little effect of it, for he began to sing a comic song as he pulled on his boots.

He threw on his coat next, and went out into the kitchen, returning soon with some hot water, with which he began to bathe the wounded boy's face and hands as tenderly as a woman.

«There; now I guess you 're in shape f'r grub—feel any like grub?—Come in,» he called in answer to a knock on the door.

Mrs. Welsh entered.

«How is he?» she whispered anxiously.

«Oh, I 'm all right,» cried Albert. «Bring me a plate of pancakes, quick!»

Mrs. Welsh turned to Hartley with a startled expression, but Hartley's grin assured her.

«I 'm glad to find you so much better,» she said, going to his bedside. «I 've hardly slep', I was so much worried about you.»

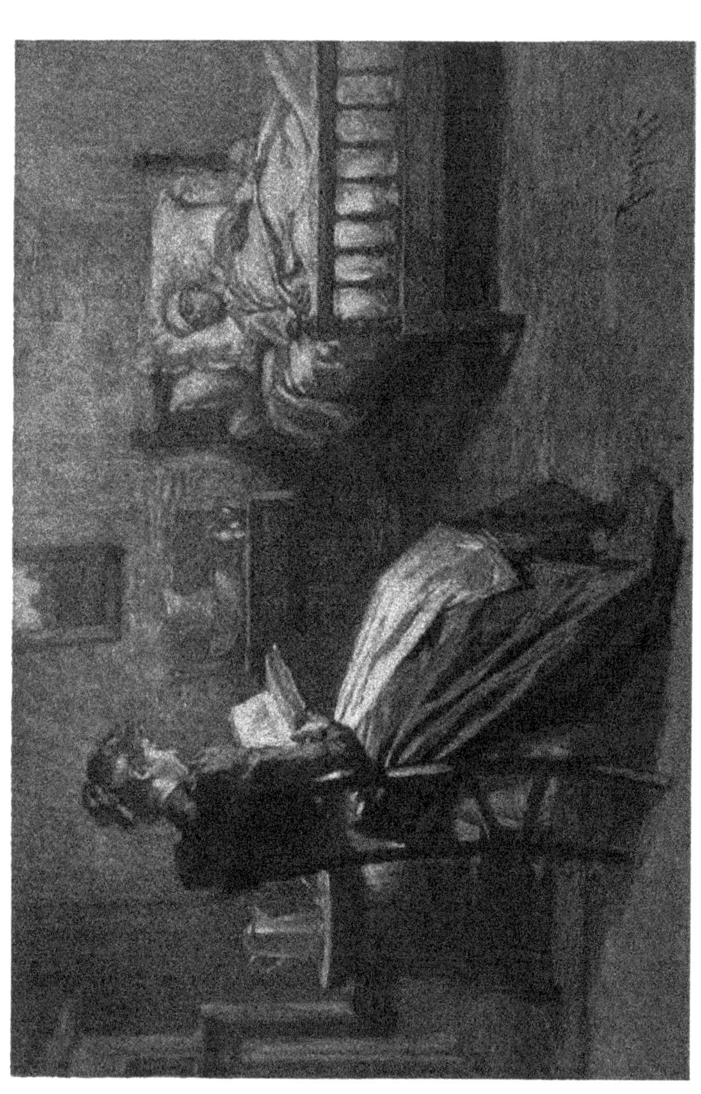

It was very sweet to feel her fingers in his hair, as his mother would have caressed him.

« I guess I had n't better take off the bandages till the doctor comes, if you 're comfortable. Your breakfast is ready, Mr. Hartley, and I 'll bring something for Albert.»

Another knock a few minutes later, and Maud entered with a platter, followed closely by her mother, who carried some tea and milk.

Maud came forward timidly, but when he turned his eyes on her and said in a cheery voice, «Good morning, Miss Welsh!» she flamed out in rosy color and recoiled. She had expected to see him pale, dull-eyed, and with a weak voice, but there was little to indicate invalidism in his firm greeting. She gave place to Mrs. Welsh, who prepared his breakfast. She was smitten dumb by this turn of affairs; she hardly dared look at him as he sat propped up in bed. The crimson trimming on his shirt-front seemed like streams of blood; his head, swathed in bandages, made her shudder. But aside from these few suggestions of wounding, there was little of the horror of the previous day left. He did not look so pale and worn as the girl herself.

However, though he was feeling absurdly well, there was a good deal of bravado in his tone and manner, for he ate but little, and soon sank back on the bed.

«I feel better when my head is low,» he explained in a faint voice.

«Can't I do something?» asked the girl, her courage reviving as she saw how ill and faint he really was. His eyes were closed, and he looked the invalid now.

«I guess you better write to his folks.»

«No; don't do that,» he said, opening his eyes; «it will only do them harm, an' me no good. I 'll be all right in a few days. You need n't waste your time on me; Hartley 'll wait on me.»

«Mr. Lohr, how can you say such cruel—»

«Don't mind him now,» said Mrs. Welsh. «I 'm his mother now, and he 's goin' to do just as I tell him to; ain't you, Albert?»

He dropped his eyelids in assent, and went off in a doze. It was all very pleasant to be thus treated. Hartley was devotion itself, and the doctor removed his bandages with the care and deliberation of a man with a moderate practice; besides, he considered Albert a personal friend.

Hartley, after the doctor had gone, said with some hesitation:

«Well, now, pard, I *ought* to go out and see a couple o' fellows I promised t' meet this morning.»



«All right, Jim; all right. You go right ahead on business; I 'm goin' t' sleep, anyway, and I 'll be all right in a day or two.»

«Well, I will; but I 'll run in every hour 'r two and see if you don't want something. You 're in good hands, anyway, when I 'm gone.»

«WON'T you read to me?» pleaded Albert in the afternoon, when Maud came in with her mother to brush up the room. «It 's getting rather slow business layin' here like this. Course I can't ask Jim to stay and read all the time, and he 's a bad reader, anyway; won't you?»

«Shall I, mother?»

«Why, of course, Maud!»

So Maud got a book, and sat down over by the stove, quite distant from the bed, and read to him from «The Lady of the Lake,» while the mother, like a piece of tireless machinery, moved about the house at the never-ending succession of petty drudgeries which wear the heart and soul out of so many wives and mothers, making life to them a pilgrimage from stove to pantry, from pantry to cellar, and from cellar to garret—a life that deadens and destroys, coarsens and narrows, till the flesh and bones are warped to the expression of the wronged and cheated soul.

Albert's selfishness was in a way excusable. He enjoyed beyond measure the sound of the girl's soft voice and the sight of her graceful head bent over the page. He lay, looking and listening dreamily, till the voice and the sunlit head were lost in his deep, sweet sleep.

The girl sat with closed book, looking at his face as he slept. It was a curious study to her, a young man—*this* young man, asleep. His brown lashes lay on his cheek; his facial lines were as placid as a child's. As she looked she gained courage to go over softly and look down on him. How boyish he seemed! How little to be feared! How innocent, after all!

As she looked she thought of him the day before, with closed eyes, a ghastly stream of blood flowing down and soaking her dress. She shuddered. His hands, clean and strong and white, lay out on the coverlet, loose and open, the fingers fallen into graceful lines. Abruptly a boy outside gave a shout, and she leaped away with a sudden spring that left her pale and breathless. As she paused in the door and looked back at the undisturbed sleeper, she smiled, and the pink came back into her thin face.

Albert's superb young blood began to assert itself, and on the afternoon of the second day he was able to sit in his rocking-chair before the fire and read a little, though he professed that his eyes were not strong, in order that Maud should read for him. This she did as often as she could leave her other work, which was «not half often enough,» the invalid grumbled.

«More than you deserve,» she found courage to say.

Hartley let nothing interfere with the book business, and the popular sympathy for Albert he coined into dollars remorselessly.

«You take it easy,» he kept saying to his partner; «don't you worry—your pay goes on just the same. You 're doing well right where you are. By jinks! biggest piece o' luck,» he went on, half in earnest. «Why, I can't turn around without taking an order—fact! Turned in a book on the livery bill—that 's all right. We 'll make a clear hundred dollars out o' that little bump o' yours.»

«Little bump! Say, now, that 's—»

«Keep it up—put it on! Don't get up in a hurry. I don't need you to canvass, and I guess you enjoy this 'bout as well.» He ended with a sly wink and cough.

Yes; the convalescence was delicious; afterward it grew to be one of the sweetest weeks of his life. Maud reading to him, bringing his food, and singing for him—yes; all that marred it was the stream of people who came to inquire how he was getting along. The sympathy was largely genuine, as Hartley could attest, but it bored the invalid. He had rather be left in quiet with Walter Scott and Maud, the drone of the long descriptive passages being a sure soporific.

He did not say, as an older person might, that she was not to be held accountable for what she did under the stress and tumult of that day; but he unconsciously did so regard her actions, led to do so by the changed conditions. In the light of common day it was hurrying to be a dream.

At the end of a week he was quite himself again, though he still had difficulty in wearing his hat, as he joked. It was not till the second Sunday after the accident that he appeared in the dining-room for the first time, with a large traveling-cap concealing the suggestive bandages. He looked pale and thin, but his eyes danced with joy.

Maud's eyes dilated with instant solicitude. The rest sprang up in surprise, with shouts of delight, as hearty as brethren.

«Ginger! I 'm glad t' see yeh!» said Troutt, so sincerely that he looked almost winning to the boy. The rest crowded around, shaking hands.

«Oh, I 'm on deck again.»

Ed Brann came in a moment later with his brother, and there was a significant little pause—a pause which grew painful till Albert turned and saw Brann, and called out:

«Hello, Ed! How are yeh? Did n't know you were here.»

As he held out his hand, Brann, his face purple with shame and embarrassment, lumbered heavily across the room and took it, muttering some poor apology.

«Hope y' don't blame me.»

«Naw; course not—fortune o' war. Nobody to blame; just my carelessness. Yes; I 'll take turkey,» he said to Maud, as he sank into the seat of honor at the head of the table.

Then the rest laughed and took seats, but Brann remained standing near Albert's chair. He had not finished yet.

«I 'm mighty glad yeh don't lay it up against me, Lohr; an' I want 'o say the doctor's bill is all right; you un'erstand, it 's *all right.*»

Albert looked at him a moment in surprise. He knew this, coming from a man like Brann, meant more than a thousand prayers from a ready apologist; it was a terrible victory, and he made it as easy for his rival as possible.

«Oh, all right, Ed; only I 'd calculated to cheat him out o' part of it—that is, turn in a couple o' Blaine's ‹Twenty Years› on the bill.»

Hartley roared, and the rest joined in, but not even Albert perceived all that it meant. It meant that the young savage had surrendered his claim in favor of the man he had all but killed. The struggle had been prodigious, but he had snatched victory out of defeat; his better nature had conquered.

No one ever gave him credit for it; and when he went West in the spring, people said his love for Maud had been superficial. In truth, he had loved the girl as sincerely as he had hated his rival. That he could rise out of the barbaric in his love and hate was heroic.

When Albert went to ride again, it was on melting snow, with the slowest horse Troutt had. Maud was happier than she had been since she left school, and fuller of color and singing. She dared not let a golden moment pass now without hearing it ring full, and she did not dare to think how short this day of happiness might be.

## IV.

AT the end of the fifth week there was a suspicion of spring in the wind as it swept the southern exposure of the valley. February was drawing to a close, and there was more than a suggestion of spring in the rapidly melting snow which still lay on the hills and under the cedars and tamaracks in the swamps. Patches of green grass, appearing on the sunny side of the road where the snow had melted, led to predictions of spring from the loafers beginning to sun themselves on the salt-barrels and shoe-boxes outside the stores.

A group sitting about the blacksmith shop were talking it.

«It 's an' early seedin'—now mark my words,» said Troutt, as he threw his knife into the soft ground at his feet. «The sun is crossing the line earlier this spring than it did last.»

«Yes; an' I heard a crow to-day makin' that kind of a—a spring noise that kind o'—I d' know what—kind o' goes all through a feller.»

«And there 's Uncle Sweeney, an' that settles it; spring 's comin' sure!» said Troutt, pointing at an old man, much bent, hobbling down the street like a symbolic figure of the old year.

«When *he* gits out the frogs ain't fur behind.»

«We 'll be gittin' on to the ground by next Monday,» said Sam Dingley to a crowd who were seated on the newly painted harrows and seeders which «Svend & Johnson» had got out ready for the spring trade. «Svend & Johnson's Agricultural Implement Depot» was on the north side of the street, and on a spring day the yard was one of the pleasantest loafing-places that could be imagined, especially if one wished company.

Albert wished to be alone. Something in the touch and tone of this spring afternoon made him restless and full of strange thoughts. He took his way out along the road which followed the river-bank, and in the outskirts of the village threw himself down on a bank of grass which the snows had protected, and which was already a tinge of green because of its wealth of sun.

The willows had thrown out their tiny light green flags, though their roots were under the ice, and some of the hardwood twigs were tinged with red. There was a faint, peculiar but powerful odor of uncovered earth in the air, and the touch of the wind was like a caress from a moist magnetic hand.

The boy absorbed the light and heat of the sun as some wild thing might, his hat over his face, his hands folded on his breast; he lay as still as a statue. He did not listen at first, he only felt; but at length he rose on his elbow and listened. The ice cracked and fell along the bank with a long, hollow, booming crash; a crow cawed, and a jay answered it from the willows below. A flight of sparrows passed, twittering innumerably. The boy shuddered with a strange, wistful longing and a realization of the flight of time.

He could have wept, he could have sung; he only shuddered and lay silent under the stress of that strange, sweet passion that quickened his heart, deepened his eyes, and made his breath come and go with a quivering sound. Across the dazzling blue arch of the sky the crow flapped, sending down his prophetic, jubilant note; the wind, as soft and sweet as April, stirred in his hair; the hills, deep in their dusky blue, seemed miles away; and the voices of the care-free skaters on the melting ice of the river below came to the ear subdued to a unity with the scene.

Suddenly a fear seized upon the boy—a horror! Life, life was passing! Life that can be lived only once, and lost, is lost forever! Life, that fatal gift of the Invisible Powers to man—a path with youth and joy and hope at its eastern gate, and despair, regret, and death at its low western portal!

The boy caught a glimpse of his real significance—a gnat, a speck in the sun: a boy facing the millions of great and wise and wealthy. He leaped up, clasping his hands.

«Oh, I *must* work! I must n't stay here; I must get back to my studies. Life is slipping by me, and I am doing nothing, being nothing!»

His face, as pale as death, absolutely shone with his passionate resolution, and his hands were clenched in a silent, inarticulate desire.

But on his way back he met the jocund party of skaters going home from the river, and with the easy shift and change of youth joined in their ringing laughter. The weird power of the wind's voice was gone, and he was the unthinking boy again; but the problem was only put off, not solved.

He had a suspicion of it one night when Hartley said, «Well, pardner, we 're getting 'most ready to pull out. Some way I always get restless when these warm days begin. Want 'o be moving some way.»

This was as sentimental as Hartley ever got; or if he ever felt more sentiment, he concealed it carefully.

«I s'pose it must 'a' been in spring that those old chaps, on their steeds and in their steel shirts, started out for the Holy Land or to rescue some damsel, hey?» he ended, with a grin. «Now, that 's the way I feel—just like striking out for, say, Oshkosh. This has been a big strike here, sure 's you live; that little piece of lofty tumbling was a big boom, and no mistake. Why, your share o' this campaign will be a hundred and twenty dollars sure.»

«More 'n I 've earned,» replied Bert.

«No, it ain't. You 've done your duty like a man. Done as much in your way as I have. Now, if you want to try another county with me, say so. I 'll make a thousand dollars this year out o' this thing.»

«I guess I 'll go back to school.»

«All right; don't blame you at all.»

«I guess, with what I can earn for father, I can pull through the year. I *must* get back. I 'm awfully obliged to you, Jim.»

«That 'll do on that,» said Hartley, shortly; «you don't owe me anything. We 'll finish delivery to-morrow, and be ready to pull out on Friday or Sat.»

There was an acute pain in Albert's breast somewhere; he had not analyzed his case at all, and did not now, but the idea of going affected him strongly. It had been so pleasant, that daily return to a lovely girlish presence.

«Yes, sir,» Hartley was going on; «I 'm going to just quietly leave a book on her center-table. I don't know as it 'll interest her much, but it 'll show we appreciate the grub, and so on. By jinks! you don't seem to realize what a worker that woman is. Up five o'clock in the morning— By the way, you 've been going around with the girl a good deal, and she 's introduced you to some first-rate sales; now if you want 'o leave her a little something, make it a morocco copy, and charge it to the firm.»

Albert knew that he meant well, but he could n't, somehow, help saying ironically:

«Thanks; but I guess *one* copy of Blaine's ‹Twenty Years› will be enough in the house, especially—»

«Well, give her anything you please, and charge it up to the firm. I don't insist on Blaine; only suggested that because—»

«I guess I can stand the expense of my own.»

«I did n't say you could n't, man! But *I* want a hand in this thing. Don't be so turrible keen t' snap a feller up,» said Hartley, turning on him. «What the thunder is the matter of you anyway? I like the girl, and she 's been good to us all round; she tended you like an angel—»

«There, there! That 's enough o' that,» put in Albert, hastily. «F'r God's sake don't whang away on that string forever, as if I did n't know it!»

Hartley stared at him as he turned away.

«Well, by jinks! What *is* the matter o' you?»

He was too busy to dwell upon it much, but concluded his partner was homesick.

Albert was beginning to have a vague under-consciousness of his real feeling toward the girl, but he fought off the acknowledgment of it as long as possible. His mind moved in a circle, coming back to the one point ceaselessly,—a dreary prospect, in which the slender girl-figure had no place, —and each time the prospect grew more intolerably blank, and the pain in his heart more acute and throbbing.

When he faced her that night, after they had returned from a final skating-party down on the river, he was as far from a solution as ever. He had avoided all reference to their separation, and now he stood as a man might at the parting of two paths, saying: «I will not choose; I cannot choose. I will wait for some sign, some chance thing, to direct me.»

They stood opposite each other, each feeling that there was more to be said; the girl tender, her eyes cast down, holding her hands to the fire; he shivering, but not with cold. He had a vague knowledge of the vast importance of the moment, and he hesitated to speak.

«It 's almost spring again, is n't it? And you 've been here—» she paused, and looked up with a daring smile—«seems as if you 'd been here always.»

It was about half-past eight. Mrs. Welsh was setting her bread in the kitchen; they could hear her moving about. Hartley was down-town finishing up his business.

Albert's throat grew dry, and his limbs trembled. His pause was ominous; the girl's smile died away as he took a seat without looking at her.

«Well, Maud, I suppose—you know—we 're going away to-morrow.»

«Oh, must you? But you 'll come back?»

«I don't expect to—I don't see how.»

«Oh, don't say that!» cried the girl, her face as white as silver, her clasped hands straining.

«I must—I must!» he muttered, not looking at her, not daring to see her face.

«Oh, what can I do—*we* do, without you! I can't bear it!»

She stopped, and sank back into a chair, her breath coming heavily from her twitching lips, the unnoticed tears falling from her staring, pitiful, wild, appealing eyes, her hands nervously twisting her gloves.

There was a long silence. Each was undergoing a self-revelation; each was trying to face a future without the other.

«I must go!» he repeated aimlessly, mechanically.

The girl's heavy breathing deepened into a wild little moaning sound, inexpressibly pitiful, her hungry eyes fixed on his face. She gave way first, and flung herself down upon her knees at his side, her hands seeking his neck.

«Albert, I can't *live* without you now! Take me with you! Don't leave me!»

He stooped suddenly and took her in his arms, raised her, and kissed her hair.

«I did n't mean it, Maud; I 'll never leave you—never! Don't cry!»

She drew his face down to hers and kissed it, then turned her face to his breast and laughed and cried. There was a silence; then joy and confidence came back again.

«I know now what you meant,» the girl cried gaily, raising herself and looking into his face; «you were trying to scare me, and make me show how much I—cared for you —first!» There was a soft smile on her lips and a tender light in her eyes. «But I don't mind it.»

«I guess I did n't know myself what I meant,» he said, with a grave smile.

When Mrs. Welsh came in they were sitting on the sofa, talking in low voices of their future. He was grave and subdued, while she was radiant with love and hope. The future had no terrors for her. All plans were good and successful now. But the boy unconsciously felt the gravity of life somehow deepened by his love.

«Why, Maud!» Mrs. Welsh exclaimed, «what is—»

«Oh, mother, I'm so happy—just as happy as a bird!» she cried, rushing into her mother's arms.

«Why, why!—what is it? You 're crying, dear!»

«No, I 'm not; I 'm laughing—see!»

Mrs. Welsh turned her dim eyes on the girl, who shook the tears from her lashes with the action of a bird shaking water from its wings. She seemed to shake off her trouble at the same moment. Mrs. Welsh understood perfectly.

«I 'm very glad, too, dearie,» she said simply, looking at the young man with mother-love irradiating her worn face. Albert went to her, and she kissed him, while the happy girl put her arms about them both in an ecstatic hug.

«*Now* you 've got a son, mother.»

«But I 've lost a daughter—my first-born.»

«Oh, wait till you hear our plans!»

«He 's going to settle down here, are n't you, Albert?»

Then they sat down, all three, and had a sweet, intimate talk of an hour, full of plans and hopes and confidences.

At last he kissed the radiant girl good night, and going into his own room, sat down by the stove, and, watching the flicker of the flame through the chinks, pondered on the change that had come into his life.

Already he sighed with the stress of care, the press of thought, which came upon him. The longing uneasiness of the boy had given place to another unrest—the unrest of the man who must face the world in earnest now, planning for food and shelter; and all plans included Maud.

To go back to school was out of the question. To expect help from his father, overworked and burdened with debt, was impossible. He must go to work, and go to work to aid *her*. A living must be wrung from this town. All the home and all the property Mrs. Welsh had were here, and wherever Maud went the mother must follow; she could not live without her.

He was in the midst of the turmoil when Hartley came in, humming the «Mulligan Guards.»

«In the dark, hey?»

«Completely in the dark.»

«Well, light up, light up!»

«I 'm trying to.»

«What the deuce do you mean by that tone? What 's been going on here since my absence?»

Albert did not reply, and Hartley shuffled about after a match, lighted the lamp, threw his coat and hat in the corner, and then said:

«Well, I 've got everything straightened up. Been freezing out old Daggett; the old skeesix has been promisin' f'r a week, and I just said, ‹Old man, I 'll camp right down with you here till you fork over,› and he did. By the way, everybody I talked with to-day about leaving said, ‹What 's Lohr going to do with that girl?› I told 'em I did n't know; do you? It seems you 've been thicker 'n I supposed.»

«I 'm going to marry her,» said Albert, calmly, but his voice sounded strangely alien.

«What 's that?» yelled Hartley.

«Sh! don't raise the neighbors. I'm going to marry her.» He spoke quietly, but there was a peculiar numbness creeping over him.

«Well, by jinks! When? Say, looky here! Well, I swanny!» exclaimed Hartley, helplessly. «When?»

«Right away; some time this summer—June, maybe.»

Hartley thrust his hands into his trousers

pockets, stretched out his legs, and stared at his friend in vast amaze.

«You 're givin' me guff!»

«I 'm in dead earnest.»

«I thought you was going through college all so fast?»

«Well, I 've made up my mind it ain't much use to try,» replied Albert, listlessly.

«What y' goin' t' do here, or are y' goin' t' take the girl away with yeh?»

«She can't leave her mother. We 'll run this boarding-house for the present. I 'll try for the principalship of the school here. Raff is going to resign, he says; if I can't get that, I 'll get into a law office here. Don't worry about me.»

«But why go into this so quick? Why not put it off fifteen or twenty years?» asked Hartley, trying to get back to cheerful voice.

«What would be the use? At the end of a year I 'd be just about as poor as I am now.»

«Can't y'r father step in and help you?»

«No. There are three boys and two girls, all younger than me, to be looked out for, and he has all he can carry. Besides, *she* needs me right here and right now. Two delicate women struggling along; suppose one of 'em should fall sick? I tell you they need me, and if I can do anything to make life easy, or easier, I 'm going t' do it. Besides,» he ended in a peculiar tone, «we don't feel as if we could live apart much longer.»

«But, great Scott! man, you can't—»

«Now, hold on, Jim! I 've thought this thing all over, and I 've made up my mind. It ain't any use to go on talking about it. What good would it do me to go to school another year, come out without a dollar, and no more fitted for earning a living for her than I am now? And, besides all that, I could n't draw a free breath thinking of her here workin' away to keep things moving, liable at any minute to break down.»

Hartley gazed at him in despair, and with something like awe. It was a tremendous transformation in the young, ambitious student. He felt in a way responsible for the calamity, and that he ought to use every effort to bring the boy to his senses.

Like most men in America, and especially Western men, he still clung to the idea that a man was entirely responsible for his success or failure in life. He had not admitted that conditions of society might be so adverse that only men of most exceptional endowments, and willing and able to master many of the best and deepest and most sacred of their inspirations and impulses, could succeed.

Of the score of specially promising young fellows who had been with him at school, seventeen had dropped out and down. Most of them had married and gone back to farming, or to earn a precarious living in the small, dull towns where farmers trade and traders farm. Conditions were too adverse; they simply weakened, slipped slowly back into dullness and an ox-like or else a fretful patience. Thinking of these men, and thinking their failure due to themselves alone, Hartley could not endure the idea of his friend adding one more to the list of failures. He sprang up at last.

«Say, Bert, you might just as well hang y'rself and done with it! Why, it 's suicide! I can't allow it. I started in at college bravely, and failed because I 'd let it go too long. I could n't study—could n't git down to it; but you—why, old man, I 'd *bet* on you!» He had a tremor in his voice. «I hate like thunder to see you give up your plans. Say, you can't afford to do this; it 's too much to pay.»

«No, it ain't.»

«I say it is. What do you get, in—»

«I think so much o' her that—»

«Oh, nonsense! You 'd get over this in a week.»

«Jim!» called Albert, warningly, sharply.

«All right,» said Jim, in the tone of a man who felt that it was all wrong—«all right; but the time 'll come when you 'll wish I 'd— You ain't doin' the girl enough good to make up for the harm you 're doin' yourself.» He broke off again, and said in a tone of peculiar meaning: «I 'm done. I 'm all through, and I c'n see you 're through with Jim Hartley. Why, Bert, look here— No? All right!»

«Darn curious,» he muttered to himself, «that boy should get caught just at this time, and not with some one o' those girls in Madison. Well, it 's none o' my funeral,» he ended, with a sigh; for it had stirred him to the bottom of his sunny nature, after all. A dozen times, as he lay there beside his equally sleepless companion, he started to say something more in deprecation of the step, but each time stifled the opening word into a groan.

It would not be true to say that love had come to Albert Lohr as a relaxing influence, but it had changed the direction of his energies so radically as to make his whole life seem weaker and lower. As long as his love-dreams went out toward a vague and ideal woman, supposedly higher and grander than himself, he was spurred on to face the terrible sheer escarpment of social eminence; but when he met, by accident, the actual woman who was to inspire his future efforts, the difficulties he faced took on solid reality.

His aspirations fell to the earth, their wings clipped, and became, perforce, submissive beasts at the plow. The force that moved so much of his thought was transformed into other energy. Whether it were a wise step he did not know; he certainly knew it was right.

The table was very gay at dinner next day. Maud was standing at the highest point of her girlhood dreams. Her flushed face and shining eyes made her seem almost a child, and Hartley wondered at her, and relented a little in the face of such happiness. Her face was turned to Albert in an unconscious, beautiful way; she had nothing to conceal now.

Mrs. Welsh was happy, too, but a little tearful in an unobtrusive way. Troutt had his jokes, of course, not very delicate, but of good intention. In fact, they were as flags and trumpets to the young people. Mrs. Welsh had confided in him, telling him to be secret; but the finesse of his joking could not fail to reveal everything he knew.

But Maud cared little. She was filled with a sort of tender boldness; and Albert, in the delight of the hour, gave himself up wholly to a trust in the future and to the fragrance and music of love.

«They 're gay as larks now,» thought Hartley to himself, as he joined in the laughter; «but that won't help 'em any, ten years from now.»

He could hardly speak next day as he shook hands at the station with his friend.

«Good-by, ol' man; I hope it 'll come out all right, but I 'm afraid— But there! I promised not to say anything about it. Good-by till we meet in Congress,» he ended in a lamentable attempt at being funny.

«Can't you come to the wedding, Jim? We 've decided on June. You see, they need a man around the house, so we— You 'll come, won't you, old fellow? And don't mind my being a little crusty last night.»

«Oh, yes; I 'll come,» Jim said, in a tone which concealed a desire to utter one more protest.

«It 's no use; that ends him, sure 's I 'm a thief. He 's jumped into a hole and pulled the hole in after him. A man can't marry a family like that at his age, and pull out of it. He *may*, but I doubt it. Well, as I remarked before, it 's none o' my funeral so long as *he* 's satisfied.»

But he said it with a painful lump in his throat, and he could not bring himself to feel that Albert's course was right, and felt himself to be somehow culpable in the case.

ALBERT and Maud still live in the homestead in Tyre. In the five years that have elapsed since that parting with Hartley he has been a hard worker as principal of the village school. His friends say he ought to be in a larger field of labor, and he has sweet dreams of doing something in the great, splendid world which he realizes at times is sweeping by him; but three little mouths have come into the world demanding bread, and three pairs of sweet, childish eyes hold him prisoner, though a willing one.

*Hamlin Garland.*

# A WOOD-BIRD'S WHIM.

HOLLOW of a dead man's breast,
In a mighty wood—
Here 's a place to make a nest
And to warm a brood!

Bees through its caressing vines,
Honey-heavy, flit;
Every star of God that shines
Sees the way to it.

Buds which at their beauty blush
Weep their dews out here;
And the snake—I pray you, hush!
Something slides a-near.

Was he poet?—he to whom
All these things have paid
Reverent rites in sacred gloom,
Loving, not afraid?

He was poet. What dark whim
Set his heart to wings?—
Oh, the song that wasted him
Now the wild bird sings!

*Sarah Piatt.*

# THE LADIES OF LLANGOLLEN.

TO the picturesque little town of Llangollen, by the Dee side, in the year 1779, came two charming Irish ladies who proposed to spend their days in the seclusion of the lovely vale.

Lady Eleanor Charlotte Butler, the older of the two, was about forty years of age, fresh, vigorous, and handsome, when she wearied of the world, and especially of matrimonial offers, and longed for a quiet residence apart from the conventionalities of the town. Just then she chanced to meet a beautiful girl who had recently been introduced to the fashionable society of Dublin, and the two soon became inseparable friends. The Hon. Sara Ponsonby listened with eager interest to her friend's romantic plan for a life of seclusion; and as one of Lady Eleanor's suitors was particularly urged upon her attention at this time, the ladies decided to take matters in their own hands. They ran away in undignified haste; but as they had neglected to take a sufficient supply of money, they readily yielded to the entreaties of pursuing relatives, and returned.

A few weeks later, so the story goes, a lady of fine presence, accompanied by a maid-servant and a tall, handsome footman in top-boots and livery, took the boat at Dublin for Holyhead; and when well on their way the footman was metamorphosed into a handsome girl, none other than the Hon. Sara Ponsonby. Mary Carryl, a faithful servant, herself a notable character, shared their flight. After some deliberation they selected a beautiful site in Llangollen, in North Wales, and built a cottage, which remains to-day as much an object of interest to readers and travelers as it has ever been since it was chosen and named «a place of sweet and blessed retirement» by the Ladies of the Vale.

Both ladies were highly connected, particularly Lady Eleanor, who was nearly related to that Duke of Ormonde who commanded the forces of Charles I in Ireland; and she was fond of recounting, in her quiet home, the stirring deeds of her illustrious kinsfolk. The attachment of the pair was ardent and strong, and their literary tastes were similar. They desired only to be allowed to live and read and study in each other's society; and after a family council of relatives had met and recognized the uselessness of further opposition, a comfortable annuity was settled upon them, and they were left to follow the dictates of their own fancy.

The ladies were of unusually fine appearance. Lady Eleanor, the stronger-minded of the two, is described as being small, brisk, plump, with a round, fair face and glowing health, when they first came to Llangollen; while her friend was tall and fair, with a graceful, elegant figure, a beautiful face, and sweet womanly features. They adopted a costume at once comfortable, serviceable, and at the time becoming, from which they never varied. Each wore a heavy dark-blue riding-habit with stiffly starched neckcloth, a gentleman's hat and boots, and a profusion of rings and brooches. On special occasions Lady Eleanor wore somewhat conspicuous ornaments—the cordon of the Order of St. Louis and a golden lily almost of natural size, presents from the Bourbon family.

The villa which they erected at Plas Newydd was unlike any known architectural construction, and the plan of it must have originated in the brains of the owners. The present-day visitor irreverently compares it to an enormous handsomely carved wardrobe. The low, two-storied front is inclosed by an oaken palisade, while doors and windows are richly ornamented with carvings of religious, historical, and mythological figures in picturesque confusion. Abraham, Venus, Julius Cæsar, and the apostles keep friendly company in the decorations of Plas Newydd. Rich carvings ornament also the interior of the house. There are only four rooms, small and comfortable: «the kitchen as elegant in its way,» writes a visitor, «as the lightsome little dining-room,» which contrasted well with the gloomy but superior grace of the library just beyond. This library, which was decorated in the Gothic style, had painted-glass windows, and was lighted by a curious sort of prismatic lantern of cut glass of various colors, in which were inclosed two lamps and their reflectors. This occupied the elliptical arch of the doorway, and, when lighted, resembled a small but brilliant volcano. A large Æolian harp was placed in one window. Books by the best authors of all lands, portraits of friends, and rare and curious articles of bric-à-brac from all parts of the world, brought or sent to them by their many visitors, were the ornaments of the little library.

The grounds of Plas Newydd were delightfully laid out with rural walks and bridges, rose hedges, fountains, temples, grottos, and a tiny but complete glen with a brook running through it. The rarest and finest fruit-trees and choice flowers were a passion with the ladies, and no weeds were permitted to grow in their small domain. A commonplace cow lived somewhere, and there were a dovecote, a house for robins, and a quaint circular dairy in which a curious churn produced a pat

FROM AN OLD PRINT.

LADY ELEANOR BUTLER AND THE HONORABLE SARA PONSONBY.

of butter every morning for the breakfast of the ladies. Lady Eleanor had charge of the estate, superintending, and often assisting in the affairs of the garden, while Miss Ponsonby looked after the house.

The daily life of the ladies was one of such originality, freedom from the ordinary cares of humanity, and indifference to fashion and conventionalities, that they soon became better known than if they had remained in society. They took long walks and drives in the country; and retained a lively interest in all the affairs of the great world, received many newspapers and letters, remembered all the births, deaths, and marriages in families of consequence, and ordered the best editions of French, English, and Italian books, which they had put into the finest of bindings, and treasured in their lattice-guarded bookcases. Lady Eleanor had been educated in a foreign convent, and shared with Miss Ponsonby a great fondness for French and Italian authors. Much time was given to drawing, painting, and embroidering.



Correspondence with distinguished people in various parts of Great Britain and the Continent formed a large portion of the daily interest of the ladies; and with commendable thrift they usually had on hand a package of envelops waiting to be franked by the first visitor who had the franking privilege at his disposal. The store-closets at Plas Newydd were filled with the familiar, agreeable letters which were a distinguishing feature of the literature of those days. The Marquis of Londonderry writes from Paris to express his admiration for the retreat in the vale; declares that should he be exiled from his country, he would certainly rebuild Dinas Bran's old castle and become their neighbor; and adds the startling intelligence that the king and queen have fled from Paris, no one knows whither. Edmund Burke writes of his delightful remembrance of the ladies' hospitality in the «elegant retirement of Llangollen.» Viscount Bolingbroke acknowledges hospitalities, and begs leave to present a few plants which he had not observed in the Plas Newydd grounds. The wife of Sir Humphry Davy tells of her friend Miss Edgeworth; of the approaching visit of Mme. de Staël, who will, she fears, find «our English opinions in trifles opposite to the full enjoyment of society»; and of Lord Byron, who talks of Greece «with the feelings of a poet, and the intentions of a wanderer,» and who is to be introduced to Miss Edgeworth at a quiet breakfast. The Hon. George Canning announces that his daughter is soon to visit Llangollen, and reminds the ladies of their kind offer to send him a specimen of Llangollen mutton, adding: «My address is Foreign Office for mutton as well as for letters.» The Earl of Darnley presents a sonnet in honor of the gentle recluses; and Southey, from Keswick, acknowledges recent hospitalities by the gift of a new poem. There are several familiar notes from the Duke of Wellington, who first visited Llangollen as a boy with his grandmother, Lady Dungannon, and who gained his knowledge of Spanish from a prayer-book in that language given him by the Llangollen ladies, which he studied during a tedious voyage. The duke's

FROM AN OLD PRINT

IN THE LIBRARY.

mother was a frequent correspondent, and several of her letters appear directed to «Miss Butler, Llangollen, Salop Post, Oswestry Bag,» in which she describes at length her various attacks of toothache, and tells of Arthur's [1] wonderful good fortune in securing an appointment as aide-de-camp to Lord Buckingham, at ten shillings a day. She has to get the future hero of Waterloo ready for his departure, and says that he is really «a very charming young man,» and «wonderfully lucky.»

«Every person of consequence traveling in Wales takes letters to the Ladies of the Vale,» says a writer of the day. Among these was Miss Anne Seward, whose poetical works were edited by Sir Walter Scott, and from whose voluminous correspondence we glean some interesting facts about the daily life at Plas Newydd. It is of interest to recall that this same accomplished Miss Seward was the author of that «Monody on the Death of André» to which General Washington felt constrained to make an explanatory reply.

Another honored visitor at Plas Newydd was Mme. de Genlis, with Mlle. de Orléans and two companions. Mme. de Genlis had

[1] The Duke of Wellington.

been told by an Englishman that an example of pure and disinterested friendship was to be seen in a valley of North Wales, and the lively Frenchwoman procured letters of introduction and journeyed thither. She writes: «We were received with a grace, cordiality, and kindness of which it would be impossible for me to give an idea. . . . I could not turn my eyes away from these two ladies. . . . Both have the most engaging politeness and highly cultivated minds.» To her the place had an air of enchantment, and she went away, as did many another, envying the friends their happy, healthful life amid beautiful scenery, flowers, and trees, with intellectual pleasures, and the joys of a friendship in which the keenest critic could not detect a trace of weariness or interruption.

Courtesies were very properly withheld from curious visitors. Proper letters of introduction were the only defense against idle curiosity-seekers.

With the advance of years the ladies seem to have developed the eccentricities which would naturally follow their manner of living. They adopted dogs, cats, and parrots, and the little villa became a storehouse for all sorts of oddities.

In 1820, when Lady Eleanor was past eighty and her friend sixty-five, Charles Mathews, the celebrated actor, was playing at Oswestry, twelve miles from Llangollen, and the two ladies went to see him, having secured seats in one of the boxes. Their appearance so distracted the actor's attention that he continued his part with difficulty. «Though I had never seen them,» he says, «I instantaneously knew them. As they are seated, there is not one point to distinguish them from men—the dressing and powdering of the hair, their well-starched neckcloths, the upper part of their habits, which they always wear, even at a dinner party, and which are made precisely like men's coats. They looked exactly like two respectable superannuated old clergymen.» He accepted an invitation to visit the ladies at their cottage, and says that he longed to put Lady Eleanor in a glass case and take her away to show to his friends.

Five years later Sir Walter Scott and his son-in-law Lockhart paid a visit to Plas Newydd, and the latter gives a graphic description of the ladies as they then appeared.

In his «Briefe eines Verstorbenen,» Prince Pückler-Muskau writes of a charming visit which he paid to the two «noble, fashionable, and handsome ladies» who had decided to dwell as twin hermits; and gives a lively picture of the home and its mistresses.

Among their visitors the ladies also counted a certain Sir Alured, a handsome and interesting, but venerable man at this period. Here is a romance within a romance; for of this gallant gentleman it is said that one of the princesses fell desperately in love with him, and her father, poor old .eorge III, sent the too fascinating young man away to India, where there was war at the time, and whence, therefore, there was some likelihood that he would not return. But at eighty he came back, still handsome and fascinating, and was received with distinguished favor by the new king, who made him a field-marshal. Of the princess and her affection nothing more is learned.

Sir Alured had long known Lady Eleanor, —indeed, for aught I know to the contrary, he may have been one of the five despairing swains mentioned in that lady's obituary,—and once a year, usually in October, he came down to Llangollen to pay his respects to the two ladies, to whom the visit was always an occasion of consequence.

The death of Lady Eleanor was a grievous blow to the old man. He came the year following, however, but was less gay than usual; and it is even said that he neglected to bestow the usual parting kiss on his fair entertainer. The Hon. Sara promptly reminded him of the oversight, for which he at once made atonement.

Mary Carryl, the faithful servant, had died in 1809, making the first change that had occurred in the inmates of the household.

Each of the friends wished a picture of the other, but neither was willing to sit for her portrait. By some stratagem of a friend pictures of the two together was secured when the ladies were unaware.

In June, 1829, at the age of ninety, Lady Eleanor passed away; and although her friends surrounded Miss Ponsonby with every possible kindness, she refused to be comforted. She was seldom seen except by her domestics, and survived in her loneliness only eighteen months.

*Helen Marshall North.*

DRAWN BY GILBERT GAUL. ENGRAVED BY SAMUEL DAVIS.

# SUMMER AT CHRISTMAS-TIDE.

WITH PICTURES BY GILBERT GAUL.

THE first of next week will be Christmas day, and I am writing this in a temperature of eighty-two degrees, beside an open door which looks out on a mountain-side wooded with a thousand trees the name of not one of which, except the palms, am I familiar with; a soft cloud is breaking in aërial foam on the hilltop. I have just come in from the pasture, where I plucked and ate three or four wild oranges, the sweetest and juiciest in the world; I could have had, had I preferred them, a bunch of wild bananas. This morning I took a bath in a swimming-tank filled with cool water from a mountain spring. I am dressed in the thinnest possible woolen pajamas, and yet the exertion of writing produces a slight perspiration. The room is a partitioned-off corner of a veranda two of the walls of which are composed of green blinds, through which the afternoon breeze is faintly drawn. I hear the low murmur of the voices of negro women below, where yams are being peeled and fresh coffee (gathered in the plantation hard by) is being pounded. This has been a remarkably cool winter, and I have the certain knowledge that it never has been and never will be, at any time of year, colder than it is now, and am equally well assured that it never has or never will be more than three or four degrees warmer. There is a big jack-buzzard perched on the top of an enormous tree out yonder, and his mate is sailing high aloft on lazy but unweariable pinions, a veritable queen of effortless and inimitable flight. At the other end of the ornithological scale is a humming-bird, a slender, supple, long-tailed, needle-beaked, gleaming jewel of iridescent green feathers and whirring wings, plunging himself in and out of the blossoms of a scarlet-flowered tree, into the cups of which his slender body just fits. The sky is of a warmer and tenderer blue than I have ever seen in the North, and the mighty sunshine which irradiates it and all things below it seems twofold as luminous as ours. And all this, and the infinite other lovely things that I can see and feel but never portray or describe, are not a dream, but an immortal reality to which nothing written, spoken, photographed, or painted can do justice. You cannot believe it, you cannot comprehend it, until you behold it for yourself, live it, and

DRAWN BY GILBERT GAUL. ENGRAVED BY HENRY WOLF.

ALONG THE ROAD.

breathe it. You may read and listen and imagine from one year's end to another, but your first glimpse of the reality will show you that all was in vain. Fancy and hearsay can issue no passport to the enchanted gates of the Caribbean, nor bear the soul across the mystic line.

The English administration of Jamaica is a thing to be thankful for: there are law and order, excellent roads, comfortable houses, adequate police, lawn-tennis and cricket, plenty of manly, companionable English army and navy officers, and a governor who is strong, able, and genial. At the same time it would be folly to maintain that the island is producing a tenth part of the wealth that is latent in the soil and atmosphere, or that most of the wealth that is beginning to make its appearance is due to anything so much as to the American enterprise and capital which are opening up railways and cultivating fruits. Another serious fact, though not necessarily an unwelcome one, is that the island's four thousand square miles contain a population of six hundred thousand persons, twenty-five thousand of whom are white.

I have referred to the view toward the mountain on the north. Turning your head the other way, you may behold a prospect that is historic as well as beautiful. A great plain, six or seven miles in breadth, slopes gradually from the front garden to the shore of the sea; here a natural harbor, long and wide, is formed by a breakwater of sand planted with cocoa-palms and terminating on the right extremity in a broader space, on which is visible a little cluster of low buildings. Nothing could be more eloquent of peace and repose than this scene, which nevertheless has been the theater of some of the bloodiest, most dramatic, and most romantic passages of human history, as well as of one of the most terrific natural convulsions ever known. For that little group of houses on the sand-spit was once Port Royal; in that noble harbor once rendezvoused the fleets of the bucaneers; there were murders done, treasure was squandered and lost, crimes were perpetrated, vices rampant on a scale never surpassed in the annals of modern history. Here human passions in their most unrestrained and diabolic forms have reigned and raged unchecked; here wealth has achieved its apogee of splendor and wantonness; and here has fallen a retribution, as moralists will call it, sudden, awful, and sweeping beyond the power of thought to reproduce. During two centuries or more, in short, an amount of human energy and vicissitude characterized the history of little Jamaica, and especially of this little corner of it, which would amply have sufficed for an entire continent.

DRAWN BY GILBERT GAUL. ENGRAVED BY S. C. PUTNAM.

LANDING IN JAMAICA.

And of it all what traces now remain? The red-tiled roofs of Kingston are so shrouded in the verdure of palms and mangos and plantains as hardly to be visible from our elevation of seven hundred feet; the Port Royal of history is underground, or under water; green plantations and luxuriant shrubbery everywhere clothe the plain and the hills; Nature has turned the red blood of men into sap and leaf and blossom; she has long since forgotten the terrible story that still darkens the pages of the chronicle. We may regard this green oblivion either as a wise hint to us, or as an ironic smile, according to our creed and temperament. For my own part, the knowledge of what has been of horror and calamity only lends a deeper charm to the omnipresent beauty, and bestows that final fascination born of the marriage of what is loveliest and most bounteous in nature with what is most tragic and hideous in humanity.

The light and the heat are the two things that most impress one on first coming to this land. The light is the more impressive of the two: from sunrise to sunset it is omnipresent and constant; the very shadows are luminous, dark though they appear by contrast. I should say that latitude seventeen was about forty-five million miles nearer the sun than latitude forty. Yet it is a tender, soft, suffused light, not a fierce and hard one. The atmosphere is not so rarefied as that of our own West; one can read here by moonlight, but one cannot read fine print easily. The remote distances of the landscape are melted in an aërial haze instead of being defined with the relentless clearness of a steel-engraving. Nevertheless, the light of the tropics is superlative; it seems to belong to a planet more recently evolved from the parental luminary than ours. So intense and pervasive is it, one would almost say it irradiates the mind as well as the body; it appears to possess a spiritual quality. I had read of blazing tropic suns, of scorching, blistering tropic heats, but I find nothing of the sort. However great the ultimate effect may be, the manner is always gentle, sweet, subtle, soothing; Harbour street in Kingston never shows so savage a temperature as Broadway in New York. But for all that, it will not do to take undue liberties with this soft-spoken climate. After walking a few

DRAWN BY GILBERT GAUL. ENGRAVED BY PETER AITKEN.

ON THE VERANDA.

DRAWN BY GILBERT GAUL. ENGRAVED BY JOHN W. EVANS.

AT THE RACES, KINGSTON.

miles along the white, undulating roads, or panting up a steep hillside, nothing could be more delicious than the touch of the northern breeze fanning you as you sit under the shadow of a broad-spreading silk-cotton, nor could anything be more dangerous. You are being fanned by the wings of death. Evaporation is wonderfully rapid; you come in from exercise drenched with perspiration, and before you can make ready for a «rub-down» your skin is already dry. In the North a slight chill may be followed by a slight cold, and that be the end of it; here your chill may turn out the end of everything for you. Moreover, the soil when dampened by rains probably exhales a miasma productive of what we call malarial fever; in Jamaica it occasionally develops into an appallingly ugly and brief disease known as black vomit. On the other hand, if you are rationally cautious, and let liquor of every kind alone, you may walk, or climb, or play tennis, or ride horseback all through the hottest part of the cloudless day, and feel only the better for it at night; in fact, you must take plenty of outdoor exercise in order to be at your best. The way to get ill is to avoid exertion and perspiration, and sit at ease in the shade absorbing cooling drinks. Such people sometimes last two years. Those who pursue the alternative regimen are not surprised to find themselves alive and alert at ninety and upward. Of course it is more difficult to get ill on the higher levels than on the lower ones; but taking the island by long and large, it is one of the healthiest places on the globe.

It was high noon, and a flat calm, when we tied up to our first tropical steamboat pier, which was fashioned after the likeness of the one we had left behind us in the North River seven days before, but the surroundings and peopling of which were so immeasurably different that it seemed like one of those grotesque dreams in which impossibilities are commonplace. Almost everybody was black, and everybody was in a perspiration. Everything was novel; even our old familiar trunks looked unfamiliar circulating in this strange environment. Order came out of the confusion gradually and, as it were, by miracle; but never before in my experience have custom-house officers been so obliging. As to the porters, there were several to each trunk, and there appeared to be as many petticoats as trousers among them. They wanted to be paid; the individual sum was infinitesimal, but began to loom larger in the aggregate. «What have *you* done?» finally inquired one gentleman of a very persistent applicant. «Oh, I ain't done nothin',» the latter hastened to reply, with an air of virtuous disclaimer. «I 's beggin'.»

One looks with all one's eyes at one's first tropical town. There were straight streets running parallel with the water-front, and straight streets crossing them at right angles, with a decided slope waterward, and with streams of water running down each. The houses were two-storied structures, brick, stucco, and wood, with a somewhat rusty aspect, as if lacking paint and varnish. It was Saturday; the sidewalks were thronged, and the roadways no less so; there were negro women in light-colored frocks of calico, with bandanas on their heads, smiling black faces, and round, shining eyes, which could give most significant glances, for there is a universal capacity for flirtation among these jolly damsels. The shop fronts were not imposing or brilliant, and their contents were not unprecedented; but they too, somehow, contrived to appear foreign. Fruit was for sale on every corner and on every woman's head. Hacks dawdled up and down the streets angling for fares, each hackman signaling to you as if he were the very old friend you had been looking for, ready to fulfil all the offices of friendship at the lowest market rates. There was a certain sort of bustle and animation in the scene, and yet there was nothing of the rush, drive, and preoccupation of America. These people were more of the butterfly temperament; they loved the sun and the warmth, they dressed in bright colors, they fluttered about a good deal; but they were not going anywhere or doing anything in particular. They looked to the right and left, and up and down, instead of only straight ahead as we do; they were all sauntering, or merely standing still and smiling and chatting, with gesticulations. The few white people in the throng looked very white,—not even tanned,—and rather out of place. They were clad unobtrusively in grays and whites, and one discerned them

DRAWN BY GILBERT GAUL. ENGRAVED BY JOHN W. EVANS.

A FRUIT-VENDER.

with some difficulty. It was market-day and steamer-day, and the following week was to be race week, and Christmas was only a little way off; so the gaiety of Kingston was at its height. But there was a lightness about the whole spectacle, an absence of the omnipresent American purpose and responsibleness and ironic seriousness,—if I may so call it,—which was vastly refreshing. And then, that sun, that warmth, that illumination, those fronds of palm and giant leaves of banana! The great brown buzzards flapped close overhead, or sat on the ridge-poles of the low houses. The sea glittered to the south like a sheet of milky turquoise, the mountains lifted themselves through the fleece of white and gray clouds to the northward, and it was midwinter all the time! I have not yet, indeed, got over the feeling that this is all some wonderful joke or dream, from which I am bound sooner or later to awaken and open my eyes on a drifting snow-storm. The enchantments of the old magicians were nothing compared with the marvelous spell worked by two dozen or so degrees of latitude.

Finally I found myself in a great, shadowy, roomy hotel, with hard-wood floors and furlongs of veranda, giving on a garden which had run somewhat to seed, but contained several palm-trees, and an assortment of lizards, green and brown, in agreeable confirmation of the propinquity of the equator. Round about this hotel and its environment we wandered till lunch was ready; there were oranges, bananas, and several other fruits which I do not specify only because I am still unable to recollect their names. As to their flavor, I can only say that I do not care much for it as yet; there was one that tasted like butter, and another that had the consistency of cream cheese and the taste of strawberry jam.

On the whole, the flavor of these Southern products strikes the Northern visitor as insipid and too sweet, and makes one understand why Englishmen always hanker after curries and the like sharp condiments in the tropics; but no doubt we are sophisticated and wrong, and ought to like what seems to us insipidity. Meanwhile, the oranges, bananas, and pineapples are all much better here than they ever are after enduring export.

As for the breadfruit and yams, of which we also had specimens, they are a mixture of the potato and the sweet potato, and are less captivating than either. They have almost no taste at all, and I should suppose that one finally would come to regard them in much the same light as bread, something usefully filling, but without character enough to inspire either loathing or devotion. With the aid of sauces and gravies, however, they go down very well.

The bill of fare included likewise fish which was good, and meat which was not very good: it has to be eaten too soon after killing to have lost its toughness. But one does not expect to eat much meat down here; vegetarians are in their element in the tropics, especially that superior order of them who favor that part of the vegetable kingdom which grows above ground. The countrywomen, who walk fifteen to twenty-five miles a day in the sun, with burdens on their heads which must sometimes weigh not less than fifty pounds, and who are never in the least tired—these ladies, it appears, live on fruit and yams only, and find them all-sufficient diet.

After dinner I went into a barber shop, and submitted myself to the ministrations of an artist there. The shop was at the rear of the little structure which bore the sign; the front part of it, if I remember right, was devoted in part to the sale of tobacco. On three sides of the room were windows protected by wooden gratings painted red and blue; through them I saw bits of intense blue sky and green fronds of palm. On a wall just outside the sash a lizard ran and hopped, and the eternal buzzard alighted on a corner of a roof within my range of vision. Close beside me a young darky with a countenance of illimitable amiability labored assiduously on an instrument in the nature of a hand-organ; but the works were in full view, and in the opinion of several bystanders seemed to vie in interest with the tunes. This music took the place of the traditional barber's conversation, though that also was abundantly available upon demand, and was, indeed, carried on with much vivacity between the various employees and some visitors who appeared to have come in for that purpose. It sounded like a mixture of Italian and French, and may have been Jamaican popular English, for aught I know. I could not understand it. I accepted all these details as being typically tropical; but, on the other hand, the chair in which I sat was made in Rochester, New York; on the wall were a large lithograph of Brooklyn Bridge and a portrait of President Cleveland. Electricity, too, has got to Kingston, and the wires run through the branches of the mangos and palms. The house in which I have taken up my abode is fitted throughout with electric bells, but I am happy to add that none of them work. In one of the larger shops, I think, there is an elevator, the only one on the island.

I said just now that the white people look out of place. That fact, so far as I can judge, is the moral of the story here. The island belongs to the colored folk, and the others are gradually being crowded out. The proportion is already about thirty to one against the latter: and while the colored race goes on multiplying, the whites are packing their trunks and moving out. Is this movement to be arrested or not? I doubt whether it will be arrested by the English. Workmen imported from the States do not succeed here; that is, they all die in two years from rum. The coolies do admirably, but they cannot be the final solution of the problem. Perhaps the best thing we can do is to become colored people ourselves.

Commerce aside, the island is beyond the reach of all competition as a pleasure-resort in winter. The sun is always warm, the nights are always cool, the atmosphere is always healthy, and you can choose your mean temperature to suit yourself: on the higher levels of the mountains you can get that of an English summer, and on the plains it will average eighty or more. The scenery of sea and mountain is, on the whole, the most beautiful in the world; and the price of most things, to our American ideas, is exceedingly cheap.

*Julian Hawthorne.*

## THE SOLITARY WOODSMAN.

WHEN the gray lake-water rushes
Past the dripping alder-bushes,
And the bodeful autumn wind
In the fir-tree weeps and hushes,—

When the air is sharply damp
Round the solitary camp,
And the moose-bush in the thicket
Glimmers like a scarlet lamp,—

When the cornel bunches mellow,
And the birches twinkle yellow,
And the owl across the twilight
Trumpets to his downy fellow,—

When the nut-fed chipmunks romp
Through the maples' crimson pomp,
And the slim viburnum flushes
In the darkness of the swamp,—

When the rowan clusters red,
When the blueberries are dead,
And the shy bear, summer sleekened,
In the bracken makes his bed,—

On a day there comes once more
To the latched and lonely door,
Down the wood-road striding silent,
One who has been here before.

Green spruce branches for his head,
Here he makes his simple bed,
Couching with the sun, and rising
When the dawn is frosty red.

All day long he wanders wide
With the gray moss for his guide,
And his lonely ax-stroke startles
The expectant forest side.

Toward the quiet close of day
Back to camp he takes his way,
And about his sober footsteps
Unafraid the squirrels play.

On his roof the red leaf falls,
At his door the blue-jay calls,
And he hears the wood-mice hurry
Up and down his rough log walls;

Hears the laughter of the loon
Thrill the dying afternoon;
Hears the calling of the moose
Echo to the early moon;

And he hears the partridge drumming,
The belated hornet humming,—
All the faint, prophetic sounds
That foretell the winter's coming.

And the wind about his eaves
Through the chilly night-wet grieves,
And the earth's dumb patience fills him,
Fellow to the falling leaves.

*Charles G. D. Roberts.*

# NELSON IN THE BATTLE OF THE NILE.

BARON NELSON OF THE NILE.

NOTWITHSTANDING the brilliant victory of the British fleet off Cape St. Vincent, the Mediterranean remained, throughout the year 1797, in the control of the French and Spaniards, virtually undisturbed by any intrusion of their enemies. French divisions came and went at their will and leisure, and the nation soon learned to look upon the sea as a French lake. Aware, however, of naval inferiority, and attaching exaggerated importance to the holding of maritime territory and fortified harbors, independent of purely naval force, many schemes were broached for strengthening their grip upon the inland sea. The Ionian Islands, Corfu and its neighbors, had fallen to them as their share of the spoils of Venice, and after peace was made with Austria the determination was reached to seize Egypt and Malta. The importance of the former need scarcely be insisted upon to men of our generation, familiar with the Suez Canal and the jealousy with which France now regards the rule of England over the country. Malta was still in possession of the Knights, but intrigues with some of their number had been initiated, and it was well understood that little resistance need be feared from the Order, which had long outlived its usefulness and its discipline.

For the seizure of these two points, of the first importance to any system of general Mediterranean control, an expedition was organized in Toulon and adjacent ports in the first months of 1798. It was to consist of 35,000 troops, to be convoyed in between three and four hundred vessels, under the protection of a fleet of thirteen ships of the line, with numerous frigates and smaller ships of war. The whole command was in the hands of General Bonaparte.

Despite all attempts at concealment, some rumor of the preparations reached the British government, by whose directions Lord St. Vincent, early in May, sent Nelson into the Mediterranean, with three ships of the line, to gain intelligence as to what was in contemplation. This force was afterward raised to thirteen ships of the line, and one of fifty guns; but the reinforcement did not reach Nelson until June 7, he being then to the westward of the northern part of Corsica. The French had already left Toulon on May 19, and proceeded leisurely by the east of Corsica, picking up on the way divisions from that island and Genoa. On June 7, when Nelson's chase of them began, they had rounded the western point of Sicily, and were steering for Malta with a fair wind. Here then began the pursuit, which ended nearly two months later in the naval battle of the Nile—called by the French Aboukir.

On the 9th of June the French armament appeared off Malta. The island was at once summoned, and after a faint show of resistance capitulated on the 12th. It is said that when General Caffarelli, the senior French engineer of the expedition, looked on the complicated pile of fortifications, the massive growth of centuries of warfare, he remarked that it was fortunate for the French that there had been some people inside to open the gates. The next day the three hundred French vessels entered Valetta harbor, and remained till July 19; then, having left a garrison of 4000 to hold the place, they again sailed for Alexandria.

Five days before they departed, Nelson, who had followed their supposed course east of Corsica, was off Cività Vecchia, and there learned on June 14 that the enemy had been seen ten days before near the west end of Sicily, steering east. On the 17th, off Naples, he heard that they had landed at Malta. Pushing hastily forward, he passed through the Straits of Messina, where, on June 20, he was informed of the island's surrender. As Bonaparte had sailed thence only on the previous day, the two fleets, pursued and pursuers, were now less than two hundred miles apart, the latter pressing in fiery haste straight for the point where the quarry at the moment was; yet six weeks were to elapse before the two met.

Though bound for Alexandria, Bonaparte ordered that the great fleet should first be steered for the south side of Crete, instead of heading direct for its port. To this was due the fact that Nelson missed it; and it is probable that the French leader, who already knew of the British having entered the Mediterranean, laid this false course for the express purpose of throwing off his enemy. As news was his great want, Nelson kept close to Sicily; and on the 22d, off the southeast point of the island, a Genoese brig from Malta was spoken, which reported, truly, that the French had sailed from Malta, but on the 16th instead of the 19th, as was actually the case. The informant added that their supposed destination was Sicily.

The British admiral was in a dilemma. That neither Sicily nor Naples was the object of the French he now had fairly satisfactory proof from his general information; and as strong westerly winds prevail at that season throughout the western Mediterranean, he argued justly that they could have gone only to the eastward, as to Corfu or to Egypt. He had already gained an inkling of their designs upon the latter country. A week before he had written: «If they pass Sicily»—the case which had now apparently arisen—«I shall believe they are going on their scheme of possessing Alexandria and getting troops to India: a plan concerted with the Sultan of Mysore,»—the most formidable of the Indian sovereigns,—«and by no means so difficult as might at first view be imagined; for three weeks from Suez to Malabar is a common passage at this season of the year.» On the other hand, he had been particularly cautioned not to let the enemy's force get to the westward of him; and how then could he, with nothing definite to allege, in reliance simply on his own insight, go to the extreme east of the Mediterranean, deliberately yielding them, in case of mistake, the advantage against which he had been warned?

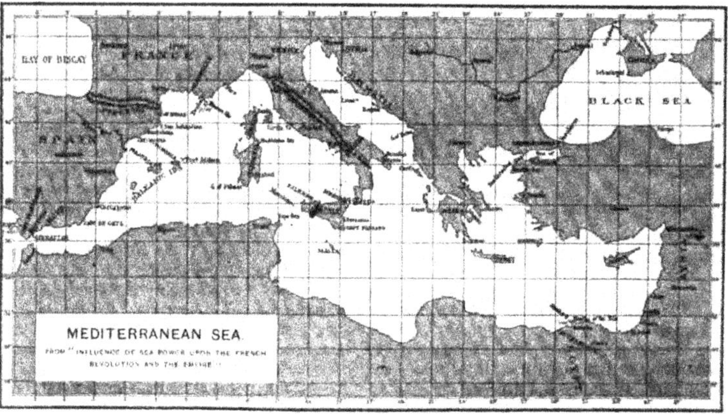


In this perplexity Nelson summoned on board the *Vanguard* four of the captains in whom he had special confidence, and asked their opinion, laying his reasons before them. They agreed with him on the propriety of going at once to Alexandria. To this conclusion the mistake in the date of Bonaparte's sailing from Malta contributed. If he had sailed on the 16th for Sicily, surely on the 20th at Messina, or on the 22d off Syracuse, they would have heard something about him. Had Nelson then known that his enemy had moved only three days before, instead of six, he might reasonably have waited for further tidings about Sicily. As it was, he decided to make the best of his way for Alexandria, «as the only means,» to use the words of the officer next in rank to him,—Sir James Saumarez,—«of saving the British possessions in India, should the French armament be destined for that country.» Another of those consulted, a man of conspicuous sagacity,—Captain Alexander J. Ball,—writing when it appeared that the pursuit had been a mistake, deliberately reaffirmed this opinion as a support to the then seemingly discomfited admiral: «Egypt appeared to be the most likely place to which they were bound. You had a prospect of overtaking them and destroying their expedition, which probably was intended against our settlements in India. But they having five days' start of you, your only chance of accomplishing this was by an immediate pursuit: a delay of twelve or twenty-four hours to have endeavored to obtain more correct intelligence would have rendered your pursuit almost useless.» It is interesting to observe that men of the first order of naval ability did not then see in Bonaparte's undertaking the absurdity which has been attributed to it by after-sight.

As the enemy, wherever bound, was believed to have six days' start, the need of haste was evident, so the British not only steered a straight course for their port, but carried all sail. Their passage, therefore, was for two reasons much more rapid than that of Bonaparte's force. A small body of well-drilled ships accustomed to work together, as Nelson's were, can under all circumstances make greater speed than three hundred such as those that composed the French armament, picked up wherever they could be had, without the habit of concerted action, and altogether too numerous to be controlled by the few ships of war, themselves not of the most efficient. Consequently, starting for Alexandria, from a point about as distant from it as Malta is, three days later than the French, but going direct and with all speed, Nelson arrived at his destination three days before they, by their roundabout route, appeared off the coast of Egypt. During this passage neither saw the other. Nelson's frigates, by an unfortunate error of their commander, had separated from him before the reinforcement joined. Having no scouts, the British could even during daylight command no wider a horizon than that over which the ships of the line could be spread without losing sight of one another; but at night they had to draw together, because the military necessity of keeping the force entire and in hand, when it would have so much work to do if the enemy were met, was even greater than that of learning the latter's whereabouts. Under these disadvantages, and with hazy weather, it happened by an extraordinary chance that, during the night after the day on which Nelson headed for Alexandria, his fleet and the French crossed the same spot without meeting or seeing, unaware of so critical a proximity, and by morning the diverging tracks and differing speeds put them again out of each other's view. Pursuing their respective courses, they continued to separate more and more, but for some days were at no time over a hundred miles apart.

On the 28th, Nelson came in sight of Alexandria. Two days before he had sent a brig, his one despatch vessel, ahead of the fleet to communicate with the British consul there. To his surprise and consternation, not only was the enemy not in Egyptian waters, but nothing was known of his movements. Overwrought with the anxiety of the past month, and feeling the full weight of the risk he had taken,—of which Saumarez, a man calm and steadfast, approving, too, what had been done, had said, «Did the chief responsibility rest with me, I fear it would be more than my too irritable nerves would bear,»—Nelson showed less than the clear judgment and sagacity that at other times so markedly characterized him. It will be remembered that this was his first independent command. Brilliant as his career had been, he had as yet no established record as a general officer upon which to fall back, or to extenuate the want of success, to which alone the public looks. Fairly arrived at the place whither his best reason had assured him the enemy was bound, he failed to allow duly for the time he might have outsailed their unwieldy numbers. «His active and anxious mind,» wrote the captain of the flag-ship, who was hourly witness of his motives and feelings, «would not permit him to rest a moment in the same place; he therefore shaped his course to the northward for the coast of Karamania» in Asia Minor. Still obtaining no information, he here, to use his own expression, «became distressed for the kingdom of the Two Sicilies,» and started back for it, keeping along the northern shores of the Mediterranean. Though his decision to quit the neighborhood of Alexandria was precipitate, the course he took in returning covered all other probable routes that the enemy's armament might have followed.

On June 29, the day after Nelson departed, the advance squadron of the French fleet sighted the sands of Egypt. Wily and calculating as usual, Bonaparte was again too shrewd to make at once for his port; and after passing Crete the course was shaped for the African coast seventy miles west of

Alexandria. Frigates had been sent ahead to ascertain if the enemy's fleet had appeared, and it is even said by a prominent French officer, one of Bonaparte's aides-de-camp, that the upper sails of Nelson's ships were still visible above the horizon as these lookouts approached the town. Be that as it may, the coming and the going of the British were now known. Skirting the coast, the expedition arrived off Alexandria on July 1, and the troops landed the same day. Pushing its conquest rapidly forward, the army entered Cairo on July 21. On the 20th Nelson had again reached Sicily and anchored at Syracuse, eight hundred miles from Alexandria. During the weary passage back, against a constant head wind, he had scarcely seen a sail, and was still, as he himself said, «as ignorant of the situation of the enemy as I was twenty-seven days ago.»

But if certainty had not been attained, the situation was clearing up. «I know,» wrote he from Syracuse to Earl St. Vincent, «that the French are neither to the westward of Sicily nor at Corfu.» This was at least something—nay, it was much; but even now in Syracuse he could «learn no more than a vague rumor that the French are gone to the eastward.» Satisfied that that general direction only could they have taken, he decided to return to the Levant, going first to the mouth of the archipelago, whence the wind would be fair to carry him to Cyprus, and finally to Egypt, a course which could not fail to bring tidings within his reach. Before pursuing, however, it was necessary to renew the water of the fleet. The kingdom of the Two Sicilies being then formally at peace with France, though secretly hostile to her, the governor of Syracuse raised many objections to supplying her enemies, as a breach of neutrality; but Nelson had orders from St. Vincent to treat a refusal as hostile, and to exact supplies by force, if necessary. This had probably been arranged to cover the liability of the kingdom to reprisals by France upon its Italian dominions. The broadsides of the British ships in a defenseless port were an unanswerable reply to the representations that the French minister did not fail to make. After a five days' stay the fleet, having been victualed and watered, sailed again on July 25. Though no time was lost, the imminent urgency that had appeared for the former chase did not now press, as the advantage it was then hoped to pluck by encountering the enemy before he landed could no longer be expected, and more thorough search could be made. More haste had once been, and might again prove, less speed. The fleet steered for the southern point of the Morea, and on the 28th the *Culloden* (seventy-four) was sent into the Gulf of Koron to seek intelligence. She returned with word that the French armament had been seen from Crete four weeks before, steering to the southeast. This could mean only Egypt, and getting at the same moment other corroborating information, Nelson again shaped a direct course for Alexandria, off which the British fleet arrived four days later, on August 1.

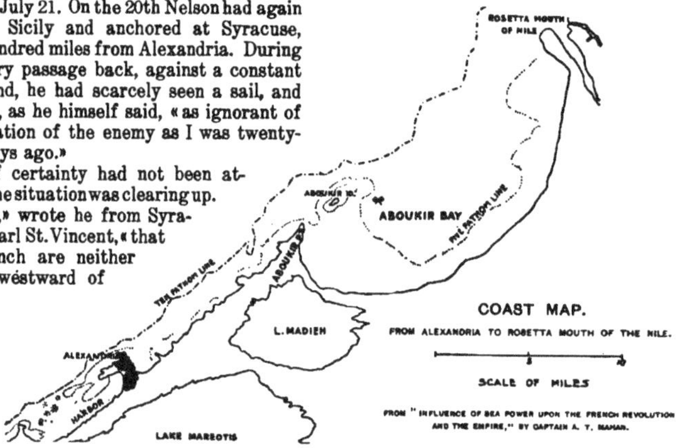

COAST MAP.

FROM ALEXANDRIA TO ROSETTA MOUTH OF THE NILE.

FROM "INFLUENCE OF SEA POWER UPON THE FRENCH REVOLUTION AND THE EMPIRE," BY CAPTAIN A. T. MAHAN.

As the French received the attack where they then lay at anchor, it is necessary to describe their preparations, and briefly the events of the month of July which had decided their movements and position.

Bonaparte had wished that the whole fleet, and especially the ships of war, should be brought into the harbor of Alexandria, where it would be out of reach of an enemy. He considered that its preservation, the mere fact of its being «in being,» would be a powerful factor in the general international situation, of which the existing enterprise, like all wars, was simply one political incident among many others. How right he was in this forecast was shown by the convulsion which the whole political fabric underwent immediately after the fleet was destroyed. In consequence of his wish, which was in fact a command, Admiral Brueys remained at anchor off the port from July 1, the day the troops landed, until July 7, seeking a channel by which the heavy ships—those of the line—could enter. Failing to find one that satisfied him, he then sent in the transports, and took the rest of the fleet to Aboukir Bay, fifteen miles east of Alexandria. The search for a practicable channel into the port was continued by skilful officers, and on July 18 these reported to Brueys that they had found one; but in the fortnight of grace that still remained he neglected to take advantage of it, having persuaded himself that the British were gone for good. «My opinion,» he wrote, «is that they have not so many as fourteen sail of the line, and, not being superior in number, have not thought fit to try conclusions with us.» In this conviction he remained passive, exposed to attack in an open roadstead. Bonaparte, who, though he shared the admiral's belief and frequently took the most tremendous risks, never did so needlessly, was urgent for him to move; but preoccupied with the land operations, and not on the spot, he could not compel compliance with instructions that were perforce somewhat discretionary.

The Bay of Aboukir, in the western part of which the battle was fought, begins at the promontory of the same name and extends eighteen miles eastward to the Rosetta mouth of the Nile. The low ground of the Nile delta, the slow deposit of centuries, continues under the sea beyond the shore line, the depth increasing very gradually, so that water enough for the heavy ships of that day (thirty feet) was not found till three miles from the coast. Two miles from Aboukir Point to the northeast is Aboukir Island,—since called Nelson's,—linked with the point by a chain of rocks. Outside the island similar rocks, with shoals, prolong this foul ground farther to seaward, forming a reef which, being covered with water, constituted a serious peril to a stranger approaching the bay. For a vessel inside, however, this dangerous barrier broke the waves from the northwest, the direction of the prevailing summer wind, and so made of the bay a fairly convenient summer anchorage. It must be noted, as one of the dangers which Nelson faced, that he had no knowledge of the place except a rough sketch found upon a passing merchant ship. Beyond the difficulties that ignorance might impose, the situation of the French fleet offered no local protection against an enemy's approach.

It was therefore incumbent upon Brueys to strengthen—fortify—by every means in his power a position so exposed. This he cannot be said to have done, although he was apparently satisfied with his own preparations; but in such a case, where the conditions demand the utmost diligence, a man must be judged not by his personal convictions, but by the reasonable criticism of others. By his own statement to the French minister of marine, the head ship—head, that is, with reference to the northwest wind, to which all would head while lying at anchor—was placed as close as possible to the shoal connected with Aboukir Island, the other twelve being formed behind her in a column, the general direction of which was from northwest to southeast, but curving a little, as shown in the diagram. The distance between two ships was five hundred feet, more than twice a ship's length. «This position,» said Brueys, «is the strongest we can possibly take in an open road, where we cannot approach sufficiently near the land to be protected by batteries, and where the enemy has it in his power to choose his own distance. It cannot be turned by any means to the southwest.» Nelson himself speaks of the French as «moored in a strong line of battle»; but however unalterably bent to dare the hazard, he could not fail to retain the deep first impression produced by the sight of the enemy's formidable array as he was bearing down upon them, nor is it to be expected of the victor to undervalue the dangers he has overcome.

Brueys's dispositions were faulty, partly in design and partly in thoroughness. For the former the distance between the ships was too great: the line could be pierced at any point. The frigates also could and should have been placed in shoal water to support the van or head ship. The latter was not placed as near as possible to the shoal ahead, for several British ships, by a wonderful exhibition of mingled skill and daring, passed between her and it. Neither was the line in general established so near shoal water as to forbid the enemy getting inside and attacking on both sides, for this too they did. By a singular misconception, also, Brueys regarded the rear of his column as the more exposed end. For this reason he placed in the van his weakest ships, upon which consequently fell the first brunt of the enemy's skilfully combined onset. At the center, the seventh vessel of the thirteen in the order of battle was the flag-ship, the tremendous *Orient*, of one hundred and twenty guns, flanked on each side by the *Franklin* and the *Tonnant*, of eighty guns each. Among the thirteen British ships of the line, properly so called, there was not one equal to either of these, nor could the *Leander* (fifty) be considered to redress in any degree the balance of aggregate force. Having thus very properly provided against his order being overwhelmed in the center, Brueys, moved by the belief already mentioned, stationed his next heaviest ships in the rear to leeward, expecting the enemy to attack there. The British admiral, on the contrary, knew, and at once saw, that with a line extending in the direction of the wind, as did the French in Aboukir Bay, it was in the power of the assailant to throw his whole force upon the ships to windward, and to destroy them before the others could work up against the wind to their aid; and this, in brief, was his plan of battle, which was virtually won, its result assured, as soon as it began. Nelson repeats a story that Brueys from the beginning of the fight declared that all was lost. Though scarcely a becoming remark in a commander-in-chief, the thought may well håve flashed across him as soon as he realized the unfolding of his opponent's plan; and if he expressed it, his heroism redeemed whatever of weakness his anguish thus betrayed.

In the order for battle thus adopted, the morning of the fatal first of August, 1798, dawned upon the French ships in Aboukir Bay. None on board of them suspected the near approach of the British fleet, of whose whereabouts they were as ignorant as Nelson not long since had been of their own. As on other days of judgment, men rose and went about their daily round, personal or public, unknowing that for so many it was their last. The cares of the admiral were numerous and varied, for the fleet was ill equipped, short of provisions, and ill manned; but among his anxieties fear of the enemy's fleet was not prominent. Hundreds of the crews were on the beach three miles away, busied in getting water, of which the supply was running short; and with them were important boats urgently needed in case of a sudden call to battle; for among the preparations postponed to the last moment was the running of cables from ship to ship, which should close the intervals against

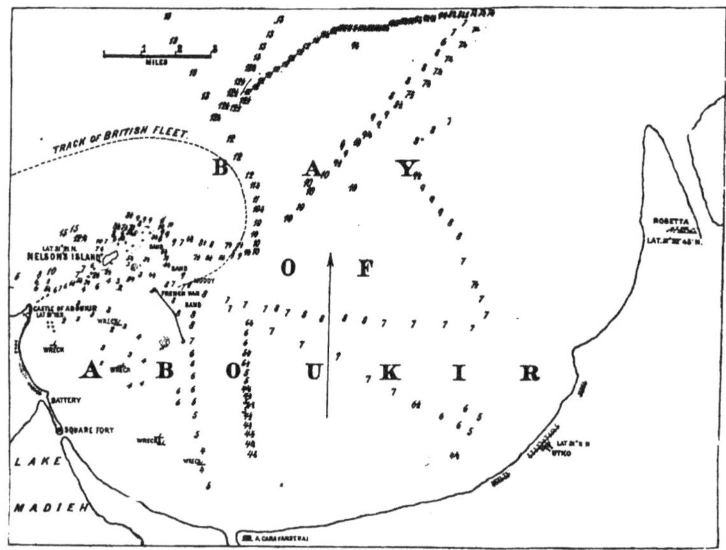


DRAWN BY AUGUST WILL.

BATTLE OF THE NILE, ABOUKIR BAY.

DRAWN BY WARREN SHEPPARD.

THE «THESEUS» ATTACKING THE «GUERRIER.»

an enemy's passing. The sun mounted to the meridian, but still no sign appeared to foreshow the destruction which was now near at hand, for at this moment the lighthouse at Alexandria was sighted from the British ships of the main body. The dinner-hour passed undisturbed, and again men turned to their appointed tasks, soon to be rudely interrupted.

When the lighthouse was reported to Nelson, the fleet was steering southeast by east for the town. Two ships, the *Alexander* and the *Swiftsure*, were ten miles ahead, having been sent forward the night before to reconnoiter. The course was at once changed to east, parallel to the shore, which brought these two to leeward of the others, and had the effect—fortunate, as it proved—of delaying their entrance into the battle. The *Culloden*, having to tow a prize brig laden with wine, which the fleet needed, was thereby seven miles astern, a fact which resulted in a bitter mortification to Trowbridge, her «nonpareil» captain, to use Nelson's word. The advanced ships saw the French flag flying on the ramparts, and the port full of vessels, but among them none of the line. Having signaled this, they were recalled; but the wind not allowing them to head high enough, they fell behind, as before said. Their news, succeeding all the buffets of adverse fortune during the last two months, caused a general feeling of depression in the fleet. «Never,» wrote Saumarez to his wife, «do I recollect to have felt so utterly hopeless or out of spirits as when we sat down to dinner» (about two o'clock); but at a quarter before three the *Zealous*, one of the leading ships of the main body, made signal that a fleet of ships of war was at anchor in the direction east by south—nearly ahead. «Just as the cloth was being removed,» continues Saumarez, «the officer of the watch came hastily in, saying, ‹Sir, a signal is just now made that the enemy is in Aboukir Bay, and moored in a line of battle.› All sprang from their seats, and, only staying to drink a bumper to our success, we were in a moment on deck,» where Nelson's appearance was greeted with a round of cheering that doubtless resounded from ship to ship. Suspense was ended.

Suspense, but for the admiral not anxiety. The waters were unknown, no officer of the fleet had ever visited them, the day was far gone, and the foe, though in view, was still distant. Three hours at least would be needed to reach him, postponing the encounter till close to night, even if its fall could be anticipated. On the other hand, off these low alluvial shores soundings are commonly regular, and give timely warning of the approach of danger. Reefs, doubtless, might exist (Aboukir Island itself showed an outcropping from the bottom); but something must be left to chance, and much might be hoped from the unexpected appearance of the British, and from depriving the enemy of the time to repair defects in his dispositions. In such a

FROM A BUST MADE IN VIENNA IN 1801, IN POSSESSION OF EARL NELSON.

HORATIO, VISCOUNT NELSON.

balance of arguments temperament commonly turns the scale, and, besides, Nelson's mind was prepared. All plain sail that could be borne was put upon the ships, which had been under short cruising canvas, and they bounded forward to a fine breeze from north-northwest. Signal was made to prepare for battle, and for the *Culloden* to join the main body, dropping the prize. An hour and a half later, as the enemy's position developed to view, the admiral signaled again that he intended to attack their van and center, and to prepare to anchor by the stern. The reason for the latter order was that ships when anchored lie head to the wind, if the cable, as is usual, runs out from the bow; and therefore they either must be turned round head to wind before anchoring or will swing round after it. In either case, at Aboukir, this would have exposed them to a raking or enfilading fire for some critical moments. Anchoring by the stern avoided this.

At a quarter before six Nelson ordered the line of battle to be formed, there being then with him ten ships of seventy-four guns and one fifty, the *Culloden*, the *Alexander*, and the

*Swiftsure* still distant. A few minutes later, as the head of the line was drawing by the island and its reef, he hailed Captain Hood of the *Zealous*, and asked if he thought they were far enough to the eastward to clear the shoal, if they turned inshore. Hood replied that he had no chart, but was then in eleven fathoms, and would, if authorized, feel his way in with the lead, and be careful not to bring the fleet into danger. This was done, the *Zealous* keeping ahead and somewhat inshore of the flagship, the *Vanguard*, which gradually dropped to sixth in the order. Ahead of the *Zealous* was the *Goliath*, Captain Foley, who from the first secured and kept the distinguished honor of leading the fleet.

The steadiness and caution of the approach, in which daring and prudence met on equal terms, led the column to make a long sweep round the shoal in water of safe depth, passing, in so doing, well beyond the head of the enemy's column, so that finally the ships had turned far enough to bring the wind on the other side. In fact, as a French spectator says, they wore in succession, and then stood down obliquely toward the van of the hostile fleet. The latter awaited the attack in the order before described. Brueys had for a moment thought of getting under way, but soon dismissed the idea. At 2 P. M., while preparing to entertain at dinner guests from Alexandria, he had received his first intimation of the British being at hand. Signals to recall the absentees and to prepare for battle were duly made, but received imperfect execution: it is even said that the guns of the broadsides toward the shore were not in all cases got ready for action. In short, though lying in a position which demanded unremitting vigilance, the French were found unready. A brig was sent to reconnoiter, and to attempt, by moving over the shoal where there was water enough for her light draft, to lure the enemy upon it; but the stale ruse had no effect. «The English admiral,» said Blanquet Du Chayla, the second in command, «doubtless had experienced pilots on board; he hauled well round all dangers.» Brueys for a time hoped that Nelson would not attack that night; but when the shoal was passed and the British continued to stand down, nothing was left but to abide the issue, the full peril of which he could not even yet perceive. According to French reports, he had said as the British approached, «They will not dare to attack us.»

It was now past six o'clock, and sunset but half an hour distant. The British column advanced with solemn stillness, broken only by the short orders of the officers, the cry of the leadsmen in the chains, the rattling of blocks and cordage when sails were handled. While still out of gunshot, canvas was reduced to topsails, the three principal sails of a ship, sufficient in such a breeze to insure managing her, without embarrassing overmuch the critical moment of coming to anchor; for upon the accuracy of the positions taken would greatly depend the fortune of the day. About half-past six the French opened fire, and broadsides were exchanged as the two vans neared. Nelson then made the signal to engage the enemy close.

The *Goliath*, closely followed by the *Zealous*, both feeling their way with the lead in the anxiously shallow water where the French line lay, passed round the bows of its leading ship, the *Guerrier*, which Brueys had thought could not be done. «Being in five fathom,» wrote Captain Hood afterward, «I expected the *Goliath* and *Zealous* to stick fast on the shoal every moment.» Foley's decision to dare this risk, which Nelson did not order, was necessarily reached at the moment of action, for not till then could he have been sure of the conditions; but it appears to have rested upon a purpose, previously entertained and maturely considered, to do so if the soundings justified him. He reasoned that the enemy, trusting to his position, would be less ready to fight on the other side, and the apparent quickness of his judgment is but the more meritorious for the alertness of mind which made it possible. As the *Goliath* passed she raked the *Guerrier*. It was Foley's intention to anchor abreast her, but the anchor hung, and he brought up on the inner quarter of the second French vessel, the *Conquérant*. Hood, in the *Zealous*, took the place on the inner bow of the *Guerrier*, whose foremast fell under his first raking broadside. The *Orion* followed, and, making a wide sweep round her two predecessors, reached the inner quarter of the fifth Frenchman, the *Peuple Souverain*, toward whom she directed most of her fire; but her after guns, bearing more efficiently upon the *Franklin* (the sixth), were used against that vessel. The *Audacious* passed between the first and the second of the French ships, and took position on the inner bow of the *Conquérant*, already attacked by the *Goliath*.

The fifth ship was the *Theseus*, Captain Ralph Willett Miller. This gentleman, whom after his premature death[1] Nelson styled

[1] Captain Miller was killed within a year of the battle of the Nile by the accidental explosion of some shells on the deck of the *Theseus*.

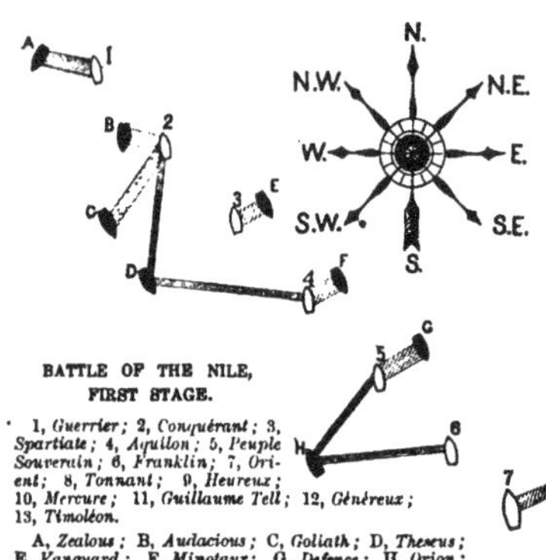


BATTLE OF THE NILE, FIRST STAGE.

1, *Guerrier*; 2, *Conquérant*; 3, *Spartiate*; 4, *Aquilon*; 5, *Peuple Souverain*; 6, *Franklin*; 7, *Orient*; 8, *Tonnant*; 9, *Heureux*; 10, *Mercure*; 11, *Guillaume Tell*; 12, *Généreux*; 13, *Timoléon*.

A, *Zealous*; B, *Audacious*; C, *Goliath*; D, *Theseus*; E, *Vanguard*; F, *Minotaur*; G, *Defence*; H, *Orion*; I, *Bellerophon*; J, *Majestic*.

«the only truly virtuous man I ever knew,» was by birth a New-Yorker, whose family had been loyalists during the American Revolution. A letter from him to his wife gives an account of the fight which is at once among the most vivid, and, from the professional standpoint, the most satisfactory, of those which have been transmitted to us. Of the *Theseus's* entrance into the battle he says: «In running along the enemy's line in the wake of the *Zealous* and *Goliath*, I observed their shot sweep just over us; and, knowing well that at such a moment Frenchmen would not have coolness enough to change their elevation, I closed them suddenly, and, running under the arch of their shot, reserved my fire, every gun being loaded with two and some with three round-shot, until I had the *Guerrier's* masts in a line and her jibboom about six feet clear of our rigging; we then opened with such effect that a second breath could not be drawn before her main and mizzenmasts were also gone. This was precisely at sunset, or forty-four minutes past six; then, passing between her and the *Zealous*, and as close as possible round the off side of the *Goliath*, we anchored by the stern exactly in a line with her, and abreast the *Spartiate*. We had not been many minutes in action with the *Spartiate* when we observed one of our ships (and soon after knew her to be the *Vanguard*) place herself so directly opposite to us on the outside of her that I desisted firing on her, that I might not do mischief to our friends, and directed every gun before the mainmast on the *Aquilon* (fourth French), and all abaft it on the *Conquérant*, giving up my proper bird to the admiral.»

Nelson, by taking this position with his own ship (the sixth), imparted by example a new and proper direction to the British movement. By the repeated raking broadsides of five vessels, the two leading French were already beaten ships; the flank of their line was crushed. Nelson himself doubled upon the outer side of the third, the inner side of the French line as far as the sixth ship being already occupied by British vessels. The rest of his column followed him. The *Minotaur* (seventh), passing just outside the *Vanguard*, anchored abreast number four; the *Defence* (eighth), covered by the fire of her two predecessors until she reached her berth, fixed herself abreast number five, already for some minutes in action with the *Orion*. The smoke and gathering darkness impaired the accuracy with which the *Bellerophon* and the *Majestic* took their stations. The former missed the sixth Frenchman, and brought up squarely abreast the *Orient*, whose force was to hers at the least as five to three, while the *Majestic* ran into the ninth ship, hanging for some minutes at great disadvantage (her captain was there killed); then, swinging clear, she anchored on the bow of the tenth French, the *Mercure*, from which position she reduced her nearly to a wreck.

While ten British seventy-fours were thus getting into battle, the *Culloden*, under a press of sail, was hastening forward to bear her needed share; for, whatever the advantage skilfully secured by the plan of attack, there were, after all, thirteen hostile ships to be handled. Coming up too late to see clearly the route followed by the others, and eager to get into position while he might yet have light to do so, her ardent captain, always prone to undervalue danger, steered too straight for the scene of action. The lead, however, was kept duly going, and a depth of ten fathoms had shortly before been reported, when the *Culloden*, fifteen minutes after sunset, brought up on the reef which the main column had so warily rounded, and there she stuck till the battle was over. The fifty-gun ship *Leander*, not yet engaged, went to her assistance, but in vain. The incident shows vividly the risks which Nelson had to confront.

The two detached ships, the *Alexander* and

the *Swiftsure*, being so far to leeward at the start, had close work to weather the reef, and the *Alexander* even had to make a tack to seaward. Thus delayed, it was already night when they turned the dangerous point. The *Culloden*, serving as a beacon, kept them clear; then the two seventy-fours, with the fifty, bore down together into the midst of the darkness, smoke, and uproar, heading toward the eastern fringe, where the British fire seemed least sustained. It was past eight o'clock when they reached the scene of battle.

By this time the *Bellerophon* had been fairly crushed by the gigantic *Orient:* all her masts were swept out of her, and two hundred of her people killed or wounded. Her cable was cut and she was dropping out of action when this welcome reinforcement came up. The *Orient* was yet unconquered, and her powerful next ahead, the *Franklin*, of eighty guns, sixth in the French order, had had no immediate antagonist, although, as the fifth ship, the *Peuple Souverain*, had been not only silenced, but, through the shooting away of her cables by shot, driven clean out of the line by the *Orion* and *Defence*, she had received some injury from each of these.

Five ships, the left wing of the French, were now subdued. On the right was going on a detached single combat between the *Majestic* and the *Mercure*, which for the moment could only be left to itself. The sixth, seventh, and eighth ships, the French center, were distinctly indicated as the point upon which the approaching reserve should direct their attack, linked thus in close support to their predecessors, whose efforts and whose injuries had left them for the moment unfit for further vigorous action. Accordingly, even in the obscurity, the *Alexander* anchored on the inner quarter of the *Orient*, and the *Swiftsure* on her outer bow, part of the latter's guns playing also on the *Franklin;* while the *Leander*, gliding into the gap left by the *Peuple Souverain*, placed herself so judiciously across the bows of the two French ships as to rake them both.

The *Orient*, which had suffered severely in her contest with the *Bellerophon*, was soon nearly silenced by the combined fire of three fresh ships. Admiral Brueys had already been twice wounded, when, at half-past eight, a cannon-ball carried away his left leg at the thigh. Recognizing that the wound was mortal, he refused to be taken below. « A French admiral,» he said, « should die at his post of command »; and he expired where he fell. Thirty minutes later it was seen throughout the field of battle that the *Orient* was in flames. Her two immediate antagonists redoubled their fire, directing it chiefly upon the scene of conflagration, frustrating the attempts to extinguish it, and insuring her destruction. All eyes were inevitably drawn to this imposing, and at the same time menacing, climax to the night's excitement. Over half an hour before Nelson had been struck on the head by a flying splinter of wood or iron, causing a wound which he for the moment thought mortal, while the flowing blood, and the cut skin falling over his only remaining eye, blinded him. He had been taken below, but when the flag-captain reported the impending catastrophe he desired to be led on deck, where he watched the outcome, and gave orders for saving the *Orient's* people with such boats as could still float.

The fire spread rapidly downward and upward, illumining the waters of the bay, and visible twenty miles away to French watchers in Rosetta, who from their distant post of observation saw the flashes of the guns, and noted by the sounds the alternate swelling and falling of the tide of battle, though unable to detect to which side were inclining the fortunes of the night. The ships near by awaited anxiously the results to themselves of the coming explosion. It was suggested

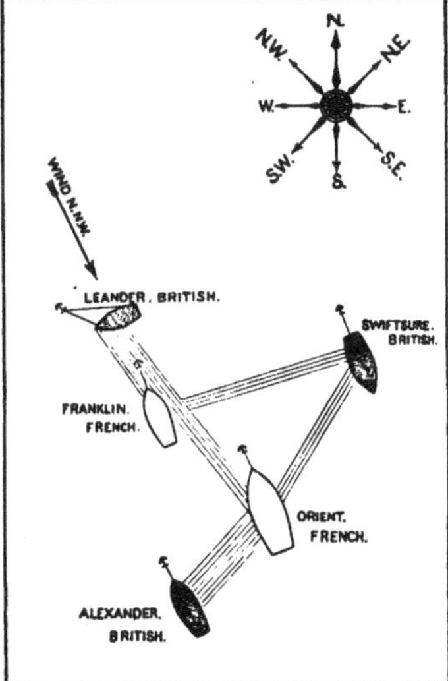


BATTLE OF THE NILE, SECOND STAGE; CONCENTRATION OF THE BRITISH RESERVE ON THE FRENCH CENTER.

to Captain Hallowell of the *Swiftsure* that she should be moved farther off; but she was already to windward, and he replied that the riven fragments would be more likely to fall far than near—an opinion that was justified by the issue. The *Franklin*, Du Chayla's flag-ship, was only five hundred feet ahead of the blazing vessel, where she likewise held on; but the three French ships astern of her slipped their cables and drifted to the rear, where two of them went ashore. The *Alexander*, after the destruction of the *Orient* was assured, also dropped astern, not so soon, however, but that she underwent the worst of the explosion, much of the burning wreckage falling on board. Her sails had been thoroughly wetted and closely furled, and all preparations against fire made, so that no serious damage was done. About a quarter before ten the *Orient* blew up with her freight of noble dead, and, it is to be feared, with many a helplessly wounded man. The hour when this occurred is closely determined by the rising of the moon, which is by one eyewitness reported to have been shortly before the catastrophe, and by another shortly after it. «Immediately after the explosion,» wrote Du Chayla, «the action ceased everywhere, and was succeeded by the most profound silence. The sky was obscured by thick clouds of black smoke which seemed to threaten destruction to the two fleets. It was a quarter of an hour before the ships' crews recovered from the kind of stupor into which they were thrown.» Some seventy of the survivors were rescued by British boats, a few made their way to the shore in French ones. The lower hull of the *Orient* sank, and to this day rests beneath the deserted waters of Aboukir Bay.

The battle now was not only won, but its aggregate results were virtually determined. Most of the ships that had been seriously engaged on both sides were too much injured for further decisive action. After the silence that followed the explosion, firing was resumed in the center and rear, and toward midnight some British ships from the van ran down by Nelson's direction to support their consorts there engaged. But all these movements, though proper and necessary, were desultory in character, and carried on by men nearly worn out by twelve hours of constant excitement, exertion, and fighting. «My people were so extremely jaded,» says Captain Miller, who bore a prominent share in thus garnering the spoils of victory, «that as soon as they had hove our sheet-anchor up they dropped under the capstan-bars, and were asleep in a moment in every kind of posture, having been then working at their fullest exertion, or fighting, for near twelve hours without being able to benefit by the respite that occurred, because while *l'Orient* was on fire I had the ship completely sluiced, as one of our precautionary measures against fire.»

At daybreak of August 2, six French ships of the line still had their colors flying. Of these, three were so badly injured that they could by no means escape, two being on shore. The three rear ships had received little injury, and they attempted with their boats to set fire to those that were aground before themselves putting to sea. The boats were driven off by the fire of British ships which had dropped down within range, and toward noon of the 2d the three got under way; but in doing so one of them, the *Timoléon*, «cast,»—that is, turned the wrong way,—and ran on shore, where she was burned by her own crew. The other two, the *Guillaume Tell* and the *Généreux*, got away, there being no adequate force of British ships in condition to pursue. The former was flagship of Rear-Admiral Villeneuve, who was in the future to command the allied fleets at the memorable disaster of Trafalgar. It has been held by French critics that he could have brought up the uninjured ships before the battle was decided, and was culpable in failing to do so. It is only fair to say that this is doubtful, though probably true. Villeneuve's personal courage was indisputable, but not his professional energy. Two frigates accompanied the flight of this scanty remnant of a great armada.

Of thirteen French ships of the line all but two were thus taken or destroyed. The fleet was annihilated. «Victory,» said Nelson justly, «is certainly not a name strong enough for such a scene as I have passed.» In completeness of immediate results upon the field, no fleet action has ever equaled the battle of the Nile. Upon the fortunes of the particular enterprise which elicited it,—Bonaparte's Oriental expedition,—the effect was absolutely decisive. It became impossible, and was by experience demonstrated to be impossible, to afford to the expeditionary force the renewal of men and supplies upon which depended not only the prosecution of the undertaking, but even the maintenance of the position already achieved.

The influence of the battle of the Nile was more far-reaching still: the continent of Europe became convulsed from end to end as soon as the news was received. Elated by Bonaparte's career of victory in Italy, and by the submission of Austria to terms of peace, the French government had entered upon a course of arrogant aggression toward other countries—of which the unprovoked Egyptian expedition was only one example—that had aroused the wrath of all nations. Even the United States was forced from its attitude of benevolent neutrality, which had depended upon the tradition of the War of Independence and the adoption by France of republican institutions. The general resentment in Europe was, however, curbed by experience of the might of the French revolutionary movement, and of the French armies when wielded by a man like Bonaparte, and there was wanting the demonstration of some power capable of imposing an absolute check upon their future progress. The battle of the Nile gave such a demonstration. As Nelson said, it was more than a victory: it was a catastrophe. The French fleet was annihilated, the Mediterranean passed into the absolute control of Great Britain, the flower of the French army and the invincible Bonaparte were cut off hopelessly from France. Turkey, previously overawed by the fleet, declared war in a month. Austria, Russia, and Naples had already drawn together in coalition. They were emboldened, as the permanence of the conditions due to the battle became evident, to pursue their military enterprises upon a scale which brought the republic to the brink of ruin, from which it was saved only by the unexpected and fortuitous return of Bonaparte, and his accession to supreme power, a year later. Before the year 1798 expired a combined Russian and Turkish fleet entered the Mediterranean from the Black Sea, and undertook to wrest the Ionian Islands from France. In India the movements against the British domination which had been fomented by French negotiations, and which Bonaparte expected to foster, fell still-born when the disaster became known there. Nelson, aware of the importance of the news to British interests, had at once despatched a special messenger overland to Bombay.

The general satisfaction, not to say exultation, was shown by the honors and rewards showered from all sides upon the victor. The Sultan and the Czar, the kings of Sardinia and of the Two Sicilies, sent messages of congratulation and rich presents, the Czar accompanying his with an autograph letter. On the part of his own country, the two houses of Parliament voted their thanks and a pension of £2000 a year. The East India Company by a gift of £10,000 acknowledged the security gained for the Indian possessions. Other individual corporations took appropriate notice of the great event; instances so far apart as the cities of London and Palermo and the island of Zante showing how wide-spread was the sense of relief.

In titular rank Nelson was raised to the lowest grade of the peerage, as Baron Nelson of the Nile. Indignant comment was made in some quarters upon the inadequacy of this advancement to the brilliancy and importance of the service done. The ministry justified its action upon the technical ground that, though no superior was within two thousand miles of Aboukir, Nelson was nevertheless a subordinate flag-officer, not a commander-in-chief.

Not least gratifying to him, with his sensitive appreciation of friendship and susceptibility to flattery, must have been the numerous letters of congratulation he received from friends in and out of the service, and especially from men whose eminence and professional standing made their praise a sound criterion for the calm after-judgment of mankind. Besides many other officers of character and reputation, the three great admirals, Lords Howe, Hood, and St. Vincent, the leaders of the navy in rank and distinguished service, wrote to him in the strongest terms of admiration. The latter two did not hesitate to style the battle the greatest achievement that history could produce, while Howe's language, if more measured, was so only because, like himself, it was more precise in characterizing the special merits of the action, and was therefore acknowledged by Nelson with particular expressions of pleasure.

«The consequences of this battle,» says a distinguished French naval officer only recently dead, «were incalculable. Our navy never recovered from this terrible blow to its consideration and power. This was the combat which for two years delivered the Mediterranean to the English, and called thither the squadrons of Russia; which shut up our army [in Egypt] in the midst of a rebellious population, and decided the Porte to declare against us; which put India out of the reach of our enterprise, and brought France within a hair's-breadth of her ruin: for it rekindled the scarcely extinct war with Austria, and brought Suwarrow and the Austro-Russian forces to our very frontiers.»

That these effects upon the course of contemporary history were not quickly productive of permanent results was due to causes in which neither Nelson nor the sea had any part; but though its immediate fruits were somewhat marred by the blunders of others, nothing can deprive this battle of its significance as announcing the existence of a force destined to limit the flight of French conquest, and ultimately to involve it in a ruin no less utter than that wrought in Aboukir Bay.

*A. T. Mahan.*

PHOTOGRAPHED BY G. C. COX. ENGRAVED BY R. G. TIETZE.

EDWARD ALEXANDER MACDOWELL.

# AN AMERICAN COMPOSER: EDWARD A. MACDOWELL.

BOSTON used to be the musical center of America, and has not yet lost all claim to that distinction, for it still enjoys more first-class orchestral concerts than New York, and has for a long time been the home of a larger number of native composers than the metropolis. This latter preëminence was, however, seriously impaired a few months ago by the departure of Mr. MacDowell to New York, where he has accepted the new professorship of music in Columbia University, founded with the gift of $150,000 made in April by Mrs. Elizabeth Mary Ludlow.[1] The fact that this honor has been bestowed on a young man of thirty-five, taken in connection with his recent triumphs as composer and pianist, and the honors conferred on him last October by Princeton University, seems to indicate that the world has at last taken to heart Schopenhauer's bitter sneer, that mankind never appreciates works of genius fresh, like grapes, but always dead and dried, like raisins. It also marks an exception to the rule that a prophet is without honor in his own country, for Mr. MacDowell has been thus honored in the city of New York, where he was born on December 18, 1861.

What distinguishes this young composer at once from most of his colleagues is the originality and imaginativeness of his work. Considering that he obtained his musical education chiefly in France and Germany, his compositions are, as a rule, remarkably free from definite foreign influences, except such traits as belong to music the world over; and some of them will doubtless mark the beginning of a real American school of music, which, like American literature, will combine the best foreign traits with features indigenous to our soil. Cosmopolitanism is the essence of American life, and cosmopolitanism was the key-note of Mr. MacDowell's musical training. One of his first teachers was the gifted and fascinating Venezuelan pianist Madame Teresa Carreño, who is not only one of the best woman pianists of our time, but who has the unique distinction, for a woman, of having written the national hymn of her native country, and who is perhaps the only woman that ever managed and conducted an Italian opera company.

In 1876 Mrs. MacDowell took her son to Paris, where, in the following year, he entered the Conservatoire, at the age of fifteen. There was one important moment during his stay in Paris when his life-work came near being diverted into an entirely different channel. One day a well-known painter called on his mother, and offered to take the boy for three years, assuming all responsibility, if he were willing to put his music away, and take painting in its place. At that time he really seemed to have more talent for that art than for music, and, boy-like, he was willing, and even eager, to make the change; but his mother, guided by a correct instinct, opposed his wishes, and made him go on with his music-lessons. He was not entirely satisfied with the atmosphere of the Conservatoire, in which there was too much of that striving for immediate effect which he had also noticed in the other arts. The professors—Marmontel, Mathias, Ambroise Thomas, and others—never hesitated to mutilate a musical work, even inserting measures of their own to make it «effective.» If they played a sonata by Schumann or Weber, and did not like certain parts, they simply left them out. If, in editing one of the classics, Marmontel came across a chord that seemed to him hard or aggressively Teutonic, he placidly altered it to suit his Gallic taste. All these things jarred on the young American's reverence for genius. His increasing dissatisfaction with his situation was brought to a climax by his personal experiences at the July *concours*. He had plenty of applause for his playing of a Weber sonata, but his reading at sight of a manuscript composition by a member of the jury was disastrous for him. He had already played more than half of this piece when the increasing hilarity of the audience (there had

[1] The musical chair to which Mr. MacDowell has been called is established upon the Robert Center Fund for Instruction in Music, based on the property of the late Robert Center, given to the trustees by his mother, Mrs. E. Mary Ludlow, with the proviso that the net income shall be «applied either to the payment of the salary of a professor of music or of other instructors in music, or to fellowships or scholarships in music, or be used in any one or more of these or such other ways as shall, in the judgment of the trustees, tend most effectually to elevate the standard of musical instruction in the United States, and to afford the most favorable opportunity for acquiring instruction of the highest order.»

been several victims before him) made him suddenly aware that he was playing the thing in minor instead of in major. Without transition, he jumped at once into major, «with an effect,» as he remarked to the present writer, «of the sun suddenly shining from a coal-hole. It was like the coping-stone of a joke, and the audience's enthusiasm knew no bounds.» He did not get a prize, for, though he had produced an «effect,» it was evidently not the kind the jury were looking for.

It may be remarked in this place that Mr. MacDowell never was, in any sense of the word, a young prodigy. His genius, like that of Paderewski and several of the old masters, was slow in developing. In his early years he used to be discouraged on finding how much harder he had to work to gain what other boys seemed to get with ease. To this day he is a hard and slow worker. He takes time to write few and short pieces. Voltaire has truly said that a writer who wishes to make the long journey to posterity should pack as little as possible into his trunk, carefully examining each article to see if it could not be spared.

The training in harmony received at the Conservatoire had proved beneficial to young MacDowell, but Paris had become distasteful to him, musically and otherwise, and his mother was at a loss what next to do with him. Some pieces he had heard played at the Exposition suggested Germany to him, and he begged hard to be sent to that country, where he hoped to find a larger horizon. Stuttgart was selected, for no particular reason except, perhaps, because it has a famous old Conservatory. But he soon found that he had got from the frying-pan into the fire. That pedantic institution may be a good training-school for pedagogues, but it is no place for a young genius who needs elbow-room and personal freedom. It took him less than a month to find out that the Lebert method (which seemed to him «to show up one's weakness through repose») was not what he had been looking for. Doubtless his instinct told him, also, that he played really better than his teachers. At this juncture the violinist Sauret, whom Mrs. MacDowell had befriended in America, wrote, advising her son to go to Wiesbaden, where he would find the pianist Carl Heymann, who was just beginning to make his name, and the eminent critic and teacher Louis Ehlert, with whom he might continue his lessons in composition. He found that Heymann was not to begin teaching till the autumn at the Frankfort Conservatory, so he remained with Ehlert at Wiesbaden during the summer.

Ehlert was an eccentric man, tall, with bent shoulders. His gray eyes looked unnaturally large on account of the magnifying-glasses he wore, but they had a shy, almost girlish expression, which was not belied by his conduct toward the young American. He was kind to him, but flatly refused to teach him, adding, however, «I shall be glad to study with you.» So they studied together, and at the same time MacDowell heard a good deal of new music at the Cursaal. His intention was to go to Frankfort in the autumn, but Ehlert thought that Heymann was not the right man for him, and wrote to Hans von Bülow, asking if he would take him as a pupil. The irascible Bülow, without having seen the boy, wrote an insulting letter to Ehlert, asking how he dared to propose such a silly thing to him; he was not a music-teacher, and «could not waste his time on an American boy, anyway.» So, after all, MacDowell went to Frankfort and entered the Conservatory.

Raff was at that time the director of that institution, and among its piano-teachers were Clara Schumann (widow of the great composer) and Heymann. Raff was very conscientious, spending part of every forenoon and afternoon in the class-rooms, besides attending the Sunday rehearsals of chamber-music. In this respect he was a strong contrast to Clara Schumann, who never entered the Conservatory. All her pupils, and those whom she turned over to her daughters, took their lessons at her house. Her pupils followed her example, and looked down on the rest of the world from a lofty height. «Some instances of their patronizing affability to Raff make my blood boil yet when I think of them,» writes MacDowell. «As for poor Heymann, he hardly existed for them. His needing the soft pedal in playing was noted once in a while with a supercilious smile. Heymann was a strange little man—very slightly built, with a large head and rather protruding forehead. His flat nose, dark, almost beady eyes, and high cheek-bones, gave him a Mongolian cast of features. His people were very strict Jews, and, in deference to his father's wishes, he would never eat at a Christian's expense or in a Christian house. I told him I was a Quaker, which seemed to satisfy him completely, and we dined together often at an old restaurant in what I would now call a back slum. Heymann is the only pianist I have ever heard who, get as near the piano as you could, remained a mystery as to how he did the things we heard. The simplest passage turned into a spray of flashing jewels in his hands. A melody seemed to have words when he played it; tone-colors that, like Alpine sun-effects, were inexhaustible, yet each one, fleeting as it was, more beautiful than the last; a technic which, while always of the ‹convulsive› order in quick passages, seemed mysteriously capable of anything. He was a marvel: he had a poor wrist, and yet sometimes he would sit down to show me a wrist passage; a kind of quiver would run over him—then, behold, the thing would be trilled off in the same supernatural way as all the rest.»

When Heymann left the Conservatory, in 1881, he proposed MacDowell as his successor, and Raff also desired his appointment; but it was opposed by Cossmann and Faelten on account of the American's «youth.» Heymann had not been popular with the professors, partly because, as MacDowell says, he «dared play the classics as if they had actually been written by men with blood in their veins.» While they were always talking about form, he adds, «when Heymann played one forgot the form in the music. A sonata was a poem under his fingers, if it was in the bounds of human possibility to make it so. If it was not possible, and the ‹bones showed through the flesh,› everywhere the struggle between poetry and prose was evident in his playing.»

More interesting still were MacDowell's relations with Raff—a true genius (think of the «Forest Symphony»!) who was compelled by lifelong poverty to squander many of his ideas on pot-boilers, and whose excessive shyness and modesty prevented him from claiming what was his due. MacDowell's first interview with him was not promising. Heymann had introduced him as having been brought up in the «French school,» which caused Raff to flare up and explain that there was no such thing as «schools» to-day, that all national musical traits were common property, and that every one made use of them according to his attainments and taste. «Raff at first sight seemed rather formidable,» MacDowell continues. «The clear-cut features, closely cropped white mustache, short, military chin-beard; above all, the slightly frowning, penetrating, keen expression in his blue eyes, made one feel as if he might be a bit tigerish. His head, which was entirely bald, save two flat tufts of hair over the ears and a very narrow fringe at the back, in some positions reminded one remarkably of Shakspere. We always spoke French together. To me, coming from Paris with, I fear, a certain amount of slang, Raff's French seemed peculiarly antiquated. He retained all the eighteenth-century terminations, and often used *y*'s instead of *i*'s in writing.»

Having failed to secure Heymann's place at the Frankfort Conservatory, MacDowell took the position as head piano-teacher at the Darmstadt Conservatory. He found it a dreary town, where music was studied with true German placidity. The pupils got all their music from the circulating libraries, which included nothing modern, the name of Saint-Saëns, for instance, being quite unknown. He did not waste much time at this place. His health was undermined by the strain of teaching about forty hours a week, and spending ten or twelve more in railway-trains going to an old feudal castle, where he had some sleepy medieval pupils of noble blood. During these trips he found time to compose nearly the whole of his second piano suite, but he soon came to the conclusion that it would be wiser to return to Frankfort. He did so, continuing with his private pupils, and beginning to devote himself more seriously to composition. He had before this played successfully at concerts in Wiesbaden, Frankfort, Hamburg, Darmstadt; but, as is well known, German orchestral societies never pay young artists a fee. If any one wishes to realize how difficult it is for a pianist to get a start, he should read the two volumes of Hans von Bülow's letters, recently published. After several unsuccessful attempts to earn his living by playing, MacDowell followed Raff's advice, and went to Weimar to see Liszt. The great pianist received him most cordially, and had D'Albert play the second piano to the first MacDowell concerto. He praised it highly, and I have heard a story to the effect that he tapped D'Albert on the shoulder, and told him he must bestir himself if he would keep pace with «the American.» Liszt, who never failed to recognize genius at first sight, was also highly pleased with «the American's» playing—so much so that he invited him to perform his first piano suite at the convention of the Allgemeine Musik-Verein, which was held that year at Zurich. This was very successful, and opened a way to the publication of his works by the leading German house, Breitkopf & Härtel.

«At this Zurich concert,» MacDowell writes to me, «I played my suite with my notes before me, as, until then, I had never waked up to the idea that my compositions could be worth actual study or memorizing. I would not have changed a note in one of them for untold gold, and *inside* I had the greatest love for them; but the idea that any one else might take them seriously never occurred to me. I had acquired the idea from early boyhood that it was expected of me to become a pianist, and every moment spent in scribbling seemed to be stolen from the more legitimate work of piano practice.»

Raff's sudden death, in 1882, was a terrible shock to his favorite pupil. «I had been with him the afternoon before, and had walked part of the way home with him from the Conservatory. As I shook hands with him it seemed to me his hand was very hot and dry, and his eyes were unusually bright. The next morning, when I went to the café down-stairs for my coffee, I was told that he had been found dead in his bed by the barber who went every morning to shave him. It seemed impossible. Hurrying up to his house, I found others before me, and the poor widow and daughter crying their eyes out.» I am indebted to Mr. MacDowell's first pupil for the sequel of this sad story: «He came to me at the hour for my lesson, looking so white and ill that I was frightened. His voice broke as he said only the words, ‹Raff is dead.› There was a sweet hero-worship of a shy boy for an almost equally shy man, and for months after Raff's death he was in a morbid condition. He gave me eighteen marks,—all he had at the time,—and said, as I knew more about flowers than he did, would I get some for him to send? So I bought a mass of roses, and, what was unusual for Germany, had them sent not even bound together; and these were put about Raff, nearer than the grand, beautiful floral things sent by the dozen. Raff had been very generous with the Conservatory, and when, in compliment to his having managed even to gain a surplus over expenses for that last year, the trustees voted it to him as a gift (it was about $275!), he added something to it from his own pocket, and built a stage in the Conservatory hall, fitted for the opera examinations. His salary was about fifteen hundred dollars a year. When he died, they engaged Bernhard Scholz of Breslau for just double! Kistner paid thirty dollars for his ‹Forest Symphony›; Templeton Strong bought the manuscript of it for nearly two hundred and fifty dollars—more than Raff got for the copyright. Raff's modesty and shyness were much to his disadvantage.»

The «first pupil,» to whom I owe this interesting communication, is now Mrs. Edward A. MacDowell. She had gone to Frankfort in 1881, attracted by the famous musicians there. First she applied to Mme. Schumann, who coolly turned her over to Raff, who, in turn, since she spoke but little German, advised her to see a young American who had just finished at the Conservatory—a young man of great talent, who, he said, was bound to make his mark in the world. In reply to her letter, the young American wrote that he was not anxious for the American pupil, who probably did not mean to do serious work, but that he would give her a trial. She was quite indignant at this «condescension,» since she had fancied *she* was «coming down» in going to so inexperienced a teacher. However, he accepted her, and gave her the most tremendously difficult things to play, all the time making her believe that they were quite simple and ordinary, which caused her to practise with truly Teutonic diligence. She is now an excellent pianist and judge of music herself, and is of great assistance to her husband—they were married in 1884—as a sympathetic friend, critic, counselor, and consoler. MacDowell is often very despondent about his work, and needs encouragement. He is sorry his first orchestral works were ever printed, but that does not signify much: Beethoven was ashamed that he had ever written the «Septet» and «Adelaide!»

After Raff's death Frankfort lost its attraction for MacDowell; so he took up his residence at Wiesbaden, where he remained with his wife several years, taking the daring risk of dropping everything but composition. They lived in a tiny suburban cottage overlooking the city on one side, with the Rhine and the Main in the distance, and a forest on the other. A frequent and welcome visitor during those days was Mr. Templeton Strong, for whose compositions MacDowell always finds room on his programs. It was an idyllic, semi-rural life, very pleasant, but ill adapted for the purpose of making material progress in life. It lasted till October, 1889, when they said farewell to Germany,[1] and came home to live in Boston, that city being chosen in preference to New York because it seemed less vast and metropolitan, and therefore a less violent contrast to their German life. Apart from social considerations, a city is to Mr. MacDowell merely a place to earn the

[1] Possibly America is indebted to Liszt for not having lost MacDowell altogether. A London friend had proposed him as examiner in Edinburgh for the Royal Academy of Music. The decision rested really in the hands of Lady Macfarren. Matters seemed to progress favorably until she asked suddenly, «I hope you have no leaning toward the school of that wild man Liszt?» He had to admit his guilt in that direction, and next morning he received a notice saying the place was not suited for him!

money that will enable him to spend the summer in the country. He is a passionate lover of Nature, and seems to need her for inspiration, for he does almost all his composing in summer. He seldom takes notes, and, as a matter of course, never uses the piano as an aid in composing. He is fond of fishing, hunting, riding, walking, which he calls «living like a human being»; and here we have the key to his music, which is as healthy and as free from any morbid taint as is his robust physique. On seeing him in his habitual golf suit, no one would fancy that his favorite companions are fairies, witches, nymphs, dryads, and other idyllic creatures of the romantic world.

Composers who are at the same time pianists labor under the disadvantage that their creative work is apt to be ignored by those who are most eager to applaud their playing. Paderewski and MacDowell are more lucky in this respect than Liszt and Rubinstein were at their age; the world has evidently learned wisdom, having found out that a pianist is never quite so entrancing as when he plays his own pieces. Mr. MacDowell's first triumph in New York was won in the double capacity of composer and pianist. He had been invited to play his second concerto with the Philharmonic Society on December 17, 1894. The result was a double success such as no American musician had ever achieved before an American audience. The Philharmonic audience, the most critical in the country, can be painfully cold; but the young composer-pianist received an ovation such as is usually accorded only to Paderewski or to a popular prima donna at the opera. The three most noticeable things about the concerto itself were that in its style and treatment of the piano it was as thoroughly *idiomatic* as if it had been written by Chopin, Liszt, or Paderewski; that its orchestration rivaled in richness and brilliancy that of the greatest living foreign masters in that field—Dvořák and Johann Strauss; and, most important of all, that it is brimful of *ideas* such as can come only from a brain born to create new ideas. I have already referred to the rarity of «reminiscences» in his compositions. MacDowell is not an erudite musician; he purposely avoids studying the scores of the great masters. He prefers to spend his time in thinking, and that is one reason why he is not a mere imitator of Chopin, Schumann, Wagner, or Liszt, like most young composers of the present day. Mr. MacDowell's concertos and orchestral pieces (among which are the symphonic poems «Hamlet and Ophelia,» dedicated to Sir Henry Irving; «Lancelot and Elaine,» «Lamia,» «The Saracens and Lovely Alda,» «In October,» and two suites) have, indeed, been played frequently in most of the foreign musical centers, and acknowledged as the best music that has come from across the ocean, while the committee that offered him the professorship at Columbia University justly stated that they considered him the greatest musical genius America has produced. Anton Seidl has declared him a greater composer than Brahms, and I myself am convinced that, with the exception of Paderewski, none of the young composers now in Europe holds out such brilliant promises of the future as MacDowell, who seems destined to place America musically on a level with Europe.

On January 23, 1896, the Boston Symphony Orchestra paid him the probably unprecedented honor (in the case of an American composer) of placing two of his longest works on the same program. They were the first of his concertos, written when he was only nineteen, and his Indian suite, completed at thirty-four, the latest of his works. The difference between these pieces was not as great as might have been expected. Indeed, this juvenile concerto seemed to me so finished in style, and so ripe in harmonic treatment and modulation, that I suspected it must have been retouched. I found, however, that, with the exception of a few lines near the beginning of the first movement, the score was exactly as it had been printed originally. After all, did not Mendelssohn write his «Midsummer Night's Dream» at nineteen, and Schubert his «Erlkönig» at eighteen? Musical genius is, like Kant's «Ding an Sich,» independent of time and space. Already in this early work do we find the conciseness, the brightness, the avoidance of commonplace and padding, which place its author's works in refreshing contrast to those of most of his contemporaries; he writes «literature,» while they seem to be content with musical «journalism.» The second movement is especially noticeable for its broad melody and dreamy harmonic coloring. The student of his works, be they for orchestra, piano, or voice, will find everywhere amid all the rich harmonic and polyphonic elaboration a broad vein of melody always distinctly marked. He will find, too, that his slow movements are usually the best, which is the surest test of musical genius.

The Indian suite played at this concert was interesting from many points of view, which I can touch on only very briefly. It is based on genuine American Indian melodies. The introduction has almost a Wagner touch thematically, but it is note for note Indian, and there is also a curious Northern ring in some of the themes. Saint-Saëns once said neatly that Liszt's rhapsodies are «civilized Gipsy music,» adapting which expression, we might say that the MacDowell suite is civilized Indian music. It must be admitted that the themes are less interesting than their elaboration, and that there is much more of the civilizer than of the Indian. However, like Dvořák's «New World» symphony, in which the spirit of negro melodies is introduced, this suite (which was sketched before Dvořák wrote his work) is an interesting contribution to the question, «Is there such a thing as an aboriginal American music?» I believe, however, that the genuine American school of music will be, like the perfect American woman, a mixture of all that is best in European types, transformed by our climate into something resembling the spirit of American literature. The atmosphere of the MacDowell suite is more Slavic than German, and in this fact we may perhaps find a hint as to the future of music in America, which has heretofore shown too exclusively the influence of Germany.

As a pianist, I would rather hear MacDowell than any professional now in Europe, excepting Paderewski. Though he is a virtuoso of the highest rank, he always plays like a composer, putting music and emotion above effect and mere brilliancy of execution. He has the rare gift of bringing tears to the listener's eyes with a single modulation, or a few notes of melody—a gift that is associated, in the minds of educated hearers, with genius only. He has his moods, and is very sensitive to the quality of his audience, playing better in proportion to the sympathy manifested by the hearers. Were he to devote himself to the piano exclusively, Paderewski might have to look to his laurels, but his extreme nervousness makes him prefer composing and teaching.

As a composer for the piano, he has twice yielded to the clamor of those who are not happy unless their music is served up in three or four courses, by writing his two sonatas, «Tragica» and «Eroica.» The first of these was played by Dr. William Mason one summer at the Isles of Shoals once a day for two months. The second even more deserves such a compliment. In these works Mr. MacDowell has shown himself a thorough master of the cyclical form of composition, which at present seems somewhat out of date. But I prefer him in the shorter, romantic forms which he loves so dearly. The essence of romanticism is that, instead of molding music, like gingerbread, into set geometrical forms, it allows the pieces to crystallize into forms of their own, thus insuring endless variety and the absence of formalism and padding for the sake of filling up a mold.

Another romantic trait of his pieces is to be found in the suggestive poetic titles he gives them. For instance, the five pieces entitled «Marionettes» have for separate titles «The Lover,» «Knave,» «Sweet Heart,» «Clown,» «Witch,» while the twelve virtuoso *études* are named «Novelette,» «Moto Perpetuo,» «Wild Chase,» «Improvisation,» «Elfin Dance,» «Valse Triste,» «Burlesque,» «Bluette,» «Träumerei,» «March Wind,» «Impromptu,» «Polonaise.» Most of his piano pieces (there are nearly eighty of them, counting separate movements) have such poetic titles, the advantages of which are fourfold: they stimulate the hearer's imagination like operatic scenery; they excite the composer's imagination; they combine the power of poetry with the charm of music; they make it easier to remember a piece and to talk about it.

I have left myself no space to speak of what perhaps I like best of all his works—the songs. It was the eight songs, Opus 47, that first convinced me that Mr. MacDowell is one of the most original composers of our time; and it was my happy privilege to be the first to call Paderewski's delighted attention to these songs, which Schubert, Franz, or Grieg could not have improved upon. Jewels of the first water are «The Sea» and «Idyl,» the finest songs ever composed in America. There are chords in some of the songs that suggest Grieg; but here we must go cautiously, for, as Mr. Huneker has remarked, «MacDowell's ancestry tells heavily in his music. His coloring reminds me at times of Grieg, but when I tracked the resemblance to its lair, I found only Scotch, as Grieg's grandfolk were Greggs, and from Scotland.» The charm of some of the songs is enhanced for us in some cases by the fact that they are set to verses by American poets, while the thrilling dramatic power of not a few of them suggests that some day, if he can get a worthy libretto, Mr. Edward A. MacDowell will write the first genuine American opera.

*Henry T. Finck.*

[*BEGUN IN THE NOVEMBER NUMBER.*]

# A ROSE OF YESTERDAY.[1]

BY F. MARION CRAWFORD,

Author of «Mr. Isaacs,» «Saracinesca,» «Casa Braccio,» etc.

VI.

ELEN had not seen the paragraph about Harmon. She rarely read newspapers, and generally trusted to other people to learn what they contained. She was more or less indifferent to things that neither directly concerned her nor appealed to her tastes and sympathies.

Her letters were brought to her before she had left the sitting-room after the colonel had gone away, and she looked at the addresses on them carelessly, passing them from one hand to the other as one passes cards. One arrested her attention among the half-dozen or so she had received. It was the regular report from the asylum posted on the first of the month. But it was thicker than usual; and when she tore open the envelop, rather nervously and with a sudden anticipation of trouble, a second sealed letter dropped from the single folded sheet contained in the first. But even that one sheet was full, instead of bearing only the few lines she always received to tell her that there was no change in her husband's condition.

There had been a change, and a great one. Since last writing, said the doctor, Harmon had suddenly begun to improve. At first he had merely seemed more quiet and patient than formerly; then, in the course of a few days, he had begun to ask intelligent questions, and had clearly understood that he had been insane for some time, and was still in an asylum. He had rapidly learned the names of the people about him, and had not afterward confused them, but remembered them with remarkable accuracy. Day by day he had improved, and was still improving. He had inquired about the state of his affairs, and had wished to see one or two of his old friends. More than once he had asked after his wife, and had evidently been glad to hear that she was well; then he had written a letter to her, which the doctor immediately forwarded. So far as it was possible to form a judgment in the case, the improvement seemed to promise permanent recovery; though no one could tell, of course, whether a return to the world might not mean also a return to the unfortunate habit which had originally unbalanced Harmon's mind, but from which he was safe as long as he remained where he was.

It was not easy for Helen to read to the end of such a letter. It shook in her hands as she went on from one sentence to the next, and the sealed envelop slipped from her knees to the floor while she was reading. When she had got to the end, she stared a moment at the signature, and then folded the sheet almost unconsciously, and drew her nail sharply along the folds, as though she would make the paper feel what she felt, and suffer as she suffered, in every nerve of her body and in every secret fiber of her soul.

She had not believed a recovery possible. Now that it was a fact, she knew how utterly beyond probability she had thought it, and immediately the great problem rose before her, confusing, vast, terrifying. But before she faced it she must read Harmon's letter.

It had fallen to the floor, and she had to look for it and find it and pick it up. The handwriting was large, somewhat ornamental, yet heavy in parts and not always regular. As she glanced at the address, she remembered how she had disliked the writing when she had first seen it, at a time when she had seen much to admire in Harmon himself. Now she did not like to touch the envelop on which he had written her name, and she unreasoningly feared the contact of the sheet it held, as of something that might defile her and must surely hurt her cruelly. The hand that had traced the characters on the paper was the hand that had struck her and left its mark for all her life. And she remembered the rest, and an enormous loathing of the man who was still her husband took possession of her, so that she could not open the letter for a few moments.

It was at once a loathing of bodily disgust like a sickness, and a mental horror of a creature who was so far from her natural nobility that it frightened her to know how she hated him; and she began to fear the letter itself, lest it should make some great change in her for which she should at last hate herself also. The spasm ran all through her, as the sight of some very disgusting evil thing violently disturbs body and mind at the same time.

The temptation to destroy the letter unread came upon her with all possible force, and the vision of a return to peace was before her eyes, as though the writing were already burned unread, and beyond her power to recover. But that would be cowardly, and she was brave. With drawn lips, pale cheeks, and knitted brows she opened it, took out the folded contents, and began to read. As though to remind her of the place where he was, and of all the circumstances from first to last, the name of the asylum was printed at the head of each sheet in small, businesslike letters.

She began to read:

MY DEAR HELEN: You will be surprised to hear directly from me, I suppose, and I can hardly expect that you will be pleased, though you are too good not to be glad that I am better after my long illness. I have a great many things to write to you, and no particular right to hope that you will read them. Will you? I hope so, for I do not mean to write again until I get an answer to this letter. But if you do read this one, please believe that I am quite in my right senses again, and that I mean all I say. Besides, the doctor has written to you. He considers me almost «safe» now; I mean, safe to remain as I am.

It is not easy for me to write to you. You must hate me, of course. God knows, I have given you reason enough to wish that I might stay here for the rest of my life. You are a very good woman, and perhaps you will forgive me for all I have done to hurt you. That is the main thing I wanted to say. I want to ask your pardon and forgiveness for everything, from beginning to end.

«Everything» is a big word, I know. There has been a great deal during these many years, a great deal more than I like to think of; for the more I think of it the less I see how you can forgive even the half, much less forget it.

I was not myself, Helen. You have a right to say that it was my fault if I was not myself. I drank hard. That is not an excuse, I know; but it was the cause of most of the things I did. No woman can ever understand how a man feels who drinks and has got so far that he cannot give it up. How should she? But you know that most men cannot give it up, and that it is a sort of disease, and can be treated scientifically. But I do not mean to make excuses. I only ask your forgiveness, and in order to forgive me you will find better excuses for me than I could invent for myself. I throw myself upon your kindness, for that is the only thing I can do.

They say that it would not be quite safe for me to leave the asylum for another month or two, and I am quite resigned to that; for the life is quiet here, and I feel quiet myself and hate the idea of excitement; I suppose I have had too much of it.

But by and by they will insist upon my leaving, when I am considered quite cured; and then I want to go back to you, and try to make you happy, and do my best to make up to you for all the harm I have done you. Perhaps you think it is impossible, but I am very much changed since you saw me.

I know what I am asking, dear Helen. Do not think I ask it as though it were a mere trifle. But I know what you are and what you have done. You could have got a divorce over and over again, and I believe you could now if you liked. It is pretty easy in some States, and I suppose I could not find much to say in defense. Yet you have not done it; I do not know whether you have ever thought of it.

If you think of it now that I want to come back to you, and try to do better, and make you happy, for God's sake, give me another chance before you take any step. Give me one more chance, Helen, for the sake of old times. You used to like me once, and we were very happy at first. Then—well, it was all my fault, it was every bit of it my fault, and I would give my soul to undo it. If you will forgive me, we can try together and begin over again, and it shall all be different, for I will be different.

Can we not try? Will you try? It will be easy if you will only let us begin. It is not as if we should have other troubles to deal with, for we have plenty of friends and plenty of money, and I will do the rest. I solemnly promise that I will, if you will forgive me and begin over again. I know it must seem almost impossible. It would be quite impossible for any other woman, though you can do it if you will.

I shall wait for your answer before I write again, though it will seem a very long time, and I am very anxious about it. If it is what I hope it will be, perhaps you will cable a few words, even one word. «Forgiven» is only one word. Will you not say it? Will you not give me one chance more? Oh, Helen dear, for God's sake, do!

H.

Helen read the letter to the end, through every phrase and every repetition. Then the fight began, and it was long and bitter—a battle to death, of which she could not see the issue.

The man wrote in earnest, and sincerely meant what he said. No one could read the words and doubt that. Helen believed all he had written, so far as his intention was concerned, but she could not cut his life in two, and leave out of the question the man he had been, in order to receive without fear or disgust the man he professed himself to be. That was too much to ask of any woman who had suffered what she had of neglect, of violence, of shame.

«No one could tell,» the doctor wrote,

«whether a return to the world might not mean also a return to the unfortunate habit» —no one could tell that. And Harmon himself wrote that most men could not give it up, that it was a disease, and that no woman could understand it. What possible surety could he give that it should never get hold of him again? None. But that was only a small matter in the whole question.

If she had ever loved him, perhaps if she could have felt that he had ever loved her truly, it would have been different; but she could not. Why had he married her? For her beauty. The shame of it rose in her eyes as she sat alone, and she could not help turning her face from the light.

For love's sake, even for an old love outraged long ago and scarred past recognizing, she could have forgiven much. Old memories, suddenly touched, are always more tender than we have thought they were, till the tears rise for them, and the roots of the old life stir in the heart.

Helen had nothing of that. She had made the great mistake of marrying a man whom she had not loved, but whom she had admired, and perhaps believed in, more than she understood. She had married him because he seemed to love her very much, and the thought of being so loved was pleasant. She had soon found out what such love meant, and by and by she had seen how traces of it survived in Henry Harmon when all thought of honoring her, or even of respecting her, was utterly gone.

A bitter laugh rang through the quiet room, and she started, for it was her own voice. She was to forgive! Did he know what he was asking, and for what things he was praying forgiveness? Yet when he had been sober he had generally remembered what he had done when he had been drunk. That is to say, he had seemed to have the faculty of remembering what he chose to recall, and of forgetting everything else. She was to forgive what he chose to remember!

«Oh, Helen dear, for God's sake, do!» She could see the last written words of his letter before her eyes, though the sheet was folded and bent double in her tightly closed hand. He meant it, and it was an appeal for mercy. She hated herself for having laughed so cruelly a moment earlier. There was a cry in the words quite different from all he had written before them. It did not touch her, it hardly appealed to her at all; but somehow it gave him the right to be heard, for it was human.

Then she went over all he said, though it hurt her. She was not a woman of quick impulses, and she knew that what was left of her life was in the balance. Even he seemed to acknowledge that, for he spoke of a possibility of freedom for her by divorce. To speak so easily of it he must have thought of it often, and that meant that it was really an easy matter, as Colonel Wimpole had said. It was in her power, and she had free will. He knew that she had a choice, and that she could either take him back, now that he was cured, or make it utterly out of the question for him to approach her. He said as much when he implored her to give him one more chance «before taking any step.» She went over and over it all for hours.

In the cool of the afternoon she opened the blinds, collected her letters, and then sat down again, no nearer to a decision than she had been at first. A servant came and told her that Colonel Wimpole was down-stairs. He had written a word on his card asking to see her again.

Her first impulse was the natural one; she would let him come in, and she would lay the whole matter before him, as before the best friend she had in the world, and ask him how she should act. There was not in all the world a man more honorable and just. She would let him come to her.

The words were on her lips while the servant stood in the open door waiting for her answer. She checked herself with an effort. She wrote a line, and gave it to the man.

She would not see Wimpole just then, for it would not be fair to him, nor perhaps quite just to Harmon. Wimpole loved her, though he was quite unaware that she knew it. She believed firmly that when he had advised her that very afternoon to divorce her husband he had been thinking only of her happiness; but he had advised it, all the same, just because he believed that Harmon might recover. He could not change his mind now that what he feared for her was taking place. How could he? He would use every argument in his power, and he would find many good ones, against her returning to her husband. He could influence her against her free will, and far more than he could guess, because she loved him secretly as much as he loved her. It was bitter not to see him, and tell him, and ask his help—it was desperately hard; but as soon as she saw that it was right she wrote the words that must send him away before she could have time to hesitate. Deep in her heart, too, there was a thought for him. Loving her as he did, it would not be easy for him either to go into the whole matter; his honor and his love would have to fight it out; so she sent him away.

Then Archie came into the room, vague and childish at first, but with an odd look in his eyes; and he began to talk to her about Sylvia Strahan in a way that frightened her, little by little, as he went on.

«Marry me to her, mother,» he said at last, as though asking for the simplest thing. «I want to be married, and I want Sylvia. I never saw any other girl whom I wanted.»

VII.

THERE are times when trouble accumulates as an avalanche, or like water in one of those natural intermittent springs that break out plentifully and dry up altogether in a sort of alternation. But the spring has its regular period, and trouble has not, and in a landslide of disasters it is impossible to say at any moment whether the big boulders have all passed in the sliding drift of smaller stuff, or whether the biggest of all may not be yet to come.

There are days in a lifetime which decide all the rest, and sometimes explain all that has gone before—happy days, or days of tears, as the case may be. On such days all sorts of things happen that never occurred before, and perhaps never occur again, and every one who has had one or two such short and eventful periods of confusion can remember how a host of unforeseen trifles thrust themselves forward to disturb him. It was as though nothing could turn out right; as if nobody could take a message without a mistake; as if the post and the telegraph had conspired together to send letters and telegrams to wrong addresses; and altogether, all things, including the most sober and reliable institutions, seem to work backward, against results instead of for them. Those are bad times. When they last long people come to grief. When they are soon over people laugh at them. When they decide a whole life, as they sometimes do, people can afterward trace the causes of happiness or disaster to some very small lucky coincidence or unfortunate mistake over which they themselves had no control.

When Colonel Wimpole was refused admittance, Helen's word merely said that she was not able to see any one just then, and he had naturally supposed that she was dressing or lying down. He was intimate enough with her to return half a dozen times a day if he pleased.

When he had gone away so abruptly, he had looked upon his leaving her as a mere interruption of his visit, necessary because he could not be sure of controlling himself just then, but not meant to last any length of time. He would have waited till the evening before going back if his sister had not been so absurdly nervous about the price of the hat, insisting that he should go at once and return the money. He had gone to his own room in rather a disturbed state of mind, and had stayed there an hour, after which Miss Wimpole, judging that he must be sufficiently rested, had knocked at his door and urged him to go at once to see Mrs. Harmon. As he had no very good reason to give for refusing to do so, he had made the attempt, and had been refused admittance. Not dreaming that anything of importance had happened to Helen, he went for a walk along the lake, and came back again after an hour, and wrote on his card a special request:

«May I see you now? It is about a rather awkward little matter.»

It was growing late. Helen reflected that he could not stay long before his own dinner-time and hers, that he evidently had something special to say, and that she was certainly strong enough to keep her own counsel for a quarter of an hour if she made up her mind to do so. Besides, it must seem strange to him to be refused a second time; he would infer that something was wrong, and would ask questions when they next met. She decided to see him.

His face was grave, and he was quite calm again. As he took her hand and spoke there was a sort of quiet tenderness in his manner and tone, a little beyond what he usually showed, perceptible to her who longed for it, though it could hardly have been noticed by any one else.

«It is rather an awkward little matter,» he said, repeating the words he had written.

Then he saw her face in the twilight, and he guessed that she had seen the newspaper.

«Are you in any trouble?» he asked quickly.

She hesitated, and turned from him, for she had forgotten that her face must betray her distress.

«Yes,» she answered, but she said no more than that.

«Can I help you?» he asked after a short pause.

«Please do not ask me.»

She sat down, and Wimpole sighed audibly as he took his seat at a little distance from her. He was sure that she must have seen the paragraph about Harmon's recovery.

« Then I will explain my errand,» he said. « May I? »

It seemed rather a relief to have so small a matter ready to hand.

« Yes; it will not take long, will it? » she asked rather nervously, for she felt how his presence tempted her to confidence. « It—it will soon be dinner-time, you know.»

« I shall not stay long,» said the colonel, quietly. « It is rather an awkward little matter. You know, Archie was with you this morning when I saw you in the shop and got that miniature.»

Helen looked at him suddenly, with a change of expression, expecting some new trouble.

« Yes, Archie was with us; what is it? » Her voice was full of a new anxiety.

« It is nothing of any great importance,» answered Wimpole, quickly, for he saw that she was nervous. « Only, he went out by himself afterward, and came across my sister and Sylvia in a milliner's shop—»

« What was he doing in a milliner's shop? » interrupted Helen, in surprise.

« I don't know,» said the colonel. « I fancy he saw them through the window, and went in to speak to them. Sylvia was trying on a hat, you know, and she liked it, and Archie, without saying anything, out of pure goodness of heart, I suppose—»

He hesitated. On any other day he could have smiled, but just now he was as deeply disturbed as Helen herself, and the absurd incident of the hat assumed a tremendous importance.

« Well, what did he do? » Helen's nerves were on edge, and she spoke almost sharply.

« He paid for the hat,» answered Wimpole, with an air of profound sorrow, and even penitence, as if it had been all his fault; « and then he went off before they knew it.»

Helen bit her lip, for it suddenly trembled. He had not told the story very clearly or connectedly, but she understood. Archie had just been talking to her very strangely about Sylvia, and she had seen that he had fallen in love with his old playmate, and she was afraid. And now she was horribly ashamed for him. It was so stupid, so pitifully stupid.

The colonel, guessing what greater torment was tearing at her heart, sat still in a rather dejected attitude, waiting for her to speak, but not watching her.

The matter which had brought him was certainly not very terrible in itself, but it stirred and quickened all the ever-growing pain for her son which was a part of her daily life. It knitted its strength to that of all the rest to hurt her cruelly, and the torture was more than she could bear.

She turned suddenly in her seat, and half buried her face against the back of the chair, so that Wimpole could not see it; and she bit the coarse velvet savagely, trying to be silent and tearless till he should go away. But he knew what she was doing. If he had not spoken she could still have kept back the scalding tears awhile. But he did speak, and very gently.

« Helen—dear Helen—what is it? »

« My heart is breaking,» she said, almost quietly.

But then the tears came, and she shook once or twice, like an animal that has a bad wound but cannot die. The tears came slowly, and burned her like drops of fire; she kept her face turned away.

Wimpole was beside her, and held her passive hand. It twitched painfully as it lay in his, and every agonized movement of it shot through him, but he could not say anything at first; besides, she knew he was there and would help her if he could. At last he spoke his thought.

« I will keep him from you,» he said. « He shall not come near you.»

Her hand tightened upon his suddenly, and she sat up in her chair, turning her face to him, quite white in the dusk by the open window.

« Then you know? » she asked.

« Yes; it is in the Paris paper to-day. But it is only a report; I do not believe it is true.»

She rose, mastering herself strongly, as she withdrew her hand and steadied herself a moment against the chair beside him.

« It is true,» she said. « He has recovered. He has written to me.»

Wimpole felt as if he had been condemned to death without warning.

« When? » he managed to ask.

« I got the letter this afternoon.»

Their voices answered each other, dull and colorless in the gloom, and for some moments neither spoke. Helen went to the window and leaned upon the broad marble sill, breathing the evening air from the lake, and Wimpole followed her. The electric lamps were lighted in the street, glaring coldly out of the gray dusk, and many people were moving slowly along the pavement below in little parties, some gay, some silent.

« That is why I did not let you come up,» said Helen, after a long time. « But now—since you know— » She stopped, still hesitating, and he tried to see her expression, but there was not enough light.

«Yes?» he said, with a question, not pressing her, but waiting.

«Since you know,» she answered at last, «you can guess the rest.»

A spasm of pain half choked her, and Wimpole put out his hand to lay it gently upon her arm, but drew it back again. He had never done even that much in all those years, and he would not do it now.

«I will keep him from you,» he said again.

«No; you must not do that.» Her voice was steady again. «He will not come to me against my will.»

Wimpole turned sharply as he leaned on the window-sill beside her, for he did not understand.

«You cannot possibly be thinking of writing to him, of letting him come back?»

«Yes,» she said; «that is what I am thinking of doing.»

She hardly dared to suspect that she still could hesitate, now that Wimpole was beside her. If he had not come it might have been different; but he was close to her now, and she knew how long and well he had loved her. Alone she could have found reasons for refusing ever to see Harmon again, but they lost their look of honor now that this man, who was everything to her, was standing at her elbow. Exaggerating her danger, she feared lest Wimpole should influence her, even unintentionally, if she left the question open. And he, for her own happiness, and setting all thoughts of himself honorably aside, believed that he ought to use whatever influence he had to the utmost.

«You must not do it,» he said. «I implore you not to think of it. You will wreck your life.»

She did not move, for she had known what he would say.

«If you are my friend,» she answered after a pause, «you should wish me to do what is right.»

It was a trite commonplace, but she never tried to be original at any time, and just then the words exactly expressed her thought; but he resented it.

«You have done more than enough of that sort of right already. It is time you thought a little of yourself. I do not mean only of your happiness, but of your safety. You are not safe with that man; he will drink again, and he may kill you.»

She turned her white face deliberately toward him in the gloom.

«And do you think I am afraid of that?» she asked slowly.

There was a sort of reproach in the tone, and a great good pride with it. Wimpole did not know what to say, and merely bent his head gravely.

«Besides,» she added, «he is in earnest. He is sorry. He was mad then, and he asks me to forgive him now. How can I refuse? He was really mad, really insane. No one can deny it. Shall I?»

«You can forgive him without going back to him. Why should you risk your life?»

«It is the only way of showing him that I forgive him, and my life will not be in danger.»

«Do you think that you can ever be happy again if you go back to him?» asked Wimpole.

«My happiness is not the question; the only thing that matters is to do right.»

«It seems to me that right is more or less dependent on its results—»

«Never!» cried Helen, almost fiercely, and drawing back a little against the side of the window. «If one syllable of that were true, then we could never know whether we were doing right or not till we could judge the result. And the end would justify the means always, and there would be no more right and wrong at all in the world.»

«But when you know the results,» objected Wimpole, «it seems to me that it may be different.»

«Then it is fear! Then one is afraid to do right because one knows that one risks being hurt! What sort of morality would that be? It would be contemptible.»

«But suppose that it is not only yourself who may be hurt, but some one else? One should think of others first; that is right too.» He could not help saying that much.

Helen hesitated a moment.

«Yes,» she answered presently; «but no one else is concerned in this case.»

«I will leave your friends out of the question,» said Wimpole. «Do you think it will do Archie any good to live under the same roof with his father?»

Helen started perceptibly.

«Oh, why did you say that?» she exclaimed in a low voice, and as she leaned over the window-sill she clasped her hands together in a sort of despairing way. «Why did you say that?» she repeated.

Wimpole was silent, for he had not at first realized that he had found a very strong argument. As yet, being human, she had thought only of herself in the first hours of her trouble. He had recalled all her past terrors for her unfortunate son, and the memory of all she had done to keep him out of his father's way in old days. He had been a mere boy then, and it had been just possible, because his half-developed mind was not suspicious. Now that he was grown up, it would be another matter. The prospect was hideous enough if Harmon should take a fancy to the young man, and make him his companion, and then fall back into his old ways.

«Why did you say it? Why did you make me think of that?» Helen asked the questions almost piteously. «I should have to send Archie away—somewhere where he would be safe.»

«How could he be safe without you?» The argument was pitilessly just.

But, after all, her life and happiness were at stake. Wimpole saw right in everything that could withhold her from the step to which she had evidently made up her mind.

«And if I refuse to go back to my husband, what will become of him?» she asked, still clasping her hands hard together.

«He could be properly taken care of,» suggested Wimpole.

«And would that be forgiveness?» Helen turned to him again energetically.

«It would be wisdom, at all events.»

«Ah, now you come back to your argument!» Her voice changed. «You are pressing me to do what is wise, not what is right. Don't do that! Please don't do that!»

«Do you forgive him?» asked the colonel, very gravely.

Again she paused before answering him.

«Why should you doubt it?» she asked in her turn. «Don't you see that I wish to go back to him?»

«You know what I mean. It is not the same thing. You are a very good woman, and by sheer force of goodness you could make an enormous sacrifice for the sake of what you thought right.»

«And would not that be forgiveness?»

«No; if you freely forgave him it would be no sacrifice, for you would believe in him again. You would have just the same faith in Harmon which you had on the day you married him. If forgiveness means anything, it means that one takes back the man who has hurt one on the same real, inward terms with one's self on which one formerly lived with him. You cannot do that, for it would not be sane.»

«No, I cannot quite do that,» Helen answered, after a moment's thought. «It would not be true to say that I had even thought I could. But then, if you put it in that way, it would be hard to forgive any one, and it would generally be foolish. There is something wrong about your way of looking at it.»

«I am not a woman,» said Wimpole, simply. «That is what is the matter. At the same time, I do not see how you, as a woman, are ever going to reconcile what you believe to be your duty to Harmon with what is certainly your duty to your son.»

«I must,» said Helen. «I must.»

«Then you must do it before you write to Harmon, for afterward it will be impossible. You must decide first what you will do with Archie to keep him out of danger. When you have made up your mind about that, if you choose to sacrifice yourself nobody can prevent you. At least, you will not be ruining him too.»

He saw no reason for not putting the case plainly, since what he said was true. Yet, as he felt his advantage, he knew that by pressing it he was increasing her perplexity. In all his life he had never been in so difficult a position. She stood close beside him, her arm almost touching his, and he had loved her all his life as few men love, with an honesty and purity that were more than quixotic. What there was left he could have borne for her sake, even to seeing her united again with Henry Harmon; but the thought of the risk she was running was more than he could bear. He would use argument, stratagem, force, anything, to keep her out of such a life; and when he had succeeded in saving her he would be capable of denying himself even the sight of her, lest his conscience should accuse him of having acted for himself rather than for her alone.

He remembered Harmon's face as he had last seen it, coarse, cunning, seamed with dissipation, and he looked sideways at Helen, white, weary, bruised, a fast fading rose of yesterday, as she had called herself. The thought of Harmon's touch was more than he could bear.

«You shall not do it!» he exclaimed after a long silence. «I will make it impossible.»

Almost before he spoke the last words he had repented them. Helen drew herself up and faced him, one hand on the window-sill.

«Colonel Wimpole,» she said, «I know that you have always been my best friend; but you must not talk in that way. I cannot allow even you to come between me and what I think is right.»

He bent his head a little.

«I beg your pardon,» he answered in a low voice; «I should have done it, not said it.»

«I hope you will never think of it again,» said Helen.

She left the window, and felt in the dark for matches on the table to light a small candle she used for sealing letters. It cast faint rays up to her sad face. Wimpole had stayed by the window, and watched her now while she looked toward him over the little flame.

«Please go now,» she said gravely; «I cannot bear to talk about this any longer.»

VIII.

AFTER the door had closed Helen stood a moment by the table motionless. Then she sat down by the feeble light of the taper, and wrote upon a sheet of paper her husband's address and one word: «Forgiven.» She looked at the writing fixedly for a minute or two, and then rang the bell.

«Have this telegram sent at once, please; and bring me a lamp and dinner,» she said to the servant.

With the lamp came Archie, following it by a sort of instinct, as children do.

«You must have been in the dark ever so long, mother,» he said; and just then he saw her white face. «You are not looking all right,» he observed.

Helen smiled, from force of habit, rather wearily. The servant began to set the table, moving stealthily, as though he were meditating some sudden surprise which never came. He was a fairly intelligent Swiss, with an immense pink face and very small blue eyes.

Helen watched him for a moment, and sighed. The man was intellectually her son's superior, and she knew it. Any one else might have smiled at the thought as grotesque; but it had for her the horrible vividness of a misfortune that had saddened all of her life which her husband had not embittered. She envied for her son the poor waiter's little powers of mental arithmetic and memory.

«What 's the matter, mother?» asked Archie, who sat looking at her.

«Nothing, dear,» answered Mrs. Harmon, rousing herself, and smiling wearily again. «I am a little tired, perhaps; it has been a hot day.»

«Has it? I did n't notice. I never do—at least, not much. I say, mother, let 's go home! I 'm tired of Europe, and I know you are. Let 's all go home together—we and the Wimpoles.»

«We shall be going home soon,» said Helen.

«I thought you meant to go to Carlsbad first. Was n't it to Carlsbad we were going?»

«Yes, dear; but—here comes dinner—we will talk about it by and by.»

They sat down to table. In hotels abroad Helen always dined in her rooms, for she was never quite sure of Archie. He seemed strangely unconscious of his own defect of mind, and was always ready to enter boldly into conversation with his neighbors at a foreign hotel dinner-table. His childish ignorance had once or twice caused her such humiliation as she did not feel called upon to bear again.

«I don't know why we should n't talk about it now,» began Archie, when he had eaten his soup in silence, and the servant was changing his plate.

«We shall be alone after dinner,» answered his mother.

«Oh, the waiter does n't care! He 'll never see us again, you know; so why should n't we say anything we like before him?»

Mrs. Harmon looked at her son and shook her head gravely, which was an admonition he always understood.

«Did you see anything you liked to-day?» she asked incautiously, by way of changing the conversation.

«Rather!» exclaimed Archie, promptly. «I met Sylvia Strahan—jukes!»

Helen shuddered as she saw the look in his face and the animal glitter in his eyes.

«I wish you could remember not to say ‹jukes› every other minute, Archie,» she said for the thousandth time.

«Do you think Sylvia minds when I say ‹jukes›?» asked the young man, suddenly.

«I am sure she thinks it a very ugly and senseless word.»

«Does she? Really?» He was silent for a few moments, pondering the question. «Well,» he resumed at last, in a regretful tone, «I 've always said it, and I like it, and I don't see any harm in it. But, of course, if Sylvia does n't like it I 've got to give it up, that 's all. I 'm always going to do what Sylvia likes now as long as I live. And what you like, too, mother,» he added as an apologetic and dutiful after-thought. «But then, you 're pretty sure to like the same things, after all.»

«You really must not go on in this way about Sylvia, my dear,» said Helen. «It is too absurd.»

Archie's heavy brows met right across his forehead as he looked up with something like a glare in his eyes, and his voice was suddenly thick and indistinct when he answered:

«Don't call it absurd, mother. I don't understand what it is, but it 's stronger than I am. I don't want anything but Sylvia. Things don't amuse me any more. It was only to-day—»

He stopped, for he was going to tell her how he had found no pleasure in his toys; neither in the blocks, nor in the tin soldiers, nor in the little papier-mâché lady and gentleman in the painted cart. But he thought she did not know about them, and he checked himself in a sudden shame which he had never felt before. A deep red blush spread over his dark face, and he looked down at his plate.

«I 'm a man now,» he said through his teeth, in a rough voice.

After that he was silent for a time, but Helen watched him nervously. She, too, saw that he was a man, with almost less than a boy's mind, and her secret terror grew quickly. She could not eat that evening, but he did not notice her. They dined quickly, and then they sat down together, as they usually did, quite near to each other and side by side. She could sometimes teach him little things which he remembered, when everything was quiet. He generally began to talk of something he had seen, and she always tried to make him understand it and think about it; but this evening he said nothing for a long time, and she was glad of his silence. When she thought of the telegram she had sent, she had a sharp pain at her heart, and once or twice she started a little in her chair; but Archie did not notice her.

«I say, mother,» he began, looking up; «what becomes of all the things one forgets? Do they—do they go to sleep in one's head?»

Mrs. Harmon looked at him in surprise, for it was by far the most thoughtful question he had ever asked. She could not answer it at once, and he went on:

«Because you always tell me to try and remember, and you think I could remember if I tried hard enough. Then you must believe the things are there. You would n't expect me to give you what I had n't got, would you? That would n't be fair.»

«No, certainly not,» answered his mother, considerably puzzled.

«Then you really think that I don't forget. You must think I don't remember to remember; something like that. I can't explain what I mean, but you understand.»

«I suppose so, my dear. Something like that. Yes, perhaps it is just as you say, and things go to sleep in one's head, and one has to wake them up. But I know that I can often remember things I have forgotten if I try very hard.»

«I can't. I say, mother, I suppose I 'm stupid, though you never tell me so. I know I 'm different from other people, somehow. I wish you would tell me just what it is; I don't want to be different from other people. Of course I know I could never be as clever as you, nor the colonel. But then, you 're awfully clever, both of you. Father used to call me an idiot, but I 'm not. I saw an idiot once, and his eyes turned in, and he could n't shut his mouth, and he could n't talk properly.»

«Are you sure that your father ever called you an idiot, Archie?»

Helen's lips were oddly pale, and her voice was low. Archie laughed in a wooden way.

«Oh, yes! I 'm quite sure,» he said. «I remember, because he hit me on the back of the head with the knob of his stick when he said so. That was the first time. Then he got into the way of saying it. I was n't very big then.»

Helen leaned back and closed her eyes, and in her mind she saw the word «Forgiven» as she had written it after the name: «Henry Harmon, New York. Forgiven.» It had a strange look. She had not known that he had ever struck the boy cruelly.

«Why did you never tell me?» she asked slowly.

«Oh, I don't know. It would have been like a cry-a-baby to go running to you. I just waited.»

Helen did not guess what was coming.

«Did he strike you again with the knob of his stick?» she asked.

«Lots of times, with all sorts of things. Once, when you were off somewhere for two or three days on a visit, he came at me with a poker. That was the last time. I suppose he had been drinking more than usual.»

«What happened?» asked Helen.

«Oh, well, I 'd grown big then, and I got sick of it all at once, you know. He never tried to touch me again after that.»

Helen recalled distinctly that very unusual occasion when she had been absent for a whole week, at the time of a sister's death. Harmon had seemed ill when she had returned, and she remembered noticing a great change in his manner toward the boy only a few months before he had become insane.

«What did you do?» she asked.

«I hit him. I hit him badly a good many times. Then I put him to bed. I knew he would n't tell.»

Archie smiled slowly at the recollection of

beating his father, and looked down at his fist. Helen felt as though she were going mad herself. It was all horribly unnatural—the father's cruel brutality to his afflicted son, the son's ferocious vengeance upon his father when he had got his strength.

«You see,» continued Archie, «I knew exactly how many times he had hit me altogether, and I gave all the hits back at once. That was fair, anyhow.»

Helen could not remember that he had ever professed to be sure of an exact number from memory.

«How could you know just how many times—?» She spoke faintly, and stopped, half sick.

«Blocks,» answered Archie. «I dropped a little blot of ink on one of my blocks every time he hit me. I used to count the ones that had blots on them every morning. When they all had one blot each, I began on the other side, till I got round again. Some had blots on several sides at last. I don't know how many there were now; but it was all right, for I used to count them every morning, and remember all day. There must have been forty or fifty, I suppose. But I know it was all right. I did n't want to be unfair, and I hit him slowly, and counted. Oh,»—his eyes brightened suddenly,—«I 've got the blocks here. I 'll go and get them, and we can count them together; then you 'll know exactly.»

Helen could not say anything, and Archie was gone. She only half understood what the blocks were, and did not care to know. There was an unnatural horror in it all, and Archie spoke of it quite simply and without any particular resentment. She was still half dazed when he came back with the mysterious box in which he kept his toys.

He set it down on the floor at her feet, and knelt beside it, feeling for the key in his pocket.

«I don't care if you see all the things now,» he said; «they don't amuse me any more.»

Nevertheless, she saw the blush of shame rising to his forehead as he bent down and put the key into the lock.

«I don't care, after all,» he said before he lifted the lid. «It 's only you, mother; and you won't think I was a baby just because they amused me. I don't care for them any more, mother—indeed I don't; so I may as well make a clean breast of it and tell you. Besides, you must see the blocks. All the blots are there still, quite plain, and we can count them, and then you 'll always remember, though I sha'n't. Here they are. I 've carried them about a long time, you know, and they 're getting pretty old, especially the soldiers. There is n't much paint left on them, and the captain's head 's gone.»

Helen leaned forward, her elbow on her knees, her chin resting on her hand, her eyes dim, and her heart beating oddly. It seemed as though nothing were spared her on that day.

Archie unpacked the toys in silence, and arranged the blocks all on one side in a neat pile, while on the other he laid the soldiers and the little cart, with the few remaining toys. Helen's eyes became riveted on the bits of wood. There were about twenty of them, and she could plainly distinguish on them the little round blots which Archie had made, one for each blow he had received. He began to count, and Helen followed him mechanically. He was very methodical, for he knew that he was easily confused. When he had counted the blots on each block, he put it behind him on the floor before he took another from the pile. He finished at last.

«Sixty-three—ju—!» He checked himself. «I forgot. I won't say ‹jukes› any more—I won't. There were sixty-three in all, mother. Besides, I remember now. Yes; there were sixty-three. I remember that it took a long time, because I was afraid of not being fair.»

Again he smiled at the recollection, with some satisfaction, perhaps, at his conscientious rectitude. With those hands of his, it was a wonder that he had not killed his father. Helen sat like a stone figure, and watched him unconsciously, while her thoughts ground upon each other in her heart like millstones, and her breath half choked her.

He swept all the blocks back in front of him, and by force of habit he began to build a little house before he put them away. She watched his strong hands, that could do such childish things, and the bend of his athletic neck. His head was not ill-shaped nor defective under the thick, short hair.

«Did he always strike you on the head, Archie?» she asked suddenly.

He knocked the little house over with a sweep of his hand, and looked up.

«Generally,» he said quietly. «But it does n't matter, you know. He generally went for the back of my head because it did n't make any mark, as I have such thick hair; so I hit him in the same place. It 's all right; it was quite fair. I say, mother, I 'm going to throw these things away, now that you know all about them. What 's the good of keeping them, anyway? I 'm sure I don't know why I ever liked them.»

«Give them to me,» answered Helen. «Perhaps some poor child might like them.»

But she knew that she meant to keep them.

«Well, there is n't much paint on those tin soldiers, you know. I don't believe any child would care for them much; at least, not so much as I did, because I was used to them. Of course that made a difference. But you may have them if you like. I don't want them any more; they 're only in the way.»

«Give them to me for the present.»

«All right, mother.» And he began to pack the toys into the box.

He did it very carefully and neatly, for the habit was strong, though the memory was weak. Still Helen watched him without changing her attitude. He sighed as he put in the last of the tin soldiers.

«I suppose I shall really never care for them again,» he said.

He looked at them with a sort of affection, and touched some of the things lightly, arranging them a little better. Then he shut the lid down, turned the key, and held it out to his mother.

«There you are,» he said. «Anyhow, the blocks helped me to remember. Sixty-three, was n't it, mother?»

«Sixty-three,» repeated Helen, mechanically.

Then, for the second time on that evening, she turned her face to the cushion of her chair, and shook from head to foot, and sobbed aloud. She had realized what the number meant: sixty-three times, in the course of years, had Henry Harmon struck his son upon the head. It was strange that Archie should have any wits at all, and it was no wonder that they were not like those of other men. And it had all been a secret, kept by the child first, then by the growing boy, then by the full-grown man, till his thews and sinews had toughened upon him, and he had turned and paid back blow for blow all at once. And last of all, the father had struck her, with a thought of revenge, perhaps, as well as in passion, because he dared not raise his hand against his strong son.

Again she saw the words of her telegram, «Henry Harmon, New York. Forgiven,» and they were in letters of fire that her tears could not quench. She had not known how much she was forgiving. Archie knelt beside her in wonder, for he had never seen her cry in his life. He touched her arm lovingly, trying to see her face, and his own softened strangely, growing more human as it grew more childlike.

«Don't, mother! Please don't cry like that! If I had thought you would cry about it, I 'd never have told you. Besides, it could n't have hurt him so very much—»

«Him!»

Helen's voice rang out, and she turned with a fierce light in her angry eyes. In a quick movement her arms ran round Archie's neck and drew him passionately to her breast, and she kissed his head again and again, always his head, upon the short, thick hair, till he wondered and laughed.

When they were quiet again, sitting side by side, her battle began once more, and she knew that it must all be fought over on different ground. She had forgiven Henry Harmon as well as she could for her own wrongs; but there were others now, and they seemed worse to her than anything she had suffered. It was just to think so, too, for she knew that at any time she could have left Harmon without blame or stain. It had been in her power, but she had chosen not to do it.

But the boy had been powerless and silent through long years; she had never even guessed that his father had ever struck him cruelly. At the merest suspicion of such a thing she would have turned upon her husband as only mothers do turn, tigresses or women. But Archie had kept his secret, while his strength quietly grew upon him, and then he had paid the long score with his own hands. Out of shame Harmon had kept the secret too.

Yet she had said in one word that she forgave him, and the word determined the rest of her life. A suffering, a short, sad respite, and then suffering again: that was to sum the history of her years. She must suffer to the end more and more.

And all at once it seemed to her that she could not bear it. For herself she might have forgiven anything; she had pardoned all for herself, from the first neglect to the scar on her forehead; but it was another matter to forgive for Archie. Why should she? What justice could there be in that? What right had she to absolve Harmon for his cruelty to her child?

She must ask Archie if he forgave his father. She could no longer decide the question alone, and Archie had the best of rights to be consulted. Wimpole's words came back to her, asking whether it could do Archie any good to be under the same roof with his father; and all at once she saw that her whole married life had been centered in her son much more than in herself.

Besides, he must be told that his father had recovered, for every one must know it soon, and people would speak of it before him, and think it very strange if he were ignorant of it. She hid from herself the underthought that Archie must surely refuse to live with his father after all that had passed, and the wild hope of escape from what she had undertaken to do which the suggestion raised.

She sat silent and thoughtful, her tears drying on her cheeks, while her son still knelt beside her. But without looking at him she laid her hand on his arm, and her grasp tightened while she was thinking.

«What is it, mother? What is it?» he asked again and again.

At last she let her eyes go to his, and she answered him:

«Your father is well again. By this time he must have left the asylum. Shall we go back to him?»

«I suppose we must if he 's all right,» answered Archie, promptly.

Helen's face fell suddenly, for she had expected a strong refusal.

«Can you forgive him for all he did to you?» she asked slowly.

«I don't see that there 's much to forgive. He hit me, and I hit him just as often, so we 're square. He won't hit me now because he 's afraid of me. I hate him, of course, and he hates me; it 's quite fair. He thinks I 'm stupid, and I think he 's mean; but I don't see that there 's anything to forgive him. I suppose he 's made so. If he 's all right again, I don't see but what we shall have to go and live with him again. I don't see what you 're going to do about it, mother.»

Helen buried her face in her hands, not sobbing again, but thinking. She did not see «what she was going to do about it,» as Archie expressed the situation. If she had not already sent the telegram it would have been different. The young man's rough phrases showed that he had not the slightest fear of his father, and he was ignorant of what she herself had suffered. Much she had hidden from him altogether, and his dullness had seen nothing of the rest. He supposed, if he thought anything about it, that his mother had been unhappy because Harmon drank hard, and stayed away from home unaccountably, and often spoke roughly and rudely when he had been drinking. To his unsensitive nature and half-developed mind these things had seemed regrettable, but not so very terrible after all. Helen had been too loyal to hold up Harmon as an example of evil to his son, and the boy had grown up accustomed to what disgusted and revolted her, as well as ignorant of what hurt her, while his own unfinished character was satisfied with a half-barbarous conception of what was fair so far as he himself was concerned. He had given blow for blow and bruise for bruise, and on a similar understanding he was prepared to return to similar conditions. Helen saw it all in a flash, but she could not forgive Harmon.

«I can't! I can't!» she repeated aloud, and she pressed Archie's arm again.

«Can't—what, mother?» he asked. «Can't go back?»

«How can I after this? How can I ever bear to see him, to touch his hand—his hand that hurt you, Archie—that hurt you so much more than you ever dream of?»

There were tears in her voice again, and again she pressed him close to her; but he did not understand.

«Oh, that 's all right, mother,» he answered; «don't cry about me! I made it all right with him long ago. And I don't suppose he hurt me more than I dreamed of, either. That 's only a way of talking, you know. It used to make me feel rather stupid; but then, I 'm stupid anyway, so even that did n't matter much.» And Archie smiled indifferently.

«More than you think, more than you know!» She kissed his hair. «It was that —it may have been that—it must have been—I know it was—»

She was on the point of breaking down again.

«What?» he asked with curiosity. «What do you mean? I don't understand.»

Helen's voice sank low, and she hardly seemed to be speaking to her son.

«Your father made you what you are,» she said, and her face grew cold and hard.

«What? Stupid?» asked Archie, cheerfully. Then his face changed too. «I say, mother,» he went on in another voice; «do you think I 'm so dull because he hit me on the head?»

Helen repented her words, scarcely knowing why, but sure that it would have been better not to speak them. She did not answer the question.

«That 's what you think,» said Archie. «And it 's because I 'm not like other people that you say it 's absurd of me to want to marry Sylvia Strahan, is n't it? And that 's my father's doing? Is that what you think?»

He waited for an answer, but none came at once. Helen was startled by the clear sequence of ideas, far more logical than most of his reasonings. It seemed as if his sudden passion for Sylvia had roused his sluggish intelligence from its long torpor. She could not deny the truth of what he said, and he saw that she could not.

«That 's it,» he continued; «that 's what you think. I knew it.»

His brows knitted themselves straight across his forehead, and his eyes were fixed upon his mother's face as he knelt beside her. She had not been looking at him, but she turned to him slowly now.

«And that 's why you ask whether I can forgive him,» he concluded.

«Can you?»

«No.»

He rose to his feet from his knees easily by one movement, and she watched him. Then there was a long silence, and he began to walk up and down.

Helen felt as if she had done something disloyal, and that he had given the answer for which she had been longing intensely, as an escape from her decision, and as a means of freedom from bondage to come. She could ask herself now what right she had to expect that Archie should forgive his father; but instead she asked what right she could have had to give Archie so good a reason for hating him, when the boy had not suspected that which, after all, might not be the truth. She had made an enormous sacrifice in sending the message of forgiveness for her own wrongs, but it seemed to her all at once that in rousing Archie's resentment for his own injuries she had marred the purity of her own intention.

Indeed, she was in no state to judge herself, for what Archie had told her was a goad in her wound, with a terror of new pain.

«You cannot forgive him,» she said mechanically, and almost to herself.

«Why should I?» asked Archie. «It means Sylvia to me. How can I forgive him that?»

And suddenly, without waiting for any answer, he went out and left her alone.

After a long time she wrote this letter to her husband:

Dear Henry: I am very glad to hear of your recovery, and I have received your letter to-day, together with the doctor's. I have telegraphed the one word for which you ask, and you have probably got the message already. But I must answer your letter as well as I can, and say a great many things which I shall never say again. If we are to meet and try to live together, it is better that I should speak plainly before I see you.

You asked a great deal of me, and for myself I have done what you asked. I do not say this to make it seem as though I were making a great sacrifice, and wished you to admit it. We were not happy together; you say that it was your fault, and you ask me to forgive you. If I believed that you had been in full possession of your senses till you were taken ill, I do not think that forgiveness could be possible. You see, I am frank. I know that you often did not know what you said and did, and that when you did know you could not always weigh the consequences of your words and actions; so I shall try to forget them. That is what you mean by being forgiven, and it is the only meaning either you or I can put upon the word. I shall try to forget, and I will bear no malice for anything in the past, so far as I am concerned. Never speak of it when we meet, and I never will. If you really wish to try the experiment of living together again, I am willing to attempt it as an experiment.

But there is Archie to be considered, and Archie will not forgive you. By a mere chance to-day, after I had sent my telegram, he told me that you used to strike him cruelly and often because his dullness irritated you. You struck him on the head, and you injured his brain, so that his mind has never developed fully, and never can.

I do not think that if I were a man, as he is, I could forgive that. Could you? Do you expect that I should, being his mother? You cannot. You and he can never live under the same roof again. It would perhaps be harder for you, feeling as you must, than for him; but in any case it is not possible, and there is only one arrangement to be made. We must put Archie somewhere where he shall be safe and healthy and happy, and I will spend a part of the year with you and a part with him. I will not give him up for you, and I am not willing to give you up for him. Neither would be right. You are my husband, whatever there may have been in the past; but Archie is my child. It will be harder for me than for him, too.

You say that I might have got a divorce from you, and you do me the justice to add that you believe I have never thought of it. That is true, but it is not a proof of affection. I have none for you. I told you that I should speak plainly, and it is much better. It would be an ignoble piece of comedy on my part to pretend to be fond of you. I was once. I admired you, I suppose, and I liked you well enough to marry you, being rather ignorant of the world and of what people could feel. If you had really loved me and been kind to me I might have loved you in the end. But, as it turned out, I could not go on admiring you long, and I simply ceased to like you. That is our story, and it is a sad one. We made the great mistake, for we married without much love on either side, and we were very young.

But it was a marriage just the same, and a bond which I never meant to break, and will not break now. A promise is a promise, whatever happens, and a vow made before God is ten times a promise. So I always mean to keep mine to you, as I have kept it. I will do my best to make you happy, and you must do your part to make it possible.

After all, that is the way most people live. True love, lasting lifetimes and not changing, exists in the world, and it is the hope of it that makes youth lovely and marriage noble. Few people find it, and the many who do not must live as well as they can without it. That is what we must do. Perhaps, though the hope of love is gone, we may find peace together. Let us try.

But not with Archie. There are things which no woman can forgive nor forget. I could not forgive you this if I loved you with all my heart, and you must not expect it of me, for it is not in my power. The harm was not done to me, but to him, and he is more to me than you ever were, and far more to me than myself. I will only say that. There can be no need of ever speaking about it, but I want you to understand; and not only this, but everything. That is why I write such a long letter.

It must all be perfectly clear, and I hope I have made it so. It was I who suffered for the great mistake we made in marrying; but you are sorry for that, and I say, let us try the experiment, and see whether we can live together in peace for the rest of our lives. You are changed since your illness, I have no doubt, and you will make it as easy as you can. At least, you will do your best, and so shall I.

Have I repeated myself in this letter? At least I have tried to be clear and direct. Besides, you know me, and you know what I mean by writing in this way: I am in earnest.

God bless you, Henry; I hope this may turn out well. HELEN.

It was ten o'clock when she had finished. She laid her hand upon the bell, meaning to send her letter to the post-office by a servant; but just then the sound of laughing voices came up to her through the open window, and she did not ring. Looking out, she saw that there were still many people in the street, for it was a warm evening. It was only a step from her hotel to the post-office, and if she went herself she should have the satisfaction of knowing positively that the letter was safe. She put on a hat with a thick veil, and went out.

(To be continued.)

*F. Marion Crawford.*

# THE ABSURDITY OF WAR.

WAR is the last remnant of man's mode of deciding disputes in the animal or savage state. As soon as he started on the road to civilization he set up judges or courts to settle controversies. Before that, when two men differed about anything, they tore or mutilated each other's bodies, and it was tacitly agreed that the man who was most mutilated, if not killed, should give way. But he abode by the decisions of courts very reluctantly. The hardest battle of the reformers of the race was to get him to submit to the judges. He always preferred in his heart some kind of mutilation of his adversary's body, and in order to give a certain dignity to this mode of settling quarrels he got up the theory that God presided over it, and always gave the victory to the man who was in the right. In England this notion lasted in the «trial by battle,» or «wager of battle,» almost down to our own time. It was held that the Deity was on the side of the man who gave most cuts and stabs.

When the wager of battle as a settlement of disputes of any kind became too absurd, the turbulent classes were driven into starting the duel. They felt that there must be some mode reserved of getting at an adversary's body with some weapon. So they established the rule that all offences against what they called their «honor»—that is, their sense of personal dignity—must be avenged by cutting, stabbing, or shooting, and that each man must decide when his «honor» was injured, and when cutting, stabbing, or shooting was necessary. This was a very cunning arrangement; for if it were left to other people to say when your «honor» was injured, you might never, or very rarely, get a chance to cut or stab or shoot at all, because they might say your honor was not injured. But there was even a better device than this; for it was arranged that the man who you said had injured your honor could not deny it or apologize without disgrace. He was held bound, no matter how trifling the injury, to give you a chance to cut him or stab him, and to do his best to cut or stab you. In what manner this mended your honor was never explained. To all outward appearance, after the theory of the interest of the Deity in the matter had died out, your honor remained after the fight exactly what it was before the fight. The cutting and stabbing had neither proved nor disproved anything; it had simply gratified an animal instinct of the primeval time. Dueling, however, has disappeared here and in England. It flourishes still, in the old barbarous, absurd form, on the Continent.

Disputes between nations, for obvious reasons, have not come as rapidly under human methods of decision as disputes between individuals. Nations have never agreed to have judges and arguments as individuals have. The result is that their mode of deciding differences of opinion has always remained the old animal one of doing as much material injury as possible to the other side; and there still lingers the belief that God is on the side of the one which does most injury; that he counts up the number of killed and wounded, and decides that the one which has most killed and wounded is in the wrong. During war he is prayed to see that the number of killed and wounded on the other side may be the larger, and after what is called a «victory»—that is, the killing and wounding of a larger number of your enemies than they have managed to kill and wound on your side—people hurry to church and sing hymns of thanks. This belief is very strong still in our day, and the enemy's dead are counted joyfully. The human plan of deciding differences of opinion by judges, proofs, and argumentative persuasion, as distinguished from the animal or feline plan of deciding by the tearing and rending of bodies, has, in fact, not made much progress, though it has begun to receive attention.

But the process of settling quarrels by mutilation and destruction of property in disputes between nations has some features of atrocity unknown in dueling, or single combat, or wager of battle. In all these cases the actual enemies, who know whatever is to be known about the cause of the dispute, meet face to face and do the cutting and stabbing on each other. They do not attack any one else, and when they have injured each other to the extent of their ability, they stop, if living. But in the case of nations vast bodies of men are employed to kill and maim one another in quarrels of the merits of which they know nothing, and which they have no power of their own to end; and they may go on fighting for years, as in the great wars of Napoleon, killing and being killed, without the power to come to terms. When this takes place it is called «war,» and really is no more human or rational than fights between animals. In fact, it is the one great trait of barbarism of the primeval world retained by modern nations. As far back as we can go we find men trying to kill each other about something, or to gratify mere hatred, on as large a scale as the tribe can afford. The Iroquois led two or three hundred men to the field because they hated the Mohicans, or because the Mohicans had something they wanted. The modern Germans led a million of men to the field because they hated the French, or because the French had something they wanted. The French do the same thing to the Germans. Nothing, or very little, is changed except the scale on which the thing is done, and the treatment of the wounded prisoners. Civilization has made its way so far that we treat them with tolerable kindness; the Iroquois used to kill and torture them.

But civilization has done another very curious thing. It has raised the business of killing enemies and destroying their property into a very honorable profession. Indeed, it has raised it in honor far above the other professions. The soldier who settles quarrels by stabbing, cutting, and rending stands higher in popular estimation than the judge and advocate who sit to decide quarrels peaceably, by reason, on the human method. The animal method has the ascendancy. With the general public this is due largely to leaving what the soldier *does* out of sight, and considering simply to what he exposes himself. He is not looked on at all as a man who kills and wounds enemies and destroys property; who makes widows and orphans by the thousand; who tramples down crops, and burns villages, and brings ruin into thousands of lives: but as a man who exposes his life for others. In the popular imagination he does not kill for his country: he is killed for his country. The active part of his business is seldom present to the mind; the passive or suffering part is what is mainly present. It is chiefly through this impression, also, that war is elevated into an improver of character, or moral elevator of the whole community. This view could hardly be maintained if war were constantly thought of as a collection of men cutting, stabbing, mutilating, and burning houses. Its success is due to the habit of fixing the imagination on soldiers as in some sense martyrs, as men who for the sake of the community sacrifice their own lives. The theory has no foundation on observed facts. Wars have raged since the dawn of civilization, but there is no record of their having improved any nation's character, of having made men more sober, or religious, or humane, or law-abiding. All that we know of the effect of war represents it as demoralizing to the many, though probably in a few cases having chastened or purified a few surviving relatives.

But the most serious charge which can be made against war is that either it does not decide things, or that it is waged over things which might be decided without it, although it is enormously costly. Take as examples the wars of this century between civilized nations. I will admit that those between civilized and barbarous nations have been just and necessary. The wars of Napoleon lasted twenty years; cost, it is estimated, the lives of three millions of men; suspended the march of civilization all over Europe; and caused enormous destruction of property. Very few of those engaged in them had any idea what they were about. They ended in leaving France exactly as they found her—much impoverished in money and population, and with the same, or nearly the same, frontiers as when they began. The next war was the attempt of France to keep a certain family on the throne of Spain. It failed: the family lost the throne. The next was the Belgian revolution. It settled what ought to have been settled without it. The next was the Crimean war. Within twenty years everything it accomplished had disappeared, and the general opinion of Europe was that it should never have been undertaken. It cost two hundred thousand lives and about one billion dollars. The next was the war for the liberation of Italy. It succeeded, but ought not to have been necessary. The next was the war of the rebellion, costing about five billion dollars, and two hundred thousand lives, and enormous destruction of property. It was of no use to those who began it. The next were the Prusso-Austrian and the Franco-German war. Both accomplished their purpose, and were enormously destructive.

Now, what is noticeable in all these is that they were about matters capable of the submission of proofs, and arguments by counsel, and judicial decisions; and that in every case, excepting the seizure of Alsace and Lorraine, wise and impartial judges would have decided the matter exactly either as the war decided it, or as the war was meant to decide it, but did not. Nearly everything in the dispute was plain, except which of the disputants had most power of destruction; in other words, the war was totally unnecessary. On human plans of expediency and persuasion, France would never have been invaded after the Revolution; Napoleon would never have fought; Holland would have let Belgium go; France would never have invaded Spain; England would never have fought Russia; Austria would have surrendered Italy, and would have concluded an arrangement with Prussia; the South would have yielded to the North for compensated emancipation; and the French would never have called the German king to account about the throne of Spain. What I mean is, that in every one of these cases an impartial tribunal would have decided the matter either in the way the war decided it, or in the way hindsight decided it. About five million men who were killed or maimed would have continued to labor and enrich their countries, and the nations of Europe would have been saved a debt which I do not put into figures because they would be so large that they would convey nothing to the reader's mind. In every case the difficulty was one which could have been settled by the human art of persuasion; by people simply saying before the war what they said after it; or, in other words, by acting like men, not like animals. If cats fought in armies, the only question they would settle which could not be settled in any other way would be, which set could do most biting and scratching. Any other question between them—such as, which was entitled to most food, which made most noise at night, which was the best climber of back-yard fences, which had the best fur—could be settled judicially by testimony and argument.

The enormous growth of armies in Europe, and the recent unhealthy outburst of jingoism among us, may seem to contradict what I say as to the growth of a more peaceful spirit among the nations—that is, as to the growth of civilization. But it must be observed that in no case is the tremendous enlargement of the standing armies ascribed to love of war or aggression. On the contrary, every nation says it is arming in the interest of peace, and that it loathes war; that it is some other nation's evil designs which render the increase in armament necessary. This is of itself a distinct advance. In the last century the increase in the army would have been boldly ascribed to a desire to conquer or humiliate somebody.

*E. L. Godkin.*

# TOPICS OF THE TIME

### A Call for Home Patriotism.

THE new year ought to be a memorable one in the work of municipal reform throughout the United States. The passing of the Presidential election, with its momentous issue, leaves the field clear everywhere for the undistracted consideration of questions which are rather local than national, and into which partizan politics should not be permitted to enter. New York City will have to decide in November whether it will go ahead with its experiment in non-partizan administration, or will slide back into the slough of Tammany misrule. Its conduct will be watched eagerly by other cities, and if the verdict shall be in favor of progress, a fresh impulse toward good government will be felt in every municipality of the land.

New York can now be looked to with profit by other cities for guidance in the work of good city government. The two years of her reform administration have accomplished one remarkable result, and many others that are valuable. The one success which overshadows all others is that of Colonel Waring in the Street-cleaning Department. For the first time in the history of the country we have a great American city whose streets are as well cleaned as those of any other city in the world. One of the most common and most humiliating charges against municipal government in this country is thus wiped out so far as our chief city is concerned. In securing this advance for us, Colonel Waring has done something even more important than to clean and keep clean the pavements of New York streets. He has shown the whole country that the most efficient kind of public service is that which has no «politics» in it. Every great city in the country had for years a street-cleaning force under the control of politics, but in no city were the streets cleaned. Colonel Waring constructed his force on new principles; he defied politics and politicians; was obliged to face bitter opposition and persistent misrepresentation because of his defiance: but he won in the end, and succeeded in doing what no «practical politician» had ever done. Herein was a victory for the «theoretical reformer» which no man can gainsay. Furthermore, while doing this he organized a force which has become a cause of public pride. Before his advent no public servant was more despicable than a street-sweeper. Now he is a self-respecting member of a uniformed force which marches in annual parade through Fifth Avenue, and is displayed with the Fire Department to distinguished foreign visitors as one of the institutions in which the city takes pride. The men feel that they are their own masters, that they hold their positions because they are fit for them, and that so long as they do their work well no political boss can harm them. In other words, freedom from political interference has made men of them, and they do their work like men, and not like slaves.

The lesson to be drawn from this is twofold. In the first place, the best municipal service is that which is thoroughly dissevered from politics; in the second place, the best results can be achieved only by a single responsible head in a municipal department. All observers agree, for example, that if Theodore Roosevelt had been the sole head of the Police Department instead of one of four commissioners, and had had as full administrative powers as Colonel Waring possesses, he would have given New York a model police force to accompany its street-cleaning force. He and his reforming associates have accomplished a great deal as it is, but they have been hampered seriously by the defective system under which they have had to work.

Back of all stands the lesson which cannot be too often enforced, that the only way in which to get model city government is to take the government of all our cities permanently out of politics—not for two years or three years, but for all time. New York has accomplished what she has by one step in this direction. If she does not follow it with a second step in November, much of the gain will disappear in a twelvemonth. Her short and fleeting taste of really civilized rule will be largely replaced by the old barbaric reign of incompetence, corruption, and political «pulls.» What must be had is not the service of a man like Colonel Waring for three years, but for life. In other words, we must have here what they have in the best-governed cities of Europe: permanent tenure for all the more important heads of municipal departments, and promotions on merit and fitness alone. In that way we shall always have in training for municipal service men who are competent to fill vacancies at the top, and to carry forward the work of government without a break. In that way, also, we shall shut and bar forever the door against the entrance of partizan politics.

In this struggle to put the government of our cities upon a thoroughgoing business basis, great progress ought to be made during the present year and the others that are to follow it, while we have a lull in national politics. Chicago, under her reform administration, has made great progress already, and is certain to make more, for a genuine public spirit has been aroused there by the Civic Federation, which has secured the thorough application of civil-service reform principles, and is exerting itself constantly to cultivate a militant civic pride throughout the city. Similar organizations ought to be formed, and indeed have been formed, in other cities, and good results are certain to follow their exertions. Let us have all over the country a genuine revival, a national awakening of home patriotism, directed at the abolition of ignorant and dishonest rule from all our cities, and in this way make the year 1897 a memorable one in our annals.

### As Others See Us.

WHY is it that foreign newspapers almost habitually accept as accurate the most unfavorable views which reach them of Americans and American affairs and doings? American readers of foreign newspapers know this to be the case, and are a good deal puzzled by it. Especially is it true of London journals. Many of these seem to be eager for news which represents this country as the land of extraordinary people and extraordinary occurrences. They revel in accounts of cyclones, of earthquakes, and of appalling railway disasters. Nothing strikes them as too unusual to be credited. The editor of a London daily who received the following cable message from his New York correspondent in August last published it in serene confidence that it was a truthful statement of facts:

> Still the heat continues, and the odor of the charnel-house reigns over the city. From hundreds of decomposing human bodies and from the rotting carcases of horses there exhales a stench that is positively sickening. Added to this horror is an epidemic of rabies. Mad dogs are running about the streets, and already more than a score of children have been bitten. The mortality due to the heat yesterday totals up 85 persons.

This was almost pure invention. If a New York editor had received from London a message ascribing such a condition of affairs to that city, he would not have accepted it as truthful. Why should a London editor be less skeptical about the probability of such things existing in New York? We are known to be a civilized community, and it is reasonable to suppose that a civilized city of a million and a half of inhabitants would have a government capable of removing dead bodies and checking the running of mad dogs through its streets. Why should not a London editor consider this when confronted with «news» like the above?

Similar credulity is shown by English journals in American political matters. The tendency almost invariably is to believe that the worst side has the best chance of winning. There must be reasons for this state of mind in regard to us as a people. Nations, like individuals, make their own reputations, and we must have a hand in making ours. Undoubtedly the long-standing view of us as an enormous country with an enormous mixed population is responsible for much of the foreign misunderstanding of us, but it does not account for all of it. For many years all the books which visitors to this country wrote about us were given up mainly to more or less exaggerated, and often largely imaginary, accounts of our peculiarities; but this is no longer the case. Most of the information which reaches the Old World in this manner nowadays is intelligent, and is calculated to depict us in our true character.

Can we be said to serve ourselves as fairly as others serve us? The two chief sources to which foreign observers look for manifestations of our civilization and progress are our press and our public men. This must be the case with every nation. Are these two reflections of our national life such always as to command high respect for our general culture, our self-restraint, our high-minded sense of justice, our broad conception of international obligations? It has been said that every nation has the kind of press that it deserves, that its newspapers reflect the tastes and mirror the intellectual standards of its people. We cannot expect to be made an exception in the general judgment of the world; and if many of our great journals place trivialities, scandal, and crime in most conspicuous position in their columns, thus assuming that American readers like that kind of news best of all, how can we complain when foreign observers accept the assumption as accurate? If some of our statesmen and politicians assume habitually a bullying tone of contempt for foreign opinion, if they habitually make light of expert knowledge, express contempt for trained intelligence, treat such grave matters as the public credit and national honor with indifference, how can we complain if foreign observers say that as a people we care little for all those things?

It is worth while to consider these matters seriously. The English editor who published the telegram about the condition of affairs in New York City had been in the habit of seeing American newspapers arrive in every mail with their columns filled with accounts of crime of one kind and another, and with groups of criminal events headed «Carnivals of Crime.» Such prominence and profusion of this kind of news in an English or other European newspaper would have meant a virtually lawless condition of society in the city in which the crime was placed. What more natural than for an editor who had been accustomed to this kind of news about New York to accept the rumors about mad dogs and dead bodies as not a bit improbable?

There is one trait of our national character which foreigners can never comprehend, and that is our unshakable faith in our ability to «come out all right in the end.» We stand idly and more or less indifferently by, and allow the country to be pushed to the verge of a financial or political precipice under the impulse of some kind of popular craze or another, entirely confident that just before it slips over we can take hold of it and pull it back. We have done this again and again, and nothing seems to shake our faith in our ability to repeat the operation whenever occasion arises. It costs us enormously, not only in reputation, but also in money, and retards our growth and progress in a thousand ways; but nothing seems likely to cure us of the habit, unless it be a great national calamity due to our failing in some crisis to take alarm quickly enough.

We must not say this much without adding that English periodicals are beginning to see the necessity of better reports both of current events in America and of the great movements of reform of various kinds that are continually being carried to successful conclusions in this country. The grotesque and sensational will doubtless not fail to have an undue share of attention on the part of the foreign, as it has with the native, press; but the deeper life of the people, the quiet, home-making, conservative, self-respecting, uplifting forces in American civilization, will not be forgotten or underrated.

### A «Law-Regarding Race.»

We have heard it said of a great English poet that he was always disappointing his admirers. It may be remarked of the great American republic that it is always disappointing its enemies. A campaign such as that through which we have recently passed, marked by such intense mental excitement and harshness of language, ought in all reason to have been accompanied by physical violence. There were, it is true, rumors of eggs thrown—that seemed to hit no one; occasionally speakers were interrupted. There was some horse-play, doubtless; but where were the shootings and riots that ought to have been reported from all parts of a country of nearly seventy millions of little and big agitated campaigners?

No; in the general good order—punctuated by not very important exceptions—the nation again disappointed those who are unfriendly to republican institutions. Riots came, indeed, neither during nor after the election. The quiet and good-natured way in which the defeated took the victory of their opponents constitutes another disappointment to our unfriendly critics.

All of which illustrates and enforces the truth of Professor Woodrow Wilson's contention that Americans have always been a law-regarding race. He holds that this regard for law was apparent in the war of the Revolution; and that, later, «neither side could have fought the battles of the war of 1861–65 until they had satisfied themselves that they had a legal right to do so»; adding with a smile: «That they both thought themselves in the right proves what subtle litigants they were.» It is this respect for law that gives the great decisions of the suffrage their acceptance and effect.

### Helen Keller at Cambridge.[1]

HELEN KELLER'S teacher, Miss Sullivan, called upon me in June last at the Cambridge School, and asked me if I would admit Miss Keller to the classes with hearing and seeing girls, and fit her for the Harvard examinations. This proposition startled me, and I replied that I thought it impracticable. However, Miss Sullivan was, as usual, deeply in earnest, and urged me not to decide at once. She afterward gave me the opportunity to discover Miss Keller's mental power, and also to learn somewhat of her educational progress. I decided that it was possible to fit Helen for the examinations, and determined to make the trial.

During the summer Miss Keller was kept free from mental effort. She was already in good health, but she gained more strength by her summer pleasures; and she appeared at her new Cambridge home in season to present herself with the other pupils at the school on the morning of the first day. She has lost no time since.

In the school we are dealing with Miss Keller as we do with normal girls of sixteen. She has the new experience of leaving her home in the morning, and of spending the usual hours in the school building, where she has her class exercises with the other members of the school. She returns to her home at the same time that the other pupils do, and mainly occupies her afternoons and evenings as they do, though naturally she takes a longer time to prepare her lessons than they do, who see.

It is our endeavor to keep her from the distractions which would arise if she were to accept social invitations; but she receives her friends, as do the other ladies of the household in which she lives, on Friday afternoons and evenings. She associates freely with her schoolmates at all times, sharing their walks and social pleasures, much to their delight. Many of them have learned to talk rapidly with her, using the manual alphabet.

I could do little for Miss Keller were it not that Miss Sullivan continues her loving superintendence, and follows her with the ministrations that she has so willingly rendered all these years. Thus, while the direction of Helen's intellectual work has been committed to me, I find it necessary to depend upon Miss Sullivan for certain assistance which no acquaintance less thorough and familiar with the past would be sufficient to suggest. I am day by day impressed by the magnitude of the work that we are called upon to perform for this marvelous girl, and I can only trust that I may be in some degree equal to the demand.

Miss Sullivan and I have always before us a sense of the novelty of the work, and we feel that we cannot lay it out far in advance. We are obliged to be constantly on the alert, watching developments, and prepared to do whatever is best at the time. While, therefore, we have the Harvard examinations before us as a goal, we are not willing to say to-day that Helen will take those examinations at any given time in the future, or that we shall not at another stage find that her nature demands a cultivation different from that which is planned for the average woman. We simply desire to feel free to take one step at a time.

In accordance with these plans, the first step was taken in October, when Miss Keller came to school with the other «new» pupils, and a rough classification of them all was made. It was at that time thought best for Helen to take up the subjects of arithmetic, English, English history, Latin, and advanced German. This work is progressing well. It was desirable, however, to get a more exact estimate of Helen's progress, and for this purpose I gave her at once four Harvard examination-papers that had been used at the college in June last by the candidates for admission. The subjects were those in which I supposed that Miss Keller was most advanced; but as she had never tried such an examination, and had had no preparation for an examination of any kind, the test would have been esteemed severe by a boy or girl in possession of all the faculties. Usually these papers are not tried until the candidate has been under special training of a technical character for a series of years. The conditions that I established were made the same as in the college, though the questions were of necessity read to Miss Keller, and the strain upon memory was greater.

The result was informally submitted to the members

[1] See also reference to Helen Keller in the article in this number on «Speech-Reading.»

of the Harvard faculty who had read the admission examination-books, and in every case I was assured that the grade was sufficient—in some respects more than sufficient—to pass the candidate. In reading these papers myself, I was struck by the literary style, which was original, and by the leisurely way in which the thoughts were brought out. Miss Keller seemed to me more willing to put a living interest into her papers than the average candidate is; and while she showed the most accurate acquaintance with the particular matter under discussion, she also showed a general cultivation which was as grateful to me as it was unusual. It was evident that the mind that was displaying itself had not been cramped by the technical training which is too often put in the place of a broader and more important instruction.

By these papers Miss Keller has shown that it would be an easy matter for her to pass the Harvard examinations in five or more hours in June next; but the question must be settled later in the year.

THESE words are written on the fifth of November. Helen has just finished her first examination in the work that her class in Latin has done since school opened. She had studied Latin only about one half of a year, and that separated from this date by two years. Her paper was marked «A,» which signifies almost perfect. It was written under my immediate personal supervision, the questions being read to her. She was allotted an hour, and she finished the paper in fifty minutes.

It is impossible at this stage of the work for us to convey to Helen all the explanations of the teachers; but in spite of this, it is within limits for me to say that she keeps up with speaking and hearing girls. I have to-day unexpectedly asked for a report from each teacher on her work. One very rapid speaker among them says that at first she was aware of a change in her way of presenting the lesson, arising from an effort to give her information slowly; but that now she does not notice Helen's presence, and treats the class as though she were not there. In replying to «snap» questions, Helen is no more ready than other girls, but when she has time she does better work than the others. This teacher, as well as the others, thinks Helen's mental processes do not differ from those of other girls.

In German it is said that «Helen has always a clear, beautiful, accurate picture of the thing that she is reading of or describing. Very often other girls give a great many words and say nothing; Helen, never.» In Latin it is reported that Helen is quicker and more accurate than the average girl, and the teacher makes no change in her methods of instruction. Helen's English teacher thinks that there is little need of further instruction in that department, at least before admission to college.

After Helen had been three weeks in school her teacher in history asked her to prepare a theme on «The Qualities Which Make a Noble Man and a Great King,» and she produced the following:

WHAT QUALITIES MAKE A NOBLE MAN AND A GREAT KING?

«A noble man!» What do I mean by «a noble man?» I certainly do not necessarily mean a man of high rank, power or wealth, as the Romans did; but, to my mind, a noble man is he who strives to attain that which is beautiful and imperishable—love. Love is the foundation on which all nobility must rest. If a man has love in his heart it will find its expression in many beautiful qualities, such as patience, courage, and charity. He is patriotic, honest and firm; he labors, not for promotion, but for the sake of the good which his work will bring to those around him. He is a true friend, whom all can trust, and all that is beautiful and good calls forth his warm enthusiasm. In a word, he is always «valiant and true.» A truly great king possesses all these qualities, and many others, which are necessary in the dischargement of his many arduous duties. He will be self-controlled, clear-headed and quick to perceive the right thing to be done, and the best way of doing it. He will be strong, honorable and just; he will respect all the sacred things of life, such as liberty, property and education; and he will encourage the pursuits of peace—science, art, literature, agriculture and so forth. When he fights, it will be to defend his country against its foes, not for the sake of conquest or vengeance. In short, he will be «like unto the King of kings.»

Such a man, and such a king was King Alfred of England. He did not seek his own glory or fame; he had but one ambition, and that was to leave his people better and happier than he found them. After having driven out the Danes, who had for many years been ravaging and plundering the country, he first.gathered the wisest, best men from all parts of his dominion around him, and then he set to work patiently to establish law, justice and order in the land. He rebuilt the old monasteries, and founded new ones, so that the people might learn to read and write, and gain useful knowledge; he himself translated some of the best books he could find from Latin into English. Consequently history tells us that he was the best and most beloved king England ever had.

Perhaps this is not a remarkable theme; but when we remember that it was written with a type-writer by one only sixteen years of age, who could not see what she was doing, who could not look back to recall the construction of a former sentence or phrase, who had never heard her teacher's voice, or when one thinks of one's self trying to do such a feat blindfolded, it takes on a different appearance. The punctuation alone is far better than that of most adults who have their eyes and ears, and who have enjoyed many years of instruction. So far as I can observe, there is but one slip. In the second paragraph, between the words «first» and «gathered,» the period key seems to have been struck instead of the space key near by it; but this many a seeing type-writer might do.

The day before the theme about King Alfred was written, Helen's teacher of English asked her to write a paper on «The Character of Rosalind,» and the following was the result:

CHARACTER OF ROSALIND.

What first strikes us in Rosalind's character is its buoyance. As soon as she begins to speak, we know that she is young, fair and lovable. When we first meet her, she is grieving over the banishment of her father; but, on being chided by her cousin, Celia, for her sadness, we see how quickly she locks up her sorrow in her heart, and tries to be happy because Celia is happy. So when we hear her merry laugh, and listen to her bright conversation, we do not imagine for a moment that she has forgotten her sorrow; we know she is unselfishly trying to do her duty by her cousin. And when we see the smile fade from her sweet face, and the light from her eyes, because a fellow-creature is in trouble, we are not surprised. We feel that we have known all along that her nature was tender and sympathetic.

Rosalind's impulses, her petulance, her tenderness and her courageous defence of her father seem perfectly natural, and true to life; but it is very hard to put in words my idea of her character. It seems almost as if it would lose some of its beauty and womanliness, if I tried to analyse it, just as we lose a beautiful flower when we pull it to pieces to see how many stamens it has. Many beautiful traits are wonderfully blended in her character, and we cannot help loving the vivacious, affectionate and charming Rosalind.

In this school-girl's theme the teacher found but one word to mark. That was «buoyance» instead of «buoyancy»; and this shows a trait of Helen's style, for she is apt sometimes to use a word in an unusual form or sense which she has met in her reading.

*Arthur Gilman.*

### Helen Keller.

SHE lives in light, not shadow,
Not silence, but the sound
Which thrills the stars of heaven
And trembles from the ground.

She breathes a finer ether,
Beholds a keener sun;
In her supernal being
Music and light are one.

Unknown the subtile senses
That lead her through the day;
Love, light, and song, and color
Come by another way.

Sight brings she to the seeing,
New song to those that hear;
Her braver spirit sounding
Where mortals fail and fear.

She at the heart of being
Lonely and glad doth dwell—
Spirit with scarce a veil of flesh,
A soul made visible.

* * *

### «Ian Maclaren» as a Theologian.

THEOLOGY and literature have not always been on good terms, and a great deal is said and done to widen the breach. It is not long since a book was published the object of which was to define the religion of a man of letters, as though it were something unlike that of other men. Not having read the book, I am unaware if it claimed that the conscience and the affections and the will of a literary man are so unlike those of other men that he requires a distinct religion, though it is difficult to imagine any other basis for one. If the claim can be substantiated, I see no reason why it should not be elaborated, and if it contemplates future existence, why it should not proceed to define the heaven held in reserve for the religious man of letters, and the particular form of hades reserved for the irreligious.

Happily, the general tide of thought does not set in this direction, and not only is the man of letters not relegated to his single category, but he is more and more counted as belonging to the ordinary run of humanity, with no need of a special religion, nor even as devoted to one vocation. It is a fortunate thing when a true man of letters turns his attention to theology, provided he rises to the height and dignity of the subject. There are enough who are ready to load it with sneers and to assail it with criticism, but an honest and earnest treatment of it is always to be welcomed; for, instead of the man of letters needing a religion of his own, it is other people who need his religion. The above-mentioned book inverted the whole business. Religion has been too much in the hands of theologians; it needs the light which can be thrown upon it by those close observers and interpreters of human life who dwell in the world of letters. The great writer is simply one who sees human life as it is, and sets it down in proper literary form.

Theology now goes half-way toward putting itself into the hands of literature by confessing that its field is largely the same—namely, life and nature. This is not a new departure, nor is it strictly an outcome of progress, but is rather a return to the beginning. The standpoint of Jesus was not in dogma, nor in ecclesiasticism, but in human life and its simple and evident relations to God and man. He found himself in life, and he made that the field of his action. Its natural and evident relations indicated his duties. The sources of the revelation of God which he made were in his own nature and in the world of human life about him. The fulfilment of his nature as the Son of the Father, and the life he lived in the world, constitute the gospel. The return to this conception is the chief characteristic of present-day theology. Hence the theologian of the new era need not be a metaphysician, nor of necessity a scholar; but he will be one who can interpret life at first hand, and follow it in all its ways; he will also have the discerning eye with which to see nature and penetrate to its meaning. We already have this order of theologians in the chief poets of the century: Browning with his direct vision of God; Tennyson interpreting the mystery of human life under the law of evolution; Whittier, the prophet of its hopes; Longfellow and Lowell, its teachers in every-day ethics. The writers of fiction have not done so well, having been insnared by a theory of realism which holds them down to one-sided and external views of life, while the poets, by the necessity of their calling, treat humanity in an ideal way, which is the only real way. But even the novelists have often rendered good service to theology by giving the final blow to some outworn dogma, or by standing sponsor for some new truth.

It is a fine service that the author of «The Bonnie Brier Bush» has rendered to theology in translating that charming cluster of stories or sketches into the form of religious teaching. «The Mind of the Master» is a straight, clear, penetrating look at Jesus, with no side-lights from other sources. Neither dogma nor church influences his touch or gives shape to a sentence. He looks upon that sacred life with the same close, sympathetic, and comprehensive glance with which he took in the Scotch parish. And here is where its value lies. The sketches move us because they are genuine interpretations of life; «The Mind of the Master» satisfies because it interprets his life.

It is needless to say of an author who is so true to himself,—a feature of Scottish writers,—that one finds in this book the same sincerity, the same soulfulness, the same keen discernment of motive and temper, which pervade his other works; «Ian Maclaren» and Dr. Watson are interchangeable names. He comes to this country as a writer of moving pictures of Scotch life; those who read «The Mind of the Master» will confess that he is also a theologian, and the two conceptions will not only not contradict, but will support each other.

*T. T. Munger.*

**«Ian Maclaren» and the Brotherhood of Christian Unity.**

A SPECIAL impulse has just come to the Brotherhood of Christian Unity from a new source. Dr. John Watson («Ian Maclaren»), in his volume of sermons entitled «The Mind of the Master," has suggested an ethical creed which so crystallizes the spirit and essence of Christianity that the Brotherhood has adopted it as a foundation for its work. It reads as follows:

I believe in the Fatherhood of God. I believe in the words of Jesus. I believe in the clean heart. I believe in the service of love. I believe in the unworldly life. I believe in the Beatitudes. I promise to trust God and follow Christ, to forgive my enemies and to seek after the righteousness of God.

It will be observed that this is in no sense a declaration of religious faith. It expresses only the ethical side of Christianity. The high Calvinist, the low Arminian, the broad Unitarian, the reverent Churchman, the Catholic, Anglican or Roman, the non-church member—all who wish to follow Christ can stand together on this platform without compromising any of their personal views concerning church or creed. To quote the words of Dr. Watson himself in suggesting the «creed»:

Could any form of words be more elevated, more persuasive, more alluring? Do they not thrill the heart and strengthen the conscience? Liberty of thought is allowed; liberty of sinning is alone denied. Who would refuse to sign this creed? They would come from the east and the west and the north and the south to its call, and even they who would hesitate to bind themselves to a crusade so arduous would admire it, and long to be worthy. Does any one say this is too ideal, too unpractical, too quixotic? That no church could stand and work on such a basis? For three too short years the Church of Christ had none else, and it was by holy living and not by any metaphysical subtleties the Primitive Church lived, and suffered, and conquered.

The Brotherhood proposes to bring Dr. Watson's sentences to the attention of the entire Christian public of America.

EAST ORANGE, NEW JERSEY. *Theodore F. Seward,* *Secretary.*

**The Kingdom of Rosenthal.**

HANS RICHTER, not long ago, presented Mr. Moriz Rosenthal to his orchestra in London as the «prince of pianists,» and since Herr Richter has chosen to pose as a Warwick in the kingdom of music, it is high time to define the boundaries of the new potentate's territory.

The first claim to royalty put forth by Mr. Rosenthal was his phenomenal virtuosity, coupled with his bravura. The development of virtuosity has proceeded in this manner: A fellow-artist once exclaimed to Dreyschock,—of whom Heine said that he was not one pianist, but *drei schock* (thrice threescore),—famous for his octaves, sixths, and thirds, but especially for his left-hand playing: «To what pitch will technic ultimately be brought! Some one will soon play Chopin's Revolutionary Étude in octaves.» Dreyschock departed meditatively, and six weeks later returned and performed the feat. Liszt, hearing the story, sat down, opened the notes, and did the same thing offhand, remarking, «Very simple!» Liszt played *études* in rapid tempo to his pupils one morning. «Can you do this?» he asked Rosenthal, after he had amused himself by exciting their astonished admiration. Rosenthal sat down and doubled his master's tempo. Such is virtuosity.

It occurred to Tausig, the unapproachable virtuoso of the next generation (he was Liszt's pupil), that Chopin's waltz in D flat major could be played in sixths and double thirds as an almost impossible feat of technic, and this he did. Mr. Rosenthal has repeated the feat plus the contrapuntal addition of the second theme simultaneously with the first. True to the instinct of virtuosity, neither artist has reproached himself for thus obviously painting the lily. Certain technical exhibitions constitute virtuosity's characteristic expression. The simultaneous delivery of the theme from «Fledermaus» by one hand and the air of a Strauss waltz by the other, in Mr. Rosenthal's «Vienna Carnival,» is the direct descendant of the waltz and galop which Moscheles used to play at once in sportive moments. But music has become such a serious business since it has assumed a religious, moral, ethical, and dramatic mission that artists no longer toss off such bagatelles with a grin, thoroughly inartistic as they are—inartistic because, though performed in counterpoint, the forced marriage of two melodies each springing from a wholly independent artistic impulse, and delivered as independently as possible, violates the first canon of art, viz., that every detail shall expand from the original poetic germ. Even at this valuation, Mr. Rosenthal's feats are considerably better than a double somersault backward on a tight rope; but he is not the «prince of pianists» on that account, although he has multiplied in geometrical proportion the difficulties that originally composed the stock of the virtuoso. He is the prince not of virtuosity merely, but of bravura (root *brav*, fine, gallant, courageous, good, kind, fierce, hardy, tempestuous). Bravura is virtuosity so applied to performance as to overcome the hearer with astonishment and admiration, and fairly to whirl him on with the motion of the music into ecstasy and madness.

The whirling is accomplished by the accent, force, and velocity of the rhythmical motion in which the almost superhuman technic is developed; and since the rhythm is wholly created by the temperament of the player, bravura playing is justly regarded as the one indispensable gift of the great concert artist. When Mr. Rosenthal by this means carried captive every audience he met in Europe, and last of all transported the great Richter also, he proved his right to his title. He is a prince, a conqueror, and the meanings that stick in that old root *brav* define his musicianly qualities exactly. Setting aside his bravura, Mr. Rosenthal's excellences as a musician are simplicity, perfection of detail, directness of technical method, good-humored temper in dealing with his subject, a tone large, musical, and of widely varied timbre, but polished rather than sweet, and a very intelligent insight into the construction and possibilities of the music he plays. With his defects it is not the purpose of this article to deal.

Born at Lemberg thirty-three years ago, he studied with Mikuli, with whom he played Chopin's rondo for two pianofortes in a concert when ten years of age. In 1875 he studied with Rafael Joseffy, himself a pupil of Tausig, remaining under the influence of this great pianist many years. Subsequently he received the appointment of pianist to the court of Roumania, a position which he still holds. In 1876 he accepted Liszt's invitation to join him in Weimar, where he learned to recognize his own genius and artistic nature. The influence of

Liszt is preëminent in the mature artist. The grand style, the impetuosity, the strength of tone, the choice of artistic effects characteristic of the Rosenthal of to-day, belong to the Weimar school. His cantabile and coloratura playing, however, have been formed on those of his earlier master, Joseffy, and the development of his tone has proceeded in large measure from the Tausig-Joseffy artistic standpoint—purity rather than warmth.

As was the case with Moscheles, Mr. Rosenthal's view of his art has steadily broadened since his preëminence as a bravura player became assured. He is a man of liberal education, and the resources of his literary culture are evident in the picturesque element which has entered his interpretation. Every piece now comes from his hands a tone-picture complete in each detail. That «kindness» which somehow crept into the old root of the term *bravura* may be trusted to save him from the intolerable dryness and hardness that so often overtake the bravura player when the fire of youth is passed. As Mr. Rosenthal's own character finds artistic expression his interpretation steadily gains in interest, power, and dignity.

Thus far he has added nothing to the stock of technical means and methods obtained from his predecessors, unless it be the magnificent development of forearm- and wrist-playing, in which in power, skill, and velocity no living pianist approaches him.

The concerto by Schytte, the most difficult piece in existence, is practically a compendium of almost impossible feats of wrist- and forearm-playing. Mr. Rosenthal's interpretation of it will remain the measure and model of virtuosity and bravura for at least one generation; and the same is true of the Brahms «Paganini» variations and the «Don Giovanni» fantasia.

*Fanny Morris Smith.*

**«The Society of Western Artists.»**

«In the natural order of things, it was to have been expected that there would arise in the West an organization of artists to occupy the vast field there presented, and to invite the attention of Western people» to the existence among them «of artists worthy of patronage.» So writes to us a Western correspondent concerning the new «Society of Western Artists» organized at Chicago in March, 1896, by artists of Indianapolis, Cleveland, Detroit, Chicago, St. Louis, and Cincinnati, with Frank Duveneck, president; William Forsyth, vice-president; H. W. Methven, secretary; and George L. Schreiber, treasurer. Long life and prosperity to the new art society!

**Benson's «Summer.»**

The picture of «Summer,» by Frank W. Benson, which appeared in the October Century, gained the Shaw prize at the eighteenth annual exhibition of the Society of American Artists, 1896, and was printed in The Century by the kind permission of Mr. Samuel T. Shaw, the donor of the prize fund.

**Partners.**

LOVE took chambers on our street
 Opposite to mine;
On his door he tacked a neat,
 Clearly lettered sign.

Straightway grew his custom great,
 For his sign read so:
«Hearts united while you wait.
 Step in. Love and Co.»

Much I wondered who was «Co.»
 In Love's partnership;
Thought across the street I'd go—
 Learn from Love's own lip.

So I went; and since that day
 Life is hard for me.
I was buncoed! (By the way,
 «Co.» is Jealousy.)

*Ellis Parker Butler.*

**A Book of Names.**

The writer recently examined a book that is perhaps the only one of its kind in the world. The volume is composed entirely of surnames, and its interest consists not only in its clever arrangement, but also in the fact that every name is genuine and well authenticated, and forms one or more English words correctly spelled.

Names are not ordinarily very entertaining reading. We can all sympathize with the old woman who found a perusal of a directory rather uninteresting because it was «arranged 'most too reg'lar.» But this volume of patronymics is an exception. All who have had the privilege of examining it have found it both curious and entertaining. In one large sanitarium it was an unfailing source of amusement to the patients, until it became so thumbed and worn that the owner was compelled to resume possession of it.

The origin of the book was on this wise. A number of years ago the compiler, then a young girl, told her uncle that she intended to make a collection of buttons or of postage-stamps. Her uncle replied: «Why do you not start something original, such as a collection of odd names? For instance, here in this newspaper are two that you might begin with—Mr. Toothaker and Mrs. Piazza.» The suggestion was immediately acted upon, and the result is a volume of some thousands of «names familiar as household words.»

During the growth of the book the collector has adhered to several well-defined rules. One, deviated from in a few instances only, is that nothing but surnames shall be used. One often hears of so-called «Christian» names that are amazingly odd. The writer knows of a father and mother who allowed their children to name themselves after they were grown up, calling them in the meanwhile simply «Bub» and «Sis,» and the result was that the two girls called themselves «Ethelial» and «Flayalva,» and the boys chose the names «Allevosto» and «Vociferi.» In compiling such a book the line must be drawn somewhere, however, and it is evident that many odd combinations of names, like «May Day,» «Constant Agony,» «Touch Me Not,» and «Westminster Abbey,» are merely the result of well-meaning though ill-advised intention.

Another strict rule of the compiler is to use none but absolutely genuine and well-authenticated names. The well-known legendary firm of «U. Ketcham & I. Cheatem» is necessarily excluded, as also the legendary Miss Rose who was called by her sentimental parents «Wild Rose,» but who by marriage with a Mr. Bull became «Wild Bull.» No names are ever selected from newspapers or other doubtful sources (the original Mr. Toothaker and Mrs. Piazza having been long since dropped); nor are any accepted upon hearsay only. The volume is composed of printed business cards, visiting-cards, and cuttings from reliable sources, where there is no probability of mistake or misspelling.

Again, no foreign names, known to be such, are used. At first the compiler of the book admitted some names that, on purely phonetic principles only, formed English words, but after a time these were culled out. «Rippe, the tailor,» is suggestive to the ear, but the eye demurs to spelling the word «rip» in so Frenchy a manner. In one instance the compiler was strongly tempted to depart from this rule, upon hearing on unimpeachable authority of the existence of a Mr. Catt whose first name was Thomas, and whose wife bore the name of Tabitha!

In turning over the leaves of this book, one becomes strongly impressed with the seriousness of the problem which confronted our worthy ancestors when they had to choose their surnames. Perhaps, though, the original surnames were distributed, and not chosen, the first applicants being awarded such charming ones as «Joy, Trust, Faith, Hope, Charity, Peace, Comfort, Bliss, Content, Delight, Goodness, Holiness, Truth,» while the unlucky wights near the end of the procession had to put up with the dregs, receiving such suggestive cognomens as «Sloth, Doubt, Folly, Blight, Dishonesty, Lies, Sorrow, Fear, Woe, Evil, Hatred.»

This theory, that surnames were awarded and not chosen, finds support in the familiar legend of the ancient Welsh prince who gathered the people of Wales together, and gave to one clan the name of Morgan, to another that of Griffiths, to another Thomas, to another Williams, and so on, until finally he became weary, and said, «Let all the rest be called Jones.»

If, however, we cling to the theory that names were voluntarily chosen, the question still remains, What principle governed our noble ancestors in their selection? Were they actuated by fitness, or sentiment, or malice aforethought, or were they simply swayed by chance? Perhaps some were governed in their choice by circumstances. Thus it may be that one man, being temporarily short of fuel, called himself «Littlewood»; another, being a brave warrior, called himself «Breakspear»; an impecunious traveler, bearing in mind the proverb, «The rolling stone has lots of fun,» selected the name of «Merrypebble»; another, whose next door neighbor was Mr. «High,» deemed it appropriate to dub himself «Dudgeon»; while still another, being in very agony at not finding any suitable cognomen for his destitute family, in sheer desperation announced himself to the world as Mr. «Agony.»

I have stated that one feature of this curious book which enhances its interest is the clever manner in which its contents are arranged. People of nearly every class, occupation, and taste may find here some topic or group of names that will appeal specially to them.

For example, anatomists should be interested in the following: «Body, Blood, Flesh, Veins, Artery, Pulse, Life, Fat, Gland, Wrinkle, Joint, Bones, Marrow, Whitebone, Rawbone, Broadrib, Head, Greathead, Fairhead, Broomhead, Lawhead, Broadhead, Redhead, Woodhead, Brain, Hair, Blacklock, Whitelock, Lovelock, Shylock, Forehead, Brows, Visage, Face, Eyes, Noseworthy, Lobe, Cheeks, Mouth, Tongue, Gums, Silvertooth, Lips, Jaw, Chin, Beard, Neck, Lung, Heart, Goodheart, Back, Firmback, Brownback, Slyback, Noback, Shoulders, Spine, Sides, Waist, Lap, Limb, Arms, Hands, Whitehand, Fist, Fingers, Thumb, Knuckles, Leg, Knee, Ankle, Foot, Barefoot, Loudfoot, Clinkerfoot, Heel, Soles.»

Turning over the leaves at random, we come to what might be called the culinary department, which will appeal to housewives and all others who are blessed with good appetite and sound digestion. This list is too long to be quoted entire, although every name is so appropriate that one hardly knows what to omit. The following are given as samples only: «Kitchen, Cook, Servant, Scullion, Range, Kindling, Fagot, Coke, Shovel, Coal, Smoke, Bellows, Sparks, Blaze, Hotfire, Burn, Clinker, Soot, Kettle, Pipkin, Meanpan, Washer, Wringer, Mangle, Irons, Laundry, Pump, Sink, Drain, Scales, Sieve, Rollingpin, Grater, Dipper, Jug, Crock, Firkins, Delf, China, Pitcher, Glass, Tins, Knife, Fork, Spoon, Cups, Saucer, Viands, Coffee, Cream, Sugar, Milk, Tea, Hyson, Chocolate, Bouillon, Butter, Bread, Yeast, Batch, Rising, Muffin, Rolls, Johnnycake, Oyster, Clam, Pickles, Olive, Gherkins, Peppers, Vinegar, Pepper, Salt, Mustard, Mace, Cinnamon, Cloves,» etc. This list appropriately concludes with the cooking directions: «Pare, Husk, Singe, Mince, Mix, Sweeten, Strain, Mash, Seasongood, Boil, Fry, Simmer, Bake, Bakewell, Pickle.»

Physicians will appreciate the following, and certainly every invalid will find in it «a consummation devoutly to be wished»: «Doctor, Doser, Surgeon, Bonecutter, Apothecary, Patient, Sickman, Paleman, Nurse, Vigil, Lint, Splint, Brace, Sling, Swab, Crutch, Bottles, Vial, Stopper, Cork, Label, Dose, Diet, Drugs, Cordial, Balsam, Bitters, Arnica, Hartshorn, Logwood, Brimstone, Morphia, Pill, Pellet, Powders, Plasters, Salve, Malady, Pain, Ache, Shiver, Chill, Cough, Grip, Croup, Hurt, Bumps, Lump, Bruise, Scar, Sprain, Blow, Clot, Warts, Splinter, Fester, Wellfinger, Shock, Gash, Gore, Matter, Rash, Cramp, Spittle, Bile, Itchings, Twitchings, Salts, Senna, Lame, Blind, Slender, Thin, Slim, Lean, Lank, Haggard, Pale, Delicate, Frail, Sallow, Faint, Sickly, Ill, Weak,

Weary, Failing, Moan, Groan, Suffer, Heal, Cure, Fat, Tall, Straight, Hearty, Well, Manwell, Heartwell, Hipwell, Bothwell, Goodflesh.»

One other list is too good to be omitted, although it can be given only in part; it may be termed the religious or ecclesiastical list: «Whitechurch, Fane, Chapel, Trinity, Church, Minster, Westminster Abbey (Westminster is a Christian [?] name), Tower, Hightower, Steeple, Spire, Cross, Vane, Belfry, Bell, Clapper, Knell, Dome, Nave, Gallery, Vestry, Pew, Organ, Pipes, Blower, Parish, Christian, Churchman, Saint, Sinner, Convert, Member, Layman, Laity, Clergy, Patriarch, Pope, Cardinal, Bishop, Archdeacon, Dean, Canon, Priest, Rector, Vicars, Abbot, Deacon, Pastor, Parson, Elder, Preacher, Ministerman, Domini, Service, Mass, Vespers, Surplice, Chant, Carol, Highnote, Mansinger, Greatsinger, Sidesinger, Creed, Text, Sermon, Alms, Silence, Pray, Divine, Blessing, Amen, Lent, Easter, Easterday, Pentecost, Wedlock, Troth, Marriage, Bridegroom, Bride, Fee, Born, Birth, Life, Die, Death, Deadman, Shrouds, Coffin, Pall, Pinecoffin, Bier, Hearse, Grave, Sexton, Bury, Tomb, Greenvault, Churchyard, Greenwood, Angel, Gabriel, Jordan, Paradise, Eden, Crown, Harp, Heaven, Demon, Hell, Godhelp, Godward.»

Having thus catered to the taste of the grown-ups, it is but fair to add this for the little ones: «Baby, Babe, Rattle, Laugh, Boo, Coo, Goo, Dollie, Linendoll, Ball, Agate, Toy, Games, Horsey, Teeter, Hobby, Horse, Mane, Lines, Drum, Swing, Jumper, Bumpus, Candy, Wink, Sandman, Nurse, Sugarwater, Supper, Barefoot, Bath, Robes, Pallet, Bolster, Sheets, Spread, Hush, Golightly.»

Among business firms we find such suggestive combinations as «Yard & Furlong, Brown & Bay, Moss & Rose, King & Page, Sweet & Pickle, Green & Wise.» Mr. «Winter» is a dealer in coal and wood; «Doll» is a toy merchant; «Wardrobe,» a dressmaker; «John Tutor,» a teacher; «Drunk,» a saloon-keeper; «Black & Green» are tea merchants.

Perhaps the most interesting pages of the book are those devoted to sentences formed of surnames. It is to be borne in mind that every name begins with a capital letter, and nothing but names are used.

«Wait! Lingo Shall Begin. Aims Are-good, Whims Only Waste. Never Say Unthank. Fallen Man-sir Will-ever Drink-wine. Gracie, Dear-love, Talks Straight-on To-her Favorite Dolly Emma All-day Long. Both-of Her-son Davids Near Neighbors Were Rather Singular Persons; Still Maybe You Will Find-later They Both Mean-well. Gouty Pat-stone, As-he Sits All-day Long Bitterly Grumbling, Fairly Grieves One-to Hear Him; But Poor Charles-with Far-less Hope Of Even Getting Out Again Will Alway Just Suffer-in Silence, Having Been Truly Blessed Therein. We-are Both Ready, Hannah, For-an Early Dinner, As-bill Will Need Thy-son Samuel Right Off Down Town, Where He-is Working Near Mountpleasant Hotel. We-dick, Ben-susan, And Fred Found Ella-by Green-tree Back-of High-tower, Far-below Rockhill, Picking Ferns. Hurry! Ben-said As-he Ran; We-are All Going Nutting About A-mile From Stonebridge. Ruths Southern Servant Works Hard, Can Wash Good-enough, Irons Nicely, Bakes Great-batch of Good-bread, Will Likewise Make Real Nice Savory Green-Apple Pies; Yet-to Wash-fish Rightly, Judy Never Will Try.»

*Charles Lee Sleight.*

**The Passing of the Widow.**

«REDDY 's got 'em again, sure,» said Canuck, jerking his thumb toward the collection of shanties, lean-tos, and tents that was dignified by the title of Boom City.

To one who knew Reddy's habits the appearances were decidedly in favor of the truth of Canuck's diagnosis. He was coming down the road at a gait that, as Dunham remarked, resembled an Indian war-dance more than anything else.

«A few more spells like that, and he will need a pine overcoat,» said Jack-pot, whose name—John Potts—was too suggestive of the national game to remain unchanged. There was a decided aversion, anyway, to calling a man by his right name in Boom City. As Reddy had put it to a new arrival, «It don't make no diff'rence what handle fitted you back in th' States; here you goes by the one what suits you best, and there 's less chance of havin' a call from th' sheriff.»

The red-headed, red-faced, red-shirted man whose predominating color had won him his sobriquet continued to wave his arms and run until within shouting-distance, when, in a voice made husky by long addiction to «the same,» he electrified the group of fortune-hunters with, «Come on! The Belcher boys hev got th' widder!»

«What 's that?» «How?» «Talk quick!» And with questions and oaths the men dropped picks, shovels, and «cradles,» and clamored for details.

«I wuz takin' a snooze in th' back of th' widder's [«Drunk,» sententiously remarked Canuck], and she was a-cleanin' th' glasses,» Reddy continued, paying no attention to Canuck's insinuation, «when I wuz woke by hearin' th' glasses smash on th' floor. I started to jump up, but sat down suddent again, fer I found myself a-lookin' into the muzzles of my own guns that Big Belcher was holdin' oncomfortably nigh my head. He says, says he, ‹You shet up and go to sleep again.› I shet, an' I seed th' widder a-goin' out th' back door 'tween th' Belcher twins.

«You fellers wuz all out here, blind and deaf to ev'rything but yer own mis'able claims, an' I wuz th' only gentleman left t' look out fer th' widder, which same I could n't do 'count o' them two guns ag'in' my head. You 're a pretty lot of galoots, you air!

«I heerd 'em a-gittin' th' widder on a hoss, an' then Big Belcher run out, and jumpin' on his pony, put after th' others.

«The feller what bought them guns paid forty dollars for 'em,» Reddy added regretfully, unconsciously emphasizing the «bought.»

«The widow» was not only the owner of the one saloon in Boom City, all rivals being forcibly discouraged by her admiring customers, but she was the one woman in the town, and as such was respected, admired, protected, and proposed to by its entire population, individually and collectively. Even Reddy himself had applied for the honor of being supported by her. To him her refusal was offset by some of «the same,» which she gave him to soothe his wounded feelings.

She was a neat, pretty little woman, who ruled in undisputed and absolute monarchy over her rough but loyal subjects, no one of whom, even in his wildest and most drunken orgies, had ever shown her aught but respect. A presumptuous tenderfoot who had attempted to kiss her had been saved from instant annihilation only by her own intercession. As it was, he was conducted to the limits of the town, where it was quietly but forcibly impressed upon him that in future the air of that neighborhood would not be conducive to his health. A nervous fingering of the spokesman's revolver added whatever emphasis was needed.

So when it dawned upon the understanding of Reddy's listeners that the widow, their sole representative of the gentler sex, the proprietor of their «hotel,» their most precious claim, and, as each man secretly assured himself, his future wife, had actually been not only roughly handled, but carried off, stolen, kidnapped, by the three «Belcher boys,» they did not lose many minutes starting in pursuit.

The «Belchers» were the proprietors of «The Palace Saloon and Road to Fortune» in Gold City, Boom City's neighbor and rival.

According to a denizen of Boom City, all that was and should not be was contained within the limits of Gold City; and the inhabitants of the latter metropolis declared that Boom City stood for all that was not and should be.

It was a quiet but determined body of men that, leaving Boom City entirely deserted, took the trail for «that one-dog town,» as Jack-pot called it.

No plan or plans had been formulated. They were simply going to Gold City, rescue the widow, and restore her to her throne (otherwise bar), or take up their abode in Gold City's cemetery, with a choice selection of their enemies for company.

It was a silent crowd that toiled along that dusty Colorado road, except for an occasional burst of swearing from some one, generally Canuck. The hot sun beat down upon them, the dust kicked up by their heavy boots filled their mouths and throats; but there was no drinking done: the work before them was of too serious a character, and even Reddy forgot to lament his parched condition.

They were surprised, as they neared their destination, not to find a delegation sent out to welcome them. They had expected a warm reception—to have to fight their way from the first shanty to the widow's side. Instead, the town sizzled along in its usual sleepy way, and, beyond a curious look or a quizzical smile from the loungers, prototypes of Reddy, no apparent notice was taken of their advent as they filed down the main and only street.

«'T ain't nateral,» said Canuck; «they must be holdin' out cards on us.»

Arriving in front of «The Palace Saloon and Road to Fortune,» the Boom City delegation halted a moment, and then, each man holding his revolver in readiness for instant use, they stalked solemnly and threateningly into the saloon. They were surprised to find it empty, and so pushed on into the gambling «parlors.»

The foremost men caught sight of the three Belcher boys standing at the farther end of the room, and in another moment the filling of the cemetery would have begun, when, to their utter astonishment, the widow stepped from behind the broad backs of her captors, and facing her subjects, said:

«Hold on, boys! Don't shoot! I want to talk with you.»

Boom City was so accustomed to obeying her slightest command that it lowered its threatening weapons, though, be it said, with marked hesitation and reluctance, and ugly glances at the Belcher trio.

«I won't take long, boys; so keep quiet. Canuck, put up that gun!»

Canuck meekly obeyed, sighing as he relinquished the thought of quietly puncturing Big Belcher. It was a sore disappointment.

«Of course I know what you boys have come for, and appreciate and thank you for your anxiety as to my safety, as well as for your past evidences of regard for me.» She smiled slightly at the thought of the way in which each of these men who faced her had asked her to marry him.

«I knew it would be no use to tell you boys beforehand; I knew you would not consent to my leaving you; so—so I had to run away. I 've agreed to take shares in this claim, and—and—let me introduce my husband, Frank Belcher, and ask you to be as good friends to him as you have to me. He could not have better ones. And remember that I think just as much of you all as I ever did [«And that 's confounded little,» muttered Jack-pot], and will be just as glad to see you.

«Now you know why I was forced to decline the honor you each offered me. I could n't afford more than one husband at a time. Won't you please forgive me?

«What will you have, boys?» said Mrs. Belcher.

And Reddy, speaking for all, replied:

«The same.»

*J. Frederic Thorne.*

A QUESTION OF SAFETY.

Ball-bearing, long and medium cranks, striped frames, guaranteed perfectly secure for one year.

THE DE VINNE PRESS, NEW YORK.

FROM A DAGUERREOTYPE OWNED BY ROBERT T. LINCOLN. SEE "OPEN LETTERS" ENGRAVED BY T. JOHNSON.

A. Lincoln

LINCOLN AS LAWYER.

"He is the true history of the American people in his time. Step by step he walked before them; slow with their slowness, quickening his march by theirs, the true representative of this continent."

EMERSON.

PHOTOGRAPHED BY BARR & YOUNG, ARMY PHOTOGRAPHERS. VICKSBURG, AUGUST, 1863. LENT BY FRED B. SCHELL. ENGRAVED BY T. JOHNSON.

GRANT AS MAJOR-GENERAL.

*MIDWINTER NUMBER.*

THE CENTURY MAGAZINE

VOL. LIII. FEBRUARY, 1897. No. 4.

# CAMPAIGNING WITH GRANT.

BY GENERAL HORACE PORTER.

## FROM SPOTSYLVANIA TO THE NORTH ANNA.

### GRANT AND MEADE.

ON the morning of May 13 [1864] General Grant expressed some anxiety as to the possibility of Lee's falling back toward Richmond without our knowing it in time to follow him up closely enough to attack him, although it was thought that the almost impassable condition of the roads would probably prevent such an attempt. Skirmishers were pushed forward near enough to discover the meaning of a movement of some of the organizations in Lee's center, and it was found that the enemy was merely taking up a new position in rear of the works which had been captured from him. There was no other fighting that day. The general busied himself principally with inquiries about the care of the wounded and the burial of the killed. He thought not only of the respect due the gallant dead, but of proper rewards for the living whose services had contributed conspicuously to the victory. He wrote a communication to the Secretary of War, in which he urged the following promotions: Meade and Sherman to be major-generals, and Hancock a brigadier-general, in the regular army; Wright, Gibbon, and Humphreys to be major-generals of volunteers; and Carroll, Upton, and McCandless to be brigadier-generals in that service. He had already promoted Upton on the field, but this promotion had to be confirmed at Washington. He said in his letter: «General Meade has more than met my most sanguine expectations. He and Sherman are the fittest officers for large commands I have come in contact with.» An animated discussion took place at headquarters that day regarding General Meade's somewhat anomalous position, and the embarrassments which were at times caused on the field by the necessity of issuing orders through him instead of direct to the corps commanders. The general-in-chief always invited the most frank and cordial interchange of views, and never failed to listen patiently to the more prominent members of his staff. He seldom joined in the discussions, and usually reserved what he had to say till the end of the argument, when he gave his views and rendered his decision. It was now urged upon him, with much force, that time was often lost in having field orders pass through an intermediary; that there was danger that, in transmitting orders to corps commanders, the instructions might be either so curtailed or elaborated as to change their spirit; that no matter how able General Meade might be, his position was in some measure a false one; that few responsibilities were given him, and yet he was charged with the duties of an army commander; that if he failed the responsibility could not be fixed upon him, and if he succeeded he could not reap the full reward of his merits; that, besides, he had an irascible temper, and often irritated officers who came in contact with him, while General Grant was even-tempered, and succeeded in securing a more hearty coöperation of his generals when he dealt with them direct. The discussion became heated at times.

At the close of the arguments the general said: « I am fully aware that some embarrassments arise from the present organization, but there is more weight on the other side of the question. I am commanding all the armies, and I cannot neglect others by giving my time exclusively to the Army of the Potomac, which would involve performing all the detailed duties of an army commander, directing its administration, enforcing discipline, reviewing its court-martial proceedings, etc. I have Burnside's, Butler's, and Sigel's armies to look after in Virginia, to say nothing of our Western armies, and I may make Sheridan's cavalry a separate command. Besides, Meade has served a long time with the Army of the Potomac, knows its subordinate officers thoroughly, and led it to a memorable victory at Gettysburg. I have just come from the West, and if I removed a deserving Eastern man from the position of army commander, my motives might be misunderstood, and the effect be bad upon the spirits of the troops. General Meade and I are in close contact on the field; he is capable and perfectly subordinate, and by attending to the details he relieves me of much unnecessary work, and gives me more time to think and to mature my general plans. I will always see that he gets full credit for what he does.»

This was a broad view of the situation, and one to which the general mainly adhered throughout the war; but after that day he gave a closer personal direction in battle to the movements of subdivisions of the armies.

General Meade manifested an excellent spirit through all the embarrassments which his position at times entailed. He usually showed his orders to General Grant before issuing them, and as their camps in this campaign were seldom more than a pistol-shot distant from each other, despatches from the corps commanders directed to Meade generally reached the general-in-chief about the same time. In fact, when they were together, Meade frequently handed despatches to his chief to read before he read them himself. As Grant's combativeness displayed itself only against the enemy, and he was a man with whom an associate could not quarrel without furnishing all the provocation himself, he and Meade continued on the best of terms officially and personally throughout this long and eventful campaign.

### FIELD DIVERSIONS.

DURING the ten days of battle through which we had just passed very little relief, physical or mental, had been obtained; but there was one staff-officer, a Colonel B——, who often came as bearer of messages to our headquarters, who always managed to console himself with novel-reading, and his peculiarity in this respect became a standing joke among those who knew him. He went about with his saddle-bags stuffed full of thrilling romances, and was seen several times sitting on his horse under a brisk fire, poring over the last pages of an absorbing volume to reach the dénouement of the plot, and evincing a greater curiosity to find how the hero and the heroine were going to be extricated from the entangled dilemma into which they had been plunged by the unsympathetic author than to learn the result of the surrounding battle. One of his peculiarities was that he took it for granted that all the people he met were perfectly familiar with his line of literature, and he talked about nothing but the merits of the latest novel. For the last week he had been devouring Victor Hugo's « Les Misérables.» It was an English translation, for the officer had no knowledge of French. As he was passing a house in rear of the « angle » he saw a young lady seated on the porch, and, stopping his horse, bowed to her with all the grace of a Chesterfield, and endeavored to engage her in conversation. Before he had gone far he took occasion to remark: « By the way, have you seen ‹ Lees Miserables ›?» anglicizing the pronunciation. Her black eyes snapped with indignation as she tartly replied: « Don't you talk to me that way; they're a good deal better than Grant's miserables anyhow!» This was retold so often by those who heard it that, for some time after, its repetition seriously endangered the colonel's peace of mind.

### SEIZING VANTAGE-GROUND.

ON the morning of the 14th it was decided to move the headquarters of Generals Grant and Meade farther east to a position on some high ground three quarters of a mile north of the Ny River, and near the Fredericksburg and Spotsylvania Court House road. The two generals and their staff-officers rode forward on the Massaponax Church road, and came to a halt and dismounted at a house not far from the Ny River. About half a mile south of that stream, at a place called Gayle's, there was a hill held by the enemy, which overlooked both the Massaponax and the Fredericksburg roads, and as it commanded an important position, it was decided to try to get possession of it.

Just then General Upton rode up, joined the group, and addressing himself to both Generals Grant and Meade, said, with his usual enthusiasm and confidence, and speaking with great rapidity: «I can take that hill with my brigade. I hope you will let me try it; I 'm certain I can take it.» He was asked how many men he had left, as his brigade had seen very hard fighting in the last few days. He replied, «About eight or nine hundred men.»

It was soon decided to let him make the attempt, and General Wright, who was supervising the movement, gave Upton orders to start forward at once and seize the position. Upton put his brigade in motion with his usual promptness, drove back the enemy in handsome style, and soon had his flags hoisted on the hilltop. But his possession of it was not of long duration. The enemy sent forward a portion of Mahone's infantry and Chambliss's cavalry, and Upton was compelled to fall back before superior numbers. However, there was no intention to allow the enemy to hold such an important position, and Meade directed Warren to send one of his brigades to recapture it. Ayres's brigade moved forward with spirit, and the position was soon retaken and held. General Grant expressed to General Meade his pleasure at seeing Warren's troops making so prompt and successful a movement, and as both officers had censured Warren on the 13th, they were anxious now to give him full credit for his present conduct. General Meade sent him the following despatch: «I thank you and Ayres for taking the hill. It was handsomely done.» General Wright then moved forward two brigades to relieve Ayres. This was the only fighting on that day.

### GRANT AND THE WOUNDED CONFEDERATE.

WHILE riding about the field General Grant stopped at a house and expressed a desire to prepare some despatches. A number of wounded were lying upon the porch and in the rooms; they had made their way there in accordance with the usual custom of wounded men to seek a house. It seems to be a natural instinct, as a house conveys the idea of shelter and of home. I walked with the general into a back room to see whether there was a dry spot which he might take possession of for a short time, to write messages and look over the maps.

As we entered, there was seen sitting in the only chair a Confederate lieutenant of infantry who had been shot in the left cheek, the ball passing through his mouth and coming out near the right ear. A mass of coagulated blood covered his face and neck, and he presented a shocking appearance. He arose the moment we entered, pushed his chair forward toward the general, and said, with a bow and a smile, «Here, take my chair, sir.» General Grant looked at him, and replied: «Ah, you need that chair much more than I; keep your seat. I see you are badly hurt.» The officer answered good-naturedly: «If you folks let me go back to our lines, I think I ought to be able to get a leave to go home and see my girl; but I reckon she would n't know me now.» The general said, «I will see that one of our surgeons does all in his power for you,» and then stepped out of the room. He told one of the surgeons who was dressing the wounds of our own men to do what he could for the Confederate. We did not hear what became of him afterward. He probably never knew that he had been talking to the general-in-chief of the Yankee armies. The despatches were afterward written in another room.

The enemy had now set to work to discover the real meaning of our present movements. In the afternoon skirmishers pushed forward on our right, and found that Warren's corps was no longer there.

### GRANT'S TOILET IN CAMP.

IN the night of the 14th Lee began to move troops to his right. Grant now directed Hancock's corps to be withdrawn and massed behind the center of our line, so that it could be moved promptly in either direction. When the general got back to camp that evening his clothes were a mass of mud from head to foot, his uniform being scarcely recognizable. He sat until bedtime without making any change in his dress; he never seemed particularly incommoded by the travel-stained condition of his outer garments, but was scrupulously careful, even in the most active campaigns, about the cleanliness of his linen and his person. The only chance for a bath was in having a barrel sawed in two and using

DRAWN BY S. WEST CLINEDINST

GENERAL GRANT AND THE WOUNDED CONFEDERATE.

(SEE PAGE 487.)

the half of it as a sort of sitz-bath. During most of this campaign the general, like the staff-officers, used this method of bathing, or, as our English friends would say, «tubbing.» Afterward he supplied himself with a portable rubber bath-tub. While campaign life is not a good school for the cultivation of squeamishness, and while the general was always ready to rough it in camp, yet he was particularly modest in performing his toilet, and his tent fronts were always tied close, and the most perfect privacy was secured, when he was washing, or changing his clothes. While thus engaged even his servant was not allowed to enter his quarters.

### IMPORTANT DESPATCHES.

THE next day, May 15, the rain continued, and the difficulties of moving became still greater. Important despatches were received from the other armies. They informed the general-in-chief that General Averell's cavalry had cut a portion of the East Tennessee railroad, and had also captured and destroyed a depot of supplies in West Virginia. Butler reported that he had captured some works near Drewry's Bluff, on the James River. The next day, the 16th, came a despatch from Sherman saying that he had compelled Johnston to evacuate Dalton and was pursuing him closely. Sheridan reported that he had destroyed a portion of the Virginia Central and the Fredericksburg railroads in Lee's rear, had killed General J. E. B. Stuart, completely routed his cavalry, and captured a portion of the outer lines of Richmond. He said he might possibly have taken Richmond by assault, but, being ignorant of the operations of General Grant and General Butler, and knowing the rapidity with which the enemy could throw troops against him, he decided that it would not be wise to make such an attempt.

The loss of General Stuart was a severe blow to the enemy. He was their foremost cavalry leader, and one in whom Lee reposed great confidence. We afterward heard that he had been taken to Richmond, and had reached there before he died; that Jefferson Davis visited his death-bed, and was greatly affected when he found that there was no hope of saving the life of this accomplished officer.

### THROUGH RAIN AND MUD.

THE continual rain was most disheartening. On May 16 Grant wrote to Halleck: «We have had five days' almost constant rain, without any prospect yet of its clearing up. The roads have now become so impassable that ambulances with wounded men can no longer run between here and Fredericksburg. All offensive operations must necessarily cease until we can have twenty-four hours of dry weather. The army is in the best of spirits, and feels the greatest confidence in ultimate success. . . . The elements alone have suspended hostilities.»

In the Wilderness the army had to struggle against fire and dust; now it had to contend with rain and mud. An ordinary rain, lasting for a day or two, does not embarrass troops; but when the storm continues for a week it becomes one of the most serious obstacles in a campaign. The men can secure no proper shelter and no comfortable rest; their clothing has no chance to dry; and a tramp of a few miles through tenacious mud requires as much exertion as an ordinary day's march. Tents become saturated and weighted with water, and draft-animals have increased loads, and heavier roads over which to haul them. Dry wood cannot be found; cooking becomes difficult; the men's spirits are affected by the gloom, and even the most buoyant natures become disheartened. It is much worse for an army acting on the offensive, for it has more marching to do, being compelled to move principally on exterior lines.

Staff-officers had to labor day and night during the present campaign in making reconnaissances and in cross-questioning natives, deserters, prisoners, and fugitive negroes, in an attempt to secure data for the purpose of constructing local maps from day to day. As soon as these were finished they were distributed to the subordinate commanders. Great confusion arose from the duplication of the names of houses and farms. Either family names were particularly scarce in that section of the State, or else the people were united by close ties of relationship, and country cousins abounded to a confusing extent. So many farm-houses in some of the localities were occupied by people of the same name that, when certain farms were designated in orders, serious errors arose at times from mistaking one place for another.

### GRANT AND THE DYING SOLDIER.

THE weather looked a little brighter on May 17, but the roads were still so heavy that no movement was attempted. A few reinforcements were received at this time, mainly some heavy artillery regiments from the defenses about Washington, who had been drilled to serve as infantry. On the 17th Brigadier-General R. O. Tyler arrived with a division of these troops, numbering, with the Corcoran Legion, which had also joined, nearly 8000 men. They were assigned to Hancock's corps.

Headquarters were this day moved about a mile and a quarter to the southeast, to a point not far from Massaponax Church. We knew that the enemy had depleted the troops on his left in order to strengthen his right wing, and on the night of the 17th Hancock and Wright were ordered to assault Lee's left the next morning, directing their attack against the second line he had taken up in rear of the «angle,» or, as some of the troops now called it, «Hell's Half-acre.» The enemy's position, however, had been strengthened at this point more than it was supposed, and his new line of intrenchments had been given a very formidable character. Our attacking party found the ground completely swept by a heavy and destructive fire of musketry and artillery, but in spite of this the men moved gallantly forward and made desperate attempts to carry the works. It was soon demonstrated, however, that the movement could not result in success, and the troops were withdrawn.

General Grant had ridden over to the right to watch the progress of this attack. While he was passing a spot near the roadside where there were a number of wounded, one of them, who was lying close to the roadside, seemed to attract his special notice. The man's face was beardless; he was evidently young; his countenance was strikingly handsome, and there was something in his appealing look which could not fail to engage attention, even in the full tide of battle. The blood was flowing from a wound in his breast, the froth about his mouth was tinged with red, and his wandering, staring eyes gave unmistakable evidence of approaching death. Just then a young staff-officer dashed by at a full gallop, and as his horse's hoofs struck a puddle in the road, a mass of black mud was splashed in the wounded man's face. He gave a piteous look, as much as to say, «Could n't you let me die in peace and not add to my sufferings?» The general, whose eyes were at that moment turned upon the youth, was visibly affected. He reined in his horse, and seeing from a motion he made that he was intending to dismount to bestow some care upon the young man, I sprang from my horse, ran to the side of the soldier, wiped his face with my handkerchief, spoke to him, and examined his wound; but in a few minutes the unmistakable death-rattle was heard, and I found that he had breathed his last. I said to the general, who was watching the scene intently, «The poor fellow is dead,» remounted my horse, and the party rode on. The chief had turned round twice to look after the officer who had splashed the mud and who had passed rapidly on, as if he wished to take him to task for his carelessness. There was a painfully sad look upon the general's face, and he did not speak for some time. While always keenly sensitive to the sufferings of the wounded, this pitiful sight seemed to affect him more than usual.

### BAD NEWS.

When General Grant returned to his headquarters, greatly disappointed that the attack had not succeeded, he found despatches from the other armies which were by no means likely to furnish consolation to him or to the officers about him. Sigel had been badly defeated at New Market, and was in retreat; Butler had been driven from Drewry's Bluff, though he still held possession of the road to Petersburg; and Banks had suffered defeat in Louisiana. The general was in no sense depressed by the information, and received it in a philosophic spirit; but he was particularly annoyed by the despatches from Sigel, for two hours before he had sent a message urging that officer to make his way to Staunton to stop supplies from being sent from there to Lee's army. He immediately requested Halleck to have Sigel relieved and General Hunter put in command of his troops. General Canby was sent to supersede Banks, this was done by the authorities at Washington, and not upon General Grant's suggestion, though the general thought well of Canby and made no objection.

In commenting briefly upon the bad news, General Grant said: «Lee will undoubtedly reinforce his army largely by bringing Beauregard's troops from Richmond, now that Butler has been driven back, and will call in troops from the Valley since Sigel's defeated forces have retreated to Cedar Creek. Hoke's troops will be needed no longer in North Carolina, and I am prepared to see Lee's forces in our front materially strengthened. I thought the other day that they must feel pretty blue in Richmond over the reports of our victories; but as they are in direct telegraphic communication with the points at which the fighting took place, they were no doubt at the same time aware of our defeats, of which we have not learned till to-day; so probably they did not feel as badly as we imagined.»

The general was not a man to waste any time over occurrences of the past; his first thoughts were always to redouble his efforts to take the initiative and overcome disaster by success. Now that his coöperating armies had failed him, he determined upon still bolder movements on the part of the troops under his immediate direction. As the weather was at this time more promising, his first act was to sit down at his field-desk and write an order providing for a general movement by the left flank toward Richmond, to begin the next night, May 19. He then sent to Washington asking the coöperation of the navy in changing our base of supplies to Port Royal on the Rappahannock.

### ATTEMPT TO TURN OUR RIGHT.

THE fact that a change had been made in the position of our troops, and that Hancock's corps had been withdrawn from our front and placed in rear of our center, evidently made Lee suspect that some movement was afoot, and he determined to send General Ewell's corps to try to turn our right, and to put Early in readiness to coöperate in the movement if it should promise success.

In the afternoon of May 19, a little after five o'clock, I was taking a nap in my tent, to try to make up for the sleep lost the night before. Aides-de-camp in this campaign were usually engaged in riding back and forth during the night between headquarters and the different commands, communicating instructions for the next day, and had to catch their sleep in instalments. I was suddenly awakened by my colored servant crying out to me: «Wake up, sah, fo' God's sake! De whole ob Lee's army am in our reah!» He was in a state of feverish excitement, and his face seemed two shades lighter than its ordinary hue. The black boys were not to be blamed for manifesting fright, for they all had a notion that their lives would not be worth praying for if they fell into the hands of the enemy and were recognized as persons who had made their escape from slavery to serve in the Yankee army. Hearing heavy firing in the direction of our rear, I put my head out of the tent, and seeing the general and staff standing near their horses, which had been saddled, I called for my horse and hastened to join them. Upon my inquiring what the matter was, the general said: «The enemy is detaching a large force to turn our right. I wish you would ride to the point of attack, and keep me posted as to the movement, and urge upon the commanders of the troops in that vicinity not only to check the advance of the enemy, but to take the offensive and destroy them if possible. You can say that Warren's corps will be ordered to coöperate promptly.» General Meade had already sent urgent orders to his troops nearest the point threatened. I started up the Fredericksburg road, and saw a large force of infantry advancing, which proved to be the troops of Ewell's corps who had crossed the Ny River. In the vicinity of the Harris house, about a mile east of the Ny, I found General Tyler's division posted on the Fredericksburg road, with Kitching's brigade on his left. By Meade's direction Hancock had been ordered to send a division to move at double-quick to Tyler's support, and Warren's Maryland brigade arrived on the ground later. The enemy had made a vigorous attack on Tyler and Kitching, and the contest was raging fiercely along their lines. I rode up to Tyler, who was an old army friend, found him making every possible disposition to check the enemy's advance, and called out to him: «Tyler, you are in luck to-day. It is n't every one who has a chance to make such a début on joining an army. You are certain to knock a brevet out of this day's fight.» He said: «As you see, my men are raw hands at this sort of work, but they are behaving like veterans.»

Hancock had arrived on the ground in person, and when Birney's troops of his corps came up they were put into action on Tyler's right. Crawford, of Warren's corps, arrived about dark, and was put in position on the left. The brunt of the attack, however, had been broken by the troops upon which it first fell. Each regiment of Tyler's heavy artillery was as large as some of our brigades. These regiments had been thoroughly drilled and disciplined in the defenses about Washington, but this was their first engagement, and their new uniforms and bright muskets formed a striking contrast to the travel-stained clothing and dull-looking arms of the other regiments. When the veterans arrived they cracked no end of jokes at the expense of the new troops. They would cry out to them: «How are you, heavies? Is this work heavy enough for you? You 're doing well, my sons. If you keep on like this a couple of years, you 'll learn all the tricks of the trade.» They were particularly anxious to get hold of the new arms of the fresh troops, and when a man was shot down a veteran would promptly seize his gun in exchange for his own, which had become much the worse for wear in the last week's rain-storms.

The fighting was exceedingly obstinate, and continued until after nine o'clock; but by that hour the enemy had been driven back at all points, and forced to beat a rapid retreat across the Ny. His loss in killed and wounded was severe, and we captured over four hundred prisoners from him. We did not escape a considerable loss on our side, six hundred of our men having been killed and wounded. A staff-officer, passing over the ground after dark, saw in the vicinity of the Fredericksburg road a row of men stretched upon the ground, looking as if they had lain down in line of battle to sleep. He started to shake several of them, and cried out: «Get up! What do you mean by going to sleep at such a time as this?» He was shocked to find that this row consisted entirely of dead bodies lying as they fell, shot down in ranks with their alinement perfectly preserved. The scene told with mute eloquence the story of their valor and the perfection of their discipline. The brevet rank predicted for Tyler was conferred upon him for his services in this engagement, and it had been fairly won.

Lee had evidently intended to make Ewell's movement a formidable one, for Early had received orders to coöperate in the attack if it should promise success, and during the afternoon he sent forward a brigade which made an assault in his front. The attempt, however, was a complete failure.

This attack by Ewell on the 19th prevented the orders previously issued for the general movement by the left flank from being carried out until the night of the 20th.

The Army of the Potomac had been embarrassed by having too much artillery. Finding that the country through which it had to move was more difficult than had been supposed, General Grant gave an order on the 19th to send ninety-two guns back to Washington.

### «BILL.»

THE next morning, May 20, the general was later than usual in making his appearance, in consequence of having overslept. Finally his voice was heard calling from his tent to his colored servant: «Bill! Ho, Bill! What time is it?» The servant ran to him, found he was still in bed, and told him the hour. In scarcely more than ten minutes the general appeared at the mess-table. We were not surprised at the rapidity with which he had dressed himself, for we had learned by this time that in putting on his clothes he was as quick as a lightning-change actor in a variety theater. When the officers at headquarters were called up particularly early to start on the march, every one did his utmost to be on time and not keep the general waiting; but, however vigorous the effort, no one could match him in getting on his clothes. There was seldom any occasion for such hurried dressing, but with him it was a habit which continued through life.

Bill, the servant who waited on the general, was a notable character. He was entirely a creature of accident. When the general was at Cairo in 1861, Bill suddenly appeared one day at headquarters with two other slave boys, who had just escaped from their former masters in Missouri. They belonged to that class of fugitive blacks who were characterized by those given to artistic comparisons as «charcoal sketches from the hands of the old masters.» Bill was of a genuine burnt-cork hue, and no white blood contaminated the purity of his lineage. He at once set himself to work without orders, taking care of one of the aides, and by dint of his force of character resisted all efforts of that officer to discharge him. When any waiter was absent, or even when all were present, he would turn up in the headquarters mess-tent and insist on helping the general at table. Then he attached himself to Colonel Boomer, and forced that officer in spite of himself to submit to his services. After the colonel had been killed in the assault on Vicksburg, Bill suddenly put in an appearance again at headquarters, and was found making himself useful to the general, notwithstanding the protests of the other servants, and before long he had himself regularly entered upon the general's private pay-roll. When his chief came East, Bill followed, and gradually took entire charge of the general's personal comfort as valet, waiter, and man of all work. He was devoted, never known to be beyond call, had studied the general's habits so carefully that he could always anticipate his few wants, and became really very useful. I had a striking illustration one morning in front of Spotsylvania of how devoted Bill was to the general's comfort. While we were camping in the region of wood-ticks, garter-snakes, and beetles, I saw Bill in front of the general's tent thrusting his hand first into one of the chief's boots and then into the other. «What are you doing that for, Bill?» I asked. «Oh,» he explained, «I allers feels around in de gin'ral's boots afore I lets him put dem on, to see dat no insec's done got into dem de prev'us night.» He followed in the general's shadow all through his Presidential terms, then he insisted upon attempting business in Washington, and afterward tried his hand at preaching; but he had fed so long at the public crib that his appetite had been spoiled for any other means of sustaining life, and he finally made his way into a government department as messenger, where he still is and where it is hoped that his eventful life may be rounded out in the quiet and comfort to which his public services entitle him. He will not be as dramatic an historical character as Napoleon's Mameluke, but in his humble way he was as faithful and devoted to his chief as the famous Roustan.

### GRANT'S UNPROTECTED HEADQUARTERS.

In discussing the contemplated movement to the left, General Grant said on the morning of May 20: «My chief anxiety now is to draw Lee out of his works and fight him in the open field, instead of assaulting him behind his intrenchments. The movement of Early yesterday gives me some hope that Lee may at times take the offensive, and thus give our troops the desired opportunity.» In this, however, the general was disappointed; for the attack of the 19th was the last offensive movement in force that Lee ventured to make during the entire campaign.

The series of desperate battles around Spotsylvania had ended, but other soil was now to be stained by the blood of fratricidal war. Torbert's cavalry division began the march to the South on May 20, and as soon as it was dark Hancock's corps set out for Milford Station, a distance of about twenty miles, to take up a position on the south bank of the Mattapony. Guiney's Station was reached the next morning, after a night march of eight miles. Hancock's advance crossed the Mattapony at noon and intrenched its position. At ten o'clock that morning Warren had moved south, and that night he reached the vicinity of Guiney's Station. Burnside put his corps in motion as soon as the road was clear of Hancock's troops, and was followed by Wright.

Generals Grant and Meade, with their staffs, took up their march on May 21, following the road taken by Hancock's corps, and late in the afternoon reached Guiney's Station. Our vigilant signal-officers, who had made every effort to read the enemy's signals, now succeeded in deciphering an important despatch, from which it was learned that Lee had discovered the movement that our forces were making. While riding forward, a little in advance of headquarters, with another staff-officer, I saw a body of the enemy on the opposite side of a stream which we were approaching. This made us feel a little apprehensive for the safety of the commanding generals, as Hancock was many miles in advance, and the head of Warren's corps was a considerable distance in the rear. Our party, besides a small cavalry and infantry escort, consisted entirely of officers, many of them of high rank. One might have said of it what Curran said of the books in his library, «Not numerous, but select.» It was promptly decided to order the regiment of infantry commanded by Colonel C. H. T. Collis, which served as General Meade's headquarters guard, to make a dash across the stream and endeavor to drive the enemy from his position on the opposite bank. This was promptly and gallantly done, and the detachment of the enemy soon beat a rapid retreat. General Grant sat on his horse quietly smoking his cigar, and watched the fight with considerable interest. It was suggested that, before pitching camp for the night, the headquarters had better move back upon the road on which we had advanced until Warren's troops should be met; but General Grant made light of the proposition and ordered the camp to be established where we were, saying, «I think, instead of our going back, we had better hurry Warren forward.» Suggestions to the general to turn back fell as usual upon deaf ears.

### GRANT AND THE VIRGINIA LADY.

While our people were putting up the tents and making preparations for supper, General Grant strolled over to a house near by, owned by a Mr. Chandler, and sat down on the porch. I accompanied him, and took a seat beside him. In a few minutes a lady came to the door, and was surprised to find that the visitor was the general-in-chief. He was always particularly civil to ladies, and he rose to his feet at once, took off his hat, and made a courteous bow. She was ladylike and polite in her behavior, and she and the general soon became engaged in a pleasant talk. Her conversation was exceedingly entertaining. She said, among other things: «This house has witnessed some sad scenes. One of our greatest generals died here just a year ago—General Jackson—Stonewall Jackson of blessed memory.» «Indeed!» remarked General Grant. «He and I were at West Point together for a year, and we served in the same army in Mexico.» «Then you must have known how good and great he was," said the lady. "Oh, yes," replied the general; "he was a sterling, manly cadet, and enjoyed the respect of every one who knew him. He was always of a religious turn of mind, and a plodding, hard-working student. His standing was at first very low in his class, but by his indomitable energy he managed to graduate quite high. He was a gallant soldier and a christian gentleman, and I can understand fully the admiration your people have for him."

"They brought him here the Monday after the battle of Chancellorsville," she continued. "You probably know, sir, that he had been wounded in the left arm and right hand by his own men, who fired upon him accidentally in the night, and his arm had been amputated on the field. The operation was very successful, and he was getting along nicely; but the wet applications made to the wound brought on pneumonia, and it was that which caused his death. He lingered till the next Sunday afternoon, May 10, and then he was taken from us." Here the lady of the house became very much affected, and almost broke down in recalling the sad event.

Our tents had by this time been pitched, and the general, after taking a polite leave of his hostess, and saying he would place a guard over her house to see that no damage was done to her property, walked over to camp, and soon after sat down with the mess to a light supper.

### A RACE FOR THE NORTH ANNA.

THE question has been asked why General Grant in this movement left so great a distance between Hancock's corps and the rest of his army. He did it intentionally, and under the circumstances it was unquestionably wise generalship. He was determined to try by every means in his power to tempt Lee to fight outside of his intrenched lines. He had in the battles of the last two weeks thoroughly measured Lee's capacity as an opponent, and he believed it would be difficult to force him to take the offensive unless some good opportunity were offered. He knew that Lee, from the distance over which he would have to move his troops, could not attack the isolated Hancock with more than an army corps. Such a force he was certain Hancock could whip; and Grant, being in close communication with the several corps, felt that he could bring up reinforcements as rapidly as the enemy, and that the chances would be greatly in his favor if he could thus bring on an engagement in the open field. There was no question in his mind as to whipping his opponent; the only problem was how to get at him.

The next morning, May 22, headquarters moved south, following the line which had been taken by Hancock's troops, which ran parallel with the Fredericksburg railroad. The officers and men had never experienced a more sudden change of feelings and prospects. The weather was pleasant, the air was invigorating, the sun was shining brightly, and the roads were rapidly drying up. The men had been withdrawn from the scenes of their terrific struggles at Spotsylvania, and were no longer confronting formidable earthworks. The features of the country had also entirely changed. Though there were many swamps, thickets, and streams with difficult approaches, the deep gloom of the Wilderness had been left behind. The country was now more open, and presented many clearings, and the range of vision was largely increased. The roads were broad, the land was well cultivated, and the crops were abundant. The men seemed to breathe a new atmosphere, and were inspired with new hope. It was again "on to Richmond," and the many miles they were now gaining toward the enemy's capital, and out of reach of fire, made them experience that buoyancy of feeling which always accompanies the prestige of success. But while the country was covered with farms and houses, there was scarcely an inhabitant to be seen. Most of the able-bodied men were serving in the armies, and the slaves had been driven farther south. Many of the non-combatants had gone away to escape the invading army, and the only people encountered were women and children and old and decrepit men.

The corps were now rapidly moving toward Hanover Junction, which is about twenty-five miles north of Richmond. Lee, notwithstanding his superior means of obtaining information, had not begun to move until Hancock's corps had crossed the Mattapony at Milford. He then started rapidly down the Telegraph road, and as he had a shorter route than the Union forces, it appears that he reached Hanover Court House at the head of Ewell's corps at 9:30 o'clock on May 22. His telegrams and manœuvers all go to show that he was entirely deceived in regard to Grant's movements. He reported at that time: "I have learned, as yet, nothing of the movements of the enemy east of the Mattapony." The day before, in speaking of the position of Grant's army, he said: "I fear [this] will secure him from attack until he crosses the Pamunkey.» Even after Grant had crossed the Mattapony, Lee spoke of the Union forces as being east of that river, and was hurrying forward troops in order to prevent Grant from crossing the Pamunkey, a stream formed by the junction of the North Anna and the South Anna rivers, while Grant was in reality moving toward the North Anna. In these movements Lee was entirely outgeneraled.

On the morning of May 22 Hancock was instructed to remain at Milford during the day, while the other corps were directed to move south by roads which would not separate them by distances of more than four miles. It appears to have been about midday of the 22d when Lee obtained information, through his cavalry, of our advance toward the North Anna. Hancock could not well have reached Hanover Junction before Lee, for Lee's route from the right of his intrenchments on the Po to Hanover Junction by the Telegraph road was about twenty-eight miles, while the route of Hancock's corps from Anderson's Mill to Hanover Junction via Bowling Green was about thirty-four miles; besides, as Hancock was advancing with a detached corps through an enemy's country and over unknown roads, he had to move with caution.

### A NOONDAY HALT AT MRS. TYLER'S.

EARLY in the afternoon General Grant decided to halt for a couple of hours, to be in easy communication with the troops that were following. He selected for the halt a plantation which was beautifully situated on high ground, commanding a charming view of the valley of the Mattapony. A very comfortable house stood not far from the road along which Burnside's corps was marching. In making halts of this kind a house was usually selected, for the reason that good water was easily obtainable, and facilities were afforded for looking at maps and conducting correspondence. General Grant never entered any of the houses, as they were usually occupied by ladies, and he did not wish to appear to invade their dwellings; he generally sat on the porch. When we reached this plantation, the escort and the junior staff-officers lounged about the grounds in the shade of the trees, while General Grant, accompanied by two or three of us who were riding with him, dismounted, and ascended the steps of the porch. A very gentle and prepossessing-looking lady standing in the doorway was soon joined by an older woman. General Grant bowed courteously and said, «With your permission, I will spend a few hours here.» The younger lady replied very civilly, «Certainly, sir.» The older one exclaimed abruptly, «I do hope you will not let your soldiers ruin our place and carry away our property.» The general answered politely, «I will order a guard to keep the men out of your place, and see that you are amply protected»; and at once gave the necessary instructions. The ladies, seeing that the officer with whom they were conversing was evidently one of superior rank, became anxious to know who he was, and the older one stepped up to me, and in a whisper asked his name. Upon being told that he was General Grant, she seemed greatly surprised, and in a rather excited manner informed the other lady of the fact. The younger lady, whose name was Mrs. Tyler, said that she was the wife of a colonel in the Confederate army, who was serving with General Joe Johnston in the West; but she had not heard from him for some time, and she was very anxious to learn through General Grant what news he had from that quarter. The general said, «Sherman is advancing upon Rome, and ought to have reached that place by this time.» Thereupon the older lady, who proved to be the mother-in-law of the younger one, said very sharply: «General Sherman will never capture that place. I know all about that country, and you have n't an army that will ever take it. We all know very well that Sherman is making no headway against General Johnston's army.»

We could see that she was entertaining views which everywhere prevailed in the South. The authorities naturally put the best face upon matters, and the newspapers tried to buoy up the people with false hopes. It was not surprising that the inhabitants of the remote parts of the country were in ignorance of the true progress of the war. General Grant replied in a quiet way: «General Sherman is certainly advancing rapidly in that direction; and while I do not wish to be the communicator of news which may be unpleasant to you, I have every reason to believe that Rome is by this time in his possession.» The older lady then assumed a bantering tone, and became somewhat excited and defiant in her manner; and the younger one joined with her in scouting the idea that Rome could ever be taken. Just then a courier rode up with despatches from Washington containing a telegram from Sherman. General Grant glanced over it, and then read it to the staff. It announced that Sherman had just captured Rome. The ladies had caught the purport of the communication, although it was not intended that they should hear it. The wife burst into tears, and the mother-in-law was much affected by the news, which was of course sad tidings to both of them.

The mother then began to talk with great rapidity and with no little asperity, saying: «I came from Richmond not long ago, where I lived in a house on the James River which overlooks Belle Isle; and I had the satisfaction of looking down every day on the Yankee prisoners. I saw thousands and thousands of them, and before this campaign is over I want to see the whole of the Yankee army in Southern prisons.»

Just then Burnside rode into the yard, dismounted, and joined our party on the porch. He was a man of great gallantry and elegance of manner, and was always excessively polite to the gentler sex. He raised his hat, made a profound bow to the ladies, and, as he looked at his corps filing by on the road, said to the older one, who was standing near him, «I don't suppose, madam, that you ever saw so many Yankee soldiers before.» She replied instantly: «Not at liberty, sir.» This was such a good shot that every one was greatly amused, and General Grant joined heartily in the laugh that followed at Burnside's expense.

### GRANT CROSSES THE NORTH ANNA.

HANCOCK'S corps had been fighting and marching almost continuously for over a week, both day and night, and the halt on May 22 was made to give a much needed rest. It was a curious study to watch the effect which the constant exposure to fire had produced upon the nervous system of the troops. Their nerves had become so sensitive that the men would start at the slightest sound, and dodge at the flight of a bird or the sight of a pebble tossed past them. One of their amusements in camp at that time was to throw stones and chips past one another's heads, and raise a laugh at the active dodging, and bending the body low or «jack-knifing» as the men called it. This did not indicate any loss of courage; it was merely an effect produced by a temporary physical condition which the men could not control, and gave ample evidence of the nervous strain to which they had so long been subjected. Dodging the head under fire is often as purely involuntary as winking. I have known, in my experience, only two men who could remain absolutely immovable under a heavy fire, without even the twitching of a muscle. One was a bugler in the cavalry, and the other was General Grant.

In the evening of the 22d the general-in-chief issued written orders directing the movement of the troops for the next day. The march was to begin at five o'clock in the morning, and the several corps were to send out cavalry and infantry in advance on all the roads to ascertain the position of the enemy. The purpose was to cross the North Anna River west of the Fredericksburg railroad, and to strike Lee wherever he could be found. To understand the topography of the country, it is necessary to explain that the North Anna and the South Anna run in an easterly direction, at a distance from each other of eight or ten miles in the vicinity of the region in which Grant's operations took place, and unite and form the Pamunkey River about five miles east of the line of the Fredericksburg railroad. This road crossed the North Anna about two miles north of Hanover Junction, the intersection of the Fredericksburg and the Virginia Central railroads. The Telegraph road crossed the river by a wooden bridge half a mile west of the railroad bridge. Farther up the river there were three fords about a mile and a half apart. Hancock marched to the Telegraph-road bridge, Burnside to Ox Ford, and Warren to Jericho Ford. Wright followed Warren; Burnside's corps used plantation roads which ran between the main roads which had been taken by the corps of Hancock and Warren.

Hancock approached the river at the Telegraph-road bridge about noon. He found the enemy holding an earthwork on the north side, and saw a force posted on the opposite bank. Seeing the importance of gaining possession of the defensive work, he determined to take it by assault, and did so handsomely, some of the enemy being captured, and the rest driven over the bridge, followed closely by our men. The retreating force was thrown into great confusion, and in the rush a number were crowded off the bridge and drowned.

Burnside, on reaching Ox Ford, found it held by the enemy strongly intrenched on the south bank of the river, and no attack was made. Warren reached Jericho Ford soon after noon, seized it, laid a pontoon bridge, and by 4:30 P. M. had moved his whole corps to the south bank. At six o'clock Hill's corps attacked Warren's line before his troops were all in position, and forced it back some distance; but the enemy was soon repulsed. Wright's corps was moved up to support Warren, but it was not deemed necessary to send it across the river until the next morning.

General Grant rode during this day, May 23, with Hancock's corps. While halting in the afternoon at a house not far from the river, he was told by the people living there that Lee had rested for a few hours at the same house the day before, and that his entire army had crossed the river. On the morning of the 24th Hancock crossed to the south side. Crittenden's division crossed the river and joined Warren's corps. They advanced against the enemy with a view of dislodging him from his position at Ox Ford, but his lines were found so strong that after a brief encounter our forces withdrew. They had not been able to take with them any artillery. That night our whole army, except one division of Burnside's corps, was on the south side of the river and close up to the enemy's lines.

### SHERIDAN RETURNS FROM HIS RAID.

GENERAL headquarters were established near Chesterfield Station on May 24. That day Sheridan returned from his memorable cavalry raid, and was warmly greeted by General Grant at headquarters, and heartily congratulated upon his signal success. He related some of the principal incidents in the raid very graphically, but with becoming modesty. In describing a particularly hot fight, he would become highly animated in manner and dramatic in gesture; then he would turn to some ludicrous incident, laugh heartily, and seem to enjoy greatly the recollection of it. It will be remembered that he started out suddenly on May 8, passed round the right of Lee's army, keeping out of reach of his infantry, crossed the North Anna in the night, destroyed ten miles of the Virginia Central railroad, together with cars, locomotives, and a large amount of army supplies, recaptured three hundred and seventy-five of our prisoners on their way from Spotsylvania to Richmond, crossed the South Anna, struck the Fredericksburg road at Ashland, and destroyed the depot, many miles of road, a train of cars, and a large supply of army stores. Finding that the enemy's cavalry were concentrating, he united his divisions, which had been operating at different points in the work of destruction, and fought a pitched battle at Yellow Tavern, about seven miles north of Richmond, capturing two pieces of artillery, mortally wounding the commander, J. E. B. Stuart, and killing Brigadier-general James B. Gordon. He then entered the advanced lines of intrenchments north of Richmond, crossed the Chickahominy, and reached Haxall's Landing, on the James, where he replenished his supplies from stores sent to him by Butler. After remaining there from the 14th to the 17th of May, he started on his return to the Army of the Potomac. He had lost only four hundred and twenty-five men in killed, wounded, and missing. One important effect of Sheridan's operations was that he compelled all of the enemy's cavalry to be moved against him, which left our large train of four thousand wagons free from their attacks.

General Grant at times had a peculiar manner of teasing officers with whom he was on terms of intimacy, and in this interview he began to joke with his cavalry leader by saying to those who were gathered about him: «Now, Sheridan evidently thinks he has been clear down to the James River, and has been breaking up railroads, and even getting a peep at Richmond; but probably this is all imagination, or else he has been reading something of the kind in the newspapers. I don't suppose he seriously thinks that he made such a march as that in two weeks.»

Sheridan joined in the fun, and replied: «Well, after what General Grant says, I do begin to feel doubtful as to whether I have been absent at all from the Army of the Potomac.» Sheridan had become well bronzed by his exposure to the sun, and looked the picture of health. It was seen at once that the general-in-chief did not intend to give him or his command any rest. He told him of the movements he had in contemplation, and Sheridan saw that all his troopers would be wanted immediately at the front.

### MEETING BETWEEN GRANT AND BURNSIDE.

THAT evening, the 24th, General Grant issued an order, which he had been considering for some time, assigning Burnside's corps to the Army of the Potomac, and putting him under the command of Meade. It was found that such a consolidation would be much better for purposes of administration, and give more unity to the movements. It had been heretofore necessary to inform Meade of the instructions given to Burnside, and to let Burnside know of the movements that were to be undertaken by Meade, in order that the commanders might understand fully what was intended to be accomplished, and be in a position to coöperate intelligently. This involved much correspondence and consumed time. The new order was intended to avoid this, and simplify the methods which had been employed. While General Grant was riding past the headquarters of Burnside the next morning, Burnside came out of his tent, and in company with several of his officers came up to General Grant, who had now halted by the roadside, shook hands with him, and said: «I have received the instructions assigning my command to the Army of the Potomac. That order is excellent; it is a military necessity, and I am glad it has been issued.» This conduct of Burnside gave the greatest satisfaction to the general-in-chief, and he commented very favorably upon it afterward. It must be recollected in this connection that Burnside was senior in rank to Meade, and had commanded the Army of the Potomac when Meade was a division commander under him; and the manner in which Burnside acquiesced in his new assignment, and the spirit he manifested in his readiness to set aside all personal aims and ambitions for the public good, were among the many instances of his patriotism and his absolute loyalty to the cause he served.

### DESTROYING A RAILROAD.

THE general headquarters were moved farther west on May 25, and established on the north side of the North Anna, near Quarles' Ford, at a place known as Quarles' Mills. That day it became evident that Lee was going to make a permanent stand between the North and the South Anna. His position was found to be exceedingly strong, and was somewhat similar to the one taken up at Spotsylvania. The lines were shaped something like the letter U, with the base resting on the river at Ox Ford. It had one face turned toward Hancock, and the other toward Warren. The lines were made exceedingly formidable by means of strong earthworks with heavy obstructions planted in front, and were flanked on the right by an impenetrable swamp, and on the left by Little River. General Grant said, in discussing the situation at this time: «It now looks as if Lee's position were such that it would not be prudent to fight a battle in the narrow space between these two rivers, and I shall withdraw our army from its present position, and make another flank march to the left; but I want, while we are here, to destroy a portion of the Virginia Central Railroad, as that is the road by which Lee is receiving a large part of his supplies and reinforcements.» He ended the conversation by directing me to cross the river and superintend this operation.

I went with a portion of Russell's division of Wright's corps, which began the work of destruction at a point on the railroad about eight hundred yards from the enemy's extreme left. A brigade was extended along one side of the road in single rank, and at a given signal the men took hold of the rails, lifted up the road, and turned it upside down. Then, breaking the rails loose, they used them as levers in prying off the cross-ties, which they piled up at different points, laid the rails across them and set fire to the ties. As soon as the rails became sufficiently hot they bent in the middle by their own weight; efforts were then made to twist them so as to render them still more unserviceable. Several miles of railway were thus destroyed.

### THE ENEMY REINFORCED.

THE reinforcements which General Grant had predicted would be sent to Lee's army had reached him. Between 12,000 and 15,000 men arrived from the 22d to the 25th of May. Breckinridge had come from the valley of Virginia with nearly all of his forces; Pickett brought a division from the vicinity of Richmond; and Hoke's brigade of Early's division had also been sent to Lee from the Confederate capital. On the 22d, as soon as Grant had learned the extent of the disaster to Butler's army on the James, he said that Butler was not detaining 10,000 men in Richmond, and not even keeping the roads south of that city broken, and he considered it advisable to have the greater part of Butler's troops join in the campaign of the Army of the Potomac. On May 25 he telegraphed orders to Halleck, saying: «Send Butler's forces to White House, to land on the north side, and march up to join this army. The James River should be held to City Point, but leave nothing more than is absolutely necessary to hold it, acting purely on the defensive. The enemy will not undertake any offensive operations there, but will concentrate everything here.» At the same time he said: «If Hunter can possibly get to Charlottesville and Lynchburg, he should do so, living on the country. The railroads and canals should be destroyed beyond the possibility of repair for weeks.» These instructions were given in consequence of the withdrawal of Breckinridge's command, which left the valley of Virginia undefended.

### A FEMALE ODDITY.

WHEN I recrossed the river and returned to headquarters in the evening, I found General

Grant sitting in front of his tent smoking a cigar and anxious to hear the report as to the extent of the damage to the railroad. About the time I finished relating to him what had been accomplished, an old woman who occupied a small house near by strolled over to headquarters, apparently bent upon having a friendly chat with the commander of the Yankee armies. The number of questions she asked showed that she was not lacking in the quality of curiosity which is supposed to be common to her sex. She wore an old-fashioned calico dress about six inches too short, with the sleeves rolled up to the elbows. She had a nose so sharp that it looked as if it had been caught in the crack of a door, and small gray eyes that twinkled and snapped as she spoke. She began by nodding a familiar «How do you do?» to the general, and saying in a voice which squeaked like the high notes of an E-flat clarinet with a soft reed: «I believe you command all these h'yah Yankees that are comin' down h'yah and cavortin' round over this whole section of country.» The general bowed an assent, and she continued: «I 'm powerful glad General Lee has been lickin' you-all from the Rapidan cl'ah down h'yah, and that now he 's got you jes wh'ah he wants you.»

Then she drew up a camp-chair alongside the general, seated herself on it, and finding that her remarks seemed to be received good-naturedly, grew still more familiar, and went on to say: «Yes, and afo' long Lee 'll be a-chasin' you-all up through Pennsylvany ag'in. Was you up thah in Pennsylvany when he got aftah you-all last summer?» The general had great difficulty in keeping his face straight as he replied: «Well, no; I was n't there myself. I had some business in another direction.» He did not explain to her that Vicksburg was at that time commanding something of his attention. Said she: «I notice our boys got away with lots of 'em Conestoga hosses up thah, and they brought lots of 'em back with 'em. We 've got a pretty good show of 'em round this section of country, and they 're jes the best draft-hosses you ever see. Hope the boys 'll get up thah ag'in soon, and bring back some more of 'em.»

The general kept on smoking his cigar, and was greatly amused by the conversation. After a little while the woman went back to her house, but returned later, and said: «See h'yah; I 'm all alone in my house, and I am kinder skeerd. I expect them Yankee soldiers of yourn 'll steal everything I have, and murder me afo' morning, if you don't give me some protection.» «Oh,» replied the general, «we will see that you are not hurt»; and turning to Lieutenant Dunn of the staff, he said: «Dunn, you had better go and stay in the old lady's house to-night. You can probably make yourself more comfortable there than in camp, anyhow; and I don't want her to be frightened.»

Dunn followed the old woman rather reluctantly to her house, and played guardian angel to her till the next morning.

### GRANT RECROSSES THE NORTH ANNA.

General Grant had now presented to him for solution a very formidable military problem. Lee's position, from the strength and location of his intrenchments and the defensive character of the country, was impregnable, or at least it could not be carried by assault without involving great loss of life. The general had therefore decided to withdraw, and make another movement by the left flank, in the hope of so manœuvering as to afford another opportunity of getting a chance to strike Lee outside his earthworks. However, a withdrawal in the face of a vigilant foe, and the crossing of a difficult river within sight of the enemy, constitute one of the most hazardous movements in warfare. There was the possibility, also, that Lee might mass his artillery on his left flank, and try to hold it by this means and with a minimum of his infantry, and with the bulk of his army move out on his right in an attempt to crush Hancock's corps. This is exactly what Grant himself would have done under similar circumstances; but he had by this time become familiar with Lee's methods, and had very little apprehension that he would take the offensive. Nevertheless, Hancock was ordered to take every precaution against a possible assault. The withdrawal of the army was conducted with consummate skill, and furnishes an instructive lesson in warfare. In the first place, the enemy had to be deceived and thrown off his guard to make the movement at all safe. For this purpose Wilson's division of cavalry was transferred to the right of the army on May 25, and ordered to cross the North Anna and proceed to Little River on Lee's extreme left, and make a vigorous demonstration, to convey the impression that there was a movement of the army in that direction with a view to turning Lee's left. This was done so effectually that Lee telegraphed to Richmond the next morning: «From present indications the enemy seems to contemplate a movement on our left flank.» During the night of the 25th the trains and all of the artillery, which was in position on our right wing, were quietly moved to the north bank of the river. Russell's division of the Sixth Corps was also withdrawn and moved in the rear of Burnside, and at daylight the next morning halted in a place where its movements could not be seen by the enemy during the day. Its position in front of the enemy had been skilfully filled with men from the other parts of the command, and its absence was not discovered. Early in the morning of May 26 instructions were issued for the withdrawal of the entire army that night. After these orders had been despatched, the general seated himself in front of his tent for a quiet smoke. In a few minutes the old woman who had had the familiar chat with him the evening before rushed over to his tent in a high state of excitement. Swinging her arms like the fans of a windmill, and screaming at the top of her shrill voice, she cried out: «See h'yah; these Yankees o' yourn got into my bahn last night, and stole the only hoss I had, and I want you to send some of your folks out to find him and bring him back.» The general listened to her story, and when she had finished remarked quietly: «Madam, perhaps it is one of those Conestoga horses you spoke of that belong up in Pennsylvania, and some of our men have made up their minds to take him back home.» The old lady at this remark was rather crestfallen, and said with a grin: «Well, I reckon you 've got me on that; but you Yankees have no business down h'yah anyhow, and I think you might get me back that hoss.» The general replied: «I 'm very sorry indeed that this has occurred, and if the army were in camp I would send you around with a guard to see whether the horse could be recognized by you and recovered; but the troops are moving constantly, and it would be utterly impossible to find the animal.» She finally went off, shaking her fist and muttering: «I 'm sart'in of one thing, anyhow: General Lee 'll just dust you-all out of this place afo' you kin say scat.»

The operations of the last two days had made the duties of staff-officers particularly arduous, and a great many of us were feeling the effects of the last week's hard work and exposure, the loss of sleep, and the breathing of a malarious atmosphere. In connection with the renewal of the work of destroying the railroad, I was sent across the river again on the 26th, and on returning that afternoon to headquarters found myself suffering severely from fever and sick-headache. About dark General Grant wished me to make another trip to the extreme right, to assist in the work of withdrawing the troops, as I was particularly familiar with that part of the lines. Sickness is no excuse in the field, so I started across the river again without making my condition known to the general. To make matters worse, a thunder-storm came up, accompanied by vivid lightning, and between the flashes the darkness was so impenetrable that it was slow work finding the roads. Babcock, seeing my condition, volunteered to accompany me, so that if I gave out, the orders I was carrying might still reach their destination. We remained in the saddle the greater part of the night. On my return to headquarters a surgeon supplied me liberally with round-shot in the form of quinine pills, which were used so effectively that my fever was soon forced to beat a retreat.

As soon as it was dark the other divisions of Wright's corps had begun the recrossing of the river. This corps followed the route which had been taken by Russell's division, while Warren took a road a little farther to the north. Burnside and Hancock next withdrew, and so cautiously that their movements entirely escaped detection by the enemy. All the corps left strong guards in their fronts, which were withdrawn at the last moment. The pontoon bridges were taken up after crossing the river, and cavalry was sent to the several fords to hold them after they had been abandoned by the infantry, and to destroy any facilities for crossing which had been neglected. The withdrawal from the North Anna had now been successfully accomplished.

(To be continued.)

*Horace Porter.*

# PLACES IN NEW YORK.

ONLY the newest comers or the dullest dwellers in New York are chiefly impressed by its size. If you know it at all, and really see it and feel it, you must marvel more at its union of individuality and heterogeneousness. It is this that makes its character, and it is this that makes that character unique. Other cities are also very big, and some of them have grown to bigness with even greater speed; but no other in the world is so big and so complex as New York, yet so distinctively itself.

I.

MORE than seventy-six per cent. of those who people New York to-day were born of foreign mothers; more than forty per cent. were born on foreign soil themselves; and many of these aliens, brought from many different lands, continue here to live in clusters with their own kin after their own kind. Yet while each of these clusters, and each of their wandering offshoots, modifies the New-World metropolis, all of them together do not destroy its cohesion; they simply intensify its curious composite sort of personality. They make it multifariously diverse, but they leave it an entity. They touch every portion of it with pungent exotic flavors, but as flavoring an American whole. They play their several parts in a civic life that is cosmoramic beyond the belief of those who have not studied it well, but they do not turn New York into a cosmopolitan town; for this means a town which, overwhelmed by its strangers, has lost, or has never possessed, a character of its own.

In the same way the architectural body of New York is a patchwork thing, structures of every size and form and color crowding together and defying all laws of harmony and concord. Yet this patchwork thing has a personality peculiar and distinct, engendered by its station on a long and narrow river-girdled isle, where land is incomparably dear, and where structures for this purpose and for that have been segregated into well-marked groups succeeding one another in a longitudinal line.

Moreover, New York is not really a modern town, although its mood is as modern as that of the youngest. And this fact, and the contrast between the fact and the mood, have helped to make it individual, and have helped to make it heterogeneous too.

The Island of the Manhattoes sent beaver-skins to Europe soon after Queen Elizabeth died. In 1626, only one year after the death of the first King James, a permanent town was established upon it. And the first great chapter in the story of this town was closed in 1664, only four years after the second Charles picked up his father's battered crown. Then New Amsterdam passed from Dutch into English hands, and was rechristened for the Duke of York twenty-one years before he began to govern it as the second James. Thus the silver tankard owned by the Schuyler family, and given to their ancestor by Queen Anne when he took five Mohawk chiefs to visit her in 1710, is by no means a relic of early New York. Who thinks of St. Petersburg as a typically modern town? Yet in 1710 St. Petersburg had been founded only half a dozen years.

Huguenots came in with our first Hollanders, and more and more of them in succeeding years. A large proportion of the so-called Dutch themselves were Flemings or Walloons of Gallic blood and speech. Englishmen, Scotch, and Irishmen arrived before Great Britain officially arrived; Portuguese, Swiss, Danes, Spaniards, Swedes, Germans, negroes, West Indians—in short, so many scraps of nationalities that in 1660, when Peter Stuyvesant ruled over some fourteen hundred people, they conversed, we are told, in eighteen different tongues. Do you wonder that in the year 1895 the pupils of a certain public school on the East Side of New York should have acknowledged a quondam allegiance, personal or parental, to twenty-nine different lands?

But very long before the war of independence we had solidified into a true English-voiced community. Our Americanism was enhanced, our personality unimpaired, by the steady immigration from New England which began soon after, and was called the «Connecticut invasion.» And all the American, European, Asiatic, and African invasions that have since been poured upon us have not left us any the less decidedly ourselves.

So it has been with our architectural body. It has never been let alone. The «progressive» builder has always worked hand in hand with the aspiring immigrant to augment the complexity of New York, and the cause of his activity has been the grandeur of our waterways. Securing our commercial supremacy, at the same time they have cramped us so upon our island that its sands have grown to be more golden than those of the richest Californian gulch; and in the struggle to get all the gold out of them our city has, season by season, rent and renewed its garments of brick and stone. Not to go back again to beginnings, it may suffice to quote Philip Hone, who wrote in 1839 just as we might write to-day: «The whole of New York is rebuilt about once in ten years.» The pulling down of houses and stores in the lower part of the city he declared to be «awful,» exclaiming, «It looks like the ruins occasioned by an earthquake.» And a little book of memoirs published by a well-known merchant, Nathaniel Hubbard, in 1875, informs us that «the city of New York has been built over two or three times during the past eighty or ninety years.»

All these foreigners could not be at once absorbed, nor could any rebuildings destroy all things of earlier dates. Thus New York has ever been a heterogeneous town, although, I must insist, it is not a truly cosmopolitan town or a mere characterless piece of architectural patchwork.

It is impossible, however, to do more than thus assert and thus insist. It is impossible to explain New York's peculiar union of the old and the new, the native and the foreign—to convey its personality or to picture its complexity. You must live within it before you can apprehend it, and even then comprehension will be long delayed. What I have written is simply meant to serve as a basis for the statement that New York is astonishingly full of places; for, of course, to be counted and remarked upon as such, a place must be something more unlike its neighbors than a cell in a honeycomb. Not only because New York is so immense, but because it is so immensely diversified, are its places impossible to count. And as for knowing them all, Mr. Bunner, who was as wise in local lore as any one may hope to be, declared that no one may hope even to know the whole of the Bowery.

Early New York has bequeathed us no architectural relics, and colonial New York only a few. Yet their spirit survives in the names of our down-town places, often in their shape and disposition, and sometimes, with modifications, even in their aspect and their uses.

I cannot tell you just how this has been effected, nor speak at all about the thousand other interesting places which have been wholly wiped off our map. I cannot venture into that fascinating region known as Old New York. My present commission bids me merely cruise for half an hour amid the places of modern New York, sketching their present coast-lines and contours. But I can heartily advise you to study elsewhere the chronicles of Old New York, for they are much richer in incidents dramatic and adventurous, patriotic, picturesque, singular, and amusing, than those of any other American town. And here, now, are two bits of good advice, to be digested before we look at a few characteristic places in modern New York.

This is the first one: Never say Manhattan Island when you mean the Island of Manhattan. The briefer term was properly applied in such a way that now it cannot be applied at all. The place that bore it is no longer discernible. Manhattan Island was a knoll about an acre in extent which lay near Corlaer's Hook, surrounded by marshes and partly submerged by high tides. Later on it became the center of a place which did us noble service, but again has been obliterated, save for the lingering nickname of «Dry-dock Village.» Here were built most of our ships in the days when no one could build them quite as well as we.

And this is the second lesson: Do not study our historic places in what you may think the logical way, beginning with their beginnings. If you do, you will often be sorely disappointed. So many New York places have been changed beyond the reconstructive power of the nimblest fancy that it is better to familiarize yourself with their present aspect, and then hunt up their histories. Thus you will protect yourself against the chill of disappointments, while securing innumerable chances to feel the pleasurable glow of surprise. Look, for example, at our pseudo-Egyptian Tombs and our pseudo-Italian Criminal Court-house, set up on second-rate commercial streets. It may pleasantly astonish you to find that they occupy the site of a once famous and very lovely lake. But if you read first of this lake, of its size and its fabulous depth, and the picturesqueness of its hilly and verdant shores; of the Indian who was murdered beside it in the first Dutch governor's time, and the wars his murder provoked; of the rural amusements it afforded, winter and summer, to many generations of Manhattanese; of the good water with which it supplied them; of the park which only a hundred years ago was imagined about it, in the interests of real-estate values, but was never decreed because the place lay so far out of town; and of the triumphant spectacle it presented when John Fitch sent his little steamboat around and around it ten years before Fulton sent the *Clermont* up the Hudson River—if you read all this, and then discover that the Collect Pond cannot now be discovered at all, or traced or imagined or believed in, why, then you may say that you would rather read fictions which do not profess to be true.

## II.

AMONG all the places in New York, which is the one that, putting thoughts of the past out of mind, best typifies to-day?

The center of the Brooklyn Bridge, you may suggest, where a miracle of modern science is stretched beneath our feet, while under our eyes lies the sweep of our all-creating harbor, and on the one hand the limitless panorama of the roofs of New York, on the other, apparently as limitless, the roofs of Brooklyn, New York's tributary twin.

Or you may declare that, as ours is the type of a commercial town, its typical place must be a place of trade; and if Wall street is too complicated to be looked upon as a single place, you may point to the Stock Exchange just around the corner, on the street which is still called Broad because it was made so to accommodate a Dutch-beloved canal.

The Stock Exchange is certainly the heart of the business life of New York. Yet there are stock exchanges in every big city in the world, and a generic likeness must pervade them. Something more distinctively American, more specifically local, we find in our towering office-buildings. There is nothing like these to be seen in Europe, and though they have spread all over America, and Chicago has taught us to build them in cleverer ways than we had found for ourselves, their birthplace was New York. They were inspired by that costliness of soil which has modified our lives and deeds in so many ways, and were made possible by the invention of the steam-elevator. Year by year they grow taller and taller, and, as rapidly growing in numbers, they are once more entirely changing the countenance of New York. Many of its down-town streets now look less like streets than like cañons cut by patient rivers between stupendous cliffs fretted and carved by a hand as vigorous and ingenious, though hardly as artistic, as the hand of Nature herself. These, I think, are our most characteristic, our most typical places.

If you enter one of the largest and go up and down and around in it, you will see that it is not a mere house, but almost a town in itself. It nearly covers the space of an entire city block. Thirty-two elevators serve the persons and the wants of its denizens and their visitors, and they carry some forty thousand passengers each day. The great business concern which owns it fills a whole floor, with halls as big as churches, and regiments of clerks. On the other floors live many another big company, and many an individual doing a big business of this sort or of that; and their number will not amaze you as much as the luxury with which prosaic tasks of money-making now surround themselves. I wonder sometimes what my grandfather would have thought of it. No one in New York did business in a bigger way than he, sending his famous clipper-ships to encircle the world and traffic in a score of ports. Yet when my father began to «clerk» for him, the first of his duties was to sand his office floor; and I can remember how small and plain was this office, even at a much later day, with the bowsprits of vessels almost poking themselves in at the window as they lay along the border of South street.

The people who dwell in the typical office-building of to-day walk about on polished marble floors; the government has given them a post-office just for themselves; a big library and a restaurant exclusively serve the lawyers among them; another restaurant generously serves whomsoever may wish to eat; there are rows of shops in the huge, barrel-vaulted main hall; there are barbers' rooms and boot-blacks' rooms, and so forth and so on. You can almost believe that a man might live in this building, going forth only to sleep, and be supplied with pretty much everything he need desire, except the domestic affections, a church, and a theater. It seems rather surprising, indeed, that a missionary chapel has not been started in one of its corners, and a roof-garden for daytime performances up on the hilltop called its roof. But on this roof was till lately the bureau which breeds our weather for us, and down in its underground stories, in the very entrails of the earth, you may confidently leave it your wealth to guard.

Truly, the steel-clad burrows of a great safe-deposit company look capacious enough to contain all the wealth of New York, and whether your share of it be large or small, your needs can be exactly met. You may hire a safe so little that a diamond necklace would almost fill it, or so big that it is a good-sized room, and its rent means the income of a good-sized fortune—seven thousand dollars or so per annum. Narrow lane after lane is walled by tiers of these safes, as streets are walled by house-fronts; there is a second story below the first, and there are other places where other things than gold and silver, precious papers, and jewels may be stored. There are rooms full of trunks, and I remember a big one with the sweat of steam glistening on its walls and ceilings, which was filled full and heaped and piled with bales of a shining cream-colored stuff—raw silk, costly and also perishable, needing to be kept perpetually moist lest it lose its pliability.

When in this treasure-house of uncountable riches we see marble floors which can be lifted by levers so that they lie against the bases of doors impregnable without them, and vents which can throw curtains of scalding steam down upon the head of any one who may try to tamper with them, it seems as though the days of Oriental magicians had returned, with conspicuous modern improvements. Of course there are rows and rows of little cabinets where Crœsus may handle his wealth very privately, and fine large waiting-rooms, too, all shut in by gates and bars and pass-words. «The ladies' waiting-room is a great convenience,» said the gray-coated guardian, one day. «When gentlemen bring their wives down town, and have business to do elsewhere, it 's a nice place to leave them in.» So it is; but if it is much used for this purpose, I hope that its niceness, not its terrific security, determines the fact.

Of course almost all the labors sheltered by these architectural colossi die down as the day dies. Even early in the night they are empty and at rest, save for the few which harbor such craftsmen as dare make no difference between night and day. Chief among these exceptions are the homes of our morning newspapers. Here it is nearly midnight before the huge presses begin to rush and roar in concert, and human activity does not reach its most strenuous point until the small hours are striking.

Even on Sunday these newspaper buildings seem alive, and, with Trinity Church and the entrance to the Brooklyn Bridge, they are almost the only things in the business part of New York which do. Its streets have not the gloomy, plague-stricken look that the City's streets in London present on the Sabbath, our air and sky are so much more cheerful, and our buildings are so much less dismally monotonous in color and in form. Yet they are almost as empty as the City's streets, and therefore this time is to be recommended if you wish to study our down-town architecture. Should you go about on a week-day, staring, and stopping, and craning your neck to look at sky-scraping cornices, you might quickly gather a throng about you, wondering whether you had lost your wits, or whether, perhaps, some one else had set off a fire-balloon.

## III.

You have heard so much of the costliness of the soil which underlies the places in New York that perhaps you may like to know what it really signifies, and how it has increased since the phenomenal development of our city began about eighty years ago.

Probably the most valuable spots on the face of the earth (as the burial-sites in Westminster Abbey cannot be bought with gold) are the four corners where Wall street touches Broad, and the two where it meets Broadway. I cannot guess how large a price any one of these might bring in the market now; but a million dollars and half a million more were recently paid for five lots on Broadway opposite Bowling Green. This was the value of the land alone, as the old buildings it bore were at once to be torn down; yet, says Philip Hone, a lot in just this place sold in 1829 for only $19,500. As late as 1840 lots on Cortlandt street could be had for $1000, or even for $700. But a year or two ago the corner of Liberty street and Nassau, measuring 79 feet along the one, 112 along the other, and about 100 feet in depth, brought $1,250,000, and this, again, for the sake of the land alone.

In 1836 Philip Hone regretfully moved from his dwelling-place at No. 235 Broadway. «I am turned out of doors,» he wrote. «Almost everybody down town is in the same predicament, for all the houses are to be converted into stores. We are tempted by prices so exorbitantly high that none can resist.» The price that tempted him was but $60,000; yet it is not strange that he thought

DRAWN BY F. H. LUNGREN.

A CITY CAÑON.

it high, for fifteen years before he had bought his dwelling-place, house and land together, for $25,000. «Everything in New York,» he wrote again, «is at an exorbitant price. Lots two miles from City Hall are worth $8000 or $10,000.» And on the corner of Broadway and Great Jones street he himself paid $15,000 for a lot 29 × 130 feet as a site for his new home. When he was choosing it he walked about in this rather remote region with his friend Mr. Swan. The latter made his purchase on Lafayette Place, and I know

FROM A WATER-COLOR BY LOUIS C. VOGT.

SOUTH STREET AT THE FOOT OF WALL STREET.

very well what a big and comfortable house he built there, for one of the best-remembered tragedies of my childhood was the drowning of my doll in one of his bath-tubs by one of his grandsons. But need I say that its aspect is no longer the same? Lafayette Place, in its turn, has become a down-town and a business street, and Mr. Swan's almost suburban residence is now the see-house of the Episcopal diocese of New York.

Two miles from the City Hall? Very much farther away than this stands the new «Herald» building, where Broadway and Sixth Avenue intersect. In 1845 the city owned its site, and sold it for $9930. The «Herald» now pays rent for it—for the land alone—at the rate of $60,000 a year. At the same sale fifty years ago a corner lot on Fifth Avenue and Forty-second street brought $1400, and in 1840 four hundred lots on Fifth Avenue above Twentieth street were sold at prices ranging from $200 to $400. Within twenty years some of these were resold for $15,000 each, and you may guess their present worth for yourselves, remembering that business and business values have now moved into this region also.

Less than twenty years ago a much more northerly district, between Fifty-ninth and One Hundred and Tenth streets, west of Eighth Avenue, would have shown you little but rocks and puddles and predatory goats and boys. Now much more than half its surface is covered with buildings, all of a very good class, and their estimated cost has been $170,000,000. Land up here is more precious than was land two miles from the City Hall in the days of Philip Hone. And it is just as easy now as then to grow greatly richer in New York if you are already rich enough to buy little bits of its soil and to hold on to them for a little while.

## IV.

THERE are nearly six hundred places of Christian worship in New York, but they would not serve its needs very well were it a church-going town, for all together they can hardly seat more than three hundred thousand persons. None is as famous as Trinity Church, four times built afresh on its present site; and not long ago it was the most conspicuous object in the city's silhouette.

Now it is scarcely discernible from afar, for many worldly structures have been carried up in their full proportions almost as near to heaven as the 284 feet achieved by its diminishing spire; nay, in very recent days many have far outstripped this spire.

But Trinity's green graveyard keeps it from being crowded very closely by examples of «Chicago construction.» Seen near at hand, it does not look (as many a church looks elsewhere in New York) like a bonnet with a slim aigrette, set comfortably down in a bonnet-box. Beheld through the sloping cañon of Wall street, it still makes a charming and a dignified effect; and no other interior that I have seen in the New World so happily suggests the general aspect and the emotional atmosphere of an old English parish church. In fact, no one since Upjohn's day, half a century ago, has built us such good Gothic churches as he. There are two more on Fifth Avenue just above Washington Square, and another on University Place near by; and small and simple and brown though they be, they have much more beauty, and much more of the true Gothic feeling, than the big elaborate white cathedral on upper Fifth Avenue.

When you have seen all the grand and gorgeous and «exclusive» or semi-exclusive places of Christian worship in New York, perhaps you may like to get a glimpse of the humble but much more inclusive conditions under which some of its souls seek their salvation. If so, you cannot do better than visit St. Joachim's, down in one of the shabbiest, most populous streets of the lower East Side. Methodists sat in its respectable pews when this was a highly respectable «residence quarter.» Now they are filled by Italian Catholics, and its plain brick front is shouldered by the cheapest of grocery-stores and lodging-houses, amid a group of all-too-cheap saloons, with only a little cross on the roof to make you quite sure that it is a church indeed. Yet few in the city can be so largely frequented—nine thousand worshipers every week, we are told. And if the largest rag-shop, wholesale and retail, in the city occupies an entire floor beneath the raised floor of the church itself, who, we may ask, more sorely need some proof that heaven at least is no respecter of trades and grades than the rag-pickers of New York? They appreciate the hospitality that is shown them. On week-days, when scores of men and women and children are bringing in and sorting their endless bundles of rags, lifting them and shifting them with great cranes and chains, their voices often join in the service that is going on overhead; and no one who wishes to profit by this service in the church itself is asked to leave the tools of even a dirty trade outside its doors. The true spirit of Christianity sends up sweet incense from St. Joachim's, mingled though it may be with the smell of garlic, of cast-off rags, and of those that still cling to unwashed humankind.

DRAWN BY F. H. LUNGREN.

AN EAST-SIDE STREET.

As for the Jews of Manhattan, who can count their places of worship, ranging from the gorgeous synagogue which looks over Central Park, with its ugly but showy big gilded dome, to innumerable little ones hidden away in the grimy upper rooms of tenement-houses?

Then, our hospitals, homes, societies, nurseries, shelters,—the charitable, benevolent, reformatory institutions which, under public or private control, try to care for the bodies and souls of our poor and forsaken, our sick and aged and crippled, our criminals and moral weaklings, and our desolate children,—they are also counted by hundreds. Some of them are enormous places, «handling» thousands of «cases» each year; and some are modest corners where only a few afflicted mortals can be tenderly entreated. The work that they do is vast in amount, and much of it is beneficial beyond the fancy of the pessimist. But even the most radiant optimist knows that much must be wasted, for many of the methods of work are patently ill-inspired. Not yet have we learned on any large scale that real help means laboring with, not laboring for, those who need assistance. But this truth has at least been perceived. There are places in New York where it is being put in practice after admirable fashions. And some day, perhaps, our civic methods will be preventive as well as punitive, while the rich and «respectable» citizens of New York will bestow charity, not in the modernized meaning of the word, but in that true meaning which the pen of St. Paul so long ago underscored.

One of the teachings of St. Paul's kind of charity is that «doing good» to our poor means sharing with them those rational pleasures which cost much money from the public or the private purse. To be made better, they must be made happier. They need not only rest and instruction, but refreshment, renewal, inspiration; and this means that they need pleasure. The fact is proved by the literal meaning of the synonymous word *recreation*.

Therefore there are no places in New York more cheerful, to the prophetic eye of the soul at least, than the little parks recently opened on the East Side in spots until lately covered by teeming tenement-houses; and it is a cheering thought that their number will soon be increased. Exhilarating, too, on a bright spring day was the sight of a great room in the Hebrew Institute, where a loan collection of excellent pictures had been gathered from far up town for the free delighting of impecunious old and young. Old and young together, more than one hundred and five thousand persons passed through the turnstile in the doorway of this room during the thirty-three days that it was open, not counting, I suppose, the many babies in arms, or the somewhat older infants who without stooping could run underneath the wheel. Conscientiously they appraised the pictures, making their hands into funnels before their eyes, after a fashion which is now out of date up town, but was still affected by elderly connoisseurs when I was a child. Accurately they knew which ones they liked, and eagerly they voted for the one that they liked best of all. A large majority of their votes was given to a picture of a mother sleeping with her babe; and in general it was sentiment, more than a sense for material beauty, that determined preferences. I cite this fact lest there be some who, disagreeing with St. Paul, doubt whether «good» is done our poor by affording them pleasures not definitely «moral,» «instructive,» or physically beneficial—who fail to see that the mere affording of innocent pleasures to people who have very few is its own sufficient excuse. Perhaps they may realize that «good» even of the strictly conventional sort must be done when pure and tender feelings that already exist are confirmed and fostered by the ministering hand of art. Send your best in the way of painting if ever you are asked to lend pictures for an East Side exhibition; but send your best in the way of sweet meanings and gentle sentiments as well. Nothing else is good enough to be shared with our poor.

V.

To see how some of our different nationalities and our different kinds of buildings are jumbled together, you may take a street-car at the western foot of Twenty-third street, and cross the town diagonally in a southward direction to the East River. For a while you will travel through Greenwich Village. Many writers have told about this part of New York because, at first an independent place, it preserved its local character long after it lost its autonomy. To-day its most distinctive traits are the crookedness of its quondam village streets, and a larger proportion of native American residents than is claimed by any other really poor quarter of New York.

When you have crossed Sixth Avenue and, rounding Washington Square, turn southward into West Broadway, and then eastward again into Spring street, you will see a more polyglot region. On the corner of the square is the Hotel Mazzini and Garibaldi;

DRAWN BY F. H. LUNGREN.

A MISTY NIGHT ON THE BATTERY.

the name of the Restaurante del' Union is loyal both to the old home and the new; and so are certain sign-boards of Italian wording which proclaim that only wines of Californian making are sold within. French restaurants are frequent, and the St. Galler Hof and the Tyroler Hof bid for Swiss and for Tyrolese patronage. *Produits français* are offered by a gentleman with an Italian name, and *charcuterie de Paris* competes with sausage-meats of German extraction. Truly American is a «Temperance Coffee-house,» elbowed by a «Pool for Drinks» announcement, and surrounded by soda-water fountains and appeals to partake of beer from Pilsen or Milwaukee, from Bohemia or Bavaria, from Jersey City or Vienna, as you may prefer. Wah Hing will wash your clothes in Chinese, and an École Française Laïque will teach your children in French if the public school is overcrowded and you do not approve of parochial instruction. Italian schools can also be discovered; more than one Banca Italiana will take charge of your money if, like many a new arrival, you have been informed that American savings-banks «alway bust-a»; and a Pharmacie Française, a Farmacia Italiana, and a Deutsche Apotheke, reduplicated on almost every block, will variously try to preserve you from the American patent medicines gaudily advertised in their despite.

All these humble places of sale are sandwiched in among shabby tenements, factories, and warehouses, while here and there a brand-new colossus shows that wholesale trade is creeping into this nondescript region, and that after a little its character will be entirely changed. And this prospect of change is what has made some of the tenement-houses in New York so vilely unfit for human habitation. What is the good of cleaning or repairing them if any day they may be sold simply to be torn down?

Cross the Bowery now, and you will enter the famous Tenth Ward—a true tenement-house district, forming part of the most crowded city quarter in all the world. As a whole, the city of New York below the Harlem River (the Island of Manhattan) is more densely peopled than any other city in the world, counting 143.2 persons to the acre, while Paris counts 125.2. Then one sixth of the entire population of all New York (reckoning now with the parts above the Harlem too) is concentrated upon 711 acres of ground. Here, on the lower East Side of our town, in the summer of 1894, there dwelt some 324,000 souls, averaging 476.6 to the acre; and a certain section of this great area—the Tenth Ward—showed a local acre-average of 626.26. The most thickly peopled spot in Europe is the Jew quarter in Prague; but it is only one fifth as large as our Tenth Ward, while it shows a density scarcely greater than that of the whole of the 711 acres in which the Tenth Ward is contained—485.4 per acre. Nor is this the worst that our 711 acres can reveal. Sanitary District A of the Eleventh Ward (bounded by Avenue B and Second street, Columbia, Rivington, and Clinton streets) contains 32 acres, and in the summer of 1894 each of them bore 986.4 human beings. This is the very thickest, blackest coagulation of humanity in all the known world. No European place of anything like the same size even approaches it, and its nearest rival is a part of Bombay where the average population over an area of 46.06 acres is 759.66.

Yet it should be remembered that, while our acres are thus more heavily burdened than any others, places can be found in European, as in Asiatic, towns where people are more uncomfortably crowded within doors. There the houses are low. But New York tenements are very lofty, and thus our floor-space to the acre is much more extensive. Moreover, although we are now more crowded than ever before, our sanitary state steadily improves. During the decade which closed with 1874 our death-rate was 30.27 per thousand; during the one which closed with 1894 it was 24.07.

God and the angels know, and the devil is quick to see, that there is room for improvement still in our tenement places, and not only room, but a bitter, crying, desperate need. But we are beginning to know it too, and to act upon our knowledge. And although it is hard to make New York look ahead at things which lie outside her money-making and pleasure-seeking routines, she does not often move backward once she has been impelled to set her shoulder solidly to any wheel.

## VI.

THE Tenement-House Commission of 1894 taught much by the «density maps» from which I have just quoted, and much, again, by a big colored map that showed—contrasting the sanitary districts established by the Board of Health—in just what places in New York the people most numerously sent us from foreign lands have chiefly established themselves.

On this map our 403,784 Germans, our 399,-

DRAWN BY F. H. LUNGREN.

MUSIC NIGHT IN A HUNGARIAN CAFÉ.

348 Irish, and our 334,725 Americans are distinguished respectively by bands of red, green, and blue; and other colors represent our 80,235 Russians and Poles, our 54,334 Italians, our 25,674 negroes, our 16,239 French, our 12,287 Bohemians, and our 60,835 «foreigners of other nationalities,» leaving «unclassified» the 111,285 remaining persons who, when the census of 1890 was taken, completed the tale of 1,515,301 inhabitants of New York city.[1]

Of course it was not possible to show on

[1] The calculations upon which this ingenious map (drawn by Mr. Frederick E. Pierce) was based counted among our foreigners all persons born on our own soil of foreign mothers—the easiest way to reckon with a population as mixed as ours. For many purposes it is a very instructive way, yet it is not a veracious way if one wants to appraise the real Americanism of New York. A foreign-born mother does not mean as much in regard to an American-born child as foreigners who have never seen America might think. In one of the most foreign parts of New York—in the heart of the Tenth Ward—I taught last winter at the University Settlement a club

this nationality map all the places where the people of a given race may be found; there is too much mingling and mixing in New York for any approach to such precision as this. In each sanitary district only those colors appear (arranged in contrasted stripes) which represent the nationalities that help to compose the most homogeneous two thirds of its population, the relative width of the stripes being determined by the numerical relation of these dominant nationalities to one another.

For example, our most crowded spot—District A in Ward 11—is striped to show that Hungary has contributed to form the characteristic two thirds of its population, that Germany has contributed more largely, and also more largely (but collectively) those foreign lands to each of which the map-maker could not assign a special color of its own. The Irish, the Americans, the Russians and Poles, the negroes, Bohemians, Frenchmen, Italians, who may reside in this district are swamped, from the statistical point of view, by the Hungarians, the Germans, and the foreigners otherwise born or mothered.

Near by there is a district where Germans and Italians mingle on almost equal terms; another where Germans mingle with Americans but exceed them in numbers; and another where Germans again predominate, but Russians and Poles stand next on the list. Then, not far away, in Ward 17, is a district that is not striped at all, but covered by a single color; and in Ward 10 is another of the same sort except for a difference in the color. These are the only sanitary districts in New York where two thirds of the population belong to the same race; and in the former it is the German race, in the latter the Russo-Polish Hebrew race. Indeed, all over this East Side elbow of New York, between the Bowery and Corlaer's Hook, the Russo-Polish Hebrews are conspicuous, chiefly mixed with Germans or, near the river-front, with Irish or Americans. The Italians live mostly to the southwestward of them, between the Bowery and Broadway, in the Ninth and Eleventh Wards, and beyond Broadway in the Eighth.

We have more French people than Hungarians, and many more negroes; but the Hungarians herd together so that their color is conspicuous in two districts of the Eleventh Ward, while the French and the darkies are scattered all over town. Not a single stripe, but only one small spot on the nationality map shows a dense little knot of Gallic people to the westward of Broadway above Madison Square; there are more of them here than on West Broadway, where to the superficial eye they seem so numerous. And only two narrow stripes show clusters of black folk: one near the Gallic spot, and one to the southwestward of Washington Square, within the borders of Greenwich Village. Then, right in the heart of the Italian region, just off the lower end of the Bowery, is another little spot, which marks the Chinese quarter—Mott street and Pell street—of which you have heard queer things, and which are also curious to see and singular to smell.

And our twelve thousand and more Bohemians? To find these you must go up town; they dwell chiefly by the East River opposite Blackwell's Island, between Sixtieth and Seventy-fifth streets. Here they have been fixed, with a considerable quantity of unspecified «other foreigners,» by the location of the breweries, where, as we might suppose, their labor is in request. But, except for this small region, the nationality map declares that above the beginning of Central Park, New York is chiefly peopled by Americans, Germans, and Irish, with Americans in the majority.

Look now at the seven successive sanitary districts which form a broad band through the very center of the map from Washington Square to Central Park, with Fifth Avenue as their axis. They are striped altogether in blue and green. A semi-American, semi-Irish quarter? Yes; but by no means in an East Side sense. This is the most thoroughly American quarter in New York, but also the richest. The green stripes stand for serving-men and -maids, quite as numerous as their masters, and mostly of Irish blood.

## VII.

NOTHING could better reveal the heterogeneousness of our people than a tour among our restaurants. There is scarcely a nation upon earth which has not eating-places of its own in New York, with its own viands and

of girls, fourteen or fifteen years of age, who were first-grade pupils in the neighboring public school. Not one of them, I think, could claim an American parent of either sex; yet in language, in manner, and in spirit they were all alike, and all as American as though their ancestors had lived here for a hundred years. German, Polish, Russian, or English, Protestant, Catholic, or Hebrew, by immediate descent, they were all decidedly, distinctively, unmistakably of New York. And just like these young girls are many thousands and thousands of the so-called foreign girls and boys, men and women, of our town.

DRAWN BY E. POTTHAST.

ENGRAVED BY PETER AITKEN.

"STANDING ROOM ONLY."

drinks, its own chatter, its own customs and subsidiary recreations. Lodging-places, of course, do not so conspicuously vary. Yet you may lodge in New York after the manner of many countries; and certainly there is room for choice among the places of repose which are characteristically American. Down on the East Side or the West Side you may buy for five cents the right to sleep for a night, among tramps and «bummers,» on a dirty piece of canvas stretched between four posts. And as your fortunes mend you may do better and better, by the most gradual steps, until on upper Fifth Avenue you sup beneath tropical palm-trees to the sound of Hungarian music, and sleep upon carved couches under canopies of Parisian silk. How much you will have to pay if you insist upon getting, even for a night, the very best that places like this can offer, I am sure I do not know. But I can tell you how big the largest of our new hotels will be when the work which is to double its present size is finished: it will then be quite as big as a medieval cathedral of the very first rank.

Cosmoramic, too, would be the scenes you would witness, Babel-like the tongues you would hear, could you mingle with all the clubs in New York. They vary from countless coteries and «lodges,» usually called by jocose or else by very ambitious names, which play an incalculable part—political or polemical, suggestive, educational, or argumentative, charitable, Terpsichorean, bacchanalian, or otherwise recreative—in the lives of our humblest folk, up to associations of our wealthiest, who, seeking club life with a view to reposeful social intercourse or else to organized athletic industry, house themselves in places as fine as the ones which bid for the custom of the plump-pocketed traveler. Even the most sumptuously ensconced among the latter class of New York clubs are by no means all composed of Americans. Some of them, as their titles confess, are formed by groups of foreigners; and they include groups of prosperous Hebrews, who must be the despair, or perhaps the inspiration, of their brother laboring in some sweat-shop down town.

And our theaters? The finest of these are much like fine theaters everywhere in the world, except that they are more comfortable, better ventilated, and better protected against accidents by fire than most of those in European cities. But visit our less aristocratic quarters, and the theaters will seem as strange as the people themselves. There are rows of them, big and little, along the Bowery. With some exhibitions that it could not profit your morals, and some that it would disgust even your curiosity, to witness, they offer you others well worth contemplation. Here the variety-show (that supplanter of the old-time minstrel-show in the lighter dramatic affections of New York) may be seen at its worst; but also sometimes at its best, because, while its «acts» are good of their kind, you will not feel, as you must up town, that the audience ought to care more for acts of some other kind.

On the Bowery, again, you may fancy yourself your grandfather in his youth, witnessing a bloody and thunderous, yet poetic and virtuous, melodrama of the brave old type. More distinctive still is the modern drama of New York life, which tries above all to be up to date, reproducing To-day in its figures, its trivial happenings, its jests, its crimes, its tragedies, and its local fads and interests with a realism which may distress you less than that of a more artistic kind—a realism so unselfconscious that you would be foolish to judge it by the canons of art at all. The acting is bad? Perhaps; but you can hardly judge it if you have not known such people, walked amid such scenes, in life. And perhaps it is not so bad when, as often happens, a genuine thief or policeman, pugilist or green-goods man, or general all-round scamp, is doing over on the stage precisely those things which he has most frequently done in life. A great deal of art in writing and acting used to be shown us in the «local» plays at Mr. Harrigan's famous theater up town, now, alack! to be numbered among the places of the past; and it taught us something as regards the way in which the «other half» of New York lives and behaves. But its witness had to be accepted with grains of salt, like that of a cleverly humorous tale or poem. The witness of the typical Bowery drama of New York life may be taken in the same spirit as the voice of the newspaper, which likewise makes no pretense to be an artistic form of speech.

Almost as characteristic are the Bowery's German dramas, adapted to the soil of New York, but played in the language of Germany; and its Hebrew dramas, given sometimes in German and sometimes in Hebrew, or, at least, in Yiddish—in that jargon composed of bad German, bad Polish, and bad Hebrew, which, developed in central Europe, is now the dominant tongue in many of our East Side streets.

Once I witnessed a benefit performance for a Hebrew lodge of some sort, when not a

Gentile except ourselves sat in the very big and crowded Bowery play-house. We saw an Oriental operetta in which most of the characters spoke or sang comprehensible German, while the pronouncedly comic ones used Yiddish. I learned two interesting facts at this performance. I learned that we have never seen an Oriental drama really well done up town, because we have never seen it done by Orientals, looking and moving and speaking and wearing their clothes as Orientals should. And I learned that when the Hebrew look, the Hebrew bearing, even the Hebrew methods of gesticulation and enunciation, are put before us in Oriental garb and setting, they no longer make a disagreeable effect upon Caucasian nerves. Once we cease to judge the Semite by Aryan standards, once he ceases to clothe himself in Aryan dress and deeds, the real beauty, the real distinction of his type makes itself apparent. You may discover this by traveling in the far East, but you may also discover it in certain places on the East Side of New York.

I ought not to feel obliged to say that, if one takes any interest in the future of our extraordinary town, none of its places should be thought more interesting than its public schools. Yet how many people in New York who do not send their own children to them have ever entered one of their doors?

Here, again, you might discover a noteworthy fact: whatever else may be well or ill taught in these schools, they are fruitful and potent nurseries of Americanism. The good they do in this direction far outranks all that can be done by all other agencies and influences put together. This is the reason —not fear of any kind of religious instruction as such—why all New-Yorkers should earnestly try to keep the children of aliens out of «national» and parochial schools. Inevitably, by gathering all kinds of children together, the public school teaches that all men are brothers under our flag; and deliberately it teaches reverence for that flag. Unconsciously it breaks down the barriers which separate race from race, and so quickly that little children speak fluent English, and broken German or Italian, whose parents cannot speak English at all; and consciously it teaches a new patriotism to these children whom our census calls foreigners. As a result the foreign child is apt to be more American—more keenly aware and more proud

FROM A WATER-COLOR BY JOHN A. FRASER.

A WINTER EVENING ON SIXTH AVENUE.

of the fact—than most of those who can trace back their Americanism for generations. Go to one of our public schools on the day before a national holiday, and you will see this flower of youthful patriotism spreading its petals very bravely; but go on any other day, and you will see the good seed that produces it being diligently sown.

VIII.

OUR most curiously peopled quarters and most singular individual streets; our parks; our great and glittering shops, and the pestiferous «sweat-shops» which so lamentably furnish some of them with wares; our ball-rooms, so cosmopolitanly conventional up town, where only Americans fill them, but down town so amusingly local, yet so national after the manner of a dozen different nations; our annual art exhibitions and our perennial waterside galleries of maritime living pictures; our museums and libraries; our police courts; our newer places up beyond Central Park; and those home interiors which, from the tenement-house to the abode of luxury, are, after all, the most important and significant places in any town—these are but a few of the many places in which I should like to linger. And certainly I ought to show you how the evil sights and odors, and even the evil acts, of our most overcrowded quarters have been lessened by our new discovery that it is possible to clean their streets. But how can I do what I wish or what I ought when editors queerly maintain that the readers of magazines demand even more «variety» than the city of New York can show?

One thought, however, makes me half content to leave some of these places for the moment mute. This is the thought that there are two New Yorks—a winter and a summer town. They are very unlike, and in many ways the city of the summer is the more individual and interesting. It deserves at least one whole chapter to itself; and in that chapter all characteristic places which are roofed by the open sky may best be discussed. These include our parks and waterways, but also many of our streets. We have highways and byways less remarkable for the buildings that line them, or the life that is led within their walls, than for the multiform activities which their pavements show. And of course the life of the pavement is most lively at seasons when the open sky is the only roof that parboiled tenement-house humanity can endure.

*M. G. Van Rensselaer.*

# THE BODY TO THE SOUL.

PURE spirit, pure and strangely beautiful,
What body fledst thou? Where in all this dull,
Unlovely world was there such loveliness
That thou couldst wear it for thy fleshly dress?

*Before this hour thou must have looked on me;*
*As men look on old friends I look on thee.*

It cannot be. Far-wandering music blown
From heaven thy voice is. In what garden grown
Wert thou, too lovely blossom? in what vale?
Who wert thou ere the flushing cheek fell pale?

*The quick winds change, and change the fields and sky.*
*Look well; thou mayest know me by and by.*

II.

What hate despatched thee out of hell
To mock me? Shapeless, smoky mass,
Thou hideous mist, I curse thee: pass!

*Time was when I was welcome to thy breast;*
*I knew it as the wild bird knows her nest.*

Thou liest! Never on *that* fell
The sight that took not instant blight.
Pass, pass! Go, blot upon God's light!

*Ay, through the portal whence this hour I stole;*
*Open thy breast to me, take back thy soul.*

*John Vance Cheney.*

# MONOTYPES.

## WITH EXAMPLES OF AN OLD AND NEW ART.

ETCHING BY HIMSELF. BY PERMISSION OF S. R. KOEHLER, BOSTON MUSEUM OF FINE ARTS

BENEDETTO CASTIGLIONE.

ONE of the most interesting of all the minor forms of the graphic arts is the monotype, which, by reason of the element of «accident» in the result, sometimes reveals an unexpected beauty of effect. The process is simple. It consists in painting a picture with plate-printers' ink on a metal plate. The plate is then put in a press, a sheet of moistened paper is laid upon it, and the roller is applied. The ink-painting is directly transferred to the paper, and the print gives the artist's drawing reversed. Unlike essays in etching, or any of the processes of engraving, mezzotint, or lithograph, a painter may work with the tools he is accustomed to—brushes. He may vary his methods by taking out lights with a rag, with his fingers, or with soft wood-points; but he is not hampered by new tools or by difficulties concerning the preparation of the plate or the printing from it. There are no acids, no bitings, no first, second, or third states, no expert printer to be depended upon, as in etching. It is in no sense a reproductive process, for the painting is entirely transferred to the paper in printing, leaving the plate blank.

The name «monotype» was given to this form of art print by Mr. Charles A. Walker of Boston, who in 1877, with no knowledge of the fact that the art was known and practised by painters in former times, discovered the process independently by an accident in proving a plate at his etching-table. The sheet of paper upon which he was taking an impression slipped in the press, and produced a blurred print which resembled a roughly indicated landscape. He took up a blank copperplate, painted a rough sketch on it in printers' ink with his fingers and a rag, and, putting it in the press, produced his first monotype. Mr. Walker has devoted a large part of his time in the last eighteen years to making monotypes, and his work has been exhibited in New York and Boston. William M. Chase, James McNeil Whistler, Robert Blum, Otto Bacher, Frank Duveneck, Henry Sandham, Joseph Lauber, A. H. Bicknell, and other American artists, have at various times produced monotypes, but have worked only intermittently. Joseph Jefferson the actor became interested in the art when its possibilities were shown to him by Mr. Walker, and he has made a number of prints; and John S. Sargent, while visiting Mr. Jefferson at his country home at Buzzard's Bay, was shown the process, and executed a single print. From time to time in recent years other painters have experimented in the art.

Hubert Herkomer, the English artist, is one of those who were favorably impressed by the results obtained in working in black and white by the monotype process. He invented and patented a process, called the «spongotype,» for reproducing monotypes made on a copperplate with German black and oil mixed with graphite. This drawing is dusted over

MONOTYPE: BENEDETTO CASTIGLIONE. IN THE "ALBERTINA" AT VIENNA

«THE ANNUNCIATION TO THE SHEPHERDS.»

MONOTYPE: CHARLES A. WALKER.

BY PERMISSION OF ARTHUR DEXTER, ESQ.

«WAR.»

A companion monotype, showing still water, is entitled «Peace.»

with a combination of bronze powder, Bath stone, and asphaltum. After drying, the face of the drawing is subjected by electrotypy to a deposit of the thickness of a copperplate, and a reversed duplicate of the original is made, which may be printed from in the manner of the photogravure, resembling the latter in texture. The results obtained in printing by this process do not differ materially from what is known as the electrotint (Palmer process), invented in London in 1844, and described in Shaw's «Manual of Electro-metallurgy.» In this electrotint a drawing is made on a surface of semi-fluid composition spread on a metallic plate. A deposit of copper is made upon this, transforming it to a metallic surface from which prints may be made in the ordinary manner. The spongotype gives the better results of the two processes, but is wanting in depth and richness of color, the «grain» changing the effect of the tints. The blacks incline to become weak, though they may be improved somewhat in quality by retouching with the roulette and dry-point. The galvanograph, still another process, was described in a work published in Munich in 1842 by Franz von Kobell. Here, as in the Herkomer process, a monotype was prepared upon the plate, and an electrotype deposit taken from the original. Eight prints which illustrate Kobell's book resemble rather closely similar subjects executed in aquatint. A galvanograph print by the Germans Freymann and Schowger, after a painting by Achterveld, is in the Boston Museum of Fine Arts, and has a complete and finished look, possessing some of the qualities that belong to lithographs.

Artists of all periods have made use of the various forms of expression in black and white. Charcoal, the pen and ink, the lead-pencil, sepia, India ink, oil- and water-color with the brush and other tools have been employed for purposes of sketching and study. Beginners are set to work to draw in black and white, so that problems of proportion and values may be made simpler than when complicated with the color-quality. Great artists have made drawings and cartoons in black and white, or in a monotint such as brown or red, that are among the most interesting pages preserved in our museums. With the Renaissance came reproductive processes, and artists' work in black and white has been given to the world by mechanical means, through engraving on wood and metal, and in our own time by photo-engraving. Book-illustration may be said to date from Albert Dürer. From the seventeenth to the middle of the nineteenth century line-engravers did not make much use of the burin for original designs, as Dürer did, but devoted their efforts principally to the reproduction of works painted in oil-color and other pictorial mediums. Rembrandt developed the art of etching, and remains the greatest master of this art. The invention of mezzotint-engraving is credited to Ludwig Van Siegen, a Hessian, in 1643; and it was more fully developed later on by Prince Rupert.

Between 1733 and 1781 Jean Leprince introduced the aquatint process. Neither mezzotint nor aquatint is much used at the present time, and both are somewhat difficult processes for the painter. Steel-engraving, a product of the present century, was formulated from the principles of etching and line-engraving. Jacob Perkins of Newburyport, Massachusetts, introduced in 1805 the use of carbonized steel as a substitute for copper in making plates; and this was followed by the invention of the ruling-machine, a labor-saving device by which large surfaces of tints could be expressed in engraving by parallel lines marked through an etching-ground on the plate with a diamond point, and bitten to varying depths by acids specially prepared for use in thus rendering such expanses as skies in landscapes. A combination of methods appears in the work of the English school of engravers, whose style was a mixed one resulting from using etching, free-line, and ruler engraving with stipple. Lithography was introduced by Aloys Senefelder in Germany in 1798. This process, allied as it is to drawing with chalk or pastels, lends itself easily to manipulation by painters.

The oldest monotypes in existence are those by Giovanni Benedetto Castiglione, who was sometimes called in Italy «Il Grechetto» and in France «Le Benedetto.» He was born in Genoa in 1616, and was a well-known painter, a contemporary of Rubens and Vandyke. He died at Mantua in 1670, about one year after Rembrandt. His studies in early life were made under Paggi and Ferrari, and later, according to some accounts, he became a pupil of Vandyke while that celebrated artist was living in Genoa. He painted in Rome, Naples, Florence, Parma, Venice, and Mantua, and is best known by his cabinet pictures, though he also painted portraits and landscapes. His work as a historical painter brought him a wide reputation, and he received some important commissions from Charles I of England. Examples of his work

MONOTYPE. WILLIAM M. CHASE.

«REVERY.»

may be seen at Genoa, Venice, and Milan, and many of his best pictures are in the Uffizi Gallery at Florence. He was a practised etcher, and left about seventy examples of his art in this field. Five prints by Castiglione were in the Albertina collection of Duke Albert of Saxony, which no cataloguer had been able to classify as to the process used in making them, until Bartsch, in his work «Le Peintre-Graveur,» wrote of them as follows, under the heading «Pieces Imitating Aquatint, made by B. Castiglione»: «Some pieces are found of which B. Castiglione is the author, and which resemble prints done in aquatint. This kind of engraving, however, not having been invented in the time of the artist, these prints must have been done by some other process. We believe we have discovered the way in which these prints were made. According to our opinion, Castiglione charged a polished copperplate plentifully with oil-color, and by means of a wooden stylus removed the color for the lights and half-tints his design required. From the plate prepared in this way he printed in the usual manner.» The titles of the five monotypes by Castiglione are: «The Annunciation to the Shepherds,» «Madonna with the Infant Jesus in the Manger,» «The Flight into Egypt,» «The Resurrection of Lazarus,» and «Three Shepherds around a Fire.»

James Nasmyth of Tunbridge Wells, who was born at Edinburgh in 1808, a manufacturer of machinery, and the inventor of the trip-hammer and the steam pile-driver, devoted his leisure hours to art, and claimed to have invented the monotypic process. It has been «invented,» as a matter of fact, half a dozen times since Castiglione employed the process. William M. Chase and some artist friends experimented with it in New York in 1879, and in 1880 Mr. Chase exhibited at the Salmagundi Club black-and-white exhibition, at the Academy of Design, two study heads done in monotype. Mr. Charles H. Miller, the American artist, purchased in Rotterdam in 1879 a monotype by Ciconi of Milan, and brought it to New York, where he showed it to his friends; and in the winter of 1879–80 the artists Duveneck, Ross Turner, J. W. Alexander, Bacher, and others amused themselves in Munich and Florence by making monotypes at the meetings of an artists' club held in the members' lodgings and studios in the evenings. Mr. Whistler and Mr. Blum made monotypes in Venice in 1880, and the former applied the monotypic principle to the printing of some of his etchings, by slightly tinting the surface of his plates in parts, and wiping out lights where needed to obtain certain effects. Nasmyth made landscapes and architectural views in monotype, and monotypes both in color and the single black tint were made by the French artist Henri Guérard, and exhibited in 1890 at the Durand-Ruel galleries in Paris. Degas has made drawings with a fat ink on plates, and printed them, and Count Lepic, a well-known French painter, made a series of monotype prints which were formerly in the collection of James L. Claghorn of Philadelphia, and afterward passed into the possession of Robert Garrett of Baltimore. Count Lepic's method of working was to etch the outlines of a landscape subject on a plate as an aid to his composition, and then, while the etched lines often completely disappeared in the ink-painting, they were left ready to be used for another effect on the same plate. In this way a given landscape motive could be rendered in an evening or noonday or a summer or winter effect, as desired—in as many variations, in fact, as the artist's fancy dictated. Peter Moran of Philadelphia has made a number of monotypes, some of his work possessing a characteristic that may be noted in the prints by Castiglione and Nasmyth—the white outlining made with a soft point of wood or with a blunt instrument. Finally, William Blake knew the process, and had worked it out by himself, and made use of it as the basis for overwork both in oil and opaque water-color. He kept his way of working secret, and enjoyed the puzzled conjectures of people who tried to guess how certain unusual effects in his drawings were obtained. In Gilchrist's biography, however, one Tatham explains his method thus: «Blake, when he wanted to make his prints in oil, took a piece of millboard and drew his design upon it with some strong, dark ink or

MONOTYPE: HUBERT HERKOMER. BY PERMISSION OF WILLIAM M. CHASE.

STUDY OF HEAD.

color, which he let dry. He then painted upon that with oil-color in such a state of fusion that it would blur well; he painted roughly and quickly, so that the pigment would not have time to dry. After taking a print on paper he finished up the impression with water-color.» When a print had been taken he used the design on the millboard to paint on again, and thus varying the details of his picture in the printing and in the water-color work afterward, he obtained results with which, we are told, he was fascinated. Monotypes

MONOTYPE. F. EUGENE.

JOSEPH JEFFERSON AT WORK AT A MONOTYPE.

may, of course, be made in black, in a single tint, or in color, all that is necessary being that the medium used in painting on the plate be such as will print well on paper. Plate-printers' ink is undoubtedly the most satisfactory medium.

It may be asked, What is the use of making monotypes, inasmuch as they are only a transferred impression of an artist's drawing or picture? To answer this question, one should see good monotypes themselves; for they lose their peculiar charm in a photograph or any other kind of reproduction. In the printing on paper effects are obtained of which there is no suggestion to the inexperienced eye in the painted design on the plate. The thickness of the ink in one part, its thinness in another, strong accents here and there, are factors that the monotype artist understands and reckons with as he works, but of which he can see the full result only when their transfer to the white paper surface is effected. The element of accident is an ever-present one, and from a plate prepared even by the most experienced worker some unexpected effect may result in the printing. Sometimes such accidental effects add much to the beauty of the printed picture; again, they may sufficiently mar it to make it necessary to do it over again. Evidently experience brings assurance, and an old hand knows better what the printing will show than a beginner. The portrait of Castiglione which forms the initial of this article is not a monotype, but an etching by himself; and it is easy to see from this example that Castiglione was much influenced by Rembrandt's work. The «Annunciation to the Shepherds» shows that his monotype work has the same general character as drawing with crayon-point or pencil. The line is particularly noticeable, and there are practically only two tones—black and white. In Mr. Chase's «Revery» the treatment is in masses with no very strong lights, and the effect is obtained by the careful use of half-tones. The brush-work in this, broad and free in the painted plate, is well preserved in the print. Mr. Herkomer's «Study of a Head» is handled in the same general way, but has far less delicacy of gradation. Mr. Lauber's «Old Woman Paring Apples» is cleverly blocked in, and the sketch portrait of Joseph Jefferson making a monotype, by F. Eugene, shows how the fugitive character of sketch-work may be agreeably utilized in

MONOTYPE: JOSEPH LAUBER.

«OLD WOMAN PARING APPLES.»

MONOTYPE: JOHN S. SARGENT. BY PERMISSION OF JOSEPH JEFFERSON.

«A DREAM OF LOHENGRIN.»

monotype-making. Mr. Jefferson's «In Louisiana Woods» has the same general character as his oil-painting, and is notable for depth of tone; and Mr. Sargent's «A Dream of Lohengrin» shows best of all our examples what an effective result may be obtained by the printing of a very broadly handled sketch, in the making of which the effect of the white paper has been well taken into account. In Mr. Walker's landscapes not much more than a suggestion of what the originals are may be obtained from the small reproductions. His monotypes are of large size (about thirty-six by forty-eight inches), and show great variety of values, and no little subtlety of tone. In the marine called «War» the transparent quality of the wave is well given, and the sky is effectively rendered. In «A Pastoral Landscape» the sky is atmospheric and delicate in tone, and the composition of stream and meadow and trees carries out the peaceful aspect sought for in the picture. In all of Mr. Walker's work advantage is taken of the quality given to the print by subtle gradation in the quantity and thickness of the ink laid on the plate, and by almost completely removing it in some portions where the lightest values appear. The results are eminently pleasing, and quite justify what he claims for the process—breadth and individuality in the impression as given in the direct work of the artist's hand on the plate, agreeable tonal quality in black and white *per se*, and truthful transcription in enduring form of the artist's impressions of nature. I am indebted to Mr. Walker for information concerning monotype processes and for historical data connected with the development of the art. In speaking of his monotype work in recent years, Mr. Walker says: «I have produced several hundred original works—all, with the exception of a few experimental studies of heads, landscapes and shore marine subjects. I have demonstrated or suggested a range of varied effects limited only by an artist's creative ability. Every gradation of color is possible, from the richest blacks to the most delicate, tender tones. The textures of trees, grass, rocks, and other things in landscape are rapidly given, while for skies there is no process in black and white so well adapted to render their airy quality and the infinity of cloud-forms. In facility for ‹wiping out› lights and alterations this medium leads all others; for by one dash of the painter's rag any portion of the painting can be removed and changed without a trace of the alteration remaining in the print.» Mr. Walker at first worked on copperplates, but latterly has made use of polished zinc, for he found the cool gray tone of the zinc a better ground to work on than the reddish tint of copper, and the effect while painting can be better judged by the eye. «Straightforwardness is the foundation of the monotype,» says Mr. Walker—as it is, we may add, of all art; «and it is a revelation to the composer, especially in landscape. With a complete chiaroscuro it is a rich, harmonious, and powerful medium; it is full of impressions and surprises; it is misty, and lends a charm to the indefinite in nature.» Mr. Herkomer says of it: «I know of no method of drawing, pencil or color, that can approach the beauty of these printed blacks. The artistic mystery that can be

MONOTYPE: JOSEPH JEFFERSON.

«IN LOUISIANA WOODS.» FROM THE COLLECTION OF «THE PLAYERS,» NEW YORK.

given, the *finesse*, the depth of tone and variety of texture, make this a most delightful medium for the painter.» The monotype, like all other mediums, has its limitations, and the secondary use of the press is one of the most important. Most painters who have employed the process have worked with such tools and appliances as they have had at hand, and most of their prints have been of small dimensions. For the best work, and to get the full advantage of its possibilities, it is essential to work on large plates and to paint broadly. With a good-sized press, and some practice, there can be no question that in the monotype the painter will find an agreeable form of expression, and a medium to work in which will interest him while at work, and please in its results.

*William A. Coffin.*

## THE SURPRISED AVOWAL.

WHEN one word is spoken,
  When one look you see,
When you take the token,
  Howe'er so slight it be,
The cage's bolt is broken,
  The happy bird is free.

There is no unsaying
  That love-startled word;
It were idle praying
  It no more be heard;
Yet, its law obeying,
  Who shall blame the bird?

What avails the mending
  Where the cage was weak?
What avails the sending
  Far, the bird to seek,
When every cloud is lending
  Wings toward yonder peak?

Thrush, could they recapture
  You to newer wrong,
How could you adapt your
  Strain to suit the throng?
Gone would be the rapture
  Of unimprisoned song.

*Robert Underwood Johnson.*

CARRYING THE MESSAGE FROM THE «ELEPHANT» TO THE CROWN PRINCE OF DENMARK.

DRAWN BY HOWARD PYLE.

# THE BATTLE OF COPENHAGEN.[1]

BY A. T. MAHAN,

Author of «Influence of Sea Power in History,» etc.

ON the 8th of October, 1798, the Czar Paul of Russia presented to Lord Nelson his portrait, set in diamonds, in honor of the brilliant victory of the Nile. Accompanying the gift was an autograph letter expressing his personal gratification at a success which, to use his words, «could not fail to attract to the victor the suffrages of the sane part of Europe.» It could scarcely then have been foreseen that within the short space of thirty months the most arduous battle of the renowned admiral would be fought with, and his most hard-won success wrested from, an ally of the same sovereign engaged in a coalition of which the chief instigator and main support was the Czar himself.

The ostensible reasons assigned for the confederation of the Northern states of Europe in 1800 to resist the maritime policy and practice of Great Britain were substantially those alleged for the formation in 1780, during the American Revolution, of the Armed Neutrality —a name also assumed by the League of 1800. The real cause, however, at the latter date was the personal policy, or, more accurately, the personal feeling and violent passion, of the Czar, who throughout his short reign (from 1796 to 1801) was in a state not far removed from insanity. Carried by paroxysms of anger from one extreme to the other, he passed rapidly from the position of the ally of Great Britain to that of an enemy, and from enthusiasm for the rights of dethroned monarchs to an equally engrossing admiration of Bonaparte, the overthrower of thrones.

In his wish to injure Great Britain he found ready to his hand the old grievance of the belligerent right to capture enemy's property under a neutral flag, and also those arising from the disputed question as to what articles were really contraband of war. It was to the interest of Great Britain, as a belligerent state supreme upon the sea, to give the widest extension to the definitions of enemy's property and contraband of war. It was to the interest of neutrals to limit the scope of restrictions which materially diminished the amount of trade that they could carry on. Denmark and Sweden, as neutral states,

[1] In preparing this article, there have been consulted, besides various British narratives, two Danish accounts, one of which appeared in the «Cornhill Magazine» a few years ago. Quotations have also been made from the article «Battle of Copenhagen» in «Macmillan» for June, 1895.

PAINTED BY JOHN HOPPNER. FROM AN ENGRAVING. BY PERMISSION OF PAUL AND DOMINIC COLNAGHI & CO., PROPRIETORS.

HORATIO, VISCOUNT NELSON.

sought continually to evade the restraints which the great maritime power claimed to enforce as a matter of prescriptive right, essential to her safety in war; but they were too weak to do so alone. In 1780 they had been backed by Russia, but in the early years of the French Revolution the instincts of her sovereigns prompted them to resist any action that tended to favor a convulsion threatening the foundations of absolute power.

The smaller Baltic states had therefore to submit outwardly, while they tried by indirection to evade the inconvenience suffered by their traders. In 1799 Denmark took a more decisive stand. She gathered her merchant ships in fleets protected by vessels of war, and claimed that the assurance of the senior naval officer, that there was in them nothing lawfully liable to capture, was sufficient to exempt the whole body from a search by British ships of war. The right of a belligerent to examine a neutral merchant ship and her cargo—the right of search—was then, and still is, admitted by all nations as a part of international law. Of this right Great Britain justly claimed she could not be deprived by a modification introduced by Denmark alone. The latter ordering her officers to resist, hostile encounters took place in the Mediterranean and in the English Channel.

In the latter, in July, 1800, several persons were killed and wounded, and the Danish frigate was carried into an English port. The British ministry then sent a fleet and a negotiator to the Baltic, and Denmark, without abandoning her contentions on other points, agreed no longer to send ships of war to convoy traders.

When this convention was signed, August 29, 1800, the rage of Paul I against Great Britain was fast approaching a climax, which was finally reached when she refused to recognize claims put forth by him to the possession of Malta, surrendered by the French to the British in September. Utilizing the maritime grievances of the Baltic states, and still more imposing upon their fears by his overwhelming power and personal irresponsibility, he drew them again into a treaty, signed toward the end of 1800, affirming a number of propositions concerning neutral rights which it was known Great Britain would not admit, and pledging the powers to mutual support by force of arms if necessary. To this treaty Prussia was also a party.

The reply of Great Britain was immediate, emphatic, and unanimous. No party in the state permitted doubts as to her claims, nor allowed any hesitancy to appear at a moment when she stood alone, almost all Europe against her, and not a single ally on her side. A large fleet was gathered at Yarmouth, the chief command being given to Sir Hyde Parker, a brave officer of excellent reputation, but who had never been tried in high command, while by a strange contrast, due primarily to the strong conservative instinct so rooted in the British, under him was placed Nelson, who had already done greater deeds and shown far greater powers than any British seaman that had yet appeared on her long roll of naval heroes. What followed was, from the point of glory, brilliant enough; but had he been in full charge, the coalition of the Baltic navies would have been to him an opportunity greater than ever fell to his lot, and it is scarcely doubtful that the results would have demonstrated his peculiar genius and energy to a degree that even the Nile and Trafalgar failed fully to do. It may here be said that Nelson had returned to England only in November, 1800, from an absence of three and a half years in the Mediterranean.

As in the previous August, a negotiator went with the fleet, the admiral having instructions to act in case the demands were not granted. On March 12, 1801, the expedition sailed from Yarmouth. It numbered twenty-one ships of the line, of from ninety-eight to sixty-four guns each, besides two of fifty guns, which bore a manful part in the battle of Copenhagen. There were attached to it twenty-five frigates and smaller vessels, needed for the shoal and often intricate waters in which operations were to take place, and also seven bomb-vessels; for the intention was to bombard the capital of Denmark, if by no less extreme measure could the country be detached from the hostile league. On the 19th of the month the greater part of the fleet was collected at its first rendezvous, off the Skaw, at the northern extremity of Denmark.

The wind was then blowing fresh from the northwest, fair for entering the Cattegat, and here first was shown the difference of spirit between the commander-in-chief and

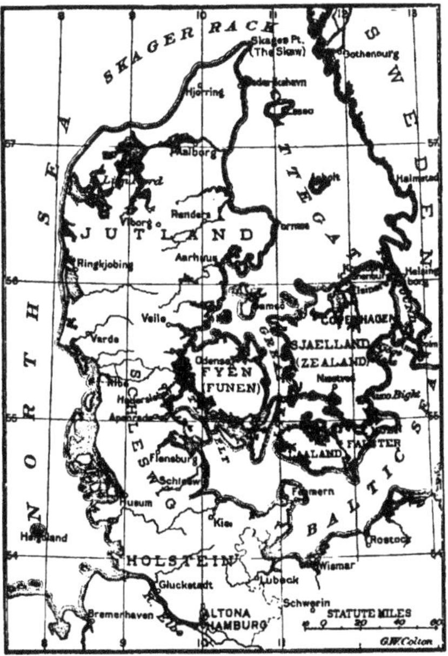

APPROACHES TO COPENHAGEN.

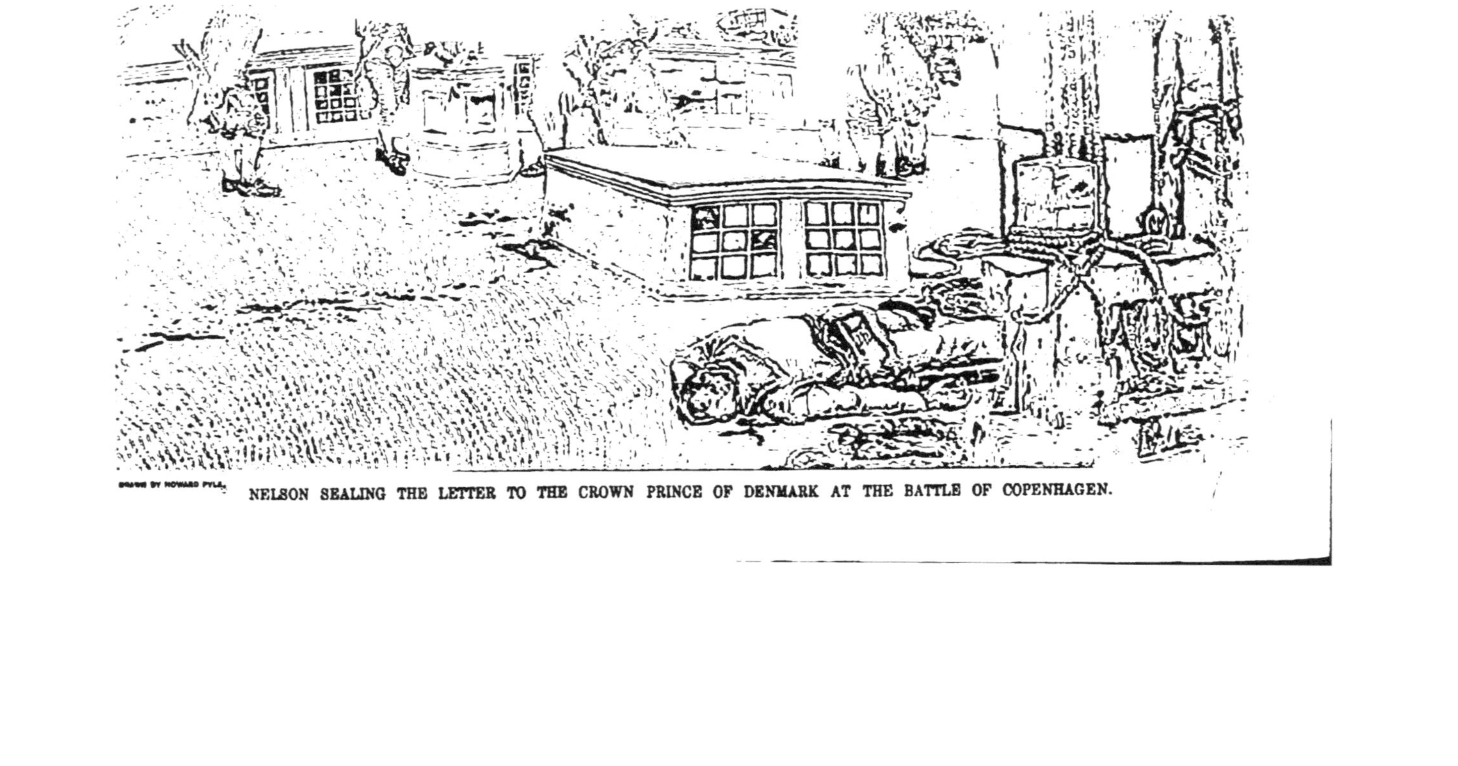

DRAWN BY HOWARD PYLE.

NELSON SEALING THE LETTER TO THE CROWN PRINCE OF DENMARK AT THE BATTLE OF COPENHAGEN.

Nelson, whose views as to the conduct of an armed negotiation were characterized by the clear incisiveness with which he went straight to the center of every question, military or diplomatic, that came within the circle of his action. «All I have gathered of our first plans I disapprove most exceedingly. Honor may arise from them: good cannot. I hear we are likely to anchor outside Cronenburg Castle» [twenty-five miles from Copenhagen], «instead of Copenhagen, which would give weight to our negotiation. A Danish minister would think twice before he put his name to war with England, when the next moment he would probably see his Master's fleet in flames and his capital in ruins; but ‹Out of sight, out of mind› is an old saying. The Dane should see our flag waving every moment he lifted up his head.» As a question of diplomacy, which was not Nelson's profession, this energetic dictum reflected accurately the temper of the ministry, whose envoy had orders to allow only forty-eight hours for the withdrawal of Denmark from the league. From the naval point of view, and especially with sailing ships that would have to pass a very narrow channel to reach their object, the need of losing no opportunity to advance while the possible enemy was still in the midst of hurried and imperfect preparations is obvious. Nelson was naturally vexed at the delay.

The fleet, however, waited off the Skaw, and of course the wind shifted. The envoy was sent ahead in a frigate, landed, and went to Copenhagen. On the 24th he rejoined the fleet, the British terms having been rejected. It was not till the 30th that the wind again served to pass the Sound, a narrow passage not over three miles wide leading from the Cattegat to the Baltic. On the Danish side lies the castle of Cronenburg (Kronborg), a work sufficiently formidable to sailing ships, the commander of which had intimated his intention to fire. The Swedes, however, had failed to fortify their coast, and consequently the British fleet, inclining to that side, underwent only a distant and harmless cannonade. At noon it anchored about five miles from Copenhagen.

Negotiations being ended, the question of hostilities alone remained. Herein the impulsive ardor of the second in command received, for the moment at least, no further check from his superior. A reconnaissance was made at once, and it was determined, in accordance with Nelson's previously expressed opinion, that the attack on the Danish defenses should be made by a heavy division, under Nelson himself, from the south instead of from the north, where the fleet then lay. This dictated the general plan of operations, to understand which a brief explanation is necessary.

It will be seen by the chart on page 530 that there are before Copenhagen two channels by which the city can be passed. Between the two lies a shoal called the Middle Ground. The inner, known as the King's Channel, lay under the guns of the defenses which had been hurriedly improvised for the present emergency. These consisted of a line of hulks, mostly mastless, ranged along the inner side of the King's Channel close to the flats which bordered it, and flanked at the northern end by permanent fortifications called the Trekroner,[1] or Three Crowns batteries. Westward of the latter there lay across the mouth of the harbor two more hulks, and a small squadron consisting of two ships of the line and a frigate, masted and in commission. This division was not seriously engaged, and as a factor in the battle may be disregarded.

The northern part of this defense was decidedly the stronger. To attack there Nelson called «taking the bull by the horns.» The southern wing was much more exposed. Nor was this all. An advance from the north must be made with a northerly wind. If unsuccessful, or even in case of success, if ships were badly crippled, they could not return to the north, where the fleet was. On the other hand, attack from the south presupposed a southerly wind, with which, after an action, the engaged ships could rejoin the fleet, if they threaded safely the difficult navigation. In any event there was risk, but none knew better than Nelson that without risks war is not made. To the considerations above given he added that, when south of the city, the British would be interposed between the other Baltic navies and Denmark. The latter, therefore, could not receive reinforcements unless the squadron were first defeated.

The King's Channel being under fire of the enemy, it was necessary to utilize the outer passage in order that Nelson's division might reach the position south of the Middle Ground uninjured. The nights of the 30th and 31st were employed in surveying the waters, in laying down buoys to replace those removed by the Danes, and in further reconnaissance of the enemy's position. The artillery officers who were to supervise the bombardment

[1] Trekroner, which was then a favorite military name in Denmark, refers to the three crowns of Denmark, Norway, and Sweden, once united.

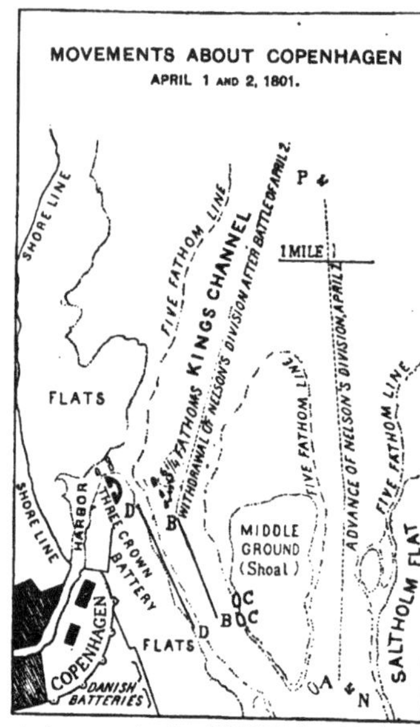


A, *Agamemnon* at anchor; BB, British line of battle; CC, British ships aground; f, British frigates; DD, Danish line of hulks; N, anchorage of Nelson's division, April 1 and 2; P, anchorage of British main fleet under Sir H. Parker.

satisfied themselves that if the floating defenses south of the Trekroner were destroyed, the bomb-vessels could be placed in such a position as to shell the city without being themselves exposed to undue risk.

But while observing such necessary precautions to insure getting at his object, Nelson's resolute temper chafed angrily against every appearance of over-prudence, of timidity, or hesitating counsels, based upon fears of the enemy's superior force. The Danes, Swedes, and Russians might aggregate a much greater number of vessels than Parker had: all the more reason to hit quick and hard before the melting of the ice in the Northern harbors released the ships of the latter two powers. «I don't care which way you go,» he said, when the drawbacks of the Sound and the Great Belt channels had been discussed off the Skaw, «so long as you fight them.» And now before the city, at a council of war held on the afternoon of the 31st, he repelled vigorously all those suggestions of possible dangers of which such meetings are ever fruitful. To the representations of the numerical superiority he replied, «The more numerous the better; I wish they were twice as many: the easier the victory, depend upon it»; meaning that masses of ships so unaccustomed to fleet manœuvers as were those of the Northern powers rather hindered than helped one another.

Nelson asked for ten ships of the line. Parker gave him twelve, but they had to be of the smaller classes, because in shallow waters surrounded by flat land and shoals each additional foot of draft adds to the embarrassment of the vessel. On the 1st of April there blew a fair though light northerly wind, with which Nelson's division passed through the outer channel. The frigate *Amazon* led the way. She was commanded by Captain Riou, who was killed in the next day's battle. Nelson, who had never met him till the day before, had been much impressed by the discipline of his ship and by a certain chivalry of bearing distinctive of the man, and in his report spoke of him as the «gallant and good»—words which the poet Campbell adopted in his well-known ode. Buoys and small vessels, carefully placed, showed where safety and where danger lay, and by dark the squadron was gathered south of the Middle Ground, about two miles from the city. As the anchor of the flag-ship dropped, Nelson was heard to say with emphasis, «I will fight them the moment I have a fair wind.» The remark summed up the spirit of his whole career—never to let opportunity slip.

There being altogether thirty-three ships of war, from ships of the line to bombs, and the anchorage-ground being contracted, the vessels lay so close together as to make a good target for mortar-firing had the Danes availed themselves of the chance. They did throw a few shells about 8 P. M., which fell dangerously near the British fleet; but fortunately for the latter, the enemy did not realize their opportunity, or were too preoccupied with strengthening their yet imperfect defenses to utilize it. For there had come upon Denmark one of those days of judgment to which nations are liable who neglect in time of peace to prepare for war; and when her honor demanded, or she thought demanded, that she should choose resistance rather than submission, there was little left but to take her beating first and to submit afterward. Her population responded to the country's call as the old Norse blood might be expected to respond. There was shouting, and singing of patriotic songs, and volunteering *en masse*, nor was enthusiasm belied by any failure of heroic performance in the day of battle; but all this did not supply the strength which preparation and training give to the latent powers of a country, as to the muscles of an athlete.

For the most part the seamen were away in merchant vessels, maintaining the trade for the immunities of which chiefly Denmark had been drawn into a contest which now concerned her honor rather than her interests. This alone would have prevented her manning the sixteen sail of the line which she might otherwise have contributed to the confederate fleet, but for the defense of Copenhagen at the moment it would have mattered less had there been available a body of fairly expert artillerists, such as at that day almost all seamen were, whether naval or merchant. The service of the guns in anchored hulks did not differ essentially from those in a covered land-battery. The necessary gunners, however, were not forthcoming, and the fight was largely fought by men unaccustomed to military exercises—peasants, mechanics, and others from all classes of life. It is told that at one gun the charge was put in after the shot, and doubtless many such mistakes were made. It is therefore greatly to the credit of the nation that the battle was the severest and most doubtful that Nelson ever fought, as he himself admitted. Accidents contributed to this result, but the fact remains.

The Danish line of defense south of the Trekroner numbered eighteen vessels. Of these seven may fairly be called ships of the line. Moored head and stern as they were, and with a shoal close behind them, so that neither advance nor retreat was possible, the strength of the center was less important than in most cases where the enemy by penetrating can cut the force in two. Here it was impossible to pass through without going aground, so the attempt would not be made. The Danes, therefore, were discreet in strengthening the two flanks, on each of which were stationed together two of the heavy ships. The remaining three were spaced between the extremes, thus affording strong points of support for the weaker vessels which filled up the line. In this position it will be remembered that the Danes had only to fight their guns; no fear for them of running aground, no embarrassment in taking position in the smoke, nor loss of power in handling sails or clearing the wreckage of spars. On the British side these difficulties must be overcome; they are those of the offensive, of the men who must cross ground and overcome obstacles before reaching the enemy; but with them, also, remained the choice of method in making the attack, and of concentrating its power. This is the privilege of the offense, and of it their chief took a wise advantage.

Parker had most judiciously left to Nelson the full direction of the attack. Beyond assigning him the force, and undertaking to make a diversion at the north end of the defense, if possible to get up to it, all was left to his subordinate. Nelson, of frail and delicate physique, rarely knew what good health was, and he suffered bitterly from the Northern cold; but the excitement of approaching battle had upon his heroic temperament the exhilarating effect which a brisk turn upon the bicycle on a bracing day has upon a man dulled and dazed with his office work. As soon as the fleet was at anchor he sat down to dinner with a large party of officers, some of them shipmates of former days, old Nile captains, and others. He was in the highest spirits, drank to the next day's success, and to a fair wind with which to attack. Be it noted that, having promptly availed himself of the north wind to reach his present anchorage, he had placed himself in the way of good luck, and good luck came. The wind shifted in the night to southeast, with which he could not have got where he now was; but, being there, it was just what he needed. «I believe,» said Farragut, «in celerity.» It is suggestive to compare this with Parker's failure to improve his first opportunity to pass the Sound, which was followed by several days of foul winds.

After dinner all the captains except Riou sought their ships. He and Foley, the flag-captain, who had led the column at the Nile, remained with Nelson while the latter perfected the details for the attack, based upon the reconnaissances of the enemy's positions already made. He was greatly fatigued by the exertions of the previous days, so much so that the officers present urged him to go to bed, in which they were peremptorily supported by one of his attendants who had long been with him, and who assumed in consequence the liberties of an old family servant. A cot was placed upon the cabin floor, and lying there, he dictated the remainder of his instructions. While this was going on, Captain Hardy, who afterward commanded the flag-ship at Trafalgar and received Nelson's last messages, was away sounding again the ground over which the next day's advance must be made. At 11 P. M. he returned, having pushed his examination up to the enemy's line, even passing with muffled oars round the leading ship. At one o'clock on the morning

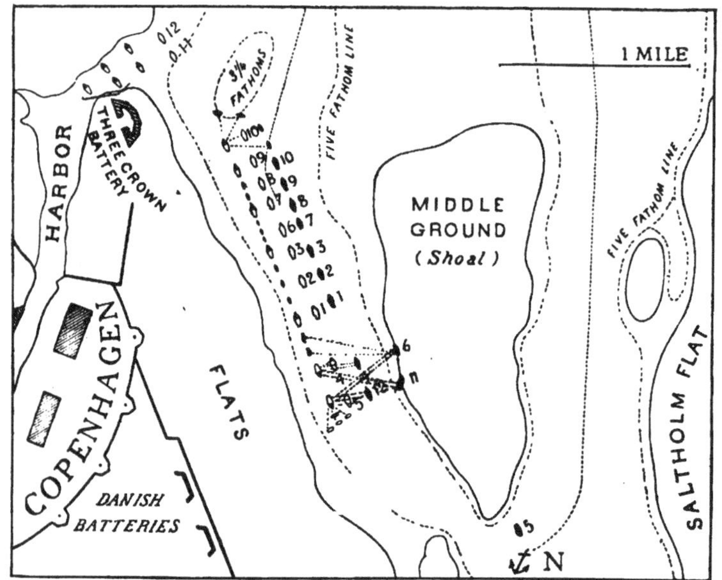


BATTLE OF COPENHAGEN, AS PLANNED AND AS FOUGHT.

Danish block-ships; British ships according to Nelson's plan; British ships as battle was fought; Danish floating batteries.

of the 2d the plan of attack was completed, and half a dozen clerks were busy making copies for the officers concerned.

A full analysis of this order is too technical for a paper of this character; yet in brief it should be shown that it was marked by that sagacity and forethought which raised Nelson very far above the level of the mere fighting man, where alone popular fame has placed him. The order in which the ships should advance having been prescribed, it was further directed that the first four should pass on, maintaining their order, beyond the extreme of the enemy's line, anchoring farther down. The Danish southern flank would thus receive the fire of four ships in succession—a powerful concentration; then, but not till then, the fifth ship, coming up fresh, would anchor abreast the first Dane, and engage this single enemy, originally her equal, but now greatly reduced by the blows already received. The second Dane, assigned to the fourth British ship, would suffer a similar but somewhat lesser disadvantage. Not content, however, with this means of overpowering resistance, Nelson accumulated still further force on this one point. Several frigates and smaller vessels were specifically detailed to place themselves so as to rake the same two flank ships. It was naturally expected that such an overwhelming combination would speedily crush resistance, and the British vessels were directed, when that happened, to move along the line and reinforce the attack where it might be necessary to do so, thus rolling up the enemy's order from south to north.

The leading British ship was to stop abreast the fifth Dane, which was the first ship of the line north of the flank ships. The rest of the British column was to pass on the off side of their own vessels already engaged, each anchoring in succession by the stern as she fairly opened the Danish line, being thus covered in her advance by her predecessors until she reached her station comparatively unharmed. In this way the British order became gradually inverted, the last ship anchoring last, ahead of the others, at the farthest extremity of the enemy's line, and getting there uninjured, as far as human foresight could provide. It appears to the writer, however, that in proposing to extend his line so as to cover not only the Trekroner but the two block-ships west of it, Nelson threw an undue and unnecessary burden upon the force he could assign to the northern flank. It is doubtful whether four ships of the line, though seventy-fours, could be considered equal to four sixty-fours securely moored and supported by permanent works of from sixty to eighty guns. That he himself was uneasy on this point is suggested by the stringent orders given to the two southern ships to cut their cables and immediately make sail to strengthen this part of the battle, when their own opponents were subdued, «which is expected to happen at an early period.»

With this possible deduction, the plan for this battle demonstrates that Nelson's conceptions of battle tactics were in strict conformity with the best principles of military art. It is simply an application of them to the circumstances before him; but it is the application which discriminates the hand of the master from that of the tyro or the student. Deeds, not words, however wise, are the proof of the warrior, and by deeds Nelson's fame as a tactician stands with the highest. Chance, for which, as Napoleon has taught us, something must always be allowed, prevented the full realization of the idea; but from the embarrassment, approaching almost to disaster, which succeeded, Nelson extricated himself with equal sagacity, and by a display of resolution and adroitness that has by some been thought to verge on sharp practice.

April 2 dawned fair, and brought a southeast wind, than which nothing could be more favorable. Nelson, who had slept little, contantly calling to the clerks to hurry their work, breakfasted before six. At seven the captains were all on board the flag-ship, and by eight were familiar with the admiral's plans, and had copies of the orders in their hands. But here a delay occurred, owing to the hesitation of the pilots. These, being Englishmen, had gained their knowledge chiefly as captains and mates of the merchant ships trading to the Baltic, which in those days were usually small. They were nervous about taking charge of ships drawing many feet more than they had ever before had to consider. At length a naval officer, the master of the *Bellona* (seventy-four), announced himself prepared to pilot the fleet. At half-past nine the signal was made to weigh, and a few minutes later the *Edgar* (seventy-four), which was to lead the column, was seen standing for the channel. Some confusion now arose, possibly from the contracted nature of the ground, for the ships did not advance in the exact order laid down by Nelson; nevertheless, as was the case in his other actions, a clear plan clearly understood proved sufficient for the guidance of capable men among the mishaps or unforeseen occurrences inevitable on a field of battle. The main and decisive lines of his admirable conception were fully observed as far as they depended upon the discretion and power of his captains. The *Agamemnon*, a ship he himself had once commanded, was unable, with the wind, to clear the south end of the Middle Ground; she was obliged to anchor, and took no part in the fight. As she was the appointed antagonist of the first Danish ship, the *Prövesteen*, it was necessary to signal another to take this essential position. Further changes followed, partly from unavoidable causes, partly from the steps taken to remedy the accidents thus occasioned.

The failure of the Danes to bombard the enemy's fleet had allowed the British seamen a sound night's sleep. The former, on the contrary, had been hard at work, pushing forward on the very eve of battle preparations that should have been completed long before. The raw guns' crews were drilling throughout the night. «We had not,» says a Danish author, «believed Great Britain was in earnest until the fleet actually sailed.» In the city few had slept. Most had relatives or friends on board the line of vessels, who, at a distance of not over half a mile from the city front, were about to fight under the eyes of their fellow-citizens; and all looked forward to the falling of shells into the town as part of the coming day's terrors. The churches were filled with women and old men at prayer; the roofs and towers which afforded a view of the scene of conflict were covered with spectators.

The *Vagrien*, which supported the *Prövesteen* upon the southern flank of the Danish line, was commanded by a captain who had served several years in British fleets—a school frequently sought in those and earlier days by young officers of the Baltic navies. Watching with understanding eye the indications of the enemy's movements, he turned at last to his officers, and said: «Gentlemen, let us get breakfast. We are sure of this meal, whatever may be the case with dinner.» Soon afterward the timeliness of his suggestion was evidenced by a signal to prepare for battle from the flag-ship *Dannebroge*, on which then flew the broad pendant of Commodore Olfert Fischer, the commander-in-chief, an accomplished seaman, but who had not before been in action.[1] The British fleet was then approaching under manageable canvas, and with a favoring current, presenting a noble and imposing sight to the onlooking enemy.

The *Edgar*, piloted by a capable man, passed safely and steadily down the channel to her appointed station, but the ships following her were not all so fortunate. An impression prevailed that the water was shoaler on the side of the city, near the enemy's line, than by the Middle Ground shoal. The two ships next the *Edgar*, shaping their course for the *Prövesteen* and the *Vagrien*, went clear; but from the opinion concerning the depth of water, they, and the British ships generally, anchored farther from their antagonists than Nelson's favorite practice demanded. The *Bellona* and the *Russell*, following them, but keeping to the eastward, struck on the Middle Ground, where they remained fast, not wholly out of action, as was shown by their losses,—especially that of the *Bellona*,—but in positions that left vacant their intended places in the contest, and made only partly effective the effort they could exert against the hostile ships at all within their reach. The British line was thus at the very outset weakened by the absence of three heavy vessels—a full fourth of its fighting force.

Lord Nelson's flag-ship, the *Elephant*, came next. He did not for the moment recognize that the two predecessors were aground. When he did, his agitation was noticeable; for, with a courage and resolution that knew no wavering, he was a man of very nervous temperament, susceptible to emotion, starting, as a contemporary has told us, if a coil of rope were unexpectedly dropped near him. It was not on this occasion, says the narrator, «the agitation of indecision, but of ardent, animated patriotism panting for glory which had appeared within his reach, and was vanishing from his grasp.» Unshaken in resolve, if distressed in spirit, as Farragut when his line doubled up at Mobile, he turned instinctively to the seaman's first resource, and ordered the *Elephant's* helm put over; at the same time hoisting a signal to «close the enemy,» which at once indicated his resolve, and tended to draw the other ships to the side where safe navigation lay. The rest of the column, under this lead of its commander, passed on without accident to take up their stations.

By this time the two southern Danes were fully engaged by the British ships *Polyphemus* and *Isis*, which had been assigned to that position. They were supported by the two grounded ships, which lay abreast, and, though too far for the full effect of their batteries, contributed materially to the concentration desired here by Nelson. The frigate *Désirée*, a capture from the French, also aided in this attack, as Nelson had prescribed. To quote the words of an eye-witness: «This service was performed by Captain Inman in a masterly style at the instant our ship [the *Monarch*] was passing. He ran down under his three topsails, came to the wind on the larboard tack about half a cable's length [one hundred yards] ahead of the *Prövesteen*, hove all aback, gave her his broadside, filled and made sail, then tacked and ran down to his station.» It is to be feared that few but seamen can understand so technical a description, but the pleasure that possible readers among seamen will derive from so clever a manœuver may excuse its insertion.

The *Edgar* also was now in position nearly abreast the *Jylland*, and engaged. North of her were ranged successively the *Ardent* and the *Glatton*. The former, a fifty-gun ship, was opposed to two of the floating batteries with which the Danes had filled the gaps between their heavier block-ships. The *Glatton* fell into place accurately, not far ahead of the *Ardent*, whence her guns played partly upon a floating battery and partly upon the flag-ship *Dannebroge*. Next to her should have come the *Bellona*; but she having grounded, the duty assigned to her of supporting the *Glatton* by engaging the batteries ahead of the *Dannebroge*, as well as the latter herself, was taken by Nelson's flag-ship, the *Elephant*, which at about eleven anchored on the bow of the *Dannebroge*, as the *Glatton* already had on her quarter.

The *Ganges*, which followed the *Elephant* in the column of attack, was hailed by the admiral as she passed the latter, and directed to anchor close ahead instead of passing on to the station first assigned her. This contraction from the line first intended was due to the absence of the *Bellona*, and was necessary in order to insure mutual support by closing the order to the rear. From this cause, also, it happened that the *Monarch*, placing herself ahead of and near the *Ganges*, occupied the berth opposite the *Sjaelland*

[1] Denmark had then enjoyed eighty years of uninterrupted peace.

(seventy-four), the heaviest ship in the enemy's line, which Nelson in the original disposition had appointed to himself. As the *Monarch* was drawing up, her captain stood on the poop scanning the position he was to take, in his left hand the card showing the plan of battle, his right raised to his mouth with the speaking-trumpet. He gave the order «Cut away the anchor,» and almost immediately was struck dead.

The action now became general as far as the *Sjaelland*. Between her and the Trekroner lay five Danish vessels, two of them being the line-of-battle ships which closed the northern flank. To these for the time there was no opponent, and but one British ship of the line remained to fill up the space originally intended for four. This one, the *Defiance*, carried the flag of Rear-admiral Graves, Nelson's second. She was somewhat later in getting into action than was the *Monarch;* it is said by Danish accounts that she was for nearly quarter of an hour engaged with the *Prövesteen*, the leading Danish ship. This, if correct, was in conformity with Nelson's general plan of first crushing that end of the line, but was unfortunate for the *Monarch*. The *Defiance*, when she came up, anchored ahead of the latter, drawing off part of the fire to which she had been exposed. She was herself within range of the Trekroner, shot from which injured her bowsprit as well as her main- and mizzen-masts.

Captain Riou had been given command of a squadron of frigates, with orders to act as he might be directed. Perceiving the vacant space ahead of the *Monarch* and the *Defiance*, he attempted to supply the place of the absent ships of the line, and engaged the northernmost enemy and the Trekroner with his light division. The heroic attempt proved beyond his strength. In making it, however, he showed as much of judgment as of gallantry; for it appears from Danish accounts that the fire of five frigates and two smaller vessels was concentrated upon the northernmost block-ship, the *Indfödsretten*, which was repeatedly raked fore and aft. The captain, Thurah, fell early; and soon afterward, also, the second in command. The crew continued to fight, sending a message ashore for a new captain. Captain Schrödersee, a retired and invalid naval officer, volunteered. He had scarcely put his foot on board when a shot cut him in two. The *Indfödsretten*, reduced to a complete wreck, struck soon after, about 1 P. M., before Parker's signal called the frigates out of action. Riou's blood was not shed in vain.

The Danes fought not only with great resolution, but with an effectiveness that is really remarkable in view of the rawness of the material hastily worked up for the occasion. They were also greatly favored by the fact that the northern portion of their line had no immediate antagonists except Riou's frigates. It is to be presumed that the ships there moored, in comparative immunity during a measurable time, managed to direct their batteries upon the northernmost British ships of the line. Such certainly was their duty, which Captain Riou's gallant effort should not have wholly prevented; and Colonel Stewart, whose contemporary narrative still forms one of our best sources of information, distinctly states that the *Monarch*, besides her broadside antagonist, the *Sjaelland*, the heaviest ship in the Danish line, was engaged by the block-ship *Holsteen* upon her bow. The loss on those British ships was accordingly heavy, that of the *Monarch*, two hundred and twenty killed and wounded, exceeding any incurred either at the Nile or at Trafalgar. A singular picture of the desolation wrought on her decks has been given by a midshipman on board of her: «Toward the close of the action the colonel commanding the detachment of soldiers on board told me that the quarter-deck guns wanted quill or tin tubes (which are used as more safe and expeditious than loose priming), and wanted me to send some one, adding, his own men were too ignorant of the ship, or he would have sent one of them. I told him I knew no one that could so well be spared as myself. He, however, objected to my going; and as I was aware of the dreadful slaughter which had taken place in the center of the ship, I was not very fond of the jaunt; but my conscience would not let me send another on an errand I was afraid to undertake myself, and away I posted towards the fore magazine. When I arrived on the main deck, along which I had to pass, there was *not a single man standing* the whole way from the mainmast forward, a district containing eight guns on a side, some of which were run out ready for firing, others lay dismounted, and others remained as they were after recoiling. . . . I hastened down the fore ladder to the lower deck, and felt really relieved to find somebody alive. I was obliged to wait a few minutes for my cargo, and after this pause I own I felt something like regret, if not fear, as I remounted the ladder on my return. This, however, entirely subsided when I saw the sun shining and the old blue ensign flying as lofty as ever. I never felt the genuine sense of glory so completely as at that moment. I took off my hat by an involuntary motion, and gave three cheers as I jumped on to the quarter-deck. Colonel Hutchinson welcomed me at my quarters as if I had been on a hazardous enterprise and had returned in triumph; the first lieutenant also expressed great satisfaction at seeing me in such high spirits and so active.»

The effect of splinters—fragments of wood, whether large or small, being technically so called—is shown by the same writer in a few scattered but graphic sentences: «Our signal midshipman was bruised from head to foot with splinters in such a manner as compelled him to leave the deck. Mr. Le Vesconte, another midshipman, who was my companion on the quarter-deck, and who was as cool and apparently unconcerned as usual, shared the same fate. I attended him to the lower deck, but could not prevail upon myself to set foot on the ladder to the cockpit.» [The cockpit is the place below the water-line where the wounded are taken.] «I left him there to make the best of his way. As the splinters were so plentiful, it may be wondered how I escaped; the fact is, I did not escape entirely. When the wheel was shot away I was in a cloud; but being some little distance before the wheel, I did not receive any of the larger pieces. . . . Our first lieutenant, Mr. Yelland, had taken care to have the decks swept, and everything clean and nice, before we went into action. He had dressed himself in full uniform, with his cocked hat set on square» [a touch which recalls Collingwood's eccentric captain, Rotheram, at Trafalgar, who, upon being remonstrated with for the exposure full dress entailed, replied, «I have always fought in a cocked hat, and I always will»], «his shirt-frill stiff starched, and his cravat tied tight under his chin, as usual. How he escaped unhurt seems wonderful. Several times I lost sight of him in a cloud of splinters; as they subsided I saw first his cocked hat emerging, then by degrees the rest of his person, his face smiling, so that altogether one might imagine him dressed for his wedding day.»

We have ordinarily too little of these small details in naval battles. On board the flagship *Elephant*, fortunately, there was a distinguished army officer who during the naval part of the engagement had little to do except to note incidents especially connected with the great admiral, near whose person he was. It had been the intention, if the full results of the attack by the ships were realized, to follow them up with an assault by troops in boats upon the Three Crowns batteries. For this purpose detachments of soldiers were on board each ship of the line, and flat-boats were towed alongside ready to land them when required. The commander of the whole, Colonel Stewart, was on board the flag-ship; but the opportunity was not obtained, owing to the accidents which kept three ships out of line, and the injuries done to the others by the desperate resistance of the Danes. The northern division of the British fleet, under Parker, the commander-in-chief, did not succeed in working up against the wind and current which favored Nelson in time to engage the Trekroner before the southern part of the fight was over. Even then the ships were at long and ineffective range. The batteries were therefore uninjured, and assault was impossible.

Stewart, being otherwise unemployed, had full time to observe. Lord Nelson, he tells us, was most anxious to get nearer the enemy, but was deterred by the strong assertions of the pilots that the ships would take the ground. Both for penetration and accuracy he relied always upon getting close alongside. Just before leaving England he had written to a friend: «As for the plan for pointing a gun truer than we do at present, I shall of course look at it; but I hope we shall be able, as usual, to get so close to our enemies that our shot cannot miss their object; and that we shall again give our Northern enemies that hail-storm of bullets which gives our dear Country the dominion of the seas.» Practised thus as the British seamen of that day were, the effect made upon their inexperienced though heroic enemies would unquestionably have been more rapid and sustained than it actually was, the contest sooner decided, and the loss less. Rapidity rather than fine sighting was then the boast of British gunnery.

At 1 P. M., therefore, the contest, after a duration of more than two hours, still raged, though with somewhat diminished fury. Men of the same blood and traditions had met in a struggle of endurance. Nelson's own name was of Norse origin. Enumerating the severe injuries already received by the British, Stewart says: «Few, if any, of the enemy's heavy ships and praams had yet ceased to fire. The contest in general, although from the relaxed state of the enemy's fire it might not have given much room for apprehension as to the result, had certainly at 1 P. M. not declared itself in favor of either side. About this juncture, and in this posture of affairs, the signal was thrown out on board the *London* [Parker's flag-ship, then four miles distant] for the action to cease.

«Lord Nelson was at this time, as he had been during the whole action, walking the starboard side of the quarter-deck, sometimes much animated, and at others heroically fine in his observations. A shot through the mainmast knocked a few splinters about us. He observed to me, with a smile, ‹It is warm work, and this day may be the last to any of us at a moment›; and then, stopping short at the gangway, he used an expression never to be erased from my memory, and said with emotion, ‹But, mark you, I would not be elsewhere for thousands.›» With this spirit may be compared his rebuke some days after the battle to a lieutenant who during the action had made a hopeless report about the grounded ships: «At such a moment the delivery of anything like a desponding opinion, unasked, was highly reprehensible, and deserved much more censure than Captain Foley gave you.»

«When the signal from the *London*, No. 39, was made,» continues Stewart, «the signal lieutenant reported it to him. He continued his walk, and did not appear to take notice of it. The lieutenant, meeting his lordship at the next turn, asked whether he should repeat it [by which, if done, the squadron engaged would retire to the northward]. Lord Nelson answered, ‹No; acknowledge it.›[1] On the officer returning to the poop, his lordship called after him, ‹Is No. 16 [for close action] still hoisted?› The lieutenant answering in the affirmative, Lord Nelson said, ‹Mind you keep it so.› He now walked the deck considerably agitated, which was always known by his moving the stump of his right arm. After a turn or two he said to me in a quick manner, ‹Do you know what's shown on board the commander-in-chief—No. 39?› On asking him what that meant, he answered: ‹Why, to leave off action. Leave off action!› he repeated; and then added with a shrug, ‹Now, damn me if I do!› He also observed, I believe, to Captain Foley, ‹You know, Foley, I have only one eye—I have a right to be blind sometimes›; and then, with an archness peculiar to his character, putting the glass to his blind eye, he exclaimed, ‹I really do not see the signal.›» Professor Laughton, whose authority on matters relating to Nelson is second to that of no one living, has lately told us in his «Life of Nelson» that this little display was but a joke, Nelson having received a message from Parker that he was to use his own discretion as to obeying the signal. If so, it is not improbable that he had in view the effect of his manner upon the many bystanders who must have witnessed the scene in the midst of a yet doubtful and desperate battle. It is the converse of the outward bearing which he reprehended in the lieutenant. The moral effect of such self-possession is indescribable. The *Monarch's* midshipman already quoted speaks thus of a wounded and disabled officer on board of her: «When the carnage was greatest he encouraged his men by applauding their conduct, and frequently began a huzza, which is of more importance than might generally be imagined; for the men have no other communication throughout the ship, but when a shout is set up it runs from deck to deck, and they know that their comrades are, some of them, alive and in good spirits.» As Parker's messenger, Captain Otway, did not reach Nelson until after the signal was hoisted, it is possible the scene witnessed by Stewart occurred before Nelson knew Parker's purpose. Parker's private secretary, who afterward served in the same capacity with Nelson for two years, has also affirmed that there was a previous understanding between the two admirals. The matter is of less consequence than appears, for the supreme merit of Lord Nelson was not the disregarding of the signal, but the sound judgment and tenacity with which he refused to incur the risk of giving ground at that moment. This was wholly his.

Nelson's second, Rear-admiral Graves, repeated the signal to withdraw; but, like his own leader, kept that for close action still flying. Not a ship of the line budged, but the repeating by Graves shows that it is playing with edged tools to hoist signals not meant to be obeyed. Situated as Nelson was, there was no safety but to fight it out till the Danish line of vessels was subdued. To retreat under the guns of the still unharmed Trekroner, through an intricate channel, would be bad enough if no ships were left to oppose him. If the ships were destroyed, his own, roughly handled as many had been, would, for the most part, be too far from the enemy's land-batteries to receive any serious additional injury. Nothing could have been more dangerous for the whole force than the attempted withdrawal of a few ships.

This the frigates proved. Riou, at the north end of the line, was being severely handled, but he was doing good service, and

[1] To *acknowledge* a signal is to hoist a flag which simply indicates that the signal has been seen and understood. To *repeat* is to transmit the signal, by repetition, to the vessels which are to execute the order.

was within touch of support if the southern ships came to him. Seeing Parker's signal, and that it was repeated by the flag-ship nearest him, he doubtless expected the whole division to retreat. The frigates hauled off, and in moving away necessarily exposed their sterns to a raking fire. «What will Nelson think of us!» exclaimed Riou, who, already wounded by a splinter, was sitting on a gun encouraging his men. His clerk was killed by his side, and by another shot several marines while hauling the main-brace. Riou then exclaimed, «Come, then, my boys; let us all die together!» The words were scarcely uttered when a ball cut him in two. «Thus,» writes Colonel Stewart, «was the British service deprived of one of its greatest ornaments, and society of a character of singular worth, resembling the heroes of romance.»

At half-past eleven the Danish flag-ship *Dannebroge* caught fire, and Commodore Fischer shifted his broad pendant from her to the *Holsteen*, the second ship from the north end of his line. The *Dannebroge* continued to fight bravely. At the end, out of three hundred and thirty-six men with which she began, two hundred and seventy had been killed and wounded. This large proportion is doubtless to be explained by the fact that reinforcements from shore were being continually carried to the ships. For a time the flames were got under, but they broke out again and again; the *Elephant* redoubled her efforts, and at length the *Dannebroge* was driven out of the line, on fire fore and aft. She drifted with the wind toward the Trekroner, within two hundred yards of which she grounded, and at about half-past four, after the battle, she blew up.

The two southern ships, the *Prövesteen* and the *Vagrien*, also suffered very severely, being overmatched and outnumbered by the force concentrated upon them. Lassen, the captain of the *Prövesteen*, became the Danish hero of the day; for long he could not appear in the streets of Copenhagen without being followed by a crowd. But popular favor passes; he died in poverty and neglect, nor is any memorial of his valor to be seen in the capital of his country. The *Vagrien*, from two hundred and seventy men, lost all but fifty killed and wounded. Both flag and pendant were shot away, and «nobody,» by a Danish account, «had time to raise a new one. The *Vagrien* fought a long time without the flag hoisted.» This irregularity has its bearings on the motives alleged by Nelson for his subsequent action in sending a flag of truce.

The block-ship *Jylland*, between the *Vagrien* and the *Dannebroge*, fought long with the *Edgar*. The floating batteries lying between her and the *Dannebroge* being at length driven out of action, the space thus left vacant was utilized by smaller British vessels to rake the block-ships lying on each side of it. This incident, which rests on Danish accounts, was distinctly in the line of Nelson's orders, and shows, as already remarked, that a plan correctly traced in its broader lines will not, in the hands of capable men, be necessarily disarranged and fail, even through mishaps and changes of conditions as serious as those which marked the British fortunes on this day.

At 2 P. M. the cables of the *Sjaelland*, next north of the *Dannebroge*, and the immediate antagonist of the *Monarch*, which suffered so severely at her hands and those of her consorts, were shot away, and the ship drifted out of position. This was a most important injury to the Danes, for she was their strongest ship. At the same hour Fischer found it necessary again to shift his pendant, going from the *Holsteen* to the Trekroner shore-battery, which had now become the center of what remained of the Danish line. The southern vessels, up to and including the *Sjaelland*, were silenced; the *Holsteen* was a wreck; and Parker's division, though not within effective range, was getting nearer.

At the same time matters had become extremely serious with the British also. Firing had indeed ceased throughout the Danish line which lay south of Nelson's flag-ship, to which circumstance is doubtless due the fact, noted by the Danish commodore, that during the latter part of the engagement she fired only occasional guns. Fischer thought from this that she had been reduced nearly to silence by her losses, whereas the legitimate inference is that, owing to the limited sweep of broadside guns, only a few bore on the enemies ahead of her and could be effectively used. «He states,» wrote Nelson, who was unnecessarily wroth over the matter, «that the ship in which I had the honor to hoist my flag fired latterly only single guns. It is true; for steady and cool were my brave fellows, and did not wish to throw away a single shot.» Naval seamen will readily understand that until springs could be run out—a long process—few guns would bear under the conditions.

But, ahead of the *Elephant*, the *Ganges*, the *Monarch*, and the *Defiance* were at two o'clock still warmly engaged, the last two especially, while the Trekroner was uninjured and injuring them. At the same time the shore-batteries on the island of Amak continued to fire from behind the silenced Danish ships; and though the flags of the latter were in many cases down, the British crews who sought to take possession were refused admission, and even fired upon, by men on board. This statement, which rests upon several British authorities, is by no means in itself incredible. Their crews knew nothing of war or its usages, and there was a scarcity of trained officers. As before quoted from a Danish source, the *Vagrien* fought some time without either flag or pendant, because no one had time to hoist others. But, however pardonable in purpose, there is no excuse in fact for any avoidable delay in replacing the tokens that one has not yielded, but is fighting. In truth, no ship should go into battle with only one flag flying. The account of the *Monarch's* midshipman is of interest in this connection: «Most of the enemy's vessels had struck their colors, in consequence of which I was desired to send Mr. Home (lieutenant), who commanded the flat-bottomed boat and launch which were both manned and armed alongside, to board the prizes opposed to us. He accordingly set off for that purpose; when almost half-way he saw a boat, which was probably sent on the same errand, knocked to pieces, the crew of which he picked up; but as the other ships and batteries still continued firing, he thought it in vain to attempt boarding the prizes, which were, moreover, prepared to resist, notwithstanding they had struck their colors.»

The time of this occurrence is fixed by the fact that Home then pulled to the *Elephant* to ask instructions of Nelson, and was by him told that he had sent a flag of truce ashore, and that if it was accepted he should remove from the action as soon as possible. Colonel Stewart's account of the flag of truce mentions that at half-past two the action was over astern of the *Elephant*, but that the ships ahead and the Trekroner were engaged, and the British repelled by force from the surrendered vessels. «Lord Nelson naturally lost temper at this, and observed that he must either send on shore and stop this irregular proceeding, or send in our fire-ships and burn the prizes. He accordingly retired into the stern-gallery, and wrote with great despatch that well-known letter addressed to the crown prince.» This celebrated and much-discussed letter ran thus:

TO THE BROTHERS OF ENGLISHMEN, THE DANES.

Lord Nelson has directions to spare Denmark when no longer resisting; but if the firing is continued on the part of Denmark, Lord Nelson will be obliged to set on fire all the floating batteries he has taken, without having the power of saving the brave Danes who have defended them. Dated on board his Britannic Majesty's ship *Elephant*, Copenhagen Roads, April 2, 1801.

NELSON AND BRONTÉ, *Vice-Admiral*, under the command of Admiral Sir Hyde Parker.

It will be observed that, whatever motives may be assumed, the words of the letter convey simply a threat that if the surrendered vessels are not given up, the admiral will throw away upon them no more shot, but instead use fire-ships, a recognized weapon of war. There is no request for a suspension of hostilities, and only the boat carrying the letter showed a flag of truce. The decks being cleared of all partitions fore and aft, and all ordinary conveniences removed, Nelson wrote in full view of all on the deck where he was, at the casing of the rudder-head, standing; and as he wrote an officer standing by took a copy. The original, in his own hand, was put into an envelop and sealed with his arms. The officer was about to use a wafer, but Nelson said, «No; send for sealing-wax and candle.» Some delay followed, owing to the man sent having had his head taken off by a ball. «Send another messenger for the wax,» said the admiral when informed of this; and when the wafers were again suggested he simply reiterated the order. A large amount of wax was used, and extreme care taken that the impression of the seal should be perfect. Colonel Stewart asked, «Why, under so hot a fire and after so lamentable an accident, have you attached so much importance to a circumstance apparently trifling?» «Had I made use of a wafer,» replied Nelson, «the wafer would have been still wet when the letter was presented to the crown prince; he would have inferred that the letter was sent off in a hurry, and that we had some very pressing reasons for being in a hurry. The wax told no tales.» It was the same sagacious regard to effect which possibly dictated the by-play of refusing to see Parker's signal of recall.

An officer who had served in the Russian navy and spoke Danish bore the letter. He found the crown prince, who was also prince regent, near the sally-port of the fortifications, encouraging his people. He sent a verbal reply by General-Adjutant Lindholm, who, upon meeting Nelson, gave the following written memorandum of his message:

His Royal Highness the Prince Royal of Denmark has sent me, General-Adjutant Lindholm, on board to his Britannic Majesty's Vice-admiral, the Right Honorable Lord Nelson, to ask the particular object of sending the flag of truce.

Nelson replied in writing:

Lord Nelson's object in sending on shore a flag of truce is humanity; he therefore consents that hostilities shall cease till Lord Nelson can take his prisoners out of the prizes, and he consents to land all the wounded Danes, and to burn or remove his prizes. Lord Nelson, with humble duty to his Royal Highness, begs leave to say that he will ever esteem it the greatest victory he ever gained if this flag of truce may be the happy forerunner of a lasting and happy union between my most gracious Sovereign and his Majesty the King of Denmark.

NELSON AND BRONTÉ.

Lindholm was then referred for further negotiation to Sir Hyde Parker, who was four miles distant in the *London;* and to that ship he proceeded, to obtain a definite understanding with the commander-in-chief.

Between the times when Nelson's flag of truce went on shore and when Lindholm reached the *Elephant,* resistance ceased upon all the Danish ships south of the Trekroner, except one small frigate which escaped. In the same interval Nelson held a consultation with the flag-captain, Foley, and Fremantle, captain of the *Ganges,* next ahead, as to the practicability of advancing the ships which were least damaged against that part of the Danish line of defense yet uninjured, *i. e.,* the Trekroner and the ships northwest of it at the harbor's mouth. «Their opinions,» says Colonel Stewart, «were averse from it, and, on the other hand, decided in favor of removing our fleet, whilst the wind yet held fair, from their present intricate channel.»

The great obstacle to this desirable end was the Trekroner, while the block-ships northwest of the latter might possibly have supported its fire. But Lindholm, either before or after his interview with Nelson, had given orders, in the name of the crown prince, that firing should cease. This order reached the Trekroner at four o'clock, according to Fischer, who was then in the battery, but before that the British ships had begun to move out. The indomitable *Monarch,* despite her tremendous losses, was engaged in springing her broadside upon the Trekroner, after the ships abreast her struck, when Rear-admiral Graves, returning to the *Defiance* from an interview with Nelson, hailed her to cut her cable and follow him out. This was done, but the sails being wholly unmanageable, the ship refused to steer, falling off broadside to the wind and current. The *Ganges,* following her, struck her amidships, and the two ships drifted, the *Ganges* pushing the *Monarch* toward the Trekroner, which opened fire upon them, showing that the message to cease had not yet been received there. It soon was, however, and Nelson's division withdrew to the northward without further molestation. On the way out both flag-ships, the *Defiance* and the *Elephant,* grounded, and remained for several hours about a mile from the Trekroner. For the gunnery of the day that was long range, but they would undoubtedly have received much harm if the enemy's fire had not been discontinued. Commenting upon this condition, Colonel Stewart says: «It should be observed, on the other hand, that measures would in that case have been adopted, and they were within our power, for destroying this formidable work.»

Nelson returned that evening to his regular flag-ship, the *St. George,* which he had left for the battle, she being of too heavy draft to participate. Lindholm's negotiations with Admiral Parker resulted in an agreement that hostilities should remain suspended for twenty-four hours, and that the Danish ships which had struck during the action should be surrendered to the British. The night and the next day were passed in getting afloat the grounded ships, and in bringing out them and their prizes. Continued negotiations followed, which ended, on the 9th of April, in Denmark signing an armistice for fourteen weeks—a practical abandonment of the Armed Neutrality, for Nelson bluntly stated that he needed that time to act against the Russian fleet. It is to be remarked that during this week of diplomatic discussion, in which Nelson was the leading British negotiator, the British bomb-vessels were being put in position for the bombardment of the city, to which the battle, by removing the southern line of block-ships, was the essential and effectual prelude.

The remark is necessary, for it bears directly upon the impression, never wholly dispelled, that Nelson, in removing his crippled ships during the suspension of hostilities on the 2d, took unfair advantage of the flag of truce. The reply is that this was done openly; that if the Danes felt that an unfair advantage was being taken, it was in their power to stop it at once; that, instead of so doing, they conceded also the surrender of the prizes which had struck but had not been taken possession of; and finally, that the active preparation for renewed hostilities in the following days, while an armistice was in force, shows that the understanding between the parties did not go further than the cessation of fighting. To all this is to be added the fact that Lindholm, the Danish bearer of the flag of truce, and thenceforth engaged through all negotiations which resulted in the fourteen weeks' armistice, wrote to Nelson a month later (May 2) in the following terms: «As to your lordship's motive for sending a flag of truce to our government, it can never be misconstrued, and your subsequent conduct has sufficiently shown that humanity is always the companion of true valor.»

The crown prince, on the other hand, has been considered weak in ordering the cessation of hostilities at the moment, seeing the disabled condition of Nelson's division. The conditions before him at 3 P. M.—the results of the fight—were these. The entire right wing of the defense, from the Trekroner south, was crushed. Nothing stood between the city and bombardment. Parker's division was uninjured, and much of Nelson's, though badly mauled, was out of range, and could refit unmolested. Above all, and this Nelson knew and reckoned upon, although Denmark had tried to carry her points about the neutral trade by a bluff, her rulers had no desire for war, but were acting under the coercion of the Czar. The glorious and desperate resistance she had made both vindicated her honor and testified to her allies that further persistence would be fruitless, except in wanton suffering. By prolonging the struggle she could gain neither in advantage nor in reputation, for nothing could place a nation's warlike fame higher than did her great deeds that day.

*A. T. Mahan.*

# INSTRUMENTS.

THE rugged cliff that faced the main
  Cherished a pine against its breast,
Whereon the wind woke many a strain,
  As 't were a violin caressed;
And souls that heard, although in pain,
  Were soothed and lulled to peace and rest.

A people strove to break their chains,
  And many bled, and strife was long,
Until a minstrel voiced their pains,
  And woke the world with echoing song;
And even the tyrant heard the strains,
  And hastened to redress the wrong.

The souls of men were dried like dew,
  And earth cried out with bitter need,
Until one said, «I dare be true,»
  And followed up the word with deed.
Then heaven and earth were born anew,
  And one man's name became a creed!

*Charles Crandall.*

# AN INLAND VENICE.

## THE SERBIAN SWAMP, VENDLAND.

WITH PICTURES BY LOUIS LOEB.

ONE of the strangest and most interesting places in all Europe is the Spreewald, not far from Berlin, and very few travelers seem to know anything about it. The tourist is supposed to have left nothing untouched on the Continent; but there are curious loops and by-ways of travel that are virtually unknown to the outsider. One of the pleasures of a foreign tour is the making of these unexpected «finds.» The Spreewald, being a little out of the line of travel, is not likely to be overtoured, so it will probably be «discovered» continually for some time to come. Its peculiarity is hinted at in the title we have ventured to prefix to the author's more precise name for the region. It is not a Venice of palaces, but of farms and country inns; not only a bucolic home, but a haunt of pleasure-seekers; a Holland far from the sea; a country where the streets are of water; an enormous network of canals and natural watercourses. A summer twilight there leaves mysterious memories. One speeds along the narrow, tree-lined water-lanes, now close to the front doors of cottages, and now through lonely farm-land stretches, the distance curtained by the evening mists, and the deep-voiced nightingales adding an imaginative charm to the haunted landscape.

*The Editor.*

Along a swift, faint-purling tide
Through farms and high-flown elms to glide,
Whilst in a copse as dark as night
One brave impassioned nightingale
Throbs like our hearts. . . .
But o'er the light,
Fresh fields beyond the swale

An anxious cuckoo cheats the ear,
Calling aloud, now far, now near,
Upon that wayward one, his wife. . . .
Sliding through dreams devoid of blame,
Within that dream fall hints of strife,
Of passionate faith and shame.

THERE is a distant rushing of water over a weir, and the boat itself, a slender, shallow punt, makes a faint, faint murmur under its shelving prow as the Vend thrusts his pole backward into the sandy bottom of the stream. Lying full length in the bows on a bed of straw, I watch the reeds and grasses nod as we pass. Reaching out my hand, I can pluck great forget-me-nots, pinks with feathery petals, yellow iris standing in stateliness against the green slope of the bank. Before me stretches the highroad of the queerest, most delightful community in all northern Germany. It is the Mühlspree, a branch of many waters that finally unite to enter Berlin, there part again, to join once more and flow by Potsdam into the Havel, thence to the Elbe, thence to the Atlantic. I am on the water turnpike between the Vendish villages of Burg and Lübbenau.

Tall trees almost meet overhead, shooting up close from the water's edge; with their overstretching branches they make a capital aërial road for chattering magpies clad in Prussian white and black, and for the more silent squirrel. Between their boles appear from time to time thatched roofs of barns, greenest green and richest yellow with moss; here the cotter's low home, with its steep roof, its stoop, and small windows, there the larger house of a village magnate, some rich peasant or landlord. Suddenly on the bank rises a tiny woman in the picturesque costume of the Vends, an envoy of the little people, it might seem, who verily must linger in such out-of-the-way spots as this! In her strange horned head-dress and bright kirtle to the knee, with her little arms, legs, and feet bare, her blue eyes most solemn, she stands stock-still, afraid to throw us the bouquet she has gathered for no other purpose than to get our *groschen*.

«Tank—Tag!» cries she, makes a little bob, and flies away with the spoil, in her glee forgetting to throw us the wild flowers till it is too late.

But what is this approaching up the leaf-swung highway? One boat, two, three—it is a pleasure party up from Lübbenau, to stop at the Bleiche, or the Black Eagle, or some other locally famous inn. On seats athwart the first punt are several rows of young men and women laughing and singing; in the second are musicians; in the third is a group about a keg of beer. This is their outing, and vociferous is their enjoyment. As quiet falls again we rush round a corner into a transverse reach shadowed dark with trees—a reach that joins one Spree branch with another; and presently a deep, rich note is heard—yes, it is a nightingale practising for his evening concert; and there again, faint and ventriloquial,—who can tell exactly whence?—comes from across a broad stretch of crops the mellow cuckoo call!

For it is June, and not yet, as some Vends still believe, has the cuckoo changed his estate and taken on the form of a hawk, nor has he ceased his monotonous but ever delightsome song.

As we pass a woman at work in the fields, her bare feet in wooden shoes, her one garment reaching just below the knee, but her head and shoulders well covered by the great *rubishko*, or horned head-dress, our boatman speaks to her in a strange tongue that sounds like Polish. She has smaller hands and feet than German peasants usually show, a small, slender figure, a plain but refined brown face, and brown eyes. She will work all day like a pony, and then think nothing of dancing half the night if she gets the chance; and dance well, too, far more gracefully than her German sisters in the cities. Her ambition is to get a position as wet-nurse in Berlin, where she will trot about the Thiergarten in a magnificent short skirt of many yards' circumference, white stockings, real leather shoes, and an immense snowy-white horned head-dress. With the money she has earned she hopes to return to the Spreewald. She hates the city, and likes her time-honored black aprons and colored skirts and many-colored headgear. The men hold less to the old and traditional, so that one rarely sees more than a hint of the remote past in their jackets and country caps. For them the army is a great leveler and eradicator of racial traits and local oddities in dress.

Now we are out of the woods, rushing down a perfectly straight *fliess* the banks of which are planted with a quick growth of willows closely cropped by the basket-makers. Here we meet two slender fellows taking a pig to market—a lovely pink pig in a new crate as clean as a pin, and as proud as that heifer of which the crazy Roman emperor tried to make an empress. Then comes another boat stacked with yellow carrots and green vegetables, broad masses of color, poled along by a peasant woman in a dark blue dress and a white, broad-spreading cap. These people speak German to the lordings as we pass, Vendish to our boatman; but the Vendish is disappearing because, for the sake of the army, its teaching is discouraged. Throughout all this district, far over into Saxony, only a few churches still offer sermons in the old tongue. Yet if the Vendish tongue disappears the names of places will tell the tale, even as such names in Brandenburg and Saxony still do. Dresden, Leipzig, these are

A CANAL-SIDE.

Vendish words—or call them Slavic, with the broader term that now means the race. And hereabout are Cottbus, Vetschau, Müschen, Brahmow, Babow, Dlugy, Raddush, Leipe,

Lehde, Byhleguhre, Straupitz, and Lübben. And the fliesses that wind or shoot straight in and out of forest and cleared fields retain Vendish names: Mutniza, Blushnitza, Rogazo, Zschapigk, Polenzo, Groblitzo, and Nabasatz. Efforts have been made to give German names to many of them, but country people everywhere are great holders to precedent, and the people who stick so tightly to their old costume are not going to give up their place-names without a struggle.

Strange indeed that so near Berlin so old-time and curious a community could have remained reasonably uncontaminated by the hordes of picknickers! The Spreewald is too near a great capital for foreigners to hear much of it. The museums and palaces of Berlin, the palaces of Potsdam, absorb all the spare energy of foreign visitors. And for convenient outflights it is a little too far for most burghers of Berlin. Some have country places in and near the Spreewald. Many visit it occasionally. It is a favorite place for people from Dresden and Leipzig who can give several days to exploring its watery labyrinths; especially for the teaching guild is it a favorite resort. Every village has its inns, and at Burg, where Vendish services are held in the old church and the costume remains the most antique, there are several famous taverns. One is the Bleachery, where Frederick the Great established a colony of dyers and weavers, who have all disappeared, although the art is still practised by private means for personal use in many farm-houses. But the fine green, orange, pink, and lilac head-dresses—the *wodzewanski rubishko*—and the turquoise, gray, and yellow skirts are now bought at Cottbus or in Berlin.

«School out» at the village school of Burg is a pretty sight. The substantial brick building overlooks the ever-murmuring highway, and the boys and girls, instead of stringing up a dusty road, tumble into punts and pole away for dear life—the boys much like other boys, but the girls reduced facsimiles of their mothers and elder sisters, clad in bright but short raiment, and visible afar off through their strange mob-caps with wings. As one moves down stream from Burg by Leipe to Lübbenau, these wings grow smaller and collapse, while the skirts grow longer and more resemble the ordinary dress of women. At a dance the Spreewälder knows instantly, by the peculiarities of her costume, from what village a woman or girl has come. At Leipe the multitudinous skirts of alarming girth are no more, the gown reaches the ankles, and the cap fits close to the head instead of resting on a framework as in Burg. Thus the dress in Leipe is perhaps more graceful, but it is more commonplace; it no longer testifies to that pride of the peasant father or husband which is shown by the number of yards in the skirts of his womanfolk and the variety of their caps, by the richness of their dress as well as their jewelry.

Swamp the Spreewald once was, and swamp it again becomes from time to time when a freshet obliterates the paths beside the streams and all the fields are wide brown lakes. To the ravens flying over, the Spreewald in its ordinary state looks much like other land, because the fliesses are scarce visible through the lines of trees, and because where the dense forest once stood ruthless nobles and landowners have felled the trees to grow hay or to plant vegetables. But let the snows melt suddenly and the rains fall, then it is a little Holland with the dikes broken.

But for its past, imagine a marsh thick with trees that annual overflows do not kill. Into this swamp human beings have fled with no hope of ever regaining the arable lands and pastures from which they were driven. Fancy them bringing with them gentler manners than those possessed who drove them to the swamp, and also habits of industry, and an inherited, inbred knowledge of water-walls, canals, dikes, weirs, and fisheries. Imagine them speaking a well-sounding Slavic tongue full of soft *s*'s and modulations, complicated in its grammar, rich in synonyms. Think of them as pagans with some few cruel rites, yet treating their women and cattle with comparative humanity, and in many other ways, such as vivacity, gaiety, and humor, contrasting favorably with their conquerors.

Such is the race that, owing to a certain querulousness among themselves, a certain tendency to envy and backbiting, an inability to agree and fight the foe unitedly, was gradually forced off the good land into the dark woods on the upper reaches of the Havel. There they fell trees, dig big and little canals, make pastures and fields, trap fish and game, and build thatched huts, not round, but square. As the world outside moves on faster, and the Teutons take on a superficial skin of civilization, and by marriage, force, and fraud enter the Spreewald and become Vends also, the original Vends of this part of northern Europe find themselves a secluded community of woodmen and fishermen, with hardly a town to show, without a literature, but not without myriad myths and superstitions; a community of men who are as lambs to the cruel Christian, ready to be gathered into the fold by threats of the sword and the auto de fe.

Such were the Serbs or Vends who dwelt in the twelfth century not far from a little town on the Spree called Kölln (from *kolna*, a shed), which, being afterward joined by another little spot called Barlin, formed the later city of Berlin. The Germans use for them the term Vends, a very old word which designates many other separated parts of one great Aryan race, such as the Veneti on the Baltic, the Veneti on the Adriatic, the Vendéans in France, the Vandals on the lower Elbe, the Pannonians of old Slav blood. Their nearer relatives were the Obotrites in Mecklenburg, the Kossubes in northeast Prussia, and the Pomorjans or Old Prussians. Like the Finns of Russia and Sweden, who speak quite another sort of language, however, they were preëminently men of the fens, amphibious, so that some have guessed none too profoundly that their neighbors called them Vends because of an old word, *wada*, meaning water. But the worst guess at the meaning of Vend is a German one, according to which they were called Vends in derision because they turned (*wenden*) in battle from the swords of the savage Teutons.

ENGRAVED BY A. E. ANDERSON.

THE BOATMAN—EN ROUTE.

And of a truth they have given way before the foe just as the old Veneti fled from the mainland into the oozy islands of the lagoons at the head of the Adriatic when the Huns grew too grievous, and lived ever after in boats, even as the Vends of the Spreewald to this day. The Venetians were of old great horsemen, and their racers took prizes at Olympia under the racing-colors of Hiero of Syracuse. The Vends have a passion for horses' heads as a decoration for their houses and barns, just as the modern Venetians love equestrian monuments. Have we here the survival of an idea in common from the earlier times when the Slavs were horsemen on the Asian plains? Vendland is better known to history as Lusatia, and the Spreewald belongs to Lower Lusatia, and contains all that is left of Vends, who speak not only the old tongue, but realize, as millions of Germanized Slavs do not, that they are a people by themselves who have manfully withstood centuries of persecution directed against their tongue, their dress, and their customs. This tongue is not unlike the Czech of Bohemia, and strongly resembles Russian and Polish.

As a rule, the older women wear white headgear; at least the big square kerchief that falls nearly to the shoulders is white, while with girls this upper part is colored like the tulip-beds of Haarlem. But on Trinity Sunday they wear the *plyachzishka:* all is white on head and shoulders, while the gown, the *wohnjanka*, is black. Then is the old church at Burg a sight that recalls Brittany. The men for the most part are in the galleries. Almost the entire floor of the church is filled with seated women, their starched caps, as white as white can be, having the effect of stiffened windrows of snow.

But on other Sundays the young women

appear in all their finery. Many of them enter the village barefoot, and put their shoes and stockings on just before assembling in front of the church. The men gather in one group, the women in another. As a gentle reminder of the uncertainty of life, the first thing one sees in the vestibule of the church is a pair of coffin-rests, past which the people troop to their German prayers and Vendish sermon. After the services a baptism may be held, when the godmothers (*kmotra*) are expected to appear in a special kind of white cap very difficult to describe. When the baptism is over the party adjourns to a tavern, and the dresses and caps are duly criticized or admired, and the proud parents are expected to do the handsome thing by the friends and godparents. Godfathers and godmothers are also given a present of money, but not a round sum,—that is unlucky,—always a little over. The child must not be left alone; at least a bird or beast must be left with it to baffle evil spirits. The elder godmother carries the child to the church, the younger from the sanctuary. But before they reënter the home some one lays symbolical tools across the threshold over which the baptismal party must pass. For a boy it may be an ax and a hoe; for a girl a spinning-wheel and a broom. As she steps across, the younger godmother, bearing the child in her arms, says aloud, «We carried away a heathen, and bring back a Christian with the proper name of John [or Mary].» In some villages children are named in a fixed order as they are born, and if the baby dies the new child is given its name. Thus in Schleifa it is customary to give boys names in the following order: Hanzo, Matthes, Juro, Kito, Merten, Lobo; and to girls, Maria, Anna, Madlena, Liza, Khrysta, Wortija, Worsula.

Next to a baptismal procession a wedding party is the jolliest sight on Spreewald fliesses, since every one is naturally decked in his or her best, and the men carry staves bound with bright ribbons, said to be a survival of the swords of an earlier period when the bride was carried off more or less by force, or at least with a show of violence. *Kozol*, the bagpipes, still survive in some parts of the forest. The bridegroom, preceded by his *druzba*, or best man, a fiddler, and a bagpiper, and followed by his friends, knocks loudly at the door of the bride, and on being admitted demands the young woman with great show of wrath, only to receive, instead of the bride, an old maid who has a false hump on her back. The men strike her on the hump, which soon breaks, since it is an old cooking-pot, and drive her back into the house. Then the bridesmaid, or *druzka*, is given up; but she also is compelled to flee into the house. Finally the bride herself is handed to the best man, who places her beside the groom, whereupon the couple turn about three times, a peculiar pagan rite known formerly to Ireland and Scotland, and the whole party enters the house to breakfast. The Turkish and Finnish tribes of Asia have similar customs of teasing the groom and his best man before surrendering the bride. At the wedding both must have money in their shoes, or they will always be poor. On the return from the wedding a newly bought pot filled with milk and beer is sent to meet the couple; as soon as they have drunk, the *druzba* seizes the pot and dashes it to pieces. On reaching her new home, the bride must feed all the animals. At the wedding feast neither groom and bride nor best man and woman must rise from the table under any pretext whatever until dancing begins in the evening at the tavern.

But to tell all that is left of heathen and medieval Christian practices in the Spreewald would fill a book or two. The water-nixy is dangerous to young women who wade into ponds to cut reeds for thatch; the sandman has his female counterpart: when a boy nods it is Hermann that has come; when a girl gets sleepy over her spinning it is Dremotka. Reapers who fail to rest for an hour at midday are in danger of a ragged female demon called Pshespolniza; she comes with a sickle bound to a pole and cuts off their heads. She seems to have been sunstroke personified, but is now, like Serpowniza, only a bugbear used to frighten children away from growing crops.

Here in the Spreewald exist many of the superstitions common to Ireland and Scotland—the changeling, the whirlwind, will-o'-the-wisp, kobold, leprechawn, and good little people generally. Have is the crafty spirit of the lake and the demon that springs on men's shoulders at night. Here especially is the banshee; indeed, no less a family than the Hohenzollerns have a private and particular white lady who appears in the unsentimental vicinage of the Schloss in the heart of Berlin and wails round the battlements when a death is to occur in the family. Connection between the British Islands and the lands drained by the Elbe and the Vistula has been constantly renewed by migration and conquest. In remote periods the race seems to have been alike in both countries.

AFTER THE CHRISTENING.

But considerations so remote and afar off in history are not suited to the fore-deck of a Spreewald punt. Better to note the picturesque royal hunting-box at the Eiche, where the dogs rush down to the bank with great show of anger, or the forester's house where one can get a cup of coffee from the forester's wife. Then we plunge into a beautiful bit of woods, and emerge on the Kanno Mill, with its little side-lock for punts; and so, descending to a lower level, spurt forward into the dark woods that still retain some of the swampy characteristics of the Spreewald as it was a thousand years ago.

A touch of the bayous of the Mississippi is here. In this oozy soil the trees have given out buttresses above their deep-lying roots, and as one rounds such a bole and a new reach of the stream opens up, one expects at least an alligator on the slimy bank to make the touch complete. This is the tragic passage in the symphony. Thence through freshly planted woods to pastures new, and with a turn into a rushing contrary tide we head for Lehde, a closely built village gathered thickly about the highway and smaller water streets, there to land for dinner at the tavern of the Jolly Pike.

In Vendland we still are: witness houses that recall the mills in Hobbema's paintings; witness the heaps of giant pumpkins by the barns, and the bare-legged maids digging the first horse-radishes for the big distant city. But Lehde is near Lübbenau, and Lübbenau is a tight little town with cobblestoned streets, and a stately castle of the counts of Lynar (who descend, according to Vend tradition, from a dragon), and a beautiful old saw-mill, and a park—and, alas! a railway. Lehde, with its tavern suited for hundreds of thirsty citizens, begins already to let one gently down from medieval Vendland into modern Germany—Lehde, with her hundred factories and hideous furniture and cheap, ugly clothes. The flowers are gone, and the nightingale and the cuckoo, and the broad arable lands brightened by the rich spot of a laboring maid's skirt, and the solemn aisles with their silvery floor and their canopy of black branches.

But the storks cling to Lehde, and the wise, thieving magpies know it, and the swallows and gnat-catchers and bats skim over its roofs of tile and thatch, while below are its fleets of white ducks and its busy barn-yard fowls. But one sad thing about Lehde is the orchestrion at the inn as it grinds out dance-measures to the infinite content of mine host of the Jolly Pike.

A BACHELOR.

The Spreewald is a «happy hunting-ground» for pedestrian and cyclist in summer. When the snow spares the great and little streams, the cross fliesses and those still smaller cuts in the meadows which just admit one hay-punt and no more, then is it a country that can be explored on skates even more delightfully than in punt or canoe. There is leisure then for the hard-worked Spreewälder and his wife and maids; merry bands glide from village to village. 'T is as if a bit of Holland had been taken up bodily and dropped between Dresden and Berlin.

THE MORNING TOILET.

Philosophy and science may be said to have begun for northern Germany with Leibnitz, a Vend; and universities with that of Prague in the land of the Czechs, who can boast of the first school of art in Germany, and of a reformer of the church before Luther, namely, Huss; yes, and the first pleader for rational education, Amos Comenius.

The handsomest officers who ride in the Thiergarten and parade on Tempelhofer Platz are apt to have Vendish names ending in *itz*, *witz*, and *ow;* they have the slim figure, smallish hands and feet, and often the pure Greek profile which is sometimes seen in the peasantry of the Spreewald.[1] The women are, comparatively speaking, less favored; but the soft, clear-cut, rather longish features, fine complexions, long, straight, thin noses, clear

[1] The Vends of the Spreewald do not call themselves Vends, but Serbjo, Serbski, or Sserski; that is to say, Servians. It has been argued that Vend is a term used by the Teutons to designate them, and attempts have been made to explain it as a Teutonic root. The fact seems to be that Vend is a very antique generic term—equivalent to, but older than, Slav—which was used in the earliest times for the whole race throughout Europe and Asia, while Slav, Slovak, Russ, Czech, Pole, Serb, and Sorb were less comprehensive terms used by various parts of the Vendic race. The Serbs on the Danube preserve the same word as the Serbs on the Spree to designate themselves in a narrow sense.

THE NIGHT WATCHMAN.

foreheads, and small hands and feet, distinguish them from their more purely Teutonic sisters. Men and women are, as a rule, handsomer than their racial relatives the Saxon Slavs and the Czechs who dwell at the head waters of the Elbe. They are great worshipers of rank and precedence; the faint tendency toward democracy which the Teutonic races in Germany are supposed to show can hardly be found among them. Faithful to their royal houses, they have borne patiently the tyranny and insolence toward weaker races which seem part and parcel of the Teuton wherever he is found; it is only very recently that there have been some stirrings of a race feeling similar to that which has always inflamed the hardier and more combative Bohemians. Last year a call went out from the Czechs of Bohemia to the Serbs (Vends) of Saxony about Bautzen and Zittau to remember their past, and read the papers which are devoted to the old literature of these disjointed portions of the Slav race. And as in Ireland the worshipers of the fetish of Anglo-Saxondom regard with distrust the endeavor to keep the Irish tongue alive, and try to boycott the Celtic elements in British speech and literature, so the Teuton in the older home of his race boycotts the Slavic elements in northern Germany, and denies their very existence if he can. There they are under his nose, but, with the obstinacy to facts which is at once his strength and his weakness, he will not see; or if he is forced to look, he explains the facts away in some fashion that suits his clumsy pride.

Some of the changes of government to which the patient Vends have had to submit may be recalled on examining one of three bells which were dismounted from a belfry in Lübbenau last summer. Cast in 1625 by Mathias Paust in Prague, it bears the inscription, «I praise the true God, call together the people, convoke the priesthood, lament the dead, drive out the devil, beautify festivals.»[1]

For one hundred and eighty years it rang for the Vendish subjects of the Saxon kings and electors, and for nearly a hundred years for subjects of Prussia. It has seen the Swede, the Russian, and the Frenchman in the streets of Lübbenau. Very little hand in the making of the government have the good people for whom it did over two and a half centuries of service. I ask my boatman if he ever votes. No; it is done, if done at all, by certain big men of his village. But does n't he vote for the Reichstag? No; he seems to

[1] «Laudo Deum verum, plebem voco, congrego clerum, defunctos ploro, Satanam fugo, festa decoro.»

have a very hazy idea what the Reichstag may be, and is quite content with the apology for representation in Prussia, without pushing political activity so inordinately far as to avail himself of the rights of universal suffrage in the empire.

The Vends are great church-goers, but if their legends mean anything, their Christianity is, so to speak, but of yesterday. It was not so long ago that Sunday was a day for heavy drinking, and the sermon a good occasion to sleep off the excesses of Saturday night in order to be ready for the bout of the afternoon. Christianity was forced upon them by the Teutons, beginning with Charles the Great.

Like the Irish, the two hundred thousand Vends of Prussia and Saxony (they of Lower and Upper Lusatia) have ever been an agricultural race, obstinate in retaining their language under the sneers of the ruling race and the violent objections of many of their own. As the half-educated Irishman of Celtic stock reviles the Irish-speaking rustic, and does what he can to prevent the old tongue from being taught in schools and used in church, so the Vends who have become partially Germanized persecute their old language more vindictively than do the Germans themselves. And again, as in Ireland some of the most effective forefighters in the cause of Irish have been Englishmen, so in Lusatia various German scholars, like Dr. Sauerwein, have been the boldest to denounce Germans for persecutions and recreant Vends for treachery to their own. Practical rising men in Lusatia, as in Ireland, oppose the old tongue because they believe that its cultivation hinders a boy from getting on materially in the world. It is this idea oftener than a dislike to keeping up the separation between Vend and German which animates these shallow-pates.

In some parts of the Spreewald the pleasant fashion of the spinning-wheel is retained. The *spinnte* or *spinne* is a room where girls work together, also a society for spinning, talking gossip, and having fun, which has taken on a certain festive air since steam-looms have driven out private weaving. Thread for sewing is still made. In the Yule week, and especially on *Fastnacht*, the spinning-room where the village girls meet is the place for mummeries carried out by the boys, such as *Baćona vozyć* (leading the stork), *Mjedweća vozyć* (leading the honey-snatcher, or bear), or *Kona vozyć* (leading the horse), in which figure boys dressed in straw or sheets to resemble stork, bear, and horse, with their attendants. Faces are smutted with soot, and practical jokes are in order. In northern Germany the word *spinnte*, originally the room where the spinsters met, has come to mean a cupboard. If some of the maids

ENGRAVED BY PETER AITKEN.

AT THE DOOR-STEP.

began to nod over their spinning, one would creep out, and putting on rags, would return as Dremotka, the sandwoman, and indulge in various pranks that waked the sleepy ones and made everybody laugh. A favorite bugbear of the Vends was a race of supernatural beings called *Graben* or *Draben*, friendly with the water-nixy, but not with mankind. They persecuted girls, and had a taste for horseflesh in that they occasionally devoured a peasant's horse. As they were reported to open the window of the spinning-room and thrust in a horse's hoof, the village boys knew just what to do in order to put the girls in a panic. The Graben or Draben seem to have been a sort of satyrs, since they had horses' legs and lived in caves in the woods and wastes, but often slipped into the villages in the form of men. They were creatures of extraordinary strength, but easily duped, and were often seen in bearskins. Evil things were said of them—cannibalism, for example. What remains in popular memory concerning them seems a condensation of memories of satyrs, bears, and robber knights.

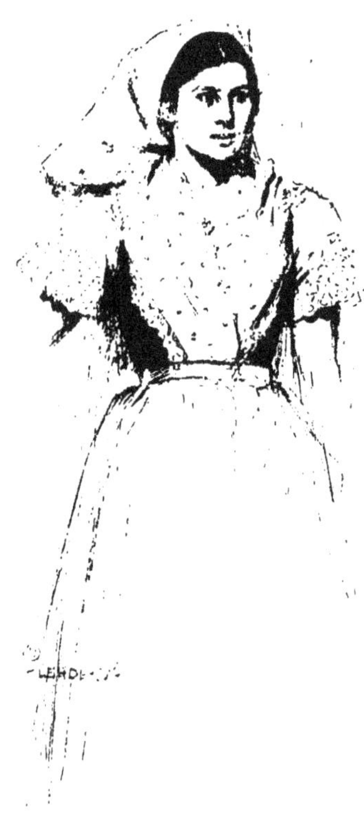

A SPREEWALD BEAUTY.

The Spreewald men have always proved docile soldiers, and when well led are dangerous foes. Even in 1848 the Vendish regiments could not be alienated from their Saxon and Prussian kings. Unfair laws and social disabilities have driven many across the ocean. Indeed, the children in some villages sing a song about the stork—a song which makes America, not Africa, the place to which the stork migrates. In Bastrop County, Texas, there was not long ago, and probably is to-day, a village called Serbin, all of Vends, who still speak the old tongue and have a newspaper in their own old language. The Vendish literature, comparatively recent, has some noted luminaries. The promising young poet Kočyk, however, emigrated to America some years ago. Emigration and stupid officials are fast ruining the Spreewald. A railway has been projected to cut straight through the heart of the swamp and destroy the last vestiges of its antiquity.

Odd and charming is the Serbian marsh in Vendland, and not less interesting when we think of its indwellers as a fragment of the great scattered Slav race that forms an important section of Austria, is well represented in Hungary, and occupies most of the eastern parts of Prussia. The remnant is very small compared with Teutons and Teutonized Slavs, but valiantly has it fought in its own silent, bovine way against the assumptions and advice of the Teutons.

These little tribes and nations have a consciousness and vigor nowadays which former centuries lacked, because science has scouted many dull pretensions and history has connected many humble peoples with a not inglorious past. Panslavists have hoped that, proceeding from Russia as a great center of population, the Russian language and religion and government would some day break their barriers and reoccupy the old territory even as far westward as the Vendish forest on the Spree. The century has proved how fantastic was this hope. Scientists know the usefulness of variety of race and language to a country, so long as the disruptive elements are not too great; but governments and official classes

HOME WITH THE DAY'S HARVEST.

are timid, and seek to destroy all such differences for fear of complications. As we are poled home through the dark fliesses, scaring with our lantern the birds that are roosting over the stream, we mourn the folly of great nations in trying to reduce everybody to the level of one tongue and one habit of ugly clothes.

The little tribes and nations of the earth,
Oh, crush them not, mortals of coarser breed!
Your beefy insolence tramples on their mirth,
Their woods and pastures melt before your greed.
Cherish the shy things in the swamp that grow;
In vain ye search the spot that once has borne
White violets of the red lip, white as snow,
Or lilies making grand some isle forlorn.

*Charles de Kay.*

## ART.

SAID Life to Art, «I love thee best
  Not when I find in thee
My very face and form expressed
  With dull fidelity;

«But when in thee my craving eyes
  Behold continually
The mystery of my memories
  And all I long to be.»

*Charles G. D. Roberts.*

JEREED PLAY.

(SEE PAGE 563.)

# IN THE DESERT WITH THE BEDOUIN.[1]

WITH ILLUSTRATIONS BY THE AUTHOR.

HASSAN-ABU-MEGABEL.

NATURE is generally credited with the making of «gentlemen» other than those born into that enviable position in life; but among the various nationalities with whom I have had personal intercourse, I have met no fitter claimants to the title than the hardy sons of Ishmael, whose hospitality, generosity, and instinctive kindness have often smoothed the difficulties, and sometimes hardships, incidental to my life in the desert of Suez while the guest of the Samana, the Hanaardi, and the Nephaarta Arabs.

In attempting to give some description of Arab life I have no intention of entering upon any critical account of the habits of the people. This is a subject already exhausted by many eminent writers, and leaves little new for me to say.

I purpose to view the Bedouin in their more picturesque aspect as presented to an artist wandering among them in search of material. Nor have I any thrilling adventures to narrate, my reminiscences being mainly pastoral, patriarchal, and pictorial.

## TOLL-GATHERER RATHER THAN BANDIT.

RATHER erroneously, I think, the Bedouin are associated in the public mind with tales of robbery and bloodshed; and though an accidental encounter with a party of wandering Arabs is not always conducive to the comfort or material advantage of the unprotected traveler, the Bedouin are far from being the savage bandits usually supposed.

Shepherds and nomads for generations, their energies are mainly confined to the rearing of flocks of sheep and goats and the breeding of camels and horses. Robbery is more or less incidental, and not a practice, and is embarked upon very largely as a variety in the monotony of their lives. Nevertheless, as the only governing power of the otherwise uninhabited wastes that they frequent, they have some justification for exacting an unwilling tribute from those traversing their country. I remember on one occasion finding a sheik's son arrayed in a lady's silk dressing-gown; and on my asking him where he got it, he rather ambiguously replied: «You see, Allah has given those dirty Egyptians all that fat land, where they can sit down and see their food grow before them. *Our* inheritance is the desert»; adding meaningly, «We take toll of the desert.»

## FIRST MEETING WITH THE BEDOUIN.

MY first meeting with the Bedouin was accidental, though fortunately unattended with inconvenience to myself. It happened in this wise.

While staying in Fakous, in the province of Sharkieh, Egypt, as the guest of the sheik Mohamed Abdoon, an Arab sheik, Hassan-Abu-Megabel[2] by name, chanced that way, and, accepting Mohamed's proffered hospitality, was seated next me at the *sanniyeh*, or tray, on which our meal was served. I was greatly struck with the unbending dignity and noble appearance of the old man, and, as I began to break the meat in orientally orthodox manner, was little prepared for the burst of excitement with which he exclaimed: «Ha! here is an Englishman who understands us; he eats with his hands.»

This little incident immediately dispelled reserve, and led to a sympathetic exchange of compliments; and an interesting conversation followed, culminating in a pressing invitation from the sheik to visit his tribe in the Gizereh of Samana—an invitation I eagerly accepted.

Some few days later there arrived at Fakous a richly caparisoned horse, several pack-animals, and an escort of mounted Arabs to conduct me and my belongings to their encampment.

Remembering the unenviable reputation possessed by the Bedouin, it was not without

[1] The author and illustrator of this article furnished the pictures for Slatin Pasha's well-known work, «Fire and Sword in the Soudan.» He spends much of his time in Egypt, and is regarded as one of the most accurate delineators of desert life.—THE EDITOR.

[2] Hassan, son of the big one.

some foreboding that I bade farewell to civilization, and cut myself adrift from all communication with the outside world. The early morning ride, however, soon dissipated any feeling save one of growing exhilaration and unbounded enjoyment of the scenery, which increased as we gradually left behind us the fertile fields and date-groves of Fakous and entered the desert. It was one of those lovely mornings peculiar to the Egyptian spring. The sun, hardly risen, was trying to pierce the delicate film which obscured the sky overhead, though low on the horizon was a streak of blue which shone with a promise of brilliance and heat later on. The desert looked soft and kind in the tender light, and the distant palms rose mistily into the genial air like the plumes of some gray bird; while against them the blue smoke of a Bedouin fire, slowly ascending, completed the scheme of silver-gray in which our little party furnished the only spot of color.

A few hours later the blinding glare of the sun beating fiercely upon sand and rock formed a strange contrast to the gentleness of dawn, and gave me my first experience of the trying nature of desert life, where shade temperature is unknown and thirst is a constant companion.

### THE BEDOUIN AT HOME.

On reaching camp my reception was most gratifying—a perfect blending of respectful solicitude and hospitable welcome. After kissing my hand, the sheik assisted me to dismount, bidding me welcome, and saying that my visit brought a blessing on his house. Conducting me to my tent, he added, «This house is yours, and all it contains; do what you will with it and with us your servants»—a truly biblical greeting, and one which immediately suggested the days of Abraham: an illusion heightened when water was brought, and hands, face, and feet were washed before I was left to rest on the cushions in the tent, and the sheik retired to prepare the evening meal.

Under the Mohammedan code three days' hospitality is a right wayfarers may demand, though in the case of accepted friends the royal bounty of the host heaps favor after favor upon the guest, without stint or limitation.

Probably the first distinct impression I received from the Bedouin was the close resemblance of their life to that of Old Testament times. Their loose, flowing robes added to their naturally tall and imposing appearance, and their strong, majestic faces, slightly Jewish in type, together with their gracious Old-World courtesies, irresistibly suggested the patriarchs of old. Their lives, thoughts, sayings, and occupations remain unchanged through all these centuries, and the incidents and conversations of my daily intercourse with them were always Abrahamic in character.

Though nomads, the Arabs are rovers from necessity rather than from choice, and where fodder and water are found in sufficient abundance they form permanent camps, surrounding their tents with a compound of

A BEDOUIN TENT.

A NEPHAARTA HORSE.

durra stalks, and frequently building stone or mud lodges for their guests.

When on the march they are content with very small tents, easily packed and carried, but in their permanent camps their homes are of regal proportions. The one I occupied covered some two thousand square feet, and was about eleven feet high in the center, sloping to five feet or so at the sides. The tent-cloth was, as usual, made of goat-hair, and party-colored in broad stripes of black, green, maroon, blue, and white, while from the seams depended tassels from which other cloths are hung to divide the tent into separate apartments when occupied by a family.

The furniture is simple. Rugs are spread over the sand, and reclining cushions scattered about them. In the corner is a *zeer*, or large water-pot, and by it a *cubiyeh*, or drinking-cup, of brass or copper. Round the side of the tent is a row of painted boxes, in which are packed the household goods and chattels when moving, while a few quaintly wrought lamps, and, half buried in the sand, a large earthen bowl used as a fireplace, complete the list.

Very domestic in their habits, everything about them has personal associations. The tent-cloths are spun, dyed, and woven by their women and children, as also are their saddle-cloths and trappings; and these are so highly prized by them that money cannot buy the simplest product of their wives' industry, though they may give them freely in token of friendship. Generally married to one wife, the Bedoui[1] regards her and her children with a devotion not general among Orientals, and I believe that the Arab word *watan* is the only real equivalent in any language for the English word «home.»

## NO «BAKSHISH.»

I HAD not much time for quiet observation, as one by one all the head men of the tribe called to pay their respects to the «stranger within their gates.» Taking off his shoes at the entrance, each one advanced with many salaams, and kissing my hand, uttered the single word, «*Mahubbah!*» («Welcome!») They then seated themselves in a long row

[1] Singular of Bedouin.

GLOOM AND GLEAM IN THE DESERT.

at the other side of the tent, discussing me in undertones. No one spoke to me unaddressed, and even the sheik himself, whose guest I was, would not sit on the carpet beside me uninvited. Literally, while the guest of the Bedouin your tent is sacred, and all the tribe are your willing servants; and though I have repeatedly paid comparatively long visits to them, I have never yet succeeded in pressing a gift upon my host.

I remember asking the sheik Saoudi el Tahoui, chief of the Hanaardi Arabs, if he knew any of the Pyramid Arabs at Gizeh. He replied, spitting upon the ground, «*They* are not Bedouin; they take bakshish»—thereby expressing his contempt for mercenary service. On another occasion, while living with the Nephaarta, the sheik Mansour Abu Nasrullah had attached to me a young Arab whose special duty it was to attend to my various wants while painting. At the end of the month I tried to induce him to accept a sovereign as bakshish. Looking very much alarmed, he exclaimed, «Oh, my master, I cannot; it is not allowed; the sheik would kill me if he knew I had accepted a gift»; and all my arguments failed to persuade him to take the «tip.»

## FOOD, TALK, AND FIRE.

DESERT life induces habits of abstemiousness. Rising with the sun, a dish of *cumis*, or mare's milk, and a small cup of black coffee are the only refreshments generally partaken of. The day is spent following one's pursuits, and with the exception of an occasional cup of coffee and some very light «snack,» one has no meal of any kind till after sundown. One quickly becomes accustomed to long fasting and abstinence from any form of drink, and the simple dinner at night is more keenly enjoyed in consequence. Though plain, the food is excellently cooked, and usually consists of a huge tray of rice over which is poured a dish of *semna*, or liquid butter; round the tray are pigeons stuffed with nuts and spices; and the pyramid of rice is surmounted by a lamb or kid, frequently cooked whole. Boiled beans, and perhaps a few fresh herbs, appear occasionally, which, with the usual flat loaves and a large dish of *riz-bil-laban*, or boiled rice-pudding, complete the meal. Salt is seldom seen,—a distinct privation,—except on the first day of your visit, and drinking-water is often scarce. After dinner a huge fire of corn-cobs, or sticks and camel dung, is lighted in the tent, about which we gather—and enjoy the after-dinner cup of coffee and a smoke, and, should we be in the mood, talk.

The Arabs have one excellent point of etiquette: Talk for talk's sake is not expected. Ever ready for a yarn, they eagerly respond should you wish to converse, but the luxury of silence is not denied if one's mood be thoughtful.

The idea of a fire in one's tent may strike some of my readers as a superfluity; but the nights are often intensely cold, and after bathing in the sun all day, with the thermometer at ninety-five to one hundred degrees in the shade, the sudden fall of temperature to little above freezing-point is very trying; and in spite of fire, blankets, and a thick ulster, I have frequently been obliged to go outside and run about in order to restore circulation to my half-frozen extremities.

### NIGHT IN THE DESERT.

NIGHT in the desert is very solemn. Surrounded by these sandy wastes melting in the gloom, the silence of nature is almost painful, and the occasional howl of a jackal or neigh of a horse only serves to accentuate the succeeding stillness, while the wonderfully rare atmosphere makes the stars appear of such unusual size and nearness that one feels oppressed with a sense of lonely littleness. I am often asked how I occupy my time in the desert; my reply is, «Painting.» Everything is paintable, and the desert is always beautiful. Infinitely varied in texture and local color, prolific of wild flowers and insect life, its interest is unending, while its trackless expanse undulating to the horizon seems like an ocean suddenly petrified into absolute rest, and impresses the mind with a sense of vastness and repose which nothing, in my opinion, can equal. Again, as the effects of varying weather pass over the silent land, how perplexing are the quick transitions from gray to gold as passing sunbeams play hide-and-seek among its billows, or when the white heat of day gives place to the violets and yellows of sunset!

Added to the intrinsic beauty of the desert itself are the innumerable «subjects» always ready to hand—now a goatherd watching his flock, or a party of Arabs exercising their horses; about the tents domestic duties in full swing: a negro slave roasting coffee over a fire of cobs; black-robed women flitting from tent to tent; or a group of gaily dressed children, the girls playing «knucklebones» in the sand, the boys, as usual, indulging in the mischief readiest to hand. Everywhere a picture! An artist's paradise indeed, the only drawbacks of which are one's utter inability to accomplish a tithe of the subjects surrounding one, and the discomforts and hardships of its life.

BEDOUIN GOATHERDS.

### THE PICTURESQUE CAMEL.

I THINK my Arab friends never quite understood the object of my work, and I am afraid I must often have tried their patience severely as, perhaps for days together, I would keep a man trotting backward and forward on a camel, while, with sketch-book in hand, I studied the action of this most peculiarly constructed but preëminently picturesque necessity of the desert. Nature seems to have specially designed the camel as an artistic accessory to desert scenes; certainly no other form of animal life is so absolutely appropriate; and I have always a feeling of real affection for them, out of gratitude for their ungainly though pictorial proportions and quaint poses which have so often solved a difficulty in a composition.

A DESERT MODEL.

Man, however, upsets the artistic intention by making them beasts of burden—an interference with prime causes deeply resented by the long-suffering animals; for who has not noticed the look of lofty scorn with which the camel regards all things human?—an attitude of disdain once aptly summarized by a German friend of mine in the remark, «I do not like the camel; he is too aristocratic.»

### PAINTING IN THE DESERT.

PAINTING in the desert is very arduous. The heat is often terrible, hands, face, and picture alike blistering under the powerful sun; and the daily mishaps, due perhaps to sudden gusts of wind which fill one's palette with dust and make one's canvas assume the appearance of sandpaper, or to the voracious onslaughts of sand-flies, are none the easier to bear for the occasional accompaniment of hunger and thirst. When working near camp, however, conditions are more favorable, as, surrounded by a group of Bedouin, all eager to render one some service,—an occasional cup of coffee, a dish of cumis, and in certain localities a cucumber or a basket of mulberries,—life is made pleasant, and one is predisposed to appreciate the unconscious humor of Bedouin criticisms. I overheard a man one day remark: «Why does the pasha sit all day in the sun? If I were he I would paint in the tent in comfort, and when I returned to England would say, ‹See, this is the desert›; but this one must have everything exact!» And another wondered why *his* tent was not in the picture: it was nearer than Mahmoud's, and I could see it quite well if I turned round! It was only when I made studies of their horses that they showed any real appreciation of my work. These they love, and could well understand my making pictures of their beauties; and I took no little credit to myself when by any chance they recognized the horse depicted.

After painting all day in the sweltering sun (for I never used an umbrella), wearied with the heat and glare, and tired mentally and physically, how I used to enjoy my evening lounge in the tent! Nor were the scenes there any less picturesque than those of the day, when, supper being finished, my dusky friends would respond to my invitation, and *t'fadd'l* round the fire. What a group they made as, only partly seen through the smoke, their swarthy features and voluminous draperies glowed in the flickering light, in bold relief against the gloom of the tent beyond—a picture of gold and rubies in an ebony frame! Weird and mysterious in the smoky air, it might sometimes have been a dream as, sitting in silence waiting for me to speak, the stillness of the scene was broken only by an occasional grunt from one of the men, or by the stirring of the embers.

### A DEMONSTRATION.

SITTING there one night, conversation turned on other countries and peoples, and I had been relating some of my experiences among the Moors, when a man called Abd-el-Messieh,[1] whom I had known in Egypt, suddenly exclaimed, «The pasha has been to Iceland!»

«*Ya, salaam*!»[2] they all exclaimed; «yesterday at the north pole, to-day in the desert! Tell us all about Iceland, *effendim!*»

As they were not to be denied, I described as best I could the volcanoes and wonderful lava flows, glaciers and huge rivers, waterfalls and geysers, peculiar to that country of geological surprises, all of which they seemed fully to understand.

Finally I told them that the sun shone night and day in summer, and never shone at all in winter. Immediately, with hand to mouth, and cries of «Impossible!» they protested that I was playing upon their credulity; for did not the sun rise every day, and set each night? Their own eyes saw it. Ya, salaam!

Without immediately replying, I called for a lamp and a gouleh, and turning the gouleh upside down to represent the globe, with an ember from the fire I marked upon it the relative positions of Iceland and Egypt.

«See,» I said, «is not the earth round just like this water-pot?»

«Yes, yes; we believe it is so.»

«Very well, then,»—and holding the lamp in one hand, and turning the water-pot in the other, I continued:

«You see that both Iceland and Egypt have half night and half day; but in summer the sun is high» (raising the lamp), «and Egypt still gets half day and half night, while Iceland gets *all* sun.»

«Salaamat!»

«But in winter the sun is low» (lowering the lamp and still turning the water-pot), «and Egypt has night and day, while Iceland has no sun at all.»

The success of this object-lesson was complete, for, jumping up excitedly, they exclaimed: «Oh, wonderful! We have read this in books, but never believed it. *You* have made it clear to our intelligence; we know it *must* be so.»

This incident struck me as a forcible proof of their ready perception and appreciation of any information, and I was somewhat surprised to learn that they had any knowledge of the existence, even, of a country so remote from their own as Iceland. Intelligent to a degree, the Bedouin have little of what we call education. Poems and tribal songs, tales of adventure and legendary lore, are handed down by word of mouth, book-learning being virtually unknown; indeed, few of them can even write their names.

### BEDOUIN AND EGYPTIANS.

LACKING education themselves, their respect for superior knowledge is great, and they eagerly listen to and absorb such information as may be gleaned in their casual intercourse with the peoples met during their wanderings. However, great as is their respect for knowledge, they hold horsemanship in still greater esteem, and I attribute much of my success in dealing with the Arabs to the fact that I could ride the half-wild desert stallions, in which my previous experience of rough-riding in Morocco stood me in good stead. Indeed, their contempt for their neighbors the Egyptians is completely expressed in their common reference to them as «those dirty Egyptians who cannot ride a horse.» I may here remark that in their habits and persons the Bedouin are a very clean people—a claim the most ardent admirer of the Egyptian can hardly maintain in their case; and I have known of Arabs who, obliged to cross the delta, have carried out with them sufficient desert sand with which to cover the ground before they would deign to pitch their tents or sit upon the «dirty soil of Masr.» Differing from the Egyptians in many essential points, their love for dumb animals is in marked contrast to the cruelty practised upon them by nearly all classes in Egypt; but perhaps in no way is the contrast more clearly shown than by the respect in which the Bedouin hold their womankind. Moslems of the strictest type, they seem to practise all that is good

[1] Slave of the Messiah.

[2] «Oh, blessing!»—a common form of expression in the East to denote surprise or incredulity.

in Mohammedanism, and avail themselves but little of its license.

While my own days were mainly spent in catching effects or studying incidents of their life, the Bedoui spends his time in the enjoyment of equestrian exercise, or in ministering to the wants of his beasts.

### HORSES.

THE Hanaardi and Nephaarta Arabs are famous horse-breeders, and take great pride in their stud. These horses are, I think, the best «Arabs» I have seen; and far from being the gazelle-like creatures usually depicted, they are strongly built, large-boned animals of from fifteen to fifteen and a half hands high. I have seen one of sixteen and a half hands, but this is unusual. Their immense neck and shoulders make them appear perhaps a little light behind; but they have plenty of staying power, and their length of hock is an earnest of the speed they undoubtedly possess. Parties from these tribes are constantly roaming the deserts of Syria and Mesopotamia in search of good brood-mares; and I have heard of as much as a thousand guineas being paid for one, and a good brood-mare is never parted with or ridden.

I remember seeing a bunch of Nephaarta horses brought in for the inspection of an emissary of the Khedive who wished to purchase a pair for his Highness. There were some twenty or twenty-five of the most beautiful colts possible, with the exception of one rather weedy-looking beast. As soon as Sheik Mansour saw it he shouted: «Take it away, and give it to the first man you meet. I will not own *that* as a Nephaarta horse!» The Khedive's agent eventually selected two, for which I saw him pay five hundred pounds Egyptian.

Entire Arab horses are always rather difficult to ride at first, though after a few days, when horse and rider have become reconciled, they are docile enough, and easily trained. Each man has virtually to break his horse to his own hand, and should another mount an apparently quiet beast, he would have to do the work all over again. It seems to be a tacit understanding between horse and rider that their joint career begins with a struggle for the mastery. To a visitor like myself, whose mounts must constantly be changing, the prospect is sufficiently alarming. One's early days in an Arab camp are frequently days of pain and tribulation, as one slowly recovers from a bout with a half-savage stallion.

Though they eventually become quiet and obedient to their masters' hand, great care must be observed, when riding in company, not to allow one's horse to approach within kicking-distance of another, or disastrous results follow. The horses are always ready for a fight, and deceitfully appear to be on their best behavior immediately before an outbreak. I was riding one day with a small party of Samana Arabs, when two men carelessly approached too close. I called out to them to sheer off a little, but before they could respond a general mêlée was in progress, and almost instantly my horse had its teeth in the neck of one of theirs, while the other was killed by a kick which burst its stomach. Fortunately we all escaped with a few bruises, though the riders do not always get off so easily. When riding at full gallop, however, the attention of the horses is concentrated upon the race, and the men may ride as close together as they like, but care must be taken to wheel apart as the pace slackens.

Nothing can exceed the intoxication of a race in the desert. Choosing a stretch of level sand, you give your horse the signal to go, and he is off with a spring that almost unseats you; and I have seen an instance where the sudden strain burst the girths, and left man and saddle in the dust, while the horse was a hundred yards away before the discomfited rider realized what had happened. The speed that these horses attain is very great, and their reach forward is prodigious, as I found on one occasion when my horse's hind hoof cut the heel clean off my boot! After a gallop, instead of breaking into a canter and then into a trot before stopping, they simply put their fore feet together and stop dead, their impetus frequently causing them to slide several yards. I understand that it is on this account that Arab horses are shod on the fore feet only.

Such riding is exciting and, until one is accustomed to it, alarming. I must confess to a feeling of abject cowardice as I have seen my steed brought up, requiring three or four men to hold it, and have realized that I must «get up» and stick there. Fortune, however, has always favored me: I have not so far been unseated, thereby acquiring a reputation for horsemanship to which I feel I have no real claim.

The Arabs themselves are beautiful horsemen, and keenly enjoy fancy riding, and delight in showing off their skill. One of their tricks is to mark out a course by water-jars placed alternately on each side some little distance apart. Urging his horse into a furious gallop, the rider, hanging from the saddle, will then with incredible rapidity pick up a gouleh, and swinging it over to the opposite side, exchange it for another, repeating this some dozen times without cracking a pot!

Another trick, rather disconcerting at first, is to charge straight at you, stopping abruptly with the horse's nose almost touching your own, while etiquette forbids any attempt on your part to get out of the way!

I have only once seen a Bedoui come to grief, and it happened to poor old Hassan-Abu-Megabel, formerly a great rider and warrior, but now an old man of eighty, who, in giving an exhibition of skill, slipped and fell heavily. «Save the throne of the prophet!» was the cry, as Hassan's turban rolled merrily over the sand. «Bother the prophet! Save your sheik!» was his indignant answer. Picking the old man up, they found him unhurt, though he seemed to feel the disgrace very keenly, and has never been the same man since.

ALMOST WAR. JEREED PLAY.

By far the most exciting of their equestrian sports, however, is their *jereed*, or short javelin, «play.» I put play in quotation-marks to express the sarcasm of it, for I never saw anything more nearly approaching war in my life. Two friendly tribes meet in a suitable bit of desert, several hundred mounted men representing each tribe, and are drawn up facing each other. Twirling his jereed, the champion of one side rides into the open, and in a loud voice and with much eloquence recounts his deeds of valor, and with many sarcasms challenges one of the other side to fight. On the appearance of an opposing champion in the arena, the first turns to flee, chased by the second, and endeavors to reach his own side before being caught by his pursuer. Should he succeed in escaping, both turn again, and the positions of fugitive and pursuer are reversed; but it always ends in a fierce fight for supremacy in the middle, in which one or the other is generally unseated, often with the accompaniment of a few broken ribs or a fractured arm or leg. Champions being eventually placed *hors de combat*, the remaining bodies charge at each other and engage, and in the excitement of the moment, when several hundred men and their horses are involved in the scrimmage, the death of several men and horses frequently results before the «sport» concludes with light refreshments and a possible funeral or two.

As I remarked before, this is the nearest approach to war possible, and is almost as exciting for the onlooker as for those engaged. No bad blood is engendered, however, whatever the casualties may be, this being an honorable exhibition of skill, where no malice is borne, and any fatality—«kismet!»

*R. Talbot Kelly.*

## THE DEATH-DREAM OF ARMENIA.

A CRY from pagan dungeons deep
  To Albion old and brave;
A wail that startles from her sleep
  The mistress of the wave.

We feel the thrill through England's soul
  Of noblest passion's birth;
We hear her drum-alarum roll
  The circle of the earth.

When mothers kiss with pallid lips
  The wounds of murdered sons,
We see the sailors on her ships
  Leap to their shotted guns.

We hear her martial trumpets blow
  The challenge of the free;
Her lean steel war-wolves howling go
  Through gateways of the sea.

The talons of her eagles tear
  The vulture from his feast;
The lion mangles in his lair
  The tiger of the East.

Ah, what a cheer from Asia breaks
  And roars along the dawn,
As rescue's battle-thunder shakes
  The walls of Babylon!

*Will H. Thompson.*

(BEGUN IN THE NOVEMBER NUMBER.)

# HUGH WYNNE, FREE QUAKER:

## SOMETIME BREVET LIEUTENANT-COLONEL ON THE STAFF OF HIS EXCELLENCY GENERAL WASHINGTON.

BY DR. S. WEIR MITCHELL,

Author of «In War Time,» «When all the Woods are Green,» etc.

WITH PICTURES BY HOWARD PYLE.

XI.

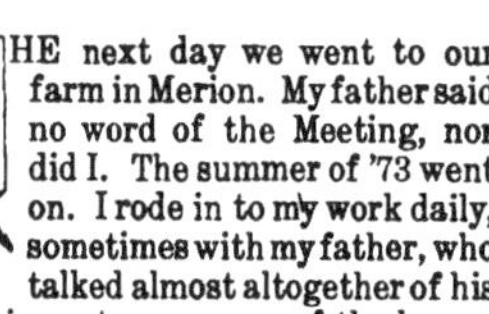

HE next day we went to our farm in Merion. My father said no word of the Meeting, nor did I. The summer of '73 went on. I rode in to my work daily, sometimes with my father, who talked almost altogether of his cattle or of his ventures, never of the lowering political horizon. He had excused himself from being a consignee of the tea, on the score of his voyage, which was now intended for September.

My aunt lived in summer on the farther slope of Chestnut Hill, where, when the road was in order, came her friends for a night, and the usual card-play. When of a Saturday I was set free, I delighted to ride over and spend Sunday with her, my way being across country to one of the fords on the Schuylkill, or out from town by the Ridge or the Germantown highroad. The ride was long, but, with my saddle-bags and Lucy, a new mare my aunt had raised and given me, and clad in overalls, which we called tongs, I cared little for the mud, and often enough stopped to assist a chaise out of the deep holes which made the roads dangerous for vehicles.

Late one day in August I set out with my friend Jack to spend a Sunday with my Aunt Gainor. Jack Warder was now a prime favourite, and highly approved. We rode up Front street, and crossed the bridge where Mulberry street passed under it, and is therefore to this day called Arch street, although few know why. The gay coats of officers were plentiful, farmers in their smocks were driving in with their vegetables, and to the right was the river, with here and there a ship, and, beyond, the windmill on the island. We talked of the times, of books, of my father's voyage, and of my future stay with my aunt.

Although Jack's father was a Quaker, he was too discreet a business man not to approve of Jack's visits to my aunt, and too worldly not to wish for his son a society to which he was not born; so Mrs. Ferguson and Mrs. Galloway made much of Jack, and he was welcome, like myself, at Clieveden, where the Chews had their summer home.

The Tory ladies laughed at his way of blushing like a girl, and, to Jack's dismay, openly envied his pink-and-white skin and fair locks. They treated him as if he were younger than I, although, as it chanced, we were born on the same day of the same year; and yet he liked it all—the gay women, the coquettish Tory maids, even the «genteel» Quaker dames, such as Mrs. Sarah Logan or Mrs. Morris, and the pretty girls of the other side, like Sarah Lukens and the Misses Willing, with their family gift of beauty. These and more came and went at my aunt's, with men of all parties, and the grave Drs. Rush and Parke, and a changing group of English officers.

In the little old house at Belmont the Rev. Richard Peters was glad to sit at cards with the Tory ladies, whose cause was not his, and still less that of Richard, his nephew. At times, as was the custom, sleighing-parties in winter or riding-parties in summer used to meet at Clieveden or Springetsbury, or at a farm-house where John Penn dwelt while engaged in building the great house of Lansdowne, looking down over trees to the quiet Schuylkill.

We rode out gaily this August afternoon, along the Germantown road, admiring the fine farms, and the forests still left among the cultivated lands. Near Fisher's Lane we saw some two or three people in the road, and, drawing near, dismounted. A black man who lay on the ground, groaning with a cut head, and just coming to himself, I saw to be my aunt's coachman Cæsar. Beside him, held by a farmer, was a horse with a pillion and saddle, all muddy enough from a fall. Near by stood a slight young woman in a saveguard petticoat and a sad-coloured, short camlet cloak.

«It is Miss Darthea Peniston,» said Jack.

«Miss Peniston,» I said, dismounting, «what has happened?»

She told me quietly, that, riding pillion to stay with my aunt, the horse had fallen and hurt Cæsar, not badly, she thought. She had alighted on her feet, but what should she do? After some discussion, and the black being better, we settled to leave him, and I proposed that Jack, the lighter weight, should ride my Aunt Gainor's horse, with Miss Peniston on the pillion behind him. Upon this Jack got red, at the idea, I suppose, of Miss Darthea's contemplating the back of his head for four miles. The young woman looked on with shy amusement.

At this moment Cæsar, a much pampered person, who alone of all her house dared give my aunt advice, declared he must have a doctor. Jack, much relieved, said it was inhuman to leave him in this case, and put an end to our discussion by riding away to fetch old Dr. de Benneville.

Miss Darthea laughed, said it was a sad thing a woman should have no choice, and pretended to be in misery as to my unfortunate lot. I said nothing, but, after looking Cæsar's horse over, gave my saddle to be kept at the farmer's, and put the coachman's saddle on my mare Lucy, with the pillion behind made fast to the saddle-straps arranged for this use. Then I looked well to the girths, and mounted to see how Lucy would like it. She liked it not at all, and was presently all over the road and up against the fence of the old graveyard I was to see again in other and wilder days.

I saw the little lady in the road watching me with a smiling face, by no means ill pleased with the spectacle. At last I cried, «Wait!» and putting Miss Lucy down the road for a mile at a run, soon brought her back quite submissive.

«Art thou afraid?» I said.

«I do not like to be asked if I am afraid. I am very much afraid, but I would die rather than not get on your mare.» So a chair was fetched, Miss Peniston put on her linen riding-mask, and in a moment was seated behind me. For ten minutes I was fully taken up with the feminine creature under me. At last I sai :

«Put an arm around my waist. I must let her go. At once!» I added; for the mare was getting to rear a little, and the young woman hesitated. «Do as I tell thee!» I cried sharply, and when I felt her right arm about me, I said, «Hold fast!» and gave the mare her head. A mile sufficed, with the double burden, so to quiet her that she came down to her usual swift and steady walk.

When there was this chance to talk without having every word jolted out in fragments, the young person was silent; and when I remarked, «There is now an opportunity to chat with comfort,» she said:

«I was waiting, sir, to hear your excuses; but perhaps Friends do not apologise.»

I thought her saucy, for I had done my best; and for her to think me unmannerly was neither just nor kind.

«If I am of thy friends—»

«Oh, Quakers, I meant. Friends with a large F, Mr. Wynne.»

«It had been no jesting matter if the mare had given thee a hard fall.»

«I should have liked that better than to be ordered to do as your worship thought fit.»

«Then thou shouldst not have obeyed me.»

«But I had to.»

«Yes,» I said. And the talk having fallen into these brevities, Miss Peniston was quiet awhile, no doubt pouting prettily; her face was of course hid from me.

After a while she said something about the mile-stones being near together, and then took to praising Lucy, who, I must say, had behaved as ill as a horse could. I said as much, whereon I was told that mares were jealous animals, which I thought a queer speech, and replied, not knowing well how to reply, that the mare was a good beast, and that it was fair flattery to praise a man's horse, for what was best in the horse came of the man's handling.

«But even praise of his watch a man likes,» said she. «He has a fine appetite, and likes to fatten his vanity.»

She was too quick for me in those days, and I never was at any time very smart at this game, having to reflect too long before seeing my way. I said that she was no doubt right, but thus far I had had thin diet.

Perhaps saying that Lucy was gay and well bred and had good paces was meant to please the rider. This woman, as I found later, was capable of many varieties of social conduct, and was not above flattering for the mere pleasure it gave her to indulge her generosity, and for the joy she had in seeing others happy.

Wondering if what she had said might be true held me quiet for a while, and busied with her words, I quite forgot the young woman whose breath I felt now and then on my hair as she sat behind me.

Silence never suited Miss Peniston long in those days, and especially not at this time, she being in a merry mood, such as a little adventure causes. Her moods were, in fact, many and changeful, and, as I was to learn, were too apt to rule even her serious actions for the time; but under it all was the true law of her life, strongly charactered, and abiding like the constitution of a land. It was long before I knew the real woman, since for her, as for the most of us, all early acquaintance was a masquerade, and some have, like this lady, as many vizards as my Aunt Gainor had in her sandalwood box, with her long gloves and her mitts.

The mare being now satisfied to walk comfortably, we were going by the Wister house, when I saw saucy young Sally Wister in the balcony over the stoop, midway of the penthouse. She knew us both, and pretended shame for us, with her hands over her face, laughing merrily. We were friends in after-life, and if you would know how gay a creature a young Quakeress could be, and how full of mischief, you should see her journal, kept for Deborah Logan, then Miss Norris. It has wonderful gaiety, and, as I read it, fetches back to mind the officers she prettily sketches, and is so sprightly and so full of a life that must have been a joy to itself and to others, that to think of it as gone and over, and of her as dead, seems to me a thing impossible.

It was not thought proper then for a young woman to go on pillion behind a young man, and this Miss Sally well knew. I dare say she set it down for the edification of her young friend.

«The child» (she was rather more than that) «is saucy,» said my lady, who understood well enough what her gestures meant. «I should like to box her ears. You were very silent just now, Mr. Wynne. A penny is what most folks' thoughts are bid for, but yours may be worth more. I would not stand at a shilling.»

«Then give it to me,» said I. «I assure thee a guinea were too little.»

«What are they?»

«Oh, but the shilling.»

«I promise.»

«I seem to see a little, dark-faced child crying because of a boy in disgrace—»

«Pretty?» she asked demurely.

«No, rather plain.»

«You seem to have too good a memory, sir. Who was she?»

«She is not here to-day.»

«Yes, yes!» she cried. «I have her—oh, somewhere! She comes out on occasions. You may never see her; you may see her to-morrow.»

I was to see her often. «My shilling,» I said.

«That was only a jest, Mr. Wynne. My other girl has stolen it, for remembrance of a lad that was brave and—»

«He was a young fool. My shilling, please.»

«No, no!»

At this I touched the mare with my spur. She, not seeing the joke, pranced about, and Miss Darthea was forced to hold to my waist for a minute.

«The mare is ill broke,» she cried. «Why does she not go along quietly?»

«She hates dishonesty,» I said.

«But I have not a penny.»

«Thou shouldst never run in debt if thou art without means. It is worse than gambling, since here thou hast had a consideration for thy money, and I am out of pocket by a valuable thought.»

«I am very bad. I may get prayed over in Meeting, only we do not have the custom at Christ Church.»

I was struck dumb. Of course every one knew of my disaster and what came of it; but that a young girl should taunt me with it, and for no reason, seemed incredible. No one ever spoke of it to me, not even Mistress Ferguson, whose daily food was the saying of things no one else dared to say. I rode on without a word.

At last I heard a voice back of me quite changed—tender, almost tearful. «Will you pardon me, Mr. Wynne? I was wicked, and now I have hurt you who were once so good to me. Your aunt says that I am six girls, not one, and that— Will you please to forgive me?»

«Pray don't; there is nothing to forgive. I am over-sensitive, I suppose. My friend Mr. Wilson says it is a great thing in life to learn how to forget wisely. I am learning the lesson; but some wounds take long to heal, and this is true of a boy's folly. Pray say no more.» I put the mare to trotting, and we rode on past Clieveden and Mount Airy, neither speaking for a while.

I wondered, as we rode, at her rashness of talk and her want of consideration; and I reflected, with a certain surprise at the frequent discovery, of late, on how much older I seemed to be. It was a time which quickly matured the thoughtful, and I was beginning to shake off, in some degree, the lifelong shackles of limitation as to conduct, dress, and minor morals, imposed upon me by my home surroundings. In a word, being older than my years, I began to think for myself. Under the influence of Mr. Wetherill I had come, as without him I could not have done, to see how much there was of the beautiful and noble in the creed of Fox and Penn, how much, too, there was in it to cramp enterprise, to limit the innocent joys of life, to render progress impossible, and submission to every base man or government a duty.

I had learned, too, in my aunt's house, the ways and manners of a larger world, and, if I had yielded to its temptations, I had at least profited by the bitter lesson. I was on the verge of manhood, and had begun to feel as I had never done before the charm of woman; this as yet I hardly knew.

As we breasted the hill, and saw beneath us the great forest-land spread out, with its scattered farms, an exclamation of delight broke from my companion's lips. It was beautiful then, as it is to-day, with the far-seen range of hills beyond the river, where lay the Valley Forge I was to know so well, and Whitemarsh, all under the hazy blue of a cool August day, with the northwest wind blowing in my face.

Within there were my aunt and some young women, and my Cousin Arthur, with explanations to be made, after which my young woman hurried off to make her toilet, and I to rid me of my riding-dress.

It was about seven when we assembled out of doors under the trees, where on summer days my Aunt Gainor liked to have supper served. My Cousin Wynne left Mrs. Ferguson and came to meet me. We strolled apart, and he began to ask me questions about the tea cargoes expected soon, but which came not until December. I said my father's voyage would prevent his acting as consignee, and this seemed to surprise him and make him thoughtful, perhaps because he was aware of my father's unflinching loyalty. He spoke, too, of Mr. Wilson, appearing—and this was natural enough—to know of my intimacy with the Whig gentleman. I was cautious in my replies, and he learned, I think, but little. It was a pity, he said, that my father would not visit Wyncote. It seemed to me that he dwelt overmuch on this matter, and my aunt, who greatly fancied him, was also of this opinion. I learned long after that he desired to feel entirely assured as to the certainty of this visit not being made. I said now that I wished I had my father's chance to see our Welsh home, and that I often felt sorry my grandfather had given it up.

«But he did,» said my cousin, «and no great thing, either. Here you are important people. We are petty Welsh squires, in a decaying old house, with no money, and altogether small folk. I should like to change places with you.»

«And yet I regret it,» said I. My Aunt Gainor had filled me full of the pride of race.

I spoke as we approached the group about my aunt, and I saw his face take an expression which struck me. He had a way of half closing his eyes, and letting his jaw drop a little. I saw it often afterward. I suspect now that he was dealing intensely with some problem which puzzled him.

He seemed to me to be entirely unconscious of this singular expression of face, or, as at this time, to be off his guard; for the look did not change, although I was gazing at him with attention. Suddenly I saw come down the green alley, walled with well-trimmed box, a fresh vision of her who had been riding with me so lately. My cousin also became aware of the figure which passed gaily under the trees and smiled at us from afar.

«By George! Hugh,» said Arthur, «who is the sylph? What grace! what grace!»

For a moment I did not reply. She wore a silken brocade with little broidered roses here and there, a bodice of the same, cut square over a girl-like neck, white, and not yet filled up. Her long gloves were held up to the sleeve by tightens of plaited white horsehair, which held a red rosebud in each tie; and her hair was braided with a ribbon, and set high in coils on her head, with but little powder. As she came to meet us she dropped a curtsey, and kissed my aunt's hand, as was expected of young people.

I have tried since to think what made her so unlike other women. It was not the singular grace which had at once struck my cousin; neither was she beautiful. I long after hated Miss Chew for an hour because she said Darthea Peniston had not one perfect feature. She had, notwithstanding, clear, large brown eyes, and a smile which was so variously eloquent that no man saw it unmoved. This was not all. Her face had some of that charm of mystery which a few women possess—a questioning look; but, above all, there was a strange flavour of feminine attractiveness, more common in those who are older than she, and fuller in bud; rare, I think, in one whose virgin curves have not yet come to maturity. What she was to me that summer evening she was to all men—a creature of many moods, and of great power to express them in face and voice. She was young, she loved admiration, and could be carried off her feet at times by the follies of the gay world.

If you should wonder how, at this distant day, I can recall her dress, I may say that one of my aunt's lessons was that a man should notice how a woman dressed, and not fail at times to compliment a gown, or a pretty fashion of hair. You may see that I had some queer schoolmasters.

I said to my cousin, «That is Miss Darthea Peniston.»

«Darthea,» he repeated. «She looks the name. Sad if she had been called Deborah, or some of your infernally idiotic Scripture names.»

He was duly presented, and, I must say, made the most of his chances for two days, so that the elder dames were amused at Darthea's conquest, my cousin having so far shown no marked preference for any one except the elder Miss Franks, who was rich and charming enough to have many men at her feet, despite her Hebrew blood.

In truth he had been hit hard that fatal August afternoon, and he proved a bold and constant wooer. With me it was a more tardy influence which the fair Darthea as surely exerted. I was troubled and disturbed at the constancy of my growing and ardent affection. At first I scarce knew why, but by and by I knew too well; and the more hopeless became the business, the more resolute did I grow; this is my way and nature.

During the remaining weeks of summer I saw much of Miss Peniston, and almost imperceptibly was made at last to feel, for the first time in my life, the mysterious influence of woman. Now and then we rode with my aunt, or went to see the troops reviewed. I thought she liked me, but it soon became only too clear that at this game, where hearts were trumps, I was no match for my dark, handsome cousin, in his brilliant uniform.

## XII.

ON September 1, 1773, and earlier than had been meant, my father set sail for London with my ever dear mother. Many assembled to see the *Fair Trader* leave her moorings. I went with my people as far as Lewes, and on account of weather had much ado to get ashore. The voyage down the Delaware was slow, for from want of proper lights we must needs lay by at night, and if winds were contrary were forced to wait for the ebb.

While I was with them my father spoke much to me of business, but neither blamed my past nor praised my later care and assiduity in affairs. He was sure the king would have his way, and, I thought, felt sorry to have so readily given up the consigneeship of the teas. I was otherwise minded, and I asked what was to be done in the event of certain troubles such as many feared. He said that Thomas, his old clerk, would decide, and my Aunt Gainor had a power of attorney; as to the troubles I spoke of, he well knew that I meant such idle disturbances of peace as James Wilson and Wetherill were doing their best to bring about.

«Thy Cousin Arthur is better advised,» he said, «and a man of sound judgment. Thou mightst seek worse counsel on occasion of need.»

I was surprised at this, for I should have believed, save as to the king, they could not have had one opinion in common.

Far other were those sweeter talks I had with my mother as we sat on the deck in a blaze of sunlight. She burned ever a handsome brown, without freckles, and loved to sit out even in our great heats. She would have me be careful at my aunt's not to be led into idleness; for the rest I had her honest trust; and her blue eyes, bright with precious tears, declared her love, and hopeful belief. I must not neglect my French—it would keep her in mind; and she went on in that tongue to say what a joy I had been in her life, and how even my follies had let her see how true a gentleman I was. Then, and never before, did she say a thing which left on my mind a fear that life had not brought and kept for her throughout all the happiness which so good and noble a creature deserved.

«There is much of thy father in thee, Hugh. Thou art firm as he is, and fond of thine own way. This is not bad, if thou art thoughtful to see that thy way is a good way. But do not grow hard. And when thou art come to love some good woman, do not make her life a struggle.»

«But I love no woman, *ma mère*,» I cried, «and never shall, as I love thee. It is the whole of my love thou hast, *chère, chère maman*; thou hast it all.»

«Ah, then I shall know to divide with her, Hugh; and I shall be generous too. If thou hast any little fancies that way, thou must write and tell me. Oh, *mon fils*, thou wilt write often, and I must know all the news. I do hear that Darthea Peniston is in thy aunt's house a good deal, and Madam Ferguson, the gossip, would have me believe thou carest for her, and that Arthur Wynne is taken in the same net. I liked her. I did not tell thee that thy Aunt Gainor left her with me for an hour while she went into King street to bargain for a great china god. What a gay, winning creature it is! She must needs tell me all about herself. Why do people so unlock their hearts for me?»

I laughed, and said she had a key called love; and on this she kissed me, and asked did I say such pretty things to other women? As to Darthea, she was now to live with her aunt, that stiff Mistress Peniston, who was a fierce Tory. «She will have a fine bargain of the girl. She has twenty ways with her, real or false, and can make music of them all like a mocking-bird. Dost thou like her, Hugh?—I mean Darthea.»

I said, «Yes.»

«And so do I,» she ran on. «I loved her at sight. But if ever thou dost come to love her—and I see signs, oh, I see signs—if ever,—then beware of thy Cousin Wynne. I heard him once say to thy father, ‹If there is only one glass of the Madeira left, I want it, because there is only one.› And there is only one of a good woman. What another wants that man is sure to want, and I do not like him, Hugh. Thou dost, I think. He has some reason to linger here. Is it this woman? Or would he spy out the land to know what we mean to do? I am sure he has orders to watch the way things are going, or why should not he have gone with Sir Guy Carleton to Quebec? It is a roundabout way to go through Philadelphia.»

I said I did not know; but her words set me to thinking, and to wondering, too, as I had not done before. Another time she asked me why Arthur talked so as to disgust my father out of all idea of going to see the home of his ancestors. I promised to be careful as to my cousin, whom, to tell the truth, I liked less and less as time ran on.

At Lewes we parted. Shall I ever forget it? Those great blue eyes above the gunwale, and then a white handkerchief, and then no more. When I could no longer see the ship's hull I climbed a great sand-dune, and watched even the masts vanish on the far horizon. It was to me a solemn parting. The seas were wide and perilous in those days, the buccaneers not all gone, and the trading ship was small, I thought, to carry a load so precious.

As the sun went down I walked over the dunes, which are of white sand, and forever shifting, so as at one time to threaten with slow burial the little town, and at another to be moving on to the forest. As they changed, old wrecks came into view, and I myself saw sticking out the bones of sailors buried here long ago, or haply cast ashore. A yet stranger thing I beheld, for the strong northwest wind, which blew hard all day and favoured the *Fair Trader*, had so cast about the fine sand that the buried snow of last winter was to be seen, which seemed to me a thing most singular. When I told Jack, he made verses about it, as he did sometimes, but would show them only to me. I forget entirely what he wrote; how a man can make verses and dig rhymes out of his head has always been to me a puzzle.

At the town inn, «The Lucky Fisherman,» I saw, to my surprise, Jack on horseback, just arrived. He said he had a debt to collect for his father. It was no doubt true, for Jack could not tell even the mildest fib and not get rose-red. But he knew how I grieved at this separation from my mother, and, I think, made an occasion to come down and bear me company on my long ride home. I was truly glad to have him. Together we wandered through the great woodlands Mr. Penn had set aside to provide fire-wood forever for the poor of Lewes.

The next day we sent Tom on ahead with our sacks to Newcastle, where we meant to bait ourselves and our horses. But first we rode down the coast to Rehoboth, and had a noble sea-bath; also above the beach was a bit of a fresh-water lake, most delicious to take the salt off the skin. After this diversion, which as usual dismissed my blue devils, we set out up the coast of the Bay of Delaware, and were able to reach Newcastle that evening, and the day after our own homes.

This ride gave us a fine chance for talk, and we made good use of it.

As we passed between the hedges and below the old Swede church nigh to Wilmington, Jack fell into talk of Darthea Peniston. Why we had not done so before I knew not then; we were both shy of the subject. I amused myself by insisting that she was but a light-minded young woman with no strong basis of character, and too fond of a red coat. It did amuse me to see how this vexed Jack, who would by no means accept my verdict. We conversed far longer on the stormy quarrels of the colonies and their stepmother England, who seemed to have quite forgot of what blood and breed they were.

As to my Cousin Wynne, with whom at first I had been much taken, Jack was not inclined to speak freely. This I foolishly thought was because Arthur laughed at him, and was, as he knew, of some folks' notion that Jack was a feminine kind of a fellow. That he had the quick insight and the heart of a woman was true, but that was not all of my dear Jack.

My aunt came back to town early in September, and I took up my abode in her town house, where a new life began for me. Letters went and came at long intervals. Our first reached me far on in October.

My mother wrote: «There is great anger here in London because of this matter of the tea. Lord Germaine says we are a tumultuous rabble; thy father has been sent for by Lord North, and I fear has spoken unadvisedly as to things at home. It is not well for a wife to differ with her husband, and this I will not; nevertheless I am not fully of his way of thinking as to these sad troubles; this, however, is not for any eye or ear but thine. Benjamin Franklin was here to see us last week. He seems to think we might as well, or better, pay for the tea, and this suited thy father; but after thus agreeing they went wide apart, Franklin having somewhat shed his Quaker views. I did fear at times that the talk would be strong.

«When he had gone away, thy father said he never had the Spirit with him, and was ever of what creed did most advantage him, and perhaps underneath of none at all. But this I think not. He hath much of the shrewd wisdom of New England, which I like not greatly; but as to this, I know some who have less of any wisdom, and, after all, I judge not a man so wise, and so much my elder.

«General Gage, lately come hither on a visit, we are told assured the king that no other colony would stand by Massachusetts, and that four regiments could put an end to the matter. I am no politician, but it makes me angry to hear them talk of us as if we were but a nursery of naughty children. It seems we are to pay for the tea, and until we do no ships may enter Boston harbour. Also all crown officers who may commit murder are to be tried in England; and there is more, but I forget.»

This was most of it fresh news to us. Meanwhile Hutchinson, the governor of the rebel State, was assuring Lord North that to resist was against our interest, and we, being «a trading set,» would never go to extremes. «As if,» said Wilson, «nations, like men, had not passions and emotions, as well as day-books and ledgers.»

Meanwhile at home our private affairs were rapidly wound up and put in good condition. My father found it difficult to collect his English debts, and so had to limit his purchases, which we stowed as they came over, declining to sell. As business failed, I was more and more at leisure, and much in the company of my cousin, whom to-day I disliked, and to-morrow thought the most amusing and agreeable of companions. He taught me to shoot ducks at League Island, and chose a good fowling-piece for me.

On Sundays I went to hear my aunt's friend, the Rev. Mr. White, preach at Christ Church, and would not go to Meeting, despite Samuel Wetherill, whose Society of Free Quakers did not come to life until 1780. Meanwhile by degrees I took to wearing finer garments. Cards I would never touch, nor have I often to this day.

One morning, long after my parents left, my Aunt Gainor looked me over with care, pleased at the changes in my dress, and that evening she presented me with two fine sets of neck and wrist ruffles, and with paste buckles for knees and shoes. Then she told me that my cousin, the captain, had recommended Pike as a fencing-master, and she wished me to take lessons; «for,» said she, «who knows but you may some day have another quarrel on your hands, and then where will you be?»

I declared that my father would be properly furious; but she laughed, and opened and shut her fan, and said he was three thousand miles away, and that she was my guardian, and responsible for my education. I was by no means loath, and a day later went to see the man with my Cousin Arthur, who asked, as we went, many questions about my mother, and then if my father had left England, or had been to Wyncote.

I had, as he spoke, a letter in my pocket writ in the neat characters I knew so well; our clerk coming from New York had just given it to me, and as I had not as yet read it, liking for this rare pleasure to taste it when alone, I did not mention it to my cousin. I told him I was sure my father would not go to Wales, both because of business, and for other reasons; but I hoped when he came back to get leave to be a year away, and then I should be sure to visit our old nest.

My cousin said, «A year—a year,» musingly, and asked when my parents would return.

I said, «About next October, and by the islands,» meaning the Madeiras.

To this Arthur Wynne returned, in an absent fashion, «Many things may happen in a year.»

I laughed, and said his observation could not be contradicted.

«What observation?» he replied, and then seemed so self-absorbed that I cried out:

«What possesses thee, Cousin Wynne? Thou art sad of late. I can tell thee the women say thou art in love.»

«And if I were, what then?»

This frankness in a man so mature seemed to me odd, when I thought how shy was the growing tenderness my own heart began to hide. His words troubled me. It could be only Darthea Peniston. After a silence, such as was frequent in my cousin, he added: «I fear that blushing friend of yours is fluttering about a certain bright candle. A pity the lad were not warned. You are my cousin, and of course my friend. I may have to go away soon, and I may ask you to do a certain thing for me when I am gone. No man or lad shall stand in my way, and you must hold your tongue too.»

I was puzzled and embarrassed. I said cautiously, «We shall see.» But as to Jack Warder, I liked not what he said, and for two reasons. I knew that, living next door to Darthea, he was with her almost daily; and here was a new and terrible fear, for who could help but love her? Nor could I hear with patience Jack so contemptuously put aside as a child.

«Cousin Arthur,» I said, «thou art mistaken in Warder. There is no more resolute or courageous man. Jack's shy ways and soft fashions make him seem like a timid girl, but I would advise no one to count on this.» I went on, hesitating, «He is an older friend than thou, and—holloa, Jack!» for here was the dear fellow himself, smiling and blushing; and where had the captain been of late? and that awkward left hand was taken, and Jack would come with us and see us play with the small sword, and would like to go after the ducks to-morrow. He seemed happy and pleased to meet us.

Pike was a little man who had a room among the shops on Second street. He wore, as I had often seen, a laced cocked hat, and was clad in a red coat, such as none wore except creoles from the French settlements, or gentlemen from the Carolinas. He had the straight figure and aggressive look all men carry who teach the sword, and a set belief that no man could teach him anything—a small game-cock of a fellow, who had lost one eye by an unlucky thrust of a foil.

I will let Jack's journal, not writ till long after, tell the story for a while. He saw more than I at the time, even if he understood it all as little.

«I saw Hugh strip,» he writes, «and was amused to see Pike feel his muscles and exclaim at his depth of chest. Then he showed him how to wear the wire mask, while the captain and I sat by and looked on.

«Hugh was awkward, but he had a wrist of steel, and when once he had caught the ideas of Pike, who talked all the time in a squeaky voice, his guard was firm. Pike praised him, and said he would learn soon. The thing so attracted me that I was fain to know how it felt to hold a foil; and saying as much, the captain, who fenced here daily, said: ‹It is my breathing-time of day, as Prince Hamlet says. By George! you should see Mr. Garrick in that fencing-scene! I will give Mr. Warder a lesson. I have rather a fancy for giving young men lessons.›

«In a minute I saw my foil fly six feet away with such a wrench of the wrist as made my arm tingle.

«‹Hold the foil lightly. Not so stiff,› said Pike, and we began again. Of course I was as a child before this man, and again and again he planted a button where he pleased, and seemed, I thought, to lunge more fiercely than is decent, for I was dotted with blue bruises that evening.

«At last I gave up, and the captain and Pike took the foils, while we sat and watched them. He was more than a match for Pike, and at last crying, ‹Take care! here is a *botte* you do not know,› caught him fair in the left chest.

«‹By George! Mr. Wynne, that is a pretty piece of play! I remember now Major Montresor tried to show it to me. He said it was that way you killed Lord Charles Trevor.›

«I was shocked to know he had killed a man, and Hugh looked up with his big mother-eyes, while the captain said coolly:

«‹Yes; a sad business, and about a woman, of course. It is dreadful to have that kind of a disposition, boys, that makes you dangerous to some one who wants what you want. He was very young too. A pity! a pity!›

«Hugh and I said nothing; but I had the odd notion that he was threatening us. One gets these ideas vaguely in youth, and sometimes after-events justify them. However, the fancy soon took me to fence with Hugh in his room, for I dared not risk asking my father's leave. As Hugh got his lessons both from Pike and the captain, and became very expert, I got on pretty nearly as fast as he.

«At times we practised in our shirt-sleeves in the garden at Miss Wynne's, or fenced with Graydon, who was later the most expert small sword we had in the army. Hugh soon became nearly as skilful, but I was never as clever at it.»

One day we were busy, as Jack has described, when who should come out into the garden but Mistress Wynne and Darthea, and behind them the captain. We dropped our points, but Miss Peniston cried out, «Go on! go on!» and, laughing, we fell to again.

Presently I, a bit distracted, for I was facing Darthea's eyes, felt Jack's foil full on my chest. Darthea clapped her hands, and, running forward, would pin a bunch of red ribbons she took from her shoulder on Jack's sleeve. Jack fell back, as red as the ribbons, and my aunt cried out, «Darthea, you are too forward!»

The young woman flushed, and cast down the bow, and as Arthur Wynne bent to pick it up set her foot on it. I saw the captain rise, and stand with the half-shut eyes and the little drop of the jaw I have already mentioned. My aunt, who liked the girl well, went after her as she left us in a pet to return to the house. I saw my aunt put a hand on her shoulder, and then the captain, looking vexed, followed after. An hour later I went to look for the ribbon. It was gone, and for years I knew not where, till, in a little box in Jack's desk, I came upon it neatly tied up.

Young as I was, I began to see that here were Captain Wynne, and possibly my friend, in the toils of a girl,—she was but seventeen,—and I, alas! no better off; but of this I breathed not a word to any. As to Jack, who hung about her and fell back when any less shy man wanted his place, I felt that he was little likely to have his way, and that neither he nor I had much chance in such a game against a man like my cousin. He had played with hearts before, and the maid listened like Desdemona to this dark-browed soldier when he talked of courts and kings, and far-away Eastern battles, and the splendour of the Orient. As to my aunt, whom nothing escaped, she looked on amused. Perhaps she did not take as serious the love-affairs of lads like Jack and me. We were like enough to have a dozen before we were really captured. That I was becoming at twenty-one more thoughtful and resolute than far older people, she did not see, and she was sometimes vexed at my sober ways. I was at times gay enough, but at others she would reproach me with not taking more pains to please her guests. Society, she said, had duties as well as pleasures. As to Jack, no one fully understood him in those days, nor knew the sweet manhood and the unselfishness that lay beneath his girl-like exterior.

One day, late in November, my aunt and I were, for a wonder, alone, when she dropped the cards with which she was playing, and said to me: «Hugh, there is something serious between that mischievous kitten and your cousin. They are much talked of. If you have a boy-fancy that way, get rid of it. I don't see through the man. He has been telling her about the fine house at Wyncote, and the great estate, and how some day he will have it, his elder brother being far gone in a phthisis.»

«There must be some mistake,» I said. «Thou knowest what he told my father.»

«Yes; I don't like it,» she went on; «but the girl is caught. He talks of soon having to join Sir Guy Carleton in Canada. And there is my dear girl-boy trapped too, I fear. But, really, he is such a child of a fellow it hardly matters. How many does she want in her net? The fish may squabble, I fear. A sweet thing she is; cruel only by instinct; and so gay, so tender, so truthful and right-minded, with all her nonsense. No one can help loving her; but to-day she has one mood, and to-morrow another. There will be a mad massacre before she is done with you all. Run away, Hugh! run! Make love to Kitty Shippen if you want to get Miss Darthea.»

I laughed, but I had little mirth in my heart.

«Aunt Gainor,» I said, «I love that woman, and no other man shall have her if I can help it.»

«If? if? Stuff! you can't help it. Don't be a fool! The sea is full of fish. This is news indeed.»

«The land has but one Darthea,» said I. «I am a boy no longer, Aunt Gainor. Thou hast made me tell thee, and, now it is out, I may as well say I know all about my cousin. He as good as told me, and in a way I did not like. The man thinks I am a boy to be scared out of going my own way. I have told no one else; but if I can get her I will, and it is no laughing matter.»

«I am sorry, Hugh,» she said. «I knew not it was so serious. It is hard to realise that you are no more a boy, and must have the sorrows my sex provides for you. I like her, and I would help you if I could, but you are late.» And she went on shuffling the cards, while I took up a book, being inclined to say no more.

That evening two letters came by the New York packet. One from my father I put aside. It was dated outside, and was written two weeks later than my mother's, which I read first. I opened it with care.

«My own dear Son: Thy last sweet letter was a great refreshment to me, and the more so because I have not been well, having again my old ache in the side, but not such as need trouble thee. I blush to hear the pretty things thy letters say; but it is love that holds thy pen, and I must not be too much set up in my own esteem. How much love I give thee in return thou knowest, but to pay in this coin will never beggar us. I love thee because thou art all I can desire, and again because thou lovest me, and again for this same dear reason which is all I can say to excuse my mother-folly. Thy father is well, but weary of this great town; and we both long to be at home.»

THEN there was more about my Aunt Wynne, and some woman-talk for her friends about the new fashions, which do not concern her, she being not of this world. «Am I not?» she says. «I love it all—the sea, even the sea, and flowers, and our woods, and, dear me! also gay gowns. I hope the last I got here will not disturb the Meeting, and my new muff,—very big it is,—and a green joseph to ride in. I mean to ride with thee next spring often—often.» And so on, half mother, half child, with bits of her dear French, and all about a new saddle for me, and silver spurs. The postscript was long.

«I saw last week a fair Quaker dame come out of Wales. I asked her about the Wynnes. She knew them not, but told me of their great house, and how it was a show-place people went to see, having been done over at great cost; and how a year or two since coal was found on the estate, and much iron, so that these last two years they were rich, and there was some talk of making the present man a baronet. Also that the elder brother is ill, nigh to death. It seems strange after what thy cousin said so often. Thy father is away in Holland. I will tell him when he is come back. Be cautious not to talk of this. I never liked the man.»

I sat back in my chair to read it all over again, first giving my aunt my father's letter. In a few minutes I heard a cry, and saw my aunt, pale and shaken, standing up, the letter in her hand.

«My God!» I cried, «what is it? Is it my mother?»

«Yes, yes!» she said. «Be strong, my boy! She is—dead!»

For a moment I saw the room whirl, and then, as my Aunt Gainor sat down, I fell on my knees and buried my face in her lap. I felt her dear old hands on my head, and at last would have the letter. It was brief.

«MY SON: The hand of God has fallen heavily upon me. Thy mother died to-day of a pleurisy which none could help. I had not even the consolation to hear her speak, since, when I came from Holland, she was wandering in talk of thee, and mostly in French, which I know not. I seek to find God's meaning in this chastisement. As yet I find it not. It is well that we should not let bereavements so overcome us as to make us neglect to be fervent in the business of life, or to cease to praise Him who has seen fit to take away from us that which it may be we worshipped as an idol. What more is to say I leave until I see thee. My affairs are now so ordered that I may leave them. I shall sail in a week for home in the ship in which I came out, and shall not go, as I did mean, to the islands.»

IT seemed to me, as I read and re-read it, a cold, hard letter. I said as much to my aunt some days after this; but she wisely urged that my father was ever a reticent man, who found it difficult to let even his dearest see the better part of him.

I have no mind to dwell on this sad calamity. I went to and fro, finding neither possibility of repose nor any consolation. I saw as I rode, or lay in my boat, that one dear face, its blue-eyed tenderness, its smile of love. I could never thus recall to sight any other of those who, in after-years, have left me; but this one face is here to-day as I write, forever smiling and forever young.

And so time ran on, and nigh to Christmas day my father came home. The weather was more mild than common, and his ship met no delay from ice. I joined him off Chester Creek. He was grayer, older, I thought, but not otherwise altered, having still his erect stature, and the trick I myself have of throwing his head up and his shoulders back when about to meet some emergent occasion. I saw no sign of emotion when we met, except that he opened and shut his hands as usual when disturbed. He asked if I were well, and of my Aunt Gainor, and then, amid the tears which were choking me, if I were satisfied as to the business, and if the tea had arrived. I said yes, and that the ship had been sent away without violence. He said it was a silly business, and the king would soon end it; he himself had been too hasty—with more to like effect.

It seemed to me while we talked as though he had just come from my mother's deathbed, whereas a long time had elapsed, and he had been able to get over the first cruel shock. My own grief was still upon me, and I wondered at his tranquillity. A little later he said:

«I see thou hast taken to the foolishness of black garments. This is thy aunt's doings.» In fact, it was her positive wish. I made no reply, but only looked him in the face, ready to cry like a child.

«Why hast thou no answers, Hugh? Thy tongue used to be ready enough. Thou hast thy mother's eyes. I would thou hadst them not.»

This was as near as he ever came to speech of her, whom, to my amazement, he never again mentioned. Was it a deeper feeling than I knew that so silenced him, or did he wish to forget her? I know not. Some deal thus with their dead. He bade my aunt take away my mother's clothes, and asked no questions as to how she disposed of them; nor for a month did he desire my return home.

What then passed between him and my Aunt Gainor I do not know; but he said nothing more of my dress, although I wore mourning for six months. Nor did he say a word as to my exactness and industry, which were honestly all they should have been. At meals he spoke rarely, and then of affairs, or to blame me for faults not mine, or to speak with cold sarcasm of my friends.

Except for Jack, and my Aunt Gainor, and Wilson and Wetherill, of whom I saw much, I should have been miserable indeed. Captain Wynne still came and went, and his strange intimacy with my father continued. I thought little of it then, and for my own part I liked to hear of his adventurous life, but the man less and less; and so the winter of '73 and '74 went by with fencing and skating and books, which now I myself ordered to suit me, or found in Mr. Logan's great library, of which I was made free.

In March my cousin left us for Canada and the army. Once I spoke before him of the news in my mother's postscript; but he laughed, saying he had heard some such rumours, but that they were not true. They did not much trouble a hungry beggar of a younger son with letters; still, if there had been such good news he should have heard it. He wished it might be so; and as to his brother, poor devil! he would last long enough to marry and have children. Were the ducks still in the river? He said no more to me of Darthea, or of what I was to do for him, but he found a way at need, I am sure, to get letters to her, and that without difficulty. At last, as I have said, he was gone to join Sir Guy. I was not sorry.

Mrs. Peniston, Darthea's aunt, usually talked little, and then of serious matters as if they were trivial, and of these latter as if they were of the utmost importance. With regard to this matter of Darthea and my cousin she was free of speech and incessant, so that all the town was soon assured of the great match Darthea would make. As to the house at Wyncote, it grew, and the estate also. Neither Jack nor I liked all this, and my friend took it sadly to heart, to my Aunt Gainor's amusement and Mrs. Ferguson's, who would have Dr. Rush set up a ward in the new hospital for the broken-hearted lovers of Darthea. When first Jack Warder was thus badgered he fell into such a state of terror as to what the madcap woman would say next that he declined all society for a week, and ever after detested the Tory lady.

I became, under the influence of this much-talked-of news, as mute as Jack; but while he had only a deep desire toward sadness, and to stay away from her who had thus defeated his love, I, neither given over to despair nor hope, had only a fierce will to have my way; nor, for some reason or for none, did I consider Jack's case as very serious,—my aunt it much amused,—so little do we know those who are most near to us.

No sooner was the redcoat lover gone awhile than, as Miss Chew declared, Darthea put off mourning for the absent. Indeed, the pretty kitten began once more to tangle the threads of Jack's life and mine. For a month Jack was in favour, and then a certain captain, but never I, until one day late in April. She was waiting among my aunt's china for her return, and had set the goggle-eyed mandarin to nodding, while, with eyes as wide as his, she nodded in reply, and laughed like a merry child.

I stood in the doorway, and watched this delicious creature for a minute while she amused herself—and me also, although she knew it not. «Say No!» she cried out to the great china nobleman; quite a foot high he was. But, despite her pretence at altering his unvaried affirmative, it still went on. My lady walked all around him, and presently said aloud: «No! no! It must be No! Say No!» stamping a foot, as if angry, and then of a sudden running up to the mandarin and laughing. «He has a crack in his head. That is why he says Yes! Yes! I must be a female mandarin, and that is why I say No! No! I wonder does he talk broken China?»

At this moment she saw my tall black figure in a corner mirror, and made some exclamation, as if startled; an instant later she knew it was I, but as if by magic the laughing woman was no longer there. What I saw as she came toward me was a slight, quiet nun with eyes full of tears.

I was used to her swift changes of mood, but what her words, or some of them, meant I knew not; and as for this pitying face, with its sudden sadness, what more did it mean? Major André said of her later that Mistress Darthea was like a lake in the hills, reflecting all things, and yet herself after all. But how many such tricksy ways, pretty or vexing, she was to show some of us in the years to come did not yet appear.

In a moment I seemed to see before me the small dark child I first knew at school. Why was she now so curiously perturbed? «Mr. Wynne,» she said, «you never come near me now—oh, not for a month! And to-day your aunt has shown me a part of the dear mother's letter, and—and—I am so sorry for you! I am indeed! I have long wanted to say so. I wish I could help you. I do not think you forget easily, and—and—you were so good to me when I was an ugly little brat. I think your mother loved me. That is a thing to make one think better of one's self. I need it, sir. It is a pretty sort of vanity, and how vain you must be, who had so much of her love!»

«I thank thee,» I said simply. Indeed, for a time I was so moved that say more I could not. «I thank thee, Miss Peniston. There is no one on earth whom I would rather hear say what thou hast said.»

I saw her colour a little, and she replied quickly, «I am only a child, and I say what comes to my lips; I might better it often if I stayed to think.»

«No!» I cried. Whenever she got into trouble—and she was ready to note the tenderness in my voice—this pretty pretext of the irresponsibility of childhood would serve her turn. «No,» said I; «I like dearly to hear my mother praised,—who could praise her too much?—but when it is thou who sayest of her such true things, how shall I tell thee what it is to me who love to hear thee talk—even nonsense?»

«I talk nonsense? Do I?»

«Yes, sometimes. I—want thee to listen to me. I have cared for thee—»

«Now please don't, Mr. Wynne. They all do it, and—I like you. I want to keep some friends.»

«It is useless, Darthea. I am so made that I must say my say. Thou mayest try to escape, and hate it and me, but I have to say I love thee. No, I am not a boy. I am a man, and I won't let thee answer me now.»

«I do not want to. It would hurt you. You must know; every one knows. It was his fault and my aunt's, all this gossip. I would have kept it quiet.»

«It will never be,» I broke out. «Thou wilt never marry that man!» I knew when I said this that I had made a mistake. I had learned to distrust Arthur; but I had too little that was of moment to say against him to make it wise to speak as I had done. I was young in those days, and hasty.

«Who?» says my lady, all on fire. «What man? Jack Warder? And why not? I do not know what I shall do.»

«It is not my dear Jack,» I cried. «Why dost thou trifle with me?»

«Your dear Jack, indeed! How he blushes! *I* might ask *him*. He never would have the courage.»

«It is my cousin Arthur Wynne, as thou well knowest. And thou art wicked to mock at an honest gentleman with thy light talk. Thou dost not know the man, this man, my cousin.»

«Only a boy would be so foolish or so unfair as to speak thus of one behind his back, and to a woman, too, who—» And she paused, confused and angry.

I could not tell her what was only suspicion or hearsay as to my cousin's double statements concerning his father's estate, or how either she or we were deceived. I had, in fact, lost my head a little, and had gone further than was wise. I would not explain, and I was too vexed to say more than that I would say the same to his face. Then she rejoined softly:

«Tell it to me. You are as mysterious as Miss Wynne; and have I not a right to know?»

«No,» I said; «not now, at least. Thou mayest tell him if thou wilt.»

«If I will, indeed! Every one is against him—you and Mistress Wynne and that impudent boy Jack Warder, despite his blushes. Oh, he can be bold enough. Is n't he a dear fellow?»

What could one say to a woman like this? I hesitated, and as I did so, not having ready anything but sad reproaches of her levity, my aunt appeared in the doorway.

«Are you two children quarrelling?» she said in her outspoken way. «You will have time to repent. Here has been your father, sir, to-day, and his affairs in Jamaica are all in a nice pickle, and you and the old clerk are to up and away in the packet for Kingston, and that to-morrow.»

«Indeed!» I cried. I was not sorry.

«I envy you,» said my lady, as demure as you please. «You will fetch me a feather fan, and come back soon. I hate all those cornets and captains, and now I shall have no one but Jack.»

My aunt looked on amused. Her news was true indeed, and with no chance to talk to any one, except to say a mere good-by to Jack, I spent the evening with my father and our head clerk over the business which took me away so hastily. At early morning on a cold day at the close of April, 1774, we were gliding down the Delaware with all sail set.

The voyage was long, the winds contrary. I had ample leisure to reflect upon my talk with Darthea. I was sure she must have known she was to me not as other women. Except for the accident of this chance encounter, I might long have waited before finding courage to speak. I had made nothing by it, had scarce had an answer, and should, like enough, have fallen back into the coldness of relation by which she had so long kept me at a distance. I had been foolish and hasty to speak of my cousin at all; it did but vex her.

Of my errand in Jamaica there is little to be said. My father's letters were of business only. Of these long months and of what went on at home I heard but little from him, and with my request to have the gazettes he had evidently no mind to comply; nor were the chances of letters frequent. I heard, indeed, from my aunt but twice, and from Jack thrice; but he said nothing of Darthea. Years after I found in his record of events:

«Hugh left us the last of April. It may be he cares too much for that wayward witch Darthea.»

I should say that it was at this time or soon after my dear friend began to keep a somewhat broken diary of events. What he says of former years was put on paper long afterward.

«If I did but know,» writes Jack, «that he is seriously taken, I should understand, alas! what not to do. But as to some things Hugh is a silent man. I think, as Mr. Wilson says, some men are made for friends, and some for lovers. I fear the latter is not my rôle. Is there—can there be—such a thing as revering a woman too much to make successful love? I think I see what Darthea is more truly than does my dear Hugh. There must come a day when she will show it. Sometimes I can hardly trust myself with her; and I yearn to tell her that I alone know her, and that I love her. I must watch myself. If it really be that Hugh cares for her, and yet I were to be the fortunate man, how could I face him again, having had the advantage of his long absence? It seems strange that I should ask myself if I am more her lover than his friend. He does not talk of her to me.

«It is now September, '74, and Hugh must soon return. Mr. Gage is fortifying Boston Neck, and we have had the mischievous Boston Port Bill, and Virginia up in a rage, which I do not understand. We, who have our commerce crippled by foolish laws, may well be on the side of resistance; but why the planters should put in peril their only tobacco market I see less well. A Continental Congress is to meet here on the fifth day of this month, and already the town is alive with gentlemen from the South and North.

«No doubt Darthea has letters from Mr. Arthur Wynne. I think Mr. Wilson judges that man correctly. He says he is selfish, and more weak as to morals than really bad, and that he will be apt to yield to sudden temptation rather than to plan deliberate wickedness. Why should he have need to plan at all? Mistress Wynne says he does not like Hugh. How could any not like my Hugh, and how do women see the things which we do not?

«It is sad to see my father's state of mind. Yesterday he was with me to visit Mr. Hancock, very fine in a purple velvet coat with gold buttons, and a flowered waistcoat. He is our correspondent in Boston. My father came home a hot Whig; and to-morrow is Meeting-day, and he will be most melancholy, and all for the king if this and that should happen. John Wynne can turn him which way he likes. If my Hugh remains of a Whig mind—and who less like to change?—he will have a hot time with his father, I fear.»

Is it any wonder I, his friend, loved this man? He seemed so gentle that all but I, even James Wilson, misunderstood him. No more obstinate fellow ever was or will be. I ought to say «determined,» for there was always a reason of head or heart for what he would or would not do, and I really think that in all his noble life he had but one hour of weakness, of which by and by I may have to tell.

(To be continued.)

*S. Weir Mitchell.*

IN AUNT GAINOR'S GARDEN.

# THE AUTHOR OF «RORY O'MORE.»

RECOLLECTIONS OF SAMUEL LOVER, BY HIS DAUGHTER.

WITH PICTURES AND AUTOGRAPHS FROM MRS. LOVER'S ALBUM.

I AM asked to write some recollections of my father, his life and his work, in particular referring to an autograph album of my mother's, which I recently sent to America as a present to my eldest son, Victor Herbert.

Samuel Lover was born in Dublin, February, 24, 1797. His father was a man of business, and, as the eldest son, Samuel was able, at sixteen years of age, to fulfil the duties of head clerk (for he was as clever at correspondence and figures as he was at everything else), and so save much expense to the firm. It was natural to wish that he should remain in it. My father, however, possessed such strong artistic talents that business was distasteful to him, and he longed to follow another path in life. He had had the misfortune to lose his mother when he was a boy of twelve. She would probably have understood and forwarded his aspirations; for the tenderest affection had existed between them, and throughout life he revered the memory of his mother as the sweetest and best of women. His talents he probably inherited in part from her, as well as his amiable and lovable character.

FROM PHOTOGRAPH OF MINIATURE BY HIMSELF OWNED BY HIS GRANDSON, VICTOR HERBERT.

SAMUEL LOVER (ABOUT THE AGE OF 35).

At sixteen years of age he left his home, in spite of the opposition of his father, and resolved to go his own way, depending solely on his own mental exertions for earning his bread. This shows his character in its true light; for although distinguished by an enchanting amiability and cheerfulness, yet he had an iron will, an untiring industry, and perfect self-dependence.

At first he managed to support himself by executing for physicians drawings, which were destined to appear in anatomical works, and had, of course, to be remarkably accurate. It is the more extraordinary that he was able to do this, as he had never been taught to draw, and had up to that time practised the art only for his amusement in leisure hours.

With patient industry, he daily improved himself in miniature-painting, and was soon able to establish himself as a portrait-painter in Dublin. This remained his principal profession through life, although he practised many branches of art besides.

Having painted everybody in Dublin who wished to be painted (as he himself used to express it), after the lapse of a considerable time he decided on shifting the scene of his efforts to London, where an endless field of action presented itself. The groundwork of all his future activity had in the mean time been laid in Dublin. He had been contributing to various magazines, and also making many charming drawings for them, which had appeared as wood-engravings.

The first and second series of the humorous and racy «Legends and Stories of Ireland» had appeared in London, and had been received with great favor by the public and the press in England as well as in Ireland.

The first song which he succeeded in selling

to a publisher he would not take money for, but arranged to take a guitar in exchange, as he had long wished to possess such an instrument, but had as yet not been able to buy one. How little he dreamed at that time of the thousands of pounds that would be made by his songs in the future! Unfortunately, the publishers got the lion's share of the profits.

I may here remark that he played both the piano and the guitar exceedingly well, although he had never had a lesson on either of these instruments. He was most eager in acquiring every sort of information, and had, for instance, out of his own scanty earnings as a youth, after he had left his father's house, contrived to pay for lessons in French from the best French teacher in Dublin, and he spoke that language fluently. It was then a still more necessary accomplishment in society than now, and at school he had learned only Latin.

After his first song had sold well, several others followed, and it was easy to find publishers for further compositions in London.

His first dramatic work was brought out at the Theatre Royal, Dublin. It treated of the principal incidents in the life of a certain real or legendary queen of Ireland, who was an Amazon and a great heroine.

Before transferring his place of residence from Ireland to England, my father had exhibited a large and beautiful miniature portrait of Paganini at the Royal Academy, London. Most portraits of Paganini were hideous caricatures, making him look like a demon, while my father's portrait of him was a wonderful likeness, representing the master as he really was, and doing justice to the spiritual and benignant expression of his extremely interesting face. The picture at once procured for my father a most honorable rank as an artist in London, and actually grounded his reputation there.

On opening my mother's album, the first names to be seen are those of Nicolo Paganini and Thomas Moore. Paganini sat for his portrait to my father in Dublin, having passed some time in Ireland. He contributed an Italian verse to the album along with his signature. Thomas Moore gave a verse of Montgomery's, which was rather ill-placed modesty, as one of his own would have been more natural and acceptable. Moore was an old friend, for the families of my parents had been long allied in friendship with his family.

Not many of the autographs date from Ireland, but there are several which were evidently contributed there.

PHOTOGRAPHED BY DAY.

SAMUEL LOVER.

Maturin, who wrote the humorous novel of «The Heroine,» an inimitable travesty of the exaggerated romantic novels formerly so popular (of which Mrs. Radcliffe's were about the best), is here represented. Maturin was one of those unusually clever men who never *did* much, and so his name is well-nigh forgotten.

Among my father's friends I may mention Bulwer, Dickens, Thackeray, Douglas Jerrold, Charles Lever, and Mark Lemon; and the artists Sir Edwin Landseer, Maclise, Henry Martin, Stanfield, Chantry, Sir Richard Westmacott, John Foley, Cruikshank, and John Leech.

In mentioning Charles Lever, I am reminded of a certain club that existed in Dublin, for it was founded by Lever, and called «The Burschenschaft,» in imitation of the students' clubs in Germany, where Lever had studied. He was a physician by profession. There belonged to this club a surprisingly large number of talented young Irishmen who afterward made themselves names in the world as authors, painters, composers, or in some other way. The club evenings were celebrated for their brilliancy. Lover was their appointed «minstrel,» and on his leaving Dublin the mem-

Daniel O'Connell M. P. for the City of Dublin

DRAWN IN PENCIL BY SAMUEL LOVER.

bers presented him with a gold snuff-box bearing the emblem of the club and the inscription, «The Burschenschaft to their Minstrel.»

I cannot resist relating here a circumstance which, although it was a case where Lover missed instead of achieved something, yet shows his character in a very amiable light.

After the portrait of Paganini had been exhibited in London, where it was very much appreciated and talked about, as I have already remarked, a letter reached him from the chamberlain of the Duchess of Kent, summoning him at once to London to paint the portrait of the Princess Victoria, now the Queen of England. Just at that time, however, there was a «happy event» expected in his own family, and he could not make up his mind to leave his home at such a moment. He therefore wrote, expressing his gratification at the honor conferred by the order, and stating that in a very short time he would be enabled to arrive in London to execute it. Unfortunately, courts are easily offended, and the order was never renewed.

On taking up his residence in London in the following year, a very agreeable time began for him, so that he had no cause to regret the pleasant social circle he had left in Dublin.

Though he did so many things well, he often regretted that not one of his talents had been thoroughly perfected by study and instruction. Had he been educated either as a painter or as a musician, there is no doubt that he would have attained a much greater celebrity; yet it is probable that it was more conducive to his personal happiness to practise all the arts he loved so well, than to be confined to the exercise of only one.

Overwhelmed with orders for portraits on his arrival in London, he painted numbers of beautiful miniatures in course of time. Celebrated men and famous beauties were among his sitters.

Two very slight sketches of his fine miniatures are in his wife's album, evidently intended as pleasant remembrances of the pictures for her. One of these is the portrait of an Indian prince who came to the British court as ambassador extraordinary from the King of Oude. The sketch stands opposite the poetical contribution of the prince. This is in Hindustani, with a line added in the Persian language. The picture itself was splendid, showing a man of fine presence in gorgeous Indian dress, and was about the largest miniature ever painted. The second sketch is of a portrait which Lover painted of Henry, Lord Brougham, in his robes of office. To my father one of the most interesting persons that he ever painted was the venerable Mrs. Gwynn, the «Jessamy bride» of Oliver Goldsmith. Mrs. Gwynn was a very old woman at the time, though the traces of her former enchanting beauty were still plainly to be distinguished. I need scarcely say that she still preserved as a sacred relic a lock of Goldsmith's hair, to cut off which for her his coffin had been opened just before he was interred.

«Sam Lover,» or «little Lover,» as his friends sometimes irreverently called him, was a great favorite in London society. Possessing an inexhaustible fund of high spirits, good humor, and sparkling wit, no one could be better company. Nor was he one of those who, as the Irish neatly express it, «hang up their fiddles behind the door» when they come home. On the contrary, he was never more happy, delightful, and entertaining than when he was at home, with only his wife and daughters about him. His truly lovable character was not only shown in gaiety: he was also deeply humane and kind, with the keenest sense of honor and the warmest heart in the world. His song of «The Four-leaved Shamrock» truly expresses his own aspirations.

Oh! thus I 'd play th' enchanter's part,
Thus scatter bliss around,
And not a tear nor aching heart
Should in the world be found!

He would have liked to see the whole world happy. Nevertheless, he was «a good hater» (such as Dr. Johnson would have loved) when he knew any one to be a contemptible character.

The songs of Lover became very popular, and he wrote a great number of them, and nearly all were set to music of his own; but sometimes he also set words to old Irish melodies. I cannot remember the names of half of these songs, and a list of them would be much too long here. I will mention the titles of only a few of the most popular: «The Angel's Whisper,» «My Mother Dear!» «The Land of the West,» «The Four-leaved Shamrock,» «What Will You Do, Love?» «The Fisherman's Daughter,» and the humorous songs «Rory O'More,» «Molly Bawn,» «The Low-backed Car,» and «The Bowld Sojer-boy.» I may say, with a truly just pride, that his songs are sung wherever the English language is spoken, and there is no danger of their being soon forgotten.

In my mother's album one song of his, «Oh, Lovely Eyes!» in his own handwriting, appears as a musical contribution. There is only one other musical addition to it, and that is a few bars of music from the hand of that gifted Irishman, Michael William Balfe. Balfe and his charming wife, a Hungarian, were frequent guests in my father's house. They had both been educated as opera-singers in Italy, and sang delightfully. Balfe was also a very good actor. He was the manager of a London theater at one time, and brought

PAINTED IN WATER-COLOR BY SAMUEL LOVER.

LORD BROUGHAM.

out several new operas and comedies, among others a little comedy of Lover's entitled, «Il Paddy Whack in Italia,» treating of artist life in Italy. In this piece Balfe played an Irish part capitally, and sang the then new song of «Molly Bawn» so charmingly that it was repeatedly encored every night.

Long before this Lover had written several comedies for the Olympic Theatre, then under the management of the celebrated Madame Vestris (afterward Mrs. Charles Mathews), who was very fond of singing his songs, which she also introduced into other pieces. Some delicately humorous songs, such as «Beauty and Time,» were written expressly for her, and she sang them perfectly.

Only one actor's name appears in the album —that of poor Tyrone Power. There are several pleasant notes of his preserved, and also a photograph of him taken at a period when photography was in its infancy.

Power was the cleverest actor of Irish parts that ever trod the stage, though, strange to say, he was not an Irishman, but a Welshman. Several dramatic works of my father's were written for Tyrone Power, among

Do you know him?

"Devil a bit," says S. L.

them the pieces «Rory O'More,» dramatized from the novel of that name; «The White Horse of the Peppers,» dramatized from one of the tales of «The Legends and Stories of Ireland»; and a little farce, «The Happy Man.» All these pieces had long runs. My father naturally delighted in Power as the man who could play his Irish parts best, and Power delighted in my father as the man who wrote him the best parts.

One of the most interesting autographs is that of Daniel O'Connell. An excellent little pencil likeness of him faces his autograph. My father drew this on the back of a letter one morning when he was breakfasting with O'Connell, which he often did when Parliament was sitting; and he also visited O'Connell on his estate of Derrynane in Ireland on one of his rare autumn holidays. Some very pretty poems by Mrs. Fitzsimon, O'Connell's amiable and talented daughter, are to be found in the album.

The following letter from Shirley Brooks, of «Punch,» also appears in the album:

1st April, 1868. 6 Kent Terrace,
S. Hugues. Regent's Park, N. W.

TOUCHING THE «ILLUSTRATED LONDON NEWS.»

And is it an old friend that can't read my handwriting merely because it happens to be disguised in print? I 'd know *his* in any verses he might put forth. But it is all the pleasanter to be thanked in a mask, when one knows the words will not be recalled when the mask comes off. «But who the devil is it yet?» says he. Now never be in a hurry. How did B. Disraeli, Esq., become Premier of Ireland and the adjacent islets, except by waiting? I am glad you are in that beautiful Jersey, which I did not know that you had (ye had) made yer Pat-mos (ha! ha!); and maybe I 'll look ye up this autumn, and will burn the incense of a cigar to St. Prelude.

> And now thou seest my soul's angelic hue,
> 'Tis time these features were uncurtained too.
> (W. T. Moore.)

Do you know *him?*

«Devil a bit,» says S. L. «Looks half asleep over his ‹Punch,› and no wonder, if he 's been reading his own contributions.» After a pause: «I think I remember some such objectionable face at the Garrick Club; but there 's a bad lot there, and I 'm not proud to remember that boiling.» Well then, look inside the envelope, and you 'll see the names? my dear Lover, of a man who is heartily glad that he has unexpectedly returned you a fraction of the pleasure you have so long given him. Ever yours,

Sam'l Lover, Esq. S. B.

The album contains also a signature of Lord Byron, which is, unfortunately, only pasted in. My mother got it, in all probability, either from Thomas Moore or from Samuel Rogers.

Notes to my father from the poets Samuel Rogers and Thomas Campbell, and from the novelists Miss Edgeworth, Harrison Ainsworth, and the gifted and beautiful Mrs. Caroline Norton, enhance the value of the book more than mere signatures would have done.

Original poetical contributions are not numerous in the album; among the well-known authors who have contributed is Sheridan Knowles. It is interesting to remember that both Sheridan Knowles and Mrs. Norton were descendants of the family of Richard Brinsley Sheridan—examples of the occasional inheritance of brilliant mental gifts.

Mr. and Mrs. S. C. Hall, Miss Austen, Mrs. Barbara Hofland, and several writers of lesser note have contributed original poems. There are also poems from the pen of the gifted but ill-fated Letitia Elizabeth Landon—«L. E. L.»

Another very talented writer, Francis Mahony, a Catholic priest who wrote under the name of Father Prout, has translated a humorous song of my father's, «Who Are You?» into French and Italian in a surprisingly dexterous manner. He was an accomplished linguist. One little unfinished water-color sketch of my father's is also there—a bard taking leave of his lady-love. Another bard, designed by Alfred Crowquill, follows soon after.

A PENCIL-SKETCH BY MILLAIS WHEN A BOY OF TEN.

A contribution in hieroglyphics by the Oriental traveler Wilkinson ingeniously sets forth my mother's name and social status.

A little original pencil-sketch, drawn in five minutes for me by «Johnny» Millais (the late Sir John Millais) when he was a boy of ten, is a pretty remembrance of his precocious talent. «Johnny» was always restless and uneasy in any company until some compassionate person provided him with a pencil and an unlimited supply of paper; then he was quite happy, and covered whole quires of paper in an hour or two with often really charming sketches from the almost inexhaustible store of his happy fancy.

My father's first novel was «Rory O'More,» and he appears to have had a great partiality for the song of that name, very likely because it was the first of his songs that attained a great popularity. I do not think that he otherwise had any particular favorites among the works of his pen or brush; but «Rory O'More» he made the hero of his first novel, and afterward he dramatized the book, thus making a threefold use of the name.

His second novel was «Handy Andy,» and this was followed by «He Would be a Gentleman.» These two were first published as serials, and illustrated with etchings «by the author.» Only people who have written works in this manner know what a severe strain it is on the mental faculties to be obliged to produce a certain amount of «copy» within a short given time; in this case two etchings had to be added, though my father had several other occupations at the same time. These two works consequently taxèd his powers to the utmost. His eyes having begun to suffer, especially from miniature-painting and etching, it became evident that he ought no longer to continue working in the same manner if he hoped to retain his eyesight unimpaired. This danger was happily averted, and he retained his keen sight to the last day of his life.

In consequence of various considerations, he determined to undertake an entirely new kind of activity, and began to give evening entertainments, which he called «Lover's

WILKINSON'S HIEROGLYPHICS.

Irish Evenings.» In these entertainments he told Irish stories, intermixed with witty and interesting anecdotes and relations of various kinds, declaimed, and sang his own songs. His new enterprise was rewarded with great success, first in London, then in the provinces, and in Ireland and Scotland. He was as zealous in this new work as he had been in all others, and in 1846 went to America, where he met with the same flattering reception as elsewhere, and had the greatest kindness and friendship shown him on all sides.

An incident of the American tour was the letter which follows:

> MY DEAR SIR: I fear that, after all, I shall not be able to attend Mr. Lover's dinner. I will be entirely frank with you: I am frightened at the idea of having to speak, which at all public dinners hangs over me like the sword of Damocles. It is this skeleton at the feast that warns me away.
>
> My warmest thanks, however, for your invitation; and believe me,
>
> Very truly yours,
>
> HENRY W. LONGFELLOW.
>
> October 2d, 1846.

Within two years he traveled through the whole of the United States, and visited the principal cities of Canada. He then returned to England, and soon gave up his «Irish Evenings» altogether, from that time forward resting upon his laurels.

Although always more or less occupied with the pencil and the pen, he did not again undertake any important literary works, and painted only for his own amusement.

The royalties on his musical, literary, and dramatic works brought him in a comfortable income, and in 1855 he was informed that Queen Victoria had granted him one of the few pensions for literary merit which are at the disposal of the British government.

To describe how he worked is no difficult task. He delighted in mental work of all sorts for its own sake, and he was of so active a mind, and by nature so industrious, that idleness was impossible to him. He was passionately fond of drawing and painting, and equally fond of music. This made the vast amount of work which he got through in his life comparatively easy to him. I may safely affirm that he did the work of several men—*industrious* men—during his active career. There is no doubt that his occupations were of so varied a nature as to make his work easier for him, and his elastic and happy temperament helped him over all difficulties.

When I remember how little time he ever allowed himself for exercise, I am astonished

AUTOGRAPH OF PAGANINI.

that his health was always so excellent. Of recreation he always had enough in society, but his holidays were rare. Only for a few weeks in the autumn, when all London is «out of town,» did he allow himself any relaxation from work. His industry was such that in the busiest years of his life he did not even grant himself time to look at the daily papers, or to read any new book that was much talked of. His wife always read the papers and the new books for him, giving him in conversation a résumé of the news of the day and the contents of the books, so that he was always well informed of everything that was going on. If anything exceedingly important was on hand in the political world, or if any part of a book was particularly interesting or well written, these she would read to him while he was painting.

My Niece is dying to see Rory O'more —
Yours very truly
Thos Campbell —

Many artists are as dumb as fishes at their easels; but he could converse charmingly while he was painting, which was a particularly pleasant quality for his sitters. In painting or in writing he worked indefatigably, and seemed to be independent of the «moods» to which many artists appear to be victims. As to his songs, he used to say himself that he never wrote a song in his life except when he could n't help it. The songs used to «come to him,» generally words and melody simultaneously, so that he had only to write them down. Frequently the idea of a song would come when he was occupied with something quite different, as, for instance, while painting. He would then leave his easel, write down the idea, and return to his work. Afterward he would return to the idea, and work it out.

Byron

He painted in water-colors and in oils, as well as in miniature, and also etched very well. He was exceedingly fond of sketching from nature, and had hundreds of beautiful sketches that he had made for his own amusement in Ireland, England, and America. In his old age he began to work in wood (in former years he sometimes carved models of ships, which he used to paint and have rigged), carving chimneypieces and bookcases adorned with Cupids, flowers, and fruits, as if he had been doing nothing else all his life!

It was not until he was nearly seventy years of age that his health began to fail. It was by no means a general break-up of the constitution, but symptoms of heart-disease showed themselves. In appearance he looked like a well-preserved man of about fifty. He was still extremely active, his curly hair was thick, though getting gray, and his teeth were as perfect and handsome as when he was twenty. Heart-disease made gradual progress, and the last year of his life he spent in Jersey, where he went to seek a milder air. He was never confined to his room, or even to the house, and he made many sketches while in Jersey.

Done in a moment
by J. Allen. R.A.
May 2nd 1842.

SKETCH OF MRS. SIDDONS.

On the last morning of his life he arose as usual. He had long known that his end was approaching, and had awaited the hour with fortitude and resignation. He was over seventy-one years of age when his unusually active life came to a close in 1868.

*Fanny Schmid.*

# MISS SELINA'S SETTLEMENT.

BY THE AUTHOR OF «SWEET BELLS OUT OF TUNE,» ETC.

«IT reads like a fairy-tale,» said Miss Selina Smith, letting fall upon her knees the newspaper containing an account of the ball just given to the great world by her cousin, the fashionable Mrs. John Sidney Stapleton of New York. «Now, mother, nobody can accuse me of being jealous or begrudging another person her good fortune; but when I think how you and I jog along through life in this dull little place, and screw and pinch to make both ends meet, and compare our lot with Elizabeth's, it does seem as if she were the most enviable of creatures. And then to remember that she and I were school-girls together, and started out upon exactly the same footing in society! She has gone up like the rocket, and I have come down like the stick.»

«I dare say Elizabeth has had her ups and downs,» replied a sweet old lady, looking away from the table-cloth she was darning in neatest old-time «basket weave.» «She has lost children, poor thing; and they say that eldest boy of hers is unsteady; and once or twice her husband has been on the brink of ruin with his speculative schemes.»

«Mother dear, do be more original!» answered Selina, laughing. «That is the conventional thing poor people always say about rich people. Everybody, rich and poor, has that sort of trouble to meet. Did n't I find my Mrs. Thompson the scrub-woman on the top floor of a wretched tenement to-day, lamenting over the habits of her son, and telling me that if Thompson did n't waste his money they would be able to move into a better room. Of course Elizabeth Stapleton does n't walk altogether upon roses—who in this life does? But sometimes, after I have gone through one week exactly like another for months at a time, when I think that I know every paving-stone in this dull little town, every article of furniture in our house, every book upon our shelves, the habits and customs and affairs and idiosyncrasies of every respectable resident of the place, I long for Elizabeth's opportunity for variety. The idea of such a life as hers—a life of ease, leisure, comfort, and yearly travel, always in touch with every phase of new movement everywhere—exhilarates me like champagne. Of course you laugh. It is natural when you hear such sentiments from a sober, steady-going little old maid like your daughter Selina; but every now and then it 's a relief to speak them out. You know better than any one, mother, that fine houses and clothes and equipages do not tempt me overmuch. It is change, scope, acquaintance with the people who influence the times, music, art of the best, such as Elizabeth has as easily as she turns electricity into her house.»

Mrs. Smith sighed faintly.

«Then why, my dear, do you not accept your cousin's invitation for a visit to them in their new house?»

«For one thing, it has been too long in coming,» said Selina, with spirit. «For another, why does not the lamp-post over the way get up and make a call upon the railway-station clock? And for a third thing, and best reason of all, I would n't leave you alone here for a kingdom, and you know it.»

«Two years ago some of these same objections came up, and were disposed of,» replied the older lady, smiling indulgently. «Now, I really believe Elizabeth feels a need of some one belonging to herself; you have proved once that you are not so deeply rooted as you think. And as to my staying alone, I had a letter this morning from my brother Joe's daughter Julia in Council Bluffs; she is evidently anxious to come East for a visit to the old town where her father was born and bred. Suppose we ask Julia to take your place while you are at Elizabeth's—what then?»

«I believe you have been planning this ‹unbeknownst› to me,» exclaimed Selina, a flush of joy mounting into her clear, pale cheek.

All at once the prospect opened to her of a renewal of the enjoyment of such mental and spiritual aliment as had transformed her dull life two years before, when Selina, with a personally conducted party of five lone women like herself, had visited the most accessible attractions of the European continent. For the sum of five hundred dollars each they had become possessors of these delights, with a glimpse of Westminster Abbey, Stratford, and Abbotsford thrown in.

«I will think of it,» she said presently, trying to be calm.

As she left the quiet little parlor in which her mother sat secretly pluming herself upon the success of an innocent manœuver, Selina was conscious of feeling already a little detached from its familiar surroundings. Nor did household cares seem to weigh upon her so heavily as usual. The old stair carpet she had long been plotting how to supplant with a new one suddenly ceased to vex her eyes. The curtains in her bedroom, which only the night before had kept her awake wondering how they would stand another laundering, now no longer occupied her mind. Even the sins of the furnace-man, for whom she had that day reserved a special rod in pickle, faded from their original scarlet, and became quite colorless. Into the periphery of Miss Smith's existence had, in truth, been introduced an overmastering new interest that jostled all others against its narrow bounds.

By the next day everybody within the radius of Miss Selina's influence in the little manufacturing town of North Colchester—and that comprised no mean number of her fellow-mortals—knew that their friend and adviser and teacher and benefactress was about to go away again, this time for a stay in the great Babylonian city. Previous to Selina's trip abroad she had remained at home for so many years at a stretch, attended upon an invalid mother, and done so many other things at the same time, that people had looked on her as an occasion for local pride. At this period a clever young doctor, possessing himself of Mrs. Smith's case, had brought to bear modern surgery upon it with such success as to make of the old lady a comparatively well woman; and Selina, released from her long service, had been induced to try the surprising flight abroad. Her mother had continued well during her absence; and upon Selina's return, fresher and brighter and prettier than North Colchester had seen her since her earliest days of maidenhood, public opinion heaved a long sigh of relief. It was then generally hoped that the indispensable Miss Smith had had «enough of action and of motion» in foreign parts. North Colchester wished to hear no more of her leaving home during the remainder of her useful life.

Naturally, therefore, the approaching departure was discussed with as much disfavor as animation. Around tea-tables, in the book club, at the Woman's Exchange, the sewing-circle, the marketman's, in the tenement-houses and dwellings of the factory hands, Selina's news was received with restraint. Old Mrs. Clancy, an opinion-maker in church circles, said she 'd «misdoubted from the first that Selina Smith's traveling in that wild way abroad had put a bee in her bonnet the girl had never really been rid of since.»

Selina went on her rounds to say good-by, with a guilty feeling that Mrs. Clancy's arrow had not sped far of the mark. For two years she had been tempted intolerably with a return, in season and out, of the exquisite ineffaceable impressions received beyond that waste of waters she might not hope to cross again. In the exercises of the sewing-circle she would be confronted by Mont Blanc rosy in the glow of sunset. During the rector's Sunday evening sermon she saw the Grand Canal by moonlight, and heard the pleading notes of the tenor's voice in the musicians' gondola. Upon her meditations the white peacock of Warwick Castle strutted without a summons, and the flashes of electricity on the trolley wires running past their house would at any time bring up the fairy vision of the old town of Edinburgh as it first burst upon her gaze after dark in Prince's street. Selina knew that it was not only the restlessness engendered by these enticing memories that made her long for the present change; but she recognized that they were primarily responsible for the impatience, bordering on morbidness, that had beset her at times since her return to her quiet life in North Colchester. What she desired was a taste—only a taste—of the atmosphere of wealth and ease from which daily toil and petty care were absent.

Whirling on her way to New York, Selina's spirits rose. She forgot the long hiatus in cousinly civilities on the part of Mrs. Stapleton toward themselves; she forgot her doubt as to whether Mrs. Stapleton's former residence was really in such a chronic condition of overcrowding by the family of its owners that a spare chamber for guests was unknown under its roof; she even forgot her small and provincial wardrobe. It was enough that she was again in motion, journeying toward a goal of experience just now more than all she desired. It would be such a luxury to look upon a woman the sacrifice of whose existence upon the minutiæ of other people's affairs was not exacted in return for the privilege of living.

## II.

ARRIVED at the station in New York, Selina's habit of travel stood her in good stead. Following the crowd of passengers who left her train, she emerged into the gloomy precinct where expectant friends stand penned. Seeing here no familiar face, she was for a moment tempted to yield herself and her luggage into custody of a cab-driver undeterred by conscience from exacting for the proposed drive to her cousin's house a sum so large as to stagger her. Had she but known that a new footman, sent by Mrs. Stapleton to fetch her, was at that moment wandering stupidly about, gazing into the wrong faces, and accosting impossible Misses Smith, the lonely lady might have felt relieved. As it was, native spirit came to her rescue, and committing herself to the hands of a policeman, she got rid of her checks, and was put duly aboard of a Madison Avenue street-car bound up town. Selina's next difficulty—that of identifying the street near which her cousin's number in Fifth Avenue was supposed to be discoverable—was by her referred to the conductor of the car, with the result that she was carried many blocks above the point desired, and finally, amid a sudden flurry of wind and snow that nearly took her off her feet, ejected upon a crossing nearly a mile beyond her destination. Toilsomely, whipped by the gust and whitened with snow, Selina plodded back down the long chill avenue of palaces facing the east side of Central Park. Once, almost blown from the sidewalk, she ventured to turn in at the basement of one of these stately dwellings, where for a moment she might recover strength under the shelter of the steps. But a couple of housemaids and a pair of lolling gentlemen in knee-breeches, whom she espied sitting in comfort by a bright fire in the room within, laughed at her forlorn figure, making signals for her to move on; and hapless Miss Smith emerged once more into the storm.

No vehicle was in sight save those of traffic or private pleasure, and, almost exhausted, she pursued her way until the broad stone steps, turned sidewise, above which an iron grille displayed the Stapletons' number, came into sight. The snow, ceasing to fall as suddenly as it had come, had not yet been removed from the steps, and up these she climbed, chill and comfortless, ashamed to touch the electric button at the showy front door until she had mustered strength to shake from her garments some of their newly added weight.

While thus employed, a man, large, important, globular, opened the door upon her.

«Come, I say; that won't do, my girl,» he remarked with authority; «you must get out of this, you know.»

A crimson flush appeared in Selina's cheek. With a dignity of manner that had at least the effect of creating astonishment in the bosom of the portly apparition she spoke:

«I am Miss Smith, Mrs. Stapleton's cousin, whom she is expecting. I lost my way in coming from the train.»

«Beg pardon, m'm, I 'm sure,» blurted the large man, suavely recovering himself. «I remember now as how the third man had orders to go to the station with a cab to meet the 4:30 train. If you will step inside, m'm, I 'll see Mrs. Stapleton's maid, and inquire what room you are to have. Mrs. Stapleton and the young ladies are out with the carriage, and expect to be home by six. Very unfortunate Thomas should have missed you, m'm, I 'm sure; but the young man is one I have only on trial, and I 'm sorry to say he 's far from giving me satisfaction. Will you please to have tea in your own room, m'm, or in Miss Stapleton's boudoir? I 'll see that it 's sent up to you directly.»

In this wise was begun the visit so eagerly longed for. Not all the luxury of the bedroom into which Miss Smith was presently conducted by a supercilious maid, whom she was glad to dismiss thereafter, could remove from Selina's spirit the chill it had received. Tea, however, and an hour's rest under the satin coverlet she found folded across a billowy couch, had so far restored her good humor that she was enabled to feel a genuine throb of pleasure when a tap on her door was followed by the entrance of Mrs. Stapleton.

«Elizabeth!» she exclaimed, springing up with open arms. «Dear Elizabeth!»

«So good of you to come,» remarked her cousin, after bestowing upon her a kiss vague of destination, and dropping exhausted into a chair. «Badley or Josephine, I forget which, told me there had been some trouble about Thomas meeting you. So tiresome of Thomas; of course we can't keep him, and I don't know why Badley is so unsuccessful this year with his footmen. But you have rested now, I hope. Josephine told me she had put one of my wrappers here for you; one is always so used up after traveling, I think. We were kept out later than I expected in all this shocking weather by the length of Mrs. Talman's program for her musicale. Afternoon musicales are a mistake—don't you think so?—when one is trying to rush around and get in just as many things as possible between four and six. And how is your mother feeling now? Such a comfort to you, her recovery; sometime you must tell me all about it—I have such an immense interest in surgical cases. And you look well, quite the same as you were five years ago when we last met—or was it longer? Really, I can't remember anything, there is so much always on my mind. What I want particularly to know now is whether you 'll mind dining with the two girls who are not yet out, and their governess, to-night? Unfortunately, Mr. Stapleton and I have a dinner engagement of three weeks' standing, and both the older girls have dinners, and my son does not live at home, you know, but has bachelor apartments; so there is no one to keep you company but Ethel and Agnes, if you won't mind. That is really the chief trouble of my undertaking to have friends stopping with me—the endless dinners, so that I have never an evening to myself. With any one else I should feel actually ashamed; but then, you always were so good.»

«You do look tired,» said Miss Smith, gravely, when her cousin had paused for breath.

«Tired is no word for it,» answered the lady, in the same hurried fashion, as if rushing for a train about to start. «I *must* go now and see the two little nursery boys before they go to bed. I have two older ones at boarding-school, you know, and Helen and Emily are in society—charming girls, and an immense success, if I do say so myself.»

«Shall I have the pleasure of seeing my cousins this evening?» asked Selina.

«They would be charmed, I 'm sure, but I 've insisted upon their going directly to their rooms to rest before dressing again. Four o'clock this morning when we left the Delmours' dance, and after the dinners to-night we have an assembly. You must ring for everything you want, and if I don't see you till luncheon-time to-morrow, Selina, I 'm sure you 'll understand. I told the girls and Mr. Stapleton how good you always are.»

«Poor thing, she was really overtasked,» observed Selina, awaking next morning to review her dull, formal dinner the night before, in company with two uninteresting school-girls and a governess altogether absorbed in them, after which she harked back to her reception by Mrs. Stapleton. «I suppose a country mouse like me must make allowance for the preoccupation of a busy woman of the world. To-day, after Elizabeth has had a good sleep, she will be more like her old self.» At this moment Josephine appeared at Miss Smith's bedside with her breakfast and a note.

So sorry, dear Selina [the note ran], that, as the morning is so fine after the storm, the girls claim my promise to go out with them to the Suburban Club for golf. I should urge you to give us the pleasure of going with us, but that I know it would bore you dreadfully. We shall be obliged to take luncheon at the club, but will be in at five o'clock for tea, and then it will be such a pleasure to chat with you. The carriage is at your service at eleven, for shopping or whatever you choose to do. To-night we have a large dinner at home and a dance after it, but there is a classical concert I thought you and the school-girls and Miss Riggs might like to go to. To-morrow I am looking forward to such a nice, long, uninterrupted day with you. Ever your affectionate E. S.

Selina looked with equal distaste upon the billet and the breakfast-tray. «I would n't have troubled you to bring this up,» she said to the maid, feeling very blank. «I never breakfast in my room.»

«Oh! but, mademoiselle, ze ladies always breakfast in bed,» replied the woman, pertly. «Zaire is only one table set for the school-room and nursery at eight, and that is over.»

Miss Smith, bowing to the inevitable, passed the day not unpleasantly amid the attractions of the large, elegantly appointed dwelling, to her for all purposes a hotel conducted upon a scale to which she was quite unaccustomed. In examining the books, pictures, and bric-à-brac, she found abundant amusement, without availing herself of the carriage for a shopping tour which she had no money to indulge in. Once, wooed out of the library by the sound of children's voices, she greeted upon the stairs two little boys equipped for the street, who, however, after bestowing on poor Selina unmitigated stares, yielded her their lifeless hands to shake, and ran off calling to their nurses to be quick and follow them.

«Is there no home atmosphere about this house?» asked of herself the old maid, who, with her slender means and fine sense of proportion, had contrived to make her own little domain a very center of cheer and comfort.

A walk after luncheon, a long, bright letter to her mother, and a return to a fascinating book, made the afternoon fly. Punctually at five there was an inroad into the library of Mrs. Stapleton and the two Misses Stapleton, upon whom, as heroines of many a paragraph of high society in the newspapers, Selina looked with curiosity.

They were tall, well-made, handsome girls, self-possessed and animated; but upon the little lady in her simple frock sitting in the corner with a book they bestowed, after perfunctory handshakes and «How d' ye do's,» no more attention than Selina had received from the others of her young kinspeople. Mrs. Stapleton, to whom this seemed a matter of course, spent the first half-hour after her return in making tea, and descanting upon the events of the day at golf, interspersed with references to the ball of the night before. Then, when the young ladies, declaring themselves perfectly worn out, withdrew from the scene, their mother turned with an air of pride to Selina.

«You see now what reason I have to be proud of my daughters,» she said confidingly. «Really, they are an immense success, and my son Arthur is run after at the greatest rate in society; poor boy, he has enough to turn his head. Now, my dear, sit right down here and tell me all about yourself. What's that, Badley?» she interrupted herself, as the butler stood at her elbow.

«A young person, m'm, who says you asked her to call about some cotillion favors.»

«Oh, dear! Tell her to come to-morrow morning, Badley—and, Badley, send these two notes to Miss Riggs, and ask her to write acceptances, and bring them here for me to see. What was it that messenger-boy came about who was waiting in the hall? What?» tearing open an envelop. «How tiresome! Mrs. Claridge and her daughter gone into mourning, and returning the opera tickets for Monday! We shall have all the trouble of getting some one else to fill our box! You can't think, Selina, how often I 've wanted to write for you to come to us. Seeing you makes me feel as I used before I was swamped in all these cares and duties. You and your dear mother were always so sweet to me, but nowadays one has hardly time to think of bygones. Yes, Badley; what is it? Speak out before Miss Smith, for I 'm quite too tired to get out of this chair.»

«It 's the kitchen-maids and the under cook and the chef, m'm,» said Badley, without ostentation of emotion. «They 've been and had a most awful row, m'm, which the kitchen is that upset I 'm afraid there 'll be no dinner ready by eight o'clock unless you could pacify the girls and persuade the chef to stop till to-morrow, m'm.»

«Good gracious! are they at it again?» cried the lady of the house, despairingly. «You see, Selina, this is one of those disgusting quarrels below stairs that I am the only one to settle. If I had two heads, and twice the amount of patience, I could n't keep those creatures in order. Tell the chef I wish to speak to him in the dining-room immediately—well, Miss Riggs, so you have written those notes for me. Let me have a look at them for fear of mistakes; yes, that is right; ring up a messenger and send them, please.»

«Mademoiselle Veltin is up-stairs waiting to see you about her benefit concert, Mrs. Stapleton,» put in the governess. «And if you will see Ethel, I think her earache is coming on again. And I am sorry to say Agnes must be spoken to about her way of answering me when I told her it was time to come in from the park this afternoon.»

Poor Mrs. Stapleton had only crossed the floor of the library to the hall when she was intercepted by the head nurse.

«Master Dick has cut his finger, madam, and as it seems to be bleeding rather bad I thought I had better let you know.»

### III.

«Decidedly,» reflected Miss Smith, as from her bed that night she heard the carriages drive up for the «dance» that was to follow Mrs. Stapleton's dinner, Selina's share of which had been confined to cold entrées and fragmentary ices served to her and the governess in the school-room—«decidedly, if I consulted my inclination, I 'd go home on the first train to-morrow. But I am sorry for Elizabeth—and besides,» here she smiled with a gleam of consolatory fun, «I should like to stay, if only with the hope of ultimately making acquaintance with my host.»

On the morrow, counting much on the promised «nice, long, uninterrupted day» of talk with her cousin about old times, Selina at ten o'clock joined Mrs. Stapleton in the boudoir, where she was rewarded by an evanescent glimpse at the master of the house—a thin, preoccupied man who, after nervously shaking hands, betook himself to his newspaper, and thence down town, where other trials awaited him.

«Sidney is so frightfully busy,» said his wife. «It is often a week before I can get hold of him to talk even about matters of not only mutual interest but importance. And when I do, he spends the time in worrying about poor dear Jack's extravagance, and the way the girls go on from one gaiety to another. Really, Selina, I think that sort of fussing over their children's habits of life is a disease among the fathers of this time. What in the world do they expect the poor things to do? Ah, here comes my secretary! Now, Selina, sit down there with the morning papers while I run over this pile of notes and cards, and give directions how they are to be answered; and after that I shall be quite at your command.»

For an hour Mrs. Stapleton was immersed in the claims of a correspondence so varied, so compelling, that Selina's brain ached in sympathy with hers. At the end of that time the two ladies went out in the carriage, Mrs. Stapleton to work off a list of engagements alternating between shopping, charities, and culture. After luncheon, at which the children were all brought to table, and had their affairs discussed like matters of national importance, there were a dancing-class, a bazaar, calls, «days,» and a crush «tea,» at all of which the great lady's presence was indispensable. When, at six o'clock, the cousins finally reached home again, and Mrs. Stapleton repaired to her nursery, Selina, tired, dizzy, confused with the variety of impressions she had received, dropped into a chair, sincerely compassionating her poor Elizabeth, who was still due that night at a dinner, the opera, and a late dance. From a mere mistaken votary of fashion, Mrs. Stapleton was now advanced in her opinion to be a monument of endurance and self-control. How was it possible that at the close of such a day—this «nice, long, uninterrupted day»!—a woman of average strength could so far subdue her own flesh and spirit as to dress again, sit jeweled like a Hindu idol through the courses of a long banquet, chat pleasantly, go on to the opera, then to a ball, where, on an uncomfortable dais, she would have to keep her post until after three o'clock A. M.? What heroism was involved in smiling while the figures of an interminable cotillion were danced, when all the time aware of an aching back, aching feet, smothered yawns, a companion as dull and weary as herself filling a place on each side! How Elizabeth could survive it, to emerge fresh the next day, and begin again the round of supervising her household, her pensioners, her daughters' toilets, partners, engagements, and accomplishments, as well as the health, education, physical training, and dress of a younger brood, passed simple Selina's ken.

No wonder, she thought, that the male head of the house, whose checks kept all this busy machinery in motion, wore a shrinking and rather distracted look. As far as the North Colchester mind could venture to sit in judgment upon upper Fifth Avenue, Mr. Stapleton's effacement of himself while at home was due to the instinct of self-preservation under the stress of a cyclone.

«You will come to me in the boudoir again to-morrow, dear Selina,» said Mrs. Stapleton, in parting with her cousin for the night. «To-day we have had absolutely no chance to talk over old times. And remember that I want especially to hear the details of your mother's case.»

It was not Josephine, but Josephine's mistress, who stood, fully dressed in a stylish tailor-made costume, wearing her bonnet, and holding an open telegram in her hand, by Miss Smith's bed at her waking hour next day.

«So sorry, dear Selina,» said the lady, breathlessly; «but I know I can count upon your amiability. Last evening we had letters urging us to reconsider our refusal to go on to Washington for the Claymores' ball to-night, and now this telegram saying they will not let us off. The dear girls have set their hearts upon the little jaunt, and so we are all ready to leave on the ten-o'clock train. But we 'll be back to-morrow, of course, as it 's my day at home, and some artists from the opera are engaged to sing for me. I can depend on you to take good care of yourself till we return; can't I? So good of you not to mind, but you see how it is.»

There was no opportunity allowed Selina to explain her own purpose of setting off for North Colchester before her hostess could resume her place as entertainer; for Mrs. Stapleton, for whom the carriage was waiting, her daughters already installed in it,—and not in the best of humors, be it said,—while a cab to follow held the two lady's-maids, hurried from the room.

Bright and early next morning Miss Smith was on her homeward way. Even as her train ran out of the unromantic gloom of the Grand Central Station a sense of peace and rest stole over her. By the time the familiar surroundings of her native town came into view she felt happier than in years. Whatever else had happened, Eve had tasted the apple, and she *knew*.

A LETTER left by the departing relative upon her cousin's table was read by Mrs. Stapleton with a few natural pangs of regret and mortification; but she resolved to send Selina a lovely present at Christmas, and the pile of correspondence with which Miss Smith's missive was accompanied soon drove the unfortunate occurrence out of her head. In a week's time she was enabled to think complacently of the pleasant little peep into gay society Miss Smith had enjoyed through her.

It is sad to have to put on record the fact that the Christmas token never went; but poor Mrs. Stapleton's own Christmas gift was the announcement of her eldest son's marriage with a variety actress who had achieved renown; and a little later everybody was talking about the misfortune of the prettier of the Stapleton girls engaging herself to an impossible foreigner, against whom Mr. Stapleton had arisen in wrath with an order turning him out of the house. With these additions to her stock of cares, no wonder the good woman forgot what she had meant to do for that dear Selina Smith, «who had certainly the sweetest temper in the world.»

«Poor Elizabeth!» Selina had remarked with real feeling, at the end of a somewhat humorous description of her visit, given for her mother's benefit—a description the details of which had been done with discretion.

«Ah, yes, poor thing!» sighed the dear old lady, comfortably.

Selina's mother never knew what her actual experience had been, and North Colchester in general congratulated itself upon the escape of its favorite daughter unscathed from the fiery ordeal of New York fashionable life.

«Don't know, but it seems to have kinder settled Selina Smith,» observed old Mrs. Clancy at a sewing-bee; and the voice of the public affirmed the judgment of their sage.

*Constance Cary Harrison.*

# ALCESTIS.

I.

I TELL you that the gods give not, they sell!
Their penalty for every golden boon,
Pitiful hucksters, they demand full soon;
And every counter grudging down they tell;
Yea, cheat us with base metal unless well
We watch them; strain the quality of our joy.
And hardest bargainer is Venus' boy:
«For so much heaven, so many hours of hell.»
Yet when I come unto that shadowy place
Of doom, and the gods taunt me with my pains,
Shall I not answer them, though with set face
And anguished eyes: «All depths of bliss I proved;
Cast from my heaven, its memory yet remains.
Yea, for I loved, and I have been beloved!

II.

«Therefore of Lethe's flood I will not drink,
O cruel gods, though it should quench for aye
This torment of fierce thirst! I thrust away
The brimming beaker. Backward from the brink
Of the dark flood wherein no star may blink
I pass with hurrying feet; I will not slay
Mine only joy! Let memory with me stay,
And from your keenest torture I 'll not shrink.
Not like yon inky waters is my soul;
The Star of Love is mirrored in my breast.
I dare your fury; on me spend the whole.
Tossed, tortured, stung to agonies of unrest,
My heart burns through my bosom like a coal—
I think on love, ye gods, and I am blessed!»

*Alice Williams Brotherton.*

ON THE WAY TO MARKET.

ENGRAVED BY M. HAIDER.

# A TROPIC CLIMB.

WITH PICTURES BY GILBERT GAUL.

OUR «pen»—for that is what country dwelling-houses are called in the island of Jamaica—stands at the foot of a group of mountains near the eastern end of the island, and overlooks the broad plain which slopes to the town of Kingston, six or seven miles distant, and six or seven hundred feet below us. Beyond Kingston, with its bay and natural breakwater, extend the blue and hazy reaches of the Caribbean Sea southward toward Central America and the equator. The view to the east and west is inclosed by the spurs of the mountain-range plunging down to the shore.

All day long great surges of white and gray cloud break on the summits three or four thousand feet above us, and pour down in vaporous spray into the upper valleys. Often they drift overhead and drop showers upon us, though Kingston just below remains dry. There is seldom a time when the sun is not shining in some part of the landscape, even when the rain-drops are pattering sharply on our red-tiled roof; and therefore, if we look northward, we see splendid arcs of rainbow spanning the ravines and resting on the acclivities in that direction. The mountains are for the most part wooded to the top with tropical forest, though here and there are peaks denuded of timber and covered with grass, concerning which I shall have more to say presently.

For every two white persons on the island there are sixty negroes. Many of the latter live in tiny cabins high upon the mountains. Perhaps they choose these sites for their dwellings because land costs next to nothing there; perhaps because the tax-collector seldom cares to climb so high to get so little; or possibly they are attracted thither because the air is fresh and the temperature always comfortably cool at such altitudes, and frequent showers give vigor to their crops. They cultivate little patches of yams, bananas, and coco (not cocoa nor coca, which are different plants entirely), and on market-days the women put in a basket whatever surplus is not needed for the family consumption, and walk down to Kingston with their baskets on their heads, sell their produce, and walk back again at night with the same springy, tireless step. The few sixpences that they get easily pay their weekly expenses, and leave a good surplus. It is a primitive and healthy life, and superb specimens of smiling ebony womanhood most of these mountain nymphs appear.

After speculating as to their domestic habits and environment for two or three weeks, I resolved to make a journey to the clouds, and see them with my own eyes. So one morning I put on a pair of buckskin moccasins and leather leggings, a flannel shirt, and a straw hat, took a bamboo staff which I had cut in the woods a few days before, and set forth. It happened to be the first day of January, 1894.

At ten o'clock A. M. the sky was cloudless, and the thermometer marked eighty degrees. Crossing the pasture above the house, I entered the forest, and followed a cow-path which presently brought me to a brook.

Already I was beyond sight and sound of civilization. The trees spread their branches overhead and shut out the sun better than any umbrella would have done it. But for the brook I should have been lost at once; for it served both as companion and guide, since it could not help leading me upward and to the neighborhood of whatever habitations the mountain might contain. Along its babbling course, therefore, I pursued my way.

Seen from a distance, these tropic woods look very like our own, save for the peculiar forms of the palms and bananas, and except that the masses of foliage are denser than in the North. As soon as you come to close quarters, however, you find that not a plant, from the gigantic silk-cottonwood to the smallest blade of grass, is identical with those at home.

Parasites of all kinds infest the tropic woods like the twisted cordage of wrecked vessels. There is a sort of silent fierceness about them that is appalling. Often you mistake them for the tree itself which they are devouring, so close and intimate is their fatal embrace. Once I saw a tree dying thus, and a second parasite upon the back of the first, which it was slowly destroying. A common sight is the liana, a vegetable rope, some no thicker than whip-cord, others inches in diameter. They hang straight down from unknown heights of tall trees, the same size from top to bottom, and of considerable strength. I was climbing down a perpendicular cliff, and had got to a point where there seemed no possibility of descending farther and still less of returning, and was wondering how it would feel to drop forty feet to the bottom of the cliff, when I saw a two-inch rope hanging down at my left hand. It was a liana. I laid hold of it and gave it a tug; it was apparently anchored fast somewhere above, and it certainly reached to the foot of the rock. It was so preternaturally convenient that I felt some suspicion of it; but there was no alternative, and I finally went down it hand under hand like a sailor, and got off safe.

Smaller parasites grow in tufts on the boughs of trees, and are no doubt species of orchid; others, again, are like bunches of grass. Ferns grow in the notches of trunks, and there is a background of lovely mosses everywhere. Upon whatever point you fix your eye, beauty reveals itself beneath beauty, and there is no end of it. There are ferns as large as ordinary trees, and others as tiny and delicate as those which the winter frost draws on our Northern panes. In several places big boles of trees had fallen across the brook, and had in the course of years become the nucleus and nourishment of an exquisite riot of emerald-hued and velvety moss and fern growth; and there were great semicircular fungi as white as milk standing out from the stem, and others hanging from delicate stalks like little silken bags. The patterns and colors of the underlying lichens would make a study for a designer of diaper patterns. Whichever way you look, and in little as well as in large, you are impressed with the evidence of a ceaseless and immeasurable energy of life, never letting go or intermitting, always encroaching and increasing. There is no winter to give pause to the endless development and multiplication; day and night, year in and year out, they go on. Ages ago, centuries hence, it has been, and will be, the same. Mortal existence seems like a shadow amidst vitality such as this.

The brook makes the loudest and the only continuous sound in the forest. Throughout these shadowy regions insects seldom hum, nor do birds sing. The great jack buzzards float overhead in silence. There are no mosquitos at this season to pipe their infinitesimal treble in your ear. The leaves of the trees stand motionless as if in a hothouse. This absence of a breeze is one of the most

ENGRAVED BY J. W. EVANS.

A NATURAL LADDER.

striking characteristics of the tropics. Puffs of wind do pass over us, it is true, during each day; now it is the Southern wind coming up from the Caribbean, now the norther descending from the mountain heights. But neither of them lasts more than a few minutes at a time, and then once more all things stand immobile in the limpid atmosphere. It is no wonder that these months of calm now and again alternate with the mad fury and screaming of the hurricane.

No forests in the world are freer from all forms of animal and vegetable peril than those of Jamaica. The mongoos has long since utterly exterminated every species of serpent; and though you may occasionally discover a miniature scorpion under a stone, its only desire will be to scuttle away, and if you force it to sting you, the pain and the danger are no greater than from a New England wasp or hornet. On the other hand, there are swarms of fireflies as big as bees, and more beautiful after dusk than anything outside of fairy-land. They come into the rooms, and float about, throwing lovely phosphorescent gleams along the walls and ceilings; or if you stand on the balcony and look out across the lawn, it is lighted all over with their soft elfin fires. But this is a digression.

The bed of the brook zigzagged upward through the ravine, keeping, however, a general direction east and west. It was not so dark in color as our brooks, nor were there weeds in its bed; its hue was a light brown, and it flowed over stones coated with a fine sediment, or in swifter reaches over coarse sand. The water was perfectly transparent, and of an agreeable coolness. It seemed as if there ought to be mountain trout in the deep pools, but I saw none; indeed, the only sign of life was a small dark crab, exactly like those that scuttle over our beaches at low tide, except that the claws of these little creatures were very small. I was surprised to find crabs in fresh water, and picked one out; he was as soft as jelly, though whether this is their normal state I know not.

The crest of the mountain on my right, ascending almost perpendicularly, hid the sun, so that the shade was even deeper than the trees alone could make it. I was in a perspiration, of course,—that is the proper condition of man in this latitude,—but I was not hot. By this time I had reached an altitude where the path threatened to abandon me. The path was a good deal of a phantom at best; if you looked away from it for a moment, you had to look twice before finding it again. It professed to follow the margins of the brook; but every few minutes it crossed the slender stream, resuming its identity at an indeterminate distance up the other side. Occasionally it would proceed directly up the bed of the brook itself, leaping from stone to stone, clambering over fallen tree-trunks or crawling underneath them, edging along an inch of strand on this side or circumventing a pool on that. Then you would arrive at an impossible ascent up a cataract or hopeless chevaux-de-frise of fallen timber. The path had vanished altogether. But just as you were about to retrace your steps and try back, your eye would light upon a gap in the bank, and there was your path again, appearing like a ghost with the silent invitation, «Here I am, comrade!» So on we went higher and higher, while the stream grew narrower and slighter, and its bed rockier and more precipitous. Glancing upward once in a while, as a gap in the foliage afforded opportunity, I saw that I was beginning to approach the clouds.

Meanwhile, I had been passing groups of plantain and banana, for the most part denuded of fruit or bearing only immature bunches. The grass beneath them was trodden down, doubtless by the feet of stray negroes who had ascended the path before me. But beyond this there had been as yet no sign of human life; the motionless forest, the babbling brook, and the blue glimpses of sky overhead had been my only companions. The bananas might have been plucked a month ago, for aught I could tell. I contrived to knock down one or two green ones with a stone, but found them wholly inedible. Just then I heard the distant barking of a dog. It seemed to come from behind me, and above on the right. I looked in that direction, but could see nothing but spheres and pyramids of green mounting one above another higher and higher. Would the brook never come to a beginning?

A little farther on I came to a standstill. The bed of the stream had narrowed, and the water was rushing down between walls of rock, completely filling the channel, and making walking along it well nigh impossible. The banks on each side were all but perpendicular. I glanced to the right and left, but the phantom path did not reveal itself. Probably I had passed the turning-off place lower down without noticing it. But I was unwilling to turn back; so I made shift to scramble up the bank, holding on by hanging roots and stems until, after an arduous five minutes, I found myself neck-deep in grass, which was not grass at all according to our notions, but a species of reed from five to eight feet tall, and with sharp edges that would cut my fingers if I gave them the chance. These reeds it was that had worn the appearance of short turf when seen from the valleys below, clothing those parts of the mountains which were free of timber. But the timber was much the easier to walk through; for the «grass» impeded the view, clung about the feet, and at the same time did not keep off the sun, which glared down upon my efforts with unrelenting splendor. All I could do was to try to plant each step higher than the last, and that was not so easy as it sounds. Time passed on; I seemed to make small progress, and I began to get uncomfortably hot. «You have got off your track entirely,» I said to myself. «You would have done better to wade up the bed of the brook; that at least would have been cool, and would probably have brought you nearer your destination.»

Here I came to a terrace so steep that I was obliged to clamber up it on hands and knees, clutching the tufts of grass, and digging my toes into the soil. After an ardent struggle I landed on the top of it, and then I was surprised.

For there I stood on a well-trodden pathway two yards in width, and bearing traces not only of human feet but of mule-hoofs. In an instant I had dragged myself up from the depths of a trackless wilderness into the midst of comparative civilization. This path was nothing less than a mountain highway, and I must be in the immediate neighborhood of a settlement. In fact, as I stood there I distinctly heard a woman's voice and laugh, followed by the prattle of a child. It seemed to come from above. The road ascended in that direction, and I followed it. In a minute I came to a fork, and chose the left hand. It led me along the brink of a precipitous valley lying between the hill which I had been ascending and another farther to the north. It was all a confusion of lovely vegetation from top to bottom and up again; and now, just beneath me, so that I could have dropped a stone on the door-step two hundred feet down, was the thatched roof of a little cabin. It hung on the side of the valley like a swallow's nest, and would have slipped down the rest of the way had not a fortunate ledge arrested it. I made up my mind to go down there and visit with the inhabitants. A narrow track presently revealed itself, corkscrewing down the face of the descent, so that at every dozen steps my head was passing the level just before occupied by my feet. In a few minutes I got to the shelf on which the cabin stood—a level space thirty or forty feet in width. I approached modestly, on the lookout for some one to whom to introduce myself; but no one appeared.

The cabin was oblong, made of wattle-work covered with clay and whitewashed. With the thatched roof it resembled a miniature copy of one of the cottages of old England. The small windows were protected by wooden slats—there was no glass; the door was closed. When I had satisfied myself that the place was empty, I made bold to look through the slats. I saw a little square room with a smooth clay floor, a table of dark wood, clean and polished, a few shelves with some chinaware on them, and two rude chairs. This room occupied somewhat more than half of the area covered by the cottage. There was a partition on the right, with a partly open door in it. That was all I could see.

Outside the front door there was a bench with a pot standing on it; half a dozen yams lay beside the bench. A very dull and time-worn hoe leaned against the side of the cabin. The space immediately about the cabin was well-trodden clay like the floor inside. Three banana plants—or they may have been plantains—overshadowed the north end of the structure, while the south was protected by a mango-tree.

At first I thought this was the whole garden, but stepping to the edge overlooking the farther declivity into the valley, I discovered a plantation sloping downward at an angle of not less than sixty degrees. Here were the huge leaves of the coco, and an array of poles like our bean-poles with yam-vines curling about them. The poles stood upright, of course, and yet so steep was the pitch of the ground that the tops of them were but a few feet distant from the upper levels. The garden was arranged in a series of narrow terraces; but there did not seem to be room enough on any of the terraces for a man to stand and work, and I could only suppose that the gardener must hang on by his nails to an upper terrace, and cultivate the one below with his toes.

ENGRAVED BY A. E. ANDERSON

A JAMAICA HOME.

The land up here is doubtless government land, which sells for about fifty cents an acre. If, however, it is measured on the horizontal, such an estate as this must come cheap indeed; for I don't believe the horizontal extent of this plantation, which might have had an area of a quarter of an acre, was more than fifteen or twenty feet. It is a perpendicular region. The most convenient way to operate such holdings would be to rig a derrick to the top, and swing the man with the hoe by a rope in front of his field of labor. He would have to be careful in gathering his produce, lest it should escape his grasp, and roll half a mile down into the depths of the valley.

In addition to the fruits above mentioned, there were a number of coffee-bushes and a little clump of sugar-cane; but in the absence of the proprietors I did not feel at liberty to help myself to anything. But where could the proprietors be? One would expect to find at least a superannuated grandfather or a brace of piccaninnies left behind to receive company. Had the family perhaps seen me coming, and, fancying I was the tax-collector, concealed themselves in the surrounding shrubbery? I peered this way and that, but nothing was to be seen. It was odd; but there must be other cabins in the neighborhood, and I set forth to explore them.

A short scramble brought me back to the main road, so to call it, and I continued to ascend. At every hundred yards or so a path would branch out to the right or left, following which I would come to a cabin in all respects similar to the one I had first investigated; but to my great perplexity, every one of them was also absolutely empty. Out of all the dozen or fifteen that I stumbled over, not one had a sign of life about it. What could have happened? Had some secret signal to disappear been passed around, and were my movements being watched by eyes to me invisible? I began to feel embarrassed, if not uneasy. There had been a good deal of talk in the local papers lately about obi. Were these vanished people working up a spell with a view to my destruction? The absence of one or two families from the community might have been explained; but that all of them should desert their dwellings at the same time seemed strange, if not ominous. I had ascended an enchanted mountain, whence I should be spirited away, and see home and friends no more.

After all, thought I, these negroes are at bottom an uncivilized race. Christianity and association with the whites have changed their outward aspect only. In their hearts they are still African savages. Their ways are not ours, and we really know nothing about them. In these mountain villages, almost utterly secluded as they are, who can tell what things are done, what religion followed, what purposes formed? The colored folk seem very childlike and amiable; but cannot one smile and smile, and be an obi-man? Suppose, now, continued I to myself, that while you are innocently scrambling about here, lost in the clouds, and out of reach and knowledge of your friends, the inhabitants of these villages should be gathered together in some savage and ominous place, with skulls and toads and caldrons of hell-broth, performing a dire incantation, the object of which is to smite you with an incurable disease or cause you to fall down a precipice and break your neck. Is not such a thing conceivable? Is it not probable? Nay, can there be any other explanation of the emptiness of this entire village of cabins? It would be clever of you, I added, to make the best of your way out of this neighborhood, and before you venture hither again to cause it to be understood by these people that your object in visiting their fastnesses is in all respects Christian and friendly.

However, I was now apparently so near the top of the mountain that I was loath to retire without having had one glimpse of the magnificent prospect which, in the nature of things, could not but be immediately at hand; besides, I hoped to find a way down shorter than that by which I had ascended, and to do that it was indispensable to see how the land lay. Accordingly I turned to the right, climbed a crooked path like a staircase, and all of a sudden I did discover an outlook over the island of Jamaica such as it was almost worth while to be the object of the wrath of the obi people to see.

I was so high up that almost the whole breadth of the great Liguanea plain was hidden from me, and the nearest object I could see was a large pen about two miles this side of Kingston. That town itself, therefore, seemed to lie almost at my feet; the harbor, capable of containing the fleets of several European powers of the first class, looked like a little pond encircled by a breakwater no thicker than a pencil stroke; the keys outside it were little dots; and beyond uprose to an immense height the horizon of the Caribbean, level beyond level melting away from blue to gray, and from gray to aërial mist, finally uniting with the sky in imperceptible gradations of delicious color. Meanwhile, to the right and left the island lay displayed, descending out of heaven into the sea with profiles bold and headlong or undulating and sweet, one exquisite hue after another changing chameleon-like in the limpid distances, steeped in glorious sunshine, enriched with the dreamy shadows of slumbering clouds. The outlines tapered away, headland after headland, point after point, refined to indescribable delicacies of form and color, until solid earth became air, and angels might become men. In the nearer reaches white villas sparkled amidst the greeny purples of the foliage, and brighter spaces showed where sugar-cane grew, while everywhere the pillars and plumes of palm defined themselves against the softly gleaming background. Overhead the zenith was pure blue with a purple depth in it, felt rather than discerned; but lower down, clouds in all imaginable shapes and shades of beauty formed a wondrous phantasmagoria of various light and dark, striving to outdo the splendor which lay beneath their brooding wings. A thousand feet below me a great bird soared majestic above the sunny slopes of the declivity, and, looking upward, still higher above me floated serene and inapproachable another king of the air, so far immersed in the remoter gulfs of the sky that he was more likely, I thought, to lose the earth altogether than to traverse again the awful spaces that separated him from it.

Could anything human or divine enhance the delight of such a scene as this? Sunshine, shadow, color, lay in silence, tropically calm—the silence of height and space. Hark! what sound was that?

Incredible as it may seem, I fancied I had caught a strain of music. It had rolled forth stately and triumphant, apparently out of the bosom of the very atmosphere about me, bringing with it unaccountable memories of boyhood and of associations immeasurably far from these, and yet uniting in harmony with them. Was it imagination—the glory of things seen seeming to utter itself to the ear? For by what means could mortal music become audible on this breathless summit unless by some miracle of the inner sense? Or had I climbed within range of choirs not of earth, and been visited by the voices of the seraphim and cherubim singing the praises of God, who made this lovely earth and us and them?

No; it was not mortal imagination nor celestial miracle; for now the strain came once more, strong, rich, and joyful, the musical harmony of many voices of men and women uniting in a hearty pæan of worship and thanksgiving. It rose and swelled and sank again, and then, in the succeeding pause, I heard a voice mellow and homely repeating words that seemed familiar, and then the song burst forth anew. Surely I knew that hymn. What son of Christendom knows it not? What reader of the book of life has not, at some period of his career, stood in the midst of the congregation on a Sunday morning, and joined with what fervor was in him in that noble human chant which bids the mortal creature of his hand «praise God, from whom all blessings flow»? Yea, verily; and now I stood here in the tropics, on the Mount of Vision, and heard Old Hundred sung again, not by angels, but by a score or two of humble, dark-skinned fellow-creatures who had left their little cabins in the ravines and on the hillsides on this New Year's morning, and were gathered together in the Lord's name, and—who shall doubt it?—with his presence in the midst of them. It was a commonplace solution of the mystery of the deserted village and all the rest of it; but somehow or other, it touched a deep and tender place in me, and standing so high above the earth as I did, I felt abashed and humbled. I had been jesting about the obi, and this was the interpretation!

A few more steps brought me within sight of the roof and windows of a neat little church perched upon the very topmost summit of the mountain overlooking the world, and, as I venture to believe, in the near neighborhood of heaven. I stayed awhile, and then turned and clambered hastily down whence I had come; for I did not feel that I could honestly look that little congregation in the face. I had forgotten that New Year's day was Sunday to them, and I had speculated idly and injuriously as to the causes of their abandonment of home and business. I went down, down, through the shadowy ravines and narrow gorges, through the silent congregation of trees and plants, stumbling over fantastic roots and clutched by serpentine creepers. I did not notice them; my mind was on other things. But the murmur of the brook, after long singing unnoticed in my ears, at length penetrated to the channel of my thought, and the discords flowed away on its current. The steepness of the descent abated; I slackened my pace, and strolled at my ease beneath the green corridors and fretted roofs. A bird sang in a bush, a green lizard glanced across a stone, the forest lightened and broke away; and I entered the broad pasture, dotted here and there with sober mangos, and hedged with the prickly leaves of the penguin, from which I had set forth on my journey. It was the first day of the new year, and, thanks to the divinity which shapes our ends and out of idle curiosity brings forth fruits of beneficence, I doubt whether I could have spent the day to better advantage than I did.

*Julian Hawthorne.*

DRAWN BY FREDERIC REMINGTON.

«HELLO, JOSÉ!»

# A MAN AND SOME OTHERS.

BY THE AUTHOR OF «THE RED BADGE OF COURAGE,» ETC.

I.

DARK mesquit spread from horizon to horizon. There was no house or horseman from which a mind could evolve a city or a crowd. The world was declared to be a desert and unpeopled. Sometimes, however, on days when no heat-mist arose, a blue shape, dim, of the substance of a specter's veil, appeared in the southwest, and a pondering sheep-herder might remember that there were mountains.

In the silence of these plains the sudden and childish banging of a tin pan could have made an iron-nerved man leap into the air. The sky was ever flawless; the manœuvering of clouds was an unknown pageant; but at times a sheep-herder could see, miles away, the long, white streamers of dust rising from the feet of another's flock, and the interest became intense.

Bill was arduously cooking his dinner, bending over the fire, and toiling like a blacksmith. A movement, a flash of strange color, perhaps, off in the bushes, caused him suddenly to turn his head. Presently he arose, and, shading his eyes with his hand, stood motionless and gazing. He perceived at last a Mexican sheep-herder winding through the brush toward his camp.

«Hello!» shouted Bill.

The Mexican made no answer, but came steadily forward until he was within some twenty yards. There he paused, and, folding his arms, drew himself up in the manner affected by the villain in the play. His serape muffled the lower part of his face, and his great sombrero shaded his brow. Being unexpected and also silent, he had something of the quality of an apparition; moreover, it was clearly his intention to be mystic and sinister.

The American's pipe, sticking carelessly in the corner of his mouth, was twisted until the wrong side was uppermost, and he held his frying-pan poised in the air. He surveyed with evident surprise this apparition in the mesquit. «Hello, José!» he said; «what 's the matter?»

The Mexican spoke with the solemnity of funeral tollings: «Beel, you mus' geet off range. We want you geet off range. We no like. Un'erstan'? We no like.»

«What you talking about?» said Bill. «No like what?»

«We no like you here. Un'erstan'? Too mooch. You mus' geet out. We no like. Un'erstan'?»

«Understand? No; I don't know what the blazes you 're gittin' at.» Bill's eyes wavered in bewilderment, and his jaw fell. «I must git out? I must git off the range? What you givin' us?»

The Mexican unfolded his serape with his small yellow hand. Upon his face was then to be seen a smile that was gently, almost caressingly murderous. «Beel,» he said, «git out!»

Bill's arm dropped until the frying-pan was at his knee. Finally he turned again toward the fire. «Go on, you dog-gone little yaller rat!» he said over his shoulder. «You fellers can't chase me off this range. I got as much right here as anybody.»

«Beel,» answered the other in a vibrant tone, thrusting his head forward and moving one foot, «you geet out or we keel you.»

«Who will?» said Bill.

«I—and the others.» The Mexican tapped his breast gracefully.

Bill reflected for a time, and then he said: «You ain't got no manner of license to warn me off'n this range, and I won't move a rod. Understand? I 've got rights, and I suppose if I don't see 'em through, no one is likely to give me a good hand and help me lick you fellers, since I 'm the only white man in half a day's ride. Now, look; if you fellers try to rush this camp, I 'm goin' to plug about fifty per cent. of the gentlemen present, sure. I 'm goin' in for trouble, an' I 'll git a lot of you. 'Nuther thing: if I was a fine valuable caballero like you, I 'd stay in the rear till the shootin' was done, because I 'm goin' to make a particular p'int of shootin' you through the chest.» He grinned affably, and made a gesture of dismissal.

As for the Mexican, he waved his hands in a consummate expression of indifference. «Oh, all right,» he said. Then, in a tone of deep menace and glee, he added: «We will keel you eef you no geet. They have decide'.»

«They have, have they?» said Bill. «Well, you tell them to go to the devil!»

II.

BILL had been a mine-owner in Wyoming, a great man, an aristocrat, one who possessed unlimited credit in the saloons down the gulch. He had the social weight that could interrupt a lynching or advise a bad man of the particular merits of a remote geographical point. However, the fates exploded the toy balloon with which they had amused Bill, and on the evening of the same day he was a professional gambler with ill fortune dealing him unspeakable irritation in the shape of three big cards whenever another fellow stood pat. It is well here to inform the world that Bill considered his calamities of life all dwarfs in comparison with the excitement of one particular evening, when three kings came to him with criminal regularity against a man who always filled a straight. Later he became a cow-boy, more weirdly abandoned than if he had never been an aristocrat. By this time all that remained of his former splendor was his pride, or his vanity, which was one thing which need not have remained. He killed the foreman of the ranch over an inconsequent matter as to which of them was a liar, and the midnight train carried him eastward. He became a brakeman on the Union Pacific, and really gained high honors in the hobo war that for many years has devastated the beautiful railroads of our country. A creature of ill fortune himself, he practised all the ordinary cruelties upon these other creatures of ill fortune. He was of so fierce a mien that tramps usually surrendered at once whatever coin or tobacco they had in their possession; and if afterward he kicked them from the train, it was only because this was a recognized treachery of the war upon the hoboes. In a famous battle fought in Nebraska in 1879, he would have achieved a lasting distinction if it had not been for a deserter from the United States army. He was at the head of a heroic and sweeping charge, which really broke the power of the hoboes in that county for three months; he had already worsted four tramps with his own coupling-stick, when a stone thrown by the ex-third baseman of F Troop's nine laid him flat on the prairie, and later enforced a stay in the hospital in Omaha. After his recovery he engaged with other railroads, and shuffled cars in countless yards. An order to strike came upon him in Michigan, and afterward the vengeance of the railroad pursued him until he assumed a name. This mask is like the darkness in which the burglar chooses to move. It destroys many of the healthy fears. It is a small thing, but it eats that which we call our conscience. The conductor of No. 419 stood in the caboose within two feet of Bill's nose, and called him a liar. Bill requested him to use a milder term. He had not bored the foreman of Tin Can Ranch with any such request, but had killed him with expedition. The conductor seemed to insist, and so Bill let the matter drop.

He became the bouncer of a saloon on the Bowery in New York. Here most of his fights were as successful as had been his brushes with the hoboes in the West. He gained the complete admiration of the four clean bartenders who stood behind the great and glittering bar. He was an honored man. He nearly killed Bad Hennessy, who, as a matter of fact, had more reputation than ability, and his fame moved up the Bowery and down the Bowery.

But let a man adopt fighting as his business, and the thought grows constantly within him that it is his business to fight. These phrases became mixed in Bill's mind precisely as they are here mixed; and let a man get this idea in his mind, and defeat begins to move toward him over the unknown ways of circumstances. One summer night three sailors from the U. S. S. *Seattle* sat in the saloon drinking and attending to other people's affairs in an amiable fashion. Bill was a proud man since he had thrashed so many citizens, and it suddenly occurred to him that the loud talk of the sailors was very offensive. So he swaggered upon their attention, and warned them that the saloon was the flowery abode of peace and gentle silence. They glanced at him in surprise, and without a moment's pause consigned him to a worse place than any stoker of them knew. Whereupon he flung one of them through the side door before the others could prevent it. On the sidewalk there was a short struggle, with many hoarse epithets in the air, and then Bill slid into the saloon again. A frown of false rage was upon his brow, and he strutted like a savage king. He took a long yellow night-stick from behind the lunch-counter, and started importantly toward the main doors to see that the incensed seamen did not again enter.

The ways of sailormen are without speech, and, together in the street, the three sailors exchanged no word, but they moved at once. Landsmen would have required three years of discussion to gain such unanimity. In silence, and immediately, they seized a long piece of scantling that lay handily. With one forward to guide the battering-ram, and with two behind him to furnish the power, they made a beautiful curve, and came down like the Assyrians on the front door of that saloon.

Mystic and still mystic are the laws of fate. Bill, with his kingly frown and his long night-stick, appeared at precisely that moment in the doorway. He stood like a statue of victory; his pride was at its zenith; and in the same second this atrocious piece of scantling punched him in the bulwarks of his stomach, and he vanished like a mist. Opinions differed as to where the end of the scantling landed him, but it was ultimately clear that it landed him in southwestern Texas, where he became a sheep-herder.

The sailors charged three times upon the plate-glass front of the saloon, and when they had finished, it looked as if it had been the victim of a rural fire company's success in saving it from the flames. As the proprietor of the place surveyed the ruins, he remarked that Bill was a very zealous guardian of property. As the ambulance surgeon surveyed Bill, he remarked that the wound was really an excavation.

III.

As his Mexican friend tripped blithely away, Bill turned with a thoughtful face to his frying-pan and his fire. After dinner he drew his revolver from its scarred old holster, and examined every part of it. It was the revolver that had dealt death to the foreman, and it had also been in free fights in which it had dealt death to several or none. Bill loved it because its allegiance was more than that of man, horse, or dog. It questioned neither social nor moral position; it obeyed alike the saint and the assassin. It was the claw of the eagle, the tooth of the lion, the poison of the snake; and when he swept it from its holster, this minion smote where he listed, even to the battering of a far penny. Wherefore it was his dearest possession, and was not to be exchanged in southwestern Texas for a handful of rubies, nor even the shame and homage of the conductor of No. 419.

During the afternoon he moved through his monotony of work and leisure with the same air of deep meditation. The smoke of his supper-time fire was curling across the shadowy sea of mesquit when the instinct of the plainsman warned him that the stillness, the desolation, was again invaded. He saw a motionless horseman in black outline against the pallid sky. The silhouette displayed serape and sombrero, and even the Mexican spurs as large as pies. When this black figure began to move toward the camp, Bill's hand dropped to his revolver.

The horseman approached until Bill was enabled to see pronounced American features, and a skin too red to grow on a Mexican face. Bill released his grip on his revolver.

«Hello!» called the horseman.

«Hello!» answered Bill.

The horseman cantered forward. «Good evening,» he said, as he again drew rein.

«Good evenin',» answered Bill, without committing himself by too much courtesy.

For a moment the two men scanned each other in a way that is not ill-mannered on the plains, where one is in danger of meeting horse-thieves or tourists.

Bill saw a type which did not belong in the mesquit. The young fellow had invested in some Mexican trappings of an expensive kind. Bill's eyes searched the outfit for some sign of craft, but there was none. Even with his local regalia, it was clear that the young man was of a far, black Northern city. He had discarded the enormous stirrups of his Mexican saddle; he used the small English stirrup, and his feet were thrust forward until the steel tightly gripped his ankles. As Bill's eyes traveled over the stranger, they lighted suddenly upon the stirrups and the thrust feet, and immediately he smiled in a friendly way. No dark purpose could dwell in the innocent heart of a man who rode thus on the plains.

As for the stranger, he saw a tattered individual with a tangle of hair and beard, and with a complexion turned brick-color from the sun and whisky. He saw a pair of eyes that at first looked at him as the wolf looks at the wolf, and then became childlike, almost timid, in their glance. Here was evidently a man who had often stormed the iron walls of the city of success, and who now sometimes valued himself as the rabbit values his prowess.

The stranger smiled genially, and sprang from his horse. «Well, sir, I suppose you will let me camp here with you to-night?»

«Eh?» said Bill.

«I suppose you will let me camp here with you to-night?»

Bill for a time seemed too astonished for words. «Well,»—he answered, scowling in inhospitable annoyance—«well, I don't believe this here is a good place to camp to-night, mister.»

The stranger turned quickly from his saddle-girth.

«What?» he said in surprise. «You don't

want me here? You don't want me to camp here?»

Bill's feet scuffled awkwardly, and he looked steadily at a cactus-plant. «Well, you see, mister,» he said, «I'd like your company well enough, but—you see, some of these here greasers are goin' to chase me off the range to-night; and while I might like a man's company all right, I could n't let him in for no such game when he ain't got nothin' to do with the trouble.»

«Going to chase you off the range?» cried the stranger.

«Well, they said they were goin' to do it,» said Bill.

«And—great heavens! will they kill you, do you think?»

«Don't know. Can't tell till afterwards. You see, they take some feller that 's alone like me, and then they rush his camp when he ain't quite ready for 'em, and ginerally plug 'im with a sawed-off shot-gun load before he has a chance to git at 'em. They lay around and wait for their chance, and it comes soon enough. Of course a feller alone like me has got to let up watching some time. Maybe they ketch 'im asleep. Maybe the feller gits tired waiting, and goes out in broad day, and kills two or three just to make the whole crowd pile on him and settle the thing. I heard of a case like that once. It 's awful hard on a man's mind—to git a gang after him.»

«And so they 're going to rush your camp to-night?» cried the stranger. «How do you know? Who told you?»

«Feller come and told me.»

«And what are you going to do? Fight?»

«Don't see nothin' else to do,» answered Bill, gloomily, still staring at the cactus-plant.

There was a silence. Finally the stranger burst out in an amazed cry. «Well, I never heard of such a thing in my life! How many of them are there?»

«Eight,» answered Bill. «And now look-a-here; you ain't got no manner of business foolin' around here just now, and you might better lope off before dark. I don't ask no help in this here row. I know your happening along here just now don't give me no call on you, and you better hit the trail.»

«Well, why in the name of wonder don't you go get the sheriff?» cried the stranger.

«Oh, h——!» said Bill.

IV.

LONG, smoldering clouds spread in the western sky, and to the east silver mists lay on the purple gloom of the wilderness.

Finally, when the great moon climbed the heavens and cast its ghastly radiance upon the bushes, it made a new and more brilliant crimson of the camp-fire, where the flames capered merrily through its mesquit branches, filling the silence with the fire chorus, an ancient melody which surely bears a message of the inconsequence of individual tragedy—a message that is in the boom of the sea, the sliver of the wind through the grass-blades, the silken clash of hemlock boughs.

No figures moved in the rosy space of the camp, and the search of the moonbeams failed to disclose a living thing in the bushes. There was no owl-faced clock to chant the weariness of the long silence that brooded upon the plain.

The dew gave the darkness under the mesquit a velvet quality that made air seem nearer to water, and no eye could have seen through it the black things that moved like monster lizards toward the camp. The branches, the leaves, that are fain to cry out when death approaches in the wilds, were frustrated by these mystic bodies gliding with the finesse of the escaping serpent. They crept forward to the last point where assuredly no frantic attempt of the fire could discover them, and there they paused to locate the prey. A romance relates the tale of the black cell hidden deep in the earth, where, upon entering, one sees only the little eyes of snakes fixing him in menaces. If a man could have approached a certain spot in the bushes, he would not have found it romantically necessary to have his hair rise. There would have been a sufficient expression of horror in the feeling of the death-hand at the nape of his neck and in his rubber knee-joints.

Two of these bodies finally moved toward each other until for each there grew out of the darkness a face placidly smiling with tender dreams of assassination. «The fool is asleep by the fire, God be praised!» The lips of the other widened in a grin of affectionate appreciation of the fool and his plight. There was some signaling in the gloom, and then began a series of subtle rustlings, interjected often with pauses, during which no sound arose but the sound of faint breathing.

A bush stood like a rock in the stream of firelight, sending its long shadow backward. With painful caution the little company traveled along this shadow, and finally arrived at the rear of the bush. Through its branches they surveyed for a moment of comfortable satisfaction a form in a gray blanket extended on the ground near the fire.

The smile of joyful anticipation fled quickly, to give place to a quiet air of business. Two men lifted shot-guns with much of the barrels gone, and sighting these weapons through the branches, pulled trigger together.

The noise of the explosions roared over the lonely mesquit as if these guns wished to inform the entire world; and as the gray smoke fled, the dodging company back of the bush saw the blanketed form twitching. Whereupon they burst out in chorus in a laugh, and arose as merry as a lot of banqueters. They gleefully gestured congratulations, and strode bravely into the light of the fire.

Then suddenly a new laugh rang from some unknown spot in the darkness. It was a fearsome laugh of ridicule, hatred, ferocity. It might have been demoniac. It smote them motionless in their gleeful prowl, as the stern voice from the sky smites the legendary malefactor. They might have been a weird group in wax, the light of the dying fire on their yellow faces, and shining athwart their eyes turned toward the darkness whence might come the unknown and the terrible.

The thing in the gray blanket no longer twitched; but if the knives in their hands had been thrust toward it, each knife was now drawn back, and its owner's elbow was thrown upward, as if he expected death from the clouds.

This laugh had so chained their reason that for a moment they had no wit to flee. They were prisoners to their terror. Then suddenly the belated decision arrived, and with bubbling cries they turned to run; but at that instant there was a long flash of red in the darkness, and with the report one of the men shouted a bitter shout, spun once, and tumbled headlong. The thick bushes failed to impede the rout of the others.

The silence returned to the wilderness. The tired flames faintly illumined the blanketed thing and the flung corse of the marauder, and sang the fire chorus, the ancient melody which bears the message of the inconsequence of human tragedy.

## V.

« Now you are worse off than ever,» said the young man, dry-voiced and awed.

« No, I ain't,» said Bill, rebelliously. « I 'm one ahead.»

After reflection, the stranger remarked, « Well, there 's seven more.»

They were cautiously and slowly approaching the camp. The sun was flaring its first warming rays over the gray wilderness. Upreared twigs, prominent branches, shone with golden light, while the shadows under the mesquit were heavily blue.

Suddenly the stranger uttered a frightened cry. He had arrived at a point whence he had, through openings in the thicket, a clear view of a dead face.

« Gosh!» said Bill, who at the next instant had seen the thing; « I thought at first it was that there José. That would have been queer, after what I told 'im yesterday.»

They continued their way, the stranger wincing in his walk, and Bill exhibiting considerable curiosity.

The yellow beams of the new sun were touching the grim hues of the dead Mexican's face, and creating there an inhuman effect, which made his countenance more like a mask of dulled brass. One hand, grown curiously thinner, had been flung out regardlessly to a cactus bush.

Bill walked forward and stood looking respectfully at the body. « I know that feller; his name is Miguel. He—»

The stranger's nerves might have been in that condition when there is no backbone to the body, only a long groove. « Good heavens!» he exclaimed, much agitated; « don't speak that way!»

« What way?» said Bill. « I only said his name was Miguel.»

After a pause the stranger said:

« Oh, I know; but—» He waved his hand. « Lower your voice, or something. I don't know. This part of the business rattles me, don't you see?»

« Oh, all right,» replied Bill, bowing to the other's mysterious mood. But in a moment he burst out violently and loud in the most extraordinary profanity, the oaths winging from him as the sparks go from the funnel.

He had been examining the contents of the bundled gray blanket, and he had brought forth, among other things, his frying-pan. It was now only a rim with a handle; the Mexican volley had centered upon it. A Mexican shot-gun of the abbreviated description is ordinarily loaded with flat-irons, stove-lids, lead pipe, old horseshoes, sections of chain, window weights, railroad sleepers and spikes, dumb-bells, and any other junk which may be at hand. When one of these loads encounters a man vitally, it is likely to make an impression upon him, and a cooking-utensil may be supposed to subside before such an assault of curiosities.

Bill held high his desecrated frying-pan, turning it this way and that way. He swore until he happened to note the absence of the stranger. A moment later he saw him leading his horse from the bushes. In silence and sullenly the young man went about saddling the animal. Bill said, «Well, goin' to pull out?»

The stranger's hands fumbled uncertainly at the throat-latch. Once he exclaimed irritably, blaming the buckle for the trembling of his fingers. Once he turned to look at the dead face with the light of the morning sun upon it. At last he cried, «Oh, I know the whole thing was all square enough—could n't be squarer—but—somehow or other, that man there takes the heart out of me.» He turned his troubled face for another look. «He seems to be all the time calling me a—he makes me feel like a murderer.»

«But,» said Bill, puzzling, «you did n't shoot him, mister; I shot him.»

«I know; but I feel that way, somehow. I can't get rid of it.»

Bill considered for a time; then he said diffidently, «Mister, you 're a' eddycated man, ain't you?»

«What?»

«You 're what they call a'—a' eddycated man, ain't you?»

The young man, perplexed, evidently had a question upon his lips, when there was a roar of guns, bright flashes, and in the air such hooting and whistling as would come from a swift flock of steam-boilers. The stranger's horse gave a mighty, convulsive spring, snorting wildly in its sudden anguish, fell upon its knees, scrambled afoot again, and was away in the uncanny death run known to men who have seen the finish of brave horses.

«This comes from discussin' things,» cried Bill, angrily.

He had thrown himself flat on the ground facing the thicket whence had come the firing. He could see the smoke winding over the bush-tops. He lifted his revolver, and the weapon came slowly up from the ground and poised like the glittering crest of a snake. Somewhere on his face there was a kind of smile, cynical, wicked, deadly, of a ferocity which at the same time had brought a deep flush to his face, and had caused two upright lines to glow in his eyes.

«Hello, José!» he called, amiable for satire's sake. «Got your old blunderbusses loaded up again yet?»

The stillness had returned to the plain. The sun's brilliant rays swept over the sea of mesquit, painting the far mists of the west with faint rosy light, and high in the air some great bird fled toward the south.

«You come out here,» called Bill, again addressing the landscape, «and I 'll give you some shootin' lessons. That ain't the way to shoot.» Receiving no reply, he began to invent epithets and yell them at the thicket. He was something of a master of insult, and, moreover, he dived into his memory to bring forth imprecations tarnished with age, unused since fluent Bowery days. The occupation amused him, and sometimes he laughed so that it was uncomfortable for his chest to be against the ground.

Finally the stranger, prostrate near him, said wearily, «Oh, they 've gone.»

«Don't you believe it,» replied Bill, sobering swiftly. «They 're there yet—every man of 'em.»

«How do you know?»

«Because I do. They won't shake us so soon. Don't put your head up, or they 'll get you, sure.»

Bill's eyes, meanwhile, had not wavered from their scrutiny of the thicket in front. «They 're there, all right; don't you forget it. Now you listen.» So he called out: «José! Ojo, José! Speak up, *hombre!* I want have talk. Speak up, you yaller cuss, you!»

Whereupon a mocking voice from off in the bushes said, «Señor?»

«There,» said Bill to his ally; «did n't I tell you? The whole batch.» Again he lifted his voice. «José—look—ain't you gittin' kinder tired? You better go home, you fellers, and git some rest.»

The answer was a sudden furious chatter of Spanish, eloquent with hatred, calling down upon Bill all the calamities which life holds. It was as if some one had suddenly enraged a cageful of wildcats. The spirits of all the revenges which they had imagined were loosened at this time, and filled the air.

«They 're in a holler,» said Bill, chuckling, «or there 'd be shootin'.»

Presently he began to grow angry. His hidden enemies called him nine kinds of coward, a man who could fight only in the dark, a baby who would run from the shadows of such noble Mexican gentlemen, a dog that sneaked. They described the affair of the previous night, and informed him of the base advantage he had taken of their friend. In fact, they in all sincerity endowed him with every quality which he no less earnestly believed them to possess. One could have seen the phrases bite him as he lay there on the ground fingering his revolver.

## VI.

It is sometimes taught that men do the furious and desperate thing from an emotion that is as even and placid as the thoughts of a village clergyman on Sunday afternoon. Usually, however, it is to be believed that a panther is at the time born in the heart, and that the subject does not resemble a man picking mulberries.

«B' G——!» said Bill, speaking as from a throat filled with dust, «I 'll go after 'em in a minute.»

«Don't you budge an inch!» cried the stranger, sternly. «Don't you budge!»

«Well,» said Bill, glaring at the bushes—«well—»

«Put your head down!» suddenly screamed the stranger, in white alarm. As the guns roared, Bill uttered a loud grunt, and for a moment leaned panting on his elbow, while his arm shook like a twig. Then he upreared like a great and bloody spirit of vengeance, his face lighted with the blaze of his last passion. The Mexicans came swiftly and in silence.

The lightning action of the next few moments was of the fabric of dreams to the stranger. The muscular struggle may not be real to the drowning man. His mind may be fixed on the far, straight shadows back of the stars, and the terror of them. And so the fight, and his part in it, had to the stranger only the quality of a picture half drawn. The rush of feet, the spatter of shots, the cries, the swollen faces seen like masks on the smoke, resembled a happening of the night.

And yet afterward certain lines, forms, lived out so strongly from the incoherence that they were always in his memory.

He killed a man, and the thought went swiftly by him, like the feather on the gale, that it was easy to kill a man.

Moreover, he suddenly felt for Bill, this grimy sheep-herder, some deep form of idolatry. Bill was dying, and the dignity of last defeat, the superiority of him who stands in his grave, was in the pose of the lost sheep-herder.

The stranger sat on the ground idly mopping the sweat and powder-stain from his brow. He wore the gentle idiot smile of an aged beggar as he watched three Mexicans limping and staggering in the distance. He noted at this time that one who still possessed a serape had from it none of the grandeur of the cloaked Spaniard, but that against the sky the silhouette resembled a cornucopia of childhood's Christmas.

They turned to look at him, and he lifted his weary arm to menace them with his revolver. They stood for a moment banded together, and hooted curses at him.

Finally he arose, and, walking some paces, stooped to loosen Bill's gray hands from a throat. Swaying as if slightly drunk, he stood looking down into the still face.

Struck suddenly with a thought, he went about with dulled eyes on the ground, until he plucked his gaudy blanket from where it lay dirty from trampling feet. He dusted it carefully, and then returned and laid it over Bill's form. There he again stood motionless, his mouth just agape and the same stupid glance in his eyes, when all at once he made a gesture of fright and looked wildly about him.

He had almost reached the thicket when he stopped, smitten with alarm. A body contorted, with one arm stiff in the air, lay in his path. Slowly and warily he moved around it, and in a moment the bushes, nodding and whispering, their leaf-faces turned toward the scene behind him, swung and swung again into stillness and the peace of the wilderness.

*Stephen Crane.*

## SURPASSED.

THE strenuous gull beats down the sweeping wind;
  The lark, aspiring, sings in viewless sky:
But I, who have so hoped and dreamed and loved—
  How less than these am I!

O silver gull, thy calm of tireless flight,
  Unresting peace, be mine;
And thou, familiar of the skies, teach me
  An ecstasy like thine.

*Grace Duffield Goodwin.*

[BEGUN IN THE NOVEMBER NUMBER.]

# A ROSE OF YESTERDAY.[1]

BY F. MARION CRAWFORD,

Author of «Mr. Isaacs,» «Saracinesca,» «Casa Braccio,» etc.

IX.

OLONEL WIMPOLE looked positively old that evening when he went down to dinner with his sister and Sylvia. His face was drawn and weary, and the lids hung a little in small wrinkles, but down in his gray eyes there was a far-off gleam of danger-light.

Sylvia looked down when she met him, and she was very silent and grave at first. At dinner she sat between him and Miss Wimpole, and for some time she scarcely dared to glance at him. He, on his part, was too much preoccupied to speak much, and she thought he was displeased. Nevertheless, he was more than usually thoughtful for her. She understood by the way he sat, and even by the half-unconscious shrinking of the elbow next to her, that he was sorry for her. At table, seated close together, there is a whole language in one's neighbor's elbow, and an unlimited power of expression in its way of avoiding collisions. Very perceptive people understand that. Primarily, in savage life, the bold man turns his elbows out, while the timid one presses them to his sides as though not to give offense with them. Society teaches us to put on some little airs of timidity as a substitute for the modesty that few feel, and we accordingly draw in our elbows when we are near any one. It is ridiculous enough, but there are a hundred ways of doing it, a hundred degrees of readiness, unwillingness, pride, and consideration for others, as well as sympathy for their troubles or in their successes, all of which are perfectly natural to refined people, and almost perfectly unconscious. The movement of a man's jaws at dinner shows much of his real character, but the movement of his elbows shows with fair accuracy the degree of refinement in which he has been brought up.

Sylvia was sure that the colonel was sorry for her, and the certainty irritated her; for she hated to be pitied, and most of all for having done something foolish. She glanced at Wimpole's tired face just when he was looking a little away from her, and she was startled by the change in his features since the early afternoon. It needed no very keen perception to see that he was in profound anxiety of some kind, and she knew of nothing which could have disturbed him deeply but her own conduct.

Under the vivid light of the public dining-table he looked old; that was undeniable, and it was really the first time that Sylvia had ever connected the idea of age with him. Just beyond him sat a man in the early prime of strength, one of those magnificent specimens of humanity such as one sees occasionally in traveling, but whom one very rarely knows in acquaintance. He could not have been more than twenty-eight years old, straight in his seat, broad-shouldered, with thick, close golden hair and splendid golden beard, white forehead and sunburned cheeks, broad, well-modeled brows and faultless nose, and altogether manly in spite of his beauty. As he leaned forward a little, his fresh young face appeared beside the colonel's tired profile in vivid contrast.

For the first time Sylvia realized the meaning of Wimpole's words spoken that afternoon. He might almost have been her grandfather, and he was in reality of precisely the same age as her father. Sylvia looked down again, and reflected that she must have made a mistake with herself. Youth can sometimes close its eyes to gray hair, but it can never associate the idea of love with old age when clearly brought to its perception.

For at least five minutes the world seemed utterly hollow to Sylvia as she sat there. She did not even wonder why she had thought the colonel young until then. The sudden dropping out of her first great illusion left a void as big and as hollow as itself.

She turned her head and looked once more, and there again was the glorious, unseamed youth of the stranger, almost dazzling her, and making the poor colonel look more than ever old, with his pale, furrowed cheeks and wrinkled eyelids. She thought a moment, and then she was sure that she could never like such a terribly handsome young man, and at the same instant, for the first time in her life, she felt that natural, foolish, human pity which only extreme youth feels for old age, and she wondered why she had not always felt it; for it seemed quite natural, and was altogether in accordance with the rest of her feelings for the colonel, with her reverence for his perfect character, her admiration for his past deeds, her attachment to his quiet, protective, wise, and all-gentle manliness. That was her view of his qualities, and she had to admit that, though he had them all, he was what she called old. She had taken for love what was only a combination of reverence and attachment and admiration. She realized her mistake in a flash, and it seemed to her that the core had withered in the fruit of the universe.

Just then the colonel turned to her, holding his glass in his hand.

« We must not forget that it is your birthday, my dear,» he said, and his natural smile came back. « Rachel,» he added, speaking to his sister across the young girl, « let us drink Sylvia's health on her eighteenth birthday.»

Miss Wimpole usually took a little thin Moselle with the cold water she drank. She solemnly raised the glass, and inclined her head as she looked first at Sylvia and then at the colonel.

« Thank you,» said Sylvia, rather meekly.

Then they all relapsed into silence. The people at the big table talked fast in low tones, and the clattering of dishes and plates and knives and forks went on steadily and untunefully all around. Sylvia felt lonely in the unindividual atmosphere of the Swiss hotel. She hated the terribly handsome young man with a mortal hatred because he made the colonel look old. She could not help seeing him whenever she turned toward Wimpole. At last she spoke softly, looking down at her plate.

« Uncle Richard,» she said, to call his attention.

He was not really her uncle, and she almost always called him « colonel » half playfully, and because she had hated the suggestion of age that is conveyed by the word « uncle.» Wimpole turned to her quietly.

« Yes, my dear,» he said; « what is it?»

« I suppose I was very foolish to-day, was n't I?» asked Sylvia, very low indeed, and a bright blush played upon her pretty face.



The colonel was a courteous man, and was also very fond of her.

« A woman need never be wise when she is lovely,» he said in his rather old-fashioned way, and he smiled affectionately at the young girl. « It is quite enough if she is good.»

But she did not smile; on the contrary, her face became very grave.

« I am in earnest,» she said; and she waited a moment before saying more. « I was very foolish,» she continued thoughtfully. « I did not understand—or I did not realize—I don't know. You have been so much to me all my life, and there is nobody like you, of course. It seemed to me—I mean, it seems to me—that is very much like really caring for some one, is n't it? You know what I mean; I can't express it.»

« You mean that it is a good deal like love, I suppose,» answered the colonel, speaking gravely now. « Yes, I suppose that love is better when people believe each other to be angels; but it is not that sort of thing which makes love what it is.»

« What is it, then?» Sylvia was glad to ask any question that helped to break through the awkwardness and embarrassment she felt toward him.

« There are a great many kinds of love,» he said; « but I think there is only one kind worth having. It is the kind that begins when one is young and lasts all one's life.»

« Is that all?» asked Sylvia, innocently, and in a disappointed tone.

« All!» The colonel laughed softly, and a momentary light of happiness came into his face, for that all was all he had ever had. « Is not that enough, my dear?» he asked. « To love one woman or man with all one's heart for thirty or forty years? Never to be disappointed? Never to feel that one has made a mistake? Never to fear that love may grow old because one grows old one's self? Is not that enough?»

« Ah, yes! That would be, indeed. But you did not say all those other things at first.»

« They are just what make a lifelong love,» answered the colonel. « But then,» he added, « there are a great many degrees far below that. I am sure I have seen people quite really in love with each other for a week.»

Sylvia suddenly looked almost angry as she glanced at him.

« That sort of thing ought not to be called love at all!» she answered energetically. « It is nothing but a miserable flirtation—a miserable, wretched, unworthy flirtation.»

« I quite agree with you,» said Wimpole, smiling at her vehemence.

«Why do you laugh?» she asked, almost offended by his look. His smile disappeared instantly.

«You hit the world very hard, my dear,» he answered.

«I hate the world!» cried Sylvia.

She was just eighteen. Wimpole knew that she felt an innocent and instinctive repulsion for what the world meant to him, and for all the great, sinful unknown. He disliked it himself, with the steady, subdued dislike which is hatred in such natures as his, both because it was contrary to his character and for Sylvia's sake, who must surely one day know something of it. So he did not laugh at her sweeping declaration. She hated the world before knowing it, but he hated it in full knowledge. That was a bond of sympathy like any other. To each of us the world means both what we know and what we suspect, both what we see and the completion of it in the unseen, both the outward lives of our companions, which we can judge, and their inward motives, which we dimly guess.

But on this evening Sylvia felt that the world was particularly odious, for she had suffered a first humiliation in her own eyes. She thought that she had lowered herself in the colonel's estimation, and she had discovered that she had made a great mistake with herself about him.

«I hate the world!» she repeated in a lower tone, almost to herself; and her eyes gleamed with young anger, while her delicate, curling lips just showed her small white teeth.

Wimpole watched her face.

«That is no reason for hating yourself,» he said gently.

She started, and turned her eyes to him; then she blushed and looked away.

«You must not guess my thoughts,» she answered; «it is not kind.»

«I did not mean to. I am sorry.»

«Oh, you could not help it, of course. I was so foolish to-day.»

The blush deepened, and she said nothing more. The colonel returned to his own secret trouble, and on Sylvia's other side Miss Wimpole was silently planning a charitable institution of unusual severity, while she peeled an orange with the most scrupulous neatness and precision.

## X.

HELEN HARMON went out alone to mail her letter. She would not have done such a thing in any great city of Europe, but there is a sense of safety in the dull, impersonal atmosphere of Lucerne, and it was a relief to her to be out in the open air alone; it would be a still greater relief to have dropped the letter into the mysterious slit which is the first stage on the road to everywhere.

No one ever thinks of the straight little cut with its metal cover as being at all tragical; and yet it is as tragic as the jaws of death, in its way. Many a man and woman has stood before it with a letter, and hesitated; and every one has, at some time or other, felt the sharp twist at the heart, which is the wrench of the irrevocable, when the envelop has just slipped away into darkness. The words cannot be unwritten any more after that, nor burned, nor taken back. A telegram may contradict them, or explain them, or ask pardon for them; but the message will inevitably be read, and do its work of peace or war, of challenge or forgiveness, of cruelty or kindness or indifference.

Helen did not mean to hesitate, for she hastened toward the moment of looking back upon a deed now hard to do. It was not far to the post-office, either, and the thing could soon be done. Yet in her brain there was a surging of uncertainties and a whirling of purposes, in the midst of which she clung hard to her determination, though it should cost ever so dear to carry it out. She had not half thought over all the consequences yet, nor all it must mean to her to be separated from her son. The results of her action sprang up now like sudden dangers, and tried to frighten her from her purpose, tried to gain time against her to show themselves, tried to terrify her back to inaction and doubt. Something asked her roughly whence she had got the conviction that she was doing right at all. Another something, more subtle, whispered that she was sacrificing Archie for the sake of her own morbid conscience, and making herself a martyr's crown, not of her own sufferings only, but of her son's loss in losing her. It told her that the letter she held in her hand was a mistake, but not irrevocable until it should have slipped into the dark entrance of the road to everywhere.

She had still a dozen steps to make before reaching the big white building that stands across the corner of the street, and she was hurrying on lest she should not reach the door in time. Then she almost ran against Colonel Wimpole, walking slowly along the pavement, where there was a half-shadow. Both stopped short and looked at each other in surprise. He saw the letter in her hand, and guessed that she had written to her husband.

«I was only going to the post-office,» she said half apologetically; for she thought that he must wonder why she had come out alone at such an hour.

«Will you let me walk with you?» he asked.

«Yes.»

He made a step forward, as though expecting her to turn back from her errand and go with him.

«Not that way,» she said. «I must go to the post-office first.»

«No; please don't.» He placed himself in her way.

«I must.»

She spoke emphatically, and stood still, facing him, while their eyes met again, and neither spoke for a few seconds.

«You are ruining your life,» he said after the pause. «When that letter is gone you will never be able to get it back.»

«I know; I shall not wish to.»

«You will.» His lips set themselves rather firmly as he opposed her, but her face darkened.

«Is this a trial of strength between us?» she asked.

«Yes; I mean to keep you from going back to Henry Harmon.»

«I have made up my mind,» Helen answered.

«So have I,» said Wimpole.

«How can you hinder me? You cannot prevent me from sending this letter, nor from going to him if I choose. And I have chosen to go; that ends it.»

«You are mistaken. You are reckoning without me, and I will make it impossible.»

«You? How? Even if I send this letter?»

«Yes. Come and walk a little, and we can talk. If you insist upon it, drop your letter into the box. But it will only complicate matters, for you shall not go back to Harmon.»

Again she looked at him. He had never spoken in this way during all the years of their acknowledged friendship and unspoken love. She felt that she resented his words and manner, but at the same time that she loved him better and admired him more. He was stronger and more dominant than she had guessed.

«You have no right to say such things to me,» she answered; «but I will walk with you for a few minutes. Of course you can prevent me from sending my letter now. I can take it to the post-office by and by.»

«You cannot suppose that I mean to prevent you by force,» said Wimpole, and he stood aside to let her pass if she would.

«You said that it was a trial of strength,» she answered.

She hesitated one moment, and then turned and began to walk with him. They crossed the street to the side by which the river runs, away from the hotels and the houses. It was darker there and more quiet, and they felt more alone. It would seem easier, too, to talk in the open air, with the sound of the rushing water in their ears. He was the first to speak then.

«I want to explain,» he said quietly.

«Yes.» She waited for him to go on.

«I suppose that there are times in life when it is better to throw over one's own scruples, if one has any,» he began. «I have never done anything to be very proud of, perhaps; but I never did anything to be ashamed of, either. Perhaps I shall be ashamed of what I am going to say now. I don't care. I would rather commit a crime than let you wreck your whole existence; but I hope you will not make me do that.»

They had stopped in their walk, and were leaning against the railing that runs along the bank.

«You are talking rather desperately,» said Helen, in a low voice.

«It is rather a desperate case,» Wimpole answered. «I talk as well as I can, and there are things which I must tell you, whatever you think of me—things I never meant to say, but which have made up most of my life. I never meant to tell you—»

«What?»

«That I love you. That is the chief thing.»

The words did not sound at all like a lover's speech as he spoke them. He had drawn himself up, and stood quite straight, holding the rail with his hands. He spoke coolly, with a sort of military precision, as though he were facing an enemy's fire. There was not exactly an effort in his voice, but the tone showed that he was doing a hard thing at that moment. Then he was silent, and Helen said nothing for a long time. She was leaning over the rail, trying to see the running water in the dark.

«Thank you,» she said at last, very simply, and there was another pause.

«I did not expect you to say that,» he answered presently.

«Why not? We are not children, you and I. Besides, I knew it.»

«Not from me!» Wimpole turned almost sharply upon her.

«No; not from you. You wrote Henry a letter many years ago; do you remember? I had to read everything when he went to the asylum, so I read that too. He had kept it all those years.»

«I am sorry; I never meant you to know. But it does not matter now, since I have told you myself.»

He spoke coldly again, almost indifferently, looking straight before him into the night.

«It matters a great deal,» said Helen, almost to herself, and he did not hear her.

She kept her head bent down, though he could not have seen her face clearly if she had looked up at him. Her letter burned her, and she hated herself and loved him. She despised herself because, in the midst of the greatest sacrifice of her life, she had felt the breath of far delight in words that cost him so much. Yet she would have suffered much, even in her good pride, rather than have had them unspoken, for she had unknowingly waited for them half a lifetime. Being a good woman, she was too much a woman to speak one word in return beyond the simple thanks that sounded so strangely to him; for women exaggerate both good and evil as no man can.

«I know, I know!» he said, suddenly continuing. «You are married, and I should not speak. I believe in those things as much as you do, though I am a man, and most men would laugh at me for being so scrupulous. You ought never to have known, and I meant that you never should. But then you are married to Harmon still because you choose to be and because you will not be free. Does not that make a difference?»

«No, not that; that makes no difference.» She raised her head a little.

«But it does now,» answered Wimpole. «It is because I do love you just as I do, with all my heart, that I mean to keep you from him, whether it is right or wrong. Don't you see that right and wrong only matter to one's own miserable self? I shall not care what becomes of my soul if I can keep you from all that unhappiness—from that real danger. It does not matter what becomes of me afterward; even if I were to go straight to New York, and kill Harmon, and be hanged for the murder, it would not matter so long as you were free and safe.»

The man had fought in honorable battles, and had killed, and knew what it meant.

«Is that what you intend to do?» asked Helen, and her voice shook.

«It would mean a great deal if I had to do it,» he answered quietly enough. «It would show that I loved you very much. For I have been an honorable man all my life, and have never done anything to be ashamed of. I should be killing a good deal besides Henry Harmon, but I would give it to make you happy, Helen. I am in earnest.»

«You could not make me happy in that way.»

«No; I suppose not. I shall find some other way. In the first place, I shall see Harmon and talk to him—»

«How? When?» Helen turned up her face in surprise.

«If you send that letter I shall leave to-night,» said the colonel. «I shall reach New York as soon as your letter, and see Harmon before he reads it, and tell him what I think.»

«You will not do that?» She did not know whether she was frightened or not by the idea.

«I will,» he answered; «I will not stay here tamely and let you wreck your life. If you mail your letter I shall take the midnight train to Paris. I told you that I was in earnest.»

Helen was silent, for she saw a new difficulty and more trouble before her, as though the last few hours had not brought her enough.

«I think,» said Wimpole, «that I could persuade Harmon not to accept your generosity.»

«I am not doing anything generous. You are making it hard for me to do what is right. You are almost threatening to do something violent to hinder me.»

«No; I know perfectly well that I should never do anything of that sort, and I think you know it too. To treat Harmon as he deserves would certainly make a scandal which must reflect upon you.»

«Please remember that he is still my husband—»

«Yes,» interrupted Wimpole, bitterly; «and that is his only title to consideration.»

Helen was on the point of rebuking him, but reflected that what he said was probably true.

«Please respect it then, if you think so,» she said quietly enough. «You say that you care for me—no, I won't put it so—you do care for me. You love me, and I know you do. Let us be perfectly honest with each other. As long as you help me to do right, it is not wrong to love me as you do, though I am another man's wife. But as soon as you stand between me and my husband, it is wrong—wicked! It is wicked, no matter what he may have been to me. That has nothing to do with it. It is coming between man and wife—»

«Oh, really, that is going rather far!»

Wimpole raised his head a little higher, and seemed to breathe the night air angrily through his nostrils.

«No,» answered Helen, persistently, for she was arguing against her heart, if not against her head; «it is not going at all too far. Such things should be taken for granted, or at least they should be left to the man and wife in question to decide. No one has any right to interfere, and no one shall. If I can forgive, you can have nothing to resent; for the mere fact of your liking me very much does not give you any sort of right to direct my life, does it? I am glad that you are so fond of me, for I trust you and respect you in every way, and even now I know that you are interfering only because you care for me. But you have not the right to interfere, not the slightest; and although you may be able to, yet if I beg you not to, it will not be honorable of you to come between us.»

Colonel Wimpole moved a little impatiently.

«I will take my honor into my own hands,» he said.

«But not mine,» answered Helen.

They looked at each other in the gloom as they leaned upon the railing.

«Yours shall be quite safe,» said the colonel, slowly. «But if you will drop that letter into the river you will make things easier in every way.»

«I should write it over again. Besides, I have telegraphed to him already.»

«What? Cabled?»

«Yes; you see that you can do nothing to hinder me. He has my message already; the matter is decided.»

She bent her head again, looking down into the rushing water as though tired of arguing.

«You are a saint,» said the colonel; «I could not have done that.»

«Perhaps I could not if I had waited,» answered Helen, in a voice so low that he could hardly hear the words. «But it is done now,» she added still lower, so that he could not hear at all.

Wimpole had been a man of quick decisions so long as he had been a soldier, but since then he had cultivated the luxury of thinking slowly. He began to go over the situation, trying to see what he could do, not losing courage yet, but understanding how very hard it would be to keep Helen from sacrificing herself.

And she peered down at the black river, that rushed past with a cruel sound, as though it were tearing away the time of freedom second by second. It was done now, as she had said. She knew herself too well to believe that, even if she should toss the letter into the stream, she would not write another in just such words. But the regret was deep, and thrilled with a secret aching pulse of its own all through her; and she thought of what life might have been if she had not made the great mistake, and of what it still might be if she did not go back to her husband. The man who stood beside her loved her, and was ready to give everything, perhaps even to his honor, to save her from unhappiness. And she loved him, too, next to honor. In the tranquil life she was leading there could be a great friendship between them, such as few people can even dream of. She knew him, and she knew herself, and she believed it possible, for once, in the history of man and woman. In a measure it might subsist even after she had gone back to Harmon, but not in the same degree; for between the two men there would be herself. Wimpole would perhaps refuse altogether to enter Harmon's door or to touch Harmon's hand. And then, in her over-scrupulousness, during the time she was to spend with Archie she knew that she should hesitate to receive freely a man who would not be on speaking terms with the husband whom she had taken back, no matter how she felt toward Wimpole.

Besides, he had told her that he loved her, and that made a difference too. So long as the word had never been spoken there had been the reasonable doubt to shield her conscience. His old love might, after all, have turned to friendship, which is like the soft, warm ashes of wood when the fire is quite burned out. But he had spoken at last, and there was no more doubt, and his quiet words had stirred her own heart. He had begun by telling her that he had many things to say; but, after all, the one and only thing he had said which he had never said before was that he loved her.

It was enough, and too much, and it made everything harder for her. We speak of struggles with ourselves. It would really be far more true to talk of battles between our two selves, or even sometimes among our threefold natures—our good, our bad, and our indifferent personalities.

To Helen, the woman who loved Richard Wimpole was not the woman who meant to go back to Henry Harmon; and neither, perhaps, was quite the same person as the mother of poor Archie. The three were at strife with one another, though they were one being in suffering. For it is true that we may be happy in part, and be in part indifferent; but no real pain of the soul leaves room for any happiness at all, or indifference, while it lasts. So soon as we can be happy again, even for a moment, the reality of the pain is over, though the memory of it may come back clearly in cruel little daydreams after years. Happiness is composite; pain is simple. It may take a hundred things to make a man happy, but it never needs more than one to make him suffer. Happiness is in part elementary of the body; but pain is only of the soul, and its strength is in its singleness. Bodily suffering is the opposite of bodily pleasure; but true pain has no true opposite, nor reversed counterpart, of one unmixed composition, and the dignity of a great agony is higher than all the glories of joy.

«Promise me that you will not do anything to hinder me,» said Helen, at last.

«I cannot.» There was no hesitation in the answer.

«But if I ask you,» she said; «if I beg you, if I entreat you—»

«It is of no use, Helen. I should do my best to keep you away from Harmon, even if I were sure that you would never speak to me nor see me again. I have said almost all I can, and so have you. You are half a saint or altogether one, or you could not do what you are doing. But I am not; I am only a man. I don't like to talk about myself much, but I would not have you think that I care a straw for my own happiness compared with yours. I would rather know that you were never to see Harmon again than—» He stopped short.

«Than what?» asked Helen, after a pause.

He did not answer at once, but stood upright again beside her, grasping the rail.

«No matter if you do not understand,» he said at last. «Can I give you any proof that it is not for myself, because I love you, that I want to keep you from Harmon? Shall I promise you that when I have succeeded I will not see you again as long as I live?»

«Oh, no! no!» The cry was sudden, low, and heartfelt.

Wimpole grasped the cold railing a little harder in his hands, but did not move.

«Is there any proof at all that I could give you? Try and think.»

«Why should I need proof?» asked Helen. «I believe you, as I always have.»

«Well, then—» he began, but she interrupted him.

«That does not change matters,» she continued. «You are right merely because you are perfectly disinterested for yourself, and altogether interested for me alone. I am not the only person to be considered.»

«I think you are; and if any one else has any right to consideration, it is Archie."

«I know,» Helen answered; «and you hurt me again when you say it. But, besides all of us, there is Henry.»

«And what right has he?» asked Wimpole, almost fiercely. «What right has he to any sort of consideration from you or from any one? If you had a brother he would have wrung Harmon's neck long ago! I wish I had the right!»

«I never heard you say anything brutal before,» said Helen.

«I never had such good cause,» retorted Wimpole, a little more quietly. «Put yourself in my position. I have loved you all my life,—God knows I have loved you honestly, too,—and held my tongue. And Harmon has spent his life in ruining yours in every way —in ways I know and in ways I don't know, but can more than half guess. He neglected you, he was unfaithful to you, he insulted you, and at last he struck you. I have found that out to-day, and that blow must have nearly killed you. I know about those things. Do you expect me to have any consideration for the brute who has half killed the woman I love? Do you expect me to keep my hands off the man whose hands have struck you and wounded you? By the Lord, Helen, you are expecting too much of human nature! Or too little—I don't know which!»

He had controlled his temper long, keeping down the white heat of it in his heart, but he could not be calm forever. The fighting instinct was not lost yet, and must have its way at last.

«He did not know what he was doing,» said Helen, shrinking a little.

«You have a right to say that,» answered the colonel, «if you can be forgiving enough. But only a coward could say it for you, and only a coward would stand by and see you go back to your husband. I am not a coward, and I won't.» Since you have cabled to him, I shall leave to-night, whether you send that letter or not. Can't you understand?»

«But what can you do? What can you say to him? How can you influence him? Even if I admit that I have no power to keep you from going to him, what can you do when you see him?»

«I can think of that on the way,» said Wimpole. «There will be more than enough time. I don't know what I shall say or do yet.

It does not matter, for I have made up my mind.»

«Will nothing induce you to stay here?» asked Helen, desperately.

«Nothing,» answered Wimpole, and his lips shut upon the word.

«Then I will go too,» answered Helen.

«You!» Wimpole had not thought of such a possibility, and he started.

«Yes. My mind is made up too. If you go, I go. I shall get there as soon as you, and I will prevent you from seeing him at all. If you force me to it, I will defend him from you. I will tell the doctors that you will drive him mad again, and they will help me to protect him. You cannot get there before me, you know, for we shall cross in the same steamer and land at the same moment.»

«What a woman you are!» Wimpole bent his head as he spoke the words, leaning against the railing. «But I might have known it,» he added; «I might have known you would do that; it is like you.»

Helen felt a bitter sort of triumph over herself in having destroyed the last chance of his interference.

«In any case,» she said, «I should go at once. It could be a matter of only a few days at the utmost. Why should I wait, since I have made up my mind?»

«Why indeed?» The colonel's voice was sad. «I suppose the martyrs were glad when the waiting was over, and their turn came to be torn to pieces.»

He felt that he was annihilated, and he suffered keenly in his defeat, for he had been determined to save her at all risks. She was making even risk impossible. If she went straight to her husband, and took him back, and protected him, as she called it, what could any one do? It was a hopeless case. Wimpole's anger against Harmon slowly subsided, and above it rose his pity for the woman who was giving all of life she had left for the sake of her marriage vow, who was ready, and almost eager, to go back to a state full of horror in the past and of danger in the future, because she had once solemnly promised to be Henry Harmon's wife, and could not find in all the cruel years a reason for taking back her word. He bowed his head, and he knew that there was something higher in her than he had ever dreamed in his own honorable life; for it was something that clung to its belief, against all suggestion of right or justice for itself.

It was not only pity: a despair for her crept nearer, and grew upon him every moment. Though he had seen her rarely, he had felt nearer to her since Harmon had been mad, and now he was to be further from her than ever before. He would probably not go so far as she feared, and would be willing to enter her husband's house for her sake, and in the hope of being useful to her. But he could never be so near to her again as he was now, and his last chance of protecting her had vanished before her unchangeable resolution. He would almost rather have known that she was going to her death than see her return to Harmon. He made one more attempt to influence her; he did it roughly, but his voice shook a little.

«It seems to me,» he said, «that if I were a woman, I should be too proud to go back to a man who had struck me.»

Helen moved and stood upright, trying to look into his face clearly in the dimness as she spoke.

«Then you think I am not proud?»

He could see her white features and dark eyes, and he guessed her expression.

«You are not proud for yourself,» he answered rather stubbornly. «If you were you could not do this.»

She turned from him again, and looked down at the black water.

«I am prouder than you think,» she said. «That does not make it easier.»

«In one way, yes. When you have determined to do a thing, you are ashamed to change your mind, no matter what your decision may cost yourself and others.»

«Yes, when I am right. At least, I hope I should be ashamed to break down now.»

«I wish you would!»

It was a helpless exclamation, and Wimpole knew it; for he was at the end of all argument and hope, and his despair for her rose in his eyes in the dark. He could neither do nor say anything more, and presently, when he had left her at the door of her hotel, she would do what she meant to do to the letter. For the second time on that day he wished that he had acted instead of speaking, and that he had started upon his journey without warning her. But in the first place, he had believed that she would take more time to consider her action, and again, he had a vague sense that it would not have been loyal and fair to oppose her intention without warning her. And now she had utterly defeated him, and upheld her will against him in spite of all he could do. He loved her the better for her strength, but he despaired the more. He felt that he was going to say good-by to her as if she were about to die.

He put out his hand to take hers, and she met it readily. In her haste to come out with her letter she had not even taken the time to put on gloves, and her warm, firm fingers closed upon his thin hand as though they were the stronger.

«I must go,» she said; «it is very late.»

«Is it?»

«Yes; I want to thank you for wishing to help me—and for everything. I know that you would do anything for me, and I like to feel that you would; but there is nothing to be done. Henry will answer my cable, and then I shall go to him.»

«It is as though you were dying, and I were saying good-by to you, Helen.»

«That would be easier,» she answered, «for you and for me.»

She pressed his hand with a frank, unaffected pressure, and then withdrew her own. He sighed as he turned from the dark water to cross the quiet street with her. The people who had been walking about had gone home suddenly, as they do in provincial places, and the electric light glared and blinked upon the deserted macadamized road. There was something unwontedly desolate, even the air, for the sky was cloudy, and a damp wind came up from the lake.

Without a word the two walked to the post-office, and as Wimpole saw the irrevocable message dropped into the slit his heart almost stopped beating. A faint smile that was cruelly sad to see crossed Helen's white face—a reflection of the bitter victory she had won over herself against such great odds.

XI.

THE two walked slowly and silently along the pavement to the hotel, the damp wind following them in fitful gusts, and chilling them as they went. They had no words, for they had said all to each other; each knew that the other was suffering, and both knew that their lives had led them into a path of sadness from which they could not turn back. They walked wearily and unwillingly side by side, and the way seemed long, and yet too short, as it shortened before them.

At the lighted porch of the hotel they paused, reluctant to part.

«May I see you to-morrow?» asked Wimpole, in a dull voice.

«Yes; I must see you before I go,» Helen answered.

In the light of the lamps he saw how pale she was, and how very tired; and she looked at him, and knew from his face how he was suffering for her. They joined hands, and forgot to part them when their eyes had met. But they had nothing to say, for all had been said, and they had only to bid each other a good night which meant good-by to both, though they should meet ever so often again.

The porter of the hotel stood in the doorway a few steps above them, and watched them with a sort of stolid interest. The lamplight gleamed upon his gilt buttons, and the reflection of them made Helen aware of his presence. Then he went into the entrance, and there was nobody else about. Voices came with broken laughter from the small garden adjacent to the hotel, where there was a café, and far away, at the end of the entrance-hall, the clerk pored over his books.

Still Wimpole held Helen's hand.

«It is very hard,» he said.

«It is harder than you know,» she answered.

For she loved him, though he did not know it, and she felt as well as he did that she was losing him. But because she was Harmon's wife, and meant to stand by her husband, she would not call it love in her heart, though she knew her own secret. She would hardly let herself think that it was much harder for her than for Wimpole, though she knew it. Temptation is not sin. She had killed her temptations that day, and in their death had almost killed herself.

The sacrifice was perfect and whole-hearted, brave as true faith, and final as death itself.

«Good night,» said Wimpole, and his voice broke.

Helen still had strength to speak.

«Neither you nor I shall ever regret this,» she answered; but she looked long at him, as though she were not to see him again.

He pressed her hand hard, and dropped it. Once more she looked at him, and then turned slowly and left him standing there.

The porter of the hotel was facing her on the steps. Neither she nor Wimpole had noticed that he had come back, and was waiting for them to part. He held a telegram in his hand, and Helen started slightly as she saw it, for she knew that it must be Harmon's answer to her word of forgiveness.

«Already!» she exclaimed faintly, as she took it.

She turned back to Wimpole, and met his eyes again, for he had not moved.

«It is Henry's answer,» she said.

She opened the envelop, standing with her

back to the light and to the porter. Wimpole breathed hard, and watched her face, and knew that nothing was to be spared to either of them on that day. As she read the words, he thought she swayed a little on her feet, and her eyes opened very wide, and her lips were white. Wimpole watched them, and saw how strangely they moved, as if she were trying to speak and could not. He set his teeth, for he believed that even the short message had in it some fresh insult or injury for her.

She reeled visibly, and steadied herself against one of the pillars of the porch; but she was able to hold out the thin scrap of paper to Wimpole as he moved forward to catch her. He read it. It was a cable notice through the telegraph office, from Brest:

> Your message number 731 Henry Harmon New York not delivered owing to death of person addressed.

Wimpole read the words twice before their meaning stunned him. When he knew where he was, his eyes were still on the paper, and he was grasping Helen's wrist, while she stood stark and straight against the pillar of the porch. She lifted her free hand and passed it slowly across her forehead, opening and shutting her eyes as if waking. The porter stared at her from the steps.

«Come,» said Wimpole, drawing her; «let us go out again. We can't stay here.»

Helen looked at him, only half comprehending. Even in the uncertain light he could see the color returning to her face, and he felt it in his own. Then her senses came back all at once, with her own clear judgment and decision, and the longing to be alone which he could not understand as he tried to draw her away with him.

«No, no!» she cried, resisting. «Let me go; please let me go! Please!»

He had already dropped her wrist.

«Come to-morrow,» she added quickly.

And all her lost youth was in her as she lightly turned and went from him up the steps. Again he stood still, following her with his eyes; but an age had passed, with Harmon's life, between that time and this.

He understood better when he himself was alone, walking far on through the damp wind by the shore of the lake, past the big railway-station, just then in one of its fits of silence, past the wooden piers built out into the lake for the steamers, and out beyond, not counting his steps, nor seeing things, with bent head, and one hand catching nervously at the breast of his coat.

He understood Helen, for he also had need of being alone to face the tremendous contrast of the hour, and to digest in secret the huge joy he was ashamed to show to himself because it was for the death of a man whose existence had darkened his own. Because Harmon was suddenly dead the sleeping hope of twenty years had waked with deep life and strength. Time and age were rolled away like a mist before the morning breeze, the world was young again, and the rose of yesterday was once more the lovely flower of to-day.

Yet he was too brave a man and too good to let himself rejoice cruelly in Harmon's death, any more than he would have gloried in his younger days over an enemy fallen in fight. But it was hard to struggle against the instinct, deep-rooted and strong in humanity ages before Achilles dragged Hector round the walls of Troy. Christianity has made it mean to insult the dead and their memory. For what we call honor comes to us from chivalry and knighthood, which grew out of Christian doings when men believed; and though non-Christian people have their standards of right and wrong, they have not our sort of honor, nor anything like it, and cannot in the least understand it.

But Wimpole was made happy by Harmon's death, and he himself could not deny it. That was another matter, and one over which he had no control. His satisfaction was in the main disinterested, being on Helen's behalf; for though he hoped, he was very far from believing that she would marry him now that she was a widow. He had not even guessed that she had loved him long. It was chiefly because his whole nature had been suffering so sincerely for her sake, during the long hours since he had read the paragraph in the paper, that he was now so immensely happy. He tried to call up again the last conversation in the dark by the river; but though the words both he and she had spoken came back in broken echoes, they seemed to have no meaning, and he could not explain to himself how he could possibly have stood there wrenching at the cold iron rail to steady his nerves less than half an hour ago. It was incredible. He felt like a man who has been in the delirium of a fever in which he has talked foolishly and struck out wildly at his friends, and who cannot believe such things of himself when he is recovering, though he dimly remembers them with a sort of half-amused shame for his weakness.

Wimpole did not know how long he wandered by the lake in the windy darkness before he felt that he had control of speech and action again, and found himself near the bridge going toward his hotel. It was less than half an hour, perhaps; but ever afterward, when he thought of it, he seemed to have walked up and down all night, a hundred times past the railway-station, a hundred times along the row of steamboat piers, struggling with the impression that he had no right to be perfectly happy, and fighting off the instinct to rejoice in Harmon's death.

But Helen had fled to her own room, and had locked the door upon the world. To her, as to Wimpole, it would have seemed horrible to be frankly glad that her husband was dead. But she had no such instinct. She had been dazed beyond common sense and speech by the sudden relief from the strain she had borne so strongly and bravely. She had been dazzled by the light of freedom, as a man let out of a dark prison after half a lifetime of captivity. She had been half stunned by the instant release of all the springs of her nature, long forced back upon themselves by the sheer strength of her conscience. And yet she was sorry for the dead man.

Far away in her past youth she remembered his handsome face, his bright eyes, his strong vitality, his pleasant voice, and the low ringing tone of it that had touched her and brought her to the ruin of her marriage; and she remembered that for a time she had half loved him and believed love whole. She is a hard and cruel woman who has not a little pitiful tenderness left for a dead past, —though it be buried under a hideous present,—and some kind memory of the man she has called dear.

Helen thought of his face as he was lying dead now, white and stony; but somehow, in her kindness, it became the face of long ago, and was not like him as when she had seen him last. The touch of death is strangely healing. She had no tears, but there was a dim softness in her eyes for the man who was gone—not for the man who had insulted her, tortured her, struck her, but for the husband she had married long ago.

The other, the incarnate horror of her mature life, had dropped from existence, leaving his place full of the light in which she was thereafter to live, and in the bright peace she saw Wimpole's face as he waited for her.

In the midst of her thoughts was the enigmatic specter of the world, the familiar tormentor of those with whom the world has anything to do—a vast disquieting question-mark to their actions. What would the world say when she married Wimpole?

What could it say? It knew, if it knew anything of her, that her husband had been little better than a beast—no better; worse, perhaps. It knew that Wimpole was a man in thousands, and perhaps it knew that he had been faithful to her mere name in his heart during the best of his years. She had no enemies to cast a shadow upon her future by slurring her past.

Yet she had heard the world talk, and the names of women who had married old friends within the first year of widowhood were rarely untouched by scandal. She did not fear that, but in her heart there was a sort of unacknowledged dread lest Wimpole, who was growing old in patience, should be patient to the end out of some over-fine scruple for her fair name.

Then came the thought of her new widowhood, and rebuked her, and with the old habit of fighting battles against her heart for her conscience, she turned fiercely against her long silent love that was crying freedom so loudly in her ears. Harmon just dead, not buried yet perhaps, and she already thinking of marriage! Said in those words, it seemed contemptible, though all her loyalty to her husband had been for a word's sake, almost since the beginning.

But then, again, as she closed her eyes to think sensibly, she set her lips to stay the smile at her scruples. Her loyalty had been all for the vow, for the meaning of the bond, for the holiness of marriage itself. It had not been the loyalty of love for Harmon, and Harmon being dead, its only object was gone. The rest, the mourning for the unloved dead, was a canon of the world, not a law of God. For decency she would wear black for a short time, but in her heart she was free, and free in her conscience.

To the last she had borne all, and had been ready to bear more. Her last word had gone at once with the message of forgiveness he had asked, and though he had been dead before it reached him, he could not have doubted her answer, for he knew her. If she had been near him she would have been with him to the end, to help him and to comfort him if she could. She had been ready to go back to him, and the letter that was to have told him so was already gone upon its fruitless journey, to return to her after a long time as a reminder of what she had been willing to bear. She could not reproach herself with any weakness or omission, and her reason told her plainly that although she must mourn outwardly to please the world, it would be folly to refuse her heart the thought of a happiness for which she had paid beforehand with half a lifetime of pain.

When that was all at once and unmistakably clear to her, she let her head sink gently back upon the cushion of the chair, her set lips parted, and she softly sighed, as though the day were done at last, and her rest had come. As she sat there the lines of sorrow and suffering were smoothed away, and the faint color crept slowly and naturally to her cheeks, as her eyes closed by slow degrees under the shaded light of the lamp. One more restful sigh, her sweet breath came slower and more evenly, one hand fell upon her knee with upward palm and fingers relaxed, and did not move again; she was asleep.

THE END. *F. Marion Crawford.*

# BILLY AND HANS: A TRUE HISTORY.

WITH PICTURES BY LISA STILLMAN.

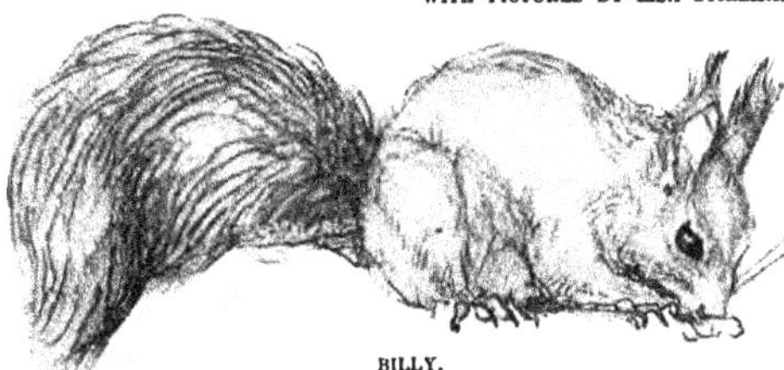

BILLY.

In my favorite summer resort at the lower edge of the Black Forest, the quaint old town of Laufenburg, a farmer's boy one day brought me a young squirrel for sale. He was a tiny creature, probably not yet weaned, a variation on the ordinary type of the European *Sciurus* (*Sciurus vulgaris*), gray instead of the usual red, and with black tail and ears, so that at first, as he contented himself with drinking his milk and sleeping, I was not sure that he was not a dormouse. But examination of the paws, with their delicate anatomy, so marvelously like the human hand in their flexibility and handiness, and the graceful curl of his tail, settled the question of genus; and mindful of my boyhood and early pets, I bought him and named him Billy. From the first moment that he became my companion he gave me his entire confidence, and accepted his domestication without the least indication that he considered it captivity. There is generally a short stage of mute rebellion in wild creatures before they come to accept us entirely as their friends—a longing for freedom which makes precautions against escape necessary. This never appeared in Billy; he came to me for his bread and milk, and slept in my pocket, from the first, and enjoyed being caressed as completely as if he had been born under my roof. No other animal is so clean in its personal habits as the squirrel when in health; and Billy soon left the basket which cradled his infancy, and habitually slept under a fold of my bed-cover, sometimes making his way to my pillow and sleeping by my cheek; and

SO long as the problem of the possession of the capacity of reasoning by the animals of lower rank than man in creation is investigated through those of their species that have been domesticated, and in which the problem of heredity has become complicated with human influence, and the natural instincts with an artificial development of their faculties, no really valuable conclusions can be arrived at. It is only when we take the native gifts of an animal under investigation, at least without the intervention of any trace of heredity and of what under teaching may become a second nature, that we can estimate in scientific exactitude the measure of intelligence of one of the lower animals. The ways of a dog or cat are the result of innumerable generations of ancestors reared in intimate relations with the human master mind. As subjects for investigation into the question of animal character they are, therefore, misleading, and the wild creature must be taken. And so far as my observation goes, the squirrel, of all the small animals, shows at once the most character and the most affection; and I believe that the history of two that I have lately lost has a dramatic quality which makes it worth recording.

he never knew what a cage was except when traveling, and even then for the most part he slept in my pocket: He went with me to the table d'hôte, and when invited out sat on the edge of the table and ate his bit of bread with a decorum that made him the admiration of all the children in the hotel, so that he accompanied me in all my journeys. He acquired a passion for tea sweet and warm, and to my indulgence of this taste I fear I owe his early loss. He had full liberty to roam in my room; but his favorite resort was my work-table when I was at work; and when his diet became nuts he used to hide them among my books, and then come to hunt them out again, like a child with its toys. I sometimes found my type-writer stopped, and discovered a hazelnut in the works. And when tired of his hide-and-seek he would come to the edge and nod to me, to indicate that he wished to go into my pocket or be put down to run about the room; and he soon made a limited language of movements of his head to tell me his few wants—food, drink, to sleep, or to take a climb on the highest piece of furniture in the room. He was from the beginning devoted to me, and naturally became like a spoiled child. If I gave him an uncracked nut, he rammed it back into my hand to be cracked for him with irresistible persistence. I did as many parents do, and indulged him, to his harm and my own later grief. I could not resist that coaxing nodding, and gave him what he wished—tea when I had mine, and cracked his nuts, to the injury of his teeth, I was told. In short, I made him as happy as I knew how.

Early in my possession of him I cast about if I might find in the neighborhood a companion of the other sex for him; and when finally I heard that in a village just across the Rhine there was a captive squirrel for sale, I sent my son with orders to buy it if a female. It turned out to be a male, but he bought it just the same—a bright, active, and quite unreconciled prisoner, two months older than Billy, of the orthodox red, just tamed enough to take his food from the hand, but accustomed to be kept with his neck in a collar to which there was attached a fathom of light dog-chain. He refused with his utmost energy to be handled; and as it was not possible to keep the little creature in the torture of that chain,—for I refuse to keep a caged creature,—I cut the collar and turned him loose in my chamber, where he kept involuntary company with Billy. The imprisonment of the half-tamed but wholly unreconciled animal was perhaps as painful to me as to him, and my first impulse was to turn him out into his native forest to take his chances of life; but I considered that he was already too far compromised with Mother Nature for this to be prudent; for having learned to take his food from a man, the first attack of hunger was sure to drive him to seek it where he had been accustomed to find it, and the probable consequence was being knocked on the head by a village boy, or at best reconsigned to a worse captivity than mine. He had no mother, and he was still

ENGRAVED BY PETER AITKEN.

HANS.

little more than a baby, so I decided to keep him and make him as happy as he would let me. His name was Hans. Had I released him as I thought to do, I had saved myself one sorrow, and this history had lost its interest.

After a little strangeness the companionship between the two became as perfect as the utterly diverse nature of their squirrelships would permit. Billy was social and as friendly as a little dog, Hans always a little morose and not over-ready to accept familiarities; Billy always making friendly advances to his companion, which were at first unnoticed, and afterward only submitted to with equanimity. It was as if Billy had accepted the position of the spoiled child of the family, and Hans reluctantly that of an elder brother who is always expected to make way for the pet and baby of the house. Billy was full of fun, and delighted to tease Hans, when he was sleeping, by nibbling at his toes and ears, biting him playfully anywhere he could get at him; and Hans, after a little indignant bark, would bolt away and find another place to sleep in. As they both had the freedom of my large bedroom,—the door of which was carefully guarded, as Hans was always on the lookout for a chance to bolt out into the unknown,—they had plenty of room for climbing, and comparative freedom; and after a little time Hans adopted Billy's habit of passing the night in the fold of my bed-rug, and even of nestling with Billy near my head. Billy was from the beginning a bad sleeper, and in his waking moments his standing amusement was nibbling at Hans, who used to break out of his sleep and go to the foot of the bed to lie; but never for long, for he always worked his way back to Billy, and nestled down again. When I gave Hans a nut, Billy would wait for him to crack it, and deliberately take it out of his jaws and eat it, to which Hans submitted without a fight, or a snarl even, though at first he held on a little; but the good humor and caressing ways of Billy were as irresistible with Hans as with us, and I never knew him to retaliate in any way.

No two animals of the most domesticated species could have differed in disposition more than these. During the first phase of Hans's life he never lost his repugnance to being handled, while Billy delighted in being fondled. The European squirrel is by nature one of the most timid of animals, even more so than the hare, being equaled in this respect only by the exquisite flying-squirrel of America; and when it is frightened, as, for instance, when held fast in any way or in a manner that alarms it, it will bite even the most familiar hand, the feeling being apparently that it is necessary to gnaw away the ligature which holds it. Of course, considering the irreconcilability of Hans to captivity, I was obliged, much against my will, to get a cage for him to travel in; and I made a little dark chamber in the upper part of a wire bird-cage in which the two squirrels were put for traveling. During the first journeys the motion of the carriage or railway-train made Hans quite frantic, while Billy took it with absolute unconcern. On stopping at a hotel, they were invariably released in my room.

Arriving at Rome, I fitted up a deep window recess for their home; but they always had the run of the study, and Hans, while never losing sight of a door left ajar, and often escaping into adjoining rooms, made himself apparently happy in his new quarters, climbing the high curtains, racing along the curtain-poles, and at intervals making excursions to the top of the bookcase, though to both the table at which I was at work soon became the favorite resort, and their antics there were as amusing as those of a monkey. Toward the end of the year Billy developed an indolent habit, which I now can trace to the disease that finally took him from us; but he never lost his love for my writing-table, where he used to lie and watch me at my work by the hour. Hans soon learned to climb down from their window-bench, and up my legs and arms to the writing-table, and down again by the same road when he was tired of his exercises with the pencils or penholders he found there, or of hunting out the nuts which he had hidden the day before among the books and papers; but I never could induce him to stay in my pocket with Billy, who on cold days preferred sleeping there, as the warmth of my body was more agreeable than that of their fur-lined nest. There was something uncanny in Billy—a preternatural animal intelligence which one sees, generally, only in animals that have had training and heredity to work on. He soon learned to indicate to me his few wants, and one of the things which will never fade from my memory was the pretty way in which he used to come to the edge of the window-bench and nod his head to me to show that he wished to be taken; for he soon learned that it was easier to call to me and be taken than it was to climb down the curtain and run across the room to me. He nodded and wagged his head until I went to him, and his flexible nose wrinkled into the grotesque semblance of a smile, with all the seductive entreaty an animal could show; and somehow we learned to understand each other so well that I rarely mistook his want, were it water or food, or to climb, or to get on my table or rest in my pocket. Notwithstanding all the forbearance which Hans showed for his mischievous ways, and the real attachment he had for Billy, Billy clearly preferred me to his companion; and when during the following winter I was attacked by bronchitis, and was kept in my bedroom for several days, after a day of my absence my wife, going into the study, found him in an extraordinary state of excitement, which she said resembled hysterics, and he insisted on being taken. It occurred to her that he wanted me, and she brought him upstairs to my bedroom, when he immediately pointed to be taken to me; and as she was curious to see what he would do, and stopped at the threshold, he bit her hand gently to spur her forward to the bed. When put on the bed, he nestled down in the fur of my bed-cover, perfectly contented. As long as I kept my room he was brought up every day, and passed the day on my bed. At other times the two slept together in an open box linéd with fur, or, what they seemed greatly to delight in, a wisp of new-mown hay, or the bend of the window-curtain, so nestled together that it was hard to distinguish whether there were one or two.

Some instincts of the woods they were long losing the use of, as the habit of changing often their sleeping-places. I provided them with several, of which the ultimate favorite was the bag of the window-curtain; but sometimes when Billy was missing, he was found in my waste-paper basket, and even in the drawer of my type-writer desk, asleep. In their native forests these squirrels have this habit of changing their nests, and the mother will carry her little ones from one tree to another to hide their resting-place, as if she suspected the mischievous plans of the boys to hunt them; and probably she does. But the nest I made my squirrels in their traveling-carriage—of hard cardboard well lined with fur—suited the hiding and secluding ways of Hans for a long time best of all, and he abandoned it entirely only when he grew so familiar as not to care to hide. They also lost the habit of hiding their surplus food when they found food never wanting.

ENGRAVED BY PETER AITKEN

HANS AT THE WINDOW.

When the large cones of the stone-pine came into the market late in the autumn, I got some to give them a taste of fresh nuts; and the frantic delight with which Hans recognized the relation to his national fir-cones, far away and slight as it was, was touching. He raced around the huge and impenetrable cone, tried it from every side, gnawed at the stem and then at the apex, but in vain. Yet he persisted. The odor of the pine seemed an intoxication to him, and the eager satisfaction with which he split the nuts, once taken out for him, even when Billy was watching him to confiscate them when open, was very interesting; for he had never seen the fruit of the stone-pine, and knew only the tiny things which the fir of the Northern forest bears; and to extricate the pine-nuts from their strong and hard cones was impossible to his tiny teeth. As for Billy, he was content to sit and look on while Hans gnawed, and to take the kernel from him when he had split the nut; and the charming *bonhomie* with which he appropriated it, and with which Hans submitted to the piracy, was a study.

The friendship between the two was very interesting, for while Billy generally preferred being with me to remaining on his window-bench with Hans, he had intervals when he insisted on being with Hans; while the latter seemed to care for nothing but Billy, and would not remain long away from him willingly as long as Billy lived. When the summer came again, being unable to leave them with servants or the housekeeper, I put them in their cage once more, and took them back to Laufenburg for my vacation. Hans still retained his impatience at the confinement even of my large chamber, and with a curious diligence watched the door for a crack to escape by, though in all other respects he seemed happy and at home and perfectly familiar; and though always in this period of his life shy with strangers, he climbed over me with perfect nonchalance. Billy, on the contrary, refused freedom, and when I took him out into his native woods he ran about a little, and came back to find his place in my pocket as naturally as if it had been his birth-nest. But the apparent yearning of Hans for liberty was to me an exquisite pain. He would get up on the window-bench, looking out one way on the rushing Rhine, and the other on the stretching pine forest, and stand with one paw on the sash and the other laid across his breast, and turn his bright black eyes from one to the other view incessantly, and with a look of passionate eagerness which made my heart ache. If I could have found a friendly park where he could have been turned loose in security from hunger and the danger of hunting boys and the snares which beset a wild life, I would have released him at once. I never so felt the wrong and mutual pain of imprisonment of God's free creatures as then with poor Hans, whose independent spirit had always made him the favorite of the two with my wife; and now that the little drama of their lives is over, and Nature has taken them both to herself again, I can never think of this eager little creature with his passionate outlook over the Rhineland without tears. But in the Rhineland, under the pretext that they eat off the top twigs of the pine-trees and spoil their growth, they hunt the poor things with a malignancy that makes it a wonder that there is one left to be captured, and Hans's chance of life in those regions was the very least a creature could have. As to the pretext of the destruction of the pine-tops, I have looked at them in every part of the Black Forest that I have visited, and have never been able to discover one tree-top spoiled. It is possible that the poor little creatures, when famished, may eat the young twigs of trees; but in my opinion the accusation is only the case of the wolf who wants an excuse to eat the lamb. Hans and Billy were both fond of roses and lettuce; but nothing else in the way of vegetation, other than fruits and nuts, would they eat. But when I remember that in my boyhood I have joined in squirrel hunts, and that my murderous lead has often crashed through their tender frames, I have no right to cast stones at the Germans, but with pain and humiliation remember my cruelty. I would sooner be myself shot than shoot another. I feel so keenly their winsome grace when I can watch them in freedom that I cannot draw the line between them and myself, except that they are worthier of life than I am. The evolutionists tell us that we are descended from some common ancestor of the monkey. It may be so; and if, as has been conjectured by one scientist, that was the lemur, which is the link between the monkey and the squirrel, I should not object; but I hope that we branched off at the *Sciurus*, for I would willingly be the far-off cousin of my little pets.

But before leaving Rome for my summer vacation at Laufenburg, the artificial habits of life, and my ignorance of the condition of squirrel health, began to work their usual consequences. Billy had begun to droop, and symptoms of some organic malady appeared; though he grew more and more devoted to me, his ambition to climb and disport himself diminished, and it was clear that his civilized life had done for him what it does for many of us—shortened his existence. He never showed signs of pain, but grew more sluggish, and would come to me and rest, licking my hand like a little dog, and was as happy so as his nature could show. They both hailed again with greedy enthusiasm the first nuts, fresh and crisp, and the first peaches, which I went to Basel to purchase for them; and what the position permitted me I supplied them with, with a guilty feeling that I could never atone for the loss of what they lost with freedom. I tried to make them happy in any way in my limited abilities, and, the vacation over, we went back to Rome and the fresh pine-cones and their window niche.

But there Billy grew rapidly worse, and I realized that the tragedy of our little menage was coming. He grew apathetic, and would lie with his great black eyes looking into space, as if in a dream. It became a tragedy for me, for the symptoms were the same as those of a dear little fellow who had first rejoiced my father's heart in the years gone by, and who lies in an old English churchyard; whose last hours I watched lapsing into the eternity beyond painlessly, and he, thank God! understanding nothing of the great change. When he could no longer speak he beckoned me to lay my head on the same pillow. He died of blood-poisoning, as I found after Billy's death that he also did; and the identity of the symptoms (of the cause of which I then understood nothing) brought back the memory of that last solitary night when my boy passed from under my care, and his eyes, large and dark like Billy's, grew dim and vacant like his. Billy, too, clung the closer to me as his end approached; and when the apathy left him almost no recognition of things around, he would grasp one of my fingers with his two paws, and lick it till he tired. It was clear that death was at hand,

and on the last afternoon I took him out into the grounds of the Villa Borghese to lie in the sunshine, and get perhaps a moment of return to Mother Nature; but when I put him on the grass in the warm light he only looked away into vacancy, and lay still, and after a little dreamily indicated to me to take him up again; and I remembered that on the day before his death I had carried Russie into the green fields, hoping they would revive him for one breathing-space, for I knew that death was on him; and he lay and looked off beyond the field and flowers, and now he almost seemed to be looking out of dear little Billy's eyes.

ENGRAVED BY PETER AITKEN.

BILLY AND HANS.

I went out to walk early the next morning, and when I returned I found Billy dead, still warm, and sitting up in his box of fresh hay in the attitude of making his toilet; for to the last he would wash his face and paws, and comb out his tail, even when his strength no longer sufficed for more than the mere form of it. I am not ashamed to say that I wept like a child. The dear little creature had been to me not merely a pet to amuse my vacant hours, though many of those most vacant which sleepless nights bring had been diverted by his pretty ways as he shared my bed, and by his singular devotion to me, but he had been as a door open into the world of God's lesser creatures, an apostle of pity and tenderness for all living things, and his memory stands on the eternal threshold nodding and beckoning to me to enter in and make part of the creation I had ignored till he taught it to me, so that while life lasts I can no longer inflict pain or death upon the least of God's creatures. If it be true that «to win the secret of a plain weed's heart» gives the winner a clue to the hidden things of the spiritual life, how much more the conscient and reciprocal love which Billy and I bore, and I could gladly say still bear, each other must widen the sphere of spiritual sympathy which, widening still, reaches at last the eternal source of all life and love, and finds indeed that one touch of nature makes all things kin. Living and dying, Billy has opened to me a window into the universe of the existence of which I had no suspicion; his little history is an added chamber to that eternal mansion into which my constant and humble faith assures me that I shall some time enter; he has helped me to a higher life. If love could confer immortality, he would share eternity with me, and I would thank the Creator for the companionship. And who knows? Thousands of human beings to whom we dare not deny the possession of immortal souls have not half Billy's claim to live forever. May not the Indian philosopher with his transmigration of souls have had some glimpses of a truth?

But my history is only half told. When I found the little creature dead, and laid him down in an attitude befitting death, Hans came to him, and making a careful and curious study of him, seemed to realize that something strange had come, and stretched himself out at full length on the body, evidently trying to warm it into life again, or feeling that something was wanting which he might impart, and this failing, began licking the body. When he found that all this was of no avail, he went away into the remotest corner of his window niche, refusing to lie any longer in their common bed or stay where they had been in the habit of staying together. All day he would touch neither food nor drink, and for days following he took no interest in anything, hardly touching his food. Fearing that he would starve himself to death, I took him out on the large open terrace of my house, where, owing to his old persistent desire to escape, I had never dared trust him, and turned him loose among the plants. He wandered a few steps as if bewildered, looked all about him, and then came deliberately to me, climbed my leg, and went voluntarily into the pocket Billy loved to lie in, and in which I had never been able to make Hans stay for more than a minute or so. The whole nature of the creature became changed. He reconciled himself to life, but never again became what he had been before. His gaiety was gone, his wandering ambitions were forgotten, and his favorite place was my pocket—Billy's pocket. From that time he lost all desire to escape; even when I took him out into the fields or woods he had no desire to leave me, but after a little turn and a half attempt to climb a tree, would come back voluntarily to me, and soon grew as fond of being caressed and stroked as Billy had been. It was as if the love he bore Billy had changed him to Billy's likeness. He never became as demonstrative as Billy was, and to my wife, who was fond of teasing him, he always showed a little pique, and even if buried in his curtain nest or in the fold of my rug, and asleep, he would scold if she approached within several yards of him; but to me he behaved as if he had consciously taken Billy's place. I sent to Turin to get him a companion, and the merchant sent me one guaranteed young and a female; but I found it a male which died of old age within a few weeks of his arrival. Hans had hardly become familiarized with him when he died. The night before he died I came home late in the evening, and having occasion to go into my study, I was surprised, when I opened the door, to find Hans on the threshold nodding to me to be taken, with no attempt to escape as of old. I took him up, wondering what had disturbed him at an hour when he was never accustomed to be afoot, put him back in his bed, and went to mine. But thinking over the strange occurrence, I got up, dressed myself, and went down to see if anything was wrong, and found the new squirrel hanging under the curtain in which the two had been sleeping, with his hind claws entangled in the stuff, head down, and evidently very ill. He had probably felt death coming, and tried to get down and find a hiding-place, but got his claws entangled, and could not extricate them. He died the next day, and I took Hans to sleep in his old place in the fold of my bed-cover, where, with a few days' interruption, he slept as long as he lived. He insisted on being taken, in fact, when his sleeping-time came, and would come to the edge of his shelf and nod to me till I took him, or if I delayed he would climb down the curtain and come to me. One night I was out late, and on reaching home I went to take him, and not finding him in his place, alarmed the house to look for him. After long search I found him sitting quietly under the chair I always occupied in the study. He got very impatient if I delayed putting him to bed, and, like Billy, he used to bite my hand to indicate his discontent, gently at first, but harder and harder till I attended to him. When he saw that we were going up-stairs to the bedroom he became quiet.



Whether from artificial conditions of life or because he suffered from the loss of Billy (after whose death he never recovered his spirits), or, as I fear, from a fall from some high piece of furniture,—for he loved still to be on any height, and his claws, grown too long, no longer held to the furniture, so that he had several heavy falls,—his hind legs became slowly paralyzed. He now ran with difficulty; but his eyes were as bright and his intelligence was as quick as ever, and his fore feet were as dexterous. His attachment to me increased as the malady progressed; and though from habit he always scolded a little when my wife approached him, he showed a great deal of affection for her toward the end, which was clearly approaching. Vacation came again, and I took him once more with me to the Black Forest, hoping that his mysterious intelligence might find some consolation in the native air. He was evidently growing weak very fast, and occasionally showed impatience as if in pain; but for the most of the time he rested quietly in my pocket, and was most happy when I gave him my hand for a pillow, sometimes, though rarely, licking the hand, for he was even then far more reserved in all his expressions of feeling than Billy. At times he would sit on the window-bench, and scan the landscape with something of the old eagerness that used to give me so much pain, snuffing the mountain air eagerly for a half-hour, and then nod to go into my pocket again; and at other times, as if restless, would insist in the way he had made me understand that, like a baby, he wanted motion, and when I walked about with him he grew quiet and content again. At home he had been very fond of a dish of dried rose-leaves, in which he would wallow and burrow, and my wife sent him from Rome a little bag of them, which he enjoyed weakly for a little. But in his last days the time was spent by day mostly in my pocket, and by night on my bed with his head on my hand. It was only the morning before his death that he seemed really to suffer, and then a great restlessness came on him, and a disposition to bite convulsively whatever was near him; but at the end he lay quietly in my hand, and when the spasm was on him I gave him a little chloroform to inhale till it had passed, and when he breathed his last in my pocket I knew that he was dead only by my hand on his heart. I buried him, as I had wished, in his native forest, in his bed of rose-leaves, digging a niche under a great granite boulder. He had survived his companion little more than six months, and if the readers of my little history are disposed to think me weak when I say that his death was to me a great and lasting grief, I am not concerned to dispute their judgment. I have known grief in all its most blinding and varied forms, and I thank God that he constituted me loving enough to have kept a tender place in my heart «even for the least of these,» the little companions of two years; and but for my having perhaps shortened their innocent lives, I thank him for having known and loved them as I have.

DRAWN BY H. D. NICHOLS. FROM A PHOTOGRAPH.
THE GRAVE OF HANS.

*W. J. Stillman.*

# «WHY THE CONFEDERACY FAILED.»

## OPINIONS OF GENERALS S. D. LEE, JOSEPH WHEELER, E. P. ALEXANDER, E. M. LAW, DON CARLOS BUELL, O. O. HOWARD, AND JACOB D. COX.

**The communications which follow from distinguished general officers who were engaged in the War of Secession have been received in reply to our request for frank comment upon the points raised in the article in The Century for November entitled «Why the Confederacy Failed,» written by Mr. Duncan Rose, son of a Confederate officer.—Editor.**

### FROM STEPHEN D. LEE, LIEUTENANT-GENERAL C. S. A.

I AM asked to give my frank opinion of the correctness of Mr. Rose's article. The writer gives three main causes of failure: «(1) The excessive issue of paper money, (2) the policy of dispersion, (3) the neglect of the cavalry,» and remarks, «The ‹sinews of war› mean specie, and nothing but specie.»

History tells us that nearly all great wars have been waged on currency that greatly depreciated in value, and yet with peace and success came full restoration of credit. This has been the case with England, France, Germany, and Russia. Finances always go wrong in failures. In our Revolution success could not even rescue the worthless paper money of our fathers from repudiation and oblivion. Alexander H. Stephens says that in the great war between the States «both sides relied for means of support upon issues of paper money and upon loans secured by bonds.» Nearly all currency issued by countries in great wars is to a certain extent «fiat money,» and depends for its redemption mainly upon the success of the issuing country. Federal greenbacks had only the faith of the government behind them, while the bills and bonds of the Confederacy had enormous quantities of cotton and tobacco, received as tithes and purchased with bonds, that were assets against its liabilities. Had the Confederacy succeeded, its ability to meet its obligations would have been recognized by financiers.

Mr. Rose says that the Confederacy provided little for taxation, and during the war «there was raised by taxation the pitiful sum of $48,000,000, and that all paper money.» Certainly the people of the Confederacy were taxed when they gave their specie (all they had) for bonds, and by law one-tenth of all their crops and of all the proceeds of their labor in every industry. This latter was better than money. *It was a tithe*, which, although money fluctuated, did not fluctuate, but furnished food, cotton, tobacco, clothing, and supplies generally in kind, and was pretty abundant even to the close of the war in the limited area not occupied by hostile armies. The trouble was that the few lines of railroad were in a worn-out condition, and were overtaxed by transportation. I do not think the statement as to the first main cause is sustained. I shall treat the second and third main causes together.

Strategically, the Confederacy was virtually exposed to combined land and naval attack. «No country could have been more fully exposed to perfectly crushing blows, both on its land and water sides.» This exposure was caused by the Mississippi River cutting it in twain, thus enabling the great fleets of Farragut from the ocean, and Foote from the North, to give their valuable aid to Grant and Sherman, virtually cutting off Texas, Arkansas, and most of Louisiana, even before the fall of Vicksburg, July 4, 1863; and by the Cumberland and Tennessee rivers, each reaching from the Ohio River with a deep southward bend into the very heart of the country, enabling the fleets to transport Grant's army to Fort Henry, and be his flank at Donelson. The control of these rivers, and others from the Atlantic and Gulf coasts, was of vital moment, and neither men nor means should have been spared to maintain control of these water highways. Certainly to do so was not dispersion.

The Confederacy had no navy worth mentioning, and when it lost control of these rivers it lost Texas, Arkansas, most of Louisiana, and most of Tennessee, for troops of the trans-Mississippi territory refused to cross the river after 1862; nor had it vessels to protect the Atlantic and Gulf coasts from combined attack, or to prevent blockade. The Confederacy for the last two years, and on the territory where the issue was decided, was composed of the States of Virginia, North Carolina, South Carolina, Florida, Georgia, Alabama, and Mississippi (seven States), and was a narrow strip from the Potomac to the Mississippi River, open to combined land and naval attack along its entire fronts —north, south, east, and west. It was all frontier, with a white population of 2,500,000 men, and it contained the supplies and means of transportation. There were really only two main armies—Lee's in Virginia, and Johnston's in Georgia. The Mississippi Army had been merged in the Army of Tennessee. This does not appear to be dispersion.

Dispersion, mainly in cavalry, was a political necessity. The battle of States' rights and local self-government was being fought. The States that furnished troops and supplies demanded protection from invasion, desolation, and pillage; and this was reasonable when we consider the character of the war as shown by Sherman's raid in Mississippi and through Georgia, and Sheridan's campaign in the Valley and in other places, the official letters and reports of these officers, and their spirit, not representing one half of the real character of their work. Why send troops to help Virginia and Georgia, and leave other States to desolation and pillage? Certainly this question is pertinent when we consider how the country was laid waste.

The cavalry, when not with the two great armies, was protecting vast granaries needed to feed troops, and defending arsenals and depots which in the narrow belt were open to attack and destruction everywhere, owing to the great odds, and the fleets holding the ocean, gulf, and rivers. The charge of dispersion does not hold good.

The writer speaks of cavalry as it existed in the days of Napoleon and the Revolution. Times had greatly changed. The rifled cannon and the Springfield and repeating rifles, arms of precision with long range, had relegated to the past the dashing cavalry charge against infantry or artillery supported by infantry. Such handling of cavalry then would have been slaughter and death to man and horse. Any splendid brigade of infantry in either army felt secure against the attack of charging cavalry. Besides, our country was more wooded than Europe. No general could watch and plan on his tower as Napoleon did. What could cavalry do in charges on the battle-field of the Wilderness, or at Chickamauga, where the fields were mere patches? Cavalry was nothing more than mounted infantry, and fought on foot even in most cases against cavalry. This arm played as important a part as it ever did in war. It covered the front, rear, and flanks of armies. By celerity of movement it met and overcame or checked isolated columns of troops. It played on lines of transportation; it overlapped armies in battle, and destroyed their trains; and in great battles even moved up along with infantry. It protected extended territory when other troops were concentrated in the great armies. No class of troops was more ably commanded or did better service in either army. The Confederate cavalry was well mounted till near the close of the war. They could not take *all* the horses from a people who had made so many sacrifices, as the Federals did from the people of the South. (See Sherman's report of his march to the sea.) The cavalry was as well equipped and armed as the circumstances permitted.

I am one of those who, like my great namesake, said: «I will not speculate on the causes of the failure, as I have seen abundant causes for it in the tremendous odds brought against us»; «the South was overpowered by the superior numbers and resources of the North.» If we compare the two parts of the country, we find the North outnumbering the South four to one in arms-bearing population, incomparably better prepared for war, having an organized government, an organized army and navy, with arsenals, dockyards, and machine-shops, and having free intercourse with the world from which to get supplies and men; while every port was sealed against help from the outside world to the Confederacy, which had to organize its government, and improvise everything for the unequal struggle from an agricultural population.

The official records show that the North had 2,600,000 men from first to last; after October, 1861, never less than 800,000, and often exceeding 1,000,000 men. 1,050,000 men in round numbers were mustered out at the close of the war.

The Confederates, who, by the most reliable records and authority, had 600,000 from first to last, surrendered

150,000 men. The effective force in the field never exceeded 200,000 men at any one time. This army came mainly from the eleven seceding States, having a population of 6,000,000 whites (3,000,000 males). It was about all that the population could do in soldiers. «The Union armies outnumbered those of the Confederacy in all cases as two, commonly as three, and during the entire time in which General Grant was in command as four, to one.» When we consider that in nearly all important battles the forces did not differ very much, the charge of dispersion might be lodged against the Union commanders rather than against the Confederate, and, considering the relative odds in enlistments, does not indicate dispersion on the part of the Confederates.

In addition to the land forces, the navy of the United States consisted of seven hundred vessels of war, manned by 105,000 sailors, with a fleet of transports, steamers, barges, and coal-floats almost innumerable, which in 1862, on the Mississippi River and its tributaries, alone numbered over twenty-two hundred vessels—a great help to General Grant and other generals in operating against Vicksburg and Port Hudson.

It was not known what was the number of vessels chartered on the Atlantic and Gulf coasts in moving the large armies to Port Royal, the North Carolina coast, Florida, Mobile, and Louisiana. The navy in its help was as decisive in results as the great armies in the field. Without its aid the armies of the Union might not have been successful. It blockaded the coast from the Potomac to the Rio Grande. It cut up the Confederacy by her rivers, in occupying these with gunboats; in establishing many depots and points of departure from the line of coasts and from the river-banks, for armies to invade, overrun, and destroy supplies in new territory; in transporting armies around territory they could not cross; and in saving armies when defeated. Coupled with the navy, I mention the great trunk railways converging in and skirting Confederate territory, connecting with powerful States full of supplies to support armies, and able to transport them in an emergency to any point.

I feel that General R. E. Lee's quotation is a good one, and none other need be sought as a cause of failure.

*S. D. Lee.*

BY JOSEPH WHEELER, LIEUTENANT-GENERAL C. S. A.

History will attribute the failure of the Confederate cause to the great preponderance of men and resources with which it was confronted.

In commenting upon Mr. Rose's article, I would say:

1. That the financial system might have been better no one will deny; but when we consider that a new-born nation equipped, furnished with ammunition, fed, clothed, and paid an army which for four years engaged a force 600,000 strong, it must be admitted that there was much in our financial management to commend.

2. I think the author goes to extremes in condemning the military policy which he terms one of dispersion.

The force with which we defended Charleston was less by far than that with which it was attacked. The surrender of 13,000 men at Fort Donelson was unnecessary. It was quite possible to have withdrawn the army after it had become apparent that the position was untenable. And it is certain that we should never have allowed 30,000 men to become penned up in Vicksburg. But these disasters cannot properly be attributed to the policy which Mr. Rose condemns.

The author is mistaken in asserting that «if every city upon the seaboard had been evacuated at the beginning of the war, the Confederacy would have been stronger.» He is also mistaken in his suggestion that we «should have learned a lesson from the war of the Revolution, whose capital was changed nine times, and the British allowed to march from one end of the thirteen colonies to the other.» In that war, and in Frederick's Seven Years' War, to which he also refers, the conditions were very different from those in our conflict. We were more dependent upon arsenals and depots and lines of communication, and we had political as well as military conditions to consider. The breaking of our railroads by which supplies were carried from Southern granaries would have made it impossible for us to hold Richmond, and the retreat of Lee's army into the Carolinas or Georgia would have been the beginning of the end.

3. The tendency in European armies during the last thirty years has been to increase the cavalry as compared with other arms, and it is true that a large proportion of cavalry generally adds to the efficiency and power of an army. Especially would this apply to a country like the South, where so many were trained horsemen; nevertheless, after careful consideration, the policy adopted by Confederate army commanders was to encourage an increase of their infantry, and to discourage and even prohibit enlistments in the cavalry. In European wars it often occurred that the weaker of two contending armies became disordered, and in this condition a charge by a large body of cavalry completed the discomfiture; but, with rare exceptions, matters were very different during the Civil War.

The first battle of Manassas and the battle of Shiloh might, however, be well cited to sustain the position taken by Mr. Rose. An organized cavalry force under a good commander at Manassas could have overtaken and captured much of McDowell's army in its retreat to Washington, and such a force at Shiloh could have intercepted much of Grant's army in its retreat to the Tennessee River; but after this the improved organization, discipline, and equipment of the Federal army, together with its numerical preponderance, gave it such strength that very few opportunities were offered for cavalry to charge upon a flying foe. At Perryville the Federal corps and divisions which became seriously engaged were defeated and driven in disorder, but night came on and ended the conflict. Our cavalry was occupied with large forces which extended beyond our flanks, and it charged upon them, and captured a great many prisoners; but the complete rout of the 70,000 men under Buell by less than one third that number was not possible. When Murfreesboro' was fought, the cavalry division of Forrest was in western Tennessee, and that of Morgan in Kentucky. The remaining cavalry did valiant service, going around the Federal rear, destroying trains, and charging with good effect upon the disordered Federal right. At Chickamauga our cavalry pursued and captured a number of the retreating enemy, but darkness and barricades stopped their advance, and the next day Rosecrans's army was behind breastworks and fortifications invulnerable to attacks from cavalry. During the last year or eighteen months of the war we did not have an army strong enough to defeat and disperse the army by which it was opposed, and opportunities for cavalry to pursue and complete their discomfiture did not arise.

In General Sherman's campaign in 1864, his force was more than double that commanded by General Johnston. Sherman's army was thoroughly organized, well equipped, well officered and disciplined. It is true that on many occasions we gained a decided victory at the point of attack, and in July, 1864, the Confederate cavalry defeated and dispersed 10,000 cavalry under Stoneman, Garrard, and McCook; but these Confederate successes in no wise disordered the Federal troops which did not engage us, and there was very seldom any flying foe for such cavalry operations as are referred to by Mr. Rose.

The important service performed by this arm was to fight dismounted as infantry, keep close up to the enemy, keep informed of their movements, cover our flanks and prevent their being turned, and frequently to raid upon the enemy's communications. Its business was also to fight the numerous cavalry of the opposing army. With rare exceptions, all these duties were well performed.

What has been said in regard to the opposing armies of Sherman and Johnston also applies to the armies under Grant and Lee. No one will controvert the fact that an increased cavalry force would have been of great service to the Confederacy; but if that increase had been obtained by taking from the infantry, it can hardly be contended that it would have added to our strength. Every thoughtful man will admit that the life of the Confederate government depended upon our maintaining the army under Lee in Virginia, and the Army of the West, commanded at different times by the Johnstons, Beauregard, Bragg, and Hood. It was evident during the entire conflict that so long as these armies were sustained without serious disaster the Confederacy would live; but that if either was disabled by defeat in battle or by loss of resources, so as to be unable to present a firm front to the opposing army, the almost immediate fall of the government would be the inevitable result.

*Joseph Wheeler.*

BY E. P. ALEXANDER, BRIGADIER-GENERAL OF ARTILLERY, C. S. A.

I CONCUR in Mr. Rose's belief that the success of the Confederacy was, for a time, not impossible; but I think it is as difficult to assign brief and general reasons for its failure as it would be to say why A has beaten B in a long and closely contested game of chess. Probably during forty moves B might have won by different play, and each move of the forty might be called the fatal one. But I do not at all think that Mr. Rose has made out his case for any one of the three moves, or causes, which he assigns.

1. Without discussing how or whether the issue of Confederate currency could have been avoided, it is enough to say that it answered its purpose; and the credit of the Confederacy was good enough, both at home and abroad, until long after the date when its last chance in the field was gone. This date, I think, can be exactly fixed as June 15, 1864, the reasons therefor being another story. Up to that date the Confederacy could *buy* anything in the world, from an ironclad in France to a horseshoe in Richmond. The trouble lay in blockades and other obstacles to getting needed articles from places where they could be procured to places where they were needed. Times were often hard in the field and camp, but this cut little figure when the trial of battle was on, and we never lost a field that I know of for lack of food, clothes, ammunition, or anything that money might have bought. Mr. Rose's deductions as to the principles of national taxation are sound enough, and there are indeed many other valuable lessons to be learned from the history of Confederate money, some of them apropos, too, to the present time; but it is not fair to hold its issue responsible for the loss of any battle having any influence upon the final result.

2. I cannot agree at all with Mr. Rose's statement that the Confederate government attempted to hold unnecessary frontier. It was bound to hold large and undisturbed agricultural districts in order to raise food for its armies; and it was bound to guard, even against bridge-burning raids, the long railroad arteries which brought up supplies to the armies; and it was bound to maintain somewhere very large arsenals and machine-shops and warehouses, and to protect them when once located. Richmond, for instance, was defended to the death, not for its being the capital, but for containing the Tredegar Ironworks, without which, it has been said, our armies could not have kept in the field two years. The capital could be moved, but the ironworks could not. These necessities seem to me to justify the defense of every foot of territory which was held after the war was once fairly joined. But had all the Confederate armies been concentrated, as Mr. Rose suggests, on the flanks of the Appalachians or anywhere else, abandoning their arsenals and sources of supply, they would soon have been out of ammunition, and would have been starved into surrender.

Had Mr. Rose, however, criticized the neglect of the Confederate government to utilize the advantage it possessed in having what is technically called «the interior lines» by transferring heavy reinforcements rapidly back and forth between the East and the West, he would have made the most severe criticism which I think can be justly made upon Confederate strategy. This was attempted only once,—in September, 1863,—and then, though under difficulties preventing attainment of the best results, Chickamauga was made a sort of a victory instead of a disastrous defeat.

The greatest opportunity ever offered for such strategy was probably in May, 1863, after Hooker's defeat at Chancellorsville. It was discussed at that time, but not adopted. Vigorously executed, it might have forestalled both the Vicksburg and the Gettysburg campaigns.

3. As to the alleged «neglect of cavalry,» Mr. Rose greatly underestimates the difficulty of supplying horses, and he entirely ignores that of getting men. Men could have been had only by diminishing the number of our

infantry man for man. Considering our inferiority in numbers, and the topography of our average battle-fields, I think no competent military critic would have advised in any of our armies exchanging any material number of our infantry for cavalry. Indeed, the general tendency, as the war went on, was to convert our cavalry into mounted infantry. For the day of decisive cavalry charges passed away with the advent of long-range small arms, breech-loaders, and improved artillery. Even at Waterloo, had half or more of Napoleon's cavalry been artillery and infantry, his chances would have been improved; for their first charge left a rampart of dead horses which broke up all renewed efforts. We may see in future armies large developments of mounted infantry (possibly two men to a horse sometimes), but cavalry, in the old sense of the term, will cut little figure in the future.

It is surely very shallow to charge West Point with depreciation of the cavalry because officers selected for branches of service requiring the most skilled application of the higher mathematics are chosen from among those who, other things being equal, are most proficient in mathematics. Any other principle of selection would be absurd.

Most of Mr. Rose's arguments and illustrations are drawn from events which happened on a different planet from the one now occupying our orbit. The old one, on which Numidians, Macedonians, Napoleon, Frederick, George III, and our forefathers adjusted their various difficulties was not fitted up, either by land or by sea, with steam and electrical appliances. Virtually the only way to go anywhere in force was to walk on land or to take small and inferior sailing-craft by sea. Consequently there were many cases where small nations got the better of large ones because the big fellow could not get at the little one. But in our case the big fellow was all about the little one from the very start, leaving him no resources but Providence and his own pluck. Which failed him, it would be invidious to inquire.

*E. P. Alexander.*

BY E. M. LAW, MAJOR-GENERAL C. S. A.

I AM loath to criticize so thoughtful and interesting a paper as that of Mr. Duncan Rose, in the November number of THE CENTURY, on the question, «Why the Confederacy Failed,» especially as it opens a field for investigation the cultivation of which may bring to light much interesting and as yet unwritten history. But I cannot entirely agree with his conclusion that «in a war for independence numbers do not count.» The history of Poland and that of Hungary are conspicuous refutations of the statement. «The little republic of Switzerland,» which he cites, «won its independence» by reason of the very fact that the kingdoms and empires by which she was surrounded *were* «in arms» as often against one another as against her, as well as because of the impregnability of her mountain fastnesses when properly defended. If we are to credit history, Frederick the Great was «at the last gasp» during the Seven Years' War, and Prussia would probably have shared the fate which overtook Poland a few years later had not the opportune death of the Empress Elizabeth and the accession of Peter III converted Russia, his most powerful foe, into a friend and ally. And, however much national pride may rebel at the admission, the unbiased student of our own Revolutionary history must confess that the American cause was well-nigh hopeless when the powerful intervention of France, and the complications of England with Spain and Holland, turned the scale in our favor. Besides the moral effect of the recognition of our independence, the fleets of France broke the strict blockade of the American ports, and provided the colonies with supplies which were of far more value to them than the few troops furnished by their ally. Had a like good fortune attended the Confederate States, had some friendly nation powerful enough to enforce its decrees recognized their independence and opened their ports, their subjugation would have been impossible, even if we admit the full force of all the reasons assigned for failure.

Our ports being closed, however, and the Confederacy being dependent entirely on its internal resources and credit, Mr. Rose's criticism of its financial system is unanswerable. The free use of the taxing power, to which as a war measure the people would have submitted as patiently as they did to the conscription, was all that could have saved its finances from the ruin that speedily overtook them through the continued issue of irredeemable paper money.

«The policy of dispersion,» which Mr. Rose assigns as another cause of failure, was from a military point of view the gravest mistake that could have been made. It prolonged the struggle, no doubt, but continued adherence to it under the conditions that existed meant certain failure in the end. Some Confederate officers, notably General Joseph E. Johnston, realized this early in the war; but their views were overruled by the Richmond government, which seemed to dread nothing so much as a loss of territory, and adhered to the end, with fatal pertinacity, to the policy of holding positions the defense of which could result only in disaster to the defenders. Whether the Confederate cause would have been won by pursuing an opposite course we cannot know; but a policy of concentration and hard blows, with the decisive results that must have followed, would at least have had the merit of deciding the struggle quickly, and saving the country the prolonged agony and the wasting effects of a four years' war.

For the third cause of failure assigned by Mr. Rose, namely, «the neglect of the cavalry,» I would substitute «the dispersion of the cavalry.» I think the records will show that the Confederacy had cavalry enough in proportion to the other arms of the service, and of a quality superior, man for man, to their antagonists. Had it been concentrated in large bodies in the vicinity of our great armies, under such leaders as Stuart, Forrest, Van Dorn, and Hampton, instead of being scattered by companies, regiments, and brigades all over the country, the many great victories won by those armies might have been as fruitful as they were in fact barren of results.

The causes that contributed to Confederate failure were many, but among them all none can be compared in potency and far-reaching influence to the failure to provide an adequate navy as well as an army; and that a far-sighted statesmanship in the beginning of the struggle could have done this there is little doubt. With open ports, foreign trade would have given the Confederate finances impregnable strength, the armies would not have suffered the deprivation of many things necessary to the efficiency of soldiers in the field, and the rivers of the South would not have been free waterways for Federal gunboats. But despite all the errors of statesmanship, financiering, and generalship, in spite of resources rendered unavailable by reason of blockaded ports, and in the face of greatly superior numbers, the valor and devotion of the Confederate soldier came «perilously near» winning the fight. On two occasions at least the cause was well-nigh won, but was lost again in such a way as almost to compel belief in the direct interposition of Providence.

*E. M. Law.*

BY DON CARLOS BUELL, MAJOR-GENERAL U. S. V.

WHY did the Confederacy fail? The comprehensive answer is that it failed for the want of ability to succeed. To say that the effort was one of the most heroic that ever miscarried, is only to emphasize the formidableness of the obstacles that opposed it.

When we look into the particulars, we find, in comparison with the government which it strove to throw off, that it was deficient in every element that could affect the result of such an enterprise but courage; indeed, we shall be amazed that four years of gigantic effort were required for its overthrow, if we lose sight of the vigor of the resistance, and the inherent difficulty of overcoming any organized revolt of such proportions. We find it completely shut in from foreign intercourse; we find it relatively deficient in men and money and resources of every sort, in military equipment, in facilities for interior communication, in mechanical appliances, in the mechanical skill which so much aided the armies of its adversary, in that material development which occupies so important a place in modern civilization, in foreign confidence and sympathy, in internal confidence as well, and in that profound popular impulse which continually strengthened the armies of its opponent, and threw the whole energy of the North into the contest.

Certainly the early stage of the war was marked by great enthusiasm and bitterness on the part of the South, especially among the upper classes, and the losing cause was followed with fidelity to the end. The Union sentiment in the North was as strong, as enthusiastic, and more general; and there was besides, in an already dominating and growing element, a motive that was stronger and more enduring than enthusiasm —an implacable antagonism which acted side by side with the cause of the Union as a perpetual impelling force against the social conditions of the South, controlling the counsels of the government, and cadencing the march of its armies to the chorus:

> «John Brown's body lies mouldering in the grave,
> But his soul is marching on!»

There was from the first but one reasonable chance for the survival of the Confederacy, and that lay in foreign intervention. Recognition alone would not have availed. How long the contest would have been protracted by such interference, and what might have been the ultimate consequences, are questions which it is not pleasant for an American and a lover of civil liberty to contemplate.

In a conflict of such magnitude as our Civil War, it followed naturally that economic and military policies should exert an important influence. Mere promissory money would be apt to cause embarrassment, but not fatally so in the isolated condition of the Confederacy so long as it satisfied the demands of interior trade. Intrinsically the greenbacks of the North were no better than the paper promises of the South; yet they constituted virtually the sole circulating medium, were received with confidence, and the country was commercially prosperous during the whole war. In the North the use of such money was a policy or device. In the South it was a necessity; for, unable to borrow money abroad, if direct taxation could have been resorted to it would have been futile: the country did not possess wealth enough in an available form for the emergency.

The failure of the financial expedient thus adopted by the South from necessity, without any foundation of material value, became inevitable as soon as it lost the confidence of the public. If there was at the time no other symptom of a distrust of their cause, the rejection of the money of the Confederacy by the people was a sufficient sign of a lack of faith. The bad money was a consequence, not a cause.

The policy of dispersion, as it is called, in the military operations has been criticized on both sides, but not with convincing argument. The conflict was not of a nature to be decided by a single campaign or on purely strategic grounds. The mission of the Federal government was to invade, put down armed opposition, and restore its authority; and the largeness of the force called to the task permitted, indeed required, its employment in different fields of operation at the same time. Correspondingly, all the circumstances of the occasion imposed upon the Confederates the general plan of a popular defensive war. Apart from the necessity of securing the resources of every portion of their territory, by just so far as the Confederate forces consolidated might by superior skill cope successfully with the superior numbers of their opponent, by so far within judicious limits might their successes be multiplied by division against their divided adversary.

There is no reason to suppose that a more extensive or a different use of cavalry would have changed the result of the war. The Confederacy was no better able to secure supremacy in that arm than in any other. The probability is strongly to the contrary, and the South had most to apprehend from rivalry in that direction.

But no explanation of the triumph of the Union cause could be more superficial and erroneous than that which would ascribe the result to military leadership, however meritorious, rather than to the immense momentum of popular will and intelligence which animated and directed the population of the North. That power found an efficient preliminary organizer in the State governments—that peculiar feature of *imperium in imperio* in our political system, which, however it may tend to preserve the liberties of the citizen, may in some future crisis prove as powerful an agent for evil to the nation as in this instance it was fruitful of good to both. It did not contribute as much to the Confederate cause in the South as it did to the cause of the Union in the North.

In these brief notes upon the chances of the Confederacy I make no reference to the so-called teachings of history, which often fail to elucidate satisfactorily the questions to which we apply them. Moreover, the conditions of the civilization of the present day—especially in their bearing upon military science and the mission of civil government—are too unlike those of even a hundred years ago to make it safe to draw comparisons of action without the most careful analysis.

*D. C. Buell.*

BY O. O. HOWARD, MAJOR-GENERAL U. S. A., RETIRED.

WHILE I do not agree with a number of Mr. Rose's postulates, his article presents important points worthy of study and thought.

It was long my favorite theory, born of my deepest conviction and expressed in a letter to the «New-York Times» at the very beginning of the war, that the Union arms would never be successful until the government aimed directly and indirectly with all its power at the extinction of human slavery. With reference to the intrinsic wrong in slavery, I believe the whole nation participated in its perpetuation, and that this fact affected the morale of our people and our armies. When, after terrible chastisement, our morale followed the divine leading, success became continuous and finally complete.

In fervor, devotion to a cause, and persistency, there was doubtless little difference between the governments, peoples, and soldiers of the South and the North.

1. The Confederate government promised to pay dollars (gold or silver) six months after recognition of the Confederacy by the United States. These promises, used as currency, naturally depreciated as their volume increased and the likelihood of success lessened. But all peoples subjected to extraordinary expenses are wont to throw part of the cost upon the future. The Union government did the same in the Civil War. It was hardly possible for the Confederacy to avoid the issue of these promises. Their reckless issue toward the end was like the straw at which the drowning man catches; it was an endeavor to keep the Confederate armies together for a little space while the government looked and prayed for European help.

At last the South was fairly exhausted. The worthless paper money was only an incident. In some localities, at every period of the war, there was much baled cotton; and though it commanded a high price anywhere outside the blockading squadron, within the Confederacy it was of little value, as it could be neither eaten nor shot at the enemy.

2. «The policy of dispersion» referred to I deem a necessity; for as soon as any portions of the seceded States were held by the Union army they contributed nothing to the Confederacy, but, on the other hand, furnished supplies to the United States. As men understood the art of war in 1861, the military administration of the South could hardly have been excelled. It is true that the armies under Lee and Johnston were hampered at times by a weak government; but all governments are human, and liable to weakness in organization and mistakes in operation.

Following a reaction against Napoleon's system, the war in the Crimea, as well as our own in its earlier stages, made much of strategic positions. After General Grant's series of demonstrations in battle, we now clearly see that the objective should have been the enemy's active army. The danger to the respective capitals was indeed a great bugbear; for as long as either side had a well-equipped army, the capture of either capital would have been only an advantage, not a conclusive victory. Certainly the strategic theory or the political situation caused the shedding of much blood and the expenditure of much treasure which from a purely military point of view was a sad waste. The endeavor should have been to destroy the opposing army.

3. It takes long training to make effective cavalry, even if raw recruits can ride. The use of horses to transport troops rapidly from point to point for the purpose of fighting on foot was developed during the war. Confederate generals found that such cavalry as they could raise was very expensive and hard to keep efficient. As soon as they had had a little experience in battle, it was not the nature of our armies to become so demoralized after defeat that cavalry could overrun and destroy them. Shiloh, Chickamauga, and Malvern Hill were hardly victories for the Confederacy, and even Fredericksburg became so only because the Union army failed to carry a position. It withdrew without loss of organization. The reason the Confederates did not gain in these more decisive advantage was not because they were weak in cavalry, but because of the stamina of the withdrawing troops. Union victories, so called, were many, but were not decisive, except in a few instances, because of the stamina of the Confederate soldiers.

During the Rebellion we lived under a Constitution which somewhat checked our raising money. These provisions were copied into the Confederate Constitution. Doubtless there was some disability here, but now we could constitutionally increase our income from the internal-revenue taxes by adding other articles to the list sufficiently to carry on a foreign war—that is, if public opinion would permit. Still, should war come, part of its expense would doubtless be thrown over to the future by the government borrowing money. In reference to losses from «the policy of dispersion,» our principal sea-coast cities must be defended as naval depots; after that, the objective should always be the destruction of any hostile army landing on our shores or entering our country from the north or the south.

Mr. Rose is mistaken in the matter of the assignment of West Point graduates. No «dullard» is *graduated* at West Point. Classes which begin with more than a hundred usually graduate less than fifty. Of these fifty not more than five go into the engineers. The other graduates are always allowed a choice of arms according to their class standing. The cavalry vacancies are generally all filled before the members of the lower half of a class have had a chance to select.

Again, I should say that an invasion of Canada, even without an extraordinary cavalry force, could be made an effective military operation, though a good cavalry force is, of course, always desirable. Its efficiency under Sheridan, however (and it would be more so now), was not so much from the old cavalry impact as from the advantage gained by transferring men with good arms from point to point with rapidity. Surely the writer undervalues General J. E. B. Stuart as a cavalry leader. His view probably arises from his partiality for the energy and enterprise of General Forrest.

*Oliver O. Howard.*

BY JACOB D. COX, MAJOR-GENERAL U. S. V.

In all great historical events the causes coöperating to produce the result are sure to be numerous—so numerous that it would hardly be wrong to call them numberless. The student of history gets so accustomed to crises in which a slight change of circumstance or of conduct would, apparently, have given a wholly different trend to affairs that he gives up the problem of the «might have beens» as one impossible of solution. Yet there is so much that is fascinating in such speculations that we may be very sure that many another son of a Confederate officer besides Mr. Rose has spent long hours of wistful thought upon his question, though not many have so persuasively presented an answer.

Yet when he dismisses the answer that it was contrary to the will of Providence that the South should win, does he not miss some of the reasons contained in that solution of the matter? Many an earnest Southern man now sees and acknowledges that all has «turned out for the best,» which is only another way of saying that a superior wisdom and a more potent will than theirs was ruling the world; and they find consolation in the thought. Then we must remember that this view does not imply a mere arbitrary fiat. Under a reign of law it means a supremely wise adaptation of means to ends and causes to effects, if we are only able to trace them out.

For instance, except for the fact that the system of slavery was in conflict with the public opinion of the civilized world, there would seem to be little doubt that both France and England would have intervened actively in behalf of the Confederacy. When we read the evidence of the embarrassment of the statesmen of those countries in the presence of the necessity of deciding whether they would join in a war to establish a new nation upon the basis of African slavery, we are made to feel strongly that a moral force was at work here that was great enough to account for the difference between success or failure in even so gigantic a struggle. The summary of facts bearing on this point which Mr. Rhodes has given in the fifteenth and sixteenth chapters of his «History of the United States» is very instructive. But this non-intervention made possible the great blockade of two thousand miles of sea-coast, depriving the Confederacy of a foreign commerce which was a vital factor both in marketing her own products and in procuring munitions of war.

Mr. Rose has sketched with no little power the mischiefs which resulted from unlimited issues of irredeemable paper money; but can we call it a principal cause of the Confederate failure? France did not fail in her struggle with Europe because of the worthlessness of her assignats. They were swept into the dust-bins, and she began again on a sounder financial basis, and carried her eagles across the Continent. We of the North also suffered from paper issued on doubtful credit, and even the statesman who issued it lived to declare, as Chief Justice, with noble frankness, that the constitutional powers of the government had been strained in doing so, and that the desperate resort to war powers must end at least when peace was achieved.

It is easy for us now to argue that the Confederate notes as well as our own were bad finance; but the true reason for their issue was that the statesmen in power on both sides did not believe that their people would stand the enormous taxation required to «pay as you go.» They looked for refusal to support war measures and war administrations when the burden of taxation should be oppressively felt. They may have been wrong, but they were able politicians, and we must not be too confident that they misjudged the situation.

To examine the causes of military success and failure on both sides is too large a task for condensation into a page, and one can only suggest that Mr. Rose, in his contention that the Confederate armies fought without necessity on «indefensible frontiers,» seems to use the term in a questionable way. The frontier in the West was virtually the Ohio River. Fort Donelson, Murfreesboro', Shiloh, Vicksburg, Chattanooga, Atlanta, made a line of interior positions in the very heart of the country from which the Confederate government must draw its resources, and which was sliced away by great breadths of territory till Sherman completed the dissevering by the march to the sea, and thence north to the capital of North Carolina.

A similar brief suggestion as to the advantage of cavalry must limit what I can say. The cavalry which Mr. Rose advocates are the horsemen of European armies, trained by years of severe drill and instruction of both man and beast to produce effects by the «shock» of galloping thousands using the lance or saber. It was well known that there was neither time nor opportunity to produce such cavalry in our Civil War, and most men of military experience still think the character of the country would have made their use in large bodies impracticable. Our use of horses was only to carry men quickly to the desired position, when they dismounted and fought on foot with carbines much inferior in range and caliber to the infantry weapons. General Forrest openly discarded sabers, and was the most pronounced advocate of dependence on the carbine and revolver in such country as our Western and Southern States.

Is it not reasonable, then, to conclude that the heavier battalions of the Northern army, persistently advancing into the Confederate States, and aided by the moral causes first mentioned, secured results which are consistent at once with military principles and with the purposes of Providence in regard to America?

*Jacob D. Cox.*

# TOPICS OF THE TIME

**The Recording Tendency and What it is Coming To.**

IT is getting to be a serious question as to how far the world shall go in the way of self-record, and after the record is made, how far it behooves the individual to acquaint himself with the record. This is not merely a question of daily journalism, or of the periodical press in general, but attaches to all the products of the printing-press, both literary and pictorial; it is a question, also, that has to do with art—literary, plastic, and theatrical.

The world's artistic record—the record in picture and sculpture of the scenes and thoughts of the present and the past—becomes constantly more extensive and minute, as shown in exhibitions, in the multiplicity of separate prints and of illustrated periodicals of all kinds. The invention of photography encourages art to be more photographic. The tendency is toward minute and literal representation of the visible world. Of late years all art has taken a realistic turn, and has gone largely into the business pure and simple of recording; we see this in fiction, in verse, in picture and sculpture, even in music. As it goes on, however, it is beginning to be discovered that the artistic record is apt to run to the trivial; that, as nature and life are infinite, we are threatened with an infinity of recording art, all fairly well executed, but gradually losing distinction, and tending finally to a false accent and an inexpressive and confusing multiplicity. Here and there reaction has been manifested against the tendency, and we have had various forms of impressionism and romanticism; but, on the whole, the last two thirds of the nineteenth century have been given over to realism in the record of humanity past and present, and of the aspects of nature. Even impressionism is simply an attempt to correct the record. This recording tendency in art is partly to be accounted for as a reaction against the conventional, partly as the effect of the great successes of science and of scientific history.

It is under this reign of recording realism that dialect has been chased up into all its myriad variations. It is the insistence of the recording spirit that has brought not merely the ugly, but the loathsome, into the record. There has been a sort of religion of the commonplace, as well as a religion of the beastly, the putrescent, and the obscene. There are books published nowadays, by men of artistic reputation, in which the record of the disgusting has been carried almost to the utmost—almost, not quite; for the most headstrong «realist» stops somewhere of his own accord. There were rooms in the two great exhibitions in Paris last year which one entered at his peril. The walls of one of these chambers of horror were covered with pictures skilfully painted, and dedicated to nightmare, despair, destruction, death, and cannibalism. The best, and we believe the biggest, painting of the whole hysterical lot was devoted to the minute portrayal of the last-named pleasing theme—a historical subject delineated with conscience and completeness. Another chamber of horrors was full of sculpture almost equally ghastly and ghoulish in character. Concerning the recording realism of the French stage, the less said the better.

The processes of chemical engraving in the lower forms of the industry have been so cheapened, and ordinary printing is also so much less costly, that there is a glut in the manufacture of pictures, books, and all periodicals. It might at first be thought that the power to print must exceed the material for printing. But it has become evident that the quantity of matter that may be printed is quite sufficient to keep all the presses going; it is only in quality that there is any deficiency. The material for record is inexhaustible.

As to the recording activity of the new journalism, its frantic attempts to keep pace with the passing human show have already arrived at the stage of epileptic contortion, partly for the reason that the material is endless. Think of it! If all the rest of the world be set aside, here in our own country are nearly seventy millions of people all daily at work at something—for even the tramp tramps. Each individual furnishes material for record—first, in his individual capacity, second, in his association with others, in endless permutation. For instance, John Jones in any one day may be the subject, we will say, of journalistic record as plain John Jones; he may have a fit, steal a watermelon, or kill his grandmother. Then this same John Jones, by association with a family, a society, a strike, a target excursion, a foot-ball team, or a philanthropic movement, may give occasion to any number of further records. The millions of perfectly commonplace and unimportant John Joneses may thus supply the press with enough material to keep it busy; but there are tens of thousands of John Joneses who have become, to some extent, notorious or distinguished. Any day of their lives may furnish material for public record; if nothing else happens, they can at least give expression to an «opinion.»

With the standard of intrinsic values lowered, with little or no selection, except a selection of the unfittest, it is no wonder that the sensational press is getting to be the epileptic press, the general excuse for sensationalism being that anything that happens may be printed. Of course it is not true that anything that happens may be printed. The courts have a word to say about that, and there is a line drawn by the publishers and by the public, though sometimes the line is lost in the mire.

You can find artists in this recording age who deprecate composition and selection. They say they are «seeking the individual.» Seventy millions of individuals, seventy million pictures, seventy million statues. But why not multiply the pictures and statues by the days of the year? No individual is the same on any two successive days.

And as for the printing-press—but that is settling itself; for the time is at hand when every man will be his own publisher, author, and editor, illustrating his own work with his own snap-shots. When this time actually arrives, every man will simply read his own writings in «proof,» and no man will have time to read the writings of any other. Then we shall all begin again, and the art of selecting from the world's thought and doings what is really worthy of record and worthy of examination will once more be exalted among men.

### Words of Helpfulness.

In addition to the great religious books—the Bible, the «Imitation of Christ,» and others—there are certain passages of spiritual literature, often of poetry, less often, perhaps, of prose, which by their noble sincerity and the intensity of their human feeling, or the boldness and sureness of their perception of realities, inspire one with the consuming wish that they might be known and read of all men. Of such are Wordsworth's «Ode to Duty» and «Ode on Immortality,» Emerson's «Threnody,» «In Memoriam,» and certain utterances of Amiel, Dean Stanley, Matthew Arnold, and Lowell. It is to such writings that the harassed and weary spirit may resort as to a valley of repose or a mountain of far-seen revelation. They constitute for us a protection alike against the induration of custom and the mold of indifference. They are the classics of the soul, nourishing in us the ideal nature by keeping us alive to the reality of the «things that are not seen.»

But on a different plane there are often struck out of the life of to-day, and sometimes seemingly published ephemerally, poignant writings on life and death which pierce the heart with a similar emotion, and become a continual source of elevated interest by reason of the sympathy always excited by deep and sincere feeling. In greater or less degree this is true of a considerable portion of serious American poetry, major or minor, while in prose there are occasional examples of inspiring writing on spiritual themes, equally removed on one hand from the indelicacy of a too personal revelation, and on the other from the coagulated dryness of a timid style. Evidences already multiply of an appreciative response awakened in our readers by Mrs. Van Rensselaer's sketch in the Christmas Century, «One Man Who was Content,» a profound and helpful study of courageous recovery from overwhelming grief. In the present number Mr. Stillman's touching narrative of the life of two squirrels, and of his divining affection for them, will likewise arouse the sympathy of readers through the love of animals which fills a large place in the human heart and has been the motive of many books. These two papers are among the writings which stir us to better moods, and leave us, as it were, enriched by the personal friendship of the writer.

There is another recent utterance of a different sort, but of similar import, which one could wish to place in the hands particularly of young men, and, in these days of friction between classes, in the hands of both rich and poor. We refer to the report of Mr. Carl Schurz's address at the obsequies of William Steinway. Mr. Schurz's words, coming as they do from one of our clearest thinkers and truest patriots, have an even higher significance than the moving tribute of a sincere friend to a good man and lamented citizen. They excite an ideal of useful living which one can never forget. Mr. Schurz, speaking in German, said in part:

«As a simple workman William Steinway began his life's activity. Through unwearying labor, honest, daring, many-sided, thoughtful, he climbed round by round till the name of the great master manufacturer resounded through all the civilized nations of the earth, and the noblest societies of art and the mightiest princes of the world decorated him with their distinguished honors. But with all the greatness of his success he remained always the simple, honest restless workman — the true, the ideal knight of labor in the broadest, noblest sense.

. . . . . . .

«And—what is in our day of special significance—he was a pattern as a rich man. I wish I could call the millionaires of the land to this bier and say to them, 'Those among you who lament that at times poverty looks with mutterings on riches, learn from this dead man.' His millions were never begrudged him. The dark glance of envy never fell upon him. Covetousness itself passed him by disarmed and reconciled. Yes, every one would have rejoiced to see him still richer, for every one knew that everything he got contributed to the welfare of all. No one fulfilled better than he the duties of wealth. There was no puffed-up pride of possession, no extravagant prank of display. Simple as ever remained his being, modest his mode of life. But he knew one luxury and he practised it: that was the luxury of the liberal hand — a princely luxury, that few of the world's greatest have indulged in more richly than he.

«I speak here not only of the gifts of large sums, of which the world knows, but of those much greater amounts that he spent quietly for his fellow-man, and of which the world knows nothing. And it was not money alone that he gave. It was the hearty joy of the genuine benefactor with which he bade the worthy welcome, and often anticipated their wants. It was the bright cheerfulness of the willing giver who could conceive no abuse of his generosity, who spared neither time nor pains, who let no business claims deter or disturb him, and who comforted and considered, thought and labored till the necessary aid was secured. How incredibly far that went, how great the number of those who looked upon Steinway as a kindly, never-failing support, how his labor of charity accumulated sometimes till the whole capacity of an ordinary man would have been exhausted, that only his closest friends ever knew; and they hardly knew it all. I have seen many men in my day, never a bigger heart. It is hard over this coffin so to speak the truth that it shall not seem exaggerated. Is it too much to say that in this man every human being has lost a brother?»

In the contemplation of such a personality one is impressed with the superiority of character over attainment, as an element of happiness either in individual or nation. The hope of humanity lies in keeping alive in each generation such a sense of its responsibilities to its time. This is the true altruism which is the mainspring of patriotism and morality.

### «384,282.»

It is not unusual to find the lawmakers of State or nation underrating the popular strength of reforms. With the lamentable but incorrigible tendency of legislators to follow rather than to lead public opinion, it has not infrequently occurred that they have waked up to find themselves very far behind the progress of public opinion. This has been the case in the matter of the abolition of slavery, civil-service reform, sound money, and other causes; and that this is equally true in the matter of forestry reform, both in the State of New York and in the country at large, there is now no reason to doubt. Instances are afforded by the favorable reception in different parts of the central West and the Pacific slope of the Presidential proclamations establishing out of the public lands forest reserves for the conservation of the timber and of the water-supply often sorely needed for irrigation purposes. Indeed, as soon as the people are led to consider this question, its far-reaching relations become evident, and with the exception of those who have something to make by the spoliation of government lands, they are sure to be overwhelmingly on the conservative side. Such has been the case with regard to the great forest reservations in the Sierra Nevada and the Cascade range, and there is every reason to believe that public sentiment will heartily support the much-needed extension of the system in other portions of the country.

But the most striking instance of public revolt against an attempt to divert a forest reservation from public uses is found in the overwhelming majority—officially given as 384,282—by which the endeavor to amend the constitution of the State of New York relating to the Adirondack Park was defeated at the election in November. Late in the campaign, under the lead of the New York Board of Trade and Transportation, a vigorous fight was made against the scheme to undo what had been gained for the Adirondacks through the Constitution of 1894, by which the framers of that instrument, in sheer despair at the prevalent vandalism, forbade the cutting of timber, or the sale or exchange of lands already reserved for public uses. The spirit of this protest may be inferred from the fact that, in the words of Mr. Frank S. Gardner, secretary of the Board of Trade, «at the first intimation of danger the people were wide awake, and in every county of the State captains eager to lead the fight were found.» The significant feature of the vote was that the counties in the vicinity of the park uniformly voted on the right side. We believe that this tremendous majority indicates that, as Mr. Gardner says, «the forests are protected in the love and intelligence of the people.»

The Adirondacks have become so largely a resort and sanitarium for the people of the United States that their preservation is no longer a matter of local concern. It would now seem, in view of this vote, an appropriate time to undertake the completion of the original plan for the reservation, the limits of which are known on the map as the «blue line,» within which, however, there is much private land, the denuding of which would largely defeat the very purpose of the reservation. Surely, the wish of the public, as revealed in the test vote on the amendment, and the fact that the acquisition of the desired territory can be made more cheaply now than at any future time, are strong arguments for seizing the opportune moment to perfect this beneficent scheme. To this end the law of eminent domain may well be invoked, and the cost of the undertaking provided for by some carefully planned scheme of gradual payment.

# OPEN LETTERS

### A Recollection of Lincoln in Court.

THOSE who knew Mr. Lincoln in the days before his contest with Douglas for the senatorial representation from Illinois, will remember that he had won reputation for legal ability and for unsurpassed tact in jury trials.

Among the most important cases in which he appeared was the Rock Island Bridge Case, which was tried in the fall of 1857.

Being then in Chicago, and meeting John F. Tracy of the Rock Island Railroad, he said to me: «Our case will be heard in a day or two. You had better look in; I think it will interest you.»

The trial was the result of a long and violent opposition of river-men and steamboat-owners to the construction of a railroad bridge across the Mississippi River between Rock Island in Illinois and Davenport in Iowa. Continued friction between the builders and boatmen finally culminated in the burning of a steamboat which ran against a pier, causing a partial destruction of one of the trusses of the bridge. Suit was brought by the owners against the railroad company, and after various legal delays was called in the District Court of the United States for the Northern District of Illinois, Hon. John McLean presiding.

The court held its sessions in what was known as the «Saloon Building» on the southeast corner of Clark and Lake streets. The room appropriated for its use was not more than forty feet square, with the usual division for the judge, clerks, and attorneys occupying perhaps twenty feet on the farther side, and provided with the usual furniture. The rest of the room contained long benches for the accommodation of the public. Near the door was a large stove of the «box» pattern surmounted by a «drum.» These were common throughout the West in those days, when modern appliances were not thought of.

Alongside the stove was drawn one of the long benches, its front and sides cut and lettered all over. Here in cool weather frequently sat idlers, or weary members of the bar, and witnesses in cases on trial.

Much time was taken up by testimony and contentions between counsel; and as the participation of the St. Louis Chamber of Commerce was openly charged, great interest was manifested in the evidence and the manner in which it was presented.

As the character of the Mississippi River was described,—the nature of its currents, their velocity at certain periods, the custom of navigators and pilots in allowance for drift, the depth of water at the «draw» of the bridge, the direction of the piers in relation to the channel, and many other points involving mechanics and engineering being drawn out,—the spectators showed their sympathies unmistakably.

Engineers in the service of the government, civil engineers, pilots, boat-owners, and river-men had testified under the most searching examination. Lincoln seemed to have committed all the facts and figures to memory, and often corrected evidence so effectively as to cause a ripple of mirth in the audience.

During a tedious examination by one of the opposing counsel, Mr. Lincoln rose from his chair, and walking wearily about,—this seemed to be his habit,—at last came down the aisle between the long benches toward the end of the room; and seeing a vacant space on the end of the bench which projected some distance beyond the stove, came over and sat down.

Having entered the room an hour before, I sat on the end, but, as Mr. Lincoln approached, moved back to give him room. As he sat down he picked up a bit of wood, and began to chip it with his knife, seeming absorbed, however, in the testimony under consideration. Some time passed, when Lincoln suddenly rose, and walking rapidly toward the bar, energetically contested the testimony, and demanded the production of the original notes as to measurements, showing wide differences. Considerable stir was occasioned in the room by this incident, and it evidently made a deep impression as to his comprehension, vigilance, and remembrance of the details of the testimony.

As the case progressed public interest increased; the court-room was crowded day after day. In due time the final arguments were made. Apparently counsel had assigned parts to one another. The Hon. Norman B. Judd, the Hon. Joseph Knox, and Mr. Stanton (of Cincinnati) preceded Mr. Lincoln, who in addressing the court claimed that the people along the river had the right to cross it in common intercourse; that the General government had jurisdiction under that provision of the Constitution authorizing Congress to regulate commerce between the States, in which power there was implied protection of legitimate means for its extension; that in such legitimate extension of commerce, which necessarily included transportation, rivers were to be crossed and natural obstacles everywhere surmounted; and that it was the manifest destiny of the people to move westward and surround themselves with everything connected with modern civilization. He further argued that the contention of the St. Louis interest was wholly technical and against public policy.

These and other points were most clearly and ably presented, and when Judge McLean gave his emphatic decision in favor of the Rock Island Railroad Company, it seemed to have received a large inspiration from Lincoln's masterly argument.

In the following year occurred the debates between Lincoln and Douglas, which abounded in amusing incidents. Lincoln's talent and tact in controversy, his deep knowledge of our institutions, his intense desire for their legitimate perpetuation, and his profound love for the people at large, for charity and forbearance—all these qualifications impressed the public mind, and prepared the way for his subsequent elevation to the Presidency.

*F. G. Saltonstall.*

### Our Frontispieces — Lincoln; Grant.

THE portrait of Lincoln which is given as a frontispiece of the present number of THE CENTURY is not new to the public; but no wood-engraving of it has before been made, and the unusual interest which attaches to it as one of the most agreeable of the early portraits of Mr. Lincoln has induced us to present here the admirable woodcut which has been made by Mr. T. Johnson. From a letter from the Hon. Robert T. Lincoln, dated November 21, 1896, we quote the following reference to the portrait:

> The proofs mentioned in your favor of the 18th inst. have come, and I am very much pleased with the work of your artist. I regret that I cannot give you any positive information as to the date of the original daguerreotype, and there is probably no one living who can do so. I was born in 1843, and can only say that I remember it as being in my father's house as far back as I can remember anything there. My own mere guess is that it was made either in St. Louis or Washington City during my father's term in Congress—which practically began in December, 1847, and ended in March, 1849. I mention St. Louis because I think it was in those days an important stage in the journey to the capital.

The portrait of Grant as major-general is from a photograph owned by Fred. B. Schell, who during the war was pictorial correspondent on the staff of «Frank Leslie's.» It bears General Grant's autograph, placed there at Chattanooga on Mr. Schell's request. It is from a negative taken at Vicksburg in 1863, and well represents General Grant's appearance at the time of his command at Chattanooga, which is the subject of the opening paragraphs of General Porter's series. It is believed that this little-known portrait has not been hitherto engraved.

### A Servant's Approval of the Training-school Idea.

WE have received a letter from a servant doing general house-work who has been in only three places in eight years. Having read in the September CENTURY the article on «Training-schools for Domestic Servants,» she expresses her opinion that it would remedy the present unfortunate state of affairs. She thinks that if such a school were established, there is little doubt that there would be plenty of capable girls willing to learn; that the present trouble is caused by a lack of knowledge of how things should be done, which makes them harder to do, and so tries the patience of the mistress. She thinks if servants had a broad training of this sort, they would then know which special line of work it would be best to follow, and they would at the same time be able to manage any branch of it; they would, moreover, thus learn that house-work is an art to be proud of.—EDITOR.

**The Ballad of a Bachelor.**

WITH PICTURES BY JAY HAMBIDGE.

LISTEN, ladies, while I sing
The ballad of John Henry King.

John Henry was a bachelor,
His age was thirty-three or four.

Two maids for his affection vied,
And each desired to be his bride,

And bravely did they strive to bring
Unto their feet John Henry King.

John Henry liked them both so well,
To save his life he could not tell

Which he most wished to be his bride,
Nor was he able to decide.

Fair Kate was jolly, bright, and gay,
And sunny as a summer day;

Marie was kind, sedate, and sweet,
With gentle ways and manners neat.

Each was so dear that John confessed
He could not tell which he liked best.

He studied them for quite a year,
And still found no solution near,

And might have studied two years more
Had he not, walking on the shore,

Conceived a very simple way
Of ending his prolonged delay—

A way in which he might decide
Which of the maids should be his bride.

He said, «I 'll toss into the air
A dollar, and I 'll toss it fair:

If heads come up, I 'll wed Marie;
If tails, fair Kate my bride shall be.»

Then from his leather pocket-book
A dollar bright and new he took;

He kissed one side for fair Marie,
The other side for Kate kissed he.

Then in a manner free and fair
He tossed the dollar in the air.

«Ye fates,» he cried, «pray let this be
A lucky throw indeed for me!»

The dollar rose, the dollar fell;
He watched its whirling transit well,

And off some twenty yards or more
The dollar fell upon the shore.

John Henry ran to where it struck
To see which maiden was in luck.

But, oh, the irony of fate!
Upon its edge the coin stood straight!

And there, embedded in the sand,
John Henry let the dollar stand!

And he will tempt his fate no more,
But live and die a bachelor.

Thus, ladies, you have heard me sing
The ballad of John Henry King.

*Ellis Parker Butler.*

**The Unfortunate Experience of a Successful Salesman.**

A TRUE STORY.

I HAD been working all winter and spring in the western part of New York State, alternately at wood-chopping and at making cradles and bedsteads, with a brief interval during which I ran a wheelbarrow express from the village hotel down to the steamboat-landing a mile and a half away, when I made my first and only flight into business as a drummer. I still think that it was a success in a way, even if it did n't work out exactly right. But that was not my fault. I like a concern, anyhow, that can stand up alone in times of prosperity: this could n't. It was an infant industry: that was the mischief.

It was this way. A lot of my fellow-workers in the factory had hit upon the idea of setting up in business for themselves on the coöperative plan. They had no capital, but they hired a shop with water-power; wood was cheap, and the oil-country close at hand, with boom towns springing up all over it like mushrooms. They wanted beds and tables and chairs down there, and had money to pay for them. All that was needed was some one who could talk to go and sell them the things; then enough could be made to establish the business before the credit of the concern gave out. They picked me for that job, and I, nothing loath, dropped ax and wheelbarrow, and started out.

An album full of photographs of furniture and a price-list made up my equipment. I was to do the rest. I remember, as though it was yesterday, the first storekeeper I struck. It was in Titusville. He was a cross old man, and would n't so much as look at my pictures; but when I poked the book under his nose and it fell open right at the extension-tables, he had to in spite of himself. I told him the price before he could get his eye off the picture, and he took another look. He turned over the leaves, while my heart beat high with anticipation, and by and by he came back to the extension-tables. If they were any good he would n't mind a dozen or so; but he had to bind me down to an iron-clad contract as to price and quality, since he had never seen me before, and did n't know our tables. I signed that contract,—I would cheerfully have signed anything just then,—and many more like it in the three weeks that followed. It was singular how suspicious they were of extension-tables, in spite of the fact that they hankered after nothing else, in that free-handed country. But then I early made up my mind that that was the way of trade.

There were others in Titusville who wanted extension-tables, and I let them have them gladly. I must have sent home an order for a hundred that night before I took the late train for Oil City so as to be up and doing with the birds. There it was the same thing, and so in Pithole Centre, in Franklin, and all the way down the Allegheny River. There was evidently a famine in extension-tables. They wanted nothing else. It seemed as if no one slept or sat down in that country, but just ate. But I made up my mind that they probably all kept boarders, oil running high in those days, and lots of people streaming in from everywhere. Before that day was at an end I had determined to let all the rest of it go, and to throw myself on the tables entirely. If tables they wanted, tables they should have, if it took the last stick of wood in Chautauqua County with Cattaraugus thrown in. A thunder-storm raged while I canvassed Oil City, and the lightning struck a tank. The oil ran down the hill, and set one end of the town on fire. But while it was burning I sold extension-tables in the other end, reasoning that they would need so many more of them when they came to rebuild. There must have been something contagious about my enthusiasm, judging from the way those tables went.

That night I went to bed happy after sending home a big order for extension-tables, all under iron-clad contract, and telling them to hurry them up. I slept the sleep of the just. I don't know what kind of a time my employers had when they got that order next morning, but I can guess. It seems that they telegraphed to my customers, and received only copies of the iron-clad contract, with assurances that it was all right—they had seen my papers. They wired for me, but no telegraph was swift enough to keep up with my progress through that oil-country. My blood once up, I swept through the region like a storm-wind, scattering extension-tables right and left, until finally I sold a dealer in Allegheny City a full thousand dollars' worth in one bill. When that order came home they gave it up. They did n't wire any more, because it was no use. Not until I brought up in Rochester on the Ohio River near the State line, my last cent gone, and sent back for fresh supplies, were they able to locate me. Every morning the mail had mapped out my trail to them, but where I might be by that time, out on the front, there was no telling.

They sent me ten dollars, and wrote me just to come back, and sell no more tables. But I was not to be balked in that way. I laid out a route which the ten dollars would cover, into Ohio a little way, and planted a few score extension-tables in every town I came to. They were just as greedy for them there as in Pennsylvania. Finally I pinched myself of a dinner or two, and wound up with a run to the city of Erie on the lake, and filled that place with tables too. Then I went home, feeling like a conqueror.

My chief met me at the depot; he wore a look of exhaustion. There was a crowd at the factory just across the canal, and a flag hung out of the window. I felt that it was not a wholly undeserved honor. I had done the best I could, and a reception a little out of the usual would not be unnatural. I asked him what he thought of it, and he said that it was great.

Lots of times since have I tried to recall what were my feelings when I found out that it was the sheriff's flag that hung out of the window. I suppose that I must have been stunned. The concern had «busted.» Too much extension-table had wrecked it. Instead of four hundred and fifty dollars of commission, I got seventy-five cents, which was just half of what the boss had in his pocket. He divided squarely. And that ended my career as a drummer, along with the firm's.

What was the matter? Why, the price-list. It seems that by some mistake the selling price of extension-tables had been put lower than the cost of working up the wood. Perhaps that also explained my sudden popularity with the trade—perhaps; I cannot say that I like to think of it that way.

*Jacob A. Riis.*

### Uncle Ezra on 'Change.

I 'D be'n readin' 'bout some fellers thet were dealin' in New York
In a brand o' wheat called «futures» an' a «fancy» breed o' pork;
An' they bought it on the «margins» of a place they called «the pit.»
So one day I traveled down there jes to take a look at it;
An' I said to Sary Ellen thet perhaps, fer all I knew,
I 'd bring home some wheat to «seed» with, an' a «fancy» pig er two.
Well, I hunted an' ast questions, an' I had the blamed-est chase,
An' I shore was disapp'inted when at last I found the place;
Fer they wa'n't no hogs a-runnin' in that lane they call «the street,»
An' you can't make bread ner flapjacks from that «future» brand o' wheat.

Why, they hain't no wheat about it, ner no pork, ez I c'u'd see—
Jes a lot o' dudes thet acted more like lunytics to me;
Fer they 'd hol' their breath a minute, sorter waitin' an excuse;
Then they 'd swing their arms an' holler like all bedlam hed broke loose.
An' I stood right there an' watched 'em fer about an hour er so,
An' I never saw no «margins» where that «future» wheat c'u'd grow;
An' they wa'n't no sort o' pastur's fer that «fancy» pork to «range,»
An' I did n't see no cattle herdin' round the Stock Exchange.
Ef you went there fer pervisions you 'd come short o' winter's meat,
An' you 'd get no bread ner flapjacks from that «future» brand o' wheat.

So I went away disgusted,—them manœuvers made me chafe,—
An' the balance of the day I watched some fellers move a safe;
An' I bought a bag o' peanuts as I stood a-watchin' it,
An' the peddler give me by mistake a quarter countyfeit.
An' I tuk the train that evenin', an' I went back home, an' then
I announced to Sary Ellen thet I 'd not go there again.
An' I told her 'bout «the street,» an' 'bout them doin's in «the pit,»
But I think I failed to mention 'bout that silver countyfeit.
An' she wondered how them city folks c'u'd get enough to eat
F'om that «fancy» breed o' pork an' that there «future» brand o' wheat.

*Albert Bigelow Paine.*

### An Irish Host.

THE door lies open and the gate swings wide;
All are made welcome—even sun and rain.
Well knows the host, and knows with conscious pride,
That all who leave his door will come again—
The refuge of the homeless and the lost;
And no one hungers there, unless it be the host.

*S. R. Elliott.*

### The Advertising Girl.

SHE was a most enchanting girl,
Rosy and plump, yet full of grace;
Her hair was perfectly in curl,
A winsome smile was on her face.
«You are so mirthful and so gay,
So free from care, fair maid,» said I,
«Life must be one long holiday
Through which you wander happily.»

«Oh, no, indeed, kind sir,» she said;
«I 've had no holiday for years;
I am the advertising maid
Who in the magazines appears.
Life is a whirl of crowded days;
Yet I am gay, and happy too,
Because I find along its ways
So many pleasant things to do.

«From morning unto night I take
My fill of change and luxury.
There are a dozen firms that make
My gowns—the latest styles, you see!
The daintiest of gloves and shoes
Are stitched for me with special care;
I 've all the kodaks I can use,
And all the furs that I can wear.

«Innumerable soaps and scents,
Candies and dentifrices, too,
I use with perfect confidence,
And recommend the same to you;
In each new style of underwear,
Braces, and waists my form is clad;
I have pianos and to spare,
And twenty tonics make me glad.

«And when these varied interests pall,
Still wider joys to them succeed—
Those swiftest, sweetest hours of all
When on my bicycles I speed.
I have at least a score of wheels,
And through each magazine I whirl.
Ah! brighter bliss no monarch feels
Than crowns the advertising girl!»

*Priscilla Leonard.*

### Aphorisms.

WHEN a man claims that he understands women, you may be tolerably sure that he has had experience with one woman whom he found he did n't understand.

EXPERIENCE is not always a good teacher. The man who has once taken a sham for a reality is apt ever afterward to take all realities for shams.

AN unhappy woman turns for distraction to «things»; but with a man the memory of love can be effaced only by a new love. Hence devotion, intense and sincere as far as it goes, to a fascinating woman is often only his surprised tribute, though genuine in its way, to her ability in helping him to forget another woman who, at all hazards, must not be remembered.

DEMAND does not always regulate supply: a lover may ask for letters at the post-office for a year without getting any.

*Alice W. Rollins.*

THE DE VINNE PRESS, NEW YORK.

PHOTOGRAPH BY GEORGE C. COX.

PHOTOGRAPH BY GEORGE C. COX.

PRESIDENT-ELECT WILLIAM McKINLEY AT HIS HOME IN CANTON, OHIO.

**This portrait and the one opposite are from photographs taken for THE CENTURY, Dec. 9 and 10, 1896.**

PRESIDENT CLEVELAND AT HIS DESK, NOVEMBER 23, 1896.
From a photograph taken for THE CENTURY.

THE CENTURY MAGAZINE

VOL. LIII. MARCH, 1897. No. 5.

# OUR FELLOW-CITIZEN OF THE WHITE HOUSE.

## THE OFFICIAL CARES OF A PRESIDENT OF THE UNITED STATES.

A PRESIDENT who should not carry into the White House a relish for drudgery, business habits of the nicest discrimination, and a constitution of iron, would be President only in name, even as regards his more important duties. His signature on the papers which he is told will not otherwise be legal might be as good as the custodian of his bank account would require, but within the meaning of the law it would be as often as not a moral forgery. Yet no complaint should be offered on this account. Presidents are made for better or for worse. Such as they are in natural faculties and strength, so they must serve—some of them leaning on official advisers and bureaucratic clerks in every step they take; and some of them putting the stamp of their own individuality on the papers and acts which make up an administration.

When a President-elect, facing the Chief Justice, has repeated the Constitutional oath, «I do solemnly swear that I will faithfully execute the office of President of the United States, and will, to the best of my ability, preserve, protect, and defend the Constitution of the United States,» he has indentured himself for four years of the heaviest servitude that ever fell to the lot of any mortal. By comparison the «hired man» talked about in the last canvass would lead a pampered existence, and a constitutional monarch is a man of leisure. A President equal to his oath is both king and premier; he reigns and he rules; he is bowed down by the crown of authority and is encompassed by the mantle of care.

A paragraph in the first article of the Constitution, and the section in the second article following the oath, define the meaning of a promise to «execute the office of President.» As commander-in-chief of the army and navy he is accountable to the people for the personnel and efficiency of both services; he is the supervisor of the acts of the members of

DRAWN BY JAY HAMBIDGE.

THE WHITE HOUSE AT NIGHT, FROM THE EAST CARRIAGE ENTRANCE.

the cabinet, who are the heads of the executive departments; with him rests the power to grant reprieves and pardons; on him devolves the responsibility of our relations with all other nations; with few exceptions among the higher officers, and not including the minor clerks, who are responsible to the heads of departments, he must select men to fill all vacancies in the vast army of public officials, from a judge of the Supreme Court to a third-rate postmaster. Furthermore, after the selections have been made he must undergo the clerical drudgery of signing every nomination and commission; and finally, it is his duty to sit in judgment on all legislation, to impart information to the houses of Congress on the state of the Union, and to suggest measures necessary to the furtherance of the domestic and foreign policy of his administration. Even in Lincoln's time, with a powerful majority behind him, the legislative feature of the President's rule was a galling care; and it is only four years since a retiring President compared that particular task confronting his successor to the driving of «a team of wild horses.» Such are the President's obligations to the government as defined in the fundamental law; yet they do not include a great many collateral cares. When the Constitution, which Mr. Gladstone has called «the most wonderful work ever struck off at a given time by the brain and purpose of man,» was framed in 1787, the population of the United States was three and a quarter millions, or only half as numerous as that of the State of New York at the present time. If it may be said that under the original instrument a President is still able to shepherd seventy million souls, it is also undeniable that a large distribution of his cares to responsible officers is inevitable and near at hand.

After a fellow-citizen has been, as it were, condemned to the herculean task, he looks about him for a man whose tact will serve for a private secretary, and whose capacity will master the crowd of the anteroom and the rushing stream of executive business. As a rule, the stress of the canvass has brought the right man to the right hand of the President-elect. This was true of Lincoln's secretary, Mr. Nicolay, who also conformed to a view which frequently commends a trained journalist to that office. General Horace Porter accompanied his war chief to the executive mansion as «military secretary,» though General Grant once said jocosely, «I suppose in a railway company he would be called Assistant President»; Mr. Phillips had been private secretary to General Arthur as collector of the port of New York; while Daniel S. Lamont is an example of a jour-

PHOTOGRAPH BY GEORGE C. COX.

PRIVATE SECRETARY THURBER AT HIS DESK.

nalist who has stood on every rung of the ladder of executive advisement. As chief clerk in the office of Secretary of State under John Bigelow during the administrations of Governors Tilden and Robinson, and as secretary of the Democratic State Committee of New York, he revealed tact and energy which marked him as the fittest man for private secretary to Governor Cleveland; and when the latter broke the spell which for a generation had barred Democratic candidates from the White House, his secretary accepted the same office with the higher responsibility. On the return of Mr. Cleveland to the White House in 1893, Mr. Lamont again became an official adviser as Secretary of War, the only other man who has passed from the laborious anteroom to executive functions being Lincoln's assistant private secretary, Colonel John Hay, who, after long diplomatic service abroad, was Assistant Secretary of State under President Hayes. In view of the unusualness of Mr. Lamont's promotion from the inner circle of executive experience, it is worthy of note that army officers give him credit for being the only civilian secretary in their generation who has mastered the complex details of that department, instead of being largely a signature clerk to the heads of the different bureaus.

For his new private secretary President Cleveland went to his own profession, choosing Mr. Henry T. Thurber, a law partner of his former Postmaster-General, Don M. Dickinson of Michigan, who has filled this difficult position with most essential cheerfulness and courtesy. When it became known that Mr. Lamont would not return to his former position, it is said that a journalistic caller undertook to do Mr. Cleveland a service by way of suggestion.

«We are hoping,» said the journalist, «that

DRAWN BY JAY HAMBIDGE.

HALL BETWEEN THE PRESIDENT'S OFFICES ON A BUSY DAY.

you will appoint a man who will be good to us newspaper men.»

«I had a notion,» replied the President-elect, «of appointing a man who would be good to me.»

Cabinet-making is a more difficult matter. A private secretary, it is safe to assume, will adapt himself to the views and methods of his chief; but the official advisers of the cabinet, according to their political stature and idiosyncrasy, are liable to have policies of their own, or even ambitions, which will not exactly dovetail one with another around the council-table. Mr. Lincoln, with a wisdom suited to a peculiar emergency, gathered about him his political rivals, who were to some extent rivals among themselves; but in discomforting one another they very largely spared him, and their abilities were so extraordinary that the work he had in hand prospered in spite of family jars. The one who persisted in presidential aspirations, Mr. Chase, finally left the cabinet, and suffered the usual failure of aspirants for the chieftaincy by way of the cabinet door. Mr. Blaine's success in securing the nomination was no exception to the rule, for he left the cabinet a few months after the tragic succession of President Arthur, and by securing the nomination in 1884 effected the latter's humiliation. A different outcome to the indomitable secretary's candidacy of 1892 was partly due, no doubt, to his position in the cabinet and to President Harrison's determination that his official family should be loyal to him or wage open warfare on the outside. Blaine's resignation came late, but none the less it placed him in the position of a secessionist whose following was in a minority.

By contrast, President Cleveland's two cabinets have proved not only free from these ambitions, but also remarkably harmonious and single in purpose. Evidently they were chosen for work. Each of his cabinets has shown the coöperation of strong individualities with complete subordination to the official head. It is safe to say that more industrious cabinets, reflecting the disposition of the President, were never gathered around the council-table.

Even when political reasons do not shape the choice of a cabinet officer, a deference to the geography of the nation is always discernible. Aspirants are expected to be as mum and as coy as a maiden pining for a young man, and as a matter of fact they are not as persistent as those who aspire to the other offices; for tradition enforces upon a cabinet officer the attitude of conferring a favor; still a President is not wholly deprived of suggestions from the friends of willing statesmen; nor are the go-betweens always on the side of the wooer; and it will be remembered that the celebrated conferences at Mentor were attended by circumstances suggestive of the negotiations of a matrimonial agency.

Still, the official family of a President-elect is seldom known with accuracy before the inaugural day. A variety of tactful reasons prescribe this, and determine also the purely formal intercourse between the outgoing and incoming Presidents. For one thing, it is felt that a dignified aloofness on the part of a successful adversary is only a proper deference to the zeal of his supporters in belittling the expiring administration; and where the latter belongs to the same political party reasons of a more personal nature are apt to prevail. But this attitude seldom interferes with an exchange of pleasant courtesies; for instance, in 1885 President Arthur invited Mr. Cleveland to dine with him the night before the inauguration, but in this case Mr. Cleveland had made arrangements which compelled him to decline. In 1889 General and Mrs. Harrison dined with the President and Mrs. Cleveland, alone, on the eve of the transfer of power; and when Mr. and Mrs. Cleveland returned to Washington to resume their life in the White House, the same courtesy was extended to them, and with the same privacy.

On March 3, 1889, at an hour privately arranged by the secretaries, and according to the established usage, General Harrison and his private secretary, Mr. Halford, drove to the White House, and were received by President Cleveland and Mr. Lamont in the Blue Room, reserved for diplomatic and official courtesies. While the chief magistrates conferred for a moment, the secretaries exchanged greetings at one side, and the interview was soon over. About an hour later Mr. Cleveland and his secretary returned the call at the hotel. Four years later these civilities were repeated exactly, with the exception that the order was reversed, and Mr. Cleveland was accompanied by Mr. Thurber, this being the only instance in our history where a retiring President has succeeded his successor.

With the shifting of such gigantic cares there is a peculiar poverty of helpful suggestion; affairs of state are avoided with graceful dexterity. In receiving Mr. Cleveland, President Arthur alluded jocosely to the daily ordeal in store for his successor, and said: «You will suffer most from two classes of visitors: the man who desires to pay his respects, and the man who wants to catch a four-o'clock train.» Mr. Arthur had the reputation of holding a firm check on fellow-citizens with such aspirations, believing as he did that the personal comfort of a President a something to do with the dignity of the office.

When a ruler of the old royal order is installed with ostentatious joy, his predecessor is comfortably dead. But a President, who wields more power than most monarchs, is forced by custom to grace his successor's triumph; unless, like John Adams, he chooses to be frank with whatever feelings of disgust he may have for the new situation, and bolts the ordeal. On the way from the White House to the Capitol he occupies the right-hand seat of honor, but when the procession is ready to return, he takes the seat of retired greatness on the left, and breathes more freely. Soon after reaching the White House the ex-President bows himself out into private life.

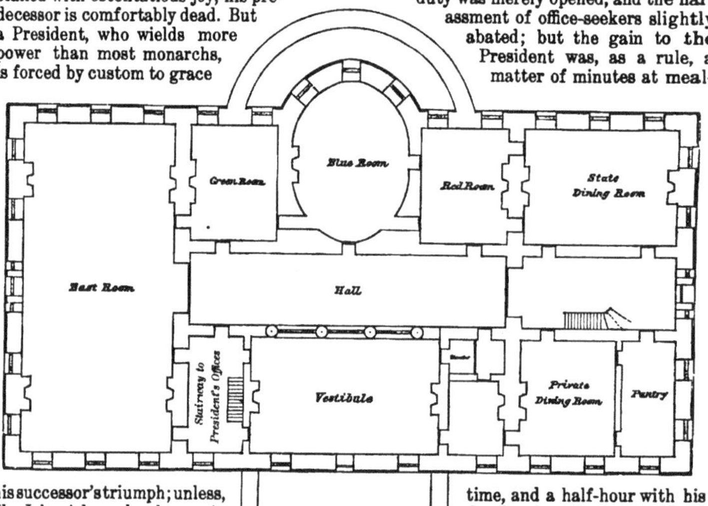

GROUND PLAN OF THE WHITE HOUSE.

After the fatigue of reviewing the vast procession that followed him «home,» and of leading the promenade at the inauguration ball, the President is left alone in his glory, the first manifestation of which is a stack of boxes reaching half-way to the ceiling, filled with applications for office. Now he is President indeed. Those preliminary boxes, nearly every caller, letters by the thousand, and large willow trunks full of papers delivered with regularity from the departments, remind him that the United States expect every President to do his duty by the party which elected him. With a large experience of this sort of thing, extending over a longer series of years than ever before fell to the lot of an American executive, Mr. Cleveland began his second term with months of labor, broken each day in the small hours of the morning. By this effort the path of executive duty was merely opened, and the harassment of office-seekers slightly abated; but the gain to the President was, as a rule, a matter of minutes at meal-time, and a half-hour with his family after dinner, with a return to his desk between nine and ten in the forenoon, while the midnight toil continued.

This habit of working in the quiet of midnight is the secret of Mr. Cleveland's ability to understand for himself the nature of every paper which receives his signature. It is a habit which he acquired in Buffalo, where his living-rooms were over his law offices, his tendency to a sedentary life heightening the attractions of midnight oil for reading and work that required quiet. First as sheriff, and then as mayor, these hours were devoted to the studious part of the public business; when he reached the gubernatorial mansion the habit had become a second nature; and on taking the reins of national government it alone enabled him to discharge his duty in the light in which he sees it—as a personal and literal responsibility. Accordingly, President Cleveland has been so little seen in Washington outside the White House for recreation or amusement, that in the minds of many credulous people his personality is shrouded in mystery. The mystery has attached even to the occasional outings for a little rest at shooting, the secrecy attending them being made necessary by the fact that little privacy is accorded him except by a dash through the pickets of the press for a government steamer and a disappearance into unsuspected waters; for if his coming were heralded, the object of the outing would be partly defeated by the well-meant attentions of the citizens of the neighborhood. In vacation time he enjoys the reputation of a devoted fisherman, whereas the daily package from the White House entails as much business, even at that season, as a man of ordinary strength would care to do in the active season. Providence and government never rest from their labors.

Within the White House there is no mystery except as to the copiousness of the work that is done. There is even little ceremony which would not be observed in an ordinary business house. The average citizen strolls up the imposing oval walk to the magnificent portico with the ease with which he would approach his own front door. His general view was indicated in the conversation of two young men approaching to examine the home surroundings of «our President.»

«It 's fine,» said one.

«*We* pay for all this,» said the other; «every time we smoke a cigar we help to keep it going.»

The only restriction on these gentle masters is that the cigar may not be smoked within the doors; and in fact there are but few freemen who do not leave their internal-revenue tobacco at the gates.

No soldier walks his beat before the portal, as before all executive offices and palaces in other lands. Several years ago, a Spanish gentleman who was being conducted over the lower floor in the hour when visitors were shown the state apartments, inquired in the dining-room after the immediate whereabouts of the President, the fact of his being in the room where that great personage actually dined implying to his mind executive absence. When told that at that moment the President was in the room overhead, he exclaimed with surprise, «But where are the soldiers?» When told that there never were any about the White House in the capacity of guards, his ideas of propriety underwent a shock.

There have been no soldiers as guardians under the shadow of the great Ionic columns since the war; and even then, on one fierce winter night, the boy in blue who was on guard was not allowed to maintain professional decorum. Mr. Lincoln emerged from the front door, his lank figure bent over as he drew tightly about his shoulders the shawl which he employed for such protection; for he was on his way to the War Department, at the west corner of the grounds, where in times of battle he was wont to get the midnight despatches from the field. As the blast struck him he thought of the numbness of the pacing sentry, and turning to him, said: «Young man, you 've got a cold job to-night; step inside, and stand guard there.»

«My orders keep me out here,» the soldier replied.

«Yes,» said the President, in his argumentative tone; «but your duty can be performed just as well inside as out here, and you 'll oblige me by going in.»

«I have been stationed outside,» the soldier answered, and resumed his beat.

«Hold on there!» said Mr. Lincoln, as he turned back again; «it occurs to me that I am commander-in-chief of the army, and I *order* you to go inside.»

At ten o'clock a hardly discernible sign against the glass of the barrier announces to the citizen who has arrived under the grand portal that the executive mansion is «open» to visitors; at two o'clock the sign is changed to «closed.» The doorkeepers swing the doors open to everybody. Within the large vestibule nothing is seen which indicates the arrangement and purposes of the different parts of the mansion. It was not always so, for originally the now concealed corridor, or middle hall, with the staircase on the right was a part of the entrance-hall; now the spaces between the middle columns are closed with colored-glass partitions, and the vestibule is simply a large square room pleasant to get out of. No way appears to open to the state apartments in the center, or to the west wing, which is devoted to the private apartments; yet glass doors are there, though as imperceptible to the stranger as a swinging panel. To the left there is a door which is always open. It admits to a small hall across which a similar door is the side entrance to the great East Room. About this splendid room, comprising the whole east end of the mansion, the visitor may wander at will before the portraits, or enjoy from the windows the beauty of the Treasury building to the east or the impressive landscape to the south, including the towering shaft of the Washington monument, and, beyond, the ever-charming Potomac spreading with enlarging curves toward Mount Vernon; and in the private garden under

DRAWN BY JAY HAMBIDGE. FROM A PHOTOGRAPH BY GEORGE C. COX.

ASSISTANT SECRETARY PRUDEN ARRANGING THE SEATING FOR A STATE DINNER.

the windows he may chance to see a merry band of little ones, two of them the President's older daughters, with a few playmates belonging to a kindergarten class.

From the small hall between the vestibule and the East Room a stairway ascends toward the medial line of the building to a wide middle hall, on each side of which are the offices of the President. The arrangement is simple, and in the floor-plan covers the space occupied below by the East Room and the Green Room, the latter being the counterpart of the small hall with the public stairway, just mentioned. At the head of these stairs, over the Green Room, is the Cabinet Room, which is the first apartment on the south side of the hall; a jog of two steps, at the private door into the President's room, marking the raised ceiling of the East Room below. The President reaches his office through the Cabinet Room, entering the latter from the library, which corresponds on the second floor with the Blue Room of the State apartments. President Arthur, indeed, used the library as his office, and the cabinet chamber for an anteroom, while his private secretary was domiciled in the traditional office of the President. During his first term Mr. Cleveland preserved the same arrangement; but General Harrison went back to the office hallowed by Lincoln's occupancy, and Mr. Cleveland, on his return, found the arrangement so satisfactory that he continued it.

Beyond the President's large square office is the corner room where Private Secretary Thurber is always either wrestling with the details of executive business or standing with his shoulder braced against the crowd struggling to see the President. It is a narrow apartment, and might be called appropriately the «Hall of the Disappointed,» the suggestion being emphasized by portraits of the greatest of presidential aspirants, Clay and Webster, to which Mr. Thurber has added, as his private property, an engraving of the closest contestant for the office, Governor Tilden.

On the north side of the hall there are two rooms which correspond to those on the south side just described, the small one being occupied by Mr. O. L. Pruden, the assistant secretary since General Grant's time, and the custodian of the office books as well as of the traditions which govern the public social routine of the executive mansion; in his room sits the telegraph clerk at his instrument, and by the window is a telephone, which saves a great amount of messenger service between the President and the departments. Occasionally a congressman, with less ceremony than discretion, attempts to get an appointment with the ear of the President over the telephone, and there is record of a stage earthquake produced in the private secretary's room by a furious congressman who found the telephone ineffective, and his Olympian style even less so.

The large room on the north side, corresponding to the President's office south of the hall, provides for the mail clerk and his assistants, and the stenographer and letter secretary; it is also a store-room for official papers and the office books, a new set of which is made ready by each private secretary for his successor.

In the hallway there are always several attendants, among them the colored messenger who was recommended to President Lincoln by Secretary Stanton.

On this historic floor the weary Lincoln buoyed desponding patriots with hearty hope and merry joke; here have been discussed and formulated the policies which have saved and maintained the republic; here the strong men of the country have chafed at the barriers to the source of appointments; and here the queue of office-seekers, stretching from the private secretary's door, has drawn its weary length, most of them departing with a hollow straw of hope, and some of them, after many calls, taking the stairs with the lingering step of despair.

More accommodation for the President is a necessity; but the White House, from the point of view of beauty and tradition, is one of the relics of our past which belong unimpaired to posterity. The perfect inadequacy of the executive offices to the present demands is apparent at a glance; nor is the lack of room less obvious at the social functions which custom as well as reasons of state impose upon the President.

At every large public reception in the White House the guests are taken in with a limited amount of style; but their departure is virtually over a stile, since the halls could not be cleared if the guests were not passed out by steps to a window-sill from which a bridge spans the basement area. These receptions and dinners occur much in the order of the winter fêtes of 1895–96, which were ushered in with the President's usual drag-net levee on New Year's day, beginning at an early hour with the cabinet, the Supreme Court, the diplomatic corps, the army and navy, Congress, heads of departments, etc., according to cast-iron rules of precedence, and finishing with the unofficial citizen.

As it happened in 1896, the cabinet dinner occurred the day after New Year's; and on January 9 the diplomatic reception, from 9 to 11 P. M., which is looked upon as the brilliant function of the year. About three thousand invitations are issued, which go to every person of some degree of responsibility in the government services and in the departments, and to the social friends of «The President and Mrs. Cleveland,» as the invitation reads. This is the reception for which every new aspirant to social position hungers and thirsts, since it is felt to be so inclusive as to leave the stamp of negative gravity on anybody of social pretensions who has been overlooked. But the number of invitations indicates sufficiently the perfunctory character of the entertainment. The members of the cabinet and their wives assemble in the private apartments on the second floor. At nine o'clock, when the Marine Band begins to play, they march down the west staircase, the President and his wife at the head of the procession. Passing from the corridor into the Blue Room, the President and his wife take position near the door leading from the Red Room, with the ladies of the cabinet at their right, the cabinet members themselves passing into the background. Meantime the diplomatic corps have assembled in the Red Room. As they are received by the President and his wife, they pass behind the line and join the cabinet. Then the members of the Supreme Court and other dignitaries are received, and afterward the invited guests in general pass in a steady stream from the anteroom by the group of honor, through the Green Room into the East Room, and crowd

DRAWN BY JAY HAMBIDGE.

A DISAPPOINTED OFFICE-SEEKER.

the halls and corridors, emerging, often with a considerable sense of relief, through the aforesaid window.

On January 16, 1896, the diplomatic dinner

was given; January 18 Mrs. Cleveland gave a large private reception; January 23 occurred the reception to Congress and the Judiciary; January 30 the Supreme Court were dined; February 1 was the date of Mrs. Cleveland's public reception, from 3 to 5 P. M.; February 6 the usual evening reception was held in honor of the officers of the army and navy and marine corps; and on February 13, from 9 to 11 P. M., the so-called «public reception» crowded the White House and marked the close of the official social season.

Thereafter Mrs. Cleveland continued to receive friends and special visitors on Mondays at 5 P. M., her day «at home,» which is made also the occasion for getting acquainted with the wives of diplomats recently accredited to Washington. According to etiquette, the ambassador or minister sends a formal note inquiring when his wife may pay her respects to the wife of the President; and the private secretary replies, in the third person, that Mrs. Cleveland will be happy to receive the lady at a given time.

For the official family dinner, so to speak, to which the members and ladies of the cabinet are invited, the state dining-room is still adequate. The ordinary table will seat thirty-six persons, and if widened at the ends with curved indented sides, fifty may be accommodated, though there will be no room between chairs for political or other animosities. As there are always officials who are wifeless or daughterless or for a time deprived of family companionship, a hostess of Mrs. Cleveland's tact and generosity will ask the necessary number of matrons and young ladies of her social acquaintance to complete the requisite couples and honor the serious gentlemen of state with their conversation. Yet this resource sometimes fails to balance the company, owing to eleventh-hour accidents.

At the Supreme Court dinner on January 30 thirty guests appeared, but the even number does not necessarily indicate that the grave and reverend signiors were all provided with partners; nor does it follow that the dignity of the Supreme Bench does not conceal a humor equal to every prandial situation. As a matter of fact, the judges always have partners, because, under the rules of precedence, they are first considered; and if a man goes in alone, it will be the Attorney-General or one of the chairmen of the Committees on the Judiciary.

An incident of one of President Arthur's dinners to the Supreme Court will illustrate some of the perplexities of such a ceremonious occasion. The Attorney-General, then Mr. Brewster, was a gentleman of decided character and brilliancy, who in society looked upon converse with the ladies as quite indispensable to his happiness and dignity. On finding that the envelop bearing his name in the gentlemen's dressing-room inclosed a table-card which merely denoted his chair at the board, his sense of a profound emergency was aroused, and instead of joining the other guests he made straight for the dining-room, where his suspicion was confirmed by the plate-cards, which showed that he was to be sandwiched between two other lone adjuncts to judicial greatness. Then he spoke in accents, not of anger, but of calm commiseration, that some one should have made so unheard-of a mistake. It was courteously explained that, owing to the limited number of ladies, some of the gentlemen must necessarily go in alone. But this did not impress him as applying logically to himself. And when it became apparent that he was not carrying the situation by storm, he proceeded to try a state of siege by dropping into a chair by the door, and near the foot of the President's stairway. His plaintive reproach, «They have even taken my wife away from me!» reached the ears of the Chief Magistrate, who, alarmed by the controversy below, had come out into the upper hall.

President Arthur summoned the assistant secretary, and on learning that the trouble had been caused at the last moment through a redistribution of the guests by the private secretary, the President exclaimed, «This is an outrage on Attorney-General Brewster, and he would be justified in leaving the house.»

But how could the fault be remedied? Only by a dash on the dressing-room, in the hope that some congressman who had been accorded a partner had not yet arrived! Fortunately, one card remained which allotted to General Logan the wife of a distinguished congressman.

«It won't do,» sighed the President. «General Logan is one of the most sensitive men in the world.»

But the strategy had to be tried; and so it happened that the card bearing the lady's name was handed to the gallant Attorney-General, who, wholly appeased, joined the company in the drawing-room and proceeded to claim his partner with the courtly elegance which always distinguished him; while General Logan, unaware of the deed, marshaled the odd guests, and helped to relieve with his jollity the seclusion of his end of the table.

An incident of this kind cannot happen at a diplomatic dinner such as was given on January 16, 1896,—at least not among the foreign guests who have seen their names printed in the «diplomatic list» provided by the Department of State, in which their rank and the date of their presentation are indicated, the two facts which determine the precedence to which, if accurately followed, there can be no demur. At that dinner sixty-six guests were present. For the second time the table was set in the long main hall which separates the Red, Blue, and Green rooms from the vestibule. Though of course not designed for such a function, the decorative effect was fine.

The seating of the guests devolves upon the assistant secretary, who has invented a table-plan which serves for all such occasions. An oblong piece of pasteboard has many slits on the four sides near the edges; into these slits are thrust narrow cards on both sides of each of which has been written the name of a guest. At the diplomatic banquet the seating begins with the President, who sits in the middle of the north side of the table, with Lady Pauncefote on his right, and Mrs. Cleveland, who sits opposite with the British ambassador at her right, since Sir Julian is at present, by priority of reception, at the head of the list of ambassadors. The other ladies and gentlemen are placed, according to precedence, alternately with reference to the President and to Mrs. Cleveland. The problem is so complicated as to be equal in the laying out to a game of solitaire; the four ambassadors are in a class apart from the ministers, and the absence of a chief relegates his representative to a less prominent place. If a mistake has been made with one of the cards, it may be moved, or by turning it over shifted to the other side. When the seating has been both proved and approved, table-cards for the gentlemen are prepared by writing in the center the name of the lady to be escorted, and checking off with a pencil the chair numbers printed on the edges of the small diagram of the table which is given to each guest; also, the name of each guest is written on a plate-card bearing a gilt eagle with stars, which is the crest of the United States and is used on the stationery connected with state ceremonies. Here and there a social difficulty appears, as when the Chinese minister and his wife, out of supporting distance of each other, convey by smiles and signs the good humor they feel, and the quips and oddities they would be glad to exchange.

It was at the entertainment to the diplomatic corps that Mrs. Hayes inaugurated her anti-wine policy. The Presidential dinner to the Grand Duke Alexis had impressed her unpleasantly; so it was decided to blend the diplomatic reception with the diplomatic dinner, and to serve a collation lavish in elegance and quality, and abounding in every kind of liquid refreshment that was free from alcohol. As a consequence the party broke up with amazing punctuality, some of the diplomats reconvening at the State Department opposite, where the waggish Secretary of State had made provision against a chilly condition of our foreign relations.

The weekly routine of executive business is at its highest pitch during the two winter months of social activity. Congress is then in session, the diplomats are pressing whatever business they may have with the government, and the capital is full of visitors, promoters, and the higher order of birds of prey. A reading of the «Executive Mansion Rules» which adorn Mr. Thurber's mantel will give the impression, of themselves, that the President leads a methodical and social existence not unmixed with the joyful consciousness of bestowing the gifts of a great father on seventy millions of grateful children; but the facts do not give credit to this view.

What could be more indicative of leisure than the first rule, which says that «the cabinet will meet on Tuesdays and Fridays at 11 o'clock A.M.»? As the eight gentlemen of the cabinet, each of whom has too much business on his mind for one man, have the entrée at any hour of any day or night, and actually avail themselves of it according to the gravity of their business, the two formal meetings of the cabinet each week are given up mainly to the discussion of questions of domestic policy and foreign relations. And as the cabinet hour approaches, as likely as not the chair by the President's desk will be occupied by some caller who is too important a personage for abrupt dismissal, and who may not dislike the sensation of seeing the cabinet officers, one by one, popping like impatient apparitions up the steps of the cabinet doorway, and receding with an air of «O Lord, how long!» Separate interviews with the members of the cabinet occur almost every day, and the difficult work, such as consultations over the papers involved in a fight for a post-office, usually takes place at night, when the President and the Postmaster-General will be closeted for hours, with the cabinet table loaded with applications and flanked by willow trunks filled with relays of papers. This is labor, and not to be compared with the deliberations of the full cabinet, which may involve a burden of care, but are often relieved by amusing incidents.

«Mondays will be *reserved* by the President for the transaction of public business requir-

DRAWN BY JAY HAMBIDGE

THE PRIVATE SECRETARY'S DOORKEEPER.

ing his *uninterrupted* attention,» is the second rule; but the raid on the private secretary's office continues just the same, and persons will call who, in exceptional cases, do get into the big room if the President happens to be alone with his never-ended task.

The third paragraph lays down this rule: «The President will receive Senators and Representatives in Congress from ten to twelve o'clock on other days, except cabinet days, when he will receive them from ten to eleven o'clock.» And what a variety of human nature and irrelevancy that rule covers! As fast as they can be passed in and listened to, the merry round of importunity goes on. A local sarcasm, that a new congressman, impressed by the importance of his surroundings, spends his first day at the Capitol wondering how he ever got there, and the second day wondering still more how his colleagues ever got there, is true enough as a key to the *raison d'être* of the «errand-boy» business of a congressman. With the eyes of his constituents upon him, the average congressman accepts as a blessing the chance of having «leave to print,» and of using the inalienable privilege of running errands to the departments and telling the President about the worthy men in his district who want, actually need, and in fact ought to have, berths in the ship of state. As the last or sixth paragraph of the rules is a gentle admonition to congressmen, it should be given here. It reads: «The President intends to devote the hours designated for the reception of Senators and Representatives *exclusively* to that purpose, and he requests their coöperation in avoiding encroachments upon the time set apart for their benefit.» And yet the impressive act of leading magnates of the cross-roads into the presence of their President goes merrily on.

Much gentleness is couched in the fourth rule: «Persons not Senators or Representatives *having business* with the President will be received from twelve to one o'clock every day except Mondays and cabinet days.» But in the working of the rule there is plenty of room for more oil, and for less sand, which the private secretary is constantly sprinkling on the cogs. It is his duty to learn if the line of callers really «*have business*» with the President, and in nine cases out of ten he discovers that they would like to have, but that a prior condition to that state is a siege of some one of the departments. He briefly interests himself in the case, points out the road to be followed, and tells them to come back when their ambition has been actually furthered as far as the President's threshold. These quixotic enterprises are frequently pitiful, and sometimes amusing; it follows, also, that oftentimes they are successful. Many a President who has dropped his fist on his desk with the vocal declaration that «if that man calls again I won't give him the place,» has been thwarted by the hypnotic influence of magnetic «cheek.»

But the majority of these visitors «having business» with the President wish merely to pay their respects. They are moved by a conscientious desire to do their duty as citizens who placed him in power. Some of them know the number of their vote in the small majority which secured him the electors of their State. «It's blanked strange I can't see *my* President,» roars some disgusted politician from the back districts, after several offered reasons for doing so have been parried. A few of this type yield grace-

DRAWN BY JAY HAMBIDGE

IN THE PRIVATE SECRETARY'S ROOM—WAITING TO SEE THE PRESIDENT.

fully, and retire with the remark, «Tell the President I called; I want him to know that I have n't forgotten him.» Then there are delegations with «organized» claims on the President's courtesy, and estimable people who bear the same surname of whom he never heard; for at this hour «relatives» are visited upon a President back to the fourth and fifth generation. Most appealing of all are the people, some of them influential in the professions, who are in Washington on their wedding trip, and would like to grasp the President's hand—it would so please the bride to observe that the President remembered her husband. Then there are the large class who accept the ear of the private secretary as a substitute, and fill it with advice on the weightiest measures of state, including suggestions for the annual message, particularly when they are told that the bar is up because it is November, when the President has to devote much time to the constitutional duty of «informing» Congress. This work President Cleveland always does with his own hand, sometimes making several drafts. He also writes his own Thanksgiving proclamation, which most Presidents have had drafted by the Secretary of State. «Tell the President to use these suggestions freely,» said one adviser on the message, adding, «*I* can't help it if people detect the ear-marks.»

A great many visitors who ascend to the offices to pay their respects are referred to the fifth rule, which says: «Those having no business, but who desire merely to pay their respects, will be received by the President in the East Room at 1 o'clock P. M. on Mondays, Wednesdays, and Saturdays.» No part of his social duties, it is said, gives President Cleveland more pleasure than this public levee, which brings him in contact with visitors to Washington from all parts of the country and from abroad. A line forms about the East Room, the President emerges from the double doors of the main hall, and without ceremony extends his hand to the head of the line, which is soon moving so rapidly as to disconcert those who have primed themselves for a chat. Often the smile on the President's face will represent more than his kindliness of feeling, for the effort of the visitor to be impressive (as in the case of the young lady who, in her self-consciousness, waltzed by) is often amusing. Recently an old lady in the line with something to say was struck dumb by the suddenness of her arrival before the President; but after she had been propelled past she recovered herself, and, turning, condensed the expression of her solicitude over a delicate international complication by shouting back, «How 's Cubay?»

In the message season there is a marked increase in the President's mail, and, indeed, every important public question calls out hundreds of letters of advice from watchful patriots. Upward of a thousand letters a day arrive in the busy season, and two hundred or more are received in the dullest times. During the first year of Mr. Cleveland's second administration the letters averaged over fifteen hundred a day. Eighty per cent. of them are referred by the clerks to the different cabinet officers, a type-written blank of acknowledgment being sent, for instance, to the applicant for office who has forwarded letters of recommendation. Polite type-written expressions of the President's inability to meet all the demands made upon his charity are mailed to the incredible number who feel that the President's salary is too large for the needs of his family. These appeals have often aggregated twenty thousand dollars in a day. Exaggerated rumors of what the President has done for some namesake always bring out letters reminding him that other namesakes, just as worthy and probably in greater need, have been overlooked; and there is a popular impression that triplets are rewarded by the government. The «baby compliment,» so to speak, and the attendant correspondence, with which every President is honored, amount almost to a special department of the public business, and more than ever when there is a baby in the White House. This is carried on by persons who are actuated by one of the finest human sentiments, but who overlook the fact that the sentiment is too general to be safely indulged in toward a public officer who is constantly in the thoughts of seventy millions of people. Nor does the President escape being taken for a very capable errand-boy. It occurs to a great many veterans that if he would drop in on the pension officer and mention their claims, it would cost him little trouble and do them a great service. The friends of a public clerk who is in difficulty appeal without compunction for the President's personal interest in the case; and a public officer in another town once asked him to run into a bank in Washington just to say that it would be safe to renew a loan, since the President was aware that the officer's official sureties were good. Not a little humor percolates through the mass, as when an office-seeker wrote: «If,

DRAWN BY JAY HAMBIDGE.

MIDNIGHT SESSION OF PRESIDENT CLEVELAND AND POSTMASTER-GENERAL WILSON WITH THE APPLICATIONS AND RECOMMENDATIONS OF WOULD-BE POSTMASTERS.

after the poor and dependent relatives of Senator —— are satisfied, there is anything remaining to the quota of our State, I would like to be considered.» Occasionally letters are received from England and Ireland inquiring as to the whereabouts of persons who emigrated to this country years before. As a matter of necessity, the President sees only a small part of the letters addressed to him; but every letter of special interest and importance reaches the private secretary, and through him receives the President's attention. The merely complimentary letters are politely acknowledged, while, with the aid of Mr. Thurber and his own pen, the President each day accomplishes a large correspondence.

The executive record-books of each administration are also an index of the vast business which burdens the life of a President. One book is a register of all appointments made by the President; and as in making the appointments for the different departments Mr. Cleveland is not in the habit of depending on the briefs of the recommendations submitted in behalf of applicants, the task of selecting from among many the man best fitted for public service at home or abroad may be imagined. Another book contains a record of recess appointments which must be renewed when the Senate reconvenes.

One book is devoted to laws approved or vetoed, and this discloses another field of labor which President Cleveland has broadened by applying for reports and opinions of the different departments as to the expediency of legislation submitted to him for approval, and when the time for his final action arrives by requiring that the reports of congressional committees on the bill shall be included with the papers for his private study. A book is set apart for the entry of congressional resolutions of inquiry, another for executive orders and proclamations, and still another for copies of the President's indorsements on the business of the several departments requiring his decision. A stick of fallen timber on a public acre or on an Indian reservation cannot be sold for the benefit of the treasury or for the relief of the wards of the nation without the President's approval of the contract. It is not long since it fell to the President to discover that the terms of such a contract implied a misapprehension of the law—a case of minor importance, perhaps, but indicative of the slips that may be made, despite the efforts of able and faithful officers, if a President discharges his duty without legal experience and in a perfunctory spirit.

A most impressive chapter of the record-book last mentioned is that relating to pardons. Prior to President Cleveland's first term it was the custom of Presidents to follow the recommendations of the Attorney-General, through whom applications for pardons and reprieves must come. In Lincoln's time a large part of the pardon business pertained to the army engaged in war, and the whole world knows how he gave it his personal attention, and how his great heart was wrung by the conflicts of mercy and duty. In President Arthur's time the pardon papers seldom, if ever, reached his table. The record of 295 cases from March 4, 1881, to March 4, 1885 (which includes a few months of President Garfield's service), does not show a single case considered by the President and «denied.» According to usage, the clerks noted that the Attorney-General recommended the pardon, and affixed the executive order, «Let a pardon issue.»

But when President Cleveland came into the White House he soon let it be known that he would assume a personal responsibility for pardons. To him «the quality of mercy» enjoined by the Constitution was one of the most sacred trusts reposed in a President; and besides, as a governor who had dealt with pardons, he felt qualified to say to his advisers: «Some of you may know more than I do about certain lines of the public business; but if there is one thing I do understand, it is pardons.»

Consequently the papers in every pardon case were sent to his desk, were exhaustively considered, the petition was granted in whole or in part, or denied, and his reasons were indorsed in his own hand on the folder.

The amount of labor which this revolution in method added to the burden of the President may be inferred from the fact that President Harrison, who followed the new custom, considered during his term 779 pardon cases (not including reprieves), 527 of which were granted in whole or in part, and 252 denied. His indorsements, sometimes extended, are often brief and pointed. On one case President Harrison wrote: «I will not act in these cases without the facts»; and a few days later, on another case: «Pardon denied. I request that the Attorney-General will in all cases hereafter insist that some statement of the facts, as developed upon the trial, shall be submitted by the judge or district attor-

DRAWN BY JAY HAMBIDGE

IN LINE AT THE PRESIDENT'S LEVEE.—I.

ney.» Again he wrote: «I will not examine a petition for pardon while the petitioner is a fugitive from the process of the court.» These are indicative of the kind of papers which under the old usage slipped through in the name of «justice tempered with mercy.»

As time goes on, offenses against the federal laws naturally increase, and the pardon cases wax more numerous. From March 4, 1893, to November 13, 1896 (a period of one hundred and ninety weeks, or four months less than his full second term), President Cleveland has considered 907 pardon cases (or an average of nearly five a week), 506 of which have been granted in whole or in part, and 401 denied; and it should be said that many cases of pardon, with all presidents, are merely slight commutations for the sake of relieving from political disability convicts who have behaved well in prison.

DRAWN BY JAY HAMBIDGE.

IN LINE AT THE PRESIDENT'S LEVEE.—II.

President Cleveland has said that «Sundays are a good time to consider pardons.» The hours, amounting to many days, spent on them, and the general character of such cases, may be indicated by a few extracts from the public record-book. It may there be easily discovered that the President has a severe front for crimes against the mails, the pension laws, and public decency. In an Idaho case of violation of the registration laws he wrote:

The pardon of this convict is recommended by the judge who sentenced him and the district attorney who tried him. This being an offense against suffrage, and committed in a locality where public interests require a firm execution of the laws passed to protect the ballot, I cannot bring myself to do more than to commute the sentence as above stated.

In a noted case of embezzling he added to his other reasons:

I confess that, in addition to other considerations, I cannot miss the fact that the granting of a pardon in this case will bring comfort to a wife and daughter whose love and devotion have never flagged, and whose affection for a husband and father remains unshaken.

To an appeal relating to aiding and abetting the abstraction of funds from a national bank, he replied:

Denied. My sympathy is very much awakened for the family of this convict, but my ideas of public duty will not permit me to grant the pardon asked.

But reconsidering two years later, he wrote:

Granted. This convict is one of five persons convicted of conspiring together to criminally obtain the funds of a national bank. All the rest have been pardoned from time to time, except one, whose sentence was so commuted that it has expired. This prisoner's term of imprisonment began about six months before any of the others, and he has now been confined almost three years and six months. The social position of these convicts and the circumstances surrounding these cases, have led to earnest efforts for their relief. If there was any difference in the degree of their criminality, this one was certainly not more guilty than the others, and considerable evidence has been presented to me, which was not adduced on the trial, tending to show that the condition of the convict's mind was such at the time the offense was committed as to render it doubtful if he should be held to the strictest accountability. In view of all the circumstances of his case, I have, upon a reëxamination, concluded that he should not remain imprisoned after his co-conspirators are discharged. I am also fully satisfied that the ends of justice have been answered by the punishment he has already suffered.

In the case of a Tennessee «moonshiner» he said:

Denied. Those who shoot at revenue officers when in the discharge of duty should be constantly taught that such offenses are serious. I do not agree with the district attorney that if those who are shot at are willing that the offender should be pardoned, their inclination should regulate the conduct of those charged with executing and upholding the law.

Two counterfeiters of Illinois, a man and wife, petitioned; and the President wrote this decision:

On the facts presented in this case, I am not clear that these convicts should be pardoned on the merits; but aside from any other consideration, I have determined to pardon the wife and mother on account of the child born to her in prison, and now less than three months old.

A Virginia case of selling liquor without a license called forth a laconic inquiry:

If the petitioner in this case went to jail, pursuant to his sentence, his term has already expired. If he did not go to jail, he seems to be doing pretty well without a pardon. Where has he been since sentence?

Another change in the business life of the White House concerns its relations to the public press. President Cleveland has not felt able to reciprocate the intimate attitude of the «new journalism,» which in its first overtures outraged the rights of privacy in a manner never before heard of, and probably never since equaled. This was followed up with betrayals of official confidences of various kinds, and finally with efforts to force the administration into cordial intimacy by the method of concerted abuse until it should cry: «Enough! Take all we know, whether public interests will suffer by publication or not, and treat us with ordinary decency.» Even this method failed. During his present term news of finished business has been given by Mr. Thurber to the two press associations, and intimations of probable events have been withheld from everybody. Little effort has been made to draw out public opinion in advance of official action by guarded revelations to journalists of ability and respectability: not because correspondents of that character no longer abound in Washington, but because such aims would be checkmated by the acts of newspapers which appear to take pride in the frustration of official purposes, and prefer sensationalism, to a judicious treatment of views and facts. The method of frustration is simple and effective. When a crisis arises a guess is made at every imaginable contingency, and all the probable moves in the case are elaborated. Some one of the guesses will be sure to impinge on the facts. By the use of such phrases as «it is intimated at the White House» (which may mean no more than that one lobe of the correspondent's brain has made inquiry of another lobe, and obtained an answer suited to the purpose), the desired amount of deception is injected into the «news.» Journalism of the old order finds it difficult to compete with such «enterprise.» And so long as it pays, men who have the guise and education of gentlemen will no doubt be ordered to do disreputable things. The latter, as a rule, do the work grudgingly, and no one pities them more than the large body of able correspondents who indirectly are the chief sufferers from the new enormity.

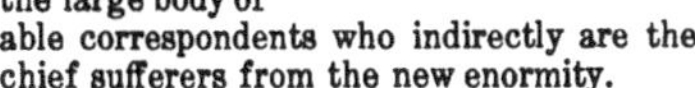

VISITORS IN THE GREEN ROOM.

While the public life of the White House is constantly open to the public view, President Cleveland has succeeded in preserving the sanctity of its home life in spite of efforts to invade it which until recently grew in recklessness in proportion as they proved to be futile. To the President, who spends twelve to fourteen hours a day in the east wing of the executive mansion, harassed by all sorts of importunities, and often worried by the duty of deciding questions involving the happiness of thousands, or even the welfare of the nation, the overshadowing importance of the home life in the west wing may be dimly imagined by the private citizen who looks to his fireside for surcease of the ordinary cares of life. And there has been vastly more of the domestic character associated with the idea of an American home in the White House, under the gracious sway of Mrs. Cleveland, than would naturally be ascribed to an official residence. The laugh-

SCENE OUTSIDE THE WHITE HOUSE DURING A DIPLOMATIC RECEPTION.

ter of romping children has rippled as merrily in the halls of the executive mansion as in any private home; and never has public sentiment been more unanimous than in regarding President Cleveland's domestic good fortune as also a public good fortune.

When cares of state have been most perplexing, President Cleveland has been known to say, in answer to inquiries concerning the welfare of his family: «There everything is well. If things should go wrong at that end of the house, I should feel like quitting the place for good.»

President Cleveland has not followed the custom of going to Congress at least once a year. His messages to the legislative branch are delivered in person by Mr. Pruden, the assistant secretary, all executive papers for the departments being transmitted by the regular White House messenger, who may be seen in the mansion burdened with a heavy budget, or on horseback without, waiting for an urgent missive. Presidents have usually occupied the President's room at the Capitol on the last evening of a session; but except in emergencies President Cleveland has declined to betake himself to the Capitol, because he believes that his duty to legislation cannot be properly fulfilled under such conditions of haste and personal pressure.

A President is the chief officer among 174,596 persons connected with what is called the executive civil service. This does not include the legislative and judicial branches, that bring the total up to 200,000. Nearly half of the executive service (80,407) are now classified under the merit system, outside of which there still remain 66,725 fourth-class postmasters, and 4815 Presidential places subject to the Senate's confirmation. It has been the privilege of President Cleveland to contribute more than his predecessors to the lightening of the President's burdens by reinforcing the merit classes through executive action. He is understood to be well pleased with the working of the system, though persuaded, by a tendency among the protected employees to combine for doubtful purposes, that some amendment of the law may be necessary. But that is one of the unsettled questions which on the 4th of March, with a meaning grasp that only an incoming Magistrate may understand, President Cleveland will hand over, with the good-will of the office, to President McKinley.

*C. C. Buel.*

(BEGUN IN THE NOVEMBER NUMBER.)

# HUGH WYNNE, FREE QUAKER:

## SOMETIME BREVET LIEUTENANT-COLONEL ON THE STAFF OF HIS EXCELLENCY GENERAL WASHINGTON.

BY DR. S. WEIR MITCHELL,

Author of «In War Time,» «When all the Woods are Green,» etc.

WITH PICTURES BY HOWARD PYLE.

XIII.

I WAS to come home earlier, but in June I got letters from my father instructing me to await a vessel which would reach Jamaica in June, and sail thence to Madeira. There were careful instructions given as to purchase of wines, and the collection of delayed payments for staves, in the wine islands.

I did not like it, but I was young, and to travel had its charm, after all. Had there been no Darthea, I had been altogether pleased. As concerned the business, I could but smile. My father was using that pretext to keep me out of the mischief which was involving most young men of courage, and creating in them a desire to train as soldiers in the organisations which were everywhere forming. He was unwise enough to say that my cousin, from whom he had heard, sent his love, and was glad I was out of our disloyal and uneasy country.

There was no help for it, and thus it chanced that not until September did I see the red brick houses of my native city. Late news I had almost none, and I was become wild with desire to learn what the summer months had brought forth.

On the fifth day of September, 1774, at seven in the morning, I saw my Jack in a boat come out to meet me as we came to anchor in the Delaware. He looked brown and handsome, reddening with joy as he made me welcome. All were well, he said. I did not ask for Darthea.

My father was on the slip, and told me that business might wait until the evening. My aunt had not been well, and would see me at once. This really was all, and I might have been any one but his son for what there was in his mode of meeting me. I walked with Jack to my Aunt Gainor's, where he left me. I was pleased to see the dear lady at her breakfast, in a white gown with frills and a lace tucker, with a queen's nightcap such as Lady Washington wore when I first saw her. Mistress Wynne looked a great figure in white, and fell on my neck and kissed me; and I must sit down, and here were coffee and hot girdle-cakes and blueberries, and what not. Did I like Jamaica? And had I fetched some fans? She must have her choice; and rum, she hoped, I had not forgot. How well I looked, and my eyes were bluer than ever! Was it the sea had got into them? and so on.

I asked about the Congress, and she was off in a moment. Mr. John Adams had been to see her, and that cat Bessy Ferguson had been rude to him. An ill-dressed man, but clear of head and very positive; and the members from Virginia she liked better. Mr. Peyton Randolph had called; and I would like Mr. Pendleton: he had most delightful manners. Mr. Livingston had been good enough to remember me, and had asked for me. He thought we must soon choose a general, and Mr. Washington had been talked of.

«Has it come to that?» said I.

«Yes; all the North is up, and Gage has more troops and is at work intrenching himself, he who was to settle us with three regiments. Mrs. Chew was here, and behaved like the lady she is. But they are all in a nice mess, Master Hugh, and know not what to do. I hate these moderates. Mr. Washington is a man as big as your father, and better builded. I like him, although he says little and did not so much as smile at Bessy Ferguson's nonsense. Darthea—you do not ask about Darthea. She is playing the mischief with Jack and her captain. She will not let me talk about him. He is in Boston with Mr. Gage, I hear. Why don't you tell me about yourself?»

«How could I, Aunt Gainor? Thou—» and I laughed.

Then she became grave. «You will have to declare yourself and take sides; and how can I counsel you to resist your father? You must think it over and talk to Mr. Wilson. He is of the Congress. Mr. Wetherill the

Meeting has a mind to bounce, and he takes it hard. Come back at eleven, and we will go to Chestnut street, where they meet, and see the gentlemen go into the Carpenters' Hall. I came to town on purpose. And now go; I must dress.»

At half-past ten—my aunt very splendid—we drove down Second street and up Chestnut, where was a great crowd come to look on. Dr. Rush, seeing my aunt's chariot, got in at Second street, and, being one of the members, enabled us to get near to Carpenters' Alley, where at the far end, back from the street, is the old building in which the Congress was to be held. Jack met us here, and got up beside the coachman. I think none had a better view than we. Andrew Allen came to speak to us, and then Mr. Galloway, not yet scared by the extreme measures of which few as yet dreamed, and which by and by drove these and many other gentlemen into open declarations for the crown.

I saw James Pemberton looking on sadly, and near him other Friends with sour aspects. Here and there militia uniforms were seen amid the dull grays, the smocks of farmers and mechanics, and the sober suits of tradesmen, all come to see.

«The Rev. Dr. Duché passed us,» says Jack, whom now I quote, «in a fine wig and black silk small-clothes. He was to make this day the famous prayer which so moved Mr. Adams.» And later, I may add, he went over to the other side. «Soon others came. Some we knew not, but the great Dr. Rush pointed out such as were of his acquaintance.

«‹There,› he said, ‹is Carter Braxton. He tells me he does not like the New England men—either their religion or their manners; and I like them both.› The doctor was cynical, I thought, but very interesting. I set down but little of what he said or I saw; for most of it I forget.

«‹There is the great Virginia orator Mr. Patrick Henry,› said the doctor. He was in simple dress, and looked up at us curiously as he went by with Pendleton and Mr. Carroll. ‹He has a great estate—Mr. Carroll,› said the doctor. ‹I wonder he will risk it.› He was dressed in brown silk breeches, with a yellow figured waistcoat, and, like many of them, wore his sword. Benjamin Franklin was not yet come home from England, and some were late.

«Presently the doctor called, and a man in the military dress of the Virginia militia turned toward us. ‹Colonel Washington,› said our doctor, ‹will permit me to present him to a lady, a great friend of liberty. Mistress Wynne, Colonel Washington.›

«‹I have already had the honour,› he said, taking off his hat—a scrolled beaver.

«‹He is our best soldier, and we are fortunate that he is with us,› said the doctor, as the colonel moved away.»

The doctor changed his mind later, and helped, I fear, to make the trouble which came near to costing Conway his life. I have always been a great admirer of fine men, and as this Virginian moved like Saul above the crowd, an erect, well-proportioned figure, he looked taller than he really was. Nor was he, as my aunt had said, nearly of the bigness of my father.

«He has a good nose,» said my Aunt Gainor, perhaps aware of her own possessions in the way of a nasal organ, and liking to see it as notable in another; «but how sedate he is! I find Mr. Peyton Randolph more agreeable, and there is Mr. Robert Morris and Jonathan Dickinson.»

Then the lean form of Mr. Jefferson went by, a little bent, deep in talk with Roger Sherman, whom I thought shabbily dressed; and behind them Robert Livingston, whom my aunt knew. Thus it was, as I am glad to remember, that I beheld these men who were to be the makers of an empire. Perhaps no wiser group of people was ever met for a greater fate, and surely the hand of God was seen in the matter; for what other colony—Canada, for example—had such men to show? There, meanwhile, was England, with its great nobles and free commons and a splendid story of hard-won freedom, driving madly on its way of folly and defeat.

Of what went on within the hall we heard little. A declaration of rights was set forth, committees of correspondence appointed, and addresses issued to the king and people of Great Britain. Congress broke up, and the winter went by; Gage was superseded by Sir William Howe; Clinton and Burgoyne were sent out, and ten thousand men were ordered to America to aid the purposes of the king.

The cold season was soon upon us, and the eventful year of '75 came in with a great fall of snow, but with no great change for me and those I loved. A sullen rage possessed the colonies, and especially Massachusetts, where the Regulation Acts were quietly disregarded. No counsellors or jurymen would serve under the king's commission. The old muskets of the French and Indian wars were taken from the corners and put in order. Men drilled, and women cast bullets.

Failing to corrupt John Adams and Hancock, Gage resolved to arrest them at Concord and to seize on the stores of powder and ball. «The heads of traitors will soon decorate Temple Bar,» said a London gazette; and so the march of events went on. In the early spring Dr. Franklin came home in despair of accommodation; he saw nothing now to do but to fight, and this he told us plainly. His very words were in my mind on the night of April 23d of this year of '75› as I was slowly and thoughtfully walking over the bridge where Walnut crossed the Dock Creek, and where I stayed for a moment to strike flint and steel in order to light my pipe. Of a sudden I heard a dull but increasing noise to north, and then the strong voice of the bell in the State-House. It was not ringing for fire. Somewhat puzzled, I walked swiftly to Second street, where were men and women in groups. I stopped a man and asked what had chanced. He said, «A battle! a battle! and General Gage killed!» Couriers had reached the coffee-houses, but no one on the street seemed to have more than this vague information; all were going toward Chestnut street, where a meeting was to be held, as I learned, and perhaps fuller news given out.

I pushed on, still hearing the brazen clamour of the bell. As I crossed High street I came upon James Wilson and Mr. Graydon. They stopped me to tell of the great tidings just come by swift post-riders of the fight at Lexington. After giving me the full details, Wilson left us. Said Graydon, very serious: «Mr. Wynne, how long are you to be in deciding? Come and join Mr. Cadwalader's troop. Few of us ride as well as you.»

I said I had been thinking.

«Oh, confound your thinkings! It is action now. Let the bigwigs think.»

I could not tell a man I then knew but slightly how immense was my reluctance to make this complete break with the creed of my father, and absolutely to disobey him, as I knew I must do if I followed my inclinations; nor did I incline to speak of such other difficulties as still kept me undecided. I said at last that if I took up arms it would be with Macpherson or Copperthwaite's Quakers.

«Why not?» he said. «But, by George! man, do something! There are, I hear, many Friends among the Copperthwaite Blues. Do they give orders with ‹thou› and ‹thee,› I wonder?»

I laughed, and hurried away. The town was already in a state of vast excitement, women in tears, and men stopping those they did not know to ask for news. I ran all the way to my aunt's, eager to tell it. In the hall I stood a minute to get my breath, and reflect. I knew full well, as I recognised various voices, that my intelligence would mean tears for some, and joy for others.

My long-taught Quaker self-control often served me as well as the practised calm I observed to be the expression assumed by the best-bred officers of the army on occasions that caused visible emotion in others. I went in quietly, seeing a well-amused party of dames and younger folk, with, over against the chimneypiece, Doctor Benjamin Franklin, now in the full prime of varied usefulness, a benevolent face, and above it the great dome of head, which had to me even then a certain grandeur. He was talking eagerly with Mistress Wynne—two striking figures.

Mr. Galloway was in chat with his kinsman Mr. Chew. The younger women, in a group, were making themselves merry with my friend Jack, who was a bit awkward in a fine suit I had plagued him into buying. And what a beauty he was, as he stood, half pleased with the teasing, blushing now and then, and fencing prettily in talk, as I knew by the laughter! At the tables the elder women were gambling, and intent on their little gains and losses, while the vast play of a nobler game was going on in the greater world of men.

To my surprise, I saw among the guests an English lieutenant. I say «to my surprise,» for the other officers had gone of their own accord, or had been ordered to leave by the Committee of Safety. This one, and another, were, as I learned afterward, on their way through the town to join General Gage. There was evidently some dispute as to the cards. I heard high-pitched voices, and «spadille,» «basto,» «matador»—all the queer words of quadrille, their favoured game.

The lieutenant was bending over Mrs. Ferguson's chair. He was a fellow I had seen before and never liked, a vulgar-featured man, too fat for his years, which may have been some twenty-eight. He played the best hand of all of them, and, as my aunt declared, that was quite enough; for the rest she could keep any man in order. I held back in the gloom of the hall, looking at their busy gaiety, and wondering what they would say to my news.

As I went in I heard Woodville, the lieutenant, say, «The king—play the king, Mrs. Ferguson.»

«No advice!» cried Mrs. Galloway.

«But I am betting,» said he. «The king forever! We have won, madam. The king is always in luck.»

I could not resist saying, «The king has lost, ladies.»

My aunt turned, and knew I meant something. I suppose my face may have been more grave than my words. «What is it, Hugh?»

«I have strange news, Aunt Gainor.»

«News—and what?» As she spoke, the talk ceased, and every one looked up.

«There has been a fight at Lexington. Major Pitcairn is beat, and my Lord Percy. The farmers were all up to hinder them as they were on their way to seize our powder and to take Mr. Hancock. The king has lost some three hundred men, and we under a hundred.»

«Good heavens!» said Mr. Galloway. «But it cannot be true.»

A pause came after, as I said there was no doubt of it.

Dr. Franklin asked if I was sure. I said, «Yes; I have it of James Wilson, and the town is already in an uproar over it.» The great philosopher remained deep in thought a moment, while the women sat or stood in fear or whispering excitement. At last he said he must go, and that it was the beginning of war, and welcome, too. Then he bowed gravely and went out. As he left, the stillness which had prevailed for a time was broken.

A dozen questions fell on me from all sides. I could only repeat my story as Jack went by me to go out and hear, if possible, more of the news than I had to tell.

At last Mr. Chew said thoughtfully, «If it be true, it is a sad business; but, really, how can it be, Hugh? How could a lot of farmers, without good arms and discipline, put to rout a body of trained men, well armed?»

«I think,» said Galloway, «we shall have quite another version to-morrow. How does it strike you, Mr. Woodville?»

«Oh, quite absurd,» said the officer. «You may reassure yourselves, ladies; such a loss, too, would be incredible even in regular war. I think we may go on with our game, Mrs. Ferguson.» He was very pompous, but none seemed inclined to take his advice.

«And yet I don't like it,» said a lady of the Tory side.

«And I do,» said Mistress Wynne. «It is as good news as I have heard this many a day.»

«It is nonsense!» said the officer; «sheer nonsense! You have strange notions, madam, as to what is good news. It is only another rebel lie.»

«I think not,» said I, venturing to add that men who could kill squirrels would rarely miss a man, and that many of the older farmers had fought Indians and French, and had, I suspected, picked off the officers.

«How horrid!» said Darthea.

Had a stray bullet found my cousin I should not have grieved profoundly.

«You see where all your neutrality and loyalty have brought you,» said Mistress Wynne. «I wish King George were with Mr. Gage; he might learn wisdom. 'T is but the beginning of a good end.»

«May I remind you,» said Woodville, very red in the face, «that I am his Majesty's officer?»

«No, you may not remind me. A fig for his Majesty!» cried my aunt, now in one of her tantrums.

«Shame!» cried Mrs. Ferguson, rising, as did the rest, some in tears and some saying Mrs. Ferguson was right, or the Lord knows what—not at all a pleasant scene; the men very silent, or vexed, or troubled.

My Aunt Gainor, as they filed out, made them each her finest curtsey. Darthea stood still, looking grave enough. Mr. Woodville, the lieutenant, lingered to the last. He made his adieus very decently, I showing him the way, meaning to be civil. On the step he said: «I do not quarrel with women; but I have heard that in Mistress Wynne's house to which, as an officer of his Majesty, I cannot submit.»

«Well?» I said; and my abominable propensity to grin got the better of me.

«You seem amused, sir,» he said.

I was by no means amused.

«I suppose you are responsible,» he added. «Miss Wynne might have better manners, and her nephew more courage. However, I have said what ought to be enough with English gentlemen. Good-evening.»

«I have half a mind to give thee a good honest thrashing,» said I.

«I dare say. You are big enough, Master Quaker; but I presume that about the weapons common among men of honour you know as much as I know of making horseshoes.»

I was now cool enough and angry enough to have killed him. «Thy friend can find me here,» said I. «I trust I shall be able to satisfy thee.»

With this he went away, and I stood looking after his stumpy figure. I was again in a broil, not of my making; just a bit of ill luck, for here was a nice business. I went in, and was caught on my way upstairs by my Aunt Gainor, who called me into the sitting-room.

Still too furious to be prudent, she broke out before Darthea. «Insolent idiots! I hope I made Mr. Galloway understand, and the rest of them too! I trust Bessy Ferguson will never darken my doors again!» She walked up and down, and at last upset the big mandarin, who came head down on the hearth.

«I wish he were Mr. Gage!» said my aunt, contemplating the fragments.

«I dare say he was a Tory,» says Darthea, who feared no one. «And I am a Tory too, Miss Wynne, I would have you to know.»

«Nonsense,» said my aunt; «it does n't matter much what you think, or what you are. You had some words with that stupid man, sir; I saw you. He looked as if he did not like it. Oh, I heard you, too.»

I vainly shook my head at her.

«Are you two going to fight? I am not sorry. I wish I could have that cat Ferguson out.»

«I hope—oh—I am sure, Mr. Wynne, it cannot be. How dreadful!» said Darthea.

«Nonsense!» cried my aunt. «A man cannot stand everything like a woman.»

I said plainly, seeing how vain my aunt had made concealment, that there had been some words, but that I trusted no harm would come of it.

«But there will! there will!» said Miss Peniston.

«Mercy upon us!» cried my aunt; for here was Darthea on the floor, and burnt feathers and vinegar at hand, servants running about, my aunt ordering «Cut her stay-strings!» as I was turned out, hearing my aunt declare, «I do believe she is in love with *all* the men. Is it you or the captain? What a shameless monkey to tumble all of a heap that way! It is hardly decent. Do go away, you goose! 'T is a way she has. Did never you see a woman faint?»

I never did, and I was scared faint myself. What between Darthea's fainting-spell, and this quarrel not of my seeking, I was uncomfortable enough. I had no one but Jack to appeal to; and here was a pair of Quaker lads, just over twenty-two, in a proper scrape. I had not the least intention of getting out of it, save in one way. The sneer at my aunt was more than I could endure. What my father would think was another matter.

Mr. Wilson used to say: «When you are in difficulties, dispose of the worst first;» and so I resolved, as I must fight the man, and that was the imminent matter, to set aside all thought of my parent until I was done with Mr. Woodville. Jack I took for granted, and so left a note with the servant asking my opponent's friend to call on Jack at an hour when he was like to be alone. Before I could leave to warn him of what was on hand my aunt came to me.

«I sent that girl home in the chaise. It was her fear lest some one may be hurt, but she really has no excuse. She talked quite wild as she came to—I mean of you and Arthur Wynne—just mere babble. And, oh, Hugh! I am a drivelling old maid, and have taught you all manner of nonsense, and now I have got you into trouble. Don't let him kill you, Hugh. Cannot it be stopped? I told Darthea to hold her tongue, and I am so miserable, Hugh; and when I think of your dead mother, and all I promised, what shall I do?»

The kind old lady penitently wept over me, as if I were run through already.

I felt, as you may imagine, the embarrassment and doubt a young man feels when about to protest by a single act against the creed of conduct which he has been taught to follow since he could remember. I smiled, too, as I recalled our first school duel, and how Jack and I ran away.

My aunt, seeing there was nothing more to be done, and having said quite enough, retired, I am sure to pray for me, and for herself as the main cause of my coming risk. She would have liked to see me well out of the affair, but I do believe would not have had me excuse myself to my lieutenant, let what might occur. Indeed, she did her best to keep Miss Darthea from betraying what, but for my aunt's rash outburst, would not have gone beyond those immediately concerned.

It was late in the afternoon when I found Jack writing in his father's house. I must have looked grave, for he rose quickly and, coming to meet me, set a hand on each of my shoulders—a way he had, but only with me.

«What is it?» he said. «Not the news?»

«No.» In fact, it had clean gone out of my mind. «I have had trouble with Mr. Woodville, and now I must fight him.» And on this I related the whole adventure, Jack listening intently.

«Thou shouldst have an older man than I, Hugh. These affairs may often be mended, I learn, without coming to violence.» He seemed a little embarrassed, and reddened, hesitating as he spoke, so that, stupidly not comprehending him as I should have done, I said hastily that the man had insulted my aunt, and that there was but one way out of it, but that I could try to get some one else, if to act as my friend was not to his taste.

«At this time,» he writes, «when Hugh came so near to hurting me, I was really going through in my mind what he had already disposed of in his. At Pike's we heard of nothing but duels. I had long been Pike's pupil. The thing had come to seem to us, I fear, a natural and inevitable ending of a quarrel. Such was the belief of my good friend Mistress Wynne's set, and of the officers whose opinions as to social matters we had learned to regard as final.

«And yet the absurdity of two Quaker lads so trapped struck me as it did not Hugh. The man must surely have thought him older than he was, but so did most. I feared that I should not do my friend justice; and then I thought of dear Mistress Gainor, whom I now loved, and for whom to lose Hugh would be as death in life; and so, quickly turning it over for one mad moment, I wondered if I could not someway get this quarrel on to my own shoulders. When I answered Hugh I must have made him misunderstand me, or so I think from what he said. When he exclaimed he could get some one else, I made haste to put myself right. We had little time, however, to discuss the matter, for at this moment came a Captain Le Clere with Hugh's note.

«Hugh was now in one of his quiet, smiling moods, when from his face you would have said there was some jest or wager in question, and from his talk, which had a kind of intensity of distinct articulation, that it was, as I thought it, most serious. He was coldly civil to Mr. Le Clere, and to me apart said, ‹Small swords, and the governor's woods by the spring,› as if he were arranging a quite familiar and every-day affair.

«I frankly declared that I was new to an office of this kind, and must trust to Mr. Le Clere's honour and courtesy. He seemed pleased at this, and thought a pity of so young a man to have such a difficulty, expressing his hopes of accommodation, which I knew Hugh too well to think possible.

«As soon as we had arranged the needed preliminaries, and Mr. Le Clere had gone, I went to borrow small swords of Pike, arranging to come for them after dark. Duels were common enough even in our Quaker town, especially among gentlemen of his Majesty's service. Although illegal, so strongly was it felt that for certain offences there was no other remedy possible, that it was difficult to escape the resort to weapons if those involved were of what we who are of it like to call the better class.

«At daybreak Hugh and I were waiting in the woods where—near to what Mr. Penn meant as a public square, a little east of Schuylkill-Eighth street—was an open space, once a clearing, but now disused, and much overgrown. We were first on the ground, and I took occasion to tell Hugh of Pike's counsels—for he had at once guessed what we were about—to watch his opponent's eyes, and the like. Hugh, who was merry and had put aside such thoughts of the future as were troubling me, declared that it was the mouth a man should watch, which I think is the better opinion. I said, of course, nothing of what Pike told me as to Mr. Woodville being a first-rate player, and only advised my friend to be cautious.

«Mr. Woodville, who came with Le Clere and a surgeon, was a short lump of a man, and an odd contrast to his friend, who was long and lank. The pair of them looked like Don Quixote and his squire. I felt confident Hugh could handle his opponent, and was surprised, seeing his build, that Pike should have declared him a good blade. Mr. Le Clere was very civil, and I followed his directions, knowing, as I have said, but little of such affairs.

«Our men being stripped to the shirt, and ready, Mr. Le Clere and I drew away some twenty feet. Then, to my surprise, the lean officer said to me, ‹Mr. Warder, shall I have the honour to amuse you with a turn? Here are our own swords of a length, as you see.›

«I was anything rather than amused. I had heard of this foolish English custom of the friends also engaging. I knew that it was usual to make the offer, and that it was not needful to accept; but now, as I saw my Hugh standing ready with his sword, I began to shake all over, and to colour. Such hath always been my habit when in danger, even from my boyhood. It is not because I am afraid. Yet, as it seems to another like fear, to feel it sets me in a cold rage, and has many times, as on this occasion, led me into extremes of rashness.

«I suppose Mr. Le Clere saw my condition, and unhappily let loose on his face a faint smile. ‹At your service,› I said, and cast off my coat.

«‹It is not necessary, sir,› he replied, a bit ashamed to engage a fellow like me, who shook and blushed, and looked to be about seventeen.

«‹We are losing time,› said I, in a fury,

not over-sorry to be thus or in any way distracted from Hugh's peril. In truth, I need have had small fear for him. For two years Hugh and I had fenced almost daily, and what with Pike and Arthur Wynne, knew most of the tricks of the small sword.

«The next moment Le Clere cried, ‹On guard, gentlemen!› and I heard the click of the blades as they met. I had my hands full, and was soon aware of Le Clere's skill. I was, however, as agile as a cat, and he less clever with his legs than with his arm. Nor do I think he desired to make the affair serious. In a few minutes—it seemed longer—I heard an oath, and, alarmed for Hugh, cast a glance in his direction. I saw his foe fall back, his sword flying some feet away. My indiscretion gave my man his chance. His blade caught in my rolled-up sleeve, bent, and, as I drove my own through his shoulder, passed clean through the left side of my neck. With a great jet of blood, I fell, and for a little knew no more.»

This account from Jack's journal is a better statement of this sad business than I could have set down. I saw with horror Jack and Le Clere salute, and then was too full of business to see more, until I had disarmed Mr. Woodville, badly wounding his sword-hand, a rare accident. And here was my Jack dead, as I thought. I think I can never forget that scene: Mr. Le Clere, gaunt and thin, lifting his late foe, the surgeon kneeling and busy, my own man hot and wrathful, cursing like mad, and wrapping his hand about with a handkerchief, clearly in pain, and I waiting for the word of death or life.

At last the doctor said, «It is bad—bad, but not fatal. How came it, Le Clere? You told me that neither you nor Mr. Woodville meant anything serious.»

I was kneeling by Jack, and was not intended to hear what all were too hot and excited to guard by bated breath.

«Damn it, doctor!» returned Le Clere. «It is no use to talk. I never imagined that youngster would take me at my word.»

«You will be in hot water here,» said the doctor. «I advise you to get away, and soon.»

«And we shall supply amusement to every mess in the army,» said Woodville, with an abundance of bad language. «Quakers indeed!»

Jack's eyes opened, and he said, «Thou art not hurt, Hugh?»

«No, no!» I answered, and, relieved a little, turned to Mr. Le Clere: «We shall, I fear, have to ask thy chaise of thee. We came afoot. I will send it back at once.»

Le Clere said, «Of course; with all my heart.»

«Thou wilt pardon me,» said I, «if I advise thee to accept the doctor's advice, and get away with all speed. I should be sorry if thou wert arrested. The feeling against gentlemen of thy profession is unhappily strong just now.»

Le Clere looked me over with a quick glance of something like curiosity, and said, as he gave his hand, «You are a gallant gentleman, Mr. Wynne. You will permit an older man to say so. I trust we may meet again. Are all Quakers as clever at sword-play?»

I said a civil word, seeing Jack smile as he lay with my bloody coat under his head. Then, as I remembered that perhaps Mr. Woodville might not be satisfied, I went up to him and said, «I am at thy service, sir, if thou art not contented to let us be quit of this matter.»

«It must needs rest now,» he replied. «Damn your tricks!»

«Sir!» said I.

«Holloa!» says Le Clere; «this won't do. Keep your temper. This way, Mr. Wynne.» And he drew me aside.

It was full time; I was beginning to get my blood up, and was in a rage.

«This comes,» he said, «of going out with a fellow that has risen from the ranks. Why do your ladies receive every one who wears a red coat? Let me help you with your friend. I am most sorry. I have a neat reminder in the shoulder. Mr. Warder has the wrist of a blacksmith»—which was true, and for good reason.

There is no need to tell of the wrath and incapacity of poor Jack's father. I got away as soon as Dr. Rush arrived, and, promising to return in an hour, went off with a smile from my Jack, and a «Thank God! Hugh, that it was not thou who had the worst of it.»

It was about seven as I knocked at my aunt's door, and, passing the black page, ran upstairs. My aunt was in the breakfast-room; she came to meet me in a morning gown, and to my astonishment was very tranquil, but with eyes that looked anxious, and far more red than common.

«Sit down, sir. I want to hear about this ridiculous business.»

«It may seem so to thee,» said I; «I am glad if it amuses thee.»

«Stuff! Talk decent English, man. That was like your father. Is—are you—is any one hurt?»

I said that was what we went for, and so told her the whole sorry business.

«And it was for me, sir!» she cried; «for me! And my dear brave girl-boy! Is it dangerous?»

I hoped not. We had both left our marks on the English officers. That she liked. Then she was silent awhile.

«Here is come a note from the kitten. Will you have it? It may be all you will ever get of her. She says she has held her tongue —I can't—I don't believe her—and asks me to let her know if any are hurt. I will. Does she suppose gentlemen go out just to look at one another? Ridiculous!»

I spoke at last of my father; of how he would take this matter, of his increasing acerbity, and of my own unhappy life, where I found nothing to replace my mother's love. My last disaster and poor Jack's wound seemed like enough to widen the gap between me and my parent, and my Aunt Gainor was troubled.

«You must be first to tell him,» said my aunt. «I think he will say but little. He has given you up as a sheep lost in the darkness of iniquity, and too black to be found easily.»

I begged her not to jest. I was sore and sick at heart.

«Eat your breakfast,» she said, «and get it over with your father.»

I hurried through the meal, and went upstairs, to find my sleeve full of blood, although no harm had been done but what was easily set right by what Dr. Rush called a bit of diachylon plaster. (I think I spell it correctly.)

As I went by Darthea's home I cast a glance up at the open window, and saw my lady looking out. She was pale, and as she called to me I could not but go in, for, indeed, she ran herself to open the door.

«Come in! Oh, just a moment!» she cried. «Your aunt has written me a note, and it tells me almost nothing—nothing.»

I was in no very kindly humour with Miss Darthea. Since our talk about my cousin she had been very high and mighty, and would have little to say to me except unpleasant things about the angry politics of the day. I said I was glad to have heard she had told no one of what my aunt's rash speech had let slip. I had better have held my own tongue. Darthea was in another mood to-day, and all at once became quiet and dignified.

«I gave my word, Mr. Wynne. When you know me better you will learn that I can keep it. Is—is Mr. Warder much hurt?»

«Yes,» I said; «he is in great peril.» I saw how anxious she was, and was vexed enough to want to hurt her.

«Oh, you men! you men!» she cried. «Will he die, do you think? Poor boy!» She sat down and began to cry. «He must not die; why did you lead him into such wicked trouble?»

It was vain to explain how little I had to do with the matter. Did she love Jack? I little knew in those days how tender was this gentle heart, how it went out, tendril-like, seeking it knew not what, and was for this reason ever liable to say too much, and to give rise to misapprehension.

«O Darthea!» I cried. «Dost thou love my Jack? I shall be the last to come in his way. I have said I love thee myself, and I can never change. But how can it be? how can it be? And my cousin? O Darthea!»

«I love no one, sir. I love everybody. I—I think you are impertinent, Mr. Wynne. Is it your business whom I love? My God! there is blood on your hand! Are you hurt?»

It was true; a little blood was trickling down my wrist. She was all tenderness again. I must not go; here was her handkerchief; and so on—till I longed to take her in my arms, she made me so sorry for her.

I said it was of no moment, and I must go.

«You will come soon again, and tell me about Jack.»

I went away, not wondering that all the world should love her.

I hastened to Jack's home, and there found Dr. Rush and Dr. Glentworth, who was later to be the physician of Mr. Washington. My aunt, preceding me, had taken possession. Mr. Warder was reduced to a condition of abject obedience, and for a month and more my aunt hardly left her girl-boy's pillow. Indeed, it was long before I was let to see him, and then he was but a spectre of himself, with not enough blood to blush with. Our officers promptly left for New York the day after our fight, and we heard no more of them.

It would have been of little use to tell this long story but for the consequences to me and to others. I should have done well to see my father at once; but I could not get away, and sat till noon, asking every now and then what I could do, and if Jack were better, despite the fact that I was told he was doing well.

Mr. Warder was one of those people who, once a crisis seems over, must still be doing something, and to be rid of him he was sent by my aunt to get certain articles the doctors did or did not need. It seemed wise to this gentleman, having completed his errands, to pay a visit of condolence to my father, and thus it was that greater mischief was made.

About two I got away, and set forth to see my parent. Already the news was out, and I was stopped over and over to explain what had happened. It was the hour of dinner; for Friends dined at two, but my aunt and the gayer set at four.

My father turned from his meal, and coldly looked me all over,—my arm was in a sling, on which Dr. Rush had insisted,—and last into my eyes. «Well,» he said, «thou art come at last. Fortunately, Friend Warder has been here, and I know thy story and the mischief into which thou hast led his poor lad. It is time we had a settlement, thou and I. Hast thou fear neither of God nor of man? A rebellious son, and a defier of authority! It is well thy mother is dead before she saw thee come to this ruin of soul and body.»

«My God! father,» I cried, «how canst thou hurt me thus! I am in sorrow for Jack, and want help. To whom should I go but to thee? O mother, mother!» I looked around at the bare walls, and down at the sanded floor, and could only bury my face in my hands and weep like a baby. What with all the day had brought, and Darthea and Jack, and now this grand old man silent, impassive, unmoved by what was shaking me like a storm, although I loved him still for all his hardness, I had no refuge but in tears.

He rose, and I sat still, thinking what I should say. «When thou art ready to turn from thy sin and ask pardon of God and of me, who am brought to shame on thy account, I will talk with thee.»

Upon this I set myself between him and the door. «We cannot part this way. It is too terrible.»

«That was a matter thou hadst been wise to have considered long ago, Hugh.»

«No!» I cried. I was as resolved as he. «I must be heard. How have I offended? Have I neglected thy business? Who can say so? I was insulted in Meeting, and I went where men do not trample on a penitent boy, and if I have gone the way of my aunt's world, is it my fault or thine? I have gone away from what, in thy opinion, is right as regards questions in which the best and purest side with me. Am I a child that I may not use my own judgment?» It was the first time in my life that I had plainly asserted my freedom to think and to act.

To my surprise, he stood a moment in silence, looking down, I as quiet, regarding him with eager and attentive eyes. Then he said, seeking my gaze: «I am to blame; I have too much considered thy chances of worldly gain. I know not whence thou hast thy wilfulness.» As I looked in the face of this strong, rock-like man, I wondered; for he went on, «Not from me, Hugh, not from me—»

«Stop!» I said. «Thou hast said enough.» I feared lest again he should reproach her of whose sweetness I had naught but a gift of the blue eyes that must have met his with menace. I saw, as his hands shook, tapping the floor with his cane, how great were both his anger and his self-control.

«It were well, my son, that this ended. I hope thou wilt see thy way to better courses. Thy cousin was right. He too is a man not of my world, but he saw more clearly than I where thou wert going.»

«What!» I cried, «and thou canst think this? Thou hast believed and trusted Arthur Wynne! What did he say of me?»

«I will not be questioned.»

«The man lied to thee,» I cried,—«why, I do not know,—and to others also. Why did he deceive us as to Wyncote? What reason had he? As he lied about that, so does he seem to have lied about me. By heaven! he shall answer me some day.»

«I will hear no profanity in my house. Stand aside! Dost thou not hear me? Am I to be disobeyed in my own house?»

I but half took in his meaning, and stood still. The next moment he seized me by the lapels of my coat, and, spinning me round like a child, pushed me from him. I fell into the great Penn chair he had turned from the table when he rose. He threw open the door, and I saw him walk quickly down the hall and out into the orchard garden.

For a week he did no more than speak to me a word when business made it needful, and then the monotonous days went on as before in the gray, dismal home, out of which the light of life's gladness departed when those dear mother-eyes were closed in death.

## XIV.

WHILE, throughout that sad summer, my Jack was slowly coming back to health, even the vast events of the war now under way moved me but little. My Aunt Gainor would think of no one but her young Quaker. Her house was no longer gay, nor would she go to the country until Mr. Warder agreed that she should take Jack with us to the Hill Farm-house, where, in the warm months, she moved among her cattle, and fed the hens, and helped and bullied every poor housewife far and near.

In a bright-tinted hammock I fetched from Madeira, Jack used to lie under the apple-trees that June and July, with my aunt for company; better could hardly have been. When I came from town late in June, with news of what the farmers and their long rifles had done at Bunker Hill, it was a little too much for Jack's strength, and he burst into tears. But Dr. Rush declared that self-control was an affair of physical health, and that he who had too little blood—and Jack was lily-white—could be neither courageous, nor able to contain his emotions. I suppose it may be true.

I went in and out of town daily, my father being unwilling to go to Merion. At times I met James Wilson, who was steadily urging me to enter the army. Wetherill had scarce any other words for me. But my father, Jack's condition, and my aunt's depending on me, all stood in my way, and I did but content myself with an hour's daily drill in town with others, who were thus preparing themselves for active service.

We were taught, and well too, by an Irish sergeant—I fear a deserter from one of his Majesty's regiments. As Jack got better, he was eager to have me put him through his facings, but before he was fit the summer was nigh over.

It had been a time of great anxiety to all men. The Virginia colonel was commander-in-chief; a motley army held Sir William Howe penned up in Boston, and why he so quietly accepted this sheep-like fate no man of us could comprehend. My aunt, a great letter-writer, had many correspondents, and one or two in the camp at Cambridge.

«My Virginia fox-hunter,» said my aunt, «is having evil days with the New England farmers. He is disposed to be despotic, says—well, no matter who. He likes the whipping-post too well, and thinks all should, like himself, serve without pay. A slow man it is, but intelligent,» says my Aunt Gainor; «sure to get himself right, and patient too. You will see, Hugh; he will come slowly to understand these people.»

I smiled at the good lady's confidence, and yet she was right. They took him ill at first in that undisciplined camp, and queer things were said of him. Like the rest, he was learning the business of war, and was to commit many blunders and get sharp lessons in this school of the soldier.

These were everywhere uneasy times. Day after day we heard of this one or that one gone to swell the ever-changing number of those who beset Sir William. Gondolas—most unlike gondolas they were—were being built in haste for our own river defence. Committees, going from house to house, collected arms, tent-stuffs, kettles, blankets, and what not, for our troops. There were noisy elections, arrests of Tories; and in October the death of Peyton Randolph, ex-president of the Congress, and the news of the coming of the Hessian hirelings. It was a season of stir, angry discussion, and stern waiting for what was to come; but through it all my Jack prospered mightily in health, so that by September 20 he was fit to leave us.

I still think pleasantly of all the pretty pictures of pale, fair-haired Jack in the hammock, with Darthea reading to him, and the Whig ladies with roses from their gardens, and peaches and what not, all for Jack, the hero, I being that summer but a small and altogether unimportant personage.

When my Jack went home again, we began at once to talk over our plans for joining Mr. Washington; I made sure that now there was no greater obstacle in my way than my father's opinions. Alas! in November my aunt took what Dr. Rush called a pernicious ague, and, although bled many times and fed on Jesuits' bark, she came near to dying. In January she was better, but was become like a child, and depended upon me for everything. If I but spoke of my desire to be in the field, she would fall to tears or declare me ungrateful. She was morally weakened by her disease, and did seem to have changed as to her character. I lamented to Jack that it was my fate to stay, and he must go alone; I would follow when I could.

It was far into April before my aunt was entirely her old self, but as early as the close of January she had decided that she was well, and that to be well you must get rid of doctors. She told the great physician as much, and he left her in vast disgust. Society she would now have had for remedial distraction, but the war had made of it a dismal wreck. The Tories had been warned or sent away; the moderates hardly fared better; and the old gay set was broken up. Nevertheless it was not until far later, in July, '77, that Mr. Chew, Mr. Penn, and other as important neutrals, were ordered to leave the city; until then some remnants of the governor's set kept up more or less of the pleasant life they had once led. But there were no more redcoats in their drawing-rooms, and our antagonists were of the last who had lingered. Even before their departure, any gentleman of the king's service was sure to be told to leave, and meanwhile was apt to find a militiaman at his door.

My aunt would have none of them that winter, and her old Tory friends ceased to be seen at her house, save only Darthea, whilst Continental uniforms and gentlemen of the Congress were made warmly welcome; but alas! among these was no match for her at piquet, and she felt that no one had sacrificed more for the country than had she.

In February of '76 a double change took place among us, and to my great discontent. I had seen much of Darthea in the fall and early winter of '75, and had come to know her better. She was fond of riding with my aunt, who had a strong gray stallion full of tricks, but no master of the hardy old lady, whom neither horse nor man ever dismayed. The good spinster was by no means as vigorous as I could have wished, but ride she would on all clear days whether cold or not, and liked well to have Darthea with us. When ill she was a docile patient, but, once afoot, declared all doctors fools, and would have no more of them «and their filthy doses.»

We rode of sunlit winter days out to Germantown, or upon the wood roads over Schuylkill, my Aunt Gainor from good nature being pleased to gallop ahead, and leave us to chat and follow, or not, as might suit us.

One fine crisp morning in February we were breasting at a walk the slippery incline of Chestnut Hill, when Darthea, who had been unusually silent, said quite abruptly:

«I am going away, Mr. Wynne.»

I was instantly troubled. «Where?» I said.

«Next week, and to New York. My aunt can no longer stand all this mob of rebels. We go to New York, and for how long I know not. Since, in September, our friend Dr. John Kearsley was mobbed and maltreated, my aunt declares you unfit to live among. I must say I thought it brutal, sir. When men of sense and breeding like Mr. Penn, Mr. Chew, and Dr. Kearsley cannot live unmolested it is time, my aunt thinks, to run.»

«No one annoys Mr. Penn or Mr. Chew,» said I. «To my mind, they are neutrals, and worse than open foes; but thy doctor is a mad Tory, and a malignant talker. I saw the matter, and I assure thee it was overstated. He lost his temper; 't is a brave gentleman, and I would he were with us. But now that both sides are sure at last that they are really at war, these men who live among us and are ready to welcome every redcoat should have their lesson. It must be Yes or No in a war like this.»

«But I hate that,» she returned; «and to be comfortable and snug, and to love ease and Madeira and a quiet horse, and a book and a pipe and a nap of an afternoon, and then to have certain of the baser sort cry, ‹Get up and kill somebody!› I think I am with Mr. Ross, and believe that, ‹let who will be king, I well know I shall be subject.› Imagine my Aunt Peniston's fat poodle invited to choose between exile and killing rats!»

«My dear Miss Darthea, for thee to preach caution and neutrality is delightful.»

«Did it sound like that Mr. Congregation?»

«No; to tell the truth, I think it did not.»

«Indeed, you are right,» says she. «I am a red-hot Tory, sir. I scare Margaret Chew out of her sweet wits when I talk blood, blood, sir; and as to Miss Franks,—she hates to be called Becky,—when I say I hope to see Mr. Washington hanged, she vows he is too fine a man, and she would hang only the ugly ones. So take care, Mr. Stay-at-home, take care; I am no neutral.»

«Thank thee,» I said, lifting my hat. «I like open enemies best.»

«Oh, I will say a good word for you when it comes to that, and you will need it. Sir Guy will have Ticonderoga soon, and Mr. Howe New York; so that, with my loyal cousins and the king in possession, we shall at least be in civilised society.»

«There is a well-worn proverb,» said I, «about counting chickens. Where shalt thou be in New York?»

«Cousin De Lancey has asked us to stay with them. When the king's troops return to your rebel town we shall come back, I suppose.»

«I am sorry,» I said. «All my friends are flitting like swallows. Poor Mr. Franks is to go, it seems, and the gay Miss Rebecca; but she likes the redcoats best, and another is of the same mind, I fear.»

«I am not over-grieved to go myself,» said Darthea, «and we will not quarrel just now. Have you seen Mr. Warder to-day?»

«I have not.»

«Then I am the bearer of ill news. He is to join your new general in a week or two. He could not find you this morning. I think he was relieved to know I should tell you. How much he cares for you! It is not like a man friendship. It is like the way we weak girls care for one another. How can he be such a brave gentleman as he seems—as he must be? I should have thought it would be you who would have gone first. Why do you not go? Here is Miss Wynne's pet girl-boy away to fight, and you—why do not you go?»

I was puzzled, as well I might be. «Dost thou want me to go?»

A light came into those brown eyes, and a little flush to the cheeks, as she said, oh, so very quickly, «I want all my friends to do what seems to them right.»

«I am glad to answer,» I said. «It seems to me my duty to be with the army; my friends have gone, and now Graydon, the last to leave, has also gone. I fancy people smiling to see me still at home—I who am so positive, so outspoken. But here is my father, with whom if I go I break for life, and here is my Aunt Gainor, who bursts into tears if I do but mention my wish to leave her.»

«I see,» said Darthea, not looking at me; «now I understand fully; I did not before. But—will you think it strange if—if I say—I, a loving and a loyal woman—that you should go, and soon?» Then there was a long pause, and she added, «When will this cruel war end?»

«God knows,» said I. «Thank thee; thou art right, Darthea.»

Another pause as long came after, when she said abruptly, and in quite another voice, «You do not like Mr. Arthur Wynne; why do you not?»

I was startled. One never knew when she would get under one's guard and put some prickly question.

«Dost thou think I have reason to like him?» I said. «I did like him once, but now I do not; nor does he love me any better. Why dost thou ask me?»

«Oh, for—no matter! I am not going to say why.»

«I think thou knowest, Darthea, that he is no friend of mine.»

«Let us join your aunt,» she said gravely.

«One word more,» said I, «and I shall trouble thee no further. Rest sure that, come what may, there is one man who loves thee with a love no man can better.»

«I wish you had not said that. There are some, Mr. Wynne, who never know when to take No for an answer.»

«I am one,» said I.

To this she made no reply, and rode on looking ahead in a dreamy way that fetched back to my memory a prettiness my dear mother had. Presently turning, she said:

«Let it end here; and—and my name is Miss Peniston, please.»

There was no pettishness in her voice—only a certain dignity which sits better on little women than on little men, and provokes no smile. She was looking at me with a curious steadiness of gaze as she spoke. It was my last chance for many a day, and I could not let her go with a mere bow of meek submission.

«If I have been rude or discourteous, I am more sorry than I can say. If I called thee Darthea, it was because hope seemed to bring us nearer for one dear moment. Ah! I may call thee Miss Peniston, but for me always thou wilt be Darthea; and I shall love Darthea to the end, even when Miss Peniston has come to be a distant dream and has another name. I am most sorry to have given thee annoyance. Forget that, and pardon me.»

«Mr. Wynne, you are a kindly and courteous gentleman. I wish—and you must not misapprehend me—that I loved you. Oh, I do not. Your aunt, who is so good to me, is a fierce wooer. I am afraid of her, and—she must be miles away; let us join her.» And with this she shook her bridle, and was off at speed, and my mare and I at her side.

If I have made those who loved Darthea Peniston and me understand this winning soul, I shall be glad; and if not I shall at least have had the pleasure of repeating words and describing actions which live in my remembrance with such exactness as does not apply to much of what, to the outer world, may seem far better entitled to be remembered. She had it in her to hurt you, help you, pity you, mock or amuse you, and behind it all was the honesty and truth of a womanhood capable of courageous conduct, and despising all forms of meanness. That she was variously regarded was natural. Margaret Shippen said she cared only for dress and the men; and the witty Miss Franks, seeing further, but not all, said that Darthea Peniston was an actress of the minute, who believed her every rôle to be real. My aunt declared that she was several women, and that she did not always keep some of them in order. It was clear, to me at least, that she was growing older in mind, and was beginning to keep stricter school for those other women with whom my aunt credited this perplexing little lady.

Before I quite leave her for a time, I must let Jack say a word. It will tell more than I then knew or could know, and will save me from saying that which were better said by another.

«At last there is certainty of a long war, and I, being well again, must take my side. It is fortunate when choice is so easy, for I find it often hard in life to know just what is right. Poor Hugh, who has gone further than I from our fathers' faith, will still declare he is of Friends; but he commonly drops our language if he is not excited or greatly interested, and the rest will go too. It is strange that his resoluteness and clear notions of duty have so helped me, and yet that he is so caught and tied fast by Miss Gainor's dependence upon him, and by his scruples as to his father. He cannot do the thing he would. Now that my own father has sold out his business, I at least am left without excuse. I shall go at once, for fear I shall change my mind.» A more unlikely thing I cannot imagine to have happened to John Warder.

«I saw Darthea to-day,» he goes on to write. «She is going to New York. She talked to me with such frankness as almost broke my heart. She does not know how dear she is to me. I was near to telling her; but if she said No,—and she would,—I might—oh, I could not see her again. I had rather live in doubt. And whether Hugh loves her or not I would I knew. Mistress Wynne does but laugh and say, ‹Lord bless us! they all love her!› Hugh is, as to some things, reticent, and of Darthea likes so little to speak that I am led to think it is a serious business for him; and if it be so, what can I but go? for how could I come between him and a woman he loved? Never, surely. Why is life such a tangle? It is well I am going. What else is left for me? My duty has long been plain.

«I did venture to ask Darthea of Mr. Arthur Wynne. She said quietly, ‹I have had a letter to-day;› and with this she looked at me in a sort of defiant way. I like the man not at all, and wonder that women fancy him so greatly. When I said I was sorry she was going, she replied, ‹It is no one's business;› and then added, ‹nor Mr. Wynne's either,› as if Hugh had said a word. In fact, Miss Peniston was almost as cross and abrupt as dear Miss Wynne at her worst. If ever, God willing, I should marry her,—there, I am blushing even to think of such a sweet impossibility,—she would drive me frantic. I should be in small rages or begging her pardon every half-hour of the day.

«What will Hugh say when he hears the Meeting means to disown us? It troubles me deeply. My father is trembling too, for since a month he is all for resisting oppression, and who has been talking to him I do not know. Miss Wynne called him a decrepit weathercock to me last month, and then was in a fury at herself, and sorry too; but she will talk with him no more. It cannot be because he has sold his Holland cloths so well to the clothier-general. I never can think that.

«When I saw Miss Wynne, and would have seen Hugh had he been in, I told her of my meaning to go away by the packet to Burlington, and thence through New Jersey. She said it was well, but that Hugh should not go yet. He should go soon. Mr. Lee, the new general, had been to see her—a great soldier, she was told. But she had not liked him, because he let her believe he came of the same family as Mr. Richard Henry Lee of Virginia, whereas this is not so. He was lank, sour, and ill dressed, she said, and fetched his two dogs into the house. When he saw Hugh, he said it was time all the young men were out. Miss Wynne disliked this, and it is reported that Mrs. Ferguson and she, meeting after church, had nearly come to blows, because Mrs. Ferguson had said the people who made the war should be in the war, and on this the old lady desired to know if this arrow was meant for her or for her nephew. Mrs. F., not lacking courage, said she might choose.

«So Madam Wynne is pulled this way and that, and I must go alone; and I shall have a lieutenant's commission, and a pretty fellow am I to order other men about. I like best the Continental line.»

I saw Jack the day after my ride with Miss Peniston. I said sadly that he was right, and we talked it all over that week, running down the river at early morning after ducks, and through the wide channel between League Island and the Neck; or else we were away to Red Bank, or to the Jersey coast, if the ice permitted, as it often did. It was a wonderful, open winter, as it chanced, and we had more than our usual share of the ducks, which were very abundant. As we lay in the gray weeds below the bluff at Red Bank, we little thought of what it was to see. Our gallant Mercer, who fell at Princeton, was to give a name to the fort we built long after; and there, too, was to die Count Donop, as brave a man, far from home, sold by his own prince to be the hireling of a shameful king.

The ducks flew over thick, and between times, as we waited, we talked at intervals of the war, of Montgomery's failure to capture Quebec, and of the lingering siege of Boston; of how the brutal destruction of Norfolk in December had stirred the Virginians, and indeed every true heart in the colonies. Jack would write when occasion served.

That last day (it was now February, as I have said) we supped with my aunt, Jack and

I. After the meal was over, she went out of the room, and, coming back, gave Jack a handsome, serviceable sword, with a proper sash and tie. Then she must make him take a hundred pounds in a purse she had netted; and when he would not she said he was going to school, and must have a tip, and would hear no more, and kissed him, at which he got very red. Indeed, she was deeply moved, as was plain to see from the way she talked, speaking fast, and saying all manner of foolish things.

This business of the sword troubled me more than it ought to have done, and I resolved that nothing should long keep me out of the field; but alas! it was many a day before my going became possible. And so my Jack went away, and Miss Peniston.

The war was dull for a time, as the armies got ready for a spring at each other's throats. At last, in March, his Excellency seized Dorchester Heights, and Boston became no longer tenable. Howe left it on March 14, and, what was as desirable, some two hundred cannon and vast stores of ammunition. Then, on Cambridge Common, our chief threw to the free winds our flag, with its thirteen stripes, and still in the corner the blood-red cross of St. George.

Late in this winter of '75–'76, an event took place, or rather the sequel of an event, which made me feel deeply the embarrassment in which the condition of my aunt and father placed me. He who reads may remember my speaking of a young fellow whom I saw at the Woodlands, a young Macpherson. I took a great fancy to him later, and we fished and shot together until he went away, in August of '75, to join Arnold for his wild march into Canada.

His father, broken and sad, now brought to my aunt the news of his son's death in the assault on Quebec, and, speechless with grief, showed her the young fellow's letter, writ the night before he fell. He wrote, with other matter: «I cannot resist the inclination I feel to assure you that I experience no reluctance in this cause to venture a life I consider as only lent, and to be used when my country demands it.» He went on to say that, if he died, he could wish his brother William, an adjutant in the king's army, would not continue in the service of our enemies. I saw, too, General Schuyler's letter of condolence, but this was later.

Nothing had moved me like this. I went away, leaving the father and my aunt. People came to this strong woman, sure of her tenderest help, and I trust she comforted her friend in his loss. This was the first officer of our own set our city lost in war, and the news, I think, affected me more than any. How, indeed, could I dare to stay when the best manhood of the land was facing death in a cause as dear to me as to any?

In June a new calamity fell on me, or I should say on my father; for I felt it but little, or only as in some degree a release from bonds which I hesitated to sever by my own act. On the morning of June 25, my father called me into his counting-room, and, closing the door, sat down, I, as was thought fit, standing until told to be seated. Since he made no sign of any such desire on his part, I knew at once that this was not to be a talk about our affairs, in which, I may say, I had no interest except as to a very moderate salary.

«Thou wilt have to-day a call from Friend Pemberton. The overseers are moved at last to call thee to an account. I have lost hope that thou wilt forsake and condemn thy error. I have worked with the overseers to give thee and thy friend John Warder time, and this has been with tenderness accorded. No good is yet come of it. If this private admonition be of no effect, thy case will come before overseers again, and thou wilt be dealt with as a disorderly person, recommended to be disowned, when thy misdeeds come to be laid before the Quarterly Meeting for discipline. Already the Yearly Meeting hath found fault with us for lax dealing with such as thou art. Thou hast ceased to obey either thy father or thy God, and now my shame for thee is opened to all men.»

Not greatly moved, I listened to this summary of what was to happen. «It is too late,» I said, «to argue this matter, my dear father. I cannot sin against my conscience. I will receive Mr. Pemberton as thy friend. He is a man whom all men respect and many love, but his ways are no longer my ways. Is that all?» I added. I feared any long talk with my father. We were as sure to fall out at last as were he and my Aunt Gainor.

«Yes,» he said; «that is all. And tell Wilson to bring me the invoice of the *Saucy Sally*.»

This time neither of us had lost temper. He had transacted a piece of business which concerned my soul, and I had listened. It had left me sore, but that was an old and too familiar story. Reflecting on what had passed in the counting-house,—and my conclusion now shows me how fast I was growing older,—I put on my hat at once, and set out to find the overseer deputed to make a private remonstrance with my father's son. I suppose that my action was also hastened by a disinclination to lie still, awaiting an unpleasant and unavoidable business.

Finding James Pemberton in his office, I told him that my errand was out of respect to relieve him of the need to call upon a younger man. He seemed pleased, and opened the matter in a way so gentle and considerate that I am sure no man could have bettered the manner of doing it. My attention to business and quieter life had for a time reassured the overseers. He would not speak of blood-guiltiness now, for out of kindness to my distressed parent they had seen fit to wait, and for a time to set it aside. My father had been in much affliction, and Friends had taken note of this. Now he had to call to my mind the testimony of Friends concerning war, and even how many had been reported to the Yearly Meeting for sufferings on account of righteous unwillingness to resist constituted authority, and how men of my views had oppressed and abused them. Had I read the letter of the Yearly Meeting of 1774, warning members not to depart from their peaceful principles by taking part in any of the political matters then being stirred up, reminding all Friends that under the king's government they had been favoured with a peaceful and prosperous enjoyment of their rights, and the like?

I listened quietly, and said it was too late to discuss these questions, which were many; that my mind was fully made up, and that as soon as possible I meant to enter the army. He had the good sense to see that I was of no inclination to change; and so, after some words of the most tender remonstrance, he bade me to prayerfully consider the business further, since overseers would not meet at once, and even when they did there would be time to manifest to Friends a just sense of my errors.

I thanked him, and went my way, making, however, no sign of grace, so that, on July 4 of this 1776, late in the evening, I received in my aunt's presence a letter from Isaac Freeman, clerk of the Meeting, inclosing a formal minute of the final action of Friends in my case.

«What is that?» said Aunt Gainor, very cheerful over a letter of thanks to her for having sold at cost to the Committee of Safety the cloth of Holland and the blankets she had induced my father to buy for her. She had stored them away for this hour of need, and was now full of satisfaction because of having made my father the means of clothing the Continental troops.

«Read it aloud. What is it, sir?» I was smiling over what a few years before would have cost me many a bitter thought.

«Give it me! What is it?» Then she put on a pair of the new spectacles with wire supports to rest on the ears. «Dr. Franklin gave me these new inventions, and a great comfort too. I cannot endure bridge glasses; they leave dents in one's nose. You have not seen him lately. He was here to-day. You should see him, Hugh. He was dressed very fine in a velvet coat with new, shilling buttons, and bless me! but he has got manners as fine as his ruffles, and that is saying a good deal—Mechlin of the best. You would not know the man.»

With this she began to look at my letter. «Hoity-toity, sir! this is a fine setting down for a naughty Quaker!» And she read it aloud in a strong voice, her head back, and the great promontory of her nose twitching at the nostrils now and then with supreme contempt:

«‹To HUGH WYNNE: A minute, this First-day of Sixth-month, 1776, from the Monthly Meeting of Friends held at Philadelphia.

«‹Whereas Hugh Wynne hath had his birth and education among Friends, and, as we believe, hath been convinced of that divine principle which preserves the followers thereof from a disposition to contend for the asserting of civil rights in a manner contrary to our peaceful profession, yet doth not manifest a disposition to make the Meeting a proper acknowledgment of his outgoings, and hath further declared his intention to continue his wrong-doing;

«‹Therefore, for the clearing of truth and our society, we give forth our testimony against such breaches, and can have no unity with him, the said Hugh Wynne, as a member of our society until he become sensible of his deviations, and come to a sense of his error, and condemn the same to the satisfaction of Friends; which is that we, as Christian men, desire.

«‹Signed in, and on behalf of, the Meeting by

«‹ISAAC FREEMAN,
«‹*Clerk.*›

«What insolent nonsense!» cried Miss Wynne. «I hope your father is satisfied. I assure you I am. You are free at last. Here was James Warder to-day with a like document to the address of my dear Jack. I was assured that it was a terrible disgrace. I bade him take snuff and not be any greater fool than nature had made him. He took my snuff and sneezed for ten minutes. I think it helped him. One can neither grieve nor reason when one is sneezing. It is what Dr. Rush calls a moral alterative. Whenever the man fell to lamenting, I gave him more snuff. I think it helped him. And so the baa-lambs of Meeting have disowned their two black sheep. Well, well! I have better news for you. Mr. Carroll was here just now, with his charming ways. One would think when he is talking that one is the only woman alive. If I thought the priests taught him the trick, I would turn papist. You should observe his bow, Hugh. I thought Mr. Chew's bow not to be surpassed; but Mr. Carroll—oh, where was I?»

«Some good news,» I said.

«Yes, yes. He tells me the Congress this evening voted for a Declaration of Independence.»

«Indeed!» I cried. «So it has come at last. I too am free, and it is time I went away, Aunt Gainor.»

«We will see,» she said. «How can I do without you? and there is your father too. He is not the man he was, and I do not see, Hugh, how you can leave him yet.»

It was too true, as my last interview had shown me. He was no longer the strong, steadily obstinate John Wynne of a year or two back. He was less decisive, made occasional errors in his accounts, and would sometimes commit himself to risky ventures. Then Thomas Mason, our clerk, or my aunt would interfere, and he would protest and yield,, having now by habit a great respect for my aunt's sagacity, which in fact was remarkable.

I went back to my work discontented, and pulled this way and that, not clearly seeing what I ought to do; for how could I leave him as he now was? My aunt was right.

Next day I heard John Nixon read in the State-House yard the noble words of the Declaration. Only a few hundred were there to hear it, and its vast consequences few men as yet could apprehend. Miss Norris told me not long after that she climbed on a barrow and looked over their garden wall at Fifth street and Chestnut; «and really, Mr. Wynne, there were not ten decent coats in the crowd.» But this Miss Norris was a hot Tory, and thought us all an underbred mob, as, I fear, did most of the proprietary set—the men lacking civil courage to fight on either side, and amazed that Mr. Wilson, and Mr. Reed, and Mr. Robert Morris, and the Virginia gentry, should side with demagogues like Adams and Roger Sherman.

And so time ran on. I fenced, drilled, saw my companions drift away into war, and knew not how to escape. I can now look back on my dismissal from Meeting with more regret than it gave my youth. I have never seen my way to a return to Friends; yet I am still apt to be spoken of as one of the small number who constitute, with Wetherill and Owen and Clement Biddle, the society of Friends known as Free Quakers. To discuss why later I did not claim my place as one of these would lead me to speaking of spiritual affairs, and this, as I have elsewhere said, I never do willingly, nor with comfort to myself.

One afternoon in September of this year I was balancing an account when my father came in and told me that Mason, our clerk, had just had a fall in the hold of one of our ships. The day after I saw him, and although his hurts were painful they hardly seemed to justify my father in his desire that now at last he should take a long rest from work.

This threw all the detail of our affairs as largely into my hands as was possible with a man like my father. I think he guessed my intention to leave him for the army, and gladly improved this chance to load me with needless affairs, and all manner of small perplexities. My aunt was better—in fact, well; but here was this new trouble. What could I do? My father declared that the old clerk would soon be able to resume his place, and meanwhile he should have no one to help him but me. Now and then, to my surprise, he made some absurd business venture, and was impatient if I said a word of remonstrance. Twice I was sent to Maryland to see after our tobacco plantations. I was in despair, and became depressed and querulous, seeing no present way, nor any future likelihood, of escape. My father was well pleased, and even my aunt seemed to me too well satisfied with the ill turn which fate had done me. My father was clearly using the poor old clerk's calamity as an excuse to keep me busy; nor was it at all like him to employ such subterfuges. All his life long he had been direct, positive, and dictatorial; a few years back he would have ordered me to give up all idea of the army, and would as like as not have punished resistance with cold-blooded disinheritance. He was visibly and but too clearly changing from the resolute, uncompromising man he had once been. Was he cunning enough to know that his weakness was for me a bondage far stronger than his more vigorous rule had ever been?

(To be continued.)

*S. Weir Mitchell.*

AUNT GAINOR.

VIEW FROM THE CAPITOL, SHOWING THE MAIN FRONT OF THE LIBRARY.

# THE NATION'S LIBRARY.

BY THE LIBRARIAN.

WITH PICTURES BY E. POTTHAST.

## I. THE NEW BUILDING.

A CONSOLE, MAIN VESTIBULE. HERBERT ADAMS, SCULPTOR.

THE monumental building provided for the extensive collections of the Library of Congress at Washington represents about nine years of construction, besides fourteen years of preliminary agitation and discussion. The act of April 15, 1886, authorizing the erection of a separate library building was the fruit of a public necessity growing out of the rapid increase, beyond all capacity within the Capitol to hold them, of the nation's books. Several proposed measures for this end had been postponed from year to year by interests deemed more important or more pressing, or by differences concerning a proper site, plan, and cost, until the act referred to secured fully two thirds of the votes of both houses of Congress.

The site selected was an ideal one in respect to elevation, salubrity, and dry, solid foundations for a massive edifice of granite. It abuts upon the park of the Capitol, being about 1500 feet distant from that building on the east, and it is surrounded by four streets with ample approaches. The white granite which forms the exterior walls of the building is from quarries in Concord, New Hampshire, and in color is nearly as light as the marble walls of the Capitol. The inner walls, facing the four spacious courts, are in part of a slightly darker granite from Maryland, and partly of white enameled brick resembling porcelain in color, and producing a light and cheerful effect. The dimensions of the library building are 470 by 340 feet, covering about three and a half acres of ground. In style the building belongs to the Italian Renaissance, and four corner pavilions, together with the central front, are moderately projected, completely relieving any monotony incident to so long a façade. The solid and massive granite walls are further relieved by many windows, the casings of which are treated in high relief, and by sixteen ornate pillars and capitals in the central front, with twelve columns in each of the corner pavilions. In the keystones of thirty-three window arches are carved in the granite thirty-three human heads, representing types of various races of men—a unique feature, furnishing an object-lesson in ethnology as well as in decoration. Four colossal figures, each representing Atlas, are carved below the roof on the central pavilion, surmounted by a pediment with sculptured American eagles, and an emblematic group in granite. Three spandrels, carved in granite above the arches of the three main entrance doors, represent Art, Science, and Literature. The whole edifice is surmounted by a carved balustrade which runs around the building. The lower story is of rough-surfaced granite, while the walls of the upper stories are of smooth bush-hammered stone, relieved at the corners of the building by vermiculated work. The height of the walls is 69 feet, and the apex of the dome is 195 feet from the ground. This dome is gilded with a thick coating of gold-leaf, and is surmounted by a lantern the crest of which terminates in a gilded finial representing the ever-burning torch of Science. The galleries of the upper story command a wide and noble view of the Virginia and Maryland heights, the city of Washington, and the river Potomac.

The combined solidity and beauty of the exterior produce an architectural effect which is generally admired. The massive granite approaches, doorway, and staircase with its heavy but finely designed balustrades, lend dignity to the edifice, instead of detracting from it, as in some notable public buildings. The grounds immediately surrounding it are laid out in a style to correspond with the spacious park of the Capitol, and a beautiful bronze fountain in the central front will contribute a refreshing adjunct to the harmonious effect. In the rear of the library building is located a granite annex with a high tower, providing for all the machinery connected with the heating of the structure—pumps, coal-vaults, steam-boilers, etc. Thus is secured within the library complete immunity from those nuisances of noise, dust, heat, and odors which are the unavoidable consequence when such plants are placed in the basement of any public building.

Entering the building, it is found to be divided into three stories besides the cellar, namely, a ground floor level with the surrounding streets, a first story, or library floor, and a second story, or gallery floor. Passing into the basement under heavy groined arches, the ceilings of which are frescoed in simple designs, we enter one of the four long, spacious corridors which extend all around the building. The feature of all these wide passageways is that they are wainscoted or are lined entirely

BRONZE LAMP-BEARER OF THE GRAND STAIRCASE. PHILIP MARTINY, SCULPTOR.

CENTRAL PAVILION, SHOWING MAIN ENTRANCE.

with American marbles coming from three different States, and embracing the handsomest colored marbles which this country produces. The western corridor (nearest to the Capitol) is of two shades of mottled blue Vermont marble from quarries at Brandon. The south wing is lined with what we may call Champlain marble, from the Swanton quarries near that lake, a very rich red-and-white stone, most effective to the eye. In the eastern corridor (360 feet in length), a Georgia marble from Pickens County, in black and white veins, has been used with beautiful effect. Finally, the north wing is lined with Tennessee marble of a light chocolate color. The arches and the walls above all these polished marble wainscotings are elaborately frescoed in harmonious colors; and when one has circumambulated the great building, he is impressed with the variety and beauty, as well as with the solid proportions, of these basement corridors. The spacious rooms opening from them are to be used for a bookbindery, packing-, receiving-, and shipping-rooms, office-rooms for the heads of the watch and superintendence of the building, and for storage purposes.

Ascending to the first or library floor, which is also entered from the outside by the granite staircase and bronze doors, the vestibule is reached, through which, decorated elaborately with white marble and gilded ceiling, one enters the foyer, or grand staircase hall. This superb apartment is constructed throughout of the finest Italian marble, highly polished. From its four sides rise lofty rounded columns with Corinthian capitals richly carved, and its heavy but very graceful arches are adorned with marble rosettes, palm-leaves, and foliated designs of exquisite finish and delicacy. The lofty height of this fine entrance-hall, rising 72 feet to the skylight of stained glass, with its ornate vaulted ceiling and grand double staircase, and its white marble balustrades leading up on each side to the galleries above, produces an architectural effect both harmonious and imposing. It has been styled «a vision in polished stone» and «a dream of beauty»; but only readers who have seen it can be expected to appreciate such terms of praise.

Entering through this spacious hall, we pass into the reading-room, or central rotunda, by wide corridors adorned with rich mosaic ceilings. This public reading-room is octagonal in shape, with a diameter of 100 feet, and is lighted from above by eight large semicircular windows 32 feet wide, bearing the arms of all the States and Territories in color. At intervals eight massive pillars rise to the height of 40 feet, their bases being of dark Tennessee marble surmounted by heavy columns of lighter red Numidian marble, and crowned by emblematic statues of heroic size. The wall-space of the reading-room is of yellow Siena marble, with numerous arches and balustrades rising to the height of the upper gallery in a double tier, and having an extremely rich and beautiful effect. There are in all seventy-seven arches, the lower tier being intercalated with pilasters and architraves carved in classic sculpture. All these beautiful architectural effects are embodied in that richest of all known colored marbles which comes from the quarries of the Siena monastery, and their soft, warm, and mellow lights and shades are a pleasure to the eye.

The reading-room is fitted with mahogany desks for about two hundred and fifty readers, allowing each four feet of working-space. In the center, slightly raised above the surrounding floor, are the desks of the superintendent and his assistants, with the card-catalogue of the library in a long series of drawers grouped about the inner circle, while the circular shelves outside the railing provide readers with an assortment of catalogues, bibliographies, and other works of reference to be used freely without the formality of tickets. Within this central desk-space, which commands every part of the reading-room, is an extensive series of pneumatic tubes communicating with the several stack-rooms in which books are stored, and there is to be introduced a system of book-carriers for the speedy service of books to readers from any part of the outlying book repositories.

Opening out from the central reading-room on each side are two extensive iron book-stacks, each of the capacity of about

THE GRAND STAIRCASE HALL, OF CARRARA MARBLE.

800,000 volumes. These stacks are nine stories in height, each tier of shelves being just seven feet high, and each stack rising 65 feet, tier over tier, to the roof. All the floors are of white marble, and every book can be reached by the hand at once. The shelves are made of rolled steel, not solid, but in open bars, very light and firm, and so coated with magnetic oxid as to render them as smooth as glass. The space between the bars secures ventilation for the books, as well as immunity in a good degree from accumulations of dust. They are adjustable by an easy movement to any height for books of various sizes. This shelf system and stacks were designed by Bernard R. Green, engineer in charge during the construction of the building. The book-stacks are lighted by windows of plate-glass without sash, each window being a single plate, and dust-proof, the ventilation of the stack-rooms being from the upper tier of windows, on the down-draft system. Three elevators are provided for the three stack-rooms, and three for public use in other parts of the library building.

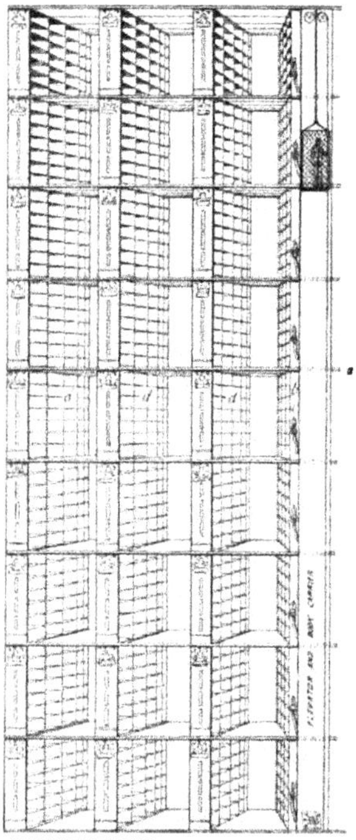

DRAWN BY WELLS M. SAWYER.

A BOOK-STACK.
*a*, flooring; *b*, pneumatic tube; *c*, carrier; *d*, shelves.

The spacious rooms on the first floor, outside the central reading-room, are designed for the copyright office, or public records, a catalogue-room, a special reading-room for the Senate, and another for the House of Representatives, an apartment for the Toner Library (presented to the Government), committee-rooms, librarian's office, etc. The Smithsonian Scientific Library, long deposited with the Library of Congress, will be placed in the smaller stack-room on the eastern side of the building, which will hold about 100,000 volumes.

The second floor of the building has four spacious open corridors surrounding it, decorated as to walls and ceilings with frescos and mural paintings, and with numerous tablet inscriptions from the great writers of the world. It contains an extensive hall designed for an art gallery, a hall for maps and charts, and three or four spacious exhibition-halls in which choice specimens of early typography, engraving, and Americana will be exhibited in glass cases.

The capacity of those portions of the library building already shelved is ample for about 1,900,000 volumes, there being about forty-four miles of shelves in position. Besides this, there is space which may ultimately be finished with book-stacks to accommodate about 2,500,000 additional volumes; and the extensive inner courts may still further serve posterity for book storage to the extent of 4,000,000 to 5,000,000 volumes more. When it is considered that the largest existing library numbers less than 2,500,000 volumes, it will be seen how extensive is the provision for future growth for at least a century or two to come.

An underground tunnel between the Capitol and the library building will transmit rapidly any books wanted for congressional use and not found in the reference library at the Capitol.

The floor-area of the library in its first story is about 111,000 square feet, that of the British Museum being a little more than 90,000 square feet, and that of the building for the State, War, and Navy departments 92,000 square feet. The ultimate cost of the entire edifice, including decorations and furnishings, will be about $6,300,000, or a little more than half the cost of the government building last named, and it will be completed within the limit of cost fixed by Congress.

SOUTHWEST PAVILION—THE EXHIBITION-ROOM.

In design and in construction the two great ends of architecture, use and beauty, appear to have been well attained in this government building, a structure erected not for the present generation alone, but for many yet to come.

## II. SPECIAL FEATURES OF THE CONGRESSIONAL LIBRARY.

WHAT is the function of a government library? is a question which becomes more than ever pertinent in view of the impending opening at Washington of the noble building to which this article is devoted. That this edifice is a permanent, fire-proof, and fitting home for the nation's books, representing the assiduous gatherings of nearly a hundred years, is already recognized by all. That the mission of the great library which it is to contain is a manifold one, reaching far beyond the limits of its locality and the present age, is perhaps less widely appreciated.

Founded in the year 1800 by the modest appropriation of five thousand dollars «for the purchase of such books as may be necessary for the use of Congress at the said city of Washington,» this collection has grown, notwithstanding the ravages of two fires, to the present aggregate of 740,000 volumes. The acquisition of the Jefferson Library in 1815, the Force Historical Library in 1865, the Smithsonian Library in 1867, and the Toner collection in 1882, all constituted specially important and valuable accessions to its stores. And by the enactment of the copyright law of 1870, followed by the international copyright act of 1891, this library

THE PUBLIC READING-ROOM.

became entitled to receive two copies of all books, periodicals, and other publications claiming the protection of copyright in the United States.

While its primary function has been and still is to furnish the national legislature with all the aids in their far-reaching and responsible duties which a comprehensive library can supply, its more extensive province has made it the conservator of the nation's literature. By the wise legislation of Congress it has been made the one designated legal repository of the entire product of the American press, so far as issued under the government guaranty of copyright. If this salutary and conservative measure had been in force from the beginning of copyright in 1790, instead of being confined to the last twenty-five years, we should now be in possession of an unapproached and unattainable completeness in every department of American books. In the absence of any central place of deposit, the copyright requirements of earlier years were most negligently and imperfectly complied with, and multitudes of books have wholly disappeared, or are found only in second-hand book-shops or in the cabinets of curious collectors. Considered in a scientific view or as absolute knowledge, the loss may not be greatly to be deplored; but, taking a single example, let the reader consider how substantial a benefit it would be to those interested in the profession of education to be assured of finding in a national collection every school- or text-book produced in the United States during the period of a century. Writers for the press may learn as much from the failures of their predecessors as from their successes. And the historian of American literature who would be thoroughly comprehensive cannot overlook the forgotten books read, and perhaps admired, by former generations. Nor can any nation claiming to hold a front rank in civilization shirk the obligation of preserving, in one inclusive and not exclusive collection open to the whole people, all the books which the country produces. From the lack of care in the past to enforce this judicious policy, the National Library of Great Britain has been for years buying up at great cost the dramas, pamphlets, chap-books, and other productions of English literature in past ages, to fill innumerable gaps in its great collection.

Where in America can one find even a respectably full collection of the pamphlet literature of which the country has been so prolific? This class of writings appears foredoomed in each generation to swift and irremediable destruction, unless preserved in public libraries. Yet its great value, as reflecting in condensed and often masterly style the real spirit of the age which produced it, with its controversies, political, religious, and social, and the ideas which moved the public mind, has been recognized by all philosophic historians as incalculable. If all authors of pamphlets would send their productions to the library of the Government, they would not only secure the preservation of their own thought, but would be found to have performed a useful public service. As an instance of the historical value of pamphlet literature, take the Thomason collection of twenty thousand pieces, covering the Cromwellian period in England. Its owner sedulously collected and laid aside every issue of the press from 1649 to 1660; and the collection, after escaping the ravages of fire and of two hostile armies, was finally bought by the king, and afterward presented to the British Museum Library. Carlyle made extensive use of this inestimable collection. In like manner, the great La Bédoyère collection of printed matter relating to the French Revolution, purchased for the National Library of France in 1863, covered exhaustively the issues of the press, including periodicals, for twenty-five years, and its 15,500 volumes were the fruit of fifty years' assiduous research by an enthusiastic and untiring collector. Another devotee to the collection and preservation of historical material, the late Peter Force of Washington, was for forty years engaged in amassing a rich library of manuscripts, newspapers, books, pamphlets, and maps illustrative of American history. He ransacked the bookshops of the cities, imported from abroad, and was a frequent bidder at auctions, where he secured the Duane and the Wolcott collections of pamphlets, representing the carefully preserved and bound gatherings of a Republican and a Federalist during many years of public and political life. The Force collection was fortunately saved from dispersion, and now forms an invaluable part of the Congressional Library.

In another field of library collection, which the Smithsonian Institution may be said to have made its own, consider the value of a complete series of the reports, transactions, and other publications of scientific bodies. Embracing as these do the results of the labors of men of science in every field of thought or investigation, they furnish material of the first importance to the student.

Through its international exchanges the Smithsonian Institution has rendered an inestimable service to the country in assembling at Washington a most extensive collection of these publications, many of which are out of print or rare. They will form a part of the rich stores open to scholars in the new Congressional Library; and as they represent more than two thousand foreign societies and institutions, besides nearly all American ones publishing transactions, they afford a

THE MAIN READING-ROOM GALLERY.

copious repository of scientific information for public use and reference.

That a library is useful and valuable in the direct ratio of its completeness is a postulate that may be termed self-evident, and fairly so. «The true university of these days,» says Thomas Carlyle, «is a collection of books.» While the vast extent of the world's literature may fill the ordinary reader with dismay, it needs only the practised eye and quick discernment of the thorough student to select the more important from the mass, and to extract in each the essential thought or fact from the verbiage that overlays it. The books which it is necessary to know thoroughly may be comprised in a comparatively small compass. The rest are to be preserved in the great literary conservatories—some as memorials of the past, some as chronicles of the times, and not a few as models to be avoided. It is easy to pronounce the great majority of the books in our larger libraries «rubbish,» and to propose, as has frequently been done, to make a bonfire of the trash which the copyright law brings into the government library at Washington. But the grave question confronts us, Where are we to begin? Are there any judgments likely to concur as to what is to be preserved? It is a common experience that the book which was nothing to us at one time came to have a most unexpected value at another. When the priest and the barber, in the immortal romance of Cervantes, sought to purge the library of Don Quixote of the perilous stuff which had bewildered his artless brain, the self-constituted censors were not agreed as to what should be condemned to the flames. Do the learned editors who would like to have the great library «weeded» ever reflect that their own works in great folio might be the first to go out, to make room for smaller books, if not better ones?

THE LIBRARIAN'S OFFICE.

A. R. SPOFFORD.

The ever-widening sphere and influence of the periodical press—one of the great phenomena of modern times—suggest the importance of preserving in our most representative libraries a copious selection from the daily newspapers, and a full collection of the literature of magazines and reviews. While no library, however comprehensive, could possibly store all the periodical publications (now amounting in the United States alone to more than twenty thousand, as against only eight thousand in 1875), it is none the less its proper function to provide full sets of the more important ones. They

THE NORTH CORRIDOR OF THE GRAND STAIRCASE HALL.

afford the completest mirror of the times to be derived from any single source. Taken together, they supply the richest material for the historian and the student of comparative civilization in all its aspects—literary, political, moral, social, religious, and economic. More and more the best thought and the inventive genius of the age become reflected in their pages. No investigator in any department whose aim is full information can afford to neglect this fruitful mine, where his most valuable material will frequently be found; and it is to be considered that unless the representative library preserves them, a very large portion of them will not be preserved in accessible form at all. The destiny of most periodicals is swift destruction. The obvious causes of their rapid disappearance are their great volume, inevitably growing with each year, the difficulty of finding room to store them in our small dwellings, the ravages of fire, and the continual demand of paper for the uses of trade. Add to these the large cost of binding sets of periodicals, and the preference of the majority of families for books, and the reasons why very few private subscribers to periodicals can afford to bind and preserve them are apparent. So much the more important is it that public libraries should not neglect a duty which is due both to their own age and to posterity. These unconsidered trifles of to-day, which are looked upon as not worth space to store or money to bind, are the very things which the man of the future, intent upon the reconstruction of the past, will search for with eagerness. Accordingly, it has been the policy of the library of the United States for nearly thirty years past to preserve and bind up at least two of the daily journals of each State and Territory, and all the magazines and reviews obtainable, with a selection of the weekly press. No department of the library is so widely used, not only for purposes of reference, but of study. When it is considered how far-reaching are the fields embraced in the wide range of these periodicals, literary, religious, scientific, political, technical, philosophical, social, fashionable, medical, legal, educational, agricultural, bibliographical, commercial, financial, historical, mechanical, nautical, military, artistic, musical, dramatic, typographical, sanitary, sporting, economic, and miscellaneous, is it any wonder that specialists and writers for the press seek and find ready aid therein for their many-sided labors?

To the skeptical mind, accustomed to undervalue what does not happen to come within the range of its pet idols or pursuits, the observation of a single day's multifold research in the great library might be in the nature of a revelation. Here one finds an industrious compiler intent upon the history of American duels, for which the many files of Northern and Southern newspapers, reaching back to the beginning of the century, afford copious material. At another table sits a deputation from a department, commissioned to make a record of all notable strikes and labor troubles for a series of years, to be gleaned from the columns of the journals of leading cities. Hither flock the ever-present searchers into family history, laying under contribution all the genealogies and town and county histories which the country has produced. An absorbed reader of French romances sits side by side with a clergyman perusing homilies or endeavoring to elucidate, through a mass of commentators, a special text. Here are to be found ladies in pursuit of costumes of every age; artists turning over the great folio galleries of Europe for models or suggestions; lawyers seeking precedents or leading cases; journalists verifying dates, speeches, conventions, or other forgotten facts; engineers studying the literature of railways or machinery; actors or amateurs in search of plays or works on the dramatic art; physicians looking up biographies of their profession or the history of epidemics; students of heraldry after coats of arms; inventors searching the specifications and drawings of patents; historical students pursuing some special field in American or foreign annals; scientists verifying facts or citations by original authorities; searchers tracing personal residences or deaths in old directories or newspapers; querists seeking for the words of some half-remembered passage in poetry or prose, or the original author of one of the myriad proverbs which float about the world without a father; architects or builders of houses comparing hundreds of designs and models; teachers perusing works on education or comparing text-books new or old; readers absorbing the great poems of the world; writers in pursuit of new or curious themes among books of antiquities or folk-lore; students of all the questions of finance and economic science; naturalists seeking to trace through many volumes descriptions of species; pursuers of military or naval history or science; enthusiasts venturing into the occult domains of spiritualism or thaumaturgy; explorers of voyages and travels in every region of the globe; fair readers, with dreamy eyes, devouring the last psychological novel; devotees of musical art perusing the lives or the scores of great composers; college and high-school students intent upon «booking up» on themes of study or composition or debate; and a host of other seekers after suggestion or information in a library of encyclopedic range.

This collection, extensive as it is, still falls far short of completeness in many important directions. While its quality is by no means commensurate with its quantity, it yet possesses a large share of the standard works in all departments of science and literature. Its greatest strength lies in the fields of jurisprudence, political science, American and British history, and what are known as Americana. Its deficiencies are most marked in books in foreign languages, and they are notably great in editions of the classics, in philology, in Oriental literature, and in many of the sciences. With all its manifold defects, it may be said that the library, so far as it is the fruit of selection, has been formed with a view to the highest utility, and with some general unity of plan. Congress may be expected, now that the expenditure upon the building has ceased, to take a more liberal view of its wants, and to make wise provision for such an increase of its intellectual stores as shall be worthy of the nation and the age. Its new and magnificent building, through the far-sighted liberality of the people's representatives, has

A GLIMPSE OF THE GRAND STAIRCASE HALL.

AN EXHIBITION-HALL, SHOWING A PORTION OF THE FRESCOS BY GARI MELCHERS.

been planned and organized to accommodate ultimately, with every convenience of administration. In the judgment of all who have seen it, its architectural and artistic beauty has been pronounced fully equal to its utility. Its gallery of art will soon be filled with an instructive exhibit of the progress of the arts of design in every form; and it may be hoped that the large-minded policy which has created this noble temple of science, literature, and art will endow it with adequate means of growth, so that its ample shelves may before long be filled with the learning of all lands.

*A. R. Spofford.*

# THE DECORATIONS IN THE NEW CONGRESSIONAL LIBRARY.

THE scene in the new Congressional Library at Washington, when I visited it in the summer of 1896, was interesting and impressive. A guard admitted me at a small door under the imposing terraces and flights of steps which form the approach to the main entrance of the building. I walked through corridor after corridor, ascended broad stairways, and found my way through spacious galleries and vestibules to the great rotunda in the middle of the vast construction. Here was an immense scaffolding rising a hundred feet or more to the base of the dome, and high above that, as I looked up, I saw the iron elliptical truss-work that swung from the platform of the scaffolding to the top of the dome, carrying ladders and landing-places to the crown of the lantern, 160 feet from the floor. Scores of skilled workmen were carving, fitting, and polishing. Some were perched high in the drum of the dome; others were setting mosaics and laying marble floors. In corridors and halls were rolling platforms and bridges full of busy

PAINTED BY KENYON COX. PHOTOGRAPH BY CURTIS & CAMERON.

«SCIENCE» (LUNETTE).

craftsmen painting in fresco on the vaulted ceilings. Four or five artists were at work on their decorative compositions in different parts of the building, and one I found, with his assistant, in the crown of the lantern of the dome. The artists, like the workmen, were in overalls, and the atmosphere of the place seemed impregnated with the spirit of art and labor. It was something as it must have been in Florence or Venice in the Renaissance.

On every side there was evidence that the decorative work had been artistically planned, and that it was being intelligently and durably executed. The interior of the new Congressional Library will be a veritable revelation when the public takes possession of it. It might have been very different if it had not fortunately happened that good brains and good culture were called upon to embellish it. Indeed, they were summoned to set right what had been but badly begun; and we may congratulate ourselves and our legislators that by timely action the country has been spared a gift that might have been an architectural failure, and obtains a great building which, whatever may be its faults of detail, is, taken as a whole, imposing and picturesque. The story of the building of the library is given in a statement prepared by the officials who have been charged by the Government with the duty of bringing the work to completion. By an act of Congress of April 15, 1886, a commission was directed to build a library building after the plans submitted by Messrs. Smithmeyer and Pelz. This commission employed Mr. Smithmeyer, with the title of architect, to supervise and manage, under its direction, the construction of the building. By an act of Congress of October 2, 1888, the act of the 15th of April was repealed, and the chief of engineers of the army, the late General Thomas Lincoln Casey, was placed in charge and directed to prepare plans for a building which should not cost more than $4,000,000. Such plans were accordingly prepared, with estimates, and submitted to Congress at the opening of the session in December, 1888. In the preparation of these plans Mr. Pelz was employed to make the drawings under the direction of General Casey and Mr. Bernard R. Green, who was appointed to the local charge of the work as superintendent and engineer. For the foundation or main lines of the design the building begun under the act of the 15th of April was used. At the same time that General Casey had the plans prepared for the building limited in cost to $4,000,000, he also had prepared a set of plans for a building

PAINTED BY GEORGE W. MAYNARD. PHOTOGRAPH BY CURTIS & CAMERON.

«DISCOVERY» (LUNETTE).

PAINTED BY KENYON COX. PHOTOGRAPH BY CURTIS & CAMERON.

«MATHEMATICS» AND «PHYSICS» (DETAIL).

which would cost about $6,000,000. These plans were evolved from the original general designs by Smithmeyer and Pelz formerly adopted by Congress, but differed from them in numerous important particulars. By an act of March 2, 1889, the design for the $6,000,000 building was adopted by Congress. Mr. Pelz was continued as architect under the direction of the chief of engineers, and construction and detail drawings were prepared. In April, 1892, Mr. Pelz's connection with the work came to an end. Upon the death of General Casey in March, 1896, Mr. Green succeeded to his duties and powers in full. In December, 1892, Edward Pearce Casey, an architect of New York, who had completed his studies at the École des Beaux-Arts in Paris, was employed to prepare the drawings for the interior architecture and scheme of decoration of the building. It is at this point that the interest of American artists was enlisted; and later on commissions were given out, under Mr. Casey's general direction, for mural and sculptural decoration. The amount of work done by Mr. Casey in designing the principal interiors of the library building is enormous. With the exception of the main portions of the mar-

PHOTOGRAPH BY CURTIS & CAMERON.

CEILING. PAINTED BY GEORGE W. MAYNARD.

ble work in the great staircase hall and the rotunda, designs have been made by him for the decoration of the entire interior. He was occupied more than three years with the work, giving all his time to it, and employing, of course, a number of draftsmen to assist him. His decorative schemes show variety of design, fertility of invention, and an excellent sense of the importance of unity in the ensemble. Under his direction all the work not given out to the artists has been intelligently and skilfully carried out by a corps of decorators, headed by Elmer E. Garnsey for the painters, by Albert Weinert for the sculptors and modelers of ornament, and by H. T. Schladermundt for mosaics and for colored glass. Praise for the excellence of the general decorative work in the building is due to the young architect who planned it and presented it in its broad aspect and in its detail forms, so that nothing might be misunderstood, and so that the execution by the hands of the craftsmen should realize his conceptions. The color-schemes chosen by the artists for their compositions will be found to harmonize with this general decoration, each of them, before making his sketches, having taken account of the prevailing general tints, and considered their color-effect as the setting for his work. The greater part of the mural pictures have been executed on canvas in artists' studios in New York, Paris, and other places. These large canvases when completed are removed from their stretchers and sent to Washington. The artist follows, and the pictures are put up under his supervision. The process employed consists in applying a thin bed of composition, of which white lead is the principal ingredient, to the wall or ceiling, and «rolling on» the canvas. In this manner it is fastened smoothly and securely. This process may naturally be most successfully employed where the surface is flat. In France, we are told, painted decoration on canvas has been rolled on concave surfaces by a clever system of goring the canvas, and in one case this was done at Washington. In almost every instance, however, where the surface is concave the painting is done directly on the material of the wall or ceiling itself. Mr. Maynard's ceiling in the southwest pavilion, where the surface is a section of a sphere, and Mr. Blashfield's work in the great rotunda, are cases in point. Both artists executed their designs in place, and spent months, with their assistants, working in the building. So, too, did Mr. Shirlaw, Mr. Barse, and others.

«The Evolution of Civilization» is the subject of the decoration by Edwin Howland Blashfield. It is composed of the collar of the dome in the great central rotunda, and the crown of the lantern. The collar is about 140 feet in circumference, surrounds the eye of the lantern, and is at the height of 125 feet from the pavement of the rotunda. It contains twelve seated colossal figures, each ten feet high. There are twelve cartouches, or tablets, inscribed with the names of the epochs or of the countries which have contributed to the evolution of civilization. These twelve tablets form rhythmical points established between the figures, and under each figure runs a banderole, or streamer, with an inscription referring to the special contribution to civilization of the country or epoch which is represented by the figure above. The wings of all the figures overlap each other and form a dominant factor in the composition, binding together the component parts of the decoration. The figures are divided into four triads. The central figure of each triad is relatively rigid, and the drapery is principally white. The side figures lean toward the central ones, and the drapery is of darker tints. Egypt, with «Written Records» on the tablet, comes first in chronological order. The figure bears the sign of immortality and a tablet inscribed with hieroglyphics. On the throne is shown the cartouche of Mena, the first Egyptian king. Judea (religion) holds stone tablets bearing Hebrew inscriptions. Greece (philosophy) bears a lamp and a scroll. Rome (administration) has a baton of command and a bundle of fasces. Islam (physics) holds a book and a glass retort. The Middle Ages (languages) bears a sword denoting chivalry, a model of a church typifying architecture, and a tiara and keys, symbols of the church. This figure has the features of Miss Mary Anderson. Italy (the fine arts) holds a palette and a statuette of Michelangelo's «David,» and rests her foot on a capital. The features are those of a young lady of New York, a sculptor. Germany (the art of printing) holds a proof-sheet, and beside her figure is a sixteenth-century printing-press. The features are those of General Thomas Lincoln Casey. Spain (discovery) has as accessories the rudder of a ship and a model of a caravel, and the head shows the features of Mr. William Bailey Faxon the painter. England (literature) bears a volume of Shakspere, the page being a transcript of the title-page of the first edition of «A Midsummer Night's Dream.» The head is a portrait of Miss Ellen Terry. France (emancipation) sits upon a cannon and holds out the «Déclaration des Droits de l'Homme.» The features of the figure suggest those of the artist's wife. America (science) is depicted with a dynamo and a book as accessories. The head is that of Abraham Lincoln. The heads of the figures are not intended to be absolute portraiture, but characterizations, the features being used because the artist thought them especially suited to the nation or contribution typified. The dominant colors in Mr. Blashfield's decoration are white (the girdle of wings), bluish green (the background of mosaic patterning), and violet (the banderoles). The drapery of the figures harmonizes with these colors, being gradated from white to violet tints, and the violet hues are shaded into yellow and orange. The composition is light in general tone, and carries with great effectiveness at the distances from which it may be seen either from the floor or from the galleries encircling the rotunda. The collar decoration is inclosed around the eye of the lantern and at the outer edge by heavy gilded moldings in the form of garlands of leaves.

The crown of the lantern, consisting of a circular ceiling, contains three figures. A female figure floating among clouds of white and gray, and lifting up a veil which almost envelops her, is depicted looking upward, and represents Human Understanding looking up from finite achievement, as presented in the decoration of the collar, to what is beyond. Two nude figures of boys float at her sides,

PAINTED BY E. H. BLASHFIELD. PHOTOGRAPH BY CURTIS & CAMERON.

«ITALY» (DETAIL).

one holding a closed book typifying the end of all things, and the other beckoning to the figures below. The drapery of the central figure is blue, darker than the portions of the sky which appear between the clouds, and the color of the veil is orange. The figure is shown as soaring upward and disappearing in the clouds. It is easy to see that Mr. Blashfield's task was a difficult one, considering the places allotted to him for decoration, the necessity of painting for effect at a great distance, and the importance of his color-scheme as the culminating point in the ensemble of the rotunda. At the ground floor the walls and bases of the piers are constructed of brownish-gray Tennessee marble. At the successive stages of the floors rising to the base of the dome the piers and pilasters are of yellow Siena and red and yellow Numidian marble. At the base of the dome, running around the drum, is a sculptured frieze composed of bay-leaf garlands and eagles, with two female figures in the round over each of the eight arches, holding up the garland and supporting escutcheons. These figures are the work of Philip Martiny, while the rest of the sculptured stucco ornament in the rotunda is by Albert Weinert. The vault is paneled in sculptured ornament and rosettes. The latter are gilded, and are relieved against a ground of greenish blue. With all these various elements of material and color Mr. Blashfield's decoration is in harmony, and possesses such individuality of itself that it counts as a dominant note in the whole. His great figures, too, are well

PAINTED BY W. L. DODGE. PHOTOGRAPH BY CURTIS & CAMERON.

«AMBITION» (CEILING).

drawn, and his composition is constructed with a firmness that gives it power while it in no way detracts from its effect, which is intended by its position to be without any heaviness of character.

In a hall about 150 feet long, to be used as a museum, Mr. Kenyon Cox has painted two lunettes of semi-elliptical form. They are at the two ends of the long room, and measure 34 feet 7 inches at the base by 9 feet 7 inches in height at the center. The prevailing color-note in the general decoration of this hall is blue. Mr. Cox's subjects are «Art» and «Science.» Each of his decorative panels is divided into three parts by two pedestals bearing flaming tripods, these pedestals coming directly over the pilasters, which are part of the architectural lines of the room. In the middle part of each lunette is a throne raised on steps; at the sides are balustrades. The panel representing «Art» contains five principal figures typifying the five great arts—poetry, sculpture, painting, architecture, and music. «Poetry» occupies of right the central throne. She is draped in white and pale rose-color, bears the lyre, and looks upward with an expression of inspiration. She is crowned with ivy, and points upward with her right hand. On the steps of her throne are two genii, one with a tablet, suggesting study, the other snapping his fingers and dancing, suggesting the gaiety of poetry. The division to the right of the spectator contains the figures of «Sculpture» and «Painting.» «Sculpture,» in pale yellow, carries a statuette in her hand, which, while an original figure, recalls the style of Michelangelo. «Painting» leans upon the shoulder of «Sculpture» in an affectionate attitude. Her type is that of the Venetian school of the Renaissance, and she is draped, below the waist only, in dusky yellow. In her hand is a palette set with white, red, yellow, and blue. On the left side of the panel are figures of «Architecture» and «Music.» «Architecture» is leaning on a Gothic column, and is simply draped in a robe of the color of terra-cotta, the long lines of which are meant to signify architectural dignity. Beside her is «Music,» in rose-color and violet, with fluttering scarf, playing on the violin, while a winged genius holds before her an open music-book. The scheme of color in this composition, based on rose and yellow, is pale and tawny. The color-scheme of the other lunette, devoted to «Science,» is based on green and blue, but with the use of some warm tints for contrast. In the middle is the figure of «Astronomy,» the

PAINTED BY WALTER SHIRLAW PHOTOGRAPHED BY G. C. COX.

«GEOLOGY.»

greatest of the sciences, leaning over a celestial globe held up by one of her attendant genii, and measuring it with a pair of compasses. She is draped in white and blue, and has a crown of stars on her head. A scarf of pale blue is disposed above her in an arch-like curve. As it was impossible to represent all the sciences in his composition, the artist has selected typical ones. To the right are «Botany» and «Zoölogy,» the sciences dealing with the vegetable and animal kingdoms. «Botany» is clad in a brocaded gown of green and gold, the forms of the pattern recalling vegetable shapes. In her hand is a small oak-tree. «Zoölogy,» a nude seated figure, points with her right hand to a peacock—introduced because of its decorative beauty, but the eyes in its tail may be thought to symbolize the curiosity of science. To the left of «Astronomy» are «Physics,» in brown and yellow, investigating the laws of weight, and «Mathematics,» type of abstract science. The latter figure is clad in salmon-pink and rich blue, and holds an abacus, while a genius at her knee reckons on his fingers the sum set by the beads. They are arranged to count 1896. While both of Mr. Cox's compositions are painted in an extremely high key, the color is suave. The necessity of raising the tints to a very light value by the use of white has not caused them to become harsh, as sometimes happens with less skilful painters. The quality of the color in this work is notable, and, as in the green robe of «Botany,» remarkably full. The artist's resources as a draftsman are especially well shown in the admirable figure of the boy holding the globe, but the drawing of the figures is erudite throughout the work. The room in which the compositions by Mr. Cox are placed has its counterpart on the other side of the building. This room contains decorations by Gari Melchers. The prevailing color in the general scheme of decoration is red. Mr. Melchers's subjects are «Peace» and «War.» The two lunettes are painted in the sound and competent manner which characterizes the work of this well-known painter, and were executed in Paris.

PAINTED BY ROBERT REID PHOTOGRAPH BY CURTIS & CAMERON

«HEARING.»

Two pavilions, octagonal rooms at the corners of the library building, are decorated by George W. Maynard and William L. Dodge. Two others contain ceilings and panels by Robert Dodge and William B. Van Ingen, the decorative schemes for these having been supplied by Mr. Casey and Mr. Garnsey. Mr. Van Ingen's work in the pavilion and elsewhere is notable for striking color quality, possessing some of the characteristics of the La Farge school. Mr. W. L. Dodge's composition has «Ambition» for its subject, and four panels on the walls represent «Science,» «Art,» «Music,» and «Poetry.» They were painted in Paris, and the ceiling was exhibited at the Salon of 1896 before being brought to Washington. There are two groups in the composition of the ceiling, one consisting of a figure typifying «Glory,» holding aloft a crown, and majestically preceding a winged horse, while another figure, symbolizing «Fame,» flies before, holding the bridle of the horse in one hand and a trumpet in the other. The other group, united with the first by a large piece of drapery, consists of a number of figures on a terrace, including one who upsets a flaming brazier at the end of the balustrade, another stretched out dead, others struggling, and a fool with cap and bells. The general aspect of the ceiling is extremely decorative. The decoration of the pavilion containing Mr. Maynard's five works, confided to Mr. Maynard, consists of a general scheme of white and gold, which has been most successfully carried out, and the room shows how satisfactory the result is likely to be when the entire decoration, if practicable, is executed with the coöperation of the artist who paints the decorative pictures. In this case a most harmonious ensemble has been achieved, and the room has an air of perfect completeness. The panels, semi-elliptical in shape, occupying the upper part of the four longer walls of the room, have as their subjects four epochs of America—«Adventure,» «Discovery,» «Conquest,» and «Civilization.» The ceiling depicts the four elements necessary for development—«Fortitude,» «Valor,» «Courage,» and «Achievement.» The figures and accessories in each of the four panels follow a general arrangement common to all, and the color-schemes, while varied, are designed to balance one another. The panel «Adventure» shows a seated female figure with a drawn sword in one hand and a caduceus in the other, symbolizing courage and daring. To her left is a female figure typifying Spanish adventure, with a hatchet and a Peruvian golden image in her hands. The image signifies booty, which was the object of the quests of the first adventurers. On the right of the central figure is a young woman of

PAINTED BY ROBERT REID. PHOTOGRAPH BY CURTIS & CAMERON

«TOUCH.»

blonde English type, a sword in one hand, and grasping with the other silver pieces of money which fall from a bag. In either corner are the arms of England and Spain. Shields on each side of the principal figure bear the images of Norse ships, and on the background, or field, appear the names of famous adventurers such as Raleigh and Hawkins. The prevailing color is yellow, and the armor of the figures is gold and steel.

In the second panel, «Discovery,» crowned with a laurel wreath of gold, grasps a tiller with her left hand and supports a globe on her knee. On the globe are the outlines of Leonardo da Vinci's map, the first one that is known to have had the name America upon it. On each side of «Discovery» are female figures, one holding a sword, but not in an aggressive position, and a Jacob's-staff, the other a paddle and a chart. In the corners are ornamental figures of mermaids growing out of the border, who hold up corals and pearls. The two shields bear an astrolabe, the primitive quadrant. On the field are the names of great Spanish, French, and English discoverers, but no Portuguese, because their exploits relate to the East Indies, and not to America. The principal colors in this decoration are yellow and blue.

«Conquest» rests her hand on the hilt of a sword, suggesting that her work is done, and her right arm, extended with clenched fist, characterizes her attitude as one of possession and defense. The side figures are in reposeful positions, and bear swords, one entwined with oak, symbolical of the North, the other with palm, symbolical of the South. The arms of Spain and England reappear in the corners, and on the shields are the Pillars of Hercules with the setting sun and the motto «*Ne plus ultra.*» The field shows the names of conquerors such as Pizarro and Standish. The prevailing colors are red and orange. «Civilization» holds an open book on her knees, and bears a torch. One of the two side figures typifying «Manufactures» and «Agriculture» holds a distaff, the other a scythe and a sheaf of wheat. In the corners are mermaids with cotton and Indian corn in their hands, and the device on the shields is a lamp. The field is inscribed with the names of humanitarians and pioneers in civilization, such as Las Casas, Hennepin, Marquette, Penn, and Eliot. The predominant tints in the color-scheme are blue and white. In the circular panel of the ceiling the field is blue, the ornament yellowish white, and the draperies of the figures yellow. «Fortitude,» with flowing robes, supports a column. «Valor» rests her hand on a sword. «Courage,» a strong Amazonian figure, is clad in a lion's skin and carries a shield and a club. «Achievement» points to the symbol of empire, a Roman standard surmounted by an eagle. The four figures, placed at points equidistant on the rim of the circle, are balanced in a symmetrical composition by ornamental designs which fill the intervening spaces and the center.

Besides the work done in this room, Mr. Maynard has painted eight upright panels around the staircase well in the second story of the staircase hall. The panels are three feet by twelve, and the subjects are the virtues — «Justice,» «Fortitude,» «Prudence,» «Temperance,» «Concordia,» «Industry,» «Courage,» and «Patriotism.» The figures are Pompeian in style, floating, and clad in drapery of whitish gray with backgrounds of vermilion. Each panel contains a single figure symbolical of one of the virtues. «Patriotism,» for example, is represented with an eagle on her arm, with wings extended as if having just alighted, and holding a bowl, from which the eagle eats. «Concordia,» the virtue of peace, carries an olive-branch and a cornucopia with wheat falling from its mouth.

Two curtain corridors are decorated by Edward Simmons and Walter McEwen. Nine heroes of ancient history form the subject chosen by Mr. McEwen, who painted his compositions in Paris. Mr. Simmons was given control of the entire decorative scheme in the corridor assigned to him, and has depicted the nine Muses. There is a tympanum at each end of the corridor, and seven others on one side, three over false doors and four over real doors. On the opposite side are windows. Besides the tympana, Mr. Simmons painted figure and ornamental subjects in the panels of the seven small domes of the corridor and in the twenty-eight pendentives. The motives are the attributes of the Muses. The tympana are nine feet long, the upper side consisting of a semicircle described by a radius of four and a half feet. «Calliope,» chief of the Muses, occupies the panel at one end of the corridor, and «Clio» the other. The color-scheme comprehends an arrangement passing from blue in the figure of «Calliope» to orange in that of «Clio.» In the row of seven tympana along the side of the corridor, three of the Muses have their arms extended, and, four between having them disposed otherwise, form a chain of arms uniting the series. The borders of the panels are formed by wreath-like designs in which roses, lilies,

PAINTED BY EDWARD SIMMONS. PHOTOGRAPH BY CURTIS & CAMERON.

MELPOMENE.

poppies, and green foliage are introduced. Grace and dignity are happily combined in these compositions, and Mr. Simmons's authoritative draftsmanship, so well shown in his decorations in the new criminal courts in New York, is here applied with force and distinction. The color-scheme is sufficiently restrained to comport well with the style of his design, while it is not lacking in such animated notes as befit the treatment of some of the details of his theme.

In the vestibule just before entering the great rotunda are five tympana painted by Elihu Vedder. The composition over the door in the middle represents «Government»; those to the right, «Good Administration» and «Peace and Prosperity»; the two on the left, «Corrupt Legislation» and «Anarchy.» Mr. Vedder's capability and good judgment are well shown in these works; for, unlike some of the other rooms given to the artists to decorate, which are fully lighted, this vestibule is somewhat tenebrous. Instead of forcing the color-scheme to a high key, an expedient which might have been adopted by a less experienced painter, Mr. Vedder has treated his compositions in sober, modified tones of an even gamut. They are in absolute harmony with their surroundings, and the restraint in color gives them depth and strength. These finely conceived designs are executed in such a manner that they do not appear as additions to the embellishment of their site, but as a part of the place itself, and nothing better in the way of fitness of placing will be found in the library. For the somewhat larger vestibule immediately preceding the one which contains Mr. Vedder's fine works, John W. Alexander has painted in Paris six tympana depicting «The Evolution of the Book.» His general color-scheme is made up of neutral tints, and the treatment, as may be seen in the illustration «The Story-teller of the Far East,» is extremely simple.

The central pavilion of the building, or the «west main,» as it is called in architectural parlance, contains the grand staircase; and on the second floor of this hall, directly in front of the visitor who mounts the steps to the mezzanine, there is to be a central panel in mosaic representing «Minerva.» The commission to make the design and color cartoon for this was given to Mr. Vedder, and it will be set in place after it has been laid in from the artist's designs. This will be done in Venice. On each side of the grand staircase is a lateral gallery, one of which is decorated by Henry Oliver Walker, and the other by Charles Sprague Pearce. The spaces in each gallery consist of two large tympana and five or six small ones. The ceilings are decorated with conventional designs provided by the artists. Mr. Pearce, whose subjects include «The Family,» «Labor,» and «Recreation,» and who has placed his figures in landscape settings, executed his work at Auvers-sur-Oise, near Paris. Mr. Walker's general theme is «Lyric Poetry.» In one of the large tympana, which is cut out in the middle by the arched top of a blind window or niche, are two female figures symbolizing «Memory» and «Joy.» An ornamental design, with an inscription over the arched space in the center, unites them. In the six small tympana are youthful figures representing concrete personages, such as Endymion, who appears as a nude stripling reclining in a contemplative attitude on a grassy bank, with the crescent moon in the twilight sky. The second large tympanum, which is free in its entire space for decoration, contains Mr. Walker's principal composition. «Lyric Poetry,» draped in rose-color and holding a lyre, occupies the center, with female figures symbolizing «Passion» and «Beauty» on her right hand. On her left are «Pathos,» in blue drapery; «Truth,» a nude figure; and «Devotion,» with robe of dull terra-cotta hue. The figures are placed in a landscape showing the bed of a brook in the middle, with trees and herbage at each side. The general tone of the picture is light, and inclines to gray in the landscape part, with great refinement of treatment in the more positive tints of the draperies. The *mise en scène* is poetic, and the great lines of the composition are graceful and effective. One of the chief qualities in the easel-pictures of the artist is facial expression, and in this composition he has striven to ally this quality with the breadth necessarily requisite in painting so large a canvas. The result is a work of genuine charm.

In the Representatives' Reading-room are two sculptured chimneypieces of Siena marble, in each of which is a mosaic by Frederick Dielman. Like Mr. Vedder's «Minerva,» they were laid in Italy, and are of rectangular shape, three feet six inches in height and seven feet six inches wide. The subject of one of the designs is «History.» A female figure in red and brown occupies the middle of the composition, with «Mythology» on her right and «Tradition» on her left. «Mythology,» in green, yellow, and purple, holds a sphere in her hand, and is intended to symbolize the phenomena of the universe. «Myths are the

PAINTED BY ELIHU VEDDER. PHOTOGRAPH BY CURTIS & CAMERON.

« GOVERNMENT. »

PAINTED BY J. W. ALEXANDER. PHOTOGRAPH BY FERDINAND ROUX, PARIS.

«THE EVOLUTION OF THE BOOK: THE STORY-TELLER OF THE FAR EAST.»

earliest recorded utterances of men concerning the visible phenomena of the world into which they were born » is the text illustrated by this figure. « Tradition,» in robes of blue and brown, listens to a nude boy who plays on a lyre and sings the deeds of ancient heroes. In the background behind « History,» a dignified figure with a book in her left hand, is a Greek temple; behind « Mythology » appears one of the Egyptian pyramids; and behind « Tradition » is the Roman Colosseum. The field is a sky of misty blue, and on columns at each side of the throne upon which « History » is seated are inscribed the names of great historians ancient and modern. The subject of the other design is « Law,» represented by a female figure enthroned, with « Peace,» « Truth,» and « Industry » on her right hand, and « Fraud,» « Discord,» and « Violence » on her left. The designs are sufficiently pictorial in character to be effective in that sense, but are composed with a certain formality that lends itself to mosaic treatment. The color-schemes are well balanced, and harmonize with the rich interior in which they are placed, the room being paneled in oak, elaborately carved, and dark in color. The seven main panels in the ceiling of the Representatives' Reading-room were decorated by Carl Gutherz, who took as his subject « The Light of Civilization.»

The figure-pieces in the decoration of the vaults of the four corridors in the second story were painted by Walter Shirlaw, Robert Reid, George R. Barse, Jr., and Frank W. Benson. The corridors are alike in dimensions, but the spaces painted by the artists are different. Mr. Reid, with five octagonal panels in the vaulted ceiling, and four circles on the walls, known as blind bull's-eyes, has for his subjects « The Five Senses » and « Poetry,» « Prose,» « History,» and « Science.» The general decoration of the north corridor, which forms the setting for these works, is similar to the famous designs in the Siena Library, and hence, in its newly painted adaptation, is rather strong and vivid. Mr. Reid has consequently pitched his color-scheme in positive tints of blue, green, red, and yellow. Each of the nine spaces contains a single draped female figure, and the artistic problems, while thus made simple in intention, do not easily admit of satisfactory solution, presupposing, of course, that variety of pose be sought for, and recognizing the inherent difficulty of making a complete and well-balanced composition with one figure in a circular space. The designs show the spaces very well filled, however, and such accessories as are introduced are of the simplest description. The lines of the figures are graceful, and the faces are good expressions of the decorative scheme—to represent each subject by a figure of a young and beautiful woman, to rely in the interpretations on natural beauty without classic convention, and to obtain grace of movement as the chief point in the different arrangements.

Mr. Shirlaw has painted designs in the spandrels between the arches of the west corridor. They consist of female figures, full length, and slightly above life-size. « Chemistry » holds a retort over the burning breath of a serpent coiled about a tripod with an hour-glass upon it. « Astronomy » bears in one hand the globe of Saturn with his rings, and in the other a lens. « Geology,» a strong figure of a type accustomed to labor, holds up a sphere and a piece of mineral, and at her feet are the earth and the moon. « Physics,» a lithe figure in flowing drapery, carries a torch, and symbolizes vital qualities. « Botany,» standing on a lily-pad, holds a water-lily in her hands, and the long stem is entwined about her body. « Zoölogy,» clad in the skin of a wild beast, and with a face expressive of animal quality, holds by his mane a lion at her side. « Mathematics,» a nearly nude figure, has a scroll in her hands on which a formula is written, and at her feet are geometrical solids. The figures are painted in a restrained color-scheme in which purple, blue, tawny-yellow, orange, and greenish hues predominate. They are drawn with special attention to the value of the great lines, and possess a fine statuesque quality.

In the south corridor three octagonal panels in the ceiling and four circular ones on the walls between the windows are painted by Mr. Benson. The subjects for the octagons are « The Three Graces,» and the color-scheme for the whole is a variation of white, blue, and green. Mr. Barse has painted eight upright panels in the spandrels of the east corridor, using as the motives « Epic Poetry,» « Lyric Poetry,» « Comedy,» « Tragedy,» « History,» « Romance,» « Tradition,» and « Fancy.» The decorations consist of a single draped female figure in each panel, painted in positive tints. The backgrounds are light, and the figures, appearing in silhouette, are strongly outlined. Simplicity of treatment, in contrast to the elaborate general decoration of the corridor, characterizes the work.

It is impossible in the space available here to give full descriptions of all the work, and only a small part of it can be reproduced in the illustrations.

PAINTED BY FREDERICK DIELMAN.

PHOTOGRAPH BY CURTIS & CAMERON.

«HISTORY.»

Commissions for mural and sculptural decoration in the new Congressional Library were given to some forty American artists. While it will be seen that the decoration undertaken is of considerable magnitude, and far more extensive than has ever before been projected in any public edifice in the United States, no adequate idea of its completeness may be obtained without mention of the large part played by the art of sculpture in the embellishment of the building. The bronze figures in the three niches of the fountain at the main approach to the library were modeled by E. Hinton Perry. In niches in the principal façade are busts of Demosthenes, Dante, and Walter Scott, by Herbert Adams; Emerson, Irving, and Hawthorne, by J. Scott Hartley; and Goethe, Macaulay, and Franklin, by F. Wellington Ruckstuhl. There are six figures in the spandrels over the main entrance by Bela L. Pratt; and there are two sets of bronze doors by the late Olin L. Warner, one of which has been completed since his death by Mr. Adams. The central doors were modeled by Frederick MacMonnies. In the main staircase are lamp-bearers, and sculptures representing America, Europe, Asia, and Africa, by Philip Martiny. In the first great vestibule are ornamental figures of Minerva by Mr. Adams. Spandrels over the door leading into the rotunda bear sculptured designs by Warner, representing students in youth and in old age. In the corner pavilions of the second story are reliefs of the «Four Seasons» by Mr. Pratt. The finely sculptured clock in the rotunda is by John Flanagan.

In the great rotunda, which will be known as the Central Reading-room when the library is occupied, there are eight colossal figures set on pedestals at the top of the piers between the arches. They are «History,» by Daniel C. French; «Art,» by Augustus St. Gaudens; «Poetry,» by J. Q. A. Ward; «Law,» by Paul W. Bartlett; «Philosophy,» by Bela L. Pratt; «Science,» by John Donoghue; «Commerce,» by John Flanagan; and «Religion,» by Theodore Baur. Sixteen bronze figures, slightly over life-size, each on a plinth in the balustrade about forty feet from the floor, and two in each arch, form another important feature of the decoration of the rotunda. Shakspere is by Mr. MacMonnies; Herodotus, by Mr. French; Columbus and Michelangelo, by Mr. Bartlett; and St. Paul, by Mr. Donoghue. Gibbon and Moses are by Charles H. Niehaus; Plato and Bacon, by John J. Boyle. Fulton is by Edward C. Potter; Kent, by George Bissell; and Newton, by C. E. Dallin. Beethoven is by Mr. Baur; Joseph Henry, by Mr. Adams; Solon, by Mr. Ruckstuhl; and Homer, by Louis St. Gaudens. The first thought that must suggest itself when we see this profuse sculptural decoration is surprise that we have so many good sculptors. Even those of us who are aware that great progress has been made by American sculptors in their art of late must be astonished at the resources shown in the work in the library. Taken together with the mural decoration, and seen in its completeness, it will surely produce a strong impression of excellence. A criticism may be recorded here that applies to the work in its ensemble, and not to any particular part. In the sculpture the subjects do not repeat one another, but in the mural decoration there are, if not too many abstract themes, at least too many similar ones. The arts and sciences, for example, have been used pretty frequently in the decoration. The point has no bearing whatever on the merit or effectiveness of the decorations in the artistic sense, but concerns only the whole of the work from the literary point of view. Historical subjects of a certain class would seem to be well fitted for use in the decoration of a library if the abstract themes do not suffice to give variety to an extensive scheme of decoration. The sculpture in the present instance, indeed, has been treated in this way, abstract subjects alternating with such historical ones as Columbus, Shakspere, and Fulton. The importance of the whole work as a step in the onward march of art in the United States must be conceded without discussion. The responsibility of the artists in the matter is not a light one. If the educated public gives as its verdict that the work has been well done, it cannot but have the effect of giving a strong impetus to the rapidly growing conviction that both public and private edifices should be made beautiful as well as convenient. It would seem as if, in the future, the best achievements of American art might be found in the field of decoration. Breadth of scope in subject, and opportunity to work without too much hurrying, are all that are needed to bring out even better evidences than exist in the library at Washington that the American artists of to-day are abundantly equal to the task of decorating American buildings, no matter how great their architectural importance, or how manifold may be the difficulties of the project. The artistic ability has been shown beyond question, and appreciation is a public duty.

*William A. Coffin.*

DRAWN BY B. WEST CLINEDINST. FROM A WAR-TIME PHOTOGRAPH.

GRANT AND HIS STAFF AT BETHESDA CHURCH.

# CAMPAIGNING WITH GRANT.

BY GENERAL HORACE PORTER.

## FROM THE NORTH ANNA TO COLD HARBOR.

### GRANT CROSSES THE PAMUNKEY.

AS soon as all the commands had safely recrossed the North Anna, General Grant set out on the morning of May 27, 1864, and marched with the troops in the new movement to the left. Sheridan, with two divisions of his cavalry, had started east the afternoon of the day before, and had moved rapidly to Hanovertown on the Pamunkey, a distance of nearly thirty miles.

On the march the general-in-chief, as he rode by, was vociferously cheered, as usual, by the troops. Every movement directed by him inspired the men with new confidence in his ability and his watchfulness over their interests; and not only the officers, but the rank and file, understood fully that he had saved them on the North Anna from the slaughter which would probably have occurred if they had been thrown against Lee's formidable intrenchments, and had had to fight a battle with their backs to a river; that he had skilfully withdrawn them without the loss of a man or a wagon, and that they were again making an advance movement. The soldiers by this time were getting on intimate terms with their commander—in fact, becoming quite chummy. One man in the ranks touched his hat as the chief rode by, and asked, «Is it all right, general?» He received a nod of the head in reply, and the words, «Yes, I think so.» Another man looked up at him, and said in an earnest tone, «General, we 'll lick 'em sure pop next time.» These remarks were not attempts at undue familiarity, but expressions of a genuine sentiment of soldierly fellowship which the men had learned to entertain toward their chief. That night general headquarters were established at Mangohick Church, about twenty miles in a southeasterly direction from Quarles's Ford.

The cavalry had been handled with great skill. It made a feint as if to cross at Littlepage's and Taylor's fords on the Pamunkey, and after dark moved rapidly to Hanover Ferry, about twelve miles farther down the stream, where the actual crossing took place on the morning of the 27th. It was followed by Russell's division of infantry. The rest of the troops had made a good march, and soon after midday on May 28 Wright, Hancock, and Warren had crossed the river and gone into position about a mile and a half beyond. Burnside had reached the ferry, but remained on the north side to guard the trains. General Grant had pushed on to Hanover Ferry, and expressed himself as greatly pleased at the success of the movement. He had abundant reason to congratulate himself upon the thorough carrying out of his instructions. In each of his three attempts to move close to Lee's troops and cross difficult rivers in his very face, Grant had been completely successful, and had manœuvered so as to accomplish a most formidable task in warfare with insignificant loss.

In the operations of the last few days General Grant had employed with wonderful skill his chief military characteristics of quickness of thought, celerity of action, and fertility of resource. While his plans were always well matured, and much thought and investigation were expended upon perfecting them in advance, yet they were sufficiently general in their nature to admit readily of those changes which often have to be made upon the instant in consequence of some unanticipated movement of the enemy, or some unexpected discovery in the topography of the field of operations. It seemed a little singular to him that Lee, after falling back behind the North Anna River, had allowed the Union army to advance across that difficult stream without any substantial resistance, and that, when across, he had made a stand with his back to another river, the South Anna, and remained there entirely passive, and that three days afterward he had permitted the Union army to withdraw across the North Anna under his very nose without even attacking its rear-guards. It was these circumstances which made Grant say at this time, and also write to the government: «Lee's army is really whipped. . . . A battle with them outside of intrenchments cannot be had. . . .»

Our base of supplies was now transferred from Port Royal to White House on the York River.

### MANŒUVERING FOR POSITION.

BEFORE describing the personal incidents connected with what is known as the Cold Harbor campaign, it is important to give the reader a general idea of the character of the country in which the manœuvering and fighting occurred. Hanovertown, near which place our army had now been concentrated, is about seventeen miles in a straight line northeast from Richmond. The country is crossed by two streams, Totopotomoy Creek and the Chickahominy River, both running in a southeasterly direction, the latter being about four miles from Richmond at the nearest point. Between these are a number of smaller creeks and rivulets. Their banks are low, and their approaches swampy and covered with woods and thickets. Three main roads lead from Hanovertown to Richmond. The most northerly is called the Hanovertown or Shady Grove road; the second route, the Mechanicsville road; the third and most southerly, which runs through Old Cold Harbor, New Cold Harbor, and Gaines's Mill, is known as the Cold Harbor road. Old Cold Harbor, half-way between Hanovertown and Richmond, consisted merely of a few scattered houses; but its strategic position was important for reasons which will hereafter appear. New Cold Harbor was little more than the intersection of cross-roads about a mile and a half west of Old Cold Harbor. It was at first supposed that Cold Harbor was a corruption of the phrase Cool Arbor, and the shade-trees in the vicinity seemed to suggest such a name; but it was ascertained afterward that the name Cold Harbor was correct, that it had been taken from the places frequently found along the highways of England, and means «shelter without fire.»

On May 28 Sheridan was pushed out toward Mechanicsville to discover the enemy's position, and after a sharp fight at Haw's Shop, drove a body of the enemy out of some earthworks in which it was posted. That night the Ninth Corps crossed the river. Wilson's cavalry division remained on the north side until the morning of the 30th to cover the crossing of the trains. General headquarters had crossed the Pamunkey on the pontoon bridge in the afternoon of May 28, after a hard, dusty ride, and had gone into camp on the south side. In the mean time Lee had moved his entire army rapidly from the North Anna, and thrown it between our army and Richmond.

On the morning of the 29th, Wright, Hancock, and Warren were directed to move forward and make a reconnaissance in force, which brought about some spirited fighting. The movement disclosed the fact that all of Lee's troops were in position on the north side of the Chickahominy, and were well intrenched.

### GRANT INTERVIEWS A PRISONER.

GENERAL GRANT was particularly anxious, that evening, to obtain information of the enemy from some inside source. Several prisoners had been taken, and one of them who was disposed to be particularly talkative was brought in to headquarters, it being thought that the general might like to examine him in person. He was a tall, slim, shock-headed, comical-looking creature, and proved to be so full of native humor that I give the portion of his conversation which afforded us the most amusement. He, of course, did not know in whose presence he was as he rattled off his quick-witted remarks. «What command do you belong to?» asked the general. «I 'm in Early's corps, and I belong to a No'th Ca'lina reegiment, suh,» was the reply. «Oh, you 're from North Carolina,» remarked the general. «Yes,» said the prisoner, «and a good deal fa'thah from it jes' now than I 'd like to be, God knows.» «Well, where were you taken, and how did you get here?» was next asked. «How did I get h'yah! Well, when a man has half a dozen o' them thah reckless and desp'rit dragoons o' yourn lammin' him along the road on a tight run, and wallopin' him with the flats o' thah sabahs, he don't have no trouble gittin' h'yah.» «Is your whole corps in our front, and when did it arrive?» inquired the general. «Well, now, jes' let me tell you about that,» said the prisoner; «and let me begin right from the sta't. I 'm not goin' to fool you, 'cause I 'm fast losin' interest in this fight. I was a peaceful man, and I did n't want to hurt nobody, when a conscript officah down thah in the ole Tar State come around, and told me I would have to get into the ranks, and go to fightin' fo' my rights. I tried to have him p'int 'em out for me. I told him I 'd as lief have 'em all, but I was n't strenuous about it. Then he begun to put on more airs than a buckin' hoss at a county fair, and told me to come right along—that the country wanted me. Well, I had noticed that our folks was losin' a good many battles; that you-all was too much for 'em; and I got to flatterin' myself that perhaps it was only right for me to go and jine our army, jes to kind o' even things up. But matters has been goin' pretty rough with us ever since, and I 'm gettin' to feel peacefuller and peacefuller every day. They 're feedin' us half the time on crumbs, and thah 's one boy in my company that 's got so thin you have to throw a tent-fly over him to get up a respectable shadow. Then they have a way of campin' us alongside o' creeks not much biggah than a slate-pencil; and you have to be powerful quick about gettin' what watah you want, or some thirsty cow 'll come along and drink up the whole stream. I thought, from all the fuss she had made at the sta't, that South Ca'lina was goin' to fight the whole wah through herself, and make it a picnic for the rest of us; but when thah 's real trouble she has to get the ole Tar State to do the solid work.»

« Are there any men from South Carolina in your brigade?» was the next question. The answer came with a serio-comic expression of countenance: « Yas; a few—in the band.» The general suppressed the laugh with which he was now struggling, and feeling that an effort to get any useful information from the North Carolinian would be a slow process, disappeared into his tent to attend to some correspondence, and left the prisoner to be further interviewed by the staff. « I tell you, gentlemen,» went on the Confederate, « thah 's lots o' cobwebs in my throat, and I could talk to you-all a good deal bettah if I only had a dish o' liquor. Thah 's nothin' braces a man up like takin' a little o' the tanglefoot.»

Thereupon a canteen and cup were brought, and after the man had poured out about four fingers of commissary whisky and tossed it off as if it were water, he looked considerably invigorated. « Nothin' as soothin' as co'n-juice, aftah all,» he continued. « I 'd like to live in Kaintucky; them Kaintucky fellers say they can walk right into a co'n-field, strip off an eah, and jes' squeeze a drink of whisky right out'n it.» « How did you happen to be picked up?» was now asked. « Well, you see, suh,» he replied, « our cap'n, Jimmy Skipwo'th, marched me out on the picket-line. Cap'n Jimmy 's one o' them thah slack-twisted, loose-belted, toggle-j'inted kind o' fellers that sends you straight out to the front; and if you don't get killed right off, why, he gets all out o' patience, an' thinks you want to live fo'evah. You can't get away, because he 's always keepin' tab on you. When he marched us out to-day I says to him: ‹ Cap'n Jimmy, thah don't 'pear to be enough of the boys a-comin' along with us. Now I tell you, when we go to monkeyin' with them Yankees we ought to have plenty o' company; we don't want to feel lonesome.› Well, we got thah, and went to diggin' a ditch so we could flop down in it and protect our heads, and could use it afterward fo' buryin' you-all in it, ef we could get hold o' you. Well, jes' then you opened lively, and come at us a-whoopin' and a-careerin' like sin; and ez fo' me, I took a header for the ditch. The boys saw somethin' drop, and I did n't make any effo't to pick it up ag'in till the misunderstandin' was ovah. The fust thing I knowed aftah that, you lighted onto me, yanked me out o' the hole, and then turned me ovah to some of you' dragoons; and Lo'd! how they did run me into you' lines! And so h'yah I am.»

After the provost-marshal's people had been told to take the prisoner to the rear and treat him well, the man, before moving on, said: « Gentlemen, I would like mighty well to see that thah new-fangled weepon o' yourn that shoots like it was a whole platoon. They tell me, you can load it up on Sunday and fiah it off all the rest o' the week.» He had derived this notion from the Spencer carbine, the new magazine-gun which fired seven shots in rapid succession. After this exhibition of his talent for dialogue, he was marched off to join the other prisoners.

### REGION OF THE TOTOPOTOMOY.

On May 30, Wright, Hancock, and Warren engaged the enemy in their respective fronts, which led to some active skirmishing, the enemy's skirmishers being in most places strongly intrenched. Burnside this day crossed the Totopotomoy. Early's (formerly Ewell's) corps moved out with the evident intention of turning our left, and made a heavy attack, but was repulsed, and forced to fall back, after suffering a severe loss, particularly in field-officers.

About noon Grant received word that transports bringing W. F. Smith's troops from Butler's army were beginning to arrive at White House; and they were ordered to move forward at once, and join the Army of the Potomac. General Grant thought that it was not improbable that the enemy would endeavor to throw troops around our left flank, in the hope of striking Smith a crushing blow before we could detach a force from the Army of the Potomac to prevent it. Sheridan was directed to watch for such a movement, and an infantry brigade was sent out early that morning to join Smith, and march back with him so as to strengthen his forces. General Grant said at this time: «Nothing would please me better than to have the enemy make a movement around our left flank. I would in that case move the whole army to the right, and throw it between Lee and Richmond.» But this opportunity did not arise.

On May 30 the general headquarters had been established in a clearing on the north side of the Shady Grove road, about a mile and three quarters west of Haw's Shop. General Grant this day sent a despatch to Halleck at Washington saying: «I wish you would send all the pontoon bridging you can to City Point to have it ready in case it is wanted.» As early as May 26 staff-officers had been sent from the Army of the Potomac to collect all the bridging material at command, and hold it in readiness. This was done in order to be prepared to cross the James River, if deemed best, and attack Richmond and Petersburg from the south side, and carry out the views expressed by Grant in the beginning of the Wilderness campaign as to his movements in certain contingencies.

It was seen by him from the operations of the 30th that the enemy was working his way southward by extending his right flank, with a view to securing Old Cold Harbor, and holding the roads running from that point toward the James River and White House. This would cut off Grant's short route to the James in case he should decide to cross that river, and would also command the principal line of communication with his base at White House. Old Cold Harbor was therefore a point much desired by both the contending generals, and the operations of the 31st were watched with much interest to see which army would secure the prize.

### GRANT SEIZES OLD COLD HARBOR.

THAT morning my orders took me to the extreme left in connection with the movements of the cavalry. Sheridan advanced rapidly upon Old Cold Harbor, attacked a body of the enemy intrenched there, and after a severe fight carried the position. The place, however, was too important to be abandoned by the enemy without a further struggle, and he soon returned, bringing up a force so large that it appeared for a time impossible for Sheridan to hold his position. Finding no troops advancing to his support, the only course which seemed open to him was to fall back; but just as he had withdrawn he received an order to hold the place at all hazards until reinforcements could reach him. With his usual zeal and boldness, he now reoccupied the enemy's breastworks, dismounted his men, and determined to make a desperate struggle to hold the position against whatever force might be sent against him. Darkness set in, however, before the enemy made another assault. In anticipation of a hard fight for the possession of Cold Harbor, General Grant had ordered Wright's corps to make a night march and move to Sheridan's relief. Lee, discovering this, ordered Anderson's corps to Cold Harbor. On Sheridan's front during the night we could distinctly hear the enemy's troops making preparations for the next morning's attack, and could even hear some of the commands given by their officers. Soon after daylight on June 1 the assault began. Sheridan kept quiet till the attacking party came within a short distance of his breastworks, and then opened with a destructive fire, under which the enemy fell back in considerable confusion. He soon rallied, however, and rushed again to the assault, but once more recoiled before Sheridan's well-delivered volleys. Wright had been instructed to arrive at daylight, but the night march had been exceptionally difficult, and the head of his column did not appear until nine o'clock. The troops were footsore and jaded, but they moved promptly into line, and relieved Sheridan's little force, which had been fighting desperately against great odds for about four hours. Grant had secured Old Cold Harbor, and won the game.

### W. F. SMITH'S TROOPS JOIN THE ARMY OF THE POTOMAC.

SMITH'S corps consisted of 13,000 men. He left about 2,500 to guard White House, and with the rest started for the front, reaching there at three o'clock in the afternoon of June 1. At five o'clock Wright's and Smith's commands advanced and captured the earthworks in their front, taking about 750 prisoners.

The enemy had made three attacks upon Warren, but had been handsomely repulsed. Hancock and Burnside had also been attacked, no doubt to prevent them from sending troops to reinforce our left.

The enemy seemed roused to desperation in his struggle to gain the much-coveted strategic point at Old Cold Harbor, and made several savage attacks in that direction during the night; but they were all successfully repelled. In gaining and holding the important position sought, the Union army that day lost nearly 2000 men in killed and in wounded; the enemy probably suffered to about the same extent.

### GRANT DISCIPLINES A TEAMSTER.

HEADQUARTERS were moved about two miles this day, June 1, to the Via House, which was half a mile south of Totopotomoy Creek on the road leading from Haw's Shop to Bethesda Church. Before starting, the general's servant asked whether he should saddle Jeff Davis, the horse Grant had been riding for two days. «No,» was the reply; «we are getting into a rather swampy country, and I fear little Jeff's legs are not quite long enough for wading through the mud. You had better saddle Egypt.» This horse was large in size and a medium-colored bay. He was called Egypt not because he had come from the region of the Nile, but from the junction of the Mississippi and Ohio rivers in southern Illinois, a section of country named after the land of the Ptolemies.

When the horse was brought up the general mounted as usual in a manner peculiar to himself. He made no perceptible effort, and used his hands but little to aid him; he put his left foot in the stirrup, grasped the horse's mane near the withers with his left hand, and rose without making a spring, by simply straightening the left leg till his body was high enough to enable him to throw the right leg over the saddle. There was no «climbing» up the animal's side, and no jerky movements. The mounting was always done in an instant and with the greatest possible ease.

Rawlins rode with the general at the head of the staff. As the party turned a bend in the road near the crossing of the Totopotomoy, the general came in sight of a teamster whose wagon was stalled in a place where it was somewhat swampy, and who was standing beside his team beating his horses brutally in the face with the butt-end of his whip, and swearing with a volubility calculated to give a sulphurous odor to all the surrounding atmosphere. Grant's aversion to profanity and his love of horses caused all the ire in his nature to be aroused by the sight presented. Putting both spurs into Egypt's flanks, he dashed toward the teamster, and raising his clenched fist, called out to him: «What does this conduct mean, you scoundrel? Stop beating those horses!» The teamster looked at him, and said coolly, as he delivered another blow aimed at the face of the wheel-horse: «Well, who 's drivin' this team anyhow—you or me?» The general was now thoroughly angered, and his manner was by no means as angelic as that of the celestial being who called a halt when Balaam was disciplining the ass. «I 'll show you, you infernal villain!» he cried, shaking his fist in the man's face. Then calling to an officer of the escort, he said: «Take this man in charge, and have him tied up to a tree for six hours as a punishment for his brutality.» The man slunk off sullenly in charge of the escort to receive his punishment, without showing any penitence for his conduct. He was evidently a hardened case. Of course he was not aware that the officer addressing him was the general-in-chief, but he evidently knew that he was an officer of high rank, as he was accompanied by a staff and an escort, so that there was no excuse for the insubordinate and insolent remark. During the stirring scenes of that day's battle the general twice referred to the incident in vehement language, showing that the recollection of it was still rankling in his mind. This was the one exhibition of temper manifested by him during the entire campaign, and the only one I ever witnessed during my many years of service with him. I remarked that night to Colonel Bowers, who had served with his chief ever since the Fort Donelson campaign: «The general to-day gave us his first exhibition of anger. Did you ever see him fire up in that way in his earlier campaigns?» «Never but once,» said Bowers: «and that was in the Iuka campaign. One day on the march he came across a straggler who had stopped at a house and assaulted a woman. The general sprang from his horse, seized a musket from the hands of a soldier, and struck the culprit over the head with it, sending him sprawling to the ground.» He always had a peculiar horror of such crimes. They were very rare in our war, but when brought to his attention the general showed no mercy to the culprit.

### GRANT'S FONDNESS FOR HORSES.

GRANT and Meade rode along the lines that day, and learned from personal observation the general features of the topography. About noon they stopped at Wright's headquarters, and the commander of the Sixth Corps gave the party some delicious ice-water. He had found an ice-house near his headquarters, and after a hot and dusty ride since daylight the cool draught was gratefully relished by those whose thirst it slaked. The previous winter had been unusually cold, and an abundance of ice had formed upon the streams in Virginia. The well-filled ice-houses found on the line of march were a great boon to the wounded. General Wright had assumed command of the Sixth Corps at a critical period of the campaign, and under very trying circumstances; but he had conducted it with such heroic gallantry and marked ability that he had commended himself highly to both Grant and Meade.

That night the variety of food at the headquarters mess was increased by the arrival of a supply of oysters received by way of White House. Shell-fish were among the few dishes which tempted the general's appetite, and as he had been living principally on roast beef and hard bread during the whole campaign, and had not eaten enough of these to sustain life in an ordinary person every one was delighted that evening, when sitting down at the mess-table, to see the general attack the oysters with evident relish, and make a hearty meal of them. Thereafter every effort was made to get a supply of that species of sea food as often as possible. At the dinner-table he referred again to the brutality of the teamster, saying: «If people knew how much more they could get out of a horse by gentleness than by harshness, they would save a great deal of trouble both to the horse and the man. A horse is a particularly intelligent animal; he can be made to do almost anything if his master has intelligence enough to let him know what is required. Some men, for instance, when they want to lead a horse forward, turn toward him and stare him in the face. He, of course, thinks they are barring his way, and he stands still. If they would turn their back to him and move on he would naturally follow. I am looking forward longingly to the time when we can end this war, and I can settle down on my St. Louis farm and raise horses. I love to train young colts, and I will invite you all to visit me and take a hand in the amusement. When old age comes on, and I get too feeble to move about, I expect to derive my chief pleasure from sitting in a big arm-chair in the center of a ring,—a sort of training-course,—holding a colt's leading-line in my hand, and watching him run around the ring.» He little foresaw that a torturing disease was to cut short his life before he could realize his cherished hopes of enjoying the happiness of the peaceful old age which he anticipated.

No warrior was ever more anxious for peace, and all of the general's references to the pending strife evinced his constant longing for the termination of the struggle upon terms which would secure forever the integrity of the Union. When he prepared his letter of acceptance of his first nomination for the Presidency, he wrote no random phrase, but expressed the genuine sentiments of his heart, when he said, «Let us have peace.»

### MOVING INTO POSITION.

THE night of the 1st of June was a busy one for both officers and men. Grant, eager as usual to push the advantage gained, set about making such disposition of the troops as would best accomplish this purpose. Hancock was ordered to move after nightfall from the extreme right to the extreme left of the army. The night was extremely dark, especially when passing through the woods, no one was familiar with the roads, the heat was intense, and the dust stifling; but notwithstanding all the difficulties encountered, Hancock arrived at Old Cold Harbor on the morning of June 2, after a march of over twelve miles. As the men were greatly exhausted, however, from hunger and fatigue, they had to be given an opportunity to rest and eat their rations, and it was found impossible to make a formidable assault until five o'clock in the afternoon. Warren and Burnside were both attacked while they were moving their troops, but they repelled all assaults, and caused the enemy considerable loss.

### THE HALT AT BETHESDA CHURCH.

AT daylight on June 2 the headquarters were moved about two miles south to a camp near Bethesda Church, so as to be nearer the center of the line, which had been extended toward the left. Upon reaching the church, and while waiting for the arrival of the wagons and the pitching of the tents, a number of important orders were issued. The pews had been carried out of the church and placed in the shade of the trees surrounding it. The general-in-chief and his officers seated themselves in the pews, while the horses were taken to a little distance in the rear. The ubiquitous photographers were promptly on the ground, and they succeeded in taking several fairly good views of the group. A supply of New York papers had just been received, and the party, with the exception of the general, were soon absorbed in reading the news. He was too much occupied at the time in thinking over his plans for the day to give attention to the papers, and was content to hear from the staff a summary of anything of importance mentioned in the press. He was usually a diligent reader of the newspapers and of all current literature. There was one New York morning journal which claimed a special previous knowledge of his movements, and made some very clever guesses concerning his plans. He used to call this paper his «organ,» and upon the arrival of the mail he would generally pick it up first, and remark: «Now let me see what my organ has to say, and then I can tell better what I am going to do.»

A large delegation of the Christian Commission had arrived at White House, and was now moving up toward the lines with a supply-train which carried many comforts for the wounded. I saw among the number a person whom I recognized as the pastor of a church which I had attended some years before. He was trudging along like the others in his shirt-sleeves, wearing a broad-brimmed slouch-hat, and was covered with Virginia dust. I presented him to General Grant and the rest of the officers, and then brought up a number of the other members of the Commission, and presented them in turn. General Grant rose to his feet, shook hands with them, and greeted them all with great cordiality; then, resuming his seat, he said: «Sit down, gentlemen, and rest; you look tired after your march.» They thanked him, and several of them took seats in the church pews near him, though, considering their professional training, most of them would have doubtless felt more at home in the pulpit than in the pews. The general continued by saying: «I am very glad to see you coming to the army on your present mission; unfortunately, you will find an extensive field for your work. My greatest concern in this campaign is the care of the large number of wounded. Our surgeons have been unremitting in their labors, and I know you can be of great assistance.»

The gentlemen replied: «We have brought with us everything that we thought could minister to the comfort of the wounded, and we will devote ourselves religiously to the work.» After the general had assured them that they should have all necessary transportation put at their disposal, they bid him good-by, and continued their march. His parting words were: «Remember, gentlemen, whatever instructions you may receive, let your first care be for the wounded.» Before leaving they expressed to the staff their great delight in having had this unexpected chat with the commander of the armies, and having been treated by him with so much consideration.

The Christian Commission, as well as the Sanitary Commission, was often of inestimable service to the wounded, and many a gallant fellow owed his life to its kindly and devoted ministerings.

### STRENGTH OF LEE'S POSITION AT COLD HARBOR.

LEE had manœuvered and fought over this ground two years before, and was perfectly acquainted with every detail of topography, while to Grant it was entirely new. There were, however, in the Army of the Potomac a great many prominent officers who had served with McClellan on the Peninsula, and were familiar with the locality.

General Grant, as usual, had not only to give direction to the active movements taking place under his own eye, but was compelled to bestow much thought upon the coöperating armies at a distance; and the double responsibility was a severe tax upon his energies. He expected that much would be accomplished in the valley of Virginia by Hunter, now that the forces opposed to him had withdrawn, and was urging him to increased exertion; but he had to communicate with him by way of Washington, which created much delay, and added greatly to the anxieties of the general-in-chief. In the afternoon of the 2d, Lee became aware that we were sending troops against his right, and was active in moving his forces to meet an attack on that flank. His left now rested on Totopotomoy Creek, and his right was near New Cold Harbor, and was protected by an impassable swamp. A strong parapet was thrown up on his right in the rear of a sunken road which answered the purpose of a ditch. On the left center the ground was lower and more level, but difficult of approach on account of swamps, ravines, and thickets. Added to this were the usual obstacles of heavy slashings of timber. General Grant had manœuvered skilfully with a view to compelling Lee to stretch out his line and make it as thin and weak as possible, and it was at present over six miles long.

### WHY GRANT ASSAULTED AT COLD HARBOR.

A SERIOUS problem now presented itself to General Grant's mind—whether to attempt to crush Lee's army on the north side of the James, with the prospect in case of success of driving him into Richmond, capturing the city perhaps without a siege, and putting the Confederate government to flight; or to move the Union army south of the James without giving battle, and transfer the field of operations to the vicinity of Petersburg. It was a nice question of judgment. After discussing the matter thoroughly with his principal officers, and weighing all the chances, he decided to attack Lee's army in its present position. He had succeeded in breaking the enemy's line at Chattanooga, Spotsylvania, and other places under circumstances which were not more favorable, and the results to be obtained now would be so great in case of success that it seemed wise to make the attempt.

The general considered the question not only from a military standpoint, but he took a still broader view of the situation. The expenses of the war had reached nearly four million dollars a day. Many of the people in the North were becoming discouraged at the prolongation of the contest. If the army were transferred south of the James without fighting a battle on the north side, people would be impatient at the prospect of an apparently indefinite continuation of operations; and as the sickly season of summer was approaching, the deaths from disease among the troops meanwhile would be greater than any possible loss encountered in the contemplated attack. The loss from sickness on the part of the enemy would naturally be less, as his troops were acclimated and ours were not. Besides, there were constant rumors that if the war continued much longer European powers would recognize the Confederacy, and perhaps give it material assistance, but this consideration influenced Grant much less than the others. Delays are usually dangerous, and there was at present too much at stake to admit of further loss of time in ending the war, if it could be avoided.

The attack was ordered to be made at daylight on the morning of June 3. The eve of battle was, as usual, an anxious and tiresome night at headquarters, and some changes in the detailed orders specifying the part the troops were to perform in the coming action were made nearly as late as midnight. Lee's position was such that no turning movement was practicable, and it was necessary that one of his flanks should be crushed by a direct assault. An attack on the enemy's right promised the better results, and Grant had decided to strike the blow there. Of course the exact strength of the enemy's position could not be ascertained until developed by a close attack, as changes were constantly being made in it, and new batteries were likely to be put in position at any time. The general's intention, therefore, was to attack early in the morning, and make a vigorous effort to break Lee's right, and if it were demonstrated that the assault could not succeed without too great a sacrifice of life, to desist, and have the men throw up cover for their protection with a view of holding all the ground they had gained. Our troops were disposed as follows: Hancock on the extreme left, Wright next, then Smith and Warren, with Burnside on the extreme right.

### A NOTABLE INSTANCE OF COURAGE.

EVERYTHING was now in readiness for the memorable battle of Cold Harbor. Headquarters had been moved two miles farther to our left, and established near Old Cold Harbor, so as to be within easy reach of the main point of attack. It has been stated by inimical critics that the men had become demoralized by the many assaults in which they had been engaged; that they had lost much of their spirit, and were even insubordinate, refusing to move against the earthworks in obedience to the orders of their immediate commanders. This is a gross slander upon the troops, who were as gallant and subordinate as any forces in the history of modern warfare, although it is true that many of the veterans had fallen, and that the recruits who replaced them were inferior in fighting qualities.

In passing along on foot among the troops at the extreme front that evening while transmitting some of the final orders, I observed an incident which afforded a practical illustration of the deliberate and desperate courage of the men. As I came near one of the regiments which was making preparations for the next morning's assault, I noticed that many of the soldiers had taken off their coats, and seemed to be engaged in sewing up rents in them. This exhibition of tailoring seemed rather peculiar at such a moment, but upon closer examination it was found that the men were calmly writing their names and home addresses on slips of paper, and pinning them on the backs of their coats, so that their dead bodies might be recognized upon the field, and their fate made known to their families at home. They were veterans who knew well from terrible experience the danger which awaited them, but their minds were occupied not with thoughts of shirking their duty, but with preparation for the desperate work of the coming morning. Such courage is more than heroic—it is sublime.

### BATTLE OF COLD HARBOR.

AT 4:30 A. M., June 3, Hancock, Wright, and Smith moved forward promptly to the attack. Hancock's troops struck a salient of the enemy's works, and after a desperate struggle captured it, taking a couple of hundred prisoners, three guns, and a stand of colors. Then turning the captured guns upon the enemy, they soon drove him from that part of the line into his main works a short distance in the rear. The second line, however, did not move up in time to support the first, which was finally driven back and forced out of the works it had captured. The men resisted stubbornly, and taking advantage of the crest of a low hill at a distance of fifty or sixty yards from the captured works, they rapidly threw up enough cover to enable them to hold that position. Another division had rushed forward in column to effect a lodgment, if possible, in the enemy's works; but an impassable swamp divided the troops, who were now subjected to a galling fire of artillery and musketry; and although a portion of them gained the enemy's intrenchments, their ranks had become too much weakened and scattered to hold their position, and they were compelled to fall back.

Wright's corps had moved forward, and carried the rifle-pits in its front, and then assaulted the main line. This was too strong, however, to be captured, and our troops were compelled to retire. Nevertheless, they held a line, and protected it as best they could, at a distance of only thirty or forty yards from the enemy.

Smith made his assault by taking advantage of a ravine which sheltered his troops somewhat from the cross-fire of the enemy. His men drove the enemy's skirmishers before them, and carried the rifle-pits with great gallantry; but the line had to be readjusted at close quarters, and the same cross-fire from which Wright had suffered made further advances extremely hazardous. Smith now reported that his troops were so cut up that there was no prospect of carrying the works in his front unless the enfilading fire on his flank could be silenced. Additional artillery was then sent forward to try to keep down the enemy's fire.

Burnside had captured the advance rifle-pits in front of Early's left, and had taken up a position close to the enemy's main line. Warren's line was long and thin, and his troops, from the position they occupied, could not do much in the way of assaulting. These demonstrations against the enemy's left were principally to keep him engaged, and prevent him from withdrawing troops to reinforce his right. Warren had coöperated with Burnside in driving Early from the Shady Grove road, upon which he had advanced and made an attack. Gordon had attacked Warren's center, but was handsomely repulsed. Wilson's division of cavalry, which had returned from destroying the Virginia Central Railroad, moved across the Totopotomoy to Haw's Shop, drove the enemy from that place, made a further advance, carried some rifle-pits and held them for an hour, but was unable to connect with Burnside's infantry, and withdrew to Haw's Shop.

The reports received by General Grant were at first favorable and encouraging, and he urged a continuance of the successes gained; but finding the strength of the position greater than any one could have supposed, he sent word at 7 A. M. to General Meade, saying: «The moment it becomes certain that an assault cannot succeed, suspend the offensive; but when one does succeed, push it vigorously, and if necessary pile in troops at the successful point from wherever they can be taken.» Troops had again pushed forward at different points of the line. General Grant had established himself at a central position, which had been made known to all the commanders and staff-officers, so that he could at that point receive promptly all reports. Some of these messages were rather contradictory, and became still more conflicting as the attack proceeded. His staff-officers were active in bringing information from every important point, but the phases of battle were changing more rapidly than they could be reported.

At eleven o'clock the general rode out along the lines to consult with commanding officers on the spot. Hancock now reported that the position in his front could not be taken. Wright stated that a lodgment might be made in his front, but that nothing would be gained by it unless Hancock and Smith were to advance at the same time. Smith thought that he might be able to carry the works before him, but was not sanguine. Burnside believed that he could break the enemy's line in his front, but Warren on his left did not agree in this opinion.

The general-in-chief now felt so entirely convinced that any more attacks upon the enemy's works would not result in success that at half-past twelve o'clock he wrote the following order to General Meade: «The opinion of the corps commanders not being sanguine of success in case an assault is ordered, you may direct a suspension of farther advance for the present. Hold our most advanced positions, and strengthen them. . . . To aid the expedition under General Hunter, it is necessary that we should detain all the army now with Lee until the former gets well on his way to Lynchburg. To do this effectually, it will be better to keep the enemy out of the intrenchments of Richmond than to have them go back there. Wright and Hancock should be ready to assault in case the enemy should break through General Smith's lines, and all should be ready to resist an assault.»

After finishing this despatch the general discussed at some length the situation, saying: «I am still of the opinion I have held since leaving the North Anna, that Lee will not come out and take the offensive against us; but I want to prepare for every contingency, and I am particularly anxious to be able to turn the tables upon the enemy in case they should, after their success this morning in acting on the defensive, be tempted to make a counter-attack upon our lines.»

### AFTER THE BATTLE.

AT two o'clock Grant announced the result of the engagement to Halleck. At three o'clock, while waiting for news in regard to the casualties of the morning and reports in detail from the corps commanders, he busied himself in sending instructions in regard to Banks's command in Louisiana, and advised a movement against Mobile.

There was a good deal of irregular firing along the lines, and in the afternoon it became heavy on Burnside's right. The enemy had made an attack there, and while it lasted he attempted to haul off some of his batteries; but Burnside's return fire was so vigorous that this attempt was prevented. In the night the enemy's troops withdrew from Burnside's front, leaving some of their wounded in his hands and their dead unburied.

General Grant's time was now given up almost entirely to thinking of the care of the wounded. Our entire loss in killed, wounded, and missing was nearly 7000. Our surgeons were able to give prompt relief to the wounded who were recovered, as every preparation had been made for this emergency, and our army was fortunately only twelve miles from a water base. Many, however, were left between the lines; and as the works were close together, and the intervening ground under a constant fire, it was not possible to remove a great number of the wounded or to bury the dead. The enemy's wounded in our hands were taken in charge by our surgeons, and the same care was given to them as to our own men.

### GRANT'S COMMENTS ON COLD HARBOR.

THAT evening, when the staff-officers had assembled at headquarters after much hard riding and hot work during the day, the events which had occurred were discussed with the commander, and plans talked over for the next morning. The general said: «I regret this assault more than any one I have ever ordered. I regarded it as a stern necessity, and believed that it would bring compensating results; but, as it has proved, no advantages have been gained sufficient to justify the heavy losses suffered. The early assault at Vicksburg, while it was not successful, yet brought compensating advantages; for it taught the men that they could not seize the much-coveted prize of that stronghold without a siege, and it was the means of making them work cheerfully and patiently afterwards in the trenches, and of securing the capture of the place with but little more loss of life; whereas if the assault had not been made the men could not have been convinced that they could not have captured the city by making a dash upon it which might have saved them many months of arduous labor, sickness, and fatigue.» The matter was seldom referred to again in conversation, for General Grant, with his usual habit of mind, bent all his energies toward consummating his plans for the future.

There has been brought out recently a remarkable vindication of Grant's judgment in ordering the assault at Cold Harbor. In a lecture delivered at San Antonio, Texas, April 20, 1896, by ex-United States Senator John H. Reagan, who was postmaster-general in Jefferson Davis's cabinet, he states that he and several of the judges of the courts in Richmond rode out to General Lee's headquarters, and were with him during this attack. In describing the interview he says:

«He [Lee] then said to me that General Grant was at that time assaulting his lines at three different places, with columns of from six to eight deep. Upon this, I asked him if his line should be broken what reserve he had. He replied, ‹Not a regiment,› and added that if he should shorten his lines to make a reserve the enemy would turn him, and if he should weaken his lines to make a reserve they would be broken.» This is a confirmation of the fact that Grant had succeeded in compelling Lee to stretch out his line almost to the breaking-point, and a proof that if our attacking columns had penetrated it, Lee would have been found without reserves, and the damage inflicted upon him would have been irreparable.

### GRANT'S «HAMMERING.»

THERE were critics who were severe in their condemnation of what Grant called «hammering» and Sherman called «pounding»; but they were found principally among the stay-at-homes, and especially the men who sympathized with the enemy. A soldier said one night, when reading by a camp-fire an account of a call issued by a disloyal newspaper at home for a public meeting to protest against the continued bloodshed in this campaign: «Who 's shedding this blood, anyhow? They better wait till we fellows down here at the front hollo, ‹Enough!›» The soldiers were as anxious as their commander to fight the war to a finish, and be allowed to return to their families and their business.

Grant could have effectually stopped the carnage at any time by withholding from battle. He could have avoided all bloodshed by remaining north of the Rapidan, intrenching, and not moving against his enemy: but he was not placed in command of the armies for that purpose. It had been demonstrated by more than three years of campaigning that peace could be secured only by whipping and destroying the enemy. No one was more desirous of peace; no one was possessed of a heart more sensitive to every form of human suffering than the commander: but he realized that paper bullets are not effective in warfare; he knew better than to attempt to hew rocks with a razor; and he felt that in campaigning the hardest blows bring the quickest relief. He was aware that in Wellington's armies the annual loss from disease was 113 out of 1000; in our Mexican war, 152; and in the Crimea, 600; and that in the campaigns thus far in our own war more men had died from sickness while lying in camp than from shot and shell in battle. He could not select his ground for fighting in this continuous siege of fortified lines; for, though he and his chief officers applied all their experience and skill in endeavors to manœuver the enemy out of strong positions before attacking him, his foe was often too able and wily to fall into the traps set for him, and had to be struck in positions which were far from Grant's choosing. When Lee stopped fighting the cause of secession was lost. If Grant had stopped fighting the cause of the Union would have been lost. He was assigned one of the most appalling tasks ever intrusted to a commander. He did his duty fearlessly to the bitter end, and triumphed. In thirteen months after Lincoln handed him his commission of lieutenant-general, and intrusted to him the command of the armies, the war was virtually ended.

### GRANT DECIDES TO CROSS THE JAMES.

THE time had now come when Grant was to carry out his alternative movement of throwing the entire army south of the James River. Halleck, who was rather fertile in suggestions, although few of them were ever practicable, had written Grant about the advisability of throwing his army round by the right flank, taking up a line northeast of Richmond, controlling the railroads leading north of Richmond, and using them to supply the Union army. This view may have been favored in Washington for the reason that it was thought it would better protect the capital. Grant said, in discussing this matter at headquarters: «We can defend Washington best by keeping Lee so occupied that he cannot detach enough troops to capture it. If the safety of the city should really become imperiled, we have water communication, and can transport a sufficient number of troops to Washington at any time to hold it against attack. This movement proposed by Halleck would separate the Army of the Potomac by a still greater distance from Butler's army, while it would leave us a long vulnerable line of communication, and require a large part of our effective force to properly guard it. I shall prepare at once to move across the James River, and in the mean time destroy to a still greater extent the railroads north of Richmond.»

On June 5, General J. G. Barnard, of the United States engineer corps, was assigned to duty as chief engineer at Grant's headquarters.

### SUFFERINGS AT THE FRONT.

THE general-in-chief realized that he was in a swampy and sickly portion of the country. The malaria was highly productive of disease, and the Chickahominy fever was dreaded by all the troops who had a recollection of its ravages when they campaigned in that section of the country two years before. The operations had been so active that precautions against sickness had necessarily been much neglected, and the general was anxious, while giving the men some rest, to improve the sanitary conditions. By dint of extraordinary exertions the camps were well policed, and large quantities of fresh vegetables were brought forward and distributed. Cattle were received in much better condition than those which had made long marches and had furnished beef which was far from being wholesome. Greater attention was demanded in the cooking of the food and the procuring of better water. Dead animals and offal were buried, and more stringent sanitary regulations were enforced throughout the entire command.

What was most distressing at this time was the condition of affairs at the extreme front. No one who did not witness the sights on those portions of the line where the opposing troops were in exceptionally close contact can form an idea of the sufferings experienced. Staff-officers used to work their way on foot daily to the advanced points, so as to be able to report with accuracy these harrowing scenes. Some of the sights were not unlike those of the «bloody angle» at Spotsylvania. Between the lines where the heavy assaults had been made there was in some places a distance of thirty or forty yards completely covered by the dead and wounded of both sides. The bodies of the dead were festering in the sun, while the wounded were dying a torturing death from starvation, thirst, and loss of blood. In some places the stench became sickening. Every attempt to make a change in the picket-line brought on heavy firing, as both sides had become nervous from long watchfulness, and the slightest movement on either front led to the belief that it was the beginning of an assault. In the night there was often heavy artillery firing, sometimes accompanied by musketry, with a view to deterring the other side from attacking, or occasioned by false rumors of an attempt to assault. The men on the advanced lines had to lie close to the ground in narrow trenches, with little water for drinking purposes, except that obtained from surface drainage. They were subjected to the broiling heat by day and the chilling winds and fogs at night, and had to eat the rations that could be got to them under the greatest imaginable discomfort.

GRANT'S VISITOR FROM THE PACIFIC SLOPE.

THE staff-officers, in their frequent visits to the front of our lines, had learned the most exposed points, and in passing them usually quickened their speed so as to be a shorter time under the enemy's fire. There was one particularly dangerous place where a dirt road ran along the foot of a knoll on the side toward the enemy. A prominent citizen from the Pacific coast, whom General Grant knew, had arrived from Washington, and was spending a few days at headquarters to see what an army in the field looked like. One morning, as the general was mounting with a portion of his staff to make one of his frequent reconnoitering trips along the lines, the visitor proposed to ride with him, but said before starting: «Is there going to be much shooting where you 're going, general? For I 've got a wife and children waiting for me on the Pacific slope, and I don't want to get pinked by the Johnny Rebs.» «Well, they 're not very particular over there where their shots strike when they begin firing. I always advise persons who have no business to transact with them to keep away,» replied the general. «Yes; but I want to see as much of this show as possible, now that I 've come here,» said the guest; and mounting a horse which had been ordered up for him, he rode along with the party. Pretty soon some stray artillery shots flew in our direction, but the visitor rode on without showing any signs of disturbance, except a very active ducking of the head, accompanied by a running comment upon the utter carelessness and waste of ammunition on the part of the enemy, and the evident disposition to mow down a mild-mannered and harmless civilian with as little hesitation as they would the general-in-chief who was crowding them with all his armies.

After a while we came to the dangerous portion of the dirt road, and the staff-officers reminded the general that it was usually pretty hot there; but he passed over it at a walk without paying attention to the warning, and stopped at the most exposed point to examine the position in front, which seemed to him to present some features of importance. A battery instantly opened, and shot and shell shrieked through the air, and plowed the ground in a most enlivening manner. The visitor, whose head was now bobbing from one side to the other like a signal-flag waving a message, cried out to the commander: «See here, general; it don't appear to me that this place could have been selected by you with special reference to personal safety.» The general was absorbed in his examination of the ground, and made no reply for a minute or two. Then looking at his guest, who was growing red and pale by turns, and rolling nearly out of his saddle in dodging to the right and left, remarked with a smile: «You are giving yourself a great deal of useless exercise. When you hear the sound of a shot it has already passed you.» Just then a shell exploded close by, scattering the dirt in every direction. This was too great a trial for the overstrained nerves of the visitor. He turned his horse's head to the rear, drove both spurs into the animal's flanks, and as he dashed away with the speed of a John Gilpin, he cried back to us: «I have a wife and family waiting for me, and I 'm pressed for time. Besides, I 'm not much of a curiosity-seeker anyway.» Just then his black silk hat blew off, but he did not stop to recover it, and was soon out of sight. He had evidently reached a state of mind when the best of hats appears to be of no special value.

That evening in camp the general perpetrated a number of jokes at the visitor's expense, saying to him: «Well, you appear to have won that race you entered your horse for this afternoon.» «Yes,» said the visitor; «I seem to have got in first.» «Perhaps,» continued the general, «you felt like that soldier in one of our retreats who, when asked by an officer where he was going, said: ‹I 'm trying to find the rear of this army, but it don't appear to have any.›» «I don't know why it was, but Lee seemed to have some personal grudge against me,» remarked the guest. «I think,» said the general, «it must have been that high hat which attracted his attention.» «Great Scott!» screamed the visitor, springing from his camp-stool as if the enemy had again opened fire on him; «do you know that that hat had a card in it with my name on? Holy smoke! If the boys get hold of it, and give me away, and the news gets out to the Pacific slope, I 'll be a dead duck in the next political campaign!»

## AN IMPORTANT MISSION.

GENERAL GRANT was now stimulating every one to increased activity in making preparations for the formidable movement he was about to undertake in throwing the army with all its impedimenta across the James. He was fully impressed with its hazardous nature, but was perfectly confident that he could carry it out without encountering extraordinary risks. The army had to be withdrawn so quietly from its position that it would be able to gain a night's march before its absence should be discovered. The fact that the lines were within thirty or forty yards of each other at some points made this an exceedingly delicate task. Roads had to be constructed over the marshes leading to the lower Chickahominy, and bridges thrown over that stream preparatory to crossing. The army was then to move to the James, and cross upon pontoon bridges and improvised ferries. This would involve a march of about fifty miles in order to reach Butler's position, while Lee, holding interior lines, could arrive there by a march of less than half that distance.

In the afternoon of June 6 the general called Colonel Comstock and me into his tent, asked us to be seated, and said with more impressiveness of manner than he usually manifested: «I want you to undertake an important mission preliminary to moving the army from its present position. I have made up my mind to send Smith's corps by a forced night march to Cole's Landing on the Chickahominy, there to take boats and be transferred to Butler's position at Bermuda Hundred. These troops are to move without their wagons or artillery. Their batteries will accompany the Army of the Potomac. That army will be held in readiness to pull out on short notice, and by rapid marches reach the James River and prepare to cross. I want you to go to Bermuda Hundred, and explain the contemplated movement fully to General Butler, and see that the necessary preparations are made by him to render his position secure against any attack from Lee's forces while the Army of the Potomac is making its movement. You will then select the best point on the river for the crossing, taking into consideration the necessity of choosing a place which will give the Army of the Potomac as short a line of march as practicable, and which will at the same time be far enough down-stream to allow for a sufficient distance between it and the present position of Lee's army to prevent the chances of our being attacked successfully while in the act of crossing. You should be guided also by considerations of the width of the river at the point of crossing, and of the character of the country by which it will have to be approached.»

Early the next morning Comstock and I rode rapidly to White House, and then took a steamboat down the Pamunkey and York rivers, and up the James, reaching Butler's headquarters at Bermuda Hundred the next day. After having obtained a knowledge of the topography along the James, and secured the best maps that could be had, we despatched a message to the general and started down the James on the 10th, making further careful reconnaissances of the banks and the approaches on each side. Comstock and I had served on General McClellan's staff when his army occupied the north bank of the James two years before, and the country for many miles along the river was quite familiar to us. This knowledge was of much assistance on the present mission. We returned by the same route by which we had come, and reached headquarters on the 12th. We had noted one or two places on the river which might have served the purpose of crossing; but, all things considered, we reported unhesitatingly in favor of a point familiarly known as Fort Powhatan, about ten miles below City Point, the latter place being at the junction of the James and Appomattox rivers. Several roads led to the point selected for crossing both on the north and the south side of the James, and it was found that they could be made suitable for the passage of wagon-trains by repairing and in some places corduroying them. The principal advantage of the place selected was that it was the narrowest point that could be found on the river below City Point, being twenty-one hundred feet in width from Wilcox's Landing on the north side to Windmill Point on the south side.

General Grant had been anxiously awaiting our return, and had in the mean time made every preparation for withdrawing the army from its present position. On our arrival we went at once to his tent, and were closeted with him for nearly an hour discussing the contemplated operation. While listening to our verbal report and preparing the orders for the movement which was to take place, the general showed the only anxiety and nervousness of manner he had ever manifested on any occasion. After smoking his cigar vigorously for some minutes, he removed it from his mouth, put it on the table, and allowed it to go out; then relighted it, gave a few puffs, and laid it aside again. In giving him the information he desired, we could hardly get the words out of our mouths fast enough to suit him. He kept repeating, «Yes, yes,» in a manner which was equivalent to saying, «Go on, go on»; and the numerous questions he asked were uttered with much greater rapidity than usual. This would not have been noticed by persons unfamiliar with his habit; but to us it was evident that he was wrought up to an intensity of thought and action which he seldom displayed. At the close of the interview he informed us that he would begin the movement that night.

### PREPARATIONS FOR A CHANGE OF BASE.

THE same day on which Comstock and I started from Cold Harbor (June 7), Sheridan had been sent north with two divisions of cavalry to break up the Virginia Central Railroad, and, if practicable, to push west and join General Hunter's force, which was moving down the valley. It was expected that the enemy's cavalry would be compelled to follow Sheridan, and that our large trains would be safe from its attacks during the contemplated movement across the James River. Nothing was left unthought of by the trained mind of the commander who was conducting these formidable operations.

On June 9 a portion of the Army of the Potomac had been set to work fortifying a line to our left and rear on ground overlooking the Chickahominy, under cover of which the army could move down that stream. Boats for making the ferriage of the James had been ordered from all available places. Preparations had been made for bridging necessary points on the Chickahominy, and a large force had been put to work under engineer officers to repair the roads. This day (June 12) was Sunday, but it was by no means a day of rest. All was now ready for the important movement.

### DEALING WITH A LIBELER OF THE PRESS.

GENERAL MEADE had been untiring in his efforts during this eventful week. He was General Grant's senior by seven years, was older than any of the corps commanders, and was naturally of an excitable temperament, and with the continual annoyances to which he was subjected he not infrequently became quite irritable. He was greatly disturbed at this time by some newspaper reports stating that on the second night of the battle of the Wilderness he had advised a retreat across the Rapidan; and in talking this matter over with General Grant, his indignation became so great that his wrath knew no bounds. He said that the rumor had been circulated throughout the press, and would be believed by many of the people, and perhaps by the authorities in Washington. Mr. Dana, the Assistant Secretary of War, who was still with the army, was present at the interview, and he and General Grant tried to console Meade by assurances that the story would not be credited, and that they would give a broad contradiction to it. Mr. Dana at once sent a despatch to the Secretary of War, alluding to the rumor, and saying: «This is entirely untrue. He has not shown any weakness of the sort since moving from Culpeper, nor once intimated a doubt as to the successful issue of the campaign.» The Secretary replied the next day (June 10), saying: «Please say to General Meade that the lying report alluded to in your telegram was not even for a moment believed by the President or myself. We have the most perfect confidence in him. He could not wish a more exalted estimation of his ability, his firmness, and every quality of a commanding general than is entertained for him.» The newspaper correspondent who had been the author of this slander was seized and placed on a horse, with large placards hung upon his breast and back bearing the inscription, «Libeler of the Press,» and drummed out of camp. There had never been a moment when Meade had not been in favor of bold and vigorous advances, and he would have been the last man to counsel a retreat.

### LOSSES.

WHILE at the mess-table taking our last meal before starting upon the march to the James on the evening of the 12th, the conversation turned upon the losses which had occurred and the reinforcements which had been received up to that time. The figures then known did not differ much from those contained in the accurate official reports afterward compiled. From the opening of the campaign, May 4, to the movement across the James, June 12, the total casualties in the Army of the Potomac, including Sheridan's cavalry and Burnside's command, had been: killed 7,621; wounded 38,339; captured or missing 8,966; total 54,926. The services of all the men included in these figures were not, however, permanently lost to the army. A number of them were prisoners who were afterward exchanged, and many had been only slightly wounded, and were soon ready for duty again. Some were doubtless counted more than once, as a soldier who was wounded in a battle twice, and afterward killed, may have been counted three times in making up the list of casualties, whereas the army had really lost but one man. The losses of the enemy have never been ascertained. No precise information on the subject has been discovered, and not even a general statement can be made of his casualties. In a few of the battles of this campaign his losses were greater than the losses suffered by the Union troops; in the greater part of the battles they were less. Our reinforcements had amounted to just about the same number as the losses. It was estimated from the best sources of information that Lee had also received reinforcements equal to his losses, so that the armies were now of about the same size as when the campaign began.

All the reinforcements organized in the North and reported as on their way to the front did not reach us. There was a good deal of truth in the remark reported to have been made by Mr. Lincoln: «We get a large body of reinforcements together, and start them to the front; but after deducting the sick, the deserters, the stragglers, and the discharged, the numbers seriously diminish by the time they reach their destination. It's like trying to shovel fleas across a barnyard; you don't get 'em all there.»

### GRANT RELATES SOME ANECDOTES.

GENERAL GRANT said during the discussion: «I was with General Taylor's command in Mexico when he not only failed to receive reinforcements, but found that nearly all his regulars were to be sent away from him to join General Scott. Taylor was apt to be a little absent-minded when absorbed in any perplexing problem, and the morning he received the discouraging news he sat down to breakfast in a brown study, poured out a cup of coffee, and instead of putting in the sugar, he reached out and got hold of the mustard-pot, and stirred half a dozen spoonfuls of its contents into the coffee. He did n't realize what he had done till he took a mouthful, and then he broke out in a towering rage.

«We learned something at Shiloh about the way in which the reports of losses are sometimes exaggerated in battle. At the close of the first day's fight Sherman met a colonel of one of his regiments with only about a hundred of his soldiers in ranks, and said to him, ‹Why, where are your men?› The colonel cast his eyes sadly along the line, wiped a tear from his cheek, and replied in a whimpering voice: ‹We went in eight hundred strong, and that's all that's left of us.› ‹You don't tell me!› exclaimed Sherman, beginning to be deeply affected by the fearful result of the carnage. ‹Yes,› said the colonel; ‹the rebs appeared to have a special spite against us.› Sherman passed along some hours afterward, when the commissary was issuing rations, and found that the colonel's men were returning on the run from under the bank of the river, where they had taken shelter from the firing; and in a few minutes nearly all of the lost seven hundred had rejoined, and were boiling coffee and eating a hearty meal with an appetite that showed they were still very much alive.»

(To be continued.)

*Horace Porter.*

# THE MAN WHO WORKED FOR COLLISTER.

BY THE AUTHOR OF «THE WONDERFUL WHEEL.»

PERHAPS the loneliest spot in all the pine-woods was the big Collister farm. Its buildings were not huddled in the center of it, where they could keep one another in countenance, but each stood by itself, facing the desolate stretches of gray sand and pine stumps in its own way. Near each a few uncut pine-trees kept guard, presumably for shade, but really sending their straggling shadows far beyond the mark. Many a Northern heart had ached from watching them, they were so tall and isolate; for, having been forest-bred, they had a sad and detached expression when they stood alone or in groups, just like the look on Northern faces when they met the still distances of the South.

In Collister's day he and the man who worked for him were the only strangers who had need to watch the pines. A land-improvement company had opened up the farm, but after sinking all its money in the insatiable depths of sandy soil where the Lord, who knew best, had planted pine-trees, the great bustling company made an assignment of its stumpy fields, and somewhat later the farm passed into the hands of Collister. Who Collister was, and where he came from, were variously related far and wide through the piny woods; for he was one of those people whose lives are an odd blending of reclusion and notoriety. He kept up the little store on the farm; and though it was usually his man who came up from the fields when any one stood at the closed store and shouted, its trade was largely augmented by the hope of seeing Collister.

The sunken money of the land company must have enriched the soil, for the farm prospered as well as the store, yielding unprecedentedly in such patches as the two men chose to cultivate. In midsummer the schooner-captains, in their loose red shirts, came panting up two sunburned miles from the bayou to chaffer with Collister or his man over the price of watermelons; and when their schooners were loaded, the land breeze which carried the cool green freight through bayou and bay out to the long reaches of the sound, where the sea wind took the burden on, sent abroad not only schooner and cargo and men, but countless strange reports of the ways and doings of Collister. At least one of these bulletins never changed. Year after year, when fall came, and he had added the season's proceeds to his accumulating wealth, —when even the peanuts had been dug, and the scent of their roasting spread through the piny woods on the fresh air of the winter evenings, making an appetizing advertisement for the store,—it was whispered through the country, and far out on the gulf, that Collister said he would marry any girl who could make good bread—light bread. That settled at least one question: Collister came from the North. The man who worked for him was thought to have come from the same place; but though he did the cooking, his skill must have left something to be desired, and after current gossip had risked all its surmises on the likelihood of Collister's finding a wife under the condition imposed, it usually added that, if Collister married, the man who worked for him would take it as a slight, and leave.

An old county road led through the big farm, and along it the country people passed in surprising numbers and frequency for so sparsely settled a region. They took their way leisurely, and if they could not afford a five-cent purchase at the store, gave plenty of time to staring right and left behind the stumps in a cheerful determination to see something worth remembrance. One day, when the store chanced to be standing open, one of these passers walked up to the threshold and stood for a while looking in. The room was small and dingy, lighted only by the opening of the door, and crammed with boxes, leaky barrels, farm produce, and side-meat. One corner had been arranged with calicoes and ribbons and threads; but though the inspector was a young and pretty girl in the most dingy of cotton gowns, she had scarcely a thought for that corner; she was staring at a man who was so hard at work rearranging the boxes and barrels that he did not notice her shadow at his elbow. Finally he glanced up of his own accord.

«Hello,» he said, coming forward; «do you want to buy something? Why did n't you sing out?»

For a little while longer the girl stared at

him as steadily as if he had not moved. Most of the people who live in the pine-woods come to have a ragged look, but this was the raggedest person she had ever seen. He was as ragged as a bunch of pine-needles; yet he had the same clean and wholesome look, and his face was pleasant.

«Are you the man that works for Collister?» she asked.

«Yes,» he said.

The girl looked him up and down again with innocent curiosity. «How much does he give you?» she asked.

«Nothing but my board and clothes,» the man answered, and smiled. He did not seem to find it hard work to stand still and watch her while her black eyes swiftly catalogued each rag. When they reached his bare brown feet she laughed.

«Then I think he had ought to dress you better, an' give you some shoes,» she said.

«He does—winters,» the man answered calmly.

She gave an impatient shake of her sunbonnet. «That is n't the thing—just to keep you-all warm,» she explained. «A man like Mr. Collister had ought to keep you looking 'ristocratic.»

The man who worked for Collister grinned. «Not very much in Collister's line,» he said. «We might get mixed up if I was too dressy.» He pulled a cracker-box forward, and dusted it. «If you ain't in a hurry, you 'd better come inside and take a seat,» he added.

The girl sank to the door-step instead, taking off her bonnet. Its slats folded together as she dropped it into her lap, and she gave a sigh of relief, loosening some crushed tresses of hair from her forehead. She seemed to be settling down for a comfortable inquisition. «What kind of clothes does Mr. Collister wear?» she began.

The man drew the cracker-box up near the doorway, and sat down. «Dressy,» he said; «'bout like mine.»

The girl gave him a look which dared to say, «I don't believe it.»

«Honest truth,» the man nodded. «Would you like to have me call him up from the field, and show him to you?»

Not to assent would have seemed as if she were daunted, and yet the girl had many more questions to ask about Collister. «Pretty soon,» she said. «I suppose if you don't call him, he 'll be coming for you. They say he works you mighty hard.»

It is never pleasant to be spoken of as something entirely subject to another person's will. A slow flush spread over the man's face, but he answered loyally, «Collister may be mean to some folks, but he 's always been mighty good to me.» He smiled as he looked off from stump to stump across the clearing to the far rim of the forest. The stumps seemed to be running after one another, and gathering in groups to whisper secrets. «You 've got to remember that this is a God-forsaken hole for anybody to be stuck in,» he said; «'t ain't in humanity for him to keep his soul as white as natural, more 'n his skin; but there 's this to be said for Collister: he 's always good to me.»

«I 'm right glad of that,» the girl said. She too was looking out at the loneliness, and a little of it was reflected on her face. «You-all must think a heap of him,» she added wistfully.

«You can just bet on that,» he declared. «I 've done him a heap of mean turns, too; but they was always done 'cause I did n't know any better, so he don't hold me any grudge.»

«Would n't he mind if he knew you were a-losing time by sitting here talking to me?» she asked.

The man shook his head. «No,» he answered cheerfully; «he would n't care—not for me. There is n't anybody else he would favor like that, but he makes it a point to accommodate me.»

The girl gave her head a little turn. «Do you think he would accommodate me?» she asked.

He looked her over as critically as she had first looked at him. «It 's a dangerous business answering for Collister,» he ventured; «but maybe if *I* asked him to, he would.»

«Well, you *are* bigoty,» she asserted. «I cain't noways see what there is betwixt you. Why, they say that whilst you 're working he comes out in the field, an' bosses you under a' umbrelly; an'—» a laugh carried her words along like leaves on dancing water—«an' that he keeps a stool stropped to his back, ready to set down on whenever he pleases. Is it true—‹hones' truth›?»

A great mirth shook Collister's man from head to foot. «Such a figure—such a figure as the old boy cuts!» he gasped. «Sometimes I ask him if he 'll keep his stool strapped on when he goes a-courting; and he says maybe so—it 'll be so handy to hitch along closer to the young lady.» Without thinking, he illustrated with the cracker-box as he spoke. «And as for the umbrella, I certainly ain't the one to object to that; for, you see, when the sun 's right hot he holds it over me.»

He leaned half forward as he spoke, smiling at her. It is hard to tell exactly when a new acquaintance ceases to be a stranger; but as the girl on the door-step smiled in answer, she was unexpectedly aware that the shrewd, kindly, furrowed face of this young man who worked for Collister was something which she had known for a long, long time. It seemed as familiar as the scent of pine-needles and myrtle, or as the shafts of blue, smoke-stained sunlight between the brown trunks of the pine-trees in the fall, or as the feathery outline of green pine-tops against the dreamy intensity of a Southern sky; and when all this has been said of a girl who lives in the «pineys,» there is no necessity for saying more. She gave a little nervous laugh.

The man began talking again. «It ain't such foolery as you would think, his wearing the stool and carrying the umbrella,» he said. «This is the way he reasons it out, he says. In the first place, there 's the sun; that 's a pretty good reason. But what started it was a blazing day up North, when he was hustling four deals at once; a man would need a head the size of a barrel to keep that sort of thing going for long, and Collister has just an ordinary head no bigger than mine. Well, the upshot of it was that he had a sunstroke, and was laid up a month; and then he reckoned up the day's business, and what he 'd gained on one deal he 'd lost on another, so that he came out even to a cent—queer, was n't it?—with just the experience of a sunstroke to add to his stock-in-trade. Then he bought himself an umbrella and a stool, and began to take life fair and easy. Easy going is my way too; that 's why we get along together.»

There was a jar of candy on a shelf behind him and above his head, and, turning, he reached up a long arm and took it down. It was translucent stick candy with red stripes round it—just such candy as every fortunate child knew twenty years ago, and some know still. In the piney woods it has not been superseded as a standard of delight, and the children expect to receive it gratuitously after any extensive purchase. Near the coast, where creole words have spread, it is asked for by a queer, sweet name—lagnappe (something thrown in for good measure). The man who worked for Collister handed the jar across to the girl, making her free of it with a gesture.

«Do you reckon Mr. Collister would want me to take some?» she asked, poising her slender brown hand on the edge of the jar. «You know, they say that when he first come hyar, an' the children asked him for lagnappe, he pretended not to onderstan' 'em, and said he was sorry, but he had n't got it yet in stock. Is that true?»

«Yes,» the man answered; «that 's true.»

«Well, *did* he onderstan'?» she asked.

He lifted his shoulders in a way he had learned in the South. «To be sure,» he said. «I told him at the time that it was a mean thing to do, but he said he simply could n't help himself; young ones kept running there from miles around to get five cents' worth of baking-sody and ask for a stick of candy. But take some; he won't mind, for he 's always good to me.»

She drew back her hand. «No,» she said, pouting; «I 'm goin' to come in some time when he 's hyar, an' see if he 'll give some lagnappe to me.»

«I 'll tell him to,» the man said.

«Well, you *are* bigoty!» the girl repeated.

«If I was to tell him to,» the man persisted, «who should I say would ask for it?»

She looked at him defiantly. «I 'll do the telling,» she said; «but while we 're talking about names, what 's yours?»

«Well,» he answered, «if you 're not naming any names, I don't believe I am. You know considerably more about me already than I do about you.»

«Oh, just as you please,» she said. To be brought blankly against the fact that neither knew the other's name caused a sense of constraint between them. She picked up her bonnet, and put it on as if she might be about to go; and though she did not rise, she turned her face out of doors so that the bonnet hid it from him—and it was such a pretty face!

«Say, now,» he began, after one of those pauses in which lives sometimes sway restlessly to and fro in the balances of fate, «I did n't mean to make you mad. I 'll tell you my name if you want to know.»

«I 'm not so anxious,» she said. One of her brown hands went up officiously and pulled the bonnet still farther forward. «Is it true,» she asked, «that Mr. Collister says he will marry any girl that can make good light bread?»

The man formed his lips as if to whistle, and then stopped. «Yes,» he said, eying the sunbonnet; «it 's true.»

She turned round and surprised him. «I can make good light bread,» she announced.

«You!» he said.

«Yes,» she answered sharply; «why not? It ain't so great a trick.»

«But—» he paused, meeting the challenge of her face uneasily—«but did you come here to say that?»

«You 've heard me say it,» she retorted.

He rose, and stood beside her, looking neither at her, nor at the fields, nor at the encircling forest, but far over and beyond them all, at the first touches of rose-color on the soft clouds in the west. He seemed very tall as she looked up to him, and his face was very grave. She had forgotten long ago to notice his bare feet and tattered clothing. «So that means,» he said slowly, «that you came here to offer to marry a man that you never saw.»

She did not answer for a moment, and when she did her voice was stubborn. «No,» she said; «I came hyar to say that I know how to make light bread. You need n't be faultin' me for his saying that he would marry any girl that could.»

«But you would marry him?»

«I allow if he was to ask me I would.»

The man looked down squarely to meet her eyes, but he found only the sunbonnet. «What would you do it for,» he asked—«a lark?»

«A lark!» she echoed; «oh, yes; a lark.»

He stooped toward her and put his hand on her shoulder. «Look up here,» he said; «I want to see if it 's a lark or not.»

«I jus' said it was,» she answered, so low that he had to bend a little closer to be certain that he heard.

«That won't do,» he said firmly; «you must look up into my face.»

«I—won't!» she declared.

He stood gazing at her downcast head. There was something that shone in his eyes, and his tongue was ready to say, «You must.» He closed his lips and straightened himself again. The girl sat perfectly still, except that once in a while there was a catch in her breath. He kept looking off into the empty, sighing reaches of pine-country, which could make people do strange things. «We have n't known each other very long,» he said at last; «but a few minutes ago I thought we knew each other pretty well, and perhaps you don't have any better friend than I am in this desolate hole. Won't you tell me why it is that you want to marry Collister?»

«For his money,» the girl answered shortly.

His face darkened as if he were cursing Collister's money under his breath; but she did not look up, and he said nothing until he could speak quietly. «Is that quite fair to Collister?» he asked. «He did talk about marrying any girl that could make good light bread; but I don't suppose he wanted to do it unless she liked him a little too.»

«I—allowed—maybe I'd like him a little,» the girl explained; «an' I was right sure that he 'd like me.»

«That 's the mischief of it,» the man muttered; «I 'll warrant he 'll like you!»

After hiding her face so long the girl looked up, and was surprised to see him so troubled. «You 've been right good to me,» she said gently, «an' I reckon I don't mind—perhaps I had ought to tell you jus' why I come. I—I don't want to be mean to Mr. Collister, an' if you don't think it 's fair I won't tell him I can make good bread; only—» she met his eyes appealingly—«if I don't, I don't see what I 'm goin' to do.»

«What 's the matter?» he asked. «Don't you have any home?»

She smiled bravely, so that it was sorrowful to see her face. «Not any more,» she said. «I 've always had a right good home, but my paw died—only las' week. You an' Mr. Collister used to know him, an' he has often spoke' of both of you. He was Noel Seymour from up at Castauplay.»

«Noel Seymour—dead?» said the man. All her light words pleaded with him for tenderness now that he knew she had said them with an aching heart. «But Seymour was a creole,» he added, «and you are not.»

«My own mother was an American,» the girl answered, «an' I learned my talk from her before she died; an' then my stepmother is American, too.» She stopped just long enough to try to smile again. «What do you think?» she asked. «My stepmother don't like me. She is n't going to let me stay at home any more. Could you be as mean as that?»

He put his hand on her shoulder. «You poor child!» he said; for gossip came in sometimes in return for all that radiated from the farm, and he could recall a cruel story he had once heard of Noel Seymour's wife. It made him believe all and more than the girl had told him. «Poor child!» he said again; «you have n't told me yet what 's your first name.»

«Ginevra,» she answered. «My own mother liked it; my stepmother says it 's the name of a fool. She thinks she 's young an' han'some; but I allow she 's sending me off because I 'm a right smart the best-favored of the two. She wants to get married again, an' thar ain't but one bacheldor up our way, so she 's skeered he 'd take first pick of me.»

«My kingdom!» said the man who worked for Collister. «If there 's somebody up your way that you know, and that likes you, why did n't you go and take your chances with him?»

A hot flush rushed over the girl's face. «Does you-all think I 'd be talkin' like this to a man I knowed?» she demanded. She stared angrily until her lips began to quiver. «An' besides, I hate him!» she cried. «He 's not a fittin' man for such as me.»

«You poor child!» he said again.

She caught the compassion of his eyes. «What had I ought to have done?» she asked. «What had any girl ought to do out hyar in the pineys if she was lef' like me? I 've hearn o' places whar girls could find work, an' my stepmother she allowed I could go to the oyster-factories in Potosi; but whar would I *stay?* An' then I went to the factories onct with my paw, an' the air round 'em made me sick. You see, I was raised in the pineys, an' they has a different smell.»

He shook his head, though kindly, at so slight a reason, and the sharp pain of his disapproval crossed her face. «Oh, you don't know anything about it,» she cried desperately; «thar ain't no man that can tell how it feels for a girl that 's had a father that 's made of her like mine did to be turned right out to face a whole townful that she never saw. Can't you see how, if you was skeered, it would be a heap easier jus' to face one man? An' then I 'd hearn no end about Mr. Collister, an' some of it was funny, an' thar wa'n't none of it very bad; so I jus' made up my mind to come round hyar an' see for myse'f what like he was. You see,» she went on, with a lift of the head, «it was for the money, but it was for the honorableness, too; an' I 'd cross my heart an' swear to you on the Bible that when I come hyar I had n't no thought that anybody could think it was onderreachin' Mr. Collister. I thought he 'd be right proud, an' before we got to talking I never sensed that it would be a hard thing to name to him; but now—» her voice trembled and broke. «Oh,» she cried, «I wished I 'd never come!»

The man looked away from her. «Don't wish it,» he said huskily. «Collister ought to be proud if he can have you for his wife; and he would give you a good home and everything your heart could ask for.»

Tears sprang into her eyes, and she dropped her head upon her knees to hide them. «Oh, I know, I know,» she sobbed; «but I 'd rather marry you!»

«O-oh!» breathed the man who worked for Collister; «I 'd so much rather that you did.» And with a laugh of pure delight he caught her up into his arms.

When they left the store a red blaze of sunset shone between the trunks of the pine-trees. The man fastened the padlock behind them, and they started in a lovers' silence along the road. The big farm was as empty and lifeless as ever, except for the lonesome neighing of a horse in the barn-yard and for a single straight blue thread of smoke which rose from one of the little houses. The girl pointed at it, and smiled.

«He 's having to get his own supper to-night,» she said; «but I 'll make it up to him: I 'll make his light bread jus' the same.»

«Yes,» he said, «you 'd better; for, whatever he 's been to other folks, he 's always been mighty good to me; an', please God, he 's going to be mighty good to you.»

A breath of land breeze had started in the pine-woods, and was going out bearing a tribute of sweet odors to the sea. The disk of the sun sank below the black line of the earth, but the trees were still etched against a crimson sky. Softly and faintly in the far distance some passing creole hailed another with a long, sweet call. They reached the edge of the clearing, and went on through the deepening twilight of the pines. There were no words in all the world quite true enough to speak in that great murmurous stillness that was in the woods and in their hearts. At last they came to a path beyond which she would not let him go, thinking it better for this last time to go on alone.

«Good night,» she said lingeringly; and he held her close and kissed her, whispering good night. Then he stood and watched her slender swaying figure as it grew indistinct between the trees; and just before it vanished he called out guardedly.

«Say,» he summoned, «come here!»

She went laughing back to him. «You-all *are* bigoty,» she said, «beginning to order me about!»

He took her hands, and held her from him so that he could see her face. «You must n't be mad at me,» he said; «but there 's something I forgot to tell you—I 'm Collister.»

*Mary Tracy Earle.*

# INAUGURATION SCENES AND INCIDENTS.

ROM the first the American people elected to make of the inauguration of a President a great national festival. They did this spontaneously, and in quiet disregard of all efforts to prevent them. Washington desired to be installed as first President without pomp or parade, as was natural in a man who looked upon his consent to serve as the greatest sacrifice he had ever been called upon to make, and who entered upon his task with a most unfeigned reluctance, and with a real diffidence, for which he did not expect to receive credit from the world.[1] Yet his journey from Mount Vernon to New York, which he wished to make as private as possible, was converted by the people, overflowing with veneration and gratitude, into an unbroken triumphal progress, which culminated in a series of public demonstrations and ceremonies that surpassed anything of the kind yet seen in the young republic. Each succeeding inauguration of a new President has been celebrated in much the same way, with a steadily increasing multitude of spectators, and a swelling measure of pomp and pageantry. In outward appearance there has been much similarity in these recurring quadrennial demonstrations; but each has had a distinct individuality shaped by the personality of its central figure and by the forces which prevailed in the election.

So long as Washington was on the scene he dominated it completely. He came much nearer to having his own way at his second inauguration, in Philadelphia, than he had been able to at his first, in New York, chiefly through the desire of his political rivals to prevent a fresh demonstration of the popular adoration for him. Jefferson's immortal devotion to republican simplicity had its origin in this desire; for he favored the abolition of all public exercises at the second inauguration, and wished to have the oath of office administered to Washington privately at his house, a certificate of it to be deposited in the State Department. Hamilton took the same view, but other members of the cabinet favored exercises in the open Senate-chamber, and their opinion prevailed. There was as large an attendance as the hall would hold, but no parade or other popular demonstration. The people went on worshiping their hero with undiminished fervor, however. They celebrated his birthday with such honors, and in so general a way, that his rivals were more distressed than ever, and began to see in this infatuation a menace to the republic, a threat of monarchy.

The chief sufferer from this condition of affairs was John Adams when the time came to inaugurate him as Washington's successor. He is the only President we have had, with the possible exception of Mr. Van Buren, who can be said to have played a secondary part at his own inauguration. The people had no eyes for him; they saw only the stately figure of Washington passing forever from the scene. The ceremonies were held in Independence Hall, Philadelphia, in the House of Representatives. Washington drove to the hall in his coach and four, and was lustily cheered both outside and inside the building. He passed quickly to his seat, as if eager to stop the applause. Adams entered a few minutes later, dressed in a light drab suit, and passed slowly down the aisle, bowing in response to the respectful applause which greeted him. He took the oath, and then delivered his inaugural address. He described the scene subsequently as a solemn one indeed, made more affecting by the presence of Washington, whose countenance was as serene and unclouded as the day. There was a flood of tears, which he sought in various ways to explain, though no explanation was necessary. There was, he said, more weeping than there had ever been at the representation of a tragedy; but whether it was from grief or joy, whether from the loss of their beloved President or from the accession of an unbeloved one, or some other cause, he could not say. He suspected that the novelty of the sun setting full-orbed, and another rising, though less splendid, may have had something to do with it. For several days after the exercises he was still bewailing the tendency to weep. Everybody was annoying him by talking of tears and streaming eyes, but nobody told him why; and he was forced to believe that it was all for the loss of their beloved. Two or three had ventured to whis-

[1] Letters to Benjamin Lincoln and Samuel Hanson.

per in his ear that his address had made a favorable impression, but no other evidence of interest in him had reached him. One thing he knew, and that was that he was a being of too much sensibility to act any part well in such an exhibition.[1]

If the tears at the inaugural exercises made Mr. Adams unhappy, what followed must have added greatly to his sufferings. When, at the close, Washington moved toward the door, there was a precipitate rush from the gallery and corridors for the street, and he found a great throng awaiting him as he emerged from the door. They cheered him, and he waved his hat to them, his countenance radiant with benignity, his gray hair streaming in the wind. He walked to his house, followed by the crowd, and on reaching it turned about for a final greeting. His countenance assumed a grave and almost melancholy expression, his eyes were bathed in tears, and only by gestures could he indicate his thanks and convey his farewell blessing.[2]

No inauguration myth has been more tenacious of life than that which pictured Jefferson, attired as a plain citizen, riding on horseback to the Capitol, hitching his horse to the palings, and walking unattended into the Senate-chamber to take the oath as President. To have done this would have been in accordance with his previous utterances, for he had strongly condemned as savoring of monarchy all public ceremony at the swearing in of a President. When the time for his own inauguration arrived, however, the case seems to have looked different to him. Whether it was because he was to be the first President inaugurated at the new Capitol, or because of an unwillingness to disappoint the large numbers of his friends and partizans who had assembled to honor him, is not clear; but the fact is that he did permit a considerable display at the ceremonies. He was met at the door of his boarding-house, which was only a stone's throw from the Capitol, by a militia artillery company and a procession of citizens, and, escorted by these, he went on foot to the Capitol. The horseback story, or «fake,» as it would be denominated in modern journalism, was the invention of an Englishman named John Davis, who put it in a book of American travels which he published in London two years later. In order to give it an air of truthfulness, Davis declared that he was present at the inauguration, which was not true. A veracious account of the ceremonies was sent to England by Edward Thornton, who was then in charge of the British legation at Washington; and in this Jefferson was described as having walked to the Capitol. These facts, together with a great mass of interesting matter about Jefferson's inauguration, are set forth in detail by Henry Adams in his «History of the United States,» and leave no doubt that the Davis version was a pure fabrication.

On reaching the Senate-chamber, in which he was to be inaugurated, Jefferson became a member of one of the most striking groups ever gathered in a public place. On one side of him stood John Marshall as chief justice to administer the oath, and on the other Aaron Burr, who was to be sworn in as Vice-President. As described by his contemporaries, Jefferson was very tall (six feet two and a half inches in height), with a loose, shackling air about his slender figure, a very red freckled face, and neglected gray hair. He was clad in a blue coat, a thick, gray-colored, hairy waistcoat with a red under-waistcoat lapped over it, green velveteen breeches with pearl buttons, yarn stockings, and slippers down at the heels—his appearance being very much that of a raw-boned farmer. Marshall, as described by Joseph Story in 1808, was tall and slender, not graceful and imposing, but erect and steady, with black hair, small and twinkling eyes, and rather low forehead, plain and dignified in manners, and very simple and neat in dress. Burr was rather small in stature, but dignified and easy in manners, and dressed with aristocratic care. The three men were alike in one respect: they distrusted and disliked one another thoroughly. Jefferson both feared and hated Marshall, saying of him that he had a mind of that gloomy malignity which would never let him forego the opportunity of satiating it on a victim. Marshall said of Jefferson, shortly before the inauguration, that by weakening the office of President he would increase his personal power, and that his letters had shown that his morals could not be pure. Both Jefferson and Marshall looked upon Burr as a political and social adventurer who was living up to his own creed, «Great souls care little for small morals.» The outgoing President, Mr. Adams, was not present at the exercises; but he undoubtedly took a grim pleasure in the presence of Marshall, whom he had made chief justice, greatly to the wrath of Jefferson, only a few weeks before. After the ceremonies the new

[1] Letters of John Adams to his wife.

[2] Personal recollections of Wm. A. Duer, once president of Columbia College.

President proceeded to the Executive mansion, or «the Palace,» as it was then styled, in the same manner as he had gone to the Capitol.

Washington set the example, which has been followed at frequent intervals by new Presidents even to our day, of wearing at the first inauguration ceremonies clothing of American manufacture. He was dressed in a suit of dark cloth made at Hartford. I have been able to find no mention of the nationality of the «light drab suit» which John Adams wore. Jefferson was inaugurated in his «every-day clothes,» which may or may not have been exclusively American; but before the end of his service as President he appeared at his New-Year reception dressed in an entire suit of homespun. Madison carried the matter a step further; for, as he passed down the aisle of the House of Representatives to be inaugurated, he was spoken of as a «walking argument in favor of the encouragement of native wool.» His coat had been made on the farm of Colonel Humphreys, and his waistcoat and small-clothes on that of Chancellor Livingston, all from the wool of merino sheep raised in the country. John Quincy Adams says in his Diary that the house was very much crowded, and that its appearance was magnificent, but that Mr. Madison read his address in a tone so low that it could not be heard. Contemporary descriptions of Madison picture him as a small, modest, and jovial man. Washington Irving spoke of him in 1812, at the time of his second election to the Presidency, as «a withered little apple-john,» and an English observer as «a little man with small features, rather wizened, but occasionally lit up with a good-natured smile.» He was habitually neat and genteel in his appearance, says another writer, dressed like a «well-bred and tasty old-school gentleman.» American wool seems, therefore, to have made its first appearance as a «walking argument» under favorable conditions.

Monroe's inauguration, in 1817, was remarkable chiefly for being the first one held out of doors since the seat of government had been moved to Washington. There had been out-of-door exercises when Washington was installed in New York, but all his successors till Monroe had been inaugurated within doors. It is said by some authorities that the proposal to change to the open air in 1817 was the outcome of a long and bitter wrangle between the two Houses as to the division of seats in the House at the ceremonies. Agreement being apparently impossible, some one suggested that by going out of doors room enough could be found for everybody, and the idea was acted upon joyfully. An elevated platform was erected for the occasion under the unfinished portico of the Capitol, and from this Monroe delivered his inaugural address to the largest assemblage that had yet been gathered there. The day was balmy and beautiful. There were no outdoor exercises at Monroe's second inauguration, the weather being stormy, rain and snow falling throughout the day. The attendance on this occasion did not exceed two thousand persons. John Quincy Adams was also inaugurated indoors four years later, and it was not till the advent of General Jackson, in 1829, that the outdoor exercises became the established custom.

Jackson's entry upon the Presidency has been likened repeatedly to the descent of the barbarians upon Rome. It was accompanied with a huge multitude of people from all parts of the land, and by an amount of uproar altogether unprecedented. Webster wrote from the capital, several days before the inauguration, that the city was full of speculations and speculators, there being a great multitude, too many to be fed without a miracle, and all hungry for office. «I never saw such a crowd before,» he added. «Persons have come five hundred miles to see General Jackson, and they really seem to think that the country is rescued from some dreadful danger.» They surged through the streets shouting, «Hurrah for Jackson!» They swarmed about Gadsby's tavern, where the general lodged, in such masses as completely to hem it in and make access to his presence nearly impossible. When inauguration day arrived, fully ten thousand people gathered about the eastern portico of the Capitol, which was to be used for the first time for these ceremonies, and a ship's cable had to be stretched across the long flight of steps, about a third of the way from the top, to keep the portico clear. It was with great difficulty that the procession which escorted the general was able to reach the Capitol. He went first to the Senate, as usual, where the chief justice and other dignitaries joined him to proceed to the outdoor platform.

An eye-witness, who took a somewhat jocose view of the day's events, wrote that the most remarkable feature about Jackson as he marched down the aisle of the Senate with a quick, large step, as though he proposed to storm the Capitol, was his double pair of spectacles. He habitually wore two pairs, one for reading and the other for seeing at a distance, the pair not in use being placed across the top of his head. On this occasion, says the eye-witness, the pair on his head reflected the light; and some of the rural admirers of the old hero were firmly persuaded that they were two plates of metal let into his head to close up holes made by British bullets. When he appeared on the portico, we are told that the shout which arose rent the air and seemed to shake the very ground. The ceremony ended, the general mounted his horse to proceed to the White House, and the whole crowd followed him. «The President,» says a contemporary writer, «was literally pursued by a motley concourse of people, riding, running helter-skelter, striving who should first gain admittance into the executive mansion, where it was understood that refreshments were to be distributed.» An abundance of refreshments had been provided, including many barrels of orange punch. As the waiters opened the doors to bring out the punch in pails, the crowd rushed upon them, upsetting the pails, and breaking the glasses. Inside the house the crush was so great that distribution of refreshments was impossible, and tubs of orange punch were set out in the grounds to entice people from the rooms. Jackson himself was so pressed against the wall of the reception-room that he was in danger of injury, and was protected by a number of men linking arms and forming a barrier against the crowd. Men with boots heavy with mud stood on the satin-covered chairs and sofas in their eagerness to get a view of the hero. Judge Story wrote that the crowd contained all sorts of people, from the highest and most polished down to the most vulgar and gross in the nation. «I never saw such a mixture,» he added. «The reign of King Mob seemed triumphant. I was glad to escape from the scene as soon as possible.»

The outgoing President, Mr. Adams, was not present. He and his father have been the only outgoing Presidents, alive at the time of the inauguration of their successors, who did not attend the ceremonies. The reason why the younger Adams did not was stated tersely in «Niles's Register» of March 27, 1829: «It is proper to mention, for the preservation of facts, that General Jackson did not call upon President Adams, and that Mr. Adams gave not his attendance at the installation of President Jackson.» This conduct must have been a cause of grief to the editor of the «National Intelligencer,» for four years earlier he had written, when describing the scene which followed the inauguration of Adams: «General Jackson, we were pleased to observe, was among the earliest of those who took the hand of the President; and their looks and deportment toward each other were a rebuke to the littleness of party spirit, which can see no merit in a rival and feel no joy in the honor of a competitor.» General Jackson was very conspicuous at the inauguration of his successor, Mr. Van Buren. The two rode side by side from the White House to the Capitol, and back again after the ceremonies, in a carriage made of wood from the frigate *Constitution*, presented by the Democrats of New York. But the general was at all moments the central figure; the crowd along the route and at the Capitol paid only slight attention to the new President.

Of the inauguration of General William Henry Harrison in 1841, John Quincy Adams says in his Diary that it was celebrated with demonstrations of popular feeling unexampled since that of Washington in 1789. It had more of a left-over campaign flavor than any other inauguration either before or since. The great «Tippecanoe» canvass, with its log cabins and hard cider, its enormous processions, its boundless enthusiasm and incessant uproar, got under such headway that it could not be stopped with election day. Enough of it was still in motion in March to make the inauguration of the general a virtual continuation of it, so far as the procession was concerned. The log cabins were brought to the capital for the occasion, and many of the clubs came with their regalia and banners. A magnificent carriage had been constructed by his admirers, and presented to General Harrison, with the expressed wish that he ride in it to the Capitol; but he declined to do so, insisting upon riding a horse instead. The crowd of visitors along the avenue from the White House to the Capitol was the largest yet seen in Washington. The procession created such enthusiasm that the novel expedient was put in operation of having it march and countermarch several times before leaving its hero at the Capitol. For two hours it went to and fro in the avenue before the spectators were supposed to have their fill of it. Mr. Adams, who saw it from his window, under which it passed, describes it in his Diary as a mixed military and civil cavalcade, with platoons of militia companies, Tippecanoe clubs, students of colleges, school-boys, a half-dozen veterans who had fought under the old hero in the War of 1811, sundry awkward and ungainly painted banners and log cabins, and without car-

THE CRUSH AT THE WHITE HOUSE AFTER JACKSON'S INAUGURATION.

DRAWN BY G. WRIGHT.

A SCENE AT WILLIAM HENRY HARRISON'S INAUGURATION.

riages or showy dresses. The *coup d'œil*, he adds, was showy-shabby; and he says of the general: «He was on a mean-looking white horse, in the center of seven others, in a plain frock coat or surtout, undistinguishable from any of those before, behind, or around him.» The day was cold and bleak, with a chilly wind blowing. General Harrison stood for an hour exposed to this while delivering his address, and at its close mounted his horse and returned to the White House with the procession again as an escort.

The inauguration ball dates from the very beginning. There was a ball when Washington was inaugurated in New York, but owing to the pressure of other demands upon his time, it did not take place till the evening of March 7. Washington attended, and performed a minuet with Miss Van Zandt, and danced cotillions with Mrs. Peter Van Brugh Livingston, Mrs. Maxwell, and others. There was no ball at his second inauguration because of its extremely quiet character, and there was none when Mr. Adams came in because of the general grief over Washington's departure. I can find no mention of a ball when Jefferson was inaugurated, but there was one when Madison came in, and since then there has been no break in the custom. There were two when Polk was inaugurated, and two when Taylor succeeded him—an administration and an opposition ball on each occasion, both very well attended. The crush was so great at the Taylor administration ball that many persons narrowly escaped injury, and there were loud complaints because of the inadequate supply of refreshments.

The crowds at Polk's inauguration were said to be the largest yet seen at the Capitol, which was undoubtedly true; for as the country has advanced in size, the number of people going to Washington to witness the advent of every new President has steadily increased. Evidence that the outdoor custom had become firmly established in Polk's time is furnished by the fact that, although rain fell steadily throughout the day, he delivered his address from the portico to a wide, moving sea of umbrellas, with no protection save an umbrella which was held over his head. The crowds amused themselves during the progress of the procession along Pennsylvania Avenue by repeating the favorite cry of the opposition in the preceding campaign, «Who *is* James K. Polk?» Roars of laughter always followed this somewhat worn but always amusing query. An interesting contemporary note of this inauguration is the following: «Professor Morse brought out his magnetic telegraph to the portico platform, close to one side of it, from which point he could hear everything that went on, having under view all the ceremonies performed, transmitting the results to Baltimore as fast as they transpired.»

There was little that varied the now well-established monotony of inauguration ceremonies when Franklin Pierce came in in 1853, and James Buchanan in 1857. Pierce was one of the most buoyantly self-poised men who ever entered upon the Presidency. He made the journey from the White House to the Capitol standing erect in the carriage beside President Fillmore, and bowing constantly to the cheers with which he was greeted. At the Capitol he distinguished himself by being the first President to deliver his address without notes, speaking in a remarkably clear voice, and arousing great enthusiasm by his handsome appearance, dignified bearing, and somewhat unusual oratorical powers.

DRAWN BY IRVING R. WILES.

THE APPROACH TO THE CAPITOL DURING POLK'S INAUGURATION. (BASED ON A CONTEMPORARY PRINT.)

Lincoln's inaugurations have been so fully described in recent years in the columns of THE CENTURY that it is unnecessary to say much about them now. Perhaps the most dramatic phase of the first inauguration, always ex-

DRAWN BY IRVING R. WILES. FROM A CONTEMPORARY PICTURE IN "HARPER'S WEEKLY."

BUCHANAN'S INAUGURATION.

cepting the address itself, was that described in Dr. Holland's «Life of Lincoln,» when the new President stood on the portico to take the oath of office, with President Buchanan, Chief Justice Taney, author of the Dred Scott decision, and Stephen A. Douglas prominent in the group about him, and the latter, his famous rival in debate, holding Mr. Lincoln's hat while he was delivering his inaugural address.

The chief characteristic of later inaugurations has been the steadily rising number of people in attendance. At both inaugurations of General Grant the crowds were enormous; but those which have gathered every four years since have shown no diminution from the standard of bigness then fixed. That standard, which stood at from five to eight thousand in the early years of the century, will have passed one hundred thousand before the century closes. The managers of President McKinley's inauguration predict the finest pageant and the greatest throng ever seen in Washington, and doubtless their prediction will be verified.

*Joseph B. Bishop.*

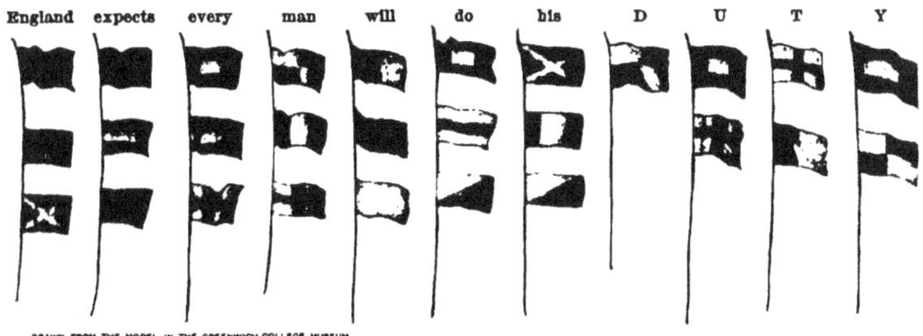


DRAWN FROM THE MODEL IN THE GREENWICH COLLEGE MUSEUM.

NELSON'S SIGNAL.

# NELSON AT TRAFALGAR.

BY CAPTAIN A. T. MAHAN, U. S. N. (Ret'd),

Author of «The Influence of Sea Power upon History,» etc.[1]

IN August, 1805, Nelson landed in England after a continuous absence of two years and three months. He remained twenty-five days, and then again departed, to die at Trafalgar. This short interval was all that the pressing exigencies of the times allowed him to spend with those who were dearest to him in the world—the woman he loved with undiminished fervor, and the only child he had. Brief as it was, it succeeded a period of tumultuous cruising and anxious care in the Mediterranean, during which, as he noted in his private diary, for more than two years he never went on shore; yet, although from the enfeebled condition of his health, always delicate, he for a great part of the time had in his hands permission to return to England, he could not bring himself to use it while any near prospect existed of the enemy's putting

[1] This is the last paper of a series by the same author, the others being, «Nelson at Cape St. Vincent,» «Nelson in the Battle of the Nile,» and «The Battle of Copenhagen.»

RESTORED AND PHOTOGRAPHED BY HENRY F. BRION, LONDON.

MODEL OF THE «VICTORY» FLYING THE SIGNAL «ENGLAND EXPECTS EVERY MAN WILL DO HIS DUTY.»

to sea. The passion which had swept before it all other obstacles was powerless to drag his frail and suffering body from the post of painful duty to the comforts of home.

The armed struggle between Great Britain, single-handed, and France in alliance with Holland and Spain was then approaching its crisis. Since the declaration of war, May 16, 1803, Napoleon had given his great energies to the preparations for an invasion of England with an army of one hundred and fifty thousand men. In July, 1805, these were collected on the coasts of France over against Dover, ready to embark at a moment's warning upon the approach of the great fleet of thirty-five ships of the line, French and Spanish, which the emperor, with profound wiliness and sagacity, was concentrating from various quarters to cover the crossing. A series of untoward circumstances, and the irresolution of its admiral, Villeneuve, brought that great fleet, not to the Channel, but to Cadiz, whence it issued again only two days before Trafalgar. On the 19th of August, at 9 P. M., Lord Nelson's flag, the symbol of his command, was hauled down at Spithead, and he left the *Victory*, the ship at the masthead of which it had so long flown. On the afternoon of the 20th, Villeneuve brought the Franco-Spanish fleet into Cadiz. This marked, in Napoleon's judgment, the failure of the scheme of invasion; but to Great Britain it remained no less imperative than before to crush the allied fleet as the sure seal and gage of future safety. There was but one man to whom with perfect confidence the heart of the nation turned as surely able to save it; upon him it called, and

DRAWN BY WARREN SHEPPARD. ENGRAVED BY JOHN W. EVANS.

A SHIP OF THE LINE UNDER FULL SAIL.

DRAWN FROM LIFE BY JOHN WHICHELO, IN SEPTEMBER, 1805, AT MERTON. OWNED BY SIR W. BIDDULPH PARKER.

PORTRAIT OF NELSON.

he, not unwilling, yet with sad foreboding, obeyed.

«At half-past ten,» wrote Nelson in his diary for September 13, «drove from dear dear Merton, where I left all which I hold dear in this world, to go to serve my King and Country. May the great God whom I adore enable me to fulfil the expectations of my Country; and if it is His good pleasure that I should return, my thanks will never cease being offered up to the throne of His mercy. If it is His good providence to cut short my days upon earth, I bow with the greatest submission, relying that He will protect those so dear to me that I may leave behind. His will be done! Amen, amen, amen.»

At two o'clock the next afternoon he embarked in a boat at Portsmouth to return on board the *Victory*. He had sought an unfrequented landing-place to elude the crowd, but one collected, nevertheless, «pressing forward to obtain sight of his face. Many were in tears, and many knelt down before him and blessed him as he passed.» With softened feelings, still fresh from his recent parting, Nelson was visibly moved. «I had their huzzas before,» said he to his old comrade in arms, Captain Hardy, who sat beside him; «I have their hearts now!» «On the 14th,» reads the *Victory's* log, «hoisted the flag of the Right Honourable Lord Viscount Nelson, K. B. Sunday, 15th, weighed, and made sail to the S. S. E.» (for Cadiz).

On the 28th of September the *Victory* joined the fleet before Cadiz, which to the number of twenty-nine ships of the line had been rapidly collected under Admiral Collingwood after Villeneuve entered the port. By Nelson's orders none of the customary salutes were exchanged, it being his object to keep the enemy, as far as possible, ignorant both of his own arrival and of the force that they might have to encounter, lest they might hesitate to come out. For the same reason the main body of the British fleet was kept fifty miles west of the port; but between the latter and it there were spaced three subdivisions, the innermost of which, composed of frigates and other lighter vessels, kept within sight of the enemy, watching every indication. Despite these precautions, however, Villeneuve could not fail ultimately to hear of Nelson's coming, and the number of his fleet, which gradually rose to thirty-three, of which twenty-seven only were present when the battle was fought. The French admiral despaired of success; but learning that the emperor, dissatisfied with his previous conduct, was about to relieve him from command, and aware that malice attributed to him cowardice, when weakness only was his fault, he closed his eyes to all other considerations than that of wounded honor, and went forth to hopeless battle. The orders to the French fleet were to enter the Mediterranean and appear off the coast of Italy, where its presence was expected to favor the great campaign, then beginning, which is identified with the name of Austerlitz.

«The morning of the 19th of October,» wrote an eye-witness from the inshore squadron, «saw us so close to Cadiz as to see the ripple of the beach and catch the morning fragrance which came off the land; and then, as the sun rose over the Trocadero, with what joy we saw the fleet inside let fall and hoist their topsails, and one after another slowly emerge from the harbor's mouth!» The movement began at 7 A.M., but there were eighteen French and fifteen Spanish ships of the line, besides smaller vessels, to take part in it, and the operation is long and intricate for a body of sailing ships in a restricted harbor, especially with unskilled men, such as were many of the allies. At 9:30 Nelson knew that the movement was begun. «At this moment,» wrote the commander of the advanced frigates later in the day, «we are within four miles of the enemy, and talking to Lord Nelson by means of Sir H. Popham's signals, though so distant, but repeated along by the rest of the frigates of this squadron. The day is fine, the sight, of course, beautiful.» Nelson at once made signal for a «general chase southeast,» and the fleet moved off to the Straits of Gibraltar, to block the suspected purpose of the allies to enter there. On that day only twelve of the allied ships cleared the harbor.

The following morning, Sunday, October 20, the remainder got to sea. The wind and weather had changed. It now blew from the southwest with heavy rain, thick and squally. With the wind from this quarter the Franco-Spanish fleet could not clear the shoals off Cape Trafalgar, and it had therefore to steer to the northwest from Cadiz. In its movements it was closely dogged by the hostile frigates, the main body of the British being then near the Straits' mouth, between Cape Trafalgar and Cape Spartel, on the African coast. In this locality it continued to work back and forth, keeping out of the enemy's sight, but observing their movements warily by the lookout ships. At five in the evening Captain Blackwood, the commander of the frigate squadron, signaled that the allies seemed determined to go to the westward. «That they shall not do,» said Nelson in his diary, «if in the power of Nelson and Bronté to prevent them»; and he replied that he relied upon the frigates' keeping track of them during the night. «The last twenty-four hours,» wrote Blackwood next day to his wife, «have been hard and anxious work for me; but we have kept sight of them, and are this moment bearing up to come to action.»

On the evening of the 20th Nelson issued special orders. Two frigates were to keep the enemy in sight throughout the night. Between them and his flag-ship communication was maintained by a chain of four ships, duly spaced, which repeated signals from end to end. If the enemy steered in one direction two blue lights were burned together; if in the other, three guns were fired in rapid succession. Thus throughout the watchful night messages flashed back and forth over the waste of waters separating the hostile squadrons. From their tenor Nelson judged that the enemy sought to keep open their retreat upon Cadiz. He was therefore careful not to come near enough to them to be seen before daybreak. From twelve to fifteen miles was the distance between the two fleets.

October 21, the day of the battle, dawned hazy, with light airs from west-northwest, and a heavy swell, a token of the approaching gale which during the succeeding days wrought devastation among the prizes. Soon after daylight Nelson came on deck. It was noticed that he wore his usual service coat, on which were stitched the stars of four different orders won by him in battle, and which he always carried. His sword, contrary to his custom, he did not wear, probably by oversight. The hostile fleet was visible in the east-southeast, forming a long irregular column, distant ten or twelve miles, and heading to the southward. Cape Trafalgar lay in the same direction, about ten miles farther off. The place where the battle would be fought was therefore dangerously near the land, if the threatening gale fell upon ships crippled in the encounter.

The British were then under easy sail head-

ENGRAVED BY T. COLE. FROM THE PAINTING BY J. M. W. TURNER IN THE NATIONAL GALLERY, LONDON.

«THE FIGHTING ‹TÉMÉRAIRE› TUGGED TO HER LAST BERTH TO BE BROKEN UP.»

DRAWN BY WARREN SHEPPARD.

THE SPANISH AND FRENCH FLEETS WEARING SHIP.

DRAWN BY WARREN SHEPPARD.

THE «BELLEISLE» APPROACHING THE ENEMY'S LINE.

ing to the northward, nearly parallel to the enemy. At 6:30 were made in quick succession the signals to «form order of sailing in two columns» and to «prepare for battle.» Ten minutes later followed the decisive command to «bear up» for the enemy, steering east-northeast. The plan upon which the battle was to be engaged, and his own share in it, were perfectly understood by every flag-officer and captain in the fleet; for it was Nelson's practice to assemble them in his cabin, to explain both his general idea and the varying phases and conditions to which it might have to be applied, as far as he could foresee them. The general idea was to throw upon the rear twelve ships of the enemy a superior number—fifteen or sixteen—under the command of Admiral Collingwood, while Nelson himself, with the remainder of his force, would act as seemed best to prevent Collingwood being disturbed. The particular application in the battle was that the attacking fleet advanced in two columns perpendicular to the enemy's line, Collingwood assailing the rear as proposed, and Nelson piercing the hostile order a little forward of the center; so that the brunt of the fight fell on the twenty-three rear ships of the allies, the ten which formed the van being for a long time untouched, and themselves remaining inactive. There is reason to believe that Nelson would have preferred to attack in line instead of column, thus bringing his ships into action simultaneously, instead of one after another; but the wind was so light that invaluable time would have been consumed in the necessary manœuvers. Obedient to his unvarying principle, he would not give the enemy time which might possibly permit them to escape battle altogether; for Cadiz was not far distant, neither were the days long, and at their best the ships, with the breeze they had, were unable to make more than two to three miles an hour.

From the same cause—the faintness of the wind—the ships advanced under every stitch of canvas they could carry, even to studdingsails on both sides. Studdingsails, commonly pronounced «stu'n'sails,» are light sails of large spread hoisted outside of the ship, and which, when not in use, are not, like the principal sails, furled upon the yards, but gathered into the body of the vessel and stowed within her. They were rarely carried when going into action, but the urgent need to gain every foot of ground and moment of time necessitated their use at Trafalgar. The ships kept them set, if not shot away, up to the instant of reaching the enemy's line, and then, according to the exigency of each case, they were either taken in, or cut adrift and dropped overboard.

Six British ships were absent at Tetuan for water. The remaining twenty-seven, while still advancing, formed as best they could into two columns, separated by a distance of about a mile. On the left were twelve, led by Nelson's flag-ship, the *Victory;* on the right, Collingwood, in the *Royal Sovereign*, headed the remaining fifteen. The wind being from the west-northwest, the former body was to windward, and has therefore been commonly spoken of in contemporary accounts of the battle as the «weather line.» It was neither possible nor desirable, with the little wind, to form the columns with great precision, ship after ship. The vessels got forward as they could, sometimes sailing in pairs; and, in fact, the need of gaining time was so urgent that faster ships were in some instances ordered to leave their regular station, and approach the head of their column by passing their slower predecessors. The great point was to get the heads of the columns into action as soon as possible. As will appear, that was not accomplished until noon, while over two hours more elapsed before the rear ships came fairly under fire.

The allied commander-in-chief, Villeneuve, was of course watching the British movements. As their plan developed he saw that battle was inevitable; and knowing that, even if total defeat were avoided, there would still be many ships too crippled to admit of his entering the Mediterranean, he looked to the safety of their retreat. This could be made only upon Cadiz, some twenty miles to the north-northeast. He therefore ordered his fleet to wear (turn around from the wind), and form its line again, heading north. This would cause it gradually to bring Cadiz more and more under the lee. The manœuver, being executed simultaneously by the allied ships, reversed their order. Admiral Gravina, commander of the Spanish contingent, had been leading. His now became the rear ship, and it was upon his portion of the field that the brunt of Collingwood's attack was to fall.

Nelson could hardly have been unprepared for this step of Villeneuve's, but he viewed it with great concern. By it Gibraltar, the British port of refuge, became less accessible, the retreat of the allies more secure, and the perilous shoals off Cape Trafalgar more immediately to leeward. He had summoned the frigate captains on board the *Victory*, to be at hand to receive in person his last commands; for, the frigates not being in the fighting line, the character of services to be required of them was too varied to admit of being laid down long before. A close and practised observer of the weather, Nelson foresaw clearly the approaching gale. He expressed his uneasiness to Blackwood; and

DRAWN BY WARREN SHEPPARD.

THE «BELLEISLE» AFTER THE BATTLE.

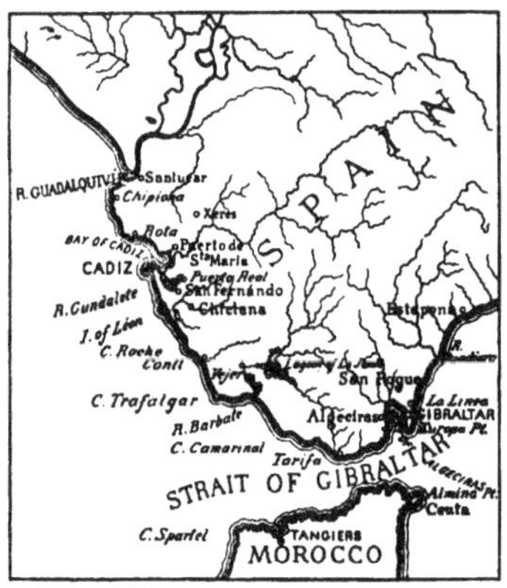


DRAWN BY A. VAN CLEEF.

WHERE THE BATTLE WAS FOUGHT.

the practical outcome was that just before the *Victory* came under fire the signal was made to be prepared to anchor immediately after the close of the day. But one more general signal followed: «Engage more closely.» With that flying the *Victory* disappeared into the smoke of battle.

The line of battle of the combined fleet was badly formed. Many of the captains were unskilful, and manœuvers were doubly difficult when wind so failed. Consequently, instead of a long and fairly straight line, in which the ships stood in close succession, each with its broadside clear to fire upon the enemy, the order assumed was that of a bow, or a crescent, with the horns toward the British. In many cases ships lay behind others, occasionally three deep, unable, therefore, to fire at the enemy except through their friends. On the other hand, British ships that entered at such points soon found themselves in a hornets' nest, and suffered severely from the successive and concentrated fires which they there underwent.

It was with these dispositions on each side that the battle was engaged, and it may here be added that Nelson's general plan received substantial fulfilment. Like Copenhagen, though from other causes, there were many variations in detail, and unlike Copenhagen, once the battle joined, it quickly passed into a confused mêlée, in which each captain acted on his own judgment, following simply the general directions before given by his commander-in-chief. How effective these were may be inferred from the fact that, of the sixteen rear ships of the allies, twelve were taken or destroyed. Of the six others captured, the principal loss fell upon the center. The place where the weight of the blow was struck, therefore, was that chosen by Nelson, but the manner of the striking he left perforce to the capable hands of his lieutenants.

Apart from its technical aspect, consequently, the living interest of the battle of Trafalgar centers upon the fortunes of the single ships, and upon the heroic figure of the British admiral, whose glorious career there terminated. Ever conspicuous and dazzling where dangers thickened, the light that at the last gathers round the closing hours of Nelson's life has lost nothing in intensity, while in radiancy and purity it has gained much. The flashing brilliancy of a star, which characterized the restless manifestations of his earlier course, gives place to the calm and settled effulgence of a sun that has run its race, triumphed over the storms that sought to obscure its shining, and now sinks to rest in a cloudless sky, secure that over the firmament of its glory neither evil chance nor lapse of time can henceforth throw a veil. The shadow of death, which hung over him with a darkness that he himself felt, softened and mellowed the vivacity natural to him, and imparted to his

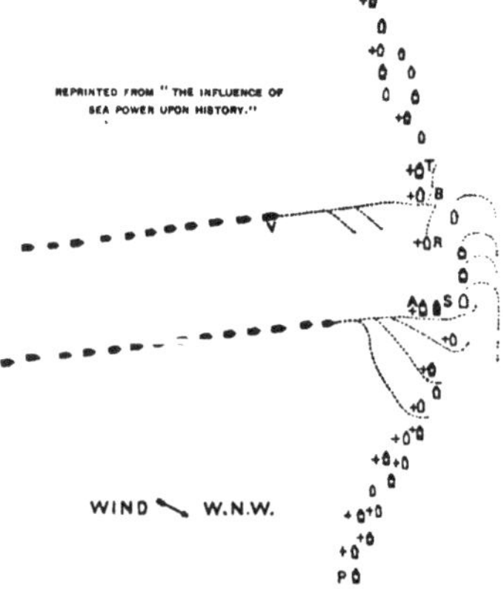


THE ATTACK AT TRAFALGAR
OCTOBER 21, 1805
FIVE MINUTES PAST NOON
BRITISH 27 SHIPS
FRENCH, 18 } 33 SHIPS
SPANISH, 15

whole bearing on that final day a solemnity, not uncheerful, yet impressive, that reflected, although without a trace of irresolution, the conscious resignation and self-devotion with which he went forward to his last battle.

The admiral in person, accompanied by the train of frigate captains, inspected the *Victory* and her preparations throughout all decks, ample time for the tour being permitted by the slowness of the advance. At 11 A. M. he was in his cabin, where the signal-lieutenant, entering to prefer a request of a personal nature, found him upon his knees writing; and it is believed that the following words, with which his private diary closes, were then penned: «May the great God whom I worship grant to my country, and for the benefit of Europe in general, a great and glorious victory; and may no misconduct in any one tarnish it; and may humanity after victory be the predominant feature in the British fleet. For myself individually, I commit my life to Him who made me; and may His blessing light upon my endeavours for serving my country faithfully. To Him I resign myself and the just cause which is entrusted to me to defend. Amen, amen, amen.»

DRAWN BY HOWARD PYLE.

THE MIZZENTOP OF THE «REDOUTABLE.»

After returning to the deck, Nelson asked Blackwood whether he did not think another signal was needed. The captain replied that he thought every one understood perfectly what was expected of him. After musing a while, Nelson said, «Suppose we telegraph that ‹Nelson expects every man to do his duty.›» The officer to whom the remark was made suggested whether it would not read better, «England expects.» In the fleet, or, for the matter of that, to the country, the change signified little, for no two names were ever more closely identified than those of England and Nelson; but the latter welcomed it eagerly, and at 11:30 the signal which has achieved world-wide celebrity flew from the *Victory's* masthead, and was received with a shout throughout the fleet.

The *Royal Sovereign*, Collingwood's flagship, leading the other column, had been recently coppered, and accordingly outstripped the *Victory*, although the latter was a fast ship. She was now about two miles distant to the southeast, a considerable interval separating her from the ship next behind in her own column—the *Belleisle*. At noon she was within range of the enemy, and the day's combat was opened by a French ship called the *Fougeux*, the nineteenth in the allied order counting from the van. At that moment, as though by signal, the ships of both fleets hoisted their colors, and the admirals their flags, a necessary yet chivalrous display, resembling the courteous salute which precedes a mortal combat. It has been said that Villeneuve's flag was not then hoisted, but the log of a British ship distinctly mentions that it was flying before the *Victory* opened fire. This she did not, and indeed could not, do until some time after the enemy had begun to fire at her. When the shots began to pass over, Nelson dismissed Blackwood and the captain of another frigate, who had till then remained, directing them to pull along the column, and tell the captains of the ships of the line that he depended on their exertions to close rapidly with the enemy, but that he left much to their discretion in the unforeseen contingencies that awaited them. As Blackwood took his hand to say good-by, he said, «I trust that on my return to the *Victory* I shall find your lordship well, and in possession of twenty prizes.» To this Nelson replied, «God bless you, Blackwood; I shall never speak to you again.»

PAINTED BY A. W. DEVIS. IN THE PAINTED HALL, GREENWICH COLLEGE.

THE DEATH OF NELSON.

The *Royal Sovereign* advanced in silence under a fire which centered upon her alone for a measurable time, until some of it was drawn off by the *Belleisle*. Nelson watched her with emulous and admiring eyes, ungrudging of her glory. «See how that noble fellow Collingwood takes his ship into action!» he cried. Beside Collingwood stood his flag-captain, Rotherham, between whom and himself there had been bad blood till Nelson in person had reconciled them a few days before. As the *Royal Sovereign* drew up with a Spanish three-decker—the *Santa Ana*, of 112 guns—to pierce the hostile array between her and the *Fougeux*, and open the day for the British, Collingwood, in keen sympathy with the old and tried friend he should never again see alive, made the like remark: «Rotherham, what would Nelson give to be here!» An instant later the guns of the port (left-hand) batteries were fired in rapid succession, as the ship's measured advance brought them to bear, pouring a double-shotted broadside into the *Santa Ana's* stern, raking her fore and aft, and striking down, by Spanish accounts, four hundred of the thousand men that manned her decks. The starboard guns were at the same time discharged at the *Fougeux*, but, being from a greater distance, with less effect. The *Royal Sovereign*, putting her helm over as she fired, now ranged up alongside the *Santa Ana* so closely that the muzzles of the guns of the two ships nearly touched. A desperate duel then ensued, much to the disadvantage of the *Santa Ana*, already dazed by the fearful first blow; but round the *Royal Sovereign* were grouped four other hostile ships, from which issued such storms of shot that it is reported they were often seen to strike together in mid-air.

For some minutes the *Royal Sovereign* was alone engaged, but before long the *Belleisle*, a large two-decker of eighty guns, came to her relief. As one of the ships most severely handled on this day, losing all her masts, the dry, brief, jerky remarks of her log possess interest; and they are typical, as by family likeness, of the experiences common to most in such a scene. «At 12:05 opened our fire on the enemy; 12:13, cut the enemy's line astern of a French 80-gun ship, second to the Spanish rear-admiral's ship (*Santa Ana*), at the same time keeping up a heavy fire on both sides; 12:40, our maintopmast was shot away. At 1 a great ship bore up to rake us, and a ship on each side engaging us. At 1:10 the mizzenmast went six feet above the deck. At 1:20 the enemy's ship on our starboard side sheered off; at 1:30 the enemy's ship which had laid itself athwart our stern placed herself on our larboard quarter; at the same time a fresh ship ranged up at our starboard side. Kept up a heavy fire on them as we could get our guns to bear, the ship being lately unmanageable, most of her rigging and sails being shot. At 2:10 the mainmast went by the board;[1] at 2:30 an enemy's ship placed herself across our starboard bow; at 2:40 the foremast and bowsprit went by the board, still engaging three of the enemy's ships; 3:15, one of our ships passed our bow and took off the fire of one of the enemy's ships laying there. At 3:20 the enemy's ship on our starboard side was engaged by one of our ships. At 3:25 the *Swiftsure* passed our stern, and cheered us, and commenced firing on the enemy, and into the enemy's ship on our larboard quarter. Ceased firing, and turned the hands up to clear the wreck. Sent a boat and took possession of the Spanish 80-gun ship *Argonaut*. The action still continuing general, cut away the wreck fore and aft. . . . At 8 P. M. mustered the ship's company; found killed in battle two lieutenants, one midshipman, and thirty-one seamen and marines, and ninety-four seamen and marines wounded.»

But we have also of the *Belleisle* one of those too rare personal accounts which let us into the human interest of such a scene. The writer [2] was a lieutenant of marines, only sixteen years old, and had but just joined the ship when called to pass through this fierce ordeal.

«As the day dawned the horizon appeared covered with ships. I was awakened by the cheers of the crew, and by their rushing up the hatchways to get a glimpse of the hostile fleet. The delight manifested exceeded anything I ever witnessed, surpassing even those gratulations when our native cliffs are descried after a long period of distant service. At nine we were about six miles from them, with studdingsails set on both sides. The officers now met at breakfast, and though each seemed to exult in the hope of a glorious termination to the contest so near at hand, a fearful presage was experienced that all would not again unite at that festive board. One was particularly impressed with a persuasion that he should not survive the day.[3] The sound of the drum, however, soon put an end to our meditations, and after a hasty, and, alas! a final farewell to some, we repaired to our respective posts. Our ship's station was far astern of our leader, but her superior sailing caused an interchange of places with the *Tonnant*. On our passing that ship, the captains greeted each other on the honourable prospect in view. Captain Tyler (*Tonnant*) exclaimed: ‹A glorious day for old England! We shall have one apiece before night!› As if in confirmation of this soul-inspiring sentiment, the band of our consort was playing ‹Britons, strike home!›

«The drum now repeated its summons, and the captain sent for the officers commanding at their several quarters. ‹Gentlemen,› said he, ‹I have only to say that I shall pass close under the stern of that ship; put in two round shot and then a grape, and give her *that*. Now go to your quarters, and mind not to fire until each gun will bear with effect.› With this laconic instruction, the gallant little man posted himself on the slide of the foremost carronade on the starboard side of the quarter-deck.

«From the peculiar formation of this part of the enemy's line, as many as ten ships brought their broadside to bear with powerful effect. The determined and resolute coun-

[1] Close to the deck.

[2] Lieutenant Paul Harris Nicolas. The account was published in 1829.

[3] This officer, first lieutenant of the ship, was killed.

tenance of the weather-beaten sailors, here and there brightened by a smile of exultation, was well suited to the terrific appearance which they exhibited. Some were stripped to the waist; some had bared their necks and arms; others had tied a handkerchief round their heads; and all seemed eagerly to await the order to engage. The shot began to pass over us, and gave us an intimation of what we should in a few minutes undergo. An awful silence prevailed in the ship, only interrupted by the commanding voice of Captain Hargood, ‹Steady! starboard a little! steady so!›[1] echoed by the master directing the quartermasters at the wheel. A shriek soon followed, a cry of agony was produced by the next shot, and the loss of a head of a poor recruit was the effect of the succeeding; and as we advanced destruction rapidly increased.

«It was just twelve o'clock when we reached their line. Our energies became roused and the mind diverted from its appalling condition by the order of ‹Stand to your guns!› which, as they successively came to bear, were discharged into our opponents on either side. Although until that moment we had not fired a shot, our sails and rigging bore evident proofs of the manner in which we had been treated; our mizzentopmast was shot away, and the ensign had thrice been rehoisted. The firing was now tremendous, and at intervals the dispersion of the smoke gave us a sight of the colors of our adversaries.

«At this critical period, while steering for the stern of the *Indomptable*, which continued a most galling raking fire upon us, the *Fougeux* being on our starboard quarter and the Spanish *San Justo* on our larboard bow, the master earnestly addressed the captain: ‹Shall we go through, sir?› ‹Go through, by ——!› was his energetic reply. ‹There 's your ship, sir; place me close alongside of her.› Our opponent defeated this manœuver by bearing away in a parallel course with us, within pistol-shot.

«About one o'clock the *Fougeux* ran us on board on the starboard side, and we continued thus engaging till the latter dropped astern. Our mizzenmast soon went, and soon afterward the maintopmast. A two-decked ship, the *Neptune*,[2] 80, then took a position on our bow, and a 74, the *Achille*, on our quarter. At two o'clock the mainmast fell over our larboard side; I was at the time under the break of the poop aiding in running out a carronade, when a cry of ‹Stand clear there! here it comes!› made me look up, and at that instant the mainmast fell over the bulwarks just above me. This ponderous mass made the ship's whole frame shake, and had it taken a central direction it would have gone through the poop and added many to our list of sufferers. At half-past two our foremast was shot away close to the deck.

«In this unmanageable state we were but seldom capable of annoying our antagonists, while they had the power of choosing their distance, and every shot from them did considerable execution. Until half-past three we remained in this harassing situation. At this hour a three-decked ship was seen apparently steering toward us; it can easily be imagined with what anxiety every eye turned towards this formidable object, which would either relieve us from our unwelcome neighbors or render our situation desperate. We had scarcely seen the British colors since one o'clock, and it is impossible to express our emotion as the alteration of the stranger's course displayed the white ensign to our sight. Soon the *Swiftsure* came nobly to our relief. Can any enjoyment in life be compared with the sensation of delight and thankfulness which such a deliverance produced? On ordinary occasions we contemplate the grandeur of a ship under sail with admiration; but under impressions of danger and excitement such as prevailed at this crisis every one eagerly looked toward our approaching friend, who came speedily on, and when within hail manned the rigging, cheered, and then boldly steered for the ship which had so long annoyed us.

«Before sunset all firing had ceased. The view of the fleet at this period was highly interesting, and would have formed a beautiful subject for a painter. Just under the setting rays were five or six dismantled prizes; on one hand lay the *Victory* with part of our fleet and prizes, and on the left hand the *Sovereign* and a similar cluster of ships; the remnant of the combined fleet was making for Cadiz to the northward; the *Achille* had burned to the water's edge, with the tricolored ensign still displayed, about a mile from us, and our tenders and boats were using every effort to save the brave fellows who had so gloriously defended her; but only two hundred and fifty were rescued, and she blew up with a tremendous explosion.»

The *Royal Sovereign* suffered even more severely than did her successor, the *Belleisle*. Her loss in men was forty-seven killed and ninety-four wounded, and although one of

[1] Orders for steering.

[2] There were three *Neptunes* at Trafalgar—one French, one Spanish, and one British.

her masts was still standing when the battle ceased, it was so tottering as to fall within twenty-four hours. It is, in fact, inseparable from all attacks in column, whether on sea or land, that the leading ships or men take the brunt of the punishment, while their followers, coming in fresh upon the havoc they have wrought or sustained, reap the fruits of the victory of which the seed has been sown by the former. This was more especially true in the days of sailing ships, because, their artillery being necessarily disposed along their sides, they had no offensive power directly ahead; nor was it practicable to support them, as a shore column often could be, by a flank cannonade before and during its advance. At Trafalgar the leaders underwent the greater injury because the sluggish breeze made the rear ships slow in coming to their aid. So it was that on the left the *Victory* and her next astern, the *Téméraire*, shared the experience of the *Royal Sovereign* and the *Belleisle*, with results the same in broad outline, but so far differing in detail as to afford themes of novel interest and peculiar excitement.

About twenty minutes after the *Fougeux* had opened upon the *Royal Sovereign*, the *Bucentaure*, Villeneuve's flag-ship, fired at the *Victory* a shot which fell short. This trial for range was repeated at intervals till the fifth or sixth shot, passing through one of the upper sails, showed the enemy that she was under their guns. Seven or eight ships then opened a tremendous cannonade concentrated upon this single vessel bearing the flag of the hostile commander-in-chief, which was powerless to reply. Nelson's secretary was killed near him among the first, all the studdingsails were stripped from the yards, and by the time the *Victory* reached the enemy her sails were riddled; but though the result could not but be to deaden her already slow progress, and though she lost fifty killed and wounded before able to return a gun, she was not stopped, nor were her powers of offense seriously impaired. When still five hundred yards from the enemy her mizzentopmast and her wheel were knocked away, and another shot passed between Captain Hardy and Nelson. The latter smiled, and said, «This is too warm work, Hardy, to last long.» At about 1 P. M. her hour of vengeance arrived.

Nelson, in his instructions to his captains, had laid particular stress upon the speedy reduction and capture of the enemy's commander-in-chief, and, following precept by example, he now aimed to make her the special antagonist of the *Victory*. Unexpected difficulties prevented. The two allied ships behind the *Bucentaure* had dropped to leeward, leaving an open space in which, though commanded by their guns, the *Victory* might have found room to manœuver, and to place Nelson alongside of Villeneuve; but the third ship, the *Redoutable*, 74, Captain Lucas, pressed into the place left by them, obtaining thus a position which, by the gallantry displayed alike in taking and holding it, has given to her and her commander a renown second to none achieved on that day of so many heroic deeds and so much heroic endurance. Thus were three ships crowded together behind and on the far side of the *Bucentaure*, while the *Santisima Trinidad*, a huge four-decked ship of 120 guns, immediately ahead of her, throwing her sails aback, drew nearer her there. To use the vivid phrase of the naval historian James, the French and Spanish ships ahead of the *Victory* «closed like a forest.»

Nelson was walking the quarter-deck when Captain Hardy, who directed the *Victory's* steering, told him it was impossible to pass through the line without running into one of the three ships there assembled. «I cannot help it,» replied the admiral. «Go on board which you please; take your choice.» At one o'clock the bows of the *Victory* reached the wake of the *Bucentaure*, the British ship passing within thirty feet, a projecting yard-arm grazing the enemy's rigging. One after another, as they bore, the double-shotted guns tore through the timbers of the French ship, the smoke, driven back, filling the lower decks of the *Victory*, while persons on the upper deck, including Nelson himself, were covered with the dust which rose in clouds from the wreck. As, from the relative positions of the two ships, the shot ranged from end to end of the *Bucentaure*, the injury was tremendous. Twenty guns were dismounted, and the loss by that single discharge was estimated by the French at four hundred men. Leaving the further care of the French flag-ship to her followers, the *Victory* put her helm up, inclining to the right, and ran on board the *Redoutable*, whose guns, as well as those of the French *Neptune*, had been busily playing upon her while she was dealing with the *Bucentaure*. At 1:10 P. M. the *Victory* lay along the port (left) side of the *Redoutable*, the two ships falling off with their heads to the eastward, and moving slowly before the wind to the east-southeast.

The *Téméraire*, 98, a three-decked ship, had followed close on the heels of the

*Victory*. The movements of the latter, and the other exigencies of the situation, had compelled her to keep more and more to the right, so that she passed through the enemy's line somewhat to the rear of the place pierced by the *Victory*, amid a heavy cannonade, and in a cloud of smoke. Here she endeavored, in accordance with the general instructions sent by Nelson through Blackwood, to haul up to the left. A slight lifting of the smoke showed her the *Redoutable* on her port side, and after a few minutes' cannonading, in which some of the *Téméraire's* spars went overboard, the two ships, now virtually ungovernable, fell together, so that the little *Redoutable*, with her colors still flying in defiance, lay between the *Victory* on her left side and the *Téméraire* on her right, the three lashed together.

The contest seemed, and was, most unequal; yet the little French vessel possessed a means of offense in which her two adversaries were deficient. The French ships, imperfectly manned with seamen, carried many soldiers, and their musketry fire was comparatively heavy. They also stationed many musketeers and men with hand-grenades aloft—in the tops—a practice to which Nelson was averse. Therefore, although the *Redoutable* could oppose but feeble resistance below decks, and received such injuries to the hull that she sank in the gale of the following day, on the upper deck her small-arm fire dominated that of both antagonists. Thus it was that Nelson met his death. He was pacing the quarter-deck side by side with Captain Hardy, the two officers having just then little to do but to await the issue of the strife raging round them. At 1:25 they were walking from aft, and were within one pace of the forward end of their short promenade, when Nelson suddenly faced left about and fell to his knees, his left hand touching the deck. Hardy hastened to him, expressing the hope that he was not much hurt. «They have done for me at last,» replied the admiral; «my backbone is shot through.» The fatal ball had come from the mizzentop of the *Redoutable*. He was carried below, where he lingered for a little over three hours, receiving before his death the assurance of a decisive victory.

Nelson fell a few moments before the *Téméraire* and the *Redoutable* came together. So destructive was the fire which claimed him as its greatest victim that the upper deck of the *Victory* was almost deserted. Captain Lucas, noticing this, conceived the bold idea of carrying his opponent by boarding. A large part of the French crew, with their cutlasses and pistols, assembled for that purpose along the side engaged; but it was found impossible to pass, because the upper parts of the ships, being narrower than the lower, were by the latter kept too far apart to permit men to leap across. An attempt was made to use as a bridge the main-yard of the *Redoutable*, which either had fallen or was lowered for the purpose; but the British improved the respite to gather a party from their lower decks to repel the attack. A sharp musketry skirmish followed, which cost the *Victory* forty killed and wounded, including several officers; but the enemy was forced to retire.

At this moment occurred the collision between the *Téméraire* and the *Redoutable*. The latter was swept by the fire of her new heavy antagonist, which, being nearly raking, struck down near two hundred of her already desolated crew. Nevertheless, the fire from aloft continued so galling that Captain Harvey of the *Téméraire* ordered his men below to escape injury and to concentrate their effort on the great guns, which the weaker vessel could not expect long to resist.

Still, among the fluctuating fortunes of the day, neither hope nor chance had yet wholly forsaken the dauntless though well-nigh prostrate *Redoutable*. The *Fougeux*, which had opened the fire upon Collingwood, had afterward stood slowly north, crossing the space separating the allied rear and center. Seeing the *Téméraire* before her, she shaped her course with the apparent intention of either raking or boarding that already crippled ship. But the latter had as yet had no occasion to use her starboard broadside, on which the *Fougeux* threatened her, the *Redoutable* being on the other. The starboard guns, therefore, were manned under charge of her first lieutenant, the captain continuing to devote his attention to the *Redoutable*. When the *Fougeux* approached within a hundred yards, incautiously confiding, perhaps, in the preoccupation of her intended victim, she received the full force of a nearly fresh broadside. The crash was by the British described as terrible, and the *Fougeux*, in confusion, ran on board of the *Téméraire*, where she was immediately lashed. A small party of boarders sprang upon the French vessel, and after a short contest she was taken into possession. Her captain had been mortally wounded by the broadside.

Thus was decided this singular encounter, in the midst of which England's greatest sea-captain met his fate. While these exciting events were occurring about him, Nelson's life was rapidly ebbing away in the cockpit of the *Victory*. Nothing could be done for the glorious sufferer but to ease the pain and thirst which harassed him, and to bring him assurance from time to time that the fortunes of the day were with Great Britain. He was from the first hopeless of recovery, nor did the surgeon, after examination, mock him with vain assurances. «You know I am gone,» said the admiral to him. «My lord,» replied he, with a noble and courteous simplicity, «unhappily for our country, nothing can be done for you.» «I know it,» said Nelson. «God be praised, I have done my duty.»

For a few minutes the four ships, *Victory*, *Redoutable*, *Téméraire*, and *Fougeux*, lay side by side; but about 2:15 the *Victory* shoved herself clear, getting her head to the northward, while the other three drifted off in the other direction. The main- and mizzenmasts of the *Redoutable* fell almost immediately. A lieutenant, with a few men, crossed from the *Téméraire* to her by one of these impromptu bridges, and took quiet possession of a ship already beaten, but whose heroic efforts, second to none in naval annals, have linked her name enduringly, if mournfully, with that of the greatest of seamen. Her loss was, by the French official returns, stated to be three hundred killed and two hundred and twenty-two wounded, out of a total of six hundred and forty-three.

The fate of the *Bucentaure*, the flag-ship of the allied fleet, was decided at about the same moment. The results of the *Victory's* attack upon her have been mentioned. The ships following in the column obeyed Nelson's injunction to concentrate their efforts on the capture of the enemy's commander-in-chief. The *Téméraire* had been unable to do so, but the *Neptune* (British) at 1:45 passed close under the *Bucentaure's* stern. Her broadside, raking like that of the *Victory*, brought down the French main- and mizzenmasts. To the *Neptune* succeeded the *Leviathan*, which raked at a distance of thirty yards. Upon the *Leviathan* followed the *Conqueror*, which, after raking, hauled up on the lee side of the crushed vessel, and in a few minutes shot away the one remaining mast. Twenty minutes of careful concentration had reduced the *Bucentaure* to absolute helplessness. Villeneuve, a man of gallant but dejected spirit, who had undergone the disasters of the day with the same hopelessness that had characterized him throughout the campaign, looked sadly upon the scene of ruin and desolation about him. «The task of the *Bucentaure* is fulfilled,» said he; «mine is not yet finished;» and he ordered a boat manned to carry him to one of the vessels in the van which, still unharmed, had viewed with strange apathy and inaction the destruction of their comrades. But no boat was left that could swim, and his brave resolve could not receive fulfilment. At 2:05 the *Bucentaure* struck to the *Conqueror*. The *Santísima Trinidad*, next ahead, lost her three masts within the next thirty minutes, and although not taken possession of for some hours, was thenceforth virtually at the mercy of the British.

This, at 2:30 P.M., completed the ruin of the allied center, its other ships having gradually moved to the assistance of the rear. The contest there was more prolonged, a much greater number of the allied ships, first and last, taking part in it. Although in that quarter occurred the heaviest of the struggle and the most copious fruits of their victory were reaped by the British, no attempt will be made to present in further detail the course of the fight there; for to do so would be but to repeat, though with much variety of incident, the fortunes of the *Belleisle* and the *Royal Sovereign*, the *Victory* and the *Téméraire*, the *Redoutable* and the *Bucentaure*.

Yet, before quitting this part of the subject, it may receive further interesting illustration from the log of a ship which for long viewed from the outside, and undisturbed, the events of which inside accounts of participants have been quoted. The *Spartiate*, 74, was the rear ship in Nelson's column, and the failing wind left her out of action, gliding imperceptibly forward, until nearly two hours after the *Victory* entered upon it. The following brief memoranda of incidents observed will, with but slight effort of the imagination, convey to the reader a striking picture of the vivid scene, which must have horne no faint resemblance to the felling of a forest:

«At 12:25 H. M. ship *Victory* commenced firing at a ship ahead of her, she then bearing down on the *Santissima Trinidada* and a French two-decker with a flag at the fore. 12:30, the *Tonnant* lost her foretopmast and main-yard. 12:31, the *Victory* lost her mizzentopmast. 12:33, a Spanish two-decker struck to the *Tonnant*. 12:45, a Spanish two-decker's mizzenmast fell. 12:51, the *Santa Anna* struck to the *Royal Sovereign*, she then making sail ahead to the next ship. 1:02, the *Téméraire* lost her maintopmast. 1:05, the *Santa Anna* rolled overboard all her lower masts. 1:15, observed the *Tonnant* had wore, and had lost her maintopmast, an enemy's ship being on board her on the quarter. 1:25, observed a Spanish two-decker, who was engaged by the *Neptune*, lose her main and mizzen masts. 1:51, observed *Santissima Trinidada's* main and mizzen masts go by the board, then engaged by the *Neptune* and *Conqueror*. 1:56, the Spanish two-decker, which had struck to the *Neptune*, lost her foremast and bowsprit. 2:03, the *San Trinidada* lost her foremast and bowsprit. 2:06, the *Royal Sovereign* lost her main and mizzen masts. 2:11, one of the enemy's two-deckers lost her main and mizzen masts. 2:23, cut away our lower and topmast studdingsails, observing the van of the enemy's ships had wore to form a junction with their center.» With this last entry the *Spartiate's* own share in the battle began.

The heads of the British columns had dashed themselves to pieces against the overpowering number of foes which opposed their passage. An analysis of the returns shows that upon the four ships which led—the *Victory* and the *Téméraire*, the *Royal Sovereign* and the *Belleisle*—fell one third of the entire loss in a fleet of twenty-seven sail. But by this sacrifice they had shattered and pulverized the local resistance, destroyed the coherence of the hostile order, and opened the way for the successful action of their followers. With the appearance of the latter upon the scene, succeeded shortly by the approach of the allied van, but too late, and in disorder, began what may be called the second and final phase of the battle.

Before the *Bucentaure* struck, Villeneuve had seen that his van was quiescent, instead of initiating the prompt steps necessary to retrieve the day, by coming betimes to the aid of the center and rear, against which it was already apparent that the weight of the British effort was to be thrown. The thought must arise whether his mind did not then revert to the catastrophe of the Nile, and his own passivity under circumstances not dissimilar, which had drawn upon him the severe reproach of a brother admiral there engaged. Be that as it may, he shortly before two o'clock made a signal, duly repeated by the attendant frigates, that «the ships which were not engaged should take the positions which would bring them most rapidly under fire.» The lightness of the breeze made it difficult for the van ships to turn round and move toward the center and rear, whither both the signal and the call of honor imperatively summoned them; but by using their boats their heads were got in the right direction before 2:30. By an inconceivable fatality, however, they did not keep together. Five passed to leeward of the line of battle, and five to windward; with the latter division being Rear-Admiral Dumanoir, the commander of the van.

The two divisions, being thus separated, met with different antagonists and different fortunes. As the farthest ships could not have been much over a mile from the *Bucentaure*, half an hour sufficed, even with the flickering breeze, to bring most of them to that part of the field where lay the shattered and glorious relics of the fight. As has before been said, several of the allied center had fallen to leeward, and not being able to regain their true positions, had made the best of their way to the rear to support their comrades in that quarter. To this is partly due the fact that Collingwood's column met much heavier resistance and loss than did Nelson's.[1] The rear ships of the latter, with two exceptions, had reached their disabled predecessors before Dumanoir's squadron put about. Passing through the line of wrecks, they fell in to leeward with the ships of the allied van that passed on that side, and captured two of them.

When Dumanoir's five other ships showed their purpose of passing to windward, the British *Minotaur* and *Spartiate* had not yet come up with the *Victory*—that is, they were still to windward of the field of battle. It is advisable here to mention that when a ship has lost her masts she no longer drifts to leeward as fast as she did; and, besides, the movement of the vessels in the mêlée would necessarily tend rather to leeward than to windward. From these causes it resulted that the dismantled ships—the *Victory* and the *Royal Sovereign* among them—lay to windward of most of their consorts, who were still under sail, and were specially threatened by the approach of these five fresh ships. At this moment Captain Hardy saw Nelson for the first time after he received his wound. «They shook hands affectionately, and Lord Nelson said, ‹Well, Hardy, how goes the battle? How goes the day with us?› ‹Very well, my lord,› replied Captain Hardy; ‹we have got twelve or fourteen of the enemy's ships in our possession; but five of their van have tacked, and show an intention of bearing down upon the *Victory*. I have therefore

[1] The heavier loss of Collingwood's column was also due to the fact that his ships distributed their efforts more widely, whereas Nelson's concentrated their efforts upon the hostile flag-ship and her two seconds. The comparative losses may be stated thus: in force, Collingwood's was to Nelson's as 5 to 4; in total loss it was as 8.2 to 4; in killed alone as 7.2 to 4.

called two or three of our fresh ships around us, and have no doubt of giving them a drubbing.› ‹I hope,› said his lordship, ‹none of *our* ships have struck, Hardy.› ‹No, my lord,› replied Captain Hardy; ‹there is no fear of that.›»

The *Spartiate* and the *Minotaur* were two of the fresh ships of which Hardy spoke. They were in a sense old comrades, having been near neighbors at the battle of the Nile, where the *Spartiate* was taken from the French. The two now hauled close to the wind, to cover the *Victory* and her disabled companions,—consorts and prizes,—and hove to (stopped), with their maintopsails to the mast and their heads to the northward, between Nelson and Dumanoir. As the latter's division went by on the opposite tack, steering to the southward, a sharp cannonade followed, in which the *Victory* joined. «Oh, *Victory, Victory!*» said the dying admiral, as he felt the concussion of the guns, «how you distract my poor brain!» and added, «How dear is life to all men!» Four of the allied ships passed without serious injury, and continued to sea to the southwest. A few days later they were all taken by a British squadron which had had no share in Trafalgar. The *Minotaur* and the *Spartiate* succeeded in cutting off the fifth ship,—the Spanish *Neptuno*, 80,—and she was added to the list of prizes.

The *Neptuno* struck at 5:15, after a gallant defense, in which were shot away her mizzenmast and fore and main topmasts—a loss which left her helpless. Fifteen minutes later firing had ceased altogether: the battle was over. Eighteen ships had struck their colors to the British, one of which—the French *Achille*—was then in a blaze, and at 5:45 blew up. With her went many of her crew, despite the efforts of British boats to save them. Four ships had escaped with Dumanoir. Admiral Gravina, the senior Spanish officer, was by Villeneuve's capture left in command of the allies. His ship, the *Principe de Asturias*, had been desperately assailed and had fought desperately. Her loss was forty-one killed and one hundred and seven wounded, among them being Gravina himself, who lost his arm, and afterward died from the effects of the amputation. She now retreated upon Cadiz with a signal flying to rally round her flag. Ten ships—five French and five Spanish—accompanied her. These eleven only, of the thirty-three that had sailed two days before, again saw a friendly port. None of those which returned to Cadiz ever went to sea again during that war.

Three years later, in 1808, the Spaniards rose in revolt against Napoleon's attempt to impose a French sovereign upon them. With that struggle we have no present concern; but one of its earliest incidents was the enforced surrender of the French ships that had taken refuge in Cadiz after Trafalgar.

Nelson's spirit had departed before the last guns of the battle had been fired, but not before he knew the probable extent of the victory. He died at half-past four o'clock, his last audible words being, «Thank God, I have done my duty.» These he had frequently repeated, making, said the medical eye-witness, every now and then a greater effort, and with evident increase of pain, to utter them distinctly.

Other men have died in the hour of victory, but to no other has victory so singular and so signal stamped the fulfilment and completion of a great life's work. «*Finis coronat opus*» has of no man been more true than of Nelson. Results momentous and stupendous were to flow from the annihilation of all sea power except that of Great Britain, which was Nelson's great achievement; but his part was done when Trafalgar was fought, and his death in the moment of completed success has obtained for that superb victory an immortality of fame which even its own grandeur could scarcely have insured.

*A. T. Mahan.*

## A DARK DAY.

GLOOM of a leaden sky,
  Too heavy for Hope to move;
Grief in my heart to vie
  With the dark distress above;
Yet happy, happy am I,
  For I sorrow with her I love.

*Robert Underwood Johnson.*

# OUR WITCH.

WITH PICTURES BY JAY HAMBIDGE.

What are these . . .
That look not like the inhabitants o' the earth,
And yet are on 't? —*Macbeth.*

WITCHES—those, I mean, that were visible, tangible, and liable to be caught at their practices—were scarce in the extreme South. Warm weather or something else discouraged immigration. Now and then an old early settler who was posted on their history was not quite sure in his mind but that ghosts of a few flitted about of nights, playing their pranks, though not to a very alarming degree. Relief of its kind was derived from the generally accorded fact that their visitations were confined to those of their own sex, and consisted in knotting manes and tails of mares, drying up milch cows, ruffling the feathers of setting hens, and spreading nightmares over the breasts of honest women who, after hearty suppers richly deserved for hard days' work, went to their beds never dreaming, until fast asleep, what was coming. Preventives were used by those who were apprehensive of such molestings of their premises. The one regarded most reliable was a meal-sieve (called sifter) hung on the outside of doors. The argument ran thus: From the very beginning of the institution of witches, one of the fixed rules of their discipline was that, when confronted by this useful domestic implement, they were to go in and out of every one of its openings before proceeding farther. Pausing to calculate that such continuous up-and-down, right-and-left movement over and through a limited circular plane, on, above, and beneath which were few objects to interest a traveler, might not be completed before daybreak, more often than otherwise they turned their backs and went away in disappointment.

Yet there was one in bodily, actively moving, even notably discernible, existence, whose suspected practices in the way of her profession wrought for a while considerable distress in a family that was living theretofore in moderate peace, at least with the world outside of itself. The witch was Mrs. Polly Boddy, and the family the Magraws. From the very start, Mrs. Magraw, whose maiden name was Nancy Tall, was plain, and she continued growing on that line until one ceased to look for any change for the better. During the good many years of waiting in her young womanhood she did not seem, except at times, painfully heartsick at the delay of suitors, and was said to have a disposition that under the circumstances was, if not remarkably good, not as bad as some. In time came along Andy Magraw, a Scotchman, two years younger, who by degrees offered himself; and she took him much as one, disappointed of something dainty and hot, takes a cold potato rather than go without dinner of any sort. He would have been regarded as plain himself except for the advantage he held of continuous comparison. They had one child; but, a weakling from the beginning, it gave way to the season of its first summer, and had no successor. As time went on, the wife, never of a cheerful spirit, seemed to grow less and less satisfied with surroundings both at home and outside of it, and learned to be quite voluble in the use of complaining words. This became particularly so of late, although she was now sixty years old.

Mrs. Boddy, on the contrary, with an excellent beginning, had kept it up surprisingly well. She had outlasted two husbands,—stout, brave men in their time,—and now, the junior of Mrs. Magraw by only four years or such a matter, looked hardly fifty. Not only that, but the bland smoothness of her cheek, the cheery beaming of her eyes, the uniform tidiness of her dress, and the cordial welcome of her voice and general manner, all made it seem that she intended to keep herself agreeable as long as possible.

They were adjoining neighbors, the Magraws living on the first rise beyond the river, and Mrs. Boddy a mile farther up the stream, and nearly opposite (on our side) Mr. Johnny Rainey, the oldest deacon in the church.

Mr. Pate, who was the first to tell me this

story, showed, I thought, that much kind compassion yet lingered in his recollection of Mrs. Magraw.

« Why, sir, it looked like a pity any female to be so unfort'nate and inmortal plain as what she were. They 's a sayin' that pootty is only skin deep, and ugly goes to the bone. It seem like 'ith Mrs. Magraw, the ugly in her cons'tootion went clean thoo and thoo, meat, bone, sinner, and muscle, and kep' itself in every single p'int of view out'ards and in'ards, and that she were jes turned loose in a flock by herself for other people to be sorry for her that had to look at her. They say she were right toler'ble mild and biddable when she were young, and even for a while arfter she got married, exceptin' when she got mad. But somehow she begun to take up the notion that things in gen'l was ag'in' her and gittin' worse a constant. Yit she were a female of powerful sperrit. She worked herself, and she made everything about her work.

« People called her a pincher. She pinched herself, and she pinched the niggers, and she pinched her husband all she could; but who, Andy Magraw, he, good, peaceable man if he were, sometimes bowed up his back, and cussed, and would n't. Some said he were too good and leniunt to her, and if he 'd take the reins in his own hand, and let her understand as the head o' the family he were goin' to keep 'em, she 'd swage down and come reason'ble. But one thing I 've noticed in my expe'unce, and it 's that them that think they know how to manage sech wives as what Mrs. Magraw were is them that ain't got 'em theirselves. Andy Magraw I no doubt done the best he knowed how accordin' to the war'ous risin's o' the case before him, so to speak. He never talked ag'in' her to t'other people, and nobody dares n't talk ag'in' her where he were.

« Now, as for the poor 'oman believin' in witches, they was other people in them times that done the same,—that is, to a' extent,—and if anybody disputed 'em, they 'd fetch in Scriptur' to back 'em up. My own sip'rate opinion is that that were a long time ago, and in a fur-away fur'n country, where the good Lord seemeth him meet to app'int 'em for the skearin' o' them hard-head Izzleites out o' their disobedience; but in these Nunited States, and special' in as healthy, peaceable country as the State o' Georgia, it 's not worth while for people to bother their brains overly much about 'em. The stand my father always took about the things it was—if you let them alone and not try to locate 'em, they 'd let you alone. The trouble 'ith Mrs. Magraw, she would n't.»

Suspicions, first vague, had been lurking for some time in the mind of Mrs. Magraw. Feeling herself Mrs. Boddy's superior in every quality except personal attractiveness, she began to speculate how it was that the cheek of a woman not far from being as old as herself, survivor of two husbands, held, and kept holding, the beauty of her youth. Instead of being marred by marriage life and widowhood, it seemed to be improved by them—specially the latter. Her gift of resilience from the loss of such companionship Mrs. Magraw for a time confessed not to understand. Particularly within this last gone year, since Mr. Boddy had been given a place under the cedars by the side of his predecessor, the woman looked, and to Mrs. Magraw's mind behaved, as if her desire were set upon going back to the period of youngest womanhood, to stay there forever. For all such as these Mrs. Magraw in time judged the cause to be preternatural, and so informed her husband. The grunt heard from his breast made her feel without any doubt that the judgment was correct.

Visiting between these ladies, always rare, for some time past had ceased. The difference was too great to let either, particularly the elder, become fond of seeing or being seen by the other. Necessarily they saw each other on monthly-meeting Sundays, and must sometimes be thrown together going or returning. It had been painful always to Mrs. Magraw that the other was so much praised by all the men, and even by some of the women who were satisfied with their own conditions and belongings. Henceforth she watched and brooded, occasionally hinting to others besides her husband the decision at which she had arrived. Lately two of the milch cows on the place suddenly went dry, both on the very same day. On the next the horn of another set in to crumple. Quickly thereafter, a middle-aged hen, theretofore as steady and sure as any the most respectable of her sex, one morning, in the very middle of her three weeks' incubation, came off the nest with every feather ruffled, and no sort of handling could make her stay there again when the back of the yard woman was turned, though she repeatedly put her upon it. Finally, Flower, a red-and-white-speckled calf of extraordinary promise, came under the spell. Irrational or not, of all the animals in the family, Mrs. Magraw's heart was set on this calf. She was a very pink of a calf, pretty, shaped to perfection, sweet-tempered, light-hearted even to frequent gaiety. Often and often, when her mistress was walking in the yard, wherein she was let to be petted, the dear little thing, making a festoon of her lovely white tail, would caper about her mistress in all sorts of exuberant fun, occasionally stopping immediately before her and gazing into her face apparently in great admiration for it. One evening, while the two were in this affectionate attitude to each other, the elder was heard to say:

«Poor innocent little Flower! Mist'ess don't seem so awful ugly to you, does she?»

The youngling licked her extended hand, and bounded away for further sport, leaving the other with a corner of her apron to her eyes.

Now even this favorite, heretofore so cheerful, so harmless, so full of goodly promise, was noticed one day looking melancholy. To fondest caressings she gave no answer but doleful cries. For four days she dwindled —if with any earthly disease, one impossible to be diagnosed. On the fifth she died. They buried her in the garden. A basket of nice pebbles was gathered, and spread over her grave.

After a day given up to mourning, of its kind earnest, even distressing, came on dire resentment. To her husband Mrs. Magraw said:

ANDY MAGRAW.

«What made me know positive in my mind it were her,—about that poor calf anyhow, if not the t'others,—when me and her were flung together on the road last meetin'-day, and I were obleeged to say somethin' to all her deceitful palarver, and I told her about Flower, she looked at me out of one eye, and she smiled at me insignificant, and said she hoped I 'd be able to raise her; and the very next day it took to drindlin'. And if you don't do somethin' about it, Andy Magraw, I will. You know I can shoot a shot-gun mighty nigh as well as you can, and I 'll go to that horrid witch's cuppen and calf parscher, and I 'll keep goin' there tell every one of 'em lays dead. What you goin' do, Andy Magraw?»

Mr. Magraw, although feeling not quite sure that occult evil influences had not been among the cattle and poultry, yet had no sort of sympathy with his wife's convictions; for, like other men, he much admired and respected Mrs. Boddy. Abundant experience, however, having taught him that argument against any opinions once risen in his wife's mind served only to fix them more firmly therein, he briefly speculated on what to do in order to appease what boded serious scandal. After some meditation he gave out that he would try to find out if anything could be done.

«In a day or two I 'll go over there and peruse around.»

«Yes, you 'll peruse around, and that 's all you 'll do.»

«Vera weel, then; I won't go.»

«Yes, you will.»

He uttered a grunt, and went out.

Brief and inarticulate as was this response, Mrs. Magraw knew very well that it contained more meaning than some other men's multitudes of words. So when he returned he found that she had moderated; for, daring and unreasonable as she had become, she must recognize, if she did not respect, the sentiment of the community that it was not becoming for a married woman to move in public with no coöperation of her husband in matters threatening collisions with outsiders. The heaviest complaint that her mind had ever lodged against him was his persistent, doggedly obstinate refusal to quarrel with her. One day her disgust for his weakness on this line had driven her to say:

«Andy Magraw, it do seem to me that when you was very born they come mighty nigh a-makin' you a fool.»

«Fool! Why, Nancy,» he answered meekly, «it 's the vera name I answer to.»

And her reply was: «Goodness gracious! To think a man would be satisfied with them conditions! I wish I was one of 'em.»

«Umph, umph! We never knaw about sic things.»

After another day's rumination, the while

making a quiet visit to the old man Rainey, which he did not mention to her, next morning, getting himself up with some smartness, he remarked that he was going to call upon Mrs. Boddy. The little confidence of his wife was somewhat enhanced when, taking down his rifle from its forks, he loaded and shouldered it.

Noting his approach, the rosy widow despatched her house-girl to gather in the garden a handful of mint. By the time the usual greetings, neighborly questionings and answerings, and a few remarks on the weather were over, there was handed to the visitor a tumbler, of the size they had in those days, brimming with a julep of a savor whose better neither eye nor nostril nor throat of man was ever regaled with. Under the influence of this king (or queen, as the case may be) of Southern potations, whatever remonstration might have been on Mr. Magraw's mind even to hint sneaked out and tried to hide behind his back. He was not an intemperate man at all. Yet from his ancestors he had inherited quick recognition of a good thing, and promptness of acceptance when thus graciously extended. As he sat and sipped, Mrs. Boddy, who merely for the sake of added grace to her hospitality had joined him in a glass smaller and paler, seemed to him to float in a very lake of loveliest innocence. When these cheering rites were over, and some moments had passed in waiting announcement of the special purport of the call, the lady, smiling kindly, said:

«'A MAN CANNA SAY ANYTHING.'»

«Mr. Magraw, of course I know what your wife sent you here for. Mrs. Magraw has been talking and making her insinuations about me for a good while. I 've stood it because I knewed she could n't stop her mouth any more than she could help some other things she 's got. I never had anything more to do with her home matters and concerns than she 's had to do with mine—that is, as I know of; and as for being the witch she tells people I am, it 's all news to me, and, of course, I some rathers she 'd stop it.»

«Why, Mrs. Boddy,» he answered, with uplifted hand, «I dunn—I—I—Mrs. Boddy—ye—ye knaw—a man canna say anything ag'in' his ain—I knaw weel ye 're na witch, but I canna—canna—»

His tone and manner were so entirely what a good man's should be in the circumstances that she was deeply sensible of them, and, interrupting him, said:

«You 're perfectly right, Mr. Magraw. No good man will open' take sides against his own wife. It is nothing. Let it go. I don't think anybody is apt to take me for the thing she names me; and now I see how it pains you, I 'm going to try and not let it trouble me any more. It has n't but mighty little. I think it must be Mrs. Magraw's health. I 'm glad to see you looking so well, Mr. Magraw.»

He gave himself a nervous shake; then, rising, said:

«Mrs. Boddy, I—thank ye, ma'am. I think mysel' somethin' may be wrang wi' Nancy, and—and—I bid ye guid day, Mrs. Boddy.»

He went away, trailing his rifle as if he were ashamed of it.

«Good man,» soliloquized Mrs. Boddy—«the best, the very best, in all this neighborhood—not hardly except' old Brother Rainey—spite of being yoked to a woman that of all in this world I do suppose is the sorrowfullest, ugliest, the foolishest, suspiciousest, the backbitingest, mouthiest, and the general beatingest, that—may the good

Lord have mercy on us all poor sinners! Amen, I pray!»

When Mr. Magraw, upon returning, reported such incidents of the visit as he deemed prudent, his mate broke out upon him with words of which the following are a few:

«Yes; it 's perfect cle'r that thing have witched you too, Andy Magraw. You never was a man that could tackle with women, exceptin' of me, that can't help herself; and I can smell on you this minute the mint-dram she give you, that before you got to the gate I see you tryin' to blow off the scent of it on your hat and on your coat-sleeve. If such as that is to go on, they 'd as well begin to season the lumber for my coffin. But I tell you now, Andy Magraw, it sha'n't go on! She may witch you in the bargain of them poor dumb cattle, but she don't tromple on me no furder. You hear me?»

«Well, now, my son,» said Mr. Pate, «good, patient man if he were, Andy Magraw could n't always stand her mouth. And so he told her plain down that Mrs. Boddy were n't no more a witch than she were, and he add that maybe the reason he want to got shet o' the julip, it were he were afeard, when the scent struck her, it might make her yit hotter with Mrs. Boddy for bein' more liber'l in the mixin' of her sperrits and sugar, and the dividin' with other people. Because she were knew to love the article well as Andy, albe' nobody ever accused her of knockin' it too heavy. My expe'unce is, mighty few people make ser'ous objection to a julip in its place, when people that makes 'em know what they 're about, which all don't, unfort'nate, and some may push the use of 'em to a too much extents. But them words of Andy made her ravin' mad, and she declared that if the good Lord have made her a man—that he, unfort'nate, did n't—she 'd raise thunder quicker 'n ever run down a skinned poplar. Did anybody ever! And she said that the very next mornin', soon as her breakfast she would git, on her head her bonnet it would go, on her horse she would mount, and then ride about 'mong the neighbors a-forewarnin' of 'em ag'in' the witch Polly Boddy. What you think Andy Magraw done then? He determ'ed in his mind that it were absolute necessity for the old man Rainey to take a hand in the business, him bein' the onl'est man in the whole neighborhood she were afeard of, because it were him that persuaded the brothern to let her in the church when they hizzitated about her high temper and the freckwent sloshin' of her tongue. He argied that if she did n't quite have grace, it might come to her arfter she were took in. Of course Andy could n't go in, because o' his cussin' sometimes, which he never denied. And so Andy, a-knowin' she would n't take his advices, sot in, he did, to beggin' her to not fetch the thing up in the church, and special' not to go to the old man Rainey about it. Fact is, Andy Magraw were one o' the sensiblest men they had in them days, spite o' bein' surrounded with sech a wife. The old man Rainey were the oldest and influentialest man in the church, and Andy Magraw knewed that if anybody could head her in her ravin' course it were the old man Rainey.»

The praise of Mr. Pate had good foundation. Immediately after the utterance of Mr. Magraw's urgent remonstrance, his wife, becoming calm, looked at him pitifully and said:

«Well, Andy Magraw, I do think, on my soul, you 're the poorest hand to help out and give advice to a body in the suffering fix I 'm in that ary poor woman ever took up with for a husband in this lonesome, perishing world. Why, man, sence you mention it, it 's the very thing for me to do; and I 'm a-goin' straight over to Br'er Rainey's if my life is spar'd tell to-morrow.»

He nodded in humble disappointment, and after dinner, resuming his rifle, remarked that he believed he would go out and see if he could not find a hawk. Returning in the evening with the body of one of these enemies of the barn-yard, he was comforted to see her in reasonable placidity of mood, in which she remained for the rest of the day.

Everybody said that Uncle Johnny Rainey had a long head, which he used for his own good and that of his neighbors, particularly those belonging to the congregation of his church. In the half-century of his diaconate he had settled a greater number of difficulties and disputes, doctrinal, social, and domestic, than any other one man in his generation throughout that whole region. Calm and conciliatory, but confident, firm, even adroit when needed, he kept his more than a thousand fellow-members in all possible harmony. The case of Mrs. Magraw had long been in his mind, and he was not surprised at the coming of its climax. On her approach, he met her at the gate, helped her to dismount, and led her into the piazza, where he had instructed his wife, after a few words of welcome salutation, to leave them together. When all preliminaries were over, and Mrs. Rainey on polite pretense withdrew, the good man began to talk. He well judged that it was best for him to take the initiative. As for his supplies of words, whether at conference meetings or other occasions, inexhaustible is hardly the word; yet with this single hearer he deemed a couple of hours enough for his purpose.

«Sister Magraw,» he began, «my mind—I don't know as you may know it, but my mind jes here lately it have been a-runnin' consider'ble on witches, and I been a-studyin' up the subjects of 'em, from the witch o' Endor down till now that they seem to be a sispicion that they is one, and maybe two, in the Jukesborough Baptis' cong'egation.»

«Two, Br'er Rainey?» Mrs. Magraw, shuddering, asked.

«Come, Sister Magraw, don't put in and interrup' me. Yes, one; maybe two; and if the thing ain't stopped, no tellin' how many more. Now, you know—if you don 't, I 'll tell you—that the onl'est way, when oncet a witch were caught, and pine-blank proved—the onl'est way laid down for her was to burn her up bodaciously. That have been done in time, more or less; yit from what I could gether in my readin' o' hist'ry, them that done it was sorry they done it arfter the thing blowed over, a-feelin' jub'ous in their mind if they did n't act hasty about the takin' in o' evidence. In my own mind—that is, in what mind the good Lord, for useful purpose, I humble hope, he have merciful putt in here—right in here»—thankfully tapping his forehead with a forefinger—«my opinion, as no longer than day before yisterday I told Sister Boddy, that I did n't believe they was a witch in the whole State o' Georgie, and special' in the cong'egation where I been app'inted deacon by the reg'lar layin' on o' hands accordin' to the Scriptur'; and I added to Sister Boddy that ef, for instance, she, Sister Polly Boddy, was to fetch up in conf'ence,—I did n't name names plain and open p'inted as some does,—but ef she was to fetch up ary 'nother female o' the cong'egation for bein' of a witch, and then could n't prove it to the satisfaction o' the brothern,—which they is no doubt she could n't,—then and in them case she might possible be turned out herself, and, what 's more, run the resk o' bein' sued for slander and scandal by the said female sister, and have her plantation and the very house over her head took for damage. Now, as for the dryin' up of milch cows, and the drindlin' o' calves, what I told Sister Boddy of my expe'unce, it were that ever sence I could 'member, and long before, milch cows and calves and settin' hens been doin' them things when the time for 'em come for doin' o' 'em, like the Scriptur' say they 's a time for all things.»

About thus on, on, and on he discoursed, occasionally turning to note upon the listener's face the effect of his words. It was plain to see that they were going straight home. She shuddered both at the intimation clearly conveyed that she herself was suspected by Mrs. Boddy of witchcraft, and at the risk of being sued by her for words already spoken to many persons. When at last Mr. Rainey saw that he could safely stop, he did so, and looked benignly into her face.

«Br'er Rainey,» she said, panting, but in a low tone, «I did n't know any of Polly Boddy's milch cows had dried up, nor any of her calves—»

«There! Of course you did n't. I knowed you did n't; and you had no more to do with 'em than I did, which of course I could n't, not bein' of a female. And it all come, like sech always in gen'l does, from neighbors not understandin' one 'nother better, and makin' 'lowances for nobody bein' perfec'. Is there anything on your mind, Sister Magraw, you wanted to open to me special'?»

«N-no, Br'er Rainey; not now. My mind has been pestered a good deal here lately; but—but I reckon maybe I 'm mistaken. But if Polly Boddy think—oh, my Lord, Br'er Rainey, what is a poor woman to do like me, that nobody ever did keer anything for her, excepting of you?»

The old man, calling in his wife, set in with words of comfort, the latter holding her hand. It was an easy task. Tears long buried at length came in her eyes. When she was slowly riding away, Mr. Rainey said:

«Poor woman! my opinion is, the climak have come on her, and I 'm thankful it ain't of the ravin' kind. Me and Sister Boddy thought that were the best way to swage her down—bein' took for a witch herself. But I tell you now, she ain't long for this world.»

I let Mr. Pate tell the rest in his own way.

«Old man Rainey were right. It come out that the poor creetur' were out her head. The doctor said she been so ev'y sence her baby died, but he never told nobody but old man Rainey, because tellin' would n't do the case no good. Soon as she got home, 'ithout sayin' a word to a soul, smilin' to ev'ybody said anything to her, she went to bed. Andy Magraw put a nigger on a horse and told him not to spar' him gallopin' for the doctor. He say—the doctor say—the egzitement about Mrs. Boddy have been too much for her head, and it have now struck her heart.

And he told Andy Magraw to prepar' his mind, and that she were n't goin' to git out that bed alive. And what time she lasted she were perfec' calm and biddable, and she talked pleasant about people and things forty and fifty year before. And when she give out final, they said it were same as a little baby goin' to sleep in a cradle. And if anybody ever see a man cry and go on about a dead companion, it were that same Andy Magraw. And that 's the end o' the tale about the witch.»

I felt much surprise at a finish so unusually abrupt. Evidently Mr. Pate had anticipated it. After a brief pause, looking down into my unsatisfied face, he said:

«Well, what is it? What more you want?»

I ventured to ask what became of them afterward.

«Of who?» he asked, in teasing delay—«of Andy Magraw or Mrs. Boddy?»

«Of both.»

«What you think? Now, jes on a ventur', what you think?»

«I think they got married.»

MRS. MAGRAW.

«There, now! Ain't it astonishin' how yearly young boys their mind 'll begin to run on marryin'? But I s'pose they can't he'p it, bein' of their natur'. Well, I 'll answer your quest'on. Look like they ought to get married, don't it? Plantations j'inin', even their very geese gittin' everlastin' mixed. Ev'ybody looked for it, same as the sun a-risin' of a mornin'. As for the old man Rainey, he told 'em both, look like to him the good Lord have jes paved the way for 'em; and they were n't any doubts but, soon as it were decent, the widder sot her cap for him. But, sir,—and there were the interestest part o' the whole business,—Andy Magraw took up the idee that maybe it were his fau't his poor wife gittin' so discontented and crazy in her mind, and nobody—not even the old man Rainey—could git him to go a-nigh Mrs. Boddy, albe' he acknowledged he loved her dear. They is people o' that kind, and I has heerd readin' people say that of all denomination of folks, a Scotmon is the stickiest about hangin' to a' idee that have oncet settled itself in the back o' his head. Some said he were crazy as his poor wife not to take up with sech a' opporchunity as Mrs. Boddy—that she were only waitin' for him to name the word. And some even add the opinion of him a-sispicionin' her bein' a witch like his poor wife 'cused her. As for her, Mrs. Boddy, she got tired a-waitin' for him, and she whirled in, she did, and she got married spite of him, and that to a monst'ous good, suitable husband. You know, havin' the expe'unce o' two of 'em, she have learnt to know how to pick and choose. But she always said Andy Magraw were as good a man as ever lived or died, and other people give their opinion the same. But, don't you know, soon arfter she got married seem like he got more and more restless and fidgety in his mind and in his gates in gen'l, and 't were n't long before he sold out and moved away—clean away—back yonder where he come from original'.»

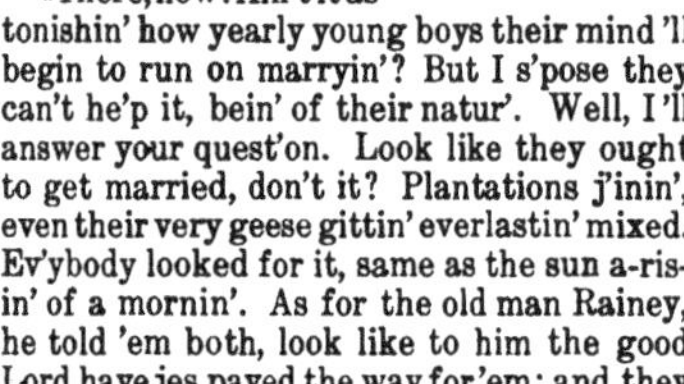

*Richard Malcolm Johnston.*

## THE STRANGER.

HE read the books that all the wise men writ;
He searched the world for knowledge, not for pelf;
He thought no man unknown, so keen his wit,
But once he met a stranger—'t was himself.

*Maurice Francis Egan.*

# THE ART OF LARGE GIVING.

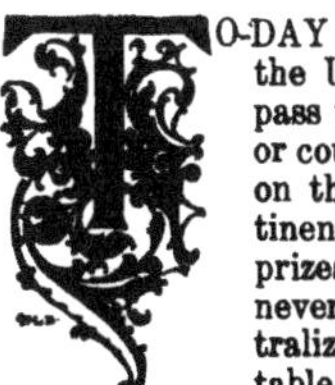

O-DAY individual fortunes in the United States far surpass those of any other age or country. The first attack on the resources of a continent has meant winning prizes such as the world never saw before, and centralizing tendencies, inevitable because economic, are bringing into fewer and fewer hands the control and the tribute of vast industries. So rapidly has all this come about that public sentiment has not yet reckoned with the problems introduced into the social and political order by the new massing of riches. The multimillionaire is usually as little enlightened as his neighbors concerning the duties bound up with the surplusage which has fallen to his lot; he is apt to inherit the ideas of a generation when property was distributed more evenly than now, when the disparity between earning and having was less glaring than to-day. In the political sphere, at the end of centuries of strife, power has been partnered with responsibility. At the present hour supremacy has passed to the chieftains of business; the real masters of the situation are the land, railroad, and manufacturing kings. Not the discontented poor alone, but the thoughtful rich, begin to feel that financial primacy creates new debts toward the public. But can these debts be legally defined and enforced? Skill and wisdom are lacking for the task, even if the question were closed as to the justice of the attempt. For many men of great possessions the voice of conscience is effective, as the contemplated grasp of the tax-gatherer could never be. Around them they see ignorance to be banished, talent missing its career, misery appealing for relief. They know that the forces of the time have brought them their huge fortunes only through the coöperation and the protection of the whole community: so, with justice in their hearts as well as generosity, they found the benefactions which are doing so much to foster the best impulses of American life; and in this response to public duty they find conferred upon riches a new power and fascination. It is the purpose of these pages to glance at a few typical large gifts in this country, showing, as they do, distinct progress in the art by which those with a great deal have come most helpfully to the aid of those with too little. Incidentally, also, it may appear that the heaping of wealth in the hands of individuals carries with it advantage in the masterfulness and singleness of aim which can transmute a vast treasure to a splendid public service.

### LARGE GIFTS ARE MAINLY FOR EDUCATION.

Of large gifts in America the chief have been devoted to education, as in the Enoch Pratt, the Newberry, and other public libraries; in institutions for original research, as the Smithsonian, the Lick Observatory, and Clark University; in industrial universities, as Pratt and Drexel institutes; and in universities proper, as Johns Hopkins and Leland Stanford. A second group of great gifts has aimed at caring for the helpless and the sick; of these Girard College and Johns Hopkins Hospital are the foremost examples. A third class are concerned with public recreation and the refinement of popular taste, as the gifts by Henry Shaw to St. Louis of the Missouri Botanical Garden and Tower Grove Park; that by William W. Corcoran to Washington of a gallery of art; and that by George Peabody to Baltimore, where the institute bearing his name, in addition to departments educational in character, furnishes musical entertainments of a high order on terms merely nominal. Only in the first of these three classes are the benefactions formally set apart for education, yet in both the others education is in large measure the purpose. Girard College not only shelters, clothes, and feeds its wards, but it instructs them for practical work and duty. Johns Hopkins Hospital maintains one of the best training-schools for nurses in existence, and is united with the Medical School of Johns Hopkins University. The Corcoran Gallery of Art conducts free classes, so well attended that the accommodation for students has recently been doubled.

In America, then, the commanding object of large giving has been education, the cultivation of intelligence, skill, faculty, and, since even enjoyment needs apprenticeship, some worthy appeal to delight, to the tastes which enrich leisure and lighten toil. As justice includes all other virtues, so wise education is regarded as bearing in its train every other benefit. An evidence of this is the growing favor in which the teaching profession is held by the men and women able to enter its ranks. To cite a case, forty-four per cent. of the alumni of Johns Hopkins to June, 1894, have become teachers and college professors. The far-sighted Baltimorean thus planted a veritable seed-plot and nursery. Baltimore, too, answers the question whether a large gift for education really does much to promote the intellectual life of a community. The doubting are apt to imagine that a university must needs be the growth of generations; that the capacity to pursue the highest inquiry is rare, and does not always appear in response to opportunity. Since 1876, when Johns Hopkins University opened its doors, a notable change has taken place in the intellectual interests of Baltimore. Nearly half the students have been drawn from the city, and even the local circles of fashion are to-day alive to questions of scholarship and criticism. Clubs have been formed among society people for the study of art and letters, and Professor Jebb, lecturing at the Peabody Institute on permanent elements in Greek literature, has attracted audiences very much larger than he addresses in Cambridge. Toward this happy result the Peabody Institute preceding the establishment of the university, and the Pratt Library following it, have undoubtedly contributed.

### PUBLIC LIBRARIES.

As a means of popular education a public library has a foremost place, especially when it is free. In June, 1894, the public library of St. Louis abolished its fees, small as they were. A fourfold increase of circulation is the result. Books and periodicals are not simply increasing in number every year, but in every province of science and art they have broken fresh ground; in the interpretation of nature they register a transformation of thought little short of revolutionary. While in the schools the training of the eye and hand is supplementing instruction from the printed page, never before were the student and the experimenter more under bonds to the last published word in science, art, and research, to the latest records of the studies and experiments of others. And, beyond its own immediate province, the spirit of science has made itself distinctly felt in literature. History and biography are now written with an exactitude wholly new. The student of taxation, of trade-unions, in care and scruple is beginning to emulate his fellow-inquirer whose thought takes form in the suspension-bridge or the alternating dynamo. To adapt the contents of shelves and tables to the specific manufacturing, commercial, and artistic needs of a community, as at Worcester; to name works illuminating the living question of the hour, as at Providence; to court helpful relations with the schools, as at Milwaukee and Detroit; and, withal, judiciously to cater to the literary recreation of the people, are among the duties which to-day fall to the public librarian. His outlook is for yet greater usefulness: last year a beginning was made by the American Library Association in giving important works a competent note of description and appraisal—a pilotage, in these days of multiplied literary wares, invaluable to the reader and the student.

In public libraries Massachusetts leads the Union: less than two per cent. of her population are unserved by public, and for the most part free, libraries. This provision has been largely at the hands of individual founders, whose cash gifts exceed $8,000,000, and who have also given more than one hundred memorial library buildings, and many valuable collections of books and manuscripts. None of these gifts in Massachusetts, however, compares with that of John Jacob Astor to New York, historic as it is in American benefaction. This library, opened to the public in 1854, to-day represents with its endowment $2,100,000. It is to form the nucleus of the projected New York Library, merging itself with the Lenox and Tilden foundations to form an institution unique in the history of great gifts. The day has dawned when the economy of united control is as clear in benefaction as in manufacturing or trade. The Astor is exclusively a reference library. A library combining a reference department with the popular circulating plan was given by Enoch Pratt to Baltimore in 1886. To bring its volumes within reach of every home in Baltimore, six branches have been established in various centers of the city; the buildings for these branches, and that of the central library, with furnishings, cost $325,000. The endowment, an additional sum of $833,333, was handed to the city on condition that six per cent. thereon ($50,000) should annually be paid for maintenance. In Chicago, Mr. Walter L. Newberry, who died in 1886, bequeathed about $2,500,000 for a reference library to serve the north side of the city. Its first librarian, the late William F. Poole, planned its buildings, bestowing each great department of literature in a room of its own. For the south side of the city provision even more generous has been made by Mr. John Crerar, who, dying in 1889, constituted Chicago his residuary legatee for the purpose. His bequest will probably realize $2,700,000. Sums much more in the aggregate than this large amount have been bestowed by Mr. Andrew Carnegie, who has founded and extended free public libraries at Pittsburg and elsewhere in Pennsylvania, at Fairfield, Iowa, and in his native Scotland.

### AID TO RESEARCH.

GIFTS which appeal less directly to popular regard than the public library may, for all that, have claims as weighty. There are many kinds of investigation which resemble forest trees, the benefits of which are only enjoyed years, or even generations, after the planting. Civilization for its advance must rely on applied science; but how, as Professor F. W. Clarke asks, can there be applied science unless first there be science to apply? This question has particular pertinence in the industrial sphere. Joseph Henry and John William Draper, in discovering the laws of electromagnetism and the chemical action of light, had no thought of the electric lamp or motor, or of the camera, which in so large a measure has superseded pencil, brush, and graver; yet all the while they were preparing the way for these triumphs of ingenuity. In the record of American science the first large gift for original research is that of $500,000, received in 1838 by the United States as a bequest from James Smithson, an Englishman, who, by the way, never set foot in this country; in 1891, Thomas Hodgkins, another Englishman, gave the Smithsonian Institution $200,000 more. This foundation has been singularly favored in the men who have presided over its fortunes. Its first secretary was Professor Joseph Henry, whose researches in electricity are classical. To him succeeded Professor Spencer F. Baird, a zoölogist famous in the science and art of fish-culture. The present secretary, Professor S. P. Langley, is an astronomer and physicist of eminence, whose studies of the sun have thrown new light on its constitution and internal disturbances, and whose «New Astronomy,» the best popular treatise on the subject extant, first appeared as a series of chapters in THE CENTURY. As an aid to the investigation of the heat radiated by the stars, Professor Langley devised the bolometer, which detects a change of temperature of one one-hundred-thousandth part of one degree centigrade. Joining this instrument to an automatic camera exposing plates sensitive to invisible rays, he has explored the solar spectrum with marvelous results. To the limited range of solar rays directly visible he indirectly maps to the eye regions more than thrice as extensive. Since 1887 he has been conducting experiments in mechanical flight. In consequence of this remarkable work, also described in THE CENTURY, actual flights of over half a mile have been made with his «aërodrome,» built of steel, and driven and sustained on the air solely by the power of a steam-engine. This achievement for the first time brings within measurable distance the annexation of the air to human pathways.



In the ordinary university practice original research is prosecuted as an incident to teaching, with but slender aid from the general fund, so that often a man who might be profitably employed in the laboratory adding new tracts to knowledge is kept in the class-room traversing a time-worn round. In a few happier cases, as at Clark University in Worcester, the man of originality, who has gained the faculty of exploration by mastery of the known field, conducts research as his primary function, teaching only that he may communicate and apply his discoveries. Perhaps because observatories are monumental, and their work appeals to the imagination as that of the laboratory cannot, astronomy has attracted the largest gifts for original research. Yet equally must we look to the investigations of the physicist, the chemist, the student of body and mind in health and disease, if science is to continue its conquests and carry its flag into territory to-day at the verge of the horizon.

In bringing the result of research to the service of the public on the lines of an industrial university, Pratt Institute in Brooklyn is doing notable work. With its endowment of $3,500,000, it represents a total gift of about $4,000,000. Charles Pratt, its founder, in his experience as a young man in business, saw that current education was unpractical, and, as fortune came to him, resolved to do what he could for reform. He devoted years to observation, conference, and thought, and the result is expressed in Pratt Institute. As THE CENTURY for October, 1893, described the institute in detail, it may suffice to say that its work groups itself into four departments: educational, pure and simple, patterned on high-school methods; normal, preparing the student to become a teacher; technical, imparting skill in the fine, industrial, and domestic arts; and supplementary courses in special subjects, domestic, social, and philanthropic.

UNIVERSITIES.

ON a plane of yet higher educational activity than that of Pratt Institute—the plane of the university proper—stands the foundation of Johns Hopkins in Baltimore, to which he gave $3,500,000. This university, inaugurated in 1876, has won distinction in the emphasis it has placed on advanced work. At the outset it established twenty fellowships for graduates who should pursue original study and research. The impulse thus given is significantly registered in its enrolment to 1896. Out of a total of 2981 students, graduate studies have been prosecuted by 2086. This result is chiefly to be credited to the academic freedom which inspires the university; to the hearty coöperation between its professors and students. The ideas embodied in its administration have, with some modification, been adopted by the University of Chicago, which, opened but five years ago, has already received about $12,000,000 as gifts. Yet a sum comparatively small may be so used as to do noble work for the higher education. Of this Cornell University affords an example in its union of individual munificence with national aid. On July 2, 1862, despite the turmoil and anxiety of civil war, Congress passed an act, introduced by Senator Morrill, evincing the nation's sustained interest in education. This act granted public lands to the several States which should «provide at least one college where the leading object shall be, without excluding other scientific and classical studies, and including military tactics, to teach such branches of learning as are related to agriculture and the mechanic arts.»

The share of this national bounty which came to New York was scrip for 990,000 acres. On April 27, 1865, its legislature incorporated Cornell University, toward which Ezra Cornell had promised $500,000, appropriating to it the proceeds receivable from sale of the land scrip. Through the shrewdness of Mr. Cornell, lands were chosen among the best pine regions of the Northwest, and were retained until they became of several times their original value, adding some five millions to the university's capital. Not content with arduous services through years of grievous commercial depression, Mr. Cornell added to his first donation the sum of $170,000. His example has been so generously followed that to-day the cash gifts to Cornell aggregate $2,738,000, the roll beginning with $1,171,000 from the Hon. Henry W. Sage, who has succeeded Mr. Cornell in administering the grants of the university. The sole gift of the State of New York, from its own treasury, has been $50,000 for an agricultural building; but the State supports a State Veterinary College, located on the campus, allied with the university. Cornell educates annually 512 students from the State of New York free of charge for tuition.

When Columbia University, New York, recently announced its intention to remove to a new site, and asked its friends for $4,000,000 to provide it with shelter, there was a general shrug of incredulity. The popular impression was that Columbia's riches were indefinitely great, and equal to all demands; the truth is that its income is wholly required for maintenance, and not a dollar of it can be used for building. Of this convincing proof appears in the gift of $350,000, for the Natural Science Building, by Mr. W. C. Schermerhorn, chairman of the board of trustees; and in the gift of $1,000,000, for the Library Building, by President Seth Low—a gift believed to form a material part of his fortune. One of the first buildings to be completed on Columbia's new grounds will be Havemeyer Hall, erected in memory of Mr. Frederick C. Havemeyer by members of his family, at a cost of $400,000. Before the new wants of the university were declared, its medical departments, certain of which are unsurpassed in the world, had received $1,970,000 from members of the Vanderbilt family. These departments are better known as the College of Physicians and Surgeons. The university during Mr. Low's presidency has so much extended and strengthened its work that its present appeal for aid is certain of response. In its services in behalf of popular culture, Columbia has placed New York deeply in its debt, and added a new argument for universities in great cities. Affiliated with Columbia is the Teachers' College. Its original site, which was presented by Mr. George W. Vanderbilt, has since been doubled by other gifts. The Manual Arts Building, completed in 1894, was constructed and equipped at a cost of over $250,000 by Mrs. Josiah Macy, Jr., as a memorial to her husband, and the western wing of the main building, the name of the donor of which is withheld, is now being built at a cost of $250,000.

AID FOR THE SICK AND DESTITUTE.

WHEN from the needs of education we turn to those of the sick and destitute, we find the stream of benefaction equally broad and deep. The superb buildings and grounds of Girard College, and its vast endowment, estimated at $15,000,000, make it in every way the most remarkable orphanage in America. Since 1848, when it first opened its gates, to the end of 1895, it had sheltered 5519 boys; in 1895 its family numbered no fewer than 1524, nurtured, too, with no stinting hand, for the average expense per boy was $330. Since Mr. Girard's time public sentiment with regard to the massing of children in vast institutions has undergone a decided change. It is urged by thoughtful critics that to withdraw children from the influences of home, and regiment them under the command of teachers and officials, is to deprive them of the best discipline of life, of that familiarity with every-day matters of work and business which an ordinary child picks up as he goes along. Still, accidents of fortune continue to cast orphans adrift, the choice for whom is not between an asylum and a home, but between an asylum and the street. The authorities of Girard, aware of the shortcomings of orphanage routine, have sought to better it in a variety of ways, and with a fair degree of success. But the aim of the foundation—to do all that can be done for children bereft of parents—will be realized only when its vast income is parceled out among hundreds of households, each caring for an orphan group, and making it possible for discipline to be attempered with affection.

As Girard is easily first among the orphanages of America, Johns Hopkins Hospital is foremost among its hospitals. Its founder bestowed for it $3,300,000. So much thought and care were devoted to its design by Dr. John S. Billings of the United States army, that it is acknowledged to be by far the most complete and admirably planned hospital in the world. Its means of warming, of providing pure air, of making easy the removal of dust and refuse, are virtually perfect. They lead the visitor to ask, Why should such appliances be reserved for the sick? Is it less desirable to maintain health than to restore it? And when shall training redeem domestic service from incompetency, as it has the calling of the nurse?

In this hospital the medical school of Johns Hopkins University receives clinical instruction, women being admitted to the classes equally with men. This is in accordance with the terms of an endowment of $500,000, gathered by a women's committee, Miss Mary Elizabeth Garrett contributing $307,000.

As this article is about to go to press it is announced that Mr. J. Pierpont Morgan has given $1,000,000 to the Lying-in Hospital of the city of New York.

### ADMINISTRATION.

In the control of benefactions a wide variety appears, each example an endeavor to meet the circumstances of a particular case. As a rule, trustees are designated by the donor, and are a self-perpetuating body. This was the course chosen by Johns Hopkins and Enoch Pratt of Baltimore. Pratt Institute, Brooklyn, is directed by three sons of its founder; it is provided that his three other sons may be added to the board. The trust deed of Peter Cooper regarding Cooper Union, New York, provides that his eldest male descendant shall be a trustee. The eldest lineal descendant of Ezra Cornell is entitled to a like honor—a seat at the board of Cornell University; its board of trustees consists of thirty-nine members, of whom nine hold office *ex officio*,[1] and the remaining thirty are elective trustees, two thirds of them being elected by the board and one third by the alumni, the term of office in all cases being five years. Of the fifteen trustees who rule Girard College, twelve are appointed for life by the Supreme Court of Pennsylvania and the Court of Common Pleas of Philadelphia; the other three are *ex officio* the mayor and the presidents of the select and common councils of Philadelphia. That the public should be represented on the board which controls a large benefaction is held by Mr. Andrew Carnegie to be a principle of cardinal importance. In the library founded by him at Allegheny, Pennsylvania, at a cost of $300,000, the majority of the committee of management are appointed by the president of the common council; this gives him virtual control of the library's policy and power to choose the librarian. That this plan needs revision is clear, and the example of Allegheny has a lesson that applies to much else than public-library management. The superintendent of a great benefaction is all the better for lacking skill in the arts by which political favor is won and kept. When once a board of trustees is satisfied that their chief officer is worthy his place, why harass him by exposure to removal unless he can

[1] The eldest son of the founder, the President of the University, the Governor of New York, the Lieutenant-Governor, the Speaker of the Assembly, the Superintendent of Public Instruction, the President of the State Agricultural Society, the Commissioner of Agriculture, and the Librarian of the Cornell Library.

ingratiate himself at the city hall? Why not let him engage his subordinates, making him answerable for their good behavior and efficiency?

To Pittsburg Mr. Carnegie has recently given $1,100,000 for a library with branches, a music-hall, an art gallery, and a museum; he has provided in addition $1,000,000 as endowment, the income to be expended mainly in the purchase of pictures by American artists. Nine of the library trustees are of his appointment, with self-perpetuating powers; the other nine are the mayor of Pittsburg, the president of the Central Board of Education, the presidents of the select and common councils, with five members chosen by and from these councils. Allegheny has not agreed to appropriate for the maintenance of its Carnegie Library any specific sum; Pittsburg binds itself to pay not less than $40,000 a year toward the expenses of its Carnegie Library. This definiteness has obvious importance.

Easy as it usually is to find fault with a trust administration in part or wholly political, the difficulty remains that a self-perpetuating body may become sluggish and irresponsive to reasonable public demands. In Worcester, Massachusetts, the admirable public library, which originated in a gift by Dr. John Green, is managed by trustees who at the end of a term of service (six years) are not eligible for immediate reëlection: this evidently with intent that there shall be no sleepy settling down into arm-chairs by men who like the honor of office without its toil. And, in truth, the duties of a board administering a large gift are far from being as easy as they may at first sight appear, especially when the founder of the trust is president. To give wisely in a small way is a severe test of good sense; to give wisely on a large scale is difficult indeed. When a difference of opinion arises, a founder is apt to be chagrined if he cannot have his way. He may have had the trouble of making the money which is being spent, and naturally he wishes to have the decisive word in spending it. It is hard for rich and forceful men to learn that they must rein their instinct for command when they enter an unfamiliar field. The tactful adjustment of relations between men who have and do not know, and men who know and do not have, is familiar enough in the sphere of business. The same adjustment arrives, sometimes after sharp conflicts, in the administration of large gifts. Confronted by the difficulty of judiciously managing a great educational or other benefaction, more than one founder has placed his gift virtually in the hands of an officer of tested ability, reserving to the board only nominal oversight.

### WHEN AND WHAT TO GIVE.

At this point in our rapid survey certain principles of the art of large giving begin to make themselves tolerably clear. First, as to *when* it is best to give. During life, by all means. The diversion of the Stewart and Tilden bequests is too fresh in the public mind to bear restatement. They are two examples among a score which might be cited to prove the folly of trying to bestow a large gift by will. And, after all, can that truly be called a gift which falls from the clutch of death? To fortunate men opportunities for amassing great wealth come earlier in a lifetime than formerly, so that it is now easier than ever for gifts to be granted during life. When, however, it would entail serious loss were a large business brought to a close or shorn of its active capital, the rich man at its head can give what he can during life, and in his will provide for strengthening such lines of endeavor as have proved most worthy. This was what, in some degree, George Peabody did.

Of large gifts, those have been by far the most fruitful which have proceeded upon the fullest information, as in the case of the University of Chicago, where President Harper began his work by an examination of the field of the higher education in both America and Europe. Experience has abundantly established, also, that unless a gift is very large, it is preferable that it add to the usefulness of an existing institution rather than that it found a new one. To roof an uncovered house is better than to dig a new cellar. A fund to be known by the donor's name is, as a rule, of more benefit than a building likely to demand for the work done in it a new outlay from the general chest. In not a few colleges, while special funds for the observatory or library or chapel are ample, the general treasury from which that forgotten man, the ordinary professor, is paid is often sadly scant. These institutions always miss the symmetry and balance which come from placing a fair margin of income at the free disposal of the governing body.

A disputed point in large giving is whether it is better to found a small local college or to strengthen a great university not local. The small college will bring the higher education to thousands who otherwise could go no further than the public school. The university, if its technical and professional departments are to be suitably manned, will need all the aid its most liberal friends can render. During the year 1894–5, the income of Harvard was $1,084,000, yet the university made ends meet only through gifts for immediate use. In the development of Harvard every college, small and great, in America has aided and shared. The question, then, is less, Which, the local college or the great university? than, Why not both? There is good reason to expect that neither need will be ignored as fortunes are multiplied among the many men whose careers have been created by what the best education has done for mother wit. Let us hope that the years of the near future will also see accomplished the end which the foremost teachers of America have at heart—the work of the universities made continuous with that of the colleges, and the creation of centers of instruction where inquiry, physical or philosophical, political or ethical, may be carried to its utmost bound. As these advances are gained, we are likely to see the public schools more and more strengthened by alliance with the universities, and gradually freed from their abounding irrationality. Harvard, Yale, Columbia, and other universities have recently created departments where the science and art of teaching are imparted in the light of the latest discoveries in informing and training the mind. In the West, where the State university crowns the scheme of public education, this bringing to the people the benefit of the most helpful word of mental science is likely to be realized more fully than elsewhere in the United States. To-day exigencies, largely due to meagerness of support, are such that throughout the country, in the higher education as in the lower, there are not enough good teachers to go round. In selecting the faculties for Chicago and Leland Stanford universities, their presidents had to introduce an element of pecuniary competition, new in university halls, and not a little disconcerting to some venerable seats of learning inadequately endowed.

### THE LARGE GIVER AS PIONEER.

WHEN a large giver has initiative in him, and can lead the way in rendering some new public service of plain value, through emulation or sheer stress of competition his work is imitated far and wide. What he directly does is vastly exceeded by what he prompts others to do. Peter Cooper, in establishing Cooper Union for New York, did much to suggest to Charles Pratt the magnificent institute which has arisen in Brooklyn; and this foundation in its turn showed a generous friend of education in a third great city how best to give form to a long-considered purpose. The original intent of Mr. Anthony J. Drexel was that the Drexel Institute should be a college for women, not in but near Philadelphia. A visit to Pratt Institute resulted in his choosing an urban instead of a suburban site, and in founding with somewhat more than $3,000,000 a college of art, science, and industry for both sexes. The president of Drexel Institute, Mr. James MacAlister, as superintendent of the public schools of Philadelphia gave them a new efficiency. His experience has suggested departments in especial for the training of teachers and for the coördination of studies. In Chicago Mr. Philip D. Armour has recently given upward of $2,000,000 for aims which first found expression in the gift of Peter Cooper to New York. Like-minded with Mr. Cooper was the late Colonel R. T. Auchmuty, who founded the New York Trade Schools for the building and allied handicrafts. With maintenance these schools cost their founder and Mrs. Auchmuty about $425,000. In 1892 Mr. J. Pierpont Morgan gave $500,000 as endowment. Colonel Auchmuty proved to be a veritable pioneer: ten cities of America have established classes on his plan; those of Philadelphia enjoyed his generous aid. In 1893, during the Columbian Exposition, Mr. Marshall Field of Chicago gave $1,000,000 to found a museum in Jackson Park. Givers of large means and small have followed his example, and, enriched by many valuable exhibits from the Exposition, the museum already stands its worthy memorial. Mr. John D. Rockefeller not only gives largely, but insures that others will follow his example. In October, 1895, he offered the University of Chicago $2,000,000, in addition to his previous gifts to that institution, on condition that an equal sum should be given to it by 1900. His offer has already resulted in a gift of $1,025,000 by Miss Helen Culver of Chicago.

Because the welfare of the bee in our complicated civilization is more and more bound up with the welfare of the hive, the sphere of action for public bodies grows ever wider and more vital. Of necessity these bodies are limited in their preparation for difficult duty, in their freedom of action, and often they are glad to take a new path of public service opened by a judicious giver. Mrs. Quincy A. Shaw of Boston for some years maintained the kindergartens of that city at her own expense. In the fullness of time the civic authorities ingrafted them upon the system of public schools. New York has had a somewhat similar experience. In 1889 a few friends of the education which begins at the beginning formed an association to maintain free kindergartens. Last October kindergartens were conducted in fifteen public schools of the city, and the Board of Education announces its purpose to extend the system to every primary school as fast as its means will allow.

A large giver, instead of leading official action for the public good, may choose to coöperate with it. Thus George Peabody gave $2,000,000 for education in the Southern States, and John F. Slater $1,000,000. The revenues of these gifts, administered by the Hon. J. L. M. Curry of Washington, serve to supplement the support locally given to the schools and normal colleges of the South. The main purpose is to promote industrial education, and to lift the whole plane of instruction, by providing more and better teachers.

There can be helpful initiative and coöperation in matters of social reform, no less than in education. In 1885 a few men of capital built a model tenement in Cherry street, in one of the worst districts of New York, limiting to four per cent. the rate of dividend sought. This tenement has aroused Cherry street to a just discontent: to-day competitive landlords find it to their advantage to provide paved back yards, good plumbing, and a degree of comfort and order unknown in the neighborhood twelve years ago.

### UNDISCOVERED WORLDS.

To educate power, to impart skill, have been the aims of many large gifts; to add to the world of the known, to the sphere in which power and skill find play, has rarely entered the mind of the large giver. Original research, wherever in America prosecuted, is commonly an incident, seldom the main purpose. And yet the area for discovery, useful and helpful, is virtually infinite. The properties of substances as familiar as iron, copper, sulphur, are yet known only in part. To determine them fully would be to broaden the foundation-stones on which rises the whole fabric of industry. American science still awaits its adequate physical and chemical laboratory for pure research. Were such a laboratory to be established,—let us say at the Smithsonian Institution,—with a corps of trained investigators, it could with success attack problems too difficult for the individual inquirer, yet problems the solution of which is eagerly awaited by the metallurgist, the working chemist, the engineer, and the inventor. Through disposing the chemical elements in family groups, Newlands and Mendelejeff detected that the law of octaves obtains as truly in chemistry as in music. Observing gaps in the chemical gamut, Mendelejeff was able to predict the properties of the missing elements; three of these elements—gallium, scandium, and germanium—have been discovered, confirming in their characteristics the law which directed the quest for them. The verification of this «periodic law» chemists are convinced is no more than the first step toward mapping the molecular motions in which consist the properties, the characteristic modes of behavior, of a substance. An approach to success in this direction has already been achieved in the study of alloys; there seems to be no reason why, within the limits of possibility, the chemist of the twentieth century may not for a special purpose produce an alloy having any degree of elasticity, conductivity, tensile strength, or lightness which he shall desire. A little carbon added to iron gives us steel; a little nickel added to steel gives us in ferro-nickel yet greater tensile strength. When results such as these have been won in the darkness of empiricism, what may we not expect when research has lighted the lamp of law?

And this question of advanced physical exploration has a very practical side in its bearing on civilization. It is a common remark that there is wealth enough in the world were it only fairly apportioned. But let us remember that were the total yearly income of this country, one of the richest on earth, allotted equally among its inhabitants, each share would be less than $200. Could this be called wealth? In truth, the world is poor, and while equity in distribution is desirable, not less desirable is it to increase the sum of divisible things.

### BOTANY A PLASTIC ART.

In the experimental farm and garden there is quite as much to be done as in the physical and chemical laboratory. Botany is a plastic art; what has been achieved with the rose, the chrysanthemum, and the so-called small fruits, is only an earnest of what can be done in perfecting and diversifying plants and their products. Professor G. L. Goodale, the successor to Professor Asa Gray at Harvard, declares that were all the cereals now used for food swept out of existence, the experimental farms of America could probably replace them within fifty years. He estimates the number of flowering plants at 110,000, utilized by civilized man barely to the extent of one per cent. As foods, as fibers for textiles, as sources of perfume and ornament, many neglected plants, he tells us, offer rich rewards to the explorer and man of experiment; while, too, our common fruits can be improved both in flavor and beauty. Professor Goodale warmly commends the work of acclimatization and experiment going forward at two splendid benefactions for botany —the Missouri Botanical Garden in St. Louis and the Arnold Arboretum in Boston. Their work, he holds, has only to be extended and linked with that of the experimental stations scattered throughout the Union immensely to enrich the resources of the country. Professor Goodale is a physician as well as a botanist, and he has a hopeful word to say concerning the remedial agents to be found or molded amid the disregarded wealth of forest and field.

### THE PREVENTION OF DISEASE.

In the sphere of medicine the rewards held out to the investigator are of even higher moment than those which tempt him in the physical laboratory or the garden. In 1892 the Laboratory of Hygiene, built through a gift of $50,000 from Henry C. Lea, and equipped through the munificence of the late Henry C. Gibson, was opened at the University of Pennsylvania, Philadelphia. The gift came on condition that the laboratory be suitably endowed, and that hygiene should be a compulsory study in the medical department of the university. The laboratory has been constructed and its work organized under the direction of Dr. John S. Billings. Here the chemistry and bacteriology of air, water, and foods are studied, with methods of detecting hurtful impurities. Diverse systems of ventilation, heating, drainage, and sewage disposal are compared. Many diseases, among them typhoid, erysipelas, diphtheria, and consumption, due to minute forms of life, are studied, as well as the best modes of disinfection, and of protection by inoculation such as since Jenner's day has banished smallpox from among civilized men. Although the laboratory has scarcely more than begun its work, it has already made valuable additions to our knowledge of the nature and effects of sewer-gases, of expired air, of dangerous dusts, of the means of destroying microscopic foes, such as the bacillus of typhoid fever.

### THE EXPLORATION OF MIND.

A LAND of promise, indeed, is it which to-day stretches itself before the investigator of the nature of the human body in health and disease; equally rich is the territory just opening to the explorer in the realm of mind. Psychology is reaping the gain which comes to a science when it adds experiment to observation, when it can surprise nature in her secrets by artificially varying the conditions of a question. Refined and subtle introspection of mental processes has well-nigh come to its limits and finished its work. To its store of discovery is being added, day by day, a knowledge of the contents and powers of the mind unimaginable in times when their study was a department of speculative philosophy, when to invoke the aid of instrumental tests would have seemed grotesque. To-day, apparatus, some of it most simple, some of it exquisitely ingenious, serves to explore impressibility, attention, the power to associate ideas; while light is incidentally thrown on the subtle play of imagination and the bonds of habit. Experimental psychology has exponents at every leading American university; one of its centers is at Worcester, Massachusetts, where Jonas G. Clark's gift, estimated at $1,500,000, has established Clark University. Here President G. Stanley Hall, aided by a corps of other investigators, is adding to the knowledge of mind with the special purpose of turning that knowledge to account in the economy of education. When a score of children are examined with regard to their quickness in recognizing tones and forms, in discriminating hue from hue, in detecting the features wherein similar flowers resemble one another, the aptitudes and deficiencies of each child are not only revealed, but may be definitely measured. The teacher is thus brought to see what areas of each mind will best repay cultivation, and what other areas, from natural sterility, require attention not less gainful. Yet more, well-contrived experiments are constantly determining just when the details of this education can best be timed, and how they can best proceed. Professor Scripture of Yale, formerly of Clark University, in a series of preliminary tests, has found reason to believe that the acquisition of a foreign language can be hastened threefold when pictures accompany the words. He looks to the psychological laboratory for definite guidance as to how all the faculties—for color, music, what not—may be elicited, and brought to their best estate. The psychologist in the class-room is thus in the way of solving the difficulty which attends the lengthiness and variety of our courses of instruction in school and college; of giving invaluable aid in making up the round of elective studies in the university. He is, in short, addressing himself to the task of both enriching and lengthening life. A generously wide curriculum, when joined to matured experimental methods of discovering aptitude and bringing it out, can put the world for the first time within reach of its truest riches, in the ability of its young minds rightly appraised and fully developed.

### TALENT-SAVING.

ONCE more emerges the need that the values in girls and boys of uncommon talent, or skill, be fully brought out in those possessed of little means or none. Despite the steadily rising requirements for matriculation, nearly every college and university in the land has constantly to turn away from its doors candidates worthy and poor. Among them, without doubt, are those who have it in them to add to knowledge, to prosecute original research. If discoverers be found and given a chance, every other discovery will follow from that. Many as are the scholarships and fellowships provided for those who seek the best education, they are all too few. Mr. Joseph Pulitzer of New York, at a yearly outlay of $15,000, enables pupils from the public schools, selected for merit, to obtain collegiate instruction. At present they are seventy in number. Such aid proceeds upon the conviction that the strength of an army lies even more in its officers than in its rank and file. Original power, inventive talent, the faculty for leadership, are rare; but need we regret that common trades and businesses are largely recruited from high schools and colleges? Rather let us rejoice that every-day men and women are brought to the utmost fullness of life, into that active sympathy with the highest work and the best thought which only cultivation can bestow.

### THE AX LAID AT THE ROOT.

EDUCATION, momentous as it is, does not fill the whole round of human need. Not only ignorance, but destitution, and destitution with disease, afflict mankind. Typical here of a revolution in the attitude of all philanthropy is the contrast between the views of the physician of to-day and those of his predecessor of the last generation. In the profession of medicine thirty years ago the conviction reigned that disease was largely inevitable; to-day there is knowledge that disease is as largely preventable. And this knowledge extends to other ills than those which fill the hospitals: in the scientific examination of chronic poverty, of drunkenness, of insanity, of criminality, the most effective means of attack are coming into daylight. Charitable agencies are scrutinized with a cool, informed eye, which often detects them fostering the very distress they would succor. In Charles Booth's masterly study of the labor and life of the London poor, we have a model of what can be done toward giving definiteness and measure to perplexing social maladies. Charity can work its will only as espoused by wisdom to show it

> What must be, and what may yet be better.

The note of the new philanthropy is not one so much of hope—that vague sentiment which is little else than desire in ignorance—as of expectation based on knowledge that certain grievous ills of society can be not abated simply, but uprooted. The wisest helper of men strives so to plan his aid that soon it may be needless.

### RECREATION FOR THE PEOPLE.

LIFE has other sides than those which touch education and the war on disease and misery: life is also for joy. In promoting healthy and refining recreation, large giving has before it a field little more than entered. With the growing domination of machinery, the more and more minute subdivision of labor, there comes a greater need than ever for the cultivation of talent and taste for art and music. In Europe the masterpieces of Raphael, Murillo, and Velasquez are public property; it is beginning to be felt by the rich men of America that the hardly less inspiring canvases of Millet, Corot, and Inness are out of place in private mansions. But in power to confer delight, the music-room is much more democratic than the picture-gallery. The love of good music is well-nigh universal, and no service has ever been rendered the people of New York, Boston, and Chicago which has evoked more enthusiasm than the high-class operas, concerts, and oratorios furnished them on nominal terms during recent winter seasons. Cincinnati, through a gift of $50,000 from Mr. W. S. Groesbeck, has for some years enjoyed free open-air concerts of a high order. The Boston Symphony, the leading orchestra in America, is supported by its founder, Mr. Henry L. Higginson, who has thus greatly served the cause of education in music. Mrs. Jeannette M. Thurber of New York has founded a National Conservatory of Music, which offers the highest order of instruction, and placed it under the direction of Dr. Antonín Dvořák, the greatest living composer. The Conservatory imposes no fee on those quite without means, whose talent promises distinction. The new movement for education in music recognizes the fact that where one student can learn to execute music well, a hundred hearers can be taught to take a heightened pleasure in an opera or a symphony; hence the increase of popular exposition as distinct from instrumental instruction. Musical education, extending as it is throughout the length and breadth of the country, has friends among the very foremost teachers, and in spheres remote enough from music. Professor Henry C. Adams, who fills the chair of political economy at the University of Michigan, and who is an alumnus of Johns Hopkins, has said: «Nothing in my life at Baltimore did me more good than the fine music I heard at the Peabody Institute. If I were a rich man, the first gift I should make to the University of Michigan would provide it with the service of Seidl, Thomas, and Damrosch. Our education to-day is lopsided: it is addressed to the intellect, and to very little else; emotion, sentiment, are almost ignored. What is the sense in taking so much pains to assure the power to command leisure; while the power to enjoy that leisure is almost neglected?» Since Professor Adams said this his university has established an excellent course of musical instruction.

### MONUMENTALISM.

In this rapid survey of the *when* and the *what* of large giving, its *how* remains to be glanced at. An allurement which has not always been resisted is that of monumentalism. A fund withdrawn from use to display can prefer only the plea of the incidental refinement of public taste. The buildings of Girard strike the visitor as much too costly and elaborate for the housing of needy orphans. In more than one temple of art reared by private munificence we have imposing architectural effects at the expense of security against fire. The frankly expressed intent of James Lick originally was to build himself a monument on some lofty peak of the Pacific coast. It was suggested to him that such a shaft could easily be demolished by a foreign foe, and that the projected memorial might fitly take the form of an observatory on an inland eminence. Accordingly his name is perpetuated, and the cause of astronomy advanced, in the noble structure which crowns Mount Hamilton. To mark the opposite pole of sentiment, we have the case of a large giver on the Atlantic seaboard, Mr. Charles Pratt, who designed his buildings in such wise that in case his educational purpose failed he might readily convert the premises into a factory.

### MAINTENANCE.

A BENEFACTION fitly housed and equipped for its work, the next desideratum is that provision be made for its maintenance. Many foundations in America lead a life of struggle, of crippled usefulness, from lack of adequate endowment. Cooper Union, New York, perhaps the most admirable benefaction in the metropolis, has an endowment of only $1,500,000; with $500,000 more its usefulness could be doubled. Its officers point with sorrow to a waiting list of more than a thousand young men anxious for admission to its classes. Lick Observatory, with its instruments built at a cost of $610,000, has an endowment fund of only $90,000. It is incorporated with the University of California. So scanty are the appropriations for its support, that while doing work which places it in the foremost rank of the world's observatories, it has the absurdly small number of seven observers, as against a working force of forty-eight at Paris, twenty-four at Greenwich, and fifty at Harvard. Only when suitably furnished with additional observerships will the Lick Observatory cease to be the most signal instance in America of a great gift merely launched, and missing much of its purpose through its work being miserably undermanned.

With an eye to the vicissitudes of even the best investments, and confident that if an institution is not to fall behind it must advance, the trustees of Pratt Institute have accumulated a large reserve fund. Apart from direct losses of property such as have befallen some great benefactions, it must be borne in mind that the earning power of capital tends to shrink by virtue of the very scientific conquest of nature which benefactions largely promote. The city of New York, in buying its northerly parks, borrowed the money at a rate which brings the investor less than two and a half per cent. per annum. When an endowment is insufficient, and particularly when an annual deficit must be referred to a founder, there is discouragement of the best work; for how can the haunting dread be banished that he who holds the purse-strings may any day prove a Mr. Ready-to-halt?

Next to making it enough as an element in the success of a gift is the leaving its trustees untrammeled. Johns Hopkins gave his board freedom to form plans as they thought proper, and to alter them at will. His wisdom has been abundantly justified. Mr. Francis T. King, the chairman, and his co-trustees, received $3,300,000 for a hospital; they erected and equipped the buildings out of the income, leaving the original fund, available for endowment, increased by $113,000. In these days of mutation in the methods of education and philanthropy, as in all else, restrictions imposed by a donor, however wise for his own day, are apt eventually to work harm where he meant to do good. In times past language, the arts of expression, held the first place in culture; as a survival of this preference there is apt to be to-day comparatively meager provision for university students of scientific bent. Yet these, were trustees always free, would, from the rarity and value of their powers, receive at least equal encouragement with youth of literary inclinations.

### ENLISTING COÖPERATION.

BECAUSE there are bounds even to the most liberal benefaction, it has always proved advantageous when its work has enlisted public sympathy. This has been chiefly the case, of course, when the administration has been able and just; and next, when no sectarian sieve has been set up between the public and the good intended to be done. Responsive to the spirit of the time, we see denominational colleges and hospitals managed with more and more relaxation of their original exclusiveness. The conviction steadily gains ground that no man or woman other than the best should direct them, and that for their benefits the only qualifications should be simple need and desert. When a benefactor is as remote and hallowed a figure as John Harvard, it becomes an honor to build on his foundation; but when days of stress befall a recent gift, help is more easily secured when the institution bears an impersonal name. Here it is necessary to distinguish between an institution as a whole and its several departments. These latter, each requiring comparatively moderate outlay, may, as in those which cluster at Yale and Princeton, fitly commemorate honored names. But with regard to the general purposes of an institution, subscribers are human, and do not like to have their donations merged in a monument which glorifies somebody else. Johns Hopkins's original intent was to found the «University of Baltimore.» Had he done so, there is little doubt that funds needed to sustain the work of his university would be forthcoming more freely than they are. The Metropolitan Museum of Art in New York, from its public character, draws to itself many donations and bequests which would never go to a museum other than public. The giver of a great gift can go beyond entitling it with an impersonal name: in a recent case the last extreme of self-effacement has been reached by a man who has taken pains that no picture, bust, memorial, or other mention of himself shall be found within the walls he reared. Almost as striking is the example of Mr. John D. Rockefeller, the founder of the University of Chicago. His gifts aggregate $7,426,000,—more than half its total benefactions,—yet he has not become even a trustee; he has not suggested a single appointment, or tried in any way to control or influence the work of organizing the university; and he has sought on its behalf large gifts from others. From unknown givers many colleges, asylums, hospitals, receive noteworthy aid. New York University is indebted for a round million to anonymous givers. A few years ago its medical school received $300,000 from a friend who wished not only to be unknown, but to have the gift unannounced to the public. The example was catching. A donor whose name is withheld has recently built a residence-hall at an outlay approaching $200,000. At the bidding of a third unnamed friend, the university is soon to enjoy a library structure to cost more than $500,000.

### TO BE RICH CAN MEAN MORE THAN EVER.

BRIEF as this glance at large giving has been, it may nevertheless suggest that superfluity to-day can do more for mankind than ever before: the paths for beneficence are broader, they are better understood. Large giving now can make the most and best of human nature in aiding education rightly timed, justly adapted to individual power and need. It can equip the explorer, and bring from the mine, the garden, the laboratory, a thousand new resources. Nor ought any narrow regard for the utilities cramp the quests it sets on foot. Were no observatory telescope to be directed to the heavens for the next fifty years, the mariner would sail the seas as securely as ever. Yet, if the astronomer with spectroscope and camera can add proof to proof that the universe is in substance one, can give it a vastly extended diameter, unfold a fresh chapter in its history, make yet clearer its immanent order, has he not done something to dignify and wing the mind of man?

Physical science, unfinished as it is on every side, is opulent with promise to the large giver; even more abounding is promise in the field of social science—the field in which individual weal becomes more implicated with every passing year. Let us take, for example, the conditions which create the large giver himself. The winds of fortune which heap up his treasure as a Northern snowdrift do so, in part, by making bare necessity yet barer. In decided measure the want to which he ministers springs from the very maladjustments which to him have brought excess. What are the causes at work here? They may well engage the skilled inquirer, whose opportunity for the work, perchance, grows out of a gift from superabundance. Have not many great fortunes been the rewards of preëminent business capacity, more gainful to the community than to itself, which fact, on proof, draws the sting of discontent? Have not other great fortunes risen through turning to account opportunities for immense profit, which profit would remain in the hands of the community could public spirit and private probity be enlisted to that end? How far has the enginery of taxation been made a means of strengthening the strong; and how can that tendency with equity be reversed, so that the disparity between what men need and what they get shall be less extreme? In advancing such inquiries as these, in promoting, as the response may indicate, the culture of the sense of social right and duty, the large giver strikes at the roots of both want and surplusage, and wins for himself the worthiest remembrance among men.

*George Iles.*

# «FLOWER BEFORE THE LEAF.»

I.

FLOWER before the leaf, boy-loved Rhodora,
Morning-pink along the valley of the birch and maple,
Now the green begins to cling about the silver birches,
Rush the maple buds and ruddy yonder hillside;
Sudden as the babbling brook or robin's whistle,
Spring-swift, thou art come in the old places,
In the hollow swamp-land, bloom on brake!

Flower before the leaf!
Ah, once here in the sweet season—
Flash of blue wings, birds in chorus,
Ere the violet, ere the wild-rose,
While the linden lingered and the elm-tree—
Years ago a boy's heart broke in blossom,
Flower before the leaf,
While he wandered down the valley loving you;
And above him, and around him,
Beam and gleam and distant color,
Waiting, waiting, hung the Spirit
To rush forth upon the world.

II.

Somewhere in the years of the dawn did I dream that a youth all boy-like stands?—
And the tender Rhodora's bloom, the first of the year, is red in his pure, sweet hands;
And in the doorway bending, dark-haired, bright-cheeked, a girlish form appears,—
A word, a smile, a blush, and out of the blue a black rook downward nears,—
And all the spirits rush to his heart, and the fragrant world, save her, turns dim,
The flowering of whose face was the glory of spring through the years of the dawn to him!

*G. E. Woodberry.*

# SOME WRITERS OF GOOD LETTERS.[1]

## EDWARD FITZGERALD—JAMES RUSSELL LOWELL—MATTHEW ARNOLD.

LAMB, in his whimsical way, talks about the «books which are no books, *biblia a-biblia.*» He drew a wry face at court calendars and directories as he wrote his anathema; at «the works of Hume, Gibbon, Robertson, . . . and, generally, all those volumes which ‹no gentleman's library should be without.›» His distaste is sympathetically understood to-day; and though it is impossible to yield him his Gibbon as belonging among biblia a-biblia, the drift of the phrase is accepted as sound. In the present instance, however, it is recalled for the sake of its admirable description of some of the best books in the language, some collections of letters. Such books are veritable biblia a-biblia. Their contents were never intended by their authors to be published. We owe their pages to the loving hands of those friends or kindred who have collected and preserved them somewhat as a woman of gentle feeling gathers old rose-leaves and puts them in a jar to achieve a fragrant immortality.

Just because there is no literature in letters, placed therein of malice prepense, they make the most exquisite literature of all. They have no professional flavor. When they have, it spoils them to a certain extent. Regnault wrote good letters; so did his countryman Berlioz; so, finallv, did Mendelssohn: but not one of these correspondents is a model, because not one was without the accent of his particular art. In the best correspondence there is rarely discovered an attempt deliberately to exploit the writer's point of view in ways that would appeal to a public audience. The true letter-writer, fascinating a whole nation of readers after his death, does so because when he wrote this or that letter he cared for nothing save the pleasure of appealing to his friend. There are, of course, letters and letters. Some of the most famous and most readable belong to times when people took as much pains over their private correspondence as over their most public acts. Goethe had a Jovian way with him even in ephemeral epistles. He always wrote in character. So also did Voltaire. Walpole, who was witty because he could not help himself, was furthermore witty because he wanted to be so; polished, courtly, artificial, because when he sat down to write the smallest note he thought of the impression it would convey, just as an actor thinks of the effect of his art upon his audience. The Earl of Orford never lets himself go. Neither does Chesterfield. Neither does Macaulay, quite, though he felt some, if not all, of the softening influences of his time; and while in Trevelyan's «Life and Letters» he is still the pontifical Thomas that he was in his conversation and in his books, he is, in spite of himself, a brilliant epistolary figure.

In so far as a man's time affects the nature of his correspondence, he must be criticized accordingly. No one counts the artificiality of Walpole against him for a sin, any more than one blames the dilettanti of France in the eighteenth century for writing like—dilettanti. But appreciation of their sincerity, such as it was, of their representative character, and of their entertaining qualities, need not blind us to this crucial fact, that theirs are not the best letters. The best letters are those in which the character of the writer is accurately mirrored and shown to be in itself delightful. In such letters the writer is frequently observed rising superior, with serene unconsciousness, to the epistolary accent of his time. Cowper offers a conspicuous example. Compared with his great contemporary Walpole, he is not so amusing a correspondent; but his letters are more cherished possessions than the earl's. Both writers give us vivid self-portraiture, but in one case the picture is

[1] «Letters of Edward Fitzgerald.» Edited by William Aldis Wright. In 2 vols. 8vo, pp. 348, 368. London and New York: The Macmillan Co.

«Letters of Edward Fitzgerald to Fanny Kemble, 1871–1883.» Edited by William Aldis Wright. 8vo, 261. London and New York: The Macmillan Co.

«Letters of James Russell Lowell.» Edited by Charles Eliot Norton. In 2 vols. 8vo, pp. 418, 464. New York: Harper & Brothers.

«Letters of Matthew Arnold, 1848–1888.» Collected and arranged by George W. E. Russell. In 2 vols. 8vo, pp. 467, 442. London and New York: The Macmillan Co.

lovable, and in the other it is not. Thus the observation of Joubert, that «Une femme qui voudrait écrire comme Mme. de Sévigné serait ridicule, parce qu'elle n'est pas Mme. de Sévigné,» may be applied to much more than the question of style by which it was provoked. The important conclusion to which it leads is that the very soul of Mme. de Sévigné is in her letters, and, style or no style, her magic cannot be renewed. There is the key to imperishable correspondence. It makes us acquainted with what is best in a noble individuality. One hears much talk about «art» nowadays, and the finesse with which a letter may be written is admired beyond measure; but the artless letters are the letters to go back to over and over—the letters in which matters of literary or artistic significance bubble up to the surface with no more suggestion of the «shop» about them than when the writer is talking about daffodils or the sea. In the correspondence of Edward Fitzgerald there are constant references to Mme. de Sévigné, whom he adored.

> She now occupies Montaigne's place in my room [he writes to Mrs. Kemble], well—worthily: she herself a Lover of Montaigne, and with a spice of his free thought and speech in her. I am sometimes vext I never made her acquaintance till last year: but perhaps it was as well to have such an acquaintance reserved for one's latter years. The fine Creature! much more alive to me than most Friends.

And then, four years later, in a letter to Mr. Aldis Wright, there comes a peculiarly eloquent reference to one source of her extraordinary charm:

> Half her Beauty is the liquid melodiousness of her language—all unpremeditated as a Blackbird's.

Unpremeditated as a blackbird's! The words may seem a little rhetorical when employed with reference to the letters of Fitzgerald, Lowell, or Matthew Arnold. Yet if those three men exert a positive fascination in their letters, it is for much the same reason that moved the first of them to admire Mme. de Sévigné. All were possessed of individuality fitted to win and hold the friendship of every one who knew them. They wrote with an absence of premeditation which makes them already as classical in the direction of private correspondence as in that of formally published literature. They were men of letters, all three, in the technical sense of the phrase; but in their correspondence they are men pure and simple—personalities, figures appreciated for their own sakes, no matter how much their literary tastes may contribute to the enrichment of their letters. Their qualities are rare. Contrast them with those which appear in the recently published «Vailima Letters» of Stevenson, in the correspondence of Dante Rossetti brought out not long ago by his brother. The nineteenth century has produced much more of the morbid kind of thinking and feeling which we find typified by Stevenson and Rossetti in their letters than it has of the lucidity and health which characterized the three subjects of this paper. It is no whimsical assumption which detaches Fitzgerald, Lowell, and Arnold from their time. Though two of them at least were nurtured by it, though Lowell and Arnold threw themselves heart and soul into the interests of their respective nations, and were modern to their finger-tips, it is surprising to see how readily they adapt themselves to Fitzgerald's remote atmosphere when the three are met together. It is surprising, because it seems paradoxical, that a busy diplomatist, a hard-working school-inspector, should speak, for all their literature and nature-worship and poetry, the same tongue as that of a hermit living among books and flowers, and forever turning wistfully to the past.

But the solution of their harmony is the explanation of their charm. They had the instincts which belong to no time. They had imagination, taste, humor. They had the love of beauty and of purity. Above all, they had the two supreme gifts, intellectual originality and human sympathy. It is astonishing how those gifts, especially the second, lift a man above his time, make him its master, keep him from ever being subdued to the stuff he works in, keep him a man and yet three fourths pure spirit. The most absurd thing in the world would be to read any of Arnold's letters merely for so-called «facts» about his life; to read Lowell's correspondence just to find out what he did on his diplomatic missions; to read Fitzgerald for «new light» on his translations from the Persian. One can imagine with what gusto the Omar Khayyám faddists turned to Fitzgerald's «Letters and Literary Remains» when they first appeared in 1889. But it is not his place in the world of scholarship, it is not his work, it is not anything concrete, that should be sought in those volumes, or in the collection of letters to Mrs. Kemble which was brought out a short time since. It is the temperament, the heart, the feeling underlying a passage like this. Writing to Mrs. Kemble on a subject that appealed closely to him, he says:

> Now once more for French Songs. When I was in Paris in 1830, just before that Revolution, I stopped one Evening on the Boulevards by the Madeleine to listen to a Man who was singing to his Barrel-organ. Several passing «Blouses» had stopped also: not only to listen, but to join in the Songs, having bought little «Libretti» of the words from the Musician. I bought one too, for, I suppose, the smallest French Coin; and assisted in the Song which the Man called out beforehand (as they do Hymns at Church), and of which I enclose you the poor little Copy. «*Le Bon Pasteur*, s'il vous plait» — I suppose the Circumstances: the «beau temps,» the pleasant Boulevards, the then so amiable People, all contributed to the effect this Song had upon me; anyhow, it has constantly revisited my memory for these forty-three years; and I was thinking, the other day, touched me more than any of Béranger's most beautiful Things. This, however, may be only one of «Old Fitz's» Crotchets, as Tennyson and others would call them.

For all that it implies, much more than for what it tells upon the surface, the foregoing passage is invaluable to a student of Fitzgerald's character. The last word is used advisedly. We have heard of his life, of his solitary tastes, of his modest and yet deep learning, of his art in translation: but it is his character of which it is interesting to hear more and more; and in the picture he draws of himself, linked quickly to the strangers about him on the Parisian street, joining so sympathetically in their spontaneous feeling — in this free confession he touches the reader's heart where otherwise he would have touched only his mind. The virtue of a man like Fitzgerald is that his sympathies are open to the movement of the times, because they are open to conviction on any subject under the sun. He was a hermit, yes, and he seems to have withdrawn himself from what we call «the active work of the world»; but as a matter of fact, he looked at public affairs as wisely and as sympathetically as the most bustling of his contemporaries. Tennyson and Thackeray, two of the most worldly-wise writers of the century, were his dear friends, and honored him profoundly. Would they have felt the tenderness that they undoubtedly did feel for him if he had been a mere indifferentist? It was Carlyle, one of the most strenuous thinkers on social and economic and spiritual matters that England has ever known, who wrote to Fitzgerald:

> Thanks for your friendly human letter; . . . One gets so many *in*human letters, ovine, bovine, porcine, etc., etc.: I wish you would write a little oftener; when the beneficent Daimon suggests, fail not to lend ear to him.

It is good for the hearts, it may be repeated, of his readers to-day that Fitzgerald went on writing his «friendly human letters.» He wakes uplifting thoughts. There is a savor as of the kindest, truest human things in every line he wrote, and this not alone in the letters of his maturity, but in those of his early manhood. Thus in his twenty-fourth year he wrote to his friend Allen a letter in which he deals with friendship almost as tenderly, certainly with as much penetration, as he shows in the letters of his old age, which chiefly make up the volume devoted to Mrs. Kemble. In his letter to Allen he says:

> Lord Bacon's Essay on Friendship is wonderful for its truth: and I often feel its truth. He says that with a Friend «a man *tosseth* his thoughts,» an admirable saying, which one can understand, but not express otherwise. But I feel that, being alone, one's thoughts and feelings, from want of communication, become heaped up and clotted together, as it were: and so lie like undigested food heavy upon the mind: but with a friend one tosseth them about, so that the air gets between them, and keeps them fresh and sweet.

Of this tossing of his thoughts Fitzgerald was very fond, and he indulged in the exercise with a wholesome freedom, a cheery frankness, which are in themselves inspiriting, leaving a pleasant memory even when the actual things said are of no great consequence. There is, for example, his bantering way whenever he refers to the forehead of his friend Spedding. To Samuel Laurence the painter he writes:

> You have of course read the account of Spedding's forehead landing in America. English sailors hail it in the Channel, mistaking it for Beachy Head.

The sensitive ear can catch the writer's laugh, merry, affectionate, the very music of innocent glee.

The last word is possibly an odd one to use in the description of a man, and yet why should it seem odd? The guilelessness of Fitzgerald, the perennial sweetness and gentleness of his nature — one returns to all this, and upon each return loves it the more. He was, on the whole, one of the most lovable men that ever lived. His modesty has passed into a tradition. Mrs. Kemble called him a man of genius who was more anxious to remain unknown than most people are to become famous. How his Omar quatrains waited for the renown which they now enjoy is one of the commonplace anecdotes of literature. And there was not the smallest suggestion of pose in his life. He meant, with all his soul, every shade of his modesty, his seclusiveness, his absorption in quiet things. When Frederick Tennyson was traveling in Italy in 1840, Fitzgerald wrote to him:

> While you are wandering among ruins, waterfalls, and temples, and contemplating them as you sit in your lodgings, I poke about with a book and a colour-box by the side of the river Ouse—quiet scenery enough—and make horrible sketches. The best thing to me in Italy would be that you are there.

That last line is no exaggeration. Fitzgerald was certainly no insensitive man, but nothing on the Continent could ever have given him the same pleasure that he got from his own country and countrymen.

> Well, say as you will, there is not, and never was, such a country as Old England—never was there such a Gentry as the English. They will be the distinguishing mark and glory of England in History, as the Arts were of Greece, and War of Rome. I am sure no travel would carry me to any land so beautiful, as the good sense, justice, and liberality of my good countrymen make this.

At first glance this may seem to mean no more than the insularity with which many of Fitzgerald's countrymen have made us unpleasantly familiar. But this would be a hasty conception of his character. His insularity is rather of the sort which may be studied in some of Lamb's essays, in a paper like «Blakesmoor in Hertfordshire,» for example. It is the insularity which is rooted in high-minded pride of race, in love of old gardens, old English books, the poetry of English life and history. Prepossessions such as Elia's, such as Fitzgerald's, may not seem defensible to the hard logician; but to any one who recognizes the right of the human spirit to be as illogical as it pleases, so that it makes for whiteness, loveliness, and the stimulation in us of what is right and fine, the calm «narrowness» of such a passage as that just quoted is simply an unmixed delight. Behind it is the affectionate heart of the writer, warm with natural and manly feeling. Neither does the spiritual placidity of the man involve intellectual stagnation. As has been said above, Fitzgerald had the great gift of intellectual originality. He wrote out of a full mind, and his independence of judgment gives to the reader a sharp sensation of pleasure: with the independence there is such maturity, such mellowness, such a sense of leisured and careful thought. For this alone Fitzgerald would be remarkable: for the fullness of his letters. There is thought in them to the brim and running over. And always it is such sane thought, so fresh, so sympathetic. He had few prejudices, and not any fetishes. He was not afraid to speak his mind in blame, and it is noticeable also that he was equally fearless in praise. His royal appreciation of Dickens is in fine contrast to the patronage which that writer has received at the hands of more recent critics. Fitzgerald's estimates are usually discriminating, and there is a heartiness about them that takes the reader captive. To read them is to feel, as has been insisted upon above, that hard thought was his persistent genius; but this fact is, after all, not the one upon which it is specially desired to concentrate attention in these pages. Enough has been said elsewhere about Fitzgerald's labors, about his literature; and whether or not he judged Dickens correctly is not now the point. The great point is that every one of his letters, whether it be devoted to Persian poetry or an English village lad, or both, is the revelation of a personality which haunts the reader with increasing tenderness as time goes on. «He hated a set dinner-party,» says one who knew him well, and he hated it for a reason suggested in lines which make him more endeared to his readers: «It is very cold here: ice of nights: but my Tulips and Anemones hold up still.» «Well: a Blackbird is singing in the little Garden outside my Lodging Window, which is frankly opened to what Sun there is.» His nature, like his window, was «frankly opened» to the sun, to the fragrance and freshness of his garden. That was why he hated a set dinner-party; that is why his letters are an immeasurable solace. It is such a relief, after all the «literary» talk which floods the world, after all the «technic» and «style» of which one hears interminable things on every hand, to find a great writer, a genius of literature, living his life out for the sake of the fresh air in its paths, the flowers in the hedge, the wind upon the heath; to find him using as his touchstone in every phase of existence not the words, words, words of the «literary man,» not the notions of modern introspection, but the divinity in things, the humanity, the infinite tenderness, of which our glib «technicians» take little account.

Whatever speaks of the inherent nobility in man touches him and wins his admiration.

Thus his friends were not Thackeray, Carlyle, and Tennyson alone. They were his Lowestoft and Woodbridge seamen; they were the country folk, the plain, honest, brave souls everywhere, even in the city, when he could find them there. They eluded him generally in London, however; and though he loved the town for his friends there, for the opera, for the theater, for a few other pleasures, the sum of his feeling in regard to it is expressed pretty closely in the following line from a letter to Mr. Norton: «What bothered me in London was—all the Clever People going wrong with such clever Reasons for so doing which I could n't confute.» There are no «clever» things in Fitzgerald's correspondence: but there are noble things; there are

High and passionate thoughts,
To their own music chanted;

and for these it is an experience to go through the three volumes of letters. What the man did, who his friends were, how many books he published and how he published them, why he became interested in Persian poetry, and how his translations from Omar, from Calderon, and from Æschylus were carried out—exactly where all these things occupied him, and for how long, may be learned from the correspondence if the reader's tastes are biographical, historical, critical. But it is a merely human sympathy which will get most out of Edward Fitzgerald.

To the enjoyment of Lowell's letters it is necessary to bring a sympathy like that which unlocks the gate to Fitzgerald's innermost charm; and all that has been said concerning the latter's exact balancing of the claims of literature with those of life—rich, sensitive life—may be said of his American contemporary and friend. But Lowell, while less eccentric than Fitzgerald, was really a more striking compound of apparently irreconcilable qualities. He had the raciness, the profound human insight and sympathy, of Fitzgerald; and added to this he had a greater number of conflicting interests. Not literature alone, but all the threads of social life were woven into the fabric of his career; and while his kinship to Fitzgerald is the one thing to which it is imperative that the reader should hold fast, there is a subtle distinction between the two which is almost equally important. Perhaps it is most succinctly stated in the observation that while Fitzgerald was Vergilian by temperament, Lowell was Horatian. With one you stand ankle-deep in the rich soil, amid the white oxen and the brown rustics who guide the plows. With the other you drive over the same fields at ease, pausing delighted from time to time to rescue a daisy that the senseless steel has thrown with the upturned sod to mingle with the loam. The scene is the same, the sky gleams with the same light, there is the same freshness, there is the same sweet smell of mother earth, and the same sense of proprietorship animates your guide. There is a difference in the latter's way of enjoying his domain, that is all.

Lowell, like Horace, belongs to the modern world; and it is perhaps easier to enter into the spirit of his correspondence than into that of Fitzgerald, with whose genuineness a certain old-world quaintness is not incompatible. Lowell could be quaint of phrase when he chose; but if Fitzgerald's charm is that he sees life across the beautiful serenity of an English garden, Lowell's may be discovered in his American alertness to every movement in modern life. This comes out not merely in his diplomatic experiences: it is proclaimed by the very texture of his «Biglow Papers»; it is revealed in the «contemporaneous» character of his letters. International copyright, civil-service reform, and similar topics, recur again and again in the two volumes edited by Professor Norton; and in one letter to Mr. Godkin there is a perfect example of the way in which his literary and political intelligences were intertwined.

By the way [he says], I found a curious misprint in the new edition of Chapman (vol. ii, p. 159), which I thought might make a paragraph for the *Nation*.

«*Caucusses*
That cut their too large murtherous thieveries
To their den's length still.»

He means *Cacus*, of course, though the editor did n't see it, for the word does n't occur in his index of proper names. It is a curious *sors castigatoris preli*, at any rate, and hits true, for the Caucus always cuts down its candidates to the measure of its robber's cave. It shows, too, that old Chapman pronounced *a au*.

The last playful line is eloquent; it marks so characteristically the return of Lowell from the political to the literary theme. For without losing any interest in the first, he was, it must be admitted, very much in love with the second, and this fact is incessantly brought forward by his letters. How spontaneously he writes to Miss Norton, apropos of his readings in early English and French literature at Elmwood in 1874: «Ten hours a day, on an average, I have been at it for the last two months, and get so absorbed that I turn grudgingly to anything else.» Yet to direct attention to this bookish absorption of Lowell's is only to inspire a swift protest against misinterpretation of it. «Do you find the real inside of him in his letters?» he wrote, with reference to Richard H. Dana. «I think not—and this is a pretty sure test.» Apply the test to Lowell. The «real inside of him» is in his letters, and it is not purely an affair of bookish absorption. It is much more the kind of nature which is reflected in the following fragment from a letter to Thomas Hughes:

And so our bright and busy-minded —— is married, and happily too. After mature deliberation with the help of a pipe, I don't think her husband's not smoking is a fatal objection. A—— would tell you that Napoleon did n't, and Goethe and several other more or less successful men. I consent, therefore, on condition that he stuff his pockets with baccy for his poor parishioners when he goes his rounds; they know how good it is. . . . I remember an old crone whom I used to meet every Sunday in Kensington Gardens when she had her outings from the almshouse, and whom I kept supplied with Maccaboy. I think I made her perfectly happy for a week, and on such cheap terms as make me blush. She was a dear old thing, and used to make me prettier curtsies than I saw at court. Good heavens, of what uncostly material is our earthly happiness composed—if we only knew it! What incomes have we not had from a flower, and how unfailing are the dividends of the seasons!

This shows, with unmistakable finality, the «real inside» of Lowell, the part of his nature which was most often in control of his faculties. For him the dividends of the seasons were always profuse, the compound interest on them gathering as they sprang from the contact of his heart with the murmuring, invisible life of the earth. Every one knows how the typical «literary man» sees nature through «literary» spectacles, and how he falls to comparing the magic of the trees with the magic of the poets, not always to the advantage of the former. Lowell could make such comparisons, but the ingenuous spirit in which he made them, preserving always his loyalty to the primrose rather than to the flower's singer, is one of his most potent claims upon the admiration of his readers. It comes out enchantingly in a letter to Professor Norton, written from Elmwood, in which he says:

The nameless author of that delightful poem «The Squyr of Lowe Degree» (may God him save and see!) gives a list of every bird he can think of that sang to comfort his hero. Here they are: (1) lavrock, (2) nightingale, (3) pie, (4) popinjay, (5) throstil, (6) marlyn, (7) wren, (8) jay, (9) sparrow, (10) nuthatch, (11) starling, (12) goldfinch, (13) ousel. On Monday the 5th I walked up to the Oaks with Stillman, and in a quarter of an hour had noted on a paper the following birds (most of which counted by dozens): (1) robin, (2) Wilson's thrush (singing), (3) chewink, (4) bluebird (warbling as in spring), (5) phœbe (doing his best), (6) ground sparrow (singing), (7) tree sparrow (singing), (8) nuthatch, (9) flicker (laughing and crying like Andromache), (10) chickadee (doing all he could), (11) goldfinch, (12) linnet, (13) jay, (14) crow (to balance his popinjay), (15) catbird. Thus I take down the gauntlet which you left hanging for all comers in your English hedge. I don't believe that hedge birds are a whit more respectable than hedge priests or hedge schoolmasters. All the while we were there the air was tinkling with one or other of them. Remember—this was in October. Three cheers for the rivers of Damascus!

Affectionately always,
HOSEA BIGLOW.

*Et ego in Arcadia*, says Mr. Wilbur.

There can be no doubt as to which Muse held conclusive possession of Lowell's heart when he wrote this letter. Nature, nature, the infinite, inexhaustible loveliness of nature—this is his never-failing resource and the root of all that is best in his letters. It kept him young. He exclaims:

Thank God, I am as young as ever. There is an exhaustless fund of inexperience somewhere about me, a Fortunatus purse that keeps me so. I have had my share of bitter experiences like the rest, but they have left no black drop behind them in my blood—*pour me faire envisager la vie en noir.*

And to the last he had the merry mood, the fairly sportive gaiety, which made life a delight to him in his prime. So late as 1891, only two months or so before his death, his note to Judge Hoar about the illness from which they both suffered is as light-hearted as though there were no such thing in the world as pain. The letter runs:

I missed you and marvelled, and am grieved to hear that you had so painful a reason for not coming. I trust you are more than convalescent by this time, and there is nothing pleasanter to look back upon than the gout—unless it be a prison. Even in the very frenzy of its attack I have found topics of consolatory reflection. Is it podagra? I think how much better off I am than the poor centipedes must be. Is it chiragra? I imagine Briareus roaring. I call *my* gout the unearned increment from my good grandfather's Madeira, and think how excellent it must have been, and sip it cool from the bin of fancy, and wish he had left me the cause instead of the effect. I dare say he would, had he known I was coming and was to be so unreasonable. . . . Convalescence is an admirable time for brooding over mares'-nests, and I hope you may hatch an egg or two. Several handsome chicks of whimsey have clipped the shell under me. Good-by and God bless you. Make the first use of your feet in coming to see me.

The touch of epigrammatic felicity in this letter is of the very grain of Lowell's character. He was a gallant spirit in more senses than one, and peculiarly in that sense which implies instinctive courtliness, a wit as charming and as graceful as it is effortless and pointed. «Good-by,» he says to Mrs. W. K. Clifford; «write when you remember me. No; not that exactly, but oftener. Is that a bull? I don't mind if it bring me Europa.»

His letters resemble those of Dr. Holmes, lately published in Mr. Morse's «Life,» in that, no matter how trivial they were, it was impossible for them to be dull, impossible for them to leave the writer's pen ungilded by the little touch of fancy, of humor, of witty mirth, which will give a man's correspondence a kind of immortality denied to his works. It would be grotesque to elevate the two volumes of Lowell's correspondence above the ten or twelve of his poems and prose; but when it is said that his letters enjoy a kind of immortality which the essays and poetry cannot claim, it is the quintessence of the man's genius that is in question, the aura, the indescribable beauty that fixes him in the deepest depths of his reader's sympathy. This is to be found in his works, but entangled with other things, equally cherishable of course, but «other things» nevertheless, not the central spring of his power. In further elucidation of this, take his criticism. It could not be finer outside of his deliberate essays than it is in them. He put his best into his work, as has been said, and his formal estimates of this man or that aim plainly at the highest ideal he knew. Yet it is unquestionable that the whiteness of his soul is made more tangible in the correspondence, in passages like this from a letter to Mr. Stedman:

I have not seen Swinburne's new volume—but a poem or two from it which I have seen shocked me, and I am not squeamish. . . . I am too old to have a painted *hetaira* palmed off on me for a Muse, and I hold unchastity of mind to be worse than that of body. Why should a man by choice go down to live in his cellar, instead of mounting to those fair upper chambers which look towards the sunrise of that Easter which shall greet the resurrection of the soul from the body of this death? *Virginibus puerisque?* To be sure! Let no man write a line that he would not have his daughter read. When a man begins to lust after the Muse instead of loving her, he may be sure that it is never the Muse that he embraces. But I have outlived many heresies, and shall outlive this new Adamite one of Swinburne. The true Church of poetry is founded on a rock, and I have no fear that these smutchy back-doors of hell shall prevail against her.

No one needs to be told how this «chastity of mind» is immanent in every line of Lowell's prose, how all that he wrote made for the same lofty goal; but the truth is more subtly alive as it falls from a man's lips than when it comes from his pen, held more or less in an instructor's mood, and that is why an impulsive protest like that against Swinburne is so precious. Stop and count over the recent collections of letters which «make for righteousness» in the healthy, happy way characteristic of Lowell or Fitzgerald. Consider the point of view from which nine tenths of the criticism published to-day is written. Reckon with the decadents, with the English and American writers who have lost their heads floundering in the dirt after Verlaine and Gabriele d'Annunzio and Friedrich Nietzsche, and similar prophets. Realize the truth, the appalling applicability to affairs at the present time, in art and literature and the drama, of Whitman's old charge, that modern men are so busy adjusting themselves to every new whim of the world that all the strong edges of the decent human being are rubbed off, and he becomes a mere chameleon, a boneless coward in everything that means spiritual and intellectual rectitude. Give all this its due weight, and then return to the «didactic» passages in Lowell's correspondence. Their importance will be better understood.

The precious character of his company as one may get it in his letters touches the imagination anew and holds the mind. The range of the man was so great, he touched life at so many points, that one might trace the Protean wanderings of his spirit through the years celebrated in Professor Norton's volumes, and never have done with citations bearing upon one subject or another. But it is the happiness, it is the stimulus as of a cool breeze across «the flower-lit plain,» that it is specially desired to indicate in this place as the first and last attraction of Lowell's letters. Like the best letters in any literature, they «drive at practice» without seeming to do anything of the sort. They do not preach. They simply show what it means to live with the sunshine in your heart, how beautiful life becomes when it is lived as Lowell lived it. Read the letters that passed between Ernest Renan and his sister when he was a young man; read the correspondence of Thackeray, of Carlyle and Emerson, of Motley, of Dickens, of Lamb, of a score of others who at once recur to the memory spurred by these few names. All bring the same inspiration, all fasten the imagination upon the nobler elements in living and thinking. And yet how rare they are! Stretch the list to its utmost, the names are still not many, the company is still a small one. That is one reason the more why it is worth while to do honor to a side of Lowell's correspondence, of Fitzgerald's, or of Matthew Arnold's, which may, from one point of view, seem to be obvious. The fine things of the world are nearly always obvious. The critics like to twist themselves into knots of metaphysical interpretation over works of art and literature, as over the works of God, which the public is willing to leave more or less exclusively in their hands, as though a technical jargon were the only fit vehicle for the celebration of such themes. But the simplicity of genius, which is often talked about in a hierophantic way, was not given to man to mystify his fellows. Like the moonlight on the sea, it appeals to the inner eye with a spontaneity that is none the less bewitching because the depths beneath silently flow on and do not ask to be considered, to be talked about. The beauty is there on the surface, where every one can see. Why ask for more? It is this splendid frankness which makes Lowell irresistible. It is no small thing for a man's thoughts to be turned inside out, as the publication of his private letters turns them, and the beauty of his nature be rendered only more beautiful thereby. He leaves in the mind the feeling which was inspired in Lowell by the spring.

> There never was such a season, if one only did not have to lecture and write articles. There never *is* such a season, and that shows what a poet God is. He says the same thing over to us so often, and always new. Here I 've been reading the same poem for near half a century, and never had a notion what the buttercup in the third stanza meant before. But I won't tell. I 'm going to have it all to myself.

He would not tell, and yet to read him closely is to begin to know what «the buttercup in the third stanza» means.

The robe of the mysterious goddess, broidered with buttercups, spurning and yet caressing the dewy grass, flutters and is gone as the reader wanders on in company with Lowell. That she could come back at Matthew Arnold's call is not surprising to those who know his poems well, and yet even to them it seems that she lends her radiance to his letters in unexpected measure. It has been difficult to discard or to modify that impression, which Lowell himself passes on in a note to the Misses Lawrence. «We have been having the coldest weather for many years,» he says; «cold and clear as a critique of Matt Arnold's.» For crystalline purity like Arnold's one expects to pay in a certain coldness that, if refreshing, is not invariably a perfect delight. But the letters change all this, and if the warm light that plays through them fails to stir the pulse of the reader, the fault must be in him. The austerity of the critic melts away beneath the tenderness of the man. Steadfastly severe his thought remains, and with the classic disposition of his genius it could not have been otherwise; but the relentless gaze of his calm, searching eyes only made life the clearer to him, its smallest joys the more to be appreciated, its most elusive sentiments the more imperious in their plea. His criticism, his satire, his poetry in some instances, have given him the reputation of a man whose every impulse was checked by serene meditation. He took pains to justify himself in many emotions and opinions over which it would not occur to the most of mankind to pause for a moment. Yet this ceases to be troublesome when a passage like this is encountered in one of his letters:

> A little brook runs into the sea here [at Bournemouth], and my great amusement was to hang upon the bridge and watch two little girls who had laid a plank across the stream below me, almost touching the water, the banks being on a level with it, and kept running across it by turns, splashing themselves by the jigging of the plank.

Where is the austerity now?

The truth is that Matthew Arnold paid the usual penalty of an author known by his works alone. Admiration of those may go a great distance, and yet fall short of divining the last fleeting secret of the spell which is laid upon the author's world. In the present instance the key is placed within the reach of every one who will recognize that what might be called the scholarship of Arnold's mind was inherent in his very nature, —was not the fruit of experience or study alone, but the natural condition of his spiritual being. Admit this, and the letters show him in the true light—show him a blithe and winning man, quick to respond to every human interest, and never losing his love of men and things because his first impulse was to know the truth about them, to pierce externals and find their hearts, with an almost impassioned eagerness and concern. His love of truth, writ across his life and works in perhaps too strenuous characters—is it not the charm of Lowell, the charm of Fitzgerald, declaring itself in another guise? Certainly his letters follow theirs with the same bracing atmosphere, the same profoundly human sweetness of tone, the same debonair animation, the same delicate humor, the same witchery as of exalted genius proving with all its might its eternal identification with the happiest and truest side of our nature. Curiously, too, he is more accessible than either of his companions in this paper. Just as Lowell's modernity creates more quickly than Fitzgerald's quaintness a bond of understanding between writer and reader, so Arnold's ultra-modern strain of feeling makes him almost instantly comprehensible and a friend. In his letters he is the type, transfigured, of the man who might be met in familiar social life. His epistolary conversation has the keen edge of talk which might have been heard yesterday, so full is it of the thought, the feeling, which is active now in the development of two nations—of more than two, for Arnold was alive to many more ideas than those of the English-speaking race alone. Because he was so original, because what he thought was so rich in sympathy, in fresh vigor and charm, he is never academic, never «literary.» But he makes literary things part of one's daily life. Beneath them, in his letters, there is the same vein of enthusiasm which declares itself in a line to Miss Fanny Arnold: «MY DEAREST FAN: It is an east wind and a gray sky, but I had meant to go to Horsley and see the daffodils.» He glides with the utmost facility from a theme as light as this to subjects of much more «solid» significance, as subjects go. He touches both with the same vivacious hand. Sometimes the easy transition from domestic topics to others, accomplished with a good-humored refusal to take the second with any more seriousness than the first, is for its own sake admirable. In a letter to his mother he writes:

Flu and I lunched with Lady de Rothschild on Sunday, and she gave us a splendid box of bon-bons for the children. Tell little Edward the box was like a trunk, and you take out tray after tray, and in each tray there is a layer of a different sort of bon-bon. Kiss that dear little man for me, and Dicky also.

Then, without a pause, the letter goes on:

On Sunday night I dined with Monckton Milnes, and met all the advanced liberals in religion and politics, and a Cingalese in full costume; so that, having lunched with the Rothschilds, I seemed to be passing my day among Jews, Turks, infidels, and heretics. But the philosophers were fearful! G. Lewes, Herbert Spencer, a sort of pseudo-Shelley called Swinburne, and so on. Froude, however, was there, and Browning, and Ruskin; the latter and I had some talk, but I should never like him.

A passage like the last would savor of professional criticism in the letters of most men living such a life as Matthew Arnold's. But, it may be repeated, his sincerity, his almost naïve seriousness, takes away the professional note and leaves his observations on books or their authors as charming as what he has to say about the less sophisticated subjects to which reference has been made. His sincerity included himself in its scope. In the whole range of autobiographical criticism it would be hard to find a judgment more reasonable, more exact, more modest in spite of its claims, than that which he passes upon his own work in a letter to his mother.

My poems represent, on the whole, the main movement of mind of the last quarter of a century, and thus they will probably have their day as people become conscious to themselves of what that movement of mind is, and interested in the literary productions which reflect it. It might fairly be urged that I have less poetical sentiment than Tennyson, and less intellectual vigor and abundance than Browning; yet, because I have perhaps more of a fusion of the two than either of them, and have more regularly applied that fusion to the main line of modern development, I am likely enough to have my turn as they have had theirs.

It would be a small-souled point of view from which this criticism could be criticized as prejudiced. It was merely impossible for Arnold to hold a brief for or against himself any more than he could hold one for or against any other writer. He practised what he preached. He endeavored to throw as much light as he could upon a subject, whether provided by his own work or another's, and then to «step aside,» in his own words, «and let humanity decide.» It is never his personal taste or feeling which serves as a basis for his criticism or his action. The episode of his pension, offered to him by

Mr. Gladstone, offers a case in point. The affair first appears within the pages of his correspondence, in the following letter:

MY DEAR MORLEY: To my surprise, I have just had a letter from your great leader offering me a pension of £250 «as a public recognition of service rendered to the poetry and literature of England.» To my further surprise, those about me think I ought to accept it, and I am told that —— thinks the same. I have written to him, but have not yet got his answer. I write to you, that, whatever his answer may be, I may be fortified (?) by your opinion also, for I have an instinct which tells me that in matters of feeling you and I are apt to be in sympathy. It seems to me that, the fund available for literary pensions being small, and literary men being numerous and needy, it would not look well if a man drawing already from the public purse an income of nearly £1000 a year took £250 a year more from the small public fund available for pensions to letters, science, and art. I feel this so strongly that I should have at once refused, if it were not for those about me. Of course, I should be glad of an addition of £250, and if I find everybody thinking that my scruple is a vain one, I shall at least consider the matter very carefully, though really I do not feel at present as if I *could* accept the offer.

The upshot of Arnold's discussion of this matter with his advisers was that he yielded to their pressure and acquiesced in the offer of his Pericles, as he picturesquely called Mr. Gladstone. But his surrender does not diminish the effect of his hesitancy, for the former was made only when he had been fairly convinced. His indecision paints again the noble constancy of the man—his inability to take a sordid or selfish view of any affair, though it might be ever so closely related to his own fortunes.

Those in the main, it is pleasant to learn more clearly from his letters, were uniformly smooth and sunny. He had griefs and uncongenial labors. To have made him a school inspector, and to have kept him at the task for the best years of his life, was one of those acts of stupidity of which «the weary Titan» has been so often guilty. If one chose to take a sentimental and perhaps strained view of Arnold's situation, it might be said that the government was as tragically blundering when it left him to waste himself over examination-papers in the smaller schools of London and the provinces as it was when it left Gordon to his fate in the Soudan. But Arnold would have been the first to deprecate so extreme a comparison as this. He kicked against the pricks from time to time, but in a buoyant manner. Like Lowell, he could say: «I have had my share of bitter experiences like the rest, but they have left no black drop behind them in my blood—*pour me faire envisager la vie en noir*.» To have escaped the blight of discouragement, of spiritual inertia, that was his greatest blessing, as it is the corner-stone of his correspondence. His parents and his children might be taken from him; tasks might overwhelm him, and with maddening triviality keep him from the real work of his life—the work he came into the world to do; cruelly bitter things might be printed against him by men who could not agree with his opinions, and forgot to confine themselves to criticism of the opinions, in wrathful anxiety to quench their author: but whatever the annoyance, whatever the sorrow, he met it with more than placid fortitude: he met it with a sweet urbanity that has been unmatched in the history of letters, and he turned from distressful things to fling his whole nature into the enjoyment of his home and his children, his garden, his animals. The last, by the way, occupy a particularly important place in Arnold's letters; and the key in which he writes of his various pets recalls the beauty of his elegiac poems. A letter to Mrs. Arnold, on the death of their pony, is full of this beauty:

Your announcement of dear Lola's death [he says] did indeed give me a pang. I have just been reading your letter again. You tell it beautifully, just all that I should naturally want to know; and all you have done is exactly right, and as I could wish. Perhaps we might have kept a *mèche* of her hair where it used to come down over her forehead, but I should have hated mangling her to take her hoof off, and should not have cared for having it when it was done. You have buried her just in the right place, and I shall often stand by the thorn-tree and think of her. I could indeed say, «Let my last end be like hers!» for her death must have been easy, though I am grieved to hear of her being so wasted and short-breathed. When I was at home at Christmas, I thought she was much as before, and she always liked her apples. I am glad Nelly went to see her. How glad I am, too, that we resisted all proposals to «put her away.» How small has been the trouble and expense of keeping her this year, and how far different is the feeling about her death now from what it would have been if we had put an end to her. There was something in her character which I particularly liked and admired, and I shall never forget her, dear little thing! The tears come into my eyes as I write.

It is in letters like this that Arnold is wholly at one with Fitzgerald and Lowell, pushing all literary things, all things of even remotely artificial temper, far into the background, and spending the entire force of his spirit upon the humane impulses, the passionately sympathetic thoughts, which spring quicker to the heart of probably every normal reader at sight of the lines on Lola's death than at the touch of the writer's finest prose. And with Arnold, as with the two men of genius whose names have been joined with his so often in this place, the purely humane mood was the common mood of his life, the one to which the reader most frequently comes back in his letters. «The real inside,» that is the test, as Lowell insists; and though Arnold is in his books one of the rarest spirits of his time, it is not until «the real inside» of him has been apprehended, not until he has been studied at home, that the extraordinary charm of his individuality is fully known. In this he is the type and ideal of what a letter-writer, and, we may add, a man also, in the noblest sense should be.

*Royal Cortissoz.*

# TOPICS OF THE TIME

### The Outgoing President.

NO President of the United States has ever taken other than a serious view of his great responsibilities; but it may be said that few of our Presidents have devoted themselves as conscientiously and minutely to the details of executive duty as has President Cleveland. The paper on «Our Fellow-Citizen of the White House,» in this number of THE CENTURY, is therefore of peculiar interest as describing accurately and freshly not only the duties of a President, but the particular methods of a particularly hard-working chief executive.

The paper referred to makes no mention of the well-known fact that the regular and constant duties of President Cleveland in his second term have been interrupted by events of unusual gravity. Certainly not since Lincoln's Presidency has any President been confronted by problems of equal difficulty, or had to meet crises of such excitement and threat. It should be remembered, too, that early in this second term there was a period of illness, occurring at a time of enormous anxiety and pressure.

It is a fact that while the career of the retiring President has been exceptional from the beginning, the period of his second term has been especially so. We have no intention to describe in detail its successes and failures, and shall mention, in an unpartizan spirit, only certain large policies with which, for praise or blame, it is sure to be identified in history. As to which of these policies shall seem from the standpoint of the future most notable, it is impossible for contemporaries to determine.

While there is difference of opinion as to the wisdom of President Cleveland's Hawaiian policy, it has been held by some experts in international relations that an ethical standard was then raised which may be cited in the centuries to come as of value to mankind.

While there is difference of opinion as to the details of the management of the Venezuelan negotiations, there is no difference of enlightened opinion as to the incomparable value of the issue of that negotiation in a treaty of peaceful arbitration between the two great nations which are the joint inheritors of the language of Shakspere and of Hampden, and of those principles of justice which, through different forms, perpetuate representative government and human freedom.

Mr. Cleveland's first term was identified, among other things, with the advocacy of a lower tariff, with the attempt to regulate pension legislation, with interest in free art, international copyright, and the reform of the civil service. His second term has been marked by a heroic struggle for that standard of value in the national coinage which exists in the most civilized nations. It stands also for a protest against high tariffs; for economy in expenditure; for defense of our harbors; for the preservation of the national forests; and for the right of the National Executive to interfere in States in certain circumstances, and without gubernatorial invitation, in the interests of law and order.

Along with the great peace treaty, which will distinguish not only an administration, but an age, must be classed Mr. Cleveland's civil-service policy. It has been his good fortune to strike the decisive blow at the spoils system. He has not gone so far as to leave no large accomplishment for his successors; but his orders extending the scope of the merit system are the most sweeping, the most damaging to the old and crying evil of our politics, that any executive has yet been fortunate enough to make.

Mr. Cleveland, with others especially of our strongly individual Presidents, has been the subject of bitter calumny. What Washington was not spared, nor Lincoln, he, too, has suffered; but perhaps in this last case the growing sensationalism of some portions of the press has added somewhat of venom and fantastic invention to the usual abuse of the partizan, the disappointed, and the evil-minded. It may be that no chief executive in a country of such diversified interests and such enormous territory can hope to be generally understood in his term of office, or even in his lifetime. Such a public servant will never be omniscient, will never be free from mistake and error; but the time comes at last, before or after the long release, when good intent is appreciated by all men of fairness and good will. In some parts of our country, perhaps, the misconception as to both man and motive has been so deep-rooted that with thousands of the present generation it may never be corrected. In answer to accusations of neglect of the claims of friendly obligation, it may be of no avail to point to numerous instances where the opportunity of reconciling public duty with private inclination has been eagerly seized. Those who charge sympathy with the « moneyed classes » rather than with the « masses » deny the necessity of promptly upholding the national credit, in the manner adopted, in behalf of all the people. Many who accuse the President of obstinacy may not acknowledge that a strong man's firm adherence to principle would be a more charitable, and in this case reasonable, explanation of conduct; and so on through the long list of animadversions.

The most extreme partizan opponent of the retiring President must acknowledge, if he knows the history of the man and if he has any fairness in him, that through Mr. Cleveland's entire public career he has taken and firmly held one position after another believing it to be right, and in total disregard of the effect of his action upon his own political fortunes. Surely no American statesman has ever more conspicuously exhibited the rare and saving virtue of civic courage.

But, as already intimated, it is not intended here carefully to weigh achievement, but rather to express those kindly sentiments which all but the most intense partizans must feel at the retirement to private life of a distinguished American, after a disinterested public service in which, often against tremendous odds, he has accomplished some things which will be « writ large » in the history of these United States.

And at such a time even an opponent should not refuse, at the very least, the meed of honest intention, and the greeting of good wishes. It was of the President who is now leaving the White House that Lowell wrote:

> Let who has felt compute the strain
> Of struggle with abuses strong,
> The doubtful course, the helpless pain
> Of seeing best intents go wrong.
> We who look on with critic eyes,
> Exempt from action's crucial test,
> Human ourselves, at least are wise
> In honoring one who did his best.

### The Incoming President.

ASIDE from partizan questions and those relating to the tariff, it is gratifying to find in the record of Mr. McKinley's service in the House of Representatives, and in certain utterances of his during the recent campaign, abundant basis for the expectation that he is likely to rise above that dead level of provincialism which increasingly in Congress has been the constant foe of progress. After all, only a small part of the questions to which a President is compelled to address his attention are related to the antecedent division of opinion which we call partizanship, and it is greatly to be desired that a chief executive should be open to the influence of that body of expert and cultivated citizens which in the last resort must shape and order events in a democracy, if they are to be shaped and ordered for the public good. The intelligence of the few is the safeguard of the many, and the chief necessity, as well as the chief difficulty, of a President is to know upon whom he may rely for such intelligence. But it is much to feel that an incoming President is animated not only by high motives, but by respect for learning and experience—a quality which, humiliating as it may be to confess, has been conspicuously wanting in recent Congresses, due partly to our machine system of nomination, and partly to the poor legislative timber brought down in recent years by unexpected and overwhelming freshets of public opinion.

Examples of Mr. McKinley's support of measures of progress are found in his votes upon the questions of civil-service reform, free art, and international copyright. On the last-named measure he voted constantly with those who took the side of civilization as against that of barbarism. With his coöperation, free art was incorporated in the original McKinley Bill as it left the Committee of the House of which he was chairman, though it was not enacted until the passage of the Wilson Bill. On the fundamental question of the merit system against the spoils system he has been aggressively right. In every platform of his party since 1872 there has been a declaration in favor of the reform, and in several national conventions he has been chairman of the Committee on Resolutions. In his letter of acceptance he said:

> The pledge of the Republican National Convention that our civil-service laws shall be sustained and "thoroughly and honestly enforced and extended wherever practicable," is in keeping with the position of the party for the past twenty-four years, and will be faithfully observed. . . . The Republican party will take no backward step upon the question. It will seek to improve, but never degrade, the public service.

This course was foreshadowed by his speech of April 24, 1890, in the House of Representatives, in which he said in part:

> Mr. Chairman: In the single moment that I have I desire to say that I am opposed to the amendment of the gentleman from Tennessee [Mr. Houk], to strike from this bill the appropriation for the execution of the civil-service law. My only regret is that the Committee on Appropriations did not give to the commission all the appropriation that was asked for for the improvement and extension of the system. If the Republican party of this country is pledged to any one thing more than another, it is to the maintenance of the civil-service law and its efficient execution; not only that, but to its enlargement and its further application to the public service.
>
> The law that stands upon our statute-books to-day was put there by Republican votes. It was a Republican measure. Every national platform of the Republican party since its enactment has declared not only in favor of its continuance in full vigor, but in favor of its enlargement so as to apply more generally to the public service. And this, Mr. Chairman, is not alone the declaration and purpose of the Republican party, but it is in accordance with its highest and best sentiment—ay, more, it is sustained by the best sentiment of the whole country, Republican and Democratic alike. And there is not a man on this floor who does not know that no party in this country, Democratic or Republican, will have the courage to wipe it from the statute-book or amend it save in the direction of its improvement.
>
> Look at our situation to-day. When this party of ours has control of all the branches of the Government it is proposed to annul this law by withholding appropriations for its execution, when for four years under a Democratic Administration nobody on this side of the house had the temerity to rise in his place and make a motion similar to the one now pending for the nullification of this law. We thought it was good then, good

enough for a Democratic Administration; and I say to my Republican associates it is good enough for a Republican Administration; it is good and wholesome for the whole country. If the law is not administered in letter and spirit impartially, the President can and will supply the remedy. Mr. Chairman, the Republican party must take no backward step. *The merit system is here, and it is here to stay,* and we may just as well understand and accept it now, and give our attention to correcting the abuses, if any exist, and improving the law wherever it can be done to the advantage of the public service.

This quotation reveals, in one who has not been wanting in stanch devotion to party measures, an underlying and statesmanlike perception of the broader ground of good citizenship upon which appeal for the merit system may be made. The same largeness of view—into which others besides Mr. McKinley have had to grow—characterized his references during the campaign to the necessity of extinguishing sectionalism, whether between North and South in its last embers, or between East and West in its first kindling. In this he has risen, if not to the measure, at least to the style of Webster, and under his administration we may look for the steady promotion of a wise, forbearing, patriotic national spirit.

Of the items upon which we may here touch without offense, there remains Mr. McKinley's uncompromising committal of himself to the gold standard. While he has shown evidences of a strong regard for party pledges, and, no doubt, feels obliged to take measures to give a fighting chance to the bimetallists in accordance with the St. Louis platform, it may be that he sees the advantage to a sound financial system of demonstrating to the country at an early day the impossibility of reaching an understanding with European countries on that delusive basis. However this may be, his personal responsibility for the practical administration of treasury affairs will doubtless force him to follow his inclination to cut loose from the present insecure system of national finance, and to do what he can to aid in the construction of a sound, firm, and stable currency in keeping with the experience of the world.

### On the Public Wearing of Political «Collars.»

SEVERAL of the chief States of the Union have recently surprised the good people of the country by conspicuous proofs of their humiliating domination by absolutely conscienceless and corrupt political machines. It would almost seem as if the great advances made of late in civil-service reform had stirred up the spoilsmen to an attack all along the line; at any rate, the notable triumphs of the merit system in the National, State, and municipal governments are contemporaneous with the manipulation of the machinery of party nominations by party «bosses» with such success as has seldom been witnessed.

But there are some consolations to be derived from the spectacle. In distributing the prizes of public office the machines have shown such baseness in their selection of many of their beneficiaries as to betray their own true natures before the eyes of the entire community. The clearest sort of object-lessons have now made the dullest comprehend the fact that this sort of «machine politics» is not politics at all, but simple corruption. The deals are made in private, but the conspirators have to come out into the open to distribute or receive their payments from the trust funds of public office. The legislators who are bought by the payment of campaign expenses, derived ultimately from the cowardly guardians of corporate interests; the «respectable» citizens who are silenced or made allies of by the distribution of honors, salaries, or «opportunities»—all are rewarded in public; all wear their collars, inscribed with the owner's name, in the light of day.

Well, either this sort of thing will not last, or the country will not last. But if vulgar and defiant corruption is not permanently to take the place of government in our States and cities, every citizen who contemplates the disgraceful travesty of free institutions, shown in so many American communities, must do his or her individual part in bringing about the better state of things that is surely coming. There is nothing that cannot be accomplished by a righteous public opinion, and there is not a man or woman in the nation who cannot help to bring that instrument into play upon the backs of public recreants and despoilers.

### A Good Example in Government Building.

THE articles devoted in this number of THE CENTURY to the new Congressional Library in Washington will give a good idea of a very notable and unusually successful example of construction under government control. Artistically, there is so much that is good that at the outset it seems ungracious to indulge in specific dispraise; and yet we may say, in passing, that some small portion of the painting now in place we hope to see removed from the walls in the interest of good taste and good art. The reproductions which we are able to give at the time of going to press by no means show forth all the excellent work of the many artists employed. There is some good work in sculpture, but on the whole the sculptors, perhaps for lack of equal opportunity, hardly seem so far to have done as well as the painters in connection with the library building.

In the matter of construction, it is to the credit of all concerned that the building, which was begun in the spring of 1889, is completed within the time limit; and, moreover, with a saving of about $140,000 on the total appropriation. It is interesting to note, by way of comparison, that the gigantic municipal building in Philadelphia, begun in 1872, is only just now being finished, and that, while the Philadelphia building has already cost not less than $1.60 per cubic foot, the library has cost but 63 cents per cubic foot, including decorations and everything else.

# OPEN LETTERS

## How to Utilize Old Magazines.

LOVERS of good current literature are often unable to decide satisfactorily what to do with their accumulation of magazines, reviews, and pamphlets. There was a time when these were not so numerous or voluminous, and the annual accumulation of two or three thumb-scarred volumes was sent by all well-regulated families to receive the bookbinder's care and attention. This done, they were placed on the library shelf with a sort of old-time parental admonition that they were not to speak until spoken to.

Much that these publications contain is of more than current interest or passing worth; then why this estrangement and neglect? Many of us value and esteem these old friends, but we approach them for the sake of lang syne, or else to remove the dust from their neglected covers. We live apart from them, so to speak, and consult them at long intervals. The gaps in these intervals are growing wider each succeeding year, and with the rapidly increasing appearance of cyclopedias, republications, and reference-books, the poor old shelf-worn bound magazines of ten, fifteen, or thirty years ago will become meaningless, except, like Mrs. Chub's picture, «for the name that 's on the back.»

By reason of the great number and variety of periodicals which nowadays come into the family, and because of their bulk and the cost involved, fewer people bind them. Another reason for not preserving them is because of the space required to accommodate their rapidly increasing numbers. Assuredly the chief reason must be their unavailability after they are bound and shelved. The name of the magazine or of the review does not suggest the subjects contained or the matter for which we are in search, and without a classified index at hand search is always laborious and often fruitless. But even with a classified index of current literature in the library the difficulty is not removed, and the proper disposition of one's magazines and reviews remains an unsolved problem. The experience of one who has given the subject some attention is here recorded, with the hope that it may act as a thought or suggestion.

There comes a time in nearly all families of the present generation when some of its members are overpowered by the enormity of «back numbers» that cover attic floors, out-of-the-way closet shelves, and sometimes deny visitors the use of a library chair or two. At this juncture the presiding genius of the household is seized with a sudden fit of charity or philanthropy, and the city hospital becomes the recipient of cast-off goods. (There have been cases when the inmates were deluged with as many as twenty sets of Congressional Records, enough to make the poor readers inmates for life!) Having been faced with such a dilemma a few months ago, the hospital decree was issued by the aforesaid feminine genius of the household, and only by a promise to make careful and satisfactory disposition of the literary property could she be dissuaded from her charitable course.

On the following evening, plans having been devised, work was begun, and it was continued through several weeks of an unusually severe winter, with pleasure, profit, and satisfaction, until the task was completed. From their dark corners came trooping forth CENTURYS, «Harper's,» «Forums,» «Scribner's,» «Nineteenth Centurys,» and «North American,» «Contemporary,» and «Fortnightly» Reviews, and these were destined to warm themselves in turn under the rich glow of the student's lamp.

The work of dissection is begun, the first step being to remove the covers and the pages of advertisements. Next, with a strong, sharp pair of nippers, the wire fastenings are clipped and drawn, or the threads cut with a sharp knife. A careful examination of the contents is now made, and the separation of the leaves is undertaken. This requires great care, and boxes of pins and small rubber bands should be kept at hand. It so happens now and then at the end of one article and the beginning of another that the leaves part easily without having to cut or tear them. The oftener this occurs the easier becomes the task, and if the printer could only be induced to arrange his matter so that the last page of one article would face the first page of another, the classification would be greatly simplified. Recognizing the inexpediency of this, the best must be made of difficulties, exercising always a little extra care and judgment. Such articles as are not to our liking, or for which we do not care, are first removed and consigned to the waste-paper basket. Serial stories, or even short storiettes if they have any merit, are likely to appear in book form, and consequently they, too, can be consigned, like some of our dear rejected manuscript, «to outer darkness.» Having disposed of stories and undesirable articles, and with still further eliminations which suggest themselves before the work of assortment and classification is begun, the original pile of publications is greatly reduced, and the undertaking seems less heroic Now classification begins, and the real pleasure of the work is fully realized. Every deposit upon the respective piles is a plunge into a world of thought or an excursion into distant lands. Like the cards in lotto, sheets of paper on which are written comprehensive headings or titles are spread out over a large table, or sometimes over several tables, and upon these sheets the respective articles are placed. In the present instance, as many sheets as there were classifications were laid, and the headings used on these were the titles adopted for the respective volumes after the classified articles had been bound. Some of these were taken from one magazine or review, and some from another, and indiscriminately mixed. However strained the relations of the editors or managers of the respective publications, no estrangement existed here. Everything was upon an equal and friendly footing, and what was best in THE CENTURY would lie down with what was best in «Harper's,» and, as if not satisfied without having all that was good, a contribution from «Scribner's,» or «The Forum,» or «The Fortnightly,» or «The Nineteenth Century,» or «The Contemporary Review» was demanded, and the demand forthwith supplied. «The North American» was in demand, but it excluded itself because of its size, which is neither so long nor so broad as it is deep and great. It, therefore, usually formed a pile of its own, but met its friends on the shelves. Thus many good things were brought together and grouped, with a view to getting kindred and congenial spirits in one another's company, giving to the reader the maximum of enjoyment, and conferring upon him the greatest benefits.

The size of the respective volumes cannot be definitely prescribed, but in thickness they should not exceed one and a half inches. A book one inch in thickness is a more convenient size, but it is not always possible to restrict it within any prescribed limit. There may be some very slight variation in the dimension of the pages in the respective magazines and reviews, but in the binding they are trimmed to a uniform size, and while there may be some variation in the margin, it is so trifling that it is scarcely noticed.

The periodicals in the present instance must have numbered five hundred or more, and after their articles were separated, classified, and bound, they numbered between sixty and seventy volumes. In a well-selected library they present an appearance inferior to few and superior to many of its volumes, and rank with the best in conferring extended wisdom and pleasure. Here are a few of their titles: «Art Papers,» «Artists,» «Architecture,» «The Stage,» «The Press,» «Clubs,» «Libraries and Museums,» «The South,» «Kentucky,» «Indian and Negro,» «International Questions,» «Biographical,» «Historical,» «Municipal Government,» «Invention and Discovery,» «Industrial Enterprises,» «Educational,» «Colleges and Universities,» «Scientific,» «Financial Papers,» «Authors and Authorship,» «Books and Book Notes,» «Great Ship Canals and Highways of Commerce,» «Government Control of the Railway and the Telegraph,» etc.

Again, the magazines are brought together in more noticeable and delightful companionship, «Topics of the Time,» «Points of View,» and «Easy Chair» commingling, comparing notes, and imparting wisdom in one group, while the «Editor's Drawer» and «In Lighter Vein» go into another, making hearts glad and driving dull care away.

It often happens that it is impossible to separate articles, for the reason that a desirable one ends on one side of a leaf and another may begin on the other side of the same leaf. One article may be on politics and another on some scientific subject, or one on politics and another on religion. This difficulty is remedied by having a volume devoted to «Politics and Religion» or «Politics and Science.» They either should not or do not generally go together in the affairs of life, but in a mute and submissive volume no harm can be done. Many other titles will suggest themselves to the reader, taste and inclination being the determining factors.

It is inconceivable to the casual reader how much literature of real and permanent value appears monthly in the magazines and reviews of the United States and England, but all doubt is removed and a clear conception is obtained after consulting the shelf of books just described. Here, for example, is the way an interesting symposium is formed by papers appearing in the volume entitled «Ships that Sail the Sea,» viz.: «Are Fast or Slow Steamers the Safest?» «The Limit of Speed in Ocean Travel,» «The Ship's Company,» «The Good Ship *Constitution*,» «The Ocean Steamship as a Freight-carrier,» «The Revenue Cutter Service,» «Ocean Passenger Travel,» «With Uncle Sam's Blue-jackets Abroad,» «With Yankee Cruisers in French Waters,» «Speed of Ocean Steamers,» «Steamship Lines of the World,» etc.

The volume entitled «The Great Ship-canals and Highways of Commerce» contains the following between its covers: «The Present State of the Panama Canal,» «Waterways from the Ocean to the Lakes,» «The Nicaragua Route to the Pacific,» «The Nicaragua Canal,» «Impediments to our Domestic Commerce,» «The International Railroad Problem,» «The Nicaragua Canal and Commerce,» «Our Lake Commerce,» «Ways to the Ocean,» «The Isthmian Ship-railway,» «Ship-railways,» «Evolution of the English Channel,» and «Speed in Railway Travel.»

It would be difficult, if not well-nigh impossible, to find any one work containing more reliable information on the subject mentioned, or one so well suited to the tastes, needs, and capabilities of the general reader.

In the volume devoted to «Studies of Sundry Subjects» are collected many odd and incongruous titles, but often a separation is impossible without destroying one or the other of such articles as end or commence on the pages of the same leaf. For example, the splendid paper on «Our Political Dangers» by Professor Simon Newcomb, and the brilliant paper of Bishop Spalding on «Froude's Historical Methods,» could not have been separated without the destruction of one or the other, and for that reason they were properly assigned to the collection in which they appear. The associations formed in these volumes are democratic, cosmopolitan, catholic, and promiscuous. All sides of all questions, and the leaders of thought representing them, are given an equal chance and an impartial hearing. Emperor, king, president, and subject, the pope, Cardinal Gibbons, Bishop Potter, John Knox, Dr. John Hall, John Wesley, and Martin Luther, Andrew Carnegie, T. V. Powderly, Henry George, Professor Ely, and David A. Wells, are brought and constantly kept together in intimate and pleasant relationship. France and Germany, England and Russia, Austria and Italy, China and Japan, form a happy union, disclosing their charms to a delighted and interested audience of impartial readers. The formality of courts, the fashion of the ball-room, the conventionalities of society, the differences of rank and condition, the bitterness of national or party feelings, personal estrangements, religious prejudices, all are here waived and made subordinate to a free and easy, united and harmonious, social and kindly spirit, much to be desired but seldom seen in the more real and less ideal affairs and conditions of human society. Thus may be instituted a modern «Thousand and One Nights'» entertainment. The occupation of arranging and assorting is in itself very pleasant, having its social side, and bringing the family together into close communion; and it is instructive, as it renews acquaintance with subjects half forgotten, and forms acquaintances with others before ignored.

Then the work itself praises its master and friends, illustrating the process of winnowing the chaff from the grain, typifying the reunion of friends and brothers separated and estranged by differences of opinion and belief, and finally establishing a union of good, wise, noble natures in an ideal republic as enduring, as delightful, and as useful as good.

*Herman Justi.*

### «One Man Who Was Content.»

A DEBT of gratitude is due to Mrs. Van Rensselaer from those who have been so fortunate as to read in the December CENTURY her sketch, «One Man Who Was Content.» This dispassionate recital of the tragedies of a life, and the triumph of personality over fate, is an inspiration to its readers. The tragedies rehearsed in the narrative are not wonderful or unprecedented. They are such as may come into any life, to be taken lightly by the irresponsible or seriously by the thoughtful and introspective soul. It is not to the light-brained, nor scarcely to the light-hearted, that the rehearsal appeals; but rather to him who knows that stinging blows can be dealt by the hand of fate, or to one who has suffered through his own mistakes or the mistakes of others. Personal tragedies are ordinary happenings to the world at large. The death of one man merely makes room for the ambition of another, and each man has his own content to seek, his own happiness to possess, and his own salvation to gain. Individual man, even amid a host of friendly souls, stands sublimely alone with his Creator. To fall by the wayside under adverse circumstances argues only a weakness which fate is justified in crushing out. Mrs. Van Rensselaer says: To dwell in resignation «is to acknowledge defeat at the hands of life, to accept it, and in passive endurance to give up the fight for happiness. . . . But the brave man, the wise man,» cannot do this; «he holds to his birthright of hope, and looks forward to a time when,» notwithstanding the enmity of fate, «in some sure way he will reconquer and reëstablish contentment.» It is the cheerful tone which commends Mrs. Van Rensselaer's story. From her position nothing, no adversity, no mistake, is irremediable. No matter what the changing conditions of life may present, there is always a chance for readjustment to new denials and new demands. Unkind fate shall not dominate, for there is always something desirable left which can be secured. Pessimism is at present so rampant in literature that optimism is to be doubly appreciated. «The mood of disdain is upon us,» but it is neither a wholesome nor a desirable state. Only that is desirable which brings content, and «the greatest good to the greatest number.» There is no surer way to make a tired, tiresome, and pessimistic people than to make their literature on that pattern. Grant that life is a struggle; grant that there is more of the minor than of the major: but do not sell the «birthright of hope» by eliminating or disabling man's power of modulating from the minor into the major.

From the most depressing situations may come the most glorious success; and the writer who inspires the world at large with this idea, who models his literature that it may build up hope, elevate character, stimulate thought, and urge to creditable and noble action—to such a one the world owes a debt. If the writer of «One Man Who Was Content» has inspired one depressed, despondent mind to vigorous action which results in accomplishment and content, then has she used her talents to great purpose.

But, some critic observes, the whole story of this one contented man is full of egotism. It puts a premium upon egotism. It is full of the all-important «I.» This criticism is granted; for in dealing with himself one always deals with an egotist. It is an egotist who says (quoting from the story under discussion): «I feel that I have indeed been successful, not because I have done all that with my chances a man might do, but because I have done absolutely all that with my abilities was possible to me.» But, egotistic as it is, it sums up all the possibilities of a life. It is a summary made by a man with sense sufficient to measure himself; and when such an example is found, be it in fiction or reality, it illustrates and accentuates the fact that when a man can measure himself, and know that he has turned all his talents to account, not burying one of them—to such belong rightfully the earnings of content.

Mrs. Van Rensselaer's story is a contribution to ethics. It defines man's duty to himself, and it tells him how to discharge that duty, in its teaching that hope and happiness are to be gained through earnest and honest development of talent, and again in the reminder of its concluding idea, that there is no «justification in a record of empty days.»

*Estelle Thomas.*

### A Scientific Basis for Liquor Legislation.

EIGHT years ago a little company of distinguished students of social problems, who called themselves the Sociological Group, took up some of the larger subjects of social welfare, and their studies (for every subject taken up was made the special study of one member, and his conclusions were discussed by them all) were published in THE CENTURY MAGAZINE in 1889 and the years following. Four years ago they decided to enlarge the group and to concentrate their study on one great subject. Thus it came about that the Committee of Fifty for the Investigation of the Liquor Problem was organized. A fund was subscribed, and an original and comprehensive investigation was begun. No more significant or more public-spirited piece of work was ever undertaken, none that showed a more serious purpose. So entangled is the subject with social and even race prejudices, religious opinions, and political purposes, that it could be investigated satisfactorily in the United States only by a voluntary association of men of the highest character and the best equipment. One of the principal lines of inquiry was into the results of our legislative experience in regulating the liquor traffic; this was undertaken under the supervision of Presidents Eliot of Harvard University and Low of Columbia University, and James C. Carter, Esq., of New York. Another was into the economic and social effects of the liquor traffic, which was intrusted to a committee of professional economists, of which the late President Francis A. Walker was chairman. In 1894 the committee on the legislative aspects of the problem sent into the field trained investigators, who, after nearly two years' work in eight States, each of which has different liquor laws, submitted their reports, which are now published («A Study of Liquor Laws») by Houghton, Mifflin & Co. These reports cover sufficient time and area and difference of conditions definitely to establish certain conclusions, which will govern all wise legislation in the future.

The most striking fact emphasized by the whole body of this work is the corruption that liquor laws bring into local politics. The corruption is not always in proportion to the severity of the law, but often in proportion to the complexity of the machinery for its enforcement, and always in proportion to the lagging of public sentiment behind the letter of the law. The worst effect in political corruption has been in Maine, in communities where public opinion has not supported the prohibition amendment to the Constitution. The investigators solemnly record as one result «a full-blown hypocrisy,» which is «nowhere so blatant as in the legislative halls.» Prohibition, which is already clearly waning as a proposed solution of the problem, can never recover from the damaging conclusions drawn by the committee from the study of its operations in Maine and Iowa. True, it has banished breweries and distilleries from Maine, but «there is no evidence that it has diminished the consumption of alcoholic drinks.» The motives of the original prohibitionists, and of many later ones, were good, and some benefits have resulted from prohibition; but «unlooked-for evils of the gravest character also are due to it,» such as «a whole generation of habitual law-breakers, schooled in evasion and shamelessness»; «courts ineffective through fluctuations in policy, delays, perjuries, negligences»; «officers of the law double-faced and mercenary»; «office-holders unfaithful to pledges»; «bribes, hush-money, and assessments for political purposes,» «used to corrupt the lower courts, the police administration, political organizations, and even the electorate itself.» The same phenomena were found also in Iowa under a prohibitory law, which, as in Maine, produced political, not to say social, immoralities out of proportion to its somewhat slight benefits.

Political evils of another kind followed the State-dispensary system in South Carolina. The army of storekeepers and State constables and commissioners that was organized under this interesting experiment produced an almost invincible political machine, with all a machine's evil qualities. The South Carolina experiment was like many other experiments in this—that the law had directly contrary results, in regard to discouraging consumption, from the results that were expected. It was expected that it would restrict drinking in the rural districts, though perhaps not in the towns; whereas in the towns it distinctly discouraged drinking and lessened crime, while in the country it encouraged intemperance. «There is,» concludes the committee, «no American legislation effective to remove the motive of private profit from the traffic.»

Measuring the success of liquor laws in proportion to their freedom from political corruption, of the eight kinds of laws the effects of which were examined in Maine, Iowa, Massachusetts, Pennsylvania, Indiana, Ohio, Missouri, and South Carolina, the most successful of all has been the simple tax law of Ohio. Under this law the traffic is not licensed, but simply taxed. No false morals creep into such frank dealing with it, and there is less chance for political corruption.

Measuring the success of liquor laws by their promotion of temperate habits, the committee has not found that «any one kind of legislation has been more successful than another.» In one community one restrictive system has proved best, in another community another system, each in proportion to its support by local public sentiment and the sincerity of the execution of the law.

One clear and helpful conclusion deduced from this wide study is that in few towns and cities has the limit of license fees been reached. Within a period of five years the fees in Boston were doubled and again increased, without diminishing the number of applicants for licenses. The revenue-producing capacity of the licensed traffic is enormous before the point is reached where the illicit traffic is encouraged in any fairly well-policed community.

In general, this thorough and illuminating study of our experience with liquor legislation establishes on a scientific basis these facts, which are as important as they are fundamental: Attempts at prohibition have been vicious failures, except in small areas where public sentiment has been virtually, unanimous and in towns adjacent to large cities; no successful method has been found in the United States to remove the motive of private profit from the traffic; the greatest success has attende restrictive laws which impose severe taxes, and reduce the number of saloons, confining them to certain localities, and requiring a separation of the traffic in liquors from all other traffic, and imposing all enforceable conditions of publicity, such as the absence of screens, as in Massachusetts; in other words, we have successfully dealt with the problem only by elevating the saloon and then by heavily taxing it. And the investigation gives overwhelming proof that this great subject of social welfare, if no other, *can be dealt with best—indeed, can be dealt with only—in small areas; local laws are the only laws worth having in regulating it, and no local law is worth having except a law that local public sentiment will enforce.* When we find these truisms scientifically demonstrated out of our wasteful and corrupting experience, they cease to be mere truisms, for they become the foundation of a real social science. And they have a many-sided significance. They show the way to the true promotion of temperance; they give a clue to effective legislation; they point to the repression of the most corrupting influence in local politics; they indicate a yet imperfectly developed source of public revenue; and they make forever plain the distinction between the real laws of social progress and the dogmas of ignorance or philanthropy. The demonstration is as clear as a demonstration can be of far-reaching conclusions about so complex a subject of social well-being.

*Walter H. Page.*

### «Trialments, Troublements, and Flickerments.»

WITH PICTURES BY JAY HAMBIDGE.

#### THE TECH. GRADUATE'S TRIALMENT.

«ONE can't do any kind of work in this world without having lots of trial,» sighed the schoolma'am of sixty-four unruly urchins; «but none of you have so much as I.»

«Oh, yes, we do,» said the half-dozen boarders in chorus; and the salesman in the engagement-ring-at-cost jewelry-store strummed on his soft-voiced guitar:

«I 'm sometimes up, and sometimes down,
Coming for to carry me home;
But still my soul feels—»

He did not finish.

«Look at me,» growled the Technology graduate in civil engineering. «Just when I 'd got engaged, and we congratulated ourselves that we could be together lots evenings, now that I had such a good position in the John Hancock Building, here I am informed by the president that ‹our plant is going to be centered,› and I am to be shipped off to Lowell to live in a ‹corporation boarding-house at $2.50 per week, or dropped from the company.›»

«Yes,» said the overworked stenographer, pensively; «but how would you like to have a woman write to ask the *same* question for the fourth time, when you had respectfully and fully answered it three times?»

#### THE PUBLISHER'S FLICKERMENT.

«WELL,» said the publisher of «Cases on Pleading,» «every few days I get an overhauling from some man who knows nothing about printing, who thinks that I am trying to gouge him out of a few dollars. He will say that he has made only half a dozen alterations from copy and he would like to know why I am so extortionate. An author has no idea of the time these ‹little› changes require. He thinks five minutes enough to squeeze in a word or two here and there, when perhaps that insert will take an hour or an hour and a half. When proof is returned corrected, it must be sent down to the compositor who set it. He looks up the number, hauls out that particular form from under a mass of heavy metal,—and perhaps that form weighs forty pounds, solid lead, too,—drags it to his imposing-stone to unlock it—or you 'll understand me better if I say knocks it apart with his mallet. You know, little wedges called quoins are rammed in alongside the type to keep the tiny bits in place so it cannot drop apart. It has got to be unlocked just right, too, or there will be a pretty kind of ‹pi.›

«It may be that the correction is at the beginning of a long paragraph; now every bit of that must be changed to get in that one word. If an author would only consider, he would see that a compositor could get in a whole line of new matter in much less time, for every character in the paragraph must be moved along to make way for the newcomer.

«Oh, we have lots of fault found with our innocent proof-readers. I tell you, it is no small matter for any one person to look after some authors' hen-tracked manuscripts, scrutinize their anachronisms, uniformity, spelling, punctuation, capitalization, notice whether there is perfect or no grammar at all in a sentence, look sharp after any historical flaws or misplaced constructions—and all this through the hottest and coldest days of the year, month in and month out, and after Labor Day not even a Saturday afternoon off in which to turn the current of mechanical thinking and prevent absolute dizziness.»

#### THE CLERK'S TRIALMENT.

«WELL, well, 't is too bad,» said a clerk; «but just let me tell you about my days. I work for the Solid Comfort Grate Company on Chickatawbut street. A customer comes in.

«‹I want a tiling round my grate.›

«‹What color?›

«‹Green.›»

«I show a dark green.

«‹Oh, no; nothing like that.›

«Then I put out a side and a half of Nile green; but that is just what a friend of hers has, and she would not copy for anything. I get a blue-green with wavy lines in the high lights.

«‹Yes, that is charming; but—› She suddenly finds that she does n't want green, but blue. Why, one woman came in, and after giving me arm-weariness for two hours dragging out tiling, said, ‹I am not at all fussy, but I must have something that suits me.›

«But I want to tell you this. The other day an old gentleman walked in with three ladies. The women proceeded to select some tiling for the library. Each had a different idea of just what color that room needed. I waltzed round there for an hour, and brought out about everything we had in the store, but they could not agree on anything. Finally the old gentleman, who had not said a word in praise or dispraise, spoke up:

«‹See here, young man; how long have you been in this business?› I told him. ‹Well, it is probable that you have got some sense by this time. Just put away or cover up all that stuff you 've taken down, and lay out what you consider would best harmonize with what these women have told you about that room.› I brought out what was, to my thinking, the prettiest thing in our stock. ‹All right,› said the old gentleman; ‹I 'll take that. Send it up to the house.› And he handed me the cash on the spot for the most costly thing we had in our establishment. You can be sure I was n't long running down to the bookkeeper to have the bill made out; and all the time I could hear the ladies chirruping: ‹That 's just too lovely!› ‹Too sweet for anything!› ‹Uncle always has such good taste!›»

THE CANVASSER'S TROUBLEMENT.

THE life of our boarding-house came in just then—a handsome man of about thirty, who several years ago, before his brother's carelessness had made him blind for life, was a clerk in the New York Stock Exchange.

«Well,» said he, «you know I 've gotten my living for some years now by canvassing from house to house with a small boy to guide me. I managed to save up a few hundred dollars, and bought a few shares flat in the Wisconsin Central. You remember it was rather shaky a while ago, and so every morning I made a point of asking my boy to read me the quotations. He had gotten quite used to opening that part of the paper first. One morning we started off in a hurry without looking at it, but the very first house we went to had a newspaper lying on the top step. I rang the bell; nobody came to the door. Rang again, and while waiting for a response the boy picked up the paper to look at the news. Just as a woman opened the door I called out to him in a jovial tone:

«‹How 's your Wisconsin Central this morning?› A more startled female, the boy said, you never saw in your life; and she slammed the door so hard that it almost threw me into a fit of nervous prostration. Though we rang and rang,—for I had been told that the woman

would be a very good customer,—never once did she come near the door. I supposed she thought I had just escaped from Bellevue.»

THE SILK-PEDDLER'S FLICKERMENT.

«IF you will bear with me a few minutes,» said a tall man who had been standing at the door listening to the salesmen's troubles, «I 'll give you an experience of mine when I was a silk-peddler in one of our New England country towns. I tell you, the farmers there have a hard tussle with mother earth for a little money, and their wives have a harder one to get a little of that, though some of them are born ‹close.›

«I had been canvassing this place about a week, and had done pretty well. Some bought because they pitied me when they saw the empty sleeve where my arm was torn off by a rebel shell, but more bought because I sold good silk, and they enjoyed taking their pick from the large assortment of big spools—one-hundred-yard spools and fifty-yard ones, with twist to match gowns of all shades of the rainbow. There was one house right in the middle of the town where I wanted to give the woman a chance to buy. I was rather curious to see her, for I had heard much of her penuriousness,—or ‹nearness,› as the folks called it,—and yet her husband was the wealthiest man in town. Rumor has it that one day at the Benevolence Society, which ‹met round› in those days, conversation turned to an aged widow who was doing her pitiful best to keep herself and invalid daughter alive on fifty dollars a year and the occasional contributions of neighbors. The lady of the house where the circle met offered to send three or four quarts of milk if Mrs. Howland, who lived only a stone's throw from the widow, would take it to her. Now ‹Gashmu saith it› that Mrs. H. kept that milk overnight, skimmed off the cream for butter, and took the rest to the widow, with two cents, which she told her she guessed would pay for the cream she 'd taken.

«Pins cost more forty years ago than they do now; and Mrs. H. had said more than once that she had fifteen pins when she was married, and never needed to buy any since. She was so devoted to her housework that she once walked almost to church before she noticed that she had neglected to put on her bonnet or take off her ‹Lancaster gingham› apron. She never would let her daughter cook because she might waste some flour; and though that girl married a street-railroad magnate, the entering wedge of the trouble that led to a separation between her and her husband was because she did not know enough about cooking to superintend a cook.

«Well, Mrs. H. was more gracious than I expected; for she said that ‹his› sister in an adjoining town had bought very good silk of me, and she did n't care if she looked at what I had. She should n't buy more than one spool anyway, for she thought ——'s thread was good enough to make any dress except a silk, and it would do well enough there for the skirt seams; but her daughter would n't hear a word to anything but silk for basques, and she supposed she 'd have to be extravagant and indulge her. She queried whether the black silk would turn gray in time.

«‹If my daughter should want to use it on the sewing-machine when she stitches the seams of the basque at her aunt Nancy's, will the silk keep breakin' and fuzzin' up?›

«I assured her that it was made in such a way that that was an impossibility.

«‹Is the silk you sell as good as the «Bon Ton» that is advertised so much?›

«I fully believed that it was.

«‹Do you think it feels as smooth as «Sewin' & Holden's»?›

«I told her I should be happy to compare the two.

«‹Wall, 'most all o' «his» folks 'cept Nancy use «Polar Star»; but Nancy told me to be sure to buy some silk from you when you came along, and I always like to oblige Nancy.›

«I told her that it was always better to keep in with one's relatives if possible.

«‹Don't you think your price is rather high for this size? Do you think there are one hundred yerds on this spool?› And she slowly revolved it in the strong sunlight.

«I told her I had never heard any complaint.

«‹Wall, don't you know they might make the wood of sixty or seventy spools thicker than the others, and kinder mix them in with the regular size, and so cheat people?›

«I told her that my firm was known all over the country for absolute honesty in its dealings.

«‹Wall, s'pose you measure the silk on this spool; it looks rather small for a hundred yerds.›

«It would have been bad enough to ask a two-armed peddler to measure a hundred-yard spool of silk! She noticed my hesitation, and ejaculated:

«‹Oh, you think there ain't a hundred yerds?›

«‹No, madam, I don't; but will you take the spool if there are one hundred yards?›

«Having assured me she would, I asked for a tape-measure; but one could not be found. She said her daughter must have been using it and put it away somewhere, but a breadth of the carpet was a yard, and I could go by that. I did n't want to disarrange the furniture too much, so I knelt down on a breadth in front of the open fire and began to unwind the silk. I measured about thirty yards, then took off my coat, and went on measuring. I am rather a large man, and I was n't used to that kind of gymnastics. The fire seemed to grow hotter and hotter, and I did n't want to overlap on the yards by the thickness of a finger-nail, for if the silk did not hold out my reputation would be lost. Now and then sparks from the crackling birchwood flew on my shirt-sleeves, and the heat from the big backlog grew greater and greater. As I neared the end of the spool my excitement grew. Mrs. H.'s keen eyes were upon me. Suppose it should n't hold out? I drew in my arm for the hundredth time, passed the silk along between the thumb and finger of my hand to the opposite end of the breadth, and—there was just enough to make one hundred yards and three quarters of an inch over.

«Since that morning Mrs. Howland has told her neighbors always to buy their sewing-silk of that one-armed peddler.»

*C. A. Brooks.*

#### In the Tea Corner.

THE curtains shut us from the night,
  The storm-beat came as from afar;
Her little hands, like waves of light,
  Flashed white around the samovar.

A swinging lantern lit the scene;
  Its crimson glow about us lay
Upon the inlaid wood between
  The service brought from far Cathay.

I followed her with half-closed eyes
  As daintily she made the tea,
Whose gracious incense seemed to rise
  Like some rare Eastern sorcery.

Yet might I have restrained my love
  But for the light that shimmered o'er
The flowing sleeves and bosom of
  The Li Hung jacket that she wore.

*Albert Bigelow Paine.*

**The Modern Cœlebs.**

I STARTED out, in hope and youth,
To find the perfect wife;
But now I doubt, to tell the truth,
If she exists in life.
I had a most complete ideal
Of gracious womanhood,
Yet not too high-flown to be real,
Too witty to be good.

I only asked for striking looks
Combined with grace and style,
Good health, good breeding, love of books,
A bright and ready smile;
Neatness, of course, and common sense,
Social position, too;
Culture, a few accomplishments,
And tact to help them through;

Perfect good temper (for I own
That mine is sometimes short);
A wise economy (I 'm prone
To spend more than I ought);
No disagreeable relatives
(For I have several such);
And a small fortune, for it gives
Ease—(and I have n't much).

Alas! for fifteen years I 've tried
To realize this dream,
And yet no nearer to my bride—
My ideal bride—I seem!
Oh! if these lines should meet the eye
Of such a model she,
My heart awaits her sweet reply
(Care of THE CENTURY).

*P. Leonard.*

**«Songs of New York's Numbered Streets.»**

«SONGS of New York's Numbered Streets» is the title of a dainty little volume of poems from the pen of that gifted poetess Rita Little More, whose «Airs of New York's Avenues» made such a stir when they first appeared a year since. The songs begin with an ode to First street, and take up successively and successfully, in an astonishing variety of rhythms, each street up to One Hundred and Twenty-third.

Miss More is not without her faults; yet she is so evidently young, and so much in earnest, that we feel sure she will improve as the years go on; and in course of time, when her complete works constitute a directory of the streets of the metropolis, her pen will have attained the cunning of an A1 bard.

As we have implied, there are one hundred and twenty-three poems in the collection, and the demands of space will prevent our printing even the shortest excerpts from each of them; but we cannot forbear quoting a few which celebrate the more noted of the numbered streets.

Especially graceful and tuneful are the verses entitled «Third Street,» beginning:

Oh, Third street! Third street! Third street! if all who pass you daily
Could look within your many homes, it would surprise them really.

And this one about Twenty-third street has a grace and freshness that are the more marked when we consider the prosaic subject:

If in town you 're ever stopping,
Here 's the street to do your shopping—
Running east and running west.
If you 've money to invest,
Particularly if female,
Stop here without fail.

There is an irregularity about the rhythm here that reminds one of Browning and Emerson.

This hits off Fourteenth street to a nicety:

Dwarfs and giants. Want to see 'em?
Go, then, to a dime museum;
You will find it quite a treat
'Most anywhere on Fourteenth street;
That is where a person goes
If he wants continuous shows.

Miss More's sonnet to East Tenth street is very delightful; but as it is one hundred lines in length, we must pass it by. A striking instance of the independence of Miss More, her freedom from the bondage of dusty tradition, is this use of one hundred lines to make one sonnet. But while we admire this quality in her work, we must protest against some of her rhymes. The fact that Wordsworth and Whittier and Keats are sometimes careless in their rhymes does not make it any the less reprehensible for her to rhyme «tea-cups» with «sea-moss,» or «soap-suds» with «words.»

Here is an original way of looking at the street that lies just north of Forty-first; we quote it entire:

It is really quite a treat
To write a poem about Forty-second street;
For it has a certain quality—
What you might term an individuality.
On it is the Grand Central Station,
Entrance to our noble nation!
Mark the hurrying crowds go by,
All of them very alert and spry,
Never stopping on account of snow or rain
As they hurry along to catch a train.
When the names of our streets are reckoned
The first is decidedly Forty-second.

Forty-third, Forty-fourth, Forty-fifth, Forty-sixth, Forty-seventh, Forty-eighth, Forty-ninth, Fiftieth, and Fifty-first streets are treated in rondeau form, in which Miss More plainly shows the influence of Austin Dobson. We think, however, that it is a mistake to repeat the refrain more than five times in a rondeau.

We understand that Volume II of «Songs of New York's Numbered Streets» is in press, and will deal with all the numbered streets lying north of One Hundred and Twenty-third. Miss More should be able to write a very noble poem upon One Hundred and Twenty-fifth street, and we look to her to do it. As we have no Alfred Austin on this side of the water, it behooves us to encourage our native talent; and as Miss Rita Little More has displayed great originality in her choice of subjects, we take pleasure in asking her to write still further.

We will conclude the review by quoting in its entirety the «Lines to Twenty-second Street»:

And what shall I say of you,
Now you 're on view?
Not so many people have heard
Of you as have heard about Twenty-third.
Yet in the economy of streets you 're necessary,
Very.
You are the back door of the shopping marts;
And the arts
Are beholden to you because studios,
As every one knows,
Abound within your confines:
Hence these lines.

*Charles Battell Loomis.*

THE DE VINNE PRESS, NEW YORK.

DRAWN BY A. CASTAIGNE.

THE TOMB OF GENERAL GRANT—RIVERSIDE DRIVE, NEW YORK CITY.

MOST OF THE DETAILS OF SCULPTURE ARE MERELY SUGGESTIVE.

# THE CENTURY MAGAZINE

VOL. LIII. APRIL, 1897. No. 6.

## OLD GEORGETOWN—A SOCIAL PANORAMA.

«THREE MILES FROM THE CAPITOL.»

WHEN the author of «The Star-spangled Banner» emerged from his quiet domicile by the Aqueduct, and went for a pensive ramble, as was his custom of an afternoon, he mounted the winding way to the heights of Georgetown to find a point of vantage there for his more comprehensive contemplation of the prospect. Here his poetic sensibility was soothed and his patriotic foresight flattered by the scene that greeted him riverward and on either hand, and even where the homely little burgh, like a happy country child, strove to spread her narrow skirts between the embowered reveries of Rock Creek and the airy gladness of the college eminence; for the legislature of Maryland, by act of incorporation in 1789, had erected into a town the erstwhile careless thorp that cuddled to the bountiful Potomac, and harbored the fishers of shad, and the fowlers of swans and ducks, and the small skippers of pinnace and pirogue lightly cruising between the Little Falls and the feeding-grounds.

Very dear to the eye of that pensive singer of piety and patriotism were the several landmarks that loomed impressively above the river mists: The Little Falls three miles up the river, whither fishing and picnicking parties resorted for hilarious junketing; Analostan Island, umbrageous and delectable, affording leafy glimpses of the fair Virginia shore, and of flashing sails that, swan-like, chased each other. Beyond the river the historic heights of Arlington, the friendly spires and homes of Alexandria, the consecrated shades of Mount Vernon; and then the nearer Rock Creek and Piney Branch, melodious haunts of birds and bees piping and humming to their floral friends—a retreat of woodland nooks and grassy glades, where twilight lingered and a parsonage nestled. Eastward of that, «Kalorama,» the once beautiful seat of Joel Barlow, patriot, poet, philosopher, whose congenial friend and guest, Robert Fulton, launched his prophetic kettle on Rock Creek; and here the remains of Decatur reposed after the fatal duel with Barron. Farther eastward showed the bold lines of the Capitol, while in the nearer west, airily seated, were the sedate university—stately memorial of Archbishop Carroll, and alma mater of many distinguished citizens of the republic, as well as of notable scholars native to the South American States, Mexico, and the West Indies—and the Convent and Academy of the Visitation, founded by French ladies of the order of «Poor Clares» when as yet the city of Washington was not.

Between the convent and the creek the heights were crowned with the mansions of prosperous and influential citizens whose names are locally historic now: «Monterey,» seat of the Linthicums, occupied by Mr. Calhoun, then Secretary of War in the Monroe cabinet; «Tudor Place,» the garden home of Thomas Peter, Esq., notable in the annals of Georgetown; the storied residence of Brooke Williams, once tenanted by Sir John Crampton, British ambassador, and later by the French minister; and other houses of much social celebrity.

Low on the incline, but slowly creeping hillward from the river, the quaint and kindly burgh looked idly out through dormer-windows on a lounging, drowsy world, and sociably shouldered the highway with all its stoops and sloping cellar doors; and comfortable little boys and girls, unembarrassed by considerations of decorum, and careless of rents and maternal rages, slid down the cellar doors, and watched the world go by—a world of shad-fishers, and fowlers of swans and ducks, and pliers of pirogues[1] and pungies; a world wherein the market-master and the hay-weigher, the constable and the town-crier, the watchman and the lamplighter, were personages of exalted privileges and mysterious powers; where a black Juliet, gaudily coifed in bandana, and hoop-ringed as to her ears, who dispensed English muffins to the outcry of a bell, and a blacker Romeo, amply aproned, who chanted on street corners the succulent glories of hot corn and baked pears, were ever the chroniclers, confidants, and oracles for the children, white or black, on Key and Congress streets and the Causeway, on Bridge and Falls streets, West Landing and Duck Lane.

A characteristic feature of the time and place was the Conestoga wagon, freighted with farm produce from Pennsylvania, ark-like under its long tunnel of canvas, and drawn by five or seven big, benevolent horses, each with a chime of bells making melodious announcement of butter, eggs, and fowls, garden truck, sauerkraut, *schmierkäse*, and apple-butter; and always a hen-coop hung at the stern, and a dog, ill-favored and unsociable, trotted between the hind wheels.

No less characteristic and picturesque was the pier, the landing-place for the lighter craft that flitted between the river-landings in excursions of business or pleasure. Hither came the fishermen to mend their great nets, and the fowlers with their ducking-guns and dogs, and the darkies, old and young, to lend a hand on the flats, or in the blinds or the boats, or in the fish-houses that flanked the beach at convenient points. Hither came country wagons from all the neighboring counties, to convey the shad or rockfish to inland markets. In April and May of 1828 Potomac shad were sold on the wharves of Georgetown for five dollars a hundred. In the early spring of 1826, rockfish weighing from twenty-five to one hundred pounds were netted in great numbers; on the Virginia side of the river, at Sycamore Landing, thirty miles below Washington, four hundred and fifty of these noble fish were taken at one draught of the seine.[2] The multitudinous fleet of small craft, bright, brisk, and bustling, that flitted to and fro between the fishing-grounds and the landings,—the boatmen shouting, singing, bantering each other,—imparted to the beautiful river the aspect of a festal panorama.

In the late fall and winter myriads of canvasback ducks, then commonly called «whitebacks,» came to feed on the small white celery that grew so abundantly in the swamps and flats of the Potomac and the Susquehanna. Formerly on James River they were known as «sheldrake»; but their favorite provender failing there, they flocked to the more bountiful fields between Craney and Analostan islands. They gathered in clouds of thousands, obscuring the river, and storming the air with multitudinous clangor, only to be fusilladed from blinds, or «tolled» within range by dogs trained to play and leap, or by the waving of a red-and-yellow handkerchief luring them by their foolish and fatal curiosity. Tom Davis, the trusty fowler of Mount Vernon, with his Newfoundland dog «Gunner,» often brought down at a single discharge of his clumsy British «piece» as many ducks as might serve the larder for a week.

Even so the snow-white swans were tolled as they floated in fleets of hundreds near the shore at the mouth of the Occoquan: superbly silly birds, spreading from six to seven feet of flashing pinions, clanging and trumpeting in melodious clamor that on still evenings might be heard by the dwellers on the creeks three miles away, and lured to their death by the diverting puzzle of a cunning puppy's antics.

Similarly spectacular was the sport that went to the taking of the ortolan[3] on dark

[1] G. W. P. Custis, in his «Recollections and Private Memoirs,» describes the «pirogue» in which Washington, with a party of his friends, made the first survey of the Potomac above tide-water, as a *canoe* «hollowed out of a great poplar tree, hauled on a wagon to the bank of the Monocacy, and there launched.»

[2] Elliot: «The Ten Miles Square.»

[3] *Sora* of Virginia, *rail* of Pennsylvania.

DRAWN BY B. WEST CLINEDINST.

THE LANDING-PLACE, OLD GEORGETOWN.

October nights on the flats near Georgetown, when the birds had settled to their perches on the reeds and wild oats. Amidships across the gunwale of a canoe stout boards were laid to make a platform, and these were sheathed with clay to form a hearth. Here a fire of lightwood was kindled, and the boat crept noiselessly to the flats, a boy feeding the flame as it glided in among the perches where the birds, stupefied by the glare, incapable of flight or outcry, and in plain sight of the hunters, were clubbed with light paddles, and so killed or captured by scores. Thirty or forty dozen were often taken by one canoe.

PAINTED BY GILBERT STUART. BORDER DRAWN BY WILLIAM H. SMITH. ENGRAVED BY R. G. TIETZE. OWNED BY MRS. GOLDSBOROUGH.

ELIZA PARKE CUSTIS.

When, in 1796, Thomas Twining, British-Indian merchant and official, alighted, cramped and sore, from the «coach with four horses» that had bumped and banged him from Baltimore by way of Bladensburg to Georgetown, he blessed the «Fountain Inn,» where a feather-bed and a bountiful supper afforded tolerable compensation for his beloved bungalow and his mulligatawny, and gave him strength to confront a great American joke; for while «in the whole course of the day he had not seen a blacksmith's nor a baker's shop,» he had been edified, while waiting for his dinner at the «Indian Queen» in Bladensburg, by the contemplation of a plan of the city of Washington that hung over the fireplace in the dining-room, and showed «all the streets, squares, and public buildings of the intended city, minutely detailed.» Next morning he took horse at the «Fountain Inn,» and rode four miles to see those squares and public buildings, and to call on Mr. Thomas Law, formerly of the Bengal Civil Establishment, who had pitched his bungalow by the Potomac, and married Eliza Parke Custis, Mrs. Washington's granddaughter.

His ride was across a level tract like an English heath. The rude beginnings of a road presently assumed the appearance of an avenue, and although no sign of habitation was visible, «I had no doubt,» writes that patient and amiable wayfarer, «that I was now jogging along one of the streets of the metropolitan city.»

Then he came out into a cleared space, where he found workmen tugging and pounding at the framework of two «somewhat imposing buildings,» and they informed him that *this* was the Capitol and *that* was a tavern. «Can such things be?» And with the thought he rides on over a trackless plain, and through a wilderness of woods and thickets and a labyrinth of bog and underbrush, until Mr. Law's chariot appears, on its way to Georgetown to meet him, and he is conducted to the bungalow by the Potomac. And immediately the wilderness blossoms like the rose; for there are the comely Mrs. Law, and her delectable sister, the vivacious Nelly Custis, and Miss Westcott of Philadelphia, «distinguished for her talents and literary attainments.» And even Talleyrand, prince, politician, diplomat, wit, was expected; for illustrious Frenchmen were entertained at the Law house from time to time, even as Louis Philippe was regaled by General Mason on Analostan Island in 1798.

Law had administered in Bengal the affairs of an extensive district, and had been trained to the discharge of important functions implying consequence and the splendor of a rajah. In England his family was opulent and distinguished. His father was Bishop of Carlisle; his uncle, «the brilliant barrister who defended Warren Hastings against the influence of Fox, the eloquence of Sheridan, and the virulence of Burke.» Now his coachman drove through a wilderness in a «trap» provided with spare shoes for the horses and an outfit of blacksmith's tools. To Twining's thinking, such nabobs as Mr. Law would have been more appropriately bestowed at «Belvidere,» the charming villa of Colonel John Eager Howard near Baltimore—a seat of luxurious shrubberies and sloping lawns, «reproducing in the wilderness the cultivated and poetic perfections of a Repton or a Haverfield.» Nor was his enthusiasm abated in contemplating the attractions of the «seat» in company with Mrs. Howard, when she took him in the chariot to make the circuit of the place; for Mrs. Howard was that redoubtable Peggy Chew whose charms of wit and person the gallant but ill-fated André had celebrated with pen and pencil.

In John Adams's time a witty French lady described Georgetown as «a town of houses without streets, as Washington is a town of streets without houses»; and Mrs. Adams, writing to her daughter in November, 1800, says: «Woods are all you see from Baltimore until you reach the City, which is only so in name—here and there a small cot without a window appearing in the Forest, through which you travel miles without seeing a Human being.» Oliver Wolcott, writing to his wife on the Fourth of July, 1800, says: «There is one good Tavern about forty rods from the Capitol, and several other houses are building; but I do not perceive how the members of Congress can possibly secure lodgings unless they will consent to live like Scholars in a college or Monks in a monastery, crowded ten or twenty in one house, and utterly secluded from Society. The only resource for such as wish to live Comfortably will be found in Georgetown, three miles distant, over as bad a Road in winter as the clay grounds near Hartford.»

But thirty years later a four-horse coach plied almost hourly between Georgetown and Washington for the accommodation of the patres (and matres) conscripti, carrying twelve inside at «a levy» each. From Gadsby's hotel, the «Indian Queen,» and the Mansion House, in Washington, stages ran to Baltimore for a fare of $2.50; there were daily steamboats to Alexandria, Norfolk, and Fredericksburg, and a «mail-stage» every evening for Pittsburg and Wheeling.

Soon after the Revolution the Conestoga wagons and the «gondolas» brought a brisk and various trade to the wharves and doors of Georgetown. The place had been largely settled by Scotch agents or factors of British houses, and British bottoms consigned to these came annually, laden with hardware, dry goods, and wines, to receive return cargoes of tobacco, or of furs brought down the Potomac by Indian traders, while sugar, molasses, and rum from the West Indies were sold on the wharves.[1] The lumbering Conestoga rolled homeward freighted with dry goods and groceries, salt and fresh shad and herring in the season, for the use and consumption of the farming folk of Maryland and Pennsylvania; and the long, flat-bottomed gondola, bringing corn and flour, pork and iron, was poled down the Potomac to the Great Falls, twelve miles above the town, and thence around the falls and back to the river by the route of a canal.

Meanwhile, Georgetown had grown to be a place of homes and congressmen's lodgings—a town of spindle-legged sideboards, tall clocks, marquetry tables, claw-and-ball chairs, screens and andirons and warming-pans. The «Union Tavern,» a hostelry of fashionable pretensions during the administrations of Jefferson, Madison, and Monroe, had the honor to entertain many imposing per-

[1] Ben: Perley Poore's «Reminiscences.»

PAINTED BY GILBERT STUART. BORDER DRAWN BY FRANK FRENCH. ENGRAVED BY T. JOHNSON. OWNED BY MRS. BAYARD

JAMES ASHTON BAYARD.

sonages, such as Louis Philippe and Talleyrand, Volney, and Baron Humboldt, Jerome Bonaparte and Lafayette. Georgetown had already become the «court end,» a trysting-place and rendezvous for persons of quality, while as yet Washington was but a huddle of booths, taverns, and gambling-houses set round about a political race-course. The more civilized and homelike little burgh had seven thousand inhabitants in 1810, and its social attractions were irresistible. Analostan Island was a romantic paradise; there were dim and whispering rambles for lovers on the slopes of the Heights, and endless were the match-making and gossip. The solicitous attention which the idle Strephon might be beguiled into offering to the idler Daphne, with the aid of much piping, twanging, and tinkling in serenades,—

> Sighing and singing of midnight strains
> Under Bonnybell's window panes,—

was construed as serious courtship, and news of it was diligently dispensed by the barber, who came on horseback, tooting on his scandalous little horn, and peddling the tattle he had cajoled from the mercenary seamstress who was supposed to be dumb for five dollars a month, or the perfidious chambermaid who vowed to be blind for three dollars and tips.

Sir Augustus Foster, secretary of the British legation in 1805, was a sort of Pepys and

Paul Pry in one for the small-beer chronicles of that time. «No lack of handsome ladies,» says he in pert staccato notes, «for the balls at Georgetown, drawn from the families of Members and others who come for the season. I never saw prettier, more lively, or better-tempered girls anywhere—mostly from Virginia and Maryland. Both Washington and Georgetown are famous marriage markets. Much dancing, much singing of popular and sentimental ditties. Small literature or improving conversation. Excess of small talk, mixed with romance derived from the high-flown novels of the period. Young married women are relegated to the background. Cards for everybody—‹loo› (pronounced with lingering sweetness) for the girls, ‹brag› for the men, for whom, likewise, toddy before dinner. Rouge and face-powder in great request.»

After the flippant secretary comes a deferential and sententious chronicler who, with becoming «predilection for the Columbian Fair,» regrets to have observed among the ladies who grace the select circles of Washington and Georgetown «a fondness for the bewitching torment of play, which, when indulged for motives of gain, and the violence of hope, fear, and even baser passions, changes the very features, in effacing that divine impression of the female countenance which is so often irresistible.»

'T is sad to reflect that it took the «Columbian Fair» about six administrations to discover that gambling reddened the nose and spoiled the complexion; but it went out at last with face-powder and the ubiquitous umbrella.

In Washington, between the «Indian Queen» and the Capitol gate, the gambling-houses appealed seductively to the heroic restlessness of members with brag and faro that were brisk, and suppers and sideboards that were free; and private play at social entertainments was eminently fashionable. A Boston matron cooed to Mrs. Clay: «How it must distress you to think that your brilliant husband gambles!» «Sometimes, yes,» replied the guileless child of Kentucky; «but really, he almost always wins.»

With its great swinging sign displaying a gaudy and theatrical Pocahontas, the «Indian Queen» tavern strove to toll strangers within range of the landlord's winning ways, as the wily hunter tolled ducks by the flutter of a scarlet petticoat. In his voluminous white apron, and with familiar cajolements, the landlord greeted his guests at the door of the dining-room, and conducted them to their favorite seats, where Moses and Columbus received them with a sort of obsequious patronage, and served them with their favorite dishes as infallibly as the barkeeper «set up» their favorite tipples. It cost about $1.50 a day to live at the «Indian Queen.» A bottle of real old Madeira imported into Alexandria was $3, and a superior grade of sherry could be had for $1.50. But the decanters of brandy and whisky that glorified the table represented «the compliments of the landlord,» and were free.

At Christmas, and on Washington's Birthday and the Fourth of July, the guests of the house were invited to partake of egg-nog or apple-toddy brewed in a great punch-bowl that had once adorned the board at Mount Vernon. The landlord's place was behind the bar, where the room bells, hung on coiled springs, rang resoundingly. Letters and cards were received by the barkeeper, who answered a thousand questions as he mixed the beguiling beverages; for he was supposed to know all the notable people, where they lived, and on what days they «received.»[1]

With the gaudy but picturesque Pocahontas of the tavern the plainer sign-board of a saddler competed for public admiration in terms of startling patriotism: «Peter Rodgers, Sadler, from the green fields of Erin and Tyranny to the green streets of Washington and Liberty! See Copenhagen; View the Seas! 'T is all blockade, 't is all ablaze! The Seas shall be Free. Yankee Doodle, keep it up!»

Peter had been banished from Cork, at the age of seventy-five, «just for appearing in a green-colored coat, and sighing for the fate of his dear native land.» How must his grateful heart have been wrung by the later satire of his melodious but spiteful compatriot, Tom Moore:

> This famed metropolis, where Fancy sees
> Squares in morasses, obelisks in trees—
> Which travelling fools and gazetteers adorn
> With shrines unbuilt, and heroes yet unborn!

Impressive and memorable were the figures of the actors who held the stage at Georgetown in those days—Clay and Webster, Calhoun and Randolph of Roanoke, Luther Martin and Aaron Burr, Robert Fulton and Francis Scott Key, John Quincy Adams, James Ashton Bayard, Washington Irving, and Major l'Enfant.

Living on the Heights (and metaphorically *in* the heights) was Vice-President Calhoun—tall and gaunt, «grand, gloomy, and peculiar,» wearing his long black hair brushed

[1] Ben: Perley Poore's «Reminiscences.»

straight back like a Drury Lane conspirator, studious of simplicity in dress, but driving four horses and giving elaborate entertainments. And daily on the Heights Calhoun encountered the man who had addressed him in the Senate as «Mr. Speaker—I mean Mr. President of the Senate, and would-be President of the United States (which may God in his infinite mercy avert!)»—John Randolph, Lord of Roanoke, precocious and pugnacious, long-limbed and lank, his hair parted in the middle, attired in an English broadcloth coat with high rolling collar and long skirts falling over knee-breeches and white boot-tops; who brought into the Senate-chamber whip and spurs and riding-gloves, and a favorite hound to crouch beneath his desk while «the gentleman from Virginia» waited for an opponent worthy of the steely eyes and the vixenish voice and the nervous forefinger.

ENGRAVED BY R. A. MULLER. OWNED BY DR. CRIM, BALTIMORE.

LUTHER MARTIN, «THE FEDERAL BULL-DOG.»

Eagerly greeted in every drawing-room from Kalorama to Analostan, where Southern senators held undisputed sway in social functions and affairs, was the magnetic personality of Mr. Clay, whose twinkling eyes and engaging smile were but gentler reflections of that restless vitality which stirred the Kentucky orator in debate, and set him «going all over»—gesticulating with arms and hands and head and feet and spectacles and snuff-box. Hither, too, came Daniel Webster, in blue dress-coat with gilt buttons, buff waistcoat, and high white cravat—«Black Dan,» stalwart and swarthy, massive as to his brow and cavernous as to his eyes, at once impressive and prodigal, majestic and convivial, heroic and hilarious. The distinguished gentleman from Massachusetts is described by one who hobnobbed with him as not really a large man. «His shoulders were broad, and his chest was burly, but his hips and lower limbs were comparatively slight. Although Clay's head appeared much smaller than Webster's, they wore the same diameter of hat.»

At Christmas, when happy darkies were delivered over to their own rousing raptures, and the generations of Maryland Catholics and Virginia Episcopalians made elegant revel between the supper-table and the sideboard, the fashionable tipple ladled from the family bowl was the «Webster punch,» brewed with brandy and arrack, or Medford rum, champagne and maraschino, green tea and lime-juice—very expensive and very neat. In Georgetown, Frederick, and Alexandria, Yule logs, Christmas carols, and mistletoe were much affected. At the houses of the cabinet and the wealthier members of the Senate and the House there were endless entertainments and evening parties in the season, with suppers, punch, and cards, and cotillions and contra-dances to the music of harp and violin.

To the assemblies, always exclusive and ceremonious, and managed by a committee who dispensed their complimentary cards with the superfine discrimination of Almack's, officers of the army and navy and members of the diplomatic corps came in regimentals and regalia, while plain citizens disported themselves in pumps, silk stockings, ruffled cravats, two or even three waistcoats of different colors, the dangling fob-ribbon with gold buckles and a big seal of topaz or carnelian, regulation frock-coats of green or claret-colored cloth with huge lapels and gilded buttons, and Hessian top-boots with gold tassels. Certain of the exquisites affected ultra-fashionable full dress, which prescribed coats with great rolling collars and short waists, voluminous cravats of white cambric, and small-clothes or tight trousers.

The costume of the ladies in the administration of the younger Adams was classically scanty; we read of skirts of five breadths, a quarter of a yard each, of the favorite India crape, coquettishly short for the freer display of the slipper and silk stocking matching the color of the gown and fastened with ribbons crossed over the instep and ankle. The low baby waist, ingenuous and frank, came to an end abruptly under the arms, which were covered with gloves so fine that they were sometimes stowed cunningly in the shell of an English walnut. The hair, dressed high, was crowned with a comb of tortoise-shell, while turbans and ostrich-feathers were the peculiar ensigns of wives and matrons.

The ball opened at eight with the *menuet de la cour*, followed by a quadrille or the «basket-dance,» and closed at eleven with a rollicking Virginia reel to the tune of «Money Musk» or «Sir Roger de Coverley» fiddled by proud and happy darkies. Cake in variety, pineapples from the West Indies, and negus of port-wine or sherry, were served to the ladies, with compliments of flowers and flowery compliments, by their cavaliers. In Jackson's administration the widow of Alexander Hamilton introduced ice-cream at the President's receptions, to «Old Hickory's» great delight. It amused him to see the rustic sovereigns «*blow* on the funny stuff.»

After the Revolution the minuet, which had long held the place of honor in the select assemblies, began to be slighted, fashionable favor turning capriciously to less exacting and more democratic styles of diversion for the fantastic toe. General Washington, whose performance in the stately dance was impressive, appeared in that function for the last time in 1781, at a ball given in Fredericksburg in honor of the French and American officers on their return from the capitulation of Yorktown. The last birthnight ball he attended was in Alexandria in 1798.

John Pendleton Kennedy, author of «Swallow Barn» and «Horseshoe Robinson,» himself a conspicuous personality in the clubs and fashionable gatherings of 1820, was wont to gossip pleasantly concerning the wits and beaus who pranced so gallantly on the streets of Baltimore, Alexandria, and Georgetown in his childhood. «Cavaliers of the old school, full of starch and powder; most of them the iron gentlemen of the Revolution, with leathery faces; old campaigners, displaying military carriage and much imposing swagger; convivial blades, too, and heroes of long stories; all in three-cornered hats and wigs and buff coats with narrow capes, long backs, and hip pockets, small-clothes that barely reached the knee, striped stockings, and great buckles to their shoes; and then the long steel chains that hung half-way to the knee, dangling with seals shaped like the sounding-board of a pulpit!»

These oppressive gentry made the little town fairly jump with the ring of their gold-headed canes on the pavement, «especially when the superfine swashbuckler accosted a lady in the street with a bow that required

ENGRAVED BY PETER AITKEN. OWNED BY MISS HOLLYDAY.

MRS. SUSANNAH STEUART TILGHMAN.

a whole sidewalk to make it in—the wide scrape of the foot, and the cane thrust with a flourish under the left arm till it stuck out behind along with the stiff cue! And nothing could be more piquant than the pretty coxcombry of the lady, as she reciprocated the salutation with a deep, low curtsy, her chin bridled to her breast.»

local pride, to induce him to part with his precious fields and orchards, he replied with unseemly flouts and gibes: «If it had not been for the Widow Custis and her niggers, you would never have been anything but a land-surveyor, and a very poor surveyor at that.» But at last, making a grace of compulsion, he yielded, only stipulating that the

PAINTED BY JOHN SINGLETON COPLEY. BORDER DRAWN BY FRANK FRENCH. ENGRAVED BY PETER AITKEN. OWNED BY COL. F. C. GOLDSBOROUGH.

ANNE FRANCIS.

Burns cottage should be spared from the encroachments of vulgar streets.

Memorable in the early annals of Georgetown society is Marcia Burns, daughter of David Burns, that obstinate Scotchman who was General Washington's *bête noire* in the infancy of the national capital. Burns owned a tract of six hundred and fifty acres, known as «the Widow's Mite,» in the heart of the projected metropolis; and to Washington's appeals, addressed to his patriotism and his

In this cottage Marcia Burns, the heiress, blossomed in a graceful prettiness. Luther Martin, the erratic and brilliant Maryland advocate, received her into his family to be educated and trained for society in the companionship of his daughters Maria and Eleanor, so that when she returned to the now famous homestead she became, by her beauty, wit, and various winsomeness, the attraction of a notable coterie of Taylors, Laws, and Keys, Lees and Brents, Calverts and Carrolls; and entertained with familiar hospitality Alexander Hamilton, Burr and Blennerhasset, James Ashton Bayard and William Wirt, Gilbert Stuart the painter, and Tom Moore the poet.

With the Mount Vernon group of Custises and Calverts, who were Marcia's occasional guests, came Washington's favorite aide and confidential secretary, Colonel Tench Tilghman, the distinguished soldier who had the honor of bearing to the Federal Congress the glad tidings of the capitulation of Yorktown and the surrender of Cornwallis. Tilghman's mother, Anne Francis, was the handsome daughter of Tench Francis, of a family distinguished in letters. One of his brothers was a barrister, and author of «Maxims of Equity»; another, the Rev. Philip Francis, translator of Horace, was the father of Sir Philip Francis, reputed author of the «Letters of Junius.» Tench Francis removed from Talbot County, Maryland, to Philadelphia, where he became attorney-general of Pennsylvania. His daughter Anne was married to James Tilghman of the «Hermitage,» afterward a member of the Provincial Council in Philadelphia. One of her kinswomen in the Tilghman connection was that beautiful Susannah Steuart, who was so admired and beloved in prerevolutionary Georgetown, also wedded to a Tilghman of the «Hermitage,» and mother of a later mistress of «Readbourne,» the hospitable seat of the Hollydays of Queen Anne's.

At twenty Marcia Burns was married to General Van Ness, member of Congress from New York, «rich, handsome, well bred and well read.» Hard by the moss-roofed cottage they built the famous Van Ness mansion, designed by Latrobe, finished in fine woods and marbles, and decorated with sculptures from Italy. Here their daughter, married to Arthur Middleton of South Carolina, died in 1822. Then Marcia went into seclusion, and in fulfilment of a vow erected an orphan-asylum and devoted her life to works of charity in schools and hospitals. At her death she was entombed with public honors in that classic mausoleum which was afterward removed to Oak Hill Cemetery in Georgetown, where the author of «Home, Sweet Home» found a home at last. Before that great bereavement converted it into a house of mourning, the Van Ness mansion had been the scene of distinguished entertainments. From its portico ships from Europe could be seen moored in the docks of Alexandria, and West India merchantmen sailed by, bound for the port of Georgetown.

BORDER DRAWN BY FRANK FRENCH ENGRAVED BY CHARLES STATE.
OWNED BY MRS. GOLDSBOROUGH.
MRS. LLOYD N. ROGERS.

Familiar as well as honored guests in the Van Ness mansion and in the pleasant homes of Georgetown were the several ladies and gentlemen who composed the «Washington group» after the house at Arlington had been built by G. W. P. Custis in 1802. With Mr. Law, already mentioned (son of the Bishop of Carlisle, and nephew of Lord Chancellor Ellenborough), came his handsome wife Eliza Parke Custis, Martha Washington's granddaughter. Mrs. Law's only child Eliza, afterward noted for her engaging felicities of mind and manner, married Lloyd N. Rogers of «Druid Hill.» I am indebted to her daughter, Mrs. Goldsborough of Baltimore, for the privilege of reproducing the miniature which so happily reflects her beauty.

Nelly Custis, delectable and wilful, ever a diverting perplexity to the household of Mount Vernon, had hardly outgrown her dolls and her Chinese pigs, her audacious rides on the awful back of the first President, and her tearful struggles with that expensive and hateful spinet, when she wrote the pert and sprightly letter in which she recounts to the stern soldier and sage her trials and triumphs in her first ball at Georgetown, and confesses «the soft impeachment» of her passion for the son of Washington's sister Betty, Major Lawrence Lewis. At her wedding on the general's birthday in 1799, at Mount Vernon, she would have had the Father of his Country attend in the gorgeously embroidered uniform of a commander-in-chief, but he preferred the Continental blue and buff, and the cocked hat with the plain black cockade. The pouting bride was consoled with the white plumes that General Pinckney had presented to him, but which were better suited for the decking of a young matron in the minuet, as when, a few years later, Mistress Lewis graced the ball-room at Arlington.

The turnpike was a diverting novelty and the steamboat a wonder, when Dolly Madison, inspiring sprite of tea-parties and loo, and idol of the common people, warm-hearted and prodigally hospitable, cleverly blending gracious dignity with a frank condescension, queened it so kindly in her spangled turbans, paradise plumes, and rosetted shoes, and ruled her little world of lovers with a snuff-box. It was at one of her receptions in Georgetown that an amusing incident occurred, remembered for the characteristic tact it illustrated. A shy young fellow from the country had come to pay his respects to the star of the hour. Mrs. Madison observed him neglected and embarrassed, and approaching him quickly with extended hand, so startled the abashed and timid lad, who had just been served with coffee, that he dropped the saucer and thrust the half-filled cup into his pocket. «How the crowd jostles!» said the delightful Dolly. «Let me have the servant bring you coffee. And how is your charming mother? We were friends, you know.» Ever «mistress of herself, though china fall,» that dazed, dumfounded boy was not less interesting to her gracious solicitude than the justices of the Supreme Court in their gowns, or the diplomatic corps in their regalia, or distinguished officers of the army and navy in the luster of full uniform—all dancing attendance at those memorable levees on New Year's day and the Fourth of July, when Dolly Madison was «at home» to kings, presidents, and the people, without distinction of persons.

The social throne that Dolly Madison had filled with historic distinction was restored and adorned by Louisa Catherine Johnson, niece of Tom Johnson, first Republican governor of Maryland, and wife of President John Quincy Adams. Mrs. Adams was born, educated, and married in London when her father was American consul there. As a bride she shared her husband's honors as senator in Washington, envoy to Russia, minister to the court of St. James, and secretary in the cabinet of President Monroe.

She was preëminently mistress of the arts of society, and her entertainments in Georgetown and Washington were events of memorable import in the political as well as in the social world. Sectional rancor or the spites of party had no place at her teas and receptions. A ball that she gave in 1824 is chronicled as the «grand ball» of that time. Webster and Clay, Calhoun, Randolph, and Jackson, were there in their pride of blue coats and gilt buttons, buff waistcoats, silk stockings, and pumps; while her democratic majesty was singular and conspicuous in a suit of steel—her gown of «steel lama,» with brilliant ornaments of cut steel in her hair and on her throat, bust, and arms. Her portrait by Leslie, a reflection from the court of Napoleon, shows an American woman of the republican court in her proper panoply of grace, culture, and distinction.

Among the ladies of honor who graced the drawing-rooms of Mrs. Adams, two daughters of Maryland were expressly admired. One of these, a cousin of «the elect lady,» was Fanny Russell Johnson, granddaughter of the governor. This beautiful young woman was born on the night and almost at the hour of General Washington's death, and that sad association endeared her to the households of Mount Vernon and Arlington. In the political and literary coteries that met at her cousin's house when Mr. Adams was Secretary of State, she was the object of competing compliments; and when Lafayette returned in 1824 to greet his brothers in arms and to salute again the patriotic ladies of whom he had written, «I am proud of my obligations to them; I am happy in the tie of gratitude that binds me to them,» his admiration for Fanny Johnson was expressed with the Gallic ardor he kept for his fair favorites. Rembrandt Peale, who made the portrait here reproduced, was never satisfied with it. He privately painted another, with which he could not be induced to part, reserving it among the happier achievements and souvenirs of his art. Fanny Johnson was married to Captain John McPherson of Frederick, Maryland, where, in her ninety-

PAINTED BY REMBRANDT PEALE. BORDER DRAWN BY FRANK FRENCH. ENGRAVED BY R. G. TIETZE. OWNED BY MRS. WORTHINGTON ROSS.

FANNY RUSSELL JOHNSON.

seventh year, she is revered and honored, as aforetime she was courted and serenaded.[1]

In those happy days in Washington and Georgetown, Fanny Johnson and Charlotte Graham Nicols were inseparable comrades and confiding rivals. Charlotte Nicols married Joseph Patterson, brother of Mme. Patterson-Bonaparte, another of whose brothers, Robert, married Charles Carroll of Carrollton's lovely granddaughter Marianne Caton, by her later marriage Marchioness of Wellesley. The portrait by Sully of Mrs. Joseph Patterson is justly coupled with that of the Marchioness by Sir Thomas Lawrence among the «counterfeit presentments» of notable Maryland women. Marianne Patterson, being widowed, went to England, and married the Marquis of Wellesley, brother to the

[1] Mrs. Carlton Shafer writes with filial love and reverence: «In the late autumn of her beautiful and honored life she shows us how gracious and charming must have been the women of her day. This venerable and beloved lady, sitting in almost total blindness, teaches us to regret the passing away of the old régime in Maryland, of which she is almost the last surviving representative.» Her family, represented by her daughter, Mrs. Worthington Ross of Frederick, Maryland, permit themselves to hope that they may be indebted to some kind reader of THE CENTURY for information disclosing the present whereabouts of the missing Peale portrait, which is supposed to be in Philadelphia.

Duke of Wellington, and viceroy of Ireland. Her sisters (Catons of Baltimore) were the Duchess of Leeds and Lady Stafford. She was for a time first lady in waiting to Queen Adelaide at Windsor, and her extraordinary beauty was the talk of court circles. The venerable Mrs. Barney, daughter of Samuel Chase, signer of the Declaration of Independence and associate justice of the Supreme Court of the United States, who had been the close friend of Marianne Caton, and was present at her wedding to Robert Patterson, once said to the writer of this sketch: «I saw her while she was living at St. John's Lodge, Regent Square, and I then thought the portrait by Sir Thomas Lawrence at her father's house in Baltimore did less than justice to her beauty. A singular grace adorned her simplest movements, and her manner was most engaging.»

A daughter of Mrs. Patterson, married to Mr. Charles Gilmor of Baltimore, inherited her mother's social charm; but stricken by the death of her two pretty boys, she died in her young motherhood.

Peale's portrait of Mrs. Rebecca Rogers is an impressive presentation of a typical Maryland matron whose occasional presence served to illustrate the affability and bounty of social life in early Georgetown. Rebecca Woodward was born at «Primrose,» her mother's estate near Annapolis, and was half-sister to Charlotte Hesselius.[1] She was wedded to Philip Rogers of «Greenwood,» the sylvan home near Baltimore of that branch of the family of Druid Hill. The gracious hospitality of its mistress made Greenwood a mansion of delight to the innumerable kinfolk and friends of the Rogers connection. As one group departed another took its place, and the house was at all times as full as it could hold comfortably or uncomfortably. On one occasion Mrs. Rogers writes: «So crowded is this house with inhabitants of the most noisy sort that I have ranged through every room in vain, seeking a respite from the chatter of children and, as poor L'Argnan used to say, the ‹chatteration› of grown people.» Postage was high in those days, and the Greenwood bills at one time amounted to five hundred dollars for the postage of guests, whose visits were neither far between nor limited as to duration: a Greenwood visit was commonly reckoned by weeks.

The fine portrait of Mrs. Rogers becomes especially interesting when contemplated in the light of a letter addressed by the lady to her friend Mrs. Walter Dulany in London, and dated at «Baltimore Town,» May 12, 1787:

PAINTED BY BENJAMIN WEST. ENGRAVED BY H. DAVIDSON. OWNED BY MRS. WORTHINGTON ROSS.

MRS. CHARLES GILMOR.

> I have for some time past been trying to get a plain mount of a Fan to paint for you, as I wished to produce something you would wear, and you know my art does not extend to miniature painting. I intend to sit as soon as possible to Mr. Peale. But, my Dear, do you prefer it a miniature? I have been thinking, when I am happy enough to have your dear Resemblance, I should choose something nearer the natural size of your Features. Unless a Face is very remarkable indeed, I think 't is never so striking in miniature; and one leading Feature, by bearing some resemblance to another person's, very often misleads the Judgment. Thus, Mrs. Sophia Carroll's, by having an aquiline Nose, is thought by some as much like me as her; but I presume you would desire something more like your friend than she is like Sophia, tho' it should not possess in a tenth degree so agreeable an Aspect.

[1] See «Certain Worthies and Dames of Old Maryland,» in THE CENTURY for February, 1896.

PAINTED BY THOMAS SULLY. ENGRAVED BY PETER AITKEN. OWNED BY MRS. WORTHINGTON ROSS.

MRS. JOSEPH PATTERSON.

Eliza, or Betsy, Hesselius, the youngest of Mrs. Rogers's half-sisters, and her protégée, was married at Primrose in 1792 to the Rev. Walter Dulany Addison, that excellent divine who had the Bible at his fingers' ends, and who in 1794 founded in Georgetown the historic church of St. John, when there was no Episcopal church there nor in the «trackless waste» that stood for Washington. But it was not until 1809 that the faithful and patient founder was called to the rectorship of the completed temple. Then the pews in the galleries were rented at high rates to persons of notable respectability, and the street in front of the church was filled with fine coaches and servants. Mrs. Madison was of the congregation, and Mrs. Calvert from Bladensburg, and the British minister—his excellency followed by two attendants in livery with drawn swords. At that time there was a small church at Rock Creek, but it had never had a floor, and the building was so out of repair that the rector was driven to holding services under the trees in the yard.

When Betsy Hesselius left school in Baltimore to return to Primrose and thence to Georgetown, her place in the house at Greenwood was taken by that delightful child Mary Grafton, whose letters afford us amusing foretastes of the ingenuous candor and the frank, engaging flings at cant and dullness that so tickled Sir Walter Scott and Dr. John Brown in the diary and letters of Marjorie Fleming. Thus, Mary Grafton to her father:

I went on Wednesday to Madame B's exhibition [a fashionable school]. There were five Crowns: the two principal Crowns for Eminence in lessons and Virtue. They were all Crowned in great style at the Assembly Rooms, in the presence of 500 Spectators. As for Mrs. Groombridge, she has postponed her Exhibition till Christmas. She says

PAINTED BY PEALE. BORDER DRAWN BY FRANK FRENCH. ENGRAVED BY HENRY WOLF. OWNED BY MRS. COMMODORE RIDGELY.

MRS. REBECCA ROGERS.

it will show the People what *her* scholars can do. She was bitterly against Crowns when she first heard of them. When I went there the next day [after Madame B's «exhibition»] she told me she would have a Crown for the most Eminent of every Class.[1]

Mary Grafton, desperately wrestling with Rollin and the Peloponnesian war, is but a forecast of Marjorie in the throes of multiplication. «I am now going,» says Marjorie, «to tell you the horible and wretched plaege [plague] that my Multiplication gives me you cant conceive it the most devilish thing is 8 times 8 and 7 times 7 it is what nature itself cant endure.»

«Aunt Brice» is delighted with the French officers; she has five or six at her house every evening. But «Aunt Rodgers» does not wish Mary to go while they are there. So that single-minded young person writes to her father:

Nancy Weems has arrived in Town, and tells me Cousin Mary will be hurt if I do not return to Annapolis with her. If I can get ready I don't know but I may, for if I wait for the French Officers to leave I may not get there till next Winter. Besides, I have not such an Invincible Hatred to them as to make me forego Cousin Mary's agreeable society.

[1] «The Life and Times of the Rev. Walter Dulany Addison,» by his granddaughter, Elizabeth Hesselius Murray.

P. S. Mrs. Twitchem, with her one eye,
A wondrous length of tail lets fly;
And as she passes through every gap,
Leaves a piece of her tail in the trap.

What do you think of that riddle? Perhaps it may seem of some consequence when I tell you it was produced by the Bishop of London.

Major Grafton's letters to his lively daughter are not lacking in the admonitions and petty maxims that were regarded as worldly wise in his time. «It has been remarked upon as a great excellence of General Washington's Writing,» says the major, «that no one c'd substitute a single Word which c'd so well express his Meaning. I have heard that for Seven years of his life he never wrote without having his Dictionary before him.»

What raptures of fun the girl's keen sense of humor most have extracted from that passage—seeing that she already spelled more correctly than the august personage whose example was commended to her!

The social atmosphere of Georgetown, hitherto placidly respectable and decorous, was sadly vitiated by the recklessness and extravagance of the Jackson period. Wine, women, and high play, social and political intrigue, and Peggy Timberlake, forced their way into retreats consecrated to sobriety, good manners, discreet deportment, and edifying discourse. Margaret Timberlake, *née* O'Neill, was the widow of a young naval officer whom she had married before she was seventeen. He died by suicide at Port Mahon in 1828, leaving this red-and-white relict, beautiful, unconventional, adventurous, much given to high spirits and boisterous assaults upon the complacent proprieties of the period. Her dark-brown hair curled naturally, and so

PAINTED BY SIR THOMAS LAWRENCE. BORDER DRAWN BY WILLIAM H. SMITH. ENGRAVED BY PETER AITKEN.
OWNED BY THE MARYLAND HISTORICAL SOCIETY.

THE MARCHIONESS OF WELLESLEY.

did her pert red lip, impatient of «preachments.» She was the spoiled daughter of a rollicking Irishman, landlord of a conspicuous public-house in Washington, who thought nothing too good for his Peggy, and was content if the company that met around his decanters were half as lively and bright as she. It was his boast that Mrs. Madison had crowned his Peggy with «the crown of beauty» at a school exhibition in Georgetown.

General Jackson, with his bosom friend Eaton, had lodged at O'Neill's tavern, where Peggy's pranks had amused them, while her impulsive, defiant temper won their hearts. Especially did she appeal to the chivalrous sentiment in «Old Hickory,» whose beloved wife had been cruelly assailed in the presidential canvass, and now he vowed vengeance against all defamers of women. Presently the widow Timberlake, whose eccentricities were tempered with ambition, became Mrs. Eaton. The respectabilities of the capital, shocked and indignant, opened fire upon her with great guns of scandal, and she gleefully reveled in the bombardment. President Jackson, her formidable champion, had her often, an honored guest, at the White House, and swore: «By the Eternal! the spiteful cats who plagued the life out of my patient Rachel shall not scratch this brave little Peggy.»

His wily ally, Mr. Van Buren, joining forces with the ministers of Great Britain and Russia, made a demonstration in force, and entertained the goddess of discord at dinners, suppers, and balls. On these occasions her audacity was as brilliant as her beauty was bewildering. Staid matrons of the cabinet and congressional set called untimely for their carriages, clergymen denounced her publicly; and Peggy danced for joy, running to the White House every day with fresh stories of delightful insults. Van Buren and Eaton pretended to resign from the cabinet. Of course the President would not accept, but he bluntly signified how willingly he would contemplate the retirement of certain of their colleagues whose sensitive consorts shrank from calling on the wife of the Secretary of War.

«It is odd,» wrote Daniel Webster, «but the consequences of this desperate turmoil in the social and fashionable world may determine who shall succeed the present chief magistrate.» The senator from Massachusetts foresaw the historical sequence—Peggy O'Neill, the widow Timberlake, Mrs. Secretary Eaton, President Van Buren!

This formidable mistress of social and political coups, who had dismembered the cabinet of a nation, and compelled the recall of a foreign minister whose wife had ventured to snub her, and who had been the bosom friend of Queen Christina at the court of Spain, died in obscure and tragic penury in Washington, in her old age the mocked and discarded wife of a young Italian dancing-master who had eloped with her money and her granddaughter.

Lest the social panorama of old Georgetown should lack aught of its intellectual harlequinade, we may not omit from the motley procession of engaging and diverting ghosts the censorious sprightliness of Mrs. Trollope, deploring the ubiquitous offensiveness of the spittoon, the fatal flimsiness of feminine foot-gear, the absence of «Punch» and the Established Church, and the superfluity of «camp-meetings»; or the sententious and rhetorical deliverances of Charles Kemble's comely daughter, she of the low Greek brow, and, like Juno, «ox-eyed,» whose fine Olympian shoulders Sir Thomas Lawrence so proudly pictured—Fanny Kemble, petulant and portentous, who disposed of the foolishness of snobs and the fate of nations with the identical oracular sweep: «It is my conviction,» said she, «that these United States will be a monarchy before I am a skeleton.»

But the social panorama of old Georgetown had its happier chronicler in N. P. Willis, whose society letters in the New York «Mirror» brewed many a tempest in a teapot: «master of Elegant Gossip, travelled, fastidious, poetic, airy»—Leigh Hunt of the drawing-rooms.

*John Williamson Palmer.*

# THE CELLO.

NOT while the cello hid its tone
 'Neath din of viol, harp, and horn,
But when it rose at last alone,
 Were faith and aspiration born.

Nor printed word, nor golden tongue,
 Nor canvases, nor statues rare,
Have led me where that last note hung,
 Dying, upon the trancèd air.

*Meredith Nicholson.*

# GENERAL SHERMAN'S OPINION OF GENERAL GRANT.

**[The letter which follows is printed from the original, in possession of the person to whom it was addressed. It is significant as representing, fourteen years after the war, General Sherman's frank and deliberate judgment of General Grant's characteristics.—The Editor.]**

Headquarters Army of the United States,
Washington, D. C., November 18, 1879.

Dear ——: . . . I don't believe Grant's head has been turned or confused one iota by the extraordinary displays in his honor at San Francisco or elsewhere. He is a strange character. Nothing like it is portrayed by Plutarch or the many who have striven to portray the great men of ancient or modern times. I knew him as a cadet at West Point, as a lieutenant of the Fourth Infantry, as a citizen of St. Louis, and as a growing general all through a bloody civil war. Yet to me he is a mystery, and I believe he is a mystery to himself. I am just back from Chicago, where he had a reception equal in numbers and display to that of San Francisco. I was president of the Society of the Army of the Tennessee, the first he commanded, with which he achieved the great victories of Forts Henry and Donelson, of Shiloh, and of Vicksburg. As such I presided at two great assemblages of people, at the theater and at the banquet-hall. In both cases I sat by him, and directed all the proceedings. He was as simple, as awkward, as when he was a cadet; but all he did and all he said had good sense and modesty as the basis. No man in America has held higher office or been more instrumental in guiding great events, and without elaborating, I 'll give you what I construe to be the philosophy of his life: a simple faith that our country must go on, and by keeping up with the events of the day he will be always right—for «whatever is is right.» He don't lead in one sense, and don't attempt to change natural results. Thus the world accounts him the typical man, and therefore adores him. Our people want success, progress, and unity, and in these Grant has been, is, and will be accepted as the type. . . .

Here at this moment crowds are assembled to unveil the equestrian statue of General George H. Thomas, another of the heroes of the Civil War, who died in California in 1870, and who now lies buried at Troy, New York. He, too, was my classmate at West Point from 1836 to '40, served with me in the same regiment for ten years, and, last, was my most trusted commander in the great campaign of Atlanta. . . .

I will be present at all, but will have a modest part, because most of the audience will think that my turn comes next, and many that I, too, ought to have died long since to make room for ambitious subordinates. But somehow I linger on—it may be, «superfluous on the stage»; but I reason that I have taken a reasonable share of chances to be killed by bullets and by sickness, and it is not my fault that I have survived Thomas and McPherson and others of my war comrades. When my turn does come I suppose that the world will have forgotten the days of 1864–5, and forget the gratitude then felt and expressed for the men who fought and won the battle for our national union and liberty. Don't forget it yourself, but be thankful that your children thereby escaped the horrors of battle, the terrible conflicts of passion and feeling, which had to be in 1861–5 or at some subsequent time. Now all is peace and glory; America now stands at the head of civilized nations, and many must exist who know the truth, and bear in honor and affectionate remembrance the men who fought that glorious peace might be possible. . . .

Yours,
W. T. Sherman.

J. W. Mackey. Mrs. M. G. Gillette. U. S. Grant, Jr. Mrs. U. S. Grant. General U. S. Grant. S. Yanada. Mrs. J. G. Fair. Gov. J. H. Kinkead. Col. J. G. Fair.

PHOTOGRAPH LENT BY NAPOLEON WELLS

GENERAL GRANT AT THE BONANZA MINES.

In October, 1879, General Grant after his trip around the world, went to Virginia City Nevada, for the purpose of going down into the mines. After they were dressed for the descent, General Grant remarked to Mr. Mackey that Mrs. Grant would not go down. Mr. Mackey said, «Oh, yes, she will—she is all ready.» General Grant then said that he knew her of old; she would go to the shaft, and then back out. Mr. Mackey again expressed his belief that she would go down, upon which General Grant said, «I will bet you a dollar in silver that she will do just as I have said.» The party arrived at the head of the shaft, and sure enough, when Mrs. Grant had taken one look down into it, she exclaimed with great earnestness, «I would n't go down in that hole for the whole mine.» Mr. Mackey told her of the bet he had made with her husband, while the latter enjoyed his discomfiture. This put Mrs. Grant on her mettle, and she at once descended with the party, declaring with much spirit that if the general had bet against her courage in that way, she would disappoint him.

*Frederick D. Grant.*

# CAMPAIGNING WITH GRANT.

BY GENERAL HORACE PORTER.

## GRANT'S DASH FOR PETERSBURG.

### THE START FOR THE JAMES.

AT dark on the evening of June 12 the famous march to the James began. General Grant had acted with his usual secrecy in regard to important movements, and had spoken of his detailed plans to only a few officers upon whose reticence he could rely implicitly, and whom he was compelled to take into his secret in order to make the necessary preparations. The orders for the movement were delivered to commanders in the strictest confidence. Smith's corps began its march that night to White House, its destination having been changed from Coles's Landing on the Chickahominy; and on its arrival it embarked for Bermuda Hundred, the position occupied by Butler in the angle between the James River and the Appomattox. A portion of Wilson's division of cavalry which had not accompanied Sheridan pushed forward to Long Bridge on the Chickahominy, fifteen miles below Cold Harbor. All the bridges on that river had been destroyed, and the cavalry had to dismount and wade across the muddy stream under great difficulty; but they soon succeeded in reaching the opposite bank in sufficient numbers to drive away the enemy's cavalry pickets. A pontoon-bridge was then rapidly constructed. Warren had kept close to the cavalry, and on the morning of the 13th his whole corps had crossed the bridge. Hancock's corps followed. Burnside set out on the road to Jones's Bridge, twenty miles below Cold Harbor, and was followed by Wright. Cavalry covered the rear. Warren moved out some distance on the Long Bridge road, so as to watch the routes leading toward Richmond and hold the bridge across the White Oak Swamp. He was to make demonstrations which were intended to deceive Lee and give him the impression that our army was turning his right with the intention of either moving upon Richmond or crossing the James above City Point. How completely successful this movement was in confusing the enemy will be seen later.

General Grant started from his camp near Old Cold Harbor on the night of June 12. Although there was moonlight, the dust rose in such dense clouds that it was difficult to see more than a short distance, and the march was exceedingly tedious and uncomfortable. The artillerymen would at times have to walk ahead of the battery horses, and locate the small bridges along the road by feeling for them.

### GRANT'S SECRETIVENESS.

AFTER the general had got some miles out on the march from Cold Harbor, an officer of rank joined him, and as they rode along began to explain a plan which he had sketched, providing for the construction of another line of intrenchments, some distance in rear of the lines then held by us, to be used in case the army should at any time want to fall back and move toward the James, and should be attacked while withdrawing. The general kept on smoking his cigar, listened to the proposition for a time, and then quietly remarked to the astonished officer: «The army has already pulled out from the enemy's front, and is now on its march to the James.» This is mentioned as an instance of how well his secrets could be kept. He had never been a secretive man until the positions of responsibility in which he was placed compelled him to be chary in giving expression to his opinions and purposes. He then learned the force of the philosopher's maxim that «the unspoken word is a sword in the scabbard, while the spoken word is a sword in the hand of one's enemy.» In the field there were constant visitors to the camp, ready to circulate carelessly any intimations of the commander's movements, at the risk of having such valuable information reach the enemy. Any encouraging expression given to an applicant for favors was apt to be tortured into a promise, and the general

DRAWN BY B. WEST CLINEDINST.

GRANT'S ARMY CROSSING THE JAMES RIVER.

naturally became guarded in his intercourse. When questioned beyond the bounds of propriety, his lips closed like a vise, and the obtruding party was left to supply all the subsequent conversation. These circumstances proclaimed him a man who studied to be uncommunicative, and gave him a reputation for reserve which could not fairly be attributed to him. He was called the «American Sphinx,» «Ulysses the Silent,» and the «Great Unspeakable,» and was popularly supposed to move about with sealed lips. It is true that he had no «small talk» introduced merely for the sake of talking, and many a one will recollect the embarrassment of a first encounter with him resulting from this fact; but while, like Shakspere's soldier, he never wore his dagger in his mouth, yet in talking to a small circle of friends upon matters to which he had given special consideration, his conversation was so thoughtful, philosophical, and original that he fascinated all who listened to him.

### STEALING A MARCH ON THE ENEMY.

THE next morning (June 13) the general made a halt at Long Bridge, where the head of Hancock's corps had arrived, and where he could be near Warren's movement and communicate promptly with him. That evening he reached Wilcox's Landing, and went into camp on the north bank of the James, at the point where the crossing was to take place.

Hancock's corps made a forced march, and reached the river at Wilcox's Landing on the afternoon of June 13. Wright's and Burnside's corps arrived there the next day. Warren's corps withdrew on the night of the 13th from the position to which it had advanced, and reached the James on the afternoon of the 14th. The several corps had moved by forced marches over distances of from twenty-five to fifty-five miles, and the effect of the heat and dust, and the necessity of every man's carrying an ample supply of ammunition and rations, rendered the marches fatiguing in the extreme.

Although the army started on the night of the 12th, it was not until the next morning that Lee had any knowledge of the fact, and even then he wholly misunderstood the movement. He telegraphed to Richmond at 10 P.M. on the 13th: «At daybreak this morning it was discovered that the army of General Grant had left our front. Our skirmishers were advanced between one and two miles, but failing to discover the enemy, were withdrawn, and the army was moved to conform to the route taken by him. . . .» It will be seen from this that Lee was occupied with Warren's advance directly toward Richmond, and made his army conform to this route, while Grant, with the bulk of his forces, was marching in an entirely different direction. On the 14th General Grant took a small steamer and ran up the river to Bermuda Hundred, to have a personal interview with General Butler and arrange plans for his forces to move out at once and make an attack upon Petersburg. Grant knew now that he had stolen a march on Lee, and that Petersburg was almost undefended; and with his usual fondness for taking the offensive, he was anxious to hasten the movement which he had had in contemplation against that place, to be begun before the Army of the Potomac should arrive. His instructions were that as soon as Smith's troops reached their destination they should be reinforced by as many men as could be spared from Butler's troops,—about 6000,—and move at once against Petersburg. General Grant returned to Wilcox's Landing at 1 P.M. He had sent a despatch from Bermuda Hundred to Washington, giving briefly the situation of the army and the progress of the movement. That afternoon reports were received showing pretty definitely Lee's present position; for Grant, with the energy and system which he never failed to employ in securing prompt information regarding his opponent's movements, had had Lee's operations closely watched.

### THE PASSAGE OF THE JAMES.

THE work of laying the great pontoon-bridge across the James began at 4 P.M. on June 14, and was finished by midnight. It was twenty-one hundred feet in length, and required one hundred and one pontoons. These pontoons were attached to vessels that were anchored above and below for this purpose. Admiral Lee's fleet took position in the river, and assisted in covering the passage of the troops. Hancock began to move his corps on ferry-boats on the 14th, and before daylight on the morning of the 15th his entire infantry had been transferred to the south side of the James, with four batteries of artillery. By 6:30 A.M. three ferry-boats had been added to the number in use, which greatly facilitated the passage of his wagons and artillery. Butler had been ordered to send sixty thousand rations to Hancock that morning. Hancock waited for them till eleven o'clock, and then started for Petersburg without them. General Grant now received the following answer to his despatch

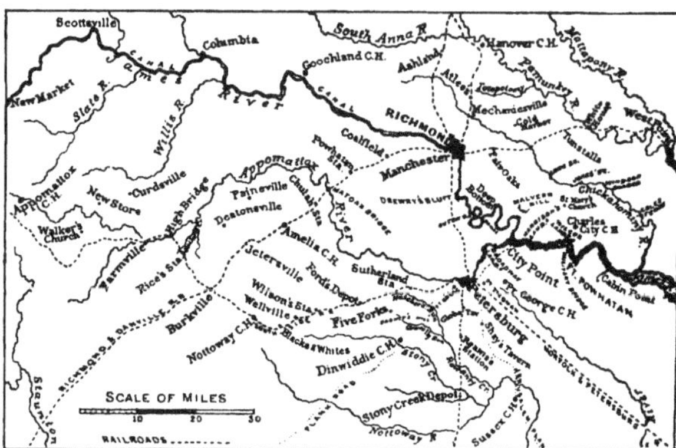


MAP OF THE PETERSBURG CAMPAIGN.

of the day before to the President: «I begin to see it. You will succeed. God bless you all. A. Lincoln.»

By midnight of the 16th the army, with all its artillery and trains, had been safely transferred to the south side of the James without a serious accident or the loss of a wagon or an animal, and with no casualties except those which occurred in the minor encounters of Warren's corps and the cavalry with the enemy. This memorable operation, when examined in all its details, will furnish one of the most valuable and instructive studies in logistics.

### A BRILLIANT SPECTACLE.

As the general-in-chief stood upon the bluff on the north bank of the river on the morning of June 15, watching with unusual interest the busy scene spread out before him, it presented a sight which had never been equaled even in his extended experience in all the varied phases of warfare. His cigar had been thrown aside, his hands were clasped behind him, and he seemed lost in the contemplation of the spectacle. The great bridge was the scene of a continuous movement of infantry columns, batteries of artillery, and wagon-trains. The approaches to the river on both banks were covered with masses of troops moving briskly to their positions or waiting patiently their turn to cross. At the two improvised ferries steamboats were gliding back and forth with the regularity of weavers' shuttles. A fleet of transports covered the surface of the water below the bridge, and gunboats floated lazily upon the stream, guarding the river above. Drums were beating the march, bands were playing stirring quicksteps, the distant booming of cannon on Warren's front showed that he and the enemy were still exchanging compliments; and mingled with these sounds were the cheers of the sailors, the shouting of the troops, the rumbling of wheels, and the shrieks of steam-whistles. The bright sun, shining through a clear sky upon the scene, cast its sheen upon the water, was reflected from the burnished gun-barrels and glittering cannon, and brought out with increased brilliancy the gay colors of the waving banners. The calmly flowing river reflected the blue of the heavens, and mirrored on its surface the beauties of nature that bordered it. The rich grain was standing high in the surrounding fields. The harvest was almost ripe, but the harvesters had fled. The arts of civilization had recoiled before the science of destruction; and in looking from the growing crops to the marching columns, the gentle smile of peace contrasted strangely with the savage frown of war. It was a matchless pageant that could not fail to inspire all beholders with the grandeur of achievement and the majesty of military power. The man whose genius had conceived and whose skill had executed this masterly movement stood watching the spectacle in profound silence. Whether his mind was occupied with the contemplation of its magnitude and success, or was busied with maturing plans for the future, no one can tell. After a time he woke from his reverie, mounted his horse, and gave orders to have headquarters ferried across to the south bank of the river. On arriving there, he set out for City Point; but he had ridden only a short distance when a small steamer came along, and as he wished to reach City Point as quickly as possible to direct operations from there, he decided to go aboard the boat. It was hailed, and took him on, with Parker and a couple of other staff-officers. The rest of us went by land, so as to take some instructions to Hancock's corps and to familiarize ourselves with that part of the country.

Upon reaching City Point, headquarters were established on a high bluff at the junction of the James and the Appomattox rivers. I have said that the passage of the James had been effected without the loss of an animal. A proper regard for strict veracity requires a modification of the statement. The headquarters mess had procured a Virginia cow the rich milk of which went far toward compensating for the shortcomings in other supplies. While preparing to ferry across the river, the cow was tied to a tree to prevent her from turning deserter, and in the hurry of embarking was entirely forgotten. The mess felt the loss keenly until another animal was procured. That evening at the dinner-table, when reference was made to the incident, the general said: «Well, it seems that the loss of animals in this movement falls most heavily upon headquarters.»

### W. F. SMITH'S ATTACK ON PETERSBURG.

GENERAL WILLIAM F. SMITH had disembarked his troops at Bermuda Hundred during the preceding night (the 14th), had started immediately upon his movement against Petersburg, and had struck the Confederate pickets the next morning, June 15. The enemy was protected by a line of rifle-pits and heavy thickets. After some hard fighting he was driven from his position; our troops then moved forward, and by half-past one o'clock arrived at a point from which it was thought that an assault could be made upon the intrenchments. Reconnaissances were made during the afternoon, and finally Smith decided that a direct assault would be too hazardous, and at half-past seven o'clock threw forward his troops in strong skirmish-lines. After a short struggle the enemy was forced back from his intrenchments in front of our center and left, and Smith's second line then made an attack upon the rest of the works. The Confederates were now driven back at all points, four guns were captured and turned upon the retreating troops, and before dark the whole line of intrenchments, about two miles long, had been carried, and three hundred prisoners and sixteen pieces of artillery captured. Instead of following up this advantage with his whole force and seizing the city, Smith again delayed until night came on. Staff-officers from Grant had reached Smith at four o'clock, saying that Hancock was marching toward him. The head of Hancock's troops reached a point a mile in the rear of Hinks's division of Smith's command about half-past six, and two divisions of Hancock's corps were ordered to push on and coöperate in the pending movement. Hancock himself rode forward to where Smith was, to learn the exact situation and participate in the attack; and though senior in rank, waived his rights in this respect, and left Smith in command of the operations, for the reason that he was more familiar with the ground and the movements of the troops up to that time. It was now after dark, and Smith contented himself with ordering up the two divisions of Hancock's corps to occupy the works which had been captured. This was not accomplished until about eleven o'clock, and the object of the movement had failed. General Grant's belief regarding the very inferior force in Petersburg proved to be entirely correct. While the works were well supplied with artillery, about the only available troops to defend them were Wise's brigade of 2500 men, and Deering's cavalry of 2000. Besides this force there was only the local militia, composed of old men and young boys, who had never seen active service, and were no match for veterans. It was a moonlight night; Kautz and Hinks were quite familiar with the country; Smith had lost only about 600 men, and a bold dash upon the city after the works had been so gallantly captured would undoubtedly have secured the prize and made a vast difference in the campaign which followed.

Instead of letting Butler, the actual commander of the forces, take charge of the operation, the commander-in-chief had especially delegated Smith for it, as he was an educated soldier, and by his intelligence had commended himself to General Grant as an officer well fitted for such a task. Grant had won all his great successes by boldness and the vigor and rapidity of his movements, and it was hard for him to understand how others could be so lacking in these qualities. General Smith said that before taking the last works that he had captured he had heard rumors that the enemy was crossing the James to reinforce Petersburg, and that he thought it best to hold on to the position he had secured, instead of advancing and taking the chance of his troops meeting with disaster and losing what they had already gained.

When the general felt that his subordinates had made a bold fight and had done their best, he always commended them for any soldierly traits they had displayed. His displeasure was aroused only when officers failed to comprehend the scope of his plans, and neglected to use to advantage the means which he placed in their hands. He had just reason to feel grievously disappointed over the failure of the admirable plan conceived for the capture of Petersburg. He had used all the arts of which he was master in preparing and conducting this memorable movement across the James, which was beset at all points by innumerable difficulties. He had thrown nearly 16,000 troops against Petersburg before Lee had sent a single reinforcement there, and had moved them by transports so that they might not arrive exhausted by a long march. With a perfect knowledge of Lee's movements, Grant had brought the advance of his army in front of Petersburg on the 15th, while Lee was still groping about to discover his opponent's movements. In reaching this point, Grant had marched more than twice the distance of Lee's route, and had crossed two rivers, one a most formidable obstacle. It was no wonder that he felt keen disappointment when Smith's command failed to seize the golden opportunity he had prepared; but brilliant generals, like eminent sculptors, in executing their best conceptions sometimes find that their tools break in their hands.

### DONNING SUMMER UNIFORM.

THE weather had become so warm that the general and most of the staff had ordered thin, dark-blue flannel blouses to be sent to them to take the place of the heavy uniform coats which they had been wearing. The summer clothing had arrived, and was now tried on. The general's blouse, like the others, was of plain material, single-breasted, and had four regulation brass buttons in front. It was substantially the coat of a private soldier, with nothing to indicate the rank of an officer except the three gold stars of a lieutenant-general on the shoulder-straps. He wore at this time a turn-down white linen collar and a small, black «butterfly» cravat, which was hooked on to his front collar-button. The general, when he put on the blouse, did not take the pains to see whether it fitted him or to notice how it looked, but thought only of the comfort it afforded, and said, «Well, this is a relief,» and then added: «I have never taken as much satisfaction as some people in making frequent changes in my outer clothing. I like to put on a suit of clothes when I get up in the morning, and wear it until I go to bed, unless I have to make a change in my dress to meet company. I have been in the habit of getting one coat at a time, putting it on and wearing it every day as long as it looked respectable, instead of using a best and a second best. I know that is not the right way to manage, but a comfortable coat seems like an old friend, and I don't like to change it.» The general had also received a pair of light, neatly fitting calfskin boots, to which he seemed to take a fancy; thereafter he wore them most of the time in place of his heavy top-boots, putting on the latter only when he rode out in wet weather.

### PETERSBURG.

ON the morning of June 16 General Grant went to the Petersburg front. He was accompanied by most of his staff, and by Mr. Dana, Assistant Secretary of War. The enemy was then constantly arriving and occupying his intrenchments in strong force. Burnside's corps had just come up, and was put in position on Hancock's left. At 10:15 A. M. Grant sent an order to Meade to hurry Warren forward, and start up the river himself by steamer and take command in person at Petersburg.

The enemy's intrenchments which protected Petersburg were well located, and were in some places strong. They started at a point on the south bank of the Appomattox, about a mile from the eastern outskirts of the city, and extended in the form of a semicircle to a point on the river at about the same distance from the western limits of the city. Petersburg had at that time a population of 18,000, and was called the «Cockade City» from the fact that at the breaking out of the war of 1812 it furnished a company which was peculiarly uniformed and in which each man wore in his hat a conspicuous cockade.

The probability of Lee's attacking Bermuda Hundred in force induced General Grant to return to City Point to direct the movements on Butler's lines. While riding in that direction he met Meade hurrying forward from the steamer-landing. In a short interview, and without dismounting from his horse, he instructed that officer to move at once to the front and make a vigorous attack upon the works at Petersburg at six o'clock in the evening, and drive the enemy, if possible, across the Appomattox. It was discovered before that hour that the enemy was advancing upon Butler's front, and General Grant directed me to ride at full speed to Meade and tell him that this made it still more important that his attack should be a vigorous one, and that the enemy might be found weaker there on account of troops having been collected at Bermuda Hundred. I found Meade standing near the edge of a piece of woods, surrounded by some of his staff, and actively engaged in superintending the attack, which was then in progress. His usual nervous energy was displayed in the intensity of his manner and the rapid and animated style of his conversation. He assured me that no additional orders could be given which could add to the vigor of the attack. He was acting with great earnestness, and doing his utmost to carry out the instructions which he had received. He had arrived at the front about two o'clock, and his plans had been as well matured as possible for the movement. Three redans, as well as a line of earthworks connecting them, were captured. The enemy felt the loss keenly, and made several desperate attempts during the night to recover the ground, but in this he did not succeed.

When I got back to City Point that evening General Grant felt considerably encouraged by the news brought him, and spent most of the night in planning movements for the next day.

### LEE MYSTIFIED AS TO GRANT'S MOVEMENTS.

AFTER further consultation with the general-in-chief I started again for the front at Petersburg before dawn on the 17th, carrying instructions looking to the contemplated attacks that day. Burnside's troops surprised the enemy at daybreak by making a sudden rush upon his works, captured his intrenchments, swept his line for a mile, and took 600 prisoners, a stand of colors, 4 guns, and 1500 stands of small arms. Attacks were also made by Hancock and Warren, and more of the enemy's line was captured, but not permanently he d.

Telegrams sent by General Lee on June 17 show, even at that late day, how completely mystified he was in regard to Grant's movements. At 12 M. he sent a despatch to Beauregard, saying: «Until I can get more definite information of Grant's movements, I do not think it prudent to draw more troops to this side of the river.» At 1:45 P. M. he telegraphed: «Warren's corps crossed the Chickahominy at Long Bridge on the 13th; . . . that night it marched to Westover. Some prisoners were taken from it on the 14th; have not heard of it since.» At 4:30 he sent Beauregard another despatch, saying: «Have no information of Grant's crossing the James River, but upon your report have ordered troops up to Chaffin's Bluff.» Grant, on the contrary, had ascertained from watchers on Butler's tall signal-tower, which had been erected at Bermuda Hundred, just how many railway-trains with troops had passed toward Petersburg, and learned from the columns of dust that large forces were marching south. From scouts, prisoners, and refugees he had secured each day a close knowledge of Lee's movements.

### A CHANGE OF COMPLEXION.

COLONEL PARKER, the Indian, had been diligently employed in these busy days helping to take care of General Grant's correspondence. He wrote an excellent hand, and as one of the military secretaries often overhauled the general's correspondence and prepared answers to his private letters. This evening he was seated at the writing-table in the general's tent, while his chief was standing at a little distance outside talking with some of the staff. A citizen who had come to City Point in the employ of the Sanitary Commission, and who had been at Cairo when the general took command there in 1861, approached the group and inquired: «Where is the old man's tent? I 'd like to get a look at him; have n't seen him for three years.» Rawlins, to avoid being interrupted, said, «That 's his tent,» at the same time pointing to it. The man stepped over to the tent, looked in, and saw the swarthy features of Parker as he sat in the general's chair. The visitor seemed a little puzzled, and as he walked away was heard to remark: «Yes, that 's him; but he 's got all-fired sunburnt since I last had a look at him.» The general was greatly amused by the incident, and repeated the remark afterward to Parker, who enjoyed it as much as the others.

### MEADE IN ACTION.

AT daylight on the 18th Meade's troops advanced to the assault which had been ordered, but made the discovery that the enemy's line of the day before had been abandoned. By the time new formations could be made Lee's army had arrived in large force, great activity had been displayed in strengthening the fortifications, and the difficulties of the attacking party had been greatly increased. The Second Corps was temporarily commanded by D. B. Birney, as Hancock's Gettysburg wound had broken out afresh the day before, entirely disabling him. Gallant assaults were repeatedly made by Burnside, Warren, and Birney; and while they did not succeed in the object of carrying the enemy's main line of fortifications, positions were gained closer to his works, and these were held and strongly intrenched. Both of the opposing lines on this part of the ground were now strengthened, and remained substantially the same in position from that time until the capture of Petersburg.

General Grant realized the nature of the ground and the circumstances that prevented the troops from accomplishing more than had been done, and he complimented Meade upon the promptness and vigor with which he had handled his army on this day of active operations. Indeed, Meade had shown brilliant qualities as commander of a large army, and under the general directions given him had made all the dispositions and issued all the detailed orders. Grant felt it necessary to remain at City Point in order to be in communication with both Meade and Butler, as Lee's troops were that day moving rapidly south past Butler's front.

My duties kept me on Meade's front a large part of the day. He showed himself the personification of earnest, vigorous action in rousing his subordinate commanders to superior exertions. Even his fits of anger and his resort to intemperate language stood him at times in good stead in spurring on every one upon that active field. He sent ringing despatches to all points of the line, and paced up and down upon the field in his nervous, restless manner, as he watched the progress of the operations and made running comments on the actions of his subordinates. His aquiline nose and piercing eyes gave him something of the eagle's look, and added to the interest of his personality. He had much to try him upon this occasion, and if he was severe in his reprimands and showed faults of temper, he certainly displayed no faults as a commander. When the battle was over no one was more ready to make amends for the instances in which he felt that he might have done injustice to his subordinates. He said to them: «Sorry to hear you cannot carry the works. Get the best line you can and be prepared to hold it. I suppose you cannot make any more attacks, and I feel satisfied all has been done that can be done.» Lee himself did not arrive at Petersburg until noon that day.

After I had returned to headquarters that evening, and had given the general-in-chief reports of the battle in more detail than he had received them by despatches during the day, he sat in his tent and discussed the situation philosophically, saying: «Lee's whole army has now arrived, and the topography of the country about Petersburg has been well taken advantage of by the enemy in the location of strong works. I will make no more assaults on that portion of the line, but will give the men a rest, and then look to extensions toward our left, with a view to destroying Lee's communications on the south and confining him to a close siege.» At ten o'clock he turned to his table and wrote the following message to Meade: «I am perfectly satisfied that all has been done that could be done, and that the assaults of to-day were called for by all the appearances and information that could be obtained. Now we will rest the men, and use the spade for their protection until a new vein can be struck. . . .»

### CONDITION OF THE ARMY.

It was apparent in the recent engagements that the men had not attacked with the same vigor that they had displayed in the Wilderness campaign; but this was owing more to the change in their physical than in their moral condition. They had moved incessantly both day and night, and had been engaged in skirmishing or in giving battle from the 4th of May to the 18th of June. They had seen their veteran comrades fall on every side, and their places filled by inexperienced recruits, and many of the officers in whom they had unshaken confidence had been killed or wounded. Officers had been in the saddle day and night, securing snatches of sleep for a few hours at a time as best they could. Sleeping on horseback had become an art, and experienced riders had learned to brace themselves in their saddles, rest their hands on the pommel, and catch many a cat-nap while riding. These snatches of sleep were of short duration and accomplished under many difficulties, but often proved more refreshing than might be supposed.

There was considerable suffering from sickness in many of the camps. It may be said that the enemy had suffered equally from the same causes that impaired the efficiency of our men, but there was a vast difference between the conditions of the two armies. The enemy had been engaged principally in defending strong intrenchments and in making short marches; he was accustomed to the Southern climate, and was buoyed up with the feeling that he was defending his home and fireside.

A controversy had arisen as to the cause of Hancock's not reaching Petersburg earlier on the 15th. Hancock conceived the idea that the circumstances might be construed as a reproach upon him, and he asked for an official investigation; but General Grant had no intention of reflecting either upon him or Meade. He assured them that, in his judgment, no investigation was necessary. He recommended them both for promotion to the grade of major-general in the regular army, and each was appointed to that rank.

### GRANT'S CAMP AT CITY POINT.

THE headquarters camp at City Point was destined to become historic and to be the scene of some of the most memorable events of the war. It was located at the junction of the James and the Appomattox rivers, and was within easy water communication with Fort Monroe and Washington, as well as with Butler's army, which was to occupy positions on both sides of the upper James. The City Point Railroad was repaired, and a branch was constructed to points south of Petersburg, immediately in rear of the line held by the Army of the Potomac, so that there might be convenient communication with that army. The new portion of the road was built, like most of our military railroads, upon the natural surface of the ground, with but little attempt at grading. It ran up hill and down dale, and its undulations were so marked that a train moving along it looked in the distance like a fly crawling over a corrugated washboard. At City Point there was a level piece of ground on a high bluff, on which stood a comfortable house. This building was assigned to the chief quartermaster, and General Grant's headquarters camp was established on the lawn. The tents occupied a line a little over a hundred feet back from the edge of the bluff. In the middle of the line were General Grant's quarters. A hospital tent was used as his office, while a smaller tent connecting in the rear was occupied as his sleeping-apartment. A hospital tent-fly was stretched in front of the office tent so as to make a shaded space in which persons could sit. A rustic bench and a number of folding camp-chairs with backs were placed there, and it was beneath this tent-fly that most of the important official interviews were held. When great secrecy was to be observed the parties would retire to the office tent. On both sides of the general's quarters were pitched close together enough officers' tents to accommodate the staff. Each tent was occupied by two officers. The mess-tent was pitched in the rear, and at a short distance still farther back a temporary shelter was prepared for the horses. A wooden staircase was built reaching from headquarters to the steamboat-landing at the foot of the bluff; ample wharves, storehouses, and hospitals were rapidly constructed, and a commodious base of supplies was established in the vicinity. The day the wharf was completed and planked over the general took a stroll along it, his hands thrust in his trousers pockets, and a lighted cigar in his mouth. He had recently issued instructions to take every precaution against fire, and had not gone far when a sentinel called out: «It 's against orders to come on the wharf with a lighted cigar.» The general at once took his Havana out of his mouth and threw it into the river, saying: «I don't like to lose my smoke, but the sentinel 's right. He evidently is n't going to let me disobey my own orders.»

### GRANT AT THE MESS-TABLE.

EACH staff-officer took his turn in acting as «caterer» of the mess, usually for a month at a time. His duties consisted in giving general directions to the steward as to ordering the meals, keeping an account of the bills, and at the end of his tour dividing up the expenses and collecting the amount charged to each officer. General Grant insisted upon paying two shares of the expenses instead of one, upon the ground that he invited more guests to meals than any one else in the mess, although this was not always the case, for each officer was allowed to entertain guests, and there were at times as many visitors at table as members of the mess. The officer acting as caterer sat at the head of the mess-table, with the general on his right.

It now came my turn to take a hand in managing the affairs of the mess. The general, while he never complained, was still the most difficult person to cater for in the whole army. About the only meat he enjoyed was beef, and this he could not eat unless it was so thoroughly well done that no appearance of blood could be seen. If blood appeared in any meat which came on the table, the sight of it seemed entirely to destroy his appetite.

(This was the man whose enemies delighted in calling him a butcher.) He enjoyed oysters and fruit, but these could not be procured on an active campaign. He never ate mutton when he could obtain anything else, and fowl and game he abhorred. As he used to express it: «I never could eat anything that goes on two legs.» Evidently he could never have been converted to cannibalism. He did not miss much by declining to eat the chickens which were picked up on a campaign, for they were usually tough enough to create the suspicion that they had been hatched from hard-boiled eggs, and were so impenetrable that an officer said of one of them that he could not even stick his fork through the gravy. The general was fonder of cucumbers than of anything else, and often made his entire meal upon a sliced cucumber and a cup of coffee. He always enjoyed corn, pork and beans, and buckwheat cakes. In fact, he seemed to be particularly fond of only the most indigestible dishes. He had been eating so little for several days just before I took my turn as caterer that I looked about to try to find some delicacy that would tempt his appetite, and after a good deal of pains succeeded in getting some sweetbreads sent down from Washington. They had been nicely cooked, and I announced them, when they came on the table, with an air of ill-disguised triumph; but he said: «I hope these were not obtained especially for me, for I have a singular aversion to them. In my young days I used to eat them, not knowing exactly what part of the animal they came from; but as soon as I learned what they were my stomach rebelled against them, and I have never tasted them since.»

When any fruit could be procured, it was placed on the table by way of helping to ornament it, and afterward used as dessert. Between the courses of the dinner the general would often reach over to the dish of fruit and pick out a berry or a cherry and eat it slowly. He used to do this in a sly way, like a child helping itself to some forbidden dish at the table, and afraid of being caught in the act. He said one day: «I suppose I ought not to eat a course out of its turn, but I take the greatest delight in picking out bits of fruit and eating them during a meal. One of the reasons I do not enjoy dining out as much as I do at home is because I am compelled to sit through a long list of courses, few of which I eat, and to resist the constant temptation to taste a little fruit in the meanwhile to help pass away the time.» Napoleon was famous for eating out of the various dishes before him with his fingers. General Grant's use of the fingers never went beyond picking out small fruits. He was always refined in his manners at table, and no matter how great was the hurry, or what were the circumstances of the occasion, he never violated the requirements of true politeness.

He ate less than any man in the army; sometimes the amount of food taken did not seem enough to keep a bird alive, and his meals were frugal enough to satisfy the tastes of the most avowed anchorite. It so happened that no one in the mess had any inclination to drink wine or spirits at meals, and none was carried among the mess's supplies. The only beverage ever used at table besides tea and coffee was water, although on the march it was often taken from places which rendered it not the most palatable or healthful of drinks. If a staff-officer wanted anything stronger he would carry some commissary whisky in a canteen. Upon a few occasions, after a hard day's ride in stormy weather, the general joined the officers of the staff in taking a whisky toddy in the evening. He never offered liquor of any kind to visitors at headquarters. His hospitality consisted in inviting them to meals and to smoke cigars.

### LINCOLN'S FIRST VISIT TO GRANT'S CAMP.

ON June 21 Butler had thrown a pontoon-bridge across the James, and seized a position on the north side known as Deep Bottom, ten miles below Richmond. General Grant had directed this with a view to divide the attention of the enemy's troops, and to confuse them as to whether to expect an attack upon Richmond or Petersburg, and because he had in contemplation some operations on the north side of the James, which he intended to carry out under certain contingencies, in which case the occupation of Deep Bottom might become important.

On Tuesday, June 21, a white river-steamer arrived at the wharf, bringing President Lincoln, who had embraced this opportunity to visit for the first time the armies under General Grant's immediate command. As the boat neared the shore, the general and several of us who were with him at the time walked down to the wharf, in order that the general-in-chief might meet his distinguished visitor and extend a greeting to him as soon as the boat made the landing. As our party stepped aboard, the President came down from the upper deck, where he had been standing, to the after-gangway, and reaching out his long, angular arm, he wrung General Grant's hand vigorously, and held it in his for some time, while he uttered in rapid words his congratulations and expressions of appreciation of the great task which had been accomplished since he and the general had parted in Washington. The group then went into the after-cabin. General Grant said: «I hope you are very well, Mr. President.» «Yes, I am in very good health,» Mr. Lincoln replied; «but I don't feel very comfortable after my trip last night on the bay. It was rough, and I was considerably shaken up. My stomach has not yet entirely recovered from the effects.» An officer of the party now saw that an opportunity had arisen to make this scene the supreme moment of his life, in giving him a chance to soothe the digestive organs of the Chief Magistrate of the nation. He said: «Try a glass of champagne, Mr. President. That is always a certain cure for seasickness.» Mr. Lincoln looked at him for a moment, his face lighting up with a smile, and then remarked: «No, my friend; I have seen too many fellows seasick ashore from drinking that very stuff.» This was a knockdown for the officer, and in the laugh at his expense Mr. Lincoln and the general both joined heartily.

General Grant now said: «I know it would be a great satisfaction for the troops to have an opportunity of seeing you, Mr. President; and I am sure your presence among them would have a very gratifying effect. I can furnish you a good horse, and will be most happy to escort you to points of interest along the line.» Mr. Lincoln replied: «Why, yes; I had fully intended to go out and take a look at the brave fellows who have fought their way down to Petersburg in this wonderful campaign, and I am ready to start at any time.»

### LINCOLN AT THE FRONT.

GENERAL GRANT presented to Mr. Lincoln the officers of the staff who were present, and he had for each one a cordial greeting and a pleasant word. There was a kindliness in his tone and a hearty manner of expression which went far to captivate all who met him. The President soon stepped ashore, and after sitting awhile at headquarters mounted the large bay horse «Cincinnati,» while the general rode with him on «Jeff Davis.» Three of us of the staff accompanied them, and the scenes encountered in visiting both Butler's and Meade's commands were most interesting. Mr. Lincoln wore a very high black silk hat and black trousers and frock-coat. Like most men who had been brought up in the West, he had good command of a horse, but it must be acknowledged that in appearance he was not a very dashing rider. On this occasion, by the time he had reached the troops he was completely covered with dust, and the black color of his clothes had changed to Confederate gray. As he had no straps, his trousers gradually worked up above his ankles, and gave him the appearance of a country farmer riding into town wearing his Sunday clothes. A citizen on horseback is always an odd sight in the midst of a uniformed army, and the picture presented by the President bordered upon the grotesque. However, the troops were so lost in admiration of the man that the humorous aspect did not seem to strike them. The soldiers rapidly passed the word along the line that «Uncle Abe» had joined them, and cheers broke forth from all the commands, and enthusiastic shouts and even words of familiar greeting met him on all sides. After a while General Grant said: «Mr. President, let us ride on and see the colored troops, who behaved so handsomely in Smith's attack on the works in front of Petersburg last week.» «Oh, yes,» replied Mr. Lincoln; «I want to take a look at those boys. I read with the greatest delight the account given in Mr. Dana's despatch to the Secretary of War of how gallantly they behaved. He said they took six out of the sixteen guns captured that day. I was opposed on nearly every side when I first favored the raising of colored regiments; but they have proved their efficiency, and I am glad they have kept pace with the white troops in the recent assaults. When we wanted every able-bodied man who could be spared to go to the front, and my opposers kept objecting to the negroes, I used to tell them that at such times it was just as well to be a little color-blind. I think, general, we can say of the black boys what a country fellow who was an old-time abolitionist in Illinois said when he went to a theater in Chicago and saw Forrest playing *Othello*. He was not very well up in Shakspere, and did n't know that the tragedian was a white man who had blacked up for the purpose. After the play was over the folks who had invited him to go to the show wanted to know what he thought of the actors, and he said: ‹Waal, layin' aside all sectional prejudices and any partiality I may have for the race, derned ef I don't think the nigger held his own with any on 'em.›» The Western dialect employed in this story was perfect.

The camp of the colored troops of the Eighteenth Corps was soon reached, and a scene now occurred which defies description. They beheld for the first time the liberator of their race—the man who by a stroke of his pen had struck the shackles from the limbs of their fellow-bondmen and proclaimed liberty to the enslaved. Always impressionable, the enthusiasm of the blacks now knew no limits. They cheered, laughed, cried, sang hymns of praise, and shouted in their negro dialect, «God bress Massa Linkum!» «De Lord save Fader Abraham!» «De day ob jubilee am come, shuah.» They crowded about him and fondled his horse; some of them kissed his hands, while others ran off crying in triumph to their comrades that they had touched his clothes. The President rode with bared head; the tears had started to his eyes, and his voice was so broken by emotion that he could scarcely articulate the words of thanks and congratulation which he tried to speak to the humble and devoted men through whose ranks he rode. The scene was affecting in the extreme, and no one could have witnessed it unmoved.

### SOME ANECDOTES BY LINCOLN.

In the evening Mr. Lincoln gathered with General Grant and the staff in front of the general's tent, and then we had an opportunity of appreciating his charm as a talker, and hearing some of the stories for which he had become celebrated. He did not tell a story merely for the sake of the anecdote, but to point a moral or to clench a fact. So far as our experience went, his anecdotes possessed the true geometric requisite of excellence: they were neither too broad nor too long. He seemed to recollect every incident in his experience and to weave it into material for his stories. One evening a sentinel whose post was near enough to enable him to catch most of the President's remarks was heard to say, «Well, that man 's got a powerful memory and a mighty poor forgettery.»

He seldom indulged even in a smile until he reached the climax of a humorous narration; then he joined heartily with the listeners in the laugh which followed. He usually sat on a low camp-chair, and wound his legs around each other as if in an effort to get them out of the way, and with his long arms he accompanied what he said with all sorts of odd gestures. An officer once made the remark that he would rather have a single photograph of one of Mr. Lincoln's jokes than own the negative of any other man's. In the course of the conversation that evening he spoke of the improvement in arms and ammunition, and of the new powder prepared for the fifteen-inch guns. He said he had never seen the latter article, but he understood it differed very much from any other powder that had ever been used. I told him that I happened to have in my tent a specimen which had been sent to headquarters as a curiosity, and that I would bring it to him. When I returned with a grain of the powder about the size of a walnut, he took it, turned it over in his hand, and after examining it carefully, said: «Well, it 's rather larger than the powder we used to buy in my shooting days. It reminds me of what occurred once in a country meeting-house in Sangamon County. You see, there were very few newspapers then, and the country storekeepers had to resort to some other means of advertising their wares. If, for instance, the preacher happened to be late in coming to a prayer-meeting of an evening, the shopkeepers would often put in the time while the people were waiting by notifying them of any new arrival of an attractive line of goods. One evening a man rose up and said: ‹Brethren, let me take occasion to say, while we 're a-waitin', that I have jest received a new inv'ice of sportin' powder. The grains are so small you kin sca'cely see 'em with the naked eye, and polished up so fine you kin stand up and comb yer ha'r in front of one o' them grains jest like it was a lookin'-glass. Hope you 'll come down to my store at the cross-roads and examine that powder for yourselves.› When he had got about this far a rival powder-merchant in the meeting, who had been boiling over with indignation at the amount of advertising the opposition powder was getting, jumped up and cried out: ‹Brethren, I hope you 'll not believe a single word Brother Jones has been sayin' about that powder. I 've been down thar and seen it for myself, and I pledge you my word that the grains is bigger than the lumps in a coal-pile; and any one of you, brethren, ef you was in your future state, could put a bar'l o' that powder on your shoulder and march squar' through the sulphurious flames surroundin' you without the least danger of an explosion.›» We thought that grain of powder had served even a better purpose in drawing out this story than it could ever serve in being fired from a fifteen-inch gun.

As the party broke up for the night I walked into my quarters to put back the grain of powder, and upon turning round to come out, I found that the President had followed me and was looking into my tent, from curiosity, doubtless, to see how the officers were quartered. Of course I made haste to invite him in. He stepped inside for a moment, and his eye fell upon a specimen artillery trace, a patented article which some inventor had left the day before in order to have it examined at headquarters. The President exclaimed, «Why, what 's that?» I replied, «That is a trace.» «Oh,» remarked Mr. Lincoln, «that recalls what the poet wrote: ‹Sorrow had fled, but left her traces there.› What became of the rest of the harness he did n't mention.»

That night Mr. Lincoln slept aboard the boat which had brought him to City Point. He had expressed to General Grant a desire to go up the James the next day, to see that portion of our lines and visit the flag-ship of Admiral Lee, who commanded the gunboats. All arrangements were made for the trip, and the President's boat started up the river about eight o'clock the next morning, stopping at Bermuda Hundred to take on General Butler. Admiral Lee came aboard from his flag-ship, and the party proceeded up the river as far as it was safe to ascend. Mr. Lincoln was in excellent spirits, and listened with great eagerness to the descriptions of the works, which could be seen from the river, and the objects for which they had been constructed. When his attention was called to some particularly strong positions which had been seized and fortified, he remarked to Butler: «When Grant once gets possession of a place, he holds on to it as if he had inherited it.» Orders had been sent to have the pontoon-bridge at Deep Bottom opened for the passage of the President's boat, so that he could proceed some distance beyond that point. His whole conversation during his visit showed the deep anxiety he felt and the weight of responsibility which was resting upon him. His face would light up for a time while telling an anecdote illustrating a subject under discussion, and afterward his features would relax and show the deep lines which had been graven upon them by the mental strain to which he had been subjected for nearly four years. The National Republican Convention had renominated him for the Presidency just two weeks before, and some reference was made to it and to the number of men who composed the Electoral College. He remarked: «Among all our colleges, the Electoral College is the only one where they choose their own masters.» He did not show any disposition to dwell upon the subject, or upon the approaching political campaign. His mind seemed completely absorbed in the operations of the armies. Several times, when contemplated battles were spoken of, he said: «I cannot pretend to advise, but I do sincerely hope that all may be accomplished with as little bloodshed as possible.»

Soon after his return to City Point the President started back to Washington. His visit to the army had been a memorable event. General Grant and he had had so much delightful intercourse that they parted from each other with unfeigned regret, and both felt that their acquaintance had already ripened into a genuine friendship.

### MOVEMENT AGAINST THE WELDON RAILROAD.

General Grant, having decided that it would be inexpedient to attempt to carry the works at Petersburg by assault, now began to take measures looking to the investment of that place by leaving a portion of his forces to defend our works, while he moved out with the other portion against the railroads, with the design of cutting off Lee's communications in that direction. Wright's entire corps had been sent back from Butler's front to the Army of the Potomac, and Martindale's command had been returned to Butler, so that Meade's and Butler's armies were again complete. Meade's corps were disposed as follows, from right to left of the line: Burnside, Warren, Birney (Hancock's), Wright.

On the morning of June 22, Wright's and Birney's corps moved westward with a view to crossing the Weldon Railroad and swinging around to the left; but they were vigorously attacked and forced back some distance. They advanced again in the evening, but nothing important was gained.

On June 23, Birney and Wright again moved out. There was great difficulty in preserving the alignment of the troops, as they had to pass through dense woods and almost impenetrable thickets, which made the movement a slow and difficult process. About four o'clock in the afternoon, while a portion of Wright's troops were at work destroying the Weldon Railroad, a large force of the enemy struck his left and drove it back. Darkness soon came on, and nothing of importance was accomplished. Wright was now given authority to withdraw his corps to the position occupied the night before, which was more advantageous. Meade had sent frequent messages to Grant, who was this day at Bermuda Hundred, keeping him advised of the movements in his front; and that night he telegraphed: «I think you had better come up here to-morrow if convenient.» General Grant felt considerably annoyed about the operations that day at Petersburg, and regarded the position of the Army of the Potomac as somewhat vulnerable. In extending to the left the center had been depleted, while the left flank was out in the air, and would consequently be weak if a heavy and determined attack should be made upon it. The enemy had made his intrenchments so strong that he could afford to move a large portion of his force to his right for the purpose of such an attack. Hancock was much missed from the command of the Second Corps. It was quite natural that Meade should ask Grant to come in person to the lines in front of Petersburg, and it was another indication of the confidence which his subordinate commanders reposed in him.

### SWAPPING HORSES.

AT eight o'clock on the morning of June 24 the general rode to the headquarters of the Army of the Potomac, accompanied by Rawlins, myself, and two others of the staff. In discussing with Meade and some of the corps commanders the events of the two previous days, he gave particular instructions for operations on that part of the line. The guns of the siege-train which he had ordered now began to arrive from Washington. Meade was told that they would be sent to him immediately, and it was decided to spend the next few days in putting the guns and mortars into commanding positions, in the meanwhile permitting the troops to desist from active operations. The heat was now intense, and the men were in much need of rest. Meade gave Grant and his staff a comfortable lunch, and late in the afternoon our party started for City Point.

Owing to the heat and dust, the long ride was exceedingly uncomfortable. My best horse had been hurt, and I was mounted on a bay cob that had a trot which necessitated no end of «saddle-pounding» on the part of the rider; and if distances are to be measured by the amount of fatigue endured, this exertion added many miles to the trip. The general was riding his black pony «Jeff Davis.» This smooth little pacer shuffled along at a gait which was too fast for a walk and not fast enough for a gallop, so that all the other horses had to move at a brisk trot to keep up with him. When we were about five miles from headquarters the general said to me in a joking way: «You don't look comfortable on that horse. Now I feel about as fresh as when we started out.» I replied: «It makes all the difference in the world, general, what kind of horse one rides.» He remarked: «Oh, all horses are pretty much alike as far as the comfort of their gait is concerned.» «In the present instance,» I answered, «I don't think you would like to swap with me, general.» He said at once, «Why, yes; I 'd just as lief swap with you as not»; and threw himself off his pony and mounted my uncomfortable beast, while I put myself astride of «Jeff.» The general had always been a famous rider, even when a cadet at West Point. When he rode or drove a strange horse, not many minutes elapsed before he and the animal seemed to understand each other perfectly. In my experience I have never seen a better rider, or one who had a more steady seat, no matter what sort of horse he rode; but on this occasion it soon became evident that his body and that of the animal were not always in touch, and he saw that all the party were considerably amused at the jogging to which he was subjected. In the meantime «Jeff Davis» was pacing along with a smoothness which made me feel as if I were seated in a rocking-chair. When we reached headquarters the general dismounted in a manner which showed that he was pretty stiff from the ride. As he touched the ground he turned and said with a quizzical look, «Well, I must acknowledge that animal *is* pretty rough.»

### SHERIDAN RETURNS.

SHERIDAN had arrived on June 20 at White House, on his return from the expedition to the north side of the North Anna River, upon which he had been sent on the 7th. As soon as Lee learned of Hunter's success he sent Breckinridge's troops to oppose him; and hearing that Sheridan had started, he ordered Hampton's and Fitzhugh Lee's cavalry commands to move against our cavalry. They were to attack Sheridan during the night of the 10th and surprise him; but that officer was not to be caught napping. He advanced promptly toward Trevilian's Station, and in a well-conceived and brilliantly executed battle defeated the Confederate cavalry, and then effectually destroyed several miles of the Virginia Central Railroad. He now obtained information from the prisoners he had captured that Hunter was in the vicinity of Lynchburg and not likely to reach Charlottesville; and as the enemy had thrown a large force of infantry and cavalry between

Hunter and him, and as he was encumbered with a large number of prisoners and wounded, and his supply of ammunition was nearly exhausted, he felt that it would be useless to try to make a junction with Hunter, and decided to return to the Army of the Potomac by way of White House, where ample and much needed supplies were awaiting him. On his arrival, orders were given that this depot should be broken up on the 22d, and the train of nine hundred wagons which had been left there was crossed to the south side of the James River, having been gallantly and successfully defended on its way by Sheridan's cavalry.

On the 26th Sheridan came in person to Grant's headquarters, and had an interview with him in regard to the results of his expedition and the further operations which he was expected to undertake at once on the south side of Petersburg. Sheridan was cordially greeted on his arrival by the general-in-chief. He was at all times a welcome visitor at headquarters, as his boundless enthusiasm, buoyant spirits, and cheery conversation were always refreshing.

The general, after learning all the details of Sheridan's expedition, told him that he fully approved his judgment in not attempting, under the contingencies which had arisen, to reach Hunter; but, as usual, the general did not dwell at length upon the past, and promptly began the discussion of the plans he had in view for the cavalry in the future.

### WHERE POCAHONTAS SAVED JOHN SMITH.

A DAY or two afterward, Grant paid a visit to Butler's lines; and while he and the staff were riding out to the front they came to the place where, according to tradition, Pocahontas had saved the life of Captain John Smith. Whether it was the exact spot or not, it was regarded in that locality as historic ground; and Virginians, who take a particular pride in well-known family names, seemed to honor Pocahontas especially, no doubt because she was largely instrumental in preserving the Smith family to posterity. In the efforts to account for the attempted execution of the prisoner, there is a story told, about the truth of which there is a lingering uncertainty. It is to the effect that, when the captain fell into the hands of the Indian chief, he was rash enough to state, in reply to questions as to his identity, that his name was «John Smith»; and that the noble red man thought he was trying to perpetrate a practical joke on him, and was roused to swift vengeance by such an ill-timed pleasantry.

In climbing a rather steep hill at this point, the party had to move along a narrow bridle-path. The general was riding in the lead, followed by the staff in single file, with Badeau bringing up the rear. The trees were soon found to be so near together that a horse and rider could not pass between them when keeping in the path, and we turned out to the left, where the woods were more open. Badeau's near-sightedness prevented him from seeing very far ahead, and he was not paying much attention to his horse, but simply letting him go along as he pleased. Suddenly we heard a cry from him: «I 'm going off! I say, I 'm going off!» On looking round, we found his horse climbing up the path with a tree on each side, between which he could scarcely squeeze. When Badeau's knees reached the trees his saddle was forced back, and as the horse struggled on his rider finally slid off over the animal's tail. Then came the cry, «See here, I 'm off!» and Badeau and the saddle were seen lying on the ground. The horse stepped out of the girth and quietly continued his march up the hill as if nothing had happened. General Grant stopped, and looking back at the ludicrous sight presented, fairly screamed with laughter, and did not recover his equanimity during the remainder of the ride. Nothing could have been more amusing to him than such an accident; for, as he was an exceptionally expert horseman, awkwardness on the part of a rider was more laughable to him than to most people. Badeau, with the assistance of an orderly, had his horse resaddled, and mounting again, soon joined the cavalcade. General Grant cracked jokes at his expense all the rest of the ride; and for two or three days afterward, when he would be sitting quietly in front of his tent, he would suddenly begin to shake with laughter, and say: «I can 't help thinking how that horse succeeded in sneaking out from under Badeau at Bermuda Hundred.»

### GENERAL JAMES H. WILSON'S RAID.

WHILE the enemy's cavalry was north of the James, and the probabilities were that it would be detained there by Sheridan for some days, it was decided to send Wilson's division of cavalry, which had remained with the Army of the Potomac, and four regiments of the cavalry of the Army of the James under Kautz, to the south of Petersburg, with a view to striking both the South Side and the

Danville railroads. This cavalry command started out on the morning of June 22. It was composed of nearly 6000 men and several batteries of horse-artillery. It first struck the Weldon, then the South Side Railroad, and afterward advanced as far as Roanoke Station on the Danville road, inflicting much damage. On the 29th, after severe fighting, it found itself confronted and partly surrounded by such a heavy force of the enemy that there was no means of cutting a way through with success; and it was decided to issue all the remaining ammunition, destroy the wagons and caissons, and fall back to the Union lines. The troops were hard pressed by greatly superior numbers, and suffered severely upon their march, but by untiring energy and great gallantry succeeded in reaching the Army of the Potomac on July 1. The expedition had been absent ten days. It had marched three hundred miles, and destroyed a large quantity of rolling stock and about fifty miles of railroad. The loss in killed, wounded, and missing amounted to about 1500 men. All the guns and wagons were destroyed or abandoned. The cavalry supposed that the infantry of the Army of the Potomac would be in possession of Reams's Station at the time of their return, but that station was still in the hands of the enemy.

The destruction of communications by Hunter, Sheridan, and Wilson gave the enemy serious alarm; but by dint of great effort he soon made the necessary repairs, and was again able to bring supplies to Richmond by rail. In the meantime the siege of Petersburg had begun, and it was now Grant's intention to make the investment as complete as possible, and to take advantage of every opportunity to inflict damage on the enemy, and give him battle whenever he could do so under circumstances that would be justifiable.

On June 29, Grant felt anxious about the fate of the cavalry and the progress of Wright's corps, which had been sent to Reams's Station to Wilson's relief, but did not reach there in time. He rode out to the Petersburg front with his staff, held interviews with Meade, Burnside, and Smith, and visited the lines to make a personal inspection of the principal batteries. He became impressed with the idea that more field-artillery could be used to advantage at several points, and when we returned to headquarters that evening he telegraphed to Washington for five or six additional batteries.

From the 4th of May until the end of June there had not been a day in which there was not a battle or a skirmish. The record of continuous and desperate fighting had far surpassed any campaign in modern or ancient military history.

### THE STAFF ENLARGED.

In view of the important operations which were to be conducted from City Point, General Grant made some changes in the organization of the staff. General Rufus Ingalls, who had distinguished himself by the exhibition of signal ability as chief quartermaster of the Army of the Potomac, was assigned to duty as chief quartermaster upon the staff of the general-in-chief. Grant and he had been classmates at West Point, and were on terms of extreme intimacy. Ingalls was exceedingly popular in the army, and both officially and personally was regarded as an important acquisition to the staff. Lieutenant-Colonel M. R. Morgan, an efficient and experienced officer of the commissary department, was added to the staff of the general-in-chief as chief commissary; thirty years after he became commissary-general of the army. Soon after General M. R. Patrick was made provost-marshal-general, and General George H. Sharpe was assigned to duty as his assistant. The latter officer rendered invaluable service in obtaining information regarding the enemy by his employment of scouts and his skill in examining prisoners and refugees. Captain Amos Webster was placed on duty as assistant quartermaster. Assistant Surgeon E. D.W. Breneman, U. S. A., was assigned to look after the health of those at headquarters; but the particularly robust condition of nearly all the officers he was prepared to attend made his work exceedingly light.

In discussing at this time the large amount of rations which had to be supplied by the subsistence department, and the system required in its management, General Grant said: «When I first had an independent command there were so few experienced men about me that I had to sit down at night and teach officers of the staff departments how to make requisitions for supplies, and fill out the blank forms furnished by the government when such blanks could be procured. I had acted at times as quartermaster and commissary in the old army, and was of course familiar with all the forms used in preparing papers. Word was brought to me one day that a new regimental commissary had gone aboard a commissary boat on the

Mississippi and presented a requisition for rations for his men. The officer in charge looked at it in amazement, and exclaimed: ‹Why, there are not half enough rations aboard this entire steamer to fill that requisition.› The commissary, who thought he had made only an ordinary demand, said: ‹Why, you 're filling requisitions for all the other regiments in our brigade!› ‹Regiment!› cried the commissary. ‹You mean a corps.› The regimental commissary then discovered that he had made out his requisition on a corps blank.»

A hospital had been established at City Point large enough to accommodate 6000 patients, and served a very useful purpose. The general manifested a deep interest in this hospital, frequently visited it, and constantly received verbal reports from the surgeons in charge as to the care and comfort of the wounded.

A telegraph line had been established on the south side of the James which connected by cable across Hampton Roads with Fort Monroe. From that place there was direct telegraphic communication with Washington. This line was occasionally broken, but by dint of great effort it was generally well maintained and made to perform excellent service.

The general headquarters had become an intensely interesting spot. Direct communication was kept open as far as possible with the various armies throughout the country, all of which the general-in-chief was directing, and information of an exciting nature was constantly received and important orders were issued. The officers on duty had an opportunity to watch the great war drama from behind the scenes, from which point they witnessed not only the performance of the actors, but the workings of the master mind that gave the directions and guided all the preparations.

(To be continued.)

*Horace Porter.*

# THE TOMB OF GENERAL GRANT.[1]

HE early part of the year 1885 found the hearts of the American people deeply touched by the certainty that a fatal disease was slowly but surely sapping the life of the illustrious citizen who had led their armies to triumphant victory, who had twice held the highest office in their gift, who in his own country had filled the largest measure of human greatness, and whose fame had extended to the uttermost parts of the earth. Tributes of affection poured in upon him from all sections of the land, and furnished the only balm which could assuage his sufferings. Congress placed him on the retired list as a general, restoring him to the rank which he vacated when called to the higher field of duty as President of the republic. Legislatures passed resolutions of sympathy; rulers of other lands telegraphed compassionate messages; church organizations, civic societies, war veteran associations, and men who had fought in the ranks of his enemies, sent touching words of condolence; and throughout the land prayers were offered, in public and in private, invoking the blessing of divine Providence upon the sufferer. Processions of school children sang anthems as they filed past his house and laid their tribute of flowers upon his door-step. Men who had voted for him and men who had opposed him, old soldiers who had served with him and strangers who had never seen him, lined the sidewalk opposite his residence, and stood for hours with moistened eyes gazing upon the windows of the sick man's room.

When the hot weather appeared, the invalid was removed to the cooler region of Mount McGregor. Every effort of devotion on the part of his family and friends ministered to his relief, and all the accomplishments of medical science were employed to assuage his sufferings and prolong the period of his life. The skill of the physicians often rallied his waning powers, buoyed up his spirits, and gained temporary triumphs over the disease; but the malady was beyond their control, and at eight o'clock in the morning of Thursday, July 23, 1885, the spirit of the distinguished sufferer passed away, and he was permitted to enjoy what he had pleaded for in behalf of others, for the Lord had let him have peace.

When the news was flashed over the wires

[1] This paper was prepared, at the request of the Editor, by General Horace Porter, who as president of the association organized the movement for completing the fund for the construction of the monument which will be dedicated on General Grant's birthday, the 27th of the present month.—EDITOR.

there was a sorrow felt in every American household akin to the grief of a personal bereavement.

The question immediately arose as to what place should be selected for his sepulture. There was a general desire to have his remains interred at Washington, either in the National Cemetery at Arlington, in the park of the Soldiers' Home, or in the crypt of the Capitol. As every previous President had been buried in the State of which he was a resident, there was an earnest plea put in by the people of New York, urging that the place of burial should be the nation's metropolis, the city which the general had selected as his permanent home. The mayor of the city, the Hon. William R. Grace, proposed to the family that if the burial should take place in the city of New York, a suitable location would be provided either in Central or Riverside Park.

A week or two before the general's death he expressed some views to his son Colonel Frederick D. Grant in regard to his burial. The disease had made such progress that his power of articulation had almost ceased, and it was only by a supreme effort that he could whisper articulate words; he therefore used a pencil and paper to communicate with those about him. When he began to write, his son, who had remained by his bedside for many months and whose filial devotion had never relaxed, bent over his father to see what he was writing. The general named Galena, Illinois, his old home, then paused, and shook his head. He then wrote West Point, but expressed the fear that the rules governing interments there would prevent the burial of Mrs. Grant by his side. He finally referred to New York, where he had found such kind and devoted friends, but added that he wished no place selected where his wife could not be buried by his side. He was apparently attempting to write more, but a paroxysm of pain seized him, and the subject was not renewed. As New York was the last place he had indicated, the fact created a sentiment in favor of that city, as it had been apparently the general's final request. The family expressed a preference for New York, as it was their home; and with their assent the site of the present monument in Riverside Park was selected. It furnished an ideal location for the erection of a monumental tomb, the ground being on the bank of the Hudson, one of our noblest rivers, at a height of about one hundred and thirty feet above the water. It was seen that a monument of suitable height would be visible from prominent parts of the city, from points many miles up the river, and from the decks of vessels in portions of the harbor.

A temporary tomb of brick masonry, of a vault-like shape, was immediately constructed. The remains were brought to New York, receiving marked tributes of respect from official bodies and the assembled masses of the people at every point along the line of the route. After the body had lain in state for a day in the Capitol at Albany, and afterward at the City Hall, New York, the funeral took place on Saturday, August 8. The demonstration as the cortège passed from the City Hall to Riverside Park was the most solemn and imposing which the metropolis had ever witnessed; and the expressions of sorrow, and the honors paid to the memory of the deceased, were manifested in a manner which signalized the profound emotion of the vast assemblage that witnessed the passage of the funeral train. It was estimated that the procession was viewed by more than a million people.

On July 28, 1885, the mayor of the city called a meeting of citizens at the mayor's office, at which a committee was appointed to initiate a movement to erect a national monument to the memory of General Grant. A committee on organization was formed which met the next day and effected a permanent organization of the Grant Monument Committee, with ex-President Chester A. Arthur as chairman. In February, 1886, the Grant Monument Association was organized under an act of the legislature, and Hon. Chester A. Arthur was chosen president. A week later, being himself stricken with a fatal illness, he resigned, and Mr. Sidney Dillon was elected to take his place. The contributions received up to this time amounted to $114,000. In April, 1887, Mr. Cornelius Vanderbilt became president of the association, and was succeeded in February, 1888, by ex-Mayor William R. Grace.

After considering various measures for providing a proper sepulcher, a number of prominent architects were invited to submit competitive designs for a monumental tomb. In September, 1890, the association adopted the plan furnished by Mr. J. H. Duncan of New York City, for a structure to cost between $500,000 and $600,000; and this design, with some slight modifications, was adhered to in the construction of the monument now completed. A contract was made for building the foundations, and ground was broken with elaborate ceremonies on the anniversary of General Grant's birthday, April 27, 1891. Comrade Charles H. Freeman, Commander of

ON A PHOTOGRAPH.

ULYSSES S. GRANT AS LIEUTENANT-GENERAL.

the Department of the State of New York, Grand Army of the Republic, was the presiding officer. Appropriate services were performed by that organization, and an oration was delivered by the writer.

A contract was afterward made for the construction of the lower course of the granite-work, which would bring the structure to a height of ten feet above the ground. The fund which had been secured now amounted to about $155,000, but all efforts to increase it beyond that sum seemed to be unavailing. When the year 1892 came, there was great public discontent manifested in consequence of the fact that there appeared to be no means of carrying out the project. In the belief that New York had failed to make good its implied promise to give to the remains of the illustrious general suitable sepulture, a bill had been introduced in Congress, providing for the removal of the body to the national capital. This led to a spirited debate in the House of Representatives, and the project was seriously resisted by the congressmen from New York, and did not prevail. The city of New York now became the target for attacks from all parts of the country for its lack of public spirit and want of generosity in allowing the ashes of so illustrious a man to lie without proper entombment for a period of seven years after his death. It was everywhere felt that this neglect was bringing serious reproach upon the fair name of the city, which had always enjoyed an enviable reputation as the most generous community of modern times. The soldiers who had served under the general's command felt the neglect most keenly, and much adverse criticism was provoked. At this period the writer was urged to take charge of the affairs of the association, with a view to devising some comprehensive means for the completion of the projected monument; and having been elected president of the association in February, 1892, he consented to assume the task.

Mr. James C. Reed accepted the position of secretary, and cheerfully contributed his time and services to the vast bureau work of the position, involving the extensive correspondence and the elaborate accounts made necessary by the manifold details of the office.

Mr. Frederick D. Tappen, president of the Gallatin National Bank, agreed to undertake the arduous duties of treasurer; and the enterprise is deeply indebted to him for his untiring labors in receiving and receipting for the numberless small sums subscribed, and for the constant care he has exercised over the finances.

The legislature was immediately asked to amend the charter of the association so as to provide for an increase in the number of trustees from thirty-three to one hundred. Such a bill was passed, and many prominent citizens were brought into the board. A by-law was adopted which provided that all the officers of the association should serve without compensation. Mr. D. O. Mills generously consented to provide offices free of charge, and the outlay for the general expenses of the association thereafter became insignificant in amount. It was deemed better to have the fund raised by a thoroughly popular subscription than by means of large contributions from comparatively few individuals. This plan involved the necessity of reaching all classes and conditions of the people, and devising means for arousing the entire community to join in the effort. It was decided to make each line of business and each profession a factor in soliciting subscriptions among its members. Investigation showed that there were over two hundred separate and distinct trades and professions in the city. Application was made to the Chamber of Commerce, to various clubs, and to many of the hotels for rooms in which to hold meetings in convenient portions of the city. These were cheerfully furnished without charge. The heads of prominent business firms and leading professional men were then requested to assemble in these meetings, and to select committees for the purpose of coöperating in the work. The committeemen thus appointed were provided with subscription-books, and urged to solicit subscriptions in their particular professions and lines of business. The number of committees soon reached 215, and the committeemen who composed them numbered 2487. Meetings were also called in the various exchanges, and public addresses delivered in all quarters of the city, day and evening, in advocacy of the cause. Urgent appeals were made to financial institutions, churches, clubs, schools, and military and civic organizations to bear their share of the work. Subscription-boxes were placed in banks, hotels, elevated-railway stations, and in stores located on the principal thoroughfares. The plans were explained to the journalists of the city, and the newspapers not only gave prompt and hearty support to the project, but also made liberal subscriptions to the fund. It was necessary to raise the sum of $350,000 at least, and public an-

ENGRAVED BY T. JOHNSON.

REPRINTED FROM "THE CENTURY" FOR DECEMBER, 1885.

GRANT WRITING HIS MEMOIRS AT MOUNT McGREGOR.

nouncement was made that the active campaign for securing this fund would be confined to sixty days, and all persons who had manifested an interest in the work were urged to complete their labors within that period. Appeals were made to the churches of all denominations and creeds to make mention of the effort to their congregations, and in many cases a hearty response was given. In the meantime fourteen generous and public-spirited citizens, upon personal solicitation, contributed $5000 each. A convention of the chairmen of committees was held once a week, in which reports of progress were received. When announcements of the additions to the subscriptions were made at these meetings, a spirit of emulation was aroused among the various trades represented, and they were stimulated to renewed efforts.

On the 27th of April, the anniversary of the general's birthday, thirty days after the beginning of the movement to complete the fund, and midway in the campaign, the corner-stone of the structure was laid with imposing ceremonies. General Harrison, then President of the United States, with members of his cabinet, came on from Washington; and he, as President of the Republic, took the trowel in hand and performed the act of laying the stone in place. The Rev. Dr. John Hall offered the prayer, the president of the association made an address, and the Hon. Chauncey M. Depew delivered the oration. In a box placed in the corner-stone there were deposited a copy of the Constitution of the United States, of the Declaration of Independence, of the Articles of Confederation, and of the Bible; the «Memoirs» of General Grant; a list of contributors of flowers; the prayer offered by the Rev. Dr. R. S. Storrs, and the address by General John A. Logan, on the occasion of the first memorial services, held at the temporary tomb, May 30, 1886; Mayor Grant's proclamation, dated April 8, 1892, to the citizens of New York, calling attention to the work of building the monument; a new American flag made of silk; a badge of the Grand Army of the Republic, and of the military order of the Loyal Legion; eleven medals struck at United States mints commemorative of events in the life of General Grant; one complete proof set of United States gold and silver coins; copies of New York City and Brooklyn daily afternoon papers of April 26, 1892, and daily morning papers of April 27, 1892; and various illustrated papers.

Upon this occasion a public announcement was made by the president of the association that in the past thirty days the sum of $202,890.50 had been subscribed. The work of completing the fund was continued actively during the remainder of the prescribed time, but the energy which had been manifested by the people began to lag somewhat, and additional methods had to be devised for stimulating public interest and arousing new vigor. Prizes were now offered to the scholars in the higher grades of the public schools in New York and Brooklyn for essays on the life of General Grant. Twenty dollars in gold were promised for the best essays, and ten dollars for the next in merit. In a few days after this announcement every school child was at work seeking information about General Grant's career. Libraries were ransacked, letters of inquiry were sent to the press, teachers were appealed to, parents were catechized at home, and policemen were stopped in the streets and asked what they knew about the subject of the forthcoming essays. The topic became the town talk, and the interest in the project was soon revived. Many of the essays proved to be of a very high order of merit. The painters and sculptors of New York made a contribution of their works, which were sold at auction and helped to swell the fund. The only loss incurred in making the collections was occasioned by the theft of a young boy who stole from a station of the elevated railroad one of the contribution-boxes containing $13. He was caught afterward, however; and although the money was not recovered, the publication of his arrest, and of all the circumstances of the act, aroused so much indignation and became such a prominent topic of conversation that the excitement caused was the means of increasing the contributions to an extent very far beyond the sum lost. Thus vice itself made an unconscious contribution to patriotism.

On Decoration Day, May 30, at the close of the usual memorial services at the temporary tomb, the president of the association was able to say that the whole of the $350,000 had been secured within the contemplated time. Subsequent subscriptions obtained during the year increased the amount to $404,000. The total number of subscribers whose names were furnished was 17,118; the number of separate coins, bills, and checks which were dropped into the numerous contribution-boxes placed throughout the city was 47,670, representing probably about that number of separate contributors. The total number of contributors to the fund may therefore be stated at 64,788, making an average of about

JOHN H. DUNCAN, ARCHITECT. DRAWN BY OTTO H. BACHER.

THE INTERIOR OF THE TOMB.

$6.23 for each contributor. The individual sums ranged from one cent to $5000. In collecting the amounts written upon the subscription-books the difference between the actual subscriptions and the amount of cash received from them amounted to less than $400. The entire amount was furnished by the people of the city of New York, with the exception of $38,115.20, which was received from citizens of Brooklyn, of the interior of the State, and of a few other States. Assuming that the average amount of the individual subscriptions to the sum of $155,000 originally secured was the same as that of the subsequent fund raised, the number of contributors to the entire fund may be said to be, in round numbers, 90,000.

During the progress of the work the unexpended balances have been deposited in four prominent New York trust companies, which have paid three per cent. interest upon the amounts. With the sum contributed, small subscriptions received from time to time since, and the accrued interest, the entire amount of the fund will reach nearly $600,000, which will fully complete the structure and sarcophagus.

After a diligent search of seven months in order to find a granite of light color which would be entirely flawless and durable in quality, a granite singularly well adapted to the purpose was found in North Jay, Maine, and this stone has been used in completing the structure. It is so light in tone that in a strong sunlight it is hardly distinguishable from marble. One of the most difficult problems presented was the selection of a

THE SARCOPHAGUS.

J. MASSEY RHIND, SCULPTOR.

FIGURES

material suitable for the sarcophagus. About a year ago there was found in the quarries at Montello, Wisconsin, a porphyry of fine texture and brilliant reddish color, which furnished a sarcophagus of great beauty and appropriateness. To comply with the frequently expressed wish of General Grant that his wife should be laid to rest by his side, a sarcophagus the exact duplicate of the one now finished will be provided, in which the body of Mrs. Grant will repose.

The work is now entirely completed. The lower portion of the tomb is a square structure of the Grecian Doric order, measuring 90 feet on a side. The entrance is on the south side, and is protected by a portico formed of double lines of columns, and approached by steps 70 feet wide. The square portion is finished with a cornice and a parapet, at a height from grade of 72 feet, and above this is a circular cupola 70 feet in diameter, of the Ionic order, which is surmounted with a pyramidal top terminating at a height of 150 feet above grade, or 280 feet above mean high water of the Hudson River. The interior is cruciform in plan, 76 feet at the greatest dimension, the four corners being piers of masonry connected at the top by coffered arches the crowns of which are 50 feet from the floor-level. On these arches rests an open circular gallery of 40 feet inner diameter, culminating in a paneled dome 105 feet above the level of the floor. The surfaces between the planes of the faces of the arches and the circular dome form pendentives which are decorated in high-relief sculpture, the work of J. Massey Rhind, and emblematic of the birth, military and civic life, and death of General Grant.

The sarcophagi will be placed in a crypt directly beneath the center of the dome. The approach to the crypt is by stairways which give access to a passage encircling the space

ON FAÇADE.

dedicated to the sarcophagi, which space is surrounded by square columns supporting paneled marble ceilings and entablature. A circular opening in the main floor gives an unobstructed view of the sarcophagi from that floor and from the gallery.

In the work of construction the fact was kept steadily in view that solidity and durability were of paramount importance, and that they should not be impaired by an effort unduly to hasten the work. To get out the large blocks of stone, new beds had to be opened at great depths in the quarry, and the dressing, carving, and transporting of the enormous amount of granite required for the construction was a tedious process. In the winter but little work could be done at the quarries, and no setting of stone was permitted for fear of damage from freezing weather. When the heavy piers of masonry in the interior were built, and large masses of concrete used, a delay of several months was insisted upon before continuing the construction, in order to allow the work to «set,» and to avoid any possibility of shrinkage or settling thereafter. Occasional delays occurred from finding specks or flaws upon the surfaces of some of the large stones after they had been dressed down to completion; and as the association reserved the right under the terms of the contract to reject such material, new stones had to be prepared to take the places of those which exhibited defects.

The time from the laying of the corner-stone to the completion of the tomb has been five years, a shorter period than has been consumed in the building of any conspicuous memorial in history. The Bunker Hill Monument, which cost $150,000, was not completed until seventeen years after the corner-stone was laid. In the case of the Washington Monument, which cost $1,187,710, the time consumed was thirty-seven years.

The next anniversary of the general's birthday, April 27, 1897, has been selected as the date of the inauguration of the tomb. The legislature has been requested to make the day a legal holiday, the President of the United States has been asked to take an official part in conducting the ceremonies, and invitations to participate in the function will be sent to all high officials of the State and city, the governors of other States, and the diplomatic representatives of all foreign governments. Naval vessels are expected to take up a position in the North River opposite the tomb and fire salutes; the regular army, the war veterans, the national guard of the various States, and many patriotic societies and other civic organizations, will take part in the services. The city of New York will assume the direction and expense of the inauguration, and the appropriation made for this purpose will be disbursed by the mayor. The structure will be delivered to the city, and will be placed in the custody of the Park Department. Since the transfer of Napoleon's remains from St. Helena to France, and their interment in the Hôtel des Invalides, there has been no similar function that will equal in solemnity and importance the dedication of the tomb in Riverside Park.

*Horace Porter.*

## SUNNY HARBOR OR STORMY SEA?

SOMETIMES I wonder which is best for me—
The sunny harbor or the stormy sea.
How may the soul woo rest, yet grow more brave;
Woo calm, yet battle with each warring wave;
Win love, yet not forget the loveless kind;
Win heaven itself, yet bear the world in mind?

*Ella Giles Ruddy.*

DRAWN BY HOWARD PYLE.

IN THE PRESENCE OF WASHINGTON.

(SEE PAGE 864.)

(BEGUN IN THE NOVEMBER NUMBER.)

# HUGH WYNNE, FREE QUAKER:

## SOMETIME BREVET LIEUTENANT-COLONEL ON THE STAFF OF HIS EXCELLENCY GENERAL WASHINGTON.

BY DR. S. WEIR MITCHELL,

Author of «Far in the Forest,» «Roland Blake,» etc.

WITH PICTURES BY HOWARD PYLE.

### XV.

MY personal difficulties were not made more easy to bear by the course of public events. Howe had taken New York. In November Fort Washington fell. Jack, who was within its walls, got away, but was slightly wounded. Our English general, Lee, had begun already to intrigue against Mr. Washington, writing, as Dr. Rush confided to my aunt, that he, Lee, ought to be made dictator. My aunt received the impression that the doctor, who loved his country well, was becoming discontented with our chief; but neither then nor later did she change her own opinion of the reserved and courteous Virginian.

He soon justified her views of his capacity. On December 1 he broke down the bridges in his rear over the Raritan, and marched through Jersey with a dwindling army. At Princeton he had but three thousand men; destroying every boat, he wisely put the broad Delaware between his army and the enemy.

Lord Cornwallis halted at the river, waiting for it to freeze that he might cross, and until this should happen went back with Howe to New York. About December 15 of '76, General Lee was captured, and, strange as it may now seem, no calamity yet come upon us created more consternation. Meanwhile our own alarmed citizens began to bury their silver plate. While the feeble were flying, and the doubtful were ready to renew their oath to the king, the wary and resolute commander-in-chief saw his chance.

To aid his courageous resolve came Sullivan and Gates from Lee's late command. «At sunset on Christmas day we crossed the Delaware,» writes Jack. «My general was in a small boat, with Knox, and two boatmen. We were ten hours in the ice, and marched nine miles, after crossing, in a blinding storm of sleet. By God's grace we took one thousand of those blackguard Hessians, and, but for Cadwalader's ill luck with the ice, would have got Donop also. I had a finger froze, but no worse accident.

«I dare say you know we fell back beyond Assunpink Creek, below Trenton. There we fought my lord marquis again with good fortune. Meanwhile he weakened his force at Princeton, and, I fancy, thought we were in a trap; but our general left fires burning, passed round the enemy's left, and, as we came near Princeton at sunrise, fell upon Colonel Mawhood on his way to join Cornwallis. I was close to General Mercer when we saw them, and had as usual a fit of the shakes, hang them! Luckily there was small leisure to think.

«In the first onset, which was fierce, our brave general was mortally wounded; and then, his Excellency coming up, we routed them finely. So away went Cornwallis, with the trapped hot after the trappers. We have the Jerseys and two thousand prisoners. I do not think even Miss Wynne can imagine what courage it took for our general to turn as he did on an army like that of Cornwallis. Are you never coming?

«It is sad that the Southern officers look upon us and those of New England as tradesfolk, and this makes constant trouble, especially among the militia, who come and go much as they please. I have had no personal difficulty, but there have been several duels, of which little is said.

«It is to be hoped that Congress will now order all enlistments to be for the war, else we shall soon be in a mortal bad way. Hast heard of Miss Peniston?»

This letter came soon after the smart little winter campaign in Jersey had made us all so happy.

«It will last a good while yet,» said James Wilson. «And when are you going, Hugh?» Indeed, I began at last to see a way opened, as we of Friends say; for now, in the spring, our old clerk hobbled back to his desk, and I knew that my father would no longer be left without friendly and familiar help. But before he could assume his full duties August was upon us—August of '77, a year for me most eventful. Darthea's letters to my aunt grew less and less frequent, and, as I thought, had an air of sadness unusual in this gladsome creature. Once she spoke of Captain Wynne as absent, and once that he, like Jack, had had a slight wound in the storm of Fort Washington. Of politics she could say nothing, as her letters had usually to pass our lines.

On July 31 Washington knew that Howe's fleet was off the Delaware capes. Meanwhile he had crossed that river into Pennsylvania, and hurried his army across country, finally encamping on a Saturday at Nicetown, some five miles from Philadelphia. I rode out that evening to meet Jack, whose troop camped even nearer to town, and close to the tents of the headquarters staff. The general lay for this night at Stenton, where our Quaker friends, the Logans, lived. He was shown, I was told, the secret stairway and the underground passage to the stable and beyond, and was disposed to think it curious.

Jack, now a captain, in a new suit of blue and buff, looked brown and hardy, and his figure had spread, but the locks were as yellow and the cheeks as rosy as ever I knew them.

Dear Aunt Gainor made much of him that evening, and we talked late into the night of battles and generals and what had gone with Lord Howe. As for me, I went to bed feeling myself to be a very inconsiderable person, and Jack rode away to camp. The next day being Sunday, the 24th of August, his Excellency marched into town by Front street at the head of the flower of his army, in all about eleven thousand. Fine men they were, but many half clad and ill shod; fairly drilled too, but not as they were later in the war. The town was wild with delight, and every one glad save the Tories and the Quakers, many of whom remained all day in their houses.

This march being made only to exhibit the army to friend and foe, the troops moved out High street and by the middle ferry across the Schuylkill, on their way toward the Delaware to meet Mr. Howe, who, having landed at the head of Elk River, was now on his way toward Philadelphia. His troops were slow, the roads bad and few, the ague in great force and severe—or so we heard. I rode sadly with our people as far as Darby, and then turned homeward a vexed and dispirited man. It was, I think, on the 4th of August that our general, who had ridden on in advance of his army, first met Marquis Lafayette.

My aunt, who spoke French with remarkable fluency and a calm disregard of accent and inflections, was well pleased to entertain the French gentleman, and at her house I had the happiness to make his acquaintance, greatly, as it proved, to my future advantage. He was glad to find any who spoke his own tongue well, and discussed our affairs with me, horrified at the lack of decent uniforms and discipline, but, like me, pleased with the tall, strong men he saw in our ranks. Later my acquaintance with French was of much use to me: so little can a man tell what value an accomplishment will have for him.

The marquis was very young, and somewhat free in stating his opinions. At this time he thought Mr. Howe intended Charleston, and, like others, was amazed at his folly in not going up the Delaware Bay to land his troops. His strange strategy left Burgoyne to the fate in store for him at Saratoga, where the latter general was to act a first part in a tragic drama much finer than those he wrote, which were so greatly praised by the fine ladies in London, and indeed by some better critics.

A letter of Jack's came to hand during this week. In it he said my aunt must leave, as he was sure we had not force enough to keep General Howe out of Philadelphia. But the old lady said, «Not I, indeed!» and I think no mortal power could have induced her to go away. She even declined to bury her silver, as many had done. Not so the rest of the Whigs. Every one fled who knew where to go, or who feared to be called to account: and none would hear of defending the town, as should have been attempted.

Jack's letter went on to say that in Delaware the general had had a narrow escape. «He rode out,» says Jack, «with Marquis Lafayette on a reconnaissance, attended by but two officers and an orderly. General Sullivan had an officer follow with a half-troop; but the general, fearing such numbers might attract attention, ordered them to wait behind a thicket. Looking thence, they saw the general ride direct toward a picket of the enemy, which from their vantage they could see, but he could not. An English officer, perceiving him, seemed to give an order to fire; but as the men raised their pieces he struck them up. As he was about to give the order to fire, the general, being satisfied, turned his back to ride away. It is a curious tale, is it not? and none can explain it.»

Long years after I myself met an English officer, a General Henderson, in Canada, and on my telling him the incident, he said at once it was he who was concerned, and that when the general turned to ride away he could not make up his mind to shoot down a man who had turned his back. He was amazed and pleased to know who it was he thus spared.

On the 11th of September, at evening, came the disaster of Brandywine, and on the 26th Lord Cornwallis marched into our city, with two batteries and the Sixteenth Dragoons and Grenadiers. They were received quietly, and that evening my Cousin Arthur appeared at our house. My father, who had been very inert of late, seemed to arouse himself, and expressed quite forcibly his joy and relief at the coming of the troops. He recounted his griefs, too: how that, refusing the militia tax, the Committee of Safety had taken away his great tankard, and later two tables, which was true enough. Then, to my amazement, my father declared Arthur must stay with us, which he was nothing loath to do.

I was cool, as you may suppose, but it was difficult for man or woman to resist Arthur Wynne when he meant to be pleasant; and so, putting my dislike aside, I found myself chatting with him about the war and what not. In fact, he was a guest, and what else could I do?

My aunt kept herself indoors and would none of the Galloways and Allens, who had come back in swarms, nor even the neutrals, like Mr. Penn, whom she much liked. The day after the town was occupied, Captain Wynne appeared early in the morning, as we were discussing a matter of business. He took it for granted, I presume, that my aunt would see him, and went past the turbaned black boy despite his small remonstrances. My aunt rose to the full of her great height, her nose in the air, and letting fall a lapful of papers.

«To what,» she said, «have I the honour to owe a visit from Mr. Wynne? Is my house an inn, that any officer of the king may enter whether I will or not?»

Although he must have been surprised, he was perfectly at his ease. Indeed, I envied him his self-possession.

«Madam,» he said, «I am charged with a letter from Miss Peniston.»

«You may put it on the table,» says Mistress Wynne. «My brother may choose his society. I ask the same privilege. It will not consist of gentlemen of your profession.»

Mr. Wynne's face grew black under its dark skin.

«Madam,» he said, «I stay nowhere as an unwelcome guest. I thank you for past kindness, and I humbly take my leave. I could have done you a service as to this business of the quartering of officers, and you shall still have my good offices for the sake of the many pleasant hours I have passed in your house. As my Cousin Hugh says nothing, I am glad to think that he is of a different opinion from that which you have put in words so agreeably.» With this he went away, leaving my aunt red in the face, and speechless with wrath.

I thought he had the best of it; but I merely said, «My dear aunt, you should not have been so hard with him.» I did, indeed, think it both unwise and needless.

«Stuff and nonsense!» says Miss Wynne, walking about as my father used to do. «I do not trust him, and he has got that girl in his toils, poor child! I wonder what lies he has told her. How does he hold her? I did think that was past any man's power; and she is unhappy too. When a woman like Darthea begins to find a man out, she can't help showing it, and some are more frank on paper than in talk; that is her way. I am afraid I made mischief once, for I told him long ago that I meant her to marry you; and then I saw he did not like it, and I knew I had been a goose. Whatever is the reason he hates you, Hugh? Oh, yes, he does—he does. Is it the woman? I will have no redcoats in my house.»

I got a chance to say—what I was sorry to have to say—how little need there was for him to fear poor me, whom Darthea wished to have nothing to do with, I thought.

«Her loves are like her moods, my dear Hugh; who knows how long they will last? Until a woman is married she is not to be despaired of.»

I shook my head sadly and went out.

I returned late in the evening, to order my horse to be saddled and sent to me before breakfast next morning; for I kept it at no cost in my aunt's ample stable. To my horror, I found a sentinel at the door, and the hall full of army baggage. In the parlour was a tall Hessian, General von Knyphausen, and Count Donop and others, smoking, much at their ease. They were fairly civil, but did not concern themselves greatly if I liked it or not. I found my aunt in bed, in a fever of vain anger.

She had the bed-curtains drawn, and when I was bid to enter, put aside the chintz so as to make room for her head, which appeared in a tall nightcap. I am unfit, I fear, to describe this gear; but it brought out all her large features very strongly, and to have seen her would have terrified a Hessian regiment.

«My house is full of Dutch dogs,» she cried. «As soon as they came they ordered bones.» In fact, they had asked quite civilly if they might have supper.

«I saw them at their feed,» says my aunt, «and the big beast, General Knyphausen, spread my best butter on his bread with his thumb, sir—his thumb! Count Donop is better; but Von Heiser! and the pipes! heavens!» Here she retreated within her curtains, and I heard her say, «Bessy Ferguson saw them come in, and must sail across the street and tell Job [the page with the turban] to congratulate me for her, and to advise me to get a keg of sauerkraut.»

I assured my aunt that fortunately these were gentlemen, but she was inconsolable, declaring herself ill, and that Dr. Rush must come at once.

«But,» I said, «he is gone with all the Congress to York.»

«Then I shall die,» moaned my aunt.

At last, knowing her well, I said, «Is it not too sad?»

«What 's that? What?»

«Mr. Howe has taken Mrs. Pemberton's carriage and the pair of sorrels for his own use.»

At this my Aunt Gainor's large face reappeared, not as melancholic as before, and I added, «Friend Waln has six to care for, and Thomas Scattergood has the Hessian chaplain and a drunken major. The rest of Friends are no better off.»

«Thank the Lord for all his mercies!» said Miss Wynne.

«And Mr. Cadwalader's house on Little Dock street Sir William has.»

«A pity that, Hugh. The fine furniture will pay for it, I fear. I think, Hugh, I am better, or I shall be soon.»

«They talk of the Meeting over the way for a barrack, Aunt Gainor.» Now this was idly rumoured, but how could one resist to feed an occasion so comic?

«I think I should die contented,» said Miss Wynne. «Now go away, Hugh. I have had my medicine, and I like it.» She was quick at self-analysis, and was laughing low, really happier for the miseries of her Tory acquaintances.

After the bedroom comedy, which much amused me and out of which my aunt got great comfort, she was inclined to be on better terms with the officers so abruptly thrust upon her. For a while, however, she declined to eat her meals with them, and when told that they had had Colonel Montresor to dine, and had drunk the king's health, she sent all the glasses they had used down to the blacks in the kitchen, and bade them never to dare set them on her table again. This much delighted Count Donop, who loved George of Hanover no better than did she, and I learned that she declared the bread-and-butter business was the worst of Von Knyphausen, and was no doubt a court custom. As to Count Donop, she learned to like him. He spoke queer French, and did not smoke. «Je ne foom pas shamais, madame,» he said; «mais le Sheneral, il foom toushours, et Von Heiser le même,» which was true. The count knew her London friends, and grieved that he was sent on a service he did not relish, and in which later he was to lose his life.

My aunt fed them well, and won at piquet, and declared they were much to be pitied, although Von Heiser was a horror. When he had knocked down her red-and-gold Delft vase, the gods and the other china were put away, and then the rugs, because of the holes his pipe ashes burned, and still she vowed it was a comfort they were not redcoats. Them she would have poisoned.

Captain André alone was an exception. When, in 1776, he was made a prisoner by Montgomery in Canada, and after that was on parole at Lancaster, I met him; and as he much attracted me, my aunt sent him money, and I was able to ease his captivity by making him known to our friends, Mr. Justice Yeates and the good Cope people, who, being sound Tories, did him such good turns as he never forgot, and kindly credited to us. Indeed, he made for my aunt some pretty sketches of the fall woods, and, as I have said, was welcome where no other redcoat could enter.

My aunt was soon easier in mind, but my own condition was not to be envied. Here was Arthur Wynne at my father's, the Hessians at my aunt's, the Tories happy, seven or eight thousand folks gone away, every inn and house full, and on the street crowds of unmannerly officers. It was not easy to avoid quarrels. Already the Hessian soldiers began to steal all manner of eatables from the farms this side of Schuylkill. More to my own inconvenience, I found that Major von Heiser had taken the privilege of riding my mare Lucy so hard that she was unfit to use for two days. At last my aunt's chicken-coops suffered, and the voice of her pet rooster was no more heard in the land. I did hear that, as this raid of some privates interfered with the Dutch general's diet, one of the offenders got the strappado. But no one could stop these fellows, and they were so bold as to enter houses and steal what they wanted, until severe measures were taken by Mr. Howe. They robbed my father boldly, before his eyes, of two fat Virginia peach-fed hams, and all his special tobacco. He stood by, and said they ought not to do it. This, as they knew no tongue but their own, and as he acted up to his honest belief in the righteousness of non-resistance, and uttered no complaint, only served to bring them again. But this time I was at home, and nearly killed a corporal with the Quaker staff Thomas Scattergood gave my father. The adventure seemed to compensate Miss Wynne for her own losses. The corporal made a lying complaint, and but for Mr. André I should have been put to serious annoyance. Our boys used to say that the Hessian drum-beat said, «Plunder, plunder, plun, plun, plunder.» And so for the sad remnant of Whig gentles the town was made in all ways unbearable.

There are times when the life sands seem to run slowly, and others when they flow swiftly, as during this bewildering week. All manner of things happened, mostly perplexing or sad, and none quite agreeable. On the 28th, coming in about nine at night, I saw that there were persons in the great front sitting-room, which overlooked Dock Creek. As I came into the light which fell through the open doorway, I stood unnoticed. The room was full of pipe smoke, and rum and Hollands were on the table, as was common in the days when Friends' Meeting made a minute that Friends be vigilant to see that those who work in the harvest-fields have portions of rum. My father and my cousin sat on one side, opposite a short, stout man almost as swarthy as Arthur, and with very small, piercing eyes, so dark as to seem black, which eyes never are.

I heard this gentleman say, «Wynne, I hear that your brother is worse. These elder brothers are unnatural animals, and vastly tenacious of life.» On this I noticed my cousin frown at him and slightly shake his head. The officer did not take the hint, if it were one, but added, smiling, «He will live to bury you; unfeeling brutes—these elder brothers. Damn 'em!»

I was shocked to notice how inertly my father listened to the oath, and I recalled, with a sudden sense of distress, what my aunt had said of my father's state of mind. The young are accustomed to take for granted the permanency of health in their elders, and to look upon them as unchanging institutions, until, in some sad way, reminded of the frailty of all living things.

As I went in, Arthur rose, looked sharply at me, and said, «Let me present my cousin, Mr. Hugh Wynne, Colonel Tarleton.»

I bowed to the officer, who lacked the politeness to rise, merely saying, «Pleased to see you, Mr. Wynne.»

«We were talking,» said Arthur, «when you came of the fight at the river with the queer name—Brandywine, is n't it?»

«No,» said my father; «thou art mistaken, and I wished to ask thee, Arthur, what was it thou wert saying. We had ceased to speak of the war. Yes; it was of thy brother.»

«What of thy brother?» said I, glad of this opening.

«Oh, nothing, except Colonel Tarleton had news he was not so well.» He was so shrewd as to think I must have overheard enough to make it useless to lie to me. A lie, he used to say, was a reserve not to be called into service except when all else failed.

«Oh, was that all?» I returned. «I did hear, Cousin Arthur, that the Wyncote estate was growing to be valuable again; some coal or iron had been found.»

«So my mother writes me,» said Tarleton. «We are old friends of your family.»

«You know,» I said, «we are the elder branch.» I was bent on discovering, if possible, the cause of my cousin's annoyance whenever Wyncote was mentioned.

«I wish it were true about our getting rich,» said Arthur, with the relaxed look about the jaw I had come to know so well; it came as he began to speak. «If it were anything but idle gossip, Tarleton, what would it profit a poor devil of a younger son? They did find coal, but it came to nothing; and indeed I learn they lost money in the end.»

«I have so heard,» said my father, in a dull way. «Who was it told me? I forget. They lost money.»

I looked at him amazed. Who could have told him but Arthur, and why? Until a year back his memory had been unfailing.

I saw a queer look, part surprise, part puzzle, go over Tarleton's face, a slight frown above, as slight a smile below. I fancy he meant to twit my cousin, for he said to me:

«And so you are of the elder branch, Mr. Hugh Wynne. How is that, Arthur? How did the elder branch chance to lose that noble old house?»

My cousin sat rapping with his fingers on the table what they used to call the «devil's tattoo,» regarding me with steady, half-shut eyes—a too frequent and not well-mannered way he had, and one I much disliked. He said nothing, nor had he a chance, for I instantly answered the colonel: «My father can tell you.»

«About what, Hugh?»

«About how we lost our Welsh estate.»

My father at this lifted his great bulk upright in the old Penn chair, and seemed more alive.

«It is Colonel Tarleton who asks, not I.»

«It is an old story.» He spoke quite like himself. «Our cousin must know it well. My father suffered for conscience' sake, and, being a Friend, would pay no tithes. For this he was cast into jail in Shrewsbury Gate House, and lay there a year, suffering much in body, but at peace, it may surely be thought, as to his soul. At last he was set free on condition that he should leave the country.»

«And the estate?» asked Tarleton.

«He thought little of that. It was heavily charged with debt made by his father's wild ways. I believe, too, there was some agreement with the officers of the crown that he should make over the property to his next brother, who had none of his scruples. This was in 1670, or thereabouts. A legal transfer was made to my uncle, who, I think, loved my father, and understood that, being set in his ways, he would defy the king's authority to the end. And so—wisely, I think—the overruling providence of God brought us to a new land, where we have greatly prospered.»

«And that is all?» said the colonel. «What a strange story! And so you are Wynne of Wyncote, and lost it.»

«For a greater gain,» said my father. «My son has a silly fancy for the old place, but it is lost—lost—sold; and if we could have it at a word, it would grieve me to see him cast in his lot among a set of drunken, dicing, hard-riding squires—a godless set. It will never be if I can help it. My son has left the creed of his father and of mine, and I am glad that his worldly pride cannot be further tempted. Dost thou hear, Hugh?»

There was a moment of awkward silence. My father had spoken with violence, once or twice striking the table with his fist until the glasses rang. There was something of his old vehemence in his statement; but, as a rule, however abrupt when we were alone, before strangers he was as civil to me as to others. My cousin, I thought, looked relieved as my father went on; and, ceasing to drum on the table, he quietly filled himself a glass of Hollands.

I was puzzled. What interest had Arthur to lie about the value of Wyncote if it was irretrievably lost to us? As my father ended, he glanced at me with more or less of his old keenness of look, smiling a little as he regarded me. The pause which came after was brief, as I have said; for my reflections, such as they were, passed swiftly through my mind, and were as complete as was under the circumstances possible.

«I am sorry for you,» said Tarleton. «An old name is much, but one likes to have with it all the memories that go with its ancient home.»

«That is true,» said I; «and, if my father will pardon me, I like still to say that I would have Wyncote to-day if I could.»

«Thou canst not,» said my father. «And what we cannot have—what God has willed that we shall not have—it were wise and well to forget. It is my affair, and none of thine. Wilt thou taste some of my newly come Madeira, Friend Tarleton?»

The colonel said «No,» and shortly after left us, my cousin going with him.

My father sat for a while, and then said as I rose: «I trust to hear no more of this nonsense. Thy aunt and thy mother have put it in thy foolish head. I will have no more of it—no more. Dost thou hear?»

I said I would try to satisfy him, and so the thing came to an end.

The day after this singular talk, which so much puzzled me, Arthur said at breakfast that he should be pleased to go with me on the river for white perch. I hesitated; but, my father saying, «Certainly; he shall go with thee. I do not need him,» I returned that I would be ready at eleven.

We pulled over toward Petty's Island, and when half-way my cousin, who was steering, and had been very silent for him, said:

«Let her drift a bit; I want to talk to you.»

I sat still and listened.

«Why do not you join our army? A commission were easily had.»

I replied that he knew my sentiments well, and that his question was absurd.

«No,» he said; «I am your friend, although you do not think so. By George! were I you, I would be on one side or the other. I like my friends to do what is manly and decisive.»

«Holloa!» thinks I; «has Darthea been talking? And why does he, an officer of the king, want me to go?»

«I shall go some day,» I replied, «but when, I know not yet. It seems to me queer counsel to give a good rebel. When does Miss Peniston return?» I said.

«What the deuce has that got to do with it? Yes, she is coming back, of course, and soon; but why do not you join your army?»

«Let us drop that,» I said. «There are many reasons; I prefer not to discuss the matter.»

«Very good,» he said; «and, Hugh, you heard a heap of nonsense last night about Wyncote. Tarleton had too much of your father's rum-punch. Your people were lucky to lose the old place, and how these tales of our being rich arose I cannot imagine. Come and see us some day, and you will no longer envy the lot of beggared Welsh squires.»

All of this only helped the more to make me disbelieve him; but the key to his lies I had not, and so I merely said it would be many a day before that could happen.

«Perhaps,» he returned; «but who knows? The war will soon be over.»

«When will Miss Peniston be in town?» said I.

He was not sure; but said I put it in his mind to say something.

«Well?» said I, on my guard.

He went on: «I am a frank man, Cousin Hugh.»

At times he was, and strangely so; then the next minute he would be indirect or lie to you. The mixture made it hard to understand what he was after.

«I trust,» he went on, «that you will pardon me if I say that in England custom does not sanction certain freedoms which in the colonies seem to be regarded as of no moment. I am not of this opinion. Miss Peniston is, I hope, to be my wife. She is young, impulsive, and—well, no matter. Some men take these things coolly; I do not. I am sure you will have the good sense to agree with me. When a woman is pledged to a man, it is fit that she should be most guarded in her relations with other men. I—»

Here I broke in, «What on earth does all this mean?»

«I will tell you. Your aunt writes now and then to Miss Peniston.»

«Certainly,» said I.

«Yes; she says, too, things concerning you and that lady which are not to my taste.»

«Indeed?»

«I have been so honoured as to see some of these famous epistles. I think Darthea is pleased to torment me at times; it is her way, as you may happen to know. Also, and this is more serious, you have yourself written to Darthea.»

«I have, and several times. Why not?»

«These letters,» he went on, «she has refused to show to me. Now I want to say—and you will pardon me—that I permit no man to write to a woman whom I am to marry unless I do not object.»

«Well?» I said, beginning to smile, after my unmanageable habit.

«Here I do object.»

«What if I say that, so long as Miss Peniston does not seem displeased, I care not one farthing who objects?»

«By George!» cried he, leaping up in the boat.

«Take care; thou wilt upset the skiff.»

«I have half a mind to.»

«Nonsense! I can swim like a duck.»

«This is no trifle, sir,» he returned. «I will allow no man to take the liberty you insist on. It amazes me that you do not see this as I do. I am sorry, but I warn you once for all that I—»

«I am at your service, sir,» I broke in.

«Pshaw! nonsense! I am a guest in your father's house. I have thought it my duty, for your sake and my own, to say what I have said. When I know that you have again disobeyed my reasonable and most earnest wish, I shall consider how to deal with the matter. I have been forbearing so far, but I cannot answer for the future.»

«Cousin Arthur,» I replied, «this seems to me a silly business, in which we have both lost our tempers. I have no hope that Miss Peniston will ever change her mind, and I am free to say to you that I think it useless to persist; but nevertheless—»

«Persist!»

«I said ‹persist.› Until Miss Peniston is no longer Miss Peniston, I shall not cease to do all that is in my power to make her change her mind.»

«And you call that honourable—the conduct of a gentleman and a kinsman?»

«Yes; I too can be frank. I would rather see her marry any other man than yourself. You have sought to injure me, why I shall tell you at my own time. I think you have been deceiving all of us as to certain matters. Oh, wait! I must have my say. If you were—what I do not think you—a straightforward, truthful man, I should think it well, and leave Miss Peniston to what seems to be her choice. You have been frank, and so am I, and now we understand each other, and—no; I heard you to an end, and I must insist that I too be heard. I am not sorry to have had this talk. If I did not care for her who has promised you her hand, I should be careless as to what you are, or whether you have been an enemy in my home while pretending to be a friend. As it is, I love her too well not to do all I can to make her see you as I see you; and this, although for me there is no least hope of ever having a place in her heart. I am her friend, and shall be, and, until she forbids, shall claim every privilege which, with our simpler manners, the name of friend carries with it. I trust I am plain.»

«Plain? By heavens! yes. I have borne much, but now I have only to add that I never yet forgave an insult. You would be wiser to have a care. A man who never yet forgave has warned you. What I want I get; and what I get I keep.»

«I think,» I said, «that we will go ashore.»

«With all my heart.» And in absolute silence I pulled back. At the slip he left me without a word, and I secured the boat and walked away, having found ample subject for reflection. Nor was I altogether discontented at my cousin's evident jealousy.

The afternoon of this memorable day I rode out on poor Lucy, whom I had put for safety in our home stables. I went out High to Seventh street, and up to Race street road, where there was better footing, as it had been kept in order for the sport which made us call it Race street, and not Sassafras, which is its real name. I was brought to a stand about Twelfth street, then only an ox-path, by the bayonet of a grenadier, the camps lying about this point. I turned to ride back, when I heard a voice I knew crying:

«Holloa, Mr. Wynne! Are you stopped, and why?»

I said I knew no reason, but would go south. I was out for a ride, and had no special errand.

«Come with me then,» he said pleasantly. «I am now the engineer in charge of the defences.» This was my Aunt Gainor's old beau, Captain Montresor, now a colonel.

«I am sorry your aunt will see none of us, Mr. Wynne. If agreeable to you, we will ride through the lines.»

I asked nothing better, and explaining, awkwardly I fear, that my aunt was a red-hot Whig, we rode south to Spruce street, past the Bettering-house at Spruce and Eleventh streets, where the troops which had entered with Lord Cornwallis were mostly stationed. The main army lay at Germantown, with detachments below the city, on the east and west banks of the Schuylkill, to watch our forts at Red Bank and the islands which commanded the Delaware River and kept the British commander from drawing supplies from the great fleet which lay helpless below.

As we went by, the Grenadiers were drilling on the open space before the poorhouse. I expressed my admiration of their pointed caps, red, with silver front plates, their spotless white leggings and blue-trimmed scarlet coats.

«Too much finery, Mr. Wynne. These are a king's puppets, dressed to please the whim of royalty. If all kings took the field, we should have less of this. Those miserable devils of Mr. Morgan's fought as well in their dirty skin shirts, and can kill a man at murderous distance with their long rifles and little bullets. It is like gambling with a beggar. He has all to get, and nothing to lose but a life too wretched to make it worth keeping.»

I made no serious reply, and we rode westward through the governor's woods to the river. As we turned into an open space to escape a deep mud-hole, Mr. Montresor said:

«It was here, I think, you and Mr. Warder made yourselves agreeable to two of our people.» I laughed, and said it was a silly business and quite needless.

«That, I believe,» he cried, laughing, «was their opinion somewhat late. They were the jest of every regimental mess for a month, and we were inclined to think Mr. Washington had better raise a few regiments of Quakers. Are you all as dangerous?»

«Oh, worse, worse,» I said. «Jack Warder and I are only half-fledged specimens. You should see the old fellows.» Thus jesting, we rode as we were able until we reached the banks of the Schuylkill, picketed on both shores, but on the west side not below the lower ferry, where already my companion was laying a floating bridge which greatly interested me.

«We have a post on the far hill,» he said, «I am afraid to Mr. Hamilton's annoyance. Let us follow the river.»

I was able to guide him along an ox-road, and past garden patches across High street, to the upper ferry at Callowhill street. Here he pointed out to me the advantage of a line of nine forts which he was already building. There was to be one on the hill we call Fairmount to command the upper ferry. Others were to be set along to the north of Callowhill street road at intervals to Cohocsink Creek and the Delaware.

The great trees I loved were falling fast under the axes of the pioneers, whom I thought very awkward at the business. Farm-houses were being torn down, and orchards and hedges levelled, while the unhappy owners looked on in mute despair, aiding one another to remove their furniture. The object was to leave a broad space to north of the forts, that an attacking force might find no shelter. About a hundred feet from the blockhouses was to be an abatis of sharpened logs, and a mass of brush and trees, through which to move would be difficult.

I took it all in, and greedily. The colonel no doubt thought me an intelligent young fellow, and was kind enough to answer all my questions. He may later have repented his freedom of speech. And now I saw the reason for all this piteous ruin. Compensation was promised and given, I heard, but it seemed to me hard to be thus in a day thrust out of homes no doubt dear to these simple folk. We went past gardens and fields, over broken fences, all in the way of destruction. Tape-lines pegged to the earth guided the engineers, and hundreds of negroes were here at work. Near to Cohocsink Creek we met the second Miss Chew, riding with her father. He was handsome in dark velvet, his hair clubbed and powdered beneath a flat beaver with three rolls, and at his back a queue tied with a red ribbon. He had remained quietly inactive and prudent, and, being liked, had been let alone by our own party. It is to be feared that neither he nor the ribbon was quite as neutral as they had been. Miss Margaret looked her best. I much dislike «Peggy,» by which name she was known almost to the loss of that fine, full «Margaret,» which suited better her handsome, up-tilted head and well-bred look.

On the right side rode that other Margaret, Miss Shippen, of whom awhile back I spoke, but then only as in pretty bud, at the Woodlands. It was a fair young rose I now saw bowing in the saddle, a woman with both charm and beauty. Long after, in London, and in less merry days, she was described by Colonel Tarleton as past question the handsomest woman in all England. I fear, too, she was the saddest.

«And where have you kept yourself, Mr. Wynne?» she asked. «You are a favourite of my father's, you know. I had half a mind not to speak to you.»

I bowed, and made some gay answer. I could not well explain that the officers who filled their houses were not to my taste.

«Let me present you to Mr. André,» said Mr. Shippen, who brought up the rear.

«I have the honour to know Mr. Wynne,» said the officer. «We met at Lancaster when I was a prisoner in '76; in March, was it not? Mr. Wynne did me a most kind service, Montresor. I owe it to him that I came to know that loyal gentleman, Mr. Cope, and the Yeates people, who at least were loyal to me. I have not forgotten it, nor ever shall.»

I said it was a very small service, and he was kind to remember it.

«You may well afford to forget it, sir; I shall not,» he returned. He was in full uniform; not a tall man, but finely proportioned, with remarkably regular features and a clear complexion which was set off to advantage by powdered hair drawn back and tied in the usual ribboned queue.

We rode along in company, happy enough, and chatting as we went, Mr. André, as always, the life of the party. He had the gracious frankness of a well-mannered lad, and, as I recall him, seemed far younger than his years. He spoke very feelingly aside to me of young Macpherson, who fell at Quebec. He himself had had the ill luck not to be present when that gallant assault was made. He spoke of us always as colonials, and not as rebels; and why was I not in the service of the king, or perhaps that was a needless question?

I told him frankly that I hoped before long to be in quite other service. At this he cried: «So, so! I would not say it elsewhere. Is that so? 'T is a pity, Mr. Wynne; a hopeless cause,» adding, with a laugh, that I should not find it very easy to get out of the city, which was far too true. I said there were many ways to go, but how I meant to leave I did not yet know. After I got out I would tell him. We had fallen back a little as we talked, the road just here not allowing three to ride abreast.

«I shall ask the colonel for a pass to join our army,» I said merrily.

«I would,» said he, as gay as I; «but I fear you and Mistress Wynne will have no favours. Pray tell her to be careful. The Tories are talking.»

«Thanks,» said I, as we drew aside to let pass a splendid brigade of Hessians, fat and well fed, with shining helmets.

«We are drawing in a lot of men from Germantown,» said André, «but for what I do not know. Ah, here comes the artillery!»

I watched them as we sat in our saddles while regiment after regiment passed, the women admiring their precision and soldierly bearing. For my part, I kept thinking of the half-clad, ill-armed men I had seen go down these same streets a little while before. «I will go,» I said to myself; and in a moment I had made one of those decisive resolutions which, once made, seem to control me, and to permit no future change of plan.

By this time we were come to the bridge over Cohocsink Creek, I having become self-absorbed and silent. The colonel called my attention to his having dammed the creek, and thus flooded the low meadows for more complete defence. I said, «Yes, yes,» being no longer interested.

Mr. Shippen said, «We will cross over to the ‹Rose of Bath,› and have a little milk-punch before we ride back.» This was an inn where, in the garden, was a mineral water much prescribed by Dr. Kearsley. I excused myself, however, and, pleading an engagement, rode slowly away.

I put up my mare in my aunt's stable, and went at once into her parlour, full of my purpose.

I sat down and told her both the talk of two days before with Tarleton and my cousin, and also that I had had in my boat.

She thought I had been foolishly frank, and said: «You have reason to be careful, Hugh. That man is dangerous. He would not fight you, because that would put an end to his relations with your father. Clerk Mason tells me he has already borrowed two hundred pounds of my brother. So far I can see,» she went on; «the rest is dark—that about Wyncote, I mean. Darthea, when once she is away, begins to criticise him. In a word, Hugh, I think he has reason to be jealous.»

«O Aunt Gainor!»

«Yes. She does not answer your letters, nor should she, but she answers them to me, the minx! a good sign, sir.»

«That is not all, aunt. I can stand it no longer. I must go; I am going.»

«The army, Hugh?»

«Yes; my mind is made up. My two homes are hardly mine any longer. Every day is a reproach. For my father I can do little. His affairs are almost entirely wound up. He does not need me. The old clerk is better.»

«Will it be hard to leave me, my son?»

«You know it will,» said I.

She had risen, tall and large, her eyes soft with tears.

«You must go,» she said, «and may God protect and keep you. I shall be very lonely, Hugh. But you must go. I have long seen it.»

Upon this, I begged she would see my father often, and give me news of him and of Darthea whenever occasion served. Then she told me Darthea was to return to the city in two days, and she herself would keep in mind all I had wished her to do. After this I told her of the difficulties I should meet with, and we talked them over. Presently she said, «Wait»; then left the room, and, coming back, gave me a sword the counterpart of Jack's.

«I have had it a year, sir. Let me see,» she cried, and would have me put it on, and the sash, and the buff-and-blue sword-knot. After this she put a great hand on each shoulder just as she had done with Jack, and, kissing me, said: «War is a sad thing, but there are worse things. Be true to the old name, my son.» Nor could she bide it a moment longer, but hurried out with her lace handkerchief to her eyes, saying as she went, «How shall I bear it! How shall I bear it!»

She also had for me a pair of silver-mounted pistols, and an enamelled locket with my mother's ever dear face within, done for her when my mother was in England by the famous painter of miniatures, Mr. Malbone.

And now I set about seeing how I was to get away. Our own forces lay at Pennypacker's Mills, or near by; but this I did not know until later, and neither the British nor I were very sure as to their precise situation. It was clear that I must go afoot. As I walked down Second street with this on my mind I met Colonel Montresor with a group of officers. He stopped me, and, after civilly presenting me, said:

«Harcourt and Johnston»—this latter was he who later married the saucy Miss Franks and her fortune—«want to know if you have duck-shooting here on the Schuylkill.»

Suddenly, as I stood, I saw my chance and how to leave the town. I said: «It is rather early, but there are a few ducks in the river. If I had a boat I would try it to-morrow, and then perhaps, if I find any sport, one of you would join me the day after.»

«Very good,» said they, as well pleased as I.

«And the boat?» I said.

The colonel had one, a rather light skiff, he told me. He used it to go up and down to look at the bridges he was now busily laying. When I asked for its use the next day, he said Yes, if I would send him some ducks; adding that I should need a pass. He would send it that evening by a sergeant, and an order for the skiff, which lay on this side at the lower ferry. I thanked him, and went away happy in the success of my scheme.

I came upon André just after. «Not gone yet?» he said.

I replied, «Not yet; but I shall get away.»

He rejoined that he would not like to bet on that, and then went on to say that if my aunt had any trouble as to the officers quartered on her, would she kindly say so? The Hessians were rough people, and an exchange might be arranged. Gentlemen of his own acquaintance could be substituted. He himself was in Dr. Franklin's house. It was full of books, and good ones too.

I thanked him, but said I fancied she was Whig enough to like the Hessians better.

On Second street I bought a smock shirt, rough shoes, and coarse knit stockings, as well as a good snapsack, and, rolling them up securely, left them at home in the hay-loft. My sword and other finery I must needs leave behind me. I had no friends to say good-bye to, and quite late in the evening I merely ran in and kissed my aunt, and received eight hundred pounds in English notes, her offering to the cause, which I was to deliver to the general. Her gift to me was one hundred pounds in gold, just what she gave to my Jack. The larger sum she had put aside by degrees. It embarrassed me, but to refuse it would have hurt her.

I carefully packed my snapsack, putting the gold in bags at the bottom, and covering it with the flannel shirts and extra shoes which made up my outfit. I could not resist taking my pistols, as I knew that to provide myself as well in camp would not be possible. The bank-bills I concealed in my long stockings, and would gladly have been without them had I not seen how greatly this would disappoint my aunt. She counted, and wisely, on their insuring me a more than favourable reception. Lastly, I got me a small compass, and some tobacco for Jack.

It must be hard for you, in this happier day, when it is easy to get with speed anywhere on swift and well-horsed coaches, to imagine what even a small journey of a day or two meant for us. Men who rode carried horseshoes and nails. Those who drove had in the carriage ropes and a box of tools for repairs. I was perhaps better off than some who drove or rode in those days, for afoot one cannot be stalled, nor easily lose a shoe, although between Philadelphia and Darby I have known it to happen.

I knew the country I was to travel, and up to a point knew it well; beyond that I must trust to good fortune. Early in the evening came a sergeant with the promised order for the boat, and a pass signed by Sir William Howe's adjutant. At ten I bade my father good-night and went up-stairs, where I wrote to him, and inclosed the note in one for my aunt. This I gave to Tom, our coachman, with strict orders to deliver it late the next day. I had no wish that by any accident it should too early betray my true purpose. My gun I ostentatiously cleaned in the late afternoon, and set in the hall.

No one but my aunt had the least suspicion of what I was in act to do. At last I sat down and carefully considered my plan, and my best and most rapid way of reaching the army. To go through Germantown and Chestnut Hill would have been the direct route, for to a surety our army lay somewhere nigh to Worcester, which was in the county of Philadelphia, although of late years I believe in Montgomery. To go this plain road would have taken me through the pickets, and where lay on guard the chief of the British army. This would, of course, be full of needless risks. It remained to consider the longer road. This led me down the river to a point where I must leave it, shoulder my snapsack, and trudge down the Darby road, or between it and the river. Somewhere I must cross the highway and strike across country as I could to the Schuylkill below Conshohocken, and there find means to get over at one of the fords. Once well away from the main road to Darby and Wilmington, I should be, I believed, safe. After crossing the Schuylkill I hoped to get news which would guide me. I hardly thought it likely that the English who lay at Germantown and Mount Airy would picket beyond the banks of the Wissahickon. I might have to look out for foraging English west of the Schuylkill, but this I must chance.

I was about to leave home, perhaps forever, but I never in my life went to bed with a more satisfied heart than I bore that night.

## XVI.

At break of day I woke, and, stealing down-stairs, took gun, powder-horn, and shot, and in the stable loft put the ammunition in the top of my snapsack; then, quickly changing my clothes, concealed those I had put off under the hay, and so set out.

The town was all asleep, and I saw no one until I passed the Bettering-house, and the Grenadiers cleaning their guns and powdering their queues and hair, and thence pushed on to the river. The lower ferry, known also as Gray's, lay just a little south of where the Woodlands, Mr. James Hamilton's house, stood among trees high above the quiet river.

A few tents and a squad of sleepy men were at the ferry. I handed my order and pass to the sergeant, who looked me over as if he thought it odd that a man of my class should be so equipped to shoot ducks. However, he read my pass and the order for the boat, pushed the skiff into the water, and proposed, as he lifted my snapsack, to let one of his men row me. I said No; I must drift or paddle on to the ducks, and would go alone. Thanking him, I pushed out into the stream. He wished me good luck, and pocketed my shilling.

It was now just sunrise. I paddled swiftly down-stream. Not a hundred yards from the ferry I saw ducks on the east shore, and, having loaded, paddled over to Rambo's Rock, and was lucky enough to get two ducks at a shot. Recrossing, I killed two more in succession, and then pushed on, keeping among the reeds of the west bank. As I passed Bartram's famous garden, I saw his son near the river, busy, as usual, with his innocent flowers.

A half-mile below I perceived, far back of the shore, a few redcoats. Annoyed no little,—for here I meant to land,—I turned the boat, still hidden by the tall reeds, and soon drew up the skiff at Bartram's, where, taking gun and snapsack, I went up the slope. I found Mr. William Bartram standing under a fine cypress his father had fetched as a slip from Florida in 1731. He was used to see me on the river, but looked at my odd costume with as much curiosity as the sergeant had done. He told me his father had died but ten days before, for which I felt sorry, since, except by Friends, who had disowned the good botanist, he was held in general esteem. I hastily but frankly told Mr. Bartram my errand. He said:

«Come to the house. A company or two has just now passed to relieve the lower fort.»

After I had a glass of milk, and good store of bread and butter, I asked him to accept my gun, and that he would do me the kindness to return the skiff, and with it to forward a note, for the writing of which Mrs. Bartram gave me quill and paper.

I wrote:

«Mr. Hugh Wynne presents his compliments to Mr. Montresor, and returns his skiff. He desires Mr. Montresor to accept two brace of ducks, and begs to express his sincere thanks for the pass, which enabled Mr. Wynne to make with comfort his way to the army. Mr. Wynne trusts at some time to be able to show his gratitude for this favour, and meanwhile he remains Mr. Montresor's obedient, humble servant.

«October 1, 1777.

«Mr. Wynne's most particular compliments to Mr. André. It proved easier to escape than Mr. André thought.»

I could not help smiling to think of the good colonel's face when he should read this letter. I glanced at the arms over the fireplace, thanked the good people warmly, and, as I went out, looked back at the familiar words old John Bartram set over the door in 1770:

'T is God alone, Almighty Lord,
The Holy One by me adored.

It seemed the last of home and its associations. I turned away, passed through the grounds, which extended up to the Darby road, and, after a careful look about me, moved rapidly southward. Here and there were farm-houses between spurs of the broken forest which, with its many farms, stretched far to westward. I met no one.

I knew there was a picket at the Blue Bell Inn, and so, before nearing it, I struck into a woodland, and, avoiding the farms, kept to the northwest until I came on to a road which I saw at once to be Gray's Lane. Unused to guiding myself by compass, I had again gotten dangerously near to the river. I pushed up the lane to the west, and after half an hour came upon a small hamlet, where I saw an open forge and a sturdy smith at work. In a moment I recognised my old master, Lowry, the farrier. I asked the way across country to Bryn Mawr. He stood a little, resting on his hammer, not in the least remembering me. He said it was difficult. I must take certain country lanes until I got into the Lancaster road, and so on.

I did not wish to get into the main highway, where foragers or outlying parties might see fit to be too curious. I said at last, «Dost not thou know thy old prentice, Hugh Wynne?»

I felt sure of my man, as he had been one of the Sons of Liberty, and had fallen out with Friends in consequence, so that I did not hesitate to relate my whole story. He was pleased to see me, and bade me enter and see his wife. As we stood consulting, a man cried out at the door:

«Here are more Hessians!» And as he spoke we heard the notes of a bugle.

«Put me somewhere,» I said, «and quick.»

«No,» he cried. «Here, set your snapsack back of this forge. Put on this leather apron. Smudge your face and hands.»

It took me but a minute, and here I was, grimy and black, a smith again, with my sack hid under a lot of old iron and a broken bellows.

As they rode up—some two dozen yagers—I let fall the bellows handle, at which my master had set me to work, and went out to the doorway. There, not at all to my satisfaction, I saw the small Hessian, Captain von Heiser, our third and least pleasant boarder, the aide of General Knyphausen. Worse still, he was on Lucy. It was long before I knew how this came to pass. They had two waggons, and, amidst the lamentations of the hamlet, took chickens, pigs, and grain, leaving orders on the paymaster, which, I am told, were scrupulously honoured.

Two horses needed shoeing at once, and then I was told Lucy had a loose shoe, and my master called me a lazy dog, and bid me quit staring or I would get a strapping, and to see to the gentleman's mare, and that in a hurry. It was clear the dear thing knew me, for she put her nose down to my side to get the apples I liked to keep for her in my side pockets. I really thought she would betray me, so clearly did she seem to me to understand that here was a friend she knew. A wild thought came over me to mount her and ride for my life. No horse there of the heavy Brandenburgers could have kept near her. It would have been madness, of course, and so I took my sixpence with a touch of my felt hat, and saw my dear Lucy disappear in a cloud of dust, riding toward the town.

«That was a big risk for thee,» said the smith, wiping the sweat from his forehead with his sleeve. «I will mount and ride with thee across country to Bryn Mawr. There thou wilt not be far from the river. It is a good ten-mile business.»

After a little, when I had had some milk and rum, the horses were saddled, and we crossed by an ox-road through the forest past the settlement of Cardington, and then forded Cobb's Creek. A cross-road carried us into the Haverford road, and so on by Ardmore to the old Welsh farms about Bryn Mawr.

We met no one on the way save a farmer or two, and here, being near to the Schuylkill, my old master farrier took leave of me at the farm of Edward Masters, which lay north of Bryn Mawr, and commended me to the care of this good Free Quaker.

There I was well fed, and told I need to look out on this side the river only for Tories. They were worse than Hessianers, he said, and robbed like highwaymen. In fact, already the Tories who came confidently back with the British army had become a terror to all peaceful folk between Norristown and our own city. Their bands acted under royal commissions, some as honest soldiers, but some as the enemies of any who owned a cow or a barrel of flour, or from whom, under torture, could be wrested a guinea. All who were thus organised came at length to be dreaded, and this whether they were bad or better. Friend Masters had suffered within the week, but, once over the Schuylkill, he assured me, there need be no fear, as our own partisans and foragers were so active to the north of the stream as to make it perilous for Tories.

With this caution, my Quaker friend went with me a mile, and set me on a wood path. I must be put over at Hagy's Ford, he feared, as the river was in flood and too high for a horse to wade; nor was it much better at Young's Ford above. Finally he said, «The ferryman is Peter Skinner, and as bad as the Jersey Tories of that name. If thou dost perceive him to talk Friends' language in reply to thy own talk, thou wilt do well to doubt what he may tell thee. He is not of our society. He cannot even so speak as that it will deceive. Hereabouts it is thought he is in league with Fitz.» I asked who was Fitz. He was one, I was told, who had received some lashes when a private in our army, and had deserted. The British, discovering his capacity, now used him as a forager; but he did not stop at hen-roosts.

With this added warning, I went on, keeping north until I came to the Rock road, by no means misnamed, and so through Merion Square to Hagy's Ford Lane and the descent to the river. I saw few people on the way. The stream was in a freshet, and not to be waded. My ferryman was caulking a dory. I said:

«Wilt thou set me across, friend, and at what charge?»

To this he replied, «Where is thee bound?»

I said, «To Conshohocken.»

«Thee is not of these parts.»

«No.»

He was speaking the vile tongue which now all but educated Friends speak, and even some of these; but at that time it was spoken only by the vulgar.

«It will cost thee two shillings.»

«Too much,» said I; «but thou hast me caught. I must over, and that soon.»

He was long about getting ready, and now and then looked steadily across the stream; but as to this I was not troubled, as I knew that, once beyond it, I was out of danger. I paid my fare, and left him looking after me up the deep cut which led to the more level uplands. Whistling gaily, and without suspicion, I won the hilltop by what I think they called Ship Lane.

Glad to be over Schuylkill and out of the way of risks, I sat down by the roadside at the top of the ascent. The forest was dense with underbrush on each side, and the hickories, and below them the sumachs, were already rich with the gold and red of autumn. Being rather tired, I remained at rest at least for a half-hour in much comfort of body and mind. I had been strongly urged by my love for Darthea to await her coming; but decisions are and were with me despotic, and, once I was of a mind to go, not even Darthea could keep me. Yet to leave her to my cousin and his wiles I hated. The more I discussed him in the council of my own thoughts, the more I was at a loss. His evident jealousy of one so much younger did seem to me, as it did to my aunt, singular. And why should he wish me to be away, as clearly he did? and why also malign me to my father? I smiled to think I was where his malice could do me no harm, and, rising, pulled my snapsack straps up on my shoulders, and set my face to the east.

Of a sudden I heard to left, «Halt, there!» I saw a long rifle covering me, and above the brush a man's face. Then stepped out to right, as I obeyed the order, a fellow in buckskin shirt and leggings, with a pistol. I cried out, «I surrender;» for what else could I do? Instantly a dozen men, all armed, were in the road, and an ill-looking lot they were. The leader, a coarse fellow, was short and red of face, and much pimpled. He had hair half a foot long, and a beard such as none wore in those days.

I had but time to say meekly, «Why dost thou stop me, friend?» when he jerked off my sack and, plunging a hand inside, pulled out a pistol.

«A pretty Quaker! Here,» and he put back the pistol, crying, as the men laughed, «sergeant, strap this on your back. Quick! fetch out the horses; we will look him over later. Up with him behind Joe! Quick—a girth! We have no time to waste. A darned rebel spy! No doubt Sir William may like to have him.»

In truth, no time was lost nor any ceremony used, and here was I strapped to the waist of a sturdy trooper, behind whom I was set on a big-boned roan horse, and on my way home again.

«Which way, Captain Fitz?» said the sergeant. «The ford is high.» In a moment we were away, in all, as I noted, about a score of redcoats.

The famous Tory chief—he was no better than a bold thief—made no reply, but rode northwest with his following for the ford below Conshohocken, as I fancied. He went at speed through the open pine forest, I, my hands being free, holding on to my man as well as I could, and, as you may suppose, not very happy. A mile away we came out on a broad road. Here the captain hesitated, and of a sudden turned to left toward the river, crying loudly, with an oath, «Follow me!» The cause was plain.

Some twenty troopers came out into the road not a hundred yards away, and instantly rode down on us at a run. Before we could get as swift a pace, they were close upon us; and then it was a wild and perilous race downhill for the river, with yells, curses, and pistol-balls flying, I as helpless, meanwhile, as a child. The big roan kept well up to the front near the captain. Looking back, through dust and smoke, I saw our pursuers were better horsed and were gaining. A man near me dropped, and a horse went down. With my left hand I caught hold of the strap which fastened me to the rascal in the saddle. He was riding for life, and too scared to take note of the act. I gave the buckle a quick jerk, and it came loose, and the strap fell. I clutched the man by the throat with my right hand, and squeezed his gullet with a death-grip. He made with his right hand for a holster pistol, losing his stirrups, and kicking as if in a fit. I only tightened my grip, and fetched him a crack under the left ear with my unengaged hand. He was reeling in the saddle when, at this instant, I was aware of a horseman on my right. I saw a sabre gleam in air above us, and, letting go my scamp's throat, I ducked quickly below his left shoulder as I swung him to left, meaning to chance a fall. He had, I fancy, some notion of his peril, for he put up his hand and bent forward. I saw the flash of a blade, and, my captor's head falling forward, a great spout of blood shot back into my face, as the pair of us tumbled together headlong from his horse. I was dimly aware of yells, oaths, a horse leaping over me, and for a few seconds knew no more. Then I sat up, wiped the blood away, and saw what had happened.

The trooper lay across me dead, his head nearly severed from the trunk, and spouting great jets of blood. A half-dozen dead or wounded were scattered along the road. Not a rod away was the sergeant who had my sack pinned under his horse, and far ahead, in a cloud of dust, that terrible swordsman riding hard after the bandit. Fitz, well mounted, got off, I may add, and, with three or four, swam the river, living to be hanged, as he well deserved.

By the time I was up and staggering forward, bent on recovering my sack, the leader, who had given up the chase, rode toward me. I must have been a queer and horrid figure. I was literally covered with blood and mud. The blood was everywhere,—in my hair, over my face, and down my neck,—but I wanted my precious sack.

«Halt!» he cried out. «Here, corporal, tie this fellow.»

«Pardon me,» said I, now quite myself. «I was the prisoner of these rascals.»

«Indeed? Your name?»

«Hugh Wynne.»

«Where from?»

«From the city.»

«Where to?»

«To join the army.»

«Your business? What are you?»

«Gentleman.»

«Good heavens! you are a queer one! We shall see. Are you hurt? No? Great Cæsar! you are an awful sight!»

«I was tied to that fellow you disposed of, and with your permission I will get my snap-sack yonder.»

«Good; get it. Go with him, corporal, and keep an eye on him.»

In a half-hour the dead were stripped and pitched aside, the wounded cared for in haste, and the horses caught.

«Can you ride?» said my captor. «By George! you must!»

«Yes, I can ride.»

«Then up with you. Give him a leg.»

I wanted none, and was up in a moment on the bare back of a big farm mare; their errand had been, I learned, the purchase of horses. The captain bade me ride with him, and, turning north, we rode away, while the big brute under me jolted my sore bones.

«And now,» said the captain, «let me hear, Mr. Wynne, what you have to say. Take a pull at my flask.»

I did so, and went on to relate my adventures briefly—the duck-shooting, which much amused him, the escape at the forge, and what else seemed to be needed to set myself right. He looked me over again keenly.

«You had a close thing of it.»

«Yes,» said I; «you are a terrible swordsman, and a good one, if you will pardon me.»

«I meant to cut him on the head, but he put his neck where his head should have been. There is one rascal the less; but I missed the leader. Hang him!»

«He will take care of that,» said I.

Then my companion said I must join his troop, and would I excuse his rough dealing with me?

I declared myself well content, and explained as to his offer that I was much obliged, and would think it over; but that I desired first to see the army, and to find my friend, Captain Warder, of the Pennsylvania line.

«Yes; a stout man and dark?»

«No; slight, well built, a blond.»

«Good; I know him. I was testing your tale, Mr. Wynne. One has need to be careful in these times.» For a few moments he was silent, and then asked sharply, «Where did you cross?»

I told him.

«And are there any outlying pickets above the upper ferry on the west bank?»

I thought not, and went on to tell of the bridging of the river and of the lines of forts, and of the positions held in the city by the Grenadiers and the Highlanders. A large part of the army, I said, was being withdrawn from Germantown, I supposed with a view to attack the forts below the city.

«What you say is valuable, Mr. Wynne.» And he quickened the pace with an order, and pushed on at speed.

It seemed to me time to know into whose company I had fallen, and who was the hardy and decisive rider at my side.

«May I take the liberty to ask with what command I am?»

«Certainly. I am Allan McLane, at your service. I will talk to you later; now I want to think over what you have told me. I tried to get into the city last week, dressed as an old woman; they took my eggs,—Lord, they were aged!—but I got no farther than the middle ferry. Are you sure that troops are being withdrawn from Germantown?»

I said I was, and in large numbers. After this we rode on in silence through the twilight. I glanced now and then at my companion, the boldest of our partisan leaders, and already a sharp thorn in the side of General Howe's extended line. He was slight, well made, and dark, with some resemblance to Arthur Wynne, but with no weak lines about a mouth which, if less handsome than my cousin's, was far more resolute.

I was ready to drop from my rough steed when we began, about nine at night, to see the camp-fires of our army on each side of

Skippack Creek. A halt at the pickets, and we rode on around the right flank among rude huts, rare tents, rows of spancelled horses,—we call it «hobbled» nowadays,—and so at last to a group of tents, the headquarters of the small cavalry division.

«Halt!» I heard; and I literally almost tumbled off my horse, pleased to see the last of her.

«This way, sir,» said McLane. «Here is my tent. There is a flask under the pine-needles. I have no feather-bed to offer. Get an hour's rest; it is all you can have just now. When I find out the headquarters, you must ride again.» And he was gone.

I found a jug of water and a towel; but my attempts to get the blood and mud out of my hair and neck were quite vain. I gave it up at last. Then I nearly emptied the flask which McLane had left me, set my sack under my head, pulled up a blanket, and in a minute was out of the world of war, and sound asleep.

I do not know how long my slumber lasted on my fragrant bed of pine. I heard a voice say, «Are you dead, man?» And shaken roughly, I sat up, confused, and for a moment wondering where I was.

«Come,» said McLane. «Oh, leave your sack.»

«No,» I said, not caring to explain why.

In a moment I was in the saddle, as fresh as need be, the cool October night-wind in my face.

«Where are we bound?» I asked.

«Headquarters. I want you to tell your own news. Hang the man!» We had knocked down a lurching drunkard, but McLane stayed to ask no questions, and in half an hour we pulled up in the glare of a huge fire, around which lay aides, some asleep and others smoking. A few yards away was a row of tents.

McLane looked about him. «Holloa, Hamilton!» he cried to a slight young man lying at the fire. «Tell his Excellency I am here. I have news of importance.»

A moment after, the gentleman, who was to become so well known and to die so needlessly, came back, and we followed him to the larger of the tents. As he lifted the fly he said, «Captain McLane to see your Excellency.»

On a plain farm-house table were four candles, dimly lighting piles of neatly folded papers; there were besides a simple camp-bed, two or three wooden stools, and a camp-chest. The officer who sat bareheaded at the table pushed aside a map and looked up. I was once more in the presence of Washington. Both McLane and I stood waiting, I a little behind.

«Whom have you here, sir?»

«Mr. Wynne, a gentleman who has escaped in disguise to join the army. He has news which may interest your Excellency.» As he spoke I came forward.

«Are you wounded, sir?»

«No,» said I; «it is another man's blood, not mine.» He showed no further curiosity, nor any sign of the amazement I had seen in the faces of his aides-de-camp on my appearance at the camp-fire.

«Pray be seated, gentlemen. Do me the favour, Captain McLane, to ask Captain Hamilton to return. Mr. Wynne, you said?»

«Yes, your Excellency.»

Then, to set myself right, I told him that I had had the honour to meet him at the house of my aunt, Mistress Wynne. «With permission, sir,» I added, «I am charged to deliver to your Excellency eight hundred pounds which Mistress Wynne humbly trusts may be of use to the cause of liberty.» So saying, I pulled the English notes out of my long stockings, and laid them before him.

«I could desire many recruits like you,» he said. «Mr. Hamilton, I beg to present Mr. Wynne. Have the kindness to make memoranda of what he may tell us.» He spoke with deliberation, as one who had learned to weigh his words, not omitting any of the usual courteous forms, more common at that time than in our less formal day. General Knox came in as we sat down.

He was a sturdy man with a slight stoop, and had left his book-shop in Boston to become the trusted friend and artillery officer of the great Virginian, who chose his men with slight regard to the tongues of the Southern officers, for whom they were too often «shopkeepers» or «mere traders.»

«Report of court martial on Daniel Plympton, deserter,» said Knox. The general took the papers, and for ten minutes at least was intently concerned with what he read. Then he took a pen and wrote a line and his name, and, looking up, said, «Approved, of course. Parade his regiment at daybreak for execution. Your pardon, gentlemen.» And at once he began to put to me a series of questions rather slowly. The absence of hurry surprised me, young as I was, and not yet apt to take in all I might see. Every minute some one appeared. There were papers to sign, aides coming and going, impatient sounds without, a man's death decreed; but with no sign of haste he went on to finish.

At last he rose to his feet, we also standing, of course. «Are you sure that Sir William has recalled any large force from Germantown—any large force?»

I knew that the Grenadiers and many Hessians had come in, and a considerable part of the artillery, but to what extent or precisely in what numbers I could not be sure. He seemed to me to be intensely considering what I told him.

At last he said: «You must be tired. You have brought much needed help, and also good news.» Why good I did not then understand. «And now what do you desire? How can I serve you, Mr. Wynne?»

I said I wished to be in the ranks for a time, until I learned a little more of the duty.

He made no comment, but turning to McLane, said: «Captain McLane, you will care for this gentleman. I trust occasion may serve, Mr. Wynne, to enable me to offer Mistress Wynne my thanks. When you desire a commission, Mr. Hamilton will kindly remind me of the service you have done your country to-day. You have acted with your usual discretion, Captain McLane. Good-night, gentlemen.» We bowed and went out.

On our way back we rode a footpace, while the captain, now ready enough to talk, answered my many questions. Yes; the general was a reserved, tranquil man, with a chained-up devil inside of him; could lay a whip over a black fellow's back if a horse were ill groomed, or call a man, and he a general, a d—— drunkard; but that would be in the heat of a fight. An archbishop would learn to swear in the army, and the general had no more piety than was good for men who were here to commit murder.

The next day I set out afoot, as I preferred, to look for Jack, and a nice business I found it. The army was moving down the Skippack road to Worcester township, and the whole march seemed, to me at least, one great bewildering confusion of dust, artillery, or waggons stalled, profane aides going hither and thither, broken fences, women standing at farm-house doors, white and crying, as the long line of our foot passed; and over all rang sharp the clink and rattle of flanking cavalry as the horse streamed by, trampling the ruddy buckwheat-fields, and through ravaged orchards and broken gardens. Overhead, in a great cloud high in air, the fine dust was blown down the line by the east wind. It was thick and oppressive, choking man and horse with an exacting thirst, mocked by empty wells and defiled brooks. No one knew where any one else was, and in all my life, save on one memorable evening, I never heard as great a variety of abominable language.



I had done my best, by some change of underclothes and the industrious use of soap and water, to make my appearance less noticeable; but it was still bad enough, because I had no outer garments except those I was wearing. Had I been better dressed, I had fared better; for in those days clothes were considered, and you might easily tell by his costume if a man were a mechanic, a farmer, a small trader, or a gentleman.

I fell at last upon an officer who was endeavouring to get his horse a share of wayside ditch water. I said to him, seeing my chance, that his horse had picked up a stone; if he would wait a moment I would knock it out. On this, and upon his thanking me, I asked where I might find Wayne's brigade, for, in it, as I knew, was my captain of the Third Pennsylvania Continental foot. He told me it was a mile ahead. Comforted by this news, I walked on, keeping chiefly in the fields, for there alone was it possible to get past the marching columns.

About eleven there was a halt. I passed a lot of loose women in carts, many canvas-covered commissary waggons, footsore men fallen out, and some asleep in the fields,—all the scum and refuse of an army,—with always dust, dust, so that man, beast, waggons, and every green thing were of one dull yellow. Then there was shouting on the road; the stragglers fled left and right, a waggon of swearing women turned over into a great ditch, and with laughter, curses, and crack of whip, two well-horsed cannon and caissons bounded over the field, crashing through a remnant of snake fence, and so down the road at speed. I ran behind them, glad of the gap they left. About a mile farther they pulled up, and going by I saw with joy the red and buff of the Pennsylvania line. Behind them there was an interval, and thus the last files were less dusty. But for this I should have gone past them. A soldier told me that this was the regiment I sought, and, searching the ranks eagerly as they stood at ease, I walked swiftly along.

«Holloa!» I shouted. I saw Jack look about him. «Jack!» I cried. He ran to me as I spoke. I think I should have kissed him but for the staring soldiers. In all my life I never was so glad. There was brief time allowed for greetings. «Fall in! fall in!» I heard. «March!»

«Come along,» he said. And walking beside him, I poured out news of home, of my Aunt Gainor, and of myself.

A mile beyond we halted close to the road near to Methacton Hill, where, I may add, we lay that night of October 2. Having no tents, Jack and I slept on the ground rolled up in Holland blankets, and sheltered in part by a wicky-up which the men contrived cleverly enough.

I saw on our arrival how—automatically, as it seemed to me—the regiments found camping-grounds, and how well the ragged men arranged for shelters of boughs, or made tents with two rails and a blanket. The confusion disappeared. Sentries and pickets were posted, fires were lighted, and food cooked. The order of it seemed to me as mysterious as the seeming disorder of the march.

After some talk with Jack, I concluded to serve as a volunteer, at least for a few weeks, and learn the business better before I should decide to accept the general's kindness. Accordingly I took my place in the ranks of Jack's company, and, confiding most of my gold to his care, kept in a belt under my clothes not more than six guineas, as I remember. A uniform was not to be had; but I was hardly worse off than half of the men who made up our company. A musket, and what else was wanted, I obtained without trouble; and as to the drill, I knew it well enough, thanks to the Irish sergeant who had trained us at home.

Our duties, of course, kept us much apart—that is, Jack and myself; but as he made use, or pretended to make use, of me as an orderly, I was able to see more of him than otherwise would have been possible. My pistols I asked him to use until I could reclaim them, and I made him happy with the tobacco I brought, and which I soon saw him dividing among other officers; for what was Jack's was always everybody's. And, indeed, because of this generosity he has been much imposed upon by the selfish.

(To be continued.)

*S. Weir Mitchell.*

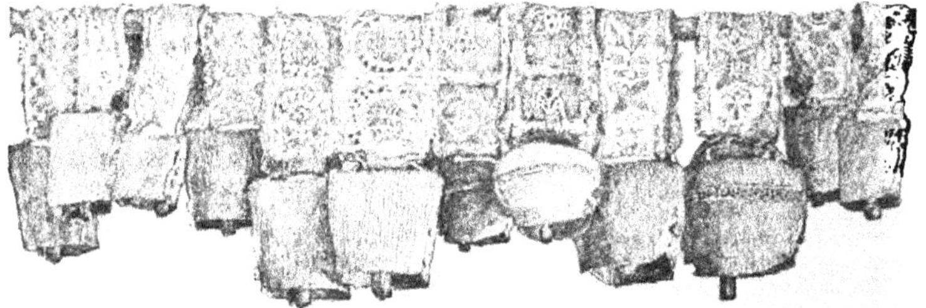

TYROLEAN COW-BELLS.

# «AL' HEIL!»—WHEELING IN TYROLEAN VALLEYS.

THE social impulse prevails in Tyrol, and the casual intercourse of life is marked by its appropriate greetings. «Guten Morgen» and «Guten Tag» are universal on the country roads and paths, when they do not give place to the more characteristic «Grüss dich Gott,» abbreviated to «Gr's' Gott,» which suggests to the American ear our familiar vulgarism «Great Scott.»

The Tyrolese Wheelmen's Club[1] would not have been Tyrolese had it not set up a call of recognition for the road. It adopted for this the cry universal among German wheelmen, «Al' Heil!» with which not only club members, but all who wheel over the smooth *chaussées* of this beautiful land, and all others who wish to greet a passing bicyclist, give forth their call of cheer, with a clarion-like emphasis on the last word. Such a custom could hardly be transplanted to America, for our habits are much more reserved and inarticulate; but in Tyrol it seems to make all wheelmen kin, and to give real charm and cheer to the intercourse of the road. We

[1] Tyroler Radfahrer Verband.

soon fell into the friendly spirit of the sport as practised here, and before a week had passed felt ourselves part and parcel of the cycling band of the Tyrolese valleys.

Knowing this land of old, and knowing what roads run through these valleys, it was a matter of course to select it for a vacation exercise of the new faculty with which modern mechanics has blessed the human race. The selection was a wise one, and the retrospect over all our four weeks of easy wheeling is filled with invitation for a return to the same field and the same diversion. The field is, in a certain sense, rather a small one, and it is marked with considerably more «grade» than a mere wheelman would choose. Those who have an ambition to scorch off a huge daily mileage, and who ride with an eye rather to the cyclometer than to the environment, should go elsewhere. The fertile flats of Holland, the plains of Berlinese Prussia, the poplar-lined *allées* of the level parts of France and of the vast plain of northern Italy, will give them what they want. Tyrol would not suit them, for it has no part where they could go fifty miles and return without fifty miles of up-grade work that would pull down the record.

But for those to whom the wheel is a means rather than an end, who care for mountain scenery, and who appreciate association with a simple, cheerful, friendly, and honest people, Italy, France, Prussia, and Holland can offer nothing to compare with it. In the first place, the scenery is most beautiful and majestic. After having run down fifty miles of the Upper Innthal (the Engadine), I wrote to a wheeling friend at home: «Except in the villages, which are interesting, every foot of the way is more beautiful than anything you ever saw or can imagine.» This was perfectly true, though my friend lives near Orange Mountain, and has wheeled up the valleys of the Delaware and the Susquehanna. I was already familiar with Tyrol as seen from the railroad, from the thread of the higher valleys, and from the alps and lower mountains and from some of the higher ones; but my experience of more than twenty years had seldom taken me along the highroads and into the towns and villages of the larger valleys. To make their acquaintance at last, and to see the great mountains deliberately and from the very bottom of the valleys, was a new sensation. It was like repeating, over miles and miles of road, the experience one has outside of Innsbruck, where the combination of cultivated plain, inclosing mountains, and great peaks had seemed to fill the full measure of possible beauty. It gave, too, time for deliberate views up the gorgeous side valleys, of which the «quick shutter» of the railway passage had left only an instantaneous picture, and not clearly defined at that. It gave frequent halts under wayside trees and frequent draughts from wayside springs; and with the certainty that we should always find within easy reach a village with clean quarters and good cheer, it invited us to take our leisurely fill of all the beauty, comfort, and enjoyment our road had to offer.

### THE COUNTRY.

It will not be amiss, for the benefit of those to whom the subject is only vaguely familiar, to give some account of the country itself. Its boundary is in the main determined by natural features. It is south of the Bavarian highlands; east of Switzerland and of the province of Vorarlberg; Italy bounds it on the south by a very irregular line which crosses Lake Garda some miles south of Riva; on the east it is bounded by Salzburg and Carinthia, which, like Vorarlberg and Tyrol itself, are Austrian. But Tyrol far more than these other Austrian provinces has always had the characteristics of an independent country. Its people are most loyal subjects of the empire, but they are first of all Tyrolese, and they hold to their territory as something better and greater than the adjoining country. The grandest and most beautiful field of the Eastern Alps lies between the Ortler and the Grossglockner (about 150 miles from southwest to northeast), and between Antelao, the most easterly peak of the Dolomites, and the Parseier Spitze beyond Landeck (about 90 miles from southeast to northwest). The chief cities are Innsbruck, Botzen, and Trent, but all the larger valleys are studded with large and minor towns, with innumerable villages, and with historic traces, often in ruins, of the successive races which have occupied the region from immemorial time. The entire population numbers about 900,000, of whom about two thirds are German and one third Italian.

Tyrol can be entered from any side only through its valleys, or over difficult and easily defensible mountain passes. Its broadest valleys—those of the lower Inn and of the Adige—are only about a mile wide. The great Alpine range runs through it from east to west, by no means in a straight line, beginning with the Ortler near the Swiss border, and including the peaks of the Oetzthal group, the Stubaithal group, the Zillerthal group, and its extension to the Grossglockner on the borders of Carinthia. The Ortler is 12,852 feet high, and the Grossglockner 12,560 feet. Many of the intermediate peaks are above the 10,000-foot line. Monte Adamello, south of this range, and many peaks between it and Bavaria, are more than 11,000 feet high. These highest points are connected by ranges which rarely go below 8000 feet. In the garden of the Pädagogium (normal school) at Innsbruck there is a large model of the whole country, which is a mass of heaped-up rock divided by very narrow valleys, mere foot-paths on the scale of the work. This shows that the entire area of Tyrol is mountainous, with only the lower parts of it valleys, many of which are steep, and its lower hills and mountain-sides susceptible of cultivation. More than one third of the whole area is above the line of vegetation, and much of it is buried under perpetual snow. By far the greater part of the remainder is covered with forests of fir and with patches of grass («alps»), which are difficult of access, and to which cattle are driven in the early summer, to be brought down in the autumn.

One evening, while waiting near Hall for the «tram» to Innsbruck, and watching a game of bowls, I fell into conversation with a sturdy workingman about the condition of the laboring population and the little emigration from the country. I enumerated some conditions which seemed to me to make it desirable for them to stay at home. He assented to these, and added that there was no other country in which the drinking-water was so good. I should have been less surprised if he had referred to the beer, which in northern Tyrol is a more conspicuous beverage, and is generally very good and cheap. As a wheelman whose thirst often came on far from sources of beer, I thought of this comment as I halted at the water-troughs which were overflowing along all the roads. Better cold water surely flows nowhere else in the world.

It was in this land of fine roads, fine scenery, and fine *Trinkwasser* that we took our vacation a-wheel. Our route lay through the entire length of the Engadine. This is not an integral part of the Tyrol of the present day, but it is so topographically, and the Lower Engadine would have been so politically had not Prince Ferdinand Carl, a spendthrift, sold it to Switzerland, about 1650, for the pittance of 123,000 gulden (about $60,000), giving up for all time forty miles of the valley of the Inn, with all its important towns and its fertile hillsides. The Engadine was then connected with Tyrol only by the deep and inhospitable gorge of Finstermüntz, but the beautiful highroad now goes zigzag over the hill, and there is nothing to mark the boundary save the custom-house at Martinsbruck.

### THE JOURNEY.

MY plans had been laid well in advance, and I had engaged a lusty young athlete with a record as a wheelman, an enthusiastic member of the Radfahrer Verband, and a prize turner, to report at Maloja two days after our ship was to arrive at Genoa. We had chosen that route of the North German Lloyd because it brought us so very near to our field of operations. We left New York by the *Fulda* on July 4. Our voyage was varied by a sail through the Azores and by two hours at Gibraltar. After a beautiful run along the coast of Spain, past the Balearic Islands and in full sight of the very hot-looking Riviera, we came to Genoa, «La Superba.» Here our bicycle experiences began. We must pay a duty of forty francs on each of our two wheels, must see them furnished with lead seals, and be ourselves furnished with official documents to identify them at the frontier, where, at any time within thirty days, we could have them unleaded and receive back our money, less a trifling fee.

We hurried on through Milan to Lecco, checking the wheels to the end of our rail route at Chiavenna. Leaving Genoa in the morning, we took boat at Lecco, and in the afternoon we were at Villa Serbelloni at Bellagio in time for an hour in its charming garden before sunset, refreshed for such a night as can hardly be passed more agreeably than there, and under the nearly full moon that rose over Lake Como.

The drive of twenty miles with our crated wheels looming up above the carriage-top through the beautiful Val Bregalia from Chiavenna to Maloja, with an ascent of 5000 feet, used up an afternoon that would have seemed long in other surroundings. At nightfall we arrived at «Maloja Palace,» a costly and expensive hotel, as far above the sea as the top of Mount Washington; but a very good hotel for all that, and large enough to house all the travelers we met in the whole Engadine.

### PERSONAL.

IN the morning we ripped the crates from about our wheels, put them into working condition, and «coupled» them. A word of personal explanation is requisite here. «We» are not two young men ready for a long, hard tour of wheeling after the manner of young men, but an elderly and somewhat ponderous gentleman—and as to wheeling a cautious one—and his wife, who is much younger than her years, but to whom the independent bicycle, with its tendency to «le zigzag et la chute,» has terrors that can hardly be overcome in the years that are left to her. So this trip was made possible only by the ingenuity of a man of Ohio, who devised a method of making a four-wheeler by cross-bracing two bicycles together, side by side and three feet apart. In this way the zigzag tendency is eliminated and the chute rendered impossible. If there comes an occasion to halt, whether to fill a pipe, to enjoy the view, or to adjust differences of opinion, we simply stop and have it out without leaving our seats, and then go on again, at will and serenely. The steering-gear is so connected that the two handle-bars work in unison. In short, it is a capital arrangement for those to whom the single machine is unsuited; and it has the great advantage that more attention may be given to the environment, as less is needed for the road. It was no slight satisfaction to be able to show an entirely new thing in wheels to the curious public. The guests at Maloja and the more numerous servants of the hotel clustered about us, and, their curiosity gratified, cheered us on our way. Thenceforward throughout our wanderings our wheels held a levee at every *Gasthaus* at which we stopped, and flashed a new idea into the minds of the people through whose villages our road lay.

Our young man proved a great success from the first, and much of the satisfaction of the expedition was due to him. He was ubiquitous. When he was needed he was at hand, but most of the time he was disporting himself much after the manner of an attendant setter dog, flying up and down impossible hills, jumping from his wheel to vault fences in quest of *Kornblumen* (which the partner greatly affected), and amusing himself by riding over piles of stones and across narrow gullies in pure boyish glee. He was of a race whose legs had been trained for generations to the scaling of long, steep mountain paths, and so simple a thing as «kicking a bike» was child's play to him. He evidently had a secret joy in his superiority to those who had had a very different muscular inheritance. One day he advised us to dismount to walk down one steep hill and up another. I suggested his doing the same. He said, «Macht mir nichts» («It does n't matter to me»), and with contemptuous ease he went down the hill like the wind and up the other side of the valley to the top. Was it to wait for us there? Not a bit of it. He came back like a shot, jumped from his saddle at full speed, and took the partner's place at guiding the four-wheeler. He was not a race-rider, only a tough-and-ready all-day wheelman. For example, it is 142 miles from Innsbruck to Maloja. The difference of elevation is 4230 feet. The grade is by no means uniform, and there are many minor hills between the towns, of which no account can be made; but the elevations at these towns are recorded, and these show descents in the road amounting to 1220 feet. Adding these, we have a total elevation to be overcome of 5450 feet. Herr L—— left Innsbruck at five o'clock on the morning of July 16, and reached Maloja at three o'clock in the afternoon of the 17th, and it rained steadily and hard all of the second day. The rise in grade is often continuous for miles and miles, and it averages thirty-eight feet to the mile. The average speed made was not great, but the strain on wind and sinew would sorely try a softer-bred man.

### «MAWK-NIX.»

OUR attendant's spirit was equal to his endurance; he was a Tyrolese Mark Tapley, and we soon came to speak of him as «Mawk-nix»; for «Es macht nichts» takes this sound in the speech of these people. His «Mawk-nix» was ready for every misadventure. If he was to turn out at an unusual hour for some special service, it was «Mawk-nix»; if he was badly bitten in the leg by a vicious hound, it was «Mawk-nix, but if I had had my revolver I should have shot him»; and he rolled on for a couple of days with an ugly red spot on his calf, saying that a healthy young fellow like him must get well anyhow. He had his people's love for beer and their hatred for Jews. His «Al' Heil!» had always been ready to greet passing wheelmen. One day a very good-looking fellow came in sight, and was passed in silence. I asked him if he greeted only members of the Verband. «Oh, no; but we don't recognize Jews.» His great complaint against them was the time-honored one that they are getting all the property and all the business. It did n't seem worth while to remind him that while he was sitting with his cronies through long hours, sipping beer or wine and bewailing Judaism, they were earning money by hard work and saving it by frugality and moderation. He confessed to twenty-seven glasses of beer at one sitting while he was with us, and he met a suggestion that he was going to the devil with his usual «Mawk-nix.» He has been in good positions and is an officer of the *Landwehr*, but the remaining end of his Tyrolese tether must be very short, for he contemplates service with the Dutch army in Borneo, with a possible decision in favor of the Belgian service in Congo. He asked my opinion. I told him that in either service he would probably die of fever. «Mawk-nix.» I said he would surely die very soon if he kept on drinking. He said he knew that, and should not drink at all. «D'rum trink ich jetzt so viel» («That 's why I drink so much now»). It was not worth while to take a more serious view of his case than he took himself, and our mission was the opposite of altruistic, so that we had no disposition to be unhappy about a fellow who was himself so entirely happy.

THE PEOPLE.

IF I could have my way, I could improve a good many things about the denizens of this mountain land; but I should probably make a mess of it and destroy their charm for their visiting friends, without adding to their own satisfaction with their lives.

From our point of view they are a delightful people, and from their own they are a happy and contented people. They are very industrious, and most of their work is in the open air. The field-work is shared by men and women alike, and a «delicate»-looking person of either sex is a rarity. Even those whose work is indoors are so good on their feet, and they are so given to walking and hill-climbing, that they seem to get their share of the ruddy health of their race. Those who do not have to work at all are so few anywhere in the world that they constitute a negligible factor of the problem. This is a land of good digestion, of sufficient food, and of the indomitable cheer that comes of good health. For my part, I should not be disposed to meddle with their ways if I could. As to the working of women in the fields, I am wholly in favor of it I have seen much of it for many years and in many places. It is not in itself degrading or injurious; and however objectionable it may be where the people are ill fed and where women are made to do the hardest work, it is far better for them and for their progeny than the grinding, ill-paid work of the ill-fed women in the sweating-shop. The Tyrolese women are not to be compared with these, but rather with the best class of female operatives in our best factory towns. If I were a woman, I would much rather do a woman's work in the house and in the fields on a high-lying valley farm of Tyrol, and eat the coarse but wholesome food on which they thrive, than lead the unventilated life of a cotton-mill damsel of Fall River. This view may easily be taken even by those who object to the female drudgery of other parts of Europe, where all the conditions of life are much harder; for in Tyrol the conditions are not hard, and girls and women seem to be on an absolute equality with their male fellow-workers. Indeed, though the whole family of useful age goes to the field early and works late, the heavier work is done by the men and the lighter by the women. The men plow, dig, and mow; the women rake, hoe, and bind the sheaves. The men pitch the hay on to the wagons, and the women trim the load. They work long and they work hard, but they go about their tasks cheerfully, and there is much more of laughter and singing than of dullness and grumbling.

DRINKING-HABITS.

I CANNOT pretend to much familiarity with the drinking-habits of these people, but they are certainly great consumers of beer and wine—more largely beer in the North and wine in the South. They drink beer almost like Germans, and they drink wine almost like water. There is virtually no obvious drunkenness. Late at night the sound of hilarity is not unfamiliar, and at other times, but rarely, one sees a party of young men who are more musical and more affectionate than is their wont. Drunken bouts are not unknown, but they are very rare indeed. One afternoon we saw an ancient hand-cart man in a fuddled sleep under his wheel. He was the only drunken man we met, and he was notorious in his village. He had a small ox to draw his cart once upon a time, but he concluded that the ox ate more than he did, and that it would be better for him to have the whole supply of provision to himself; so he sold the beast, ate all he could and drank all he would, until the ox's forage and the ox's price were all consumed. He still manages to earn enough drink before nightfall to lay him under his cart until he gets sober.

«Temperance» as we know it not only does not exist, but the people listen with wonder when we tell them of it. Temperance as we desire it is well-nigh universal, as is shown by the rarity even of tipsiness. Their outdoor life and exercise enable these people to drink with comparative impunity more than would be possible with us, and their cubical capacity is far greater than ours. Their immunity from drunkenness is due to their immunity from «treating,» and to the fact that strong drink is not a beverage with them. They cannot easily get intoxicated on the amount of beer and light wine they are capable of drinking or of paying for. Each orders and pays for what he wants. «Let 's have another» is never heard. I used sometimes to go with «Mawk-nix» into a wayside Gasthaus, and at first I paid for what he took. I soon found that this was unusual, and that he did not understand it; he had a look as though wondering if I thought he could not pay for his drink. I suppose he would have had the same feeling had I offered to pay for his bed. We generally went into the peasants' room, and this gave me a chance to watch their ways. Perhaps three or four would come in together, women and men indiscriminately. Some would order beer or wine, and some schnapps, which is as strong as whisky. This is served in a very small liqueur-glass, hardly more than a couple of thimblefuls, and costs only two or three cents. It is tossed off at a gulp, and followed with a glass of water, a pipe of tobacco, and a long talk. Those who took wine or beer were much more apt to repeat it, but they always drank very slowly, and eked out their rest with conversation.

The wine of the country, red or white, is good, sound, thin wine of very fair quality. The Emperor Augustus preferred the red wine of Tyrol to any other that he could get. The people are all connoisseurs, and a house that serves poor wine is sure to be neglected. It is brought in white glass decanters of standard size, liter, half liter, quarter liter, or eighth liter. A party might club together for a liter, but they would divide the cost. The usual order is, «Ein viertel Roth» or «Ein viertel Weiss.» It is served with a tumbler and a carafe of cold water, which is often mixed with the wine. The charge is eight kreutzers, and the change out of a ten-kreutzer piece (four cents) is given to the *Kellnerinn*, who carries at her belt a well-filled money-bag, and is the familiar but very well-behaved gossip of the establishment, and in social position a little below the Kellnerinn in the *Herrschaft's* room.

I have never seen a bar-room in Tyrol, and I have never seen a man, except at a railway-station, drink standing or drink in haste. All sit at tables and sip their glasses slowly, always reading or talking. If all the «saloons» in New York could be suppressed, and if the customs and the drinking-habits of the Tyrolese towns could be made universal, we should accomplish all that is possible of the reform at which prohibition aims so uselessly, and we should substitute temperance for the present intemperance. There would be no drinking-place which women would not frequent with their men, and without degeneration.

Were it practicable, it would be a blessing to the human race if all strong drink were abolished. It causes infinite injury with no compensating benefit. But its use cannot be prevented; it can only be modified. It can be modified by a controlling public opinion; it cannot be modified, it can only be aggravated, by legal restriction. Dr. Rainsford's bold suggestion that the church should attempt to guide what the law cannot curb, was wise and of good promise. True reform lies in that direction, and the customs of Tyrol justify his counsel.

### WHEELING IN TYROL.

As a country for wheeling, Tyrol has the advantage of such roads as can hardly be found elsewhere, so far as their surface goes. They are so narrow that the lateral flow of water does not make the cross gullies near their sides which are so annoying on our wider roads, such as the main drives in Central Park; they are kept in constant repair, and those which are most traveled are as smooth as a floor. The less frequented ones have a decided wheel-track, which our double machine had to straddle; but a single wheel would meet with no inconvenience from this condition. The grades, except in the higher valleys, are rarely too steep to ride; but in going up-stream they are apt to continue so long as to be fatiguing to a novice. Some of the higher hills are surmounted by serpentine roads, the turns of which are so short as to require caution in going down. Often the bicyclist will find that «the longest way round is the shortest way home»; that is to say, the direct road may have grades or obstacles which it is worth while to avoid by taking a route with more mileage.

The tourist finds every facility ready to his hand for making the most of his opportunity. The railroads carry wheels safely and cheaply, and this is a great help. For instance, in going over the Brenner road from Innsbruck to Botzen, or the reverse, the road up to the pass from either side can be ridden only by an expert, while nothing is finer than the road down in either direction. Our double machine was taken to the summit, two hours by rail, for twenty-eight cents.

For reasons already suggested, we were disposed as far as possible to eschew uphill work, and there were uphill roads where no railway could help us. In preparation for this I had brought from home a towing-line, with which we could call in the aid of an *Einspänner*, getting enough help in this way to make the pedaling easy on any hill up which the Einspänner could go. The two ends of a loose bridle were buckled to the posts of the two wheels, and at the bight there was fastened a very strong india-rubber « health-pull.» From the other end of this a long rope ran to the carriage. This elastic attachment took up any sudden change of tension and worked well in every way. The chief caution needed was to have the change from a walk to a trot made gradually. A sudden start would stretch the rubber to a length of five or six feet, and the recover made back-pedaling necessary for a moment. The trick of it once learned, it was, ignominy apart, very satisfactory, and it enabled us to make many a mile together where otherwise the partner must have been driven while «Mawk-nix» and I worked the machine. This we often did with great satisfaction. His original contempt for it gradually changed, and we had some long rides together, which gave him a very high regard for it. He even came to enjoy a run up-grade in the tow of a team.

It will be understood, of course, as I did not do very much single-wheeling, that my observation must be worth more than my experience, and younger riders will be glad to know just what they will be able to do on the varied roads of this country. Mr. Yandell Henderson of the Sheffield Scientific School at New Haven, a young American who had passed the summer in Germany, was a passenger with us returning on the *Ems*, and he rode all the way from Göttingen to Genoa. He left Murnau, in the edge of the Bavarian highlands south of the Starnberger See, on the morning of September 9. Late on the evening of the 11th he reached Bellano on Lake Como, which is at the Italian foot of the mountains. His road lay through Partenkirchen, Leermos, Nassereit, Imst, Landeck, Nauders, Mals, Traffoi, the Stelvio pass, Bormio, Sondrio, and Colico. The recorded elevations run as follows: 2250, 2152, 3243, 2345, 4900, 3430, 9039, 4018, and 720 feet. But there are many high elevations and considerable depressions between these points. It would have been shorter and much easier to go through the Engadine and over the Maloja pass; the route was selected because it crosses the highest wagon-road in Europe. The whole distance was 211 miles, and the daily runs were 61, 57, and 93 miles. The last day began at Traffoi at an elevation of 4979 feet, with a push of fully two hours to the pass (9039 feet), and a run of eleven hours down to Bellano. There is hardly a three days' route anywhere through these mountains that would be harder than this. The three days from Bellano to Genoa, over the Apennines, were much easier.

### TOURING IN TYROL.

I CANNOT refrain from saying again that Tyrol seems to me to be the most satisfactory country, all things considered, in which one can make a vacation tour with the wheel or otherwise. Switzerland is very different. Its mountains are higher, its scenery is even grander, and it is much better known; but the trail of the traveler is over it all. Its hotels are much more costly, and its exactions as to wardrobe are greater. One's intercourse is more with the sight-seeing and self-showing stranger, and with a native population of less genial character, trained to the financial exploitation of the traveler. Tyrol, out of sight of its few fine caravansaries, is still unspoiled. Its wonderful beauty need not be enlarged upon. The illustrations scattered through this and the final article were selected not because they were exceptional, but because they were well suited to reproduction. Thousands of equal beauty and interest could be taken, and there is hardly a view that would not be worth perpetuating. Castles and churches, in use and in ruins, abound everywhere in the larger valleys; the life and occupations of the people are a constant source of interest, and one soon gets into such touch with it as to forget the occupations of home, which it is so useful to lay aside during a period of recuperation.

The cost and conditions of living are interesting to all travelers, and important to most of them, so that some account of our experiences in these matters may be useful. We did not go to the hotels in Innsbruck save for casual meals. Some of them are said to be very good and not extravagantly costly, but the larger ones are devoid of «local color.» They are substantially the same as the finer houses all over Europe. We did stop for one night at the Victoria in Botzen, and another at the Erzherzog Johann in Meran. Their luxury was not unwelcome for a

DRAWN BY E. POTTHAST.

GOING UP THE HILL. THE COUPLED BICYCLES.

change. At the latter we had a beautiful large room, an excellent table-d'hôte dinner, a bottle of Munich beer, and fruit with our *café complet* in the morning. The bill for two persons was $4.07. This is surely moderate for a famous and most excellent house. At the Victoria we were equally well cared for at the following rate:

| | |
|---|---|
| Room | 2.50 |
| Light | .60 |
| Roast beef | .60 |
| Tête de veau en tortue | .80 |
| Potatoes | .30 |
| Spinach | .30 |
| Kraut | .20 |
| Pfannenkuchen | .60 |
| Wine | .95 |
| Demi-tasse | .20 |
| Cafés complets | 1.20 |
| Fruit | .60 |
| Sandwiches for the road | 1.60 |
| Service | .60 |
| | Gulden, 11.05=$4.24 |

I made an excursion to a high point of outlook across the river, where I had an *Achtel* of very good red wine, a plate of bread, and a carafe of wonderfully good water, all for 12 kreutzers (5½ cents). At an ordinary village Gasthaus our bill, with the usual fees, would be about $2.40; for a single person it would be about $1.60. Good quarters and good food may be had for materially less, and it would not be easy to spend $2.50 per person without extravagance.

At Hochfinstermüntz there is a charming but rather costly little house facing an amazingly fine view, where we arrived for the evening dinner, leaving after breakfast. This was our bill:

| | |
|---|---|
| 2 Soups | .30 |
| 1 Roast capon | 2.30 |
| 2 Salads | .24 |
| 2 Potato | .24 |
| 2 Cheese | .24 |
| 2 Bread and butter | .26 |
| 1 Coffee | .15 |
| ½ Bottle of wine | .36 |
| 1 Bottle of aërated water | .45 |
| 1 Foot-bath | .10 |
| Room | 3.40 |
| Light and service | .30 |
| 2 Cafés complets | 1.00 |
| | Gulden, 9.34=$3.87 |

Our lunch that day at Ried—a very good one, with an abundance of wild strawberries, wine, and aërated water—cost 2.70 gulden, or $1.12.

At Zernetz, a beautiful village in the Engadine, we committed the extravagance of having for luncheon a big dish of brook trout, which, though abundant, are dear. I saw them taken with a net from the dark-flowing tank in which they were stored. The whole luncheon, with wine, cost 3.40 gulden, or $1.41.

At the Aquila Nera in Cortina, a great resort of English and American visitors to the Dolomites, our bill for two averaged about $3.75 per day.

### SCHLOSS WEIHERBURG.

AT Innsbruck I am an old frequenter of Schloss Weiherburg—a *pension*, it is true, but a pension of a unique sort. From 1490 to 1505 it was the favorite hunting-castle of the Emperor Maximilian I. He had taken it in exchange for Schloss Tratzberg, twenty miles farther from the town, but intrinsically more valuable. The main part of the building is as he left it, and all additions have been made in appropriate style. The chapel with the ancient hole in the wall through which the emperor performed his devotions is still unchanged, and there are stories of one or two rather attractive ghosts who still frequent the venerable shades. The main hall, occupying the entire floor of the body of the house, and now used as a dining-room, still sports the canopy that distinguished the imperial dais, and under it hangs a good portrait of the emperor himself. His *Trinkglas*—he must have been a large drinker—still stands on the sideboard. The balcony of this room looks out over the beautiful city and the mountains which border the flat valley on the south. Through the gap of these we look up the valley of the Sill, bringing the floods of the north slope of the Brenner to join the Inn. This view is closed by the Serles Spitze, which is one of the most perfect mountain forms in Tyrol—a vast bare peak of limestone rising beyond the fields and forests of the nearer range. We occupied Maximilian's room under the imperial hall. It reaches across the whole front, and has windows on three sides. The beds are better than they knew how to make four hundred years ago, but the furniture, the curious old colored prints, and the porcelain stove, have not a discordant note. The tone of the room and of the whole house is the tone of the middle ages. It is open to those who seek it, but it is sought only by those who can appreciate it. The same persons come to it year after year, and these seem to count a summer visit to the Weiherburg as an essential part of their lives. Deep down in its foundations there is a summer place of casual entertainment, and its inclosed plateau («schöne Aussicht») is a favorite resort for afternoon strollers from the town. At times service is held in the chapel, and crowds are drawn to it at certain seasons, because a pilgrimage there buys «full absolution» for all one's sins. What with this attraction, the view from the grounds, and the beer in the cellar, crowds of people came to it in St. Ann's week, while we were there. It is twenty minutes' walk or drive from the town, and it stands two hundred feet higher on the side of a mountain that is rich in beautiful walks. The fare is all one could ask, and is much better than is usually to be had in a pension, and the charges are low. Maximilian's room costs, and is worth, a gulden more; but for two persons in other good rooms the rate is 5 gulden a day, and a gulden is 41½ cents. All meals not taken are deducted.

I have hesitated long about making this disclosure, for I do not want to help spoil the Weiherburg for my future use; but I have concluded that those who would appreciate this somewhat remote resort have a right to be told about it. Its approach is *unfahrbar:* it cannot be reached by wheel. In fact, the best way to get a wheel to it would be to carry it over the shoulder. There are good old Tyrolese Gasthäuser in the town, where moderate wheelmen may gladly go, notably the Hotel Post in the broad Maria Theresien strasse, and the Grauen Bär in Universitäts strasse. Into neither does the air of modern Europe penetrate very deeply.

I am not writing a guide-book, and I must refer the reader elsewhere for an account of Innsbruck; but there is something about it which no book can convey, which grows on one with increasing familiarity, and which makes it, for one who knows it as I do, the most charming town in Europe. Cortina and Meran and many other places have their own great attractions; but it seems to me that, taken all in all, Innsbruck is the best center for the Tyrolese tourist.

I have wandered over many parts of this country for many years, and I have never gone to a Gasthaus in Austrian Tyrol where I have not found a clean and good bed, good coffee, good bread, and good wine. In the remote valleys beer is not always to be found, nor very good when found. Sometimes there is no meat, and the chicken is often too young; but eggs and milk are generally to be had. The *Pfannenkuchen* is solid food when other things fail, and such bread and coffee as one finds here make a more substantial meal than those may think who have not had to depend on it. It is only the

DRAWN BY MALCOLM FRASER.

SUNDAY EVENING MUSIC IN A HIGH PASTURE.

mountaineer who is often out of sight of a village, and it is a rare village that has no Gasthaus. This is usually kept by one of the larger farmers of the place, and he is a person of importance. As a rule, he has little contact with his guests. The Kellnerinn represents him below, and the chambermaid rules on the upper floors.

Outside of the principal towns, and generally within them, English is an unknown tongue, so that a little knowledge of German is requisite, but very little will suffice. The people can all read, and a phrase-book will be a good interpreter. Familiarity with the German of Berlin is not enough to enable a stranger to converse with these people. They will understand him, but their rasping, guttural dialect does not immediately find its way to his untrained comprehension. The talk of a group of peasants among themselves is not easily followed by a born German who has not passed some time among them. It is well, in spite of one's inability to talk with them, to consort with the peasants in their own haunts rather than with the rarer visitors in the better quarters. They are seldom so rough as to be unpleasant, and they respond with a very good nature to any advance that does not savor of patronage. The visitor's more interesting memories will run back to these people and their ways rather than to those of the commercial travelers and summer visitors at the house. This is said with special reference to the short stops of a wheelman, who rests for a few hours at a wayside inn, and is off again on his journey. There is a very short limit to the social range of the peasant man or woman. They have not much to say, nor have they much capacity to receive ideas not connected with their daily lives; but they have a great capacity for good feeling and hospitality, and to a tired man this is better. As a rule, they are exceedingly bigoted. Many of the younger men are «getting ideas in their heads»; but the older men, and most of the women of all ages, are of very limited education, and they are intensely devoted to the church and its teachings.

The exhibition of relics, and the presentation of the horrors of the hereafter, which are so much used as

> . . . a hangman's whip
> To haud the wretch in order—

these do not, after all, make the real intercourse between the priesthood and the people. They are perfunctory in performance and superficial in effect. The priest is generally the friend and companion of his people, especially in the country, and he often enters freely into their festivities and lighter pastimes.

Some years ago I was sitting over my coffee in the inn garden at Absam when a wedding-party from Schwatz marched in and occupied a long table in front of me. There were the bride, in a French bonnet, and the bridegroom and the family and friends, including the notary and other dignitaries from their town. Among them was the Franciscan monk who had performed the marriage ceremony. After the usual formal health-drinkings and congratulations they turned to song and mirth. The priest was as gay as the best-man, and more natural in his gaiety. As I left he was taking a vigorous part in the well-known «Musikant aus Wien,» and his

> Ting-a-ling, dass ist Triangel;
> Boum, Boum, Boum, dass ist mein Trommel,

was full of boyish glee. Everything was perfectly decorous, perhaps the more so because he was there; but evidently because of him the whole party had a much better time. The influence of a good priest on the people of a small village is often seen to have its fraternal as well as its pastoral side.

*Geo. E. Waring, Jr.*

# BY CONTRARIES.

THAT day my hurrying heart proclaimed thee near,
  Fate mocked my hope, and thou cam'st not to me.
Now, when my heart is but one siege of fear,
  Let Fate still mock me—then thy face I 'll see!

*Edith M. Thomas.*

# A NEW AMERICAN SCULPTOR.

## GEORGE GREY BARNARD.

«BOY.»

AT the Salon of the Champ de Mars in 1894 a very prominent place was given to a group of works by a sculptor whose name was new to the Paris public. The chief work was a colossal group bearing the title «*Je sens deux hommes en moi*,» taken from one of Victor Hugo's poems, and generally given in English as «I feel two natures struggling within me.» The other sculptures were a single figure, «Boy»; two fragments of a Norwegian stove showing in decorative relief the struggle between man and the elements as described in the Scandinavian sagas; a group called «Brotherly Love»; a portrait bust of an elderly lady modeled from memory; and a portrait bust of a man. The «Two Natures,» «Brotherly Love,» and the bust of a lady were sculptured in marble; the bust of a man was cast in bronze. These works were acclaimed by the jury of the Société Nationale des Beaux-Arts, and the sculptor was elected an associate member. His success was instantaneous with the artists, the critics, who wrote of the work with enthusiasm, and that portion of the public which gives the word for or against a newcomer in the Paris world of art. It was soon learned that the sculptor, George Grey Barnard, was a young American, a pupil of M. Cavelier, and that he had come to Paris a few years before, a novice in the art in which he then showed such masterly ability. He was totally unknown in America, for, although he had been a pupil in the Chicago Art School, he had not gone far enough in his studies to feel like exhibiting, and he had no acquaintance in the art coteries of the Eastern cities. In the autumn of 1896 Mr. Barnard showed this same group of works, with some additional pieces, in New York, at the Logerot in Eighteenth street; and during the three or four weeks that it was open the exhibition was visited by a large number of people. His sculpture was widely discussed in art circles, but did not receive much appreciative comment from the press. The artists, I think, pretty generally admitted his power, and some of them spoke in superlative terms. The young sculptor now stands at the threshold of a career in his own country, and it is to be hoped that his remarkable talent will receive full recognition and encouragement.

It is plain to be seen that Mr. Barnard's ideas and those formulas and principles generally accepted as essential parts of beauty of form and composition do not agree. Like Rodin, he seems to delight in the natural and the accidental, and to be more susceptible to impressions of force than of grace. The «Two Natures» has an uncouth, rugged aspect as a whole. It is soon seen, when the group is looked at in detail, that it is amazingly good in technical treatment, and that characterization in the heads of the two figures has been thoughtfully conceived and truthfully rendered. The great lines of the group cannot be said to build up well, and the effect is not unified. The standing figure presents a long perpendicular line on one side that is not balanced by any other. The under figure in the struggle, half raised up and supported by one arm, is full of movement, as in life. The group gives an impression of unrest that entirely befits the motive of the title, it is true; but we are accustomed, and rightly accustomed, to expect repose or dignity, or some quality that is not disturbing, in sculpture. But this conception or choice of subject may be excused, because the sculptor has made of it a means of showing such masterly treatment of marble with the chisel as few men have shown us. It is pure modeling without tricks, and it is varied, firm, vigorous, and skilful all at once. I should say, in looking at this group and the other pieces in the exhibition, that the sculptor has a hundred ways of expressing texture, color, and effect, and that

«BROTHERLY LOVE.»

«'I FEEL TWO NATURES STRUGGLING WITHIN ME.'»

he must have made a special study of his art in this respect. He has painted a good deal, and has evidently brought the knowledge gained in that way to bear on his modeling without permitting it to lead him into elaboration of detail.

The «Boy» is in every way admirable; it is complete and it is beautiful. The «Brotherly Love» violates some of our traditions, but it is beautiful, too, and possesses a weird, indescribable charm. It is a group intended for a tomb, and shows the nude figures of two young men whose heads are partly buried in the roughly hewn marble which forms the bulk of the monument, and whose hands seem to have forced their way through it and to be searching each other's grasp. I suppose that the marble mass may typify rock or darkness or eternity, or something else tangible or intangible, and that the brothers are groping through it to join each other after death. I did not think to ask the sculptor

A FIGURE FROM «TWO NATURES.»

the meaning, or if it had any. The meaning is unimportant, and it would add nothing to my delight in looking at the work to know what it is beyond what I conjecture. I should like it still better if the hands were a little more manly in character, and I should mention the fact that certain small indentations which appear in several places are not eccentricities of modeling, but are due to errors in «pointing»; for the «Brotherly Love» exhibited in New York is a reduction of the original, which has been put in place in Norway. The fragments of the sculptured decoration of a Norwegian stove show much originality of conception, and the illustrative quality of the work is interesting. Man is shown struggling in the waters with the elements, typified by a great serpent, the Hidhoegur of the sagas. The uncanny types that the artist has represented, and the fine decorative way in which the work is treated, produce a fascinating effect. The handling is very broad; but in parts, as in the heads of man, the modeling is of the subtlest and most sensitive sort. The great figure of Pan, designed when cast in bronze to surmount a fountain, possesses many of the virile qualities of the «Two Natures,» but is even more simply treated. The head of Pan, with one ear raised and the other flopping down, the eyes aslant, and the great mustaches turned up, revealing the grin which distorts the lines of the mouth and the base of the nose, is unlike any other Pan, and extremely individual. The characterization as shown in this head, in the noble type of the good nature, and in the evil, lethargic head of the bad nature, is one of Mr. Barnard's strongest merits outside of his masterly treatment of surfaces with the chisel. The possession of this faculty, joined to his able equipment in technical expression, constitutes a good omen for his future work, in that it will enable him to go far in the realm of subjective creation. Among the works shown in New York by this young sculptor, none was more complete in itself or more enjoyable than the small bust of a Norwegian lady. If it has any defect, it is a lack of precise construction; but it was modeled from memory, and no doubt is more tentative than it would have been if it had been done from life. It is a marvel of treatment of facial texture and color with the chisel. The cheeks are absolutely flesh-like, the forehead suggests the thinly covered skull, and the hair is unmistakably white; yet the modeling is superlatively simple.

It is interesting to hear of the boyhood and early training of this young artist, and we find some traits of character and some facts in his occupations that have had their influence on his present development. Barnard is the son of a Presbyterian clergyman, and was born at Bellefonte; Pennsylvania, May 24, 1863. While a small boy he went to school in Bellefonte; but his father accepted a call to Chicago later on, and young Barnard met there an old sea-captain who had a fine collection of stuffed birds, shells, specimens of stone and mineral, and other natural objects. He used to offer the boy prizes of shells if he would learn and remember the Latin names of the specimens, and led him to study conchology in a systematic way. He promised his pupil a copy of Dana's «Manual of Geology» as a grand prize; and when the lad had obtained this he spent two years reading it and hunting specimens in the suburbs of Chicago. He was devoted to geology until he was ten years of age, but then began to feel that the science was too cold and unsympathetic for his taste, and, the family removing to Iowa, he experimented in taxidermy. He went to school in Iowa for three years, studying birds and nature generally meanwhile, and formed a collection of stuffed specimens, twelve hundred in number, all mounted by himself, and including all kinds of birds and animals, from a humming-bird to big deer. At thirteen he began to engrave, and made two books of plates. Then he took to modeling birds and beasts in clay. At sixteen he made a bust of his little sister, which excited the praise of the neighbors; and leaving school, he went to work to learn engraving, for it was thought that he should have a regular trade to enable him to earn his livelihood. His first master was a man who had been engraving thirty-five years, but his pupil soon surpassed him in his work. Afterward he had some lessons from the best engraver in Chicago, and did decorative designs. In 1881, when he was eighteen, he entered the Chicago Art School, where he drew from casts, but did not model. Later on he received orders for two busts, and started for Paris on the proceeds in November, 1883. He worked three years and a half in Cavelier's atelier, and then set up a studio at Vaugirard, near the Porte de Versailles. Here he worked unremittingly, and modeled his «Boy» in clay. It was seen by some of his artist friends, who praised it highly, and he received an order to execute it in marble. After his success at the Champ de Mars in 1894, with the recollection of the cheers of the jury and of the honor of several receptions given for him by great people in Paris, he came back to America, and settled himself in a studio in the upper part of the city of New York.

There is a sufficiently wide range of subject and treatment in the group of works shown by Mr. Barnard to admit of a summing up of his qualities as a sculptor. Strength and breadth are evidently his. In interpreting his perception of what is before him in nature his hand is wonderfully skilled. He is an analyst in thought and a synthesist in execution. His work shows a decided psychological bent. He apparently cares more for force and virility than for so-called beauty. This preference has led him, in the «Two Natures,» to disregard certain things that seem to me essential in the making of a great work of art, or has prevented him from feeling the necessity of their presence. It might have been possible to give all the force and power that he has obtained in the «Two Natures,» and at the same time to bring the group within lines of composition that would have produced an effect more unified and beautiful. I mean beautiful in its best sense, as relating to the ensemble, not that I could wish to see the figures themselves modified by softening or refining them in any way whatever. Delicacy and refinement are attributes much more commonly met with in the works of artists of Anglo-Saxon origin than true virility. Mr. Barnard's sculpture is full of the healthful, living force of nature, and the desire to see it include other things may be repressed for the moment, for the splendid vigor and pure artistic power of his work entitle it to be received with enthusiasm.

*William A. Coffin.*

## EVEN AS THE WAVE.

A STORM at sea; though here, undimmed, the sun
In silver dazzles from bright-burnished dunes,
While, through the wooded uplands faintly spun,
Low winds bring even to the salt lagoons
Memories of goldenrod and yellowed leaves.
Yet, white with wrath, the heavy-handed surf
Lashes the beach, not heeding how it grieves
The tender autumn day. Torn kelp and scurf
Of thick-churned spume strew all the curving marge
Where, blind with strife, the sand and breaker close.

Strong from mid-ocean, rolling to the charge
A billow gathers. Darker, greener grows
Its steepening slope, while fast the rearing crest
Flickers to froth and foam. By sudden wind
Whirled high in air, a misty woven vest,
Smit with the sun's seven colors, streams behind.
Broad-based beneath, on comes the ponderous sheet,
Shoaling from green to emerald; arching o'er—
Crash! The great cataract falls. A burst of sleet
Leaps with a boom, and, seething toward the shore,
Shimmers the wide white field of hissing foam.
Broadening and spending, crossed with marbly bands
Of fading surge, its whispers softer come,
Till but a lapping ripple lips the sands
Before my feet.

Then through my heart there stirred
A dream of brave resolve, of strenuous deeds
And heart-sick failure. Turning thence, I heard
A sad-tongued sea-bird mourn among the reeds.

*George De Clyver Curtis.*

# THE DAYS OF JEANNE D'ARC.

BY MARY HARTWELL CATHERWOOD,

Author of «The Romance of Dollard,» «The White Islander,» etc.

I.

ALL France was lighted by an early rising moon, and the village of Bury-la-Côte, seated on a high ridge, seemed to glitter just beneath the sky. There was frost on the square, low church tower, on tight-shut windows, and on the manure-heaps carefully raked into place beside the doors, and held by stone barriers to mellow for the spring fields.

It was a cold night even for January. Durand Laxart decided, as he unchained his horse, to let the cart stand outside the archway, and lead the poor beast directly into its snug stable in the end of the house.

He came out again into the moonlight and walked around the muck-barrier to his own door. He was proud of his new house. It had an ogival portal, and above the little window was an ornament in stone shaped like a clover-leaf. But no light shone through this window, for a long, dark passage led to the inner room, where his wife and new-born child lay asleep in their cupboard bed. Durand took off his wooden shoes, and carrying them in his hand, tiptoed over the hard, white earthen floor. The woman's brown peasant face, strangely bleached and refined by motherhood, awed him by its contrast with the coarse wool of her bed. The bed doors stood wide open, their clean panels shining in the firelight. A whole bundle of fagots blazed in the chimney. The white stone mantel, shaped somewhat like a penthouse, and the scoured hearth flags, brightened the dark room, for there was only one window, looking toward the valley of the Meuse.

He scented his supper in an iron pot on a tripod before the fire. The table stood near the hearth, holding a large knife with which to cut his bread, a wooden drinking-cup, and a flask of red wine; for in this valley of the Meuse contending armies had not trampled down the vines.

The woman and the baby continued to sleep. Durand slipped on his wooden shoes again, and opened a back door into his garden. There was a steep flight of stone steps, down which he thumped toward a tile-roofed oven. The garden sloped downward, and though it had the desolation of winter upon it, his eye selected the very spot where he would soon begin to dig and plant. Pausing, with his wooden shoes wide apart on the slippery descent, he gazed down the south-stretching valley, the loveliest valley of the Vosges, streaked with ribbons of stubble left by the scanty crops. Plowing and sowing had been irregular work since the English began to trouble France. The soil had a whiteness not given to it by winter rime; but in the next villages, hid from him by a shoulder of the hill,—Goussaincourt and Greux and Domremy,—there were black gaps made by raiding Burgundians. The Meuse, in summer almost hid among its marshy islands, now spread from bank to bank, showing a line of ice along its edges. The course of the Meuse was called the march of Lorraine and Champagne, and had long been a place of contention between kings of France and dukes of Burgundy, lying as it did between the two portions of Burgundy. The people of this march had no feudal lord between them and the king; they were vassals to the King of France alone. This bred a serious and stubborn loyalty, which kept them bound to their sovereign, though isolated from him. For in that year of grace 1429 the kingdom of France had receded before the invading English until its northern line lay far below the ancient capital of Paris, and included only the provinces of Dauphiné, Languedoc, Bourbonnais, l'Auvergne, Berri, Poitou, Saintange, Touraine, and Orléans. And some of these were crumbling before the incoming tide. All the richest provinces and nearly all the seaports were held by the English. To go into France from the march of Lorraine at that day meant to traverse a wide country overrun by aliens.

The far ridge beyond the Meuse seemed to draw near in moonlight. All at once there was a sweet clamor of bells drifting from Greux and Domremy, and the church of Bury-la-Côte joined in, chiming the angelus. The man pulled at his cap with a gesture of reverence, and slouched into an attitude of devotion. He felt constrained to pray, for at the sound of the bells his wife's cousin, Jeanne d'Arc, came out of the oven-shed with a huge ring of bread in her hands. She slipped the ring upon her arm and joined her palms, bending her forehead to them. While the angelus rang no man could speak a word to little Jehannette. Though she was full of life, Durand sometimes thought her unnaturally religious for so young a creature. But it made her very handy when one had sickness in the house. He was better pleased to have her take care of his wife than to have his own loud-voiced mother continually about.

As the bells ceased, a faint wailing in the house called them. Jeanne put her ring of bread on the table, and took up the baby, while the mother, roused from sleep, answered her husband with yawning responses:

«It is nothing but drowsiness that keeps me abed. I shall be up at my spinning by to-morrow.»

«Not to-morrow, Aveline. Isabel Romée says we may keep Jehannette two weeks more. Let her spin for thee. She can spin and sew as well as any maid of her age in the Meuse valley.»

«But if I am able to spin, why should n't I? A man never thinks any woman can get tired of waiting on him. Jehannette may like to stir from the house while she stays.» Aveline drew her hand down his winter-reddened cheek.

«Lie still yet to-night,» he insisted; so she dozed again, while he cut his black bread and emptied the pot into his platter. Then he sat down comfortably to his supper. The earthen floor, as hard as rock, had been brushed speckless with a broom of soft river-grasses. Small joists, crossed by large beams overhead, so low that they almost touched his hair when he stood up, were rich brown in the firelight. There was no candle lighted. Threads of flame wove themselves among the fagot sticks and rushed up the chimney-back. Jeanne sat with the child's swaddled feet toward the blaze, and after blinking at the joists it sunk into the stupid content of its kind. Her face was so young that this maternal care was like the attitude of a child nursing its painted doll.

Durand poured out his wine, and plunged his fingers into his dish. He glanced at the girl, but her eyes were on the fire, and suddenly he noticed under them the hollows made by weeping. Her face was oval in shape, and the outline of the cheek never changed, but firelight showed the pallor of dejection. The laced bodice of her red peasant dress did not cover the top of her neck; it was white and childlike compared with the neck of her cousin in the bed. Her hair was twisted into a long knot, but it flew out in halos. The hollow between lower lip and chin was deeply indented, and her chin was pointed rather than round.

«What ails thee, Jehannette?» inquired Durand, with quick sympathy and some dread that she had grown tired of waiting on him.

Jeanne visibly repressed herself. Instead of answering she inquired of him:

«Did you see my father in Domremy to-day?»

«I saw him; he is well.»

«And my mother?»

«Yes; she is well.»

«And Pierrelo?»

«Yes; he sent a kiss for each cheek.»

«Mengette and Jacquemine, you also saw them?»

«I saw them all, and they all asked when you were coming home; but Isabel hath promised you to us a little longer. It is not so far from Domremy to Bury-la-Côte,» argued Durand; «not two leagues, though they be slow leagues through stiff clay across the prairie. Your footpath along the hills is quicker.»

«But it is farther to Vaucouleurs,» said Jeanne; «I must go to Vaucouleurs to-morrow.»

«And what would you do at Vaucouleurs?» Durand's eye twinkled. «Would you go to take back what you said at Toul?»

Jeanne's hazel eyes reflected his image with simple candor.

«No; I will never take back what I said at Toul.»

«But Bertrand de Poulengy is a fine young fellow. I have heard if we knew more about him it would turn out he was born in a château.»

«He should have learned to speak the truth there. He did a wicked thing to take a public oath I had given him my word. I had to go to Toul to deny it before the magistrate. It was very cruel of Bertrand de Poulengy.»

«He wanted thee,» chuckled Durand. Nothing amuses a man so much as another man's discomfiture in courtship. «And thy father and mother they were willing.»

«But I cannot cumber myself with marriage,» said Jeanne. Her repressed weeping broke out. «Compère[1] Durand, I must go into France.»

The man paused in his eating, holding the meat between his jaws. He had heard of this matter before; but it had not pierced his

[1] Godfather, friend, or crony.

marrow with that sweetness of voice and that cry of necessity. «I must go into France!» Jeanne's voice was spoken about in the valley. When she called to one at a distance, the bell notes expanded, filling the air; but in talk she spoke low. The woman in the cupboard bed was aware only of the man's hoarser note.

«Jehannette, thy father has told me he would drown thee with his own hands rather than have thee go away with men-at-arms.»

Jeanne put out one palm to stop him. The firelight showed her long fingers and compact wrist. Tears rushed down her face.

«My father—my dear father! I would rather be in the fields with him, or by my mother's side spinning, than anywhere in France. But I can no longer help it. For three years I have been commanded, and now I must go.»

«Who commanded thee?» asked her relative, holding a black bit of liver in his fingers.

«Attend,» said Jeanne, in the manner of the peasants of Domremy. Her childish face stiffened with awe. «I was about thirteen when I had a voice from God to help me rule myself. The first time I heard it I was very much afraid. It was in my father's garden at noon in the summer. I had fasted the day before. The voice came from the right hand of the church, and there was a great light with it. Afterward, if I was in a wood I heard the voice coming to me. When I had heard it three times I knew it was the voice of an angel. It has always kept me well, and I understand perfectly what it says.»

«What does it say?» whispered the man. He obeyed habit, and put the bite into his mouth, but held it there with the other meat. Old Choux in Domremy, Jeanne's nearest neighbor, who was so old that people had forgotten his age, was claiming to have a voice also.

«It says,»—she lifted both hands and threw them out before her,—«‹Daughter of God, go, go! I will be thine aid.›»

The baby slept in its bands on her lap. The fagots showed that her face was white. Durand ground his food and swallowed it with a gulp; he leaned his elbows on the table.

«Pucelle,[1] did you see anything in the light?»

Jeanne's voice became a thread of sound, one chord, on which she vibrated to him:

«I saw St. Michael; I saw St. Catherine and St. Margaret.»

«But how did you know it was St. Michael, or St. Catherine and St. Margaret?»

«At first I did not know, but St. Michael told me; he said: ‹Go into France; St. Catherine and St. Margaret will aid thee.› I said on my knees: ‹How can I go? I know nothing of arms.› He answered: ‹Daughter of God, go, go! I will be thine aid.›»

Though Durand Laxart had never seen visions, and his wife Aveline had never seen visions or heard voices, he felt a surging of the blood which seemed to clear his brain for new impressions. Jeanne saw that he believed in her. The strained whiteness of her face became a softer pallor, and she wiped her eyes.

«Compère, have you not always heard that a woman would ruin France, and a maid from the march of Lorraine would rise up and save it?»

Durand nodded his head. He had heard this prophecy all his life, and it had already become a common saying that Isabel of Bavaria, the queen, was that woman.

«The Queen of France is that woman,» said Jeanne; «she has denied her own son, and sold us all to the English. Compère, myself—I am that maid from the march of Lorraine. I was born for this purpose. You must take me to Vaucouleurs, to Robert de Baudricourt, and ask him to send me into France. I have to raise the siege of Orléans and take the Dauphin Charles to be crowned at Rheims.»

Durand sat staring at her without speaking. He poured out a cupful of the thin, sour wine, and drank it down.

She had to raise the siege of Orléans, and take the Dauphin Charles to be crowned at Rheims!

It was high time the dauphin was crowned at Rheims, that ancient city of coronation, where nearly every king of France since Clovis had been consecrated. No subject accepted a king until he had been crowned at Rheims. The loyal people of Poitiers had put a crown upon Charles's head, but his enemies laughed at him, and called him the little King of Bourges. And it was high time some power raised the siege of Orléans—Orléans, the heart of France, the key to the southern provinces, the last stronghold of the loyal party.

News traveled slowly, but in those days political facts were stamped on a peasant's mind by the horse-hoofs of raiders. The Duke of Orléans was a prisoner in England. His people, in their extremity, had appealed to his enemy and kinsman, the Duke of Burgundy, to stand betwixt them and the English, and make their territory neutral. The Duke of Burgundy attempted to do this, but his distrustful allies permitted him to protect no French territory except his own. It was

[1] Maid.

hard to be the greatest peer of France, the one whose right it was to place the king's crown on his head and do him first homage, and yet to be constrained by personal revenge to join hands with hereditary foes and invaders. The Duke of Burgundy was now sulking in his own domains, and the English intrenchments were closing around Orléans.

«Compère,» continued Jeanne, «when I found my family would never consent, I started by myself one day to go into France; but when I had gone some leagues I knew it was no use. I must be sent by the Captain of Vaucouleurs; St. Catherine and St. Margaret have told me what to do.»

«Do you ever see their faces?» inquired Durand, sinking his voice.

«I see their faces,» spoke Jeanne; «I see them always in the same form. I do not know if there is anything in the shape of arms or other members figured. They are crowned with beautiful crowns, very rich and very precious. Of their raiment I cannot speak. I know them by the sound of their voices. They are sweet and humble. They speak very well and in beautiful language, and I understand them perfectly.»

It was an age in which supernatural things were heard of on every side: but Durand had a well-compacted body, and lived near the soil; he had never troubled himself about spiritual mysteries. This new attitude of his mind, when he noticed it, astonished him. He did not know why he believed in Jeanne; he felt as if he were in church, and obliged to do what he was told to do. The baby slept on her lap, with the rapid breathing of infancy. He looked at his little child with an emotional puckering of his face, and at the larger child holding it. His wife had played with Jeanne d'Arc about the spring behind Bermont chapel. His wife was now a young matron; but this other girl, of unusual physical growth, had yet an innocence like that of a babe. St. Michael, the terrible archangel of battles; St. Catherine, the martyr of Egypt; and St. Margaret, the Greek virgin, might have shown themselves to such a being.

«But if I take thee to Messire de Baudricourt, Jehannette,» Durand objected, «what will Jacques d'Arc and Isabel Romée say to me?»

«They will forgive you.»

«They will say I have made them a poor return for the nursing of my wife and child,» he continued.

«If you cannot take me, compère, I must set out by myself on foot to-morrow,» she responded.

«No; that will never do. I must go along.»

Durand sat frowning over his folded arms while he deliberated. He glanced toward the cupboard bed, and leaned forward to speak between nearly closed lips.

«Attend, Jehannette. When my mother comes in to-morrow to help Aveline with the child, we will say nothing about Vaucouleurs. They might send word to Jacques and Isabel. I will say I go again to Domremy. When you get into the cart they will think you are going home.»

Jeanne heard this proposed deceit without any answering smile of caution.

«I must go, no matter who tries to prevent me. They will forgive you, compère, and they will forgive me when they understand that I was obliged to go.»

«The horse and the cart and I, we will have to stay in Vaucouleurs overnight. Attend, Jehannette,» continued Durand, twitching the lid of one of his pleasant eyes. «I will say that I may have to go even as far as Neufchâteau to-morrow. It is a bad time of the year to travel, and I cannot get back the same night.»

As he laid plans to hoodwink his family, Durand's big finger traced a map on the table, with the villages in their actual position, leaving out the intermediate ones which had nothing to do with the matter: Vaucouleurs first, in the north; then Bury-la-Côte; Domremy farther down the valley of the Meuse; and farthest south of all, Neufchâteau. The cunning expression on the honest man's face made Jeanne laugh. The tears were scarcely dry on her cheeks, but her whole figure was elastic with relief.

«We must tell the truth, compère; I think Aveline and your mother ought to know that we go to Vaucouleurs.»

Durand regarded her attentively, and nodded his head. «Eh, well; if you think it best, I will tell Aveline and my mother. But the next thing to be considered is, where will you stay at night in Vaucouleurs?»

«I have thought about the wife of Henri Royer the wheelwright,» answered Jeanne. «She was my mother's friend when they were both pucelles in Vauthon.»

«Her house will be the place for you. Have you ever seen her?»

«Only once, when she came to Domremy in a new cart, before men-at-arms overran the country. It was before our Catherine died. Aveline and I were not old enough to tend the sheep. She gave us all a good welcome to her house.»

«It will do,» said Durand, with satisfaction;

«and now go to bed, Jehannette, for we must get up early to make this journey.»

Drawing the child's clumsy cradle to its place beside the cupboard bed, Jeanne tucked the little bundle in, and put away the remains of Durand's supper on the shelves of a closet beside the chimney. She then washed the ware which he had used, and set the cup back on the clean table beside the unfinished bottle.

To reach her bed she was obliged to go out of the back door into the garden and enter another room. She went without any light except the abundant splendor of the moon. It was to a fireless best chamber, as chill as the walls of a tomb; but her face laughed in the closing doorway as she bade her kinsman and helper good night.

«Good night, Jehannette,» answered Durand, and he poured out another cup of the thin wine, and leaned over the dying fagots. «Oh, yes; I will tell Aveline and my mother,» he said to himself, rubbing his knee, and grinning; «but I will tell them what I please, and it will not be that I go in the direction of Vaucouleurs. A man ought to have at least one lie on his conscience when he goes to confession. I have recently been too good myself.»

It was not the lie which troubled him most all next day.

Vaucouleurs,—valley of colors,—built on a hillside above the Meuse, was a walled town, one of the faithful little citadels holding out for the Dauphin Charles. The river-meadows below are wide, and clouds seem always to be leaning on those Vosges hills, which roll in undulating uplands against the sky. The early blue twilight of winter had already begun to blur leafless thickets on the islands and those ribbons and squares of stubble which showed where the valley crops had been and the plowman had not, when Durand Laxart drove his horse between the southern gate-towers. Flakes of stiffened mud fell from the cart-wheels on the small paving-stones of the principal street; dirty water stood chilled in the stone gutters. Vaucouleurs, like other towns, threw its worst out of the front door, and saved its best for the garden at the back. Crooked and winding streets, so narrow that a cart filled them from wall to wall, ascended and descended in every direction. The château of the Captain of Vaucouleurs was up the height, and its battlements and square towers could be seen far down the valley. Jeanne had watched it while horse and cart plodded over stretches of the white mire into which those stony hills dissolve their dust. She still looked upward, half muffling her face in her woolen wrappings, as Durand stopped in an open square and searched for Royer's house.

«They told us at the gate that it faced north—a high, narrow house with a yellow door. There it is,» said he, indicating a door with his whip. He turned the horse's head.

«But I must go first to Messire Robert de Baudricourt,» said Jeanne.

«Not without a bite to eat or a fagot to warm by?»

«I am too warm, compère; I am full of blood. And I cannot eat until Messire de Baudricourt has heard what I have to tell him.»

«Eh, well,» grumbled Durand; «but consider the horse. I say nothing; fasting is good for my soul: but the poor beast has no soul to be benefited, and he needs stable and provender.»

«Then, compère, let me stand here while you stable the horse and take a message to Henri Royer's wife. I cannot speak to any one before I have spoken to Messire de Baudricourt.»

Durand would have descended from the cart, but Jeanne let herself lightly down by the iron step. Then he rattled across the square, and she stood waiting.

Some children in wooden shoes made a great noise in the street as they ran past with a dog. They looked at her, but felt too abashed to say good day to a stranger who did not appear to see them. Few women looked out of the closed windows. Candles began to show.

Robert de Baudricourt, the Captain of Vaucouleurs, was sitting at his supper when a soldier came in and made salutation. Enjoyment of his fire and cheerful table never relaxed this portly captain of an isolated and dangerous post. The Burgundians were more to be dreaded than the English in his part of the kingdom, but matters were growing so bad that everything was to be dreaded.

«News, my man?» he inquired, with an alert turn of the head.

«There are two peasants at the gate, messire the captain. The woman says she has an urgent message for you.»

«Troopers are probably out over the valley again. Bring her in and let us hear what she has to say.»

He went on hastily with his supper, for arming and saddling might be the very next business. At the sound of wooden shoes he looked up, and saw a bareheaded peasant, abashed and reluctant, leading into the room a young maid in a bodice and petticoat of the coarse cloth spun and woven in the valley. Her bodice was laced up toward her neck. Baudricourt noticed that her face was white even to the lips. He expected to hear of a house sacked and a family slaughtered.

«Good evening to both,» said the captain; «I hope you bring no evil news.»

«No, messire the captain,» spoke Jeanne; «I bring you good news. St. Michael and St. Catherine and St. Margaret have sent me to you.»

Baudricourt wheeled around in his chair. In all his military experience he had never had any dealings with saints. It was his opinion that the beneficent powers, if any existed, had washed their hands of France. There was not a more distressed kingdom on the face of the earth. The very princes of the blood had trampled it in their quarrels. For years a lunatic king and a dissolute queen had represented its government. And now that Charles VI was dead, his heir the dauphin was disinherited by the treaty of Troyes, which bound the queen and the Duke of Burgundy to the party of young Henry of England. Paris was the capital of invaders. The whole realm was desolated by long-continued war. And now Orléans was about to fall into the hands of the enemy.

«Who are you?» inquired Baudricourt, bending his eyebrows at Jeanne. Robert de Baudricourt never seemed a clean-shaven man; he bristled fresh from his toilet.

«I am the maid sent from God.»

«What 's your name?»

«Jeanne d'Arc; but in my country they called me Jehannette.»

«What do you want?»

«I want you, messire, to send me to the Dauphin Charles. I have to raise the siege of Orléans, and take him to be crowned at Rheims.»

«Stuff and nonsense!» roared Baudricourt. «Why do you come to me with such a tale as this? You fellow with her, who are you?»

«I am her cousin, messire the captain.»

«Her relative, are you? Has she no father and mother?»

«Yes, messire the captain.»

«Then take her home to them, and tell them to give her a good whipping. St. Michael and St. Catherine and St. Margaret!» repeated Baudricourt, cutting his bread with a blow. «Go home and spin and mind your sheep, and don't come to me with your archangels and saints and coronations! Tell her father and mother to give her a good whipping!»

II.

The winter air of the courtyard did not cool Durand's burning chagrin at having taken a step which brought a young pucelle to such treatment. The peasants of the Meuse valley had never learned to cringe to a feudal lord, but Robert de Baudricourt represented the king among them. Durand took Jeanne by the elbow to lead her away. Her father's resentment, which had followed him all day, now approached and hung over him. Domremy and Vaucouleurs were almost the extreme boundaries of his world. He was angry; yet nothing kills faith in the unseen like ridicule.

Durand could see the quaking of Jeanne's figure, and hear the indrawing of her breath, as she wept in her wrappings. Twilight lingered here when darkness lay in the lap of the valley. The soldier who had led them into the château could also see her going with bowed head from Baudricourt's abuse. He looked after her with a puzzled smile, but Durand's compassion was like a woman's.

«Come home to Royer's house, pucelle; they are ready to give thee good treatment there. I blame myself for this. Such a thing shall never happen to thee again.»

While he talked at her side, Jeanne turned to the chapel which stood facing Baudricourt's quarters. Durand followed her, his shoes clumping on the flags. He was afraid Baudricourt would send some curt envoy after the maid and hale her out, and was glad that the open door showed little except a dusky interior. But when Jeanne saw there was no light, she turned and followed some steps which led down into a crypt. Durand felt along the wall as he clumsily kept on her track, and descended to a corridor which ended beside an arched door. The crypt chapel had floor and vaulted ceiling of white stone, and he could distinguish small carved faces set like rosettes around the supporting pillars. Walls swam in dimness, but there was a cup of crimson light on the altar between the statues. Jeanne was kneeling before it. That was always her way. Aveline had told him that Jeanne used to leave her playmates dancing by Bermont spring, or listening to some delicious tale like «The Red Children,»—as red as melted iron,—and slip up to Bermont chapel to pray. «And what was there in Bermont chapel?» said Aveline. «Nothing but a painted wooden image of the Virgin and Child, the Child holding a bird in his hand.»

Durand stood by the door and waited until

his charge was ready to rise up and come away. As for himself, he felt more like swearing than praying.

They were both silent as they went down hill; but when they reached the square before Royer's house he suggested:

«We must get up early in the morning to start to Bury-la-Côte.»

«Yes, you go back, compère; Aveline expects you; but I have to stay here until Robert de Baudricourt sends me into France.»

«He will never do it, Jehannette.»

«Yes, he will do it; I must go to him until he does do it.»

«You shall not stay here among strangers, to be railed at by the Captain of Vaucouleurs; that I will not myself allow.»

«Compère, I have to go into France. Robert de Baudricourt will be obliged to send me. St. Catherine and St. Margaret have told me that.»

«Jehannette, come home; I do not know how to face Jacques and Isabel.»

«You must let me be, compère; I cannot turn back.»

Merely walking in her company seemed to infect him again with her visions; every step took him farther from Baudricourt's contempt.

«Royer's wife has a good welcome ready for you; but Jacques d'Arc shall never say I brought his maid here, and left her to shift for herself. I am obliged to go home, but I will come back again in a week.

«Tell my father,» said Jeanne, quickly, «it will be no use to follow me.»

«I shall keep myself out of the way of Jacques d'Arc till this business is settled.»

«But if Aveline sends him word he will surely follow me.»

«I do not think she will send him word, Jehannette. My opinion is,» added Durand, under his breath, «she has no word to send.»

In a week Durand Laxart came back to Vaucouleurs, and found Jeanne spinning by the side of Royer's wife. The shadows were heavier under her eyes, and the oval of her face had grown more wan.

«She is the best pucelle I ever saw,» declared her guardian to Durand, after taking him into another room and setting food before him. «All day she is either spinning with me or on her knees in the chapel.»

«Has she been to messire the captain again?»

«My faith, yes! And I never thought to stand by and hear such railing as he put upon her. But to-day he came down here with the priest and a censer, and they exorcised her for an evil spirit. *Par exemp'!*» cried Royer's wife; «did you ever hear of such a thing as exorcising a child like that for an evil spirit!»

«She is no more under possession than is my baptized infant,» said Durand, with strong disapproval.

«And that messire the curé saw when he bade her approach. She fell on her knees, and went so across the stone floor, and she laughed in their faces, the dear child, at their foolishness.»

«Have you heard whether messire the captain will send her into France?»

«He says he will not, and he will have her punished if she comes up to the château to trouble him again. But my husband has told me a messenger went out several days ago to the dauphin at Chinon, giving information about her, and asking what shall be done with her.»

Durand felt his heart sink, for in every Christian realm the fate of accused sorcerers was the stake.

He did not talk much with Jeanne, but sat and looked at her silently. The week had changed her. She noticed her surroundings less. She was waiting with all her body and spirit. Durand felt hurt that she did not inquire about the baby; all the children in Domremy and Bury-la-Côte used to hang about her petticoat, she took such pleasure in them.

Next morning he walked the streets of Vaucouleurs instead of going to chat in Royer's shop. Vaucouleurs was his great capital. He never expected to see anything finer. The gray-tiled roofs were more venerable to him here than the same kind of roofs in Bury-la-Côte. There was a white glare from the white soil which smote on the eyes even when the sun did not shine out. Beyond the western wall he could see the Meuse in its meadows, and then the long ridge beyond, bearing up sear vineyards which in a month would begin to quicken with vines.

On the terrace of street where Durand clumped aimlessly along some public theme fermented. The air had a mild and springlike touch, and people came out of their houses. He saw through an open window half a dozen or more maids sitting close together with their little wheels, and caught the names St. Catherine and St. Margaret.

He saw two women with children in their arms meet on a corner, and nod white caps, as one of them pointed toward Royer's house.

The street was choked with huge wagons woven of unpeeled boughs into the shape of enormous baskets, oblong and rounded, heaped with charred sticks. Three horses with bells on their high yokes were hitched in a line before each load. The charcoal-burners were bringing in the product of their labor, thankful to be within closed gates, safe from wanton despoiling. They marched bare-headed beside their horses, cracking their whips, each with a black smock over his woolens descending almost to his wooden shoes. The first man encountered a group in mid-street that the touch of a horse's nose did not scatter. He shouted warning, but the foremost horse was willing to halt, and yoke after yoke ceased swaying and filling the narrow track with melody. The drivers all came up open-mouthed when they had rested a few minutes; for the talk was about raising the siege of Orléans, and taking the dauphin to be crowned at Rheims, and a maid who wanted to be sent into France.

« She says she must go,» declared a mercer, who had his shears hanging to his neck by a cord. He also was smocked for his labor behind the counter. « I never heard anything so strange as a young pucelle wanting to leave her family to go where there is so much bloodshed.»

« There will be more bloodshed, and one will not have to go far to see it,» said a man who carried a quill behind his ear, and wore instead of the blouse or smock a short, close garment called a hardy-coat, buttoned its entire length in front. « If the dauphin could get soldiers from Scotland, what port is there open to land them in?» He moved his large, light eyes from face to face.

« What pucelle wants to leave her family and go into France?» inquired one of the charcoal-burners.

« It is a young pucelle from Domremy,» answered a baker, pushing his white cap awry with the back of his hand. « The women in Vaucouleurs say there is nothing to be spoken against her. She pays no attention to anything but her prayers and her spinning. She wants Messire de Baudricourt to send her to the dauphin.»

« Is there not an old saying,» asked the charcoal-burner, « that a maid from the march of Lorraine is to save France?»

The men all turned as if surprised by an echo. The old saying had been many times repeated that week in Vaucouleurs. The man in the hardy-coat took the quill from behind his ear, and poised it as if about to write his words on the faces of the others. He was a distinguished person: he could both read and write. Writing legal papers was his business; and though among nobles his calling was despised, it gave him some authority in a remote place like Vaucouleurs. « I believe she is the maid. It will be as little as the town of Vaucouleurs can do to fit her out for the journey.»

« *En nom Dé!* » exclaimed a smith, « if the saints send her into France, let her go! Here is the fist that will shoe her horse free of charge.»

« It is Messire de Baudricourt who will decide that,» said the mercer; « but I have good gray Flemish cloth on my shelves.»

« There she goes to the chapel crypt again to pray,» said the baker. Dough stuck to the nail of his pointing finger. « They let her in at the fortress gate for that. She goes three times every day.»

They all stood silent, watching Jeanne ascend a flight of stone stairs to the winding track by which the château was reached. Her shrinking, muffled figure had already taken on for them a kind of religious sanctity.

As she turned the wall she came face to face with a middle-aged knight. He wore no armor except a heart-shaped cuirass or breast-plate buckled with leather straps over the front of his close-fitting habit; a sword hung from his belt. Jeanne held her woolen covering by one hand under her chin; not a bit of her hair showed. The face, with its clear eyebrows and delicate, round-lipped mouth, was so sweet and determined that if he had not taken up its cause before he must have been moved to do so now.

« Pardon, pucelle,» said the knight. He put his hand on his cap. « I am Jean de Metz, seignior of Novelopont, one of Captain de Baudricourt's officers. I know why you are here, and I would willingly help you.»

« Messire, everybody in Vaucouleurs knows why I am here. I am waiting for Robert de Baudricourt to send me into France. I must reach the dauphin before Easter, if I wear off my legs to my knees.»

Her low voice stirred De Metz like a call to arms. He stood looking at her with his cap off. His hair, betwixt black and gray in color, was cut straight around below his ears, and being of a strong growth, flared outward. The dazzling light of the uplands printed benevolent wrinkles about his eyes. His chin stood forward even when he lowered it toward his breast, and it gave force to his smile and words.

« Pucelle, I will, on my own venture, take you to the dauphin. Messire the captain will not forbid that.»

« Messire de Metz, I thank you for your good will; but I must be sent from the governor of my own country. Bitterly have I learned that. My counsel have bid me to wait.»

«And who are your counsel?»

«St. Michael and St. Catherine and St. Margaret.»

«Do you hear their actual voices, pucelle?»

«Yes, many, many times. But it is when the church bells ring that they speak to me clearest.»

«But how can you hear voices through a clamor of bells?»

The reticence of one whose dearest secret is touched appeared in Jeanne's face. Her eyes pitied him for not understanding.

«The voices are clearest then,» she repeated. «They often come among Christians who do not hear or see them.»

De Metz had never served in the dissolute rabble of Southern soldiers and mercenaries. He thought it was his own softness which melted before her. Yet he realized all the enormous force carried by a person with one idea.

«When you go to the dauphin,» he offered, «I will be your knight, and commander of your party.»

«Messire knight, you have given me comfort; but I have no comfort to send to Robert de Baudricourt. Tell him that my counsel has told me this day the French have suffered a defeat near Orléans, and it might have been prevented. And worse will come unless I am allowed to do what I am sent to do.»

She made him a peasant's reverence, and went on up the hill; and he went down, resting his left hand on his sword-hilt, and staring at the stony soil. The walls made a sheltered reservoir in which air settled warm from the sun.

De Metz passed the staircase which Jeanne had ascended, and winding on, he came to a narrow turn between houses. A young man whom the knight did not know stepped before him there. The young man pulled off his cap. If he had not been well dressed in a close hardy-coat belted around his hips, and the same kind of long cloth trunk-hose and leather shoes as De Metz himself wore, the knight might have taken him for a bold footpad. Yet at second glance he had a handsome young face. He was well made and he was blue-eyed, an unusual thing in rugged Lorraine.

«Messire, I want to speak a word with you,» said the young man.

«Speak,» responded De Metz. He was at first not inclined to stop, but he did stop.

«Messire, I know you to be the knight of Novelopont. I am a free-born man. My father has a holding of land in Neufchâteau. Before my time we were better than innkeepers. My name is Bertrand de Poulengy. You were talking yonder with a young pucelle.»

De Metz glanced backward as if the shadows of Jeanne and himself were still standing by the wall.

«Do you know her?» he inquired. «I thought she was from Domremy village, not Neufchâteau.»

«She is from Domremy village, messire. I am going to tell you the truth. I was a fool. When the raiders came two years ago, and the people were driven from Domremy to Neufchâteau, her family lodged with us. You may not know it, messire the knight, but there is no one like her in the world. She helped my mother when we were thronged, and she was so humble and so kind that even before they went home again I began to think I should die if I could not get her. But we were both young, and my father obliged me to wait awhile before he made the proposals. Messire, her family were willing, but she would not marry at all.» He hung down his head.

«Never mind, my lad; never mind. There are plenty of maids for wives in the world. This one has set her heart on other things.»

«That is not it, messire. I was like a crazy man. Some said she was so timid and modest that if I took oath she had given me her promise she would not dare deny it, and everything would go well after we were once married. I thought about it day and night. Then I went to her mother, and her mother was so terrified by the pucelle's talk about going into France that we both thought such a sin might be forgiven. So I went to Toul and took oath before a magistrate.»

«My faith, you were a persistent man,» said De Metz, with contempt.

«Yes, you will find me that,» answered Bertrand, lifting his head. «Messire, she went to Toul herself, and on her oath denied it. It was a hard thing for a young pucelle to do. I put that mortification upon her. There is no excuse for me. I was a fool to think I could get her. Messire, I want to be her squire or servant if she is sent to Chinon to the dauphin.»

«Do you think a man who has perjured himself is a fit man to be squire and servant to a good maid?»

The boy's appealing eyes took all the sternness out of De Metz's question.

«Messire, if you had ever been—that way, you would not judge me at my worst.»

«But if you were in her party you

might grow worse—that way,» suggested the knight.

«I can never think again, messire, that if she would take a husband she would ever look at me. But even my father and mother understand I have to go to the wars. You are older than I am, messire, and perhaps you have wife and children?»

«No, I have none,» said Jean de Metz.

«I have taken another oath,» said Bertrand, «and this oath is a true one. I will follow her if she goes to the wars, and take all the care of her that a man may. She is more than wife and children and friends and home to me. Messire, she is religion to me now.»

Though De Metz's experience extended little further than Bertrand's, he dimly recognized the cry of that age in the boy's declaration. It was the exalting of a virgin, chivalry and religion strangely met. Political divisions had resulted from it. Dominican friars, who opposed the dogma of the immaculate conception, had been expelled from the court of the late king; while Franciscans, who zealously upheld the dogma, became identified with the loyal party. The Duke of Burgundy protected the Dominicans, and they turned with him to the English cause.

«I will do this much, my lad,» said De Metz; «I will recommend you to messire the captain. But a man makes his own reputation in arms. Have you a horse?»

«Yes; I came here on a horse of my own. My father gave me enough to fit me out. There is no other child at home.»

«That is hard for your father and mother.»

«But they were willing to let me go.»

«Did you hear of the maid so far down the valley?»

«No; I did not know she was here until I came to Vaucouleurs. But her family have been afraid for two years that she would go into France.»

THE news was spreading, however, as far down the valley as Domremy. Durand Laxart's wife got down from a cart, and took her child from the hands of the neighbor who had given her the lift. Her uncle, Jacques d'Arc, came from the fagot-stack to meet her. He had gentle, dark eyes and a face of lovable keenness. The winter day was so mild that he had been at work bareheaded, and his yellow-ivory skin showed hundreds of little cross-lines enmeshing his small mouth, which was like his daughter's, with a sweet and wistful expression. This look changed to apprehension as he carried Aveline's baby in.

The house was a shed-shaped stone cottage with the roof sloping from a height on one side half-way to the ground on the other. At one corner of the low side Jeanne's little window looked directly at the church. Aveline noticed the church while she followed her uncle. The door was partly charred, and there were patches in the roof. A new low tower replaced the high square tower which had been there before the Burgundians swept the valley.

Aveline's small forehead was drawn with puzzled anxiety, and it tightened as Jacques d'Arc inquired:

«But where is Jehannette?»

She hurried before him into the house, and looked about as if she must find the answer there. The earthen floor and the stone mantel were white. There was a wrought-iron plate to keep the back of the fireplace from crumbling with heat, and it glowed rosy behind the fagots. Isabel Romée's andirons, which were her pride and inheritance,—three feet high, with cups at the top for brewing posset, and hooks in front for bars,—held the fagots in place and some meat suspended from a bar roasting for dinner. The father had watched Jeanne's head rise year by year and overtop these andirons. He remembered more than one night when she had slept on the floor before the great guardians of the hearth, giving up the daughter's chamber to refugees made houseless by raiders. With the self-control of habit, he stooped and turned the meat before laying Aveline's precious bundle in her arms.

«Here is your child; now where is mine?»

«My uncle Jacques, is Jehannette not here at all?» persisted Aveline, turning her head like a hen.

«How could she be here and also in Bury-la-Côte? We lent her to you,» accused Jacques.

«Did not my husband bring her home more than a week ago?»

«She has not been seen in this house since she went to nurse you.»

Aveline began to cry.

«Then it is true that Durand Laxart went to Vaucouleurs the first time as well as the second time. I heard them talking about Vaucouleurs while I was asleep, but he told me he was going to Neufchâteau and would bring Jehannette home. She herself told me nothing. I thought she wanted to see her mother.»

Jacques set his hands in his thin hair. His face bleached while she spoke, nostrils and jaw-lines showing for a moment as in a death's-head.

«My child has gone into France! Durand Laxart has taken my child to Vaucouleurs, and let her go into France!»

He flung the door open, and ran toward the Meuse, his wisp-like legs threatening to snap with the weight of his wooden shoes. Aveline, rolling in her short petticoat, ran after him, holding the baby, and making audible noises as her tears increased and her breath shortened.

The ice was gone from the edges of the Meuse, and a practised eye might note reviving life in the flat islands. Near the bridge was a deep pool, and two women had set their box-shaped washing-tables, open at one side, in the water's edge, and were kneeling at their labor. The sound of their paddles could be heard along the valley, as they beat and turned and dipped and beat again the coarse, dark woolens of their families. One was a large-framed woman; she wore a white cap on her auburn-and-gray head. The other was a girl, and though the winter sun shone directly in her face, she kneeled bareheaded. She had a countenance which seemed to shine with rapturous contentment, and impressed the beholder as purely blonde. It was afterward a surprise to see that her hair was black and her skin really dark, and that it was only a whiteness of expression.

«How do you get along, Mengette?» inquired the woman.

«It is nearly clean now. I wish I could put Choux in the river and wash him.»

«He grows fouler as he grows older,» remarked the woman. «This water, is it not cold for thee?»

«No colder for me than for you, godmother Romée,» answered the girl. A woman kept her own name in marriage, and the wife of Jacques d'Arc was always called Isabel Romée of Vauthon.

«But I am hardy. I can cleanse woolens at the river when most other women keep the house. I would rather spread garments on the bushes when snow flies than have them lying foul.»

They heard a cart rolling over the bridge, and looked up. It was a stranger's head passing along the parapet. Cart-wheels were not so startling as the sudden clatter of horsemen. Every villager lived ready to seize his goods and drive his flocks for safety up in the hills.

«That was Jehannette's way also,» said Mengette; «we have had many a good time bleaching clothes together at the river. Her cousin keeps her too long, godmother. Why don't you command her home again?»

«We foolishly promised Durand; but I am going to-morrow to see her myself.»

«Are you going in the cart?»

«No; the lads must get more fagots in while this weather holds good. I am going by the hill path.»

«Then let me go with you, godmother. I can set Choux's dinner for him on the table, and we can reach home by twilight.»

«It will be very good to have you,» said Isabel, and their paddles brought echoes from the hills opposite.

«I will tell Aveline that when her little maid grows up she will find how hard it is to lend her and doubly lend her out of the house. Jehannette must come home with us; it will not do any longer.»

She heard a noise in the alluvial hollow, and turned, to face Aveline and Jacques and the calamity.

Isabel struggled to her feet.

«Where is Jehannette?» she demanded.

«I am going to Vaucouleurs,» answered Jacques.

Isabel flew at her husband, and caught his wrists, falling on her knees. She begged him not to tell her that her child was gone. Her bare red arms and hands, and her face burned by many a day in the fields, lost their strength in a moment, and hung on the slighter man. Jacques held her against him as she kneeled, hushing her cries, and straightening her cap, while he formed his lips piteously for an ungiven kiss.

«I am going to Vaucouleurs,» he repeated; «I am going to saddle the horse. Pierre and Jacquemine will stay here with thee.»

«Oh, Aveline, it is not true that my child has gone into France! You have not let her poison our old age and kill us! We lent her to you in a time of need. Give me back my Jehannette!»

Aveline, suffering for her husband's act, hid her face from Isabel, and mourned aloud. Mengette helped Isabel to stand up, and supported her on one side. That serene look which had made Mengette Jeanne's favorite did not pass from her face with the dripping of tears. The quick and helpful little creature put her nervous strength to the mother's sagging body, and when the wretched procession was in the house Mengette returned to finish the clothes and carry them away to spread. The blow was heavy upon her. Mengette had not much in the world which she could afford to lose. She was a step-child of fortune, but she had always cheated the sour dame by her own temperament, and got the best out of everything.

Jeanne had slept with her in her own bed, and she looked back now at their simple talks about life and religion and angels. Neither girl knew that maids usually talked more about men than about angels. It made Mengette very comfortable to be with Jeanne. But lately she knew her friend had gone beyond her. She could not understand herself how any maid could feel impelled toward war; and as to being spoken to by saints, Mengette prayed that such a thing might never happen to her. She could take care of the house and her geese, and sew and spin, and tend Choux as long as it pleased Heaven to let him last; but if a saint had spoken to her out of the clouds she must have died of fright.

Jacques d'Arc was on his horse galloping to Vaucouleurs, and Isabel lay prostrate in the cupboard bed, with Aveline to wait on her. The lonely little worker kept to her double task at the river. At noon it was growing colder, and her heart was heavy. The pleasure of washing in the villages was in the meeting of many women, and chattering and laughter and news-telling between the thump, thump of the clothes-beater.

When everything was wrung out she piled the large pannier up until it towered over her head, then she lifted it to her back, thrusting her arms into the plaited handles. Mengette was obliged to steady herself carefully to keep from tipping backward. As she turned her face to the ascent she saw Jeanne's two brothers coming over the bridge with a cart-load of fagots. Oxen drew the cart, moving almost silently between parapets where it was impossible to run aside or rebel against the head-yoke. The labors which belonged to other seasons were done then as men had opportunity to do them. Sowing and reaping, tying up vines, burning charcoal, and bringing in fuel, had not the old regularity. Though the valley of the Meuse was remote from the track of the invaders, it was the direct route between the two portions of Burgundy. And there were armed bands gathering in all parts of the kingdom, mercenaries who had shaken off military service and really taken to the trade of robbers. Some of them yet wore the badge of the Armagnacs, as the dauphin's party was called, and others wore the badge of the English. These wolves of war penetrated everywhere. What Domremy had suffered from the Burgundians was never forgotten.

Pierre walked ahead of Jacquemine, cracking the whip. It was always Pierre and Jacquemine, never Jacquemine and Pierre, though Jacquemine was the eldest of the family. Jean, the second brother, was already married and settled in his mother's house at Vauthon. He seemed no longer to be of the family, for his wife's people had absorbed him; Pierre and Jacquemine were the sons at home. Pierre was a large fellow with rich, dark, rosy color, and gray eyes that laughed inside their black lashes. He held his head back, and his cap usually slipped to one side upon it. The girls in Domremy liked him, but he was fonder of his sister than of any of them. He was two years older than Jeanne, and Jacquemine was four years older than he was. Yet he could lift Jacquemine up by the girdle and smock; and though Mengette had little to complain of in the world, it disturbed her to have Pierre do this. The helpless, wrathful look on Jacquemine's face as he struck and kicked against the indignity aroused her. Jacquemine had always come to her to talk about his troubles, which consisted of slights put upon him. There seemed to be too little of his darkly freckled, sandy, and wizened person. He wept as easily as a girl, and this wrung Mengette's heart and first attracted her protection. A betrothal had been arranged between them by the two families before her father and mother died, but it was understood that they were not to marry while Choux lived. They would not have enough to support a family with Choux also to provide for, though by themselves they might be fairly prosperous. Jacquemine's father was to give him a field and some cattle. Mengette had a house and garden and a flock of geese. She herded the geese herself, and exchanged their feathers for wool; and being a thrifty maid, gathered her own fagots,—for Choux would not work,—and weeded and tied vines in vineyards whenever the chance offered. Besides, Mengette had the caps and petticoats her mother wore, waiting in a chest until she should need them. She had carried them with her when the villagers fled to Neufchâteau from the Burgundians.

Jacquemine sulked across the bridge without seeing her until Pierre called down a good day. She made a sign for them to halt, and ascended with her load, dreading to speak her news, yet obliged to spare Isabel. The oxen swayed to one side, the foremost one running obstinately down the bank. Pierre had some trouble to bring them to a stand beside a wall without upsetting the load. Jacquemine waited at the end of the bridge until Mengette struggled up to him. He did not reach down his hand to her as

Pierre would have done: for Pierre was always quick to notice when a pannier was heavy, and to help a maid, especially his sister and Mengette; but Jacquemine seldom noticed anything except his own feelings. He was the kind of man that women wait on; masculine strength was not expected in him.

Jacquemine was stung because she rested the bottom of the pannier on the parapet and waited until Pierre came back. If Mengette had anything to say, he was the person to say it to. This individual resentment entered his grief when he heard the news.

« I always knew Jehannette would disgrace the family,» he exclaimed, coloring darkly; « if you do not want to marry me after this, Mengette, I shall say nothing.»

« She has not disgraced the family,» retorted Mengette, with heat. « She is better than I am. You ought to be ashamed of saying she has disgraced the family.»

Jacquemine's eyes filled with tears. « You can take her part against me if you want to.» And he turned his back and sobbed. Mengette herself wept again, understanding and pardoning his misery. But Pierre stood without a sound. He did not hear them, or Mengette knew he would have shaken Jacquemine over the parapet. Rings of dark hair had been formed about his forehead by the heat of walking. He held the whip across his shoulder, and stood stunned, taking the news into his mind. The long stretch of road and meadow and hill rising toward Neufchâteau was behind him. The January sky was soft and gray with gathering clouds. One could hear the wind begin to sing up in the leafless oak woods where Jeanne used to run about with him.

He spoke out huskily:

« Does anybody know that she has yet gone into France?»

« No; but it is certain she has gone as far as Vaucouleurs. Aveline says Durand Laxart is in Vaucouleurs now; and she heard them talking about it. Your father is already on the road,» repeated Mengette.

« I am going with my sister,» determined Pierre.

The habit of his life was first to assert itself. From the time Jeanne was old enough to run in the fields, Pierre had run after her and let her dictate the course.

« Your father told your mother that Jacquemine and you would stay with her.»

« Jacquemine can stay, but I am going with my sister.»

« Go, go! » said Jacquemine, showing an indignant face over his shoulder in the act of wiping it with his sleeve. « By the time all the family have run off but me, my father and mother will find who is really a child to them.»

« But, Pierre,» pleaded Mengette, « godmother Romée is struck down in her bed. If you go now it may be the death of her. She said to Aveline, ‹ You have let my child poison our old age and kill us.› »

« Go, Pierre! » repeated Jacquemine, fiercely; « I can do all the heavy labor, and take care of the family and the cattle in case the Burgundians come again. Run after the Armagnacs, you and Jehannette.»

« We will,» responded Pierre.

« But wait, Pierrelo, until your father comes back,» still pleaded Mengette; « he may find her and bring her home.»

« He will not find her; he should have sent me.»

« Yes; he should have sent big Pierre,» venomously hissed Jacquemine.

He snatched the whip, and ran clattering on to start the oxen. They were not used to his guidance, and swayed in a zigzag course from wall to wall, while he cracked the whip and let his trouble out in noisy abuse of them. Mengette lifted her pannier and trudged directly after him. She was a pucelle of spirit, but Jacquemine's rages always woke her motherly compassion, like the helpless suffering of a child. She felt it necessary to quiet him before he went into the house and increased the disapproval which he had long resented there.

Pierre sat down on the parapet of the bridge and stared at the washing-place, where open-sided box-tables and paddles yet remained. The Meuse curled about its islands and rippled among the naked bushes. He was not sure that it was a calamity which had fallen on the family, but it was certainly a grief. To be entirely separated from his sister was out of nature and not to be endured. He had a vague and careless knowledge of Jeanne's visions and of what she intended to do if she went into France. Pierre was not spiritual-minded. He had almost to be flogged to his prayers when he was younger. He enjoyed the world; but more than everything else he enjoyed loving. Jeanne would draw him after her as certainly as the bell-sheep drew the flock. But when he had thought awhile he decided not to set out on foot along the hills to Vaucouleurs without seeing his mother, as he would be obliged to do if he went at once. He would not forsake his mother while she lay prostrated by the loss of Jeanne. But he had a conviction that his father would never bring Jeanne back.

And when Jacques d'Arc reached Vaucouleurs he did not find his daughter. He was the last man to enter the gates that night, haggard and splashed with hard riding; but a strange experience met him there. He had scarcely mentioned the maid he was seeking when a lantern was lifted by a passer-by, and men came together in a bunch like bees to hum about her. She was as well known in Vaucouleurs as the captain there. They escorted him like a guard of honor to Royer's house.

«Here is the father of the maid,» they said to Royer's wife, when they had struck on the door and she opened it. «We have told him that she has gone to Nancy with her cousin and the knight of Novelopont, being sent for by the sick Duke of Lorraine.»

Jacques leaned his head on his hands and listened to Royer's wife when he was in the house. It was plain that the people in this part of the country believed Jeanne ought to go into France.

«But she shall come home,» said Jacques, feeling the tightness at his heart relax, since she was gone in the opposite direction, and he might yet intercept her. «She is my little maid. As to raising sieges and crowning the dauphin, we have a hearth for her in Domremy, and she was always contented there until these troubles grew so bad. Her mother is struck down in bed on account of her. If the saints send her into France, I will say the saints have little regard for family ties. We have no other maid: our Catherine is dead. From the time Jehannette could clip her little hand around one of my fingers, she would toddle at one of my legs and Pierrelo at the other. I say she shall not go; and she was always obedient. What! would I let my innocent child go among men-at-arms, and be spoken to by any vile follower of the camp? I would kill her before she should suffer such things.»

He waited several days in Vaucouleurs, wrenched from his accustomed places, and divided between Jeanne and Isabel. The journey was an education to a peasant who had never stirred before, except from his native village to Domremy, and afterward to Neufchâteau. He felt the pulse of the world, and realized the growth of his child. But he was more than ever determined not to give her up; and when the strain of his absence grew unendurable, he saddled his horse in haste, and said to Royer's wife:

«I am going back to Isabel, and Pierre will come in my place. Tell Jehannette I command her home with her brother. Tell her that I forbid her to go into France. The curse of the disobedient will fall on her if she goes. My maid is a good maid, and I blame the people of Vaucouleurs for encouraging her in this strange desire. Her innocent dreams about angels and saints, what would they avail her among bloody men-at-arms? Her place is at home with her mother and me.»

But before Pierre reached Vaucouleurs the dauphin's messenger from Chinon had galloped in, and Jeanne had gone.

Jacques's horse fell lame. He led it and walked, stumping among the stones in his sabots, and reaching Bury-la-Côte late in the night. There he slept in the house of Aveline's mother, and borrowed another horse. But the delay made Pierre too late.

It was a poor, powerless maid who threw herself across a bench and cried aloud on her knees when she returned from Nancy, and was told that her father had been seeking her, and the messenger from Chinon was already there.

«Oh, my father, my dear father! How can I endure not to see my father and mother and Pierrelo again! But I must go—I must go!»

Jeanne ran from the house up the stone stairs leading to the chapel crypt. It was her last heartbreak before the altar, weeping to be sent, and weeping because she must be sent.

There was excitement both in the château and the town. Nobody in Vaucouleurs except Baudricourt had doubted that the dauphin would send for the maid. Candles burned all night in the shop where her outfit was finished, and the people of Vaucouleurs, who bore the expense of it, looked in crowds at the busy workmen as a public spectacle.

«The maid is to ride forth in man's apparel,» said women to one another, in consternation. «She says she has been counseled so to do. Is that decent?»

«I call it decent myself,» decided a dame in authority. «What would she do with petticoats astride of a horse, riding a hundred and fifty leagues, and having no woman of her party? Even messire the captain had nothing to say against it when she begged for the habit of a man.»

«Messire de Baudricourt has changed his opinion of her since the dauphin's messenger came in with news of the defeat near Orléans.»

«Yes; they say the maid knew it, and sent him word the very day the battle was fought.»

In Vaucouleurs Jeanne was the maid who out of the march of Lorraine was to deliver

France. She was to have a knight and a squire, two common soldiers as their servants, an archer, and the dauphin's messenger, as her escort. Durand Laxart himself pledged payment for a horse. It would be a hard ride to Chinon—from this northeast corner of the ancient realm a hundred and fifty leagues diagonally southwestward across France. The party would have to avoid cities held by the English, and slip between marauding bands. They had five large rivers to cross. Wherever they dared use the old Roman roads good speed could be made; but much of the journey lay across trackless spaces full of the dangers of war.

It was the first Sunday in Lent, and people flocked to the château early in the morning to see her start. The maid had been brought there by Royer's wife and other women, to be dressed for her undertaking.

Every citizen of Vaucouleurs raised his cap in the air and cheered as she came out into the court, a supple, easily moving creature with a radiant face, in the suit of a man-at-arms, the jacket and tunic of gray cloth, the cuirass of leather thongs. Her long hose, cut and shaped from the cloth, were laced over her body-garment, and strong leather shoes were on her feet. The women had cut her hair off about her ears, and put the cap of a man-at-arms on her head.

The horses were standing ready. The men of her party waited her mounting. There was nothing male about her. Though she looked smaller than in her maid's dress, no person said to another, «She is like a boy.» She was simply the maid dressed to ride like a man.

«What have you there, pucelle?» inquired Baudricourt, meeting her, and taking her packet to fasten behind the saddle.

«My red peasant dress, messire the captain.»

«What would you do with your peasant dress on a journey to court?»

«Unfold it and look at it sometimes, messire. I love what I wore in my home.»

«Let come what may come of this,» said Baudricourt, «Heaven knows I don't understand these things, or how you should be able to tell me there was a battle over some herrings and camp supplies near Orléans the very day it was fought. But go your ways, pucelle, my friend; it is no longer my affair.»

«Good-by, messire the captain; have no fear for me. I shall be taken care of.»

«If you be not, God he knoweth it will be through no fault of mine; for every man in this party hath sworn an oath to me to deliver you safely to the dauphin.»

Jeanne laughed as she put her hand on the bridle. Her squire knelt to take her foot and lift her into the saddle.

«I am a peasant,» she said; «I do not know anything about mounting as grand dames mount. Let me find a block of stone.» Then she looked at the squire with sudden scrutiny.

«Not this man, messire the captain. Has this man also taken oath?»

«I have,» the young man answered, on his knees; «and this oath is a true one, maid of France.»

Jeanne believed him. She had no grudge against Bertrand de Poulengy. Her open, bright look accepted at once his atonement and their new relations. She mounted the horse from the château steps. Her eyes moved gratefully from face to face in the crowd. She lifted her cap; her forehead was white in the sun, a girl's smooth forehead, with the hair blowing back from it. Men and women felt their hearts swell. This tender young being was going out to fight for them. It was the strangest thing that had ever happened. For a hundred years France had given her sons to war, but now a daughter was demanded—a maid was necessary for sacrifice. Jeanne leaned down and grasped hand after hand. Women kissed her fingers, which had not yet touched anything more deadly than needle or spindle. She was their dear child, whom they were themselves giving up.

«Good-by,» said Jeanne, looking into her cousin Durand's faithful face; «I am glad you christened the baby Catherine. Give my love to them all—my father, my mother, my Pierrelo—»

She touched the spurs to her horse, and the party rode out through the gate, which is called to this day the Gate of France.

(To be continued.)

*Mary Hartwell Catherwood.*

# NEWLY DISCOVERED PORTRAITS OF JEANNE D'ARC.

PORTRAIT OF JEANNE D'ARC WITH HALO, IN MANUSCRIPT OF FIFTEENTH CENTURY. BRAUN PHOTOGRAPH.

Notes of "plein chant" on the reverse of the above.

TWO interesting miniature portraits of Jeanne d'Arc have recently come to light in Alsace. They are in the collection of M. Georges Spetz of Isenheim, to whom THE CENTURY is indebted for permission to reproduce them in black and white. M. Spetz informs us that the two portraits have been cut out of manuscripts which are said to have been found in Italy, but which are certainly French. He at first thought that the artist was of Lorraine, but his researches since have led him to relinquish this attribution, while he holds to the theory that the type of face is that of Lorraine.

The first of these miniatures is painted upon parchment, and ornaments an initial letter of an antiphon of the fifteenth century. The head of the maid is surrounded by a saint's halo. On this point M. Spetz says in a letter to the Editor: «The artist certainly

[1] This is the only periodical publication of them permitted by M. Spetz, except in the «Notes d'Art et d'Archéologie» issued by the Société de Saint Jean in Paris.

painted this picture after the trial of rehabilitation; and there exist contemporaneous pictures which similarly represent her, proving that already in the fifteenth century she was considered a saint.» The long hair is not peculiar to this portrait. The heroine's locks were cut short during her martial career, but Here the hair is short and the head is inclosed in a helmet.

With regard to the coloring of these paintings, M. Spetz informs us as follows: «According to tradition, Jeanne d'Arc was a brunette; the hair is a dark blond (‹blond foncé›) in the miniatures. The blue eyes in

PORTRAIT OF JEANNE D'ARC IN HELMET, IN MANUSCRIPT OF FIFTEENTH CENTURY. BRAUN PHOTOGRAPH.

this and some other early representations dignify her with the long hair belonging to the woman, to the virgin.

On the back of this initial letter and portrait appear some notes of sacred music («plein chant»), which are reproduced here at the beginning of the article.

The second portrait is from a fifteenth-century manuscript recounting the history of Jeanne d'Arc. Upon the back the parchment has been mutilated, but the following words in Gothic characters are legible:

ins de hardiment . . .
gloire de France . . .
dez hardiz côbatant . . .

the portrait which has the halo are those of one who sees visions.» He says that the miniatures are evidently not portraits from life, but that they have the great value of being contemporaneous or of belonging to a time when the memory of her was still fresh. M. Spetz adds: «The Baron de Braun, of the collateral line of descent of Jeanne d'Arc, who knows all the iconographic documents which have appeared, writes to me that these miniatures recall none of the types of the maid, and that he knows no picture of the great heroine having so much character and approaching so near his own idea of Jeanne d'Arc.»

*The Editor.*

# NEW CONDITIONS IN CENTRAL AFRICA.

## THE DAWN OF CIVILIZATION BETWEEN LAKE TANGANYIKA AND THE CONGO.

EXTRACTS FROM THE JOURNALS OF THE LATE E. J. GLAVE.

LAKE TANGANYIKA, September 19, 1894. Reached Kinyamkolo, the London Missionary Society's station, a splendidly situated place. The natives are not coddled by the missionaries, but are taught to work and are kept busy. At present the staff is the Rev. Mr. Thomas, in charge, and Mr. A. Purvis and wife; besides, there are Mr. Hemans and wife, colored missionaries from Jamaica, he being a school-teacher. The educated blacks have not been found to be so successful as white men. Instinctively the natives acknowledge a white's authority, but they have not the same respect for a black, unless his unusual intelligence and learning are backed up by physical force. What a difference the presence of a white woman makes to a household in Africa! Her presence checks a white man's tendency to become brutal. With barbarous surroundings even the mildest character often becomes brutal. This is pardonable, as, living among the African natives, there is never anything to suggest the finer feelings, gratitude, pity, mercy, charity being unknown to them. You may aid a native even to the extent of saving his life; he takes it as a matter of course, even though you are put to expense and trouble. He expects the winds to be favorable, rain to fall at the proper season to refresh the crops, game to be abundant and not dangerous, and in war to suffer no losses. When the smooth run of his life is checked by accident or misfortune, the blame is placed on evil spirits.

About one thousand people are settled within the stockade. During the last few years the general health has much improved; a few years ago there was so much sickness and so many deaths that the home society thought of abandoning the station. There seems to be a good deal of jealousy in the mission; in fact, throughout this land one

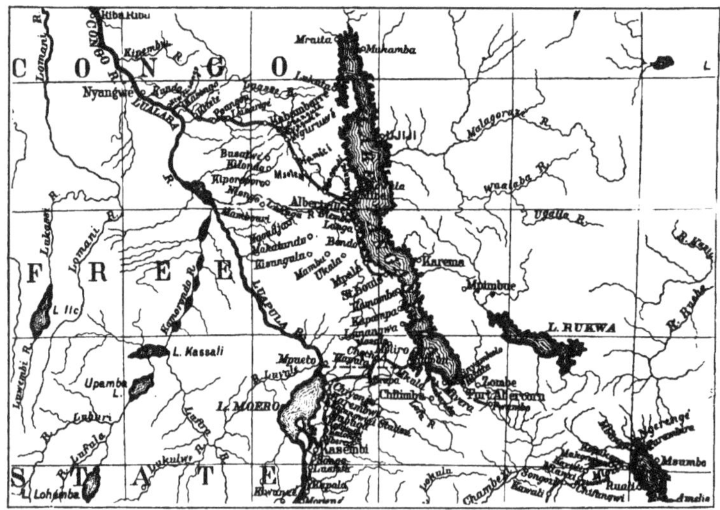


MAP OF GLAVE'S JOURNEY IN THE TANGANYIKA REGION.

VIEW IN THE NATIVE QUARTER OF FWAMBO, A SECTION OF THE VILLAGE STOCKADE IN THE REAR.

hears one missionary speak of another in anything but brotherly terms. The one feeling of Christian fellowship, of disregarding one another's small faults, is very noticeable among the Catholic missionaries, who in times gone by have purchased hundreds of homeless little slave boys and girls; these have been brought up in the Catholic faith, knowing no other, and knowing no friends save their masters, the white fathers.

September 21. I left Kituta early this morning, and after four hours' marching reached Fort Abercorn, a sturdy stockaded little place with houses built of white clay from the ant-hills. Locusts are hovering about in tremendous swarms, and during the coming season they are expected to play havoc with the new crops. Leaving Abercorn, I marched for three hours to Fwambo. When Stanley visited the south end of Tanganyika the rocky mountains came down to the water's edge; but now the waters in the lake have diminished, and large flats stretch out half a mile from the foot of the mountains. I am assured by careful observers that, although the lake is gradually receding generally, there are places where the waters are gaining on the land, suggesting a local sinking.

About fourteen thousand people are gathered within the palisades of the Fwambo mission. All of the boys and girls must go to school, and many make rapid progress. I saw one youngster, not more than seven, who wrote a splendid hand, and another, ten or eleven, did some difficult sums. Mr. Alexander Carson, in charge of the mission, believes thoroughly in the industrial cultivation of the African, and in sufficient Christianity to come within the grip of their understanding. There is a good carpenter-shop, well stocked with tools, where boys make chairs, tables, etc. There are native iron-foundries in the immediate neighborhood; iron is smelted in native furnaces, and the mission employees shape out very cleverly large nails, bolts, screws, hinges, catches, and latches. Brick-making also is successfully carried on.

Some time ago Rumaliza showed Mr. Swann a piece of quartz bearing free gold, and said he knew where there was plenty on the east shores of Tanganyika. I have seen none, although I have seen plenty of good quartz. There is any amount of iron, which is easily worked by the natives. Coffee is the best means of developing the land. Good peat is said to have been found at Kinyamkolo, also an excellent fiber for rope. Cattle thrive on the Tanganyika plateau. The land must be developed by whites and blacks in company.

The natives want cloth; they are ashamed to wear bark cloth. Once natives have been in the employ of whites and have earned cloth, they always return and continue to work. Women without beads are looked down on. The natives possess a certain honest jealousy among themselves; they like to have good cloth and other possessions like their neighbors, and are ambitious even to possess more than others. At present more merchandise means the ability to marry more wives to enhance their importance. Those who have joined the church, of course, may not have more than one wife, but others have several. Few natives are really converted; most are found after a while to be breaking the laws which they have solemnly sworn to respect. The argument which I have often heard advanced, that after a time there will be so much cloth in the land that the natives will no longer take any interest in obtaining more, does not hold good. Where a labor-market has been established the number of workers increases year by year.

THE SCHOOL-HOUSE AT FWAMBO.

KINYAMKOLO, October 9. A miserable fever tucked me into the blankets to-day.

October 10–12. The wretched fever returns every day. I cannot eat anything. I have taken any amount of quinine, which has the effect of giving me grotesque visions as soon as I close my eyes. Mr. and Mrs. Purvis and Mr. Thomas have done everything for me.

October 14. I am truly grateful for the kindness of the missionaries. At about ten at night we left Kinyamkolo in the *Morning Star*, en route for Sumbu, and hoisted the sail with a favorable breeze.

October 16. Early this morning we had a strange experience. Several large fish, over four feet long and very thick like salmon, came about our slow-moving boat and grappled vigorously at the paddles, showing no fear. I shot two with my Martini, but unfortunately they sank before we could pick them up. Whether we were considered an enemy in their waters, or whether we were looked upon as food, I don't know, but this lasted for an hour at intervals. We could have shot several, but desisted from useless slaughter, as we could not regain the creatures before they sank—very much to the disgust of the boatmen. If we had had a boat-hook or gaff we might have obtained a few. At ten this morning we reached Sumbu.

October 17. Went down to see Teleka to-day, and took his photograph. After returning I was attacked by fever and had to turn into blankets. Purvis is in the same condition.

October 19. Left Sumbu at five this morning. I still have fever, and turned into the cabin. We journeyed by paddle and oar close along the coast, steep and rocky, sparsely wooded, with scrubby, gnarled bush dropping to the water's edge, and here and there good, sandy landing-places. We reached Moliro at nine in the evening. M. Demol came off in his canoe and offered me a room, which I accepted for that night. I covered myself up in blankets. In the morning the fever was gone, but I was still without appetite. Demol speaks very little English, Purvis no French; my slight knowledge of French comes in very handy. The station here (Poste de Moliro) of the Belgian Antislavery Society is built on a slope rising gradually from the lake. There are groups of low, rocky, sparsely wooded hills to the southwest, fine, rich, undulating land extending toward the north, with hills in the distance. The lake at this point curves into an immense, picturesque bay.

October 21. Purvis left in the *Morning Star* this afternoon. Only a good, seaworthy boat

CONSPICUOUS TREE AT MPALA PRESERVED BY THE NATIVES BECAUSE DR. LIVINGSTONE CAMPED UNDER IT DURING HIS FIRST VISIT TO LAKE TANGANYIKA.

M. DEMOL, IN CHARGE OF POSTE DE MOLIRO, FEEDING A BUSHBUCK AND A DOG.

can stand the wind at present blowing. M. Demol is making extensive gardens of manioc, sweet potatoes, peanuts, *mtama*, *kaffu* corn, and maize, and hopes to have enough to feed all his men next year, in spite of locusts, which are bound to appear. In the morning men and women fall in for work. The women go to the gardens under the superintendence of women; they leave off at ten, so as to have time to cook for their husbands. The men drill till eight, and afterward work in the gardens till twelve; then rest till three, and work till six. They are very orderly. Two long lines of huts, well built, with a street between, lead to the lake. Two other parallel lines of huts extend from the back gate. All except ten Zanzibari are liberated slaves. Slaves have to serve seven years, being well cared for, fed, and clothed, during that time; afterward they are at liberty to go where they will. The soldiers are clad in a blue drill shirt, knickerbockers, and red fez; they carry chassepot rifles. Many have recently deserted. The Belgians are rather free at flogging; even women are not exempt. It was my original idea to wait here at Moliro for Descamps; but I cannot afford the time it must of necessity take before he returns from Lake Mweru. The Belgians are conceited about what they have done, and about their capabilities generally. Of course they compare most favorably with the British authorities south of Tanganyika, but they have not a better officer than Captain Edwards, and if the British Central Africa Company had an efficient staff in the district, things would be very different.

October 27. Demol is very kind-hearted and hospitable, but I don't think the released natives are very happy with the Belgians; there is too much stick for the slightest offense. Attacked by another fever to-day, the third in three weeks. Have arranged to leave here by canoe for Mtoa next Tuesday. Demol is having the canoe renovated, a mast put in, a sail made, and a small part roofed.

October 28. Demol finds great difficulty in getting me sufficient paddlers; when his men go out with the request, the natives leave their villages and run to the mountains.

November 2. Obtained a scratch crew, and left this morning; ran a few hours with sail, when a north wind sprang up, compelling us to seek shelter.

November 9. Made about six hours to-day, owing to adverse wind and rough water. Under such conditions I put in to the beach and wait till there is no danger; and when it

GATEWAY OF THE STOCKADE, POSTE DE MOLIRO.

rains I put in and without delay get everything under cover. Why lose everything for the sake of a few hours? Not I. Our boatmen will run a canoe till she swamps and rolls bottom up; they will then clamber on top, and paddle ashore with their hands if paddles are lost; they have nothing to lose but a few roots of manioc, and in a quarter of an hour their scrap of clothing is all the better for the washing and drying. Take no black man's advice, unless he has property to lose or has your confidence by past experience.

November 11. At eight reached Captain Joubert's at St. Louis. He is living in a large, airy, comfortable clay house, with his black wife Yanese, an Itawa girl, to whom he was married by the missionaries at Mpala. He has been married about five years; his first child, a girl, died at the age of two; he has another pretty little girl, Louise, now two and a half years old, strong and healthy, to whom he is devotedly attached. He is a citizen of the Congo Free State, fifty-three years old, and well preserved. He was first in the service of the mission for three years. He is very religious, and has done great good, rendering the land secure.

November 16. This morning Père Roehlens sent me down a donkey to ascend the hills to his station, called Baudoinville. The trail was, generally speaking, fairly good; but there were one or two steep climbs where I had to dismount. The mission has a fine situation on the plateau, about one and a half hours from the lake. Many rough clay buildings serve every purpose till the government buildings are finished. A very fine dwelling-house is in course of construction, also a hospital built of fire-burnt bricks and stone, of very artistic design. There are magnificent plantations of rice, sweet and European potatoes, onions, haricots, and ground-nuts, and good vegetable gardens, besides fruit-trees, including the mango, fig, papaw, and pineapple. The coffee-plantation is worked by mission boys and redeemed slaves, three or four hundred of both sexes; and the school is attended by many youngsters. The village is flourishing; three *pères* and three *frères* superintend the work, and a company of sisters are expected next year. The men are living on good terms, and are altogether of a jolly disposition, intelligent, hospitable, and charitable. They teach the youngsters to work, as well as give religious teaching. They are much liked by the people.

November 7. Spent the morning with Père Roehlens, and took photographs of the mission. Of these Catholic missionaries one has been in Africa eighteen years without returning home; Roehlens, eleven; Père Guillemet, nine; Herrboert, six. The frères work for the cause of religion merely for their clothes and food. Nearly everybody about Tanganyika is subject to hematuric fevers, Jacques and one or two pères alone escaping; but of late, owing to successful treatment, they are not regarded as very dangerous. In the afternoon I returned to Captain Joubert at St. Louis. He is very hospitable, but a very indifferent cook, and is content without any service. Without trouble he could surround himself with a few comforts to make life more pleasurable. He has decided to stay here, and leave his bones. Why not do so gracefully? He does not care for European things, except coffee, tea, sugar, and sardines.

November 8. Père Herrboert arrived this morning, and at eleven we embarked in his boat, the *Bwana Edward*, with all my loads aboard, and my canoe following. It is a splendid dugout, with a good sail and sixteen paddlers, and will stand any sea; it was made by the missionaries; a cabin could be fitted aft. We reached Mpala past midnight, and had a slight lunch of omelet and fruit at 2:30 A. M., the missionaries good-naturedly insisting on making something, and I must say I was very hungry and made no violent resistance. Mpala has a fine brick boma, and a building roofed with tiles. A great many natives are settled in the neighborhood, under the protection of the missionaries. In 1885 the Pères Blancs settled on Tanganyika. If their methods, so faithfully applied, do not have good results, then I shall think the case of the Africans hopeless. The pères are light-hearted, jolly fellows, devoted to their own religion, and not frantically opposed to others differing from them in views; they are on good terms with the English Protestant missionaries.

In combination with the expedition of Dhanis from the west,

GATEWAY AND ROOFED WALL OF THE MPALA MISSION.

the whole country from the Congo to Lake Tanganyika has been swept clear of Wangwana and Arab slavers, all, including the greatest of all slavers, Rumaliza, so magnificently beaten that they will never recover power in this part of the world. These men, especially the Wangwana, who were the slaves of the Arabs and were doing their dirty work, are now allies of the whites, and have been successfully employed against their old masters.

November 9. Had but little favorable wind; arrived at Mpala at 2:30 A. M., and unmercifully woke up Père de Beerot. Père Guillemet, the chief, is absent. The mission has a splendid station, surrounded by a high stone-and-brick wall, which with another wall forms a superior tembé construction. The house covers three sides of a square, with open court in the center and wide verandas all around. It is built of brick, with tiles for the roof; the carpenter work is good—all, of course, done by the mission. Their church was decorated by Frère François, an ingenious man, and has an altar made of odd scraps of wood and empty cans.

I find that fevers, dysentery, etc., have lately seriously affected my nerves. After firing one shot from my rifle I tremble abominably, and cannot hold the gun steady even with

NEW BUILDINGS OF THE FRENCH CATHOLIC MISSION AT MPALA.

a rest. I hope this is not going to last any length of time.

November 11. Went to mass to-day to please the missionaries, who thought the natives would think it strange if all whites did not attend the same

A CORNER TOWER OF THE WALL OF THE MPALA MISSION.

religious rites. There was a lot of formality which I did not attend to. Nearly the whole service was in Latin. There was very good singing, and the natives were attentive. Dozens of candles were burning about the altar.

About eleven o'clock Père Guillemet arrived from his journey. He was interested to know all about my journey, especially the finding of the Livingstone tree. He paid a great compliment to the Antislavery Society for their work in ridding the land of slavers. Spent the day with the pères, and late at night bade them good-by, reluctant to leave. They loaded me up with fresh vegetables and fruit. If I make any money I shall certainly do something for this mission.

Ujiji—but all to no avail: the force against him was too thoroughly managed, too determinedly conducted, to admit of his armed slaves offering any resistance. If coöperation had been carried out, the Germans would have kept Rumaliza east of the lake, powder-caravans and other ammunition would not have been permitted to leave the east coast, and Teleka would not have been permitted to supply the slaves of Abdallah with supplies to carry on the war against Captain Descamps. If Portugal and the British would do their part, slavery would at once become a thing of the past. The Belgians have driven out the slavers from their domains, and have done it well. To-day from Tanganyika to the Congo it is as safe as in the streets of Brussels.

WEST SHORE OF TANGANYIKA NEAR MOLIRO, LOOKING NORTH

WEST SHORE OF TANGANYIKA NEAR MPALA, LOOKING SOUTH.

November 15. Arrived at Mtoa, the station which was completely destroyed by fire a few weeks ago. I found Miot very much disheartened at the loss of the station. Altogether he has had little luck. Before the expedition of Dhanis and the operations of the Antislavery Society, slaves in chains and forks were constantly tramping through Manyema to Mtoa, and then by canoe across to Ujiji. While out hunting here the other day for a few hours in the vicinity of this station, I passed ten skeletons in the course of my tramp. These I saw by walking haphazard through plain and forest. But thousands have died here: many, too ill to be worth the passage-money across the lake, were knocked on the head; many ran away or died of starvation. Dhanis, only thirty-two years old, who has had supreme control of the war against Arabs on the Upper Congo, pluckily drove the slave-raiders from point to point, whipping them at every turn, driving them from their depots, occupying their tembés, his own force embracing as allies the native tribes, till Rumaliza, thinking his influence and name enough to give fresh courage to the lawless, arrived from

November 21. Not feeling well. When I feel better I shall get men together and make a start for Kasongo *via* Kabambarré, and with as little halting as possible shall get down to the Atlantic and home.

November 30. I am fortunate in obtaining from Miot thirty Wanyamwezi porters to accompany me to Kabambarré. These men have been in the service of the Antislavery Society, and are full of good spirits and fun, careless of everything so long as they have wife, food, and drink, but loyal; something can be made of them.

December 1. Left Kasanga [near Mtoa] at 6:30. Got men to help carry the loads across the Lufumba River, where the water was up to the armpits. My men were afraid of the water; could not carry their loads across. The

CAPTAIN JOUBERT, IN COMMAND OF STATION ST. LOUIS, HIS NATIVE WIFE, AND HIS CHILD LOUISE.

natives had to arrange this, and then take the big Wanyamwezi by the hand and lead them over.

December 4. A good trail; thick clumps of matted tropical forest; immense trees festooned with creeper; plenty of rubber of two kinds—one vine with yellow fruit like the orange, one tree with small red-cheeked fruit like little apples. At first a gradual ascent, then a gradual descent, the trail winding about over the hills; no open spaces, all wooded more or less, on the tops of hills sparsely; small timber generally in the hollows, and a mass of tropical foliage roofing the trail, supported on massive columns; a great many butterflies of the ordinary sorts. It is a fine soil, and the immense country is now almost uninhabited.

December 6. Left Mselem's at six, and reached Hamici's at eleven. Splendid trail, but not having been used much, the foliage has grown very thick, and carriers with loads have difficulty in breaking a passage through. The natives tell me that before the Wangwana came into the country there were flourishing villages and any amount of food from Mtoa to Kasongo; but now they have all been driven away by the Wangwana slavers, and no permanent villages are met, only a few new villages springing up since the whites took decisive measures against the slavers. But I do not think the Belgians are going the right way to work. When the whites asserted their power the slaves belonging to the elephant-hunters ran away and joined the native villages. The white men were appealed to, and the chiefs to whom the slaves had fled were bound and retained until they had delivered back all the slaves to the Wangwana. This they did to regain their liberty; but when they were told that they must leave their mountain retreats and come and build their villages near the caravan road, they naturally failed to carry out their promises.

The British are more successful than the Belgian officials in gathering natives about them. A native told me to-day that formerly a Mgwana caravan, seeing a man, would catch him, give him a load to carry, cloth to wear, and shave his head, and immediately ship him across Tanganyika, sometimes in chains or fork. West of the lake he was called *rafiki* (friend), but once aboard a dhow he was *mtumwa* (slave).

The road from Mtoa is infested with wretched dark-brown and black ants, which bite most unmercifully; they are found in swarms, covering the trail for fifteen yards, and even with the most hasty dash some of the insects manage to get on you, and if you do not attend to their removal with despatch you will have their angry little nippers buried in your flesh. This whole land appears to be a low, undulating plateau with no open plains of any size.

December 7. It is said, but I must have it corroborated, that the white officer at Kabambarré has commissioned several Mgwana chiefs to make raids in the country of the Warua, and bring him the slaves. They are supposed to be taken out of slavery and freed, but I fail to see how this can be argued out. They are taken from these villages and shipped south, to be soldiers, workers, etc., on the State stations; and what were peaceful families have been broken up and the different members spread about the place. They have to be made fast and guarded for transportation, or they would all run away. This does not look as though the freedom promised has any seductive prospects. The young children thus «liberated» are handed over to the French mission stations, where they receive the kindest care; but nothing justifies this form of serfdom. I can understand the State compelling natives to do a certain amount of work for a certain time; but to take people forcibly from their homes, and despatch them here and there, breaking up families, is not right. I shall learn more about this on the way and at Kabambarré. If these conditions are to exist, I fail to see how the antislavery movement is to benefit the native.

December 8. Six hours' marching from Nguruwé's to Mpianmsekwa's, the easterly limit of the Arab zone under the Kabambarré authorities. Saw gray parrots for the first time day before yesterday.

The Belgians are employing the Wangwana and their followers to fight the natives; and if captives are taken they are handed over to the authorities at Kabambarré. State soldiers are also employed without white officers; this should not be allowed, for the black soldiers do not understand the reason of the fighting, and instead of submission being sought, often the natives are massacred or driven away into the hills.

To-day I met in Sungula's village thirty-five Baluba soldiers bound on a fighting expedition against the natives to the south of here.

LES PÈRES BLANCS (THE WHITE FATHERS) OF THE FRENCH CATHOLIC MISSION AT BAUDOINVILLE NEAR STATION ST. LOUIS.

FREED SLAVE GIRLS AT THE BAUDOINVILLE MISSION POUNDING CORN.

because these people do not consent to send tribute ivory to the whites at Kabambarré. Sungula is a tall, wiry coast man who has killed eighty elephants and owned three hundred slaves; two hundred have run away and joined the natives. He says some of his slaves he bought; others had trouble in the villages, and, fearful of punishment, gave themselves up; some were caught in fights against the natives. Sungula tells me that previous to the last fight of Rumaliza and the Belgians he was invited to join the campaign by Sefu, son of Tippu Tib, who came to Sungula's village, and wrote letters to Rumaliza, who was at Ujiji. When Rumaliza fled he called at the village of Sungula, and advised the latter to remain in the country and accept the Belgian flag. Sungula gave me enough corn to feed my men, also fowl and eggs for myself. I gave him a return present.

At Mpianmsekwa's the Manyema soldiers complain that the native hunters do not go off after elephants. Sungula says the reason is that when the hunters are absent the Manyema soldiers take their wives. This is a heinous offense in the eyes of the natives, who have a superstition that if the wife does not remain constant when the husband is away fighting or hunting dangerous game, the hunter will be sure to suffer serious failure, wounds, or death. The natives of the Congo have the same idea, which prevails generally throughout central Africa.

All the ivory that Sungula now gets he sends to the white men at Kabambarré, and receives cloth in exchange. He seems fairly contented with his lot. His people are all hungry-looking creatures; they are having a time of short rations till the corn ripens, when there will be plenty. Now they live chiefly on wild fruits, the oily nut of the fan-palm, the acid fruit of the rubber-vine, and certain insipid roots known to the natives. Sungula is very intelligent, and does not badger one by begging. He does not seem pleased with the big party of Baluba soldiers without a white man; thinks the natives, upon seeing the forces brought against them,

NATIVE DUGOUT CANOE IN WHICH GLAVE TRAVELED FROM MOLIRO TO MTOA, WITH TWENTY PEOPLE ABOARD AND A TON OF CARGO.

will submit and pay the desired *hongo;* but the black soldiers are bent on fighting and raiding; they want no peaceful settlement. They have good rifles and ammunition, realize their superiority over the natives with their bows and arrows, and they want to shoot and kill and rob. Black delights to kill black, whether the victim be man, woman, or child, and no matter how defenseless. This is no reasonable way of settling the land; it is merely persecution. Blacks cannot be employed on such an errand unless under the leadership of whites.

December 10. Very glad to reach the village of Lobangula. He makes the following complaint against the Manyema soldiers who arrived at his village two days ago: The soldiers saw one or two guns leaning against the huts loaded and capped; fired off two of these in the air; then went searching through the village, and found in the huts other guns loaded and capped. In two huts where guns were found two natives were made fast and beaten, one very badly lacerated, his shoulders being cut most unmercifully; the other bears marks of the chicot on his back and a swollen eye as the result of beating. The chief arrived on the scene, and asked the reason of this treatment. The Manyema replied that the villagers had been arming to fight against the whites. The chief replied that this was not so. He had acknowledged the whites, and hoisted the flag given to him by the white men at Kabambarré; moreover, he was engaged in collecting rubber for the whites. He explained that he was menaced by his near neighbors, and as a matter of precaution his people kept their guns in readiness. The soldiers were not satisfied with this explanation. The chief was seized and bound, and kept so for several hours, and released only after he had consented to pay to his persecutors one goat, ten fowls, and two slave girls; then he was set free and the eight guns were returned. Then the hut of Lobangula was rifled. The brutal action of the soldiers so terrified his people that many fled into hiding and have not returned. Yesterday the sergeant of the soldiers gave me two fowls; evidently they were of the lot received as ransom; and my servant saw the skin of a goat which was spread on the ground to dry. Lobangula says that in the future, when he hears of the approach of a party of soldiers without white men, he and his people will go into hiding till they have passed, as he is afraid of them.

Lobangula asks, What became of all the slaves who were taken over the road by Tippu

SLAVE BOY WITH CARVED CHAIR, AND IDOL FROM THE RUA COUNTRY WEST OF TANGANYIKA.

Tib, Rumaliza, and Nzige? Formerly a marriageable girl could be bought for sixteen yards of white cloth, a very young girl for ten, and a man for the same price. Kasongo was a great slave-market. Bwana Nzige has fled to the coast with Rumaliza. Lobangula says Tippu Tib and Nzige were the first to «bore a hole through» the country between Tanganyika and the country of the Manyema. In collecting rubber the natives cut the rubber-vine into small pieces, put the rubber-juice first on the chest, then take it off and make it into a ball.

December 11. After five hours' hard marching from Lobangula's I reached Bwana Msa's place, in a hollow surrounded on all sides by wooded hills. After the fight with the whites he remained quiet, and when the white men came to Kabambarré he asked for a Congo Free State flag. After receiving it he thought he would be free from attack; but a party of black soldiers, under a head man, Furahani, attacked the village, looted the place, and killed three of his people. Since then the State soldiers have inflicted repeated persecution on him, stealing everything he has. He has given them food each time they have passed. Not content with this, they steal everything on the plantation and in the houses. If the rightful owners object, they are beaten; the women are taken by force. Msa says he is afraid to complain to Kabambarré for fear that out of revenge the soldiers will inflict persecution worse than ever. The whole country is being upset by the brutal and thoroughly unjustifiable conduct of the soldiers.

TRUMPETERS, DRUMMERS, AND WHISTLERS AT KABAMBARRÉ.

Msa has lots of slaves, as have all his people; and they seem to be happy enough. Slavery is finished in this part of the world, so far as raiding is concerned; but the Wangwana are allowed to retain the slaves which they own. In fact, it would be difficult to put them back in their own villages; and once in the hands of the Wangwana, under the white man's government, their chief troubles are over. They are compelled to work, but that is always good for Africans; it is the only way to elevate them. Slaves who have been a long time with the Wangwana do not wish to return to their villages even if given the opportunity.

Msa is very intelligent; he wears spectacles, and reads Arabic fluently. I showed him the letters given me by Tippu Tib in Zanzibar. He read them, and told me the contents. Tippu asked everybody to show me kindness, and if necessary give me cloth or anything I might want, and he himself would stand security for the payment. Had

VENDERS OF POTTERY ON MARKET-DAY IN NYANGWÉ.

I got into a tight corner, these letters would have proved very valuable.

December 12. I am visiting at Bwana Msa's to-day. My men are tired, footsore, and hungry, and some sick, and I myself have a very sore heel; a day's rest is desirable for everybody. My sick men are suffering from sore heads and maimed feet. They got their stomachs full of mtama flour and fish to-day, and have been standing on their heads and dancing. There is no better remedy for African ailments than a full belly. African travelers nearly always have crow's feet sprawling from the outside corners of the eyes, which should be credited to the constant blinking caused by the sun's rays, and by the long grass drooping over trails in the wet season, the sharp-pointed blades cutting, spatting, and flicking one's face.

December 14. Reached the Kabambarré station at noon; met very kindly by Lieutenant Hambrusin and Mr. Sinade, his second, just arrived.

December 16. Spent a very quiet day in Kabambarré. Hambrusin has been here since April last [1894. The place was captured on the previous January 25]. He has a good substantial brick house in course of construction and nearly finished, needing only doors and windows and plastering. He has a big force at the station: four hundred soldiers, with their women and children—in all over one thousand people. From the open square in front of the station-house a most picturesque street forty meters wide runs away, lined on each side by well-built clay huts of uniform size, made for two men and their families. There are one hundred of these huts in one street already occupied; another long street is in course of construction to accommodate the remainder. Banks of banana-trees and clumps of tropical forest make the place very picturesque. The plantations are superb, and Hambrusin is still busy making other plantations. Fruit is brought in from the neighboring Wangwana settlements.

December 17. Yesterday the natives in a neighboring village came to complain that one of Hambrusin's soldiers had killed a villager; they brought in the offender's gun. To-day at roll-call the soldier appeared without his gun; his guilt was proved, and without more ado he was hanged on a tree. Hambrusin has hanged several for the crime of murder.

December 18. The tribute exacted from the natives consists of rubber, ivory, and labor. From six till about seven Hambrusin himself gives instruction to the soldiers, who march headed by a band of drummers beating native instruments and whistling. The bugle-call is understood and very well produced by the soldiers.

Hambrusin was through all the fighting against Rumaliza; he says that Dhanis and Pontier are to receive the credit of the campaign. Pontier mastered the country between Stanley Falls and Kasongo, and Dhanis that between Lusambo and Kasongo, and as far as Kabambarré.

All the troops here are Baluba, and from the neighboring tribes, men taken in the fights; they are to serve seven years at a small salary, cloth and provisions; after seven years they are free to go where they like; here the men and women are married. Hambrusin is a stern master, but without that the spirit of this big horde of men would be decidedly rebellious. He has been alone for several months; one of his agents returned home, and two died here of hematuric fever.

I do not think the natives are making much out of this partition of Africa; something should be done to permit their earning a living, to give them comfort and content. Formerly an ordinary white man was merely called *bwana* or *mzungu;* now the smallest insect of a pale face earns the title of *bwana mkubwa* (big master). During the campaign against the Arabs by the soldiers of the Congo Free State many cannibals were to be seen, so officers tell me, provisioning themselves from the killed.

This antislavery movement has its dark side also. The natives suffer. In stations in charge of white men, government officers, one sees strings of poor emaciated old women, some of them mere skeletons, working from six in the morning till noon, and from half-past two till six, carrying clay water-jars, tramping about in gangs with a rope round the neck, and connected by a rope one and a half yards apart. They are prisoners of war. In war the old women are always caught, but should receive a little humanity. They are naked, except for a miserable patch of cloth of several parts, held in place by a string about the waist. They are not loosened from the rope for any purpose. They live in the guard-house, under the charge of black native sentries, who delight in slapping and ill-using them, for pity is not in the heart of the native. Some of the women have babies, but they go to work just the same. They form indeed a miserable spectacle, and one wonders that old women, although prisoners of war, should not receive a little more consideration; at least their nakedness might be hidden. The men prisoners are treated in a far better way.

December 21. To-day I saw an old woman prisoner who had died, being dragged to burial by her fellow-prisoners in the rope gang.

December 23. No work to-day, as the men on the station received an advance during the week. Natives came in crowds to trade; certainly several hundred natives are at the station with maize, bananas, potatoes, fowls, etc. The market lasted from seven in the morning till four in the afternoon. Hambrusin will encourage the natives to this, and hopes to have a market every Sunday in the future.

When Hambrusin took over the station the men were in a rebellious state, ill-treating the natives, robbing, and even killing. Hambrusin executed a few, and the natives, seeing that they would have justice from the whites, remained friendly. There are dozens of villages about Kabambarré, all friendly and submissive, and with large, flourishing plantations. The natives pay tribute by working, gathering rubber, and carrying loads to and from Kasongo.

December 25. Spent another Christmas in Africa to-day—a very pleasant one. I must not forget the kindness of the Belgians. Everywhere they have rendered me kindly aid and saved me all sorts of bother and expense. Their hospitality has been unbounded. Nobody, however, has pleased me so much as Hambrusin, Belgian lieutenant of artillery, who was all through the war, did valuable work as an artilleryman, and was always in the thick of the danger. With his Krupp gun he played a most important part in the downfall of Rumaliza.

There is one blemish on the generally admirable aspect of the Kabambarré station—the miserable, hard-worked, half-starved prisoners, under control of brutal sentries, who delight in every opportunity of ill-treating the wretches placed in their care. But this will end now that Hambrusin has the help of white men. When he was alone for so long he was helpless to attend to everything himself, and had to leave the most responsible work in the hands of his black leaders.

Everything is done in military style, and the discipline is splendid. The men arise at the bugle-call in the morning, and form in line two deep; the roll is called, and then they drill for two hours under the supervision of the whites. They march well, each forty men under a corporal, who instructs his men by word of command in French. After morning drill there is an hour's repose; then the bugle sounds again, and the men turn out for work. Hambrusin inspects the line, sees that all are there, and in response to a bugle-call the head men file in front of their officer, salute respectfully, and receive instructions for the respective squads; they retire to their places, half turn, and march away in order, headed by the buglers, who conduct them to their particular work.

December 26. Left Kabambarré this morning. Lieutenants Hambrusin, Sinade, and Steeman saw me on my way. Marched from the station on the main road, flanked on each side by the soldiers' huts; the men off duty turned out and saluted me as I passed; and *moyo*, the friendly salute of the Baluba, was exchanged with my men. Hambrusin engaged for me forty-two Wabangobango carriers, two for each load; good, strong, willing fellows. Hambrusin has the natives well in hand. I sent word yesterday that I needed carriers, and they turned up in force to-day, quite prepared, and no grumbling. I pay them one fathom Amerikani each to carry a load to Kasongo. Hambrusin also supplied me with an escort of five soldiers and a corporal, two boys as servants, and a cook, the last three to go as far as Nyangwé. I am most grateful for the kindness; if I had been denied aid, I should have been put to great expense and trouble. Hambrusin informed me that he had received orders to prohibit strangers from passing from Tanganyika to the Lualaba *via* Kabambarré and Kasongo; but that he did not think the regulation applied to me, as I was an ancient employee of the Congo Free State, and, moreover, my recommendations were a sufficient passport through the newly acquired land.

December 29. Last night camped at the village of Kestro. Kibonge, who ordered the assassination of Emin Pasha, is being deserted, and one of his own people, in consideration of cloth, is leading Lothaire to Kibonge's hiding-place. The district of Piana Kitetė (Piana means «successor of») is said to be full of incorrigible thieves and bravados, who have attacked caravans several times; but I am assured that Kitetė's people have been most unmercifully persecuted by the State soldiers, who arrive in the villages, and without any payment save blows and curses, take fowls and bananas, destroy cooking-pots, etc.

December 30. All the natives on Tanganyika Lake and from Mtoa to Kasongo speak more or less Swahili, most of them fluently. Natives who have first been under the Wangwana element are the best people to deal with; they have been taught by harsh lessons not to humbug their superiors, and they are taught to be clean besides. They learn to desire good cloth, to build good houses, and to make plantations extensive enough to guard against a drought. I camped near the village of Piana Kitetė to-day. He is in a sad frame of mind; says that he and his people have been fought and raided now four times for no reason that he knows of. Nearly all the women and children have been taken from his villages by Kibangula, Kalombola, and Falabi, the *nyamparas* of Kasongo. Kitetė swears he has done the whites no harm, nor have the Congo Free State soldiers or porters been molested by him. On the contrary, he received the Congo Free State flag, and sent goats to Kasongo. The last goats he sent to Kibangula, and also some slaves; and the slaves were accepted, and the guardians of the goats were also retained as captives. He says his people's huts have all been burned, and they have been so hunted that they have not made new huts. A soldier on the trail has women, and always a boy servant; his wife carries his sleeping outfit, food, etc., cloth, and sandals; his boy carries his cartridges and gun. Often a wife carries the gun. Some of the soldiers have several wives, and are quite large insects. Piana Kitetė says all his people want to emigrate to more peaceful regions, but he restrains them.

A native accompanying a white man, even as ordinary porter, an occupation as humble as that of a pack-donkey, calls other natives *wachenzi*, a scornful word for «savage.» A military spirit prevails through the whole settlement of Kabambarré. My escort are constantly whistling the bugle-calls, and shouting out military commands in French. Experience proves that youths of fourteen and sixteen are as useful and as plucky as matured soldiers.

January 1, 1895. Marched from Myula's village, near the Lulindi River, to Piana Mayengé's village. The land traveled over is undulating; we are constantly marching over grass-covered hills with sparse growth of stunted bush. The natives are all friendly to the whites, and peaceful among themselves. *Mandiba* (small mats of the fiber of palm-trees) are the current coin from Piana Lusangé to Kasongo.

We see people who carry knives in sheaths, worn over the right shoulder and slung to the right side, the handle of the knife just below the armpit. Also, we see more spears than have been present for a long time. Guns are scarce; probably they have them, but the power is now in the hands of the whites. The Wangwana and Arab traders are not yet allowed in the country by the Congo Free State—a wise precaution, I think; they would smuggle powder into the country, and intrigue with the natives, and the Congo Free State would have their battle against the lawless element to fight over again. Besides, if the Wangwana traders are permitted, the profit goes out of the hands of the Congo Free State. Piana Mayengé has built a fine large house to entertain travelers; it is made of clay, with broad verandas and five large rooms.

I learn that Sefu, Tippu Tib's son, left the boma at Ogella, and joined the fighting outside. He was using a short Winchester, fired three shots, then had his arm shattered; he retired into the boma, and handed his gun to Bwana Jama. Sefu died a few days afterward. Tippu Tib did not want the Wangwana and the whites to fight; he knew the inevitable conclusion of such a contest, and sent letters to Raschid, Sefu, Rumaliza, and Nzige, telling them how to come to terms with the whites and open up trade relations. Nzige was the only one who wished for peace; the others tore up Tippu's letters in rage.

Kasongo was built on two parallel slopes facing each other, with a gentle ravine between large clay or brick buildings. Limes, oranges, bananas, papaws, pomegranates, and guavas are growing everywhere. Some establishments were surrounded by a tembé wall; others consisted merely of one big house. There were immense plantations. It was the most important ivory-mart in central Africa; all agree that it was far bigger and more important than Ujiji. Many Arabs were permanently settled here in the past; now they are all gone to New Kasongo to be under the eye of the whites. Many ivory-traders here were immensely rich.

Kasongo shows signs of having been a most important town, certainly the largest I have yet seen in Africa. For a square mile the ground is covered with masses of large clay or sun-dried brick of houses which contained numerous rooms. Each Arab *mgwana*, or man of any importance whatever, had a large house for himself and wives; their followers and slaves lived elsewhere. The houses are now in utter ruins. A broad road running from west to east, thirty feet wide, was kept clear of grass when Kasongo was occupied. The large houses were built on each side of the way. Now a prolific outburst of foliage threatens to hide every vestige of this famous place. Only a few Wangwana of minor importance are now here; all others have gone to settle, by order, near the Congo Free State station at New Kasongo, on the Lualaba. The roofs have been pulled off the bomas, and all wood-work of any value, such as doors and windows, has been taken by the white man for building purposes. New Kasongo is four hours west from here.

January 3. Reached New Kasongo, and was kindly received by Lieutenant Francken and Messrs. De Corte and Perrotte. The station is surrounded by villages that pay tribute in different ways. Some do paddling; others build; others, again, bring in wood for building purposes. The chiefs to the west of here supply mandiba mats as their tribute. Some bring in ivory and rubber.

The place has a population of fifteen thousand, nearly all slaves. I left New Kasongo, and followed the right or east bank of the Lualaba to Nyangwé, which is built on a treeless plain; all the timber for building purposes comes from the opposite bank of the river. Lemery has done good work here. He has a herd of forty head of large-horned cattle. Magnificent avenues of forest trees are seen, and clean roads lined with mango, guava, palm, and banana. A small island opposite the station has five hectares of rice in perfect condition, and in other places are maize and manioc; besides there are the plantations in the vicinity of the station. Lemery says Nyangwé can be made to produce fifteen tons of rubber a month when more tribes are brought under control. Also a good deal of ivory is brought in as tribute and for sale.

In connection with the station there are five thousand auxiliaries, who are sent all over the country to beat the natives into submission to the State. They go in bands of one thousand men, women, and children, and all belongings, settle upon a suitable spot in a rich district, then bring the natives under their control, and prepare the way for a white man to establish a post. The natives, who are all cannibals, are persecuted till they submit; then there is no more trouble.

*E. J. Glave.*

# THE FALL OF THE HOUSE OF ROBBINSON.

«IT is really history, my dear,» Miss Camilla Robbinson would say—«unwritten history, which is so much the most interesting, is n't it? And these family traditions and letters and things correct so much that is in the books. For instance, I don't believe one half of the stories about Lord Dunmore,—though, of course, he *was* very loyal to the king,—because he was a friend of my great-grandfather's, and my great-grandmother thought him charming. And surely he could n't have been such a monster! That picture over there—the little dark one in the oval frame—is said to be of him, but you can't see the face now. Certainly he was n't as black as he is painted there, at any rate.»

Miss Camilla had an oddly charming little laugh, and the brightest play of eyebrows as she spoke or listened. So mobile was her face that even the tiny, scattered rings of pale-brown hair that curled lightly about her white forehead seemed to nod and quiver with sympathy and attention.

With all her quaint charm and fragile beauty, Miss Camilla had early and easily slipped into the ranks of spinsterhood, for the ladies of the house of Robbinson had never been given to matrimony; but she loved graceful little vanities of attire, and wore roses in her hair as she presided in the evening over the worn silver, and thin, mismatched china of the Robbin Hall tea-table. It must be confessed that Robbin Hall, like Dotheboys Hall, was a hall only in name, being in fact the brick kitchen of the old Robbinson mansion, which fully fifty years before had been destroyed by fire; but it had, with some alterations and additions, sheltered the family for half a century, and it was ample for Miss Camilla and the widowed fifth cousin who was her sole companion.

It was a not unattractive dwelling, with its overhanging roof making a narrow porch in front, and with its small many-paned windows; but it looked curiously out of proportion to the great oaks which stood about, and to the gaunt, towering locusts of the old avenue.

A climbing rose, as somber green and as persistent as ivy, matted and tangled itself over the trellis which shut in one end of the porch, and broke out yearly into a wealth of small yellow-white, half-blighted blossoms, with a faint, earthy fragrance, and a peppery something within their pallid folds which made one sneeze.

Within, the staircase was steep and narrow, it cannot be denied, and the old portraits were crowded together upon the walls in a way to suggest that these darkling shadows of dead Robbinsons held themselves so stiffly for want of elbow-room. But all was atoned for by the subtle thing called «atmosphere.» One looked about with a sense of mellow distinction, and absorbed a reverence for the Robbinsons from the very walls.

Perhaps it was the stillness of the place which caused a lull in the levity of the most thoughtless when the door of the narrow parlor had shut upon them, and old Aunt Viny had crept off to find Miss Camilla out among the sweet-williams and mottled balsams of her sunny, old-fashioned garden, and to warn Miss Betsy, lying on the sofa in the long west room up-stairs, to get ready for company.

Miss Betsy had once made a feeble dash into matrimony, but the incident soon closed with the death of the perfectly helpless and ineligible groom, and made little or no impression upon the community, to which she continued to be Miss Betsy Ashby to the end of her days. Only in Miss Camilla's heart rankled the recollection that she was Mrs. Jaggs.

KENYON P. ROBINSON, late of Texas, and purchaser of the Robbin Hall Low Grounds, glanced about him not without interest as he waited, looked down upon by all the goodly company upon the walls.

A fanciful observer might have seen something especially stony in the stare which they bent upon the possessor of so many of their hereditary acres, and the occupant of their old overseer's house; but his clear gray eyes roved easily and unconsciously over them all. It was a good face, with a firm mouth and chin, half hidden by the short brown beard; but a boyish blush suffused it as a light step was heard outside, and he stirred a little nervously in his chair.

Miss Camilla gave him her hand with a

smile. Her large hat was hanging by its strings from her slender arm, and she carried in her hand a bunch of winter violets.

There was a fine gradation in Miss Camilla's smiles, and she did not smile upon Mr. Robinson without a delicate reserve. For who was he? That was the question. She had been able to cast aside the natural prejudice which arose from his being in possession of a part of the family estate; she had overlooked, after a little struggle, his living in the old overseer's house: but she could not forget that she knew nothing of his antecedents. The very fact that his parents had left Virginia to go to Texas was against him. The First Families do not leave Virginia.

His name told nothing. A Robinson might be anybody. He might have blue blood—or he might not. They had once had an overseer named Robinson!

It was indeed an old grievance of Miss Camilla's that Robbinson and Robinson were so often confounded, and she had acquired a distinct dislike to the latter name.

«I am not related to any Robinson,» she would say, with a stress born of stifled irritation, when questioned as to her relationship to such and such a one. Just as invariably a wave of remorse would sweep over her as soon as the words had left her lips, and she would hasten to add:

«Though there are a great many of them that I should *like* to be related to—oh, a great many of them! One branch, to my certain knowledge, is descended through the female side from one of the Signers. And there was a Robinson who was a friend of my great-grandfather's, and of General Washington's, and of a great many people like that—I have some of his letters now. But my name really is n't Robinson at all. It is Rob-binson—with two *b*'s, not one. I can hear that second *b* distinctly myself when it is properly pronounced, but most people say that they can't at all, and so it is very natural that the mistake should occur. But even if our names were spelled alike, there would be no relationship; for my father and my grandfather and my great-grandfather were only sons, and so there could n't be, you know. I am the last of the name,» she would add almost casually. But though she let fall this remark like an afterthought,—for she was never sure whether there was not a trace of boastfulness in saying this,—it was clear from the gentle complacency of her face that she knew it was no trifle to be the whole Robbinson family.

So she smiled upon Mr. Robinson her smile of gracious aloofness as she greeted him that morning for the second time beneath her roof. This, it seemed, like the first, was a purely business visit. He had heard, he said, of the famous Robbinson recipe for curing hams, and he had come to beg a copy.

She went to her little spindle-legged desk, and wrote it for him in her slim, flowing hand.

He took it with a profusion of shy thanks.

«I am going on to the station» he said. «I should be very glad to take any letters, or attend to anything.»

Miss Camilla thanked him, but she had no letters. He looked into his hat and meditated.

«If I can be of any use to you»—he hesitated—«at any time, I shall be very glad. You see, I am so near—»

She murmured her acknowledgments, but her smile was a little strained. So near indeed! The bitterness of it all came over her as he spoke.

There had never been anything of the sordidness of poverty in the hereditary tangle of affairs which, according to a cherished family tradition, began when the first Taggart Robbinson mortgaged his plantation and melted his plate to help Bacon in his rising against Berkeley, and which the successive Robbinsons had long looked upon much as they did upon the family gout.

Heavily encumbered as the estate was, it had remained intact until now. Poor Miss Camilla had had many a bitter struggle with herself before she could accept the offer for the Low Grounds; but there had seemed no help for it.

After all, it was not unpleasant to have a neighbor, and it *was* convenient to have a gentleman about, as Miss Camilla admitted to Miss Betsy, in the mere matter of getting the mail, for instance, for old Uncle Madison was woefully slow and irregular. But there were a hundred other things in which Mr. Robinson rendered the friendliest services.

He hived her bees, dosed old Bess the mare, trimmed the fruit-trees, and discovered so many ways of making himself useful that Miss Camilla wondered sometimes how she had ever got on without him. But his own place did not in the mean time suffer, for the Low Grounds were the wonder of the county.

New books and magazines found their way to the round table in the narrow parlor, new flowers to the garden. Mr. Robinson himself had a love of flowers not inferior to Miss Camilla's own, and delighted her by innumerable clever devices for raising slips and starting seed. Altogether, things are rarely so bad as they seem at first, Miss Camilla reflected.

She was even moved to confess to Mr. Robinson that it was pleasant to have a friend at hand.

«But suppose I am not a friend,» he said.

She glanced at him with something like fright, and looked away.

The firelight shone upon their faces and across the waxed floor, and rows of painted eyes stared down upon them. Her look passed rapidly from the short-waisted lady leaning upon the harp to the slim-handed gentleman with the lace ruffles, from the red-faced colonel of the French-and-Indian war to the double-chinned dame with the pearl necklace; and her face was pale and storm-swept.

«But I hope,» she faltered, «that you will be.»

«I would rather,» he said huskily, «be something else.»

She tightened her hands together as if they shook, and she did not speak for a long, long time.

«There is nothing else,» she answered, «that you could be.»

AND then how frightfully she missed him! He brought her mail, but he did not come in. He helped her into her carriage at church, but he no longer rode beside it. And Robbin Hall was stiller than ever; for Miss Camilla's sweet, reedy little songs ceased somehow, and she dusted the miniatures over the mantel or rubbed the thin silver in silence. But once she astonished Miss Betsy beyond measure by asking her, not without gentleness, about the deceased Mr. Jaggs.

Perhaps it was the discovery of a new cause of anxiety which brought the line between her blue eyes during those dismal November days, when the rain pattered upon the roof, and even oozed through the plaster of wall and ceiling. A white blur had appeared upon the judge's black-silk sleeve, unsightly specks marred the beauty's white-satin gown!

Miss Camilla stood transfixed before them. Why—why had she not noticed! Why had she not prevented it! But how could she?

MR. ROBINSON looked about him with surprise, and Miss Camilla smiled faintly.

«I have sent most of my pictures away, you see,» she said; «some to the State Library, some to the Association for the Preservation of Virginia Antiquities. I had intended to do so at my death; but they were getting mildewed, and I was afraid to keep them.»

«I am glad you kept that young lady,» he remarked, looking up at an old-time beauty above the mantel. «She is rather like you, by the way.»

«Is she?» she said. «I should be glad to think so; but we have never thought as much of that picture as of some of the others. It is a Gilbert Stuart, but she—my great-aunt—displeased the family by her marriage, and for a long time her portrait was turned to the wall.»

«And so there is a story to that picture,» he mused.

«No—only a commonplace one. She fancied some one who was not quite—who was her inferior in birth—or her family thought so—and she would marry him—»

«And lived happily ever after?» he finished.

Miss Camilla smiled.

«Yes; it is n't much of a story.»

«I don't suppose it seemed commonplace,» he said, «to him and her.»

A curious little pause came upon them, which he broke.

«I have been finding out something about my ancestors since I was here last.»

«Ah, indeed?»

Miss Camilla was interested.

«Yes; I have been turning over some old papers during the rainy days, and I came across rather a curious bit of information about my grandfather. I have often as a boy heard my father and mother talking about their life in Virginia; but if they mentioned this fact, it made no impression upon me. It is rather interesting. My father's father once lived on this very estate.»

Miss Camilla looked at him in blank bewilderment.

«But how *could* he?» she exclaimed.

«It is quite a remarkable coincidence. He lived, as I suppose, in the very house in which I am living now!»

Miss Camilla's lids fluttered and fell, and the blood beat in her cheeks. Then she lifted her eyes to his face, and held them steadily there.

«Indeed?» she murmured. «That is very—interesting.»

He smiled.

«Or very shocking? Don't think that I care about my grandfather. He seems to have been an honest man, and a man not to be ashamed of, if he was an overseer. But I love you so—that for anything more—to come between us—»

He set his lips as if half angry at the unsteadiness of his own voice, and waited to regain his mastery of it.

«And I know the traditions of your family—»

Miss Camilla looked at the fire.

«I am afraid,» she said softly, «that I have talked to you a great deal about my family.»

«You could not talk to me about anything,» he said, «that I would not care to hear; but some things—the story of that young lady's picture, for instance—have been rather discouraging to a plebeian who wanted to ask you to be his wife.»

Miss Camilla still studied the blazing logs almost as if she had not heard, but a faint rose crept into her face.

«We were speaking just now of the portraits,» she said. «While they were hanging on the walls, with their eyes always following me about, I could think only of my ancestors as they were painted there—in wigs and ruffles and satin gowns; and when I tried to do as I ought as the last of the name, I remembered how much they thought of the family, and how particular they had been about—everything; and it seemed to me that for their sakes I must be careful about the same things, and not do anything—different.»

She paused for a moment, with his eyes fixed eagerly upon her face. His own face was tense almost to haggardness.

«I am glad those pictures of them are gone, for now I can think of them as being in heaven, and—not caring.»

Miss Camilla's lashes were still wet, but she broke into a bright, tremulous laugh, letting her hands drop restfully into her lap, and looking up at Mr. Robinson.

«I shall be so glad,» she said, «to stop telling people about those two *b*'s!»

*Annie Steger Winston.*

# THE RED COLUMBINE.

FAIR, fragile daughter of the ledge,
  Thou shakest in the breezes free
Thy gold-rimmed bells along the edge
  Of headlands looking out to sea,

Or climbest up the rugged face
  Of inland boulders high and steep,
Or fringest with thy airy grace
  The precipice whence waters leap.

Fair herald of the race of flowers,
  Daintiest of all the springtime knows,
Fresh with the chill of April showers
  Or breath of late-dissolving snows,

The secret places of the rocks
  Wherein no human foot may stand,
The overhanging crag that mocks
  The bravest climber's reaching hand;

The inaccessible ravine,
  Shadowed and dewy all day long,
Where at the bottom, dimly seen,
  The unsunned brook repeats its song;

The cliff unscaled by daring feet,
  The glen concealed in twilight gloom,
These offer thee their safe retreat,
  And look upon thy hidden bloom.

Thou lovest to climb the highest rock
  Seamed by a finger's breadth of soil,
And thence look brightly down, and mock
  The lover who would seize and spoil.

Uncloistered nun among the flowers!
  Thou keep'st thy virgin pride and state,
Kissed only by the winds and showers,
  From all the world inviolate.

The winged banditti of the air
  Who plunder through the summer hours,
The insect thieves who everywhere
  Rob and despoil the helpless flowers,

Are yet asleep; the chrysalis
  Still in his branch-hung hammock swings,
Unconscious of the coming bliss
  Of sunshine, liberty, and wings.

Ah, flower that virgin-hearted dies!
  Whose heart no butterfly has stirred,
Whose honey-laden nectaries
  Have never known a humming-bird!

Ere wasps forsake their cradling clay,
  Or night-moths haunt the apple-bough,
Thou livest thy brief and lonely day,
  And when the bee comes, where art thou?

*Elizabeth Akers.*

# THACKERAY IN WEIMAR.

WITH UNPUBLISHED DRAWINGS BY THACKERAY.[1]

EIMAR, the old residence town of the grand dukes of Saxony, yearly attracts a large number of strangers. They are not drawn thither by any extraordinary natural beauties or mineral springs, nor by old art treasures, or the fashionable life of modern summer-resorts. What attracts so large a multitude of travelers is the desire to visit the place where German thought blossomed and ripened into a classic beauty never before known. Well has the small town on the Ilm been called «Ilm-Athens,» and the ruling house been compared with the Medicis. For it was not a mere coincidence, but the cautious choice of the intellectual and benevolent Grand Duchess Anna Amalia, that brought together in Weimar the greatest German poets and thinkers as teachers and companions for her son Carl August, who in his turn knew how to appreciate them, to increase their numbers, and to retain them in Weimar.

Among the visitors to Weimar are representatives of all the civilized nations of the world; but particularly numerous since the beginning of this century have been travelers from England, and recently from the United States. Goethe's biographer, Lewes, was received there in the most kindly and cordial manner; there Bayard Taylor pursued his studies for his beautiful «Faust» translation, and gave lectures on American literature. It was through him that many of the inhabitants of Weimar first became acquainted with Edgar Allan Poe's «Raven.» In like manner, Professor Thomas of Ann Arbor, one of America's best Goethe students, who has now been called to take the place of the late H. H. Boyesen at Columbia University, studied there in the Goethe-Schiller Archives and the Goethe National Museum.

The existence of the Goethe-Schiller Archives and the Goethe National Museum is due to the generous bequest of Goethe's last grandchild, who died in 1885; and they have lately become objects of great interest to admirers of art and literature.

But many of those who come to Weimar unattracted by the classic peace of the past find the social and intellectual atmosphere of the place most agreeable. The worthy descendants of Anna Amalia and Carl August, mindful of the noble traditions of their house, are continually striving to keep fresh the artistic and literary atmosphere. The Weimar Court Theater was one of the first to produce the great works of Wagner; Liszt made the cosy little cottage near the park, given him by the Grand Duke Carl Alexander, his permanent home, and hundreds of his pupils carried with them from Weimar into the world the art taught them by this great master. The Art School and the Conservatory of Weimar boast of a well-earned reputation.

The opening of the Goethe National Museum offered the layman an opportunity to glance into the workshop of this universal genius; and the manuscripts and correspondences of the «Poet-Archives» put in new light the commanding position held by Goethe in the literary and artistic life of his time. Contributions to his art and natural-history collections were sent him from all sides, and his opinion was asked on all questions of literature, art, and the natural sciences. Artists and scholars of all nations came to Weimar in the first decades of this century in ever-increasing numbers to form a personal acquaintance with Goethe, and to rejoice in his kindly appreciation of their works and interests.

They received at the same time stimulus and encouragement in the intellectual and friendly intercourse which was carried on both at court and in private houses. In this respect the salons of Frau Johanna Schopenhauer, and of the witty, fantastical daughter-in-law of Goethe, Ottilie (née Von Pogwisch), particularly distinguished themselves. Ottilie, with her husband August von Goethe, and their children, Walther, Wolfgang, and Alma, occupied the top floor of Goethe's house on the Frauenplan. She stood at the head of Goethe's household, cared for her father-in-law with the greatest assiduity and self-sacrifice, and entertained her guests in the most agreeable and graceful manner imaginable.

The rooms on the first floor were used only

[1] Printed by permission of Smith, Elder & Co.

for large parties, while Goethe's study and bedroom, which looked out upon the spacious garden in the rear, remained undisturbed in the midst of the liveliness and gaiety often going on in other parts of the house.

With advancing age, Goethe had retired more and more from the whirl of society; and often again, as in the beginning of his stay in Weimar, he lived in the idyllic little cottage in the park, and there received his visitors in quiet and friendly intercourse.

Henry Crabb Robinson, the friend of Charles Lamb and William Wordsworth, who until the middle of this century traveled extensively through the Continent and became acquainted with all persons of intellectual or artistic renown, describes a visit to Goethe's cottage in the year 1829. He writes in his «Diary, Reminiscences, and Correspondence»:

> He [Goethe] generally eats and drinks alone, and when he invites a stranger it is to a tête-à-tête. This is a wise sparing of his strength.

HONI SOIT QUI MAL Y PENSE

To his Britannic Majesty's Consul in Weimar. These drawings of his Britannic Majesty's subjects are dedicated by An Individual.

Thackeray

In the course of a second visit they talked much of Byron, and of the similarity of Burns's «Vision» and Goethe's «Zueignung.» Afterward the conversation turned more in detail to Byron's life and works.

> It was a satisfaction to me to find that Goethe preferred to all other serious poems of Byron the «Heaven and Earth.» He added: «Byron should have lived to execute his vocation, to dramatize the Old Testament. What a subject under his hands the tower of Babel would have been!» In this way I spent five evenings with Goethe. I saw much of his daughter-in-law; he is said to have called her «ein verrückter Engel» (a crazy angel), and the epithet is felicitous.

At Ottilie's Robinson often met Samuel Naylor, the clever translator of «Reineke Fuchs» into English, and the son of his friend Thomas Naylor. Samuel Naylor, it seemed, was a favorite of Frau von Goethe. In fact, during those years a considerable number of young Englishmen were shown particular favor by the ladies of Weimar.

A member of the English colony at Weimar in 1830 was Mr. W. G. Lettsom, who was then the English minister's attaché at Weimar, and later became her Majesty's chargé d'affaires in Uruguay. While a student in Cambridge he had been a friend of William Makepeace Thackeray, and seems to have given him most enticing descriptions of the charms and attractions of the society life at Weimar. For when Thackeray, then but nineteen years of age, had, without the permission or knowledge of his pastor and masters, undertaken a trip to Paris during his vacation in the summer of 1830, and had overcome his first scruples about this escapade, he extended his journey to Weimar, and remained there the entire winter, captivated by the pleasant and stimulating life.

Through his friend he was soon introduced into the best social circles, and above all, of course, into Goethe's house. Wherever he went, he met with a friendly and hearty welcome, as did every well-recommended Englishman. But Ottilie von Goethe particularly rejoiced at this splendid addition to her English retinue. She had expressed her affection for the sons of England before this, calling herself in jest «the British consul at Weimar.» As such she extended her protection to young Thackeray, who, though unknown at the time, soon became through his talents a general favorite.

We gain further knowledge of Thackeray's visit to Weimar from his own hand. He writes in a letter dated Wednesday, the 20th of October:

> I saw for the first time old Goethe to-day. He was very kind, and received me in rather a more distinguished manner than he had used to other Englishmen here. The old man gives occasionally a tea-party, to which the English and some special favourites in the town are invited; he sent me a summons this morning to come to him at twelve. I sat with him for half an hour, and took my leave on the arrival of ——. And Madame de Goethe was very kind. When I went to call on her I found her with three Byrons, a Moore, and a Shelley on her table.

At about the same time Thackeray ordered from a bookseller in Charterhouse Square «a liberal supply of the Bath post paper, on which he wrote his verses and drew his countless sketches. On certain sheets of this paper, after his interview with Goethe,

A COACHMAN.

we find the young artist trying to trace from recollection the features of the remarkable face which had deeply impressed his fancy.»

There is to be found in «Thackerayana,» a collection of notes, anecdotes, and drawings which have been put together from the works left by Thackeray, rather an unsuccessful portrait sketch. This, it seems, partly served as a model for the illustration by Daniel Maclise (under the pseudonym of Alfred Croquis) which appeared in the March number of «Fraser's Magazine» in 1832, almost simultaneously with Goethe's death.

Goethe received from Thackeray the first numbers of this magazine, founded in February, 1830; and Thackeray writes to Lewes:

> Any of us who had books or magazines from England sent them to him, and he examined them eagerly. «Fraser's Magazine» had lately come out, and I remember he was interested in those admirable outline portraits which appeared for a while in its pages. But there was one, a very ghastly caricature of Mr. R——, which, as Madame de Goethe told me, he shut up and put away from him angrily. «They would make me look like that,» he said; though, in truth, I can fancy nothing more serene, majestic, and healthy-looking than the grand old Goethe.

Goethe's unfavorable judgment unfortunately did not deceive him, for the portrait by Maclise unintentionally became in the reproduction a very striking caricature, like that of Mr. R——. The original drawing, however, which is now in the South Kensington Museum, in spite of its sharp characterization and painfully realistic treatment, makes a striking and noble impression, and thus realizes far better the enthusiastic description which Carlyle gave it in «Fraser's Magazine» of March, 1832:

> Reader, thou here beholdest the Eidolon of Johann Wolfgang von Goethe. So looks and lives, now in his eighty-third year, afar in the bright little friendly circle of Weimar, «the clearest, most universal man of his time.»

Maclise, who had never seen Goethe, undoubtedly used Thackeray's sketch for the profile drawing, which explains its awkward and bent figure. For the full face he made use of an engraving, widely known in England, after the admirable Goethe portrait by Stieler in Munich. Later Carlyle himself says, in a note to the Fraser portrait:

> The copy in «Fraser's Magazine» proved a total failure and involuntary caricature, resembling, as was said at the time, a wretched old clothes-man carrying behind his back a hat which he seemed to have stolen. (Carlyle's «Miscellanies,» vol. iii, p. 93.)

On November 17, 1830, Thackeray writes, still from Weimar:

> I have read «Faust,» with which, of course, I am delighted, but not to that degree I expected.

It is natural, of course, that, owing to his youthfulness, the pathos and dramatic power of Schiller appealed to him in a greater degree, as one can see from his letter of February 25, 1831:

> Talking of Schiller, I am in possession of his handwriting and of his veritable court sword, and I do believe him to be, after Shakspere, «The Poet.» . . . I have been reading Shakspere in German. If I could ever do the same for Schiller in English, I should be proud of having conferred a benefit on my country.

The best description of Thackeray's subsequent life in Weimar is found in the above-mentioned letter to Lewes, of April 28, 1855:

> Five and twenty years ago at least a score of English lads used to live at Weimar for study or sport or society, all of which were to be had in the friendly little Saxon capital. The Grand Duke and Duchess received us with the kindliest hospitality. The court was splendid, but yet most pleasant and homely. We were invited in our turns to dinners, balls, and assemblies there. Such young men as had a right appeared in uniform, diplomatic and military. Some, I remember, invented gorgeous clothing—the kind old Hof-Marschall of those days, M. de Spiegel (who had two of the loveliest daughters eyes ever looked on), being in no wise difficult as to the admission of these young Englanders. Of the winter nights we used to charter sedan-chairs, in which we were carried through the snow to those pleasant court entertainments. I, for my part, had the good luck to purchase Schiller's sword, which formed a part of my court costume, and still hangs in my study, and puts me in mind of days of youth most kindly and delightful.
>
> We knew the whole society of the little city, and but that the young ladies, one and all, spoke admirable English, we surely might have learned the very best German. The society met constantly. The ladies of the court had their evenings. The theatre was open twice or thrice in the week, where we assembled, a large family party. Goethe had retired from the direction, but the great traditions remained still. The theatre was admirably conducted. . . .
>
> In 1831, though he had retired from the world, Goethe would nevertheless kindly receive strangers. His daughter-in-law's tea-table was always spread for us. We passed hours after hours there, and night after night, with the pleasantest talk and music. We read over endless poems and novels in French, English, and German. My delight in those days was to make caricatures for children. I was touched to find that they were remembered, and some even kept until the present time; and very proud to be told, as a lad, that the great Goethe had looked at some of them.

A small collection of sketches of this kind he had, at this time, dedicated to Frau von Goethe, under the joking title, already mentioned, of «British consul in Weimar.» The loose leaves are carefully pasted together, and on each one Ottilie von Goethe has testified in her own hand to Thackeray's authorship; and the name Thackeray which stands below the dedication given on page 921, and which serves more or less as identification of «An Individual» immediately above it, is written by Ottilie.

These drawings were handed down with the greatest care by inheritance to Goethe's grandchildren, and so on down to the author, who takes pleasure in presenting them to the public as valuable aid for the appreciation of Thackeray's artistic talent, and as a remembrance of one of the happiest episodes in the life of the great novelist.

Most readers know Thackeray as an artist only from the drawings he has made for his novels; but in these, as well as in the Goethe sketch, he shows himself by no means to the best advantage; for, on the one hand, the sketch suffered, as did that of Maclise, in course of reproduction; and on the other hand, the great knack of his artistic talent lay in his very sketchy though highly characteristic treatment of lively and preferably humorous scenes or funny types and personages.

Frau von Gustedt, who as Jenny von Pappenheim was a friend of Ottilie von Goethe, tells in her memoirs how Thackeray used to caricature himself:

> As we sat about the tea-table and conversed he drew the most humorous sketches. He always drew himself by beginning at the feet and completing the picture without taking his pen from the paper. He used to draw a little street boy next to him, making fun of him because of his queerly shaped nose, which had once been broken while boxing. Otherwise he was of good appearance—tall, with fine eyes, and thick curly hair. He belonged to the most popular set of Englishmen who made Weimar their temporary home, and of these there were a great many.

Pictorial puns can be found in Thackeray's Charterhouse school-books, in which there is a drawing called «In a State of Suspense.» Still more numerous are his similarly humorous treatments, while a student, of legal definitions, such as «Fee Simple,» «On Freeholds,» «A General Clause,» «A Rejoinder,» «An Ejectment,» etc.

Further details concerning his visit to Goethe, and his impressions of court and of Weimar society, Thackeray describes from memory:

The Grocer & the House-Maid.

> Of course I remember very well the perturbation of spirit with which, as a lad of nineteen, I received the long-expected invitation that the «Herr Geheimerath» would see me. This notable audience took place in a little antechamber of his private apartments, covered all round with antique casts and bas-reliefs. He was habited in a long greydrab redingote, with a white neck-cloth, and a red ribbon in his buttonhole. He kept his hands behind his back, just as in Rauch's statuette. His complexion was very bright, clear, and rosy, his eyes extraordinarily dark, piercing, and brilliant. . . . I fancied Goethe must have been still more handsome as an old man than even at the days of his youth. His voice was very rich and sweet. He asked me questions about myself,

which I answered as best I could. . . . *Vidi tantum:* I saw him but three times—once walking in the garden of his house in the Frauenplan, once going to step into his chariot on a sunshiny day, wearing a cap and a cloak with a red collar. He was caressing at the time a beautiful little golden-haired granddaughter, over whose sweet fair face the earth has long since closed to. [Alma von Goethe died at the age of seventeen years, while on a visit in Vienna in 1844.]

Though his sun was setting, the sky round about was calm and bright, and that little Weimar illumined by it. In every one of those kind salons the talk was still of art and letters. . . . At the court the conversation was exceedingly friendly, simple, and polished. The Grand Duchess, a lady of very remarkable endowments, would kindly borrow our books from us, and graciously talk to us young men about our literary tastes and pursuits. In the respect paid by this court to the patriarch of letters there was something ennobling, I think, alike to the subject and sovereign.

The most interesting document of the international literary pursuits cultivated by the social circle grouped about Ottilie von Goethe is «Das Chaos» («The Chaos»), a publication printed for this same small company. J. D. Gries, the talented translator of Tasso and Ariosto, had described the confusion of languages then spoken in Weimar in a stanza which, freely translated, would read:

Often time full many a thing can show,
 Which once we thought was but a fable;
Weimar as «German Athens» we did know,
 But now they call it «German Babel.»

And the origination of «The Chaos» points, if only in a trivial way, to the polyglottism which later reigned throughout its pages.

In the year 1829, when the French sculptor David visited Weimar for the purpose of making his famous bust of Goethe, and Mickiewicz, the Polish Byron, was also there, a small circle of intimate friends of Ottilie met together in her living-room one rainy afternoon. Among the gentlemen were Councilor Soret of Geneva, the instructor of the present Grand Duke Carl Alexander; Mr. Patrick Parry, a popular Englishman who had settled down in Weimar; and Eckerman, Goethe's secretary. The conversation had come to a standstill, something which very rarely happened, when Eckerman remarked with a sigh, «Es regnet»; «It rains,» said Parry; and «Il pleut,» laughed Soret.

«Go home if you don't know anything better to talk about,» said Ottilie, moodily; «it seems to me, anyway, that our company is falling asleep. It is the highest time to shake them up with something of particular interest.»

The proposition met with general applause, and after diverse expressions of opinion it was finally decided to found a Musen-Verein, (Society of the Muses), with an Apollo at its head. The club was to meet once a week to furnish contributions for a journal to appear only in manuscript form. Ottilie succeeded in interesting Goethe in the undertaking, but could not persuade him to act as Apollo. The nine Muses soon met, and were compelled to take a tenth into the club. «The old gods will gladly suffer this from us good people of Weimar,» Ottilie explained. In a few days the manuscript journal appeared. The contributions were not signed; Ottilie alone knew their authors, and took good care to keep their names in secrecy.

The Society of the Muses was heard from as such but once, and forthwith disbanded. «The Chaos» took its place, as the contents of the future printed pages were to be chaotic. According to the rules, only such persons were admitted to «The Chaos» as had lived in Weimar at least three days, had contributed at least one original but still unpublished article, and had promised to keep it secret from all non-members. Ottilie, as editor, was assisted by Parry and Soret. These three carried out the original undertaking with much tact and discretion; and by and by the greater portion of society also took part. Young and old were interested

and excited in trying to guess the authors of the different articles, and in the hope of being guessed themselves, and of having replies. On Goethe's birthday, August 28, 1829, the first printed number appeared.

It opened with a German prologue, by Holtei, explaining the appearance of «The Chaos,» and «invoking the good graces of the great master.» In the «Letter-Box,» which begins in the next number and is continued in the succeeding ones, one «Elvira» replies in French to an Englishman who writes for news from Weimar. One «Henry Davantry» writes from London warning a friend against visiting Weimar, against the German «malaria» sentimentality, the tobacco, the moonlight, and the dancing-craze of the women. The writer of the «Elvira» letter was Mr. Plunkett, son of Lord Dausany, and Ottilie was the author of the letter signed «Davantry.»

The second number opened with an English prologue by Mr. Charles Knox, the twelfth son of the Bishop of Derry; while a prologue in French, written by Soret under the pseudonym of «Plainpalais,» served as introduction to the third. The same number contained an answer, also by Soret, to a letter by «Elvira.»

After the appearance of a fourth prologue in Italian, a correspondence in French by the Russian Larazin, and English poems by Charles des Voeux, the translator of Goethe's «Tasso,» Gries, under the pseudonym of «Alikuin,» again complained of the predominance of the foreign element in verses a free translation of which is:

British, Gallic, and Italian
  Seem to be in fullest sway;
If I knew some Kamchadalean,
  Satisfied I 'd go my way.
With happiness supreme I 'd smile
  If Turkish I could murder; oh,
But German now is out of style,
  And only German 's all I know.

Goethe, too, contributed several poems, which were marked with a star, and by his graceful verses «To Her» evoked a contest of skilful retorts «To Him,» written by four ladies, among them Ottilie, each one of whom claimed for herself the compliments of his verses.

It was generally taken for granted that Thackeray, too, had contributed to «The Chaos» during his stay at Weimar; for Ottilie von Goethe could not permit such a talent, although only later fully developed, to escape her undertaking. But nothing has ever been discovered which might lead to the identification of any pseudonym which he may have used. Two contributions, however, have been found among the manuscripts which are carefully kept in the «Poet-Archives» in Weimar, which doubtless were written by the same hand as the above dedication and the titles of the other illustrations. They were surely, therefore, written by Thackeray.

The first is a merry drinking-song, without title or signature:

I pray not for riches, I ask not for fame;
  Let madmen and soldiers go seek her;
But honesty needeth no Sir to his name,
  And a little 's enough for good liquor.
I state him an ass who, despising his glass,
  For place or preferment will quarrel;
My creed I do hold with the lyric of old,
  For he stuck all his life to his barrel!

When goblins and ghosts 'mong the children of men
  Were permitted by Satan to riot,
Our priests laid them deep in the Red Sea, and then
  The poor exorcised devils were quiet!
Now all dæmons are rare, save the one that 's called care;
  But we 've need of no priest to dismay him.
Right simple 's the spell the dull spirit to quell—
  In the red sea of wine you should lay him.

St. Peter in heaven hath charge of the keys,
  If his brother St. John 's a truth-teller.
When an angel in heaven, how gladly I 'd ease
  The old boy of the keys of the cellar!
Or if banished elsewhere as a sinner who ne'er
  Has listened to prayer or to preacher,
Then may I be cursed with perpetual thirst,
  And to quench it an emptiless pitcher!

Numerous translations from Goethe's works appeared in «The Chaos.» Count Alessandro Poerio in Florence translated «Die Braut von Corinth» into Italian, and Count Casa Valencia «Die Spinnerinn» into Spanish. Lord Leweson contributed to «The Chaos» parts of his «Faust» translation, which, however, did not please Goethe very much. But all the more satisfactory were the translations of «Meine Ruh' ist hin» from «Faust,» and «Nur wer die Sehnsucht kennt» («Mignon»), by Samuel Naylor, and of other selections by Mr. Lawrence under the pseudonym of «St. Ives.»

To this category belongs Thackeray's second contribution, entitled «Translated from Faust,» and signed «Rosa»:

Once on a time there lived a king,
  And he did keep a flea.
Now he did love this little thing
  As though his sire was he.

The tailor was called by the king's desire,
  And he bid the man of stitches
To make a coat for the young squire
  And an elegant pair of breeches.

Silks and velvets rich and rare
  Did this flea each day now put on;
Ribbons, too, on his coat he did wear,
  And a gold cross at his button.

A minister next was this little flea,
  And wore a star which made his
Brothers and sisters at court to be
  Great gentlemen and great ladies.

They bit the court, and they bit the queen
  And the wretched maids of honor;
But not one of them all might scratch, I ween,
  Though a dozen were upon her!

Now ladies and lords are more at ease,
  For nothing does prohibit 'em,
When bitten by nasty little fleas,
  To kill them all ad libitum.

In a letter also published in «The Chaos» Ottilie von Goethe characterized the general tone of Weimar society which then reigned, and which to some degree still reigns:

We speak to each other frankly and openly about every feeling and sensation. Even if Weimar were a place in which few strangers were seen, or where these were widely scattered, we would, according to custom, fight our way up the entire ladder which has to be climbed with a stranger, beginning with the first question, « Is this your first visit to Weimar? » and ending with remarks on the weather and the theatre. But as so many different countries sent us their inhabitants, we all silently resolved to throw off the awful chain of monotony which in consequence would surely weigh upon us every hour of the day; and then, after the first phrase had been uttered as payment on account, quietly to continue in our customary way, as if no stranger were present. . . . Wherein consists the great difference in feeling one's self out of place or at home? Surely only therein, that one approaches one's old acquaintances with confidence and without all ceremony. So one acts and talks as if one could not be misunderstood, whereas one treats strangers in their places in a way which really is nothing but politely expressed distrust.

It was no wonder, then, that the charm of such an unceremonious and cordial intercourse, and the cultivated amiability of the members of society, induced Thackeray to interrupt his university work for a considerable time. With joyous gratitude he in later years remembered his sojourn in Weimar and the friends he had won there. After twenty-three years he returned thither for a short visit with his daughter, to show her the dearly loved town where he had spent so happy and so instructive a period of his youth.

I passed a couple of summer days in the well-remembered place, and was fortunate enough to find some of the friends of my youth. Madame de Goethe was there, and received me and my daughter with the kindness of old days. We drank tea in the open air at the famous cottage in the park, which still belongs to the family, and had been so often inhabited by her illustrious father.

Thackeray closes his letter to Lewes with the words:

After a five and twenty years' experience since those happy days of which I write, and an acquaintance with an immense variety of human kind, I think I have never seen a society more simple, more charitable, courteous, gentlemanlike, than that of the dear little Saxon city where the good Schiller and the great Goethe lived and lie buried.

And Lewes adds from personal experience:

Thackeray's testimony is not only borne out by all that I learn elsewhere, but is indeed applicable to Weimar in the present day, where the English visitor is received by the reigning Grand Duke and Duchess with the same exquisite grace of courtesy, and where he still feels that the traditions of the Goethe period are living.

*Walter Vulpius.*

*(Translated by Herbert Schurz.)*

# EASTER FLOWERS.

THE roses were the first to hear—
  The roses trellised to the tomb;
Bring roses—hide the marks of spear
  And cruel nails that sealed His doom.
The lilies were the first to see—
  The lilies on that Easter morn;
Bring lilies—crowned with blossoms be
  The head so lately crowned with thorn.

The roses were the first to hear:
  Ere yet the dark had dreamed of dawn,
The faintest rustle reached their ear;
  They heard the napkin downward drawn;
They listened to His breathing low;
  His feet upon the threshold fall.
Bring roses—sweetest buds that blow,
  His love the perfume of them all.

The lilies were the first to see:
  They, watching in the morning gray,
Saw angels come so silently
  And roll the mighty stone away;
They saw Him pass the portal's gloom;
  He brushed their leaves—oh, happy dower!
Bring lilies—purest buds that bloom,
  His face reflected in each flower.

The roses were the first to hear,
  The lilies were the first to see;
Bring fragrant flowers from far and near
  To match the Easter melody!
«Rabboni!» be on every tongue,
  And every heart the rapture share
Of Mary, as she kneels among
  The roses and the lilies fair!

*Clarence Urmy.*

# NANCY.

WITH PICTURES BY E. W. KEMBLE.

WHEN Maitland and I arrived at the Café Durand, at the corner of the Rue Royale and the Place de la Madeleine, the little tables were already far out on the sidewalk. Surrounding them, here and there, were many apathetic sippers of absinthe and many garrulous bock-drinkers, sunning themselves and gossiping of the last escapade of a famous actress. We had walked leisurely from the Rue d'Argenson, where for several years I had established my studio. We had seated ourselves at one of the little tables, and were enjoying the amusing spectacle of the Paris street, intending later, possibly, a visit to the florid canvases of Rubens in the Louvre.

It was about the hour of noon; the sun was very mild and pleasant, for the May of this 1891 had been extremely cold in Paris. Maitland offered me a cigar, and ordered some coffee. Like many of his rich fellow-countrymen, he was dressed like an Englishman, and might very well have been taken for the younger son of some wealthy lord. He fell to chatting and laughing, as was his wont, and commenting upon the myriad faces—sad, gay, stern, and flippant—of the crowd that passed us. He told me that there was not here the variety of Broadway, nor the beauty. I remember I replied that there was not even the beauty of Regent street. There were many sad instances of vagabondism; there were many women with hectic complexions and blonde hair; there were, also, many specimens of the Paris dandy: but there was in all the faces no freshness, no purity. I fancied my young American friend secretly regretted the absence of the pert young miss of Fifth Avenue, who is able to lighten the heaviness of the passing show by her open-eyed trustfulness. I have never had the good fortune to travel in the States, but I fancy that to watch the promenade from a café on Broadway, if they have these affairs in New York, would be extraordinarily amusing. I fancy the people dress much more showily even than here; that there is a greater exhibition of millinery and a more generous display of color, a fondness for which is probably to be traced to the influence of their brilliant autumnal foliage.

Maitland amused me by his newly acquired *fin de siècle* pessimism. He affected to find nothing of interest in the throngs of well-dressed men and women who were moving in either direction; he pretended to give me his opinion that the faces of the Parisians betrayed a marvelous lack of *esprit!* Suddenly he became very silent. His attention was fixed upon the sad, white face of a nun who passed. She wore, I believe, the garb of the order of Sacré Cœur. Her face, pale and set, had a strained, painful quality, as if she were silently brooding over some secret grief. Maitland frankly stared at her as she moved by our table; then, excusing himself, he rose and hastened on to a point on the boulevard, where he stopped and again scrutinized her features more closely. When he returned to his seat he was silent a long time. He appeared to have entirely lost interest in the gaiety of the street. Maitland was usually such good company that I was beginning to be afraid that I had probably wasted an afternoon when at last he said abruptly:

«You Englishmen imagine that you know American characteristics very thoroughly. You know and are fond of certain optimistic American types; you introduce them into your plays and novels; you solemnly assure yourselves that you have, in the vulgar phrase, ‹sized us up.› It will therefore surprise you, I presume, when I tell you that the face of the cloistral nun who passed is quite typical of many of our New England women; that it is the exact counterpart of one which has been indelibly stamped on my memory, which I saw but once, and which betrayed, as did the nun's, a sadness beyond words.»

«I fancy that you knew the handsome nun from the way you stared,» I said with a smile, sipping my coffee leisurely.

«No; only the face. I knew that—it was familiar to me.»

«She reminded you of the typical New Englander? She certainly appeared anemic to a degree. I hope in America you are not in the habit of starving your typical women. Perhaps you starve them—the types—to preserve them.» I laughed.

Maitland was silent a moment.

«That is the word—*starved*,» he said. «They are starved—their emotions allowed to wither away of inanition. I can't take this thing lightly, because the life of some of these mistaken women, with their horrible self-repression, comes so vividly before me. I have lived much in New England; I know whereof I speak; I can give you an instance.»

Maitland glanced about at the gay scene before us with a quick glance, and then, as it were, with a gesture put it far from him—the passing throng, the pretty kiosk with its illustrated papers, the array of carriages, the glitter of a parade of soldiers. In the distance the magnificent if irreligious Madeleine seemed to rise from an enormous bank of roses, for there was in the place before the church a flower-show of unusual proportions. On all sides the gaiety of the Paris afternoon was beginning. The city was festal,—it is always festal,—playing the part to the nineteenth that Venice did to the seventeenth, that New York will perhaps, to the twentieth, century. Within the Café Durand a skilled musician played a lively waltz. Some very charming Americans came and took a table near us—a handsome mama, and a daughter with the frankest blue eyes, who demurely sipped her little glass of Madeira, and glanced at my friend. Maitland saw and heard nothing of it all. «I have half a mind to tell you,» he said, «the story of Nancy Brandon.»

The waltz the musician was playing was a very pretty trifle. I made a mental note to learn its name, buy it, and send it to my little niece in Devonshire.

«Go on!» I laughed; «I want to hear if there are nuns to be found in your puritan New England, and to learn that your typical woman there is a recluse. Let me tell you that the type you send across the water for us to admire is talkative, lively, rapid, *brave*. Are there, then, also the other sort—?»

«I assure you what I say is true,» he interrupted. «Consider me, if you please, an ancient mariner. I must tell my story to get rid of it.»

«To be rid of the face?»

«Yes; that is it.» Maitland did not smile.

«I see. The nun reminds you of—the New Englander?»

«It is the likeness of two minted coins, of two casts of a statue; the white face of stone, the dying soul within the eyes; the nun's and Nancy Brandon's were the same. There were the same traces of faded beauty in each of their delicate, flower-like features, and the same repression and the same repellent hauteur in their eyes.»

I said nothing, and after a moment's hesitation he continued:

«About three years ago I spent a week with a friend in the hills of Vermont for the trout-fishing. It was just about this time, in May. Our luck was not of the best, and I resolved to fish a stream hitherto untried. It led me through a wild country, a primeval forest, through the gorge of a mountain, and so down into one of those remote valleys which seem to be entirely shut out from the world.

«I remember that I had fished all day with some success, and it grew to be dusk before I realized my distance from home. I came upon a road which appeared to have fallen into complete disuse. The grass was growing between the tracks of the wheels, and brambles and raspberry-bushes entirely obscured the old rail-side fences on each. I came to a farm-house, and found it locked and deserted. Three or four apple-trees were in full bloom at the north side and in the meadow. The old barns near by were rotting, with their open doors hanging half off. Across the valley, upon a hillside, gleamed a light. I determined, if possible, to reach the house which contained it. As I came out into the road again, I remember, it began to rain a little.

«I passed many other deserted farms—you see, the soil in parts of New England cannot compete with the fertile Ohio and Mississippi valleys. I had happened upon a district where nearly all the farmers had sold out or died out, and the later incoming foreigners—the Irish, the French Canadians, and others—had not yet arrived.»

«But you astonish me, Maitland,» I said, interested; «is it possible that your Yankees are dying out in New England?»

«Yes; the change has been silently going on for some years. It is quite true that the old ‹first-settler› population is disappearing; also that the differences between the rich and the poor are becoming much more marked. The cities are growing, but the rural districts are becoming depopulated, the small farmers moving West. It is noticeably so in the Connecticut valley and in Vermont. Farm after farm that I passed presented the most wretched appearance; the low, white wooden houses were overgrown with rank vines, the fences broken down, the windows in many instances boarded up. At one house, which had the stately white pillars of the classic architectural period in America and seemed finer than its neighbors, I observed a swarm of dirty Irish children about the door, playing a noisy game among the old box-bordered flower-beds in the quaint garden. I pressed on, and at last, chilled by the rain, arrived just as darkness was setting in at the house on the hill farm whose light I had observed from the valley.

«There was an air of neatness about the yard as I entered, and I felt sure that the hill farm, for some reason, was still being cultivated by the descendants of the original settlers. The house was of the common New England type, two stories in front, and straggling out in the rear to a number of low sheds and outhouses. I knocked at the side door, and it was immediately opened by a tall, middle-aged farmer-like man with a long, brown chin-beard. He was dressed in his Sunday black doeskin. I asked him if I could obtain lodging for the night. He answered me with a question.

«‹Be'n fishin'?› he asked in a loud voice and with a cheery manner. ‹I reckon you ken stay, ef Nancy don't mind. Come right in, sir; it 's a bad night fer to be out.›

«The door opened into the great farm kitchen. By the stove, in a stiff wooden chair, was seated an old man, who held his skinny hands out over the fire, looking at me suspiciously over his shoulder. A large Newfoundland dog sniffed at my heels and growled. The younger man, who had every appearance of being from the West, placed a chair for me by the stove, and I had leisure to tell them of my successful fishing venture and to show them my basket of trout. I had leisure, also, to observe the third figure in their household—a delicate, slight little woman, who was busy setting the table near a window. Her back was turned toward me. She seemed to have no curiosity concerning my arrival, but to be completely engrossed in her affairs. When at last she turned and approached the stove for some purpose, she scarcely lifted her eyes from the floor.

«‹Nancy,› said the younger man, briskly, ‹ken ye make room fer a stranger to-night?›

«‹It 's nothing to me,› she answered in a low, dull voice, which possessed too little interest to be forbidding.

«‹I guess ye ken stay,› said my host, winking at me as who should say, ‹You see, *I 'm* willing enough.›

«I saw Nancy's face—a tragic face, like the nun's, as white and cold as marble, with faint traces of a past beauty, and a sweet, solemn purity of profile like a Greek cameo. She gave me an impression of outline without color or life.

«‹Huh! Ef it had be'n to-morrow night, now, guess you 'd not found no light here nuther. It jest happed father an' Nancy here is goin' West with me to-morrow. Ye see, most the folks in this valley has moved away long afore this; but ye 're welcome to stay the night here.› He observed my glance about the neat kitchen.

«‹No; we ain't need to pack. Sold out as she stands to the bank folks to Equinox—everythin'. I made a clean sweep. Yes, house, barns, cattle, furnitoor, beddin', pictyers,—everythin'; guess they think they got a bargain. They was mighty ready to bid a lump sum.›

«NANCY.»

«‹Some o' the furnitoor in this house is nigh goin' on a hund' fifty ye'rs old,› said the old man, not looking at me, but with an attempt, I thought, to be agreeable. William smiled contemptuously, and went on:

«‹Wal, the bank folks did n't hev fer to go down deep fer it, true; but how was we to take it West? Folks out in my kentry ruther prefer modern furnitoor, an' wife she would n't hev the old stuff in the house. Whar be you from? New York? Guess likely you would n't be hevin' the old stuff in New York, nuther;› and he laughed heartily.

«His laughter seemed to irritate his father. The old man shifted himself on the edge of his chair, then pushed back again.

«‹There 's most folks nowadays gettin' too high an' mighty,› he said. ‹William, it wa'n't right to sell the old mahogany table yer mother used ter set such a store by.›

«‹Thet table fetched ten dollars,› said William, laconically; ‹an' mother she 's beyond where she needs tables, I reckon.›

«His father did not reply. He was a lean old man, white-haired and clean-shaved except beneath his chin, where his whiskers grew out from his collar in a sort of fringe. His whole appearance was neat and well cared for; he seemed to partake of the general tidiness of the place. It came over me that this neatness was due to the quiet little woman setting the table—that she had performed her whole duty in that household, and yet she had done no more.

«What is the cause of every one's deserting the valley?» I asked, feeling that I had hit upon a domestic dénouement.

«‹Because—no one 's willin' ter be content an' thank God for what they 've got,› quavered the old man, irritably. ‹Because they 're always wantin' an' wantin', an' ain't ready to stay settled down.›

«William winked at me. ‹Why, it 's because farmin' don't pay up here on these hill farms, thet 's why. An' you 've got to git up an' git. I writ father fifteen year ago to hustle an' sell out an' come live wi' me, an' I kep' writin' an' writin'; did n't do no good. I told him to sell out when he 'd a chance, the year the slate folks took to minin' slate over to the holler. I told him to sell out then, and I guess likely he wishes now he 'd took my advice. I reckon Nancy and him hez hed 'most enough on it up here all alone winters. No; it 's played-out kentry; might 's well own up to it. I guess he 's hed enough.›

«The old man had the discomfited air of one who admittedly has the joke turned against him at last. He kept on warming his hands over the stove, for the evening had come on raw and cold, and varied his movements by occasionally touching the hot tea-kettle. Over his stern face there flitted a senile grin, then disappeared. He seemed to me to have been a large man once, like his son, but latterly to have shrunken down hard and small upon his bones. He moved uneasily in his seat, then said, as though to change the subject to an impersonal one:

«‹I guess likely it 's a-goin' to storm all night.›

«He walked over to the window and looked out. The rain was driving in on an eastern wind. He gazed vacantly out into the storm a moment, and the window reflected his old withered face. Then he turned about, his eye, I thought, meeting Nancy's. He said quickly, ‹Guess—ye won't want to start to-morrow, William, in the rain?›

«I noticed that Nancy paused a moment as if listening for her brother's reply.

«‹Rain 'r shine, father; I 've been a week longer now than I expected. It 's time I was gettin' back—so it 's rain 'r shine.›

«The look that came over Nancy's face was one I never shall forget. Her expression settled down into a rigid, tragic despair. She sighed, and went out of the room with a soft step.

«‹Why,› said William, with a confidential smirk, ‹it does beat the Dutch how they fought ag'in' goin' away from the farm! They kep' a-gittin' stiffer an' stiffer. Now,› said the honest fellow, ‹it will be doin' me a favor, sir, if, you bein' from the city, you should try an' persuade 'em that it 's no place up here alone—them two; a word from you, bein' from the city, might go a great way to make 'em feel satisfied to go. Why, sir, they do remind me of these 'ere lichens that grow about this 'ere farm on the stun fences! Nancy she sees plain it 's fer father's best good, an' so now she jines in an' does her best; but there was a long time when she done her best t' other way.›

«‹She loves the old Vermont farm too well to leave it?›»

«‹Dunno; guess not; don't believe, ef you should ask her, she 'd know why. She 's got to be an old maid, an' she 's set in her way; I guess that 's it.› William gave a great yawn. There was no tragedy here for him.

«Presently supper was ready. I was rather surprised at its delicacy, expecting only coarse farmers' fare. There were light, delicious biscuit, gooseberry preserves, and slices of thin cold pork. The tea was fragrant, the cakes and gingerbread such as I remember long ago at home. I noted places in the table-cloth where it had been darned with exquisite skill, presumably by Nancy's patient fingers.

The old man moved toward his seat at the table, and held out his cup to Nancy, who waited on us, not taking a seat herself. She poured him a cup of steaming tea, and I said, rising:

«‹I 'm afraid I have Miss Nancy's seat?›»

«‹Oh, no,› William laughed; ‹Nancy she never sets down.› Then he added: ‹When she gets out West she 'll have more time. I intend fer her ter be a lady.›

«William looked at his father, and even at Nancy herself, as if for some reward for this gracious speech; but Nancy said nothing.

«The old man appeared to ponder over this remark, and ate his supper in the same nervous, hurried manner his digestive organs had contended against since boyhood, and pushed back his chair. Nancy's face still betrayed no sign. It was only after he had bolted his supper and regained his seat by the stove that her father said with severity, by way of doing justice to his silent daughter:

«‹I guess Nancy hain't no cause to move West ter be a lady.›

«‹Well, she won't hev ter wait on folks,› said William.

«His father hitched his chair a peg nearer the stove. It was as if one of the old-fashioned customs of his house was being attacked—the custom of toilsome house duties for the women, inherited from the early settlers, from the old puritan customs of his fathers.

«‹Women-folks don't need ter be idle,› he said. ‹Nancy she 's like her mother; I 've seen her mother git up off a sick-bed ter churn.›

«They proceeded to discuss Nancy slowly and laboriously in her presence, as if they had often done so before, and had come to regard her as virtually absent. She sat in a distant corner of the kitchen, as though afraid of intruding. When we rose from the table she came forward and began quietly removing the dishes. I noticed for the first time that she had a slight limp as she walked. I wondered how much her lameness had to do with her strange reticence. In the semi-darkness of the great shadowy kitchen I watched her as she moved noiselessly about, performing her gentle offices in the old farm-house for the last time. It seemed to me that she lingered caressingly over the old blue china and the table-cloth, so spotless and so white.

«I had happened upon a strange catastrophe in her narrow, arid life. Yet her face was so utterly devoid of emotion that I almost believed the sadness of the situation lay in my own mind, not hers. I was heartily glad they were going to take her West, where, as William coarsely and humorously said, his boys 'd ‹romp the old maid frills right out 'n her.› I thought of the long days, immured in the bleak snows of winter, that she had passed in the bleaker society of the old farmer. Alone! For it is not the habit with these arid farm-folk to interchange opinions save upon the weather. All else is fixed and settled—religion, patriotism, duty; they have no qualms, no fears, no hopes, and what affections they may have they bury deep within their souls, as if ashamed to own them!

«As the evening wore on it was evident that hidden in the old man's heart was a secret satisfaction at leaving the old hill farm which he could not entirely suppress. He began to ‹thaw› a good deal, as they say in Vermont. An odd Gargantuan humor betrayed itself in his sallies at William—reminiscences of days, long past, spent in taverns or about the village store. His mirth was almost dreadful, for it seemed an unconscious acknowledgment of an emancipation, as if he had been cold and hard, but Nancy harder still, and the day of his release had come at last.

«‹A nice pair, you two!› laughed William, noisily; ‹you two a-farmin' it! Say, between you an' the old horse, s'pose ye plowed one furrer a day!›

«‹Huh! guess we made out ter live, me an' Nancy. When I wuz about I did my share, an' when I wuz took with the quinzy—wal, Nancy she done everythin'.›

«They both chuckled at this sally, while little Nancy sat silent and mute, knitting at the other end of the room as if not listening.

«‹Why, one night she thought I wuz a-goin' ter die. She hitched up an' druv over to Equinox, fifteen mile, for a doctor. I never see her so excited. I see her cheeks flush up, an' I see tears in her eyes. She took on 's if I 'd been a babe!›

«William rocked in his chair with laughter.

«‹Me a babe!› echoed the old man, joining in the laughter with his high treble. Presently Nancy rose and went out of the room, and William fell to boasting quietly about his Illinois farm and belongings. It was the usual bragging of the successful Westerner. He boasted of his town, of its railroad, of its enterprise. I myself said very little. I felt somehow oppressed, tired, and out of sorts. William was too triumphant over these two poor creatures, who had clung so long and so bravely to the little sterile hill farm in Vermont; for of this kind of faithful, queer human stuff, as it seems, are martyrs born and heroes made.

«The storm grew in power as the night advanced. The wind tore down the narrow valley from the uplands to the north with the velocity of a legion of broomstick witches. We could hear the branches of the maples before the house swish and thrash in the rain and blast, and could feel the old house groan and tremble as if about to fall and bury with it in revenge all who meditated treason to the hillside farm. At first I could not sleep. I kept seeing Nancy's stony, soulless face before me—beautiful, yet so hard, so cold. Toward daybreak I fell into a dull, lethargic forgetfulness.

«The next morning, as you may readily believe, I came down a trifle late for their rigorous farmers' six-o'clock breakfast. William and his father had been up at daybreak, getting ready the few trunks and parcels they intended taking West with them. When I entered, the kitchen floor was swept and garnished. The tin coffee-pot was smoking on the table with cheerful invitation. Father and son stood by the window waiting for me. As I approached him the old man allowed that he thought ‹likely› it would ‹clear,› after all. He stood motionless, looking off at the massive broken clouds flying at great height across the valley from the west. Far above, the wind was blowing half a gale; in the valley the air seemed dead and still. The vast procession of high cumulous clouds seemed to fascinate the old farmer. He did not change his gaze at the clouds when I approached. He would see the same clouds and sunlight in Illinois, yet to him they would never be quite the same. The clearing wind there might be from the east or north, not west. A thousand signs of weather would be useless to him in Illinois. The long compilation of facts about farming in the rocky hill soil would be worthless now. Even the moon, my friend, looks down at us so differently in Illinois!

«William motioned me to a seat at the table, and as we sat down pointed in his father's direction and grinned.

«‹Takin' a last look!› he said, chuckling in a low voice. ‹Jest watch him—ain't he seen it long enough?›

«The old man suddenly gave a startled cry and half turned. ‹I 'm a-comin', Nancy,› he cried, looking in our direction.

«‹Why, Nancy—she ain't spoke,› laughed William, with brisk cheeriness. ‹She 's went out.›

«The old man looked about, dazed for a moment. ‹Why, why, I thought I heerd her callin', jest as she always called. Why, where *is* Nancy?›

«William looked about vacantly then said: ‹I guess I 'll jest go call her. She don't never eat, an' she 's got a long journey ahead.›

«William went to the door and called twice. There was no response. His father had just taken one of Nancy's light, delicate biscuits,—and you know how much the character of a woman goes out into her cookery,—but he laid it down again as if listening. The Newfoundland dog was barking far down the slope of the hill.

«‹Nancy! we 're a-waitin' fer you,› called William, who had gone to the kitchen porch. Then we could hear his loud voice calling her name out in the field near by. The old man began to fidget about; he could not eat. He rose from his seat and went about the rooms on the first floor—into the parlor, cold and damp with long disuse, and tenanted by the somber haircloth furniture and solemn stove. He climbed up into the second story, and I could hear his quavering old voice calling, ‹Nancy—Nan-cee! where be ye, my gal—where be ye?›

«Presently he came stiffly down the stairs, muttering to himself, his face betraying a helpless sort of anxiety. He extended his hands, as if his sight were failing and he was groping to find his daughter, on whose quiet strength he had leaned so many years. He went out of the door, not noticing me, and I followed with a nervous dread of some catastrophe. I was more alarmed by the expression in the old man's face than by anything else. Men of his long isolation seem always to be prepared for and to live in expectation of great crises, and when they grow terror-stricken it is a sign that the catastrophe is at hand.

«I followed him out to the barns, black with weather-stain, and in ruins. They leaned one against the other as if feeble with old age, weak skeletons of joists and beams covered loosely with boards. One of the great doors was hanging by one hinge, half ajar. There was a rotten, wormy flooring, from which as we entered a troop of rats scampered in fright. These wooden ruins have a deathly human significance in their integral decay. They are on their way, like ourselves, to impalpable dust. A ruin of stone gives no such disagreeable impression. In time the old barns would become but a mound of earth, a grave. I shuddered as I glanced upward among the shadowy rafters and down in the gulf-like disused haymows. The rain had beaten in on all sides, and there was a continual drip, drip from the roof. The old hay smelled musty and wet. We made our way through the old stables. Nancy was not to be found. I cannot forget the keen sense of relief I experienced as we came out.

«Just then we heard again the deep bark of the Newfoundland far down the meadow. ‹Oh, Nancy—she can't be far away,› quavered the old man; and so we went back to the house.

«William was awaiting us at the porch of the kitchen door with a perplexed air. ‹She 's run off some'eres; I dunno what started her off. Why, I knowed she 's stood by father not wantin' ter go West; but I can't understand her a-hidin' this way, an' not wantin' to start. She 's awful freakish, an' she 's hid.

I s'pose the best thing we ken do is to s'arch all through the house—she ain't outside nowher's. Let 's begin in the garret; it's the only thing we ken do. She 's freakish, an' she 's went an' hid.›

«I followed William up-stairs, as his father sat down on the porch feebly, and said, ‹I guess I 'll jest set here till she comes back.›

«In the garret we saw in the half light some old dresses hanging, and on the same nail a faded bonnet; they sent my heart into my throat. Near by was a half-opened trunk, and many little articles that women value were scattered over the floor.

«‹SHE CAN'T BE FAR AWAY.›»

«‹She 's be'n here,› said William, picking up a bundle of old letters, which he threw back into the trunk. ‹She 's be'n here s'archin' fer suthin'.›

«We continued our search through the house, floor by floor. We went into Nancy's own room—a spare, sad little chamber, the small white bed neatly made, a tiny chest of drawers, and one looking-glass, bright and clean. There was but one stiff wooden chair. Her chamber reminded me of the cell they show in Florence once used by Fra Savonarola. The floor was bare like his, and to make the place seem nun-like, a small worn Bible lay on a little table by the bedside.

«‹I guess Nancy 's took and run away,› said William, cheerily. ‹Huh! she 's down on the West; mebbe she did n't like the teasin' I give her about gettin' married!› But then we happened upon her little bonnet and shawl, and William seemed again perplexed.

«Once more we heard the dog barking far down the field.

«‹Where ken he be, a-barkin' so?› said William. And I followed him down-stairs and so out of doors.

«His father, who had restlessly gone inside, came out now, trembling as with a palsy. ‹Oh, she can't be far away—not far away,› he repeated; but fright had taken possession of his face. He knew, as did we all, that Nancy was the most systematic little person in the world, the most methodical, the most precise, and that any deviation on her part from the ordinary was laden with dreadful possibilities.

«‹No,› said William; ‹she 's jest stepped out—that 's all.›

«‹Why, Nancy she *had n't* a care,› the old man quavered with a dreadful meaning. ‹She can't be far away.›

«‹Father!› replied William, as if angrily; ‹you go in the house. Me an' Mr. Maitland 'll go find where she 's gone. She 's about somewher's.›

«The old man turned obediently, then followed us afar off. He looked as if he had shrunken very small and thin as he stood in the path watching us. Perhaps if little Nancy had seen him then she would have perceived in his attitude the keen fatherly affection which for some reason he had been so scrupulously careful to conceal from her all the long years.

«We walked down the hill through an orchard, fragrant and snowy-white with apple-blossoms, and through a small piece of woods, in silence, William glancing furtively here and there along the old stone walls among the brambles. The black Newfoundland dog came running up and barking, as it seemed, leading us on. We came presently upon a little old-fashioned burying-ground. It was quite overgrown with raspberry-bushes, wild honeysuckle, and clematis in bloom. It was one of those little ‹neighbor› burial-places common among the old New England hill farms. A broken wall of stone surrounded it. We caught sight of a gray dress, a sleeve, and a small white hand that lay on the grass palm upward, like a camellia.

«William and his father stood still like frightened animals. I advanced to the wall and looked over it. Lying there, her head fallen back among the briers, was Nancy. Her features had relaxed in death, her lips were slightly parted, and she almost seemed to smile. There was a small empty vial in her hand, showing clearly the medicine to which she had resorted to relieve herself of life's burden. The dog kept barking, and William called to it angrily. Then they both advanced to where I stood, removing their hats unconsciously.

«‹Never wa'n't a-goin' fer to leave the old farm,› said William, in an awed whisper, nodding his head.

«‹Nancy!› called out the old man, in his high treble. ‹She 's took sick.› But he did n't move from where he stood.

«William began to cry like a young boy, and shake his head from side to side. He strode over the stone wall, pressing the briers out of his path. I followed him. He stood a moment looking down at the upturned face. Then he very gently lifted the slender little figure in his strong arms. She was quite dead. As he bore her up I fancied I perceived a smile of contentment on her pure maiden face. There was certainly a change from the night before. It seemed that Nancy was happy.

«William carried her across the upland pasture, making his way through the tall grass, stooping here and there among the low branches thick with white apple-blossoms, through the trees, and so across the meadow toward the old farm-house. Her hair broke loose upon his shoulder, wavy and light like that of a young child. I can see his strong, huge figure now, with its burden, and the old man slowly following, mumbling and muttering to himself. I can see them as they disappeared, with their dead, amid the fragrant boughs.

«I waited for some time, hesitating to intrude upon their grief. I turned to the burial-ground. The headstone of the grave where she had lain was overgrown with luxuriant vines. I pushed them away, and read the simple inscription:

Here lies the body of
John G. Bradley,
Private, Co. —, Eighteenth Vermont Infantry.
Killed in the battle of the Wilderness,
May 5th, 1864.
Aged 19 years, 4 months.

«Near by in the brambly grass I found a letter, crumpled and worn. It was dated ‹Fredericksburg, Virginia, April 26, 1864,› and it began, ‹Dear Miss Brandon.› It was simply an amusing account of the soldier's camp life, in a lively boyish hand. Nancy had loved him. She had kept her secret well all the years; I believe she had kept it even from the soldier she had loved.»

There was a short silence before Maitland called out quickly: «*Garçon, garçon! l'addition!*»

A moment later we rose and strolled in silence over to the galleries of the Louvre, through the laughing, chattering throngs. The streets were crowded with life, and the sun shone down with blinding glare upon the full flood-tide of the splendid Paris afternoon.

*John Seymour Wood.*

# «THERE IS A PEACE THAT COMETH AFTER SORROW.»

«THERE is a peace that cometh after sorrow,»
  Of hope surrendered, not of hope fulfilled;
A peace that looketh not upon to-morrow,
  But calmly on a tempest that is stilled.

A peace which lives not now in joy's excesses,
  Nor in the happy life of love secure;
But in the unerring strength the heart possesses
  Of conflicts won while learning to endure.

A peace there is, in sacrifice secluded;
  A life subdued, from will and passion free;
'T is not the peace which over Eden brooded,
  But that which triumphed in Gethsemane.

*Jessie Rose Gates.*

# GENERAL GRANT'S MOST FAMOUS DESPATCH.

«I PROPOSE TO FIGHT IT OUT ON THIS LINE IF IT TAKES ALL SUMMER.»

IN the January number of THE CENTURY General Horace Porter gives the origin of the famous message from General Grant which electrified the country—«I propose to fight it out on this line if it takes all summer.» As General Porter's article shows, it was a passage from a letter, and not a laconic message as was supposed when the extract first appeared in the newspapers.

General Grant and his army had been «lost in the Wilderness» for three days. Rumors had reached Washington of terrific fighting and fearful loss of life; the people of the whole nation were almost breathless with anxiety and fear of a terrible defeat, with consequences more disastrous than ever before.

Then came this letter from Grant to Halleck. He at once took it to President Lincoln, to whom it was a great relief. He joyfully exclaimed, as he read the terse sentence aloud, «We will give that to the country!» and the next morning the people learned that Grant and the army were safe. Remembering that other laconic message at Fort Donelson, «I propose to move immediately on your works,» the country applauded, and fully believed that we had a soldier and a fighter at the head of the Army of the Potomac.

For many years this famous letter has been in my possession, and this is how it came into my hands: I was the «attorney in fact» and business agent of General Halleck, had charge of his property and money, and was the executor of his estate. When he returned to California after the war, to assume command of the Division of the Pacific, he brought with him a chest containing his personal correspondence and copies of most of the army papers that passed through his hands. It was his intention then to write a history of the rebellion. And let me say here, it would have been a true history; there would have been very little romance in it; his enemies would perhaps have discovered that their causes of grievance were not of his volition or instigation, but that he had fearlessly carried out the orders and wishes of his and their immediate superiors.

When General Halleck was ordered to Louisville, Kentucky, in 1869, to command the Division of the South, the chest of papers was left in my care. I expended some time in arranging them as a preliminary to the work on the proposed history. While on a trip to the East I visited General Halleck. This was a few months previous to his death, which occurred on January 9, 1872. To my inquiry, «When are we to begin our history, general?» he replied emphatically:

«Never! History is a falsifier.»

He had become disgusted with those already written.

On my return to San Francisco, I placed the papers in the bank vault of Montgomery Block, where they remained for several years. When Colonel Robert N. Scott, formerly of Halleck's staff, was appointed government historian in charge of the publication of the War Records, he asked me for them. Upon receipt of an order from General Halleck's widow, then the wife of General Cullum, I forwarded the chest to Colonel Scott, in Washington.

Three or four years ago, in overhauling and destroying the old and worthless papers in the vault, I found a bundle of letters marked, in General Halleck's writing, «Personal.» They were from various persons in civil and military life, and among them I found the famous letter. My first thought was, «I will send it to Washington»; but Colonel Scott was no longer living. I also argued, «Why not let the people continue to believe that it was a short message?» Then it occurred to me that most certainly a copy of the letter had been retained at the headquarters of the army, which proved to be the fact, since it is printed in its proper place in the Official Records.

I shall hold the letter, subject to an order from the proper authority. If not so called for, then it should be placed in the National Museum at Washington.

*G. W. Granniss.*

Near Spotsylvania C. H. Va.
May 11th 1864. 8.30 A.M.

Maj. Gen. Halleck,
Chief of Staff of Army,

General,

We have now ended the sixth day of very heavy fighting. The result to this time is much in our favor. But our losses have been heavy as well as those of the enemy. We have lost to this time eleven General officers killed, wounded or missing, and probably twenty thousand men. I think the loss of the enemy must be greater we having taken over four thousand prisoners, in battle, whilst he has taken from us but few except stragglers. I am now sending back to Belle Plaines all my wagons for a fresh supply of provisions, and Ammunition, and propose to fight it out on this line if it takes all summer.

The arrival of reinforcements here will be very encouraging to the men and I hope they will be sent as fast as possible and in as great numbers. My object in having them sent to Belle Plaines was to use them as an escort to our supply train. If it is more convenient to send them out by train to march from the rail-road to Belle Plain or Fredericksburg send them so.

I am satisfied the enemy are very shaky and are only kept up to the mark by the greatest exertion on the part of their officers, and by keeping them entrenched in every position they take.

Up to this time there is no indication of any portion of Lee's Army being detached for the defence of Richmond.

Very respectfully
Your obt. svt.
U. S. Grant
Lt. Gen.

# A BLUE AND GRAY FRIENDSHIP.

## GRANT AND BUCKNER.

ABOUT fifteen years ago I visited Lookout Mountain with a party of gentlemen, and stood with them on the pinnacle overlooking the beautiful valley of east Tennessee, and range after range of mountains visible from our point of vantage, from the Great Smokies of North Carolina to the Cumberland of Kentucky. The battle-field of Missionary Ridge formed the immediate foreground of this vast panorama. In our party were men who had served with distinction as officers in the opposing armies in that battle, and naturally the incidents of the conflict formed an interesting subject of conversation between them, with much good-humored badinage and friendly interchange of views. Mr. Thomas Hughes, the author of «Tom Brown,» who had listened with an expression of surprised interest to the conversation between these friendly foes, turning to me, said: «Why, this is extraordinary—most extraordinary!» «What?» I asked. «Why, that these men, standing in full view of the field where, only a few years ago, they were trying to slay each other, should be discussing the incidents of that battle, calmly, kindly,—I might almost say in a brotherly spirit,—with no trace of bitterness or ill feeling. Now, I doubt if we in England could discuss the Wars of the Roses, or the Cromwellian wars, with such an entire freedom from antagonism.»

Could Mr. Hughes have witnessed, a few years later, the funeral cortège of the great general who had hurled the successful columns against the Southern lines along the crest of Missionary Ridge, and who had brought final defeat to the Southern arms in Virginia, his astonishment would have been greater, and his pride in the «kin beyond sea» would have increased, on seeing that there were no more sincere mourners than the Southern generals who came from faraway homes to pay a last tribute of friendship to the memory of Grant.

One of these Southern generals, who served as a pall-bearer at the funeral, was General Simon Bolivar Buckner of Kentucky; and I have had the opportunity of learning the story of the friendship between these two soldiers.

The two men had many characteristics in common—faithfulness to duty, loyalty to friends, gentle, dignified, unostentatious simplicity of manner, directness of purpose, and firm persistence. They were together for three years at West Point, and served in the same division through the Mexican war, where they were much associated. They were in most of the battles of that war, and both were promoted for gallantry. Grant resigned from the regular army in 1854, and Buckner in 1855.

Then came our Civil War, and the two met again for the first time at Fort Donelson, as generals on opposing sides. The capture of Donelson laid the foundation of Grant's subsequent success, culminating in the command of the largest armies of modern times and his election as President of the United States. The surrender of Donelson consigned General Buckner to months of inactivity as a prisoner of war, at a time when others less able were winning promotion in the field. But Buckner was the hero of Donelson on the Southern side. He was in no wise responsible for the blunders of his two superior officers in command—blunders made against his repeated protests, as is well shown by the official records. He advised against allowing the army to be cooped up in the trenches, and took his command there under protest. On the morning of February 14, before the investment was complete and before expected reinforcements had joined the Union forces, it was decided, upon the advice of Buckner and Floyd, to force a way out through the then weak right flank of the Union army, General Buckner making disposition to form the rear-guard and cover the movement. Before the orders were put in execution they were countermanded at the instance of General Pillow. On the night of the 14th it was again decided to make a sortie in force on the Union right early the next morning, Buckner's force to form the left wing and to protect the rear on the retreat. The movement on the morning of the 15th was successful: the Federal right wing was doubled back, and the road to Nashville was open. General Grant was absent from the field, having been summoned to a consultation with Commodore Foote on his gunboat beyond the extreme Federal left. Pillow had halted twenty pieces of artillery that had been ordered up by Buckner. There remained nothing to do but to

Hd Qrs, Army in the Field
Camp near Donelson, Feby 16th 1862

Gen. S. B. Buckner,
Confed. Army,

Sir; Yours of this date proposing Armistice, and appointment of Commissioners to settle terms of Capitulation is just received. No terms except an unconditional and immediate surrender can be accepted.

I propose to move immediately upon your works.

I am sir, very respectfully
your obt. sevt.
U. S. Grant

FACSIMILE OF THE ORIGINAL « UNCONDITIONAL SURRENDER » DESPATCH. FROM « PERSONAL MEMOIRS OF U. S. GRANT.» (THE CENTURY CO., NEW YORK.)

In order to show this despatch on the present page the word «Sir» has been lowered to the line beneath, and the words «I am, sir, very respectfully,» have been raised to the line above, and the words «Brig. Gen.,» under the signature, have been omitted.

begin the march toward Nashville, which Buckner was expected to cover, when he received an order from Pillow to withdraw to his former position within the works. While hesitating to obey an order which did not come from the first in command, and which was so at variance with the agreed plan, a second order to withdraw at once was received. Buckner sought Floyd as he began the execution of the orders, and protested that its execution meant the loss of the army. Floyd ordered him to hold his position while he hastened to consult Pillow. He yielded to the arguments of Pillow, who had lost his head by the success of the morning, and, thinking the works could be held, had sent a grandiloquent despatch claiming a great victory. Buckner was again ordered to resume his former position, and the wise plan, so gallantly executed, was abandoned. The Union right was reinforced, their former position reoccupied, and the chance to save the Southern forces thrown away.

General Grant, in his «Memoirs,» says that General Floyd «was no soldier, and, possibly, did not possess the elements of one»; and shows that he held General Pillow's ability as a soldier in light esteem. He adds: «I had been at West Point three years with Buckner, and afterward served with him in the army, so that we were quite well acquainted. In the course of our conversation, which was very friendly, he said to me that if he had been in command I would not have got up to Donelson as easily as I did. I told him that if he had been in command I should not have tried in the way I did.» One of General Grant's first questions on meeting General Buckner was: «Where is Pillow? Why did n't he stay to surrender his command?» «He thought you were too anxious to capture him personally.» «Why,» he answered, with a humorous smile, «if I had captured him I would have turned him loose. I would rather have him in command of you fellows than as a prisoner.» It was not, at this early stage of the war, known what course the Federal government would take with regard to prominent officers who should be captured, and Generals Floyd and Pillow were not willing to take the risk. Turning the command over to Buckner, they escaped on the only transport available, Buckner informing them that he considered it his duty to stay with his men and share their fate.

During the Washington Centennial in New York in 1889, when Buckner, as governor of his State, rode up Broadway at the head of the Kentucky troops, as he passed a line of the Grand Army of the Republic the veterans broke ranks and crowded about him to shake the hand of the gray-haired soldier who, years before, had chosen to stay with his men at Donelson and share their fate.

It was one of General Grant's peculiarities that he never forgot a favor. Some years before the war it had come in Buckner's way to do him a kindness. After the surrender, and when General Buckner had gone aboard the transport that was to convey him North, General Grant took him aside, and said, in his gentle, half-diffident way: «Buckner, you may be going among strangers, and I hope you will allow me to share my purse with you.» Buckner thanked him for his kindness, and told him that he had made provisions so that he would not require financial assistance.

The following anecdote, here first published, shows General Buckner as a participant in similar courtesies between Northern and Southern soldiers after his exchange.

When Bragg invaded Kentucky in 1862, Chalmers, commanding the advance, attacked a Federal force strongly intrenched on the hills on the south side of Green River at Munfordville, where the Louisville and Nashville Railway and the turnpike both cross that river. Bragg was greatly incensed at this repulse, and ordered a large force to march at once and take the position by assault. General Buckner advised against this as a needless sacrifice of life, stating that he had an intimate knowledge of the surroundings, having hunted over the ground when a boy, and that a force could cross at another ferry, and by placing artillery on hills on the north side of the river could command the works in a manner to force a surrender. His advice was taken, plans were put into execution, and orders given to open fire on the following morning at daylight. About midnight Colonel (afterward General) John T. Wilder, commanding the Union forces, came under a flag of truce to General Buckner's bivouac in front of Wilder's position, and the following conversation, unique in the history of war, took place. Colonel Wilder informed General Buckner that, as he was a volunteer officer, he did n't know much about the usages, regulations, and proprieties of war; and knowing General Buckner to be an educated soldier, an old army officer who understood such matters, and esteeming him as a high-minded gentleman who would deal honestly and frankly with him, he had come to ask his advice. «Now,» said he, «I know that I have a strong position, and can put up a good fight. I want to do my whole duty to my country, but I don't want to sacrifice my men unless there is a chance of making a successful resistance. Those men back there are my neighbors and friends, and I don't want to do anything that will bring disgrace upon them. You know what is right and proper under such conditions. You know my force and the strength of my position, and you know what force you have to bring against it. Now, I ask you, as a soldier and a gentleman, to tell me whether you think, under the circumstances, I should surrender or fight.» His voice trembled with emotion when he spoke of his men being his neighbors and friends. General Buckner, realizing the helplessness of Colonel Wilder's situation, was deeply impressed by his earnestness, his sincerity, and his patriotic spirit, and especially by the confidence Wilder had reposed in him; and he felt that he must treat him with perfect frankness and fairness. He told him that he could not advise him as to whether he should surrender or fight, but would give him accurate information respecting his force and its disposition, and that he must then decide for himself. He told him that he had a force amply sufficient to take the place by assault, but gave him to understand that it was not at present his intention to assault the works. He told the position and number of guns on the north of the river, with orders to open fire at daylight, and that he was satisfied these guns would render his position untenable; that, as an evidence of his good faith, he would send Colonel Wilder with a staff-officer to visit the batteries. After some further conversation, Colonel Wilder said that he accepted General Buckner's statement without visiting the batteries; but he yet hesitated, and was evidently suffering from conflicting emotions, whereupon General Buckner said: «Colonel Wilder, I think it but right to say to you that if you have any information that would induce you to believe that a prolonged resistance would materially aid the movements of the Federal forces elsewhere, I think it is your duty to hold your position as long as possible, even, if necessary, to the sacrifice of your command.» Colonel Wilder finally said that he had no such information, and that he would surrender his command early the following morning. A staff-officer then presented to Colonel Wilder, as his vindication for surrendering, a map on which was shown the position of the guns commanding his position. Early the next morning General Buckner visited Colonel Wilder's camp, and the arrangements for the surrender were completed. The Union forces, about four thousand strong, marched out and grounded arms, as we used to see in the pictures of the Cornwallis surrender in the old-time school histories. Colonel Wilder handed his sword to General Buckner, who returned it with a complimentary speech. Colonel Wilder served with distinction through the war. He was one of the gentlemen with Mr. Hughes on the visit to Lookout Mountain referred to above, and took part with the ex-Confederates present in the friendly discussion of the battle. Only a few years ago he came to Frankfort, Kentucky, while General Buckner was governor of the State, and while dining with him at the executive mansion I heard the story from the two officers.

The war over, the Union restored, Grant was hailed as the successful general, and was twice chosen President. Then came his triumphant journey around the world, in which he was received everywhere with distinguished marks of homage. Then the clouds gathered. Defeated for renomination for a third term, he suffered political vituperation from his own people and financial disaster. Stricken with an incurable malady, long and patient suffering followed. Was the great general's life to pass away in gloom? His calm endurance, and his heroic struggle to complete his «Memoirs» before his death, touched the nation's heart. From the South, remembering his magnanimity in his hour of victory, came expressions of sorrow and sympathy.

General Buckner, who had chosen the life of a country gentleman after the war, honored and beloved by the people of his native State, who fondly called him the «gray eagle of Glen Lily,» after the name of his picturesque country home, and recently married to a beautiful and accomplished woman, was traveling in Canada when he learned that General Grant had been carried to Mount McGregor, and that the end was approaching. Wishing to carry to him a message of kindly remembrance from Southern soldiers, he telegraphed to Colonel Frederick Grant his desire to visit his father. Colonel Grant met him at Saratoga, and accompanied General and Mrs. Buckner to Mount McGregor. General Buckner found General Grant in his sitting-room, in the adjustable chair, furnished with wheels, which served him as a bed. Though pale and somewhat emaciated, he preserved the calm courage that was his most marked characteristic. General Grant, who was unable to articulate, replied to General Buckner's cordial greeting by writing on a small pad of paper, from which he removed the

I have witnessed since my sickness just what I have wished to see ever since the war; harmony and good feeling between the sections. I have always contended that if there had been nobody left but the

slips after writing on them. He wrote: « I appreciate your calling very highly." And: « You look very natural, except that your hair has whitened, and you have grown stouter.»

General Buckner said that, aside from the gratification of a feeling of personal friendship, he had a special object in view in paying this visit. It was to assure General Grant that every Confederate soldier held him in kindly remembrance, not only for his magnanimity at the close of the war, but for his just and friendly conduct afterward in interposing to prevent the violation by his own government of the terms of the military convention which he had entered into, at the surrender, with the Southern soldiers, which secured them from molestation so long as they complied with the terms of their parole. To this General Grant wrote an answer which is a last message of friendship to the South and to the whole country, and part of which is published in facsimile in this article for the first time:

« I have witnessed since my sickness just what I have wished to see ever since the war: harmony and good feeling between the sections. I have always contended that if there had been nobody left but the soldiers

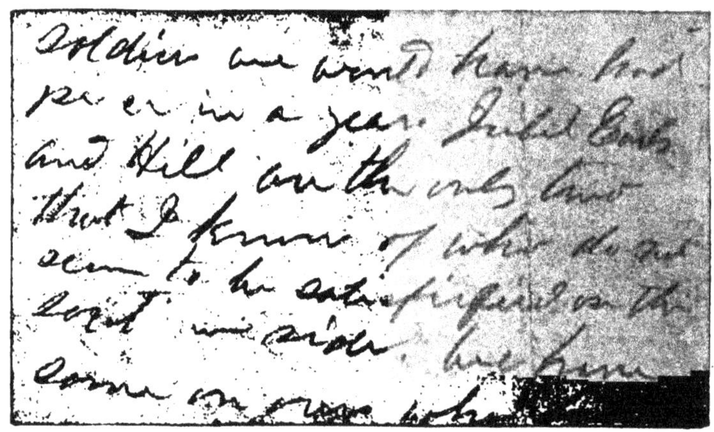

soldiers we would have had peace in a year. Jubal Early and Hill are the only two that I know of who do not seem to be satisfied on the Southern side. We have some on ours who

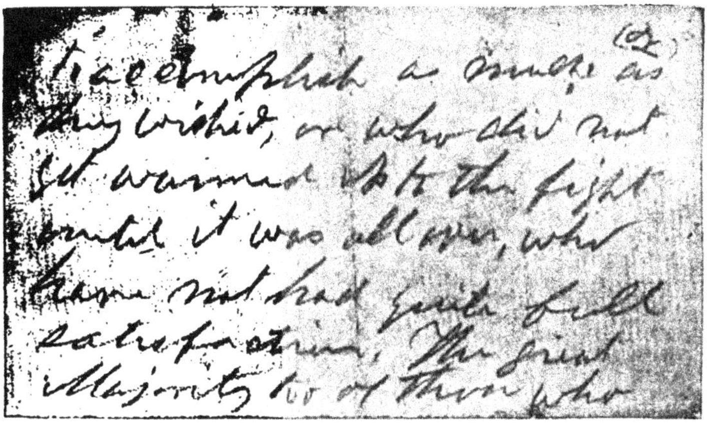

(2)

to accomplish as much as
they wished, or who did not
get warmed up to the fight
until it was all over, who
have not had quite full
satisfaction. The great
majority too of those who

we would have had peace in a year. Jubal Early and Hill are the only two that I know of who do not seem to be satisfied on the Southern side. We have some on ours who failed to accomplish as much as they wished, or who did not get warmed up to the fight until it was all over, who have not had quite full satisfaction. The great majority too of those who did not go into the war have long since grown tired of the long controversy. We may now well look forward to a perpetual peace at home, and a national strength that will secure us against any foreign complication. I believe myself that the war was worth all it cost us, fearful as that was. Since it was over I have visited every state in Europe and a number in the East. I know, as I did not before, the value of our inheritance.»

General Buckner expressed himself as fully in accord with the views in regard to the friendly feelings of the actual combatants, and said that if the chief political promoters of the war on both sides could have been assembled between the lines of the two armies, with instructions to arrange all differences in a few hours, or else to fight out the differences to a finish among themselves in sight of both armies, the result would have

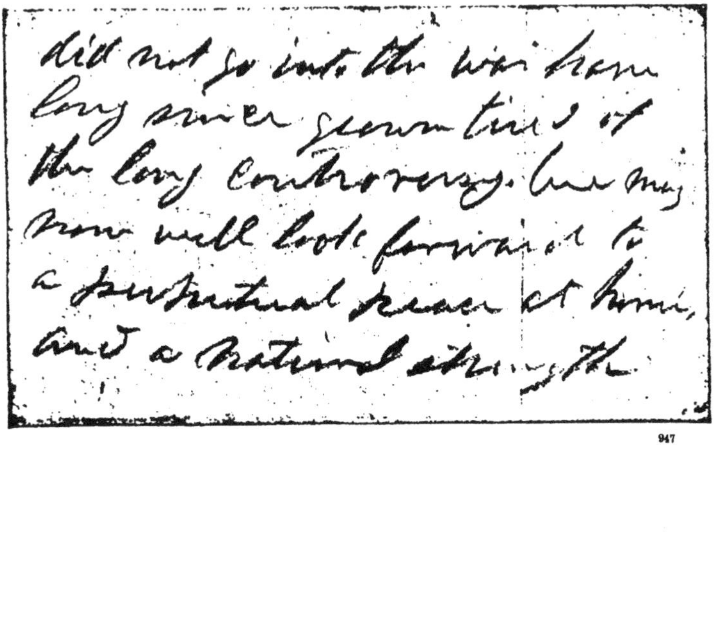

did not go into the war have
long since grown tired of
the long Controversy. We may
now well look forward to
a perpetual peace at home,
and a national strength

(3)

strength that will secure against any foreign complication. I believe myself that the war was worth all it cost us, fearful as that was.— Since it was

been an arrangement satisfactory to all sections in a short space of time. This suggestion seemed to amuse General Grant. After some further remarks by General Buckner, he said that he was unwilling to credit the newspaper accounts of the serious character of General Grant's illness; that he could no more abandon hope in his case than he could in that of Captain W. H. T. Walker of the Sixth Infantry, who was desperately wounded at Molino del Rey, and who, though abandoned by his physicians, had completely recovered his health. General Grant wrote in reply: «I remember Walker's condition well. He was, as I remember, many months unable to help himself. In my case I have not been confined to bed a single day; but there cannot well be a cure in my case.»

After talking for some time, General Buckner proposed taking his leave, fearing a longer interview might prove fatiguing to General Grant, who then wrote:

«I am very glad to see you indeed; and allow me to congratulate you. I still read the papers, and saw a full account of your recent marriage.» And: «Is Mrs. Buckner here at the house with you?» To which an affirmative reply being given, he added:

me I have visited every State in America and a number in the East. I know as I did not before, the value of our inheritance.

«I would be very glad to see Mrs. Buckner, if she can come in and see me as I am now. Where you see me has been my bed for more than four months.»

After greeting Mrs. Buckner, he wrote:

«I knew your husband long before you did. We were at West Point together, and served together in the Mexican war. I was with him on a visit to the top of Popocatepetl, the highest mountain in North America. Your husband wrote an account of that trip for publication at the time. I have just written my account, which will be published in my forthcoming book.»

The conversation lasted for fifteen or twenty minutes longer, and the friends separated, to meet no more. They had met in battle as worthy foemen; they met for a last farewell as loving friends. A few days later General Buckner was summoned by telegram to attend as a pall-bearer at the funeral of General Grant in New York.

The bitterest passions are engendered by civil wars, and our great conflict was no exception, being the terrible culmination of years of political and social strife, followed by complications incident to race problems and political reconstruction. But as Americans we can well take pride that the soldiers of the South and the defenders of the Union now unite in rejoicing in the glories of a common country. There is no Southern soldier who does not hear with a thrill of patriotic pride the story of Keenan's charge at Chancellorsville, or of Cushing's deed of daring in blowing up the *Albemarle;* while the best, the most appreciatively generous tribute to the enduring courage and fortitude of the soldiers of Lee's army was written by Colonel Theodore A. Dodge, a Union officer who had been crippled for life facing those soldiers on Cemetery Hill.

It was a Southern soldier who wrote the immortal lines, since cast in enduring bronze and placed in the national cemeteries where lie the soldiers who fell for the Union:

On Fame's eternal camping-ground
  Their silent tents are spread,
And Glory guards with solemn round
  The bivouac of the dead.

*John R. Procter.*

# A VETO BY GRANT.

THANKS to THE CENTURY, and to General Porter, for responding to the wishes of a waiting people to know more about their hero Grant. A character so modest and undemonstrative very slowly impresses its real grandeur upon the popular mind. That impression, however, has now so far progressed that we look eagerly for every new line penciled in the portrait with proper authentication. I beg to add one strong line.

While in Vienna on his tour around the world, ex-President Grant stayed at the American legation. In one of our long evening talks I said to him that I knew of no braver civil act in our history than his veto of the fiat money («inflation») bill, which had passed both houses of Congress, and to which many of his warmest friends had committed their political fortunes. He quietly replied:

«I will tell you about that. During the progress of the discussion I followed its course, but expressed no opinion. After the bill came to me I was visited by both its friends and its opponents, urging their views. To none of them did I express any judgment of the measure, nor did I bring it before my cabinet. When the time for its consideration was nearing its end, one night when I was alone in my room I took up the bill. I thought it admitted a construction which would obviate the evil effects alleged against it, but resolved not to sign it without communicating to the Congress that view. I proceeded to write out such a message to accompany the notice of my approval.

«After finishing the draft I took up the sheets to read them over. At the conclusion of the review I said to myself, ‹This is evasive and a strained construction. It is not my honest conviction.› I gathered the sheets, tore them up, and cast them into the wastebasket. Then I wrote out my veto message. Next day I advised my cabinet of it, and sent it to the Congress.»

The line I seek to add to his coming portrait is that of a silent man, in the night, in the solitude of his chamber, aware of his great power over the welfare of his country, watching his own debate between inclination and duty, and resolutely deciding with his conscience against an eager popular demand.

*John A. Kasson.*

[*Ex-U. S. Minister to Austria.*]

# THE MIRACLE OF THE GREEK FIRE.

HOLY WEEK IN JERUSALEM, 1896.

THE bare but richly colored landscape—the rocky hills, the caravan tracks, the narrow, rushing river, the shaggy-coated shepherds with their flocks—on the railroad from Jaffa to Jerusalem was all that we expected; but the carful of tourists and the scene at the railroad station utterly spoiled the longed-for «first view.» I tried to arrange it so that we should stop at a station on the way, and take horses for the city, but without avail. Never shall I forget the baggage-master's deliberate fury. With the entire traveling public demanding its baggage,—sometimes with the wailings of native women,—he would cease his frantic work of assortment, and keep the world waiting while he stormed, raged, and imprecated. Then he would seize a trunk, and tug at it with the face of a madman, stopping everything now and again to declaim in shrill and spurting sentences, or dashing at a bag with contorted features and the rage of a Turkish soldier clutching an Armenian. On the whole, perhaps it was not unfortunate; if there was to be nothing about it but the modern, the diversion might as well be noisily complete.

It was not till the next morning that we *felt* the place. Starting from our hotel just inside the Jaffa Gate, near David's Tower, we went on donkeys around the city, devouring with eager eyes and hearts the landscape so strange and so familiar—past the Pool of Siloam, along the edge of the valley of Jehoshaphat over against Gethsemane, past the Golden Gate, till we came to the barren hilltop that some think is the true Calvary. The identification has no certainty—Dr. Bliss, the young archæologist who is tracing so skilfully the old walls, says that when you abandon tradition you are lost till there is something actual to lead you. And yet at least this is now more like Calvary than is the little chapel inside the Church of the Holy Sepulcher—this lonely hilltop, dismal and unperverted, with its native graves, uncared for, unwalled, strangely spotted with blood-red anemones. We were not sorry that for the time being it appealed to us as the very scene of the immeasurable tragedy. Opening the New Testament, my eye caught a sentence from the well-known story, and I felt as if my heart were struck.

Anxious, dangerous, murderous now, all this part of Asia was a bloody country in the days of Moses, in the days of Christ; doubt, suspicion, and threat, murder in religion's name, are in the air now as they were of old. One day (our first Friday here), on the way to the Wailing-place of the Jews, an old Jewess was knocked down by a camel. The drivers grinned, and went on. There seemed little pity for the bemoaning old creature even among her own people. Another time I saw a woman run to a girl of about eight years, and drag her home, biting the tender flesh of the child's arm like a vicious dog. The traveler is entirely safe here if he or she knows and submits to the ways and regulations, and refrains from journeys that are for the time being pronounced dangerous. But when you ask what would happen if a Christian should visit the Mosque of Omar at certain sacred seasons, or if a Jew should enter the Church of the Holy Sepulcher, the answer is not, «He would be put out,» but, «He would be killed.» The sad eyes of the Armenians here hide sorrows and anxieties that no one dares to tell.

Any of the sacred places themselves may be scenes of violence at any moment. Not long ago the Dalmatian cavass in charge of some Russian tourists who were visiting the Grotto at Bethlehem resented the interference of the sacristan monk who was clearing the way before the Latin procession, drew his revolver, and shot him dead on the spot; after that, firing four shots wildly at the procession, he wounded a priest in the arm and rib.

At the miracle of the Greek Fire in the Church of the Sepulcher there is always violence: in 1834, in a horrible panic, hundreds of pilgrims and others were crushed, beaten, or bayonetted to death.[1] In 1895, at this same ceremony, the Greek crowd pushed back the

[1] See a graphic account of this extraordinary catastrophe in «Visits to Monasteries in the Levant,» by the Hon. Robert Curzon, Jr. London: John Murray, 1849.

Armenian patriarch who was going into the Chapel of the Angels to take his usual part with the Greek patriarch. The bugle sounded, and the Turkish soldiers who are always present there to keep the peace came to the rescue. They themselves are said to have behaved well, but the rival Christian factions fought with desperation. No lives were lost, but injuries were inflicted, and the patriarch's miter was knocked from his head.

In the old days, as now, there were lepers and misery; then, as now, there was a city beautiful, worthy of love and tears; then, as now, there were goodness and brutality, envy and hypocrisy, and many a faithful heart. Jerusalem, Syria, this Ottoman empire, — yes, and the unchristian Christian world, — need a Redeemer now as then, a Prince of Peace. All this comes upon one here with new and tremendous force.

A city beautiful! On Palm Sunday, from the stairway near the spot where Mary stood when the body of her son was taken from the cross, I saw the Greek procession in the Church of the Sepulcher. Then I went over to the Mount of Olives. Looking back from a field well up on the hillside, the whole city lay beneath — the temple area, with the great mosque in full view across the valley of Jehoshaphat. From here Jerusalem, with its clear and stately outline of walls, the domes and minarets of the mosques, and the old towers and churches, has a singular completeness. Perhaps even in Solomon's time, from the outside, though different, it was not more lovely. The warm gray of the stones of the city is the color of the unbleached wool of goats; the hills are darker, with a delicate bloom over them, spotted with gray olive-orchards, and melting in the distance into violet. It is indeed a city set upon a hill, isolated, distinguished. The picture realizes one's lifelong dream of the city of God.

The sunset sky was wild and cold, with streaks of sunshine. The rain ceased, and the air grew warm. In the rich, low light all blemishes were lost, and the City Beautiful was spread before the pilgrim's eyes. Perhaps it was here that Christ wept over Jerusalem; along or near this path he must have come on the day of his «entry» on the first Palm Sunday, whose feast was being kept that very day throughout all Christendom. There were no other travelers; a few Syrians passed by. I gathered some flowers by the wayside, and turned again homeward.

You see that we did not find the Holy Land disillusioning. There are many things that confound the Western mind; there is filth and degradation and superstition. But here is the same sky, the same landscape, the same dominating Orient. The painter who knows the Holy Land best said to us in Jerusalem: «At times when I look at these fields, and realize that this very picture was reflected in the eyes of Jesus, I feel myself shiver.» The Bible, no matter what one's theology or philosophy, here takes on a vitality and meaning beyond the power of conception hitherto. Are the places real? Jerusalem, all Syria, is real, and some of the «sacred places» are unquestionable. But you do not have to be sure that the place is exact when you listen, with a new emotion, to the words of Jesus repeated by the French monk on Good Friday, and at that «station of the cross» where Christ cried out, «Daughters of Jerusalem, weep not for me, but weep for yourselves, and for your children.»

Even the terrible rounds of the «sacred places» in the Church of the Sepulcher, all bedizened, and ridiculous with fantastic impossibilities — is it not all given a true holiness by the passion of believing worshipers through the ages? Bent under the unescapable burdens of this life, hither from every part of the earth they have come, only that they might touch the footprints of the Man of Sorrows. Crawling on the worn pavement, they have kissed reality into every sacred lie.

The warring of emotions in the breast of the onlooker from another civilization is something indescribable. You might expect to feel nothing but indignation at some of the scenes of Holy Week; but the human element gives pathos and dignity to ceremonies which otherwise would be shocking indeed to the Protestant mind. Do you know that on Good Friday evening, in the small up-stairs Chapel of the Holy Sepulcher, which is called the true Calvary, the scene of the descent from the cross is reënacted? The Latins borrow the altar built over the very spot of the crucifixion. There is a large crucifix on the altar, flat, and painted to represent life; but the Latins bring their own small jointed crucifix; the crown of thorns is removed with iron pincers, a sheet is passed under the arms, the long nails are withdrawn one by one and kissed, the arms are turned down, and the body is laid upon the altar. There is chanting, most melodious and moving, and a sermon in French. Pilgrims, in various costumes and of various Christian beliefs, are bowed in worship in the low-ceiled room which was once «Golgotha.»

I shall not attempt to describe the effect of such a scene at such a place. The part which sounds grotesque and painful is lost from sight; the mind rushes back to the event, and realizes it in a way which can only be hinted at in words.

But the most startling scene of Holy Week is the miracle of the Greek Fire on the Saturday before Easter Sunday.

In the center of the rotunda of the Church of the Sepulcher is the Holy Sepulcher itself, a hexagonal structure, divided into the Chapel of the Angels and the tomb proper.

The night before we had seen the pilgrims, most of them Russian peasants, lying in the places to which they would cling till they should receive the fire. With two cavasses leading the way, we arrived at about 11 A. M. The soldiers examined the natives for arms as they went in. We were led around the Greek chapel, through the pilgrims thick upon the floor, and taken to our outlook in the gallery. The armed Moslem soldiers encircled the Sepulcher, the crowd packed eight or ten deep between them and the walls. In harsh and piercing tones they were shouting their songs, some religious and some secular, with clapping of hands and excitement that grew apace. The Arabic was translated for us as the chanting went on:

O Jews, O Jews,
Your feast is the feast of devils.
Our feast is the feast of Christ—
Christ who has redeemed us,
And with his blood has bought us.
We to-day are happy
And you are sorrowful.

Then it would be

The resurrection of Christ has redeemed us from our sins,

given out with antiphonal yells, and with hand-clappings. Sometimes they shouted working-songs and sometimes a Bedouin war-song.

At about one o'clock some Armenian monks formed a small procession. At this moment a youth in white was lifted on the shoulders of the crowd.

This is the tomb of our Saviour!

first the youth shouted, clapping his hands, and pointing to the tomb; then the crowd responded antiphonally,—this over and over.

Now the youth is hoisted higher in the air to the top of a pyramid made with three men on the shoulders of the level crowd.

Our candles are in our hands,
And to the tomb we are praying—

still antiphonally. Now the youth drops down, and five men are raised in a circle, and, chanting, move around, from left to right.

A man wearing a pink shirt, red waistband, and white trousers is standing with his arm in the oval window of the Sepulcher. The shouting and clapping continue:

O the Jews! O the Infidels!
Your feast is the feast of the dead,
And our feast is the feast of Christ.

It is like college foot-ball games, negro camp-meetings, the Salvation Army, the boatmen on the rapids of the Nile. An American presidential nominating convention is a quiet gathering in comparison with all this hysterical yelling, pulling, pushing, and gesticulating.

But if the ear suffers, the eye has a feast beyond the power of words to picture. The processions of Greeks, Armenians, Copts, and dark-faced Abyssinians—one sect following another, and each vying with the others in splendor—are like chains of jewels drawn through a box of precious stones. For there is color everywhere, not only in the glowing marbles, and the jutting ornaments of the architecture, and all the unmoving background, but in the whole swaying mass below: the red fezzes and gleaming guns of the Sultan's troops; the fezzes and turbans and flowing robes of the Syrians, red, white, blue, and orange. The black dress of certain of the Greek priests serves as a foil to the magnificence of their dignitaries. Gorgeous indeed are the jeweled miters of the chief ecclesiastics, and their vestments of blue, white, and pink, stiff with embroidery of gold and silver.

The surging to and fro of the crowd below; the swinging of the lamps, the strange and outlandish odors, mixed with the smell of incense; the straining of the gaze past the archways into the chapels where mass was continuously chanted; the waiting for some strange new thing to happen, made us at times faint and dizzy.

Occasionally a big, black drinking-jar is passed over the heads of the people, and eagerly seized.

The Armenians waiting at the window on the other side of the tomb seem more quiet.

Now there are high-pitched yells that sound like catcalls; now it is «God save the Sultan!» sometimes joking and laughter: but there is no cessation of the clapping and singing, though at some moments louder than at others, and more antiphonal and concerted.

To the right from where we stand, in the corner made by the tomb and the little Copt chapel, is a group of Copt women in robes of black, with children, and some older men, looking sedate and devout, a pleasant contrast to the clamor.

For a few minutes the shouting has ceased; but I cannot note the fact before they have begun again, clap, clap; yell, yell, yell.

Now the time of the miracle approaches. A flame from heaven is to be communicated to the expectant world. As a preliminary to this sacred manifestation there is a new, wild outburst of cries and screams. We are told that it is the Jerusalem worshipers, who pound with their fists their fellow-Christians of Jaffa, and drag and jerk them away one by one from the window where the celestial fire is to appear.

At about two o'clock the Greek patriarch approaches with banners and attendants. He comes from the Greek chapel, near the door of the Holy Sepulcher. The excitement intensifies. The noise is frightful, and the vociferous scrambling in front of the Greek window of the Sepulcher is a thing of amazement. Men, standing on the shoulders of the crowd, screech words of religious greeting,—

This is the tomb of Christ

darting a finger at the tomb itself with every repetition.

Now the procession moves; those nearest the crowned patriarch join hands about him to prevent violence or accident. Three times they wind about the tomb. Two officially appointed carriers of the light appear in front of the window, and the man who has stood with his arm extended into it gives place to them, and stands by, shouting with the rest. Increasing noise. A seeker of the divine fire climbs up on the side of the Sepulcher, supporting himself by a rope around a pillar. The roar and screams are louder. The procession has halted in front of the door of the tomb. The crown is removed from the head of the patriarch and carried back into the Greek chapel. Now he enters the tomb. He leaves, we are told, in the outer tomb, or Chapel of the Angels, a Greek bishop and an Armenian bishop or priest; he then goes into the inner tomb, where the visible divinity is to be communicated to him. He is to hand the light from heaven to both of the attendant priests, and they are to give it out through the two windows at the sides.

The noise swells like a tempest. A burst of sound—the clanging of bells and stricken bars of metal! A flash at the Greek window. The fire has come! One wild rush, one high-pitched, multitudinous scream, still the excited clanging, and out springs the light over the frantic human mass, leaping from hand to hand, as if each flame were lightning and music. Around and up and over and through, till flame is added to flame, spreading from candle to candle, and floor to gallery. Now a priest appears on the roof of the Sepulcher itself, and the flame runs round the top like a crown of fire. Higher it springs—drawn by a rope up to the people at the base of the dome. It illuminates the most distant and dungeon-like vaults, the chapels above and below, every vantage-ground where the spectators have stood or crouched on the floor, or in temporary lodgments in mid-air.

On and on sounds the clangor and the shouting; men, women, and children are mad; they pass their hands over the flame,—is it not from heaven? how can it do harm?—and then draw their hands over their faces, taking the celestial touch in ecstatic adoration. Over a path made clear for the runners from the window already the fire is on its way to the ends of the earth.[1]

The Armenian patriarch declared to us later, and without hesitancy, that the Greek patriarch simply had a lamp on the tomb proper, which he blessed. This kindly old Armenian said to us that it was not miraculous. It was rumored that a prominent visitor was told by the Greek patriarch that he told the people it was only a symbol, and not a miracle. I asked the visitor whether this was true, and was answered: «No! How could he tell them that? He would be torn to pieces.» Intelligent Greeks assure you that it is a symbol, that «holy fire» is the same as «holy water.» The Latins will have nothing to do with this, one of the most venerable ceremonies and the most appalling scandal of the Christian world.

At the height of the frensy, as the flame leaped through the rotunda and lighted the encircling chapels, making more rich and glittering the altars, the gorgeous vest-

[1] An account, which I have from a resident, states that three bunches of candles are given first by the Greek patriarch to the Greek community, through the window on the side of the Latin chapel. After that a bunch is given by the Armenian priest to his people through the window on their side. The last two bunches are for the Copts and Syrians. They are handed to their priests, who wait for them at the door of the Sepulcher. My informant adds that the Greeks say that the Armenian priest does not enter inside the sepulcher proper, but only as far as the Chapel of the Angels; and the Armenians claim that their priest goes in as far as does the Greek patriarch.

ments, the whole ecclesiastical paraphernalia, the arms and uniforms of the troops, and the many-colored costumes of the mad and motley crowd, the thought flashed upon me: Was there ever anything in all Christendom so beautiful and so blasphemous?

### THE ANGER OF CHRIST.

I.

On the day that Christ ascended
To Jerusalem,
Singing multitudes attended,
And the very heavens were rended
With the shout of them.

II.

Chanted they a sacred ditty,
Every heart elate;
But he wept in brooding pity,
Then went in the holy city
By the Golden Gate.

III.

In the temple, lo! what lightning
Makes unseemly rout!
He in anger—sudden, frightening—
Drives with scorn and scourge the whitening
Money-changers out.

IV.

By the way that Christ descended
From Mount Olivet,
I, a lonely pilgrim, wended,
On the day his entry splendid
Is remembered yet.

V.

And I thought: If he, returning
On this festival,
Here should haste with love and yearning,
Where would now his fearful, burning
Anger flash and fall?

VI.

In the very house they builded
To his saving name,
'Mid their altars, gemmed and gilded,
Would his scourge and scorn be wielded,
His fierce lightning flame.

VII.

Once again, O Man of Wonder,
Let thy voice be heard.
Speak as with a sound of thunder;
Drive the false thy roof from under;
Teach thy priests thy word.

*R. W. Gilder.*

## TOPICS OF THE TIME

### The Right Place for an Expert.

When, in January last, it was made known that President McKinley had selected Mr. Lyman J. Gage of Chicago to be Secretary of the Treasury, the announcement sent a thrill of confidence and hope throughout the channels of trade and industry in all parts of the country. Why was this? Simply because business men and financiers everywhere knew Mr. Gage to be preëminently fitted for the post. They knew him to be a financial expert of the first rank, in whose hands the finances of a great nation could be trusted, with entire confidence that they would not be mismanaged. Various other men had been suggested for the place, but none of them had commanded the wide approval which the first mention of Mr. Gage's name had called forth. Some of them were excellent men, of long experience in public life, but they did not possess the expert qualification which distinguished Mr. Gage.

We count it a piece of great good fortune that such a man should be at the head of the financial department of the government at the present time. As our readers are aware, we have urged for many years that in no branch of the public service is expert knowledge more essential than in the conduct of our finances. The whole country realized this last year, when uncertainty about the future financial policy of the nation plunged us into a more acute period of anxiety and alarm than we had experienced since the Civil War. An incompetent man at the head of the treasury would only prolong this period. We must have assurance of safe leadership there, and this Mr. Gage's reputation gives us. It is as comforting as the entrance of a tried and trusted physician to a sick-chamber. We know that in the latter case everything possible for the restoration of the patient to health will be done, and in the best way.

That this nation has been sick nigh unto death from financial distempers was admitted by all of us last year.

Since we have emerged from the crisis in safety there is some disposition to forget that we were sick at all, and to exclaim in the old, familiar way, «Oh, we 're all right; we are the greatest nation on earth, and nothing can hurt us.» But the business men do not take this view. They do not desire a repetition of last year's slow panic, and are anxious to avoid it by removing its cause. For this reason they wish to see some plan of currency reform adopted which will put our financial system on so sound a basis as will make another national «scare» impossible. It was with this end in view that they desired an expert financier at the head of the treasury, and hence their hearty satisfaction at Mr. Gage's selection. They know that he will carry forward the firm, intelligent policy which the Cleveland administration upheld with such courage and steadfastness during the trying times of the last four years, and which Secretary Carlisle explained from time to time with such admirable clearness and force; for Mr. Gage's ideas are identical with those upon which the Cleveland policy was based.

It is from this point of view that his advent is especially beneficial. There have been many plans of currency reform suggested, and the authors of them differ in regard to methods which should be used in carrying them out; but we believe it to be a fact that they will all agree in saying that Mr. Gage's judgment as to methods can be followed implicitly. There are few other men in the country of whom this could be said. His influence, therefore, both in the formulation of a plan and in persuading its adoption by Congress, will be very great. He is on record in favor of having the government go out of the banking business, of having the greenbacks retired, and of establishing some well-guarded system of bank-note circulation, broader and more elastic than that of the present national banks. He regards our present monetary system as the outcome of makeshift legislation and unscientific compromises, and thinks it should be reformed utterly.

In these general propositions Mr. Gage is in complete harmony with all other intelligent advocates of currency reform. The impressive monetary conference which assembled at Indianapolis in January last occupied the same ground. It declared with absolute unanimity that the maintenance of the gold standard, the retirement of the greenbacks, and the establishment of a better and more elastic banking system, are the first and absolutely necessary steps toward reform. The machinery which this conference set in motion will work in cordial harmony with Secretary Gage, and thus the national administration and the most intelligent sentiment of the country will be united in the effort to aid Congress in the best solution of the problem. This is representative government in its ideal form, for it brings to bear upon a great public question the best intelligence of the nation, thus at once commanding the respect of the people by giving them the benefit of the wisest action.

What we have said applies only to Secretary Gage's fitness for office as an expert financier. He has another qualification, which is scarcely inferior to this, and which may be said to be its natural ally. He is an earnest believer in civil-service reform, saying soon after his selection for office that his chief aim as secretary would be to give the country a businesslike administration, making all his appointments on merit alone, and without regard to political obligations. This is the natural policy for a trained and experienced bank president to follow. He knows that a private financial institution can be managed successfully only on that basis, and as a faithful public servant he will not consent to manage the financial department of the government in any other way. This again demonstrates the value of an expert in office. He believes in the best talent available in private business, and can see no reason why inferior talent should be employed in public business. With a government by experts,—that is, by men of real fitness in all its branches,—civil-service reform would be established without a struggle and without a law.

### The Value of Dignity.

It is the opinion of some observers that the American sense of humor, combined with the confirmed American disposition to take a good-natured view of everything, has tended to a lack of seriousness and of dignity in our attitude toward public affairs. It is held that our public speakers, especially at banquets and other festive occasions, treat us to chaff and jokes, with little or no effort to appeal to our intellectual tastes. They say that many of our newspapers are no longer our instructors, but avowedly our entertainers, giving us only such brief and furtive instalments of genuine instruction as are necessary to keep up the pretense of guiding public opinion. These, and other like manifestations, are pointed to as signs of a change in national character; but we do not think that they reflect accurately the true feeling of the American people. Certainly in the recent political crisis the press and our public speakers showed a capacity for serious and able discussion.

Any one who moves about much among his fellows knows that there is a wide-spread weariness of the flippant after-dinner oratory of the period. Whenever, at a public banquet, some speaker makes a thoughtful, serious, earnest speech, the response of the audience is invariably so quick and hearty as to give evidence of a keen appetite for wholesome intellectual diet of this kind. So, too, in the press and in public life. The real instructor and leader of public opinion was never surer of a following than he is to-day. The whole country is, in fact, straining its eyes eagerly over the political field in search of true statesmen, real leaders, who take a dignified view of their place in politics—that is, an elevated and worthy one.

We believe firmly that our public men have sometimes underestimated the public taste in this matter. Surely the American statesmen who are held in highest veneration were men of dignity, having that elevation of character, deportment, and speech which was worthy their office. Washington was the ideal of dignity. Lincoln was a most impressively dignified man in his public acts and utterances. What nobler dignity can be found than exists in his inaugural addresses and in the Gettysburg oration? Long before he delivered those immortal productions, in his speeches in the famous Illinois campaign with Douglas,—notably in that at Springfield, in which he defined his attitude toward the slavery question,—this same high dignity was revealed.

True dignity in a public man means a full sense of his responsibility as a statesman. It means masterful knowledge of the subjects discussed, and elevation of tone and repose of manner in their discussion. Charles Sumner, though often irritating in tone, had this quality in greater perfection than almost any other of our modern American statesmen. To equal his treatment of public questions, we have to go back to the days of Hamilton and the «Federalist.» No one will deny that a strong case is made all the stronger by dignified presentation of it, or that a weak one is put in the best possible light by the same treatment.

John Stuart Mill said at the close of the Civil War that what we needed for our future greatness was «men of a caliber to use the high spirit which this struggle has raised as means of moving public opinion in favor of correcting what is bad and of strengthening what is weak in [our] institutions and modes of feeling and thought.» That is another way of saying that we need men with a sense of the value of dignity, of the responsibility of statesmanship. Instead of following blindly what is bad and weak in our modes of thought and feeling, the work of the true statesman is to correct the one and strengthen the other.

Mr. Mill declared that if we were to develop such men among us, we should prove that the war had been a permanent blessing to our country, and a «source of inestimable improvement in the prospects of the human race in other ways besides the great one of extinguishing slavery.» There can be no doubt on this point. We are making in this country the greatest experiment in free government that has ever been tried. The eyes of the world are upon us at every stage of our progress, to see in what way we meet the demands which the problems of enlightened government make upon our system. If we meet them worthily and wisely, the cause of popular government, which is the cause of human progress, gains everywhere. This opens a field of labor for American patriotism which has no equal. It includes all branches of the public service, and extends from the halls of Congress, through all the State legislatures, down to the municipalities of our cities. In all of these popular government is on trial, and in all of them the greatest want of the time is men who know the value of dignity, and who feel the full responsibility of statesmanship.

### «Speech and Speech-Reading for the Deaf.»

A CRITICISM.

I NOTICE with regret that in the interesting article on teaching the deaf to speak, which appeared in your January issue, a number of inaccuracies occur, likely to mislead those of your readers who are not familiar with the processes of educating the deaf. I am sure you will allow me a little space to point out these errors.

It is true that statistics of schools for the deaf in the United States report twenty-five hundred pupils as being taught «by speech»; but no one acquainted with the facts would venture to say that the children «are taught as wholly by means of speech as the children of our public schools.» In their instruction adjuncts, such as natural gestures, writing in the air, the manual alphabet, and other means of conveying ideas to the mind, are in constant use to supplement the inadequacy of speech, which are never even thought of, much less employed, in the instruction of normal children.

A reference to the college at Washington with which I have had the honor to be connected for more than thirty years would lead the reader to suppose that an orally taught deaf-mute entering the college would be likely to lose his speech therein, and that no instruction in lip-reading was afforded in the college. Nothing could be farther from the truth than that any student has ever «lost his speech» because of his connection with the college at Washington. More than half the students speak fluently; every student desiring instruction in speech has it; a corps of eight teachers gives constant and special attention to the preservation and improvement of the speech of the students.

The system of educating the deaf introduced by my father into the country in 1817, when he founded the first school at Hartford, was very much more than one of «conventionalized signs.» It included from the start a thorough training in verbal and written language, providing successfully for the full mental development of the pupil, which in very many cases the oral method does not secure.

The Hartford method was adopted without exception by the schools springing up all over the country during fifty years following 1817; and though speech was little cultivated, thousands of deaf boys and girls received the essentials of a common-school education, including industrial training, and, with scarcely an exception, became self-supporting, even wealth-producing, and always happy members of society. Not a few of them have risen to high positions in the learned professions, becoming lawyers, editors, clergymen, and scientists, attaining «literary prominence» even, which Mr. Wright says he is not aware that orally taught deaf persons have done. And in this connection it should be said that the statement concerning the writing of poetry by the deaf is inexcusable in one who assumes to speak *ex cathedra*. Among the manually taught deaf a score of writers of verse can be named, whose poems ask no partial consideration on account of the «infirmity» of their authors; and even among the orally taught deaf a number have given to the world poetic effusions of a high order of merit.[1]

Mr. Wright's statement as to the various methods now in use in the schools for the deaf in the United States is incorrect, since he makes no mention at all of the only existing *system*—that is to say, one that includes all *methods*. Nine tenths of the deaf children at present

[1] *Vide* an article on "The Poetry of the Deaf," "Harper's Magazine," March, 1884.

under instruction in the country are in schools conducted on a «combined system» which includes a judicious adaptation of means to ends, according to the varying capacity of individuals. In the «combined schools» a much greater aggregate of speech is taught than in the «pure oral» schools, and a greater number of pupils are successfully taught «by speech.» But in these schools is recognized the fact, abundantly proved by the so-called «failures» which have come to them in large numbers from the «pure oral» schools, that very many deaf children are by nature unfitted to succeed with speech, and therefore require other methods for their education.

Nowhere does Mr. Wright show his lack of knowledge more conspicuously than when he speaks of the language of signs as one of the «tools of savagery,» and says «it is unfit for representing grammatically constructed language.» He certainly would not have made such statements had he seen me interpret, a short time since, through the language of signs to the students of our college, a most eloquent and interesting lecture by General Greely on arctic explorations and recent discoveries in Africa. Mr. Wright is doubtless unaware that such interpretations are of frequent occurrence in our college; and I am certain he has little knowledge of the graceful and expressive language the use of which he condemns.

PRESIDENT'S OFFICE, COLLEGE FOR THE DEAF, WASHINGTON, D. C. *Edward M. Gallaudet.*

### REJOINDER.

AMONG the twenty-five hundred deaf pupils reported by statistics as «taught by speech,» there may be some in the «combined» schools, of which Dr. Gallaudet speaks so highly, whose instruction by speech is supplemented by the devices to which he refers. I have not visited all the schools for the deaf in the country; but in our own school the children are taught as wholly by speech as those of any public school, and I know from personal observation that this is true of hundreds upon hundreds of deaf children in the other oral schools. If the «combined» schools, in their eagerness to make a good showing of oral work in their reports, put too liberal an interpretation upon the term «taught by speech,» as Dr. Gallaudet would seem to infer, it is a pity, since it invalidates official statistics, but it may result favorably by inciting them to live up to their reports.

The point which I suspect to be the principal *casus belli*, however, is the reference in the article to the College for the Deaf in Washington, of which Dr. Gallaudet is the honored head. The reference consisted simply in the statement made to me by a graduate of that institution concerning his unaided struggles to retain his speech during the period of his residence there; and I took special pleasure in being able to add that, owing largely to the pressure brought to bear by the advocates of the oral method, this unfortunate state of affairs is rapidly becoming a thing of the past.

Dr. Gallaudet's dissent from my statement that no graduate of the schools for the deaf has attained literary prominence may easily be due to a different standard of what constitutes «literary prominence.» That many deaf persons have reached literary excellence I stated in my article, and a great honor it is to them. I am proud to have had two of this class among my own pupils. But «literary prominence» is quite another matter.

That there are more deaf children in the «combined» schools than in the oral schools is true. This may possibly be explained on the ground that there are more «combined» schools, and the reason for this may be connected with the fact that the «combined» schools had fifty years the start, and that the expense of running an oral school is greater than of a «combined» school. A glance at the statistics quoted in my article will show the remarkable growth of the oral method since its introduction into this country; and it does not take half a prophet's eye to see that the end is not yet. It is the method of the present and the future, as distinguished from that of the past. The «combined» school is only the first step toward oralism.

Dr. Gallaudet is mistaken in assuming that I did not know that interpretations of spoken addresses in gestural signs were often given at his institution. I have several times had the pleasure of myself witnessing these interpretations, both by himself and others. I am astonished that Dr. Gallaudet has the temerity to dissent from my very conservative statement that the language of signs is «unfit for representing grammatically constructed language.» That this statement is not wholly without foundation, the following literal translation from signs into English may show. It is the «blessing» that the elder Dr. Peet, one of the ablest teachers of the deaf America has ever had, was accustomed to sign before his pupils began their repast. The words are given in the exact order in which the gestures were made.

«Father our, heaven in, again we assemble, bread, meat eat, drink receive; while we all things receive, thou blessing give, so we all strength receive; command thy love obey. We ask all Christ through alone. Amen.»

I purposely avoided in my article any statement concerning the sign-language that I thought could be considered extreme; and I will not add such here, but will content myself with quoting Dr. Gallaudet's own words as uttered in an address before a convention of instructors of the deaf. He then said: «I must say that for the deaf-and-dumb children in schools, striving to master the English language, it [the sign-language] is a very dangerous thing. . . . Then, if we want the children in our institutions to master the English language, what have we to do with the sign-language? I answer, as little as possible. I would bear in mind every hour of the day, and every minute of the hour, the sign-language in a school for the deaf is a dangerous thing. . . . The use of the sign-language, except in cases where it is absolutely essential, is pernicious. It hurts; it pulls down; it undoes; it brings forth groans and grunts and expressions of dissatisfaction and disappointment from teachers.»

*John Dutton Wright.*

THE WRIGHT-HUMASON SCHOOL, NEW YORK CITY.

### Acknowledgments.

MR. DODGE'S ceiling decoration in the Congressional Library, entitled «Ambition,» was reproduced in the March CENTURY from a photograph by Davis & Sanford.

In the same number «Trialments, Troublements, and Flickerments» was illustrated by George Varian.

# IN LIGHTER VEIN

## On the Road.

I 'S boun' to see my gal to-night—
 Oh, lone de way, my dearie!
De moon ain't out, de stars ain't bright—
 Oh, lone de way, my dearie!
Dis hoss o' mine is pow'ful slow,
But when I does git to yo' do'
Yo' kiss 'll pay me back, an' mo',
 Dough lone de way, my dearie.

De night is skeery-lak an' still—
 Oh, lone de way, my dearie!
'Cept fu' dat mou'nful whippo'will—
 Oh, lone de way, my dearie!
De way so long wif dis slow pace,
'T 'u'd seem to me lak savin' grace
Ef you was on a nearer place,
 Fu' lone de way, my dearie.

I hyeah de hootin' of de owl—
 Oh, lone de way, my dearie!
I wish dat watch-dog would n't howl—
 Oh, lone de way, my dearie!
An' evaht'ing, bofe right an' lef',
Seem p'int'ly lak hit put itse'f
In shape to skeer me half to def—
 Oh, lone de way, my dearie!

I whistles so 's I won't be feared—
 Oh, lone de way, my dearie!
But anyhow I 's kin' o' skeered,
 Fu' lone de way, my dearie.
De sky been lookin' mighty glum,
But you kin mek hit lighten some,
Ef you 'll jes say you 's glad I come,
 Dough lone de way, my dearie.

*Paul Laurence Dunbar.*

## Jean the Chopper.

WHERE Jean de Chambeau swings his ax
The snow is crushed in panther tracks,
Ghostly the flap of the great white owl,
Lonely and grim the wolf-pack's howl;
Yet, to ax-stroke keeping time,
His yodel rings a laughing rhyme:
To-day the depths of the shadowy wood
To Jean the Chopper seem gay and good.

A moose runs by, and he lets it go;
A bear that 's floundering in the snow;
A panting deer whose desp'rate flight
Has led the wolf-pack through the night.

«Run on!» he cries; «go on your way!
I harm no living thing to-day.
This night at Père Thibault's we feast.
He 's called the neighbors, called the priest;
His Lise is tall, like a white-birch tree,
And her black eyes have called to me!»

*Francis Sterne Palmer.*

## The Dialect Store.

«I SUPPOSE I dreamed it; but if there is n't such a store, there might be, and it would help quill-drivers a lot,» said the newspaper man, as he and his friend were waiting to give their order in a down-town restaurant yesterday noon.

«What store are you talking about, and what dream? Don't be so vague, old man,» said his friend the magazine-writer.

«Why, a dialect store. Just the thing for you. I was walking down Fifth Avenue, near Twenty-first street, and I saw the sign ‹Dialect shop. All kinds of dialects sold by the yard, the piece, or in quantities to suit.› I thought that maybe I might be able to get some Swedish dialect to help me out on a little story I want to write about Wisconsin, so I walked in. The place looked a good deal like a dry-goods store, with counters down each side, presided over by some twenty or thirty clerks, men and women.

«The floor-walker stepped up to me and said, ‹What can I do for you?› ‹I want to buy some dialect,› said I. ‹Oh, yes; what kind do you want to look at? We have a very large assortment of all kinds. There 's quite a run on Scotch just now; perhaps you 'd like to look at some of that.› ‹No; Swedish is what I 'm after,› I replied. ‹Oh, yes; Miss Jonson, show this gentleman some Swedish dialect.›

«I walked over to Miss Jonson's department, and she turned, and opened a drawer that proved to be empty. ‹Are you all out of it?› I asked. ‹Ja; but I skall have some to-morrer. A faller from St. Paul he baen haer an' bought seventy jards.›

«I was disappointed, but as long as I was there I thought I 'd look around; so I stepped to the next counter, behind which stood a man who looked as if he had just stepped out of one of Barrie's novels. ‹Have you Scotch?› said I. ‹I hae joost that. What 'll ye hae? Hielan' or lowlan', reeleegious or profane? I 've a lairge stock o' gude auld Scotch wi' the smell o' the heather on it; or if ye 're wantin' some a wee bit shop-worn, I 'll let ye hae that at a lower price. There 's a quantity that Ian Maclaren left oot o' his last buke.› I expressed surprise that he had let any escape him, and he said: ‹Hech, mon, dinna ye ken there 's no end to the Scots?› I felt like telling him that I was sorry there had been a beginning, but I refrained, and he went on: ‹We 're gettin' airders fra the whole English-sp'akin' warld for the gude auld tongue. Our manager has airdered a fu' line of a' soorts in anticipation of a brisk business, now that McKinley—gude Scotch name that—is elected.›

«I should have liked to stay and see a lot of the Scotch, as it seemed to please the man to talk about his goods; but I wanted to have a look at all the dialects, so I bade him good morning, and stepped to the next department—the negro.

«Here an unctuous voice called out: ‹Fo' de Lawd! Ah don' b'leeve you 'll pass me widout buyin'. Got 'em all hyah, boss—Sou' Ca'lina an' Ten'see an' Virginny. Tawmas Nelson Page buys a heap er stuff right yer. Dat man sut'n'y got a great haid. He was de fustes' one ter see how much folks was dyin' ter git a leetle di'lect er de ra'ht sawt, an' Ah reckon Ah sol' him de fus' yard he evah bo't.›

«‹Do you sell it by the yard?› I asked, just to bring him out. ‹Shuah!› and pulling down a roll of black goods, he unrolled enough dialect to color ‹Uncle Tom's Cabin.› But I said, ‹I don't want to buy, uncle; but I 'm obliged to you for showing it to me.› ‹Oh, dat 's all right, boss. No trouble to show goods. Ah reckon yo' nev' saw sech a heap er local col'in' as dat. Hyah! hyah! hyah! We got de goods, an' any tahm you want to fix up a tale, an' put in de Queen's English in black, come yer an' as' fer me. Good day, sah.› And I passed on to the next—Western dialect.

«Here I found that James Whitcomb Riley had just engaged the whole output of the plant. The clerk had an assistant in his little son,—a Hoosier boy,—and he piped up: ‹We got 'ist a littul bit er chile's di'lec', an' my popper says 'at ef Mist' Riley don't come an' git it soon 'at I can sell it all my own se'f. 'At 'd be the mostest fun!› and his childish treble caused all the other clerks in the store to look around and smile kindly at him.

«In the German department the clerk told me he was not taking orders for dialect in bulk. ‹Zome off dose tayatreekalers dey buy it, aber I zell not de best to dem. I zell imitation kints «made in Chairmany.» Aber I haf der best eef you vant it.›

«I told him I did not care to buy, and passed on to the French-Canadian department. The clerk was just going out to lunch; but although I told him I merely wished to look, and not to buy, he said politely: ‹I try hall I can for get di'lect, but hup in Mon'réal dat McLennan he use hall dere is; but bymby I speak for some dat a frien' have, an' 'e sen' me some. An' 'e tell me I 'll get hit las' summer.› I expressed a polite wish that he might get his goods even sooner than ‹las' summer,› and walked to the Jew-dialect counter, over which I was nearly pulled by the Hebrew clerk. ‹You 're chust in time,› he said. ‹Say, veepin' Rachel! but I sell you a parkain. Some goots on'y been ust vun veek on der staich; unt so hellep me cracious! you look so like mein prudder Imre dat I let dem go› —here he lowered his voice to a whisper—‹I let dem go fer a qvarter uf a darler.›

«I resisted him, and hurried to the Yankee department. There was tall hustling going on there, and a perfect mob of buyers of all sorts and conditions of writers; and it took half a dozen men, women, and children, including three typical farmers, to wait on them; and they were selling it by the inch and by the car-load. ‹Wall, I 'm plumb tired. Wisht they 'd let up so 'st I could git a snack er sump'n' inside me,› said one; and he looked so worn out that I passed on to the Irish counter. A twinkling-eyed young Irishman, not long over, in answer to my question said: ‹Sure, there 's not much carl fer larrge quantities av ut. Jane Barlow do be havin' a good dale, an' the funny papers do be usin' ut in smarl lots, but 't is an aisy toime I have, an' that 's a good thing, fer toimes is harrd.›

«I paused a moment at the English-dialect counter, and the rosy-cheeked clerk said: ‹Cawn't I show you the very litest thing in Coster?› I told him no, and he offered me Lancashire and Yorkshire at ‹gritely reduced rites›; but I was proof against his pleading, and having now visited all the departments but one, went to that.»

«What was it?» asked the writer for the magazines.

«The tough-dialect counter.»

«Tough is not a dialect,» said he.

«Maybe not, but it sounds all right, all right. Well, whatever it is, the fellow in charge was a regular Ninth-Warder, and when I got abreast of him he hailed me with, ‹Soy, cully, wot sort d' yer want? I got a chim-dandy Sunny-school line er samples fer use in dose joints, or I k'n gi' yer hot stuff up ter de limit an' be-yon'. See? Here 's a lot of damaged «wot t''ells» dat I 'll trun down fer a fiver, an' no questions ast. Soy, burn me fer a dead farmer if I ever sol' dem at dat figger before; but dey 's some dat Townsen' did n' use, an' yet dey 's dead-sure winners wit' de right gang. See?›

«And then I woke up, if I was asleep; and if I was n't, I wish I could find the store again, for I 'd be the greatest dialect-writer of the age if I could get goods on credit there. Say, waiter, we came for lunch, not supper.»

*Charles Battell Loomis.*

DRAWN BY W. D. STEVENS.

A SEIZURE IN THE JUNGLE.

«I say, Uncle Boon, what 's the row?»

UNCLE BOON: «Why, the elephant owes my sister for cocoanut milk, and Bab is going to hold his trunk until he pays.»

### A Maid of '96.

OUT from the narrow, gilded frame,
  Eyes like bluets and lips aglow,
Grandmama's face smiles, fair and young
  As when it was painted years ago.

Grandmama, with her snow-white hair,
  Then was a beauty—some said a flirt;
Dressed in the fashion of 'ninety-six,
  With wide, full sleeves and a flaring skirt.

Danced the two-step and waltz at balls,
  Rode in a heavy, old-time coupé
Drawn by horses: in 'ninety-six
  That was considered the modish way.

One can guess how she might have smiled—
  Old-time belle with her stiffened stock—
Could she have seen the modern girl
  Stepping free in her loose-hung frock.

How she 'd have marveled beyond belief,
  Chancing to raise her eyes to the sky,
Over the din of the noisy street
  To have seen an air-coach sweeping by!

Grandmama had a lover then,
  Far away in a distant land;
Letters he wrote her must travel days
  Before their message could reach her hand.

Grandmama treasures those letters still,
  Yellowing sheets of a long-past day,—
«Darling,» «sweetheart,» «my own dear love,»—
  Faded writing half kissed away.

Little she dreamed that the time would come
  When over land and ocean wide
Voices could sound, and faces smile,
  Clearly as though they were at one's side.

But eyes of love in those dim old days
  Could hold the image as true and clear,
And voices of loved ones far away
  Sweetly could sound in memory's ear.

And still from the narrow, gilded frame
  Grandmama smiles serenely bright,
And the satin gown with the filmy lace
  About the neck is her bridal white.

*Katharine Pyle.*

### An Up-to-Date Sweetheart.

I LOVE her for her infinite variety;
  She does everything my fancy can desire.
'T is impossible to tire of her society,
  For there 's always something novel to admire.

She 's a graduate of Cornell University,
  And can talk on solid themes like a review;
She has pretty gowns in flowerlike diversity,
  And she wears a dainty Cinderella shoe.

She 's the leader of a cooking-class of twenty,
  Rides a wheel as well as any in the park;
When she dances she has eager swains in plenty,
  And she sings as clear and sweet as any lark.

On the golf-links she is quite a star performer,
  And at whist she plays the best and newest leads;
She 's a fervent college-settlement reformer,
  And knows all about the masses and their needs.

She can talk in French or German or Italian;
  She can row and swim as well as any boy;
She can work in clay or model a medallion
  In a way to fill a sculptor's soul with joy.

Yet her versatility, though I adore it,
  With this drawback my bewildered heart confronts:
That—it does not seem quite fair to blame her for it—
  She 's engaged herself to six of us at once!

*P. Leonard.*

### Hunting-Song.

HAH! list to the drumming of horses' feet on the dry-baked, frost-bit ground;
And hark to the laugh of the morning breeze as it tosses the rhythmic sound.
    «Swing away! Swing away!»
    It seems to say,
  «From the sorrows that pale your life;
Let your soul sit straight in the saddle to-day, unweighted by thoughts of strife.»

«Tarra-rum! Tarra-rum! Tarra-ralla-lah-lah!» the whipper-in's bugle sings;
'T is enough to waken the pulse of life in the dust of long-dead things.
    «Break away! Break away!»
    It seems to say,
  «From the sorrows that crush your days;
And gallop away with us to-day, through the rime-touched morning haze.»

Look! over the hills where they reach the sky, mounts up the red-faced sun;
In an onrush of light on the mists he swoops and scatters them one by one;
    Ride away! Ride away!
    Oh, life 's but a day;
  Your gallop will soon be o'er.
If you 've never been in at a death, my lad, you 'll fear your own the more.

Soho! Soho! there 's Reynard in sight—may the gods grant him speed to-day,
And may the devil put thought in his heart to lead us some perilous way.
    Tally-ho! Tally-ho!
    And on we go—
  We 've got no time to quail:
Put your trust in fate, take each five-barred gate, and ride home to roast and ale.

*Thomas D. Bolger.*

THE DE VINNE PRESS, NEW YORK.

CPSIA information can be obtained
at www.ICGtesting.com
Printed in the USA
BVHW04*1340230818
525056BV00051B/2248/P

9 780260 126207